Timeless Regency Romance

COLLECTION

Books by Julie Klassen

Lady of Milkweed Manor
The Apothecary's Daughter
The Silent Governess
The Girl in the Gatehouse
The Maid of Fairbourne Hall
The Tutor's Daughter
The Dancing Master
The Secret of Pembrooke Park
The Painter's Daughter

Timeless Regency Romance COLLECTION

JULIE KLASSEN

Three Regency Romances
From a Bestselling Novelist

Lady of Milkweed Manor

The Apothecary's Daughter

The Silent Governess

BETHANYHOUSE
a division of Baker Publishing Group
Minneapolis, Minnesota

Previously published in three separate volumes:
Lady of Milkweed Manor © 2007
The Apothecary's Daughter © 2008
The Silent Governess © 2009

Published by Bethany House Publishers
11400 Hampshire Avenue South
Bloomington, Minnesota 55438
www.bethanyhouse.com

Bethany House Publishers is a division of
Baker Publishing Group, Grand Rapids, Michigan

Printed in the United States of America

ISBN 978-0-7642-1834-7

Library of Congress Control Number: 2015950662

Unless otherwise indicated, Scripture quotations are taken from the King James Version of the Bible.

3-in-1 Edition cover design by Eric Walljasper
Original cover designs by Jennifer Parker
Cover photography by Mike Habermann Photography, LLC
Front cover background photograph for *The Silent Governess* by Mary Harrsch © 2006

Author is represented by Books & Such Literary Agency

16 17 18 19 20 21 22 7 6 5 4 3 2 1

Gods Precious Grace Is All Sufficent !!!

Contents

Lady of Milkweed Manor

To my dear parents,
whose unconditional love
paved the way.

To the Milkweed

NONE call thee flower! I will not so malign
The satin softness of thy plumëd seed,
Nor so profane thee as to call thee weed,
Thou tuft of ermine down,
Fit to entwine about a queen . . .
. . . Ah me! Could he who sings,
On such adventurous and aërial wings
Far over lands and undiscovered seas
Waft the dark seeds of his imaginings,
That, flowering, men might say, Lo! look on these
Wild Weeds of Song—not all ungracious things!

—*Sonnets by Lloyd Mifflin*

Prologue

When first I knew her, I thought her an amusing scrap of girl, silly and a bit grubby from her mornings spent in the gardens. When not pottering about out of doors, she seemed always to be reading some poetic nonsense or other and loved nothing more than to pose the most disturbing questions. Still, I liked her even then and, I think, she admired me. But her father took notice and pronounced me unsuitable, effectively pruning our young friendship before it could grow into anything. I soon forgot about Miss Charlotte Lamb. Or so I convinced myself.

Years passed, and when I saw her again she was altogether changed. Not only her situation, which had changed from privileged to piteous, but also her very substance. At least it seemed so to me.

Others would look at her with much different eyes. They would see, perhaps, a fallen woman at the deepest point of humiliation. A woman to be flicked off one's sleeve like a disgusting worm. Or an insect to be tormented. Cruel, overgrown schoolchildren that many are, they seem to delight in ripping off one wing, then another, watching in morbid glee as she falls helpless to the ground.

To the gentler observer, she is a creature to be scorned at worst, ignored at best, but certainly not one to watch in hopeful anticipation. Day by day to witness her transformation amid the grime and cloying weight of her surroundings, not to wither nor shrink, but to unfurl, to become all that is sun and wind and flower and grace.

I, of course, can only watch from a safe distance—safe for us both. For me, now a married man, a physician of some note, a man of standing in town. And for her, whose reputation I am determined will suffer no more—not if it is in my power to prevent it.

Yet, as I watch her there among the milkweeds, I confess all these thoughts fade away. I think only of her.

How lovely she looks. Not abstractly beautiful, but perfectly fitted to the landscape, etched into a painting of purest golden glow above, and mad, overgrown garden below—gold, green, purple—heaven and earth. And there at the center, her still figure, looking not at me but at the distant horizon, where the sun is spilling its first fingers over the milkweed, over her milky skin, her hair, her gown.

The light moves toward me and I am stilled, speechless. A sharp barb of waiting fills my chest and I can barely breathe. If I don't move, the light will touch me, the painting encompass me. If I step away, retreat into the shadows, I will be safe, but I won't be there to see her when she finally flies away. . . .

Dear God. Please guard my steps. And somehow bless Miss Charlotte Lamb.

Part I

That exquisite thing, the seed of milkweed,
furnished abundant playthings.
The plant was sternly exterminated in our garden,
but sallies into a neighboring field provided supplies
for fairy cradles with tiny pillows of silvery silk.

—Alice Morse Earle, *Old-Time Gardens*

Alas! And did my Saviour bleed,
And did my Sovereign die?
Would he devote that sacred head
For such a worm as I?

—Isaac Watts

1

> The common milkweed needs no introduction. Its pretty pods are familiar to every child, who treasures them until the time comes when the place in which they are stowed away is one mass of bewildering, unmanageable fluff.
>
> —19th century naturalist, F. Schuyler Mathews

Twenty-year-old Charlotte Lamb laid her finest gowns into the trunk, pausing to feel the silken weight of the sky blue ball gown, her favorite—a gift from dear Aunt Tilney. With one last caress, she packed it carefully atop the others. Then came her promenade dresses, evening dresses, and gayer day dresses. Next were the coordinating capes, hats, and hair ornaments. Finally the long gloves, petticoats, and the new boned corset. Definitely the corset.

Turning back to her rapidly thinning wardrobe, her hand fell upon a plain muslin in dove grey. It showed wear in the elbows and cuffs. She tossed it on the bed. Then a thought came to her and she stopped her packing and left her room, stepping quietly down the corridor to her mother's room. Looking about her and seeing no one yet awake, she pushed the door open as silently as she could. She stepped into the room and, finding the shutters closed, walked to the windows and folded them back, allowing the grey dawn to illuminate the chamber. Then she returned to the door and closed it. Leaning back against the wood panels, she closed her eyes, savoring the stillness and peace she always felt in this room. It had been too long since she'd been in here.

From somewhere in the vicarage she heard a noise, a clang, and she jumped. Though why she should fear being caught in here she had no idea. Most likely it was only Tibbets lighting the fires. Her father would probably not be awake for hours. Still, the thought of someone up and about reminded her that she needed to hurry if she wanted to depart with as little to-do as possible. She stepped purposefully to the wardrobe and opened its doors. Yes, her mother's clothes were still here. She raked her fingers through the fabric, the lace and velvet and silks, but did not find what she was looking for. Had her father or Beatrice discarded it? She pushed the gowns aside and looked at the bottom of the wardrobe, at the slippers lined up neatly in a row. Then a flash of brown caught her eye, and she reached down and pulled out a crumpled wad of clay-colored material that had fallen to the bottom of the cabinet. She shook out the simple, full-cut dress—her mother's gardening dress.

Tucking it under her arm, she ran her fingers across the books on the bedside table. She didn't dare take the Bible her mother had used, knowing it was from the vicarage library. Instead she chose the *Lady's Pocket-Sized New Testament and Psalms*, as it was smaller and lighter. It was a lovely edition with a canvas cover embroidered with birds and flowers worked in silk and metallic thread. It had been a gift from her mother's sister, and Charlotte didn't think her father would object to her taking it.

With one last look at her mother's things—hairbrush and combs, cameo necklace and butterfly brooch—she left the room and walked quickly back to her own. She rolled her mother's dress as tightly as she could and stuffed it into a leather valise. Then she shoved in the worn grey gown, shifts, stockings, slippers, drawers, and a pair of short stays. Into a carpetbag she placed a shawl, dressing gown, gloves, and the New Testament. Two of her most serviceable bonnets went into her bandbox. Handkerchiefs and what little money she had were secured in a reticule which would hang from her wrist.

She looked at the trunk, filled with her beautiful years, her happy vain youth, and firmly shut the lid. Pausing to secure a traveling hat over her pinned-up brown curls, she left her room with only her valise, carpetbag, reticule, and bandbox—all she could carry. She quietly made her way down the stairs and glanced at the silver tray resting on the hall table. Yesterday's letter lay there still, unanswered. Their cousin had written to tell them of her "blessed news" and how she looked forward to the "great event to come this autumn." Beatrice had curled her pretty lip and said it sickened her to read of such private matters, especially from a woman of Katherine's advanced age. Charlotte had said not a word.

Now Charlotte paused only long enough to run her fingers over Katherine's elaborate script and the smeared London Duty date stamp. She took a deep breath and walked on. She was nearly to the door when she heard her father's voice from the drawing room.

"You're off, then." It was not a question.

She turned and, through the open doors, saw him slumped in the settee by the fire. His greying hair was uncharacteristically disarrayed and he still wore his dressing gown. She felt her throat tighten. She could only nod. She wondered if he would soften at this final moment. Would he hold out some offer of assistance, some parting words of conciliation or at least regret?

In a voice rough with the early hour and disdain, he said, "My only consolation is that your mother, God rest her soul, did not live to see this day."

The pain of it lanced her, but it should not have. He had said the like before, worse even. Willing tears to remain at bay, Charlotte stepped out of the vicarage, quietly shutting the door behind her. She walked through the garden, committing it to memory. There were the neatly trimmed hedges that Buxley still coaxed into the shape her mother preferred. There, the exquisite flower beds with their cleverly mixed color palettes, graduating heights and varying textures—delphinium, astilbe, cornflower, Canterbury bells, lemon lilies—all of which Charlotte had tried to maintain in her mother's honor, at least until now. She took a long deep breath, then another, savoring the dew-heavy fragrances of sweet violets and purple pincushions. She had no intention of picking a flower to take with her, a flower that would wither before she reached her destination, but then she saw it. A vile milkweed in the border of sciatic cress, which Buxley called Billy-come-home-soon. How had she missed it before? She strode to the weed and pulled at it with her free hand, but the stalk would not give. She set her bags and box down and pulled with both hands until the whole stubborn thing was unearthed, roots and all. She would leave her mother's garden in perfect order. But for how long? *Who will tend your gardens, Mother? Buxley will try, I suppose. Though he is not getting any younger. With the horses and all the heavy work falling to him, the garden suffers. And Beatrice has no use for a garden, as you well know.*

On nostalgic impulse, Charlotte snapped off a cluster of small purplish flowers from the milkweed plant and held it briefly to her nose—it smelled surprisingly sweet—then slipped it into her reticule. She tossed the stalk onto the rubbish heap on her way down Church Hill. Glancing over her shoulder at the chalky white vicarage, a face in an upstairs window caught her eye. *Beatrice.* Her sister wore a stony expression and made no move to wave. When Beatrice turned from the window, Charlotte turned as well, wishing for a moment that she had turned away first. Two minutes later, just as she knew it would, the post wagon approached.

"Hallo there, Miss Lamb," the driver said as he halted his horses.

"Good morning, Mr. Jones."

"Care for a ride into the village?"

"Yes, thank you."

He took her bags from her and helped her up. "Off to visit your aunt again, are we?" He settled her carpetbag beside her.

She did not wish to lie any more than necessary. "I am always so happy in their company."

"And why not. Such fine people your aunt and uncle are. Never knew the better."

"You are very kind."

She clutched her carpetbag as the wagon started off again, her generous pelisse shielding her from the damp morning wind, from curious onlookers—and even from the full brunt of her father's farewell, such as it was. She would not cry—not now, not here, where villagers she knew might see her and guess she was leaving not on another holiday but rather on a much darker journey.

When the driver helped her alight at Chequers Inn, she took not the coach headed for Hertfordshire and Aunt Tilney, but rather a coach bound for London.

The black enclosed coach bumped and jostled its way to the west side of London. When the driver called his "whoa" to tired horses, Charlotte arose from her seat, clutched her belongings, and pushed her way out of the conveyance before the coachman might help her alight.

She stepped down and made haste up Oxford Street, past the stationer and paper hanger, china and glassman, and linen drapers. Walking north on busy Tottenham Court Road, she passed silversmiths, chemists, and dwelling houses that were clearly less than fashionable. Then she stepped off the cobbles and crossed the damp and narrow Gower Mews. At the alley's end, she paused between market wagons and rubbish carts to look over her shoulder, assuring herself that no one was watching. Then she slipped in through the rear door of the Old Towne Tea Shoppe and, with an apologetic nod toward the proprietress, stepped out the front door onto Gower Street, opening her black umbrella against the slight mist and any prying eyes. Head lowered, she stepped over a refuse-filled gutter, then walked crisply on. Coming upon a sign bearing the name Store Street, Charlotte checked the directions her aunt had written down for her. This was it.

Charlotte glanced up and immediately saw an old manor house looming against a border of shadow and trees. It was a grey hulk of a building with two dark wings at right angles to each other, a boxy garret at their apex, standing guard over a formidable, arched door below. Perhaps a great house a hundred years ago, the structure looked sound but bleak—mottled stone, severe lines, the absence of adornment save a hedgerow lining the edge of a mossy stone walkway. She saw no sign, no plaque naming the manor, and somehow that made her all the more sure she was in the right place.

It was only then that she allowed the tears to come. Here, the street behind her streaming with people who knew her not and cared less, she felt the sting of her father's rejection and the loss of her home. But she could not agree with his assessment. He might be glad that her mother was not here to witness this day, but Charlotte was not.

She thought of her dear mother, the well-loved Lillian Lamb, who had brought warmth and moderation, cheer and steady calm to the vicarage, and especially to Reverend Gareth Lamb himself.

Charlotte hoped her memories of her mother, gone these five years, would not fade in this absence from all that was familiar—her mother's room, her portrait, the far-off look in Father's eyes that meant he was thinking of her. His parting words echoed again through Charlotte's mind, and she flinched—envisioning the disappointment that would certainly have clouded her mother's face—but yet she wished her mother were here with her, walking this rutted path, consoling her as she always had that all would work out in the end.

I wish I had your faith, Mother. I wish I were half the fine lady you were—or half as proper a clergyman's daughter. Would you have forgiven me, even if Father will not?

As Charlotte drew closer to the looming grey edifice that was to become her temporary home, she could not help but notice the secretive shuttered windows of the ground floor.

Then she noticed the milkweeds.

No formal gardens here, or if there once were, they had long since given way to islands of tall grasses and unchecked patches of milkweeds running the length of the wall facing Charlotte.

Her father would be horrified, and even her mother would not have approved of the tangled mess. Charlotte sighed. She supposed that for the women within these grey walls, the gardens outside were the least of their problems. *And the same is true of me.*

But milkweeds? What a bane they were to gardeners, their stubborn roots sending out crafty runners, the offspring only slightly easier to pull than the mother plant herself. And they spread not only by runners, but by their prolific seeds that filled the air every autumn. Apparently that was what had happened here—milkweed had been introduced and, left unchecked, had taken over most of the lawn.

Couldn't they at least hire some boy with a scythe to come and cut the pests down? Charlotte wondered. Milkweeds were pretty enough when the flowers bloomed, but when the grey-green pods aged to a dull silver, the reedy stalks held little aesthetic value at all.

Perhaps that solicitor friend of Uncle's had given false information about this place. Or Aunt Tilney had gotten it wrong somehow. Her aunt had confided in hushed tones that this place was of better quality and more discreet than others like it. Charlotte gathered their London solicitor had procured the recommendation for her. Her father knew nothing of the arrangements, other than to exact Charlotte's promise of secrecy and anonymity for as long as possible. Otherwise he seemed to care little of where Charlotte was to go or how she was to provide for herself. It was clear he could barely wait to get her out of his sight.

Charlotte wondered if her mother would recognize the man she had been married to for so many years. Not that Gareth Lamb had changed so much physically, except to grow a bit grey in his sideburns and a bit paunchier around the middle, but his demeanor was markedly changed. He had been stern—self-righteous even—before this happened, and now was all the more. The whole of his concern revolved around two points: how such a thing would likely ruin his career and how it would ruin Bea's chance at a suitable marriage.

I am dreadfully sorry for it. I am. I suppose Father's anger is right and just. But it does not feel like it. If only you were here to soften him. To accompany me.

But her mother was dead. So Charlotte walked alone.

A single knock brought to the door a thin, plain-faced woman a few years Charlotte's senior who quickly led her from the entry hall, through a large dining room, and into a small study with the words, "The matron shall be in directly." And, indeed, not two minutes later, a severe but attractive woman in her forties wearing a dark dress and tightly bound hair walked in, her officious air proclaiming her title. The woman's stern appearance brought Charlotte some disquiet, but when she settled her gaze on Charlotte, there was grim kindness in her expression.

"I am Mrs. Moorling, matron of the Manor Home. May I be of assistance?"

Charlotte arose on shaky legs and pressed a letter from the London solicitor and a bank note into the woman's hand. This was her only reply.

Mrs. Moorling slipped the money into her desk drawer without comment or expression, then glanced briefly at the letter the solicitor had written at her uncle's request. "I see. I'm afraid we haven't a private room available at the moment, but you shall have one as soon as possible. In the meantime, you will need to share."

"I understand."

"Your name is—" the woman scanned the letter—"Miss . . . Smith?"

"Yes, Smith. Charlotte Smith."

Mrs. Moorling paused only a moment before continuing, again with no change in her expression, though Charlotte had the distinct impression the woman knew she was lying about her name. "Before I can admit you, there are a few questions I need to ask."

Charlotte swallowed.

"Is this your first occasion availing yourself upon such an institution?"

"Yes, of course."

"Not 'of course,' Miss Smith. There are many who do not learn from experience. I must tell you that the Manor Home for Unwed Mothers is a place for deserving unmarried women with their first child. Our goal is to rehabilitate our patients for a morally upright life."

Charlotte looked down, feeling the heat of embarrassment snake up her neck and pulse in her ears. She heard the sound of paper rustling and knew the matron was again reading the letter.

"This letter attests to your character and background, though I haven't the time to verify it at the moment."

"Mrs. Moorling. I assure you. I have never been in such a predicament before . . . never conceived myself in such a predicament."

Poor choice of words, Charlotte thought grimly.

She forced herself to meet the older woman's eyes. Mrs. Moorling looked directly at her for a moment, then nodded.

"Gibbs will find a place for you to sleep."

Gibbs, the plain, painfully thin young woman, led her back through the entry hall and to the right, to the street-facing wing of the L-shaped building. Hurrying to keep up, Charlotte followed her through the long corridor to a door midway down its length. Charlotte looked into the dim room—once a portion of a fine drawing room, perhaps—with a high ceiling and broad hearth. The bedchamber held only one narrow bed, the width less than Charlotte's height. A small table with a brass candlestick sat on either side of the bed, and one chair stood against the nearest wall. Three simple wooden chests lined the opposite wall, no doubt used to store the belongings of the room's temporary lodgers.

"You'll be sharing with Mae and Becky. Both slight girls—you're a fortunate one. They must be off visiting in one of the other rooms. They'll be in by and by. We have a water closet below stairs. But there's usually a wait for it. Chamber pots under the bed for late-night emergencies. We know how you lying-in girls get toward the end. You're responsible for emptying your own, at least until your ninth month or so. Our physicians believe activity is healthy. All the girls have duties, long as you're able. You'll get your assignment at breakfast tomorrow. Eight o'clock. Any questions?"

Charlotte's mind was whirling with them, but she only shook her head.

"Good night, then." Gibbs let herself from the room.

2

There is no sense in crying over spilt milk.
Why bewail what is done and cannot be recalled?
—Sophocles

She is dreaming or remembering—she isn't sure which, but the sensation is delightful. She is dancing with a young gentleman at Sharsted Court, a gentleman whose name she can't recall, or perhaps never knew. She feels the polite pressure of his hand on her gloved palm and sees the warm admiration in his shy glances. In fact, she feels admiring glances follow her as she moves effortlessly through the patterns and steps of the dance. She feels not, she hopes, bloated vanity but rather surprise and pleasure at the attention paid her. Her sister, Beatrice, is not in attendance this night. Beautiful Bea, home with a cold. She is sorry, but really, how heavenly to feel so sought after, so desirable, all loveliness in her sky blue silk. Suitors aplenty, all her life ahead of her.

The music ends, and the young gentleman, golden eyelashes against thin pale cheeks, escorts her from the floor. She catches a glimpse of green eyes and rust-gold hair, but when she looks again, another partner has already taken his place. This one boldly thrusts his hand toward her, his brown eyes gleaming confidently, impudently. She turns away but feels his hand fall against her shoulder and turn her back around. She wants to flee, to refuse the presumptuous hand.

Instead, she wakens.

There, in the dimness before Charlotte's eyes, dangled a hand. Someone in bed beside her had thrown an arm across her shoulder. Bea? *No*, her mind told her. *You're not home any longer.* Dread and black fear swelled and sank deep within her.

Please. Please, let it all be a dream. Oh, God, please . . .

She reached under the blanket and ran her hand across her midriff, hoping it would still be smooth and flat.

Please.

Her hand found the hard rounded mound and she winced her eyes tightly shut.

It cannot be. It cannot be.

But it was.

Charlotte, lying on her side on the edge of the droopy bed, again opened her eyes. The hand was still before her, eerily like the one in her dream. Gently, she pushed the arm off her shoulder and scooted farther still, until she feared she might fall off the bed. Her back ached. Unable to get comfortable, she turned over again, the effort creaking the bed and taxing her more than imaginable a half year before. She found herself nose to nose with Mae, who had obviously eaten onions for supper. Another young woman clung to the opposite edge of the bed. Three women, six souls, in one small bed. Like sausages being turned, one after the other in a pan, Mae turned over to her other side, and the third woman followed suit without waking. Charlotte couldn't recall the younger woman's name. A girl, really.

Charlotte had met Mae not long after she had gotten into bed, plumping, then folding the pillow to try to get comfortable. The pretty, petite woman, near her own age, Charlotte guessed, had come in, mumbled her name, and promptly climbed in beside Charlotte as though they had been sharing a bed their whole lives. Charlotte surprised herself by falling asleep soon after. She did hear the second girl come in some time later, but was too tired to acknowledge her. All she wanted was sleep. Because in sleep she could return to her old life.

Charlotte was just drifting back to sleep when she heard a scream in some distant part of the manor. She sat up so suddenly that Mae awoke beside her and groaned.

"Lie still, would you?"

"I heard something."

"What?"

"Someone screaming."

"Better get used to it." Mae turned over, her long auburn plait landing on Charlotte's pillow. "Babies always gettin' born in the night here."

"What?"

"Never heard a woman in childbirth afore?"

"Oh. No, I haven't."

Mae didn't respond, and Charlotte surmised that the woman had fallen back to sleep already. Charlotte sat still, listening. But she heard no more and lay back down for a few more hours of fitful rest.

In the morning, Charlotte awoke to find herself alone in bed. She arose and dressed quickly in her grey day dress, then followed the sound of footsteps and feminine voices through the entry hall and into the large room she had passed through yesterday on her way to Mrs. Moorling's study. The room had doors on either end and was filled with tables—serving, apparently, as both dining room and workroom. At a long table against one wall, Charlotte followed the example of the others and filled a small plate with bread and a stringy hunk of cold mutton. She also poured herself a cup of weak but, thankfully, warm tea. She sat at a table alone, dreading the questions that would undoubtedly come from the other girls. She had barely eaten half her bread when Gibbs, the assistant who had shown her to her room the night before, stopped before her, a ledger of some sort in her hands. She spoke with cool efficiency, her dull eyes glancing only briefly at Charlotte before returning to the bound ledger before her.

"What use are you, then?"

"Pardon?"

"What are you fit for? Laundry, cooking, sewing . . . ?"

"I am skilled enough with needlework, I suppose. Embroidery and the—"

"Very well. Mending stockings for you, then. Second table—off you go."

Charlotte took another bite of bread, skipped the congealed mutton altogether, and drank the rest of her tea. She took her time returning her cup and utensils to the sideboard and then, when she could think of no other excuse, stepped toward the table Gibbs had indicated. As she walked, she looked at the women's heads, pulled in close like a tightly cinched drawstring purse. She heard their whispers and laughter and feared they were talking about her. The first to raise her head and look in Charlotte's direction was a fair-haired woman with a long, angular face and surprisingly kind eyes.

"Here you are, love. Have a seat." She moved her darning things, clearing a place for Charlotte beside her.

"Thank you," Charlotte said quietly, eyes downcast.

"You're a new one."

"Yes." Charlotte forced a smile and bent to her task, trying to find a stocking with enough sound material left to mend.

"I'm Sally. Sally Mitchell." The blond woman smiled a toothy smile, her prominent front teeth protruding and not quite straight. Still it was a friendly smile. Unlike the narrow-eyed scrutiny she felt aimed at her from the others.

"I am Miss Charlotte . . . Smith."

"*Miss* Charlotte, is it?" a second woman broke in.

Charlotte glanced up quickly and took in a mop of tight brown curls, a sharp nose, and thin mouth.

"And I'm *Lady* Bess Harper." The woman affected a haughty voice and dramatically extended her hand as though for a kiss.

The other women laughed.

Bess slumped back in her chair and gave Charlotte a hard look. "I wonder you're here at Milkweed Manor, then, and not up the road."

"What do you mean?"

"Queen Charlotte's up the road at Bayswater Gate. I would have thought you'd go there, what with your name and all."

"Queen Charlotte's?" Charlotte repeated, confused.

Mae, her pretty bedmate from the night before, said, "Maybe she thinks one queen is enough in a place, and she wants to be ours."

"No, I . . ."

At this, Bess Harper leaned in, her thin lips disappearing in a frown of disdain. "Queen Charlotte's Lying-in Hospital. Telling me you never heard of it?"

"No. Should I?"

Bess looked pointedly at her middle, and Charlotte fought the urge to look away in shame. She threaded her needle and said weakly, "It is my first time."

"Sure it is," Mae said, "just like the lot of us."

Bess grinned wickedly, "Oh, me too. You never heard me say otherwise."

Sally leaned toward Charlotte and explained gently, "They only takes girls what haven't gotten themselves caught breeding before."

"They aim to reform us here," Bess said. "Put us on the straight and narrow and all that."

"One fall they can forgive." Sally sighed. "But two and you're done for."

"Yes," Charlotte said. "I believe the matron said the Manor Home was for 'deserving unmarried women with their first child.'"

"Deserving? I'm deserving all right," Bess said. "How 'bout the lot of you?"

Mae nodded her head. "Very, very."

"I believe we're all deserving a cup o' tea about now, don't you agree?" Bess said.

"Aye." Sally grinned and rose to fetch some. "And jam tarts besides."

From time to time, Charlotte glanced around the workroom, taking an inventory, of sorts, of the two dozen or more girls. She was curious as to why she hadn't seen the young girl who had shared her bed last night. Surely her time had not already come.

"Mae, might I ask the name of the other girl who shares our room?"

"Young Becky, you mean."

"Yes. I don't see her about, do I?"

"No. It's her morning, I'm afraid."

"Her morning? She's delivering right now?"

"Nay. Her morning to be examined by one of them blood and bone men, you know."

"Oh . . ."

"Better her than me." Mae shuddered.

"What do you mean?"

"You'll find out soon enough."

Gibbs approached the table and tapped her ledger with a blunt, ink-stained finger. "Miss Smith, you will be seen next."

"Pardon me?"

"For your examination. All the girls must be seen by one of our physicians."

"Oh. I see."

"He is just finishing up with another patient. Wait here, and I'll call you when he's ready." Gibbs strode briskly away.

Charlotte sat without moving, watching her go.

"Why, you look frightened half to death." Sally laid her hand on Charlotte's. "'Tis nothin' to be scared of."

"Unless she gets Dr. Preston," Mae said. "That man's like an orphan in a candy shop, all eyes and hands and lickin' his lips."

"S'pose he figgers, why not—ain't the jar been opened already?" Bess's sharp face was expressive. "A bit more used up won't do any harm."

Charlotte swallowed. "Are you suggesting this . . . Dr. Preston . . . takes advantage of the girls here?"

"I'm not suggesting a thing," Bess said. "Only sayin' you best watch your backside, underside, and all the rest like."

"He's never bothered me," Mae said.

"Well, you're not half the looker I am, are ya?"

"Well, then, I'm thankful I'm not."

"Have they no midwives here?" Charlotte asked.

Bess smirked. "Oh, a country girl, ey?"

"They once had some," Sally answered. "But not at present."

"Do they . . . ? I mean, I have never been 'examined' before. Not . . . like that. Do they . . . ? I mean, will I be asked to . . . ?"

"Take off your drawers?" Bess grinned.

Charlotte inclined her brow and swallowed nervously.

"I hate to break it to you, birdy, but when the babe comes, you won't be wearing drawers or petticoats or much of anything else for that matter."

"Hush, now," Sally interrupted. "Don't scare her more than she already is. Don't fret, Charlotte. They let you wear your nightdress, though 'tis likely to be spoilt."

"As for the examination," Mae said, "it depends on which man you get."

"Are there two physicians?"

"And a surgeon."

"The young physician is real gentleman-like," Mae said.

Bess snorted. "Green, you mean. He's barely more than a boy. I don't think he's ever seen a woman in all her natural glory."

"'Course he has," Mae said.

"Can't tell it the way he turned red as a robin when he looked me over last month." Bess crossed her arms smugly.

Mae ignored this. "But if you get the other, Dr. Preston, I'm afraid you're in for it," she said. "He seems to like dressing us girls down."

"Undressing us down, you mean."

Just then Charlotte recognized young Becky as she walked quickly through the room, head down, face flushed red, shawl and arms pulled tight across her bosom like a shield of wool and adolescent muscle. Sally followed Charlotte's gaze and clucked sympathetically.

"Becky, poor girl, come sit with us," Sally called. "Can I pour you a cup o' tea?"

But the girl only shook her head swiftly, eyes on the floor, as she walked past them and out the other door.

"Whatever is the matter?" Charlotte asked. "Is she ill?"

"She was right as rain before her appointment," Mae said.

Gibbs reappeared in the doorway and Charlotte's heart began thudding in her chest. The needle slipped in her sweating hands and she set her work down, wiping her palms across her lap. If this man did not conduct himself properly, she would give him a piece of her mind. Just because she had made one mistake did not mean she would make another. She took a deep breath. Still she could not calm herself. She felt so vulnerable, so removed from those who would protect her.

Gibbs walked toward her, and Charlotte took another deep breath. The woman's face was a mask of somber efficiency, but Charlotte thought she glimpsed some darker emotion there as well. Anger? Annoyance? Had Charlotte done something wrong? When Gibbs stopped at the table Charlotte rose from her chair.

"You may return to your work, Miss Smith. Dr. Preston has been . . . called away suddenly and cannot see you this morning after all. We shall reschedule for tomorrow."

"Oh, I see." Charlotte exhaled. "Thank you."

Gibbs turned on her heel and strode back toward the offices. Charlotte sank back into her chair, feeling foolishly relieved. Across the table, Sally winked at her.

Charlotte returned to her stitching but found herself thinking about her mother, who had spent a great deal of time in the company of surgeons and physicians in the final years of her life. Her mother had enjoyed a friendly camaraderie with her physicians and never feared their presence. Portly Dr. Webb, a respected and kindhearted doctor, had called on her so often as to become nearly a friend to the family. The only thing Charlotte had feared from him was a final diagnosis for her mother.

Dr. Webb had brought to the Doddington vicarage a succession of colleagues and apprentices. The colleagues were stuffy older men—Cambridge professors or renowned London physicians come to offer their opinion on her mother's condition. These men offered benign greetings to Charlotte in passing. The apprentices were young men who seemed determined to prove themselves, so most rarely condescended to speak with a young girl, and of course, Charlotte was never examined by any of them. Actually, Charlotte had been such a healthy girl that she had rarely been treated by anyone. Her mother had cared for her minor ailments, and she had never broken a bone. The only time she had seen a surgeon was when she had fallen into a fox hole while running through the sheep pasture behind the churchyard. Her parents had feared her ankle broken, but the surgeon—she didn't recall his name—declared it only sprained.

There was one apprentice who did speak with Charlotte, though granted, he was a bit older than most of Dr. Webb's apprentices. Daniel Taylor was his name. He was tall and very thin, with reddish-blond hair and the palest of skin. She could not think of him without both a smile and a painful wedge of guilt pressing against her stomach. She always seemed to say the wrong thing, and inevitably his boyish face would blush a deep apple red, a brighter hue than his rust-colored hair. But still, he must have admired her. She was certain he did, at least until her father made his disapproval so mercilessly clear. Mr. Taylor left Kent with barely a good-bye and, she feared, the impression that her own opinion of him matched her father's. Something the vicar had no doubt implied.

Charlotte pricked her finger with the needle and gasped. Eyes from around the table rose up in question. She held up her finger, the spot of blood growing big as a beetle. She smiled dolefully at the others. "One should never daydream with sharp implements in one's hand."

Bess rolled her eyes and the others returned to their work, but Charlotte found herself morbidly fascinated with the mounding blood. She lifted her finger and watched the blood run down into her palm. *Life-giving liquid*, she thought oddly. *God's milk.*

3

Poor woman! how can she honestly be breeding again?

—Jane Austen, letter to her sister, 1808

The next morning Charlotte awoke before either Mae or Becky, driven by nerves to prepare herself for the visit with the dreaded Dr. Preston. Would he really require her to remove her clothing? She shuddered. Worse yet, would he question her about how she came to be in this place?

She bathed herself with a rough cloth and cold water from the washbasin, cleaned her teeth, and brushed and pinned her hair. It crossed her mind that she should attempt to make herself appear as unattractive as possible, considering the girls' comments about Dr. Preston's character. But she doubted anyone could find her attractive in her present condition. Rather, she felt the need to arm herself with good grooming and her best dress, as though to show the man that she was not just another poor, uneducated girl he could manipulate. The thought pricked her conscience as surely as the needle had pricked her finger. Did she feel herself above the other girls? Yes, she admitted to herself, she did—even as she acknowledged the hypocrisy of the thought. *Forgive me*. Wasn't she just another poor—though not uneducated, certainly naïve—girl, alone in the world and at men's mercy? She shook off the unsettling thought. *Please protect me, almighty God*.

After breakfast, Charlotte again joined the other women at the sewing table. She glanced around nervously and was relieved when she didn't see Gibbs anywhere about. Perhaps the doctor was still indisposed. But no sooner had she begun her second stocking than Gibbs and her ledger appeared before Charlotte.

"The doctor will see you first this morning." Gibbs glanced at the clock on the mantel. "He is expected directly. I will let you know the moment he's ready."

Charlotte swallowed and nodded.

Bess and Mae exchanged knowing looks. Bess snorted and Mae covered a giggle with her freckled hand.

"Hush, now," Sally admonished gently. "Dr. Preston is gentleman-like most of the time. If you ask me, 'tis that other doctor what gives me the shivers."

"The old one or Dr. *Young*?"

"Young. He looks at you with those cold eyes and 'tis as if they've got no feelin' in them. Ice like. Like he's . . . gutting fish instead of tending people."

"Better cold eyes than warm, roamin' hands," Bess muttered.

"Here he comes," Mae whispered.

"Which one is it?" Bess shifted in her seat to try to see past Sally.

"Young," Mae supplied.

Charlotte turned her head with dread to look at the man entering. She took in a tall, thin man in coat and hat, with hard, pointed features and somber expression, neither much softened by the small round spectacles he wore. Even before she could get a good look at his face, something about his demeanor made her stomach clench. He removed his hat just as he pulled open a door partway down the passageway. When the sunlight from a nearby window shone on his rust-blond hair, a jolt of recognition stunned her. Mr. Taylor.

It had to be. Mr. Taylor, here? Now? To examine her? It could not be! She pressed her fingers to her brow and groaned as he swept out of view.

Sally leaned close. "Did I not tell you? Ice."

"At least it's not Preston," Mae said.

"I cannot," Charlotte whispered.

"You 'ave to, love," Sally soothed.

"But I . . . know him."

"Know him?" Bess asked sharply. "Biblically-speakin', you mean?"

"Of course not."

"I thought you said you hadn't been here before," Mae said.

"I haven't."

"Then how'd you know him?"

An inner plea for caution rose up in Charlotte and she changed tack. "Perhaps I am mistaken. Perhaps I do not know him." Perhaps her eyes had played tricks with her mind. After all, no one had actually mentioned the name Taylor.

"Dr. Taylor will see you now, Charlotte." The matron, Mrs. Moorling, appeared and her no-nonsense voice dampened Charlotte's spirit yet pulled her to her feet. "Dr. Preston has yet to appear this morning—I've sent Gibbs to find him. Come, come, we haven't all day." The woman should command armies rather than this sorry gaggle of expecting females. Hurrying to catch up, Charlotte followed the older woman down the passageway.

"Mrs. Moorling. I am sorry," Charlotte said, struggling to keep pace, "I don't mean to be difficult, but I really cannot be examined by Mr. Taylor. . . ."

"And why not?"

"Because I . . ." She hesitated. What would be gained by telling the matron that she knew Daniel Taylor? Would that somehow risk her anonymity? Would the matron ask more questions than Charlotte wanted to answer?

"It does not seem, well, proper. He is so young, and I . . ."

"Miss Smith. Dr. Taylor may look young, but I assure you he's well educated—more than most. He is also a married man and completely respectable. Again, more than most." Her voice carried a hard edge.

But Charlotte was still striving to grasp what the matron had just said. Mr. Taylor was married. Somehow that both troubled her and eased her mind greatly, for the present predicament as well as the past.

"If it were another physician, I might offer to stay in the room with you, but I have a long list of duties that require my attention and, I assure you, you are in perfectly good hands."

Terrifying choice of words, Charlotte thought.

Mrs. Moorling opened the office door for her, and taking a deep breath, Charlotte stepped inside.

He was sitting at a plain but large desk, reading some documents on its surface. She took a few steps forward, then stood silently before the desk, waiting for him to address her. He squinted at the paper before him and did not look up.

"Miss Smith, is it?"

"Ah . . . um . . ."

"Miss Charlotte . . ." He glanced up at her then, and his lips parted slightly. " . . . Smith?" The question in his tone was obvious, and in that moment in which he sat there, unmoving, staring at her, she saw the ice of his expressionless blue-green eyes melt and then freeze over again.

"Miss Smith. Do sit down." His eyes fell back to the papers, and he picked up his pen and dipped it into the ink.

She sat and primly folded her hands in her lap. Did he not recognize her after all? She felt relieved yet mildly hurt at the thought. Was she so changed in the years since they had last seen each other? He had changed but was clearly the man she had once known. His hair was a bit thinner at his forehead, the rust-brown stubble on his cheeks more noticeable, the shoulders broader, but his face was still as angular as ever. What had changed most were his eyes. Gone was that teasing spark she remembered so fondly, and all warmth with it, or so it seemed.

"Age . . . twenty?"

She found her voice. "Yes," she whispered.

"And this is your first pregnancy?"

She cringed with shame at the baldness of his words. "Yes."

"When was your last monthly flow?"

Never had a man broached such a topic with her! Never had a woman, for that matter. Such things were not spoken of. She was too stunned to speak.

At her obvious hesitancy, he rose to his feet, but his eyes seemed trained beyond her. "Look here, I heard your little conversation with Mrs. Moorling. If you'd rather wait and see Dr. Preston, that is perfectly all right by me. I shall tell Mrs. Moorling myself."

"No!" The urgency with which she spoke surprised them both, and he silently sat back down. Embarrassed by her outburst as well as the whole mortifying situation, Charlotte sat staring at her hands, yet felt the man's silent scrutiny.

She took a deep breath and whispered, "The second of January."

She heard the scratching of his quill.

"And Smith. That is your . . . married . . . name?"

She swallowed, completely humiliated. This man who, she believed, had once admired her was now—if he recognized her at all—thanking the Lord above that her father had so thoroughly discouraged him. And she couldn't blame him. "I am . . . not married."

Dr. Taylor hesitated, eyes on the paper, then put down his pen. He looked up at her, his professional facade gone, his expression earnest.

"Good heavens, Charlotte, what on earth are you doing here?"

Charlotte sighed. "I should think that painfully obvious."

He winced. "Forgive me. I only meant this is not a place for you, a girl with your family, your connections."

She opened her mouth, but the words "I no longer have either" wouldn't form over the hot coal lodged in her chest and the tears pooling in her eyes. She bit her lip to try to gain control over herself. She would not seek pity.

"As bad as all that, then?"

She bit her lip again but only nodded.

"I am very sorry to hear it. I suppose your father, being a clergyman, took it very hard."

Again, she nodded.

"Still, there's not a one of us who hasn't made some foul error or other. All like sheep astray and all that."

She could only look at him, speechless.

"I've had a taste of your father's rejection, if you remember. I mean no disrespect, but I cannot say I'd wish that on anyone, much less you."

She managed a slight smile through her tears.

"I don't wish to insult you, but I assume that every attempt has been made to garner some arrangement, some responsibility or recompense?"

"Please. There is nothing to be done, and even if there were, I should not like to pursue it."

"Still, there are legal actions in such cases, if the man—"

She shook her head.

"You claim no injury, then?"

She closed her eyes against the shame her answer brought with it. "I cannot."

"Still, though you be a party to it, there remain courses of action to secure your support."

"Please. I do not wish to speak of it further. You can be assured that my father and my uncle, a solicitor himself, have discussed these matters with me thoroughly. Exhaustively."

"I am sorry."

"Everyone has urged, even begged me to reveal the man so they might *work* on him."

"You have not told them who the man is?"

She shook her head.

"Why on earth not?"

"Because it will do me and my child absolutely no good . . . and it will harm others."

"A married man, then?"

She swallowed. "He is now."

"Miss Lamb. Charlotte. Have you considered—"

"Mr. Taylor, excuse me, *Dr.* Taylor, I have already told you far more than I should. More than I've told anyone else." She looked up at him, then back down at her hands. "You always did have that effect on me."

"Make you chatter on? I'd rather have had a different effect on young ladies in those days."

She smiled in spite of herself. "Then let us speak of it no more. Though I do appreciate your concern."

"Yes, well." He cleared his throat. "We have an examination to conduct."

"Yes," she murmured, feeling her heart begin pounding again.

"Well, first of all, I need to ask you a few questions about your medical history and the like."

"All right."

"If I remember correctly, you were a most healthy girl. Any medical problems since? Illnesses, serious injury?"

She shook her head.

"And, since your . . . condition. Any pain, light-headedness, swelling of extremities?"

She thought of her ankles, not as thin as they once were. "Nothing to speak of."

"You have been seen by another physician prior to coming here?"

"Only one time."

"Dr. Webb, was it?"

She shook her head again. "Father wouldn't hear of me seeing anyone local. He was sure word would get out. I saw a surgeon, a Mr. Thompkins, when I was in Hertfordshire with my aunt."

"And how long ago was this?"

"Three . . . nearly four months now. He was brought in only to confirm that I was indeed, well, as I am."

"Well, here we examine patients weekly once they're as far along as you are."

"I see."

"Now, I notice that you are showing surprisingly little for someone as progressed as you are."

"Which has been a blessing until now."

"Yes, I can understand that. But, have you had difficulty eating, keeping foods down?"

"I haven't much appetite lately, but I do try to eat."

"All right. Now I do need to do a physical exam. To start, I will auscultate you."

"Pardon me?"

"Sorry. Listen to your heart."

He tapped the tall table. "Please, have a seat here."

She complied and sat as straight as she could, rearranging her skirts around her, self-conscious of her bulging middle, her plain dress, her hair escaping its practical pinning. She had a sudden flash of memory, of peering through the keyhole as a young girl and seeing Dr. Webb lying over her mother's body, head on her chest. Charlotte had been quite shocked and had burst into the room, ready to defend her mother's honor.

"What are you doing?" she'd cried, her affront ringing in the room. Dr. Webb sat up quickly, stunned at her outburst. But mother only smiled gently. "It's all right, my dear. Dr. Webb is only listening to my heart, to see if the old thing is still working."

Understanding dawned on the man's kind face and he, too, smiled gently at her. "Come here, if you like, Charlotte. Would you like to listen to your mother's heart?"

She nodded, all seriousness, and walked to the bed. She sat beside Dr. Webb and laid her ear on her mother's bosom.

"A bit higher—there. Do you hear it?"

Charlotte had closed her eyes and listened, and there, a dull *ta-toom, ta-toom, ta-toom.* "I hear it!" she'd declared proudly, relieved in more ways than one.

As delightful as the memory was, when Charlotte imagined Dr. Taylor pressing his head to *her* chest, her palms began sweating.

From his case, he extracted a wooden tube, a device she had never seen before.

"A physician friend of my wife's made this. He's still working to perfect the design. Still, it's amazing how much better I can hear with this simple tube than I can with my ear alone."

He stepped closer and bent near. He looked into her face. "It also lends a bit of propriety, which patients seem to appreciate." He lifted one side of his mouth in an awkward grin, then bent to his task. Charlotte took a deep breath and held it, aware of his nearness, aware of the strangeness of the situation—to be alone with Daniel Taylor, unchaperoned, so close to him—all of which would be highly inappropriate in any other setting. She felt the tube press against her chest, just above her left breast, and she involuntarily started. The device was not terribly long, so he had to bring his head to within six or seven inches of her body to listen. She released a ragged breath and drew in a shallow one in return, finding it difficult to breathe.

"Fine. Now I will attempt to hear the heart of the fetus as well. Has the babe been active?"

"Yes, quite."

He pressed the tube with firm pressure against her abdomen and listened intently. He repositioned it slightly and listened again. "There he is." He listened a moment longer. "Strong and steady."

Charlotte smiled. "Do you call all unborn babes 'he'?"

"I don't know. Don't think so."

"I do think it is a boy. Just a feeling I have. I suppose all ladies in confinement say such things?"

"Yes, and they are often right."

"Are they?"

He grinned. "About half of the time." Then his grin faded. "Well, next I would normally palpate the"—he waved his hands over her abdomen—"uh . . . area. And examine . . . other areas as well." He swallowed, "However, I think, considering your general health and the quickening of the babe, that this has been sufficient for today." He stepped back, and Charlotte slumped a bit on the table, relieved.

A soft knock sounded at the door, and Dr. Taylor leapt eagerly to answer it. Charlotte couldn't see whom he spoke with through the partially opened door, but she could hear much of the muted conversation.

"You're wanted above stairs."

"Is there a problem?"

"I'm afraid . . . quite upset."

"I see. I shall be up directly."

He shut the door and looked back at Charlotte. "I'm wanted elsewhere, Miss Lamb—excuse me, Miss Smith."

Charlotte lowered herself from the table.

"Gibbs will alert you to our next appointment."

She nodded.

"Good day," he said, and turned to leave.

"Good day," she answered, but he was already gone.

4

> The poor collect milkweed down and with it fill their beds, especially their children's, instead of feathers.
>
> —Peter Kalm, 1772

Charlotte read the letter in the garden, which, mess though it was, offered her a bit of privacy—something sorely lacking within the manor itself. Gibbs had handed it to her with a simple, "Letter, miss." And while Charlotte should have been pleased to receive it, especially because the fine, feminine handwriting was clearly her aunt's, she trembled as she carefully peeled it open. Somehow she knew it bore ill tidings. What else could she expect at present? Surely her father hadn't forgiven her, asking through Aunt Tilney for Charlotte to come home. She knew this, and still her hands trembled as she read.

My dear niece,

It is with deep sadness that I write to you today. Your father has asked that I sever all connection with you, something I am loathe to do. You know I hold you in the highest esteem and dearest affection, positions unaffected by recent revelations. I hope you will in time learn to forgive your father. He has always held the good opinion of others too dearly, as you well know, and I fear this has laid him very low.

There is some small hope, I believe, that your sister may secure the affection of a certain gentleman, whom you well know, before news reaches the ears of those who would compel him to withdraw any connection with your family. Your sister, especially, longs to conceal the unhappy truth as long as possible.

It pains me to write so plainly, but there it is. Your father bids me to beseech you to confine yourself away from the public eye, and to conceal your identity until an engagement is secure. It is too much to hope this could extend past a longed-for wedding date, but all put every confidence that the gentleman's long association with your sister might withstand, nay, even overshadow, other less happy events.

Do not give up hope, my dear. There is goodness in your father, and I will fervently pray that he will soften toward you in time. For now, I have little choice but to abide his edict. Perhaps if your dear uncle stood with me, but alas, he feels it is not our place to come between father and child. You know he would do all he could to assist you were he only allowed to do so.

Still, I cannot rest without at least offering this olive branch. Likely you have been too upset to think too far into the future, but I am plagued with worry over your situation. I offer you this—while not grand nor fashionable, it will at least assure a roof and bed and food to eat once your time in London is at an end.

As you may recall, I have in Crawley an elderly aunt. You can well imagine how old she is if I, your aunt, describe her thusly. Still, she lives in a snug cottage a short distance from the village proper on Crawley's High Street. I have not seen her these many months, but at Michaelmas she was in good health and spirits. I have every confidence she would welcome you and that the two of you would get on well together. I daresay she would be quite happy for some companionship. Her own grown son lives in Manchester and, as I understand, rarely visits. I shall write her directly and introduce you.

If some impediment to this arrangement arises, I shall find some way to let you know. Otherwise, my dear, this must be my last letter, at least for the foreseeable future. My heart aches to think of it. Rest assured, you shall never be far from my thoughts or prayers.

Your Loving Aunt

Charlotte wiped at the tears with her free hand, then quickly refolded the letter and tucked it into her dress pocket. She strode back inside the manor and into the workroom, determinedly putting on a cheerful face.

"What is that you're working on, Becky?" she asked, sitting beside the young girl at a fabric-strewn table.

"'Tis a swaddling blanket, mum."

She eyed the square of coarse cotton. "How nice. Will you have it done in time, do you think?"

"Oh! 'Tisn't for my own babe. Least I don't think 'tis."

"Oh?"

"Same as your mending stockings for the girls here, I'm stitchin' blankets for the foundlings next door."

Charlotte looked in the direction of the girl's nod.

"You didn't know about the foundling ward?" Becky asked.

Charlotte shook her head. "I did wonder what was in the other wing."

"Sure and what did you think happened to all the babes born here?" Bess asked brusquely, coming to the table with a teacup in her hand.

"I don't know. I had not thought . . ."

"They just keep infants here 'til they're weaned," Becky explained. "Then they're moved to the big foundling hospital up on Guildford Street."

"Don't some girls take their infants home with them?"

"Is that what *you're* going to do?" Bess asked skeptically, sitting down across from her.

"No. Not home. I am not . . . quite sure where yet."

Two other girls walked to the table together, tall flaxen-haired Sally towering over petite auburn-haired Mae. They sat down on either side of Charlotte.

"Well, I know where I'll be," Becky said. "Back in the workhouse soon as my time's up."

"But . . . what about . . ."

Bess broke in, "Don't you be judging her or any of us."

"I did not mean to. I am only surprised."

"Some of us haven't any choice," Sally said quietly, eyes on her tea.

"But . . . to leave one's child in the care of strangers. It is something I could never do."

"Oh, don't be too sure," Bess said. "Never can tell what a body might do for love or money."

"Or to keep body and soul together," Mae added.

"My mum can barely feed my brothers and sisters," Becky said. "She sure don't need another mouth to feed."

"How old are you, Becky?" Charlotte asked.

"Fourteen."

"So young."

Becky shrugged. "About my mum's age when she had me."

"And you, Sally," Charlotte asked, "what will you do?"

"I already had me boy two months ago now. I'm a wet nurse in the foundling ward. Didn't you know?"

"No, I . . ."

"Guess I haven't me figure back if you thought me still in my lying-in! I best lay off those jam tarts."

Bess and Mae laughed.

"Forgive me, Sally."

"Never you mind, Miss Charlotte. I've been a big girl me whole life—I'm used to such."

"Your boy, is he . . . ?"

"I'm blessed to have a sister who looks after my wee lamb. I'm nursing here until I find a better post."

"A post?"

"Wet nurse, o' course. Pays good, sleepin' in the nice warm nursery of some fine house. Yes, that's the life for me."

"But who nurses your own child?"

"I told you. Me own sister. She's always breeding and has a little ankle-biter right now what's got her milk flowin' but good. 'Tis no bother to her to nurse another."

"You're lucky," Mae said. "My sister had to put her child out to take a wet nurse post. One of them baby farms, like, where the nurse had three or four others to feed. Poor thing near starved to death."

"Then why would she do it? Why leave her own child to nurse a stranger?"

"A bit daft this one," Bess murmured under her breath—but loud enough for all to hear.

"The *money*, dearie," Sally explained. "If she don't work, she starves—and her own child with her."

"I'm sorry. I suppose I have never known that depth of want. I could never do that, leave my own to nurse someone else's baby."

"Careful what you say, Charlotte," Sally warned gently. "I'll wager a year ago you never thought you'd find yourself in a place like this either."

"You are quite right."

"How . . . did . . . you end up here, Charlotte?"

"Same way as everyone else I suppose." But she could feel her face heat with a fierce blush.

"Somehow I doubt that," Mae said. "Who was the bloke? A baron, was it? Some scheming lord what promised you a wedding?"

"Maybe she fell in love with the footman and her father forbade them marry," Becky said wistfully.

"Girls, don't tease Charlotte so," Sally urged. "You can see plain as anything she's a lady."

Bess snorted. "*Was* a lady more like."

Sally put her hand over Charlotte's. "Don't listen to her, Charlotte. You're still a lady in my eyes. All your handsome words and polite ways . . ."

"Handsome words and polite ways won't get her very far 'round here," Mae said.

"Won't make a bit o' difference when her time comes neither. I can just hear her now." Bess began imitating an upper-crust accent. "I say, Dr. Preston, would you be so kind as to remove this melon from my middle?"

Mae joined in. "Pardon me, but the pain is such that I fear I must yell my fool head off."

The others laughed good-naturedly, and Charlotte couldn't take offense. She did continue to blush, however. And the first prickling of fear for the delivery itself began to work its way through her being.

Charlotte was just about to blow out the bedside candle that night when the sound of a scream snaked beneath the door. Beside her, Mae groaned and young Becky slept on. Pulling her dressing gown around herself, Charlotte arose and stepped tentatively out into the passageway, holding the candle before her. She paused, listening. The draft in the old manor led the flame in an erratic, swaying dance. She heard no more screams, but she did hear footsteps approaching. She hesitated. Should she duck back into her room? How foolish! She was doing nothing wrong. No doubt some girl was in the pains of labour somewhere in the manor. Dr. Taylor appeared at the end of the passage his face drawn, rust-stubbled and weary.

"Is everything all right?" she asked.

"Miss Lamb. You startled me."

"Forgive me. . . . I thought I heard someone crying out."

"Did you?"

"Yes. Is someone delivering?"

"Um . . . no. False alarm as it turns out."

"Oh, I see. Are you quite all right, Mr.—excuse me—*Dr.* Taylor. I'm afraid that will take some getting used to."

"That's all right. And . . . yes, I am well, thank you. And you?"

She nodded. "Are you always here this late?"

"Yes. Though not always awake, thankfully. I keep a small apartment above stairs here. Makes night duty less interminable."

"You are very dedicated."

He looked at her sharply, as though weighing the sincerity of her statement.

"Truly." She smiled to reassure him. "It is a comfort to know there's a physician about the place."

He smiled then too. "Even if the physician is me?"

"Yes. I have heard some things about the other man that are not comforting in the least." She said it lightly but saw his eyes widen and his mouth set in a hard line.

"What are you implying? Wait. Let us step into Mrs. Moorling's office, where we won't disturb anyone."

"Very well." She followed him to the matron's office beyond the workroom.

"You were saying?" he prompted.

"Well, from the sound of it, the girls here do not trust him, in fact they are quite frightened of him."

"Frightened? That is absurd. He isn't perfect, I realize, but is certainly not as bad as all that."

"I'm sorry, I am only repeating what I've been told."

"Well, in the future I suggest you don't besmirch a man's reputation based on rumor alone."

She looked at him, stung. His reaction seemed too strong, and she wondered if there was more at play here than collegial loyalty. "You are quite right. But I had no reason not to believe them. In fact, I saw one young girl shaking when she took leave of Dr. Preston."

"Preston?" he asked, clearly surprised.

"Yes." *Who did he think I was referring to?*

He hesitated, seeming to study his shoes.

Charlotte felt compelled to continue. "Forgive me—are the two of you friends?"

"Colleagues certainly. Are you implying that he behaves . . . inappropriately with his patients?"

"Yes, or at the very least humiliates them."

"Well, humiliation is no crime. It's difficult to maintain modesty in such situations. As far as the other . . . well, I'd wager it's just gossip, but if you personally have any difficulty whatsoever with Dr. Preston, please let me know immediately."

"Thank you. I shall."

The tension in his face faded, and they stood there for a moment in mildly awkward silence, Charlotte trying to think of a way to excuse herself, when she saw the side of his mouth lift in a boyish smirk.

"And what do they say about *me*?"

She smiled at him, then said imperiously, "Oh, you are the worst of the lot. Ice, they say. Distant. Impersonal. One girl compared your bedside manner to that of a man gutting fish."

His brows rose. "Dreadfully sorry I asked."

She regarded him a moment, then said tentatively, "You do seem changed. Though I suppose that is only natural after so many years."

His expression became somber indeed. "If you had seen the things I have—death, piteous creatures, loved ones lost . . ." He hesitated, seemingly adrift in thoughts too bleak to share. She guessed he was speaking of more than his medical duties alone, of losses infinitely more personal.

"Yes," he continued, "perhaps I have distanced myself. Become harder."

"Colder," she added helpfully. "More aloof."

"There are worse things." He looked directly at her, and Charlotte ducked her head.

"Miss Lamb, I did not mean . . . I was not referring to you, to your condition."

And there he was again. The Mr. Taylor of old, teasing but reassuring, comforting her.

Charlotte kept her eyes lowered. "I confess when I first saw you here, I was quite mortified."

"I can imagine."

"I think now the worst of the shock has passed, I shall be glad to have a friendly face about."

"A cold face, you mean."

"One that improves upon acquaintance. Or in our case, reacquaintance."

"I am glad to hear it."

Charlotte suddenly had the disquieting thought that he might think her forward, so she asked, "Might I have the privilege of meeting Mrs. Taylor sometime?"

"Well, I . . . I don't think . . ."

"Of course. Forgive me. I am in no position to be introduced to anyone. How foolish of me."

"Miss Lamb, I—"

"It is Miss Smith for now. Good night, Dr. Taylor."

She left the office and walked quickly down the passageway, embarrassment burning at her ears. *Stupid girl,* she remonstrated herself. She imagined Dr. Taylor saying to his wife, *My dear, please meet the ruined Miss Charlotte Lamb. Can you believe I once admired her?*

5

> If the milk of a wet nurse could give a child a loud laugh or a secretive disposition, what kind of influence would be derived from the milk of a goat or a cow?
>
> —Janet Golden, *A Social History of Wet Nursing in America*

The next few weeks passed slowly and Charlotte grew weary of stitching. She stood before the matron's desk, feeling like a wayward schoolgirl.

"Mrs. Moorling. I wonder," she began, "might I help in the foundling ward?"

The matron's eyes narrowed with near suspicion. "Why?"

"Well, I . . . I am sure sewing is no doubt beneficial. It is only that I thought . . . well, with my own child on the way, some experience with infants might do me good."

Still the woman stared at her.

"I might enjoy it, actually."

Mrs. Moorling shook her head, an odd bleakness in her eyes. "I would not plan on it."

"Then I may not—?"

"You may. I only meant that you should not plan to enjoy it. You really are naïve, aren't you?"

"I suppose so. Still I see no harm. . . ."

"Go on with you, then. Use the entrance through the scullery. Be sure the door latches behind you."

"But what shall I do once I get there?"

"Just ask for Mrs. Krebs. She oversees the foundlings and is always in need of another pair of arms."

Charlotte thanked the matron, then walked through the dining room and down the scullery passage. The large white door with an old-fashioned swing bolt stood at attention, its X-shaped cross boards reminding Charlotte of a guard with his arms crossed, barring the way. She swallowed back the silly notion and reached for the bolt, only to have the door swing open in her face. Charlotte stepped back quickly as Sally and another girl came through the door, Sally balancing a tray of used plates and teacups in her hands.

"Oh, Miss Charlotte! Sorry, love, nearly ran you down."

"Hello, Sally." Charlotte looked up at her. She had never known such a tall woman.

"You're not thinking of goin' in, are you?"

"Yes. I was."

"Well, I suppose Mrs. Krebs might need some mending done, or some cleaning."

"Could I not help with the children? I have never been around babies and I should like to learn."

Sally stood silently a moment, studying Charlotte seriously. Then swiftly, she swiveled and placed the tea tray in the other girl's hands. "Take this into the kitchen for me, Martha. There's a love."

The girl disappeared and Sally was still staring down at Charlotte, her frequent smile noticeably absent.

"If you're set on it, I had better go in with you."

"All right . . . thank you," Charlotte murmured, but she was confused.

Sally took Charlotte by the arm and led her through the doorway, latching the door firmly behind her. Then she escorted Charlotte down a whitewashed passage, through a small galley, and into an entry hall.

"This is where the babies first come in. Admitted, they calls it." She pointed to an odd revolving shelf built into the outer wall. "See that turn there?"

"Yes. It looks like one we had at home between the galley and kitchen. The servants used it to pass through dirty dishes."

"'Tisn't dirty dishes passing through there. 'Tis babies what no one wants. This way the poor mother don't even need to show her face. She puts her baby on the shelf and rings the bell. Then Mrs. Krebs turns the shelf and the baby comes inside."

"Poor things."

"Yes. 'Tis a desperate girl who abandons her baby."

Charlotte had meant the babies left behind were the "poor things," but she didn't argue.

"Sometimes mothers what's starving leave their babies in the turn, then come to the front door soon after, asking for work as a wet nurse, hoping to feed their own babe and get food and some small pay in the bargain."

"But why would they do that?"

"'Cause they's starvin' or have no place to live, no money, no job. How can they work with a newborn to feed every few hours?"

"Oh."

"Come on."

They walked down the long passageway, past a dim room on the left filled with cribs and another room filled with rocking chairs. On nearly every one sat a woman nursing an infant, sometimes two babes at once. Charlotte had never seen a woman do such a thing, and though most were fairly well covered with blanket or babe, Charlotte felt her cheeks redden at the intimate sight.

"And see them doors on the other side of the passage? That's where we nurses take turns sleepin'."

"Sally! Good, you're back. I need your help." An older woman in her late fifties stepped forward, her ash-grey hair in a loose knot at the back of her neck and a large stained apron over her ample figure in a simple black dress.

"Mrs. Krebs, this is Miss Charlotte Smith."

"How do you do, Mrs. Krebs." Charlotte stepped forward, offering her hand. "I would like to help too, if I might."

Glancing back down the passage, the woman didn't seem to notice her hand. "Well, you're just in time to help with the goats."

"Goats?"

"Yes, yes, follow me."

Charlotte looked at Sally, who sighed and nodded and followed Mrs. Krebs, who was already marching purposefully toward the end of the passageway.

"You were brought up on a farm, weren't you, Sally?" Mrs. Krebs asked over her shoulder.

"Aye."

"And you, Miss Smith?"

"No, I'm afraid not."

"No matter, a pair of willing hands is always welcome." She stopped at a small table beside a closed door. "But do put on these masks and gloves. Dr. Taylor's orders."

Sally began pulling tight leather gloves onto her long fingers and explained, "This is the syphilis ward, Miss Charlotte. All these babies have syphilis and must be kept away from the rest."

Mrs. Krebs handed Charlotte another pair of gloves and began tying a cotton mask over her own nose and mouth.

Charlotte hesitated.

"Is it safe? For my own baby, I mean."

"Dr. Taylor assures me the nasty business is only transmitted by direct contact with the sores," Mrs. Krebs said. "'Course these poor lambs caught it from their own mothers afore they was even born."

Mrs. Krebs pushed open the door and walked in. Sally and Charlotte paused at the threshold, taking in the scene.

Cribs filled the room and cries filled the air. In one corner, a nun was standing hunched over a crib, trying to get an infant to suckle from some sort of tube. Dr. Taylor stood beside her, arms behind his back, quietly instructing the woman. He looked up when the door opened. His eyes narrowed for a moment when they lit on her.

A knock came on a wide, stable-like door on the other side of the room.

"That's Rob now, I wager."

Old Mrs. Krebs strode with impressively youthful vigor past the cribs with their pitiful infants. She opened the door and a young man came in with two goats, one black and one white, at his heels.

"What are they doing with the goats?" Charlotte whispered.

"You'll see," Sally said and stepped into the room.

Charlotte, still concerned, stood in the doorway and watched a sight she would never forget. The goats pranced with seeming eagerness into the room, bleating as they came. The black one trotted down one row of beds, the white down the other. Suddenly, the white goat jumped nimbly up on top of the first cot and gingerly straddled the infant. Charlotte gasped. Sally stepped forward and helped lift and position the waiting infant onto the goat's teat. The hungry babe latched on and began nursing. Charlotte was stunned, horrified, yet fascinated at the same time. She stepped forward tentatively and stood behind Sally, peering over her bent back.

"Why in the world . . . ?" Charlotte began.

"No one will nurse these poor souls. The syphilis is catching that way. They try to feed the babes by hand, but it ain't natural like. This ain't either, but it seems to work a bit better."

Mrs. Krebs, who was helping another swaddled infant suckle the black goat, said from her position a few strides away, "I was as stunned as you no doubt are, Miss Smith, when Dr. Taylor first suggested it. Thought he was off his bean. Said the Frenchies do it all the time and it might be worth a go here as well."

As Charlotte watched, the white goat jumped down and moved to a cot at the end of the row and eagerly hopped up again. Sally followed, again helping the waiting babe reach the goat's teat with her gloved hands.

Dr. Taylor came to stand next to Charlotte. "It's as if the goats actually know and remember which babes are hers to nurse. The white one always feeds these and the black the others. Even if we put the babe in a different crib, the goat finds her own to feed."

"Amazing."

"It is, isn't it? Still, it's a pity. Most of these children have little hope of seeing the month through."

"Really?" Charlotte felt herself take a step back even before she realized what she was doing.

"It's a sad business. But we try."

Charlotte's cheery visions of singing lullabies to healthy pink babies seemed foolish now. She felt as though she might be ill.

"Can nothing be done?" she asked.

"Well. Pray, of course. And thank God for goats."

6

> The [milkweed] root, which is the only part used, is a counter-poison, both against the bad effects of poisonous herbs and the bites and stings of venomous creatures.
>
> —Nicholas Culpepper, 17th century herbalist

A few hours later, Daniel was standing in the manor hall directing the flow of volunteers bearing crates and bundles of donated supplies. He looked up and saw Charlotte walking toward him, coming from the direction of the foundling ward. He immediately stepped forward, hoping to shield her from view.

"Miss Smith," he said, keeping his voice low, "might I suggest a sojourn in the back garden? A horde of ladies-aid types are swarming about the place, and I understand several are from Kent."

Her eyes widened as she glanced at the hall beyond him, expression sober. "Thank you, I shall."

She turned at once and quickly retreated the way she had come. But not quite quickly enough.

Daniel turned and nearly collided with a thin-faced socialite in burgundy velvet and plumed hat.

"That woman you were just speaking with—that was Charlotte Lamb, was it not?" She craned her neck to see past him.

"Lamb? I do not believe we have anyone here by that name."

"Yes, yes, that was Charlotte. I am sure of it."

He shrugged. "There are so many here today, with your group, as well as our staff and volunteers . . ."

"But you were just speaking with her."

"Was I? I believe the last lady I spoke with was a volunteer, donating blankets. She is not with you?"

"No."

"Well, we are blessed to have so many generous souls such as yourselves come to visit. I cannot keep track."

She opened her mouth to speak again, her expression clearly skeptical. But instead of questioning him further, her mouth curved in a feline smile. "I know what I saw. Or shall we say, *whom*." She turned on her heel and swept across the hall.

Charlotte walked through the manor's garden, breathing in the outdoor air, forcing away the images she had seen in the syphilis ward. Reaching into her dress pocket, she ran her fingers over the letter from her aunt, which she carried with her as a comfort, a sort of lifeline. She knew whom her aunt was referring to in her veiled reference to Bea's "gentleman" suitor.

Charlotte remembered well the first time she had met William Bentley. That is, the first time in many years. She had seen him on several occasions when they were young children, but not for a number of years since, when he unexpectedly appeared at their drawing room door three or four years ago.

"Mr. William Bentley," Tibbets had announced and then backed from the room, pulling the doors closed as she went.

The young man who stood before them was slight and not much taller than the maid who had shown him in. He was about eighteen, Charlotte estimated, a year above her own age at the time, though he bore the confidence of someone far older.

"How do you do?" he asked, hat in hand. Tibbets had forgotten to take it.

Charlotte glanced at Bea, saw from the frown line between her brows that she had no idea who the young man was. Charlotte glanced next at her father, whose place it was to greet the man and make introductions, but he wore an expression that would have been comically similar to his daughter's, were not the situation so awkward.

"Bentley . . . Bentley . . ." he began, obviously trying to place the mildly familiar name.

"You remember, Father," Charlotte offered. "Mr. Bentley is nephew to Mr. Harris."

"Is he now? Oh, yes, I think I remember hearing something of a nephew. Let's see, Harris has an older brother . . ."

"Sister, actually, Father. Mrs. Eliza Bentley. Of Oxford."

"That's right, thank you." The young man smiled at Charlotte. "You seem to know the family quite well, Miss—?"

"Charlotte Lamb."

"Of course." He nodded, his eyes widened in a knowing expression that left her feeling unsettled.

Her father stood at that moment, casting a disapproving glance at her. "I am the Reverend Mr. Gareth Lamb, Vicar of the Parish Church of Doddington, Dedicated to the Beheading of St. John the Baptist."

Mr. Bentley's eyebrows rose. "How unusual." A hint of a smile lifted the corner of his mouth, but her father did not seem to notice.

"Yes, it is. One of the rarest dedications in England, shared only with the Church of Trimmingham in Norfolk."

"Ahh . . ." Mr. Bentley uttered the universal sound of the duly impressed. When her father's grave expression remained fixed, Mr. Bentley continued, "I am very pleased to make your acquaintance. My uncle speaks highly of you, sir."

"As I do of him. And may I present my elder daughter, Miss Lamb."

Beatrice merely dipped her head.

"And Charlotte has already introduced herself," her father added as he reclaimed his seat. He tossed a sour smile toward Charlotte but did not quite look at her. "Do sit down, Mr. Bentley."

"I thank you."

"Of Oxford, sir?" her father asked. "The university or environs?"

"Both, of late."

"You must know my friend Lord Elton, then. He is quite the patron of Pembroke."

Charlotte winced at her father's boast. Lord Elton was Uncle Tilney's friend, not his.

"Who has not heard of him? His son is also quite well-known. I have not had the pleasure of meeting either man, I'm afraid. My studies keep me quite occupied."

"Excellent. And what will you take up?"

He hesitated, then oddly looked at Charlotte, then Beatrice. "I have yet to make up my mind, sir."

"The church is as noble a profession as you might aspire to, sir, if you have a taste for servitude and humility."

William Bentley smiled, clearly amused, then straightened his expression into sobriety. "I'm afraid I haven't your fortitude, good sir. Nor your modesty."

"Well, you are yet young." Her father sighed. "I'm afraid the church calls to me even now." He pushed himself cumbrously to his feet. "I'm to meet the churchwardens to discuss repairs to the south chapel and nave. If you will excuse me."

Mr. Bentley rose.

"No need to get up on my account. Do stay and have your visit with the ladies. Beatrice, perhaps you could play something for Mr. Bentley?"

"It seems a bit early in the day . . ."

"Oh, would you, Miss Lamb? I'd be delighted to hear it."

Bea looked at Mr. Bentley as if gauging his sincerity. "Very well."

Their father left and Bea walked slowly across the room and sat at the pianoforte. She flipped through some pages of music on its ledge and began playing a moody piece, the somber tone darkening her already stern countenance. Then, seeming to remember her guest, she stopped.

"Forgive me, that's not quite fitting."

"Quite powerful though," Mr. Bentley said, his eyes full of admiration.

Tibbets knocked once and entered. "Begging your pardon, Miss Charlotte, but Digger says it's time."

Charlotte rose, but Bea answered for her. "Tibbets, we have a guest, as you know. Tell him to wait."

"Actually, I will go," Charlotte said gently. "Thank you, Tibbets. Tell young Higgins I shall be out directly."

"Very good, miss."

Bea shook her head in disapproval. She spoke to Mr. Bentley but her gaze remained narrowed on her sister. "Charlotte seems to love nothing better than playing with dirt and plants all day. She spends more time out of doors than in."

"Your grounds here are lovely," Mr. Bentley allowed. "But why go out of doors when there is so much beauty to appreciate within?" He smiled significantly at Bea.

Charlotte bit back a wry smile of her own. "I am sorry, Bea, but I did ask Ben Higgins to fetch me just as soon as the tree arrived for the churchyard. Forgive me, Mr. Bentley. You must think us terribly rude, first Father rushing off, and now me."

"Think nothing of it, Miss Charlotte. My visit was unplanned, after all."

"Thank you. Perhaps you might come again. Are you staying with your uncle long?"

"I'm not sure. A few days at least."

"Then please do call again." It wasn't Charlotte's place to invite him, she knew, and she could feel Bea's silent censure from across the room.

But the young man smiled brightly. "Thank you. I shall."

He bowed to Charlotte and she smiled at him. Bea glared at her over the man's bent head. Charlotte simply shrugged, then left the room.

Charlotte sat down in the entry hall, on the bench between the drawing room and the outside door. She leaned down to remove her slippers and begin the arduous task of fastening all the buttons on her calfskin gardening boots. From the nearby drawing room doors, she heard Bea run her fingers experimentally over a few keys.

"Please excuse my sister, Mr. Bentley," Bea said. "I don't know what she could be thinking, leaving on account of a tree."

Charlotte started. She had not realized she would be able to hear their conversation from here. Evidently Bea did not realize it either.

"What is so important about this tree?" Mr. Bentley asked.

"Oh, some tree she wants to plant by our mother's grave."

"That is very sentimental of her."

"I suppose." Bea began playing a cheerful quadrille.

William Bentley spoke more loudly to be heard over the music. "You know, my uncle has often described what a lovely girl Miss Charlotte Lamb has become. So, when I first entered the room, I thought you must be she."

A sour note, a half step off-key, reverberated through the doors as Bea abruptly stopped playing. "Mr. Harris finds Charlotte . . . lovely?"

In the hall, Charlotte froze mid-button.

"I suppose that's what he meant, a lovely girl, a lovely young girl. But you, Miss Lamb, are a beautiful woman."

Charlotte expelled the breath she'd been holding. She could imagine Bea's reaction, the red-cheeked pleasure that must be coloring her face.

"I believe Uncle is quite fond of your sister," Mr. Bentley continued, "though it must be tedious for a man of his age to always be warding off the infatuation of one so young."

Humiliation filled Charlotte, and she quickly pulled on her other boot without bothering to finish buttoning the first.

"Did he say that?" Bea sounded as appalled as Charlotte felt.

"No, no, heavens no. I am only reading between the worry lines as it were. Fret not, beautiful Beatrice, Uncle holds you all in great affection."

Charlotte did not wait to hear more. She made her way quietly out of the vicarage and strode across the narrow lane to the churchyard. Ben Higgins, a lad of fifteen who assisted his father with grave digging and upkeep of the church, was waiting for her. He had already maneuvered the young tree, its roots bound in a ball of dirt, to a spot near her mother's grave. Charlotte picked up a shovel and thrust it into the ground with more vehemence than necessary.

A few minutes later, William Bentley came walking across the churchyard. "Your workman desert you, Miss Lamb?" he called.

Charlotte looked up at him from the hole she was digging. She paused in her work, leaning on the shovel with one hand and pushing a stray hair from her face with the other, though she did not realize until later that her muddy glove had left a smear of dirt on her forehead. Nor why Mr. Bentley had bit back a smile as he drew near.

"I sent him to ask our gardener for some manure. He shall return directly."

"Manure? Lovely. You could wait and let him do that, you know."

"I do not mind a bit of work. Do you?"

"I confess I am not really the digging-in-the-dirt type."

She grinned. "I cannot say I'm surprised."

"Really?"

At his feigned chagrin, she felt her smile widen.

His eyes danced with pleasure. "You do indeed have a lovely smile, Miss Lamb."

"Thank you."

He nodded toward the sapling resting beside the hole. "What sort of tree is that?"

"A French lilac. *Syringa vulgaris*."

"Looks like a stick to me."

"I suppose it does. But in a year or two, it will boast the most fragrant lilac blossoms."

"Your mother. She's been gone—?"

"Two years." She felt her smile fade.

"Forgive me. I'm sorry."

"That is all right." She sighed. "I went traveling with my aunt in the spring, as I often do. Our carriage passed a long stand of lilacs in full bloom, and I remembered how much Mother loved their fragrance. But this variety doesn't spread like the more common English lilacs. I ordered this all the way from Limoges."

"That's a very dear gesture."

Charlotte shrugged. "She was very dear to me."

Resuming her work, her shovel clanged against something solid, and Charlotte bent low to pick a large stone out of the hole. As she did, she had the discomfiting realization that William Bentley enjoyed a lingering look down the bodice of her dress.

"Mr. Harris speaks very highly of you, Miss Lamb. I know I said the same of your father, but in all truth I think my uncle holds you in the highest regard of all."

"I'm sure you are mistaken," Charlotte replied, straightening. "Mr. Harris has long been a friend to our entire family. Even Mother was fond of him."

"And you, I think, are not indifferent to him either."

Remembering what Mr. Bentley had said to Bea, Charlotte could not hide her embarrassment. "Of course not. Mr. Harris has always been very kind, the best of neighbors, almost like a son to Father."

"A son? I shouldn't think so. That would make you brother and sister, and I don't think either of you should like that."

"Mr. Bentley, please don't speak so. It isn't fitting."

He appeared genuinely chastised. "You are quite right, Miss Lamb. Forgive me."

"If you are implying what I think you are, you are quite mistaken."

"Am I? Then I confess myself relieved."

"Relieved? Why so?"

"Well, it is just that I should be disappointed were you already spoken for."

"I am not spoken for, Mr. Bentley. I am only seventeen."

"Seventeen. And my uncle is, what? Five and thirty?"

"Not so old as that, I don't think."

He studied her face, and her discomfort grew under his close scrutiny.

"In any case," she hurried on, "I've no thought of marriage. My sister is two years older and has no thought of it either."

William looked up at the vicarage window and Charlotte followed his gaze. She saw Beatrice standing there frowning down at them. When she saw them look up, she spun away.

"I wouldn't be too sure of that, Charlotte," Mr. Bentley said, then lowered his eyes back to her. "May I call you Charlotte?"

"Yes, please do."

"And you must call me Mr. Bentley."

She looked at him dumbly, taken aback.

He smiled, reached out, and rubbed an immaculate gloved finger across her forehead. She allowed him to do so, standing like a submissive schoolgirl. Then he showed her the dirt-stained glove. "Dirt doesn't suit you, Charlotte. You should remain unsullied by the earth you love."

In the manor garden, Charlotte stooped awkwardly over her rounded middle to pick up a stone. She wondered briefly where William Bentley was now and if he truly planned to marry her sister. Had his intentions ever been honorable? Rising gingerly, she hurled the stone into the mossy pond, where it landed with a dull plop.

Unsullied indeed.

That very afternoon, Charles Harris rode his horse from his estate toward the Doddington vicarage.

A young lad herded a dozen sheep across the pasture path, so he had to slow his horse to allow them to pass. The boy tipped his hat to him, but Charles Harris only gave a terse nod in return. In no mood to be hindered, Charles pulled the reins up short and urged his horse up the embankment and around the walled churchyard. He was irritated to see his nephew's grey gelding in front of the vicarage, old Buxley attempting to hold the jittery horse by its bridle. *What is that boy up to now?*

Here William came in his green coat and cravat and fine hat, his smile decidedly self-satisfied.

"Hello, Uncle. Sorry I cannot stay and chat. Pressing business calls."

The young man was a dandy and a conniver. Charles should have discouraged his visits to the vicarage, but it was too late now.

Astride the horse now, William turned in the saddle and said with seeming innocence, "Miss Charlotte seems to have disappeared utterly. You haven't any idea what that's about, do you?"

Charles stared, dumbfounded at the boy's insolence. He opened his mouth to fashion some feeble reply, but the young man was already spurring his mount down the lane.

Buxley took his horse with a "Good day to you, Mr. Harris." Charles entered the vicarage and Tibbets took his hat and showed him into the drawing room. Gareth Lamb sat on one of the satin settees, staring off into space while his elder daughter, Beatrice, picked at tinny melodies on the pianoforte.

"There you are, Charles," the vicar greeted him gloomily. "We despaired of ever seeing you again."

"Yes . . . Katherine prefers town to country living, I'm afraid. I've just come round to check on the place and visit my mother and all of you."

"Do come and sit down."

But Charles hesitated, looking around the room for some clue that what he had heard was true. Beatrice looked up at him with a brief nod.

"Good day, Beatrice."

"Mr. Harris." She played on, seemingly unconcerned with or unaware of his agitated state or her father's pale stupor.

"And . . . where is Charlotte this fine day?" He attempted a weak smile.

"Who?" Mr. Lamb asked, his expression blank.

"What do you mean, who? Your younger daughter, of course."

"I have only one daughter, and here she sits." The Reverend Mr. Lamb waved vaguely in Bea's direction.

"I am speaking of Charlotte."

"She is lost to me. It pains me to speak of it."

"I beg you forgive me. But if you could only speak a bit more and tell me where she has gone . . . I only want to help."

"I know not."

"You . . . *don't know* where Charlotte is?" he asked in disbelief.

A discordant clang shuddered through the pianoforte, and Bea glared at him over the fading notes. "We do not wish to speak of it, Mr. Harris. I believe Father made that quite clear. And pray do us the kindness of not speaking of her to others either. Charlotte is off"—she waved her hand with dramatic flair—"visiting friends. Gone to Brighton, I believe. Or was it Bath? In any case, we don't expect her anytime soon." She began playing again.

"That young man who was just here," Gareth began, frowning. "I know he is your nephew, but I have to say, I do not trust him."

"Father!" Bea exclaimed.

"I am sorry, my dear, but I cannot help but think he had something to do with the whole infernal affair."

Bea stood quickly. "Mr. Bentley is a perfectly amiable gentleman, and I will not sit by and hear him maligned in my presence." She flounced out of the room, and Charles was relieved to see her go.

"She's pinned her hopes on him." Mr. Lamb shook his head, his eyes still on the open door though Bea was no longer visible. "I know I should encourage it, but something does not sit right with me. You do not think Bentley had anything to do with . . . Charlotte's leaving?"

"I . . . I shouldn't think so. Did you ask him?"

"Not in so many words, but yes, I did inquire of his dealings with her."

"And how did he respond?"

"Perhaps I had better not repeat it. . . ."

"I insist. What did he say?"

"It shames me to speak of it." Still, the older man went on. "He said he was not altogether surprised at Charlotte's 'troubles,' that he saw her being very familiar with more than one man on several occasions."

"He said that?"

"Well, you know how he talks, all hints and innuendo and you didn't hear it from me."

"Insolent fool!"

"You do not think it the truth? The evidence certainly bears him out."

"I am afraid my nephew has motives of his own that no doubt colored his report."

"Have you never seen her cavorting with men?"

Charles hesitated, and the old man set his face bitterly.

"No, my friend," Charles hurried on. "You mustn't think the worst of Charlotte. I have never seen her act in any untoward manner with anyone."

"Then who was it, man? Have you any idea?"

Charles sighed and shook his head. "I am so sorry. If there was anything I could do, I would do it. You know I would."

"Of course, of course. You have your own future to think of. You don't suppose there is any hope of convincing young Bentley to redirect . . ."

"I am afraid not. Not any longer. Has he . . . made any offer that you know of?"

"No. Though Beatrice seems nearly to be holding her breath in hopes of one."

7

The name of the Milkweed, *Asclepias*, comes from the Greek god Aeskulap, the god of healing.

—Flower Essence Society

Through a grated window in the foundling ward door, Daniel Taylor watched Miss Lamb. She was standing alone in the tangled garden behind the manor, and he couldn't help but remember her in a garden far more grand. She had often been there when he'd come with Dr. Webb to call on her mother.

He had spent a few years in Doddington as an apprentice to Dr. Webb before he'd gone off to the University of Edinburgh to complete his studies. He'd enjoyed his time in Kent and had a great deal of respect for Dr. Webb, who seemed never to tire of visiting patients, consoling families, and doling out physic and other remedies as needed.

Mrs. Lillian Lamb was one of the patients he visited most frequently. In truth there seemed little the good man could do for her, though Webb never said as much. Mrs. Lamb was a lovely, serene woman who seemed more concerned with making them welcome and comfortable than with her own prognosis. It was the Reverend Mr. Lamb who insisted on such regular visits. He seemed quite convinced his wife would "be her bonny old self one day soon, now that you're here." Daniel had both admired and feared his optimism.

As was often the case with female patients, Dr. Webb shooed his apprentice from the room soon after the preliminary pleasantries were dispatched and the physical examination commenced. Dismissed and with nothing to occupy him, Daniel would poke through the many books in the vicarage library or wander through the modest grounds or even into the more sprawling expanse of the great estate abutting the churchyard. Fawnwell, he believed the estate was called. But for its more modest size, the Lambs' garden was among the finest he'd seen, and he knew from his pleasantries with Mrs. Lamb that gardening was her dearest pastime. Evidently her younger daughter shared this enthusiasm.

On one of these occasions Charlotte, who must have been fourteen or fifteen at the time, hailed him from where she stood in the garden. Dropping the shears into her basket, she ran toward him, hand atop her bonnet to keep it in place.

"Mr. Taylor," she panted, out of breath, "there you are. And how fares my mother today?"

"Better, I think. And you? I trust you are well?"

"Yes, very, I thank you." Charlotte searched the lawn behind him. "And where is Dr. Webb?"

"Still in with your mother."

"I see." Though from her wrinkled brow it was clear she did not. "Then why are you not with him?"

"It seems Dr. Webb feels that it would be more discreet, more comfortable for your mother, were I absent."

"I am sure Mother said no such thing."

"Of course not. It is assumed, I suppose. I gather the examination was of a delicate nature."

"Delicate?"

Daniel had felt the blood heat his cheeks and silently cursed his tendency to blush.

"Your mother's ailment is of a . . . feminine nature, and being a man . . ."

"Dr. Webb is a man."

"Yes, but I am young."

"Not so young. I understand his last apprentice was much younger."

"Be that as it may, I must bow to Dr. Webb's greater experience."

"But however are you to gain such experience wandering about my mother's garden?"

"An excellent question, Miss Lamb. Most perceptive."

"I can only hope Dr. Webb is not away should I need a physician."

"Yes, well . . ."

"Forgive me. I meant no offense."

"Of course. I understand."

Daniel smiled grimly at the memory. Indeed, Charlotte would soon need a physician and Dr. Webb was nowhere near. He pushed through the foundling ward door and walked out into the garden, in time to see Charlotte bend over and begin pulling on a milkweed with great effort.

"Careful there, Miss Lamb. Do not overtax yourself."

"Dr. Taylor, do please try to remember to call me Miss Smith."

"I shall try, but we are alone here, so I thought it would be all right. May I ask what you are doing?"

"This garden is overrun with milkweeds, as you can well see. I understand gardening is not a priority in such a place, but—"

"You are quite mistaken, Miss Lamb. This garden is one of my priorities indeed."

"There is little evidence of that."

"Ahh . . . that is only because you are looking at it with the wrong eyes."

"Wrong eyes?"

"Yes, the eyes of a formal English gardener who adores box hedges and lilies and other lovely useless things."

She opened her mouth, but he lifted a hand to ward off her rebuttal.

"Wait until you have heard me out. What do you know of milkweeds, Miss Lamb?"

"I read an article about them in one of Mother's journals. It said French people actually plant them in their gardens. But I think most people do their best to eradicate them."

"Yes, you look here and see a patch of pestiferous weeds—is that right?"

"Of course."

"Yet I look here and see a plethora of elixirs and natural healing compounds that aid my work and soothe my patients."

"Really?" Charlotte looked back at the milkweeds with skepticism.

"Really. The down of the seed can be used to dress wounds, and the milky sap creates an instant bandage that can be applied to various skin eruptions. A good root tea serves as a diuretic, expectorant, and a treatment for any number of medical conditions—including respiratory ailments, joint pain, and digestive problems. It serves as an invigorating tonic and helps with stomach problems, headaches, uterine pains, influenza, typhoid fever, and inflammation of the lungs. The sap can even heal warts with topical application."

"You have memorized that entire list?"

He smiled. "You are not the first to question my garden."

"I would imagine not." She smiled back at him.

"Come, I will show you how to harvest the root."

They had dug up only one plant, Dr. Taylor on his haunches to show her where to sever root from stalk, when Sally bolted out the foundling ward door waving her arms.

"Dr. Taylor, do come quick!"

Charlotte noticed he did not question Sally. The urgency in her tone was enough for him to leap to his feet and run toward her. Charlotte followed, though more slowly, the uprooted plant hanging limply in her hand.

Once inside, she heard a woman crying out and shrieking, and old Mrs. Krebs giving orders in her lower-pitched tones.

"What's happened?" Charlotte asked a white-faced Sally.

"Her baby's died."

"Oh no."

They tiptoed forward and saw Mrs. Krebs trying to console a distraught young woman Charlotte had never seen before.

"Who is she?"

"She came to the door last night, asking to be a nurse," Sally began earnestly. "But both Mrs. Krebs and Mrs. Moorling was out for the evening, and Gibbs told her she'd need to come back in the morning. I thought she looked desperate-like, even offered to work without wages, but Gibbs wouldn't hear of it and sent her on her way. Well, this morning she comes back first thing and Mrs. Krebs takes pity on her and lets her start right away. I was helping hand-feed, you know, and I watched her. I seen how she went from crib to crib, looking not at the babes' faces but at their feet! Mrs. Krebs comes and puts a baby in her arms and points to the first rocking chair, and the poor dear sits down and starts to nurse the little one, and I see her work the wee one's foot out of its bundling and look close-like at the heel. That's when I figgered it."

"Figured what?"

Dr. Taylor reappeared and gave the woman a dose of laudanum.

"Just this morning I had to wrap up a babe what died in the night," Sally continued. "And for some reason, I found myself looking at the little angel's perfect wee hands and perfect wee feet. That's when I seen the little black mark on 'er heel. Tar, most like. Marked by its mama, so she could find her own again."

Charlotte watched as Dr. Taylor and Mrs. Krebs ushered the woman, still weeping and moaning, into one of the small sleeping rooms down the passageway.

"I shouldna told her, Charlotte. I should've found some tar or coal and marked some other poor babe's heel. She wouldna known and the both of them be better off now."

"It's not your fault, Sally. You did what you thought best."

Sally swiped at a tear and shook her head, clearly not convinced.

Charlotte had difficulty sleeping that night. She turned slowly and heavily in the swaybacked bed, trying in vain to find a comfortable position and to lure the sweet spiral of sleep.

She heard a muffled call from somewhere in the manor, followed by running footsteps down the corridor. Thinking again of the poor babe who died in the night, Charlotte arose from bed, lit a candle, and made her way to the foundling ward. As soon as she opened the heavy door, the sound of crying reached out to her. She stepped in quickly, shutting the door behind her.

Was this the crying she had heard those other nights? Not likely this far from her room. She moved to the first room of sleeping infants. One was crying, and another awoke to join the first, the cries mingling in an ear-piercing refrain. Charlotte stepped back into the hall and saw a mobcapped

Mrs. Krebs struggling to fix a feeding tube with sleep-smeared eyes. "Go and fetch Ruthie for me, will you, Charlotte? It's her turn. Second door on the right."

Charlotte soon returned with the sleepy red-haired woman, who sat down and began nursing the two crying infants. Charlotte walked down the row of cribs and saw another infant lying awake, a boy according to the small card with the child's sex and date of admission pinned to the side of the crib. Occasionally a card contained a name, if the child had been given one, but it was rare. This little boy lay on his back, looking around the room peacefully, taking in the commotion with calm ease. Charlotte paused, looking down at the child, his eyes bright in the candlelight.

Mrs. Krebs sighed. "Fixed the feeder up for nothing, looks like. Usually when one cries a whole choir wake with it. But only two so far, and Ruthie can manage a pair on her own."

"Would you mind if I fed this one?" Charlotte asked quietly.

"Isn't fussing."

"I know, but he's awake and so am I."

"Suit yourself." Mrs. Krebs set the feeding tube on the table and left the room.

Charlotte picked up the swaddled infant, who seemed light as a kitten in her arms. She sat with him in the rocking chair nearest the table, and he immediately turned toward her, molding himself to her body. At first she pulled away, back pressed hard against the chair, feeling embarrassed as the infant rooted against her nightdress. She looked around, feeling guilty, though of what she wasn't sure. But no one was watching. Ruthie was facing the other direction and seemed to have nodded off even while she nursed, and Mrs. Krebs had taken herself back to bed.

Charlotte relaxed and allowed herself to draw the infant close. She felt a sharp longing, and wished she could nurse this little one. She ran a finger along his smooth cheek and he turned toward it, taking its tip between his lips. The force of the suction was surprisingly strong. He took her finger farther in until she felt the wet ridges of the roof of his mouth and his tongue tugging along the underside of her finger. She wondered how it would feel, if it would hurt or be pleasant, when she finally nursed her own child.

"You'll have to settle for goat's milk tonight," Charlotte whispered. She pulled her finger from his mouth with a slick popping noise and picked up the feeding tube from the nearby table. She adjusted it, lowering the open end toward the baby's mouth.

"Here you are," she murmured and smiled when the little one began drinking the milk in earnest.

"If you were my handsome boy, I would not let you out of my sight." She closed her eyes as she fed the baby. *Dear God in heaven,* she silently prayed, *please watch over this dear, helpless child.*

Daniel Taylor stood in the darkness, watching Charlotte. Unable to return to sleep after a trying day and worse evening, he had roamed the manor's corridors. As he passed through the quiet ward, he had been surprised to see her there, especially at this hour. Aware of his hasty dress and need of a wash and shave, he did not make his presence known. He had seen many women hand feed or nurse infants over the years—from beautiful young girls to ancient nuns—why did he feel so oddly transfixed by the sight of Charlotte Lamb feeding a foundling?

8

> Milkweeds are considered field pests, hard to eradicate and a threat to stock. But many people would just as soon have a patch of milkweed. . . . The French, in fact, imported them to their gardens in the 19th century.
>
> —Jack Sanders, *The Secrets of Wildflowers*

Daniel Taylor helped his father into his Sunday coat, dusting off, then smoothing the shoulders and sleeves. His hands lingered a moment on his father's upper arms. When had he become so slight? He felt the tremor running through the older man's body and bit his lip. Today was no day for lectures.

"Come now, Father. Wash a bit and then we'll go."

John Taylor appeared far older than his fifty-five years as he hobbled over to the washbasin and bent low to wash his hands and face.

"Give your mouth a rinse as well."

His father paused in his ablutions, then did as he was bid. When he finished he said quietly, "Perhaps I ought to stay in this morning."

"No, Father. You know the service does you good."

"I'm not sure I'm feeling up to it."

Daniel sighed quietly. He was torn between the temptation to feel relieved and go alone, knowing his association with his father would not help him build a thriving practice—at least not among those who could pay—and, of course, guilt at such a thought. He looked at his father, sitting on the edge of his bed now, and felt a combination of feelings too complicated to separate: mild revulsion, pity, anger, protectiveness, love.

"Let's see," Daniel began softly, stepping close to his father and lifting his chin gently, looking into his aging face. His eyes, though tired, were not bloodshot. He then laid his wrist against his father's creased forehead. Warm but not feverish. From this angle above him, he noticed how thin his father's hair was becoming on top and how several white tufts stood in disarray. Carefully, he smoothed down the errant hair, as methodically as if he were performing some important medical procedure.

"There now. The picture of health and decorum."

John Taylor's grin was bleak. "If only that were true, eh, my boy?"

"Come now, Father, we do not wish to be late."

Daniel and his father sat on the high-backed bench in a box near the middle of the church—a box generously shared with them by the widow Mrs. Wilkins, originally with the evident purpose of introducing her grown daughter to an eligible physician. She had been too polite to rescind the invitation once she learned Daniel was already married. An easy mistake to make, he realized, considering no one in that church had ever seen his wife.

As the man in black began his sermon, Daniel's attention wandered, as it usually did. If asked, he would likely acknowledge that he attended church because that was what respectable people did, and what a respectable physician was expected to do. His spirit received little nurture—nor conviction—from the lofty sermons and formal hymns. He did not blame the Church of England. He knew the problem lay within his own soul.

As he sat there, his father listening attentively beside him, the hard bench digging into his spine, the man's deep baritone took him to another church, another time.

How long ago was it? Five years, perhaps. He had just come from seeing Mrs. Lamb. Dr. Webb, eager to return home in time for tea, hurried on but urged him to take his time. He no doubt guessed Daniel was feeling low—first from having been called by a teary-eyed lad to a dismal thatched cottage just that morning, only to find the grandmother already dead, and now the disappointing visit with Mrs. Lamb. Daniel was grateful to the older man and, indeed, felt the need for some solitude.

Walking away from the vicarage, Daniel passed the church and, on impulse, walked inside the empty, echoing old building. The age of the place continued to astound him—sections dated back to the twelfth century. He never tired of gazing upon the unique ornaments of the otherwise humble church—chancel arch, double squint, mullioned windows, wall paintings of St. Francis and Henry the Third outlined in red ochre. He had attended services there the past Sunday and for a moment imagined he could still hear Mr. Lamb's booming baritone reverberating within the stone walls as he delivered his sermon from the raised pulpit. But no, the place was utterly silent but for the crisp turning of a page. He turned his head and there, in a rear pew of the nave, in a spot clearly chosen for its wide swath of sunlight, sat a teenaged Charlotte Lamb.

"Miss Lamb."

"Hello, Mr. Taylor. How fares my mother?"

"A bit weaker than usual, I'm afraid. But she seems in good spirits."

"Mother always is. I only wish her health were as good as her spirits."

Knowing it was not his place to reveal Dr. Webb's prognosis, he changed the subject, nodding to the black book the girl held against her chest. "May I ask what you are reading so intently?"

"Well, it's the Bible, as you see."

"And do you like reading it?"

"Yes, of course. Don't you?"

"I'm afraid I find some of it rather dusty, but there are parts I am quite fond of."

"Which parts?"

"Oh, I like the Gospels, the Proverbs, and some of David's Psalms—the desperate ones. And of course in secret . . ."

"Secret . . . ?"

He felt his face heat and knew he was blushing, "I was going to say the Song of Solomon, but I should not say it to you."

"But you have already said it."

"Forgive me."

She turned to scan the south chapel, then looked back at him and whispered, "You have told me a secret. Now I shall tell you one. Shall I show you what I am truly reading?" She pulled out several folded pages that had been tucked into the Bible. "I am supposed to be reading the book of Numbers, but instead I am reading this letter over and over again."

"It must be a very interesting letter."

"More interesting than Numbers at any rate."

"Is it . . . a love letter?"

"A love letter?" She ducked her head. "No. Not at all."

"But you do . . . receive love letters . . . from time to time?"

"No. I have never."

"I'm sorry."

"Whatever for? I am only fifteen years old."

"Quite right. Those should wait until you are at least . . ."

"Sixteen."

"I quite agree."

"This is only a letter from my dear aunt. I'm to stay with her the month of August, and I long for it. I am reading what she says we shall do and whom we shall likely see . . . all the while pretending to read *this* to please my father. Do you think me very wicked?"

"Never, Miss Lamb."

"Father would. He says if we are all very good, and pray hard, Mother will get better. Do you think it true?"

"It's certainly not fair."

"Fair?"

"For your father to put that responsibility on you. Forgive me, I mean no disrespect, but do you really think God works that way? If we do the things we ought, He'll preserve those we hold dear, but if we forget or neglect our duty, He'll bring down calamity upon us and those we love?"

"I think perhaps you need to read the Old Testament more often."

"Perhaps you are right. But I prefer the New."

"Except for the Proverbs and most desperate of Psalms?"

He smiled, "And that other book, which shall remain nameless."

Now Daniel became aware of the congregation standing around him and quickly joined them, glad to rise from the hard bench. He felt himself smile again at the memory, a smile quite out of place with the serious benediction.

That night, Charlotte dreamt that Dr. Webb was again listening to her mother's heart. And, as she remembered him doing before, he asked her if she would like to listen as well. Smiling, Charlotte climbed up onto the bed, returning her mother's serene smile, and laid her head against her mother's chest. But her mother's smile soon faded. Try as she might, Charlotte could not hear the heartbeat.

"Do you not hear it?" Dr. Webb demanded sternly.

"No," Charlotte cried. "I cannot."

It was her fault. If only she could position her head correctly, find the right spot to listen, if only she could hear it . . . but she could not, and so it beat no longer.

Charlotte awoke, her own heart pounding, a nauseous dread filling her body as the images and cloak of guilt filled her mind. The images soon faded, but that familiar, nauseating guilt remained. It expanded, accompanied now by new pressure in her abdomen, a pressure which soon grew into pain.

Charlotte rose gingerly and removed her nightclothes to dress for the day—and that was when she saw the small, dark red stain.

On shaky legs, she made her way to breakfast, ate little, and was soon sitting at the table with the other women, attempting to finish the blanket she was embroidering for her child. She found it difficult to concentrate. Then a second wave of pain struck.

At the urging of the other women, Charlotte made her way carefully to Mrs. Moorling's office. When she had confided to the matron about the pains and the slight but frightful bleeding, Mrs. Moorling had immediately gone off in search of a physician to see her.

By now, Charlotte had been sitting in the office for a quarter hour or more, shifting on the hard chair, trying to get comfortable, rubbing her abdomen, hoping to somehow ease the tightness, the strange new pains.

Gibbs appeared in the doorway. "Dr. Preston has just arrived. He will see you directly."

"Dr. Preston? Perhaps I could wait . . . see how I feel tomorrow."

"Miss Smith. If you are bleeding, you had better not waste time."

"Is it so serious?"

The woman shrugged. "Can be."

Charlotte felt sick. "Very well."

Gibbs led her down the corridor, through the workroom, and to the examination room. She opened the door and announced without expression, "Miss Smith," before stepping out and letting the door shut Charlotte into the room. Charlotte saw Dr. Preston straightening from a slouched position in the desk chair. He was a very handsome man, she could not deny. His clothes were rumpled, however, as was his hair—even though it was but midmorning. Had he slept in those clothes? She saw him lift the lid of a Smith & Co. tin and pop a "curiously strong" mint into his mouth. Charlotte found it ironic. She, who had grown up in a home that abstained from strong drink, might very well not have identified the odor, but the cure he had taken for it was a telltale sign. He smoothed down each side of his moustache before rising. It was not a dandy's gesture, she judged, merely a very tired-looking man trying to smooth on a professional facade. His next words, however, dispelled the image before it could fully form.

"Remove your frock, if you please."

She felt her mouth drop open. "I beg your pardon."

"Your frock. Remove it. Come, come. I haven't all day."

"But is that really quite necessary?"

"There's no need to feign modesty with me, Miss Smith."

"I am feigning nothing . . ."

"I am a physician, Miss Smith. I assure you the female form holds no mysteries for me."

No mystery she could well believe, but still!

"Perhaps I only imagined the pains. Really. I feel quite, quite well now."

"Do not flatter yourself, Miss Smith. A female body in this distended shape does more to repulse a man than entice him, I assure you."

Now she felt shame heaped atop her embarrassment and irritation. Did he really think she thought he might be interested in her as a woman?

He went on, "I have a beautiful wife at home with blond curls and an eighteen-inch waist." Here he paused. "Of course she also has a tongue to rival King Arthur's sword."

"The two often go together, I find," Charlotte murmured, thinking of Beatrice. She did not move but felt his eyes studying her.

"Do I know you, Miss Smith?"

"I do not believe so."

"You seem familiar somehow. Where do you come from?"

"I . . ." What had she told Mrs. Moorling? She realized he could check her file. "I am lately of Hertfordshire."

"Hertfordshire? Hmm . . . and we have not met before?"

"I do not believe so, no."

"Ah well, it will come to me. Now, do you wish to know if your babe is all right or not?"

She squeezed her eyes shut, swallowing. "Oh, very well." She reached around and began unfastening her buttons. Of all days to wear a frock that buttoned down the back.

"Here, here." He walked up behind her and impatiently began working the buttons. "I'll miss my hunt at this rate."

At that moment, the door burst open and Dr. Taylor strode in. He stopped suddenly, clearly startled to see the room occupied. His bespectacled gaze went from Preston to Charlotte and back again. He frowned.

"What's all this, then?"

"I should ask the same of you, barging in here."

"Mrs. Moorling sent for me. Said you had yet to make it in."

"Well, clearly she was mistaken. For here I am, seeing a patient."

Dr. Taylor opened his mouth, then apparently thought better of what he was going to say. Instead, he tossed his case casually on the desk and said lightly, "I thought you were off hunting grouse today."

"I depart this afternoon."

"Well, why not leave early. Make a day of it."

"But I have women to see. Patients."

"I'll see them for you. My day is already spoiled. No point in both of us being indoors on such a fine day as this."

"Well, I—"

"Off with you, man. I'll see to Miss Smith myself. I saw her when she first arrived."

"I'll wager you did."

"Go on. Before I change my mind."

"I shall. Before I change mine."

Dr. Preston grabbed his bag from the desk, his coat from the back of the chair, and strode from the room without so much as a glance her way. The slamming door punctuated the tension in the room, which didn't fade as quickly as the sound. Charlotte felt unaccountably guilty, awkwardly trying to reach around herself and refasten her frock.

Dr. Taylor stood there, staring at the desk. Then he looked at her, evidently unaware of her struggle.

"Why were you seeing Preston? I saw you only last week."

"Mrs. Moorling insisted. I am having pains."

Instantly his strained demeanor snapped into professional concern. "What sort of pains?"

"Cramping pains, here. And I . . . I am . . ." She could barely make herself say the word aloud to him.

"Any bleeding?"

She nodded, relieved to have it out. "A bit."

"And the babe, when was the last time you felt movement?"

Charlotte felt tears fill her eyes. "Not once all day."

"Do not be alarmed, probably just enjoying a bit of slumber. Still, I ought to give another listen."

He again retrieved the wooden tube from his bag, and Charlotte sat on the table as she had before, but this time she was praying. *Please, God, please, God, please, God. . . .*

He pressed the tube to the center of her abdomen and stared blindly in concentration. Then he repositioned the tube to one side . . . and the other. Charlotte studied his expression with growing trepidation.

"Do you hear anything?"

He moved the tube lower.

"Can you not hear it?" she tried again.

"Not with you talking."

He moved the tube again.

"I suppose some would say I ought to be relieved, but I am not."

"Of course not. Shh."

Charlotte bit her lip. "Do you suppose this is God's punishment?"

"Charlotte, please lie down on the table." He ignored her question. "I need to listen lower, but it's difficult with you sitting up." When she complied, he pressed the tube very low indeed, where the underside of her rounded belly nearly met with her hipbones. He listened intently, his face growing, she concluded, terribly grim. Tears fell down Charlotte's temples and into her hair. He moved the tube above the opposite hip bone and pressed it in deep, nearly painfully so. This time he closed his eyes as if to focus on his sense of hearing alone. Or perhaps he was wincing, realizing the painful truth.

"Well, hello there."

"What?"

"I hear your little lad a'way down here."

"You do?"

He nodded, set his tube down, and lifted his hands above her abdomen. "May I?"

Charlotte appreciated his consideration. She guessed he would not ask permission before examining other patients who came to him. She swallowed but nodded. He put his hands firmly around the lower portion of her belly, feeling and gently pushing.

"Here is his little rump right here."

"You can feel that?"

"He is all curled up down here, bottom side up. No wonder I had difficulty auscultating his heart."

"He is all right, then?"

"Seems so. About the bleeding though."

"It is only a little."

"Yes, and it does not necessarily mean there are any problems. Still, I ought to examine you . . . internally, to see if your body is readying to give birth."

"But it is too soon!" She sat up on the table.

He looked at her quizzically, and Charlotte saw the question in his eyes. *Too soon to examine you or too soon to give birth*? She looked away from his raised-brow gaze.

"Charlotte?"

She squeezed her eyes closed and reached behind herself again, attempting to undo the remaining buttons, unable to look at him as she did so.

Would it be less terrible to disrobe before Dr. Taylor than Dr. Preston—or worse? Eyes still winced shut, she was surprised to hear the door open. She looked and saw him standing at the threshold, his hand on the latch.

"There's no need to remove your gown," he said over his shoulder.

He called for Gibbs and whispered instructions to her in the corridor. In a few minutes she returned, Mrs. Krebs in tow.

Dr. Taylor said, "Mrs. Krebs will have a look at you, Char . . . Miss Smith."

"I will," Mrs. Krebs grumbled, "but I'm no surgeon, mind."

"A finer midwife I have never known."

"That's been a few years now, Dr. Taylor."

"You remember the rudiments, no doubt."

"I suspect so."

To Charlotte he said, "If she sees anything worrisome, I will need to examine you myself, but if not, we shall wait a day or two and see if the bleeding ceases on its own. All right?"

"Yes. Thank you."

He left the room, and Charlotte wondered which of them was more relieved.

Mrs. Krebs found nothing amiss and helped Charlotte refasten the buttons she could not reach earlier. "Dr. Taylor must have taken a shine to you, miss," she said.

"No! Nothing of the kind. It is only that he . . . that he is known to my family. That is, when I was quite young. It is a bit awkward, is all."

She tutted, then said, "As you say, miss." She left the room, leaving Charlotte quite sure the woman didn't believe a word she had said.

9

Our milkweed is tenacious of life. Its roots lie deep as if to get away from the plow."

—John Burroughs

Charlotte added a few more pieces of coal to the fire, washed her hands and face in the basin, cleaned her teeth, and climbed into bed. She checked to make sure the candlestick was on the night table, within reach. Pulling the rough blanket up under her chin, she waited for sleep—or a scream—to come.

Sleep must have come first, for when the scream came Charlotte awoke with a start, forgetting her plan for a moment. Quietly, so as not to awaken Mae beside her, she crawled out of bed and wrapped her dressing gown around her. Carrying the candlestick to the mantel, she took a match-straw from the tinderbox and lit it in the fire, using this to light the wick. Then she tiptoed to the door. Letting herself out and closing the door quietly behind her, Charlotte listened. Hearing nothing, she lifted her candle high, grateful for the light, hoping it would chase away the fear and ease the raw nerves eating at her heart.

The scream sounded again—and her nerves moved on to her stomach.

Charlotte crept down the dark corridor, her candle flickering against the grey walls and the stone floor beneath her stocking feet. The chill night air seeped through her stockings, through her nightdress and dressing gown. But her shivering had little to do with the cold. It had to do with the scream. Such an unearthly sound. Charlotte had lived in the manor long enough to have heard any number of shouts, cries, and groans of women delivering babes. Those were earthy, striving, determined sounds—awful to hear yet bearable for the sweet relief that followed and, Lord willing, the responding cry of a newborn that rose up to wash away memory of pain and struggle.

This cry was met with no relief, no answering cry of new life. This cry did not rise and fall with the regularity of birthing pains—increasing, building, then abruptly sighing into silence. These cries were clapped off, silenced for hours, days even, only to escape, to rise up in shrill desperation, in anger sometimes, in woeful distress, only to cut off mid-cry a few minutes later. No gradual fading, no sense of the cries having accomplished, nor brought forth, nor delivered anything or anyone. These were the cries Charlotte had come to dread, the ones that brought gooseflesh to Charlotte's skin and darkness to her soul. She longed to banish both.

She continued down the corridor—the opposite direction from the common rooms and foundling ward—to its end. She knew the staircase to the upper floors stood in the center of the building and serviced both wings. So when she reached the far wall and the corridor simply ended, with the cries seeming still quite distant, Charlotte was confused. Had the drafty old house played tricks on her ears, her mind even? The cry rose again, closer yet still muffled. She tried one of the doors, which opened to a small cleaning pantry. Then she tried another door, which opened onto an empty chamber. Why hadn't it been offered her? She extended the candle farther into the room and saw it housed neither hearth nor bed but only a few old chairs and a wardrobe. Without bothering to close that door, she tried the last—a narrow, plain thing, a linen closet, perhaps.

She lifted the latch and the door flew out at her with surprising velocity. Charlotte gasped and nearly dropped her candle. She cupped her hand around the flame and only just managed to keep it alight. She looked inside the door. This was no closet. This was a second set of stairs. And from its narrowness she guessed it had been designed for servants' use in the building's original design. A servant might silently disappear and reappear in the corridor, bearing coal for the upstairs bedrooms or bringing down chamber pots and the like, she supposed.

And that's when she heard it again—the scream, darting down the staircase and piercing her with its nearness, its wildness. What was this? All the girls were on this floor, as far as she knew. The higher floors were more difficult to heat, and the Manor Home had insufficient staff to manage all the available space. She had heard Gibbs complaining of having to haul down a chest of drawers from above stairs, and gathered that some of the upstairs rooms were still furnished while others were used for storage. And Dr. Taylor, she knew, kept rooms up there when he was on duty during the night.

When she heard a door open above her, Charlotte stepped back quickly from the doorway, hand to her heart. Whoever was coming down the stairs was descending rapidly. She knew she would never make it back to her room undetected. She quickly slipped into the empty chamber she had so recently inspected, setting her candlestick on the floor in the corner, hoping her body would block its small light.

Footsteps hit the landing and entered the corridor. Charlotte held her breath. Candlelight preceded the shadowed figure past the open doorway. Charlotte peered out from behind the door and made out the figure of a man. The familiar smell of antiseptic and herbs confirmed the identity of the man more readily than his fleeting figure. Dr. Taylor. Not surprising. He made no secret of sleeping above stairs. Then why was she so frightened?

Charlotte stood there, heart pounding, trying to quiet her breathing as the candlelight and footsteps faded and she was alone again. But for how long? Did she have time to sneak back to her room before he returned from whatever errand or mission took him from his room this late at night? She wasn't sure she wanted to return to her room without knowing who was screaming yet neither was she certain she wanted to know. Did she have the courage to ascend those black stairs alone? Retrieving her candle, she stepped into the corridor and listened once more. Silence. Surprising herself, she took a deep breath, reopened the stairway door, and closed it behind her, allowing it to swallow her whole.

She paused at the top of the stairs, listening. She heard—what was it? Sobbing? Yes, a woman was sobbing now. The same woman who had been screaming? Or another? How many people were up here? And why? Charlotte slowly pushed the door open and held forth her candle to illumine the upper floor. She saw door after door on either side of a long, dim passageway. Midway down its length, one door on the left gaped open, faint light leaking out to blend with the glow of an oil lamp on a small table on the opposite side of the corridor. She could hear the crying more clearly now, but still could distinguish no words.

She had taken two steps down the passageway when she heard the door open and close below. She gasped. Caught. Blowing out her candle, she looked wildly about her, but where could she go? She tried the handle of the door closest her. Locked. She had no time to check every door, and something told her they would all be locked as well. Grateful for stockinged feet, she hurried down the corridor as quickly as her additional girth would allow. Knowing nothing else to do, she bustled through the open doorway and stepped behind the door.

What was she doing? She had stepped into the one lit room, like a moth to a flame. And now she was trapped. Dr. Taylor would come in and find her there in but a few seconds. What would she say? What *could* she say? Foolish girl! She should have stayed in the corridor and simply said she'd heard a scream and came to see if help was needed. She'd done nothing wrong . . . until now. She stole a quick look about the room. Rumpled bedclothes, a coat tossed over a chair. On the chest a leather case, a bulky medical bag, a hat, gloves. A Bible. A miniature portrait of a woman in wedding clothes. She couldn't see it well from this vantage, but she knew it must be Dr. Taylor's wife. Good heavens! What if Mrs. Taylor had been lying there in bed, gaping at this stranger who barged right in and hid behind her door? Then there would be screaming indeed! Relieved, she remembered that Dr. Taylor had mentioned he and his wife had a townhouse some distance away, which they shared with his father.

The footsteps in the corridor were coming closer. Then they paused right outside the door. Did he sense her presence? Had he heard her? She would just step out and tell him the truth. *Forgive me, Dr. Taylor, you gave me a fright. I heard a scream and . . .* She heard the jiggle of a door handle, a key in a lock. She stepped out. Dr. Taylor was unlocking the door across the way. His back to her, he opened it a crack, hesitating, apparently listening. He retrieved an apothecary bottle from his coat pocket and checked the label by light of the table lamp, before tucking the bottle back into his pocket. Then he took hold of the lamp itself. With his free hand, he pushed the door open just enough to allow himself in. In that flash of moment, before the door shut behind him, Charlotte saw a figure fly at Dr. Taylor. Charlotte put her hand over her mouth, stifling a gasp, and stepped into the corridor.

She heard a thud, then a voice—a woman's voice, but strange—crying out a string of syllables. "Nonononon . . . !"

"Stop it!" Dr. Taylor boomed, in a voice so strong and commanding, Charlotte would not have believed it from Daniel Taylor had she not seen him just enter the room. She felt chilled, stunned, as if he were shouting directly at her. Never would she have imagined him speaking to anyone, let alone one of his patients, in that manner. But then the sobbing started again, and she heard the more familiar sound of Dr. Taylor's soothing voice rumble through the closed door.

Charlotte stood there a moment more, too confused to move. Knowing he might come out at any moment, she stepped back into his room and relit her candle off the one burning low on a bedside table. Beside it was the miniature she'd seen from across the room. She picked it up and quickly studied the portrait. The woman was truly beautiful. Thick dark hair, a wide perfect smile, delicate features, white lace and cameo at her throat. The clothing, the pose, were traditional, but there was something unusually appealing, something nearly exotic about the woman. Charlotte supposed it was the broad smile, deemed so unfashionable in formal portraits. The artist had rendered a nearly playful light in Mrs. Taylor's dark eyes, hinting at some secret happiness. Was she at home now, missing her husband terribly?

Remembering herself, Charlotte quickly lowered the portrait. *I've no business poking about.* She hurried from the room and made it back down the stairs and into her own room without incident. With a sigh of relief, she slipped into bed, which had never seemed more comfortable.

At the sewing table the next morning, Charlotte asked in what she hoped was a casual tone, "Have any of you ever seen Dr. Taylor's wife?"

"I never 'ave," Sally said.

Mae shrugged. "Me neither."

"Maybe he isn't really married," Bess said. "Just says so, so's us girls will trust him."

"So you won't fawn all over 'im, more like," teased Sally.

"Well, Dr. Preston has a wife too, by all accounts, and that don't make me trust him none," Mae said.

"Dr. Taylor sure doesn't go about like a married man. Here all hours instead of a'tome," Sally mused.

Bess snorted. "Sounds like most men I know. Gone all hours. Comin' and goin' as they please."

"I still say he hasn't a wife. Looks barely groomed half the time. Needs a wife to dress him I'd say." Mae grinned.

"Don't be foolish, ladies," Gibbs interrupted, stopping at their table. "I have seen Mrs. Taylor with my own eyes I have. More than once."

"Have you, Miss Gibbs?" Charlotte asked.

"Indeed I have. Dr. Taylor once brought her around to see the place. Right fine lady, by the looks of her. Very handsome, with the finest feathered hat I've ever seen. Hair dark as night and eyes twinklin' like stars. Glowed she did. Like she was eating up every word her husband said. Never seen two people so in love."

"Goodness, Miss Gibbs, I've never heard you string together so many words at one time," Charlotte said with an appreciative smile.

The woman frowned and bit her lip. "Well, I could not stand here and not put you to rights. Not about good Dr. Taylor's wife."

"How long ago was this," Charlotte asked, "since you saw Mrs. Taylor?"

"Oh, I don't know. Few months now . . . maybe half a year."

10

In common milkweed, white juice, which oozes out of the stems and leaves when broken . . . clots, like blood, soon after exposure to air.

—Jack Sanders, *The Secrets of Wildflowers*

After two weeks of caring for the little foundling boy, Charlotte sat on the bench in the manor garden at dusk, tears streaming down her face.

She became aware of Dr. Taylor standing near. When she glanced up at him, his expression grew alarmed.

"What is it?"

"Dr. Taylor! If only you had been here earlier. Dr. Preston said there was nothing he could do, but had you been here, I know you would have at least tried. . . ."

"Slow down, please. What has happened?"

"The little boy—he's gone."

"The one you'd taken to feeding?"

Charlotte nodded, wiping at her eyes with a handkerchief.

"I'm sorry." He sighed in frustration. "I'm afraid it happens more often than I can stand . . . or explain."

"Dr. Preston said, 'Get used to it. I have.'"

"Unfortunately it's a natural response. One must harden oneself or work elsewhere."

"I should never get used to it."

He nodded. After a moment he stepped closer and murmured, "Come, Charlotte." He offered his hand. Her brain mildly noted his use of her Christian name, but at that moment she was beyond caring.

She allowed him to help her to her feet. Her time was drawing near and she would have found it difficult to get to her feet unassisted, even had she not been in so distressed a state.

"Come," he repeated. "I shall help you to your room."

He held her by her arm and guided her inside and down the passage.

"Did I do something wrong?" she asked tearfully. "Is that why . . . ?"

"No, Charlotte, no. I'm sure that little boy lived longer than he would have had you not cared for him so."

"For all the good it did him."

"Of course it did. How much better to leave this world loved and cared for." He opened the door to her new bedchamber. She had gotten her private room at last. "Now, off to bed. You'll have your own little one soon, and you need your rest."

Charlotte was unaware she had sat in the garden so long and that it was evening already. "Very well. Good night."

"Good night."

She went inside and sat down on her bed. She was vaguely aware of him closing her door and the sound of his footsteps fading away, but Charlotte's tear-streaked eyes were filled with another scene, another death. She wrapped her shawled arms tightly around herself and remembered.

"She's gone," young Mr. Taylor had said, looking at her over her mother's still form.

Charlotte gasped. She felt her insides collapse, like a cocoon flattened by a careless boot.

Mr. Taylor stepped forward, as if he might take her in his arms, but at that moment Charles Harris swept into the room, his stride urgent, his handsome face nearly fierce in its grimness.

"Oh, Mr. Harris!" Charlotte cried and turned on her heel, stepping into his arms. He pulled her close against him.

"Dear, Charlotte. Dear, dear, Charlotte . . ." He murmured against her hair. "I am so sorry."

She sobbed against him and felt him stroke her back as he whispered words she knew were meant to comfort her, but no words could diminish the flaming, burning pain inside of her. She was vaguely aware of Mr. Taylor letting himself from the room but was too devastated to care.

Daniel Taylor did not venture to the club as often as he once had. He went not to drink and play cards, as did the other men, but to further his reputation and, he hoped, his private practice. But tonight, he had no thoughts of business in his weary mind, only a few minutes relaxation before taking himself home.

A group of regulars, gathered tightly around a table, were jesting with two well-dressed newcomers. Daniel looked over and recognized both men immediately, although he knew them from another time and another place.

"So the great Charles Harris is finally married," silver-haired Mr. Milton said, raising his tumbler in salute to the older and darker of the two newcomers.

"Well, yes, for more than half a year now."

"Many are the lasses still crying over it, I can tell you," a second gentleman with a wax-curled moustache agreed cheerfully.

"Miss Lamb is among them, I assure you," a younger voice said.

The young man—perhaps now twenty years old—was another person Daniel had last seen in Kent. William Bentley was sitting beside Mr. Harris—his uncle, if Daniel remembered correctly.

Harris stared at his nephew, clearly astonished. "Miss Lamb?"

"I believe she was brought especially low by your marriage."

"No. I am sure you are mistaken."

"Come, Uncle. You cannot tell me you did not know it."

"Well, then," the mustachioed man interjected wistfully. "This Miss Lamb was not alone in her hopes of catching the most eligible bachelor in Kent. My own Nellie spoke very highly of you."

William ignored the man, keeping his half-lidded gaze on his uncle. "Miss Lamb has had her sights set on you for years," he insisted.

"I do not think so. I have merely been a friend to the family."

William snorted. "Miss Beatrice was hoping for more than friendship, I can tell you."

"Beatrice?"

"You're barking up the wrong tree, young man," Mr. Milton interrupted. "Your uncle here has always been like an older brother to the Lamb girls and feels most protective of them. Do not risk his ire by speaking ill of either of them. Especially now he's married a cousin of theirs."

"A rich one at that," the mustachioed man said, wagging his eyebrows meaningfully.

"And how do you like your wife's townhouse in Manchester Square?" Mr. Milton directed the conversation to more comfortable topics.

"Fine, fine."

"And how do you find life in London?"

"A far cry from Kent, no doubt."

The discussion calmed and continued, but Daniel found himself remembering the first time he had seen Charles Harris—and the way Charlotte had looked at the man. They had been standing in the vicarage garden, as they often did, when the man came riding up on his big black horse, the tails of his greatcoat nearly matching the gleaming ebony flanks. But Daniel's attention was soon pulled from the admirable horse to the equally gleaming look in young Charlotte Lamb's eyes. And as Daniel looked from girl to horse, from girl to man, he realized she was admiring not the fine animal, as he had been, but rather the man astride it. Her attention was completely captured by him, her eyes, always cheerful, had taken on a glow as though she were gazing on a candlelit Christmas tree, or the first snowfall, or . . . he admitted to himself grudgingly, an exceedingly handsome man.

"Who is that?" he asked her.

She laughed a sudden, surprised laugh, as if amused that someone in the world should not know who this astounding man was. "Why, that is Mr. Harris. Our neighbor."

"And where is Mrs. Harris?" he asked somewhat peevishly.

"Mrs. Harris? There is no Mrs. Harris. Unless you mean his mother."

The man rode close and reined in his horse in an impressive show of hooves and horsemanship. "Hello, Charlotte. You are looking lovely as usual. Your father about?"

"In the church."

"And Bea?"

"Not in the church."

He grinned a knowing grin, and Daniel wondered at the meaning of that little exchange. Was there something between Charlotte's sister and this dashing neighbor—older though he was?

Harris touched the brim of his hat and quickly spurred his mount off again in the direction of the church. Daniel noticed he barely looked his way.

"He is a bit old for your sister, is he not?"

"Yes, he is much too old for Bea. But not for me."

"But—she is older than you are!"

"Oh, I am only teasing, Mr. Taylor. You will have to forgive me. I have learned that art from Mr. Harris, and I am afraid it is a habit deeply ingrained."

"You spend a great deal of time with him, do you?"

"No. Only small bits of time, but in regular doses over many years."

"Your father approves?"

"Of Mr. Harris? Completely. He rather thinks of him as the son he never had."

"And your sister?"

"Bea has long been smitten with him."

"And you?"

She shrugged. "She would say the same of me."

"And would it be true?"

"Oh, Mr. Taylor," she soothed, touching him lightly on the arm, "we are all smitten with him—every last one of us, from Father to Cook. Who would not be? But we do not expect anything to ever come of it. Well, except perhaps for Bea."

The second time Daniel saw Charles Harris was the day Charlotte's mother died. He remembered that day all too well.

Dr. Webb had been called away that morning to another patient's home, so

Daniel alone had attended Mrs. Lamb when she breathed her last. He had felt a heavy mixture of failure and grief, sharpened by the caved-in expression on Charlotte's face. He had stepped forward, intending to take her in his arms, to try in some small way to comfort her, when Mr. Harris swept in. Harris immediately took Charlotte in his own arms, enfolding her in his greatcoat, which looked to Daniel at that moment very much like bats' wings. The man whispered words of familiar comfort, as if it was the most natural thing in the world to hold her in his arms.

Unnoticed and unwanted, Daniel had silently let himself from the room.

A few days later, Daniel found Charlotte alone after her mother's funeral. She was sitting in the garden. Not weeding or cutting anything, just sitting on a little lawn rug. He could remember but few times he had seen her idle. He cleared his throat, clutching his hands behind his back.

"I am terribly sorry, Miss Lamb."

"Thank you."

"We did everything we could for her. But there was so little—"

"Of course you did. We do not blame you."

"I'm afraid your father does."

"Father is wrong. We all knew it was coming. Even Mother knew. Father was nearly cruel with her when she tried to raise the subject. In any case, it is not you he blames."

"What do you mean?"

"How do you think Mother got this ailment? Father told me himself she was never the same after birthing me. She was never able to bring another babe to term—her pain often left her too weak to stand. And here I was, forever tiring her with my questions and tempting her to the garden when she ought to have been indoors resting. She'd been ill so long, I guess I stopped believing just how ill she was. Or was too selfish to care. I should have made her rest. I should have prayed harder. I should have—"

"Charlotte, stop. You did all you could do. You loved her better than any daughter I've known, and it was perfectly obvious she loved you as well. There was nothing more you could do."

"I want so badly to believe this isn't my fault."

"It isn't your fault. Charlotte, it isn't. Don't take guilt upon yourself that isn't yours to take. There's too much of the deserved variety to go around."

He paused long enough to fish out his handkerchief from his pocket and hand it down to her before continuing. "Why does it have to be anybody's fault? I'm no theologian, but I don't suppose it's God's fault either. Allowed it to happen, perhaps. Who's to say? Our medical knowledge and skill is not all it could be—much of it still remains a frustrating mystery.

Even if we deduce that some organ has quit functioning, and even if we understand why, that does not mean we have an inkling of how to repair the thing. There was nothing we knew to do for your mother that we did not do. And I don't think God withheld a miracle because you did not read the book of Numbers."

11

> In the early nineteenth century a new term—"puerperal insanity"—would find its way into medical texts. . . . Women were believed to be particularly at risk shortly after childbirth . . . but they could also become mad during pregnancy.
>
> —Dr. Hilary Marland, *Dangerous Motherhood*

The entry hall was empty as Charlotte walked through it, passing the manor's main staircase. There was normally a chain strung from between the wall and banister, but at the moment it hung limply from the wall. She thought she heard voices above stairs and paused to listen. It was afternoon, and bright sunlight filled the hall from the high, unobstructed windows over the main door. There was nothing sinister about the setting this time, but still, when the cry came, chills coursed through Charlotte's body—accompanied by pity for whatever poor creature had uttered it.

Charlotte put her hand on the banister and took a slow step up and then another.

Suddenly a male voice burst out from above, "Moorling! I'm waiting!" The voice startled her. It was Dr. Preston's voice, angrier than usual. She shouldn't have been surprised, she supposed. She knew Dr. Taylor was not usually on duty during the afternoons—that daytime hours were primarily the reign of Dr. Preston. Still for some reason it perplexed her to hear him up there. She had assumed that it was Dr. Taylor's on-duty residence—and domain—alone.

She heard footsteps clicking across the marble of the ground floor and looked over the railing to see Mrs. Moorling approaching. She was carrying a tray laden with lances and glass vials, iodine and bandages. Charlotte recognized it immediately for what it was. A bloodletting tray. One of Dr. Webb's colleagues had treated her mother with similar instruments over a course of days, and it had weakened her so badly that Dr. Webb forbade its use ever again.

Carefully balancing her tray, Mrs. Moorling had not yet seen Charlotte, but as soon as she reached the foot of the stairs and glanced up, her already drawn expression took on a sharp edge.

"May I ask what you are doing, Miss Smith?"

"I thought . . . I heard voices."

"Of course you did," she snapped. "We have occasional patients on the upper floors as well. Did you not see the sign?"

Charlotte shook her head.

Mrs. Moorling looked over and saw the dangling chain. "Someone's let it down. Put that back up for me after I pass, will you? And please stay on the ground floor."

Mrs. Moorling started up the stairs. Charlotte realized the matron would likely have given her a longer lecture had Dr. Preston not been waiting so impatiently. Charlotte sighed and reached down awkwardly over her bulky middle for the chain. She fingered the small engraved plaque that hung at the chain's midpoint. The plaque read: *Staff Admittance Only.*

Well, there was someone up there who was not on staff and who was not happy about being there.

Why she stood there, she did not know. But she felt oddly rooted to the spot. A few minutes later, she again heard footsteps on the marble—duller male steps. She looked across the hall and saw Dr. Taylor approaching, peering at a document of some sort as he walked. When he looked up and saw her there, he smiled easily. "Good day to you, Miss Smith."

"And to you, Dr. Taylor."

"I say, this place is a tomb. Um, rather, I cannot seem to find anyone about. Have you seen Mrs. Moorling or Preston, by chance?"

"Yes, as a matter of fact. They are both above stairs right now."

He stopped where he was. "Are they indeed?" His expression was both thoughtful and perplexed.

"Mrs. Moorling was taking up some things Dr. Preston must have ordered."

He lowered the document in his hands. "What sort of things?"

"If I am not mistaken, lances and such for bloodletting. I saw that at home on more than one occasion before Dr. Webb forbade it."

His expression transformed from perplexity to alarm and, she thought, anger.

"Thank you," he murmured tensely and jumped over the low chain easily and bounded up the stairs two at a time. He disappeared around the corner hollering, "Preston!" as he ran.

There was something troubling going on above stairs. Quite troubling.

She thought to follow Dr. Taylor, but a quick look at that little plaque, still swinging from a flick of Dr. Taylor's shoe, stopped her. That and the thought of Mrs. Moorling's censure.

Charlotte walked quickly back down the corridor, past her room and to the servants' stairs. Looking back and seeing no one, she opened the door and stepped in, closing the door behind her. She climbed the stairs as quickly as her taxed body would allow, and when she reached the top she heard the unmistakable sounds of Dr. Preston and Dr. Taylor shouting at each other, as well as Mrs. Moorling's low, admonishing tones. But then the other voice sounded, the high, plaintive wail Charlotte had heard before. The cry seemed more distressed than ever, and the volume and panicked pitch of it were mounting by the second.

Charlotte cracked the door open and peered down the corridor. The windows up here were unshuttered, so the passage was light enough for her to see clearly. She could also hear clearly as Dr. Taylor exclaimed, "Good heavens, Preston. You have frightened her nearly to death."

"I am only attempting what you hadn't the courage to do."

"Yes, and see how much it has helped her."

"I was not finished."

"Yes, you are."

The fevered wailing rose again, and Dr. Taylor barked a command, "Get out of here, Preston. Now."

"Fine. Moorling, come with me."

Preston marched away down the corridor toward the main stairs, Mrs. Moorling following less assuredly behind him. Charlotte saw the woman glance back.

Dr. Taylor's voice called out, "Mrs. Moorling, please hand me that sponge."

"Mrs. Moorling, you will come with me," Preston insisted. "That room is no place for you."

Charlotte was surprised to see Mrs. Moorling obey the man. The two turned the corner and disappeared, Charlotte knew, down the main staircase.

"Mrs. Moorling!" Dr. Taylor's voice had taken on new urgency. "I need you here!"

The wail broke off into short cries and curses and Charlotte heard the unmistakable sound of struggle.

"I need some help here!"

Dr. Taylor's plea pulled Charlotte into the corridor. She stepped both rapidly and timidly down its length to the open doorway. She peered in and put her hand over her mouth to stifle a gasp. Chills prickled her skin. Dr. Taylor held a wild-haired, half-dressed woman in a wrestling hold against the far wall of the room. In one hand, raised above her head, the woman held a lance like those Charlotte had seen on the tray earlier. Dr. Taylor held her wrist to keep the lance at bay and with the other hand held the woman still as she struggled to free herself. The woman, Charlotte realized, was cursing in French.

Dr. Taylor must have heard her footsteps, because he said, without being able to turn around enough to see her, "The opium sponge on the corridor table. Quick!"

Charlotte turned and found the sponge in a bowl. She picked it up carefully and quickly stepped back into the room, dripping water and who knew what else and swallowing back her fear of recrimination. Dr. Taylor pressed the woman's body with his shoulder and awkwardly stuck out his hand behind himself to receive the sponge.

Charlotte walked closer and laid it in his waiting palm. At that moment she stepped into his peripheral vision and he glanced up at her, and his eyes sparked with—what? Anger? Astonishment? Mortification? She wasn't sure. Charlotte glanced quickly at the woman, and even through the dark hair strewn across her face, there was no missing the fury in her expression.

The woman began yelling at her, lip curled in disdain, obsidian eyes flashing. Charlotte's familiarity with the French language did not extend to whatever vile words the woman was spewing—words that were cut off when Dr. Taylor pressed the sponge against her nose and mouth. Charlotte backed away slowly, watching the woman struggle in vain to turn her face away. Just as Charlotte reached the door, the woman slumped against Dr. Taylor, clearly sedated. He picked her up and laid her on the room's lone bed. Only then did Charlotte realize that the woman was with child.

Dr. Taylor looked over at Charlotte in the doorway. "You are not supposed to be up here, you know."

She nodded. "I know."

She stood there a few seconds longer. He offered no explanation and neither did she.

He covered the woman with a blanket, grumbling as he did so, "Blast that Preston. I have told him never to try that with her. Arrogant fool . . ."

In repose, the woman's face relaxed into lovely lines and features somehow familiar. Recognition flitted within reach and away again.

"There, she will rest quietly now." Rising, he led Charlotte from the room, locking the door behind them.

"I suppose you wonder why I don't have him discharged. What with things like this and those other charges you brought to my attention."

"I was not . . ."

"I cannot release him, though I likely should. He knows too much. And now, so do you. I don't suppose I have any right to ask you to keep silent about what you have seen this day."

"What . . . have I seen?" she asked softly.

He looked at her, then away. He sighed deeply. "A woman who suffers from puerperal insanity."

"What is that?"

"A type of melancholy mania. In her case it commenced with conception. More typically it develops after birth."

"I have never heard of it. Do many suffer from it?"

"More and more it seems. And I have yet to figure out why." He ran a frustrated hand through his hair, then seemed to notice Charlotte's hand pressing against her own chest. "Do not fret, Charlotte. I am sure you will be fine. Mania runs in her family, I discovered, but not in yours, as I remember quite well."

"How can one be sure?"

"There are many early symptoms. Inability to attend to any subject, indifference to one's surroundings, fear, melancholy, suicidal thoughts. . . ."

"Good heavens."

"Yes, good heavens indeed. One might wonder what God is doing up there in those heavens of His when so many could use Him down here."

She stood there watching as he walked away toward the main stairs. Then she made her own retreat down the servants' staircase, pressing a hand to her newly aching back and shaking her head as she relived the details of the startling encounter. So shaken was she that it wasn't until she reached her own room that she fully realized that the wild-haired French woman was the bride in the wedding portrait—Dr. Taylor's wife.

The next morning Charlotte arose from bed and immediately groaned, thrusting her hand into the small of her back. The pain she'd first felt the previous night was now visiting her tenfold. Had she injured herself climbing the stairs? She paced her room, hoping to warm her muscles and ease the ache.

A new belt of painful cramping seized her underbelly. Charlotte stopped her pacing and leaned over the bed, supporting herself with her hands, panting. This was no mere backache. This was something altogether new. Altogether frightening. When the constriction abated, she walked gingerly to the door and opened it. Looking down the passage, she saw Gibbs walking across the entry hall.

"Miss Gibbs!" Charlotte called.

"Yes?" The woman paused, and then quickly strode toward her. Taking one look at her face, Gibbs said, "Your pains have begun?"

Charlotte nodded.

"Very well. I shall alert Dr. Preston."

"Is there no one else who might—?"

Gibbs shook her head, "I am afraid not. Dr. Taylor has gone home."

Charlotte sighed and returned to her room. Why must her babe come now, early in the day, with only Preston on hand to deliver her? Woe filled her at the thought of putting herself in such a vulnerable position in his harsh presence. She would prefer Dr. Taylor to attend her, although she would still be mortified to assume the birthing position—on her side, knees up, facing away from him, according to Sally's whispered description. Was there no one else to help her? Another pain struck. *Lord, please help me,* she breathed.

Hat in place and newspaper tucked under his arm, Daniel locked the door to his private medical office on the street level of his townhouse on Wimpole Street. He had no idea where his father was. He had still been abed when Daniel had left early this morning to pay a house call but was not at home when Daniel returned. He hoped his father hadn't broken down and headed out to a tavern somewhere. Hungry, but with little interest in eating alone, Daniel decided to walk down the street for a quick meal at the Red Hen before his next appointment at two.

He was startled to see Preston rounding the corner and heading toward the Red Hen as well. Wasn't the man supposed to be on duty?

"Hello there, Preston."

"Taylor. Hello. I'm rather surprised to see you here."

Daniel was about to icily tell him the same, and to remind him of the office hours for which the Manor was compensating him, but the man's next words stopped him.

"How fares Miss Smith?"

Daniel pulled a grimace. "Fine last I saw her. Why?"

"She's delivered, has she not?"

"Has she? When?"

"Well, beg me, I am confused. Mrs. Moorling told me to head on home, that Taylor was on duty, helping Miss Smith as we spoke, or some such."

"I haven't been to the manor since last night."

"Something afoul there, then. Shall I go back and sort it out?"

"No. I'll go."

He thrust his paper into Preston's arms and strode quickly down the street, worry pushing aside his hunger. Had there been some misunderstanding? Had Mrs. Moorling sent Preston away, thinking Daniel had spent the night and was still above stairs when Charlotte's time came? Had Charlotte been left alone, to deliver her child unaided? Was she suffering still? Or worse, what if complications had arisen as they had with Charlotte's mother? Fear prodded his heart, and soon he was running down the street, over the manor lawn, and pushing through the doors. It was too quiet, deathly quiet. Was he too late? His shoes slapping against the floor echoed as he ran to Charlotte's room. He knocked but didn't wait for an answer as he pushed the door open and barreled inside. Charlotte looked up at him, clearly surprised at his abrupt entrance. But far from looking distressed, Charlotte smiled a wide, contented smile. Heart pounding in his ears, Daniel bent over, resting his hands on his knees to catch his breath. He looked around the room, trying to deduce the situation. Charlotte was sitting up in bed, fresh nightdress and bedclothes around her, bundled babe asleep in her arms.

"Are you . . ." He panted. "Are you well?"

Charlotte nodded, eyes bright.

"But . . . how? When?"

"About an hour ago. As to the 'how,' I think you should know that better than I." Again she smiled at him, a heavy-lidded, peaceful smile.

"But who delivered you? You were not alone, I trust?"

"No, thank goodness. When Gibbs did not find you at home, your father offered to come in your stead."

"My father? Did he? But was he—That is . . . was his attention . . ."

"He was quite wonderful, Daniel. A godsend."

A quick knock sounded and his father walked in, looking the part of the regimental surgeon he once was—dressed in shirtsleeves, black waistcoat and linen apron, drying clean hands on a white cloth. Only his snowy hair, standing here and there out of place, detracted from his competent appearance.

"Daniel. There you are. Have you ever seen such a stout, healthy lad?"

Daniel looked at Charlotte's babe, which he had yet to examine. "Perhaps I should have a look at him."

"Go on, feast your eyes if you like. But I checked him over myself, I did. A perfect specimen, if I say so myself."

Charlotte grinned up at his father. "I must say I quite agree with you, sir."

"May I?" Daniel asked.

Charlotte nodded, and he began his examination of the plump, pink babe.

His father said mildly, "Miss Charlotte here tells me she knew you when she was a girl."

"Yes, I had the privilege of meeting Charlotte's family during my apprenticeship in Kent."

"And now here you meet again. God looks after His lambs, now doesn't He?"

Charlotte's lips rose in an attempted smile, but Daniel could see she doubted the sentiment. For his part, he did not miss the irony of his father referring to Miss "Smith" as a "lamb."

"You are both correct," Daniel pronounced. "Perfect indeed." He rebundled the infant and returned him to Charlotte's arms.

"And what will you call him?" his father asked.

"I have not decided."

"Well, no great hurry." His father picked up his bag and packed away his last few things. "You rest awhile, miss. You've had quite a day already."

"Thank you. I shall."

Mrs. Moorling knocked at the partially opened door and stepped inside. "I've brought Ruth to nurse your child for you."

"I planned to do that myself."

"In time you shall."

"But—"

Charlotte glanced from Mrs. Moorling to him, clearly embarrassed to discuss such matters in front of two men, but still he didn't feel he could leave without explaining. "Prevailing opinion is that a mother's first milk is not suitable for her child. Most women have nurses for the first few days."

"And you agree with this 'prevailing' opinion?"

"Frankly, I do not. Nor does Father."

"You go right ahead and nurse that bonny boy yourself, if you like, miss," his father soothed. "Won't hurt him a bit. After all, the good Lord knew what He was doing when He designed the whole affair."

"Dr. Taylor?" Mrs. Moorling, clearly disapproving, looked to Daniel.

"I see no problem with it. Perhaps Sally Mitchell would be so good as to instruct Miss Smith on proper positioning."

He noticed Charlotte's face and neck became splotched red with embarrassment.

"We shall leave you for now," he said, wanting to end her discomfort. "Come now, Father."

"I shall return on the morrow to check on you, miss," his father offered. "And I will sign the birth record as soon as you settle on a name."

"Thank you."

Once in the corridor, Daniel took his father's arm and leaned close as they walked away. "What are you doing, Father? You do not really mean to return?"

"I always check on my patients."

"She is not your patient . . ."

"Of course she is. I delivered her son myself."

"Yes, and I appreciate your stepping in to assist when I was not available. But I can check on Miss Smith and the others."

"Daniel, I have not felt this good, this useful, in a long time."

"Yes, I am sure. But remember, I agreed to take your place with the condition that you would stay home and . . . get better."

"Get sober, you mean."

Daniel sighed.

"I am sober, Daniel. Have been for some time. I am ready to return."

"I am glad, Father. I am. But for how long? This institution operates on public funding. We cannot afford any more pocks on its reputation." His father's pained expression lanced his conscience. "Father, I did not mean . . ."

But the older man was already walking past him down the corridor, a bit less steady on his legs than he seemed only moments before.

12

> Lord Clarendon, British foreign secretary, reported that Queen Victoria was hostile to maternal breastfeeding. "Our Gracious Mistress," Lord Clarendon wrote, "is still frantic with her two daughters making cows of themselves."
>
> —Judith Schneid Lewis, *In the Family Way*

When Charlotte first attempted to nurse her son, she quickly realized it wasn't as easy as it appeared to be. As Sally helped her position her baby, and herself, she felt awkward and humiliated. When Sally then showed her how to coax the child's small mouth open and compress her flesh to fit more fully inside, she was quite relieved no one else was in the room, that she had her private room at last.

She was just beginning to think she'd been dreadfully wrong in insisting she nurse her babe herself when finally, wonder of wonders, he latched on with a lusty mouthful and began suckling greedily. Seems they'd both figured it out at about the same time. Charlotte giggled with relief and satisfaction, and Sally smiled at her in return.

"There you are now—that's how 'tis done. You shall be an old hand in no time, just like me."

Charlotte opened her mouth to say she had no plans to become an experienced wet nurse as Sally was, but she thought better of it. She smiled at Sally instead.

"You have been such a help to me. To us."

Us . . . the single syllable was an unexpected salve to her soul. She who had lost her family now had her own. The memory of birthing pains began fading more rapidly at the thought.

"Well, I'd better toddle back to the ward. Just you let me know if you 'ave any trouble, Miss Charlotte."

"Thank you."

Sally left, closing the door softly behind her.

Charlotte closed her eyes. "Thank you," she murmured, but she was no longer thanking Sally.

Her son suckled a few minutes more, his pink-fair skin and red lips bowed over her white bosom. His little hands, which had bundled into fists, now relaxed open. Eyes closed, he fell asleep, his mouth popping off in a wet sigh of satisfaction.

"My sentiments exactly," she whispered and held him close. She leaned down and kissed his temple with the fine, downy brown hair. She studied his profile. So like his father. Was it possible for an infant to so resemble a man, or was she imagining it?

"If circumstances were different I should have named you for him. But as it is . . ."

Tears filled her eyes and, though she squeezed them shut, hot wet streaks escaped and seared paths down her cheeks, alongside her nose, rolling under her chin.

Oh, dear God, she silently entreated. *Please, please make a way. I know I do not deserve your mercy, but this little one does. Please watch over him. Please show me how to provide for him—make a life for him. I cannot do it without you. Please, make a way.*

Daniel sat on the periphery of a group of gentlemen. The club was busy this night. He had met with the secretary of the Manor Home for Unwed Mothers earlier about the reduced funding over the last six months and possible ways to cut expenses. One of Daniel's least favorite topics. The man had just bid him good evening and Daniel drank the last of his tea, somehow enjoying the disjointed hum and drone of deep male conversation though not participating himself.

"How is your wife, Harris?" someone asked. The voice was familiar.

Daniel looked up. Charles Harris must have come in during his meeting with the secretary—he had not noticed him there before. Harris was seated with a group of men, speaking with Lester Dawes, a physician who had been a year ahead of Daniel at university and with whom he had a passing acquaintance.

"Katherine is . . . well, how are we putting it delicately these days? Great with child."

"Let's see, you two have been married, what—eight months? Nine?" Dawes said. "Someone did not waste any time."

Harris, perhaps hoping to direct attention away from himself, caught Daniel's eye across the narrow room. "And you, Taylor, how is that lovely French wife I've been hearing about?"

Daniel was dismayed when all those dark and silvery heads turned his direction. He swallowed. "Fine, I thank you."

"I am beginning to believe Mrs. Taylor is just a creation of our dear friend's imagination." Dawes grinned indulgently. "I have not laid eyes on her this half year at least."

Daniel felt compelled to speak. "Mrs. Taylor is also expecting a child."

"Well, well," Harris said.

"Lot of that going 'round these days," a portly man muttered meaningfully.

Then a clearly inebriated dapper gentleman, a Lord Killen, Daniel believed, spoke up. "I say, Taylor, my wife tells me she saw you, em, consulting with that vicar's daughter, Miss Lamb. Is it true?"

"Is what true?" Daniel realized this must be the husband of the ladies-aid volunteer who had seen him talking with Charlotte at the Manor.

"You know, what they are saying about her. Laid up, you know, ruined and all that."

Daniel brought his empty teacup to his lips to buy himself a moment. When he spoke, he feigned a casual tone. "I am not personal physician to the Lambs, but I have, as you say, consulted with Miss Lamb on a few occasions about a simple malady. And when I saw her, she appeared quite the same as ever."

"What?" the portly man asked in disbelief. "When was this?"

"I'd say the occasion in question was about two months ago." He turned to Lord Killen, whose wife had reported the meeting. "Does that seem right to you?"

"About so long ago, yes."

Harris was looking at him closely. "This malady you saw her for. Is she quite recovered?"

Daniel stared at him, no doubt severely, then forced himself to take a deep breath. "Yes. When last I saw her, she was recovered quite nicely. The picture of health."

"And when was that?"

He looked at the man meaningfully. "Six days ago now."

"She is . . . back to her old self?"

"As much as one can be, yes."

"Well, I for one am glad to hear those rumors put abed," Harris pronounced. "I was always so fond of Miss Lamb."

"As am I," Daniel agreed quietly.

"I still say there is something afoot," Killen said. "I have not seen her these many months. And when I asked her father, he was quite rude in not answering me."

"Her father is always rude when not making sermons," Daniel said.

"Even then on occasion," Harris added.

The gentlemen began talking of other things, and Daniel soon left them.

Mr. Harris followed him out into the gallery. "Charlotte told you, then?"

"What do you mean?"

"Do not play me for a fool. You know what I mean. Miss Lamb. She told you."

"Miss Lamb has not uttered your name, Harris. She has told me nothing, but this very evening someone revealed your part in her fall."

"Who?"

"You did. Your words, your looks have said it all."

"It is not as it appears, Taylor."

"And how does it appear? That a supposed gentleman has ruined a young gentlewoman, then left her to fend off the wolves for herself and his child? That not one thing has been done to make amends?"

Harris glared at him, anger beading in his dark eyes. "My hands are tied here, man. If but I could, I would. You force me to say what I would conceal from everybody . . . from every man in that room."

"I force nothing."

"You force me to admit I have no money. Nothing. I am holding on to my family estate by the thinnest thread. The fire, the repairs have brought me to the end of my means. The only cash I have is what my wife sees fit to allow me of her father's money and that is but a pittance, doled out in careful drops to keep me on a short tether."

"Bit late that. Why not tell her? Charlotte is her young cousin. Would she not feel some pity for her sake if not for yours?"

"You do not know my wife. I would lose everything. I would be in even less of a position to help Charlotte than I am now. Perhaps in time . . ."

"You could give the child a name."

"I cannot. As I said, Katherine is expecting her own child any day."

"Congratulations," Daniel said dryly.

"Thank you. Contrary to appearances, I am looking forward to being a father."

"You already are one."

Harris studied the floor for a few moments, then asked quietly, "I have no right, I realize, but could you tell me . . . the babe is healthy?"

"Yes, extremely so."

"A . . . girl?"

"A son."

Harris stared at nothing, shaking his head. "A son," he breathed.

"Yes, a son who will grow up in shame and poverty while you play at cards and live in comfort in a fine house—no, make that two fine houses."

Anger flashed in the man's eyes. "Taylor, you overstep yourself."

"No, sir. It was you who overstepped yourself some nine months ago when you took advantage of a girl half your—"

"Lower your voice! She is not *half* my age, and I will not stand here while you throw out unmitigated charges against me. Has she accused me of anything?"

"No. She refuses even to identify you. That girl has idolized you for as long as I have known her—though I cannot fathom why."

"That's right. You wanted her for yourself, but she refused you."

"Her father refused me, yes, but that is neither here nor there."

"Well, here is your chance, then. Perhaps you ought to set her up somewhere, support her yourself."

"I am a married man, as well you know."

"As am I, but you would have me do the same."

"*I* am not the child's father."

Three older men came out, putting on their coats and eyeing the two of them curiously. Harris glanced at the men, then back at Daniel, saying a bit too loudly, "Well, who can say with women today. One never knows."

Daniel swung at the man's face, but Harris was quicker and stronger and caught Daniel's hand in a grip strengthened with constant horsemanship, no doubt, and rough compared to Daniel's sensitive, skilled hands. Harris squeezed Daniel's hand painfully tight.

"A pity to break a surgeon's hand—do you not think?"

"Physician," Daniel said through gritted teeth and stomped on the man's foot.

Harris howled and reared back. He released Daniel's hand and pulled back his arm, thick hand clenched in a fist.

"Mr. Harris!" A young manservant ran up the salon steps, clearly panicked.

Mr. Harris faltered and swung around to face the newcomer. "What is it, Jones?"

"It's her ladyship, sir. The babe's come early, and she's having a hard time of it. That man-midwife says something isn't right."

Fight forgotten, Harris winced. "I told her to have a physician. But she insisted on Hugh Palmer, some *accoucheur* popular with her friends."

"Please, sir," the servant Jones begged. "He says come at once."

Harris paled. Clasping Daniel's arm he urged, "Taylor, I know you despise me, but please, for my wife's sake . . ."

"Of course."

They arrived to screaming. Charles Harris cringed and his expression faded to an ashen mask of panic. "Good heavens." He swiveled to face Daniel. "Please help her."

Daniel took the stairs by threes, his medical bag swinging with each upward lunge. Harris followed close behind.

Hugh Palmer, an elfin-faced beauty of a man, met them at the door, his expression grim. "You are too late."

"Too late!" Harris exploded.

"The child has come," the accoucheur announced, "after much struggle."

Daniel noticed the blood on the man's hands and the fatalism in his voice.

Harris cringed again. "Then, why is she still screaming?"

"The child is . . . I did my best to revive him, but I fear he is not long for this world."

"No." Harris bolted past the accoucheur, through the sitting room and into the lying-in room. Daniel followed. A monthly nurse was trying to keep a wild-faced Lady Katherine from leaping from her delivery cot.

"Where is my baby? Give me my baby! Charles! Oh, thank God you are here. They have taken our baby, Charles. They have taken our baby!"

Harris rushed to his wife's side, and Daniel looked around the room. The nurse nodded toward a table near the door. Daniel jogged over and laid his ear on the chest of the swaddled babe. The skin was warm but he could hear no heartbeat. He struck the soles of the infant's feet to stimulate crying, to no avail. He began blowing small puffs of air into the tiny mouth and lungs. Laying his long hand on the child's abdomen, he applied gentle pressure at regular intervals to mimic exhalation.

"What is he doing? Is that my baby? What is he doing to him?"

"Hush, Katherine. Lie back. That is Dr. Taylor. He's an excellent physician. Everything is going to be fine."

Daniel doubted the words.

The nurse approached and quietly suggested they move the baby to the sitting room, out of view of the missus. Daniel complied.

"The physician is going to examine the babe in the other room, missus," the nurse soothed. "He'll be back soon."

Daniel carried the newborn to the sitting room and took a chair near the fire to keep the babe warm. He continued his attempts to rouse the child. There was little hope of success, but he had to try. For the devastated mother, for Harris even, and for himself.

Daniel bitterly assumed the male midwife had disappeared, far from the wrath of father and misery of mother. He wondered if the man even had any hospital training. Accoucheurs were all the rage with the aristocracy, and Daniel, like most physicians, found them a threat—to their own practices, yes, but also to the medical hierarchy and standards of care.

The nurse paused in the doorway. "Shall I give her some laudanum, sir?"

Daniel paused momentarily in his task and sighed. "Please do. And do not be stingy."

The nurse disappeared into the other room, and a short time later Lady Katherine's heartrending shrieks quieted to pitiful sobs.

Harris joined him. "Well?"

Daniel shook his head. "Only the faintest of heartbeats. I am afraid we are losing him."

Harris stared blindly at him. "Dear God, no."

The accoucheur reappeared in the doorway, leather bag in hand. "Do not blame providence. I find women who live in affluence and luxury often endure prolonged suffering and more difficult births than the lower orders of women."

"How dare you . . ."

Harris lurched forward, raising his arm to strike the man, but Daniel called out, "Harris, don't."

Slowly, Harris lowered his fist and his voice. "Get out of my house this instant," he growled.

The young man inclined his nose, turned on his heel, and left the room.

Daniel continued his ministrations on the child. "If we were at the lying-in hospital with my warming crib and stimulants, maybe, but in any case, there is so little I can do."

"Go then, in my carriage. Or send my man for whatever you need. Spare no expense."

When Daniel did not move, Harris exclaimed, "Good heavens, man, why do you sit there?"

The nurse reappeared. "Her ladyship will sleep 'til morning I'd wager. I gave her a hefty dose. Poor lamb."

Charles Harris swung his gaze to Daniel, steely resolve and desperation flinting in the candlelight. "Take my son to that hospital of yours, Taylor. Take us both."

13

After the copulation concludes, butterflies fly away
[to] areas with an abundance of milkweed. . . .
—Morgan Coffey, Coronado Butterfly Preserve

Charlotte sat up in bed. She'd heard a sound, a moan. This was not the wail from the French woman above stairs; this was a male cry. The sound vibrated with anguish. It struck her deeply somehow, as though she'd heard the sound before. But how could that be? She didn't think it was Dr. Taylor. And she barely knew the other men about the place.

She looked down at her little son, asleep beside her, a feather pillow keeping him close. She'd retrieved him from the little crib at the foot of her bed for his last feeding and they had fallen asleep together. She had awakened only long enough to secure the spare pillow on his other side to make sure he would not fall from bed. He slept peacefully still, undisturbed by the sound. She stroked his head lightly, needing to touch him but hoping not to wake him.

When the sound didn't come again, she settled back against her pillow. What was it the cry had reminded her of?

Then she remembered. And that memory she had so often pushed away reasserted itself. Lying there, looking down at the profile of her newborn child in the moonlight, she let the memory come.

That night Charlotte had also awakened to a sudden sound. Someone had called out in pain, she was sure, and her mind quickly identified the familiar voice. *Mr. Harris.* Lightning flashed in her bedchamber, and for a moment she hesitated. Perhaps she had imagined it or it had only been the wind. She should stay in bed. Safe. But she couldn't sleep, wondering if Mr. Harris was ill.

He had come to stay at the vicarage two weeks before, after the Christmas Eve fire at Fawnwell. What a night that had been. Fire brigades and people from all over Doddington had come to help. Charlotte herself had run over and was soon put to work hauling pitchers of tea and water for the volunteers. There was little they could do to stop the fire tearing at the south wing with fiery claws. In a matter of hours, the south wing was a black, smoking heap of rubble and skeletal ribs. At least they had managed to keep the fire from spreading to the north.

Still in her bed, Charlotte heard Mr. Harris moan once more. Rising, she quickly wrapped her white dressing gown over her nightdress, quietly opened her door, and stepped out. The upstairs rooms were arranged around a square court, open to the ground floor. She stepped to the balcony railing. A faint light from below drew her eye and compelled her toward the stairs.

She found him slumped in a chair before a dying fire in the drawing room, staring at a sheet of paper.

"Mr. Harris?" she whispered.

But at that moment, a loud clap of thunder shook the vicarage and he didn't hear her. He crumpled the letter in his hand, dropped the tumbler he'd been holding in his other, and held his face instead.

"Mr. Harris!" She flew to his side, kneeling before his chair, reaching for the spilled glass and turning it aright on the floor.

Her hands were tentative on his knee, entreating him to notice her presence. "Are you ill?"

He looked at her with strange wonderment. "Charlotte? Did I wake you? Pray forgive me."

"There is nothing to forgive. Has something else happened? Mr. Harris, you look very ill. Should I send Buxley for Dr. Webb?"

"No. There is nothing he can do for me."

"What, then?" She spied the crumpled letter. "Have you received bad news?"

"Yes. Bitter news."

"Your mother?"

"No. Mother is fine—still staying with friends in Newnham. Doing as well as can be expected for a woman forced from her home." He rubbed both hands over his face, clearly distressed.

"Is there nothing I can do? Is there something you might take for your present comfort?"

"If you mean brandy, I have had plenty . . . with little relief to show for it."

"Shall I call Father?"

"No. Let him sleep."

"Shall I leave you alone, then?"

"Stay, Charlotte, if you will."

"Of course."

"You are a comfort to me," he said idly, still staring at the embers in the grate. "Always have been."

Lightning flashed, filling the room with light, then leaving it more shadowed than before. Wind howled, holding the curtains aloft on the breath of its wail.

"You must be freezing!" She rose and rushed to the window, wondering why on earth it had been opened on such a cold January night.

"I had not noticed . . ."

She closed the window firmly, pausing to look out at the swaying tree limbs and swirling snow. "Thunder and lightning in January." She shook her head in wonder. "This is going to be an incredible storm."

She walked to the hearth and tossed a few scoops of coal onto the fire, then turned to him. Seeing him shiver, she pulled her father's wool lap robe from the back of the chair and laid it across his shoulders.

"Is it Fawnwell?" she asked, straightening the robe over his arms.

He didn't answer, so she continued. "You shall rebuild—"

"In time." He straightened in his chair. "Though it is not Fawnwell alone which weighs on my mind this night."

She again knelt before him. "It is not the wind, is it?" She attempted a mild tease. "I have never known you afraid of a coming storm."

But his answer was contemplative, serious. "Afraid? Why be afraid when there is nothing I can do. This I know, but still—I detest my utter helplessness to stay its hand. I dread its power over me. I dread the . . . damage . . . it will certainly havoc."

She squeezed his hand and he looked down at her, as if suddenly realizing she was there.

"Good heavens, you look beautiful like that."

"Like . . . what?"

"Your hair down around you, the firelight . . ."

His eyes fell from her face to her neck, and Charlotte for the first time was aware of her own state of dress. But rather than the rush of embarrassment she would have expected, a strange feeling of power filled her instead. She had come into this room a little girl, to comfort her dear Mr. Harris, with no care for her dress or decorum, only to soothe the man she loved most in the world. It was as if, as she knelt there before him, she grew from little girl to desirable woman in a space of a few aching heartbeats. And, if she was reading his expression rightly, he was witnessing the same startling transformation as well. But perhaps it was only her view of herself that had changed, because she had indeed seen that look in his eyes before—that admiration, that desire—but had been blind to its meaning.

He leaned nearer, inspecting her closely. He lifted his hand to touch her face, tenderly outlining her jaw, her chin, with his fingers.

"I always knew you would be beautiful, Charlotte. But you always were to me. Promise me you will forget all my foolishness in the morning—chalk it up to lightning and brandy—but now I feel I must say what I very soon will no longer be able to speak of."

She opened her mouth to speak, but she feared whatever she might say would break this pleasurable spell. He ran a thumb over her silent, parted lips and her heart throbbed within her.

"I have loved you since you were a little girl, Charlotte—I suppose you know that—and I love you still. To me, you are the dearest creature God ever made. You have always been so kind, so affectionate to me—more than I deserved. When I see myself in your eyes, I am the best man on earth. Or at least in Kent."

His mouth lifted in the crooked half grin she'd always admired, and in thoughtless response to his warm words, she leaned close and placed a quick kiss on his mouth, and instantly his grin fell away.

He stood suddenly, awkwardly, and since her hand was still clutching his, pulled her to her feet with him. He looked down at her, then away. "You had better go back to bed."

He stood rock still, but made no move to turn from her nor to turn her out. She stood before him, wishing she might kiss him again, to wipe that bleak look from his face, to see him smile once more. But he was too tall for her to reach, her head reaching only to his shoulders.

"Go on," he repeated in a rough whisper, and for a moment she wasn't sure if he wanted her to leave or to continue with her unspoken desire. Rather than feeling dismissed or rejected, she felt instead emboldened, sure at last of his attachment to her and feeling the pleasure, the intoxicating sweetness of it. How could she not, after a lifetime of thinking him the most handsome and cleverest of men? After endless years of loving him, of dreaming of him, of believing him out of reach, here he was, right here now, loving her.

She lifted his hand, caressed it in both of hers and kissed it. He winced as though she were hurting him.

"Leave me."

She looked at him, wild emotions coursing through her. "How can I?" She pressed his hand over her heart. "When I love you as well?"

"But"—his eyes fell to the discarded letter—"I cannot love you."

"You already do."

Slowly his hand slid lower and she could barely breathe. She leaned closer to him.

He whispered, "Charlotte. You are killing me. I am only a man."

She lifted her face toward his, and he pulled her into his arms, lowering his lips to hers, kissing her deeply. He half sat, half fell into the chair behind him, lifting her onto his lap, holding her close, still kissing her.

Then once again he pushed her aside, standing and twisting away, leaving her sprawled in the chair alone. He ran his hand over his face. "Charlotte, go. We cannot be together like this."

Though his back was to her, she reached around and took his clenched hand in hers and turned him back around to face her. Gently, she pulled him down to his knees before her and, for the second time in their long relationship, their positions were reversed. His eyes were wide, desperate, full of desire. She felt the cold night air on her neck, her limbs, her shoulders, she felt his hand in hers and wanted to feel more. She did not truly think, made no conscious decision to cross the threshold; she was not versed in such things. She knew a woman could comfort a man, though she knew not how. And she knew she loved this man. She thought only of lengthening this time together, of holding him close as she had never been allowed before. When she pulled him toward her, he peered at her closely.

"This is your last chance, Charlotte."

But she pulled him into her arms and kissed him, feeling, foolishly, as if she, too, were helpless to stop the coming storm.

She knew little of the rudiments of physical love. She had been told only that some men were not trustworthy and that is why she must never be alone with a man without a proper chaperone. But she had always trusted Mr. Harris implicitly and knew her father did as well. Mr. Harris was not "some man"—he was looked upon practically as relation. She had not known a moment's fear in his presence, even alone with him, until this moment. Only when he leaned against her and she felt her nightdress begin to slide up did the warning bells finally go off in her desire-drunk mind. She tried to pull her mouth from his, to pull herself away, but the back of the chair pinned her in. She finally wrenched her mouth free and entreated, "Wait, I—"

He halted immediately, staring down at her in growing apprehension, suspended. Frozen.

But somehow, though she felt no pain, the damage was done.

In the morning, Charlotte awoke with the dreadful hope that she had somehow mistaken the events of the previous night. She was not completely certain that what she feared transpired actually had. But in the cold, dark hours she had lain alone in bed since, she knew without doubt that she had left behind all modesty, all rules of polite society, and, she feared, lost all virtue as well. Worse yet, she felt she had lost Mr. Harris, his esteem and his love. She sat up in bed and in so doing, spied the letter, which had apparently been slid under her door. She knew better than to hope for a love letter now. So this was how it was to be—worse than she thought.

With fatalistic numbness she arose and picked up the folded stationery. She climbed back into bed and cocooned herself beneath the featherbed, shielding herself from the cold reality she knew awaited her. She opened the letter and read the single line:

Somehow, someday, please forgive me.

It bore neither salutation nor signature. *Cold indeed.* But at least, it seemed, it bore no blame either.

A mere fortnight later, Charlotte had been shocked, sickened, and scared to death when another letter came. Her father read it aloud during breakfast.

"Well, well, a letter from your cousin Katherine."

"What does she say, Father?" Bea asked, spearing a sausage. "Do read it to us. She is ever so amusing."

Father's face looked anything but amused as he scanned the inked script. "I fear you will not enjoy it, my dear."

"What is it?"

"An announcement of her upcoming wedding."

"Wedding? You are joking! Katherine has long proclaimed herself a determined spinster."

"Well, she has clearly changed her mind."

"Who is the brave soul who finally convinced her?"

He didn't immediately answer.

"Do we know him?" Bea persisted, sausage forgotten.

"Yes. We know him quite well. Or at least I thought we did."

Charlotte clenched her hands together beneath the table. Bea's face began to grow concerned.

"Not Bentley," Bea breathed. "He's too young."

"No, not Bentley. Charles Harris himself."

Bea's expression barely had time to clear before it blanched, her mouth falling open, slack.

Charlotte was stunned but kept her expression as blank as possible, seeing her own feelings mirrored in her sister's face. She knew her own desolation, her humiliation, must be deeper, more complete, than Bea's, but she willed herself not to show it.

"But . . ." Bea protested. "There was no reading of the banns in church. . . ."

"Applied for a license no doubt. Never one for public displays, your cousin."

"I cannot believe it."

"I have never approved of these licenses," their father began. "The banns are not merely tradition, they serve a purpose, allowing anyone with a preexisting marriage contract or other cause to object, to 'speak or forever hold their peace.'" He sighed. "Now a few pounds to a bishop and one may forgo the banns altogether."

"But it isn't right!" The words burst from Charlotte, surprising them all.

"Why not?" Bea glared at her. "Would you have stood up in church and spoken against it had you the chance? Have you some reason to object to Mr. Harris marrying our cousin?"

The bile rose in Charlotte's throat and she stood on shaking legs. "Please excuse me," she mumbled, putting her hand over her mouth and walking quickly from the room.

Bea called after her, "You never seriously thought he would marry you, did you?"

Charlotte threw open her bedroom door and made it to the chamber pot just in time to lose her breakfast.

A few hours later, Charlotte was in the garden when the man she was trying not to think about came thundering across the grounds on his horse. She turned and ran.

"Charlotte, wait!" Charles Harris leapt from his horse, not bothering to tether it, and ran after her. Charlotte hurried through the garden gate and across the lane to the churchyard, hoping to hide herself there. She did not think this rationally—her core instinct simply told her to flee this man. To be close to him was to invite another mortal wound.

She had made it through the church doors when he grabbed her shoulders, swinging her around to face him.

"Let go of me," she commanded.

Panting from his run, his face was stricken, his hair disheveled.

"Only if you will listen to me."

She pulled out of his grasp and stepped back, but didn't run. A foolish part of her still hoped he would tell her it was all a mistake, that he had no intention of marrying Katherine.

"I had no idea she would send the announcements so soon," he began. "My mother received one as well, and I rushed over here the minute I realized. I had hoped to tell you myself, to explain. . . ."

She only stared at him, offering him no encouragement.

"Charlotte. I realize that, considering what happened between us, you might have expected . . ." He pushed his hair off his forehead with a stab of his hand. "That is, under normal circumstances, I would have behaved differently. . . ."

"Do you mean that night, or afterwards?" she asked, her tone pointed.

He sighed heavily. "Both actually. I was stupid and selfish that night. I had just gotten a letter from the bankers, you see, and I was so desperate . . ."

"Yes, I remember."

"I should have tried harder to put a stop to it."

"It was all my fault, then, was it?"

"Of course not. I am to blame. I knew better."

"Yet you accept no responsibility."

He studied her sharply, clearly worried. "Is there . . . something for which I need bear responsibility?"

Mouth open, she shook her head, stunned at the stupidity of the question.

Did he not realize she was forever changed? Her future like a candle without a wick?

But clearly he took her shake of head as a longed for answer and blew out a rush of air, relieved. "Good."

Good? "Tell me this. That night—were you already engaged to her?"

He lowered his head. "Not . . . exactly. She had proposed an alliance . . . a marriage of sorts, prior, but I had put her off. But then the fire occurred. . . . Charlotte, you have no idea what it's like, the responsibility I bear for Fawnwell. I was hanging on by a thread before the fire. After it . . . it was all but lost. That letter from the bank confirmed it. I had neither the funds to repair nor rebuild. My mother had no idea. She assumed we would simply rebuild, maybe even improve on the original structure. I hadn't the heart to tell her the truth. I promised my father I would keep the place going, make it prosper. . . ."

"So you are marrying Katherine for her money."

"I am sorry. Truly I am. But there is nothing else to be done."

Now, lying there in the manor, his child in her arms, Charlotte remembered what her parting words to him had been: "*Your house has been destroyed . . . but I must pay the price.*"

14

> Because of the deep roots, successful transplantation of mature plants is difficult. Attempt it only with small offspring of the mother. . . .
>
> —Jack Sanders, *The Secrets of Wildflowers*

In his office in the manor, Daniel rested his palm on the infant's small chest in silent benediction. "I am sorry," he said quietly to the child's father. "There is nothing else to be done."

Harris stared up at him, clearly not able or not willing to comprehend.

"He is gone," Daniel added gently.

"Give him to me," Harris ordered tersely, and for a moment Daniel feared the man might continue with vain attempts to breathe life into his son's small body. Daniel wrapped the child securely in a donated blanket and reverently handed him over to Charles Harris, who reached both hands out to receive the bundle.

When the weight of the infant's body filled his hands and arms, it seemed the child became real to the man all at once. He stared down at the little face and buckled over as if struck hard. He cried out in anguish. A cry that must certainly be echoing throughout the manor. The man sank to the nearest chair and held the bundled child to his chest, face contorted, tears streaking from his eyes. A different man indeed from the smug man Daniel had sparred with only a short time before. His heart tore for the man, his loss. He could not help but imagine himself in the same situation, if his own wife or soon-to-arrive child should die during childbirth. His answering tears were for himself as well as for Charles Harris.

"Katherine will not bear it," Harris whispered.

"Of course the loss is terrible, but in time . . ."

"No, you don't understand. Katherine feared this might happen. She insisted I should plan to have her locked away immediately should the child die. That she would go insane with grief—want to die herself. I promised her everything would be all right. Nothing would happen to our child. . . ." The man's grief rendered him unable to continue.

"It is not your fault, man. You did everything you could."

"I did nothing."

"Your wife will want her time to say good-bye to him. We should take him back to her before—"

"No! Did you not notice her state? I have never seen her like that. I cannot bring home a . . . lifeless . . . child. . . ."

"It will be painful, yes, but in the end it will help her overcome her grief."

"No." He spoke the word with less vehemence, shaking his head thoughtfully, staring at nothing. Suddenly he looked up, startled, his face alight with manic purpose.

"Where is Charlotte?"

Instantly, panic, dread, and profound fear struck Daniel Taylor with full force. He could see what was coming, should have foreseen it an hour before. "Mr. Harris, whatever you are thinking, I beg you to put it from your mind."

"What am I thinking?"

"I forbid you to approach Miss Lamb on this. You are grieving, I realize, but—"

"You cannot keep me from seeing Charlotte."

"Actually I can. I am her physician and she is still in recovery."

"She will want to see me."

"Will she? Even when she discovers your purpose? I cannot believe you are thinking to . . . I cannot conceive of a more cruel offer."

"Cruel? What is cruel about offering my son—my other son—a decent life? You said it yourself, if I do nothing, he will grow up with nothing—no advantages, no opportunities, let alone the basic necessities of life."

"I never said . . ."

"How many other fatherless children could hope for such as I, as *we,* could provide?"

"But your wife . . ."

"Need never know!"

"You offer only because your own son is dead. Had he lived . . ."

"Then you and I would not be having this conversation, I grant you. But he did not live, did he? And here I stand, not—what?—a few steps from my own flesh-and-blood living, breathing son? I say it's providence."

"I say it's heartless and selfish."

"But it does not really matter what you say. It only matters what Charlotte says, does it not?"

Daniel shook his head, arms crossed, head pounding.

"Please, man, I beg of you. Let me at least see her!"

Daniel stared at the man, but instead saw a younger Charlotte, smile beaming, looking up into the face of this man before him. *Would she want to see him? Consider his wretched offer?* Daniel longed to protect her, but who was he to make such a colossal decision?

Daniel insisted on entering Charlotte's room first, on having a few moments alone with her. To prepare her, somehow—as if such a thing were possible.

He sternly waved Harris back, waiting until he was hidden in the shadows several steps down the corridor, before knocking softly on Charlotte's door.

"Yes?" she answered after only a moment's hesitation.

Pinning Harris with a "stay there" stare, he opened the door a few inches. "Charlotte? It's Daniel Taylor. May I come in a moment?"

"Of course."

He stepped into the room, closing the door behind him, his lamp held low at his side, hopefully providing her some modesty should she need it.

"Good evening," he said, striving for normalcy. "Please forgive the lateness of the hour."

"I was still awake, watching him."

He noticed that a candle burned on her bedside table. He set his small oil lamp atop the chest near the door, causing large shadows to quiver on the room's walls.

She sat up on the bed, facing him. "Is everything all right?"

He stood awkwardly clenching his hands, then realizing he was, stuffed them into his pockets. In the bed beside Charlotte the babe awakened, fussing a bit. Charlotte leaned over and picked him up. She leaned back against the headboard, bouncing him gently in her arms.

"There, there. You cannot be hungry yet, little one."

When the infant relaxed back to sleep, Charlotte smiled up at Daniel, her tired eyes alight with a look of maternal wonder at, perhaps, her unexpected skill with her child. Her smile held a touch of pride; her face, glowing in the golden light of the candle, beamed with deep contentment. What a lovely portrait she and her babe made at this moment. He smiled at her in return, and felt another pricking at the back of his eyes and a tightness in his throat. He feared that this was the last time she would ever look this happy again.

"Have you decided what to call him?" he asked, putting off the inevitable.

"I believe I have. I found the task much more difficult than I would have imagined." She laid the child on the far side of the bed beside her, securing him with a pillow.

"Why is that?" The moment the question left his mouth, he knew it was a stupid one and wished it back.

"Well, because normally I should name him for . . . his father. At least that is customary. But there is little customary about this situation." She straightened a blanket over the babe. "Or I should name him for my own father. But given the circumstances. . . ."

"Yes, I see what you mean."

He cleared his throat.

She turned to him. "Is something the matter?" she asked gently.

"Yes, I am afraid there is something. Something that might—potentially—trouble you."

"What is it?"

"There is someone here who wishes to see you."

"Now? Who is it?"

"It's, um . . ."

"My father?" she asked, surprise and, he could not miss, a note of hope in her voice. His heart ached dully at disappointing her.

"No, I'm sorry. Not your father."

She stared at him but didn't reply. He took a deep breath and continued.

"It's Charles Harris."

"Mr. Harris?"

"Yes, you see, his own child . . . that is, his wife Katherine's child was born this night."

He saw Charlotte's face harden at his words, and for a moment he was relieved. He hoped she might rebuke the man without a second thought.

"But he lived for only a short time," Daniel continued. "I revived him but was not successful in keeping him alive."

"Poor Katherine."

"Yes, though Mr. Harris is distraught as well."

"Is he?"

The door creaked slowly open and both turned to look.

"Charlotte?" Harris's voice was both plaintive and determined. "Sorry, Taylor, I could not wait any longer." He stepped into the room, closing the door quietly behind him. "Charlotte, I had to see you."

He approached the bed, hat in hand. "What has Taylor told you?"

Charlotte stared up at him. "That your . . . that Katherine's newborn child died this night."

"Oh, Charlotte. I am laid low indeed." Charles dropped to his knees beside the bed and grasped her arm, his hat falling unnoticed to the floor. Now he looked up at her with tear-streaked eyes.

"A little son—did he tell you?"

Charlotte nodded mutely.

"I held him in my hands as he died. . . ." A sob broke through his throat, and Daniel looked away from the painful scene. Still, Harris must have suddenly remembered that he was standing there. "Taylor. Give us a moment, will you?"

Daniel wanted nothing more than to flee from this room, filled with one man's pain and likely to soon flood with another's. But he feared the older man might pressure Charlotte, who was clearly susceptible to his persuasion. And given her fragile emotional condition as a new mother . . . No, he couldn't leave her to face this alone.

"I am staying."

Charlotte looked over at him, clearly surprised. She opened her mouth as if to argue but then closed it, saying nothing. She returned her gaze to Charles Harris.

"Katherine will be insane with grief as you might imagine."

"Any woman would be."

"She does not yet know. The nurse sedated her while Taylor here tried to revive him."

She stared at the man, clearly perplexed. "I am sorry for your loss."

"Thank you. That means a great deal to me. I know I made an immense mistake where you are concerned. That you could still say that, well, I thank you."

Her brow wrinkled as she listened to him, perhaps trying in vain to follow his line of thought.

"And you, Charlotte? How do you fare?"

Harris was evidently avoiding the issue—that is, the baby—a mere arm's length from his nose. Waiting, most likely, for Charlotte to bring him into the conversation.

"Quite well, actually. Everyone here has been very kind to me, and my son and I are in good health."

"Your son, yes. Taylor mentioned him."

She looked up sharply at Daniel, eyebrows high. "Did he?"

"Well, I asked him about you. How you were . . . and everything. He deduced the rest himself."

"I see."

"And your son. What do you call him?"

"Dr. Taylor and I were just discussing that very topic. I have decided to call him Edmund, after my grandfather."

"That was my father's name as well."

She looked away from both men's gazes. "Yes," she murmured.

Charles Harris smiled through fresh tears. "You honor me."

Charlotte's gaze shifted to her sleeping son. "It was not my intention."

"May I . . . see him?" he asked.

She looked at Harris, clearly confused by his attention, but she complied, shifting the little bundle to her other side. Harris laid out both forearms on the bed to receive him. In the lamplight, Harris studied the small face, the tiny hands, and a new wave of sorrow stole over his features.

"He is beautiful . . . perfect . . ." He forced words over his tears. "Like his mother."

Charlotte's eyes filled with tears of her own at the man's obvious awe layered over raw grief.

She smiled, causing a tear to run down each of her cheeks. She whispered, "Actually, he looks a great deal like you."

Charles nodded, tears coursing down his face too.

Daniel stood there feeling the worst of interlopers and had just decided to leave the sad pair to themselves when Charles changed tactics.

"I cannot help wondering . . . how will the two of you get along? I would help you if I could, but you know I haven't any money of my own at present. Perhaps in time, but for now . . . how will you live?"

"I do not know exactly, but we will manage."

"Will you? Charlotte, forgive me, but I must ask. You are young, you might yet marry and have more children. Katherine, as you know, is much older. The pregnancy was very difficult for her and she has vowed never to bear another child should anything happen to this one."

Charlotte stared at him. "What are you saying?"

"Charlotte . . . think about it before answering."

"Before answering what?" Her voice rose.

"Charlotte. Think. You could go back to your old life. Reenter society. I would raise him as my own."

"He is your own! And that has never tempted you to any duty before now."

"I do not deny I have treated you ill. But I would treat Edmund very well. You know I would be a good father to him. And Katherine . . . You would be saving your cousin from a broken heart, from the brink of insanity."

"It is you who is insane. Do you think I would just give my child to you? How dare you ask such a thing? He is my son!"

"He is mine as well."

"He is yours no longer. You gave him up when you married my cousin." She gathered her infant back into her arms and held him close.

"I had no choice."

"You had a choice. And you made it. Now leave us alone. Leave, this instant."

Daniel took a step forward, ready to escort Harris from the room, feeling none of the satisfaction he had anticipated now that Charlotte had refused him. There was no happy ending for such a situation as this.

Harris rose to his feet, clearly shaken and chagrined. "I am sorry, Charlotte. I had no right to ask."

She shook her head, wonderingly, despairingly. "Again you would choose your own happiness—and Katherine's—over mine. *Again.*" Her voice shook as she spoke. "You would have me take on Katherine's heartbreak, to suffer in her stead. I cannot have her place in your life, but I can have her intolerable grief?"

Mr. Harris looked at the floor. "You are right, Charlotte," he said quietly. "It is too much. Forgive my asking."

Harris turned toward the door, Daniel a few paces behind him. He opened it and gestured Daniel through. As Harris was about to shut the door behind him, Charlotte called out, "Wait."

Charlotte swallowed as Mr. Harris stepped cautiously back into the room.

Dr. Taylor stood near the door, searching her face. "I shall wait just outside the door," he said. "If you need me, you need only call."

Charlotte nodded mutely, and Dr. Taylor closed the door behind him. Mr. Harris took a tentative step back toward the bed, arms behind his back, head bowed.

Charlotte looked away from him, away from her son. She stared toward the window, its shutters folded back. From across the room, the light of the moon outside drew her gaze. She was silent for several minutes. Unable to think. Only to feel.

"You know I want what is best for him," she began, her throat tight and burning. "But this . . . this is too much, too sudden."

From the corner of her eye, she glimpsed his nod, but he said nothing. She turned from the moonlight to look at him.

"Do you have any idea what you are asking of me? He is my son—my heart! I love him more than my own life. Have you ever felt that way about anyone? Or do you love only yourself . . . and that estate of yours?"

"That might have been true once. But no longer."

"You really do love her, then—Katherine?"

"Yes. Not at first, perhaps. But now . . ."

"And would she . . . love my son?" Sobs racked her entire body.

He did not answer immediately. When he did, it wasn't the answer she expected. "Charlotte, you know my wife. Katherine is very loving, but she is also very proud, very jealous, and very possessive."

"Yes, I know her well."

"If we act now, and give Edmund to her, she will believe him her own and he will grow up with every advantage, free from scandal, with both a father's and a mother's love. But if she knows he is not her own flesh and blood, I fear she will reject him, or at best be bitter toward him—and me—all his life. While Katherine has her failings, she is capable of great love, great loyalty and devotion, and I can promise you Edmund will have all these things from her."

"She will not mistreat him?"

"Of course not. He is my own son! And she will believe him hers as well."

"*If* I were to consent to this, would you be willing to promise me something?"

He nodded cautiously.

"If she does realize Edmund is not her own, if she cannot love him utterly, I beg you please, return him to me. Promise me you would not let him suffer."

"I give you my word."

"Would you give me some time to think about it?"

"We haven't much time, Charlotte. If I take Edmund home now, or at the very least in the next few hours, when Katherine is just waking from the sedatives, I can easily persuade her that this little boy is her own, home safe and well from his trip to the hospital. If we wait and she suspects, not only is her devotion in question, but my ability to bequeath my land and holdings to him as my legal heir would also be at risk. If we are to do this, it must be now. Tonight."

"But how . . . ?"

"Taylor!" He startled her by shouting.

Dr. Taylor opened the door, behind which he had been standing at the ready as promised.

"Come in, man, and close the door."

When Dr. Taylor had complied, Mr. Harris said in a low, conspiratorial voice, "Is there any reason—should Miss Lamb agree, of course—if I left here tonight with this child, that anyone would know he is not my own? The one I arrived bearing?"

Daniel Taylor's face looked ashen and angry behind his grim mask. "For that to work, Miss Lamb would need to falsely claim your, pardon me, deceased son, as her own. And I should also have to lie to verify that somehow a perfectly healthy infant in my care has died during the night. The death certificate would need to be forged and the birth certificate falsified. And then there is the problem of the accoucheur and the monthly nurse who witnessed your son's struggle. But beyond these minor inconveniences"—his tone was acid—"I see no reason whatever."

Mr. Harris ignored his sarcasm. "The accoucheur will be so relieved his patient has a living child—that his own reputation will not suffer—he will raise no alarm. And I am quite certain he completed neither birth nor death certificate. Remember, my poor child was still alive, though just barely, when we left the house."

"And why would I lie for you and risk my own reputation and career?"

"You would not for me," Mr. Harris said, "but you would for Charlotte. You'd do anything you could to help her."

Dr. Taylor paused but did not deny the man's words. "If it was what she truly wanted." He looked at her, and the panic and nausea that rose in her while they discussed details of an act that would surely kill her now made her whole body tremble.

"How can I? How can I part with him?"

Mr. Harris searched her face earnestly. "I shall appeal to you only once more, Charlotte, and then torment you no further. But think on this. You do not know how you would provide for Edmund, though I've no doubt you would try admirably. With Katherine's wealth and, God willing, a return to prosperity for Fawnwell, Edmund will have the best of everything—the best doctors, the best tutors, the best schools. When Katherine and I die he will be our heir. He will know no want and want for nothing."

"And he will never know me."

"A terrible loss to be sure, but he will not know what he is missing."

"But I shall know what I am missing."

"Yes, dear Charlotte. You will know."

They stayed as they were for several moments, none of them speaking. Charlotte thought not so much on Mr. Harris's promises of abundance for her child but rather on the alternatives. What flashed before her mind were not idyllic images of Edmund romping about the croquet lawn in a fine suit of clothes, but rather the things she had seen at this place. She saw the perfect brown-haired boy she had fed die for no apparent reason. She saw the desperate young woman who put her infant on the turn beg for a wet-nursing post hoping to be reunited with her baby—only to find her heel-marked daughter dead by morning. She thought of women like Becky's mother, who couldn't afford to feed her children, of Becky herself, who would likely have to give up her baby and go back to work or starve.

But surely she had more options. Wouldn't Aunt Tilney help her? She'd already offered her a place to live, and she could nurse Edmund herself for at least a year, if her milk held out. But what then? How would she buy him food, let alone all the other things he'd need? Would her uncle allow her aunt to help further against her father's directives? Not likely. What sort of post could she get with an infant to nurse every few hours? The words she had so naïvely spoken to Mae echoed back at her, *"I would never give my child to someone else to feed . . ."* And here she was, considering doing just that. *I must be insane.* She shuddered.

Dr. Taylor cleared his throat. "Perhaps, Miss Lamb, there might be something I can do. I haven't a large income, but I am sure I could find a way to help you out of this predicament."

Dr. Taylor clearly had no idea how inappropriate his offer was, but she knew he offered with the best intentions.

"I thank you anyway, Dr. Taylor, but you have a wife and your own child to think of."

Charlotte looked down at Edmund's small face, which had instantly become so precious to her. Sobs overtook her again. "Must I decide right now? I cannot. I cannot."

She held her tiny son close and glared up at the men. "Can you both please excuse me? I need a few moments alone. I cannot think with the two of you staring at me."

Charles looked at his pocket watch. "But—"

"Of course," Daniel overrode him, leading the other man from the room. "We shall return directly."

When the door closed behind them, Charlotte got up, one hand on Edmund to keep him safe, and fell to her knees beside the bed. Tears dripped from her face onto the blanket she'd embroidered as she looked down at her bundled son. *I cannot do it, Lord, I cannot. When I prayed for you to provide a way for him, this is not what I meant! This is too hard. Too cruel. Is it truly the right course? Your way out of this muddle? If so, you will have to help me. I cannot do this alone. . . .*

Her prayers turned to thoughts of her son, and she whispered through her tears, "Oh, my little one, you will never remember me. But I will always remember you. Always love you. Never think I did not love you . . . or want you. Oh, God, it is too hard. . . ."

Charlotte Lamb laid her head down on the bed beside her son and cried, knowing she must somehow do an impossible thing.

15

The milkweed pods are breaking,
And the bits of silken down
Float off upon the autumn breeze
Across the meadows brown.
—Cecil Cavendish, *The Milkweed*

Daniel left his carriage in the lane and walked across the Doddington churchyard just as dusk was falling the next eve. Two men were digging a grave beneath a yew tree near the cemetery wall.

He called out as he approached, "I am looking for a Ben Higgins."

The younger of the two men looked his way without ceasing his labors. "You found him. Though folks call me Digger."

Not very original, Daniel thought grimly. "Might I speak with you?"

Digger straightened. "Well, I am a bit busy, man. What's on yer mind?"

Daniel didn't answer, but still the young man laid his shovel aside and climbed from the hole. He walked forward, removing his floppy hat as he came, revealing a mop of chestnut hair in need of cutting.

"You're that doctor's boy," Digger said. "Apprentice, rather."

"Yes, I was." Daniel walked back toward the carriage, where the horse was tied to a post. Digger followed.

"Haven't seen you 'ere since I was a lad."

"I am relieved you remember me."

"And why is that?"

Daniel turned toward the wooden box on the carriage floor, and Digger followed his gaze. The young man's eyes became wary and his mouth pursed.

"Oy, if that's what I'm thinkin' it is, you best move along. I'd be losin' me job if I was caught doin' any buryin' not approved by the vicar."

"I am not asking for myself." Daniel pulled the sealed note from his pocket and handed it to the young man. He took it reluctantly.

"I am told you can read."

"And who told you that?"

Daniel didn't answer.

The young man read and his eyes widened. "Miss Charlotte . . . merciful heavens. Miss Charlotte's own wee one. We did wonder what become of her. The vicar won't even speak her name."

"Which is why no one must ever hear of this."

"I'll take it to the grave with me. . . . Oh, sorry. Fault of the trade."

Daniel reached over with a wad of folded bank notes. But Digger waved it away, then swiped at his eyes with the same hand.

"You tell Miss Charlotte for me. You tell her rest easy. Ben Higgins will take care of her wee one. A boy was it?"

He nodded.

"You tell her Ben Higgins will watch over her little lad. Never fear. You tell Miss Charlotte that for me, will you?"

"Yes, thank you. I certainly shall."

My dear Aunt,

I know I should not write to you, but I feel I must. You have long been my most trusted confidante. As you have been asked not to correspond with me, I will not expect an answer. But still, I must tell you. Must share this awful weight or I fear I shall go mad.

My child is gone . . . lost to me. But it is I who feels lost. The pain, the self-recrimination presses on me until I cannot breathe. I cannot bear it. I must away. I feel the loss too keenly in this dreadful place. The milkweed pods have all broken, the soft white down flown away. Only empty wombs and dry stalks remain.

I feel I must soon depart for the place you offered me. Might I prevail upon you to see me one more time before I go? I so desperately need the comfort and counsel only you can give.

But no, I do not want you to risk condemnation from my father. Did he not threaten to prune you from the family tree along with me? One of us cut off is more than sufficient. . . .

Seeing Charlotte's door ajar, Daniel looked in and saw her writing furiously at the little desk in the corner. She laid down the quill only long enough to swipe at the tears on her cheeks, then picked up the pen and dipped it again. In truth, he was surprised to see her out of bed. When he had last seen her the day before, she had seemed almost incapable of movement, of thought beyond her grief. It reminded him pitiably of his own dear Lizette, and the thought of Charlotte sinking in similar fashion made him feel physically ill. He wondered to whom she was writing. Had Charlotte already changed her mind—was she writing to Mr. Harris?

Suddenly, Charlotte dropped her quill and sat very still. He was just about to make his presence known and step in to speak with her when she picked up the single sheet and crumpled it into a small ball. Her expression was bleak. She laid her head on her arms on the desk and gave way to great shoulder-shaking sobs. He longed to rush to her, to comfort her, but he knew that such an action would be not only inappropriate but also futile. No man could ease a pain as tormenting as this. Only time and only God. Still, he wished there was something he might do.

At that moment, the tall nurse, Sally Mitchell, walked into the passage and he gestured her over. He nodded his head toward the room and Sally followed his gaze. Pausing only long enough to give him a grim nod, she hurried into the room.

"There, there, love . . ." he heard her murmur.

Daniel decided then and there, if ever he could do some good for Sally Mitchell, he would.

After Charlotte had finally cried herself into a grief-exhausted slumber that night, she was awakened by screaming from down the corridor. The screams were familiar and yet different. Dr. Taylor's French wife, yes, but this time crying out with the regularity of labour pains. Charlotte turned over in bed, feeling aware but dulled in her senses. She couldn't bear to give too much thought to another baby at the moment.

Then she heard the matron barking orders and people rushing about in the corridor. Feeling a sudden pull, Charlotte rolled back over and climbed out of bed. She put on her dressing gown and stockings and opened her door, peering out. Lamps were lit and shadows and echoes danced off the walls as people ran past on their way above stairs.

Gibbs marched past, clean linens in her arms.

"Gibbs, what is happening?"

The normally aloof, efficient assistant had been unusually warm and consolatory toward Charlotte since the news of Charlotte's loss.

"The doctor's got hisself a little girl," Gibbs said matter-of-factly. "But the missus . . . Oh, Miss Smith, she is utterly changed. I wouldn't have known her! I best get back up there. Go to sleep, Miss Smith. Nothing you can do."

Of course there was nothing she could do. Even so, and not knowing why she did, Charlotte made her way to the servants' stairway at the end of the corridor, as she had on those other nights that now seemed so long ago. She walked as one sleeping, without aid or need of a light, knowing the way well enough by now. She felt her way up the stairs and cautiously pushed the top door open.

From here, the screaming was even louder. And now came the clamor of things being thrown and smashed as well.

Charlotte winced.

"Take eet away from me!" the woman cried in her accented English.

Charlotte took a few tentative steps down the corridor. Mrs. Moorling suddenly emerged from Mrs. Taylor's room, a bundle in her arms. Someone inside the room slammed the door shut behind her.

Charlotte walked closer and, by the light of the oil lamp, saw a long angry scratch on the matron's cheek. Her brown hair had come all but loosed from its knot.

"Mrs. Moorling?"

"Oh, Charlotte!"

"Are you all right?"

"I will be."

From behind the closed door, Dr. Taylor barked out, "Bring the restraining device—hurry!"

Mrs. Moorling's flushed face grew even more strained. She took a step closer to Charlotte and thrust the baby toward her. Charlotte shrank back and opened her mouth to protest. Then she caught a glimpse of the little face, clearly resembling Daniel, just as her own son resembled his father. Had God planned it thusly—designed to garner paternal support? She accepted the baby into her arms and Mrs. Moorling ran toward the main stairs.

Charlotte stood there, staring down at the tiny infant whose eyes were wide open, looking at her. Then the babe began nuzzling her, instinctively looking to nurse. Charlotte's pent-up milk let down in response. She looked down at the front of her wet dressing gown in growing horror. Then another voice startled her. Mobcapped Mrs. Krebs had come up the stairs and was striding toward her in the same militant style of Mrs. Moorling.

"The babe, is she all right?"

"Yes. Mrs. Moorling gave her to me. Here." Charlotte started to hand the baby over to Mrs. Krebs but then pulled the infant back against herself to cover the mortifying stains.

"I am . . . forgive me. I did not mean to . . ." Charlotte stammered. "She cried and it just happened."

"Perfectly natural. Do nurse her for me. There's a love. I've got me hands full now."

"But . . . I cannot. I should not."

"Come now, you know how it's done."

"Yes, but this is Dr. Taylor's baby. His wife might . . ."

"His wife's a raving loony at the moment, dearie. Best thing for that wee one is to be as far away from her as possible for now. Go on, nurse the wee one. Nurse your own grievin' heart as well."

Charlotte saw the compassion, the understanding in the older woman's eyes, and her own eyes filled with tears.

"If you think it would help her," she whispered.

Mrs. Krebs smiled a sad smile and squeezed Charlotte's arm. "It will help, Charlotte."

Using the better-lit main stairs, Charlotte returned carefully to her room. She sat in her chair and loosened her gown and offered her heavy breast to the baby. After a few awkward tries, the little girl latched on and began nursing. Charlotte wept the whole while. Blood and tears and milk were flowing out of her at such a rapid rate that Charlotte felt as though her very life were being drained from her . . . yet returned to her at the same time.

Daniel Taylor shuffled through the corridor, exhausted and defeated. His wife was worse than ever. The delivery had sent the puerperal mania to new heights. Or was it depths? His poor little daughter! Would she ever know the bright, loving woman he'd married?

Mrs. Krebs came out of the infant ward, closing the door behind her.

"Mrs. Krebs. Have you found someone to nurse the baby?"

"Aye."

He headed toward the foundling ward.

"She isn't in there. I asked Miss Smith to nurse 'er."

"Miss Smith? Why on earth?"

"I have me reasons."

"And she agreed?"

"That she did."

"Where is she?"

"Told her she could take the wee one back to her room. Poor lamb—never seen a girl so modest-like."

He walked quietly back through the manor to Charlotte's room. The door was closed. Through it, he could hear Charlotte Lamb singing to his infant daughter in a tear-cracked voice. It was not a lullaby she was singing. He recognized the tremulous melody of a hymn:

> " . . . To thee in my distress, to thee,
> A worm of earth, I cry;
> A half-awakened child of man,
> An heir of endless bliss or pain,
> A sinner born to die. . . ."

He leaned his forehead against the smooth wooden door, to absorb the sound, the sadness . . . if he could.

Part II

It has long been customary to provide facilities for ladies requiring wet nurses to obtain them at the Hospital on payment of a small fee. Many ladies are accommodated with wet nurses in the course of the year, and the Hospital is, in this way, a great convenience.

—T. Ryan, *Queen Charlotte's Lying-in Hospital from its Foundation in 1752 to the Present Time* (London 1885)

No object, however beautiful or interesting, gives pleasure to their eye, no music charms their ear, no taste gratifies their appetite, no sleep refreshes their wearied limbs or wretched imaginations; nor can they be comforted by the conversation or kindest attention of their friends. With the loss of every sentiment which might at present make life tolerable, they are destitute of hope which might render the future desirable.

—Thomas Denman, celebrated man-midwife, describing melancholia following childbirth, 1810

16

> Now, in chusing of a Nurse, there are sixe things to be considered: Her birth and Parentage: her person: her behavior: her mind: her milke: and her child.
>
> —James Guillemeau, *Childbirth or The Happy Deliverie of Women*

A few days after the birth of little Anne Taylor, a knock sounded on the door of Charlotte's bedchamber. She rose gingerly from bed and opened it.

"Hello, Dr. Taylor."

"You needn't have gotten up."

"I do not mind."

"Most physicians insist on a full month's recovery. But I see it as a good sign that you are up and about already."

She nodded, briefly attempting a smile. "I suppose you are wanting your daughter?" Charlotte retreated back into the room toward the cradle. "Let me bring her to you. Mrs. Krebs asked me to nurse her or I should never have presumed . . ."

"Nonsense. I am most grateful."

"Your wife. She is . . . ?"

"No better, I'm afraid. I regret you had to see her in that state. But that is not why I am here."

Charlotte lifted wide eyes and waited.

"I thought you would like to know. Mrs. Harris wants a wet nurse for your . . . for the newborn child."

A swell of hope rose within Charlotte, which she immediately realized was vain and foolish. She could not apply to nurse her own son. Katherine would know the truth at once.

"Mr. Harris has asked me to recommend someone," Dr. Taylor continued. "Have you a preference?"

She smiled gratefully. "Indeed I do."

There was comfort, at least, in choosing someone to care for Edmund.

"Oh, no, Miss Charlotte," Sally protested. "I'd never get hired in such a great house, not the likes of me."

"But you have the kindest heart of anyone I know, Sally. If I were choosing a nurse, you would be my very first choice."

"Thank you, miss. But them likes the pretty, genteel girls, not some big baggage like me."

"Nonsense. I shall help you. I shall show you exactly what to say and how to act. Please, you must at least try! It would mean the world to me to know you were there, looking out for him."

"Are they family to you, miss?"

Charlotte swallowed. "Only distantly . . . but if I could help them, I would."

"I don't know . . ."

"Dr. Taylor has a list of qualifications for a wet nurse. He will let us borrow the pamphlet and we shall have you ready in no time."

"Oh, very well, Miss Charlotte." Sally smiled, her front teeth protruding as always. "I'm afraid I'm a beetle-headed burdock, but I shall give it me best try."

Charlotte stood outside the door to Mrs. Moorling's office, waiting while the matron made the introductions inside.

"Well, I shall leave you to it," she heard Mrs. Moorling conclude. Then she exited the room. Seeing Charlotte there, Mrs. Moorling left the door ajar. She knew Charlotte had helped Sally prepare for this interview but not the reason why. Charlotte smiled her gratitude and took up sentry at the narrow opening, watching the proceedings with nervous hope.

Katherine Harris sat with perfect posture, her back to the door. Charlotte could see her profile as she turned to whisper something to her husband seated beside her. Charles Harris nodded stiffly and shifted in his chair, clearly uncomfortable. Before them stood Sally, petrified into stony stillness. She was dressed in one of Charlotte's gowns, its hem lengthened with six inches of material taken from forgotten curtains in the unused room at the end of the corridor. Hugh Palmer, the man-midwife, stood beside Sally, facing the Harrises. In his hand, he carried a small booklet, which he held open, referring to it as he spoke.

"First, concerning lineage," Hugh Palmer began, in his somewhat nasally voice. "Have any of your kindred, whether it be parents, grandfather, or grandmother, ever been stained, or spotted, either in body or mind?"

Sally silently shook her head no.

"And what is your age?"

"Five and twenty."

He glanced at Katherine. "Between five and twenty and five and thirty is the best age, wherein women are most temperate, healthful, and strong."

Katherine nodded her understanding and he continued. "And your child's age?"

"A half year."

"Good. If her child be above seven or eight months old, then her milk will be too stale. It would also call into question whether she would have milk enough to nurse your son."

Katherine again nodded, and Hugh Palmer continued, walking around Sally and eyeing her as one would a gown in a dress shop.

"She is a little tall perhaps. Not too fat nor too lean, however. Arms good and fleshly . . ." He suddenly reached out and pinched Sally's arm, and she gasped. " . . . and firm."

He returned his gaze to the book. "'She must have a pleasing countenance, a bright and clear eye, a well-formed nose, a ruddy mouth, and very white teeth.'" He paused before Sally. "Open your mouth, if you please. Now smile. White, yes, but not very straight."

He read on. "'Her hair should be between yellow and black, ideally a chestnut color. But she especially should not have red hair.'"

Sally self-consciously touched her golden hair, pinned up in a classic twist by Charlotte herself.

"'She must deliver her words well, and distinctly, without stammering.' Please tell us something about yourself."

Taking a breath and swallowing hard, Sally began in careful, practiced tones, "My name is Miss Sally Mitchell. I am five and twenty years of age . . ."

From behind the door, Charlotte held her breath. Sally had already told her age. Charlotte hoped they wouldn't find it odd that she was repeating it.

"I have one child. His name is Dickie. He's a rascal but I loves him."

Oh dear. She was extemporizing now.

Sally, apparently seeing the fine lady frown, returned to the rote speech Charlotte had prepared for her.

"My son is a half-year old and is in the care of my dear sister . . ."

"Thank you. Moving on . . ."

But Sally wasn't finished yet. "Leaving me free to seek employment as a nurse."

"As we see. Thank you." The haughty man returned his focus to the book. "'She must have a strong and big neck, for thereby, as Hippocrates said, may one judge the strength of the body.'"

Sally swallowed as three pairs of eyes studied her neck. She lifted her chin higher as though to accommodate them.

"'She must have a broad and large breast. . . . '"

His gaze lowered and Sally's strong neck turned bright red.

Katherine dipped her head, touching gloved fingers to her temple, her lowered hat brim no doubt concealing her face. Charlotte noticed that Mr. Harris had the good grace to turn his face away. He cleared his throat. Mr. Palmer looked up, oblivious to their discomfiture.

Mr. Harris said, "We shall leave it to you to examine, um, that aspect of her nature. We need not hear those particulars."

"Ah . . . yes. Very well." Palmer moved on to the next page.

"'She ought to be of a good behavior, sober, and not given to drinking, or gluttony, mild, without being angry or fretful: for there is nothing that sooner corrupts the blood, of which the milk is made, than choler or sadness.'"

"Yes, well, we have letters from a physician and the matron testifying to her character on those accounts," Mr. Harris said dismissively.

"Indeed. 'She must likewise be chaste.' Miss Mitchell, are you married?"

"No, sir."

"'She must not desire the company of her husband or strange men, because carnal copulation troubleth the blood, and so by consequence the milk.'"

Sally blushed once more, and again Katherine's hand went to her temple.

"Yes, yes." Mr. Harris rose, agitated. "Mr. Palmer, do try and remember there is a lady in the room."

"I am only trying to determine if this woman is a suitable choice."

"I understand that. And what is your conclusion?"

"Well, I have yet to examine her breasts or her milk for the correct color and consistency . . ."

Charles Harris lowered his head and bit out, "And how long does that require?"

"Not long. For the milk, I shall have the nurse express a small quantity onto a looking glass. It should be pure white, have a sweet smell, and be neither too thick nor too thin."

"Then get on with it, man." Mr. Harris sat back down.

The accoucheur and Sally disappeared behind a curtained partition, placed there for this use.

Even from her position of modest safety, Charlotte felt her heart pound, her face and neck heat at the thought of what poor Sally must be enduring on the other side of that partition. The only sounds were the rustling of fabric and an occasional murmur of "Mmm-hmm . . ." from Mr. Palmer.

Five minutes later the man reappeared, a square of glass in his hand. He tilted it gently from side to side. "The milk flows in a leisurely fashion, not too watery, nor too thick."

"So?"

"She will do," Hugh Palmer announced. "The height and crooked teeth are not ideal, but overall an acceptable specimen."

Stepping back into view, Sally beamed at the words, as though they were the finest compliment a woman could receive.

Charlotte sat on the garden bench, a swaddled Anne Taylor asleep in her arms. She remembered how her mother believed fresh air and sunshine were as important as mother's milk for a child. Dr. Taylor came out the side door and waved to her. She tucked the child into the handled basket beside her and rose as he approached.

"Miss Lamb, may I say you look like a woman who has borne many a child."

She looked at him quickly, then away, her hand moving self-consciously to her midriff, still somewhat rounded.

Dr. Taylor's pale cheeks turned pink beneath the sandy stubble.

"What I mean to say is . . . you look quite the experienced. . . . That is, quite . . . as if you know what you are doing." He rubbed his eyebrows with thumb and forefinger. "Though I obviously do not."

Charlotte wondered why he seemed so nervous.

"Do you still plan to depart for Crawley soon?" he asked.

"Yes. Unless I hear otherwise from my aunt."

Hands behind his back, he studied the earth. "Miss Lamb, I wonder if you might consider another course." He cleared his throat. "That is, I do not suppose you would do me the honor of, um . . ."

He left off and began again. "You see, I'm afraid I know not when my wife will be sufficiently recovered to return home. I should only hope it will be soon. But, as my wife must, I fear, reside here longer, I would be eternally obliged . . . Of course I shall understand completely if you refuse. I know it is terribly presumptuous, that you no doubt would rather be rid of this whole business forever, but . . ."

Charlotte furrowed her brow, trying to follow his rambling. Then she understood. He was asking her to continue on as his daughter's nurse. She recalled Sally's examination and interview with humiliating clarity. She swallowed.

"But any of the women here would be happy to oblige. I do not . . . That is, why would you ask me?"

Dr. Taylor seemed to calm at the question. "Common wisdom dictates that a nurse passes on not only nutrition but her very character, her qualities, her good and vice through her milk. I do not believe science bears this out, but if there is any truth in it at all, I certainly believe that the care of a kind, loving, and honorable woman can only be to my daughter's benefit."

"How can you say such things of me. After everything . . . ?"

He took a step closer to her and looked directly into her eyes. "There's not one of us who passes through this life without making a mistake, Miss Lamb," he said gently, "but it's a rare soul who redeems one so utterly. I have never known a more noble, more honorable, more worthy woman . . . and if my daughter can glean any of those qualities, well, I should be exceedingly grateful."

She stared up at him, seeing the sincerity shining in his blue-green eyes.

She opened her mouth to give an answer, but at that moment she heard a familiar voice call out her name.

"Charlotte?"

She turned and saw a finely dressed and wonderfully familiar woman at the garden gate. She excused herself from Dr. Taylor and strode quickly up the garden path, hardly noticing that Dr. Taylor quickly stepped back inside the manor.

"Aunt Tilney! How I've longed for you to come!"

The two women embraced, and then Charlotte led her aunt to the garden bench. Amelia Tilney's eyes widened as she looked into the basket at the sleeping infant.

"Is this *your* child?"

"No."

"I thought not."

Charlotte looked at her aunt, brows raised.

"The tone of the letter suggested something was amiss here."

"But I did not send a letter."

"A letter from a physician, a Dr. Taylor."

"Dr. Taylor wrote to you?"

"Yes." Her aunt sat beside her, withdrew a folded note from her reticule, and handed it to her. "Very wise, really. Your uncle would have recognized your hand and chastised me. He might have read *this* directly and not known it pertained to you."

Charlotte read the brief note quickly.

To Mrs. Amelia Tilney,

Madam, I thank you for your interest and support of our work at the Manor Home in the past. I am writing to inform you of a new development here which will be of particular interest to you. In fact, we are in need of the wise counsel that your past association uniquely equips you to offer. We understand you are a person with innumerable commitments and restraints upon your leisure, but do urgently hope you will find the time. Our facilities are open to you at any hour. Please do call on us as at your earliest convenience.

Most sincerely,
Dr. Daniel Taylor
Physician, The Manor Home
for Unwed Mothers

"I never asked him to write," Charlotte said, still staring at the letter. "I do not see how you understand anything from these few lines."

"I read between them, as they say. What has happened?"

Charlotte handed back the note. "I had a child. A son. But he is gone. Lost to me."

The tears that sprang immediately to her aunt's large brown eyes were salve to Charlotte's soul. Her mother's sister sat next to her on the bench and laid gloved fingertips on Charlotte's hand. "My dear girl. How long ago?"

"He was born ten days ago. I had him for six days. Six very short days."

"I am so sorry, my dear. So very sorry. How this loss must pain you."

"Indeed it does. At times I can barely breathe for it."

"I understand. And yet, who can question God's will? Perhaps He allowed this so you might return to your family."

"I do not see how this changes anything."

"But it does! The evidence is—"

"Evidence! He was not evidence—he was my son. My precious little boy, my heart."

"My dear, forgive me. I do understand." Her aunt wrapped her other arm about her shoulders.

"I am so glad you are here."

"May I ask, then . . . whose child this is?" She nodded toward the basket.

"Dr. Taylor's daughter."

"And why are you . . . ?"

"His wife is ill. He has asked me to be the child's nurse."

Amelia Tilney lifted her gloved hand from Charlotte's and laid it across her lace-covered chest.

"Can you seriously be thinking of accepting this offer?"

Charlotte nodded.

"You know what disgrace such a thing would bring to your family were it known?"

"More disgrace than I have already brought?"

"Substantially. My dear, if you must have a post, be it that of a governess."

"And who, pray, would hire me to teach and mold their children?"

"Many families would. Many fine families."

"Now that I haven't a babe with me, you mean. I shall not lie about it."

"I understand your scruples, my dear—though some might wonder where they were in other matters."

"Aunt—"

"Forgive me. You know I only want the best for you."

"I do know that."

The older woman squeezed her hand again, and the two sat quietly for a moment. Then her aunt continued, "I think your secret is still safe, my dear. Your father and sister know, of course, and the people here, but they are not likely to be in contact with the type of family with whom you would seek a situation."

"Surely others have guessed . . . or at least suspect."

"Suspicions do not allegations make. Of course there is the . . . father. Does he know?"

"Yes."

"And is he trustworthy?"

"Evidently not. If you mean, will he keep my secret, then, yes, I believe he will. Now more than ever."

"Are you absolutely certain there is nothing that can be done in that regard?"

"No, Aunt. Nothing."

"But certainly a gentleman. . . . He is a gentleman?"

"Aunt, I told you. I will not reveal his identity, so please do not fish about for hints."

"I only want . . . Please tell me it wasn't that young gravedigger who ogles you so rudely."

"Ben Higgins? He doesn't ogle me. Heavens no, Aunt. You can rest on that score."

"But someone, at least, of your station in life?"

"Aunt, please. I will tell you this, and then let it be the end of the matter. Our family would suffer no further from either the man's name or connections, were they known. All right?"

"A gentleman. I knew it. Then why . . . ? Forgive me. We will speak of it no more."

"Thank you." Baby Anne began to fuss, and Charlotte drew her forth and cuddled her close. "I am sorry you disapprove of my course, although I am surprised by the vehemence of your objections."

"My dear, wet nurses are infamously ill-bred, uneducated, immoral creatures . . ."

"Thank you."

"I mean, in general, of course. You will be little higher than a scullery maid. The mistress of the house will treat you with ill-concealed contempt so long as her infant needs you. If you vex her, there is nothing to stop her from putting you out on the street as soon as another nurse might be found."

"The mistress will not be in residence, at least not for some time."

"What? But that is worse yet. Really, my dear Charlotte, I must put my foot down here. You cannot live in a house with a man if his wife is not living there with him."

"Servants do so all the time."

"But Charlotte Lamb does not."

"His father lives there as well."

"Two men, Charlotte?"

"But his wife is in hospital. She is indisposed and may be for some months. Dr. Taylor hopes for less, but he cannot be sure."

"Why can he not care for his wife in his own home? He is a physician, is he not?"

"Yes, but she . . . Well, it is not for us to question. Dr. Taylor wants only what is best for his wife, I am sure."

"What's best for her . . . or for him?"

"Aunt. I am certain he is completely selfless in this situation."

"But what is best for you? Certainly not this. My dear, I beg you reconsider. If it becomes known, you will not be able to secure a position as governess, I am quite sure. Your father and sister would be mortified, and I confess, I should not be far behind. But think, Charlotte, even if it is not known, could you really bear another parting? And you will be parted from this child—make no mistake."

"I know this," Charlotte said dully.

"Can you really bear it? Would it not be better to leave this place now, to make a new start?"

"I do not know. All I know is . . . I need this. I feel as though I am standing on a ribbon's edge over a black pit, and this is the only way I can keep my balance. Why should I not use this God-given sustenance to nurture this child?"

"It is not your child."

"I am very aware of that Aunt. Painfully aware. I know this will not bring my son back, if you fear I am suffering from that misapprehension. But this little girl needs me."

"No. She does not. Any of a dozen women in this place could care for her needs."

"But who will care for mine?"

"God will."

"I believe that, Aunt, I do—or I would be in that pit already. But I cannot hold God, smell or caress God. His cries do not drown out my own as hers do. She gives me a reason to get out of bed, to keep living, for today, for a little while longer."

"There are other ways to cope."

"How do you know? Forgive me, but you are not a mother. You have no children of your own."

"I did." She stared off, a sudden sheen of tears brightening her eyes. "I had a little girl many years ago, long after your uncle and I had given up hope of children. She lived but a few days."

"Oh, Aunt. I am sorry. I had no idea."

"She had dark curls, just like you. I suppose that is one reason I have always felt close to you."

Charlotte gazed at her aunt's profile, but instead saw bits of memory like pieces of colored glass, a beautiful jumble of special moments and little kindnesses collected over a lifetime. "How did you get past it?" she asked quietly.

"I am still getting past it. Every day. The pain is dimmer now, but still there. The first days, weeks, were torture—like being skinned alive. But it is not something we talked about. Infants die all the time. Women are supposed to be strong and try again as soon as possible. But there was no trying again for me. I lost my womb along with my babe."

"Dear Aunt. How dreadful for you."

"Yes. And for you."

"But . . . you always seemed so cheerful. So happy when you visited us."

"I was happy. In many ways. Especially when your mother was alive. Although visiting your family was a joy with a slice of pain all its own. My sister with her two beautiful daughters. And you, with your dark hair and eyes . . . I could never look at you without thinking of my own daughter. How old she would be, what she would be like, how similar and how different from you."

"I never knew."

"I did not wish to spread my sorrow."

"Yes, but we might have shared the burden with you."

"Yes, well. That is why I am biting my puritanical tongue and having this conversation with you. I would share this sorrow with you, if you would allow me."

"Of course. You have done so much for me already."

"Tosh. I have done nothing. Would that I could take you into my own home had your father not forbidden me. But do you not see how this situation in a man's home could open your family to more talk and scandal?"

"Dr. Taylor is not much out in society. He certainly does not entertain in his home, where people might see me. But I do see your point."

"Do you? Then you do feel some . . . unease about the man?"

"No. Not about Dr. Taylor. I believe his intentions are honorable. But still there is something . . . a discomfort at the thought of living in his house."

"You fear he would not treat you well?"

"No. I think he would treat me very well. As he does here. But you see, Dr. Taylor is some acquainted with our family. He attended Mother during her illness."

"Did he?"

"Yes. Dr. Webb was mother's physician, but Dr. Taylor was one of his apprentices before he went to university."

"So he is a young man, then?"

"I suppose he is but five or six years older than myself."

"All the more reason."

"Dr. Taylor holds nothing but respect for me—even after everything he has learned about me. Do not look at me so. I mean only that he treats me like a gentleman's daughter—a lady—even after I have proven otherwise. Still, I see the wisdom in what you say. . . . Do you think your old aunt would still welcome me if I brought a baby not my own?"

"Oh yes, I am sure of it! She wrote back directly to assure me of her pleasure in having you and the babe come, and I do not think this will sway her, once I explain . . . I know you will not wish to lie to her. Nor do I, but perhaps the villagers need not be told that the babe is not your own."

"Better for them to think me an unmarried mother than a wet nurse?"

"Yes. I am afraid so. Others might insist you pass yourself off as a recent widow, but I will not suggest such a ruse. We shall hope the distance from Doddington and my aunt's solitary life will provide all the shield you require. I shall write to her directly and apprise her of the situation."

"Thank you."

"Still, I must beseech you one last time. Let me call for the matron. She will find another fine woman to suckle this child, and I shall take you to Crawley in my own carriage."

"Aunt, I appreciate your concern. And I am sorry to disappoint you. But I could no more give up this child than my own, had I to do it over again."

"But you did not give him up—the good Lord took that situation out of your hands. He has something else in store for your future. He knows what is best."

"I do feel Him, somehow. A bit of comfort amid this . . . broken glass slicing at my heart. I am clinging to the hope that He is in this. That He will redeem this, me, my son."

"Of course He will. Your son is with his loving father right now."

"Yes." Charlotte nodded. "Yes, he is."

After Aunt Tilney left, Charlotte found Dr. Taylor in the foundling ward. Together they walked to the far end of the entry hall—out of earshot of the other nurses.

Charlotte began quietly, "It would not be appropriate for me to live in your house without your wife present."

Dr. Taylor lowered his head. "Of course you are right. I had not considered that. My father does live with us, but still . . . I understand." He nodded, resigned.

"I could take Anne with me to Crawley," Charlotte continued, knowing she sounded too eager, "and nurse her there for as long as you need. My aunt assures me we would both be welcome."

Daniel's face brightened. "You know, it was very common until recent times for infants to be sent to the country for a year or so. It was believed the fresh air away from London would benefit the children, and some families still hold to this practice. Would you really be willing to take her with you? To care for her?"

Charlotte nodded. "Unless, of course, you cannot bear to be apart from her. . . ."

"Crawley is not so far off, you know," he said. "If I might visit Anne from time to time, I should think it an excellent plan. I wonder I did not think of it." He tapped his thumb against his lip as he thought. "I would ask that you postpone departure for a fortnight. Give both you and Anne time to gain strength for the journey. The roads can be treacherous at times."

"Very well."

"You are quite certain you are willing?"

"Yes. I will care for her as if she were my own. Until your wife is recovered, of course."

"You do not know what this means to me, Miss Lamb. You will be recompensed well and have my eternal gratitude."

Charlotte smiled weakly. *Now if only I shall be able to bear another parting. . . .*

17

The Hospital Foundling came out of they Brains
To encourage the Progress of vulgar Amours,
The breeding of Rogues and the increasing of Whores,

While the Children of honest good Husbands and Wives
Stand expos'd to Oppression and Want all their lives.
—Porcupinus Pelagious, *The Scandalizade,* 1750

"Miss Lamb." Dr. Taylor stopped her in the corridor the following week. "May I ask how Anne is faring?"

"Fine. I have just come from her. She is sated and sleeping peacefully."

"I am glad of it." He hesitated. "I don't suppose . . ."

"What is it?"

"It's just that I am in a bit of a bind. I need to make a brief call on a patient, one who is quite adamant about needing a female chaperone, and neither Gibbs nor Mrs. Krebs can get away at present. I have just come from Mrs. Moorling's office, though it would have been quite presumptuous to ask her such a thing, but she is out for the evening."

"You need me to accompany you?"

"I know it is difficult for you to get away . ."

"Anne will most likely sleep for another two or three hours. I am sure Mae would be happy to listen and tend her should she awaken. How long would we be?"

"Only an hour or so. But I don't want to impose on you. And while we are both aware of how insensitive I can be on points of propriety, I realize it would not be proper to ask you to ride alone with me in the carriage."

"Is it urgent?"

"Not really. Some stitches I need to attend to, make sure no infection sets in. I promised I would be by tonight and the night is nearly gone. It really should not wait until tomorrow. But perhaps she will forgive me arriving on my own this once. When I explain."

"She lives alone, then?"

"Well, not alone exactly. She has three children in her care. Two are her own, one she wet-nurses for hire."

"I see."

"Well, I must away. Pardon me for speaking before I thought through the notion."

He bowed and walked past her, setting his hat upon his head and lacing his arms through the sleeves of his coat.

Charlotte turned and watched him go.

"Might I have a moment to collect my wrap and speak to Mae?" she called after him.

He turned and looked at her, his face weary. "Of course. If you are certain you do not mind."

She shrugged and smiled blithely. "I shall wear my most concealing bonnet."

And she did.

They rode through the cobbled streets of London in relative silence.

"Do you often make calls at this late hour?" Charlotte asked lightly. She was unprepared for the thick silence which answered her question. She glanced over and saw Dr. Taylor's eyes narrow. He took a corner rather more sharply than needed and urged the horse forward with a click of his tongue.

"No," he answered dully.

She nodded but kept her eyes forward. His tone invited no further inquiry. She did wonder, though, what was special about this particular patient to bring him out for a call this late in the evening—and having to bring someone with him too. The patient was a wet nurse, was she not? No genteel nor wealthy lady that she should have such influence over a physician.

When they halted in front of a worn three-story tenement and Dr. Taylor did not even offer his hand in helping her descend, Charlotte knew his mind was preoccupied and the task ahead an unpleasant one. She lifted her skirts a bit more than she would have liked, but managed to step down to the filthy street without mishap.

"Dr. Taylor!" She was obliged to call, for he was already inside the doorway without her, as if he had forgotten she was behind him.

He looked back, winced, and then held the door open for her as she stepped through. He stopped at the first door on the left.

"You needn't say anything," he whispered. "Just stay near the door."

She nodded in feigned understanding. She was dumbfounded when he extracted a key from his breast pocket and, after but a slight knock on the door, unlocked and opened it. He stepped in and indicated that she ought to follow and stand in the small cramped entry.

"That you, Taylor?" a husky female voice called.

"It is," he answered, setting his hat on a cluttered bench.

"Mrs. Krebs with you?" the voice called again.

"A nurse tonight."

"Pity, that."

With a nod to Charlotte, Dr. Taylor disappeared into a room a few feet away.

"Let's check those stitches, then," she heard him say.

"Let me get a look at her you brought first," the woman said.

After a pause, Daniel called, "Miss Smith, would you mind stepping in here a moment? Miss Marsden would like to meet you."

Charlotte stepped forward and paused in the doorway. An attractive though fleshy woman of thirty or so years lay in bed, propped up with pillows and a mobcap over her blond curls. An infant suckled each breast and a toddler lay asleep, curled up peacefully at her side. The woman somehow managed a free hand, from which she was feeding herself a biscuit.

Mouth full, the woman said, "Hoy . . . a pretty one. And young."

"That will be all, Miss Smith."

Charlotte took a step back, but the woman's voice stopped her. "Wait on. What's your hurry." She turned a calculated gaze on him. "Does she know?"

He began to form what must certainly be the word "no," for what other answer could he utter, but instead he closed his mouth, then tried again. "Miss Smith has . . . She knows my father, yes."

Charlotte felt a smile touch her face at the thought of Daniel's gentle father. "Yes, he delivered my own babe."

But instead of the answering smile and empathetic chat she expected, the woman's face fell into a coarse scowl.

"Oh, did he? And just when was that?"

Before Charlotte could reply, Daniel cut her off. "Only because Miss Smith is a family friend. I have known her since she was a girl. Is that not so, Miss Smith?"

"Oh yes!" she said, grasping the plea in his voice, though not entirely sure how to answer. "Since I was quite young. Dr. Taylor has long been a friend of the family."

"Just so," he said, clearly relieved. "His sole patient. Now, then, please let us proceed. I want to make sure all is healing nicely."

"'Course you do." the woman said superciliously. And Charlotte wondered at the sarcasm in her tone.

Back in the carriage a quarter of an hour later, Charlotte could not keep herself from asking, "Has that woman some sort of hold on you?"

Daniel stared straight ahead, his face bleak. "Yes."

This was all he said, but his grim expression, and what she had seen this night, told her much more.

She nodded, and the two fell into silence.

Several minutes later, Charlotte realized they were taking a different route on the return trip. Suddenly Dr. Taylor pulled the reins up sharply.

"Dear me," he said. "I turned on the very street I meant to avoid. Or my horse took the way she knows best without consulting me."

"What is the matter?"

"Carriages ahead. We've just crossed into Pentonville." He leaned over to try to see past the fine tall carriage in front of them. "There are a couple of grand manor houses ahead. One of them must have something going on tonight."

"Awfully late in the season for a ball," Charlotte mused. "Must be someone's birthday."

The carriage ahead of them pulled forward. "There we go." They rode alongside the broad stone manse just in time to see a finely clad couple allowed entrance by a black-suited butler.

"Just the one carriage holding up traffic. Good. Latecomers by the looks of it."

"Could we stop for a moment?"

She knew he looked at her in surprise, but Charlotte's gaze was focused on the manor and the golden light streaming from the windows.

"I have been here before."

He reined the horse to the right and halted the rig along the side of the street.

"Yes, I was here with my cousin Katherine during my first season. I cannot recall the family name. But I remember something she said, about the place being 'on the very edge of decent society.'" Charlotte began parroting an upper-crust accent. "'If the building were one street over, we should have declined the invitation. But since the family throws the most lavish balls in town—perhaps to make up for their lack of pristine location—we shall condescend to taste their fine meal and dance with their handsome guests.'" Charlotte chuckled dryly. "I had no real idea where I was at the time, or how true her words."

She stared off, remembering. "Please. I'd like to get closer. Just for a moment."

"But—"

She half rose from her seat, giving Dr. Taylor little choice but to step down from the carriage, pausing only to tie down the reins. Before he could step around to her side to help her down, she was already lowering herself from his side. He offered his hand and she accepted it.

She preceded him across the street, quiet now. She was aware of his footsteps behind her. Then he caught up and walked by her side.

She did not go up the steps to the door but instead daintily lifted her skirts and stepped up over the brick gutter and onto the lawn. She took a few steps closer to the facade, then paused. She looked up, and side to side. The windows were like moving paintings in gold-leaf frames. The light spilling from the windows pooled close to where she had paused, but she did not step into that light. Instead she stood at a distance and watched. Across one window passed couples dancing, swirling gowns of every color flowing by, men in black-and-white smiling solicitously to partners pink-cheeked with pleasure. In another window, people mingled, drinking tea and punch, talking and laughing with one another as though they hadn't a care in the world beyond the quality of the musicians, the strength of the tea, or the quantity of sugar buns.

Though her view was limited, Charlotte was relieved to see no one she knew. No sign of Bea or William, Charles or Katherine—though Katherine, no doubt adhering to the prescribed month of bed rest, would surely not be in attendance. Charlotte's breath caught at the sight of Theo Bolger and Kitty Wells. Kitty had always been an attentive friend, and Theo had never failed to seek out Charlotte for a dance. Now, the two danced on without her. She was on the outside, separated forever by glass, by choices.

"Charlotte . . . ?" Daniel began.

"Let us leave," she said, turning abruptly and brushing past him without meeting his eyes.

A couple was coming up the street, arm in arm. The man hailed her. "I say, is that Charlotte Lamb?"

Charlotte glanced over and was chagrined to see William Bentley with a girl she did not recognize. Mr. Bentley's smile was wide in obvious surprise and inebriation.

"It *is* Charlotte Lamb, and looking . . . well, quite herself. But I thought—"

"You thought wrong," Dr. Taylor said brusquely and gently took Charlotte's arm, leading her across the street. She stole a glance back over her shoulder.

"Not going so soon, I hope? I hadn't even one dance with you . . ." He tripped and the girl caught his arm. "'Course I am a bit unstable on my feet at present."

Behind them, the girl laughed. "You'll be a danger on the dance floor tonight, that's for certain."

He must be drunk indeed to not notice neither Charlotte nor her companion was dressed for dinner, let alone dancing.

As he helped Charlotte back into the carriage and urged the horse down the dim street, Daniel recalled the last time he had seen William Bentley.

It was at a ball held at Sharsted Court in Doddington more than three years ago now. Daniel had been standing awkwardly in an archway, drinking tea, when two young ladies passed and he thought he heard his name. He stepped back into the shadows, hoping to avoid blatant humiliation.

"I do not see why he's here," Beatrice Lamb was saying, her lip curled. "A bone and blood man at a ball—it's revolting. What were our hosts thinking?"

"The man is not a surgeon, Beatrice," the friend consoled, "he's a physician, or plans to be."

"Still, it turns one's thoughts in a most gloomy direction, seeing him."

"He's treated their little nephew, I believe, to most satisfactory results."

"Well, send him home with an extra guinea, then, but don't dress him in tails and expect me to dance with him. Just imagine what those hands have touched."

The two girls passed out of earshot, and Daniel stepped forward, embarrassed and contemplating the quickest route to claim his coat and make his exit when a more pleasing voice called to him.

"Mr. Taylor. I am surprised to see you here."

He turned and saw the welcome face of Charlotte Lamb. "Yes. I am not often invited to such as this."

"And why not, I wonder?"

"It seems people do not like reminders of illness and death—and I'm afraid that's what people think of when they see me. Do you?"

"Well, I don't know. I—"

"Forgive me, Miss Lamb. I had no intention of raining on your pleasure this evening."

"Now I see why many a wise hostess has left you off her guest list." She smiled at him, clearly teasing, hoping to put him at ease.

"If you wonder if seeing you brings my mother to mind," she continued, "I suppose it does. But you needn't worry that you have ruined my evening. My mother is never very far from my thoughts."

"You miss her a great deal, do you, Miss Lamb?"

"I do. But it is not a morbid missing, I hope. I think of her often and strive to remember her. I plan to tell my children all about her someday."

"I have little memory of my own mother—she died when I was quite young."

"I am sorry, Mr. Taylor. Why have you never told me this before?"

He shrugged.

"And worse, why have I never asked?"

"Do not make yourself uneasy. You have had your own worries."

"You must think me a terribly self-interested person."

"Caring for your mother is not selfish, Miss Lamb. Or if it is, it is the best kind of selfishness, I think."

"You know, my mother was the least selfish person I think I've ever known. She would do anything for anybody, especially her children. I should like to be a mother like that someday."

"I am certain you shall be, Miss Lamb."

The music started, and after a glance at the musicians, Mr. Taylor looked back at Charlotte, clearly unsure of himself.

"I am a terrible dancer, Miss Lamb, but if you would care to . . . ?"

"I would, Mr. Taylor. Very much. It's only that . . . I'm afraid I have promised the first two dances to another gentleman."

At that moment, emerging from a sea of feathered hats and swishing gowns, young William Bentley appeared, looking dapper in a fine tailcoat, striped waistcoat, and extravagant cravat that had no doubt cost ten times what his own had. At least Daniel had the pleasure of looking down at the boy, whose height barely surpassed Charlotte's.

"There you are, Miss Lamb," Bentley said with a bow. "I've come to claim you."

"Mr. Taylor," Charlotte said, turning to him, "may I present Mr. William Bentley, Mr. Harris's nephew. Mr. Bentley, this is Mr. Daniel Taylor, physician's apprentice and long-time family friend."

"Physician, eh? And you have known Miss Lamb for some time?"

"A few years now, yes."

"So you are uniquely qualified to give me your professional opinion about her."

"How so?"

"Is it just me, or is she not absolutely perfect?"

"Mr. Bentley, please," Charlotte protested. "I am not perfect, as Mr. Taylor knows very well."

"Do you, man? Has she some hidden flaw, some malady I've yet to discover?"

"Mr. Bentley, you are speaking utter foolishness. Come, the other couples are starting."

"Very well. Excuse us, Taylor."

While Charlotte danced with William Bentley, Daniel went to retrieve his coat, then sought out the host and hostess to say his thank-yous and farewells. He felt the coward, running off with his coat tails between his legs, but he had used up his courage for one evening. He was just making for the door when the music paused. He glanced over and saw Bentley escort Charlotte from the dance floor and bow, excusing himself to claim his next partner. He noticed Charlotte's head swivel as she looked about the room. She must have seen him and guessed his route of departure, for she crossed the room at a diagonal and met him at the foot of the stairs.

"Mr. Taylor, you are not leaving, I hope?"

"I am afraid so." He lifted slightly the coat over his arm.

"Oh dear. I was hoping to see if you are as terrible a dancer as you claim."

He laughed. "I can assure you on that point, madam."

She looked at him steadily. "I would rather judge that for myself."

At the time he was unaware that her words had been rather forward, nearly a breach of etiquette. But clearly she was aware, for her face turned a pretty shade of pink. "Though I realize it is bad form, begging a partner this way."

He laid his coat and hat on a nearby chair and offered his arm. "Very well. But you have been forewarned."

Daniel soon proved that his assessment of his dancing skill was honest indeed. He was painfully aware that his steps were ungainly, his form inelegant. He did not pretend to enjoy the sneers from the other couples he inadvertently jostled, nor the dance movements themselves. What he did enjoy, however, was being with Charlotte Lamb, holding her lightly in his arms and gazing into her lovely face. When she smiled up at him, he felt as though he was not *such* a poor dancer after all.

When the music ended, Daniel escorted Charlotte from the dance floor. "You know," he said, "when you said you had promised your dance to another gentleman, I immediately assumed you meant Mr. Harris."

"Did you? I wonder why. Mr. Harris rarely dances, and when he does, it is only with the finest, most handsome lady in the room."

"Charlotte, there you are." Charles Harris appeared, looking elegant and confident in black-and-white evening attire. "Would you do me the honor of dancing with me?"

Charlotte swallowed, clearly stunned.

Smiling at her hesitancy, Mr. Harris slanted a glance at him and said, "Unless you are otherwise engaged?"

"Mr. Taylor and I have just been dancing."

"Taylor, is it? Oh, yes, Webb's apprentice. How do you do."

Daniel opened his mouth to reply, but Harris had already returned his attention to Charlotte. "Come, Charlotte, we have not danced since you were a girl."

"I was just telling Mr. Taylor that you dance but rarely."

"Not so rarely." He held out his hand to her, and she looked at the hand, the slight bow, the wry grin. She placed her white-gloved hand in his.

"If you will excuse us," Harris said to him.

Charlotte looked back at Daniel, lips parted, clearly wanting to say something to him, even as she was being drawn away by the charming Charles Harris.

"Mr. Harris rarely dances, and when he does, it's only with the finest, most handsome lady in the room," Charlotte had said.

Well, his record is unchanged, Daniel thought, wondering at the leaden disappointment in his stomach. What had he expected, for her to refuse Harris? And why should she?

A week after that long ago ball at Sharsted Court, Daniel had walked briskly from the study and presence of the Reverend Mr. Gareth Lamb, hat in hand, disappointment in his chest.

He had made it out the vicarage door, past the garden, and onto the road toward the village when he heard rapid footfalls behind him. He knew who it was, of course. He had hoped to take his leave without this encounter. He did not wish to share his humiliation with anyone. Nor could he forget the triumph on the vicar's face as he assured him that his daughter shared his views. Daniel took a deep breath before turning around.

She looked more like the girl-Charlotte again, rather than the poised young woman he'd danced with last week. Cheeks flushed, eyes wide, hair loose from her run, falling around her face, more concerned for the feelings of others than proper appearances. The girl he'd fallen in love with in the first place.

"You're leaving?" she asked between breaths. "For keeps, I mean?"

"Yes."

"Without saying good-bye?"

"I thought it best, under the circumstances."

"Oh . . . I suppose I should apologize for spoiling your dignified parting by chasing after you in a most undignified manner."

He smiled at this in spite of himself. "Your father would not approve."

She looked at him meaningfully, her earnest eyes sad. "No, he would not."

He looked away from her, toward Doddington, grasping his hands behind his back. He felt her gaze on his profile.

After an awkward moment, she asked, "Are you sure you must go?"

"Charlotte, I am sure of very little. Except that I need to improve myself. I am determined to complete my studies at the University of Edinburgh and become a licensed physician."

"But Oxford or Cambridge would be so much closer."

"I am afraid I haven't the status nor means for either of those institutions. Dr. Webb recommends Edinburgh—it is where he studied."

"You admire Dr. Webb."

"Yes. My own father is a surgeon, but I want to do more than set bones and cut out offending bits . . ." He paused. "Forgive me. That was terribly unfeeling of me."

She gave him a tiny smile. "You certainly do not have Dr. Webb's discretion."

"Quite right. Another thing I shall have to improve upon."

"My mother was quite fond of you—just as you are."

"Thank you. I am honored."

"Father, however . . ."

"Yes, Miss Lamb. I quite understand. Your father himself has made his opinion of me quite clear."

She opened her mouth as if to say more, to apologize, perhaps, but instead she pressed her lips primly together and said no more.

Knowing there was little more he could say on that subject, or any other, Daniel Taylor bid farewell to Miss Charlotte Lamb and to Doddington, determined to rarely think of either of them again.

18

Since they may be hindered by sickness,
or for that they are too weake and tender,
or else because their Husbands will not suffer them,
it will be very necessary to seeke out another Nurse.

—James Guillemeau, *Childbirth or The Happy Deliverie of Women*

In the London townhouse of Lady Katherine and Mr. Harris, Sally sat in a rocking chair in the third-floor nursery, holding the small boy in her arms, enjoying the warm weight of his compact body against her bosom. Holding him both comforted and pricked her heart. She missed her own dear boy, a few miles away with her sister. She had only seen him once since coming here the previous month. *'Tis for you I'm doin' this,* she thought. *I'm savin' every shilling. We'll have us a better life, Dickie. You see if we don't.*

The lady of the house entered without knocking, and Sally sat up straighter in the rocking chair, quickly making sure her frock was properly done up.

"Good evening, m'lady," Sally said quickly.

"And how is my son this evening?" Lady Katherine asked, eyes only for her boy.

"His belly is full and his dreams sweet."

Lady Katherine slanted a wry glance at Sally. "And how would you know the content of his dreams?"

"Oh, just look at him, m'lady. He's got the look of peace about him. He sleeps the sleep of one with no worries. No twitchin', no moanin'."

"Well, let us hope he is this quiet during the churching tomorrow."

Sally lifted the boy gently from her lap, offering him up to his mother. "Would you like to hold him?"

"Not tonight, I fear. We're off to a small dinner party and I haven't time to clean spittle—or worse—from my gown. You understand."

"O' course."

Katherine turned and stepped back to the door, then paused. "Just listen to that wind. It will ruin my hair. Do find Edmund an extra blanket for the night. This house is so drafty when the wind blows."

"Yes, m'lady."

The townhouse *was* drafty, especially up on the higher floors. It was tall and narrow, like those adjoining it. Sally guessed their interiors were similar too, though she had little to base this on, as she had barely been out of the house since hiring on as Edmund's nurse.

The warmest room in the house was the kitchen below stairs. Its high windows looked out onto a small herb garden, ruined this late in autumn. The dining room was on the main level, with large windows facing the street. On the first floor up were the drawing room, sitting room, and library; and on the second, the master and mistress's bedchambers and dressing rooms. Above that were the nursery and two other bedrooms, and on the top level, the servant's quarters. It had taken Sally weeks to get used to all the climbing of stairs. Her appetite since coming here had grown, and she'd overheard the cook grumbling more than once about how much she ate. *'Tisn't my fault*, Sally thought, *what with the milk I must give and all this added exercise.*

Sally laid the sleeping child in his cradle and went searching for another blanket as her mistress had bid. This child already had more belongings than Sally herself had owned in her entire life. She dug through the wardrobe, then lifted the cover of the cedar chest behind the settee. She soon discovered a thick wool tartan and a small satin quilt. She ran her hands over each for the sheer pleasure of feeling the fine materials and textures. The silky ivory quilt felt cool to her touch, the wool scratchy but substantial. Surely the poor thing would sweat under either of those.

She dug farther. Near the bottom, she found a small blanket rolled up like a sausage. Curious, she pulled it from beneath the layers and unrolled it. The material was coarse—ordinary unbleached cotton. Just like the material the girls at Milkweed Manor used to stitch up blankets and nappies. She was surprised to see such a homely article in this chest of treasures. Had some poor relative given it as a gift, only for the thing to be stuffed to the bottom of the heap, with no hope of touching Edmund Harris's delicate skin? She felt embarrassed for the foolish pauper, whoever she was.

But then the lamplight fell on the corner of the blanket and Sally's fingers flew to trace the unusual stitching. She lifted the corner and inspected it closely. Why, she recognized this embroidery, this flower and pod. This was Charlotte's work, surely. Wasn't that the faintest hint of her initial C in the leaf of the flower? But how had Charlotte's blanket . . . the one she had stitched for her very own child . . . ended up here, at the bottom of Lady Katherine's cedar chest?

The door creaked open and Sally jerked awake. She had fallen asleep rocking Edmund. Lady Katherine and Mr. Harris stepped into the nursery, no doubt to check on their son after their evening out.

"What is that?" Censure obvious in her tone, Katherine stood beside the chair, looking down her nose at Sally.

"What?" Sally looked down at herself, then at Edmund, asleep in her arms.

"That filthy thing you've wrapped him in?"

"'Tisn't filthy, m'lady. Only plain."

"Wherever did it come from?"

Mr. Harris stepped closer, quickly looking from the blanket, to Sally, to his wife, and then back to Sally. His face was somber.

"Perhaps Nurse brought it with her," he suggested.

"No, sir, I found it in the chest."

The father shrugged. "It might be from the hospital. It was cold that night, and I believe the physician might have sent Edmund home bundled up in an extra blanket or two."

"The hospital? Well, get it off him, then. Who knows how filthy the thing is."

"I'm sure it's been laundered," Mr. Harris assured her. "During your recovery."

"Still . . . we have all these fine lovely blankets," Katherine walked to the cedar chest herself and lifted its lid. "Please use these."

"Yes, m'lady." Sally bobbed her head.

Lady Katherine selected the ivory satin quilt, and realizing her mistress meant *now*, Sally quickly unwound the hospital blanket from the infant. Lady Katherine handed her the quilt and took the embroidered blanket from her with two fingers held far from her body. She furrowed her brow and brought it closer to her face. "That's odd . . ."

"What is?" Mr. Harris asked.

"This stitching. I have seen something very like it before."

"All stitching's alike to me. It's late—come to bed."

"Very well. Dispose of this for me, please."

"Yes, m'lady."

Sally folded up the offending blanket but could not bring herself to discard it. After her employers left the room, she shoved it back down into the bottom of the chest.

Charlotte hired a hansom using the few bank notes her aunt had slipped into her hand prior to her recent departure. She knew she should not go. But she couldn't seem to stop herself. Once more leaving Anne in Mae's capable hands and donning her large brimmed bonnet, she stepped into the hansom and gave the driver the simple directions.

She had received her aunt's note just yesterday. Knowing now that her niece had an ally in Dr. Taylor, Amelia Tilney had sent him a brief letter of gratitude, thanking him for alerting her to Charlotte's situation and within that note, enclosed another addressed to Charlotte herself. Her aunt had thought to cheer her, Charlotte supposed, with her news. But she had not.

My Dear Charlotte,

I thought it might please you to know that two you have long held dear are celebrating the joyful occasion of the birth of a son. We all feared how your cousin Katherine would do, considering her somewhat advanced age and the discomfort she experienced late in her lying-in. But I know you will be happy to hear that all is well and Charles and Katherine have a little son they have named Edmund. I understand Katherine is to be churched this Wednesday at St. George's Hanover Square. They have even graciously included your uncle and I in their plans for a christening dinner in honor of the occasion. Our old friend Lord Elton will also attend, so it will no doubt be a grand celebration. I am sure if things were different, you would have been invited as well. But let us think only on the joy of such news, in hopes that you will glean hope that life indeed goes on. It was a difficult lesson for me, but I hope to ease your way a little if I might. So please take this news with the happiness intended. . . .

The letter went on to explain that after her recent visit to the manor, Aunt Tilney had instructed her driver to take her directly to Crawley to speak with her aunt personally, and yes, Margaret Dunweedy was still perfectly happy and willing to receive Charlotte and the child. But Charlotte's mind was focused on the news of the churching to be held not so very far from the manor.

Charlotte arrived at St. George's early, passed between the columns of the portico, and entered the grand church through a side door as discreetly as possible. She tiptoed through the entry hall, hoping to diminish the echo of her boots on the stone paving, and climbed the curved rear staircase to the upper gallery. Selecting a box to the rear, where she could see but hopefully remain unseen, she quietly opened its latch and sat on the bench. Below her, she saw a portly cleric lighting candles near the front altar, but otherwise there seemed to be no one about.

A quarter of an hour later, the center doors opened and a small group of gaily-dressed women entered, chattering and laughing like a clutch of hens. Charlotte recognized one of Katherine's friends but none of the other regal ladies. There was Katherine in the center of them, wearing a pale blue walking dress and a fur-trimmed cape. A blue hat ornamented with feathers crowned her head. In her arms, she held a babe . . . Charlotte's babe, gowned even more lavishly than his attendants, in flowing white satin. As the women chatted amongst themselves, Charlotte heard bits of their plans to visit an elegant tearoom after the churching.

An Anglican priest in flowing robes entered and the women hushed. He directed them to a small chapel beside the chancel, its size conducive to the intimate gathering. There Katherine kneeled, as directed by the *Book of Common Prayer*, and the service began. Having grown up a vicar's daughter, Charlotte knew the service was formally named the "Thanksgiving of Women after Childbirth."

"'For as much as it hath pleased Almighty God of His goodness to give you safe deliverance, and hath preserved you in the great danger of childbirth: you shall therefore give hearty thanks unto God,'" the priest intoned.

Katherine responded, "'I am well pleased that the Lord hath heard the voice of my prayer. The snares of death compassed me round: and the pains of hell got hold upon me.'"

Charlotte unconsciously mouthed the familiar words along with her cousin. She was touched by the unexpected humility of Katherine's audible response. She had long known Katherine to be cynical of religion, but her declaration seemed wholly sincere.

"'Oh, Almighty God,'" the priest continued, "'which hast delivered this woman thy servant from the great pain and peril of childbirth: Grant, we beseech thee, most merciful Father, that she through thy help, may both faithfully live and walk in her vocation, according to thy will in this life present . . . '"

This part of the service did not apply to her, Charlotte realized with a dull ache. Katherine was being exhorted to remain faithful to her husband and to bear other heirs for him. Charlotte swallowed back remaining dregs of bitterness.

"' . . . and also may be partaker of everlasting glory in the life to come: through Jesus Christ our Lord. Amen.'"

Would Katherine bear more children? Even though she was older and had experienced such a difficult childbirth? Katherine believed a healthy child had resulted from the ordeal . . . so would Edmund yet have a brother or sister? Or would he grow up an only child?

"'Children,'" continued the priest as he delivered the liturgy, "'are an heritage and gift that cometh of the Lord. Happy is the man that hath his quiver full of them.'"

Charlotte sat and waited as Katherine's friends filed cheerfully from the church, their heels and laughter echoing in the lofty space. Katherine paused to thank the cleric, then turned and followed after the others. Charlotte watched until Katherine and Edmund disappeared from view beneath the gallery railing.

Then her tear-filled gaze fled to a carving of Mary holding the infant Jesus and, above, the magnificent painting of Jesus at the Last Supper. She stared at the images as Katherine's footsteps faded away below. Charlotte felt her lips part and her chest tighten. She had spent her life in a church not unlike this one, but this was the first time she had been so deeply struck by the immensity of what God had done in giving up His only Son. *How did you do it?* she breathed, tears running down her cheeks. Of course she knew the situations were beyond compare. God's sacrifice had saved countless multitudes. Hers, only one precious child.

A few days after the churching, Katherine pulled the long-forgotten handkerchief from beneath the sachet in her drawer. How long had it lain there, concealed? The smell of musty lilac was heavy on the material, its folds now permanent creases. She turned it over and there it was. The unusual flower, the pod, the curve of the leaf resembling the letter C. Yes . . . this was a C and now she remembered. This was Charlotte's signature. Cousin Charlotte, who detested needlework but had nevertheless made a pretty handkerchief for Katherine as a gift for some birthday or Christmas many years ago now.

Clutching the handkerchief, Katherine marched up the stairs to the nursery.

Sally jumped when she entered.

"Where is that blanket? The embroidered one?"

"I . . . I'm not . . ."

"Did you dispose of it as I asked?"

"Well, I . . . I meant to put it out with the children's aid donation. But let me see . . ."

Sally lifted the lid of the chest and flipped through the linens.

"There 'tis."

"I knew it." Katherine snatched the blanket from her and walked to the window, comparing the two items in the light.

"Do forgive me, m'lady."

"Look. They are so similar, are they not?"

Sally approached cautiously and leaned close. "Seems so."

"Do you know who made this?"

The nurse hesitated. "Well, I . . ."

"My cousin Charlotte, that's who."

"Charlotte?"

"Yes, Charlotte Lamb, my young cousin. I've been wondering where's she gone to."

"Charlotte Lamb?"

"Yes, yes."

Katherine strode from the nursery, both pieces in hand. She found Charles in the library.

"I knew it. Look."

"What am I looking at? Not the confounded blanket again."

"Yes . . . and the handkerchief. See—they were made by the same person."

"I do not see that they are so alike."

"I asked and asked, and no one would tell me. I detest secrets! I have had my suspicions, but I did not want to believe—"

"Katherine," he said sternly. "What are you talking about?"

"Charlotte Lamb, of course."

"What of her?"

"She made this blanket, just as she made this for me years ago. That could only mean one thing."

"What are you suggesting?"

"You said you got this from a hospital. Which hospital?"

"What does it matter?"

"Was it a lying-in hospital? The Manor Home? Queen Charlotte's?"

"I had my mind on other things. The physician directed the driver to the nearest facility . . ."

"Yes, yes. Which was it?"

"Why do you need to know?"

"Because Charlotte is there . . . or was. And I have the proof of it." She lifted the blanket.

"You have nothing of the kind. All sorts of ladies aid societies make blankets for hospitals and foundling wards and other worthy charities. If, and I repeat *if,* Charlotte Lamb stitched that blanket, that by no means proves anything other than her stitching hasn't improved."

"Can you imagine Charlotte sitting around stitching with some ladies aid society? And with such cheap material? I for one cannot."

"For a good cause . . ."

"Yes, for a very good cause—her own. I tell you she has disappeared, and my uncle will not speak her name nor hint at her whereabouts. Neither will her trying sister."

She suddenly looked at him, staring baldly at him, daring him to lie. "You do not know where she is, do you, Charles? Tell me honestly."

He replied levelly. "I do not know where she is."

"I should ask Amelia Tilney. She would know if anyone would."

"Why do you want to know?"

"Why do you think? So we can help her."

"Even if what you are suggesting is true . . . that she's had a child out of wedlock?"

"Yes. Not publicly, of course. But if she's been left to fend for herself, there must be something we can do."

"That is very kind of you, Katherine."

"Do look into it for me, won't you, Charles?"

"Very well. If it's important to you, I shall."

Daniel's father, John Taylor, looked at him sadly from across the table. "But to send your child away . . . ?"

"What would you have me do?" Daniel asked.

"I could help care for her. Have the nurse stay here."

"What sort of woman would live alone with two men?"

"Plenty would."

"Not the sort I want nursing my daughter."

"Anne is my grandchild."

"And my daughter. Do you not think I shall miss her as well?"

"But Lizette will want her near . . . once she is sufficiently recovered."

"I pray that will be so."

"May I ask what—" his father hesitated—"what course of treatment you will try next?"

"I do not know."

"Allow me to help you, Daniel."

"You are not to practice, if you'll remember."

"It was one mistake. And even then both child and mother survived."

"Yes, I thank God I happened by."

"She was not expected to deliver for a fortnight at least. If I'd had any indication her time might come sooner, that I might be called into duty, I should never have allowed myself to . . . to . . ."

"Get drunk?"

His father winced.

"Forgive me," Daniel said. "That was uncalled for."

"I have not taken a drink since," his father said quietly. "But if I'm not allowed to work, to help people . . . I do not know . . ."

"Perhaps in time, Father. Once that episode is forgotten. Do not forget Miss Marsden threatened to go to the courts with her charges if she caught wind of you practicing."

"I have not forgotten. Still, I might be of use to my own granddaughter or daughter-in-law. . . ."

"You saw how Lizette was while she was still here with us. You would barely know her now. The mania is completely out of control. If you have some idea . . ."

"I confess I have never treated a case so severe."

"Nor I, Father. Nor I."

The following week, Katherine again raised the topic of Charlotte's whereabouts. "I was speaking with my accoucheur and he remembers a physician by the name of Taylor being on hand the night of Edmund's birth."

"Yes, that's right."

"Well, where does he practice? Have you contacted him?"

"What do you plan to do once you know?"

"To inquire after Charlotte, of course."

"I'm sure such information is confidential. For obvious reasons."

"Oh, I have my ways—as you well know." She smiled at him.

"Have you considered for a moment, my dear, that if Charlotte were in such a place, she might not like the fact to be discovered?"

"Bah. I am sure it is only that preening vicar-father of hers that sent her into exile. Charlotte has always been very fond of me. I am sure she would be happy to see me, once she knows where my sympathies lie."

"I am sorry, Mrs. Harris." The matron, a Mrs. Moorling, was either ignorant or refused to address her properly. "But I cannot divulge the name of any of our girls—neither current nor past residents. Surely you understand."

"Normally, yes. But I assure you this instance is different. I only want to help my cousin."

"Very noble, I'm sure."

Katherine sighed. "Very well, I shall leave my card." Katherine handed one across the desk. "Perhaps you might deliver it to her and ask her to contact me, if that would be more suitable."

"I told you, there is nothing I can do." Mrs. Moorling rose. "I trust Sally Mitchell has proven herself a suitable nurse?"

Katherine had little choice but to rise as well. "Yes. Quite suitable, thank you."

Unaccustomed as she was to being refused anything, Lady Katherine's departing smile was quite false.

As she left Mrs. Moorling's office, she saw a thin, plain, officious woman with a sheaf of papers in hand.

Katherine smiled at her. "You look a very knowledgeable, helpful sort."

"I do?" The plain woman curtsied. "Thank you, mum."

"I would be ever so obliged if you could help me. I am looking for my dearest cousin, sent here by her tyrant of a father. Poor dear thinks she hasn't a friend in the world, when here I am ready to offer hearth and home."

"'Tis good of you."

"So. If you could just direct me to Charlotte's room . . ." She took a tentative step toward the stairs.

"Charlotte?" the young woman asked.

"Yes, Miss Charlotte Lamb." Katherine paused on the first step.

"Oh . . . I'm afraid we haven't anyone by that name. We did have a Charlotte not so long ago by another surname. But I'm afraid she's left and I know not where. Poor soul."

Katherine arched a brow.

"Lost her wee babe, she did."

"How dreadful."

"Yes, mum. A finer young woman I've never known."

"But not . . . a Miss Lamb?"

"No. I'm afraid not."

Discouraged, Katherine was just leaving the manor when she heard a voice call out a familiar name. "Afternoon, Taylor. Any new patients I should know of?"

Katherine whirled around. Two men stood talking in low tones on the other side of the hall. Both looked up as she approached, her shoes clicking on the marble floor. One was handsome—dark hair brushed back from his forehead with a touch of silver in his sideburns. The other man was taller, but thin and pale.

"Dr. Taylor?" she asked.

The thin one inclined his chin and answered, "Yes?"

She introduced herself. "Lady Katherine Harris."

Before Taylor could respond, the handsome man bowed. "Lady Katherine . . . a pleasure. Allow me to introduce myself. Jeffrey Preston, esteemed physician. May I be of service?"

"Actually I'd like to speak to Dr. Taylor." She turned to him. "That is, if you have a moment?"

"Of course. Excuse us, Preston."

Dr. Preston bowed curtly before turning on his heel and stalking away.

"You must forgive me," Katherine began once they were alone. "I am told you were on hand the night my son was born, but I am afraid I don't remember meeting you . . . or little else for that matter. I was not myself that night."

"Perfectly understandable. It is a pleasure to see you looking so well."

"Thank you."

"And how does young Edmund fare?"

"Very well." She beamed. "I am surprised you remember my little son's name." Then her pleasure transformed into a question. "But how do you know his name, I wonder? We had not yet decided what to call him."

"Oh. I don't know. Someone told me. Your husband, perhaps. I've seen him by chance a time or two since."

Her eyebrows rose. "Have you really?"

"Only in passing."

She looked at him closely, opened her mouth as if to say more, then closed it again. She smiled. "I have not thanked you for everything you did for my son that night."

"You needn't thank me."

"Of course I do. You saved his life."

"Well . . ." Dr. Taylor looked down at the floor, clearly uncomfortable.

"Let me tell you why I'm here," she began. She told him of her quest and the man's discomfiture only seemed to increase.

"I am afraid I cannot help you. The Manor Home has strict policies—"

"Yes, yes, your Mrs. Moorling has explained all that already. But I thought, perhaps since you are some acquainted with my family . . ."

"I'm sorry."

She pulled a small paper-wrapped bundle from her reticule. "I have funds here I was hoping would help my cousin. Shall I be forced to roam the corridors, calling her name?"

"No. That will not be necessary. You have my word that Char . . . that no one by that name is in residence."

"But she was here."

"I cannot say."

Katherine sighed in frustration, then forced a smile. "Very well." She returned the bundle to her bag and turned to leave.

Dr. Taylor called after her. "If I were to . . ."

Katherine turned around.

" . . . to somehow come into contact with this person. Can you tell me, what exactly is the money for? Is it . . . in payment for . . . something?"

"Payment? Goodness, it isn't payment for anything. I simply want to help her and never imagined I would have so much trouble doing so."

Dr. Taylor again studied the floor. Katherine closed the distance between them.

"It is clear you know more than you let on. I know—I will give you a . . . donation. If you can get it to Charlotte, wonderful. If you cannot, use it for the worthiest cause . . . or woman . . . you know. Surely you cannot reject such an offer."

"It is indeed generous and there are many needs."

She pressed the money into his hand.

"I trust you to help her, if you can."

19

Wanted, a child to wet nurse.

A healthy young English woman having abundance of milk, wishes to take a child to wet nurse at her own house—every attention will be paid to the comfort of the child, as she is living in a quiet and healthy house. . . .

—*Philadelphia Public Ledger,* 1837

Charlotte and young Anne were established in Margaret Dunweedy's snug cottage in the village of Crawley, not far from The George Inn—a midway stop on the coach route between London and Brighton.

Margaret Dunweedy, Charlotte's great-aunt, was a small, wiry woman with surprising vitality for one of her advanced years. Her hair was white and twisted around the crown of her head in a long plait. Her eyes were the color of cornflowers, as were many of the veins around her eyes, making her irises appear even bluer. She was rarely still. She received Charlotte and the baby with great warmth and enthusiasm, bustling about, making tea, bringing extra blankets, exclaiming over the joys of having someone sharing the old place again. Her husband had been gone twenty years, and her son, Roger, was living in Manchester and too busy with his post to visit very often.

Margaret Dunweedy's sole fault, Charlotte soon surmised, was her inability to cease speaking. The cheerful woman seemed never to run out of things to say. For the first few weeks, this was quite a pleasant relief, for Mrs. Dunweedy felt no need to question Charlotte, happy to simply relay countless tales of her own life. But as the long months of winter wore on, Charlotte began to grow weary of the constant chatter.

Otherwise, the winter passed in relative ease and comfort. Dr. Taylor visited his daughter every fortnight or so, as his schedule and road conditions allowed. His wife was somewhat improved, he'd reported, but was still suffering.

Anne began sleeping through the night, and so did Charlotte. She was amazed at how much better she felt, how much lighter the anguish, the pressing weight of her grief. It was still there, of course, like a hooded cloak about her head and shoulders. The cloak had at first been fashioned of barbed chain mail that threatened to knock her to her knees. Over the winter months, it had become a cloak of heavy grey wool, its hood falling over her eyes and blocking out the light, encasing her in darkness, suffocating her. But as winter gave way to spring, so too the cloak lightened as if to a dense velvet or thick damask. She could still feel it with every fiber of her skin, her being, but now it let in the light and allowed her, finally, to breathe. Even so, there was not a waking hour in which she didn't think of Edmund. And rare was the night when she did not dream of trying to find him, or of him about to fall from some dangerous precipice. How she tried to get to him, but he was always out of reach.

As soon as the weather allowed, she took to bundling up Anne and taking the baby outside with her in the untidy remains of last year's garden and beyond, to the damp fallow field behind the cottage, parroting her mother's wisdom about the benefits of "fresh air and exercise." She closed her eyes and breathed in the loam, the wilted sage, the rare silence.

On one such day in March, she noticed a carriage coming to a halt on the road on the far side of the meadow. Something about the horse and rig seemed familiar, but at such a distance she could not see the driver. As the carriage sat there on the open road, Charlotte saw a glint of light, as off glass. *Strange*, Charlotte thought. Was someone watching her?

On the first day of April, Gareth Lamb, her brother-in-law, stared at her incredulously over his teacup. "Are you suggesting she might yet be recovered?"

Amelia Tilney nodded, taken aback by his sharp tone.

Across from Amelia, her eldest niece said between clenched teeth, "I suggest we discuss this no further."

"Beatrice, please," Amelia began. "I have reason to believe she's lost the child."

"Must we speak of it! The indecency . . ."

"The babe lives," Gareth Lamb said flatly.

"What?" Amelia asked, stunned.

"I saw them with my own eyes."

Amelia's heart began to beat painfully within her. "You did? When?"

"I was in Crawley for a clerical meeting Monday last. Drove by your aunt's cottage, and there she was in the back garden, babe in arms."

"Will my mortification never end!" Bea flopped herself down on the settee in a most unladylike manner.

Amelia realized her hand was over her heart. "I confess I am speechless . . ."

Gareth gave her a knowing look. "I am sure you are."

"Did Charlotte see you?"

"No. I was too far off. I—" He shifted uncomfortably. "I happened to have an opera glass with me."

"Well, she cannot return here," Bea stressed. "Really, Father, it is too much."

"If only the man would do his duty," Mr. Lamb shook his head somberly. "Plenty of other children have come into the world in such a manner. Many have been granted educations and gone on to marry well. Some have even been given titles . . ."

"Father. I doubt *this* father has any title to bestow beyond that of assistant gravedigger."

"Beatrice!" Amelia gasped.

"Have you another theory, Aunt? Another explanation?"

"She assures me the man in question is a gentleman of good repute."

"How can that be?"

"She declines to blame him, but it seems clear that he must have chosen to marry another."

"She said so?"

"Not directly, but I gathered this from her certainty that there was no way to bring him around."

"I have another theory," Gareth Lamb said with a frown. "Perhaps the bounder has intentions for her sister and refuses to yield."

It was Bea's turn to gasp. "Father! I forbid you to speak so of Mr. Bentley! It's slanderous!"

"Well, the young man has yet to ask for your hand. Has all but disappeared. Have *you* another explanation?"

Bea raised her chin. "If it has anything to do with Charlotte, it is that our family's disgrace has somehow come to his attention."

Bea flounced out of the room, more for escape than out of any true emotion. She was off to meet her friend Althea. They were to attend a reading together in the bustling market town of Faversham. Buxley was already waiting for her outside with the carriage as she had requested.

Arriving in Faversham a quarter hour ahead of schedule, Bea asked Buxley to let her down near the town center. She would walk to the library from there. It was a market day and vendors filled the streets surrounding the old guildhall, their carts, baskets, and makeshift tables overflowing with sausages, cheeses, bread, fish, and fruit. Taking her time, she strolled past the booths, then paused to look at the hats displayed in the milliner's window, noting with disdain that they were terribly out of fashion. She sighed. It was too bad they did not live closer to London town.

Ahead she saw a tearoom. Outside its doors, several tables stood beneath a striped awning. She noticed two couples enjoying refreshment *al fresco*, taking advantage of the unseasonably warm spring day.

"Mr. Bentley!" Bea called before the scene fully registered. Then her breath caught and she nearly stumbled. There was no mistaking the smile William was giving the young lady across the table from him, how close he was leaning . . . that light in his eyes. Bea had seen all these before. She knew. It was either slink away, ashamed, and hope he had not heard nor seen her, or mount an offensive. Beatrice Lamb had never slunk away from anything in her life, and she decided not to start now. She wouldn't give him—or her—that satisfaction. She squared her shoulders and waved a handkerchief. His handkerchief.

He saw her and quickly excused himself from the redhead. Squire Litchfield's daughter, if she was not mistaken. Pretty, yes. Dumb as a mule. That her father had more money than hers, there was no doubt.

Did she imagine the slight sheepish expression, the flush of his fair cheeks? The awkward smile now as he approached? Surely she had, for the man clearly had no shame.

She summoned her most confident smile and stood tall. "How fortuitous to happen upon you, Mr. Bentley."

"Yes. Miss Lamb, um, how good to see you again. How do you fare?"

"Wonderfully well, I thank you. And so relieved to see you out enjoying yourself on such a fine afternoon."

"Yes?"

"I have been hoping for an appropriate time to return this to you. Trite thing, this, but how glad I am to happen upon you in a public place. There you are. Now I am relieved of that obligation. I do thank you, sir. And wish you well."

She turned to leave, smile stiff but resilient. If only she could manage not to trip and disgrace herself on her departure.

"Bea!"

She started, which she hoped he did not notice, and forced herself to turn around slowly at his unexpected call.

"Yes, Mr. Bentley?" she began, but fearing she sounded too hopeful, added breezily, "Did I forget something? Oh, forgive me, please do give my regards to your companion. I must hurry to a reading with a friend or I would adore meeting her."

"You must know her. It is Amanda Litchfield."

"Oh, one of the Litchfields. Do say hello for me."

"Bea . . . Miss Lamb. Are you certain you are all right?"

"Of course I am."

"And . . . your family?"

"Better than ever, I thank you. Now I really must fly."

He looked at her, clearly perplexed. There was a speculative look in his eyes that told her he might suspect her act but wasn't quite sure what to believe. It would have to be enough.

Amelia Tilney studied the stern face of her brother-in-law. He had moved on from tea to port, though she knew he was not given to drink. She felt only mildly guilty for driving him to its solace this day. "Gareth, I must say your coldness surprises me most unhappily."

"Madam. There are consequences to be reckoned with, and certainly we are all aware that there is no happy outcome in such a situation."

Amelia leaned forward and adjusted the framed miniature of her sister on the table. She said softly, "You are a man of God, Gareth. You of all men should know that God is forgiving, a God of mercy—"

"He is also a God of wrath. And of consequences."

"But must Charlotte pay such a dear price—the loss of her entire family? She has already suffered greatly. She was a mere shadow of herself when last I saw her."

"Was she?" He seemed to contemplate this. "Is she repentant? Sorry?"

"Oh, a sorrier girl I have never seen."

"And is she being well provided for by your aunt?"

"Well, there is not much money for coal or meat, but she has a nice kitchen garden and preserves all she can for winter. I am afraid Margaret's son is a mean sort who provides little for her upkeep. My husband and I send what we can. If you would but allow us, we would do more, now that Charlotte is there."

"No. You have done enough. I must ask you to do nothing further. And to speak no more of this."

"You may depend upon my discretion. I only speak now because I feel Charlotte's plight so keenly—"

He halted the rest of her sentence with a dismissive wave of his hand. "Yes, yes." He rose. "Now I really must bid you good day."

Amelia rose as well. Though stung by her brother-in-law's rudeness, she believed him not quite as unmoved as he appeared.

A week later, the bell jingled as Margaret Dunweedy pushed open the butcher shop door. The gust of wind that accompanied her sent the hanging fowl and sides of meat to swaying on their hooks. The smells of sausages, strong English cheeses, and meat-pie pastries greeted her, as did the cheery butcher with his ready smile and crisp apron. "A good day to you, Missus Dunweedy."

"And to you, Mr. Doughty. What have you today for sixpence per pound?"

"No need for soup bones today, ma'am. Not with your account bulging with a good two pounds to spend."

"Two pounds—you are surely mistaken, Mr. Doughty. On my account?"

"No, ma'am. No mistakin' it." He winked at her. "You've got yourself a secret admirer, I'd say."

"Don't talk foolishness, man. At my age."

"Not foolishness at all. Well, then, what will it be. A fine leg of lamb? Or perhaps a stuffed goose? A roast of beef?"

"You are quite sure?"

"Sure I'm sure."

Margaret Dunweedy would have liked to believe the gift from her son, Roger. But she knew better. She guessed the two pounds had more to do with her lodger than with her, but she was grateful to be able to provide the sweet lass something finer than the stews and soups she'd been preparing.

"I haven't had a roast of beef since I don't know when," she admitted.

"Roasted with potatoes and onions . . ." The butcher closed his eyes, savoring the thought.

"The roast it is, Mr. Doughty."

"Excellent choice, ma'am. Excellent choice." He wrote himself a note.

She raised a brow at the paper he scribbled upon.

"I'm to account for how the pounds is spent, ma'am. Seems your admirer has more generosity than trust in an old scuff like me. Afraid I might take your two quid and leave you none the wiser."

"Then he doesn't know you, Mr. Doughty. A more trustworthy butcher I've never known."

"Thank you, ma'am. And here you are. You enjoy that, now." He handed her the wrapped package.

"Indeed we shall."

"You've company, then?"

"Oh, just my niece come to call."

"Ah, that explains it."

It didn't. Not fully, Margaret knew. But she was wise enough to know the village butcher didn't need to know her great-niece's troubles. He might not cheat on the fair weight of meat, but he wasn't above handing out juicy gossip along with his chops.

Tibbets announced Lady Katherine's arrival and her father stood. Bea merely laid aside the book she had been reading. Her cousin strode into the room, looking—Bea noted begrudgingly—elegant in a feathered hat and a full pelisse that did not quite conceal her figure, still somewhat rounded from her confinement last autumn.

"Lady Katherine. Niece!" Father boomed.

"Good day, Uncle. You're looking . . . well, rather tired, actually. Are you not well?"

"I am not getting any younger. But I cannot complain."

"And Beatrice. How nice to see you again."

Beatrice merely nodded.

Her father smiled in her stead. "What an unexpected pleasure."

"Is it unexpected? Surely you heard that we were returning to Fawnwell."

"We did hear that the repairs were nearing completion, but not that you—"

"Yes. I've shut up my London home for the season. We're doing everything quite the wrong way round this year. Now that most of our friends have left their country homes and are returned to London, we have quit town to stay here for the spring and summer. I detest the thought of missing the London season, but Charles believes the country air will be so much better for Edmund. Oh! You must meet him." She turned to the servant. "Do ask the nurse in as soon as she's done changing the child."

"Yes, m'lady." Tibbets curtsied and left the room.

"Won't you sit down?" Beatrice offered coolly.

"Thank you. That gown . . . Rather severe, is it not? Yet it fits you somehow."

"I think so." Bea liked the high-necked frock in a color she thought of as storm grey.

"I would have called sooner," Katherine chatted on, filling the silence. "But first I had my recovery, of course, and then this dreadful winter. Did you not find it so? I do detest traveling in inclement weather. The roads get so rough and rutted. How glad I am that spring is here at last and I can be out calling again."

Tibbets returned a moment later with a tall horse-faced woman holding a chubby baby in a satin gown. The nurse bobbed a curtsy, then carried the child to his mother and placed him in her outstretched arms.

Katherine, smile bright, turned the baby around to face them.

"This is our Edmund. Is he not the image of Mr. Harris?"

Bea stared. For a fleeting moment, she saw Charlotte in the child's features, his upturned nose and fine brows above large brown eyes. Was she really feeling so guilty about her? Or missing her so keenly? The little boy smiled a toothless grin in Bea's direction. She did not return the gesture.

"He looks like Charlotte," her father said dully, staring too. He'd said her name, as he'd vowed not to.

"You mean Charles, Father, surely," Bea rushed to correct.

"Oh, yes, yes. Charles. The names are so very similar. I meant to name my son Charles if I'd had one."

Katherine's brows were furrowed as she looked from one to the other.

From the corner of her eye, Bea noticed the ungainly nurse staring at her from across the room, where she stood in wait behind her mistress. *Why had Katherine even brought the sorry creature?*

"Speaking of Charlotte . . ." Katherine began.

"We were not," Bea said. "In fact we prefer other subjects."

"Yes, do tell us about Fawnwell," Father added. "Is all as it once was? Before the fire, I mean."

Katherine stilled, only her eyes moving between them, scrutinizing. She opened her mouth, closed it, and changed tack.

"Beatrice, Charles and I are thinking of hosting a house party this summer to celebrate the restoration of Fawnwell, and of course, to introduce Edmund. We are considering inviting many of our London friends down, many eligible . . . persons you might enjoy meeting. Has that any appeal for you?"

Beatrice shrugged. "Perhaps." *Why is that nurse still staring at me?*

"And you, Uncle, certainly you would not mind a little variety in society? A chance to debate theology with like-minded men of rank?"

Bea did not miss the patronizing choice of words, but Father did, and beamed.

"I should not mind at all. Sounds grand. When is it to be?"

"Why, just as soon as you tell me what I wish to know."

20

> Wet nurses are unfortunately a necessary evil. Without them the children of the better classes . . . would suffer very materially.
>
> —T. C. Haden, *On the Management and Diseases of Children,* 1827

She had no warning.

Charlotte was pacing Mrs. Dunweedy's small parlor with Anne in her arms, hoping to lull the child to sleep, when she heard the familiar sound of a carriage on the street outside. It was pulled by a team of at least four horses, she judged, by the thunderous beating of hooves. Being this close to the High Street, that sound did not alarm her—in fact it barely registered. It was the sound of the hooves slowing, the coachman shouting "Whoa" to his horses that caused Charlotte to walk to the window. She shifted Anne to her left arm and parted the curtains with her right hand. Her heart began pounding, faster and faster even as the pounding hooves slowed, then ceased. A fine carriage indeed. Tall and enclosed. A carriage made for traveling some distance in speed and comfort. Lady Katherine's carriage.

Oh, God, help me. . . . The breathed prayer was automatic. What else could she do? She couldn't flee. How had her cousin found out where she was? Had Aunt Tilney told her? No, she would never do such a thing, loathe as she was for anyone in the family, or in their general acquaintance, to discover Charlotte's position as a wet nurse. Then who? And how was she to honor her aunt's fervent plea and keep that fact hidden?

The coachman helped her cousin alight. There she was in fine, full-length cape and plumed hat. Had she—*Oh, dear Lord*—had Katherine brought her son? *Her* Edmund? How would she hide her feelings?

Behind Katherine, a second woman alighted on the coachman's hand. This one far taller and more simply attired. Sally! Sally—here, now? Charlotte was elated and dread-filled all at once.

Sally will know Anne is not mine.

That thought pushed Charlotte into action. Hurrying, she gently laid Anne in her little cradle in the guest room, wincing in anticipation but breathing deeply when the child did not cry. She then quickly opened the front door and stepped out onto the path, not waiting for her visitors to knock.

"Lady Katherine! What a lovely surprise!"

Both women, still standing beside the tall carriage, turned to look at her. But it was Sally who sprung into movement first, handing her bundle to Katherine and hurrying over to Charlotte, arms outstretched, her thin face overwhelmed by her crooked, toothy smile.

"Bless me, Charlotte! I didn't know it was you we was visiting!"

Sally threw her arms around her and held her tight.

Charlotte took the opportunity to whisper urgently. "Sally. Please. Don't say a word about . . . my son. I've a baby here, a girl. Please don't say anything. They all think she is mine."

"But . . . I don't understand . . ."

"Please. I'll explain when I can."

"Well, I gather you two have never met," Katherine said wryly. Charlotte and Sally pulled apart. Katherine was looking at them with a speculative grin.

"Sally and I met in London."

"Oh?"

Charlotte took a deep breath. "Yes. She worked at the lying-in hospital where I . . . spent my confinement."

Katherine shook her head, lips pursed. Charlotte lowered her focus to the ground.

"That father of yours . . ." Katherine grumbled. Charlotte looked up at this unexpected response. "Well, cousin"—Katherine raised a brow—"are we to be invited in for tea or not? I am dying to show off my son."

Charlotte glanced quickly at the bundled child in Katherine's arms, where she had been trying to avoid settling her gaze.

"Yes! Forgive me. Please do come in."

Once they were all inside, Charlotte began the introductions. "This is Margaret Dunweedy, my great-aunt on my mother's side. And this is Lady Katherine, my cousin on my father's side."

"And this is my son," Katherine added. "Little Edmund Harris."

"Oh, he's lovely," said Mrs. Dunweedy appreciatively. "How old is he?"

"He was born October . . ." Katherine thought for a moment.

Staring at him, Charlotte whispered, "The second . . ."

Katherine looked at her, puzzled. "The seventh."

"So, six months old," Margaret went on quickly, smiling and glancing at one, then the other of them.

"And this . . . ?" Margaret nodded toward Sally.

"Oh." Katherine waved her hand dismissively. "This is Edmund's nurse."

"Sally Mitchell," Sally supplied with a friendly smile.

Katherine sat on the worn, stuffed chair, holding Edmund on her lap. She turned sideways a bit in her seat to show her child off to the fullest vantage. "What say you, Charlotte? Is he not absolutely perfect?"

Charlotte swallowed, her eyes drinking in the still-familiar face—the prominent, upturned nose, the crease between the faint eyebrows. Yet how changed he was! He was able to sit up now, with a bit of support. His cheeks were rounder, his close-set, serious eyes more alert. Her heart ached. Her arms ached to hold him.

"Yes, perfect," she mumbled, then forced a smile. Edmund gave a toothless grin in response, and Charlotte had to bite her lip to hold back tears.

"I think he looks just like Charles. Do you not agree, Charlotte?"

"I could not say . . ."

"Of course you could, for you've known my husband longer than I have."

Charlotte's mouth went dry, and she studied the child's face again, glad for the excuse to savor the sight of him.

"Yes, I see the resemblance," Charlotte said quietly. "Indeed."

Charlotte excused herself and she and her great-aunt went into the kitchen to prepare tea. Charlotte helped her hostess bring out the tray of tea things and served their guests, trying in vain to keep her hand from shaking as she poured tea and passed the plate of scones. She was relieved Margaret had decided to purchase an unaccustomed sweet from the baker in addition to their usual sparse fare.

Katherine handed Edmund over to Sally and placed one of the damask napkins in her lap in his place. Katherine took a sip of tea, barely covering a grimace—Margaret made their tea weak to conserve—and began filling the awkward silence with her articulate speech, telling how they had closed up their London home for a few months and returned to Charles' estate.

"Charles feels the country air will be so much better for Edmund. I am not so sure how I shall fare, so isolated from the rest of the world. How I shall miss the season in town. But you know how it is—maternal sacrifice and all that. Whatever is best for my Edmund."

Charlotte's stiff smile began to waver, and she brought her teacup to her mouth just in time to cover the quiver of her lips.

Katherine took a bite of her scone, with a somewhat more approving expression, leaving the room silent again. Even Margaret was not her talkative self for once. Perhaps she found having a titled lady in her home somewhat intimidating.

Then, above the dainty clink of china cups on saucers and the clicking of the mantel clock, a baby's single cry pierced the silence. For a moment it seemed everyone froze, or didn't appear to have heard. Charlotte kept her eyes on her teacup, praying Anne would fall right back to sleep. Another cry arose. Margaret looked over at her first. Sally looked down at Edmund—sitting happily on her lap—then glanced up at her, questioningly. Katherine looked around the room at them all.

Charlotte got to her feet and said brightly, "Well! That was a short nap." She walked to the guest room and looked down into the cradle at Daniel Taylor's daughter. Anne's face was a wrinkled peach of need, which relaxed into contentment as soon as Charlotte lifted her into her arms.

"Forgive me. I don't know what else to do," she whispered and returned to the parlor.

"And this is Anne," she said, returning to her seat on the settee and holding the child close to her. She attempted to move the conversation along. "We were all so dreadfully sorry about the fire. Have the repairs been completed?"

"Yes, for the most part," Katherine said, eyes on Anne.

"And Mrs. Harris. That is . . . Mr. Harris's mother. She is well, I trust?"

"Yes. Quite well. Pleased to be back in her beloved home and delighted with her new grandson."

"Of course she is."

"You are familiar with her other grandson, are you not?" Katherine asked.

"Yes. Mr. Bentley visited the vicarage on occasion."

Katherine looked at Charlotte closely, then her gaze dropped again to the child in her arms. She set down her plate.

"Here, let us see her. Anne, was it?" Katherine held out her hands, leaving Charlotte little choice but to rise and place the child in her arms for inspection.

"Hello there, Miss Anne," Katherine began, situating the girl on her lap. "Was that you making all that fuss? Not very ladylike, are you? Oh, that is better. I believe she has fixed her eyes upon my feather." No conventional platitudes about the child's beauty nor perfection from Katherine Harris. "She is so different from Edmund. They look nothing at all alike."

Was that relief in her voice? Had she suspected, somehow, her own husband?

"Well, that is not surprising," Charlotte said. "You and I are not so closely related. And though they were born only a week or so apart, boys and girls are often so different—"

"She is a bit on the small side, is she not?" Katherine interrupted.

"Perhaps a bit," Charlotte allowed.

Katherine seemed to study the child more closely. She looked from the babe to Charlotte, then back again.

"We have not seen William for quite some time," she said quietly, not lifting her eyes from Anne's face.

Charlotte did not answer immediately, for she had not seen him nor anyone from home these many months, save Aunt Tilney and Charles. Neither of whom she could mention.

Just when Charlotte decided Katherine expected no response, that she had merely mentioned William idly, Katherine looked up at her, eyebrow raised in question.

Charlotte shrugged. "Nor I."

Only belatedly did she remember that she *had* seen Mr. Bentley, though only in passing—and him very drunk on his way to a ball with another woman. But, considering, well, everything, she thought it not worth reporting.

Katherine looked back at the infant. "Yes, I see the resemblance," she announced finally.

Charlotte's stomach lurched. Was she really suggesting the child resembled William Bentley?

"Resemblance?" Charlotte asked weakly.

Katherine smiled at her. "She looks a great deal like her mother."

Charlotte smiled stiffly, steeling herself as Katherine went on.

"You forget—and some days I should like to—that I had already seen my first season when you were born. She reminds me very much of you as a baby. The big eyes and something about the mouth . . ." Katherine waved vaguely about the child's face in a circular motion.

Charlotte swallowed. "Thank you."

She could feel Sally's eyes, wide and questioning, on her profile, but she kept her own gaze straight ahead.

Charlotte refilled teacups, although Katherine refused with another wave of her hand. When Charlotte had set the pot back down, Katherine handed Anne back to her.

"I went through no small ordeal to find you, Charlotte. I trust you do not mind the invasion?"

"Of course not," Charlotte said halfheartedly, returning to her seat.

"I even asked after you at that lying-in hospital back before Christmas. But neither the matron there nor Edmund's own physician would acknowledge you had been there, nor give me a clue to your whereabouts. All very private."

Charlotte's mind was whirling. *Edmund's own physician?*

Suddenly Charlotte remembered, and her palms began to perspire and her breathing escalated. She had to get Katherine out of here!

"It was your own father who finally tipped me off," Katherine continued. "And I had to all but threaten him with social ostracism before he would."

Father knows where I am?

"Why?" Charlotte asked with a half smile and a broken laugh.

"Why indeed! To help you, of course."

"Thank you, but . . . how?"

"Well, for starters, I shall be sending over more tea."

Anne began to fuss in earnest. Charlotte had put her off as long as she could, bouncing her and offering her little finger to suck on, but the child would have no more of that and was burrowing her face into Charlotte's bosom in a most humiliating manner.

"Please excuse me. Anne needs to be fed."

"Sally, do nurse Edmund as well. Then we really must be going."

"Yes, m'lady." Sally nodded.

"Why not join me in my room, Sally?" Charlotte offered. "That way these ladies may remain where they are."

Sally nodded again and, when Katherine didn't object, followed Charlotte to the guest room down the short passageway.

Both women busied themselves with their gowns and helping their charges latch on and begin nursing. When Anne was settled against her, Charlotte looked up. Sally, already nursing Edmund, was watching her, her eyes moving from Charlotte to the child and back again.

"Who is she?" Sally whispered.

Charlotte, sitting on the small chair near the door, cocked her head, listening, before responding. Hearing Katherine's voice as she regaled Margaret Dunweedy with an enthusiastic description of Edmund's christening—"The finest London has seen in many a year, I can tell you"—Charlotte reached over and pulled the door nearly closed. "Sally . . . I . . ."

"Is she a foundling?"

"Well, in a manner—"

"Bless your heart, Charlotte, I guessed it! You're motherin' a wee one from the foundling ward in place of your own poor lad gone to heaven. What a saint you are."

"I'm no saint, Sally. Far from it."

"Well, I think you are."

She opened her mouth to tell Sally the truth. But how could she admit she had lied to avoid the immense shame it would bring her family if it were known she was a wet nurse—Sally's own chosen profession?

"Well, all I can say is that this little girl needed a mother's care. So I'm caring for her—at least for a time. But, please, Sally, don't say a word to Katherine or anyone about my son. Please. I cannot tell you why, but it's very important. Promise?"

"But if she knew, she could—"

"No, Sally. No one must know. Ever."

Sally looked at her, eyes wide, searching. Finally she said, "Very well, Charlotte. If that's what you want."

"It is. It is what I need."

Charlotte looked down at Anne, who had nursed for only a few minutes before falling into a deep sleep. "Oh, Anne . . ." Charlotte mumbled, gently trying to rouse the baby.

"No use." Charlotte sighed. "She's hardly nursed all day. Too tired, I suppose." Charlotte rose and laid the sleeping child in the cradle. "She didn't sleep well last night. I think the poor thing had an earache."

"Would you mind, then?" Sally looked at her, then away, almost too casually.

"Hmm?"

"Well, you're needin' to nurse and I'm needin' a rest. This lad is never satisfied, and I want to have enough milk fer the long ride home."

Charlotte was stunned. A warm ache of need pooled within her as she stared at Edmund. Sally pulled him gently from her breast and stood, child in arms. Charlotte sat down, speechless, and Sally handed him to her.

"Mind if I take a lie on your bed?"

"No, of course not," Charlotte whispered, still staring down at Edmund.

Sally left her peripheral vision, but Charlotte didn't pay attention. Her mind barely registered the creak of the bed ropes as Sally reclined—her eyes were focused on her son. She guided him to her breast and cuddled him close. She felt his wet little mouth, the tug of his tongue, the sweet sting of milk coursing through her, the bittersweet flow of tears on her cheeks. She glanced up and saw Sally lying on her side on the bed, watching her all too closely.

Daniel Taylor alighted the horse drawn London-Brighton coach at The George, then began the walk down Crawley's High Street. As he strolled, he pulled out the schedule pamphlet and double-checked the return departure times. Looking up with the barest glance, he made the turn through Mrs. Dunweedy's gate and nearly walked straight into Katherine Harris.

"Well, Dr. Taylor, imagine meeting you here."

He dropped the schedule.

"Lady Katherine!" He gulped a deep breath. Then he bent over to pick up the pamphlet, and as he raised back up, took in her traveling clothes and just then saw the large carriage in the lane. He silently berated himself for his inattention. "I am surprised to find you here."

"I imagine you are. And here I thought you said you had no idea where Charlotte was."

"Well, I . . . I am not here to see Charlotte. I am here to see my—"

"Dr. Taylor!" Mrs. Dunweedy interrupted with a great burst of voice and smile as she hurried from the cottage and took his arm. "How good you are to come all this way to see me. My poor back has been hurting dreadfully. So good of you to come."

Katherine looked from Mrs. Dunweedy to Dr. Taylor, skeptical brow rising. "You are here to see Mrs. Dunweedy?"

"Oh yes, Dr. Taylor has offered to come look in on me," Margaret Dunweedy said. "He's a good friend of my son. School chums, they were."

"An awfully long way for a house call, is it not?" Katherine asked.

Dr. Taylor looked at the cottage and saw Charlotte in the window, her face pale and somber, eyes pleading.

"Not so great a distance," he said. "I come this way now and again on business."

Katherine Harris followed his gaze and no doubt caught a glimpse of Charlotte before she stepped away from the window. "What sort of business, I wonder."

"Dr. Taylor, I should tell you," Mrs. Dunweedy interjected, "I've taken a boarder since you were here last."

"Oh?"

"Yes, her name is Charlotte Lamb, but I believe you knew her in hospital as Charlotte Smith. She has her daughter with her. Poor fatherless angel . . ."

Lady Katherine appeared incredulous. "You mean to tell me you are not here to deliver . . . to act on my behest of last autumn?"

"But of course I will," Daniel said. "Now that I am here."

As soon as Lady Katherine's carriage disappeared down the road, Charlotte turned away from the window and faced him, her expression downcast.

"Dr. Taylor, please forgive me." Charlotte all but pressed young Anne into his arms and took three long steps back. "I had no right to presume . . . to claim your child as my own. How awful that must have made you feel."

"And you would know," he said softly.

She glanced up at him quickly, as though fearing censure. He smiled grimly, hoping to put her at ease.

He looked down at Anne for a moment before saying, "I had no idea, until this moment, just what an awkward predicament I placed you in, asking you to do this."

"It is not your fault."

"Still, I am not sure if what I am about to tell you will be a relief or a greater trial."

Her gaze flew to his face. "What is it?"

He chewed on his lower lip. "Lizette is better."

"That is wonderful. You—" she began, but he cut her off soberly.

"She wants Anne home with her."

Charlotte's mouth opened, but for three full ticks of the clock no words followed.

Then she said quickly, "Of course. How wonderful. I am happy for you. And for your wife. And, Anne—Anne should be with her mother."

"Thank you," he said with a single nod, then studied the floor. "Considering . . . what just happened here—how difficult this is for you—and the fact that it will become, I'm supposing, only more difficult, I won't ask you to come with us," he said. "I will find another nurse and release you to find a more appropriate post . . . or to return home."

"I shall not be returning home," she said.

"What will you do, then?"

"I do not know. I imagined I would be occupied with Anne for the foreseeable future. I should have been better prepared."

"I'm sorry."

"Don't be." She smiled admirably, then asked, "Are you returning to London?"

"Yes, for a time. Though I've been offered a seaside cottage for a few months and am considering taking it. I think a change of scenery might do Lizette good."

"Where is the cottage?"

"Not far from Shoreham on the south coast. Nothing very fashionable, I'm afraid."

"I don't know a soul there . . ."

"Of course it is not that we do not wish you to come. If you wanted to continue on, we—"

"I would. I would like to continue on as Anne's nurse."

"Really? Well, wonderful."

"I do not like to leave my great-aunt so suddenly, but I am sure she will understand."

"Yes. She seems a loyal friend." He smiled, thinking of the old woman's enthusiastic falsehoods, as though she were playing a part in some Shakespearean farce.

"Now that Katherine knows I am here . . . well, should she return and find Anne gone, I would have to explain. I am not prepared to go through another false mourning. Although neither would be truly false."

He nodded.

"And seeing Edmund like that," she continued, "with her. I don't know. It is both nourishment and deprivation. Pleasure and pain."

He bit his lip. "But if you stay here . . . you would be more likely to see him now and again."

"Yes. No doubt you are quite right. And yet, I know myself. I would both hope—and fear—that someone would see a resemblance, or some inexplicable quality in my manner of looking on him. I know I should give myself away. Give him away." She expelled a puff of dry laughter. "Poor choice of words, that."

"You hope still to amend your arrangement?"

"Only every other moment. Most of the time I remain convinced I have done the right thing."

He ran his long hand over his face. "I feel so responsible—"

"Dr. Taylor," she said almost sternly. "We have been through this before. You are not to blame. Not for any of it. Not even for this." She nodded toward Anne as a new thought struck her. "Perhaps it is I who should be releasing you to go home without me, back to your former, trouble-free life. As long as you must see *me* you will always be reminded of how I came to be in your employ, will always feel responsible somehow."

"A *trouble-free* life." It was his turn to laugh dryly. "I am afraid my former life is as far from me as yours is from you. Though there are days when I am tempted to hope. Like now, when Lizette seems almost herself."

"Well, then, let us not tarry." Charlotte smiled bravely. "Let us get this dear one back to her mama. One cannot help but be cheered by her sweet presence."

"I quite agree. And I am pleased you will meet my wife now that she is recovered." He hesitated, then continued awkwardly, "It might be better if we did not mention her . . . time . . . in the manor."

"Of course. I understand."

Soon, farewells said and bags packed, Charlotte sat across from Daniel Taylor in the London-bound coach, Anne asleep in her arms. Two other passengers rode with them, an elderly couple with expressions as worn as their faded traveling clothes and drooping hats. The old woman smiled politely.

"How old is she?" she asked.

"Five-and-a-half months."

The woman glanced at Dr. Taylor, who was already reading a medical journal. "She looks a great deal like your husband."

Charlotte felt her cheeks warm. "We are not . . ."

But Dr. Taylor looked up from his book and interrupted her, saying kindly, "Thank you, madam. Though I dearly hope my daughter shall grow more handsome in time."

He smiled at the woman, and she smiled in return, not seeming to notice anything amiss.

Later, when both the man and the woman had nodded off, Charlotte leaned across the aisle and asked quietly, "Do you think my cousin suspected anything . . . about your coming to my aunt's as you did and, well, everything?"

"I cannot say," Daniel whispered back. "I fear I am not the thespian your great-aunt is. It's quite possible my expression gave something away. What do you think? You know her better than I."

"I think the questions are even now parading through her mind."

21

WANTED

A NURSE with a good Breast of Milk, of a healthy Constitution and good Character, that is willing to go into a Gentleman's Family.

—*Maryland Gazette,* 1750

Charles Harris attempted to read while his wife paced the length of Fawnwell's newly restored sitting room.

"Really, Charles. A journey of that length to pay a house call? On a widow who cannot have more than a hundred pounds a year?"

"What did the woman say?"

"Something about her son and Dr. Taylor having been at school together."

"Well, then." Charles flipped over his newspaper.

"I do not believe it. I cannot imagine the Dunweedys affording Oxford or Cambridge. Which did Taylor attend, do you know?"

"I do not."

"I think I shall find out."

"To what purpose?"

"Clearly something is amiss with the entire situation."

Charles looked at her over his paper. "Of course there is. Did you not find your unmarried cousin with a child?"

"Yes, yes. I do not mean that. I mean with Taylor showing up there."

"Did you not ask him to get the money to her?"

"Yes, but I had the distinct impression he was there as a course of habit."

Charles shrugged, resuming his reading. "Even if he was there to check on Charlotte, a former patient, I don't see that as so unusual."

"Do you not?"

Keeping his tone casual and his eyes on his paper, Charles said, "You said Charlotte has a girl . . . a daughter?"

"Yes. Calls her Anne. Little thing. Not at all as robust as our Edmund."

"And what did Charlotte have to say about Edmund?"

"The usual niceties, I suppose. Though without the enthusiasm I might have expected. She did agree he looks like you."

Charles nodded but said no more.

"I also admit, I studied her child quite closely, thinking to see a resemblance to someone we both know quite well."

He looked up at her, feeling suddenly anxious. Had Katherine suspected the child would resemble *him*? He shifted uncomfortably in his seat.

"Of course she admitted nothing about William. Still I wondered. But then this Taylor showed up, all the way from London. You don't suppose . . . ?"

"Taylor is a married man."

"We both know that is no guarantee of anything. He traveled alone."

"Common enough. Besides, I heard his own wife was expecting a child. Taylor is likely a father already."

"Indeed?"

"Indeed."

Katherine shrugged, her pretty lips screwed up in thought. She seemed satisfied. For the time being.

The Taylors' London townhouse was a tall narrow building sandwiched between a dozen others just like it. The medical offices were housed on street level, above the kitchen and beneath three floors of living quarters above. When they arrived, Daniel preceded Charlotte into his offices, where he dropped his medical case and picked up a few pieces of correspondence. He gave her a reassuring smile. "This way."

Holding Anne, while he carried her heavier bag, she followed him up the stairs. Up on the first floor, he stepped into an adjoining room, the sitting room most likely. Charlotte hesitated on the landing.

She heard the happy, accented voice of Mrs. Taylor call out, "Daniel! *Mon amour. Tu m'as manqué!*"

Charlotte stepped forward tentatively. From where she stood in the doorway, she could see Dr. Taylor's back, his arms wide, and a brief view of Mrs. Taylor's dark hair and bright smile before she disappeared into her husband's embrace. Charlotte averted her gaze and stepped back into the corridor.

"I've missed you too. More than you know."

"Have you brought her? *Notre fille?*"

"Of course, my love."

Charlotte stepped forward just as Daniel reached the doorway. She handed Anne to him carefully but swiftly and again stepped back.

She heard Lizette Taylor's gasp, followed by a moan that was at once joyful and mournful.

"Annette! *Ma petite. Ma fille. Chair de ma chair.*" The words were a warm litany of love and loss. *"Tu es très grand."* Charlotte heard laughter mixed with unseen tears. *"Quel bébé dodu!"*

"Yes, she has been well fed," Daniel said.

"*La nourrice?*"

"Yes, my dear, I should like you to meet her."

Again, Charlotte stepped forward, hands clammy, stomach churning. Her eyes were downcast as she entered the sitting room.

"May I introduce Miss Charlotte Lamb. Miss Lamb, my wife, Lizette."

Charlotte glanced up quickly at Daniel's wife. His beautiful wife.

"*Madame Taylor*," the woman corrected pleasantly, slanting a look at her husband.

Charlotte looked back at the floor and bobbed a quick curtsy.

"*Enchantée*," Charlotte mumbled, unsure whether her use of French would please her new employer or not.

When Charlotte darted another look, Mrs. Taylor smiled graciously at her. And with her smile she was even more beautiful. Charlotte could hardly reconcile this poised, exquisite woman with the howling, pitiful creature she had seen at the Manor Home.

Lizette Taylor's eyes narrowed. "Have we met?" she asked.

Charlotte swallowed, instantly knowing the correct answer. "No, madame. We have not been introduced."

Mrs. Taylor scrutinized her a moment longer, then turned her head.

"Marie!" she called out.

A maid with red-chapped cheeks entered, greying hair fringing out from her mobcap, "*Oui, madame?*"

"Please show Nurse to her chamber, would you?"

"*Bien sûr, madame.*"

"Welcome, Miss Lamb," Mrs. Taylor said. "I hope you will be happy with us."

As do I, Charlotte thought.

Charlotte did not see Mr. John Taylor, Daniel's father, that first evening. But the next morning, while she breakfasted alone, he joined her in the dining room and greeted her with a warm smile.

"Miss Smith! How good to see you again. Oh, forgive me—it's Miss Lamb now, if I understand correctly."

"That's right. And a pleasure to see you again, Mr. Taylor."

He poured himself a cup of tea from the sideboard and sat across from her at the table.

"I was so sorry to hear of your loss."

"I thank you, sir."

Keeping his gaze on his teacup, he asked timidly, "It wasn't anything I did, or failed to do, was it . . . ?"

"Oh no, of course not, Mr. Taylor. I could not have asked for a kinder, more skilled surgeon."

"Thank you, Miss Lamb. You are most kind to say so. What a blessing for Anne to have been in your care. Where is the little mite this morning?"

"Still asleep. Tired from the journey, I suppose."

"Yes, and what a boon to have you here with us. With three beautiful ladies under our roof, well, I don't see how Daniel or I could be happier."

She smiled at him. "And you, sir, how do you fare?"

"I miss the work, I must say. I take great pleasure in feeling useful, helping people, you know. I miss it."

"Of course you do. Is there no hope of returning?"

"Daniel says not." He looked about the room, as if to reassure himself they were alone. "That Miss Marsden has quite a hold on me, I'm afraid. Says if I ever practice again, she'll bring me up on charges."

"But certainly your word, sir, against such a woman's . . ."

"That's right, Daniel mentioned you met her." He sighed. "It's not her alone who holds power over me. It's her patron, the father of her child, or so she says. Some rich and revengeful lord, to hear her tell it."

"May I ask who the man is?"

"A Lord Phillip Elton."

"Lord Elton . . ."

"You know him?"

"The name is familiar. I think he might be known to my uncle."

John Taylor shook his head sadly. "Well-known and well-connected, I'm afraid. There's naught I can do. For myself I might risk it, but I would not endanger Daniel's career any more than I have done already."

"Would you mind, sir, if I made a few inquiries on your behalf?"

"I would not *mind*, but do not trouble yourself, my dear. I shall be happy again now that I have my granddaughter here at home."

Charlotte and Anne were to share the nursery on the third floor. It wasn't a large room, but it would do nicely. John Taylor hauled up an old screen from one of the exam rooms in the office downstairs. With her permission, he set it up between the door and Charlotte's bed, to give her some semblance of privacy should one of the family wish to come in and pick up Anne, whose cradle was on the other side of the room.

During those first days they were all in London, Lizette Taylor seemed happy indeed. Happy, especially, to have her daughter back in her life. She held Anne for hours on end, bouncing her on her lap, speaking to her in French, singing French ditties and lullabies. Anne, for all her unfamiliarity with her own mother, was delighted with this enthusiastic attention and went happily from Charlotte's arms to Lizette's with little fuss. Charlotte was relieved for Mrs. Taylor's sake.

Anne was slower to take to her grandfather, unaccustomed as she was to male attention beyond the occasional visits her father had made over their months in Crawley. But still, after the first few days, her lower lip no longer quivered when he spoke to her—though she watched him carefully whenever he came near.

Sensitive to how Daniel's wife must be feeling, having missed those first precious months of her daughter's life, Charlotte was careful to stay in the background as much as possible, only offering to take Anne when she began to fuss or it was clearly time for another feeding.

So she was not sure of the cause of Lizette Taylor's growing moodiness.

"You take her, Miss Lamb, I feel a headache coming on," she began to say nearly once a day. Or, "There you are, back to Nurse. *Ta mère* must lie down and rest."

The spring that year was gloomier than usual, and during the last half of April it rained five out of every seven days. *Such weather could make the cheeriest person morose,* Charlotte thought.

Mrs. Taylor began spending hours in the sitting room alone, reclining on the settee, staring off into nothingness. Often she would neglect to raise the shades in the morning, or to light a lamp when darkness fell. With only one servant about the place, there was often no one to do it for her. Charlotte helped as much and as quietly as she could. She prayed as well.

"I am worried about Lizette," Daniel's father said quietly as the two men sat in the dining room over lukewarm tea. Gone were the days of after-dinner port for this household.

"As am I," Daniel confided. "I have been wondering if a change of scenery might do her good. I've been offered a seaside cottage for a few months."

"Where?"

"The south coast. In France she lived by the sea."

"But . . . the Manor Home—what of your work there?"

"I don't know. Perhaps I can find someone to take my place for a time. I know how important the Manor is to you, but I can only do so much."

"It is important, Daniel. It is my life's work."

"It *was* your life's work, Father."

Daniel saw the light dim in his father's eyes and immediately regretted his words. "Again, I ask your forgiveness, Father. I have no right to take my exhaustion out on you."

"You are distraught, son. I understand. I know I have disappointed you. Truth is, I have disappointed myself. I have been weak—not the brother I should have been, not the father I should have been, and not the surgeon I should have been. . . ."

"Father . . ."

"But I have done some good. I have. Mothers who would have died, lived. Children too. That is why the Manor Home is so important. Promise me—keep the place going if you can. If not for me, for your poor aunt Audrey—God rest her soul."

Daniel squeezed his eyes shut, the guilt pouring over him as it always did when his father mentioned Aunt Audrey—a woman Daniel had never known. His father's sister had died as a young woman in a disreputable lying-in hospital. Until recent years the standards of care and cleanliness at such facilities meant fatalities were all too common. It was in his sister's honor that John Taylor had joined forces with other surgeons, physicians, and charity groups to establish the Manor Home for Unwed Mothers in the first place. Of course that was before he fell into disrepute.

"The Manor is not going to close if I take a leave."

"We cannot be sure. Did you not mention donations were down?"

"Yes, and expenses rising." Daniel ran a weary hand over his face. "I shall see what I can do. Perhaps I can carry on at the Manor during the week and travel to the coast at the weekend."

"Thank you, Daniel." John Taylor's hand trembled as he brought his teacup to his lips, then returned it to its saucer, untasted. "When my time comes, I can go thinking of the Manor Home and the lives saved there. May the good Lord forgive the rest. And you, Daniel. I pray you forgive me as well."

A few days later, Daniel was disconcerted to find his father and Miss Lamb waiting for him in his study. "What is it?" he asked.

His father glanced at Charlotte. "Miss Lamb has some news she wishes to share."

Daniel took in her anxious expression. *She's not leaving, I hope.*

"I fear you will mind," Charlotte began. "But I took the liberty of writing to my uncle—who is a solicitor—about the situation with Miss Marsden."

"What?" Daniel's relief that she wasn't announcing her resignation was quickly replaced by anger.

"Forgive me, I know it was presumptuous."

"Father, you were not to divulge—"

"Please," Charlotte interrupted. "Allow me to explain."

His father studied his hands, folded together in his lap as he sat. Daniel lifted his own hand, gesturing in irritated compliance for her to continue.

"Your father did not offer the information, Dr. Taylor. I asked for the man's name, this Phillip Elton."

Daniel groaned and shook his head.

"I thought the name was familiar but not for the reasons I guessed. In any case this man's father, Lord Elton himself, has long been a friend to my aunt and uncle. It was his name I had heard spoken with fondness over the years. I have even dined with him at my uncle's home on one or two occasions. However, this Phillip Elton is Lord Elton's son, and my uncle has had to wrest him from trouble more than once.

"I wrote to my uncle to inquire—do not fret, I did not mention your names nor the details of the situation but only asked whether this Miss Marsden was known to him. My uncle has written back." She lifted a letter she held in her hand. "In all truth, I wondered if he would, what with my father asking my aunt to cut off communications with me. But since I wrote with a 'professional' question, he thought it within his rights to reply. In any case, he assures me that not only is this woman no longer connected in any way to Phillip Elton nor Lord Elton himself, but that the Elton family has disowned the child she claims is his. They have severed all relationship with her. Beyond that, Phillip himself has had his privileges reduced and hasn't the money to pay his club tab, let alone take anyone to court. So you see, the woman has no hold on either of you any longer."

She smiled triumphantly—first at his father, who, Daniel noticed, did not meet her gaze, and then at him. Clearly, theirs was not the reaction she had expected.

"Perhaps my father forgot to mention that the woman's allegations were not unfounded. He *was* guilty of negligence during the delivery of her child."

Charlotte's smile faded, but she did not answer.

"Yes. Father is very skilled in garnering sympathy but less so in staying sober. Had I not happened along when I did, the child might have died."

"Daniel, I told you. I have not taken a drink since. It has been over a year. Will you never trust me again?"

Hands on hips, Daniel shook his head. "I don't know, Father. I want to, but I just don't know."

Dr. Taylor arranged to take Lloyd Lodge for the months of May, June, and July. His wife and the servant Marie, a maid-of-all-work, journeyed to Shoreham a week earlier than the rest of the family to set up housekeeping.

Charlotte enjoyed those days, alone in the house much of the time with Anne and John Taylor. Aunt Tilney would not have approved had she known, but Charlotte felt not a moment's unease in the kind man's company. He treated her more like a daughter than a servant. And his gentle fondness was a warm salve that filled in the injured places, the jagged cracks in her heart, left there by her own father's cold indifference.

And to his delight—and Charlotte's—Anne grew quite attached to her grandfather during that time. His son, however, remained cool.

"I am sorry, Mr. Taylor," she said to Daniel's father one afternoon as they sat together in the sitting room during Anne's nap. "It seems I have succeeded only in making things worse between you and your son."

"Do not fret, my dear. I was touched by your efforts to help me. I know you acted with the best intentions. Daniel knows it, too, but is struggling to admit it. You see, he takes my failure quite personally. He resents that my disgrace has cast a pall on his reputation. I fear my son has always been overly sensitive to the criticism of others—real or perceived. I am sure he believes more censure has befallen him due to my failings than actually has. He has not the confidence some men do. I do not know why. Perhaps it has to do with his mother dying so young. Finding out his sole-remaining parent was fallible was a blow to him. I suppose it is always difficult for a child to realize his father's flaws do not reflect on him. That he—or she—must make the best of the life God gave him."

Charlotte felt tears sting her eyes but smiled at John Taylor nonetheless, knowing he could have little idea why his words affected her so.

"You will join us at the coast, will you not?" she asked.

"I do not believe I will. Daniel needs some time alone with his wife without his father hanging about. And I think I shall see what needs doing about the foundling ward. Mrs. Krebs will put me to work washing nappies if nothing else. Daniel cannot object to that." He smiled warmly at her. "Especially not now, after what you have found out for us."

When the week passed, they all stood in the entry hall, Charlotte holding Anne on her hip.

"I cannot change your mind, Father?" Daniel asked, picking up the last of the baggage to carry down to the waiting hansom.

"And who would water your gardens if I leave?" John Taylor bent his head to Anne's eye level and rubbed her cheek. "*Someone* has to work around here." He winked at Charlotte.

"Very well. I shall see you Monday week. Write or send a messenger if you need anything before. You have the directions?"

"Yes, I have everything I need. Do not worry about me, my boy. Just go and have a grand holiday—rest and rejuvenation for everyone, that's what I prescribe. And I shall be praying for you all as well."

"Thank you, Father." Daniel walked out the door.

Charlotte stepped forward and offered the dear man her hand.

"We shall miss you, Anne and I."

He took her hand in both of his. "And I shall miss you. But the summer will fly quickly, as it always does in soggy ol' England, and we shall all be together again soon."

If only his words could be true.

22

> Wet nurses earned twelve dollars a month, paid five dollars for the care of their children, and netted an impressive seven dollars. This was top dollar in the New York City servant market.
>
> —*Harper's Weekly,* 1857

The seaside cottage Dr. Taylor had taken for the summer was a boxy Georgian of blond stone. From the village, where they had alighted the coach, they hired a boy with a pony cart to take them the rest of the way, across the Adur River bridge and west along the coast. It would have been a taxing walk with Anne and all their things. The road approached the cottage from the rear, and Charlotte could see neither beach nor sea as they walked up the cobbled path. The boy carried their baggage to the back porch, where Daniel paid him and waved him on his way. As Charlotte held Anne and waited quietly, she thought she heard the distant cry of gulls.

"We're a hundred yards or so from the sea. You cannot see it from the cottage, but I understand it's an easy walk down the hill."

Daniel preceded her inside, dropping his medical case in the entry porch as he went. Taking a deep breath, Charlotte followed.

Mrs. Taylor seemed in good spirits and received Daniel and Anne warmly, taking the child and kissing her repeatedly. She offered a reserved but cordial greeting to Charlotte.

The French servant, Marie, led her upstairs, pointing out the rooms where the master and mistress would sleep, then preceded Charlotte up another set of stairs. Huffing and puffing, the woman pointed to two doors close to each other.

"For you and for ze nursery."

Charlotte opened the first door and saw it led to a small but pleasant room with a narrow, canopied bed, dresser, and walls of white planking. *A child's room,* she thought. Then she opened the nursery door and stepped inside, instantly noticing that it was much larger than her bedchamber. It was a lovely room with a white cradle made up with cheery pink bedding, two chests of drawers and two chairs, one of which was occupied by a doll and a stuffed rabbit.

"We are not to share, then?" Charlotte asked, wondering what to make of it. This room was certainly large enough to accommodate another bed.

"*Non*," Marie answered haughtily. "Madame does not wish to bother you every time she wants to see her own baby."

Charlotte raised her eyebrows. Perhaps it was only her accent, but the maid's tone made Charlotte wonder if what she really meant was Madame did not wish to *bother with* her.

But Charlotte said only, "I see," and forced herself to smile at the woman, who, had she been young or pretty, might have found easier, higher-paying work as a ladies' maid—a post for which French women were in much demand. But Marie was neither. Charlotte wondered if this explained her sour and resentful disposition.

In short order, Charlotte established a daily routine. She nursed, bathed, and dressed Anne. Then, when the weather allowed, she bundled her up and took her for walks along the sea. Charlotte ate her meals with the servants: Marie and Mr. and Mrs. Beebe, who maintained the place for its absentee owners and were the doting grandparents to six children who lived nearby. Elderly Mr. Beebe took care of the simple grounds and what repairs he could, though judging by the worn condition of the place, he was no longer equal to the task. Mrs. Beebe, a few years his junior, was a decent, no-nonsense woman who cooked and did basic cleaning, though she made it clear she expected Marie to help with the housework and laundry while they lodged there.

On her first Sunday in Shoreham, Charlotte nursed Anne and handed her off to the Taylors as they prepared to leave for church, dressed in their finest clothes. The Taylors would drive together in the gig kept at Lloyd Lodge for tenants' use. Charlotte also planned to attend services, but she would go on foot. Together with Mr. and Mrs. Beebe, she walked across the bridge to the Old Shoreham Church.

When they arrived, she saw the Taylors already seated near the front of the church. Charlotte sat near the back, next to Mrs. Beebe, whose head kept lolling against Charlotte's shoulder during the long sermon. At one such moment, she noticed a broad-shouldered young man across the aisle, looking her way. He was a head taller than anyone else in the building and had a strong, square face and long nose. His light brown hair was short and tousled. He was not handsome, Charlotte decided, but was a very pleasant-looking young man. He looked from Charlotte to Mrs. Beebe in repose, and then back at Charlotte, smiling at her in amused empathy. It was a boyish, friendly expression, and Charlotte smiled in return.

After the service, when they had shaken the curate's hand and walked out of the church a dozen paces behind the tall man, Charlotte asked Mrs. Beebe, "Do you know that young man?"

Mrs. Beebe followed her gaze. "Can't say I'm surprised you'd notice him, Miss Charlotte. He does stand out in a crowd."

"Indeed."

"His name's Thomas Cox. His family lives up coast from us a bit. One of his younger sisters is at school with our granddaughters."

"Are his sisters tall as well?"

"No. He's the biggest of the lot. But a gentler soul you'll never find. Shall I introduce you, Miss Charlotte?"

"Oh, no. I only wondered." Charlotte changed the subject, lest Mrs. Beebe misinterpret her interest as something it was not. "And what will you and Mr. Beebe do on your Sabbath day of rest?"

"We're to dine with my daughter and her husband. They're the ones with the four little girls. It's my son in Worthing what's got the two older boys. We'll see them Sunday week."

"How blessed you are to have your family so close at hand."

"Indeed, Miss Charlotte. And close in heart." The woman surprised Charlotte by reaching out and squeezing her hand. "Someday you will as well, my dear."

A few days later, Charlotte borrowed Mr. Beebe's pride and joy—the baby carriage he had built for his own grandchildren. It was much lighter and simplier than the large, ornamental conveyances afforded by only the very rich. His was fashioned after the invalid chairs he had once seen in the spa town of Bath, with a hood and push-handle. Promising to be careful, Charlotte put Anne securely inside, and together they strolled along the sea. The large wheels of the carriage turned more easily on the water-worn pebbles of the shingle beach than they likely would have on sand. Enjoying the breeze and the rhythmic roar of the waves, Charlotte walked for nearly a mile, she reckoned, passing the rooftops of several houses on the ridge as she did. In the sky ahead, she saw a kite flying. The sight cheered her somehow, the colorful diamond, soaring on a wind. She picked up her pace, hoping to catch sight of the child flyer.

She soon realized the flyer was not on the beach but up on the ridge, hidden from view. As she passed a path leading up to the nearest house, the kite came crashing down beside her. So startled was Charlotte that she shoved the carriage to the side too quickly and it struck a large stone. She heard something snap.

Oh no . . .

Charlotte sunk to her haunches between the injured carriage and the fallen kite and almost immediately heard feet crunching over the pebbles toward her.

Looking up, she saw a boy of nine or ten years, spool of thread in hand, brown curls flopping up and down on his head as he ran.

"I didn't brain you, did I?" the child called, worried.

"No. Not quite." Charlotte smiled, and as the child stepped closer she realized it was not a boy after all, but a girl with hair cropped short around her face and dressed in boys' trousers.

"When I saw you down on the ground like that, I thought I must have."

"I was just examining this wheel. I seem to have knocked it from its, em, rod there."

"Axle."

"Right."

The girl peeked beneath the carriage hood to look at Anne. "What's your baby's name?"

"Her name is Anne. But she isn't mine. I'm her nurse."

"She's lovely."

"As are you. I like your hair." Charlotte looked at the loose, springy curls, much like her own hair would be, she guessed, if she cut it that length. "Must be less fuss short."

"That's what Mother says. Keeps all our hair short."

"All?"

"My sisters and brothers. I have three of each."

"I see. Shall I help get your kite back up?"

"Do you know how to fly a kite?"

"No. My mother and I tried once, but there was insufficient wind."

"Plenty today."

"What shall I do?"

"Well, if you'll hold the kite while I take out the slack and start running . . ."

Charlotte was already picking up the kite and flicked a piece of lichen from it.

Over her shoulder, the girl called, "Just let it go when I say."

Charlotte saluted. "Aye, aye."

The girl ran, the string grew taut, the girl shouted, and Charlotte released the kite. It struggled low to the ground for several seconds, then wavered. Just when she feared it would crash to the rocks, it caught the wind and leapt up. It rose higher and higher in the sky, level with the ridge, then beyond. It danced in the currents and reached higher still, straining at its tether. Watching the bright thing fly, Charlotte felt unexpected tears prick her eyes.

"Woo-hoo, Lizzy, that's the way!" A man stood high on the ridge, his fist and face raised to the sky. The girl's father, she assumed.

A few moments later, there came the man bounding down the steep hill, a broad smile on his face. He was younger than she would have expected. Wait, she recognized the man—the very tall man.

"Hallo there," he called.

She waited until he jogged closer. "Hello. I was just admiring your little flyer there."

"That's Lizzy, my sister. I'm Thomas Cox."

"Charlotte Lamb. I believe I saw you at church Sunday last."

His eyes widened in recognition. "That's right. And has your shoulder recovered from serving as Mrs. Beebe's pillow?" He smiled his boyish smile.

"Indeed, there was little recovery needed."

"I am surprised to hear it. But don't let on I suggested Mrs. Beebe has a large head or I shall never hear the end of it. Nor enjoy those apple tarts of hers anytime soon."

"Thomas! Thomas, look how high!" Lizzy Cox called from her position up the beach. Her brother turned to look her way. Again he whooped and raised a triumphant hand in the air.

Charlotte bent to reexamine the wheel. She really should be getting back. Mrs. Taylor might worry.

"Broke, did it?" With one large step, Thomas drew near and hunched beside her, hands on his knees.

"I'm afraid so. I feel terrible—it belongs to Mr. and Mrs. Beebe."

"Never fear. I helped Mr. Beebe build the wee gig. We'll have 'er fixed up sharp." Thomas loped back up the hill, as if the incline were no effort for his long legs.

A few minutes later, Lizzy jogged over, winding the twine back around its spool. "Thomas can fix anything," she confided.

"Did your kite fall again?"

She shrugged. "No, I reeled it in. I need to finish my work in the garden."

"That's your home there?" Charlotte asked, looking up the ridge.

"Goodness no. That's Shore Hill House. Thomas works there."

"He's their gardener?" Charlotte asked, watching Thomas return across the pebbled shore.

Again Lizzy shrugged. "Gardener, carter, cooper, surgeon, and all around repair boy."

"Surgeon?"

Thomas clearly overheard at least part of their conversation. "Lizzy, don't abuse Miss Charlotte's ear so—and you know I'm not a surgeon." He bent to the task of repairing the baby carriage.

"Did you not set Johnny's arm and put a cast on it? And make those poultices for Mother that set her to rights last winter?"

"Yes, but you're family."

"You stitched up the McKinleys' dog when it got into a fight last week. And Mrs. Moody says you're better at getting her boy's shoulder back in place than that surgeon in town."

Thomas looked at Charlotte apologetically. "Not everyone can afford to call a surgeon for every ache and injury." He shrugged, the gesture charmingly similar to his sister's. "I just do what I can."

"How do you know what to do?"

"I read a great deal. One of the families I work for—and have for some eight years now—the grandfather was a physician. When he died they gave me a few of his books."

Charlotte nodded her understanding, wondering though, what Dr. Taylor would think of an uneducated man setting bones and stitching wounds. Of course she knew there were plenty of men who worked as surgeons or apothecaries who had never read a single book on the subject.

"The family I work for—the father is a physician."

"The family letting Lloyd Lodge?"

Charlotte nodded.

"Is he planning to practice here?"

"I do not believe so. We're only to be here for a few months."

He looked oddly disappointed.

"But if you wanted to see him for something . . ."

"I should not like to trouble him on his holiday."

She wanted to say more, but Thomas abruptly rose to his feet, and to his full impressive height.

"There you are, good as new."

"Thank you so much. I shall tell the Beebes of your noble service."

"Please do—perhaps I shall earn an extra tart from the telling." He smiled.

"I should like to pay you something for your time, but I haven't my purse. . . ."

He waved her offer away. "Don't give it a second thought, Miss Charlotte. It's what neighbors do."

"So you do live nearby?"

"Yes, a modest cottage further inland. About midway between here and Lloyd Lodge, I'd say. Wouldn't you, Lizzy?"

"About that, yes."

Charlotte began pushing the carriage. "Well, then, perhaps I shall have the pleasure of seeing you again sometime, Lizzy. And Thomas."

He smiled again. "The pleasure, Miss Charlotte, would be ours."

Mrs. Beebe looked up from the buns she was brushing with egg-water. "There you are, Miss Charlotte. The missus was looking for you."

Regret filled her. "I feared as much. Where is she?"

"She and her maid went into the village to do some shopping, though I don't suppose she'll find much there to her fancy. She wanted to take Anne along, but I told her, I did, 'Mrs. Taylor, I have six grandbabies. So believe me when I tell you, you shall have a much more pleasant outing without a babe in arms.'"

Mrs. Beebe winked at Charlotte.

"Thank you." Charlotte smiled, relieved. She could ill afford to anger Mrs. Taylor. "I happened upon Thomas Cox and his sister Lizzy on my walk."

"Did you now?"

"Yes, I understand Thomas works for several families in the area."

"That he does. Does an odd job for Mr. Beebe now and again as well. That boy can fix anything he puts his hand to, whether it be an object or growing things, animals, even people."

"Lizzy said he set her brother's broken arm."

"That'd be Johnny, the rascal. Always gettin' into some mischief or other."

"And I'm afraid I broke a wheel of Mr. Beebe's carriage—but Thomas repaired it."

"That's a mercy. No one likes to see the old man cry." Mrs. Beebe grinned. "Thomas has the touch, he does. What a blessing he is, especially to his mother—what with the mister out to sea fishing for days on end."

"I wonder he's so much older than his sister."

"Than all the others, aye." Mrs. Beebe looked as though she might say more but seemed to think better of it.

"Do pass me that sugarloaf, will you? There's a love."

On a fine afternoon the following week, Charlotte again took Anne for a walk on the shore. She looked up hopefully but saw no kites in the sky. She enjoyed the wind—though the arrangement of her hair did not—and she relished the freedom of being out of the cottage and the atmosphere of malaise that seemed to indwell it. So, too, the relief of being out from under the watchful eye of Mrs. Taylor. Her mistress was certainly not cruel, but she was exacting in her expectations of how Anne should be cared for—how she should be dressed, upon which side of her head the bow should be fastened in her small tufts of hair, and so on. It was tiresome to always be on one's guard against a misstep. And unsettling to realize one's livelihood and lodgings depended on a mistress who was both particular and changeable.

"Miss Charlotte!" a voice called down to her from the ridge above. There was Lizzy Cox, in those same trousers, waving down to her. "Come and see!" she called excitedly. "Come and see!"

Charlotte did not relish the prospect of pushing the baby carriage up the steep incline, so she maneuvered it off the side of the path, picked up Anne, and carried her up the slope. Lizzy met her halfway. "You're just in time!"

"For what?"

"Lambs!"

She followed Lizzy around a fine house and to a timbered outbuilding. Inside, the smell of hay and grain and animals was strong, but not unpleasantly so. In the straw bed of a stall, Thomas sat cross-legged beside a ewe, on her side breathing rapidly. Thomas held one lamb in his arms, a second draped over his leg. "That's it, then. Hello, Miss Charlotte."

"Hello, Thomas."

"Always best to be on hand during lambing. Tend to have trouble, they do. This girl is late—and see how big her lambs are." He held up the one in his arms for her inspection.

"She was having trouble at first," Lizzy said, "bellowing something awful. But Thomas helped her along."

"Old Bob is a friend of mine. Had to go to town for his daughter's wedding, so I said I'd watch this ewe for him."

He stuck a piece of straw into the lamb's nostrils. The lamb sneezed. Thomas wiped at its nose with a rag, then wiped down the rest of the lamb as well. "Sneezing helps them breathe."

He offered the lamb in his hands to Lizzy. "Would you like to hold this little lad?"

"Yes, please."

She took the lamb into her arms and held him gently against her chest. "How soft he is."

"Would you like a turn, Miss Charlotte?" Thomas asked. "I'd offer to hold Anne for you, but my hands are soiled."

"Here, I shall hold her, Miss Charlotte." Lizzy handed her lamb back to Thomas, wiped her hands on her trousers and held out her hands to receive Anne. Anne, one fist in her mouth, opened her mouth even wider, forming a smile around her hand. Drool leaked out, but Lizzy didn't seem to mind. She held Anne as if she had held many babies before. And likely had.

Thomas handed Charlotte the lamb and she held it and stroked it.

"You're right, Lizzy. He is soft indeed."

Little Anne's eyes lit up as she watched the baby animal. She babbled happily and reached both hands toward the lamb.

"Not this time, moppet," Charlotte said gently. "He's not to put into your mouth."

She handed the lamb back to Thomas, who set it on the floor near its mother, followed by its sibling. The ewe scrambled to her feet and began licking first one lamb, then the other. Stretching their necks eagerly, the lambs began to nurse.

"They'll be all right on their own now," Thomas said, and rose to his feet. Charlotte took Anne from Lizzy, and they all stepped outside into the sunshine. Thomas washed his hands in a bucket and wiped them with a clean rag.

"I'm off to finish picking the beans," Lizzy announced, running off.

"Care to see the garden, Miss Charlotte?" Thomas asked.

"Very much. I love a garden."

They strolled through the gardens inland from the house. In the vegetable garden, Charlotte grinned at the sight of Lizzy, tongue between her lips in concentration, carefully plucking bean pods from the vine. They also toured a kitchen herb garden and several flower gardens, all very well kept.

She was surprised to spy several milkweeds along the garden wall, near the hollyhocks. "Do you mind if I take some milkweed back with me?"

He looked at her, an amused grin on his face. "Have a wart, do you?"

Embarrassed by this, she laughed. "No! But my employer is quite fond of milkweeds—uses them to treat a whole list of ailments."

"Does he now? I should like to know the contents of that list."

"You shall have to come by the cottage. I know he would be happy to tell you."

From the garden, Charlotte and Thomas walked to the top of the ridge, overlooking the sea. "Care to sit for a moment and enjoy the view?" Thomas asked.

"Thank you."

He reached out his hands to take Anne, and Charlotte was surprised when the child went to the big man willingly. Charlotte sat on the edge of the lawn and straightened her skirts around her. Thomas plopped down not far from her, easily holding Anne in the crook of one arm as he did so.

She lifted her arms to take Anne back, but Thomas shrugged. "I'll hold her, if neither of you mind."

Lizzy bounded up and sat beside Charlotte. "Cook gave me a sixpence," she said proudly.

"My goodness. For picking beans?"

"Well, there were the peas and lettuces this morning too."

"What a hard worker you are. So, Lizzy, tell me about your brothers and sisters—three of each, I believe you said?"

"Right. There's my sisters: Hannah, Hester, and Kitty. They don't like the out-of-doors as I do. Then my brothers: Thomas here, of course. And Johnny and Edmund."

"Edmund? That is my very favorite name. How old is he?"

Thomas leaned closer to Charlotte and said in a low voice, "We lost Edmund as an infant, but Lizzy still counts him."

Charlotte looked at Lizzy, who was staring down at her lap. Feeling tears spring to her eyes, Charlotte put her arm around the girl's shoulder and gave her a squeeze. "Of course she does."

Lizzy looked up, and Charlotte smiled gently at her. "And so do I."

Lizzy smiled shyly in return.

A few minutes later, Lizzy ran off to find a litter of kittens a mother cat was reported to have hidden somewhere about the place.

"She's a lovely girl," Charlotte said, craning her neck to watch her go.

"Yes."

"Is she the youngest?"

"No, Edmund would be nearly five now, had he lived. Kitty is seven. Lizzy there is ten. Johnny's twelve. Hannah and Hester are twins at fourteen.

"It's a wonder there are so many years between you and the others."

"Not such a wonder, really." Thomas tossed a twig out over the ridge. "Our mum took me in when I was already a lad of nine. Adopted me as one of her own. Hannah and Hester were but a year old at the time."

"Were you relations?"

"No. My first mother was only a neighbor. Died in childbirth, the baby girl with her."

"I am sorry."

"Do not make yourself unhappy. I feel blessed to have Rachel Cox as my mother. And these children to call brothers and sisters."

"How well do you remember your first mother, as you called her?"

Thomas's eyes stayed on the distant sea as he thought. "Quite well, though I cannot recall her features as clearly as I once did." He picked up a pebble and tossed it as well.

Charlotte swallowed the lump in her throat. She asked quietly, "Do you miss her?"

He looked at her, clearly surprised by the question, or her shaking voice. No doubt he saw the tears in her eyes as well. He returned his gaze to the sea. He was silent for some time, picking at the pebbles near his legs, gathering them into his large hands. Finally he said, "I have all I could wish for with my family here. But . . . yes, there is a . . . a quiet longing for her. I am a man of two and twenty but still I sometimes dream of her. In the dreams, I cannot see her face, but I can feel her arms about me."

Charlotte nodded, biting her lip. Tears rolled down her cheeks. Thomas looked at her, his expression serious and aware. He said nothing but simply waited.

She opened her mouth then closed it again. Finally, voice quivering, she whispered, "My son . . . is being raised by another."

Slowly, he nodded his understanding. "Edmund?" he asked quietly.

She nodded, and neither said more.

As soon as Charlotte stepped into the parlor, Mrs. Taylor rose from the settee. "You have been gone a long while, Miss Lamb. I was beginning to fear I would never see you—or my daughter—again." She smiled as she spoke, but an understandable mixture of relief and displeasure strained her features.

"Please pardon me, madame. I took Anne for a walk and lost track of time."

Only then did Charlotte notice the older woman seated across from Mrs. Taylor, half hidden by the wings of the tall arm chair. The lady appeared to be in her fifties and had a beautiful coif of silver grey hair under an elegant black hat.

"Mrs. Dillard has been waiting for nearly an hour to meet Annette."

"Forgive me. I did not realize you were expecting guests." Charlotte handed the little girl to her mother.

"Here she is, Mrs. Dillard. Is she not beautiful?"

The older woman rose and Charlotte saw that her attire, though practical, was finely made. Mrs. Dillard stepped across the carpet with dignified ease. "Yes, lovely." She patted the child's head with jeweled fingers. "Very like you."

"Thank you. Please, do sit down again, Mrs. Dillard. I shall call for more tea."

But the woman remained standing. "Now that I have met your charming daughter, I really must be going. Ladies' Charity meeting begins—" she lifted the watch pendant hanging from a chain at her waist—"dear me, half an hour ago."

"I am so sorry to have kept you waiting, Mrs. Dillard."

"No need to apologize. I understand how difficult it is to find a dependable nurse." The woman spoke as though Charlotte were not standing there in the doorway. "My daughter has been through two in the last four months. The first one nearly ate the larder down to the walls." She pulled on her gloves. "Thank you for the kind invitation, Mrs. Taylor. I do so hope you enjoy your holiday here."

Mrs. Taylor's smile was forced. "You are very kind. Thank you."

The woman bid her good-day and Charlotte held her breath, preparing for the worst.

The door closed, but Lizette Taylor still stared after the woman. "There will be no answering invitation, I can promise you."

"I am sorry, madame."

"Yes—you did not help me impress the ladies." She sat down heavily on the settee, jostling Anne, and waved her hand in a fatalistic gesture. "But they would not be impressed in any case. The other two ladies left before tea was even served. They remembered some church meeting they 'simply must attend.' I am surprised Mrs. Dillard stayed as long as she did."

Before Charlotte could form some consoling response, Mrs. Taylor continued, "They were eager enough to respond to my written invitation. And how they smiled when they first arrived—surprised to find a doctor's wife so finely dressed, I think. But then I began to speak and how their smiles fell from their faces. When they realized I was French, they could not leave quickly enough."

"Perhaps they really did have obligations."

Again the dismissive wave.

"Mrs. Taylor, I cannot tell you how sorry I am. I never considered how it must be for you to—"

Lizette Taylor held up her palm, ceasing Charlotte's words midsentence. "I may be a French woman living apart from my country and my family . . . but you are in no position to pity me, *Nourrice*."

Charlotte looked down and Mrs. Taylor followed her gaze, until her eyes widened.

"Your hands . . . what has happened?"

Charlotte looked down at her dirt-streaked gloves.

"I stumbled upon a patch of milkweed and wanted to bring some back, but I fear they proved too stubborn."

"Why?"

"Well, the roots as you may know are very strong and run very deep, so I settled on bringing back the one."

"No. I meant why would you want to bring this back. This weed?"

"The milkweed has medicinal qualities, as you are no doubt aware. I thought Dr. Taylor might find it useful, having none in the garden here."

Mrs. Taylor continued to look at her, her gaze scrutinizing. So Charlotte continued, "I have always loved a garden, but I confess I thought milkweed a mere nuisance. But then I saw your husband's garden in London—all the varieties of plants for this medicinal purpose and that." The more Charlotte prattled on, the less she recognized her own voice. She realized too late that Mrs. Taylor knew how to use silence to her advantage. That by saying nothing, Charlotte felt compelled to blather on, chipping away at her own dignity with each word. "Quite the man of science, your husband."

"Indeed? Well, here is the man of science now."

"Hmm?" Daniel looked up from the post in his hand to smile amiably at his wife and then at Charlotte. "What have I missed?"

"My dear, tell me, where did we find such a nurse?" Her voice sounded pleasant enough, but Charlotte detected suspicion in Mrs. Taylor's tone.

"From the Manor, as I believe I told you. But I knew Miss Lamb's family a long time ago as well."

Her rather thick eyebrows rose. "And how were you acquainted with this woman's family?"

"It was during my apprenticeship in Kent. I called often on her mother with Dr. Webb."

Mrs. Taylor turned again to Charlotte. "And your mother, how is she now?"

"I'm afraid she died. Many years ago now."

"And how is it you came to be a nurse? I don't mean . . . the particulars. I mean, where is your own child?"

Charlotte swallowed. "I'm afraid he . . . he is gone as well. I had him but a few days."

Mrs. Taylor looked at her husband, eyes wide under tented brows. "And *this* is the fit woman you would have nurse my child?"

"Lizette. You have no cause for concern. I can attest to Miss Lamb's character and her health. She has cared for Anne these many months while you were . . . indisposed."

"If madame prefers, I can leave on the morrow," Charlotte quietly interjected.

She could feel the woman's stare on the top of her bowed head. Charlotte was mortified, but if she wasn't wanted, she would leave. Even if it meant saying good-bye to Anne.

"No, do not be foolish. I meant no offense, Miss Lamb. I am simply a mother concerned for her child. You understand, *non*?" Suddenly the woman's face brightened. "Of course you must stay. Clearly my daughter needs you, and who knows how long it would take to find another suitable nurse? Please. Consider this your home. For as long as Annette needs you."

She said it graciously, but Charlotte did not miss the message. Accented or not, her English was skilled . . . and pointed.

23

And every one knowes how hard a thing it is,
to finde a good [nurse], because they have been
so often beguiled, and deceived therein.

—James Guillemeau, *Childbirth or The Happy Deliverie of Women*

Sitting in the nursery at Fawnwell, Sally held little Edmund close, studying the shape of his nose, his brows, his mouth. "The image of yer mum, you are," she cooed, running a finger over his smooth cheek.

"What did you say?"

Sally looked up, startled. She hadn't heard the mistress, but there she stood, looking sternly down at her.

"Nothing, m'lady," Sally said, panicked. Had she broken her promise so quickly? What would become of her little charge . . . of herself?

"I heard you. Repeat what you said," Lady Katherine demanded imperiously.

"I . . . I only meant . . ." Sally stammered.

"You said he looked like his mother," Lady Katherine supplied.

Sally lowered her head, waiting for the hot words to rain down.

Instead the mistress took a step closer. "Between you and me, I quite agree."

Sally looked up at her, trying to discern the meaning, the mood behind Lady Katherine's pensive expression.

"Do you?" she asked weakly.

"Yes. I always make a point to say how much he resembles his father—I think it wise to offer such comments to build a man's esteem, his bond with his offspring."

"Oh . . ." Sally whispered, still not at all sure what the woman was saying.

"Still, I do see hints of myself in his features. The arch of his brows, the coloring of his fair skin . . ."

"Aye . . ." Sally murmured, slipping back to a word Charlotte had advised her not to use. Still, she thought Charlotte would not mind, considering her secret, it appeared, was still safe.

Sally looked with wide eyes around Chequers, Doddington's crowded, noisy inn. Through the haze of smoke from many pipes and the inn's fireplace, she took in the tables ringed by men drinking ale and laughing. She felt out of place, sitting there with her new friend, the two of them the only women in the place, save for the innkeeper's wife.

She'd met Mary Poole when she'd been out walking with Edmund. Mary worked as a nurse for the Whiteman family down the road, in a house that lay between her master's estate and the village itself.

"Your first night out?" Mary said, aghast. "Sally girl, you must make your conditions known."

"Conditions?"

"Conditions of employment. 'Tisn't right they shouldn't give you a night out each week."

"But I need to be on hand to nurse the child. 'Tisn't anyone else to do it."

"Aw, he's not going to starve in a few hours, now, is he?"

"I suppose not."

From over her cup, Mary slanted a look across the room. "My, my—two gents are looking this way."

Sally followed her gaze and saw two men near their own ages standing at the bar.

"Sit up straight," Mary whispered sternly, "and do close your mouth."

Sally only then realized she was staring at the men, mouth drooping open. She hurried to close it and sat up straighter on the bench.

"The fair one's mine," Mary whispered through smiling lips.

But it soon became obvious that the fair one had set his sights on Sally.

The slight, wiry man with light hair and dark eyes was handsome indeed. He smiled boldly at Sally as he walked over, and she felt her face, already warm from the ale, burn red.

"Name's Davey. And my mate here is George. Mind if we sit with you lovelies?"

Mary giggled coyly and scooted over on her bench. Sally still stared dumbly at the man named Davey.

"I'm Mary and this is Sally," Mary said and kicked her under the table. Sally again closed her mouth and followed Mary's lead in making room on her bench. Davey sat down right next to her.

"Evenin', Miss Sally. Yer a sight for these weary eyes, I can tell ye."

Sally looked away from his admiring stare, biting on her lip to keep from smiling too broadly.

As the evening wore on, Sally's cheeks glowed warmly from Davey's many compliments and the second glass of ale he bought for her. Not since Dickie's father had a man given her such admiring attention. And Sally drank it in.

Sighing, Mary gave up and turned her focus to the bearded, dark-haired man named George.

A week later, Sally and Mary met out in the lane as planned, each with their respective charges.

"You're coming out again tonight, I trust," Mary said, bouncing little Colin Whiteman in her arms.

"I cannot. They only gave me the night out last week because it was my birthday."

"I'm surprised the new missus gave you that much."

"Well, it was the master who did it. I let the day slip in his hearing."

"Very clever."

"I suppose I was desperate for some time away."

"'Course you were. And the way Georgie tells it, Davey is very desperate indeed to see you again."

Sally tried to close her lips around her teeth, but she could not help the smile that overtook her.

"Is he?"

"Yes. Says you are the handsomest girl he's ever seen."

"He didn't."

"He did."

"Must have had too much ale that night, then."

"Don't be foolish, Sally. You have very pretty . . . hair. Just—well, try to keep your mouth closed. And don't stand up quite so . . . tall."

Sally bit her lip. "I shall try."

"Well, then, meet me here tonight at nine o'clock and we'll walk into the village together."

"I don't know. The master and missus are going out for the evening. I don't know who could look in on Edmund for me."

"One of the other servants?"

"Perhaps."

"Listen, love. You're not the first nurse to find herself in this fix. But if your charge sleeps till you get back, who's to be the wiser?"

"Oh, but Edmund will want his eleven o'clock feeding. If he wakes the whole house, I shall have the devil to pay by morning."

"Well, what if you could make sure he sleeps quiet as a mouse right through the night?"

Sally laughed dryly. "By what magic?"

Her new friend's eye lit up with a mischievous gleam. "By this." She pulled from her skirt pocket a small corked bottle.

Sally felt her eyes widen. "What is it?"

"Just a bit of laudanum."

"Where did you get it?"

"Never you mind."

"Does it make babes sleep?"

"Aye. Surgeons use it all the time—it's quite safe."

"Is it?"

"Yes, I've used it several times myself."

"Really?" Sally's eyes seemed fixed on the small vial.

Mary held it out to her. "Go on, then."

"But—how do I . . . ?

"Just put a bit into his mouth before you nurse him."

"How do I know how much to give him?"

"Oh, I'd say half a teaspoon ought to do it."

"You sure it shan't harm him?"

"'Course I'm sure. When did sleep ever harm anybody?"

Sally looked at her friend's earnest face and back to the bottle.

"Here, take it." Mary pressed the vial into her hand.

Sally gingerly took hold of it.

"Go on, then, and meet me back here at nine. Wear that pretty blue frock of yours."

"You're certain?"

"Yes, your eyes look so blue when you wear it. I am quite sure Davey shan't be able to look away from you."

Sally had not been asking about the dress but did not correct her. "I did so like Davey."

"'Course you did. Any girl would be a fool not to. Quite a looker, he is."

"Aye . . ."

"Well, then, see you back here tonight."

"All right."

Sally turned to go, then turned back. "Wait. Won't you be needing some o' this yourself?" She held the vial aloft.

"I have another in my room." She grinned archly. "My last employer was a surgeon."

For some reason, the face of Dr. Taylor appeared in her mind. Unsmiling, soft-spoken Dr. Taylor. He was a physician. She had often assisted him in the ward. Had he ever used the stuff? Yes, she believed he had on one or two occasions, when an infant had been inconsolable in pain or had arrived in the turn injured.

Would it be all right, even though Edmund was quite healthy?

Mrs. Taylor requested a morning alone with her daughter, and Charlotte gladly obliged, offering to go into the village to do a bit of shopping and pick up a spool of wicking Mrs. Beebe wanted from the chandler's. Daniel said he was going in, as well, and would give her a lift in the carriage.

"Thank you, but actually, I long for a walk," Charlotte said.

"As you like."

But instead of harnessing the horse, Mr. Taylor caught up with Charlotte on the road, medical bag in hand. "I've decided to walk in as well. Exercise is good medicine, and I have taken too little of late. Do you mind?"

She shook her head, supposing it was appropriate to share a public road with her employer but still hoping neither Marie nor Mrs. Taylor was looking out a rear window.

They walked more than the proper distance apart, she with her hands behind her back and he switching his bag from hand to hand as his arm tired.

After walking in silence for several minutes, he asked, "And how do you like the coast?"

"Very well indeed."

"Glad to hear it." He cleared his throat. "I hope things are not too . . . strained . . . between you and Mrs. Taylor?"

She faltered, "Umm, no. Not really."

"She is still not quite herself. I wish you could know her as I do, happy and loving and full of life—"

"But how improved she is!" Charlotte interrupted. "That is something to be thankful for."

"I am. Still, I had hoped the two of you might become friends."

"Dr. Taylor, you and she are my employers. I do not expect friendship." Charlotte hurried to change the subject. "Are you leaving for London again this week?"

"Yes. I shall put in a few days at the Manor and visit my father."

"Do greet him for me."

"I shall."

They had just crossed the wooden bridge over the river and were on the path leading into Old Shoreham when a well-dressed man approached from the opposite direction. His head was tilted down as he walked, evidently preoccupied. Blond curls shown from beneath his hat. Charlotte fell behind Dr. Taylor to make way for the other man to pass.

Ahead of her on the path, Dr. Taylor stopped short.

"Kendall? Richard Kendall?"

The man with the golden hair looked up. His heart-shaped boyish face broke into a wide smile.

"Taylor! Is it really you?" The two men strode toward one another, shook hands vigorously and slapped one another's shoulders. Charlotte stood to the side, off the path, where she could observe without intruding.

She had rarely seen Daniel Taylor smile so warmly, with such genuine delight. She felt unexpected tears prick her eyes at the happy sight of good friends reunited. And perhaps the slightest twinge of envy.

Two workmen were walking toward the bridge now, crates of fish on their shoulders. One looked at her boldly. Unconsciously, she took a step closer to Dr. Taylor.

"I thought you were practicing in London," Dr. Kendall said.

"I am."

"What brings you to our fair village, then?"

"My wife and I let a seaside cottage not far from here."

"Well, do introduce me."

Following his friend's gaze, Dr. Taylor looked over his shoulder in her direction. "Oh, no this isn't my . . . That is, Mrs. Taylor is at the cottage with our daughter. This is Miss Charlotte Lamb. Our . . . friend of the family."

"Miss Lamb." The man's smile was guileless, which Charlotte found both relieving and charming. He bowed, then looked up at Daniel, brows raised.

"Oh!" Daniel started. "Forgive me. Miss Lamb, may I present Dr. Richard Kendall, physician and friend."

"How do you do, sir." Charlotte curtsied.

"Very well indeed. Pleased beyond reason to run into old Taylor here. We were at university together, did you know?"

Charlotte shook her head.

"Miss Lamb, you never saw poorer, sorrier excuses for candidates, I can tell you."

"None poorer, I assure you," Daniel agreed.

"Miss Lamb . . ." Kendall eyes lighted as he repeated her name. "Not *the* Miss Lamb, surely."

Charlotte cocked her head to one side, uncertain. "I am not sure . . ."

"Of Kent. Doddington, was it?" He looked at Daniel, whose face began to redden.

"Yes," Charlotte said, uneasy.

"Taylor here spoke quite highly of you at Edinburgh, I can tell you."

Daniel cleared his throat. "You have quite the memory, Kendall."

"Yes. Helps me sort out my many patients and their various complaints."

"I'm sure you do so admirably."

"I try. Now do tell me exactly where you are staying. I probably know the place. Probably set a bone there or bled somebody nearby." He smiled teasingly at Charlotte.

"It's an old stone cottage west of here. Owned by the Lloyds."

"Lloyd Lodge? On a cliff overlooking the sea? Yes, I know it! Well, Taylor, you must be doing well for yourself."

"I am afraid not. I treated the Lloyd's granddaughter, and in lieu of payment they let us have the cottage for the season."

"Generous."

"I suppose. Though by the looks of the place, it is evident they don't use it much anymore. It has seen better days."

"Haven't we all? Still, when my patients are low on quid, I get mutton and codfish. I would say a seaside cottage is not too shabby—even if it is."

Dr. Taylor smiled. "Well, come see for yourself, then. Yes, come for dinner, Kendall. You must."

"I should be delighted. Just name the date."

"Would Saturday week suit? That should give Lizette time to prepare."

"Lizette . . . ?"

"Yes. I hope you are not opposed to French cuisine, nor French wives."

"If she is your wife, I have no doubt she is all a lady should be."

"Indeed, she is very lovely," Charlotte felt compelled to say.

"And will you be there, Miss Lamb? Or will your holiday conclude by then?"

"I . . . that is . . . I shall be there . . ." *But not at a formal dinner!* She looked at Daniel for help, but he was still smiling at his old friend.

"Then, I shall look forward to seeing you again as well," Kendall said gallantly, offering another brief bow.

When they had bid Richard Kendall farewell and were walking alone again, Charlotte asked quietly, "Why did you not tell him I was your daughter's nurse?"

"I did not think you would want me to. Did you?"

"No, but he will find out for himself when he comes for dinner. Then I shall feel doubly foolish."

"I am not sure I follow. . . . But I am awfully sorry to have upset you."

"I should not have minded otherwise."

"Otherwise?"

"Do you not see? He knows of the other Charlotte. Charlotte of Kent. The vicar's daughter. The young lady you once spoke highly of . . ."

"But I still—"

"But I am not that person anymore," Charlotte interrupted him. "And now I shall have to see your friend's opinion of me undergo that awful transformation." Charlotte sighed. "I shall have to fall all over again."

Sally could not rouse the child. She removed his blanket, tickled his bare feet, stroked his cheek. No response. She picked him up gently, hoping the movement would wake him. He lay limp, his little arms drooping down and swaying as she swayed, bouncing as she bounced. She went to the pitcher and basin on the dressing table and dipped her fingers in, rubbing the cool water on his forehead and neck. Nothing.

Sally groaned. "And I haven't even given you the stuff yet." She had planned to give him one last feeding, with the laudanum, before she left, but the groggy biter couldn't be bothered to wake up. She thought of getting dressed first, putting on the blue frock as Mary suggested, but she feared Edmund would spit up on it, or worse, that his nappy would leak and spoil it. Could she somehow get the stuff into his mouth without waking him? Then he could just go on sleeping. Shifting him into the crook of her left arm, she picked up the vial on the dressing table. She'd need both hands to uncork it. Setting the vial down, she went to return the child to his crib, then walked back to retrieve the vial. She uncorked it and peered down its narrow shaft. She pulled the silver teaspoon from her pocket—she had snatched it from the tea service on her way upstairs—and poured a bit of the liquid onto the spoon, until she reckoned it was halfway full. Should she try to get the spoon into his mouth? Small though the delicate utensil was, it seemed too large for Edmund's little buttonhole mouth. Should she put the little vial itself into his mouth? But how, then, would she measure the amount? It would surely spill all over and she'd have to clean that up too before she could sneak out again.

She stood there with the teaspoon in her hand, debating. The image of Davey's bonny brown eyes flashed in her memory. Such a handsome man, Davey was. And to think, he admired *her*! *Just do it and be done,* she bolstered herself.

But she hated the thought of letting the baby go hungry for so long. She looked at the mantel clock. She had only a half hour more before she should be on her way. She walked purposely to the cradle, spoon in hand. She looked down at the babe and was surprised to see the child's eyes open, watching her. *Charlotte's eyes*, she thought.

Daniel watched Lizette's reflection in the dressing table mirror as she brushed the thick dark hair that fell past her shoulders.

"And how are you feeling tonight, my dear?"

"Do you ask as my husband or my physician?"

"Take your pick. Both are very happy to see you in such good health and spirits."

"You seem happy as well, I would say. Happier than I have seen you in some time."

He unfastened his collar, grinning. "Why should I not be? I have a beautiful wife I adore, a healthy daughter, a rent-free home by the sea . . ." He leaned down and kissed her cheek.

"Do not forget the nurse."

"Hmm?" he asked, wrinkling his brow.

"I mean that Annette is so well looked after . . . all through the night." She smiled, a suggestive lift to her eyebrows. Then she stood and leaned against him. She kissed his cheek, his chin, his mouth.

He kissed her back. He knew he should be thrilled. Physically, emotionally, he was thrilled. It had been so long. But his mind leapt to the potential consequences, the terrifying possibility of another pregnancy. Another nightmare.

He pulled gently away and cupped her exquisite face in his hands. He looked at her, relishing, delighting in her contented, loving expression. Before him was the woman he had fallen in love with.

"Come." He sat on the bed and took her hand, slowly pulling her to lie next to him. He wrapped one arm around her, holding her tight to his side. With his free hand, he brushed the long dark hair from her face. When her hand began to caress his chest and then move lower, he clasped his hand over hers, stilling its path. He knew from painful experience that speaking of her condition directly would only stir up in his wife a cauldron of defensiveness, denial, and anger.

"I just want to hold you," he murmured, bending his neck to kiss the top of her head.

The truth was much more complicated.

24

The practice of dosing young infants with proprietary medicines, usually containing opiates, increased during the nineteenth century. . . .

—Valerie Fildes, *Wet Nursing: A History from Antiquity to the Present*

Sally picked up little Edmund, his eyes now open, his drooling little mouth working, showing his pink gums, his soft fair cheeks plump with health. Going a few extra hours without a nursing wouldn't harm a stout boy like him. She took him to the dressing table and changed him into a dry nappy. Back in her arms, his pleasant expression wrinkled in restlessness as he began rooting against her. *Put a bit in his mouth,* Mary had said, something like it anyway. Then follow with his feeding. He was definitely ready to nurse now.

Her thought should have been, *finally the little biter's awake. Now I can give him the stuff, nurse him, and be off for a night o' fun with Davey.* But it wasn't. Instead she thought of her own Dickie. Had her sister ever done the likes to keep him quiet? She supposed it was possible, but she believed her sister had genuine feeling for the boy. They were relation after all. This boy was no relation to her, so why did she feel such a strong urge to protect him? She thought again of the embroidered blanket she'd stubbornly refused to toss on the rubbish heap. She knew why.

Sally sighed.

Still, she hated the thought of disappointing Davey. She longed to see him again. Perhaps if she hurried she could still catch Mary.

Sally ran down the lane as fast as she could, pressing her arm over her heavy bosom to protect herself from the jarring pace. Mary would be put out with her indeed, for she was a quarter hour late. Ahead, she saw her friend's shape in the shadows of the moonlit hornbeam tree.

Mary must have heard her approaching and no wonder, she must sound like a big mule thundering down the hard packed road, eager to win some race.

"I'd about given up on you," Mary called. "I was just now heading in without you."

"Sorry, Mary." Sally panted, hands on her knees to catch her breath.

"I thought I told you to wear the blue," she said peevishly. "You're still in that same soiled dress?"

"I'm not goin'."

"What?"

"I'm not goin'. Here." She thrust the vial into Mary's hand, making her take it.

"Whyever not?"

"I couldn't do it."

Mary expelled a loud humph, clearly vexed. "But I told you how."

"I know." Sally shook her head, already backing away. "Please tell Davey I am sorry and maybe we can meet up another time."

"I shall tell him no such thing. If you don't come with me right now, Sally, all bets are off. A man like that doesn't stay unattached for long, and I'll be hanged if I don't take a try at him myself."

Sally paused, then nodded sadly. "Good-bye then, Mary." She turned and began trotting back toward the house.

"You're a bigger fool than I thought," Mary called after her. "Giving up your own chance at happiness to wet-nurse the brat of some stranger what don't give a farthing about you."

The words burned at her ears and heart like stove irons. *I am a fool*, Sally thought. But still she ran up the lane, as fast as her large feet would carry her, as though wild dogs were on her heels.

In the morning, Sally awoke to fierce pounding on the nursery door. She'd already given Edmund his early feeding and had fallen back to sleep, his warm form still beside her. The little biter had woken up three times in the night, fussing and crying. She'd barely gotten two hours of sleep put together. She'd nearly come to regret not giving him the sleeping stuff. When the child had seemed to stare at her, eyes wide, she'd murmured, "Oh, don't pay me any mind. I just gets cranky when I don't gets me sleep." And clearly, she thought wryly, she also forgot how to speak properly when she was overtired.

"Hang on—I'm coming," she called now, quickly pulling her dressing gown around her. But the door banged open before she could get to it. She jerked the tie into a rushed knot and stared, shocked as first the missus and then the master rushed into the room and to Edmund's cradle.

"Where is he?" he asked.

"What have you done with him?" she accused.

"Edmund's right here. In my bed." She pointed to where Edmund lay propped between a pillow and a rolled-up blanket.

"Is he all right?" the lady asked, breathless.

"Seems to be," her husband said, bent over to peer at him.

"Oh, thank God," Lady Katherine exclaimed and picked him up, cuddling him close. She gave Sally a sharp look. "Why isn't he in his cradle? You might have suffocated him!"

"I fell asleep after his last feedin'. The little thing kept me up half the night."

"Did he indeed?" she asked pointedly.

"Yes, m'lady."

Lady Katherine lifted her chin toward the open door. "Search the room," she ordered.

"What is it?" Sally asked as men from the place—the butler, the groom, the manservant—strode into the room. "What's happening?"

"As if you don't know!" Katherine snapped.

"I don't."

"The Whitemans' baby was found dead early this morning," Mr. Harris said. "The nurse was apprehended, clearly intoxicated, with laudanum on her person. It is assumed that she drugged the infant."

"It is more than assumed—she killed him!"

"My dear, allow me," he soothed, and then turned a hard gaze on Sally. "You are familiar with this nurse, this . . . What was her name?" he asked the groom searching through her drawers.

"A Mary Poole, I believe, sir."

He turned back to Sally.

"Yes, I know 'er." Sally swallowed. "A little."

"Did you not, in fact, see her yesterday?" he demanded.

"Only for a moment . . . I'm sure she did not mean for it to happen. She told me it was quite harmless."

"Did she? She claims the laudanum found on her person belongs to you."

"'Tisn't true!"

"Was it not in your possession?"

"Well, she did give it to me, but I gave it right back."

"Did you bring it into this house?" Lady Katherine interjected.

She swallowed again, dread filling her, and nodded.

"Into the nursery?"

Sally nodded again, eyes downcast. "She told me it wouldn't hurt him. Surgeons use it, you know. Well, I believed her."

"I shall give you one chance to answer this question truthfully," Mr. Harris said. "Did you or did you not give any to Edmund?"

She looked at him then, meeting his eyes directly. "No, sir, I did not. Not one drop."

"How can we believe her?" his wife asked. "She had it with her. In this very room."

"Aye, but then I ran down to the road and gave it back."

Katherine turned toward the butler. "Call for the physician. He must come at once and examine poor Edmund."

"Why did you?" Harris asked Sally.

"I don't know. It's a hard life sometimes, never getting an hour to yourself, never seeing people your own age . . ."

"I meant, why did you not give it to him? You certainly intended to. You no doubt had plans to meet up with this Mary, to go to the inn with her, as she clearly had from the state of her, I gather. You brought it up here with the intention of drugging my child so you could have this 'hour to yourself.' But you want me to believe you didn't follow through with it. And if you expect me to believe you, to not have the police come and haul you off straightaway, I need to know why."

She looked at the man, the child's father, obviously shaken and angry, yet trying so hard to control his emotions. Oddly, she thought fleetingly of other occasions when he had shown some kindness to her, and understood what a certain young lady had once seen in him.

She stared directly at him and said quietly, "For the sake of his mother."

As dusk fell, Charlotte sat on a bench overlooking the sea. She held Anne on her lap, for the two had fled the cottage and the frenzy of preparations for company and Lizette Taylor's shrill orders. Charlotte was sure Daniel's wife did not mean to be demanding nor difficult. But it was clear she was tense and determined that everything about the place and the meal should be perfect. Anne's fussing had only added strain to the woman's agitated nerves, and Charlotte had been relieved when asked to "take the child away somewhere."

The walk and the cool evening air had quickly calmed Anne, and now the two sat in peaceful silence, listening to the tumbling of the sea and the call of gulls.

She was surprised when Richard Kendall walked briskly up the slope from the sea path. She had not expected to see him—nor anyone—on this side of the cottage and felt disquieted to meet him again. She rose to greet him.

"Miss Charlotte Lamb," he called. "How pleased I am to see you again."

"And I you, Dr. Kendall." The two bowed politely to one another.

"And this is Taylor's daughter, I take it? I'd recognize that bit of strawberry hair anywhere."

Charlotte smiled. "You have a keen eye, Dr. Kendall. Yes, this is Anne Taylor."

"Hello, little lady. Let's hope your father's hair is all you've inherited." He put his face close to the child's and wrinkled up his nose. The baby smiled, releasing a stream of drool down her cheek. "That's very like her father as well," he joked. Then he smiled warmly at Charlotte. "Nice of you to look after her. Mrs. Taylor busy overseeing preparations, I suppose?"

"Well, yes, and well, you see . . ."

"Does Mrs. Taylor care for the baby herself or do they have a nurse for her?"

"They have a nurse. In fact, I—"

"Kendall!" Dr. Taylor called out from the back stoop. "You found us! Do come and meet Mrs. Taylor."

"On my way, old boy."

Daniel waved and stepped back inside.

Kendall turned back to Charlotte. "You're coming in as well, I hope."

"No . . ."

"Joining us for dinner later, then?"

"No, I'm going to watch over Anne here. You go on ahead."

"Better let the nurse do that. It's what she's paid for, isn't it?" He began to walk toward the cottage, smiling at her over his shoulder.

"I am the nurse, Dr. Kendall."

"What?" He paused, turning back to face her.

"I am Anne's nurse. It is why I am here."

"I don't . . ."

"Your friend Dr. Taylor was a great help to me when my own child . . . was lost to me. And since Mrs. Taylor . . . needed someone, well, here I am."

"I see."

"I am sorry for the deception the other day."

"No need to apologize." He nodded thoughtfully, then cleared his throat. "Well. I best be getting in."

Yes, yes, hurry away. "Please do."

Daniel led Kendall into the parlor, where Lizette waited.

"My dear, allow me to present my old friend Richard Kendall. Kendall, this is my wife. Madame Lizette Taylor."

Kendall's eyes widened at the sight of Lizette, resplendent in her ivory gown, her hair piled high on her head, her black eyes shining. It was a reaction Daniel was used to, even enjoyed. He still sometimes found it difficult to believe he had such a lovely wife.

"*Enchantée*," Lizette said, smiling coyly before dipping her head.

"I am delighted to make your acquaintance, Mrs. Taylor." Kendall bowed. "You are even more beautiful than your husband described."

"You are very kind, Dr. Kendall. Now, please come and sit down. Dinner will soon be served."

Both men instinctively offered their arms. She laughed, her smile brilliant, and she crooked her arm first through Kendall's, then Daniel's. The three walked slowly together to the dining room, arm in arm.

After dinner, the two men sipped their port in Daniel's study.

"Why did you not tell me?" Kendall asked.

"Hmm?"

"About Miss Lamb. Your *nurse*?"

"Oh. How did you . . . ?"

"She told me herself. Outside, before I came in."

"Well, I saw no need to humiliate her—you are a stranger to her. I was not thinking ahead."

"You might have sent a note and saved us both the embarrassment."

"I am sorry. She berated me as well for not telling you. I only meant to spare her feelings."

Kendall looked at him closely. "Were you and she . . . ?"

"What?"

"She mentioned a child."

"Heavens no. I had not seen her in several years when I came upon her in hospital, quite far along in her lying-in."

"I must say I find this situation highly unusual."

Daniel shrugged. "My daughter needed a nurse. Miss Lamb needed a post."

"Does Mrs. Taylor know?"

"She knows I am acquainted with Miss Lamb and her family from my time in Kent."

"But not how you felt about her?"

"I saw no need. It's years ago now."

"Is it?"

"Yes. Kendall, I am devoted to my wife."

"Of course you are. I did not mean to imply anything untoward. It is the irony of this situation—do you not recognize it? You have Charlotte Lamb in your service, living under your roof, nursing your child, looking as lovely as ever I imagined from your descriptions—"

"And what is your point?" Daniel asked in growing irritation.

"I am only pondering. I take it the bloke responsible has offered no marriage, no arrangement?"

"No. He is married." Daniel took a sip. "As am I."

"Yes, yes. And Mrs. Taylor is very beautiful, I grant you." Kendall shook his head. "Here I am a year your elder with no woman in my life and you have two."

"I do not have two women!" Daniel heard the anger mounting in his own voice.

"Look, I know you to be a man of honor and all that. Always have been.

But you know, Daniel, these things *are* done. It is nearly respectable these days to support a beautiful lady in such a situation. Though I suppose the word *lady* must now be applied rather loosely."

"Richard. You know not of what you speak. I have been and shall remain faithful to Lizette. I took vows. Sacred vows. And, well even if I had not. I am devoted to my wife!"

"Yes, so you have said."

Daniel turned away, on the verge of ordering this man from the house. He forced himself to relax his fisted hands flat against his trouser legs and take several deep breaths.

"Forgive me," Kendall said. "I have clearly overstepped and misspoken. You are not the only one who disgraces himself socially, you see." Kendall sighed. "I shall see myself out. Do thank Mrs. Taylor again for the excellent meal."

Daniel nodded stiffly without turning.

Later, when they were preparing to retire, Lizette smiled at herself in the dressing mirror as she let down her hair.

"Your friend could barely keep his eyes from me all evening."

"I noticed."

She glanced at him. "You do not seem afflicted with such difficulties."

"My dear. You know I consider you absolutely beautiful."

"So you say."

"You do not believe me?"

"You do not prove your words. I do not *feel* that you find me desirable or irresistible. Nor understand why you should want to resist."

"It is only out of consideration for your . . . health."

"Unless," she went on as if she had not heard, "some other woman has captured your attention?"

"Of course not, Lizette. You know better. You have been my only lover."

She stepped close to him. "But we do not live as lovers. I need to *feel* that you desire me. I need to feel you . . ."

She pressed herself against him, her breath hot on his neck, and he found he could resist no longer.

Daniel sat in the study in the cottage, refolded the letter, and laid it on the desk. He removed his spectacles and rubbed his eyes. Replacing them again, he saw Charlotte walking past his door.

"Miss Lamb? Might I have a word?"

"Of course." She stepped into the study and stood before his desk. "What is it?"

"I've had a letter from Charles Harris."

"Yes?" Worry stretched itself across her features.

"Your . . . the family is all well. He wrote to tell us that he's had to let Sally Mitchell go."

"Go? Why?"

"It seems she was given laudanum by a neighboring nurse—meant to drug the child—"

"Dear God, no . . ."

"Put yourself at ease. Edmund is fine. There is every indication that she did not give him any, but it appears the neighboring nurse administered a fatal dose to the infant in her care."

"Merciful heavens."

"He says, given that I personally recommended Sally, and considering the continuing health of his child, he is prepared to believe her innocent of all but considering the act. But that is enough that his wife cannot bear the thought of keeping the child in Sally's care. She has hired a—" he briefly consulted the letter again—"a Mrs. Mead from the village to replace her."

"I know her. A kind, honest woman from what I remember. But still, poor Sally—what must she have been thinking?"

"That is at least one purpose for Harris's letter. To alert me to the fact that the nurses coming from the Manor may be under the misapprehension that the drug is suitable for such purposes. It is clear that I have some reeducating to do when I return. I can rest, at least, in the knowledge that the neighboring nurse was not a resident of our institution."

"What will become of Sally?"

"They are not pursuing legal redress. Though I'm afraid the other nurse will not be as fortunate. I suppose Sally will be free to return to her own home, her own child."

"But how will she support herself and her son?"

He sighed. "I do not know. That continues to be a problem for many."

25

The moral character of the future man may be influenced by the treatment he receives at the breast and in the cradle.

—Almira Phelps, *Godey's Lady's Book,* 1839

After Sunday services a few weeks later, Thomas Cox caught up with Charlotte as she stepped through the churchyard gates into a fine summer's day.

"Good morning."

Charlotte smiled up at him. "Hello. How fare the lambs?"

"Very well, and how fares Miss Lamb?"

"Very well, I thank you."

"I noticed Mrs. Beebe took pity on your poor shoulder this morning."

"Yes. I was careful to refill her teacup twice at breakfast."

He chuckled and they walked on.

"Miss Lamb!"

She was surprised to hear Mrs. Taylor call out to her. Lizette Taylor gestured for her to stay where she was and, taking her husband's arm, all but pulled the man over to where Charlotte and Thomas waited.

When they drew near, Mrs. Taylor smiled brightly from Charlotte to Thomas. "Miss Lamb, you must introduce us to your new friend."

"Of course. This is Thomas Cox. My employers, Dr. and Madame Taylor. And you know Anne."

"Yes, of course. How do you do?" Thomas gave an awkward bow and a charming smile.

"Dr. Taylor is a physician, as I mentioned," Charlotte said to him, then turned to Dr. Taylor. "Mr. Cox is very interested in your uses of milkweed."

Thomas quickly added, "Oh, that and other plants as well, sir."

"Mr. Cox is known as quite the local healer," Charlotte explained.

"No, no," he demurred, "purely amateur. I do what I can for my family. But I am interested in learning more."

She noticed Dr. Taylor look from her to Thomas, then back again.

"Well, then, you must come by the cottage this afternoon and take tea with us. I shall tell you all I know, and you shall be left with the better part of that hour to enjoy Mrs. Beebe's cakes."

"Thank you, sir. But I should not like to intrude on your holiday."

"No bother at all, Mr. Cox," Dr. Taylor said.

"Of course you must come," Mrs. Taylor added cheerfully.

Charlotte had hoped to arrange such a meeting but was a bit bewildered at how it had all come about so quickly. And with so much enthusiasm on the part of Mrs. Taylor.

Since Marie took her half-day on Sunday, Charlotte sat at the work table with Mrs. Beebe that afternoon, helping her arrange buns, biscuits, and small cakes on a silver plate. Thomas, still wearing his Sunday suit, knocked on the kitchen door, hat in hand. Rising, Mrs. Beebe wiped her hands on her apron and opened the door for him.

"Hello there, Thomas."

"Mrs. Beebe."

"I half expected you to come 'round to the front door."

"And when have I ever?"

She returned to her work, *tsking* her tongue against the roof of her mouth. "Taking tea with the tenants. My, aren't we rising in the world."

"Now, now, Mrs. Beebe, you know I am only here for your apple tart."

Mr. Beebe, drinking tea at the three-legged chop block, winked at him. "I figgered that was the way of it. Any time to help me with the hedges this week?"

"Would Tuesday suit?"

"That it would. Any time before two or after three."

Mrs. Beebe shook her head. "Heaven forbid you should interrupt the old man's nap." She smiled begrudgingly at her husband, then nodded to Thomas. "Well, then, off with you into the parlor. But don't expect me to call you 'sir.'"

"I wouldn't know who you were addressin' if you did."

Mrs. Beebe took his hat from him, then swatted his backside with it as he passed through the kitchen door.

Mrs. Taylor insisted that Charlotte join them for tea, which was a first. In many ways, Charlotte would have preferred to stay in the kitchen with the Beebes. But Anne was still napping and she had no excuse to decline. Besides, she would enjoy the time with Thomas and looked forward to witnessing his discussion with Dr. Taylor firsthand.

As she had imagined, the two had a great deal to talk about. Dr. Taylor gladly told him all about the medical uses for milkweed—as well as costmary, foxglove, wood sorrel, comfrey, candytuft, and several other plants.

Thomas asked question after question, and Dr. Taylor never seemed to tire of answering. Mrs. Taylor, however, tired of the conversation and soon rose and excused herself, saying not to get up, she would just go check on Anne.

Charlotte relaxed in Mrs. Taylor's absence, knowing how closely the woman had been observing her and Thomas during the afternoon.

At one point, Charlotte interjected, "Tell Dr. Taylor about the poultices you made for your mother."

Thomas reddened, embarrassed, but described the herbs and method he had used.

"Very well done," Dr. Taylor said. "I could not have prescribed better."

Thomas beamed with pleasure.

Two hours later, the men parted, shaking hands. Under his arm, Thomas carried two books that Dr. Taylor insisted he borrow.

"That's quite a young man," he said to Charlotte as the two stood near one another, watching from the window as Thomas walked away down the path.

"Yes," Charlotte agreed.

Feeling his gaze on her profile, she added, "Though not so young, really. Only four years or so younger than you yourself."

"Really? Feels like more. Some days I feel quite ancient."

At week's end, Lizette Taylor insisted Charlotte take the morning off—walk into the village or visit that "*très grand* friend of yours." She smiled meaningfully and Charlotte felt the need to correct her.

"He is not my particular friend."

"*Non? Tant pis.*"

Too bad, she had said, though Charlotte had the distinct impression it was Mrs. Taylor herself who was disappointed. Charlotte admired Thomas and enjoyed his friendship, his easy acceptance, and their shared love of growing things—but friendship was all she felt for him. Wasn't it?

"Are you certain you want me to go? You will be all right?"

"I do know how to care for my own child."

"Of course you do. I only meant . . . Well, she has been fed, so you should be fine."

Thomas had mentioned he would be visiting cousins this day, so Charlotte didn't take the sea path but instead walked into the village. There, she walked from shop to shop, idly taking in the displays in the windows. She planned to stay away from the end of the street where Dr. Kendall kept his offices.

Turning, she walked right into the man.

"Oh! Dr. Kendall, you startled me."

"Miss Lamb." He bowed. "Do forgive me."

She dipped her head. "Good day, Dr. Kendall." She turned her face back toward the milliner's window, effectively dismissing him, allowing him to walk on without appearing rude. She felt his gaze on her, but feigned interest in the bonnets, hats, and hair ornaments on display. He stepped past her. After their last awkward encounter, he was no doubt relieved to have this unexpected meeting done with as quickly as possible.

His footsteps halted. "I say, Miss Lamb?"

Surprised, she turned toward him as he retraced his steps to stand before her.

"I am on my way to take tea at the little shop on the corner. I do not suppose you would care to join me?"

She pursed her lips, but her brain didn't know quite what words to form. Finally, she managed, "Why?"

"I know things may be a bit awkward between us at present, but I see no need for us to continue so. Your current . . . station . . . in life might be somewhat of a shock to a proper Londoner, I suppose. But here, in this small village, well, such things are quite ordinary and need not form a barrier between us."

She looked down at her hands, clasped before her.

"Come now, Miss Lamb. Have we not a dear friend in common? Are we not two educated gentlepeople, free to take tea together in a public place?"

"I wonder you did not miss your calling, Dr. Kendall. Politics would have suited you." She could not keep a hint of a smile from softening her words.

"Is that a yes?"

"Very well."

He grinned.

But before they had taken four steps, a young voice called out, "Dr. Kendall! Dr. Kendall!"

They turned and watched a young boy running toward them at full speed, panic evident in his features. "Mrs. Henning says come quick! She needs you something awful."

Kendall's expression grew grim. He turned briefly. "The midwife. Forgive me, Miss Lamb—perhaps another time."

"Of course you must go."

"Would you mind coming with me? I may need an extra pair of hands."

"Of course."

"Mrs. Collins, is it?" Dr. Kendall called out to the boy, who was already turning back.

"Yes, sir."

"Bring this lady along, if you please." And to Charlotte he said, "I'll run on ahead."

She nodded, but he was already jogging up the street.

"This way, miss," the boy said.

They arrived at a small tidy cottage with thatched roof. The boy went in first, leaving the door open for her. When she stepped in, she was stunned to see Thomas there, holding a swaddled infant in his large hands. She thought instantly of the lambs.

"Bring another blanket, Freddie," he said. "We've got to get your sister here warmed up."

Thomas looked at the boy—her escort—then his gaze rose to her. "Miss Charlotte?"

"Dr. Kendall asked me to come along."

"He's in there with her now." He shook his head, clearly worried. "She's strugglin', I'm afraid."

"The mother?"

He nodded. "Twins. Seems they're having a terrible time with the second one. Mrs. Henning handed this one to me and told me to keep her warm."

Freddie jogged back into the room holding a wool blanket.

"Here, let me help." Charlotte took it from the boy and helped Thomas wrap the blanket around the tiny baby.

She said, "I thought you were off visiting cousins today."

"Betsy is my cousin."

"Miss Lamb?" Dr. Kendall appeared in the doorway, rolling up his sleeves. "Please, if you will."

She gave Thomas a look of empathy before following Dr. Kendall into the bedroom. In the bed, Betsy Collins looked exhausted. The midwife standing nearby did as well.

"Mrs. Henning. Do rest yourself," Dr. Kendall admonished.

"But—" The grey-haired woman paused in her mopping of the patient's brow and shoulders.

"You cannot help if you faint on me." He turned to Charlotte. "Miss Lamb, please."

Charlotte gently took the bowl and rag from the elderly midwife and began wiping Betsy's forehead. She was sweat-soaked and clearly weak. Charlotte smiled at the woman, who was close to her own age. "I saw your new daughter in the parlor. What a beauty she is."

"Is she?"

"Oh, yes."

Betsy smiled faintly.

"I shall have to attempt to reposition the baby," Dr. Kendall announced sternly.

Betsy grimaced and squeezed her eyes shut.

"Take her hand, there, Miss Lamb," he instructed.

Mrs. Henning had already risen from her stool to take the other.

He pushed and strained against the woman's abdomen, sweat pouring off his forehead. "I cannot . . . quite . . ."

"Thomas can help," Charlotte said. "Thomas!" she called without thinking.

Thomas strode into the room, babe in arms.

"Give her to me," she ordered. "The doctor needs your help."

When Dr. Kendall looked at Thomas and hesitated, Mrs. Henning said, "He's good, he is. He can help."

"Just tell me what to do," Thomas said.

"You push on her abdomen, here, when I tell you."

Together the two men struggled and Betsy cried out and moaned.

"Hang on, Betsy," Thomas said, looking pale as he glanced at his cousin's contorted face.

Dr. Kendall looked again beneath the sheets. He swore beneath his breath. "I shall have to use the forceps."

"No! Please, no . . ." Betsy moaned and began sobbing. They all knew the dangers for both mother and child with the dreaded instrument.

"Mrs. Henning . . . ?" Betsy beseeched.

The older woman shook her head grimly. "Nothing else I can do, love."

Betsy turned her head toward her cousin. "Thomas, please. Do something," she begged.

Thomas nodded and said to Dr. Kendall, "May I try?"

Before Dr. Kendall could answer, Thomas was already moving into position at the foot of the bed, leaving Kendall little choice but to step aside.

"There now, Betsy, relax. Everything's going to be all right. Just relax now—ease those muscles."

Hunching low, one hand propped on the bed and the other reaching under the sheet, Thomas's face was gripped in concentration.

"Sorry, Betsy, won't be long. Try to relax."

"All right, Thomas, all right," Betsy panted.

"There's the little one. I feel his head and neck. Come on, little one, come on . . ."

His expression tightened with the effort of tempered strength.

Betsy cried out.

"Not yet, not yet. Now push!"

Betsy gritted her teeth and pushed.

"Here he comes. Here he comes."

Thinking swiftly, Charlotte pulled out the bottom drawer of Betsy's dresser and laid the first baby into it. Then she leapt forward to hand Thomas a clean sheet left there for this purpose.

"That's it—get ready to catch him, Miss Charlotte."

With a final cry, Betsy pushed and Thomas retracted his arm and together he and Charlotte guided the slick infant into the sheet.

Relieved and revived, Mrs. Henning hurried over and helped Charlotte rub the infant dry and clean out her mouth and nose before handing her to Dr. Kendall.

"It's another girl, Betsy," Mrs. Henning announced.

"Is she all right? I don't hear anything—is she breathing?"

Dr. Kendall carefully turned the child upside down. When she didn't respond, he swatted her gently on her bottom, then once again more smartly. The baby whined, then broke out in an angry cry. Dr. Kendall handed the child to Betsy, and her tears became those of joy.

"Oh, thank you. Thank you, all."

Charlotte turned to look at Thomas. Dr. Kendall was staring at him too, clearly impressed. "How did you know to do that?" he asked.

Thomas shrugged. "Works with sheep."

"Indeed?"

"I'll go brew some yarrow tea for Betsy," Thomas said quickly and left the room.

Dr. Kendall watched him go, amazement on his face.

"Who *is* that young man?"

"His name is Thomas Cox."

"Ah yes . . . I've heard of him. Friend of yours?"

"Yes."

"Has he ever considered the medical profession?"

"I believe he has."

"I wonder if he would be interested in an apprenticeship."

"I believe Dr. Taylor wonders that as well."

Charlotte returned to Lloyd Lodge two hours later, only to hear the baby's piercing cries before she had reached the door. Charlotte hurried inside. Mrs. Taylor was pacing the parlor, bouncing the child in an attempt to soothe her. Lizette's face was flushed red, and it was clear both mother and daughter had been crying for quite some time.

"*Ici*. Take her." Mrs. Taylor thrust the child toward Charlotte. "I cannot make her stop crying. It seems only you have such power."

"No power, madame," she said gently, taking the child in her arms. "Only milk."

"*Non*. It is clear my daughter prefers you. My husband as well . . ."

"No, madame. Anne only wants me when she's hungry." She sat down and skillfully unfastened the hidden front flap of her nursing frock, discreetly allowing the child to nurse with minimum exposure of her person. "There you are." She looked back up at Mrs. Taylor, hoping to assure her. "As for Dr. Taylor, he was a friend to my family long ago, and I appreciate his offer of employment. I am grateful to have a position with such a respectable family as you are."

New tears filled the woman's eyes. "You say the right words. I know I should believe you. I should be thankful that you are here, taking care of my child. But I am not. I want to nurse her myself. But I cannot."

"I am sorry."

"My body, my mind, betray me. My husband . . ."

"No, madame. Never your husband."

"*Non*? Then, why am I so angry? *Je pleure de rage*."

Lizette Taylor turned and strode from the room, the echo of her words capped with a sob. *I am so angry I weep*.

After laying Anne down for her nap, Charlotte knocked softly on Dr. Taylor's study door, her heart pounding painfully.

"Yes?"

She stepped inside, leaving the door ajar.

"Good afternoon, Miss Lamb."

"Good afternoon." She cleared her throat. "Dr. Taylor, I am afraid the time has come for me to leave your employ."

"Pardon me?"

"Do not think me ungrateful. I do appreciate all you have done for me. But it is time I moved on. I wonder if you might consider sending a messenger to find Sally? If you find her quickly, before she takes another position or her milk fades, she would serve you well, I have no doubt. Or if that does not suit, perhaps another nurse from the Manor."

"But why? Has Lizette said something?"

"No. But I am certain Mrs. Taylor will understand my decision."

"Charlotte. You have done nothing wrong."

"Thank you. But I want you—both of you—to be happy, and I do not wish to be a hindrance to the peace of your family."

"You are not—"

She lifted her hand to stop him. "Dr. Taylor, I know how your wife feels about me. In many ways, I understand her fears, her jealousy . . ."

He looked at her, eyes wide. "You do?"

But she was not referring to him. Tears shimmered in her eyes as she whispered, "I know what it feels like to have my child look at another woman as his mother."

He swallowed. "But this will be the case with any nurse."

"Dr. Taylor . . ."

"Forgive me. Of course that is not entirely true. She has no doubt seen my . . . regard for you. Careful as I have been to conceal it. Have I not treated you with the utmost propriety?"

"Utmost."

"I'm afraid Lizette is, by nature, a jealous person. I cannot deny I am concerned for your well-being, but of course, other aspects of our relationship are long over."

"Of course," she echoed. "Still. I feel it would be best if I leave. As soon as possible."

He rubbed his hand over his eyebrows. "Do you think Sally would come?"

"I do. And it would put my mind greatly at ease if she did."

"Very well. I shall do my best to find her."

"Thank you."

Charlotte walked from the room, still in control of her emotions. She walked quickly from the cottage to the seashore, where the waves could swallow her cries and a bit more salt water would not be noticed.

26

> She was melancholy and . . . dissatisfied with herself constantly, incapable of attending to anything, and entirely indifferent to things around her. She felt at times as if she were nobody, and would rather be dead than have that feeling.
>
> —L. Shafer, M.D., *Case of Puerperal Insanity,* 1877

As soon as Dr. Taylor sent out his messenger, Charlotte began to regret her decision. She almost hoped he would not reach Sally or that she would be unable or unwilling to come. Charlotte doubted Dr. Taylor would strive to find another unknown nurse, though Mrs. Taylor might wish it, especially while they were in temporary lodgings. But even as Charlotte entertained such thoughts, she knew it was foolish to think staying would make her—or anyone—happy. She supposed it was the dark unknown future that caused her to long for things to remain as they were.

When the return message arrived, Charlotte held her breath. She tried to find some small satisfaction in being right—as she had predicted, Sally would come. In fact her letter reached them just ahead of Sally herself, who wrote to say she would be arriving in Old Shoreham on the late afternoon coach.

From Sally's few hastily written lines, Dr. Taylor ascertained that he had located her the first place he tried—with the Harrises in Doddington. Mrs. Mead, it seemed, had needed a few more days to wean her own child and had arrived at Fawnwell the same day as Dr. Taylor's messenger. Sally had secured passage on the next morning's coach.

Now that it was settled, Charlotte felt the block of sadness begin to break up and sift out through all the broken places in her heart, replaced with a numb pragmatism. There was nothing she could do about it now. It was the right thing, whether it felt like it or not.

That afternoon, Charlotte took a basket of clean laundry to hang on the line outside. She had offered to help Marie, reasoning that keeping busy might take her mind off her impending departure. But as she began hanging little nappies and sweet little bed gowns, she realized she ought to have volunteered for some different task.

Suddenly Thomas was there beside her, bending low and coming up with a pair of knitted socks barely large enough to cover his thumbs. She was immediately relieved the basket held none of her own undergarments.

Charlotte watched as he hung the tiny socks in mock concentration. "Hello, Thomas. Here to help Mr. Beebe again?"

"Why—are these his?"

She shook her head, amused.

"Actually, Miss Charlotte, I am here to ask you to take supper with us at the week end. Mother wants to meet you."

"She does?"

"Well, Lizzy has been going on about you. And, I confess, I have as well."

She smiled quickly, then bit her lip. "Thank you, but I am afraid I will be gone by then."

"Gone?"

"Yes. I am leaving my post here. There's to be a new nurse. In fact, she arrives today."

"But—" He stared down at her in dismay. "This is a blow. Is . . . is this what you want, Miss Charlotte, or . . . ?"

Mrs. Taylor appeared on the lawn, looking from Thomas to Charlotte and back again. "Good day, Mr. Cox. You have heard the news—Miss Lamb is leaving us?"

"I have just."

"But you will still come to visit us, will you not?"

"I—"

"Of course you must. Now, I shall leave you to your farewells." She returned to the cottage, humming a seaman's tune.

Thomas looked back at Charlotte, his eyes sparking with uncharacteristic emotion. Was it anger?

Charlotte answered his question as though they had not been interrupted. "I am learning, Thomas, that what I *want* is not always the wisest course."

"Miss Charlotte . . ."

She forced a bright smile. "Actually, it is quite a happy turn of events, for the new nurse is a friend of mine. I know you will like her. She was raised on a farm and will so enjoy all the things Lizzy enjoys. I am certain you will all get on famously."

Thomas had been looking down at the ground while she spoke but now glanced up at her earnestly. "You cannot be so easily replaced, Miss Charlotte."

Again she bit her lip. "Thank you. You are most kind."

"Might I at least accompany you into the village to meet the coach?"

She hesitated. "I should not like to trouble you—haven't you work waiting?"

"The work will always be here, Miss Charlotte. You will not."

Mrs. Beebe insisted they take the gig to the inn. Leaving Anne with Marie, Charlotte and Thomas rode into Old Shoreham, halting only long enough to pay the shilling-per-horse toll to the boy at the bridge. When they arrived, Thomas helped her down in front of the Red Lion.

"I'll tie up Old Ned. You go on and greet your friend. I'll be waiting when you're ready."

"Thank you."

When the coach arrived, Charlotte stood back while the dust and horses settled and the innkeeper ran out to meet prospective guests. When she saw Sally's fair head duck low to descend the carriage on the coachman's hand, she stepped forward to meet her.

"Miss Charlotte!" Sally cried as soon as she saw her, but she did not offer her usual toothy grin. Instead her long face looked forlorn and she clearly had difficulty meeting Charlotte's gaze. "Please believe me, Miss Charlotte. I didn't do it—I swear I didn't. I would never even have thought of it if I'd known it might harm him."

"I believe you, Sally."

"Oh, thank you, Miss Charlotte. God bless you." The two women embraced. Then Sally stood back, her hands on Charlotte's shoulders, regarding her. "Now, tell me you haven't gone and gotten yourself sacked too."

"Not exactly. But it is time for me to leave."

"A fussy one is she?"

"No. Anne's an angel."

Sally stuck her elbow into Charlotte's side. "I meant the missus." Sally's smile was back, her front teeth protruding over her bottom lip.

"Let us just say it might be best if she did not know you and I are so fond of one another."

Sally nodded her understanding.

"I've told Mrs. Taylor I knew *of* you at the Manor and that she would be very pleased with you."

Thomas appeared, already bending low to pick up Sally's two carpetbags before standing to his full height beside her. Sally's gaze followed his upward movement with a slight opening of her mouth.

"Sally, this is my friend Thomas Cox. Thomas, this is Miss Sally Mitchell."

Thomas gave an awkward bow, then looked at the newcomer. "A pleasure it is to meet you, Miss Sally."

Charlotte did not miss the admiration in his expression.

Sally shook her head in wonder. "I'll be bobbed, but you're tall," she said, then giggled, teeth splayed as she did so.

Thomas smiled in return. "Yes, we have that in common." He looked back at Charlotte beside him. "As well as a dear friend."

Charlotte pretended not to notice his blush nor the question in Sally's eyes as she looked at them both.

When they arrived back at Lloyd Lodge, Mrs. Taylor welcomed Sally warmly. As Charlotte had predicted, the mistress seemed very pleased with her replacement. There was something about the large, simple woman that seemed to put people, perhaps especially jealous wives, at ease.

Charlotte helped Sally carry her carpetbags up to the room Charlotte had used. She moved her own packed bags off the dressing table to make room for Sally's things.

"You're not leaving already, Charlotte, surely?"

"Not today. Dr. Taylor said I might stay as long as I like."

"Stay, then. I don't mind sharing."

"I shall stay just long enough to see you settled with the Beebes and the Taylors, and with little Anne, of course."

"Won't it be difficult for you, Charlotte?"

Charlotte chose to ignore the deeper implications of the question. "You have just arrived. Of course I want to spend a day or two with you before I go."

"Will you see Thomas again . . . after you leave, I mean."

"I shouldn't think so. Why?"

"You don't, that is, the two of you are not . . . ?"

"No, Sally, we are not."

"You don't . . . love him, then?"

Charlotte took a deep breath and exhaled slowly. She heard Anne, who had been napping, gurgling happily to herself in the next room.

"She's awake," Charlotte said. "Please excuse me." She walked to the nursery and picked up Anne.

Sally followed her. "It's all right if you do. I just want to know how things are between you."

Charlotte lifted Anne into her arms. "There is someone here for you to meet, Miss Anne."

"Isn't she a gorgeous thing. And so much grown since I seen her last."

"Yes." Charlotte stroked Anne's cheek. Then she sighed and placed Anne into Sally's arms. "I will miss Thomas and he will miss me, but that is the end of it."

"But I saw the way he looked at you."

Charlotte smiled gently at her friend. "And I saw the way he looked at you. Something tells me he will not be missing me for long."

Unlike Mrs. Taylor, young Anne was slower to hand over her loyalties. She wouldn't nurse from Sally that first night and cried and reached for Charlotte.

Charlotte sat in the rocking chair with her, nursing her and soothing her—and herself. She knew she ought to refuse and let off nursing all at once, but she felt unable to do so, unable to withstand Anne's pitiful tears.

Finally, when Anne awoke at dawn, crying to be fed, Charlotte laid her in bed at Sally's side. While nurse and child were both only half awake, hunger won over and Anne nursed. Sally's sleepy eyes filled with tears as she looked at Charlotte in silent understanding.

Richard Kendall stood before the writing desk in the study that served as Daniel's office.

"Have you no objections, then, were I to offer her some . . . situation?"

Daniel stared at the man, wanting very much to throttle him. Instead he said in controlled tones, "You will offend her."

"Quite possibly. Beyond that risk, have you no objections?" When Daniel made no answer, Richard continued. "You said yourself she has few options. That the man who should have made some recompense, should be providing for her, has failed to do so. You are not in a position to do so, but I am."

"Yet you do not offer marriage."

Kendall frowned and sighed. "No. I am afraid not. Not at this point. We are not so well acquainted."

"But acquainted enough to ask her to become your mistress?"

"Well." He cleared his throat. "The particulars are yet to be agreed upon, of course, and will be strictly between Miss Lamb and myself. You can be assured of my discretion."

"She will refuse you."

"I am aware of that possibility."

"I would ask that you dispense with this line of thinking altogether. But I have no authority to stop you."

"No, being merely her former employer . . ." He nodded thoughtfully. "Though I am beginning to understand why you chose not to tell Mrs. Taylor about your *past* regard for Miss Lamb."

Richard Kendall found Charlotte Lamb strolling along the path parallel to the sea, swinging a stick of driftwood in her hand. He fell into step beside her.

"Where will you go now, Miss Lamb?"

"To Crawley. I have a great-aunt there."

He nodded. "A pleasant prospect, then?"

She shrugged. "Pleasant enough."

She seemed pensive, her eyes far away on the grey water, the distant gulls and beyond. "If I could go anywhere I liked, I suppose I would return to Doddington. Though I am no longer welcome in my own home. Still, I would steal back to that dear place if I could. I was just imagining that very thing: strolling through the village and up the lane, past the churchyard and into my mother's garden."

"Your family would not approve of such a visit?"

She shook her head. "My father would not likely see me, spending so much time in his library as he does. Beatrice, my sister, is so often at her pianoforte, or lost in the pages of a book, that the world outside the vicarage windows holds little appeal and she would not likely see me either."

"What would you do there?"

"I would walk along the garden paths, pausing at every flower bed and ornamental tree, taking in which have flourished, which are languishing, and which have died. I should no doubt cry foolish tears over their loss. And feel just the slightest satisfaction that my absence has left some small mark on the place. Then, when no one was about I would find dear Buxley, our gardener, and see if he could, with every kindness and attention, save those suffering from neglect. And perhaps even coax the lost to return once again."

She paused to toss the stick of driftwood into the sea. "But, as that is not a real possibility, I suppose my second choice would be to return to the home of my aunt and uncle in Hertfordshire. I have spent many happy hours in their company and would find much solace in doing so again. Of course, I doubt my uncle would see fit to have me out in society, but even confined to their home, I believe I should be happy. My aunt has the most comforting way about her. Everyone who meets her says so."

Charlotte stopped and turned toward him, hand over her mouth. "Do forgive me! I have used a week's worth of words on your poor ears."

He grinned. "Think nothing of it."

"I suppose it's due to spending so little time in adult company."

"I am happy to oblige." They continued walking. "So—why not away to Hertfordshire, then?"

She sighed. "My father has forbidden my aunt and uncle to shelter me. So"—she straightened her shoulders—"I shall return to Crawley. I am sure I shall enjoy it."

"You did enjoy your time *here*—before recent conflicts, that is?"

"Yes indeed. I am sorry to leave such a beautiful place and such fine company."

"I am happy to hear you say so. I had thought of a possible solution to your dilemma, if I may be so bold as to make a suggestion?"

"Of course."

"I had thought that I might offer another alternative."

"Yes?" She turned to look at him and they stopped walking.

"Yes. That is . . . Please forgive my presumption. I realize we are not so well acquainted, but it did occur to me that you and I enjoy one another's company."

"Yes," she agreed, but her brow began to wrinkle in growing confusion.

"As a physician, I have some means—not an overly grand income but sufficient, I believe, to offer you a comfortable living here."

Her eyes lit, as if with pleasure, but, just as quickly, the hint of a smile evaporated and her mouth opened, then closed, then opened again.

"For a moment I thought you were offering me a post." Her chuckle held no mirth.

He shifted on his feet and cleared his throat. "Well, in a manner of speaking . . ."

"As a midwife. Or monthly nurse . . ."

"Oh . . ."

"I suppose I should be flattered. Or offended."

He laughed nervously. "So, which is it to be?"

"Both, actually. I'm afraid you have rather stunned me."

He found the blush in her cheeks charming. He asked timidly, "But you do not find the idea . . . totally repugnant?"

She swallowed, looked at him and then away. "I do not find *you* repugnant, Dr. Kendall. But the nature of the offer . . . yes, I'm afraid I do."

"Well," he said, and looked down at his boots. He forced himself to swallow the sting of her rejection, relieved for her manner of delivering it, the concession to his person. "Then, do forgive me. It was not my intention to offend you, though I cannot say I am overly surprised at your response."

An awkward silence ensued.

"I do not suppose there is any hope of your forgetting the former portion of this conversation and allowing me to begin anew?"

She smiled tentatively. "If you like."

He returned her smile and straightened. They began walking back toward the cottage. "I am sorry I had not thought to offer you a more, shall we say, traditional post. In all truth, the midwives and nurses I know are older, work-hardened women with little education—very different from my perception of you. Still, I have no doubt you are more than capable, should such a position truly appeal to you."

"I should never have guessed so until recently. Though I suppose a position of governess or lady's companion is more in keeping with my upbringing."

"I'm afraid I have no need of either at present." He smiled wryly. "I also have a quite competent monthly nurse at the moment. And there is a local midwife as well—Mrs. Henning, whom you met—though she is getting up in years. Perhaps I might call on you in the future, should the need arise?"

"Indeed you may. Though I would have much to learn."

"As do we all, Miss Lamb. But I have no doubt you would be a most able student. Have we an understanding, then?"

She nodded. "We do."

"And may we . . . part as friends?"

She smiled. "We may."

Daniel watched the discussion from afar. The exchange took longer than he would have thought and she did not strike Kendall nor stalk off as he'd guessed she would—hoped she would. And now there was no mistaking the nod of her head, the slight bow the two exchanged, the smile on his friend's face. She had agreed. Daniel did not wish to think about what it would mean . . . or to ponder why his chest felt like it might cave in on itself.

27

> You will suckle your infant your self if you can; be not such an ostrich as to decline it, merely because you would be one of the careless women, living at ease.
>
> —Cotton Mather, *Ornaments for the Daughters of Zion,* 1692
>
> (Note: Mather's own children were wet-nursed.)

Before the assembled family and staff, Charlotte bid Mr. and Mrs. Taylor a formal, somewhat stiff farewell. She was careful to only glance briefly in Sally and Anne's direction, lest she give too much away. She had sat up rocking the little girl half the night, so those farewells had already been endured. Ignoring Marie's smirk, she smiled at Mrs. Beebe, who had earlier that morning embraced her in the kitchen and stuffed a bundle of food and jingling coin into her reticule, brooking no objection. Now Charlotte bit her lip to keep it from trembling, turned, and left the cottage, reticule in hand and heart in her throat.

Thomas walked with her into Old Shoreham this time, carrying her bags as though they weighed nothing.

As they crested the bridge, a family approached from the other side—father with child in arms, mother holding a little boy's hand—and she and Thomas stepped close to the rail to allow them to pass. When they had, Charlotte walked on but quickly noticed Thomas stayed where he was.

Retracing her steps, she looked at him questioningly. "What is it?"

He stood stiffly, and in a voice nearly petulant said, "I wish there was something I could do."

She studied his face, so unusually somber. "Thomas," she soothed, "there are some things even you cannot fix." She smiled gently. "It's all right."

He turned and gripped the bridge rail, still refusing to go farther.

She stood at the rail beside him, an arm's length away. Staring at the river below, she sensed his agitation, his deliberation.

But what could he do? She knew any money he made went to help his mother provide for his many siblings. Even if he began working as an apprentice, he would have little money of his own for several years. He was surely not yet thinking of taking a wife—not her, in any case. Was he?

Charlotte squeezed her eyes shut, realizing that if she did not speak, he would. Without turning to face him she said cheerfully, "I told Sally how it was, between us."

She heard him move a step closer to her. His voice was uncertain. "Did you?"

She stole a glance at him before returning her gaze to the water. "Yes, I told her that you could never think of me the way I do you."

"Charlotte—"

She went on quickly, "For you already have four sisters, but I have never had a brother."

Turning toward him, she self-consciously lifted her gaze to his. "And I have always longed for one."

His eyes glimmered. He lowered his head, bringing his face close to hers. "I should be honored to be yours."

They stood that way for a moment, in a silence heavy with unspoken things.

Charlotte took a deep breath. "Sally is dear to me, as you know. I hope you . . . and Lizzy . . . will be kind to her." She put her fist to her heart. "It will please me if you show her every attention."

Quietly, he asked, "Will it?"

She nodded. "Yes."

He straightened but continued to peer down at her for a long moment without speaking. He reached out his hand toward her. It was not customary, to say the least, but Charlotte understood the impulse behind it. Some culmination of feeling must occur. It was either shake hands or embrace. But that, of course, would be inappropriate and foolish and unfair to them all. So instead, she gripped his hand with her smaller one and felt his answering squeeze. She held tight a moment longer, then let go.

Charlotte sipped her tea in the dining room of the inn, waiting for her coach to be announced. She had insisted that Thomas return to his work, that he need not wait with her. He had gone, though reluctantly.

Dr. Kendall came in, hat in hand and out of breath. "Miss Lamb. I am so glad I found you before you left. I wonder if I might trespass on your kindness for some time longer?"

"Of course. Please, do have a seat, Dr. Kendall."

"Thank you." He sat down and leaned across the table to speak in confidential tones. "A couple has come to me in dire need of a nurse for their infant son. The young mother is unable to nurse him properly, and the father fears his son will suffer."

"What is the problem?"

"Well, that is rather delicate to discuss here. But if you could come to my offices and meet them . . ."

"But my coach—"

"They pass through for London with stops in Crawley twice each day, Miss Lamb. If you could postpone at least until the afternoon's coach, or tomorrow's, I am sure the couple would pay for your lodgings. Or I shall, if you would allow me."

"I had not thought to continue on as a nurse."

"This would only be a temporary position. I am certain the mother will, in time, be able to nurse her son herself as she desires to do."

He leaned closer yet. "You are still . . . able, do you think?"

She looked at the table, self-consciously slouching a bit to diminish her swollen breasts. She nodded.

"If you could relieve the child's distress and hunger even for a few hours, I am sure the couple would be most grateful."

Charlotte had no real desire to wet-nurse another child. But neither could she stand the thought of an infant suffering hunger when she could help. "I shall come."

"Thank you. I have already told them about you. In fact, they are waiting on us as we speak. If you would not mind . . . ?"

"My bags . . ."

"I shall ask the innkeeper to stow them for you. Until you decide?"

"Thank you."

They walked quickly through town to Dr. Kendall's offices, where he lost no time in making introductions. "Mr. and Mrs. Henshaw, may I present Miss Charlotte Lamb."

Charlotte curtsied.

Mr. Henshaw was older than she would have imagined, in his early fifties, perhaps. He was well dressed with craggy features and light brown hair combed to one side. He remained seated, legs crossed, impatiently bouncing his knee. His wife was young indeed. No more than seventeen or eighteen, Charlotte guessed. She was a lovely, dainty girl, with fair hair pulled into a fashionable coil and wide, pale blue eyes—eyes which looked terribly concerned. In her arms, she held a baby, wriggling and red-faced. Yet he made no loud cry, merely whined in high-pitched bursts of protest every half minute or so.

"Poor dear. How old is he?" Charlotte asked.

"A week tomorrow," Mrs. Henshaw answered quietly.

"If he lives that long," Mr. Henshaw snapped. "Now, let's not waste time, Kendall. You've found us this nurse in haste. How do we know she even has sufficient milk to nurse my son?"

"I can attest to the robust health of her last charge."

"She might have dried up since then."

Charlotte recoiled at the man's bald words.

"No, sir. She left my friend's employ only this morning."

"Why was she sacked?"

"It was nothing of the kind. I can vouch for her character and dependability, sir. Rest assured."

"Well, have you examined her yourself?"

"Examined? Not in so many words."

"Then do your job, man, and let's be done. If she's fit, I want her to nurse little Crispin here before he starves."

Charlotte felt the blood rushing to her face and neck.

"Miss Lamb is a naturally modest girl," Kendall muttered, biting his lip.

"Then use that screen there. I don't know a thing about this girl. Is it not reasonable to want some proof of her health, that she isn't ill or infected with some foul sores that would harm my boy?"

Dr. Kendall opened his mouth and closed it again. He looked at Charlotte soberly.

"Miss Lamb, would you mind stepping behind the screen? It won't take but a moment."

Charlotte opened her mouth to protest further, but the infant's whines grew into pitiful squeals that tore at Charlotte's heart—and threatened to cause her milk to let down on its own.

She stepped behind the screen and waited as Dr. Kendall adjusted it to enclose them more fully. He looked at her and mouthed the words *Forgive me.*

He looked from her face down to the neckline of her gown meaningfully. Heart pounding, face burning, she looked away from him and worked her bodice down until it pooled at her waist. Then she lowered one strap of her chemise from her shoulder, then the other. She had forgotten she had bound her breasts with muslin, to alleviate the pain and swelling since she was still full of milk. She swallowed, then unpinned the cloth where she had fastened its end. As she began to unwind the long strip, she glanced surreptitiously at the doctor and saw that he endeavored to maintain a detached, officious expression.

"Make sure her milk is still flowing," the dreadful man called from the other side of the screen.

Wincing, Charlotte paused. Would Dr. Kendall expect her to express milk in front of him? How mortifying.

At that moment the infant began crying in earnest. As she had feared, her milk let down in response, wetting through the remaining layers of muslin before she could wrap her arms over herself. Dr. Kendall lifted a hand, silently motioning for her to cease unwinding.

"Milk flow is excellent," he called over his shoulder. "The . . . everything . . . looks quite perfect."

He returned his gaze to her face. Although Charlotte was relieved beyond words not to have to expose herself fully, she was still too embarrassed to meet his eyes.

"You may redo your things, Miss Lamb. I apologize for the inconvenience."

Charlotte quickly repositioned her gown. "Why do I not nurse him right now?" she said, attempting to regain her composure. "Have you another room I might use?"

"Yes, of course."

Charlotte sat in a chair in a small examination room, nursing the babe who suckled with desperate voracity. The sensation was both relieving and slightly painful. She hoped he would be gentler in subsequent feedings.

The young wife watched with eyes wide, not averted as politeness might have dictated. "You *are* perfect," she breathed.

Charlotte did not know how to respond to such a shocking remark. The young woman clearly realized what she had said, for her face flushed pink. "I only meant, compared to me . . ."

"I'm sure you are fine."

"No. I am not."

When Charlotte next glanced up from Crispin's fuzz-covered head, she was stunned to see that Mrs. Henshaw had unfastened the nursing panel of her gown. Charlotte glimpsed dark purple bruises before the young woman closed the panel again. Charlotte's shock was replaced by compassion.

"Oh, you poor dear! No wonder you cannot nurse Crispin. How painful that must be!"

"The physician thinks I may have some infection. All I know is that I cry out in pain when I try to nurse my son. Crispin starts crying then, too, and Mr. Henshaw starts shouting."

Charlotte shook her head in pity.

"I do not blame him," Mrs. Henshaw said. "What kind of woman cannot nurse her own child? He says his own mother nursed him, and he would not have his son farmed out to some crude, greedy peasant. Oh! Forgive me, I did not mean you—"

"It's all right. I have heard such opinions before. You know, you are not the only woman to have trouble, Mrs. Henshaw."

"Please. Call me Georgiana."

"Very well, Georgiana. And you may call me Charlotte."

"Thank you."

"I have seen that once before. At the lying-in hospital."

"You have? Is it curable?"

"Of course it is. I shall nurse Crispin for you for a few days while you heal. It appears that he has not been latching on properly." Georgiana lowered her head and Charlotte hastened to add, "But how would you know if no one showed you? I realize women have been doing this since creation, but it does not always come as naturally as one might think."

Georgiana attempted a smile. What a lovely, gentle expression she had. Charlotte liked Georgiana Henshaw very much, felt nearly as maternal toward her as she did toward little Crispin. Her husband, however—she'd prefer to have as few dealings with him as possible.

"My own mother is gone, I'm afraid," Georgiana said wistfully.

"As is mine."

"I have one sister. But she is far off in Newcastle. Have you a sister?"

"Yes. But she is far away from me as well."

28

[Milkweed] has also been used in ancient times to poison arrows.
It also induces vomiting in birds that eat the Monarch butterfly.

—Jack Sanders, *The Secrets of Wildflowers*

His wife vomited daintily into the basin, then wiped her mouth with a lace handkerchief. It was a graceful act, nearly ladylike. At least until she swore.

"What is wrong?" Daniel asked.

"Nothing. I am only sick of this foul English food."

"Are you all right now?"

"*Oui—maintenant*. Why will Mrs. Beebe not allow Marie to cook our meals? If I must eat that wretched cabbage fried in mutton fat one more time, I shall spew out my soul."

He chuckled and helped her to her feet.

"This is not funny. *C'est terrible*."

"It isn't that bad."

"Not for you. You are here only at the week end. She saves the tripe mash and greasy cabbage until you are gone to London."

He smiled. "Why do we not go to the inn in the village tomorrow. Kendall said the food there is fine."

"I doubt they have anything that resembles cuisine in that little fishing village."

"Well, let us venture there and find out, shall we?"

"I do not know if I shall feel up to it, Daniel. Let us see what tomorrow brings."

"Dr. Taylor?"

He opened his eyes. Mrs. Beebe stood in the parlor doorway.

"Hmm?" He had fallen asleep in a chair, tired from the coach trip and the long nights at the Manor before. He glanced at the mantel clock. He'd been asleep for nearly an hour.

"I thought you should know—the missus has gone out in the rain."

"What?" He looked toward the window. The rain that had been pouring down all afternoon had slowed to a steady drizzle. "When?"

"A quarter hour or more."

"Did she say—?"

Mrs. Beebe shook her head. "Didn't say a word. I thought of sending Mr. Beebe, but after the way your missus chewed my ears after supper, he isn't feeling too charitable toward her—if you know what I mean."

"I understand. And I am sorry for it. I will go. Do not trouble yourself further. Mrs. Taylor has always liked the rain."

This was not true, and he felt guilty for the lie as well as the motive behind it. He didn't want others to realize—didn't want to realize it himself. *It is happening again. . . .*

He found his wife sitting on the bench overlooking the sea.

She sat perfectly still, her hair, dress, and face thoroughly soaked.

"Lizette, my love, what are you doing?"

"Trying to see France. Smell France. And, after that wretched supper, *taste* France. I cannot see it by day with this country's ever-present fog and rain . . ."

"The channel is too wide here. I wish I could take you, but things are still too volatile—"

"But tonight I saw a light," she said urgently, as if he hadn't spoken. "On the horizon. I thought, *voilà! Bien sûr!* At night I can see France. I watched the light for a long time. It did not move. Just winked at me, called to me. I felt so happy. But then the light moved. Sailed closer and away down the coast. Just another stinking fishing boat. Bringing more stinking cod for your Mrs. Beebe to fry in her mutton fat."

"You might have spoken more kindly to her."

"I should repay with kindness the poison she feeds me? I can feel it, Daniel, filling my bowels and flowing through my veins. Poisoning me. Changing me. I used to be so . . . so different. So alive, so lovely."

He knelt beside her. "You are still."

"I used to be so happy too—remember?"

Tears filled his eyes. "I remember," he said quietly. He laid his hands on her knees. The hot tears trailed down his cheeks, mingling with the cool raindrops on his face. "You will be happy again, my love. *We* will be happy again."

The following afternoon, Marie brought in a tray of tea things, but Lizette waved the servant away. She picked up the book, glanced at a single line, and tossed it down again. She rose from the settee and stalked about the room, as restless as a creature caged.

Daniel lowered his own book. "Shall we go for a walk, my dear? Some exercise might do us both good."

"What is the use?"

"We'll take Anne. She always seems to enjoy a stroll in Mr. Beebe's carriage."

"Sally and Thomas Cox have already taken her for a walk."

"Well, have you thought any more about having the neighbors over for tea?"

She expelled a dry laugh and rolled her eyes.

"Kendall assures me Mrs. Dillard and her lot are the worst of the village snobs. Our neighbors would be far kinder."

"Why would they accept an invitation from me? I am nobody."

"That is not true. You are a fine woman—you are my wife."

"You are nobody as well."

"Granted."

"And you leave for London tomorrow, again, leaving me caged up in this strange house."

"I shall stay if you prefer." He paused. "One of my patients is expecting twins and I fear it shall be a difficult birth, but I am sure Preston can manage it."

"That man is not fit to deliver goats. No, go. Go and do what you must."

Five days later, the front door of Richard Kendall's offices opened and in strode Lizette Taylor, beautifully turned out in crimson gown and feathered hat.

"*Bonjour*, Dr. Kendall."

"Mrs. Taylor. This is a pleasant surprise. What brings you by?"

"Are we not well enough acquainted that I might visit without an appointment?"

"But of course we are. Is there something I might help you with?"

She looked at him, opened her mouth, hesitated, and then said, "Yes, there is. It is silly, really, a trifling complaint, but if you would not mind . . . ?"

"Of course not."

She glanced toward the old man sitting near the door. "Should we not step into your private office?"

He followed her gaze. "Of course." Then more loudly, to the man, he said, "I shall be with you shortly, Mr. Dumfries."

He showed her into his office. "Now, what seems to be the problem? Are you not feeling well?"

"Do I not look well?"

"You look very well indeed. As usual."

"You are very gallant to say so." She lowered her dress from one shoulder. "There. Do you see?"

"Ah . . . what am I looking at?"

"I am usually more modest, but I suppose, being a physician, you are unmoved by the sight of the female form?"

He swallowed. "Usually, yes."

She stroked the exposed skin below her clavicle. "This patch of skin—does it not look red to you?"

He stepped closer, peering down at the spot. He cleared his throat. "What has Daniel said about it?"

"I have not asked him. He is away in London again at that precious lying-in hovel of his."

"I hear the old Manor Home is quite well run."

"Manor indeed."

"How would you describe the irritation? Does the area itch? Burn?"

"Yes, I burn . . ."

He looked from the mild rash up to her face, into her smoldering eyes.

"Do I not feel warm to you?" She let her dress fall farther down her shoulder, exposing a hint of cleavage.

He hesitated, feeling beguiled and perplexed. He forced his gaze away and focused again on her face. This time he saw that, indeed, her complexion looked flushed, her eyes nearly fevered. He looked once more at her lovely neck and shoulders. He reached out and pressed his fingers to the side of her throat. Then he lowered his hand across her bodice, to her abdomen, resting there, kneading, exploring. She shivered.

Again he cleared his throat and stepped back. "Yes, well, I believe I have all the information I need. You may do up your frock now."

He turned his back to her and picked up a pen and prescription booklet.

"That is all?" Her tone was bitter.

"Yes. I shall write up a prescription for some salve that should help." He ripped the script from its binding and turned to hand it to her. "I am sure the chemist will have this in supply."

"That is all you great physicians are good for. You write your orders like a housekeeper with a list for the greengrocer." She held up the paper and crumpled it into a ball. "But you *do* nothing." She let the wad fall to the floor.

Stepping nearer, she grabbed a handful of his coat in one fist and pushed her face close to his. "You do not help us. You do not give us what we need."

Swallowing hard, he stepped back, pulling his coat loose from her grasp. "You must excuse me, Mrs. Taylor. I have another patient waiting."

He turned, opened the door, and stopped abruptly. Daniel Taylor stood waiting, hat in hand.

"Taylor! How good to see you," Kendall enthused rather falsely, though his relief at his friend's sudden appearance was genuine enough. "We thought you were in London. That is, Mrs. Taylor here was just telling me that you were. But how could you be, for here you are."

Daniel's pleasant expression faded and his brow furrowed. Kendall self-consciously smoothed down his coat. Glancing over his shoulder, he noted that Mrs. Taylor had shrugged her gown up higher on her shoulder, but it was still not properly done up.

"I've only just returned by the afternoon coach," Daniel said flatly.

"How fortuitous. You are just in time to offer a second opinion on my diagnosis. Mrs. Taylor has a skin irritation she was just pointing out to me."

Daniel looked at him a moment longer, than swung his gaze to his wife, to her exposed shoulder.

"You have not mentioned this to me," he said, stepping into the office. "Is this a new affliction?"

She looked at him pointedly. "I have suffered for some time."

"You knew I was on my way. Could you not wait?"

Lizette Taylor narrowed her eyes. "You have shown little interest in my skin of late, Dr. Taylor."

Daniel glanced up and Kendall shook his head slightly, forcing himself to meet his friend's stare. He had done nothing wrong, whatever fleeting thoughts had flitted across his mind. He hoped Daniel would believe him.

Dr. Kendall asked Lizette to wait in his office while he spoke to Daniel in the other room. Mr. Dumfries took himself home, saying he would return on the morrow.

Once they were alone, Kendall began somberly, "I believe it is as you feared."

Daniel stared at the man without seeing him, dread filling his gut. "Are you sure?"

"No. But she has symptoms—accelerated pulse, itching, and, um, certain uncharacteristic behaviors. . . ."

"It's true she has not been herself—demonstrated again this afternoon by the looks of it."

"Daniel, I hope you do not think—"

"I don't know what to think. Why now? Our child is more than seven months old. Lizette seemed so recovered from the postnatal mania. Yes, she's been melancholy, but not nearly as out of control as she was before."

"You don't know?"

"Know what?"

"Well, I did only a preliminary examination, but I do believe your wife is pregnant."

Daniel squeezed his eyes shut as if to block out the truth. He had been so determined to avoid intimacy with Lizette that he had barely allowed himself to look at her nor touch her for months, save that one time. The signs he had noticed, he had tried to ignore or explain away. *Not morning sickness, surely—merely Mrs. Beebe's greasy food. . . .*

His friend must think him an idiot.

"The symptoms of puerperal insanity often start with conception," Kendall said. "Whereas for other women, it doesn't make itself known until after delivery. Did it strike her during her first lying-in?"

Daniel nodded, the fear beginning to grow.

"Good heavens, man, how bad was it?"

He looked at Richard, too devastated to lie. "Very."

"Did she try to harm herself?"

Daniel nodded.

"How did you treat her?"

"Herbs, purgatives, blisters. . . . Nothing worked. When she became violent I resorted to laudanum for a time and finally had to institutionalize her."

Richard stared at him, horror and pity a terrible pall on his face. "I am sorry, Daniel."

"As am I."

"What will you do?"

"The best I can. For now, she is melancholy and restless but has yet to become violent. I will find someone to cover for me in London. I will stay with her and keep her here as long as I can."

"If I hear of anything . . . any new developments or treatments . . ."

"Thank you, Kendall."

29

> Women turned against their husbands, neglected themselves and the household, bullied their servants, broke the china . . . displayed an overt sexuality, making vulgar and suggestive comments to complete strangers. Yet so common was this disorder . . . that it came to be seen as an almost anticipated accompaniment of the process of giving birth.
>
> —Dr. Hilary Marland, *Dangerous Motherhood*

After dinner, Lizette began scratching her arm, then her neck. He watched calmly at first, but when she began scratching with great vigor, he rose to his feet and took her by the arms to still her. Already she bore long streaks of red down her white neck. "Come, I shall give you something for that."

"Nothing helps."

"I shall find something. Come."

Pausing to pick up his medical bag, he led her upstairs to their bedroom and closed the door. She flounced down on the bed while he set the bag on the dresser and began looking through its contents. "Here we are."

He sat on the bed beside her and began applying the ointment to her neck, lowering her gown from one shoulder to avoid getting the sticky medicine on the fine material. He smoothed the ointment onto her throat, then bent to kiss her bare shoulder. She had been trying to seduce him for weeks. Now, the damage done, why not enjoy his wife while he could? He kissed her clavicle and slid the gown off her other shoulder, his hand moving lower to stroke her exposed skin. His lips moved lower as well.

"*Non.*"

She shoved him with startling strength and he fell away from her. Stunned, he looked up at her, surprised to see tears streaming down her face.

"Can you not see how I suffer? And yet you force yourself on me!"

"I . . . I thought you wanted . . . I am sorry."

"Yes, you are sorry indeed."

The next night, Daniel found Lizette sitting alone in the dark parlor, weeping. He lit a lamp, forcing optimism into his voice. "Dr. Kendall sent this tea for you. He thinks it might help."

"There is no use in doing anything, as I shall die soon."

"Please do not say that. Think of Anne."

"Why? Is it not she who ruined my body and my mind?"

"Lizette. It isn't her fault."

"Nor is it mine! You behave as though it is all in my mind. As though I am insane!"

"Shh . . . calm yourself. I know what ails you is real. And you are not the only woman to suffer from it."

"Do you think that helps me? Do you think that makes me want to live?"

"No, you live for us, for Anne and for me and for the babe to come."

"I do not care about any of you." She rubbed her forehead roughly. "I just want this to end."

"My dear. I think it's time we thought about returning to London."

"*Non!* I will not go back to that place. That hospital, that dark little room."

"Only until the baby comes."

"*Non!* Please, Daniel, I beg you. I shall be fine. I will get better. I like it here by the sea. I can breathe here. I can smell France."

Daniel looked at her beautiful, pleading face. "Very well. For now. But you must try to calm down, to control yourself."

"*Oui, mon amour.* I shall."

But a few days later, Daniel heard Lizette and Marie shouting and swearing in French. He leapt up from his desk and sprinted into the parlor.

His wife held a large brass candelabra in her hand and was about to strike the windowpane. Marie tried to wrest it from her.

"Lizette! Put that down!" he shouted.

"It will not open. I need air."

"Then ask me to help you."

"I can help myself."

"Allow me." He took the candelabra from her and placed it on the table, then tried pulling and shoving at the old window. "It is painted shut."

Marie nodded, "*Oui, monsieur.* Zat is what I tell madame."

"I am trapped in this old ruin of a place," Lizette cried. "I need air!"

"Take hold of yourself! Calm down."

"I am so sick of those words—that patronizing way you speak to me! You are not my father. Do not speak to me as if I were a child."

"You are acting like one."

"*Non.* Having a child is making me this way. I cannot stand it. I want out of this body . . . this skin!"

He gave up on the window and took hold of his wife's elbows, motioning the maid out of the room with a lift of his chin. "Lizette."

"It is my life, *non?*"

"No," he said gently, shaking his head. "You are not God."

"Well, neither are you. Some great physician you are, *Doctor* Taylor. You cannot even heal your own wife."

"I am trying. I am doing all I know to do."

"It is not enough!" She pulled away, grabbed the candelabra and threw it across the room, shattering the gilt mirror over the fireplace mantel.

He froze.

Marie reappeared in the doorway and hesitated there, frowning at the broken mirror and then at him.

"Stay with her, please," he instructed. Then he dashed from the room, leapt the stairs three at a time, and knocked on the nursery door. Sally opened it, white faced. She had obviously heard the commotion from below.

"Sally, please collect Anne and whatever things you need. I am taking you into the village. I want you to stay at the Red Lion. Here—" He pulled several bank notes from his wallet and handed them to her. "That should do for a night or two."

"Yes, sir."

After seeing Sally and Anne safely to the inn, he drove the carriage to Kendall's office.

"Richard," he began, hat in hand before his friend's desk, "I do not know what to do. I am at my wits' end. Lizette has begged me not to take her back to the Manor Home, but now with Anne to think of . . . I may even have to find a more equipped asylum."

"There are one or two I might recommend."

"Please. Come one more time. See if there is anything I have left undone."

"Of course." Richard rose and followed him outside.

But the scene that greeted them was not at all what either gentleman expected. The cottage had been restored to rights. Although the mirror was missing, the glass shards had been taken down and discarded, and the late afternoon sun lit the room in a peaceful, golden glow. Lizette looked up at them from a pristine table laid with a full tea service, as well as plates of sandwiches and cakes. Lizette herself looked serene and lovely, dressed in a pink silk gown, her hair done up properly, her face powdered. She even had the strand of pearls around her neck that Daniel had long ago given her but she seldom wore.

She greeted them warmly. "Welcome, gentlemen." Dumbly, Daniel stepped forward, Kendall close behind.

"Hello, darling." She rose and smiled at him as he approached, eyes glowing, then reached up and kissed his cheek.

"Dr. Kendall, how pleased I am to see you again. Do sit down."

Both men were speechless. They laid their hats aside and sat as they were bade, watching in awe as Lizette poured tea with practiced precision and grace.

"Dr. Kendall, how do you take your tea?"

"Uh . . . milk will do nicely, thank you."

She complied and handed him the cup and saucer with a steady hand.

"And I know my husband likes sugar in his. There you are, my dear."

"Thank you."

Daniel stared at her, and then he and Kendall exchanged a look, brows raised. Hopes too.

"It does happen," Kendall said to him later, behind the closed doors of the study. "Some remedy creates a delayed effect or a woman's balance somehow restores itself on its own."

"But will it last?"

"I don't know. But it seems quite possible."

"Thank God."

"Indeed."

"Will you do me a favor and stop by the inn and let Sally Mitchell know she may return?"

Kendall paused, then nodded. "Of course. I shall tell her she may return . . . in the morning." Kendall smiled at him and turned on his heel, donning his hat.

For an unmarried man, Kendall was quite astute.

30

> "When puerperal mania does take place, the patient swears, bellows, recites poetry, talks bawdy, and kicks up a row. . . . Every precaution must be taken to prevent her doing injury to herself, to the infant, or her friends."
>
> —Robert Gooch, early 19th century physician

The next morning, Daniel came down the stairs whistling, knowing all the while how cliché it was to do so. Still, he could barely keep the smile from his face. The day was sunny and so were their prospects for the future.

In the kitchen, he found Sally Mitchell eating a biscuit.

"You're returned early. How is Anne?"

"She fell asleep on the way home. Already laid her down for an early nap. 'Fraid the inn was awful noisy last night. Neither of us got much sleep."

I know how you feel. "Sorry to hear it," Daniel said, though the cheerful tone did not match his words.

"The missus really has turned the corner, then?"

"Yes, it seems she has, thank God. Though we must still monitor her progress."

"That is good news, sir. Your friend said as much, but I was afraid to believe it."

"I understand."

"I told Charlotte as well. She was most relieved, I can tell you."

"Charlotte?"

"Yes, she stopped by the inn this morning."

"Oh? She did not return to Crawley?"

"Nay. She's staying on in Shoreham for a time."

"Is she?"

She nodded. "Something to do with your Dr. Kendall, but I didn't hear the particulars. Place was too loud to hear much of anything."

Daniel swallowed. "I see."

Taking a deep breath, he changed the topic. "Mrs. Taylor is still asleep. Peacefully at last. Do your best to keep Anne quiet so as not to disturb her. I am just going to ride into town and send a message to my father. I shan't be long."

"Yes, sir."

When Daniel returned an hour later, he opened the door gingerly and was relieved at the peace and quiet that greeted him. He laid aside his hat and went in search of his wife. No one was in the parlor or dining room. She wasn't still sleeping, surely—although they had lain awake together until the early morning hours.

Upstairs, he found their bedroom empty, the bed neatly made. Peeking into the third-floor nursery, he saw it, too, was empty. Stepping down the passage, he tapped lightly on Sally's door, thinking to check on Anne. Sally answered the door, sleep etched plainly on her features, her mouth stretched wide in a yawn. "Must have fallen asleep," she said.

"Is Anne awake?"

"I believe so."

"She isn't here with you?"

"Mrs. Taylor wanted to have her to herself. Poor dear said it felt like a month of Sundays since she'd held her little girl."

Daniel smiled. Had Lizette's maternal feeling been restored, along with her affection—and desire—for her husband? Nearly as quickly, his smile faded.

"Where are they? I saw no one downstairs."

"Off to get some fresh air, I believe she said. Oh dear, have I done wrong?" Sally's expression grew pained. "She told me to go on and have a rest. And after last night, I was happy to oblige."

"I'm sure all is well," Daniel muttered, already heading for the stairs. But he wasn't sure at all.

"Should I start packing, sir?" Sally called after him.

"Packing? Why?" He paused midway down the staircase.

"Mrs. Taylor said something about going home."

He froze. "Home?" But he had assured her he would not yet take her back to the Manor.

"Aye. Are we returning to London soon?"

"I . . . I don't know," he called over his shoulder as he rushed down the stairs.

He found Mrs. Beebe in the kitchen.

"Have you seen Mrs. Taylor?"

"Yes, sir. She went outside with the little one."

"When was this?"

"Oh, about a quarter of an hour ago."

"Where were they headed?"

"Toward the sea, I suspect. And a lovely day for a stroll it is."

The sea? Panic gripped him. *Oh, dear God . . .*

Daniel ran outside, across the wide lawn, down the rocky decline and onto the pebbled shore. He looked wildly about, up and down the coast. Then, out on the channel, he glimpsed a lone, dark-haired figure swimming with clumsy strokes, then disappear below the surface.

"Lizette!" he cried. *God, help me!*

He ran across the rocks and splashed into the water, pausing only long enough to haul off his boots and throw them back on shore, then he swam out after her. He tried to gauge where he'd seen her go under. At least he thought—feared—it was her.

When he reached the spot, he dove down. He searched frantically through the cold, dark water. When his lungs forced him, he lurched up and sucked in air. He searched the surface, desperate to see her.

Hearing a shout, he spun around. There were Thomas and Kendall on the shore. Remembering Kendall had never learned to swim, Daniel dove back down, scarcely giving thought to the men. He swam deeper, deeper, his long arms stretching, his fingers combing the water. There! He caught a handful of fabric. He held on and kicked closer, wrapping one arm around the figure and trying to drag her to the surface. At first he could hardly lift her, but then she began to rise. He kicked and pawed at the water with all his might. He felt her moving, kicking beside him, and rejoiced. She was alive!

He broke through the surface and filled his burning lungs with air. Only then did he realize that Thomas was there, had swum out and helped him pull up Lizette. His gratitude was quickly suffocated by the realization that it had been Thomas's movements, not his wife's, he had felt beside him.

The long, full gown Lizette wore, sodden with water, had become a weighted anchor dragging all three of them back down. Slowly and painfully, the two men kicked, paddled, and pulled themselves back to land. Together they hauled Lizette carefully toward shore. Richard Kendall waded into the surf to help them, and together they laid her carefully down onto the pebbled beach.

Richard leaned close, listening for breath. He turned her on her side and began compressing her abdomen, releasing a stream of water from her mouth.

"I've got to find Anne!" Daniel ran over the surf and dove back into the water. Thomas followed after him.

Back and forth they swam, pawing the dark water, coming up with only handfuls of shale and debris. After seemingly endless, exhausting dives, Daniel fell back on shore, panting. Thomas crawled out after him.

"She's gone," Richard said.

"I know. We could not find her."

"I mean your wife. She's gone. I could not revive her."

Daniel fisted his hands and pressed them to his forehead and down into his eye sockets. Then he forced himself onto his hands and knees and crawled over the wet pebbles to the prone body of his wife.

He laid his head on her chest, then looked up at her face and stroked her damp cheek.

"I am sorry, Daniel," Kendall said quietly.

"She was going home. To France. She was trying to swim there." Daniel's voice broke.

Richard laid a hand on his shoulder.

Daniel moaned and sat down, pulling Lizette onto his lap, into his arms. "I could not find Anne. I know you did not mean to lose her. I tried, I did . . ."

Kendall sent Thomas to the cottage to fetch some blankets. One to warm him, Daniel supposed. Another to cover his wife's body. His own body was wracked with shivering, his muscles tight and convulsing. The waters of the channel were cold, even this time of year. Had the cold stolen her consciousness, even before she drowned?

For a moment, he was struck with the desire to walk back into the sea that had claimed his wife, daughter, and unborn child. Let it claim him too. Anything to stop this crushing pain.

But even as he entertained the thought, his own words to Lizette echoed in his mind, *"You are not God."*

"Oh, God . . ." He moaned and began sobbing. How could he go on? It was all his fault. How could he ever forgive himself?

"Daniel," a voice spoke softly behind him. Or maybe he had imagined it.

"Merciful heavens!" Kendall exclaimed beside him. "Is that Anne?"

Daniel turned. There was Charlotte, the sun at her back, casting a golden glow around her. He winced. His mind must be numb, or hallucinatory.

"Yes," the Charlotte-image said. "I found her asleep up the shore. Surrounded by rocks and driftwood."

"Thank God," Kendall said. "Daniel! Anne's all right. She's alive. Do you hear me?"

Daniel sat mutely as Charlotte walked toward him, tears streaming down her face as her eyes darted to, then away from Lizette's still form.

She knelt beside him and gently handed Anne to him. Then she rose and stepped back.

Daniel stared down at Anne, who was awake now and seemed pleased to see him. She wriggled and babbled, her little fists moving from her mouth to clasp his nose.

"Yes . . . I seem to have lost my spectacles. Do you still recognize me?"

The little girl opened her mouth in a toothless grin.

"Your *maman* is gone. I am so sorry, dear one. She loved you—never think she didn't. She just . . . could not stay. I tried to help her, but I could not. . . ."

Thomas and Sally returned with blankets, and Kendall wrapped one around Daniel's shoulders. Then he laid the other one carefully over Lizette. Sally took Anne and headed back toward the cottage.

"Come, my friend," Kendall urged gently. "Let's get you into the house and out of those wet clothes."

Daniel looked over at his wife's shrouded form. "I cannot leave her."

"I shall see to her," Kendall assured.

Together Charlotte and Thomas helped Daniel up and into the cottage.

The day after the funeral, Charlotte found Daniel sitting on the bench, staring out at the sea. Wordlessly, she sat down as well, careful to leave a proper amount of space between them. He acknowledged her presence with the slightest nod before returning his gaze to the sea.

"You never really knew her, Miss Lamb. Not really. Not the woman she once was."

She asked softly, "How did the two of you meet?"

"She was working as a governess in Edinburgh when I was at university there. I first saw her in the park, swinging her little charge around and around until the sound of their laughter filled the square. I can still see her in her green-striped dress, her dark hair escaping her straw bonnet, her smile so bright—the only brightness to be seen on that grey Scottish day. She told me she had left her home in Normandy, looking for adventure.

"Only later did I find out she was looking for escape, that her mother was afflicted in much the way Lizette was, at the end." He leaned over, elbows on his knees. "I don't think she meant to deceive me. I think she truly believed, or at least desperately hoped, that she'd left all of that far behind her, that she could avoid the same fate. We traveled to Caen only once to meet her family. I suspected how it was with her mother, but by then it was too late. I was in love with Lizette. I could not have stopped myself from marrying her, even had I known what was to be."

After a few minutes of silence, Daniel sighed. "Still, I should have seen it coming. Should have prevented it somehow."

She glanced over at him, saw him shake his head dolefully.

"I wanted to move her someplace safe, but she begged to stay. She said she loved it here—felt closer to home. Too close, it turns out."

"How could you know? She was much improved."

"So we thought. Or so she wanted us to believe. But I should have known better."

"Mr. Taylor . . ." Without intending to, she had slipped back to his former address.

"If only I had found a more effective treatment. Or insisted we return to London a fortnight ago."

"Mr. Taylor . . . do you not remember what you said to me when my mother died?"

"No."

"I was sure that if only I had been a better daughter, or prayed harder, or insisted she not tire herself in the garden, then she would have lived."

He shrugged.

"But you told me God does not work that way. Remember?"

"And I believe you told me I needed to read the Old Testament."

"*That* you choose to remember." She smiled gently. "It is not your fault."

It had taken a long time for Charlotte to believe this herself. She feared Daniel Taylor would prove no quicker a student.

He took a deep breath, then straightened. "Thank you again for finding Anne. I don't know that I could have gone on if—"

"Shh . . . Someone else would have found her had I not happened along."

"I can only hope so. How did you happen to be here that day?"

She took a deep breath. "I awoke with the darkest foreboding that morning. Even though Sally assured me at the inn that all was well, I had to come. I should have walked, but Dr. Kendall and Thomas passed by on their way here and offered me a ride."

"And what were they about? I never asked, and after, well, everything, I quite forgot."

"Dr. Kendall brought Thomas out with the intention of convincing the both of you that Thomas should remain here as *his* apprentice. But after he saw Thomas's loyalty to you that day, I believe he quite gave it up."

"Yes. That boy has a place with me for as long as he wants one."

The two sat for several more minutes without speaking before Daniel said, "I shall be returning to London soon. Letting go of this place early. You are welcome to stay on here until I do. That is, unless Kendall . . . unless you have made other arrangements."

"I have made other arrangements."

"I see." He rose abruptly. "Of course that is none of my affair."

"My arrangements are not with Dr. Kendall, however," she said.

"No?"

"I have taken a post with a family in Old Shoreham."

"May I ask in what capacity?"

"As their nurse."

"Oh . . . I had not realized you planned to continue in that vocation."

"I had not planned to do so. But they were in need and, well, there I was. It is only temporary."

In fact, Georgiana Henshaw was well on her way to nursing her son herself. She had begun nursing him once or twice a day as her recovery allowed while Charlotte kept up with the other feedings. But the young mother was quickly assuming the majority of nursing. Mrs. Henshaw had assured Charlotte she would be welcome to stay on as long as she liked, but Charlotte doubted Mr. Henshaw would agree to such generous terms.

"And after?"

She shrugged. "Return to Crawley, I suppose. As I intended to do before."

But the next morning, Sally received a letter that changed Charlotte's plans once again.

Charlotte had returned to take breakfast with Sally and, privately, to assure herself that Mr. Taylor was all right. As they sat visiting, Mrs. Beebe came into the kitchen with the morning post. "Letter for you, Sally."

Sally took the letter and studied the direction with surprise but none of the happiness Charlotte might have expected.

"'Tis from my sister."

Dr. Taylor came in for a cup of tea while Sally opened the missive and read as quickly as her skill allowed. After a moment, she propped a hand on the table as if to support herself.

Alarmed, Charlotte asked, "Sally, what is it?"

"'Tis Dickie. She says he's very ill. Oh! I must go to him at once."

"Steady on," Dr. Taylor said. "What else does she say?"

"He's weak, high fever, won't eat. . . . She fears the worst. And this was written days ago now! Dr. Taylor, please help him. You will come, won't you? Please."

He hesitated a moment, in which time Charlotte feared he was offended by Sally's presumption that he should drop everything to help a child he barely knew, or that, in his morose state, he felt ill-equipped to save anyone.

Instead, he set his cup down. "We shall go directly."

In a flurry of plans and instructions, Charlotte agreed to remain at Lloyd Lodge for a few days to nurse Anne and give notice to the Henshaws. Marie would return with Sally and Dr. Taylor to prepare the London house, which had no doubt gathered dust during their absence with only John Taylor to care for it. Charlotte would stay behind long enough to see to the packing and help the Beebes set the place to rights. Then she would escort Anne back to London, to the home Dr. Taylor shared with his father. After that . . . she did not know.

It wasn't within her to refuse any help Anne Taylor—or her father—needed.

Still it chafed her a bit to realize she was allowing her course to be set by the winds of circumstance. Yet again.

Forcing thoughts off herself, she set to work and prayed fervently for the recovery of Sally's son.

31

What will you think when I tell you she is not yet weaned? How to set about it is more than I know . . .

—1765 letter between friends, from *The Gentleman's Daughter* by Amanda Vickery

Mr. John Taylor met her coach with broad smiles for both Anne and herself.

"How good to see you again, Miss Charlotte. And little Anne! How much you have grown!"

Anne's little lip trembled as her grandfather put his face close to hers. "Forgot me already, did you? We shall soon put that to rights."

"I am sure you shall—if you can catch her. She has just learned to creep about."

"Has she indeed. Well, there'll be no rest for any of us now. All those tempting staircases."

He gestured to the hackney driver he had hired to take them the rest of the way to the Taylor residence. The bulky man came and gathered her baggage and carried the load to his carriage. They followed and Mr. Taylor held Anne while Charlotte climbed in. The child looked at him warily but did not cry.

Once they were all settled and Anne back in Charlotte's arms, Mr. Taylor looked across at them and said, "You look as well fed as a stuffed goose at Christmas. I mean Anne, of course. I must say you look far too thin. You are in good health, I hope."

"I am. Thank you."

"What a trying time this has been for all of you, no doubt. Daniel looked positively dreadful upon his return."

"And little Dickie?"

Mr. Taylor shook his head gravely. "I'm afraid the lad is very ill indeed. Still, Daniel hasn't given up hope."

Coming to a halt at the Taylors' offices and residence on Wimpole Street, Mr. Taylor paid the driver and asked him to bring the baggage to the living quarters above.

Marie, looking worn and apathetic as usual, met them on the first floor up. "You and ze child will be in ze same chamber as before." She turned her back without offering to help carry up their things.

"I must say that having you back with us is the one bright spot in the whole dismal affair," John Taylor added kindly. "Though I would not have chosen the circumstances for the world."

"No, of course not."

"I'm afraid we won't see much of Daniel for some time, between his work at the Manor, his own practice, and seeing the Mitchell boy. But we'll do quite nicely on our own, I trust. Do let me know if there is anything you need."

"Thank you. You are very kind." Tears filled Charlotte eyes as she spoke the words, and she didn't stop to wonder why.

"You are certain you do not wish your post back?" Charlotte asked Sally over tea in the Taylors' sitting room a few weeks later.

"No. My place is with Dickie now."

"How does he fare?"

"He's fully recovered, I am happy to say. Thanks to your Dr. Taylor."

"He is not my Dr. Taylor."

The look Sally gave her said she begged to differ.

"And how is your Thomas?"

"'Tisn't mine." She hid a toothy grin behind her hand. "Yet . . ."

Charlotte smiled. Soon after her return to London, Thomas had arrived to begin his apprenticeship to Dr. Taylor. The young man slept either in one of the manor's upstairs chambers or on a cot in the offices on the street level, depending on where Dr. Taylor needed him on a given day.

"Why not come out with me and Thomas sometime?" Sally asked. "Thomas loves going to hear lectures and concerts and the like, and he is determined that I should learn to like such as well. Come along with us. You'd enjoy a night out now and then, wouldn't you?"

"You are thoughtful to include me. But Anne . . ."

"My sister would watch her and Dickie both. I know she would."

"Anne is still nursing. It is difficult to get away. You remember how it is."

"Aye." Sally's eyes clouded.

"I did not mean . . ."

"'Tis all right, Miss Charlotte. I remember my blunder whether anyone reminds me of it or not."

"It is forgotten, Sally."

"Not by the Harrises, 'tisn't. And not by me."

"Oh, Sally . . ." Charlotte reached over and squeezed her friend's hand. "Someday soon I should be delighted to accompany you for an evening out."

Charlotte glanced up and saw Dr. Taylor standing in the doorway, his expression dour. How much of their conversation had he overheard?

A few days later, Dr. Taylor approached Charlotte as she sat spooning porridge into Anne's open, bird-like mouth. When she glanced up at him, he cleared his throat. "I've been wondering, Miss Lamb, if it might not be time to wean Anne? She has begun eating other foods now."

She glanced at the spoon in her hand. "Yes, I know. But I had thought to nurse her for a full year or more."

"Ah, well. As you wish." He started for the door.

Charlotte turned, spoon still poised midair. "But if you want me to cease, then, of course, I shall."

"I was only wondering . . ."

Then it struck her. He wanted to be rid of her. Her heart pounded dully, painfully.

She would not overstay her welcome.

She had not expected the process to be so difficult. In fact by the next morning, breasts full, she had already resigned herself to continuing on. But Anne was fussy and restless and wouldn't nurse properly. She pulled off again and again as Charlotte encouraged her to latch on.

"You must be hungry. . . ." What was the trouble? Had Charlotte eaten something that had spoilt her milk? She did not believe so. Charlotte grimaced. "One would almost think you understood your father's suggestion about weaning . . ." Finally Charlotte gave up, hoping the little girl wasn't coming down ill.

The next morning was much the same. Anne nursed fitfully, pulled away, tried again. Charlotte stroked her little tummy. "What is it, dear? What pains you?"

A sharp pain struck Charlotte's breast. Charlotte cried out and jerked back. Startled, Anne began to wail. Tears welled in Charlotte's eyes at the stinging pain. As Anne cried, mouth wide, Charlotte saw the white kernel protruding from her pink gums. Her first tooth. "Well, you needn't have bitten me. That hurt."

Anne cried louder yet.

"There, there now. It's all right. I know you did not mean to. At least I hope not."

After that, both of them seemed resigned to wean each other. Charlotte steeled herself for each of the few nursings that followed. Anne must have felt her apprehension, for she too seemed tense and nursed very poorly. Still, nights were the most difficult for Anne, when she rooted against Charlotte, wanting to nurse for comfort, to ease into sleep. Charlotte obliged her. Mornings were most difficult for Charlotte, when she longed for the relief of pressure nursing brought. Gradually she realized, however, that the morning fullness was diminishing. By evening, when Anne grew most fussy, it seemed Charlotte had very little milk to offer her, for Anne pulled away quickly.

Though she had set out to wean Anne, now that the reality of its imminence dawned on Charlotte, a strange panicked sadness stole over her. She knew once she was through, there was no going back. Her unique role in this child's life would be over. She would be more replaceable than ever. Anne would not need her anymore. How would Charlotte support herself now? True, she had never wanted this vocation, but what would she do?

Her breasts lost some of their fullness, which seemed sad too. She began to feel as empty as they. She would need to take in her gowns.

Knowing each might be her last, she began to cherish every nursing—and concerns for her livelihood were not uppermost in her mind. She would miss this. The warmth and satisfaction of holding this little one close to her body. Anne's little face relaxed and content, now and then opening her dark eyes to look up at Charlotte as if to greet her or thank her. Her little hand, lying against Charlotte's breast or stomach. The sweet sting of milk coursing through her, the tug of the curled tongue and rough-ridged mouth. The sounds of drawing, of swallowing, of nourishing. Of life.

Charlotte stroked Anne's hair, the soft curve of her neck. "Very soon, you will not even remember this time together. But I shall always remember. And I shall miss it. And you . . ."

Even as Charlotte's milk stopped flowing, her tears began, running over to take its place.

Two weeks after Sally's teatime visit, Charlotte stood before Dr. Taylor's desk, hands clenched together. "I will be leaving in a week's time, Dr. Taylor. Does that give you sufficient notice to make other arrangements for Anne's care?"

"Leaving? But why?"

"I have weaned Anne, as you requested."

"I only suggested it to afford you a bit of freedom."

"Well, I am free. You will not have need of me any longer."

"But we do. Anne is quite dependent on you."

"I am only the nurse, Dr. Taylor. My post here is finished."

"Well, that part may be ended. But there are other . . . capacities in which you might stay."

"Such as?"

"Well, however you like. That is . . . I know it's too soon to talk of . . . such things, and I haven't any right to presume on your time, but all I know is that, that . . ."

He stopped then, catching his breath and running his hand across his face.

"All you know is, what?" she prompted, trying to be gentle but feeling unaccountably frustrated.

He swallowed, then stuttered, "I want . . . I wish . . . I would like you to stay."

She was oddly touched by his stammering, his obvious nervousness. But no, she was foolish to read anything into his manner. His wife was not long in her grave, and he'd clearly loved her. Though the last years of their lives together had been wretched, that did not erase his pain, his mourning. He was not offering anything other than a position, and she'd do well to remember so.

"Do you wish me to be Anne's governess?" she suggested tentatively.

"Governess? She's a bit young for that, but . . . would you want that? I mean, eventually? Of course I would like you to keep caring for her as you do."

"Nursery maid, then?"

"Well, I don't like the sound of that. That's beneath you, Miss Lamb."

"No it isn't." *Not anymore.*

"What I mean to say, is that a woman of your character and education could do so much more, could be anything she wanted."

"But you need a nursemaid."

"Anne needs a nursemaid. I . . ."

"What?"

"For Anne's sake, I wish you would stay on as nursemaid, governess, what have you. But quite frankly, I don't."

"You don't want me to be Anne's nurse."

"No."

Charlotte felt as though she'd been slapped and drenched with icy water at the same time. She'd thought he admired her way with his daughter—that he admired her in general.

"I shall leave immediately."

"No!" he all but shouted.

She looked at him, stunned by his uncharacteristic outburst.

He sighed and said more gently, "Forgive me. I know I am a broken shell of a man with little to offer you. But still, I ask you."

"Ask me what?"

"To stay."

"As what?"

"Why must we define it? Can you not give me more time?"

"I'm afraid I do not understand, sir. I am an unmarried woman. I cannot stay under your roof unless I am employed by you in a legitimate capacity. Tell me you are not asking me to be your . . . to be your . . ."

"To be my what?" he said defensively.

"Do not make me say it."

"Say what?" He looked nearly angry now. "What is it that is so odious to you?"

"Dr. Taylor!"

"No, tell me. Be my what?"

She frowned, looked about her, then whispered tersely, "Mistress."

The man looked stricken. "Oh, Miss Lamb. Forgive me. No wonder you looked so ill. Certainly you know by now how highly I think of you. I would never make such a proposition to anyone, least of all to you."

She knew he meant it as a compliment; still, it hurt her feminine pride. She was not the sort of woman he would want for himself. At least, not anymore.

"Your friend Kendall had no such scruples, so I feared . . ." She let the mortifying words drift away.

"Yes, I am sorry for that. And I see why you might think—" He rose to his feet. "Miss Lamb, Charlotte, forgive me. I am handling this very poorly."

"No need to apologize. You are distraught. You still mourn your wife, and you have a young daughter to raise alone."

"Yes. But none of that changes the fact that I want you to stay. Anne and I would be adrift without you."

"As . . . ?"

He sighed. "I suppose I prefer the term nursery-governess. For now."

Though she dreaded the possible repercussions, Charlotte decided she was obligated to write to apprise her cousin Katherine of her change in situation. She did not like the thought of placing Mrs. Dunweedy in an awkward predicament should Katherine write or call there. So she wrote a rather brief note to let her cousin know that she had taken a position as governess and was no longer residing in Crawley. She did not inform Katherine that she was in the employ of Daniel Taylor, for several reasons. She had seen the speculative gleam in Katherine's eyes when she had seen him arrive at her great-aunt's cottage. Though she might have imagined that. Worse, she had foolishly passed off Anne as her own daughter. If Katherine were to inquire—or heaven forbid, take it upon herself to call upon the Taylor home—how would she explain that Anne was, after all, Dr. Taylor's daughter and not her own? Katherine's shock and censure would be too awful to imagine.

So Charlotte had omitted the name of her employer and his address on the first letter, only to be mortified when Daniel Taylor delivered a return letter from Katherine the following week.

"Lady Katherine asked me to give this to you when I saw you next," he said. "She came by the Manor today."

"She did?"

"Yes, she seemed certain I would know how to find you."

"Did you tell her . . . ?"

"I told her nothing. Knowing my shortcomings in the tact and discretion department, I thought it best."

"But she must know something, to ask you to deliver this to me."

"True. She did not seem surprised when I agreed to the task. I suppose she remembers that I had delivered that . . . other . . . parcel for her when last I was in Crawley."

Charlotte knew he was referring to the money he had long ago delivered to her on Katherine's behalf—most of which Charlotte had given to Margaret Dunweedy to cover her living expenses.

"She did mention she had stopped by the Manor on two other occasions with the intention of asking me to get some message to you, only to be told the first time that I was away on holiday, and on the second, that I had taken leave and no one knew when I would return. Must have been while we were on the coast."

She knew he did not like to recall that grim time. None of them did. Quietly, she thanked him for the letter and slipped up to her room before opening it. She held her breath as she read Katherine's curt reply.

. . . I am trusting Dr. Taylor, who seems to know your whereabouts better than anyone, to get this to you. Goodness, Charlotte, why on earth did you not write to me sooner? I had grown concerned. I called round at Margaret Dunweedy's on Whitsunday, but she could not—or would not—tell me where you had gone. She said something about you being off on holiday, but of course, given your situation, I did not believe it.

Katherine went on to write several blunt questions.

Governess? Could be worse, I suppose. In whose employ are you? Do I know the family? I certainly hope they allow Anne to stay with you. Where in the world am I to write you should the need arise? Do not be foolish, Charlotte. Send me your directions by return post.

Did Katherine guess she had been with Dr. Taylor all along? Was that why she was so certain he could contact her? But then, why hadn't she acquired Dr. Taylor's home address—it would certainly not be difficult to discover, since he had a fairly well-known medical practice. In any case, Charlotte knew she could not put her cousin off any longer. And so, with no small trepidation, Charlotte wrote back:

I am in the employ of Dr. Daniel Taylor, with whom you are some acquainted. I am content in my post, and the Taylors are kind and generous employers, though Dr. Taylor is away a great deal with his work as a physician. And, yes, Anne is here and enjoying excellent health. I do hope the same is true for your family. . . .

After this, Charlotte and her cousin Katherine began exchanging brief, occasional letters. Charlotte found it a mixed blessing of pleasure and deprivation to read Katherine's chatty reports of Edmund's growth and antics and "how dear Charles dotes on the boy." Still, Katherine had not suggested paying a call, and Charlotte had not offered.

32

And let this feeble body fail,
And let it faint or die;
My soul shall quit this mournful vale,
And soar to worlds on high.
—Charles Wesley, *Funeral Hymns*

The Doddington churchyard was quiet in the late afternoon sun. White willow trees hung low in perpetual sorrow, paying homage to the departed. Field maples, whose leaves were just beginning to turn at the edges, shone orange-red. Blood-red too.

Charles Harris walked slowly through the churchyard, past the ancient yew tree and mottled graves whose inscriptions were worn unreadable, to a row of newer graves along the far wall.

Stepping over fallen leaves and yew needles, he stopped before a small grave.

A child's grave. It was marked by a simple, hand-hewn cross. There was no inscription to give away the identity of the one buried there. But he knew who it was and mourned. Kneeling before the small marker, he reached out a trembling hand and gently touched the wooden surface, wondering again who had made it, who had placed it there, knowing such graves rarely had a marker of any kind.

Tears began flowing down his face, as they often did when in this place. When confronted with this loss.

"I shall never forget you," he whispered, then rose.

A door creaked open somewhere not far off. Charles turned sharply, startled. From around the corner of the church came Ben Higgins with a shovel over one shoulder and a bunch of chrysanthemums in his other hand.

The young man paused when he saw Charles Harris standing there.

"I'm sorry, sir," Ben Higgins said. "I didn't know anyone was about the place."

"Nor I. Did you put that cross there—on that grave?"

Charles pointed and the young man looked in the direction he indicated.

Ben nodded sheepishly. "That I did, sir. But on my own time."

"I am not reprimanding you. Merely asking."

Ben nodded again, standing there awkwardly, flowers drooping from his hand.

"Well, go about your work. Do not let me hinder you."

Still the young man hesitated.

Realization dawned, and Charles nodded toward the flowers. "Are those . . . for that grave?"

"Yes, sir," Ben admitted, still clearly uncomfortable.

Charles nodded, biting his lip. "You are a kind soul, Ben Higgins."

Charlotte opened her eyes in the dim light and was surprised to see Dr. Taylor leaning over her bed. He held a candle lamp and wore his dressing gown. Startled, she instinctively pulled the blankets higher on her neck.

Daniel winced. "Forgive me. I had hoped not to wake you. I wanted to check on Anne."

Only then did she recall that little Anne was in bed beside her. "Oh. Of course." She remembered now. Anne's fitfulness, the burning skin—too hot to merely signal the emergence of more teeth.

"She cried so in her cradle," Charlotte whispered. "I finally brought her into bed with me."

Dr. Taylor pulled the baby blanket lower and tenderly felt Anne's forehead, cheeks, and chest.

"She is still warm. Too warm."

"I shall go fetch cloths . . ."

"Shh . . . stay as you are. Let Anne sleep. I shall fetch them."

He returned in a few minutes with a small ceramic basin and several face cloths. Gently he dipped one in the water, wrung it out, and laid it over his daughter's forehead.

"I'm afraid I shall get your sheets damp. I should have brought something to lay underneath her."

"I don't mind. I can do that if you like."

"Allow me. How many nights am I at the Manor and you must tend to her alone?"

"It is my responsibility."

"I'd say it is mine as well." He continued his ministrations, whispering more to sleeping Anne than to her, "What's the use of having a physician for a father if he cannot care for his own child?"

He untied his daughter's nightdress and laid another cool cloth across her chest. The little girl tossed her head, whining at the intrusion.

"If this doesn't work, we shall have to set her in a tub of cool water. She shall like that far less, I fear."

"What do you think is wrong?"

"Hard to tell at this point. Stomach is relaxed—no distension. Has she been pulling on her ears at all?"

"No."

"There is quite a lot of sickness going around. Hopefully nothing serious, just something that must run its course."

Charlotte watched him continue to touch a third cloth to his daughter's face and arms.

He looked at her suddenly. "How are you feeling, Miss Lamb? I do hope you are well."

"Yes, I think so. A bit tired, but that is to be expected."

He reached his hand toward her, then, seeing her surprise, hesitated, hand midair. "May I?"

"Oh, of course."

He gently touched her forehead, his fingers tracing down her cheeks before returning to the basin. "You feel fine. I never stopped to think Anne might have something contagious. Perhaps I ought to take her to my room."

"I do not think that necessary. And I am quite certain that if Anne has anything catching I should already have caught it in any case. Or perhaps even passed something along to her."

"I doubt that. You are so rarely out alone. When would you have occasion to come into contact with some ill person?"

"At the park or market, I suppose, though Anne is always with me. Or church. No, she goes with me there as well . . ."

"No wonder you are tired. It's amazing you are not exhausted."

"It is nothing compared to your days and nights. You so rarely sleep in your own bed, or at all for that matter."

"I usually find at least a few hours of sleep at the Manor. My own bed holds little appeal for me these days."

Charlotte could feel a blush warm her cheeks at the implication of his words. An awkward silence hung between them.

"Forgive me. I'm tired. I did not think. . . ."

"It is understandable," she whispered. "You miss Lizette, and no wonder."

"Perhaps. Still . . ." He shook his head.

Trying to lighten the tension, she said, "For my part, I rarely slept the night through at the Manor. All the noise and having to share my bed so."

"You—" he hesitated, eyes on his task—"object to sharing your bed?"

Her cheeks burned more furiously, and she was relieved he kept his gaze on his daughter.

"Not on principle, no. But before I moved to a private room, I slept with five others."

He looked up. "Five? Surely not as bad as all that?"

She smiled, "Two other women and three unborn children."

"Ah . . . crowded indeed." He returned her smile before again lowering his gaze. "At least here you have your own bed. Except when my daughter shares it with you. She has no idea how fortunate she is. . . ." He looked up, startled at his own words. "I mean, to have you care for her so. . . ."

She could not meet his eyes, nor stop the slight lift of her lips. "I know what you meant," she whispered.

Walking with Anne through nearby Russell Square on a fine autumn afternoon, Charlotte almost collided with a young boy running past, pulling a Chinese-dragon kite behind him. "*Regardez-moi! Regardez-moi!*" the boy yelled in perfect French accent.

"*Très bien*, Jonathan."

Charlotte glanced over and saw an elegantly dressed young woman sitting on a park bench, her gaze fixed on the running boy.

Two finely dressed ladies walking together approached from the other direction. They, too, seemed to be watching the elegant young lady and her charge.

"I have contracted with an agency in Piccadilly to arrange for a French governess for Henry."

"I know you will be pleased. I would never go back to an English governess. They are so dour, and usually not as well educated as the French girls who come over."

Charlotte looked more closely at the elegant young woman. She had dark hair in a fashionable coil, and her dress seemed as fine as those the English ladies wore. As Charlotte passed by she looked at the woman's face more closely. She was reminded of Lizette Taylor.

The next morning, as Charlotte sat at the kitchen table enjoying a cup of coffee and the quiet of a morning in which she had arisen before Anne, Marie dropped a section of newspaper before her.

"*Voilà*," the woman said, the paper slapping the tabletop. She had already turned back to the blood sausage and tomatoes she was frying before Charlotte could respond.

She looked at the paper. Folded in quarters as it was, she could not miss the bold print Marie wanted her to see.

French Governesses. Highest education.
Excellent references. Qualified to teach
literature, music, French, and etiquette.
Paris Agency, 212 George-court, Piccadilly

Charlotte knocked on Dr. Taylor's study door.

"Enter."

As she pushed the door open, he looked up from the thick book he was reading. "Hello, Miss Lamb."

"Have you a moment?"

"Of course." He closed his book, and as he did, she noticed it was a Bible.

Inclining her chin toward the volume, she asked, "Old Testament or New?"

He grinned. "Old. Someone once told me I should read it more often."

She smiled and then bit her lip, remembering her mission. "Dr. Taylor. It has come to my attention that many English families are hiring French governesses to care for their children."

He looked at her blankly.

"It seems the fashion now," Charlotte added.

"I care little for fashion, as you know."

"Yes. But I was thinking you might desire a French education for Anne."

He looked at her, clearly perplexed.

"She could grow up speaking both English and French," Charlotte continued. "Mrs. Taylor would have liked that."

He shrugged. “True. But you speak French.”

“Very ill. My accent is far from authentic.”

He stared at her, clearly unsure of her meaning.

“I understand there is an agency in Piccadilly for French governesses.”

“Miss Lamb, I don’t understand. Are you suggesting I replace you?”

“I am only thinking of Anne, what is best for her.”

“What is best for her . . . or you?”

The implication stung.

He sighed. “I am only saying that if you wish to leave us, come out and say so.”

“I do not wish to, but nor do I wish for you to feel obligated. You must think of Anne’s future. Do what is in her best interests.”

“I have. I believe *you*, Miss Lamb, are in Anne’s best interests.”

She lowered her head. “Thank you.”

“But—”

She looked up. He was regarding her with an intensity that made her want to look away again. “There is another position I would offer you. If you were willing.”

As she took in the longing, the trepidation, even the passion in his eyes, realization dawned. She had been a fool these last few months. He did want her, in every way a man wants a woman.

He rose and walked around his desk. Reaching past her, he shut the door quietly behind her. That done, he did not move away but stood close to her.

“You could become my wife.”

For Anne’s sake, for hers, for his own even, he would marry her. Even though he was not through mourning his wife. She ought to be relieved, she ought to be happy, but she was not. As the dread, the sudden irrational urge to turn and flee washed over her, she saw the reason clearly.

“What is it?” he asked, obviously not seeing the reaction he’d hoped for in her expression. “Have you no regard for me? Or is your father’s approval still so important to you?”

“Of course not. I long ago gave up hope of winning Father’s approval. As far as my regard for you, it is of the highest order.”

“Then why do you hesitate? I realize it is too soon for me to make a proper offer, but I thought, in the circumstances—”

“You do me a great honor, Dr. Taylor. But—” And here she paused, taking a deep breath. “You see, as long as I can tell myself that I am in no suitable state to raise my son, then I can bear his absence. I can console myself with the wisdom that he is better off where he is, that I can barely provide for myself, let alone another. But if my situation were to suddenly change . . . if I were in a position where I could reasonably provide for him . . . and still . . . still

I could not have him with me . . . that I could not bear. Do you understand? Does that make any sense at all?"

"I don't think . . . Are you saying that you must remain alone in order to bear his loss?"

She swallowed. "Yes."

"But would not the support of another make the loss more bearable? Or the possibility of another child someday?"

"I cannot think of that. He can never be replaced."

"Of course not. Still, the loneliness would be abated, would it not?"

"Perhaps. But I will always want him back. Always long for him."

"Perhaps there is something we can do. Your uncle is a solicitor. Perhaps—"

"No. I gave my word."

"Yes, but you were distraught, desperate. You thought you had no other choice, but now you do."

"Even if my circumstances change, I have not."

"But you have. You had just recently given birth. Changes occur in a mother's psyche, in her nerves, her mind, as I know all too well."

"But I knew what I was doing. Terrible as it was."

"Yes—then. But now—"

"I *gave* my word."

He opened his mouth as if to argue further, then closed it again. Frustration was evident in his stance and features.

"In any case, I could not do it to Edmund. How confusing and cruel it would be to rip his world, his very concept of himself, asunder. I cannot do it. I won't."

"But still . . . will you not reconsider . . . ?"

She looked at Daniel and felt tears filling her eyes. Slowly, she shook her head. "I cannot."

Was she making a terrible mistake? She remembered bemoaning the realization that she had let circumstances and the will of others set her course on many occasions. But now she had made a decision of her own, rejecting the only offer of marriage she had ever received, or was likely ever *to* receive. But she had made the only decision she could at present. She had chosen to stay her present course.

She could only hope fate would concur in the months and years ahead.

Part III

Surely 'tis better, when summer is over
To die when all fair things are fading away.

—Thomas Haynes Bayly,
I'd Be a Butterfly

Monarch butterflies are not native to Great Britain, but individuals are found in the south each year. . . . blown there by strong winds.

—Journey North

33

> The butterfly is at the center of numerous superstitions the world over, and in some parts of Germany it is called "milk thief."
>
> —Anatoly Liberman, *The Oxford Etymologist*

Two years had passed since Charlotte returned to London with the Taylors.

She walked slowly up the cobbled street toward the old Manor Home on Store Street. *Milkweed Manor*, she thought wryly of the moniker by which the place was infamously known. She could hardly believe it had been more than three years since she had first walked this way, carrying her child within her. This being autumn, the day was colder, and beneath Charlotte's wool cape, a bulge was mildly noticeable, much as it had been then.

She did not knock on the front door of the manor, but instead went around the back and let herself in the garden door. Gibbs looked up from her desk as she entered, then looked down at her rounded middle in question.

From beneath her cape, Charlotte retrieved her bulging reticule.

"Not safe to walk this neighborhood with one's purse dangling in plain sight," she said.

Gibbs gave her a rare grin. "It's good to see you, Miss Charlotte. Sally's expecting you."

"Charlotte. There you are," Sally called, coming down the corridor. "Right on time."

"Missy!" Anne Taylor shouted gleefully. The little girl, now nearly three years old, broke away from Sally's side to rush up and throw her arms around Charlotte's legs.

Charlotte bent to embrace her. "Goodness, I've only been gone an hour." She glanced up at her friend. "Thank you for watching her for me."

"I was pleased to."

"How is that new girl getting on?"

"The ginger-haired girl?"

"Yes—Meg."

"Oh, she has the way of it, she does. Nursin' her wee one like an old hand. Says you are a fine teacher."

"Good. I shall visit her tomorrow."

"And how did you fare shopping?" Sally asked.

"I found some fine new things for a girl who's growing far too fast."

"Let me see!" Anne cried.

"You shall, but let's wait until we get you home, all right?"

"Is Grandfather home?"

"I believe so."

"Then let us go, do!"

"In a moment . . ."

"That's all right, Miss Charlotte—you go on ahead. Thomas is off duty in a few minutes and we're to walk home together."

"How is Thomas?"

Sally smiled, her eyes glowing. "Wonderful, as you well know. Adores working for Dr. Taylor. Adores me." She sighed. "Never thought I'd have such a man for my husband—or any husband for that matter. And such a fine father he is to Dickie."

"I am so happy for you, Sally."

"As I always say, it's you I have to thank for it."

Charlotte shook her head. "I only introduced you."

"Still, I cannot help feeling guilty, Miss Charlotte. Should have been you before me. I cannot help thinking—"

"Go on, Sally. Do not worry about me."

Anne reached her hands high, wanting to be picked up.

"I am fine. We are fine." Charlotte held one of Anne's hands and put her other on top of the girl's head. "Is that not right, moppet?"

In the dining room of the Taylors' townhouse, Charlotte reigned over breakfast.

"Now, now, Mr. Taylor, sit down and have your porridge," Charlotte urged.

"Aw, Miss Charlotte," John Taylor said, "I haven't any appetite this morning."

"Breakfast is important, as you well know, being one of the most renowned surgeons in London. . . ."

"That was a long time ago."

"And becoming so again, to hear Mrs. Krebs tell it. Now, please sit with us and eat. We'd like that, Anne, would we not?"

"Yes, Grandfather. Eat! Eat!"

"Oh, very well. I cannot disappoint two such lovely girls."

Just as the three of them sat down to porridge and tea, Daniel Taylor walked in, rumpled and red-eyed from a long night of duty at the Manor Home.

"Good morning, Dr. Taylor," Charlotte said. "Did you have a pleasant evening?"

"Not at all."

"I am sorry to hear it."

"Finances at the Manor improving any?" his father asked.

"The pressure has let up some, yes."

"Capital!"

"I should not go that far."

"Here. Sit down." Charlotte spooned out another bowl of porridge. "Have some breakfast."

Dr. Taylor sat down with a grateful smile.

"Are you working in the foundling ward today, Father?"

"Yes. And Mrs. Moorling has asked me to look in on one of the new patients as well. Poor thing is frightened to death of Dr. Preston."

Shaking his head, Daniel Taylor shared a knowing look with Charlotte. Then he turned to his daughter. "And what will you two do today?" he asked, spooning treacle into his bowl.

"We're going to the *moo-zeeum*."

He chuckled. "How marvelous."

"I know she is too young to enjoy it," Charlotte explained. "But I have been longing to see the Egyptian exhibit."

"I hear it is impressive indeed."

"And we're to have cherry ices after. Do come with us, Papa!"

He smiled at his daughter's enthusiasm. "Not this time, I'm afraid. I did not manage much sleep last night. I am in great need of a nap before I see patients this afternoon."

"Missy says naps are good for you."

He smiled at Charlotte over Anne's head. "She is quite right."

One afternoon in late September, Charlotte was playing backgammon with John Taylor during Anne's nap, when Marie handed her a letter from the day's post. From the return address, she saw it was from her cousin Katherine. She opened the letter and read it slowly. Then she glanced up and saw John Taylor looking at her with concern in his hound-dog eyes.

"Not bad news, I hope?"

"No. An invitation, actually."

"To a hanging?"

"No." She sighed. "To a birthday party."

"Well, then, that's cause for a smile, my dear, not a frown. Where is the party to be?"

"Manchester Square." What had prompted this sudden inclusion? Why had Charles not convinced Katherine to exclude her from the invitation list? Did he think that would rouse suspicion, after all this time? He certainly could not want her to attend.

"Worried about Anne, are you?" John Taylor asked. "Do not be. I shall watch over her myself."

"You are very kind."

What would it be like to see Edmund after all this time? Could she go and satisfy herself with a glimpse or two, or would the seeing only reignite the burning desire for more contact with him? Perhaps it was better to stay away.

"You have not had any entertainment in far too long, Miss Charlotte. You go and enjoy yourself. I shall pay for the hansom myself. I insist upon it." He beamed at her, and she felt she had little choice but to agree.

"When is the party to be?" he asked.

She looked again at the invitation. The date read *Friday the 7th.*

"On Saturday," she answered.

When Charlotte arrived, Katherine was reclining on the settee, one hand on her forehead, the other on her rounded abdomen. She glanced over at her guest before again closing her eyes.

"The party was yesterday, Charlotte," she said dully.

"Yes, I know."

"Forgive me for not standing to greet you. I am perfectly exhausted. I overdid yesterday—Charles is quite put out with me for it. This time is worse than the last. I suppose that means it is a girl. How was your lying-in with Anne?"

"Actually, Anne is not—"

"I am sorry you could not attend the party, Charlotte," Katherine interrupted. "What a to-do it was. Edmund was quite beside himself. Too many presents and too much cake. Went to bed with a tummy ache. And he's to have a pony when we return to Fawnwell besides."

"How exciting."

"Mrs. Harris came to town for the party, but she looked very ill indeed. What a wretched hat she wore. Oh, and William was here with his new wife—Amanda or Althea or something. I forget. Had you heard he married? I had thought he would marry you or your sister, and here neither one of you has wed. I must say Bea looked positively grim-faced upon seeing the two of them here together."

"Bea was here?"

"Yes. I suppose I hoped to throw the two of you together—force a reconciliation. Is that why you did not come—had you gotten word Bea planned to attend? I suppose your Aunt Tilney let it slip. . . ."

"I had not heard, actually."

Katherine rang a little bell beside her. "Celia!" she called. "Do bring me some ice, would you?" Then to Charlotte she explained, "It seems to help my headaches."

"Is . . . Edmund here?" Charlotte asked, palms damp. "I have a gift I hoped to give him."

"Oh . . ." Katherine waved her hand vaguely in the air before returning it to her forehead. "He's about the place somewhere. Do be a dear and find him, will you? My physician says I should keep off my feet as much as possible."

"Of course. I hope you feel better soon."

Charlotte walked out of the sitting room just as a maid was rushing up the stairs with an ice bucket.

"Have you seen Edmund?" she asked the girl.

"No, ma'am. But you might try the nursery upstairs."

"Thank you."

Charlotte trotted up the stairs to the third floor. As she looked in both directions, trying to decide which corridor to try first, she saw a red ball roll from an open doorway to her right.

The ball came to a stop beside a Greek statue, and Charlotte stooped to pick it up.

A little boy stepped into the corridor, then hesitated, clearly surprised to see her there.

"Hello," she said, suddenly breathless. "Could this be what you are looking for?" She held out the ball with a smile.

"Yes, thank you." He took the ball, then looked up at her with his father's brown eyes framed by a tousle of dark curly hair so like her own.

"You are very welcome, Edmund."

He cocked his head to one side. "Who are you?"

"I am your . . . your mother's cousin Charlotte."

"Cousin Charlotte?"

"Yes. And you are the birthday boy." She pulled a small wrapped rectangle from her reticule. "I have a gift for you."

"I know what that is—it's a book."

"Yes, and you probably already have it."

She stooped down, sitting on her heels, so that she was at eye level with him as he ripped open the paper and looked at the cover. "Yes." He shrugged. "I do have it."

"Well, it is such a good book, it won't hurt to have another."

He looked up at her, little brows crinkling up—so like his father. "Why are you sad?"

"I don't know. I suppose it is because I cannot believe you are already three years old. It is silly, really. Birthdays are to be happy times, and you are a very happy boy, are you not?"

Again he shrugged. "Yes."

"I am so glad."

He lifted the book. "Read to me?" he asked.

Her heart fisted hard within her, and she bit her lip to hold back bittersweet tears. She opened her mouth to answer when a woman's voice called down the corridor, "Come now, master Edmund, your father will be home any moment." A prim-faced young woman in grey dress appeared, shaking out a miniature frock coat before her. "Time to dress."

Charlotte stood and the woman paused.

"Oh, pardon me I did not know Edmund had a guest."

"That's all right. I was just leaving."

The woman passed by them and into Edmund's room.

She felt Edmund tug at her sleeve. "Father is taking me to the circus."

"How nice."

"But you can read to me first."

She smiled at him. "I would love nothing more, but I am afraid I must take my leave."

"Oh. Then Papa shall read it. It's his favorite."

"Yes, I know," Charlotte said softly. She reached a tentative hand toward him and touched his shoulder briefly. "Happy birthday, dear Edmund."

Charlotte could not sleep. She turned over yet again. Her stomach growled. She should have eaten more at supper. Giving up, she reached for her dressing gown at the foot of her bed but could not find it. She must have kicked it to the floor with all her tossing and turning. Oh well. She wouldn't light a candle to find it and risk waking Anne. Besides, the house was warm and there was no one to see her at this time of night.

She tiptoed out of her room in her nightdress. In the corridor, she could hear John Taylor's soft snore as she passed his room. She picked up the candle lamp on the landing table and used it to guide her down the many stairs and into the kitchen. There, she set the lamp down and opened the icebox. She retrieved the bottle of milk and set about lighting a fire in the stove and pouring some milk into a pan to warm. Then she selected an apple from the vegetable bin. Taking it to the work table, she slid a sharp knife from its slot and set to work slicing off a few wedges of fruit.

The door opened behind her and Charlotte started. The knife sliced into her left index finger. She gave a little cry, more from fright than pain. She half-turned from the table, surprised and relieved to see Dr. Taylor standing there, medical bag in hand.

"You frightened me."

"Forgive me. I did not expect to find anyone up."

Charlotte became aware of throbbing in her finger. She put it to her mouth, tasting blood.

"I've cut myself."

"How badly?"

She stepped closer to the candle lamp and he did as well. Her relief that the late-night intruder was Dr. Taylor now faded as she remembered she wore nothing but a thin nightdress.

"Let me see it."

"I am sure it is nothing."

He took her left hand in his, her palm forward. With his free hand, he gently examined her index finger. Her heart pounded in time with its throbbing.

"Here, let's clean that." From his bag, he deftly retrieved a bottle of antiseptic. He held her hand over the basin, released her only long enough to open the bottle, then poured antiseptic over the wound. The stuff stung, and she wrinkled her nose at its smell.

"Let me wrap that for you," he said quietly.

He retrieved a small rolled bandage from his bag and then stood again before her. He guided her hand closer to the light and leaned near. She realized she was breathing in shallow, rapid breaths as he skillfully and gently wound the bandage around her finger and secured it. Still, the process seemed to take quite a long time, as he reexamined his work, still holding her hand in one of his. She hoped he did not guess how affected she was by his nearness.

Without releasing her hand, he looked up from her finger to her face. His eyes shone with intensity, his pupils large in the dim light.

Did she alone feel this tension, this delicious, terrifying ache?

To dispel it, she said shakily, "Who is minding the Manor?"

"Thomas is filling in. Said I looked dead on my feet."

She smiled and said awkwardly, "You do not . . . look so to me."

His eyes roamed over her features. "Nor you."

She swallowed and said needlessly, "I could not sleep."

He looked down at her hand again, as though just realizing he still held it.

"Will the patient live?" she asked lightly.

He did not smile. Instead he turned her hand over and lifted it to his cheek. He pressed his lips to the back of her hand and looked into her eyes. Charlotte could hardly breathe.

Without warning the kitchen door again opened, and they both turned to see John Taylor standing there, candlestick in hand. Charlotte took a sheepish step away from Daniel.

John Taylor looked from one to the other, a speculative gleam in his eyes. "I thought I smelled something burning," he said.

Charlotte turned. The milk was boiling out onto the stove.

34

> Right after emergence from its chrysalis, the Monarch is extremely vulnerable to predators because it is not yet able to fly.
>
> —Journey North

At the breakfast table one morning in November, Charlotte announced to Dr. Taylor and his father, "Anne and I are planning quite the celebration tonight, and you are both invited."

"What is the occasion?" Dr. Taylor asked.

"Your birthday, silly!" Anne laughed.

"Today *is* your birthday, is it not?" Charlotte asked tentatively.

"Well, I guess it is. I had quite forgotten."

"I hope neither of you will have to work late tonight."

"I'm going to help make a cake!" Anne announced proudly. "Just like the one Missy made for my birthday!"

"How nice. I shall look forward to it."

"As will I," John Taylor said. "Though I'm afraid I haven't a gift for you, my boy. Unless you'd like a new ear horn or scalpel?" He winked.

"Do not trouble yourself, Father. You and I have gotten out of the habit of celebrating birthdays."

John Taylor folded his napkin and stood. "Well, I'm off. I promised Mrs. Krebs I'd be in early this morning."

His son turned his head to watch him leave. "If I did not know better, I would think he was taken with her." He looked at Charlotte and smiled self-consciously. "And I *would* recognize the symptoms."

Charlotte bit back a smile. "Do finish your breakfast, Anne, so we can begin our preparations."

Porridge dripped off Anne's chin as she said eagerly, "We are to wear our new gowns, and you must wear your green coat, Papa."

"Try not to speak with your mouth full, dear," Charlotte admonished.

Daniel bowed his head toward his daughter. "As my lady wishes."

"Do you not think Papa most handsome when he wears his green coat?"

Charlotte smiled, clearly embarrassed. "I . . . yes, quite handsome."

"Well, then"—he held her gaze—"your wish is my command."

How differently it all might have gone had he not stopped by the club on his way home. He had left the Manor sufficiently early, leaving Thomas and his father on duty, and only dropped by in hopes of finding Preston, who had not shown up to relieve them as scheduled. His father had insisted Daniel go home and not miss his own birthday celebration. He would stay until Preston arrived. Not seeing his colleague in the club, Daniel turned to leave. That's when he saw Lester Dawes. He might not have stopped at all, had his old acquaintance not looked so miserable, hands holding up his head, several empty tumblers before him.

"Dawes?"

The man looked up, bleary-eyed and desolate. "Hello, Taylor."

"What's wrong, man? You look dreadful."

"You haven't heard?"

Daniel shook his head.

"Lost a patient."

"I am sorry. I know how that feels."

"It's a double blow. I hate to be mercenary, but this will be death to my practice as well. It is always a gamble, having prominent patients."

"May I ask who?"

His answer hit Daniel like a fist. The sensation a sickening combination of true grief and pity along with several self-centered emotions far less noble.

"I am sorry," Daniel mumbled again, and ducked out of the room before the man could respond.

When he arrived home, Charlotte was there to greet him. "Happy birthday," she said shyly, adding tentatively, "Daniel."

She was dressed in a lovely rose-colored gown with a flattering, feminine neckline. Her hair was arranged in a pretty crown of curls, several framing her face, now flushed and expectant. He did not miss the intentional use of his Christian name, her attention to her appearance, nor the blush in her cheeks. No, he had not misread the situation. Her feelings had changed and she wanted him to know it. He should be relieved and pleased, but he felt a nauseating ball of dread in his stomach instead. Why did such a thing have to happen now? When she was finally ready to receive his affection? It seemed to Daniel a cruel and ironic twist of fate.

"You look beautiful," he said, an empty sadness stealing over him.

She smiled at his words, but her smile quickly faltered. "Is something wrong?"

He opened his mouth to answer. Must he tell her? Now? Could he not wait until . . . until there was an understanding between them?

"Happy birthday, Papa!" Anne shouted, running out to meet him, throwing her arms around his legs. "Doesn't Missy look like a princess?"

"Yes. She does. As do you." He smiled at his daughter, touching her fancy, curled hair and taking in her bright blue frock. "Your new gown is almost as lovely as you are."

Anne giggled and pulled his hand, urging him to follow her into the dining room. "I helped make the cake, but I fear the icing is rather a mess."

Daniel breathed a silent sigh. *A mess indeed.*

While Anne knelt on a chair at the dining room table, happily poking little sugar petals onto the icing of the cake, Charlotte joined Daniel in the sitting room. "Daniel, are you sure nothing is amiss? I hope I have not offended you."

"Offended me, how?"

"Well, by my presumption, my familiarity in arranging this birthday celebration. If I have overstepped—"

"I am the opposite of offended, Charlotte. I am pleased by your . . . familiarity, as you say. In my mind, you are part of this family already."

Even with her head bowed, he could see the pleasure in her pink cheeks and concealed smile.

"Charlotte," he said, suddenly intense, "my feelings for you, my intentions, remain unchanged."

Her head rose and she looked at him shyly, expectantly. How lovely she was, how fondly was she regarding him. Would it be so wrong to postpone the news that would wipe that look from her face forever?

"If your feelings," he added more gently, "were no longer hindered . . ."

"They are no longer hindered, Daniel," she whispered.

"Then I would ask you . . . what I have longed to ask you . . ."

She smiled warmly, her body leaning toward him ever so slightly. What agony this was. To be so close to her, to realize she was ready to accept him. But only because she remained in sweet ignorance.

He winced, then said, "But I cannot."

Her smile fell. "What has happened? Have I done something to . . . ?"

"You have done nothing. Nothing but make us all completely devoted to you. You have not only become beloved mother to my daughter, but beloved daughter to my father as well."

"But you do not share their . . . affliction?"

"Oh, I am indeed afflicted, Charlotte. But . . ."

"But?"

"I am afraid I have dreadful news. I thought to wait until after . . ." He waved his hand in direction of the dining room but guessed they both knew he included much more than the festivities in his statement. "But I find in good conscience that I cannot keep it from you a moment longer."

"What is it?"

"Your cousin Katherine is dead."

Charlotte gasped.

"She died in childbirth, her infant with her."

Charlotte sat, stunned, her hand covering her mouth.

After a few silent moments, Daniel rose. Charlotte still sat there, unmoving. She did not ask him to stay, nor assure him the news had no bearing. He knew too well that it had changed everything.

Although society did not expect women to attend funerals, Charlotte knew Katherine would expect her to be there. So, dressed in black, her face concealed behind a veiled hat and umbrella, Charlotte walked slowly past ranks of rain-speckled headstones, toward her cousin's gravesite. She watched from a distance as four black horses with black feathers on their heads brought the hearse into the churchyard, followed by a long procession of mourners. Six strapping men, William Bentley among them, carried the lacquered coffin to its final resting place. Charlotte slowly joined the rear of the congregation. In front of her, the mourners wore black—the few other women in black gowns and mantles and swarms of men bearing black armbands and gloves.

There were so many people in attendance that she barely caught a glimpse of Charles through the crowd and didn't see Edmund at all. The church bells tolled their sharp death knell, and with each clang, Charlotte felt her heart bang against her ribs. *Poor lamb*, she thought, the epitaph seeming to fit not only Edmund but Charles, and even Katherine as well. Her cousin wouldn't be there to nurture the little boy she loved, nor see him grow to manhood. And being so young, how much would Edmund even remember of the woman he'd called mother—a year from now? Five years hence? Charlotte's mother-heart grieved for Katherine's loss as well as that of Charles and Edmund.

The same priest who'd conducted Katherine's churching only a few years ago now officiated over her funeral. From her place in the back, Charlotte could not make out much of anything he said. A talented soprano sang a hymn so beautiful and haunting that the mourners wept more under its power than the cleric's words preceding it.

> Why do we mourn departing friends?
> Or shake at death's alarms?
> 'Tis but the voice that Jesus sends,
> To call them to His arms. . . .

Charlotte wept as well.

She had not planned to go to Katherine's home in Manchester Square with the honored gentry, close friends, and family members who were traditionally invited to do so after the ceremony, to partake of a cold supper and a "cheerful glass." But she felt oddly compelled to do so. She was family, after all, a close cousin to Katherine. Tradition would expect her to wear black mourning clothes for six weeks for a first cousin; would it not expect her to pay her respects in person as well? Frankly, she was surprised she had the courage to ring the bell.

She certainly had no intention of approaching Charles. In fact her hands shook at the thought of it. She did not want him to think she was "waiting in the wings" nor expecting anything from him. She merely felt it was her duty, and yes, her right, to attend, if only for a few moments. Knowing her cousin as she had, she knew Katherine would be affronted beyond words if Charlotte did not at least make an appearance.

So with trembling hands she handed the butler her wrap and umbrella but kept on her veiled hat and followed the man up the stairs. Still holding her things, he said apologetically, "I'm afraid we've an overflow of coats, m'um. I shall have to put your things there, behind that screen, with the others. If you need help finding them again upon departure, I shall endeavor to aid you in your search."

"Thank you."

The drawing room was already filled with people huddled in small groups, some talking soberly and others less so, clearly enjoying the promised glass of cheer. Charlotte sat in a row of chairs near the door, content to observe the gathering. She did not see Charles or Edmund. They were perhaps in the adjoining sitting room. Nor did she see her father, which she found puzzling. She wondered if he was ill—could not imagine another reason why he would not attend. She recognized several people, but no one it seemed had recognized her. She breathed a sigh of relief.

Relaxing a bit, she allowed her head to swivel as she surveyed the remainder of the large room. Her heart pounded. There was her sister, Bea, holding Charles' arm as the two walked into the room. And there, his head barely visible through the assembled throng, was Edmund. Several mourners clustered around Charles as he entered, clearly offering condolences. Even from this distance, Charlotte could see there was a terrible pall over his features.

Bea leaned close to Edmund, her arm resting across his shoulders as she whispered some confidence. Her sister comforting *her* son? For some reason the idea of it—the reality of it—made her feel queasy. Edmund ran off suddenly, disappearing through the crowd, and Bea returned her attentions to Charles.

Charlotte realized she could walk right up to Charles and say a few kind words. If she could manage to ignore her sister's inevitable icy glare, she might even accomplish the feat with her emotions under rein. She sighed. Even if Bea were not standing guard at Charles' side, Charlotte knew she would not have the courage.

She rose from her chair and turned to leave. As she stepped briskly into the passage, she nearly ran right into Edmund. He looked at her, head cocked to one side.

"You're Cousin Charlotte."

She lifted her veil off her face. "That's right. What a wonderful memory you have."

"My mother died," he said somberly.

She nodded. "Yes, I know. I am very sorry."

"That's what everybody says."

Charlotte lowered herself to his eye level, sitting on her heels. "But even though she is gone, you are not alone."

"I know. I still have Father."

"Yes, and there are others, too, who love you."

"Do you mean Bea?"

Charlotte swallowed. "Bea?"

He shrugged and said matter-of-factly, "Mummy lives in heaven now."

"That's right. What a smart little boy you are."

"I am not little."

"All right, Edmund. You are very big. And far too wise."

"Haven't you any children?"

"I . . . not at present, no."

"You're crying."

"Am I?"

"Father cries sometimes. I do too."

"Of course you do."

She smiled at the boy through her tears and allowed herself to reach out and briefly touch his head. Then she retrieved her hand and stepped back.

She watched as Edmund walked through the doorway she had just exited—then realized he was heading directly toward his father and Bea. Charlotte quickly stepped behind the door. Out of sight but not out of earshot.

"Cousin Charlotte is here, Father," she heard Edmund say.

"Charlotte? Where?"

"Oh . . . I don't see her anymore."

"What did she say to you?" Charles asked.

She could not make out Edmund's reply.

Charlotte risked a glance back into the room and saw Charles bent over Edmund, his hand lying on his son's head, much as hers had done. When she saw Charles look abruptly in her direction, she instinctively ducked from view. Moving quickly to the temporary "coatroom" to retrieve her wrap, she stepped behind the oriental screen flanked by potted palms that served to conceal the untidy pile of coats from view. It concealed her as well.

Hearing footsteps nearby, she peeked from between the slats in the screen. From her hiding place, she watched Charles stride quickly into the passage and look in both directions. How foolish she felt behind the screen. Should she step out and offer her condolences?

But then Beatrice appeared beside him and took his arm. "Do not trouble yourself, Charles. I suppose she had the right to come and pay her respects, but I do wish she might have stayed away and not sullied the day for you. At least she had the decency to be unobtrusive. Though I wonder what she was thinking, speaking to Edmund?"

Charles stood still, alert without moving, as though trying to hear her . . . to sense her presence. Was he angry she had come?

Threatened that she would speak to his son? Afraid or furious she would dare make herself known to Edmund, and at such a vulnerable time?

I told him nothing, she thought defensively.

"Come, Charles. Come back in. There is no harm done. Forget about her."

He turned and gave Bea a brief smile, patting her hand, which was placed on his arm. "I am sure you are right. How good you are to us."

Yes, Charlotte thought. *Mr. Harris seems to have no problem following Bea's advice. No doubt I am long forgotten.*

She wondered if her sister would finally have what she'd always wanted. The thought depressed her. *I would not have chosen you to mother my son, but I have lost my say in the matter. You will do your best by him, I know—for Charles' sake, if nothing else. What would you say if you knew? Will Charles tell you, if he marries you? If he never told Katherine, I doubt he will. Probably best that way. You were never especially fond of me.*

Waiting a moment more, Charlotte stepped away from the screen and toward the stairs—just as William Bentley reached the landing.

"Miss Lamb!"

"Mr. Bentley," she answered, heart pounding dully. She wished she had remembered to reposition her veil.

"I am surprised to see you," he said with a knowing smile.

"Why should you be? Katherine was my cousin, as you must recall."

"Yes. And my uncle's wife." He cleared his throat. "You are here alone?"

"I am."

"Beatrice did not come?"

"She is inside. With your uncle."

"Ah, offering comfort. How good of her. I would have thought you—"

"I came only to pay my respects, Mr. Bentley. And now if you will excuse me." She quickly began to descend the stairs.

"Miss Lamb, forgive me. I did not mean . . ."

She turned back to face him. "Oh yes, Mr. Bentley. You most certainly did." With that, she smiled as knowingly as he had, she hoped, and walked sprightly away.

Charles watched his nephew stride toward him, eyes bright with some new trouble.

"I was surprised to see Charlotte Lamb here."

"You saw her?"

"Yes, she was leaving as I came in. First in line to offer comfort, I suppose?"

"William. I am tired of your innuendo and disrespect. Miss Lamb—Charlotte—did not even speak to me. I did not even know she had been here until Edmund mentioned it."

"Edmund knows her?"

"Apparently Katherine and Charlotte kept in contact over the last few years."

"I did not realize. And certainly I meant no disrespect to anyone. Especially at such a time. But do be warned, Uncle. The spinsters and widows are already lining up, ready to offer the grieving widower solace and care for his poor orphaned son."

"Edmund isn't an orphan."

"Motherless, then."

"You are a fool, William."

"Mr. Bentley." Beatrice came and stood at Charles' side, making her familiarity evident by her proximity and proprietary air. "How kind of you to come."

He bowed stiffly. "Beatrice . . . Miss Lamb. How pleasant to see you again."

"And what are you two gentlemen discussing?"

"Your sister, actually," his nephew said, clearly relishing her disapproval.

"Really."

"Yes, I have just seen her, and I must confess, I have never seen her looking lovelier. A bit tired perhaps—black doesn't really suit her. But still, as handsome as ever."

"Yes, well," Bea said briskly. "I must check on Edmund. Poor dear is exhausted with grief and attention."

She dipped her chin. "Mr. Bentley. Charles."

Both men bowed briefly as she walked away.

"My, my. That did not take long."

"William, please. Bea is like family."

"Or very much wished to be."

"Do shut up, William."

35

Grant us the pow'r of quick'ning grace,
To fit our souls to fly;
Then, when we drop this dying flesh,
We'll rise above the sky.

—Isaac Watts, *A Funeral Thought*

Months passed as Charles and Edmund grieved. They spent the Christmas holidays at Fawnwell before returning to London to begin the depressing task of going through Katherine's things and disposing of all but the most meaningful mementos. When they next visited Fawnwell in the spring, Charles brought several trunks of clothing to donate to Doddington Church for distribution to the poor. Leaving Edmund in the care of the boy's grandmother, Charles and his man drove over to the churchyard in a horse-drawn wagon.

Beatrice met him in the south porch of the church and in her sober and industrious fashion, helped direct the unloading. "This is very kind of you, Charles. I shall see to it that every piece is put to good use."

While his driver went back to the wagon for another load, Charles set a second trunk on top of the first. Bea opened the lid and pulled out several gowns—one with an expandable laced-vent bodice, and two others with billowing waistlines.

"These must be the gowns Katherine wore during her confinement."

"Yes, well . . . perhaps I will leave you to it."

"Of course, Charles. This is hard on you. Come to the vicarage for tea. I can do this later. Father, I know, will want to see you."

"Very well. Thank you."

He paused to direct his man to finish the unloading, then followed her across the churchyard and into the vicarage. There was no sign of Gareth Lamb. "I do not know where he has gotten to. I shall have Tibbets ask him to join us when he arrives."

They took chairs in the drawing room and Bea ordered tea. While they waited, Bea mused, "A whole trunk of gowns suitable for confinement. Perhaps I shall donate them to one of the lying-in hospitals." She added sardonically, "In honor of Charlotte."

"Beatrice . . ."

Tibbets entered with a tray, and when she had left again, Beatrice poured tea for the both of them. "I certainly hope she has not put in another appearance since the funeral, Charles."

"No, she has not."

"Thank goodness. I hate to think of her becoming a nuisance to you and Edmund, especially during your mourning period."

"Charlotte is not a nuisance, Beatrice." He hesitated, then turned to her, his face set. "What has your sister done to you to earn such bitter contempt?"

"I should think that obvious. She . . . she ruined my chances when she ruined herself."

"Come, come, Bea, you despised her long before that."

Beatrice shrugged her thin shoulders.

"One might almost assume you jealous of Charlotte."

"Jealous? Hardly."

"But of what?" Charles wondered aloud, as if he had not heard. "You are, classically speaking, more beautiful. You held your father's approval whereas Charlotte did not. William favored you, though that lad's opinion is worth less than I'd imagined. What is it you begrudge her?"

Bea's chin quivered.

"What did she have that you did not?"

Bea stared down at her hands, then lifted her gaze. "Your admiration."

He took a deep breath. "Beatrice." He sighed. "You have long held me in too high of a regard. And your sister in one too low."

"I do not think my opinion unjust. She has never named a villain in her fall. Can we not surmise his low status? We know he could not be a gentleman."

"Do we indeed? Did it never cross your mind that she might have another reason for withholding his name?"

"No."

"Beatrice. I know you foster some idea of a future alliance between the two of us."

She gasped. "I have never said—"

"Come, come. I tire of this game playing. You would have no objections to an alliance with me—is that not so?"

"I suppose, in theory, I would have no objections."

"Well, I do. And you should as well."

"What do you mean?"

"You despise Charlotte. But I admire her. You condemn the man responsible. But I am he."

"What?"

"Yes, Beatrice. I am that man. And Charlotte did not reveal my part in her fall because I had already chosen to marry Katherine. Needed to marry Katherine to keep Fawnwell afloat."

"You . . . and Charlotte . . . ?" Bea sputtered.

"Yes. And I could never join myself with a woman who despises someone I hold so dear. Someone *she* should hold dear as well." He sighed again and sat back. "Nor do I expect you will ever want to see me again now that you know."

Tears filled Beatrice's eyes. She squeezed them shut and the tears streamed down her pale cheeks. "Go," she said miserably.

It was the first time in twenty years he had seen her cry.

When Charles made his exit from the drawing room a few moments later, the vicar was sitting on the bench in the entry hall.

"So it was you all along," Gareth Lamb said flatly. "Yet you did nothing to help her."

Charles paused, realizing all that Charlotte's father had overheard. He took a deep breath, resigned. "Yes. I did nothing then. You and I have that in common. But now I can. And I will."

"Do not tell me you will marry my daughter in some foolhardy attempt to make restitution for past sins?"

Charles exhaled a dry puff of breath. "Is that not exactly what we are supposed to do—*Reverend*?"

When Charles returned with his young son to their London townhouse, he greeted the servants as politely as his exhaustion would allow and instructed the governess to put Edmund to bed straightaway. Weary from the journey and the encounters preceding it, Charles stepped toward the library, intending only to take a cursory look through the post to make sure nothing required his immediate attention before taking himself to bed. Passing by the sitting room doors, he was surprised to see his nephew William sprawled on the sofa, cravat askew and tumbler in hand. The young man did not bother to stand when Charles entered the room.

"William? I did not expect to find you here."

"That sweet housemaid of yours let me in. Said I could wait for you."

"I hope you've not been waiting long."

William shrugged. "Two days." He sipped from his glass.

"What do you want?"

"To help myself to your port, as you see. As well as a little holiday from the missus. I haven't the luxury of two dwellings as you do."

Charles bit back his annoyance. "I see."

"And how fares Fawnwell? I suppose you saw Beatrice Lamb?"

"I did."

"As cold and serious and delicious as always, I suppose?"

Charles sighed in frustration. "I do not understand you, William. You had your chance with her and gave it up."

"Yes. A pity. She is one of those rare women who is more attractive stern than smiling. Have you noticed that?"

Charles walked back to the doors and shut them carefully before turning again to face him. "Did you never have serious intentions toward Miss Lamb?" he demanded.

"Oh yes. I seriously intended to preempt your intentions."

"What do you mean?"

"I should think that evident. You know I had always counted on being your heir—back when I still thought you had something to inherit, that is." William reached for the bottle on the side table and refilled his glass. "I had believed you a confirmed bachelor, which was jolly good for me. But then I heard you were showing a great deal of interest in one of the vicar's daughters. Thus, I decided to deduce which of them it was and to win the lady—and keep the inheritance—for myself." He raised his glass in mock toast.

"Of all the presumptuous—"

"Yes, yes." He waved away Charles' censor with a casual flip of his free hand. "And I deduced it was young Charlotte you admired within ten minutes of stepping foot inside the vicarage."

Charles stared at him, silent anger building in his chest.

"You *did* plan to marry Charlotte Lamb, did you not?" William asked.

Charles made no answer.

"While I found Charlotte charming, with her lovely smile and generous . . .

nature, I admit it was Beatrice I preferred. So prim. So tightly wound I was sure every moment she must come unsprung." He sighed wistfully. "How I miss those afternoons in Doddington, listening to beautiful Bea play. But of course, all that was before Fawnwell burned and I came to realize the dire straights you were in. Still, I must admit your marriage to Lady Katherine took us all by surprise. One of the Miss Lambs was especially devastated, as I am sure you know."

Charles clenched his fists at his sides.

"And after that I had no choice but to change course and begin pursuing a wealthy wife."

"But you still called on Bea after that, letting the poor girl think—"

"I deluded myself, hoping Lady Katherine might not be spring chicken enough to lay the golden egg. I was wrong—drunk on wishful thinking, I suppose."

"You're drunk now."

"Quite tolerably, yes. It's the only time I am this honest."

"So, when our son . . . when Edmund was born, you had no use for Bea anymore."

"Precisely. And regret it though I did, I would regret more being poor." He sighed theatrically. "Marrying the dreadfully cheerful Amanda Litchfield with her five hundred a year is a burden I must bear up under somehow. You know all about marrying for money, do you not, Uncle?"

On a lovely summer day, Charlotte and Anne were sitting on a blanket in the small garden behind the London townhouse when Dr. Taylor came upon them.

"There you are," he said.

"We are having a picnic, as you can see," Charlotte explained.

A basket and Anne's miniature tea set were spread out neatly on the blanket.

"A picnic in the garden. How lovely. Might I join you?"

"Of course, Papa," Anne said. "But I shall have to fetch another cup. Constance is using the pink one, and Missy and I the other two."

"I do not believe Constance and I have been introduced," Daniel said, nodding toward the porcelain doll seated before the pink cup and saucer.

"Of course you have, Papa." The three-and-a-half-year-old sounded mildly peevish. "You see her every night when you tuck me in."

"Forgive me. My mistake."

Anne jumped to her feet. "I shan't be long. But do not blame me if the tea is cold, Papa. You did not tell me you would be joining us today."

"Do not hurry on my account, sweetheart. I am quite fond of cold tea."

He sat down on the blanket and folded his long legs, knocking over the tiny sugar bowl as he did.

Charlotte righted it again and confided quietly, "The sugar is make-believe but the tea is quite real."

He grinned. "Then I shall endeavor to be more careful." He looked about him. "Such a small bit of earth we have here. Barely worth calling a garden."

"How fortunate, then, to have such a large plot at your disposal at the Manor."

"Yes." he said distractedly, then cleared his throat. "There is something I wish to discuss with you."

"Yes?"

"I've had a letter from our old friend, Dr. Webb."

"Dr. Webb? It is good news, I hope?"

"Yes, rather. He has decided to retire—plans to move north to be nearer his grown son and grandchildren." He plucked a forget-me-not from the grass and twirled the stem in his fingers. "He has offered me his practice. His home in Doddington, his offices, all for a very reasonable sum."

She stared at him, but he kept his gaze on the weed in his hand. "But—that would mean giving up your practice here and your work at the Manor."

"The Manor Home is my father's life's work. Not mine. I merely stepped in while he was unable. I can leave it in his hands now. He and Thomas can manage the place—and Preston—quite nicely without me."

"Have you told him yet—your father?"

"No, not yet. I wanted to speak with you first."

She was not prepared to ask why. "You would really leave London?"

"Yes. I tire of city life. And, in truth, there are too many memories here—in this house and at the Manor both—and not all of them pleasant. I quite enjoyed my time in Kent. It is so peaceful and lovely there on the north downs. So much open land. So much green." He lifted his face and smiled at her. "And, as you may recall, I was quite fond of its residents as well."

She smiled briefly in return, but felt a surge of fear rising within her. Were Dr. Taylor and his daughter leaving her behind? Or was he assuming she would return to Doddington with them?

"Your father will not be pleased at my return. But should I allow the opinion of one man to keep me from something which, I believe, will bring much happiness?"

She assumed it a rhetorical question, but then saw he was studying her, waiting for her response. Waiting for her to answer the same question of herself.

"Charlotte?"

She studied her hands, tightly clutched in her lap.

"Charlotte. I will not take you back to Doddington as Anne's governess."

She looked up at him, oddly relieved. She had inwardly cringed at the thought of returning to her home village as a servant. Of facing the disdain of her former acquaintance—especially her father and sister. Though at least governess was one of the more respectable positions of service. No, easier to remain in anonymity in London. Perhaps with Sally and Thomas, or Sally's sister. Or she could return to Crawley, as she had once thought she might do.

"You will find another governess, once you are settled in Kent?"

"Yes. I will."

"I understand."

"No, I do not think you do. I would not take you back to Doddington as a governess. But I would take you there—as my wife."

She stared at him, saw the grim determination on his face, and her heart pounded dully, a dozen different emotions flooding her mind.

"Here it is!" Anne sang, running back to them and plopping back down. "Now I shall pour you some tea."

As she did so, Charlotte felt Daniel's intense gaze on her profile.

"Will you, Charlotte?"

She looked up sharply from her thoughts. "Hmm?"

"Yes, Missy, will you have more tea?"

"Thank you."

As Anne refilled her cup, Charlotte glanced at Daniel, tilting her head in his daughter's direction, silently indicating that their conversation would have to wait.

That evening, after Charlotte had gotten Anne into her nightclothes and her teeth cleaned, Daniel came in as usual to tuck in his daughter and hear her prayers.

Charlotte silently hung the girl's dress in the wardrobe and gathered up her soiled stockings. As she did, she heard, without meaning to, Anne's sweet prayer:

"Thank you for Papa and Grandfather and Missy. And Constance too. Tell Mother not to be sad because we are all happy together. Amen."

His arm around his daughter's shoulders, Daniel looked at Charlotte over Anne's little bowed head. "Amen," he echoed, his gaze still holding hers.

After breakfast the next morning, Charlotte glanced at the mantel clock and saw it was nearly nine o'clock. Daniel sat at the head of the table still, nursing his third cup of coffee and rustling distractedly with the newspaper.

"May I be excused to go play, please?" Anne asked.

"Yes, you may," Charlotte answered and watched her skip from the room.

She finished her tea, then looked at Daniel again. "Are you not seeing patients today?"

"Not as yet. I am certain I should not be able to concentrate in any case." He put down the paper. "I am still waiting for your answer."

She opened her mouth. Closed it. Then opened it again. "I—"

"Tell me you have not forgotten the question." He attempted a smile.

"No," she laughed weakly. "I have thought of little else since."

"And?"

"And, I think—"

A loud knock sounded on the door.

Charlotte rose to her feet. "I will answer that."

"There is no need for you—"

"Marie has the day off."

He sighed and rose. "Very well. But we *shall* discuss this tonight."

Charlotte went down and opened the door, expecting to find a messenger or delivery of some sort. She froze—except to quickly close her mouth, which had fallen open. Mr. Harris stood there, elegantly dressed as usual, but his eyes, which she remembered nearly always dancing with merry teasing, looked frightfully serious. He removed his hat and smiled at her, but his smile was brief and did not cheer his expression.

"Miss Lamb."

"Mr. Harris." She stood looking at him dumbly, and then the realization struck her that he wasn't there to see her at all and she felt mortified at her own presumption. "You are here to see Dr. Taylor?"

He shook his head. "No, Charlotte, I am here to see you."

She put her hand to her chest. "Is something wrong with Edmund?"

"No. He is fine—missing his mother, of course."

Charlotte swallowed. "Of course."

"Forgive me. I am handling this very ill."

"Do come in."

He followed her up the stairs to the sitting room. "Please, sit down."

"Thank you."

She sat in the chair opposite him. He crossed one leg over the other, then uncrossed his legs and spread his feet on the carpet before him, resting his elbows on his knees and playing with his hat. "I had every intention of merely paying a social call to begin. But . . ."

Sitting back, he ran his hand through his hair. "But, seeing you now, I cannot pretend to a casual call."

"Mr. Harris, you are frightening me. Are you certain Edmund is all right?"

"Well, fine in health and spirits. But it's no good. He needs . . . he needs a woman's influence."

"He has a governess. I met her once. She seemed quite capable."

"You know that isn't what I mean."

Did she? He could not mean—Her mouth felt instantly dry. "Mr. Harris. I am not sure my presence in your home would be in Edmund's best interest. I fear word about me has circulated, rumors at least. Many of your acquaintance do not hold me in the same esteem they once did."

"You do not suppose *my* esteem has been affected by all this. How could it be?"

She lowered her head. "No, but it might not reflect well on Edmund. Nor you."

"So be it. I refuse to be driven by the opinions of others any longer. You have no idea how often I have thought of you, grieved for you. Forced to work in a post beneath your station. Torn away from your family and friends—your child, worst of all. What a burden it has been, knowing it was all my doing. Do you think you might ever find it in your heart to forgive me?"

Charlotte answered quietly, "I have forgiven you. Long ago."

"Then, this is my chance—do you not see? At last I am able to right my wrongs as best as I can."

"You need not feel obligated. I have a comfortable place here."

"Charlotte, this is not about obligation."

She rose quickly, clutching her hands and walking away from him. She was trembling with nerves, afraid to presume. To hope. "Are you asking me to be Edmund's governess?"

She heard him bolt from his chair behind her. "Blast the governess, Charlotte. Edmund has that. He needs . . ."

She turned around to face him.

"He needs you."

Her heart ached at the words.

He stepped closer. "And not only Edmund. I—"

The sitting room door opened and Daniel strode in, pulling on a glove. "Charlotte, have you seen my other—Oh . . ." He glanced up and stopped abruptly, looking from Mr. Harris to Charlotte and back again.

When he said nothing for several awkward seconds, Mr. Harris said, "Hello, Taylor."

Daniel paused, breathed in and exhaled before responding. "Harris."

"Forgive the intrusion, old boy." Mr. Harris smiled and added lightly, "I have just been trying to persuade Miss Lamb here to make young Edmund and I the two happiest males on earth." His smile faded, and it was his turn to look from Charlotte to the other man. "That is, unless you . . ." He swung his gaze back to Charlotte. "You two are not . . . You have worked for him so long with no word, I just assumed . . . But . . . *is there* an understanding between you?"

Charlotte's face burned. She found it difficult to breathe. She could hardly raise her head, let alone meet the gaze of either man. It was not her right to speak first. But Daniel remained silent. Finally, she lifted her eyes to meet his. He looked at her a moment, his chest rising and falling in exaggerated effort. And although he answered Mr. Harris's question, his eyes remained fixed on hers when he said, "No. There is no understanding."

They stared at one another a moment longer. Then Daniel nodded curtly to Harris, said dully, "I wish you both the best," and quickly bowed and left the room.

Once he was gone, Charles said, "Forgive me. I did not intend to put you on the spot in that manner. I fear there is something between you after all."

"There is a great deal between us." Charlotte sighed, stepping to the window and watching as Dr. Taylor appeared on the street below and strode away. "We have been friends for nearly as long as you and I have been. I was there when his wife died, and I have nursed and cared for his daughter for more than three years. But he spoke the truth. There is no understanding between us."

"But there might be, someday?"

She hesitated only a moment. "Yes."

"Well, then, Charlotte. You have a choice to make. I am proposing marriage now, today. I am asking you to be my wife and Edmund's mother."

She looked at him.

"I suppose that last bit is quite ironic, since you have always been his mother."

"No. That was Katherine's privilege, in every way that counts. To Edmund, in any case."

"Yes. About that. I'm afraid I would have to ask you to keep the true nature of your relationship with Edmund a secret."

The statement felt like a blade between her ribs, but of course he was right.

"I am not saying we can *never* tell him, but . . . out of loyalty to Katherine's memory and sensitivity to Edmund's reputation and feelings . . ."

"Of course. I understand completely. I won't pretend it is not a painful mandate, but you know I want whatever is best for Edmund."

"Yes, I do know that. You have proven that over and over again. If only Bea could see—"

"Bea?"

"Yes. She, too, has taken quite an interest in Edmund. Though I am not convinced her motives are purely maternal."

"I take it she would not be pleased to know that you are here."

"You are quite right. She does not know I am here, but she does know . . . about us."

"She does?"

"Yes. I was quite tired of hearing her disparaging remarks about you, and the slanderous suppositions about the ill-bred scoundrel that must have ruined you. I confessed *I* was that man. Scoundrel, perhaps, but ill-bred on no account."

"You didn't."

"I did."

"Is that why you are here? Did she refuse you?"

"Bea refuse me? I asked nothing of her. It is you I am asking, Charlotte. You."

"Did you did tell her . . . everything?"

"I did not tell her about Edmund, for obvious reasons. She still believes your child passed on."

She touched his arm. "When it was your own son who died—yours and Katherine's—it must have been difficult for you, having to grieve in secret. Alone."

He nodded. "You know a great deal about that." He grasped her elbows. "Let us put an end to it, Charlotte. Let us neither one be alone anymore."

She looked up into the long-held-dear face of Charles Harris. He was still so very handsome. And he was, finally, offering his name, his protection. Perhaps even his love. She realized he hadn't mentioned that. But what did she expect? Outpourings of romance and devotion when his wife was not long in her grave? She knew he cared for her on some level. He always had. And oh! to be near Edmund. Her own son. To be his mother, whether he knew it or not.

But what about Daniel? She admired and respected him. Perhaps even loved him, his daughter as well. True, they had as yet no formal understanding, but he had made his desires clear enough. At least before today. Why had he not spoken? She could guess why. He knew how deeply she longed to be with Edmund.

Could she forego a future with Daniel in order to be stepmother to her own son?

But the alternative seemed even more difficult to conceive. For to refuse Mr. Harris would mean giving up Edmund all over again.

36

> Oh, poor little butterfly, bound by so many fetters, which prevent you from flying whithersoever you will!
> Have pity on her, my God . . . so that she may be able to fulfill her desires to Thy honour and glory.
>
> —St. Teresa of Avila

Time passed quickly, as time is wont to do.

Daniel Taylor worked alone in his garden in Doddington, thinking back yet again to that day fifteen years ago when Charles Harris had come to his London home and changed his life forever.

Daniel had been aware, of course, of Charlotte's long affection for Harris, and knowing how she longed to be with her son, Daniel had despondently guessed which man she would choose. Loving her as he did, and wanting her much-deserved happiness, he had excused himself from the situation. He did not come home from the Manor all that day. He slept, albeit poorly, in his rooms there, knowing his absence would make things easier for Charlotte. And hopefully, less painful for him. He placed an ad in the newspaper for a new governess, confident Marie would suffice until one could be found. And he wrote to Dr. Webb, agreeing to take over his practice. He knew he might come into contact with the Harrises in Doddington, but since he surmised Charles would still be splitting his time between London and Fawnwell, he did not think it would be too often to be borne. He was ready to leave London and its memories behind. He would leave the Manor in the care of Thomas and his fine, understanding father.

Voices disturbed Daniel's memories, and he looked up to see a group of Doddington school children running onto the lawn nearby, kicking a ball. He hoped they would not trample his prized specimens nor his entire garden with it. He recognized most of the children and knew several by name. With the numbers of children scampering about the village these days, his practice stayed busy indeed.

He was on his knees beside a swamp milkweed plant, searching each leaf, when the ball flew over the low garden wall and landed with a puff of dust beside his patch of sciatic cress. A girl—his favorite among the village children—leapt the wall neatly and went in search of the ball. Watching her, he could not help but be reminded of Charlotte Lamb as a girl.

"Near the sciatic cress, Lucy," he said, returning to his examination of the chrysalis he had just found.

"The what?" she asked, bent low.

"The candytuft. There." He pointed toward the small bushy plants with clusters of flat white flowers.

"Voila!" The girl held up the ball triumphantly and tossed it back over the wall to her friends. But instead of clambering back over the wall herself, she came and squatted on her haunches near him.

"What are you doing?" she asked.

"Examining this chrysalis." After a moment he glanced at her. "Do you not wish to rejoin your chums?"

She shrugged. "Not especially." She knelt there beside him amid the milkweeds.

Now, close up, he thought Lucy reminded him a bit of Anne at that age, but Anne was all grown up now.

"You do know about milkweed, do you not?" he asked.

"I know Mr. Jarvis wishes you'd pull it from your garden."

"That's only because he doesn't understand how important milkweeds are. Besides a whole host of medicinal uses, monarch butterflies lay their eggs on milkweeds, which is the only plant the larva eat."

Lucy looked at him blankly, clearly not impressed.

"Monarchs are not native to England. But once in a while—every decade or so—they are sighted. Blown here by powerful winds."

"From where?"

"The Canary Islands, or even as far away as the Americas, where they are as common as black flies."

"From so far?"

"Yes. But look here—this is really amazing." He lifted another leaf, exposing a beautifully luminous jade-green pod. "I do believe this is a monarch chrysalis. Right here in my garden. If I am correct, some monarch stopped here long enough to lay her eggs on my milkweed. The caterpillars hatched, ate this bitter weed to grow—and for protection from those who would destroy them. Then hid themselves away."

"In a cocoon, right?"

"Yes, that is the common term."

"Is there really something growing in there?"

"Oh yes. It might appear lifeless or trapped, but only for a time. Inside it is secretly growing and changing until it will emerge strong enough to live in the world and ride the wind."

A magnificent black and orange butterfly alighted on a neighboring plant, and Lucy gasped in admiration.

"Is that a monarch?"

"Yes," he said, equally awed, and watched as it fluttered and rose in the air. They both looked up, following its flight. Over the girl's head, Daniel saw Charlotte, the former Miss Lamb, in the distance, walking down the lane from the direction of Fawnwell. Out paying calls, no doubt. Watching her, he said wistfully, "See how beautiful she is when she emerges."

Gaze still on the butterfly, Lucy asked, "How do you know it's a girl?"

Daniel shrugged, not shifting his focus. "She is a survivor. Strong and beautiful. A creature reborn."

Someone called out to Charlotte, and Daniel saw her pause and lift her hand in greeting. Eighteen-year-old Edmund Harris came trotting down the lane, smiling as he caught up with her.

Even from a distance, Daniel saw the way she looked at her son, her brilliant joy that they were together at last, and he thought his chest might break for the flood of gratitude and pain he felt.

At that very moment, Charlotte looked across the garden at him. Though they were far apart, they shared a knowing look filled with wistfulness and poignant understanding.

Daniel was happy for her. Truly happy. But with the happiness came the sting, the awareness of all Charlotte had sacrificed. How had she done it? Why?

He knew the why, but sometimes he still struggled to believe it.

Charlotte, too, was thinking of that long ago day when Charles Harris had proposed to her. On this day of days, how could she not?

She still remembered Mr. Harris's earnest face as he awaited her answer. She remembered the surprise she had felt upon realizing her girlhood infatuation with him had faded. She had become too aware of his weaknesses, his previous, though regretted, betrayal. Still, she considered accepting Mr. Harris for Edmund's sake, if not her own.

When Daniel did not return home all that day, Charlotte realized he already supposed she had accepted Mr. Harris. After putting Anne to bed, Charlotte sat in the sitting room, waiting for him. At nine o'clock the door opened below and she heard footsteps on the stairs. She rose and went to the sitting room door.

But it was John Taylor who ascended. "Oh. Hello, my dear."

"You worked late." She forced a smile. "Was Daniel there?"

"Yes, shut away in his office."

"Do you know if he plans to remain at the manor all night?"

"No. I am afraid I don't know." He looked as though he might say something more, but did not. His weary face rose in a brief, sympathetic smile. "Well, good night, my dear."

"Good night."

She sat back in the armchair nearest the door.

Sometime later, she awoke suddenly. Dim light shone through the sitting room windows. The clock showed half past five. She heard cautious footsteps on the stairs, and with each step her heart seemed to beat faster. She rose and walked to the door, her hand on her stomach in an attempt to ease her nerves.

Daniel, drawn and tired, stepped onto the landing, loosening his cravat. When he looked up and saw her there, he hesitated. "Oh. Forgive me. I did not expect you up this early. I need only a clean shirt and I shall be gone again." He paused. "Tell me you have not been sitting there all night?"

She touched her hair self-consciously. "When you did not return, I grew anxious."

Daniel crossed his arms over his chest, his face wooden, eyes averted. "Is there something you needed to tell me?"

"Daniel," she began gently, moving closer. "If you are avoiding me because you think I shall marry Mr. Harris, then you are mistaken. I do not wish to marry him." How could she, when she loved Daniel, as well as Anne, so deeply?

Daniel stood frozen, clearly as stunned as Mr. Harris had been at her refusal. But though disappointed, Mr. Harris had wished her every happiness and assured her they parted friends.

Daniel's brow furrowed. "But . . . Edmund . . ."

"I know." She squeezed her eyes shut, then opened them again. "But it cannot be helped. I cannot have him and you both." She smiled tentatively. "And I want you."

When Daniel did not respond, she reached out and touched a button on his waistcoat, giving it a gentle tug. He released a long, jagged breath. "Charlotte . . . are you quite certain?"

She nodded.

Shaking his head in wonder, he slowly reached out and cradled her face with his long, sensitive fingers. He leaned close, his blue-green eyes wide through his spectacles. He whispered, "I am afraid to believe it."

She looked into those eyes and urged, "*Believe.*"

His gaze melded with hers for a long moment before lowering to her mouth. His eyes drifted closed behind a curtain of golden eyelashes and he kissed her gently. Then more deeply. Then again.

They were married by special license a mere fortnight later. Daniel's father was there with them, of course, proud and happy, Mrs. Krebs at his side. Aunt and Uncle Tilney also attended, as did Thomas and Sally, who smiled and wept throughout the entire ceremony.

Though invited, the Reverend Mr. Lamb did not attend, nor did Beatrice. Charlotte felt their absence, but not too keenly. She was busy embracing all the joy and passion of her wedding day and married life.

Even so, Charlotte regretted that she was never able to reconcile with her father. The Reverend, as distant and unforgiving as ever, died shortly after she and Daniel moved to Doddington. A kindly new vicar took his place and gladly welcomed Charlotte back into the church of her childhood.

Beatrice also remained distant. Through Mr. Harris, Charlotte learned that Bea married a naval officer many years her senior and resided in London. Bea did send a brief note one Christmas, enclosing their mother's butterfly brooch. Charlotte's thank-you note and other letters remained unanswered.

Charles Harris did not remarry. His mother, Mrs. Harris, rallied and provided Edmund a healthy regimen of maternal influence and nurturing over the years. Edmund spent a good deal of time with his grandmother in Doddington, and Charlotte was able to see him at village events or on the rare occasion Daniel was called upon to treat some childhood ailment or other.

Edmund had even played with Anne now and then when they were young and seemed to enjoy the company of Daniel and Charlotte as well. If he ever wondered at the reason for their heightened interest and many kindnesses, he never voiced the question.

He remained, of course, completely unaware of his relationship to Charlotte. Hearing her son call her merely "Mrs. Taylor" was always bittersweet, but she resigned herself to living with that particular ache for the rest of her days.

Charlotte's close relationship with Anne did a great deal to soothe that ache. Daniel's daughter knew about Lizette but had recently confided that Charlotte had always been mother to her, even before she and her father had married. At Daniel's encouragement, Anne had long ago stopped using the endearment "Missy" and began calling Charlotte "Mother." Every time she heard it, she paused to savor the sound and think, *What a lovely word.*

Epilogue

When Edmund Harris found me in my office and asked permission to marry my daughter Anne, I was at first astounded, then utterly amazed. The poor lad took my expression as hesitance and looked quite miserable. For one flicker of a moment I saw Charles Harris in the young man's face and thought of disappointing him in some sort of belated revenge for the obstacles his father had placed between Charlotte and me. But I quickly banished the petty thought. Thinking instead of Charlotte, as well as Anne, I warmly assured him of my blessing.

I follow behind now as Edmund goes to find Charlotte to tell her the news himself. I want to witness this moment from afar, so as not to intrude on their reunion.

I see them in the garden, standing close in conversation. Stepping nearer, I am just in time to hear Edmund's words to Charlotte.

"May I call you Mother now?"

She looks at him, stilled. Then her face blooms into a radiant smile. "Nothing would please me more."

Anne comes out of the house, and I blink away unexpected tears, stunned all over again at what a lovely young woman our daughter has become. She walks, tall and graceful, to join Charlotte and Edmund in the garden. She laces her arm through Edmund's, and Edmund offers his other arm to Charlotte.

"He's told you our news, then, Mother?" Anne asks.

Smiling, Charlotte nods. She links her arm through Edmund's, placing her free hand on his, as if drawing as much physical contact as possible deep into her healed but forever scarred soul.

Lucy, our youngest, comes up behind me and puts her hand in mine. "Why is Mummy crying?" she asks.

"Those are happy tears."

"She is happy?"

"Yes, she is soon to be the mother of the bride." To myself I add, *and groom. . . .*

So we are to be related to the Harrises after all. Not the relationship any of us anticipated all those years ago, but the one God saw, designed even.

Charlotte Taylor is my wife, my dearest friend. And as I stand here at the edge of the garden she has helped me tend so beautifully here in Kent, watching her bright eyes flit from daughter to son, son to daughter, I see joy transform her countenance, her spirit soar to heights beyond earlier imaginings. I see her lift her face to heaven and I know she is thanking God. From where I stand I join her prayer, thankful that He has transformed all the pain and sacrifice of the past into something so beautiful. I leave my solitary post and step into the garden, into the sunlight. Thankful, especially, that I am here with Charlotte, to watch her, finally, fly free.

Author's Note

When I first began researching *Lady of Milkweed Manor,* I had never been to England. Through Web sites and old maps, I chose Doddington (Kent) as my character's birthplace—charmed by what I'd read about the place and how relatively unchanged it seemed (compared to say, London or Crawley). The old vicarage, however, had fallen out of church use by then and into private ownership. Even if I visited Doddington someday, I reasoned, I could do no more than look upon its exterior and try to imagine its rooms and what it might have been like to live there.

Two years later, when the book was finished and I learned it would be published, I decided I could finally justify my long desire to travel to England to see the places I'd written about. How serendipitous to discover that the old vicarage had just become a bed-and-breakfast! I could barely believe I would be able to stay in "Charlotte's childhood home." Nick and Claire Finley were wonderful hosts, and our stay with them was a highlight of our trip.

The people of Doddington were so kind and welcoming. Many thanks to you all—and especially to Pier Vousden, my first contact in the village, and the Rev. George Baisley, who graced us with a warm and inspiring Easter Sunday service that will long live in our memories.

Please note that while Chequers Inn, the Parish Church of Doddington (Dedicated to the Beheading of St. John the Baptist), and the old vicarage are real places, most of the other settings in the book are not. There are two fine manor houses in Doddington, but fictional Fawnwell is not among them. Nor are the book's characters based on real people.

There were several lying-in and foundling hospitals in London in the early 1800s, but Milkweed Manor is only a fictionalized composite of those real institutions. For those readers shocked by details like babies left in "the turn," and goats nursing syphilitic babies, be assured those details are all-too-real pieces of history. I found them fascinating and moving, and I hope you did as well.

In fact, I found the entire wet-nursing profession fascinating. The practice seems foreign to most of us now, but it was very common in the 1700s for infants to be sent away to be nursed, and in the 1800s for wet nurses to be brought into one's own home. Jane Austen herself was sent to live with (and be nursed by) a woman in the country for most of the first two years of her life!

While I enjoyed researching and writing about life in early 19th-century England, I no doubt made my share of errors. I am indebted to my talented editors, Rachelle Gardner and Karen Schurrer, for limiting these to as few as possible. Please forgive any remaining inaccuracies. One I am aware of is that the lambing season is actually earlier than I have it here, but I hope you will indulge the liberties I took to include it in the book's timeline. If you would like to read more about (and see photos of) the research and settings of *Lady of Milkweed Manor*, please visit my Web site at *www.julieklassen.com*.

In closing, I would like to thank my families—my husband and sons, and my Bethany House family, for all the support and encouragement that have made this book possible.

Reading Group Discussion Questions

1. After reading *Lady of Milkweed Manor,* do you view the foundling hospital "turn" as a compassionate practice, or one that was too easy on fallen ladies?

2. Was the topic of wet-nursing new to you? What surprised you about its history and practice? How would you have felt about having a stranger living in your home, nursing your infant for you?

3. Did you learn anything new about milkweeds or monarch butterflies? How did you feel about the imagery in this novel and epigraphs at the beginning of each chapter?

4. Reverend Lamb remained unforgiving, but did you notice a possible act of compassion toward Charlotte? How would it feel to grow up without a father's love and approval? How did Charlotte's relationship with Daniel's father serve to fill this hole in her life?

5. How is the historical "puerperal insanity" Daniel's wife suffered from similar to or different from modern postpartum depression? Have you or someone you know suffered from this very real condition?

6. In the early 1800s there was much competition among medical practitioners for the delivery of infants (physicians, midwives, accoucheurs). Does this same competition exist today? Is competition in this field beneficial, or not?

7. It is much more common (and economically feasible) for a single mother to raise a child on her own today than it was in the 1800s. Faced with Charlotte's decision for the future of her infant son, what do you think you would have done?

8. Which of Charlotte's various suitors throughout the novel did you like most? Would you have made the same choice Charlotte did?

9. Did the revelations about the character's lives in the final chapter and epilogue surprise you? Were you satisfied with the ending?

10. How would you describe the book's theme or message? What effect did the book have on you?

The Apothecary's Daughter

In memory of my funny, creative, hardworking father

HAROLD "BUD" THEISEN

October 1937—August 2008

Shepherd's Purse

This plant is a remarkable instance of the truth of an observation which there is too frequently room to make, namely, that Providence has made the most useful things most common and for that reason we neglect them. . . .

—*Culpeper's Complete Herbal & English Physician*

Prologue

I remember it clearly, although it was years ago now. For I remember everything.

The year was 1810. I was a girl of fifteen, standing on the arched Honeystreet Bridge—which I often did when I was not needed in Father's shop—gazing upon the brightly painted boats that floated past. There a blue barge, and there a yellow-and-white narrowboat. In reality, I was searching. Searching the face of every person on every narrowboat that passed by on the newly completed K and A Canal. There were not many women, but a few. For though men worked the canals as pilots, navigators, and merchants, entire families sometimes lived aboard—as wives and children made for less costly crews.

My mother had disappeared on one of those narrowboats two months before, or so the villagers whispered when they thought I could not hear. I suppose I hoped she would return as she left, declaring her absence a lark, an adventure, a mistake . . . anything. How many hours had I stood there? How many boats had I seen pass beneath that bridge—boats with names like the *Britannia*, *Radiant*, or *Perseverance*? Where had they come from, I always wondered, and where were they bound? What cargo did they bear—spices from the West Indies, perhaps, or tea from China? Coal from the Midlands or timber from as far away as Norway? How often I dreamt of stowing away and leaving Bedsley Priors for the bright unknown beyond.

That day, however, I watched the yellow-and-white narrowboat for another reason. A gangly boy with a cinched bag slung over his shoulder climbed unsteadily from the moored boat. My father, standing on the bank, extended his hand in greeting, just as the boy leaned over and was sick.

I winced. Not a very propitious beginning for a new apprentice. Father's shoes were likely spoilt.

I sighed. I knew I should go down to them. Father had not seen me there or he would have called for my help. He always did. With Mother gone and my only brother slow of mind, many responsibilities for both the household and shop fell to me.

But no. I would wait and meet young Mr. Baylor later, once he'd had a chance to collect himself. I would brew ginger tea for him and find an old cloth for Father's shoes. But first I wanted a few more moments on the bridge.

Several minutes later, a red-and-blue narrowboat approached from the west, from as far away as Bristol, perhaps, on its way to the Thames and then to London some eighty miles east. A man led one boat-horse along the towpath. A lone person sat in the curved bow deck. Far behind, aft of the cabin, two crewmen stood on the tiller deck.

As the boat drew nearer, I saw that the figure in the bow was a woman, head low, as if in prayer. Or perhaps she was reading. A wide bonnet concealed her face from the sun, from me. My heart leapt. Something about the woman's posture and tilt of her head struck me as familiar. *Mother loved to read.*

I leaned across the wide brick ledge, peering hard, heart beating. The boat drew closer. I saw that the man leading the horse was deeply tanned and broad-shouldered. *The man she left us for?* As he led the boat-horse along the strip of land beneath the bridge, he disappeared from view. The bow of the boat reached the shadow of the bridge, and one of the crewmen gaped up at me. I barely saw him. Instead I read the vessel's name painted in decorative lettering on the side, *The Gypsy,* and I thought, *How apt.* Still, I could not see the woman's face.

I whirled and raced to the other side of the bridge, hoping my angle would be better, that I would see her from that side as they passed.

Perhaps she does not even realize where she is, I thought, engrossed as she was in her reading. *Should I call to her?*

I only stared, afraid to be a fool before this woman, before the men labouring at the nearby timber mill. *If only I could see her face. . . .*

I squinted. Tried to focus. Dimly, I heard a voice. Someone was calling my name.

"Lilly!"

The boat passed further down the canal and she began to disappear all over again. *Look up!* I urged silently. *See me.*

The woman stood and looked up, but away from me—ahead toward the man and horse. The back of my mind registered pounding footsteps. The voice grew urgent. *Is she calling me?*

"Lilly!"

"Here I am!" I called.

The woman turned around. She held a hand to her forehead, shielding her eyes from the sun. Her brow wrinkled in perplexity as she stared back. I raised my hand and waved.

The woman slowly, tentatively, raised her own hand. Not in greeting, but in somber salute. The motion revealed her face—a stranger's face—kind and plain. In her hand, not a book but a rumple of cloth. Mending.

A hand shook my shoulder. "Lilly?"

Numbly, I tore my eyes from the fading sight of the woman and turned. My younger brother, Charlie, stood before me, clearly agitated and breathing hard. "I called you. Why did you not answer?"

"I . . . thought . . ." I blinked away the pathetic vision of what I had thought and in its place saw his wide eyes, his frightened tear-streaked face. "What is it, Charlie?"

"'Tis Mary. Oh, how she shakes! Father sent me. He needs—" He paused, eyes searching the air above me.

"He needs what?" Pulse accelerating, I grasped him by both arms, frustrated at his limited ability to focus, to remember.

He winced and bit his pronounced lower lip.

"Valerian?" I prompted. "Hyssop?"

He shook his head, still squinting in attempted concentration.

"Musk pod? Peony?"

"Peony!" he shouted. "Yes!"

I was incredulous. "But we have syrup of peony on the shelf. The jar marked *S: Poeniae.*"

"Father says 'tis empty!"

Dear Lord, no.

"Oh, Lilly! How she jerks about! Will she die?"

"No," I bit out. Running from the bridge, I yelled over my shoulder, "Tell Father to set water to boil!"

I knew of only one place to get peony root. One nearby garden where it grew. I began perspiring—not from exertion, but from fear. Fear for my oldest friend. Fear for myself. For to trespass in this garden was to break the law and risk *his* wrath. But he was far away at university, was he not? *Lord, let him be far away. . . .*

I ran.

I had always loved to run, across the vale, or up the chalk hills beyond Bedsley Priors. But this time I felt no pleasure in the exercise. I ran because I had no other choice—it would take far too long to return home and hitch up the gig. True, Mrs. Mimpurse had often admonished me not to go running about the village, that I was practically a young lady now and ought to behave as such. But I knew our kindly neighbor would not blame me for running this time. For Mary was her daughter.

I ran up the Sands Road and veered right onto the High Street, nearly colliding with a man coming out of the wheelwright's.

"Sorry, Mr. Hughes!" I called, without breaking stride.

I sprinted across the village green, around the enclosed churchyard, past the Owens' farm, and up the lane to Marlow House. Once there, I darted around the stone garden wall, ducking to keep out of sight as I ran toward the closed garden gate. Fear gripped me, but I had only to imagine Mary, writhing in pain, and I pushed the gate open, wincing at its high-pitched screech. Rushing across the path to the gardener's shed, I threw back the door and grabbed the first spade I saw. Dashing to the cluster of staked peonies—the late Lady Marlow's *prized* peonies—I swallowed, realizing I had no time to be neat or exacting.

As I lanced the soil with the spade, I heard the first cry of alarm. A man yelled "Stop!" but I shoved the spade in again, deeper now. I heard footfalls and cursing on the other side of the wall. Mr. Timms, the surly gardener, I supposed. Another few seconds and I would reach the roots. I put all of my slight weight on the spade and jerked the handle back and forth. *Come on. . . .*

Just as I pulled up the plant by its roots, a man's head and shoulders appeared over the garden wall. Not surly Mr. Timms. Worse.

"Stop where you are," the young man ordered. "Those are my mother's."

Steady . . . I tried to find my voice, to explain, but found I could not speak. I knew Roderick Marlow put peony blossoms on his mother's grave every spring. I knew he was infamously cruel.

"I need one . . ." I finally croaked out, "for a friend."

"Do not move! I am calling the constable."

I had no time to explain and no time to wait for the constable. I darted across the garden, and again I heard him curse. Over my shoulder I glimpsed him hauling himself up and over the garden wall. Heard his feet hit the ground and pebbles fly as he bolted after me, his long stride stretching no doubt twice the length of my own. I ran through the garden gate and slammed it closed with all my strength. His exclamation of pain and anger chased me across the lawn. There I glimpsed a groom leading out a tall black horse—already saddled.

No.

The gate screeched open behind me. Roderick Marlow whistled and shouted, "Bring my horse. Quick!"

Immediately, I changed course. I knew that if I followed the open road as I had come, he would overtake me seconds. I could not let that happen. Instead I headed for the wood, pushing past branches that scratched at my arms and legs. Horse hooves beat the ground behind me as I wove through the trees. I left the wood and ran across a narrow pasture—a sheep fence crossed the landscape ahead. I vaulted over it, stumbled, but ran on. Behind me horse and rider cleared the fence without pause. One chance left. Ahead of me stood the tall privet hedge around the churchyard. And beyond it, the village. My pursuer galloped closer. *Does he plan to run me down?* I wondered wildly. *For a simple plant Father will happily repay him for?* He would, I did not doubt.

I ran along the hedge, and there it was. I stopped abruptly, my back to the seemingly impenetrable wall of privet. Far too tall to jump. Too dense to push through. Roderick Marlow leapt from his horse and came striding toward me, anger in his eyes and riding crop in hand. I swallowed, suddenly grateful that my long frock covered the bottom reaches of the hedge behind me. *Wait until he is a little further from his horse. One second more. . . .*

Suddenly I turned and dove into a hole in the privet, the tunnel barely large enough for a child to wriggle through. Dug, I knew, by the vicar's hound. Terror gripped my heart as I felt Roderick's hand trying to grip *me*. Fingers clawed at my skirt hems as I scrambled through the hedge and stumbled to my feet on the other side. He swore in frustration, and I knew he was not giving up. *If only the horse would bolt.* But I doubted such a well-trained beast would dare. At least it might take a second or two for him to regain his mount. I dashed across the churchyard and out its front gate, and ran down the High Street. I saw the sign for my father's shop ahead, just as I again heard pounding hooves behind. *If I can just make it inside and deliver the root, he can do what he likes with me then. Just let me reach Mary in time.*

I ran through the door and gave it a shove. But Roderick Marlow caught it and pushed in behind me, the shop bell jingling crazily. He grabbed my arm before I could hand the plant to my startled father.

Roderick raised the crop in his hand.

"Roderick Rupert Marlow!" Maude Mimpurse commanded. "Put that down and unhand the girl. Lillian Grace Haswell. What have I told you about running through town like a stray?"

Roderick froze, and I was stunned to see him lower his arm in mute submission. *That's right*, I remembered to my immense relief. Our robust, dark-haired neighbor had once worked as the Marlows' nurserymaid. Her powers of persuasion were legendary.

"She is a vandal and a thief!" the furious Marlow shouted. "She trespassed upon our garden."

"I sent her for peony root, young sir," Father explained, concern straining his features. "It was an emergency. Miss Mary has had her worse case of falling sickness yet."

The rest of the room came into focus then. I spun about and, through the surgery door, saw my dear friend lying still on the cot. Deathly still.

"Am I too late? Is she . . . ?"

"The fit has finally passed," Father said. "I believe the valerian took effect after all."

"She's fallen asleep, poor lamb," Mrs. Mimpurse said, her voice returning to its customary softness. "So exhausted was she."

I held up the peony—stalk, root, and all. "Then . . . I stole this for nothing?"

"Stole? Good gracious." Mrs. Mimpurse tutted. "We are all neighbors, are we not?"

"I will reimburse your family, young sir," Father offered, reaching up to lay his hand on the young man's shoulder. "We still need to distill a batch of syrup in any case. Or we can endeavor to replant the peony, if you prefer."

Roderick Marlow shook off Father's hand. "No. Just stay away from our gardens." He aimed his blazing glare in my direction and a chill ran through my body. "And away from me."

I would obey that command for almost three years.

Not nearly long enough.

Part I

The apothecary's house should [have an] inner chamber, wherein he may prudently observe through some lattice window whether his apprentices spend their time idly or faithfully. . . .

—C. J. S. Thompson,
Mystery and Art of the Apothecary

Thou art gone from my gaze like a beautiful dream,
And I seek thee in vain by the meadow and stream.

—George Linley, composer

1

LILY OF THE VALLEY
Strengthens the brain, recruits a weak memory,
and makes it strong again.

—Culpeper's Complete Herbal

Knowing she faced a long day indoors, Lilly Haswell arose early to take in the crisp, fragrant air of a Wiltshire autumn morning. With a quiet greeting to Mrs. Fowler, already busy at the stove, Lilly left by the rear garden door and walked sedately out of the village. As soon as she rounded the corner of the vicarage, however, she picked up her pace. When she reached the hill just beyond Bedsley Priors, she began a loping climb, tripping over turf grass from time to time, relishing the burning in her legs and lungs. She did not stop until she crested modest Grey's Hill. As she leaned over to catch her breath, her long russet brown hair fell around her shoulders. She'd not taken the time to pin it up properly, though she knew she should, especially now that she was eighteen years old.

She straightened, taking in the view across Pewsey Vale, with its rolling chalklands, scant trees, and in the distance, the newly carved white horse on the ridge between Milk Hill and Walker's. She had heard that the rector of Alton Barnes often took his telescope up to Adam's Grave, the ancient mound atop Walker's Hill, and with it could see as far as the Salisbury Cathedral. Lilly wished she might climb that hill for herself some Sunday after services when she had the entire afternoon to herself. She would like to see the Salisbury spire. She would have given just about anything to see such places in person—and far more besides. She wondered what sights and delights her mother was experiencing, wherever she was, now these three years gone.

Lilly forced her gaze down to the village at the foot of the hill, with its Saxon churchyard, sleepy streets, and rectangular village green dotted with grazing sheep. How peaceful Bedsley Priors looked. How small and insignificant.

When her mother had first disappeared, Lilly had felt a roiling tincture of emotions—bewilderment, grief, guilt—certain her leaving was due to something Lilly had said or done. But in her secret heart, she had also felt a shameful thrill. Something had changed. Change begot change, she knew, and she longed for more. Though Lilly still prayed fervently for her mother's return, somehow she knew that had her mother not left, her life would go on as it always had. She would ever be trapped, working in an inconsequential shop in an inconsequential village. And Lilly was certain that would never be enough.

Sighing now, Lilly began the jarring downhill slog home. Back to the endless duties of an apothecary's daughter.

Again rounding the vicarage, she slowed to a stroll, passing the butcher's, the chandler's, and the coffeehouse. Inside, Mary looked at her through the window and motioned for her to wait. Lilly paused as her friend hurried to the door. Her friend who had thankfully not had a fit in nearly a year.

"Morning, Lill." Mary thrust a warm, paper-wrapped bundle into her hand. "I insist. You need sustenance after your long . . . *mmm*, walk." Mary's grin was all too knowing, and her pale blue eyes gleamed beneath faint strawberry brows.

Lilly smiled and accepted the scone. "Thank you. Currant?"

"What else? Now, go on. I shall see you later."

She gave Mary a mock bow and continued across the mews to her father's shop. She noticed the sign bearing the apothecary's rose and *Charles Haswell, Apothecary* was looking worn, and the white paint of the many-paned bowed window was beginning to flake. She would have to suggest Father hire someone to repaint it.

For a few moments she stood there, peering through the shopwindow as a customer might, while she ate her scone.

Upon the inside ledge of the bowed window stood her grandfather's tall, ornate apothecary's jar, bearing the Haswell coat of arms. Around it were displayed colorful carboys and ready-made remedies with gilded labels: *Royal English Drops, Gaskoin's Powder, True Venice Treacle*, and many more.

Three walls of the shop were lined with shelves of blue-and-cream Lambeth delftware pottery. Upon each was inscribed its contents in Latin: *C: ABSINTHII*—conserve of wormwood, useful for dropsy. *O: VULPIN*—oil of fox, distilled in spring water, good for chest complaints.

And below these shelves were rows of knobbed drawers for small simples, such as leaves, seeds, and roots.

The front counter was clear for pressing tablets, and rolling and cutting pills. The rear counter held the tools of the trade. Open for reference were several books, such as Lewis's *New Dispensatory*, and Culpeper's *Complete Herbal*. Mortars and pestles of various sizes stood at the ready, as did scales, syrup jars, scarificators and bowls for bleeding, and leeches in their jar of water, always kept hungry.

To the left of the rear counter was the door to the laboratory-kitchen, where her father heated and distilled physic through snaking copper pipes. To the right was the door to her father's surgery, the private office where he consulted with or bled patients.

Already, the shop was busy and full of life. Father had his hand on Arthur Owen's shoulder, talking to the old pig farmer in gentle admonition. Her brother, Charlie, three years her junior, dusted the shelves. Her father's seventeen-year-old apprentice, Francis Baylor, stood behind the front counter, busy with mortar and pestle. She was pleased to see both young men engaged in such industrious fashion.

She pushed open the shop door, barely hearing the familiar bell. The usual rush of voices and aromas greeted her. Treasures from distant lands and nearby meadows, dried, crushed, and distilled, filled the air with powerful, exotic appeal. It was only during these moments, coming in from the windy hills, that she could really smell their complex and ever-changing fragrance.

From the beams that striped the ceiling, strings of poppy heads, chamomile, sage, and mint hung in bunches to dry. An ancient alligator hung among them in macabre pose, teeth bared. Several missing teeth rendered him less menacing.

Once inside, Lilly realized the probable cause of the apprentice's unusual dedication. He was serving the flirtatious Dorothea Robbins, whose father owned the timber mill and the new barge yard in the neighboring hamlet of Honeystreet.

"It is not for me, of course," Miss Robbins was saying. "For I am perfectly well."

Francis Baylor shook his head in near wonder. "As I plainly see."

The girl giggled and Lilly rolled her eyes. Francis glanced up and, seeing her expression, had the decency to flush. "If you will excuse me one moment, Miss Robbins?"

"Of course."

The gangly young man walked around the counter and paused beside Lilly. Quietly, he said, "You might wish to change your frock, Miss Lilly. You would not want Mrs. Mimpurse to catch you with muddy hems."

She looked down. "Oh! I did not realize . . ."

But a glance told her pretty Dorothea Robbins *had* realized. The honey-haired girl in a charming bonnet was regarding Lilly's frock with a condescending smile.

The sound of shattering pottery brought Lilly around. Charlie stood frozen, feather duster in hand.

"Suds!" He sank to his haunches and began picking up the sharp pieces of a broken ointment jar. "Not again . . ."

Lilly hurried to his side. "It's all right, Charlie. Only an accident. I shall help you clean this up. Mind your fingers."

Dorothea Robbins strolled past them, a small parcel in gloved hand and an aloof smile on her pretty lips. Francis nearly tripped over them in his hurry to open the door for her.

Shaking her head in disgust, Lilly carried the broken pottery through the rear door into the laboratory-kitchen, where Mrs. Fowler was washing up the breakfast dishes. She thought to dash upstairs to change her frock and pin up her hair, but she had barely dumped the pieces and wiped her hands when she heard the shop bell jingle, announcing the arrival of another customer.

"Good day, Mrs. Kilgrove," she heard Francis call. "And welcome to Haswell's."

"You need not behave as though you own the place, young man," the old matron reprimanded. Mrs. Kilgrove was known for her sharp tongue, which she seemed to wield on everyone save Charlie.

"Of course not, ma'am. I am only grateful to be apprenticed to such a respected apothecary. Now, how may I help you?"

"You? I'd not tell *you* my troubles for all the prince's ponies. Nor give you leave to sell me a single lozenge. Where is Miss Haswell?"

Lilly sighed. So much for changing her frock.

That afternoon, while Francis used the cork borer to fashion bottle stoppers, Lilly was bored indeed. She cleaned the front counter, all the while daydreaming about some gentleman traveler—wounded, ideally—falling into the shop, and in love with her. She had just reached the part where he begged her to run away with him when her cloth reached the bear-shaped pottery jar on the counter's far end. She paused, fanciful images fading. She wondered once more why her father insisted on stocking the useless remedy.

"Have we sold any bear grease lately?" she idly asked.

Francis paused in his work. "Yes, to several gentlemen yesterday."

"Would you try it, had you the need?"

He grimaced. "Why would I? I have a full head of hair."

A bit too full, Lilly thought, taking in his brown, wavy mop of hair.

Her father came in and stood, arms crossed, before his apprentice. "Mr. Baylor," he demanded sternly, "did I not ask you to compound another batch of Pierquin's Diuretic?"

Lilly saw the young man blanch.

"Right. Sorry, sir."

"You *do* recall the instructions I gave you only last week?"

Lilly held her breath.

"Of course I remember, sir. It was, after all, only last week." He stole a glance at Lilly, the plea for help evident in his wide eyes.

Stepping away from the counter with the cleaning cloth, Lilly said with as much nonchalance as she could muster, "That one is simple at least, as it has only three ingredients."

"Three, right," Francis parroted. "Very simple."

Lilly felt her father's gaze on the back of her head as she began polishing the shopwindow. "I cannot bear to compound Pierquin's," she continued, keeping her eyes focused upon her task. "It is"—she wiggled her fingers dramatically, hoping Francis was watching—"a *thousand* times worse than any other."

Behind her, Francis caught on. "Which of course it would be, with all those . . . millipedes."

"Exactly," she replied casually. "Which is why I am so relieved Father asked *you* to prepare it."

Glancing over her shoulder and seeing that her father was again facing Francis at the counter, his back to her, she breathed on the window glass and with her finger wrote *berry*. "I have not had to do so since *June*." She then held up her little finger, miming the act of drinking daintily.

After watching her surreptitiously, Francis announced, "Pierquin's Diuretic: macerated millipedes and juniper berries boiled in tea."

"In white *wine*, Mr. Baylor," Charles Haswell said between clenched teeth. "Tea, indeed. You had better study harder, young man, if you want to excel as my pupil." He threw Lilly a flinty look of two parts irritation to one part paternal pride. "*Professor Lilly* will not always be on hand to rescue you."

"Right. Sorry, sir."

Shaking his head, her father left them, taking the day's post back to the surgery to do a bit of reading and, she guessed, a bit of napping.

Francis looked at Lilly, shoulders drooping. "How do you do it? I must read and reread things ten times over before I remember them. It all comes so easily to you."

She shrugged. "It is in my blood, I suppose."

"It is more than that. Is there nothing you cannot remember?"

She strolled over to the old globe on its stand in the corner. Foregoing the cloth, she ran her fingers over its surface. "Probably a great many things."

"I do not believe it. Quick—Godfrey's Cordial."

"Francis. That one is easy. You know it is so popular we must prepare it every week—sassafras, aniseed, caraway, opium, sugar . . ."

"Stoughton's Bitters?"

She traced her finger over the West Indies. "Gentian root, orange peel, cochineal powder . . ."

"On what page in Culpeper's *Herbal* would you find, say, *saffron*?"

"I don't know. . . ." She glanced up. "Maybe, one hundred forty-four?"

"And what is listed after *saffron*?"

"Do you not wish to check my answer?"

He shook his head, waiting.

She sighed. "Well, *meadow saffron*, of course, then *scurvy-grass* in all its varieties, *self-heal, sage, saltwort* . . . It is in alphabetical order for the most part after all."

He stared at her, shaking his head. "You should be the apprentice. Not I."

Walking back to the counter, she said, "You know girls cannot be apothecaries. I can only assist."

"Lucky for me, or I'd be out of a post."

She tossed the dustcloth onto the rear counter. "Never fear. Even if I could, I should not want to work here all my life."

He looked nearly stricken. "But, Lilly, with your abilities—"

She cut him off. "You heard Father—even he realizes I shall not always be here to help."

Much to Lilly's relief, the shop bell rang, putting an end to the uncomfortable conversation.

When nearly an hour had passed and her father had still not come out from his surgery, Lilly grew concerned. His afternoon naps never lasted for more than half an hour.

She knocked softly on the surgery door. There was no answer. She pushed the door open anyway. "Father?"

Her father sat at his desk, head in his hands.

"Father, what is it? Are you all right?"

"No. I don't believe I am."

Alarmed, Lilly stepped inside the small room, closing the door behind her. "What has happened?"

He lifted his head. "I've had a letter."

Lilly regarded the fine piece of stationery upon his desk. "So I see." She swallowed. "From . . . Mother?"

The look he gave her held equal measures of surprise, incredulity, and pain. "No."

She bit her lip and waited.

He sighed. "It is from Mr. Jonathan and Ruth Elliott."

"Elliott?" None of their acquaintances bore that name.

"Your aunt and uncle Elliott. Your mother's brother."

She almost blurted, *Have they seen her?* but thought the better of it. She did not want to conjure that look upon her father's face again.

Instead she said, "I do not remember an aunt and uncle Elliott."

"How could you? You have never laid eyes on them. But you shall. They are coming all the way from London to pay a call this Friday—whether I like it or not."

"Why should you not like it? They are family, are they not?"

He looked away, toward the surgery window. "I suppose that depends upon your definition of the term."

"But you have met them?"

"Yes, many years ago." He frowned. "It was not a happy occasion."

"Do they know . . . ?" There was no need to spell out the painful subject her father habitually avoided.

"Yes. I wrote to them some time afterward."

"What do you think they want?"

Her father's features were pinched. "I shudder to think."

Seeing his distress, she laid a reassuring hand on his shoulder. "Perhaps they merely wish to reestablish bonds with us."

He looked up at her, his blue eyes glinting in the late afternoon sun slanting through the window. "I admire your hopeful outlook, my dear. But I would caution you against it. Mark my words, Lilly. We will rue this visit for years to come."

2

> When [Jane's brother] Edward was 16, the Knights adopted him as their heir. It was not uncommon for wealthy relatives to take in a child from a less fortunate branch of the family.
>
> —Jane Austen Society of North America

Lilly watched from an upstairs window as a post chaise pulled by two matched bays came to a halt before the shop. When the postillion clambered down from his mount and opened the carriage door, a tall, portly man in hat and greatcoat stepped out. He then turned and assisted a dainty woman in fur-trimmed cloak and hat. Lilly hurried down the stairs and peeked through the door of the laboratory-kitchen as Father opened the shop door.

"Elliott. Ruth," he said. "Welcome."

The man took her father's measure. "Haswell. You are looking fit, I must say."

"Benefit of the profession, I suppose. Do come in." He took their coats and gestured them inside.

Taking in her surroundings, Ruth Elliott asked tentatively, "You live here, in your shop?"

"Why, yes—behind and above it."

"Is that common with men of your trade?" she asked.

"Yes. I believe it is common with men of most professions. Now, please, come into the sitting room."

Taking her cue, Lilly hurried to precede them up the stairs. Straightening her mother's miniature portrait on the end table, she stood nervously behind the settee as her father escorted their guests inside.

"Here we are. Do be seated—anywhere you like. Oh, there you are, my dear. May I introduce my daughter, Lilly. Lilly, this is your aunt and uncle Elliott."

Lilly curtsied. "How do you do. I am pleased to meet you both."

"Lilly?" Ruth Elliott repeated skeptically, arranging herself in an armchair.

"Yes," Lilly said. "Short for Lillian."

"Ah, yes, after Mother," Jonathan Elliott said, taking a seat. "That is, your grandmother."

Lilly smiled. She had not known. "But almost nobody calls me that."

"Lillian, a young lady ought to use her given name," her aunt said. "You are too old for pet names, do you not think?"

Lilly felt her smile waver. "Well, you must be tired and hungry from your journey. Will you have tea?" She gestured toward the tea service and tray of assorted tarts, scones, and biscuits.

"You employ a cook, then?" Aunt Elliott asked.

Lilly nodded. "Mrs. Fowler cooks and cleans, but these were provided by a kindly neighbor. An old friend of Mother's, actually. Here, let me pour the tea." Lilly began to serve, hoping to put into practice all that her mother had taught her long ago. She had even rehearsed yesterday, heeding Mrs. Mimpurse's gentle admonitions, but still her hands shook now.

She felt her aunt's gaze upon her every move as she handed her the first cup.

"And where is the boy?" Uncle Elliott asked. "A young Charles, I believe, you mentioned in your letter?"

"Yes," her father answered, accepting a cup from Lilly. "I expect him any moment."

"And young Charles is what age now?" Jonathan Elliott asked. "Thirteen? Fourteen?"

When Father hesitated, Lilly supplied, "Fifteen."

"Fifteen," Uncle Elliott repeated. "And do you plan for him to take over your shop one day?"

Charles Haswell studied his teacup. "I had hoped, but now I am not certain."

The Elliotts glanced at one another, and Jonathan Elliott smiled. "Well, that is good to hear."

Her father frowned. "Why on earth would it be?"

"Well, Haswell. We need to meet the boy first, of course, see how we three get on, but I can say that it has occurred to Mrs. Elliott and myself that it might be time to adopt an heir. Providence has not blessed us with a child of our own, and I at least"—he smiled at his wife—"am getting up in years. One must think of the future."

Lilly nearly spilled her tea. "But Charlie has a family," she said quickly. "Us."

"Of course he has, my dear," Aunt Elliott soothed. "And that would not change."

"It is done, you know," Uncle Elliott said. "Legal adoption for inheritance purposes. Quite common."

Lilly murmured, "I had not realized."

"It is not as if we would take him from you completely," Aunt Elliott assured her, then shifted her gaze to her brother-in-law. "Between us, we could determine a visiting arrangement that suits us all. Assuming you and young Charles are amenable, of course."

"Have you no other close relatives?" Lilly asked, feeling panic begin to rise.

Uncle Elliott shifted uncomfortably on the saggy settee. "I do have one young cousin who might suit—if he were not such a despicable character. But a nephew would be my first choice. And, well, Charles is my sister's son." He beamed at them both, as if this would dissolve their disbelief and despair.

As Lilly looked at the smiling face of Jonathan Elliott, she thought how odd it was that this portly man of middle years was her own mother's brother. He appeared years older, for Rosamond Haswell had always been so youthful, slender and pretty. Beyond the man's dark hair and brown eyes, she could find no resemblance to the portrait—nor her memory—of her mother.

The thought of Charlie leaving them, visits home not withstanding, filled Lilly with dread. Her little brother living in London without their father? Without Mary or Mrs. Mimpurse? Without *her*?

She looked to her father for help, expecting at any moment for him to refuse the Elliotts in no uncertain terms. Hoping he would. But then another line of thought presented itself. Might this be the opportunity she had prayed about for Charlie? With her aunt and uncle's resources, could they not find a specially equipped school, although Father insisted none existed for boys like Charlie? Or even a learned tutor who might help Charlie grasp new ideas, adapt to his limitations, and, well . . . grow up?

Lilly stood. "Father, might you help me downstairs a moment?"

"Hmm? Oh, of course." He rose. "Excuse us a moment."

He followed her down to the laboratory-kitchen.

"I know what you are thinking, Lilly," he began, speaking in low tones.

"Do you? I am thinking this might be a wonderful opportunity for Charlie."

He looked at her askance.

"Yes, I know," she continued. "My first instinct was to refuse them and keep dear Charlie here with us. But that would be selfish, would it not? Should we not give Charlie every opportunity to learn, to improve himself? Mr. Marsh did little for him. You and I try, but in London there might be new schools, new tutors, or methods that will take decades to reach us here in Bedsley Priors. Please do not reject their offer for the sake of revenge."

He snorted. "Another man might seek revenge for his wife being cut off from her family simply for marrying him." His voice began to rise. "Followed by nearly twenty years of cold silence, only to have them show up now and ask for one of his most treasured—" He broke off, ran a hand through his thinning reddish-brown hair, and forced his voice back down to a whisper. "But if I truly thought they would do Charlie good . . ."

"Father, I know you will worry, but—"

He grasped her arms. "Lilly. I do not worry about Charlie. Not in the way you mean. I do not worry about him leaving us, for he never shall. Rather, I worry about his hopes being raised and his feelings crushed."

"But—"

"Lilly. The Elliotts will never adopt him as heir. Not once they realize—"

"Hallo, Father!" Charlie bounded through the garden door, dirt on his sleeves and a smile on his face. "Mrs. M. said I was to hurry home. I was at Mr. Fowler's. He has a litter of puppies. Are 'em very nice?"

Lilly bit her lip and smiled gently at her brother. "They are very nice. Now do wash your face and hands and put on a clean shirt. All right?"

Her father moved to the door. "Then join us in the sitting room."

"And Charlie?" Lilly added. "Do your best to remain calm and speak slowly. Let them see how sweet and polite young Charles Haswell is."

Her brother wrinkled up his face. "Who's he?"

"Here we are." Lilly brought in another plate of tarts and currant scones, though no one had touched the first. "May I pour more tea for anyone?"

"None for me." Aunt Elliott touched a linen cloth to her thin lips.

Uncle Elliott held out his cup. "Thank you. I know it must be quite a shock—Rosamond's family showing up after all this time. If it is any consolation, we both regret having remained distant so long."

Father, taking his seat again, nodded. "I will say I was surprised to receive your letter, especially when I had written to let you know that Rosamond was . . . no longer with us."

"Yes. . . ." Uncle Elliott looked down at his hands, and his wife studied her own as well, leaving Lilly to wonder if they knew something about her mother or had been in contact with her.

Father cleared his throat. "I believe your intentions toward Charlie are sincere and honorable, but I must tell you, I do not think an arrangement likely."

"But why?" Aunt Elliott raised her eyes, clearly stunned. "Surely you realize what you are denying your son?"

"I deny him nothing. You see, my son is the dearest, sweetest-natured boy you will likely ever meet, but—"

The sitting room door banged open and Charlie strode in, looking quite presentable in a clean white shirt tucked into his breeches and a wide smile on his boyish, handsome face. He had even combed his coppery-blond hair.

Her father rose. "And this is my son, Charlie. Charlie, say hello to your aunt and uncle Elliott."

Charlie stuck out his hand toward Aunt Elliott. She smiled, but eyed it skeptically, finally touching it with gloved fingers.

"Hallo," Charlie said. "I've never had an aunt and uncle before. Our friend Mary has two of each, if you can believe it."

The Elliotts smiled and exchanged pleased glances.

"So, young Charles," Mr. Elliott began, "your father has been telling us that you are fifteen years old."

"'At's right. But all the lads say I look younger—act it too." Charlie laughed as though he'd made a fine joke.

"Well, you have a good many years ahead of you to grow up. Have you given any thought to what you will take up?"

Charlie tilted his head. "Take up?"

"Yes, for your profession. The law, for example, or the church?"

"Oh, no. I can barely fink what I am to do tomorrow, or remember what I did yesterday. But Lilly remembers everyfing." He turned to her. "Don't you, Lilly?"

She began to demur. "Well . . ."

"'Tis true," Charlie insisted. "Francis—he's Father's apprentice—tested her, like. Picked a number from one of Father's books and she remembered everyfing on the page!"

"Not everything, Charlie, I am sure," Lilly said, embarrassed. "Aunt and

Uncle Elliott have not come all this way to hear fibble-fable about me. Now, do tell them about your work in the physic garden."

He shrugged. "I just do what Father says I ought."

"But our garden has never looked as fine as it did this year." She looked at the Elliotts. "If it were not so late in the season, I would show you." She squeezed her brother's shoulder. "You have a way with plants, Charlie. Do not be modest."

Before he could respond, Mrs. Elliott asked, "Are you in school, Charles?"

"I was. But I guess I learnt all Mr. Marsh knows, for he said 'ere was nofing more he could do wi' me."

"Yes, well, Charlie," Father said kindly, "some lads are gifted at book learning and others at working with their hands. That is where you excel, my boy. I show you how to do something in the garden or in the laboratory, and you work harder at it than any lad I know."

Charlie smiled at his father's praise, and Lilly felt tears prick her eyes. Her father did not praise him often enough. Nor did she.

Aunt and Uncle Elliott did not smile, however. They looked at each other, then at her father with question—and disappointment—in their expressions.

Charles Haswell took a deep breath. "Charlie, why don't you run over and thank Mrs. Mimpurse for her delightful sweets?"

Charlie eagerly stood. "I had better eat one first if I am to tell her how good 'em are!"

"Of course. Take the whole tray."

"Careful!" Lilly rose quickly and helped Charlie pick up one of the trays, then opened the door for him. When he was gone, she closed the door behind him, shutting in the awkward tension in the small room.

From the stairwell came the sound of a crash—metal tray on plank floor. Followed by a muffled call of, "I'm all right!"

When the din faded, Jonathan Elliott cleared his throat. "I am afraid we have been rather hasty. We did not realize . . ."

"Of course you did not," Father interrupted. "How could you?"

When both Elliotts sheepishly lowered their heads, Father hastened to add, "I meant only that, when I wrote, I simply mentioned that Rosamond had left me with . . . that is, left behind . . ." He sighed in frustration. "That she *had* two children—a daughter and a son. I never thought to mention Charlie's . . . limitations. Never dreamed you'd need know." He leaned his elbows on his knees. "You see, Rosamond suffered an extremely difficult lying-in with Charlie. He was far too long in reaching the air he desperately needed. I believe it was this, and no innate defect, that caused his delayed mental development."

"But he isn't, well, an imbecile or anything," Lilly hurried to explain. "Just a bit slow, I suppose you would say. In time, he might very well catch up."

"Lilly, we do not know that," Father admonished. "It would be unfair to offer that hope to others, however dearly we cling to it ourselves."

"But with education, and special tutoring . . ." Lilly looked imploringly at the Elliotts. "I am certain in London, there must be many opportunities for a boy like Charlie."

"I doubt that is the case," Uncle Elliott said, his expression sober. "And even if it were, I must be honest and tell you that I do not feel I can name your son as my heir. While he would no doubt reap some benefit, I have my own estate to think of. I must choose someone who can manage it well."

It was Lilly's turn to hang her head.

"My dear." Her aunt's voice was surprisingly warm. "May I say your concern for your brother is most admirable and touches me deeply. A lesser girl might have begrudged her sibling such an opportunity."

Looking up, Lilly slowly shook her head. "Never."

"I promise you this," Ruth Elliott said. "If we hear of any special school or teacher for boys of Charlie's, well, special qualities, I shall write you directly."

"Thank you."

Her aunt's gaze lingered. "Do not take offense, my dear, but I cannot help but wish that *you* were a boy."

They shared a rueful smile.

"Now, are you really as bright as your brother boasts?"

3

> In Bartholomew Lane, the drink called coffee—which closes the orifice of the stomach, fortifies the heat within, and maketh the heart lightsom . . . is to be sold both in the morning and at three in the afternoon.
>
> —*London Public Advertiser,* 1657

In the coffeehouse the next morning, Lilly sat on her usual stool in the kitchen. It had been her place for as long as she could remember, which was long indeed. From the adjacent scullery came the rhythmic *rustle, rustle, rustle* of scrubbing and an occasional tinny clang as the kitchen girl, Jane, went about her work. Over this mild clatter, Lilly recounted the Elliotts' visit to her friend

Mary, who stood at the worktable, cutting ginger biscuits. Paying no heed, Charlie hunched at the little table in the corner, picking out the caraway seeds from a piece of seedcake. He counted each seed and laid it neatly on a plate beside the others.

"If you don't like it, Charlie, you needn't eat it," Mary said. Her voice and round, pale blue eyes emanated irritation and affection both.

"Ninety-seven seeds, Mary. 'At's fine, fine."

With the back of her hand, Mary pushed a strand of dull strawberry hair from her milky round face. "You know I don't like to see my good baking wasted. At least feed it to the birds, all right?"

Charlie nodded. "Birds likes seeds." He put on his coat, then carried the plate out the door to the kitchen garden.

"Mind you bring back the plate," Mary called after him.

Though it was an autumn day, it was always warm in the kitchen, so the window stood ajar. Lilly realized her brother had settled himself on a bench beneath it, for through it, they heard him begin counting all over again. "One, two, tree . . ."

Lilly shook her head, chagrined.

Mary said quietly, "Don't fret about Charlie. Probably find a post in a counting house one day and end up richer than the Marlows."

From the open window, Lilly heard quick footsteps on the stone garden path. A female voice, in tense, pinched tones said, "Charlie Haswell, you are a sneak and a spy."

Lilly's mouth fell open and she turned toward the door. But Mary placed a staying hand on her shoulder and shook her head, finger to her lips.

"If you tell anybody what you saw—"

"I saw nofing," Charlie said. "I was behind a tree."

"Heard then. Or thought you heard." The girl attempted to whisper, but in her agitation her voice rose. Lilly recognized it as Dorothea Robbins's voice. "I will have you know I did not allow him to so much as kiss my glove. Do you understand?"

"Yes, miss."

"And you must promise that you won't say anything. That you will not even mention my name."

"All right, miss."

Frustration heightened her pitch. "What were you doing in the wood anyway?"

"Nofing. Just sittin' and countin'."

"Counting? Counting what?"

Lilly and Mary exchanged knowing looks.

"Red leaves on the trees."

"What on earth for?"

"Just like to is all."

Miss Robbins sounded incredulous. "But it's not natural."

"Oh yes, miss. Very natural, trees are. 'Tis why I likes 'em."

The footsteps marched away as they had come. When the sound faded, Mary stepped to the door and held it open.

"Everything all right, Charlie?"

Lilly could hear the hesitation in his voice. "Uh . . . yes, Mary."

"Did you get the birds fed?"

"Oh . . . yes."

Lilly rose and joined Mary at the door. She saw Charlie on his feet, dusting seedcake crumbs from his breeches.

"Well, good-bye," he said and lurched away in his awkward gait.

"Charlie?" Lilly called after him.

He turned and looked at her, clearly troubled.

Lilly bit her lip. "Nothing. I shall see you later."

The two young women returned to their places at the worktable.

Lilly began picking at her own piece of seedcake. "The man Miss Robbins was with in the wood. I suppose it was Francis."

Mary kept her eyes on the biscuits as she placed them on the pan. "Do you? I shouldn't think so."

"You would if you saw them flirting with one another in the shop."

Mary shrugged. "It is her nature to flirt, I think. Perhaps after this she'll be more circumspect."

"I doubt it," Lilly said, then recalled that Francis had taken ill the previous day. Miss Robbins had not mentioned when the tête-à-tête had occurred, but likely quite recently. So perhaps it had not been Francis after all. . . .

"You aren't going to ask Charlie about it, are you?" Mary asked.

Lilly hesitated.

"Lill, don't. You wouldn't want him to break a promise to a lady—no matter if the lady is Dorothea Robbins."

"I suppose you are right. Must you always be right, Mary?"

Mary put a dough-crusted hand to her brow in mock melodrama. "It is a curse I must bear up under somehow." She eyed Lilly's plate. "Now, are you going to eat my cake or not?"

That afternoon, diminutive Jack Dubin stepped into the shop, a wax-sealed missive in his hand.

"Letter by special messenger—that's me—for one Miss Lillian Haswell. You wouldn't know anybody by that name, now, would ya?"

Cheeky boy. Stepping around the counter, Lilly swiped the letter from him. "You know very well who I am, Jack." She tossed him a coin. "Here is a little something for your trouble."

He looked at the coin in his palm. "A very little!"

"Well, try delivering with less wit next time."

Lilly retreated through the back door and took her time slitting open the red wax seal. It was the first time she had ever received a letter by messenger. Or any letter, addressed specifically and solely to her. How she had once longed for a letter from her mother. But none had ever come.

She opened it and saw it was from Aunt and Uncle Elliott, written from their lodgings across the canal in Honeystreet, just a short stroll away.

My dear niece,

We very much enjoyed meeting you yesterday, though the circumstances were no doubt trying for you all. Would you please do us the honor of dining with us this evening here at The George at seven? We would very much like to deepen our acquaintance with you before we return to London.

Sincerely,
Mr. and Mrs. Jonathan Elliott

Still holding the letter, she wandered back into the shop, and was surprised to see Jack Dubin still there.

"What's it to be, love?" he asked. "I'm to take back your reply."

"Oh." She hesitated. Should she refuse out of loyalty to her rejected brother? For the sake of her long-spurned father and mother? After all, these people were strangers to her—strangers by choice.

But by choice no longer.

"Tell them I accept."

Lilly had eaten at The George before, though not recently. During the first few months after her mother's disappearance, her father, dazed and struggling to care for his children as well as his shop, had taken them to the then-new establishment whenever Mrs. Fowler had a day off. Finally he and Lilly, under the tutelage of Mrs. Mimpurse, had learned to cook simple meals for themselves.

During her mother's absence, the kitchen had slowly transformed into a laboratory-kitchen, as the distillation and compounding apparatus slowly made their way into the room Mother had doggedly declared off limits before.

Now, despite Mrs. Fowler's protests, stove, cupboards, and table saw double duty in food and medicinal preparation. Lilly often wondered how long it would be until they accidentally sat down to a meal of arsenic or digitalis while their patients languished with cure-alls of cod and leek soup.

Mary, who had a knack for such things, had come over earlier to dress Lilly's hair, coiling and pinning her long plait atop her head, curls at her temples. Now donning her best gown for the occasion—the printed muslin with lace tips, normally reserved for churchgoing—Lilly descended the stairs at a quarter before the hour, cloak over her arm.

The door of Francis's bedchamber was open and she looked in on the miserable young man, who had lain abed ill since yesterday. Lying propped on his pillows, his brown eyes widened and brows rose when he saw her. "Where are you off to?"

"Supper with my aunt and uncle. At The George."

"Oh. Right." Still, he stared at her.

Stepping into the pantry that had long served as the apprentice's bedchamber, Lilly sat on the edge of the narrow bed and removed the cloth from his forehead. "How are you feeling?"

"Two parts dizzy and a drachm of weak."

She touched his forehead. "Your fever has abated somewhat."

She rose to her feet and dipped the cloth in a basin of water on the room's single chest of drawers. "Your color is better also. I believe Father is right—the patient will live."

"Is he relieved or disappointed at that prognosis?"

"Relieved, of course." She added with a grin, "Otherwise he should be obliged to return your apprenticeship fee."

He did not grin back. "I thought he might be disappointed, considering I am not the cleverest apprentice he has ever had."

"Shh. You improve every day." She wrung out the cloth.

"And you, Lilly, are you relieved not to be rid of me?"

She cocked her head to one side. "Well, it would be nice to have this pantry back, and I should not mind a better balance of males to females in this house. I am sorely outnumbered."

Francis, whom she was so used to teasing, did not seem to find this amusing. Instead he looked crestfallen.

"Francis, forgive me. I see you are not your old thick-skinned self at present, ready to serve up your own share of teasing in return. Of course I am pleased you are feeling better. And that we shall have you with us for years to come."

Francis smiled ruefully and closed his eyes. "You are never so kind to me when I am well. I shall have to fall ill more often."

"I pray not, Francis. You know what Father says. . . ."

He ducked his chin and mimicked Charles Haswell's low, stern voice, "'It does not do for a medical man to take ill.'"

"See? You remembered." She replaced the cool cloth on his forehead. "And as soon as you are fully recovered, we shall have you remembering herbals and remedies as well."

When she entered The George's dim, lamplit dining room, her uncle rose from a table in a quiet corner. Jonathan Elliott was tall enough that when he stood to greet her, his head rustled the dry hop flowers hanging from the beamed ceiling. "Lillian, we are so pleased you could join us."

Still seated, her aunt extended her hand and Lilly took it in hers. "I am pleased to do so."

"How nice you look. Your hair is lovely like that."

"Thank you. My friend Mary arranged it." Lilly took her seat and Uncle Elliott pushed in her chair.

Sitting once more he said, "We have taken the liberty of ordering supper. I hope you like beefsteaks and artichokes?"

She could not remember the last time she'd had either. "Sounds delicious."

Two old farmers sitting near the fire with tankards of ale were the only other patrons. Mrs. Dubin, who looked from Lilly to her well-dressed companions with unconcealed curiosity, served them with pragmatic efficiency.

Once their meal was before them, her aunt began. "As you know, we came here with intentions toward your brother which, sadly, are not feasible. However, your uncle and I both believe that we have not made the trip in vain, for meeting you—and of course your father and brother—has been delightful. We are especially impressed with you, my dear."

"Thank you." Lilly felt undeniable pleasure at this warm praise.

"Now, as you know, your uncle must name a male relative to inherit his entailed property. However, we do have some discretion in the distribution of personal effects, such as jewelry, furniture—even an annual allowance may be left to, say, a special young lady. I do not mean to bribe you, Lillian, but I would like you to consider an opportunity. We would like you to come live with us in London. We would hire the best tutors for you in deportment, drawing, language, and dance, and teach you all you need to know to be a proper, accomplished young lady."

Lilly's pulse accelerated. Her own days at Shaw's private girls school had ended when her mother left. Might she now finish her education as she'd longed to do?

Her aunt continued, "You might even bring that friend of yours as lady's maid if you like. We would count it a privilege to host you through a London season or two and introduce you to society . . . and perhaps even to your future husband."

"Now, Ruth, let us not get ahead of ourselves," Jonathan Elliott admonished.

Lilly's heart and head were pounding with such exhilaration, hope, and fear that she found herself speechless.

"Would you not like to see London?" Aunt Elliott asked. "To fill the gaps in your education? See the best museums, hear the finest concerts, dance at the most exclusive balls? Perhaps even travel to Italy or Spain?"

Travel. An image flashed before her mind's eye. Her younger self and her mother, heads bent over an old world map . . .

Still Lilly said nothing, just stared at the kind face of her aunt as though the woman were speaking a language Lilly could not quite make out.

Finally Lilly managed to sputter, "W-why?"

"Why?" her aunt repeated, not understanding.

"Why would you do this for me? Why would you want to? I have nothing with which to ever repay you."

Her aunt's delicate features became earnest. "I do not believe that, Lillian. Not for one moment. Your happiness, your success shall be all the repayment we ever need." She reached across the table and took her hand. "If you come to feel some fondness for us, well, that would be more than we could ask for."

Lilly battled to contain the excitement building within her. Was this not what she had long wished for? But would Father ever allow it? Tentatively, she asked, "Have you spoken to my father about this?"

Uncle shook his head. "There was no need to until we knew if you were even interested. But we shall, if you think you might be."

Aunt Elliott studied her, obvious hope in her eyes. "Shall we, Lillian? Shall we speak to him?"

Lilly took a deep breath, inhaling the hundred questions warring within her. She asked only one.

"When?"

4

> An apothecary first of all should be a lover of piety, one that fears God, void of envy and malice, of good competency . . . and not given to corpulency.
>
> —C. J. S. Thompson, *Mystery and Art of the Apothecary*

Upon her return from The George, Lilly found her father standing in the laboratory-kitchen, using a scraper of horn to clean one of his mortars. He set down the instrument and wiped his hands on a cloth.

"Lilly, good. You're home. I need you to come with me to Marlow House."

Whatever excited words she might have spoken died on her lips. "Marlow House? Whatever for?"

"Sir Henry's man summoned me. Seems his master is in a great deal of pain."

"But, Sir Henry has been calling for Dr. Foster of late."

"Yes, but Foster is home in bed with the very malady that has laid our Mr. Baylor low." He added a vial to his medical case and snapped the lid shut.

She took a deep breath and blew it out between puffed cheeks. "I see."

"Why so forlorn? This is good news for us. Have I not told you that it does not do for a medical man to fall ill? It costs business—patients. Which is why I never get sick." He grinned at her, but she did not return the gesture.

"Perhaps I ought to stay here in case Francis—or Charlie—needs anything."

"Mrs. Mimpurse is on her way over. Come along. You need only carry two species jars. I cannot have them jostling about the gig while I drive."

Her natural curiosity trumped her trepidation. "What remedy do you propose?"

"I prepared traditional gout powder, of course."

Unbidden, her mind flashed the ingredients: *birthwort, red gentian root, leaves of germander, and centaury.*

"But depending on his symptoms," her father continued, putting on his greatcoat, "I may need to prescribe something stronger."

"James's Powder?" she asked.

"Too strong."

"Compound powder of ipecacuanha?"

He narrowed his eyes in thought. "Do you mean . . . ?"

Opium, potassium nitrate, vitriolated tartar, liquorice, ipecacuanha. She gave him the outmoded name. "Dover's."

"Ah. Right. I have both."

Lilly looked about her, intertwining and twisting her fingers. "I could transfer smaller amounts to vials, Father. Then you could carry them in your case."

"I prefer not to delay."

"But—"

He eyed her keenly. "You are not still afraid of Sir Henry's son, are you?"

"No. That is, not as long as you shall be there with me."

Mrs. Mimpurse, buxom and energetic, arrived from next door and shooed them out, clucking like a mother hen. Lilly climbed up into the gig, and her father handed her the clunky jars, then circled the rig and climbed up into the seat beside her. Urging Pennywort, their mare, into a trot, he drove through the dark, windy night the short distance to Marlow House. Unlike his daughter, Charles Haswell was not fond of walking. Especially in chilly weather.

Lilly thought of a dozen ways to bring up the astounding offer her aunt and uncle had made, but she could not force out a single syllable. Not yet. In any case, the howling wind would only swallow her words. There would be time later, once the current crisis was passed and she'd somehow found the courage to withstand the hurt that would surely appear in her father's eyes when she told him she longed to accept.

When they arrived, Sir Henry's butler, Mr. Withers, greeted them and took their coats. He then led them through the large manor and up the long curved staircase. Following her father, Lilly carefully carried the two pottery jars. At the far end of the corridor, Withers knocked softly on a closed door and then opened it to them.

They passed through the outer dressing room and then entered the inner bedchamber. From the canopied bed, the baronet lifted his arm in a weak gesture of welcome.

"Haswell, good of you to come."

"Of course, Sir Henry. And this is my capable assistant, Miss Haswell."

Even in his pain, the grey-haired man smiled politely to her, the expression lifting the bushy silver sideburns. She knew the baronet was in his fifties, yet he looked older. "Ah yes, your daughter. How do you do?"

Lilly dipped an awkward curtsy.

"Very pretty," Sir Henry said, then shifted his gaze to her father. "More and more like her mother, is she not?"

Her father looked at her, then quickly away. "Yes, rather."

Sir Henry studied her father's averted face. "Still no word?"

Setting down his case, her father drew himself up briskly. "No word. Now, let us see what we can do to alleviate your discomfort. . . ."

Lilly waited at a polite distance from the bed while her father questioned the baronet in low tones about his symptoms. Twice at her father's bidding she retrieved vials or instruments from his case and once filled a water glass at the bedside table.

When her father began lifting the blankets from the man's legs, he paused. "Lilly. I think you've done all I need. Perhaps you might take yourself to the kitchen and wait for me there? If Mrs. Tobias is still awake, she might offer you a cup of chocolate. And if not, at least the fire will keep you warm."

"Very well, Father."

"Take a candle."

Nodding, she took the candle holder and let herself from the room.

She did not admit she did not know the way to the kitchen from Sir Henry's room. She had been to Marlow House before but had always waited in the kitchen while her father went up to see Sir Henry, or Lady Marlow, before her passing.

Lilly held the candle high and started down the dark, broad corridor. High upon its walls were formal portraits of Marlows past—men in coat and cravat, or military regalia; ladies in fine gowns and jewels—as well as paintings of the hunt, rearing horses, hounds with bared teeth, and foxes with hideous wide-eyed expressions of pain and fear.

In the light of the candle, those eyes seemed to glare at her. The dogs, to growl at her. She shivered.

She passed the main staircase and continued to the corridor's end, assuming she would there find the servants' stairway down to the kitchen.

Suddenly she heard a noise behind her. She spun around, holding her candle before her like a sword. But the corridor was empty.

She continued on until she heard footsteps to her left. She whirled. But her candle only illuminated more paintings and tapestries upon the wall.

She walked faster.

Nearby she heard a scrape, saw a dark stab of movement before her, then felt a rush of air. Her candle was out before her mind could identify what she had seen. And then she saw nothing at all. Nothing but blackness.

"Who is there?" she demanded in an airy croak.

She took a tentative step backward, toward her father and safety, but an arm grabbed her from behind and a hand cupped her mouth, catching her cry and rendering it useless.

"Shh . . ." a male voice whispered. "Did you hear something?"

For one tense second, the arm remained clasped about her waist and the other hand covered her mouth, but then, as quickly as it came, the contact was broken, the hands gone from her.

Indignation chased away fear. Those had not been phantom hands touching her. "Yes. I heard something. You, no doubt. You enjoyed frightening me, did you not?"

A door opened nearby; footsteps receded and promptly returned. Roderick Marlow appeared in a doorway, carrying a glowing candle lamp he had apparently retrieved from the nearby room. With it, he lit a wall sconce. In its light she could see that he was taller and broader than he had been when she had last seen him. His hair and brows just as dark. How old was he now—three and twenty? Four?

"Why are you wandering about in the dark?" He cocked his head to one side, regarding her. "Are you lost?"

"No. Merely on the way to the kitchen."

One dark brow rose. "And where you live, the kitchen is abovestairs?"

She exhaled sharply. "Of course not. I was on my way down."

"You passed the staircase."

"I was looking for the servants' stairs—"

"Are you a servant?"

"No. The apothecary's daughter."

"Ah, I remember. The bran-faced thief."

Irritation surged at this ungentlemanly reference to her freckles.

Before she could respond, he continued. "That explains why you are sneaking about. Perhaps I shall have to search your pockets." He took a step closer. "See if you have helped yourself to any valuables."

She backed away again. "I have never stolen anything in my life!"

"Except a peony?"

"Except a peony," she allowed.

He parted his lips, then paused. "What is your name? I forget."

"Lilly Haswell."

"Ah. Haswell. Of course."

He continued to step forward while she backed away, as if in some slow, inelegant dance.

"And do you do miracles, Lilly Haswell, as your father supposedly does?"

She hesitated, shook her head. "No."

"You do not believe in miracles?"

"I do."

"Why? Have you not prayed for your mother's return?"

She swallowed the painful lump in her throat. "Yes."

"And has she?"

"Not as yet."

He barked a laugh. "Still hoping?"

"Every day."

He stopped where he was. "Such faith . . . such fervency. And yet, nothing. Is it any wonder I do not believe?"

"No wonder. But sad if true." She ceased moving as well.

"I prayed for my mother, too, you know. But that did not stop her from dying. Where were your father's miracles then?"

"I am sorry," she whispered. "We can only do so much."

"Which is why we must take what we want in this life, Miss Haswell. Make our own way. Not wait for some fat, hairless angel to deliver our whims on a silver platter." He lifted the candle lamp and peered at her. "Do I offend you?"

"Yes. As you no doubt intend to."

He laughed again. "True, I am a skilled offender. Whereas my father is a skilled . . . ingratiator. And yours a healer or pretender—I am not certain which. And you, Miss Lilly Haswell, what are you?"

When she hesitated, he smirked and turned away dismissively, clearly not expecting an answer from a frightened girl.

"A rememberer."

He turned back to her, studying her face in the flickering light. Surprised, perhaps, to see how serious and somber she was.

"How so?" He asked, his smirk gone.

She swallowed and answered quietly, "I remember everything. Whether I wish to or not."

They stared at one another. He took another step closer. Suddenly a door opened far down the corridor from which she had come. He grasped her wrist and pulled her through a narrow door she had not even known was there. She gasped, but did not scream.

"This old place is full of secret passages and trapdoors," he whispered, leading her along a dark narrow passageway, holding the candle lamp to light their way.

"Where are you taking me?"

"You said you sought the kitchen."

He pushed open a timbered door and paused to light the lamp at the top of a steep set of stairs. Growing anxious about being alone with him, Lilly stepped around and preceded him down the narrow stairs, even though her own shadow made it difficult to see. When she reached the bottom door, she lifted the latch but could not make it release. When she turned, he was right there.

"It sometimes jams." But he made no move to open it. He brought the light closer to her face. His eyes glinted oddly in the candle's glow, the right eye appearing a deeper shade than the left. "You know, Lilly Haswell," he said in a low voice, "freckles or no, you might be handsome one day."

He reached around her to give the latch a sharp jerk, the action bringing his hand close to the small of her back and his face near to hers.

Feeling the door give behind her and imagining the safety of a bright fire and no-nonsense Mrs. Tobias beyond, she smiled sweetly up at him and said, "Well, that makes one of us."

She pushed her way backwards into the kitchen. Her smile of triumph immediately fell away. The kitchen was empty, the fire but embers.

In two strides he was before her, anger in his eyes. She took a step back. He, another forward.

"Lilly?" Her father came into the kitchen and Roderick stopped midstride.

"Oh! Father! You frightened me."

"Did I?" He looked from her to Roderick and his brow furrowed at seeing the young man looming so close.

"Are you . . . all right?"

She swallowed. "I am perfectly well. My flame blew out, but Mr. Marlow kindly lit another and showed me the way."

Her father looked at her, then turned to scrutinize the young man. "Did he indeed?" He held Roderick Marlow's bold stare a moment longer, then clasped Lilly's hand. "Come, my dear. It is time we took our leave."

On the ride home, her father was quiet but obviously not at peace. The wind had died down, but she still had not found the courage to bring up her aunt and uncle's offer.

"The Elliotts," her father said suddenly. "They want you to go to London?"

Nerves quaking, she forced her gaze to meet his and nodded solemnly.

But instead of the arguments and cautions she expected, he returned his eyes to the road. He drew in a long breath and said, "Perhaps it is well that you leave for a time after all."

She studied his profile for several moments, but he did not explain further. Giving up, she laid her head on his shoulder for the rest of the journey home.

5

> DALBY'S GENUINE CARMINATIVE
> Superior to all other remedies for the wind. . . . This invaluable cordial medicine is prepared by Frances Gell, daughter of the late Mr. Joseph Dalby, apothecary.
>
> —*The Edinburgh Evening Courant*, 1815

On Monday morning, Francis was feeling like his old self again and joined Lilly in the shop. She watched as he worked with the mortar and pestle, ineffectively swishing and tamping the simples within. *Must I again demonstrate proper technique?*

"Hold the pestle with a light grip, Francis," she said. "Like a quill. And press firmly in a circular motion." The swishing continued. Frustrated, she stood at his shoulder and reached her right hand over his. "Like this." She held his larger hand beneath her own, guiding his motions.

Though a year younger, he was already taller than she. When he looked down at her, standing close as she was, Lilly felt his warm breath tickling the hairs at her temple. He leaned closer yet, his brown eyes alight, and whispered, "I so enjoy your demonstrations."

She pulled away, irritated at his cheekiness, and decided now was a perfect time to tell him of her plans.

"Leaving?" Francis's voice rose. "Only two days ago you said, 'We'll have you remembering herbals and remedies in no time.'" He repeated her words with syrupy sarcasm.

She had never seen Francis so agitated and was relieved the shop was empty. "I cannot help you forever, Francis. I know you can succeed on your own if you only take your post more seriously."

"I try."

She huffed, "You spend more time learning to amuse Dorothea Robbins than learning your trade."

He ignored that. "Remember what else you said . . . ? Of course you do, for you remember everything. You said, 'I am glad you will be with us for years to come.' What about that?"

"How could I have guessed the Elliotts would offer such an opportunity?"

"An opportunity for what? To wear silk frocks and drink tea with your small finger in the air—and your nose as well?"

"No! I want to see the world, or at least London. I want to learn new things. I want to sleep in a room that does not smell of cat mint, comfrey, and rue." She thought of adding, *I want to find my mother*, but left those words unspoken. "It is different for you. You *want* to work here. I do not want to stay here my entire life, forever the apothecary's daughter, cutting pills and sweeping Father's shop. I thought you would understand. *You* left your home to pursue what you wanted. Are you sorry you did not stay in Saltford all your life?"

"No, I am not sorry to be here. At least I have not been, until now."

His reaction surprised her. "I do not understand you, Francis."

"No, Lilly. Clearly you do not."

Mary Mimpurse came into the shop that afternoon without her customary apron. Her mother's coffeehouse closed at one o'clock on Mondays, giving her the afternoon free. She dragged a stool beside the dispensing counter and watched as Lilly counted liquorice pastilles and packaged them into small paper boxes. Mary reached out and popped a liquorice lozenge into her mouth.

"These are for medicinal purposes." Lilly feigned reprimand. "You do not appear to me to have a cold, Miss Mimpurse."

Mary blithely shrugged. "Put a fancy label on it and call it medicine. I call it a sweet. Sugar or honey?"

"Honey."

"Delicious."

While Mary enjoyed her liquorice, Lilly shared her London plans and the proposed departure after Christmas. Like Francis, Mary responded with less enthusiasm than she had expected.

Eyeing her friend's piqued expression, Lilly asked, "What is the matter?"

"Nothing. I am happy for you. Truly." Mary's tone was snappy, her mouth a thin line. "You'll no doubt have a grand time and forget all about us."

"Nonsense. I don't forget anything and certainly not my oldest friend."

Mary would not meet her gaze.

Lilly laid a hand on Mary's forearm, strong, she noticed from all her stirring and kneading, much as Lilly's own were from many hours spent with mortar and pestle. "I shall miss you, Mary," she said.

Mary acknowledged this with a nod and briefly laid her hand atop Lilly's. "And I you."

"Come with me, then." Lilly slid a box toward Mary and began sealing one herself. "Aunt Elliott said I might bring you along as lady's maid."

Mary froze mid-seal. Her small mouth gaped. "Did she? Well . . . I am surprised. Surprised your aunt even knows who I am."

"She admired my hair. I told her you had done it—and about your many other talents." Lilly reached out and tweaked Mary's nose.

Her friend did not smile or seek playful revenge. Instead she rose and said officiously, "Then you must have also told her that I am much too busy slaving away in a poor coffeehouse to come to London. In fact, I had better hurry." She turned toward the door. "No doubt the *mistress* needs floors scrubbed or potatoes peeled. . . ."

"Mary! Do not take offense. You know I do not view you as my servant."

Mary turned back. "Do you not? I know you've always thought yourself above me, when in reality—"

"I do not!"

"How ironic." Mary shook her head, eyes clouded. "That *she* would suggest such an arrangement, I do not mind, but that *you*, my own—"

"Mary. I did not think. I only wished you might come with me. I am sorry! Please forgive me. . . ."

But sweet, docile Mary had already stalked from the room.

Ignoring the October chill, Lilly stood on the Honeystreet Bridge, staring far off down the canal in the fading light of evening. A ginger tabby lay curled up on the bridge, enjoying the warmth the bricks had absorbed during the day. Enjoying, too, the occasional scratch Lilly administered to its furry chin. She sighed. *If only my day had been as pleasant.*

She could see lantern light gleaming on the water, though she could not make out the shape of the vessel. Was it a narrowboat approaching, or a barge already moored for the night? She would stand there just a little longer in case it came closer. A sudden thought startled her. Perhaps she should not leave. What if Mother finally returned, only to find her gone?

She sensed someone beside her and looked over to see Charlie, his elbows on the bridge ledge, his eyes trained on the distant light.

"Were you looking for me?" Lilly asked.

"I always look for you here." He glanced at her, then away. "I want you to stay."

Father must have told him. "But, Charlie, I cannot always live with you and Father, keeping house for the two of you. I know it sounds selfish, but I want more. I am only going to Aunt and Uncle Elliott's in London. You liked them, did you not?"

"Very nice," he mumbled.

The cat rose, arched its spine, and rubbed itself against Charlie's arms. Lilly was grateful for the interruption. When Charlie reached out to stroke its back, she reminded him, "Gently."

He nodded, petting and addressing the tabby, "I know you. You're Mrs. Kilgrove's puss."

The cat relished the attention with purring and half-lidded eyes.

Lilly smiled. "He likes you."

Watching her brother pet the cat, Lilly remembered something she had not thought about in a long while. Perhaps it was seeing the cat and Charlie together, here on the bridge. Here where she searched the boats.

As if the same memory had also been invoked in him, Charlie said, "I had a cat once. Ran away."

Not wanting to dwell on the sad aspect of the memory, she asked, "Do you remember that Christmas when Father gave you the little cat? I think you were eight years old."

"Yes! In a bandbox. Holes cut for air. And his little paws pokin' out, lookin' to play."

Lilly knew her father had mostly wanted a mouser for the shop, but she had rarely seen Charlie as happy as he had been that day.

Charlie bit his lip. "Then he ate the leg off the Christmas goose, and she was angry."

She? It had only been three years since Mother left, but Charlie's memory was often poor. How much did he recall? "Do you remember what Mr. Mimpurse said, when you showed him your new cat?"

"Mr. Mimpurse . . ." Charlie suddenly looked troubled. "He's gone now."

"I know."

Mr. Mimpurse had died more than six years before. Hoping to divert Charlie, she continued, "But do you remember what he said?"

When Charlie shook his head, she supplied, "He said, 'That's a jolly good puss, Charlie.' Remember?'"

"'At's right."

"And so you named him Jolly."

"Jolly," Charlie breathed, his eyes growing soft at the memory.

Poor Jolly, Lilly thought. How Charlie had clung to that cat, always trying to hold it on his lap, to make it sleep in his bed, forever picking it up and squeezing it so tightly, Lilly feared he'd suffocate the increasingly skittish creature. Charlie was not cruel; he merely tried too hard. Cats want to come *to* you. They need time alone, time to hide away, time for daytime naps and nighttime hunts. But Charlie was young and Charlie was Charlie, and he didn't understand, no matter how often and gently their parents had tried to explain.

Lilly started. *Is that what we did?* she wondered. *Did we try too hard to hold on to Mother? Fail to give her the solitude she needed? Suffocate her with affection?*

When spring had come that long ago year, and the windows and doors began to open more often, Jolly had darted outside and was never seen again.

Not a week had passed before Charlie began bringing home strays with a vague resemblance to Jolly, or sometimes even a neighbor's cat, to the garden door for Mother to inspect.

"Is it Jolly?" he would ask, eyes shining with hope.

"No, Charlie, I am afraid not." Mother would smile with sympathy and return to the kitchen.

Soon he was presenting tabbies, then striped cats, then cats with spots. It was clear he no longer remembered what his cat had looked like. But Mother did and continued to inspect and renounce the would-be Jollies that Charlie dragged to the door all that summer and fall.

Lilly remembered wondering what it would really hurt for Mother to lie just once and say, "Yes, Charlie, you found Jolly," the next time he brought home some stray. But she never did.

Now, on the canal, the distant boat began to move. As it drew near, Lilly saw it was a narrowboat, its lantern casting flickers and shadows along the canal bank and bridge as it passed beneath them. Lilly watched carefully, studying the crew of work-roughened men talking and jesting with one other. From their boisterous laughter it seemed clear they had been moored at The George for some time, drinking a few too many ales.

No women were aboard.

It struck Lilly then. She was as pathetic as Charlie had been back when he was eight or nine, searching out every cat in the village and beyond, hoping to find his lost Jolly. Here she was, eighteen years old, still inspecting the faces of every woman she saw, hoping to find the mother she had lost. But even Charlie had eventually given up and quit searching. Father and Mother had never given Charlie another pet for fear of repeating the drawn-out melodrama. Soon they had all put it from their minds and gone on. Why could she not do the same? She would, she decided. She would go to London. Right after Christmas.

In silence, she and Charlie turned and watched the lantern light until it disappeared.

Suddenly Charlie reached over and grasped her hand—a rare gesture. "Stay."

Tears filled Lilly's eyes. "You are not making this easy." She squeezed his hand. "Do not be sad, Charlie. It won't be forever. I will come back and see you."

He stared off in the distance once more. "'At's what she said."

Lilly's pulse quickened. "What?"

Charlie kept staring, but did not reply.

"Do you mean Mother? *She* told you she was leaving?"

"No more leaving," he whispered.

"What else did she tell you? Do you remember?"

"Don't leave, Lilly."

Lilly was torn, wishing she might extract every fragment of her brother's memory, yet not wanting to further upset him.

She drew herself up. "Come, Charlie. Father will be wanting his supper."

She returned home to find the laboratory-kitchen in more disorder than usual.

"Father, you left the large alembic on the stove again!" she called. "Please help me move it if you want any supper tonight."

Charles Haswell wandered in from his surgery, hands full of rumpled letters and bills of lading. "Sorry, sorry. Lilly, where is that order for Shipton's?"

"I put it on your desk two days ago." Lilly brought the soup pot from the cold cellar.

"Did you? I cannot find the dumble thing."

"Perhaps if you put things away instead of stacking them all over your desk."

"But I have looked everywhere."

"Father. I do not wish to spend two more hours writing it again."

"Then would you please find it for me?"

"Yes, yes. After I heat our soup. Can you find the ladle?"

He began clanging around, removing the alembic and pulling out pots and kettles from the cupboard. "I cannot find a thing in here! Heaven help us after you leave."

Lilly sighed. "Not you, too, Father. I have argued with three of the people I care about most today. I cannot stand to disappoint you as well. If you want me to stay, just say so."

"Stay? Stay here and clean after me and sort my mess because I am a disorganized fool? Absolutely not. Go."

"You truly want me to go?"

"Well, I don't want you to stay and become like your mother."

Lilly gasped. "Father!"

He paused in his search to look at her earnestly. "What I mean is—I do not want you to stay here and always wonder, always long for what you might have missed. Find out now, before . . ."

"Before?" she asked.

He sighed. "Before there is a husband—and children—to leave behind."

"Oh, Father." Tears filled her eyes for the second time that evening. She squeezed his arm, and the two shared a rare moment of silent empathy. Then he cleared his throat and resumed his search.

Lilly moved to the cupboard and pulled out a quarter loaf of stout brown bread. She forced a light tone. "Charlie told me that Mother spoke to him before she left. Said she would come back, that she would not be gone forever. Do you think it possible?"

"That she planned only a short absence?" He shook his head. "I do not know. She was here one day and gone the next. Told me nothing. Perhaps she lied to Charlie to ease her conscience. Or Charlie might have remembered incorrectly or imagined the exchange. I doubt we shall ever know."

Finding a clean wooden paddle, Lilly used it to stir the soup, but her mind was far away. "I think perhaps she did lie, only meaning to comfort him. For I told Charlie I wouldn't be gone forever, and that was a lie as well. Was it not? For I really do not know that. If I return soon, it will only be because I am an utter failure. Unable to learn what the tutors try to teach me, an embarrassment to the Elliotts."

"Which of course you will not be."

"I pray not, but what if the opposite is true. If I succeed, even modestly, will I not stay two years or more? She mentioned two seasons."

"And if you have the ultimate success . . ." He let the thought trail off.

"What do you mean?"

"Why, to find a suitable husband, of course."

Lilly felt a thrill of anticipation at his words. "I had not thought of that as my principle aim, but I suppose you are right."

"In your aunt's eyes, what else could it be? If you are a success that means you will be sought after by several eligible men and married to the richest or best connected among them. And assuming he is a London man, you might very well live there forever."

Still blindly stirring, Lilly bit back a smile. Her daydreams of a handsome gentleman falling in love with her no longer seemed so foolishly fantastic.

"Which is a sad prospect for your old father, but that is life, and we cannot stop it. Thankfully there are decent roads between here and London, and there is always the canal." He pulled out the ladle from the cupboard with triumphant flourish. "Now, when are you to depart?"

Part II

The apothecary of this country is qualified by education to attend at the bedside of the sick, and, being in general better acquainted with pharmacy than the physicians of English universities . . . is often the most successful practitioner.

—Jeremiah Jenkins, *Observations on the present state of the profession and trade of medicine,* 1810

For seeing that our frail mortal bodies are subject to a vast multitude of diseases, it hath most graciously pleased almighty God, of his infinite mercy, goodness, and compassion to sinful man, to plant remedies in our gardens, before our doors, and even on every side of our paths, in order that we might put forth our hands, and duly receive the healing balm. . . .

—*Culpeper's Complete Herbal & English Physician*

6

> She was certainly not a woman of family, but well educated, accomplished, rich, and excessively in love. . . .
>
> —Jane Austen, *Persuasion*

In the room that had been hers for more than a year, Lillian Grace Haswell stared at herself in the dressing table mirror. Her aunt's lady's maid placed the last ornament in her elegant crown of russet hair, copper highlights gleaming in the candlelight.

"There you are, miss."

"Thank you, Dupree."

Rising, Lilly smoothed the bodice of her jonquille gown where it skimmed over her slight figure and flowed to the floor. The maid handed her long white gloves and helped arrange a light mantle over her shoulders. A heavy cloak would not be needed on such a fine early-May evening.

As she carefully descended the stairway of the Elliott home, her aunt and uncle watched from the hall with evident delight.

"My dear Lillian, how lovely you look!" Aunt Elliott cooed.

"Very handsome indeed," Uncle Elliott added, his hands grasping lapels which did not quite cover his girth.

Aunt Elliott smiled at her husband. "Is she not a vision of perfection?"

"A vision to be sure. But not quite perfect, dear lady."

Her aunt tilted her head to one side. "Oh?"

"Something is missing."

Lillian paused on the landing, looking down at herself. She considered the gloves, the reticule, the slippers peeking from under her skirts. What had she forgotten?

"I know just the thing." Jonathan Elliott turned to the hall table behind him and a moment later walked purposefully toward Lilly.

He stood before her and brandished a brown velvet case. "Now, mind your expectations, my dear. It is not the 'latest thing,' as they say. I am afraid it is rather old."

The Elliotts shared a smile that revealed her aunt's awareness of her husband's intent.

He opened the hinged lid of the jewel case and displayed its contents.

"How lovely!" Lilly's exclamation was sincere. For within the silk lining was a stunning saffron-yellow pendant on a gold chain with a matching topaz bracelet.

"These belonged to Lillian Elliott," her uncle said. "Your grandmother."

Her heart squeezed at this show of affection. "They are beautiful. I wish I had known her."

"I have no doubt she would have been very fond of you."

Her aunt stepped behind her and fastened the necklace while Lilly slipped on the bracelet.

"I shall take great care and return them safely."

"They are yours now, my dear. Although it would be wise to lock them in the jewelry chest when not in use. One can never be too careful."

"I am happy enough to be borrow them, Aunt—you needn't give them to me."

"Nonsense. We have had every intention of giving them to you for some time. Why do you think I counseled you to select a gown of this color?"

"They *are* perfect together. Thank you, Aunt. You are very kind." She kissed Ruth Elliott's soft cheek. "And you too, Uncle." The big man leaned down to receive her kiss.

"There, there. You are most welcome, my dear. Now, shall we be off?"

The Price-Winters family was hosting the ball, and Lilly had long been looking forward to it, for she had become acquainted with both son and daughter during the previous season.

"Mr. and Mrs. Price-Winters, good evening," Jonathan Elliott began. "You remember our niece, Miss Haswell."

"Of course. She and our Christina often enjoy one another's society."

Lilly noticed Mrs. Price-Winters had not included their son, William, in her mention of *society*. Aunt Elliott had tried to match her with Christina's brother last season and was disappointed when he married another. Still, Lilly curtsied and smiled at the parents of her friend. The sole friend she could claim after sixteen months in London.

She followed alongside her aunt and uncle, past their hosts and around the perimeter of the crowded ballroom. Lilly smiled and curtsied her way through a long series of introductions, her eyes straying around the room in hopes of seeing Roger Bromley, a current admirer whom her aunt highly favored.

A silver-haired gentleman in uniform bowed before her. "Miss Haswell. You probably do not remember me, but—"

"Admiral Asher, of course I do. How fares your Dora?"

Admiral Asher was uncle to Roger Bromley, Lilly knew, and she was careful to speak kindly to him. The older man smiled and informed her that his daughter had just presented him with a charming granddaughter and that both were getting on extremely well. Lilly assured him she was happy to hear it and moved on.

Her aunt joined her at the refreshment table. There, they were approached by an elegant matron. Lilly did not miss the wrinkle between Ruth Elliott's eyebrows as she began, "Lillian, have you met—?"

Lilly smoothly supplied, "Mrs. Langtry. Of course. We met at the Willoughbys' last summer."

The matron's eyebrows rose. "How kind of you to remember. And I am pleased to see you again, Miss . . ."

"Haswell."

"Quite."

When her uncle went off to acquire something other than punch or ratafia to drink, Lilly also excused herself, stepping away from her aunt and Mrs. Langtry to greet her approaching friend.

"Christina, there you are. What a lovely gown."

"It is nothing to yours, and you know it."

"Nonsense."

A year older than Lilly, Christina Price-Winters was plump and well-endowed, and her mauve dress dipped low to reveal more cleavage than Lilly would have felt comfortable exposing—even had she that much to expose. Christina's face was broad, with prominent eyes and expressive brows that often rose and fell in dramatic punctuation during conversation. Her wide mouth was given to smirks and sardonic one-sided grins.

"Zee gown eez mag-nee-fee-sawwnt," Christina said, mimicking her French dressmaker. "Ew-la-la, eet transforms *votre fille*, madame. So svelte. So graceful . . ." Christina snorted. "She is more skilled in opening Mother's purse than in stitching seams—that much is certain."

"That explains why your neckline is so low," Lilly quietly teased. "Or perhaps Madame Froissant ran out of material?"

Christina grinned. "This is my current scheme to encourage Edward to propose. Do you think it will succeed?"

Lilly glanced at the balding but highborn lord who was staring at Christina with frank admiration. "I believe it already has."

Though not a beauty, Christina's family, connections, and deep dowry supplied her with a promising number of most eligible suitors. Far more than Lilly enjoyed.

Christina's ginger-haired brother, William, walked across the room toward them. Secretly, Lilly had shared her aunt's keen disappointment when he had announced his plans to wed last year. He had been the first man in London to catch her eye and raise her hopes. She found him amusing and sweet-natured and had briefly believed he admired her as well. Perhaps he had. But with Will, and the few suitors that followed, she had quickly learned that she had neither the rank nor wealth to hold the interest of a gentleman of quality—nor of his parent with the purse strings. Men enjoyed dancing with her and flirting with her, but in the end went on to marry girls with better connections and richer dowries.

Will Price-Winters bowed before her. "Miss Haswell."

She curtsied. "Good evening, Mr. Price-Winters. What a fine ball this is. And where is your lovely new wife?"

He shrugged. "Some earth-shattering calamity with her hair, I understand. No doubt she shall be down directly." He frowned at something over their heads. "I say, who is that?"

Christina followed his gaze and rolled her eyes. "Mr. Alban."

"Your old tutor?"

"And recently Lillian's as well." Christina hunched over, rubbing her hands together in imitation of Mr. Alban, parroting his stammering speech. "Miss . . . Miss Has-s-s-well. Do decline the vairb *to be* onc-c-ce more."

"Christina, please," Lilly admonished. Christina's imitation was spot on, but Lilly did not wish to injure the man's feelings or reputation.

"What is he doing here?" William asked.

Christina shrugged. "He all but begged an invitation, and Mother hadn't the heart to refuse him."

Mr. Oscar Alban was educated, mild-mannered, and patient. He was also short, balding, and wore thick spectacles and ill-fitting clothes. It was little wonder parents trusted him with their daughters.

Mr. Alban bowed before Christina's parents, who now stood conversing with Lilly's aunt and two older couples. "Mr. and Mrs. Price-Winters. Thank you for your generous-s-s invitation. I cannot remember when I've enjoyed mys-s-self more."

Mrs. Price-Winters was reserved in her reply. "You are welcome, Mr. Alban."

The tutor turned to those assembled around his host and hostess. "I had the privilege of instructing Miss Price-Winters s-s-some years ago. And now

Miss Has-s-well also. It as been a rare honor indeed to teach two s-s-such fine and gifted ladies."

"Thank you, Mr. Alban."

"Miss Has-s-well's progress with the romance languages has s-s-surpassed every expectation, although Miss Price-Winters can proudly claim the s-s-superior accent."

"That is Christina," Mr. Price-Winters interjected. "Our little myna bird."

"But Miss Has-s-well has memorized French and Italian vocabulary more quickly than any s-s-student I have ever had the pleasure of teaching."

William leaned near Lilly and teased quietly, "Bluestocking."

"I s-s-suppose her background and her familiarity with Latin—"

Aunt Elliott interrupted abruptly. "Mr. Alban, why do you not dance with my niece? I am sure she would benefit from instruction there as well."

"Ah . . . well . . . I do not claim to be a dancing master. But, of course, I s-s-should be pleased to dance with Miss Has-s-well." He turned toward her. "If she would oblige me."

Lilly forced a smile. "Of course."

As he escorted her to the dance floor, he asked quietly, "What was it I s-s-said to offend?"

"Please forgive my aunt, Mr. Alban. It is only that she prefers as little as possible said of my background. Not everyone sees knowledge of Latin and physic as a credit to accomplished young ladies."

"I s-s-see."

"I ought not to have mentioned my past to you. It was just . . . you struggled so to account for my progress, and I didn't want you to think—"

"That I am a more gifted teacher than I truly am?" he wryly supplied.

"No! I did not mean—"

"There, there Miss Has-s-well. I understand. Do not fret—I shall take all the credit for your amazing progress from here on."

When the dance ended, Lilly excused herself from Mr. Alban and rejoined Christina and her brother.

"And where is Mr. Bromley this evening?" Christina asked.

"I have yet to see him," Lilly said. She still held out hope for this suitor. Roger Bromley did not seem put off by her lack of title or sizeable income. But then again neither he nor his parents likely knew her father was in trade, nor were they aware of her mother's disgrace. Lilly wondered how long his interest would last once they knew.

"I see the swell," Will said, "there by the door."

Lilly followed Will's gaze and saw Mr. Bromley, stylishly dressed in black tailcoat and white waistcoat. He stood before a willowy blonde in blue satin with an overdress of white netting. "Who is that he is talking to?"

"Susan Whittier . . ." Will breathed, staring.

Lilly stared as well and felt a stirring of dread. "I have never seen her before."

"She was away much of last season," Christina explained. "Touring Italy, I believe."

"She is very beautiful," Lilly acknowledged, and swallowed a lump of envy.

"Is she?" Will said innocently. "I had not noticed."

Lilly was unsuccessful in restraining her sarcasm. "And neither, I see, has Mr. Bromley."

With a dismissive wave, Christina said, "Oh, he tried to engage her affections two years ago but was soundly rebuffed. You have nothing to fear from her, Lillian."

Had she not? Lilly saw Mr. Bromley's awestruck expression and did not feel reassured.

As they watched, Roger Bromley offered Miss Whittier his arm. She patted it as though it were the head of a child, laughed, and twirled away in a flutter of blue satin. Even from across the room, Lilly could not miss the man's crestfallen countenance.

He glanced their way.

To pretend they had not witnessed his rejection, the three quickly feigned engrossed conversation. By the time Bromley had crossed the room and stood before them, a bright smile had transformed his handsome face.

"Price-Winters, you old hound," he began. "Monopolizing the two handsomest ladies in the room, I see. The missus would not approve." He bowed to Christina. "Miss Price-Winters."

"Bromley."

He turned toward Lilly. "And Miss Haswell. What a delight. I do hope you have saved at least one dance for poor me?"

She answered warmly, "Of course I have."

Mr. Bromley had become one of her most frequent partners. He was an elegant, slim young man of middling height and excellent bearing. Straight brown hair framed classic English features. He was also the only son of a wealthy family, as her aunt often reminded her. As though Lilly needed reminding.

"Excellent," he said. "Then I shall have the next and the last and as many as I can in between, when the chaperones aren't looking."

She smiled at him, and his answering smile almost reached his eyes. She studied his face, wondering just what was between him and the lovely Miss Susan Whittier.

At the end of the evening, Lilly found herself alone, surreptitiously searching the crowd for Mr. Bromley, who had requested the last dance with her. The first notes of a slow, ceremonious minuet began.

William Price-Winters hurried by. Seeing her, he paused. "Miss Haswell. Not sitting this one out, I hope? Oh, that's right. Bromley claimed the final. Where is that chap?"

"I do not know."

At that moment Roger Bromley and Susan Whittier walked past and joined the dance.

Will saw them too. "Oh. Well, I say."

"She has agreed to a dance after all," Lilly said. "How nice for Mr. Bromley."

Will was not fooled. "I am sorry, Miss Haswell. My wife is waiting, or I—"

"Think nothing of it, Mr. Price-Winters. I have enjoyed a great deal of dancing this evening."

"Wait," Will said triumphantly. "Graves here will dance with you."

"Really, I am fine—"

Will grabbed the arm of a nearby man she had never seen before and turned him around to face her. And a very handsome face it was. Thin nose. Pale blond hair swept over his right temple. A faint moustache, not in present fashion, shadowed his upper lip. "May I present Adam Graves. We were at Oxford together. This is Miss Haswell. Most sensible girl in the room, I assure you." Will winked at her. "Even if she is my sister's friend."

Lilly curtsied to the newcomer. When she looked up, the blond-haired man still stood as he was, stiffly staring at her with startled blue eyes. After a tense moment, he gave a jerky nod.

Will clapped Graves on the shoulder. "Good man." Will walked away to find his wife, who had finally made an appearance.

Still the man made no move. Did not offer his arm nor open his mouth. An awkward silence followed, and Lilly felt her cheeks burn. *How mortifying.*

She turned slightly so that she was facing at an angle between Mr. Graves and the dance floor. Blindly, she gazed toward the other couples moving gracefully through the delicate steps of the dance.

"It is all right, Mr. Graves," she said without looking his way. "You needn't dance with me. Mr. Price-Winters was only acting the part of protective brother. I do not mind sitting out."

"Graves!" Will hissed as he and his wife stepped near, then away again.

Finally, Mr. Graves woodenly offered his arm. "Will you dance?"

She had long ago promised herself never to reject a man who'd gathered his courage to ask for a dance. The automatic response, "I'd be delighted," would not come forth, however. She took a deep breath and forced out a quiet, "Very well."

They joined the minuet in progress. He led her to an open space in the ballroom and took up the movements with stiff, minimal precision. She tempered her own steps accordingly. He kept his gaze averted.

She sighed inwardly. Throughout the previous season and now this new one, she had danced with dozens of gentlemen she secretly found disagreeable or unappealing. But never, she hoped, had she made her disinterest as plain as Mr. Graves made his now. Everyone in the room undoubtedly saw how loath he was to dance with her.

She discreetly glanced around at the other dancers. There at the front were Roger Bromley and Susan Whittier. Roger beamed at his partner, though Susan stared aloofly off in the distance. *Miss Whittier and Mr. Graves ought to be dancing together,* Lilly thought, since both appeared to be enjoying themselves equally.

Suddenly, over Roger's head, Lilly glimpsed a familiar profile. She started, drawing in a breath and turning her face away quickly. There was no mistaking that imposing figure nor those sharp features. *Roderick Marlow?* Here? Now? To witness her humiliation? To reveal, to her aunt and uncle's mortification, her identity as an apothecary's daughter, which to most in attendance, granted her the status of a mere shopkeeper's daughter?

On the next turn of the dance, she stole another glance. Roderick Marlow stood talking to Mr. and Mrs. Price-Winters. On his arm was a stunning woman with splendid maple-leaf-red hair. Mr. Marlow glanced up and his eyes narrowed. Again she averted her face. Had he seen her?

As the musicians reached the final stanzas, Lillian stepped closer to her partner. "Please excuse me, Mr. Graves. I fear I must take my leave."

He stopped dancing and stood there. He opened his mouth, but she was already turning away. She was several yards away from him when his "Of course" reached her ears. Normally she would have hated to be so rude, but in this case she assumed her partner would be relieved to be free of the duty to escort her back to her place and falsely thank her. She again glimpsed Mr. Marlow's face above the heads of the crowd. She could not be certain, but—was he trying to weave his way toward her? She walked quickly away to the safety of the ladies lounge.

Her aunt found her there several minutes later. "There you are, my dear. Are you all right?"

"Yes. Merely tired."

"Your uncle and I are ready to depart, if you are certain you do not wish to remain longer?"

"I am ready."

Gathering their wraps, they made their way to thank their hosts near the door. A man's hand touched her gloved arm and she started. But it was only

Will Price-Winters. His usually cheery face was serious. "Miss Haswell, I hope you will not take my friend's reluctance as an affront toward your lovely person. Graves is the most reticent chap I know."

She quickly skimmed the crowd around them. "Think no more of it. Good night, Mr. Price-Winters."

He eyed her closely. "You are certain you are all right?"

"Quite, I thank you. Do say good-bye to Christina for me."

"I shall."

On the carriage ride home, Aunt Elliott squeezed Lilly's hand. "Well done, my dear."

"Pray what do you mean?"

"Roger Bromley favored you with more dances than any other lady present."

Perhaps not by choice, however, Lilly thought. "Yes, he was very kind."

"More than kind, my dear," Aunt Elliott said. "He is evidently quite taken with you. And as a gentleman of means, Mr. Bromley is under no compulsion to find a wealthy wife of the ton. I know we were disappointed last season, my dear, but I trust we shall prevail this time."

Lilly only smiled meekly. She had thought so, too, before tonight. Before she had seen the way he looked at Miss Whittier. Had her aunt not noticed? Had she seen only what she wished to see?

Ruth Elliott continued, "I *was* a little concerned when I saw you dancing with that fair gentleman at the last."

"Were you. Why?"

"Chap with the moustache, you mean?" Uncle Elliott interrupted. "Someone ought to tell him it isn't all the crack, no matter what some officers seem to believe."

Her aunt continued undeterred, "Have you met him before?"

"No. Christina's brother introduced us. A Mr. Graves, I believe. They were at Oxford together."

"Ah . . . Graves," her uncle said. "Mr. Price-Winters told me he is awaiting licentiateship in the Royal College."

She stared at her uncle, not comprehending.

"The Royal College of *Physicians*, my dear," Uncle Elliott clarified.

Lilly felt oddly stunned. "I did not even realize."

"Good gracious, I trust the two of you did not spend the evening discussing ailments and diseases." Her aunt shuddered.

"We discussed nothing," Lilly said. "We barely spoke."

"Good." Her aunt relaxed against the seat. "Then no harm done."

7

So modern 'pothecaries, taught the art
By Doctor's bills to play the Doctor's part,
Bold in the practice of mistaken rules,
Prescribe, apply, and call their masters fools.
—Alexander Pope

The following evening, the Willoughbys hosted a musicale in their stately Grosvenor Square home. The performer was a young soprano Lilly and the Elliotts had heard perform the previous season. Lilly did not appreciate the ingenue's cathedral-high vibrato but resisted comment. She knew her aunt would never dream of declining an invitation from the Willoughbys.

Dressed in an elegant gown of pearly nacre satin, her upswept hair ornamented with pearls, Lilly followed her aunt and uncle into the impressive home. Several servants were kept busy taking guests' wraps, and by the time Lilly turned after handing over her hooded cloak, she realized she had become separated from the Elliotts in the throng. No matter. She knew where to find them. Front and center before the soprano.

Following slowly with the crowd, Lilly made her way through the double doors into the great drawing room. There the crowd thickened as gentlemen greeted one another and ladies searched for the best seats to regard one another's gowns and to spy potential suitors for their daughters. Lilly paused and stepped to the side, out of the flow, while she searched the room for her aunt and uncle. From the corner of her eye, she glimpsed a gentleman standing against the wall, arms crossed. She glanced over and was disconcerted to see Mr. Graves standing there, looking at her. One could not miss his pale blond hair.

Not knowing what else to do, she nodded at him and returned to her search. Where *were* they? A moment later, she still felt his ponderous eyes upon her. The last thing she wanted was for him to believe she loitered there in hopes he would take notice and address her.

She glanced coolly at him over her shoulder. "I am looking for my aunt and uncle. We came together, and I seem to have lost them."

He nodded stiffly but said nothing.

"Why do you stare?" Lilly asked tartly. "If you are trying to place me, I am the lady you danced with last evening."

"I had not forgotten. But nor would I call what I did *dancing*."

She looked at him sharply. "Dancing it was, though you were coerced into doing so."

He blinked his blue eyes. Opened his mouth. Blinked again.

Crossing her own arms, she turned her back to him, attempting to resume her search, though anger coursed through her and she felt unable to focus with his cold eyes pricking her.

A moment later she was surprised when he stepped to her side and said quietly, "I meant only that I am aware my poor attempt can hardly be called dancing."

"You seemed familiar enough with the steps," she challenged.

He dipped his chin. "True. I can claim no lack of training."

"But you clearly did not enjoy it."

"No. I am—" He cleared his throat. "Miss Haswell, please forgive my conduct of last evening. There is not a man alive who should require coercion to dance with you."

She looked at him, stunned. She felt her lips part, but now it was she who could not seem to speak. And by the time she could, he had already slipped away into the crowd.

It was all Lilly could do to keep from wincing as Miss Augusta Fredrickson hit the climactic note of her aria. However, she could not keep one eyebrow from lifting higher and higher with each screeching half step as the soprano trilled up the score in a piercing octave. The scream, when she first heard it, sounded like more of the same. It took her a few seconds to realize that the scream came from behind her and from a more pleasing voice. She whirled in her seat as the soprano sang on. Clearly others had not realized the shriek had not been part of the performance.

Lilly left her chair and, ducking a bit, hurried to the back of the room. A woman screamed again, this time adding words to her emission. "Somebody help! Call a doctor!"

It was Mrs. Price-Winters, kneeling beside her husband, who lay prone and gasping on the floor.

The singer broke off at last.

The hostess, Mrs. Willoughby, rose. "Is there no doctor in the house?"

Crouched beside Mr. and Mrs. Price-Winters, Lilly searched frantically, but there was no sign of Mr. Graves.

One liveried footman ran to send for a doctor. A second stood nervously at the double doors of the drawing room.

"You there," Lilly called to him. "Please bring me the house medicine chest."

The footman stared at her.

"The mistress does have one?"

He nodded.

"Then hurry!"

The young man rushed away, and Lilly bent to examine Mr. Price-Winters.

In less than a minute, the footman ran back in and set a mahogany box beside the prone man. Kneeling there, Lilly threw open the hinged lid. Square bottles with labels on their shoulders proclaimed their contents—*turkey rhubarb*, *fever powder*, *ipecacuanha*, *laudanum*. Lilly recognized the chest as an older model of one they sold in their shop at home. She pulled open the bottom drawer—lancet, blistering plaster, double-ended measure, and . . . There! The probang. A long flexible device used to dislodge anything stuck in the gullet.

The first footman rushed back in. "Doctor's on his way."

"How long?" Lilly asked.

"A few minutes yet, I'd reckon."

Mr. Price-Winters's face was turning blue.

"He hasn't got a few minutes! Here, help me roll him onto his side." The servant complied. Mrs. Price-Winters was too hysterical to help, and the others seemed frozen—an audience transfixed. It was left to her. She knew what to do. Had done so for Mary more than once. Inserting the probang, she used it first to fully pry open the man's mouth, then to peer down his throat. "Step aside, please. I need more light!"

Someone held an oil lamp above her. There it was. A white object lodged in his throat. She gently but quickly slid the device alongside the obstacle, careful not to push it further down his throat. Pressing the top of the device like a lever, she pushed and pulled simultaneously. This, combined with his gag reflex, was enough to expectorate the obstacle.

"There," she announced, as the object—a round peppermint by the looks of it—popped out.

Mr. Price-Winters coughed and gagged and sucked in a breath, quickly regaining consciousness. His wife embraced him awkwardly there on the carpet. "Oh, thank God!"

Amen, Lilly silently added, grateful Christina's father not been denied life-giving air any longer.

She became aware of murmuring voices, of people staring at her with looks both censorious and amazed. She glanced up, hoping to see her aunt and uncle, but instead saw Mr. Graves. Standing in the back, stone-faced and pale. Had he been there all along? Why had he not come forward?

A distant voice shouted, "Doctor's here!"

A foppish gentleman in evening attire bustled in, carrying his black leather case. "Make way, make way!"

His eyes widened as he took in the open medicine chest, the probang, and the young woman kneeling beside his patient.

"What has happened here?"

Lilly smelled alcohol on the doctor's breath. He had clearly been called away from a supper or party.

"Mr. Price-Winters had a peppermint lodged in his throat," she calmly explained. "He could not breathe."

Mrs. Price-Winters gestured with a limp hand. "She used that thing and got it loose."

"A probang? Good heavens, girl, what were you thinking? You might have punctured his esophagus!"

"I am all right," Mr. Price-Winters whispered hoarsely. "Throat hurts like hades, though."

"And no wonder!" The doctor turned on Lilly. "Who do you think you are to operate on a man?"

Lilly was stunned. Why was he so angry? Was inebriation clouding his judgment?

"I am sorry, Dr. Porter," Mrs. Willoughby soothed. "None of us knew what to do."

Lilly hesitated. Surely she had not done anything so wrong. "I saw no other alternative—"

"Had we known you would arrive so soon," Mrs. Willoughby continued, sending a cool glance her way, "we might have stopped her."

Dr. Porter glared at Lilly. "You could have killed him."

"On the contrary, sir." Adam Graves now stood above them. "He could have died had she not acted."

"Graves . . . you approved this?"

"Not exactly . . ."

His words trailed off and were lost in Dr. Porter's mutterings and instructions for a heavy dose of laudanum, which Lilly thought quite more than necessary.

The crisis past, the crowd began to drain away toward their coats and carriages.

Mrs. Price-Winters offered Lilly her hand. "Thank you, my dear."

Lilly leaned forward and embraced her friend's mother. "I am only glad he is all right." Then she added quietly, "Have him rinse with salt water and a drop of laudanum thrice daily and his throat shall heal quickly."

"Come, Lillian," Aunt Elliott called. "Let us depart."

Even as she stepped away, she heard Dr. Porter ask, "What did she tell you?" Lilly did not hear Mrs. Price-Winters's answer but did hear the doctor call after her, "Who do you think you are? First to operate on a man and then to prescribe treatment?"

Mr. Graves cleared his throat and began weakly, "I must say, Dr. Porter, the young lady acted more quickly than I, but she acted well. Do not abrade her for saving the man."

Lilly silently wished Mr. Graves had found his voice earlier, when the critical crowd was still around to hear it.

"Saving the man? The chit near skewered him."

Her aunt took her arm and said between clenched teeth, "Keep walking, Lillian."

In the carriage, Aunt Elliott sighed emphatically. "Lillian, I know you acted from the heart, but really, could you not have resisted?"

"What would you have had me do? Sit by and do nothing? No one came forward to help, or I would have gladly stepped aside."

"One of the men would have come forward were you not so . . . forward. That Graves fellow was there, it turns out, and the doctor was on his way. You usurped their rightful position as learned medical men."

"He might have died."

"Do not be so dramatic. It was only a peppermint, for goodness' sake."

"Probably choked on it when that soprano hit her high note," Uncle Elliott said dryly. "I know I almost did."

"Mr. Elliott. There is nothing amusing about this. All the dressmakers and dancing masters, all the hours of language, drawing, and deportment. All our efforts, ruined."

"Dear lady, now who is being dramatic? It cannot be as bad as all that. Our Lillian will be a heroine, at least among those with brains in their heads."

"You don't know what you are saying, Mr. Elliott."

"Come now. Even if a few mavens look down on her actions of one evening, they shall forget soon enough."

"I would not depend upon it." Her aunt's voice was haughty and defeated at once. "In that regard, society and Lillian have much in common. They both remember everything."

8

The art of medicine consists of amusing the patients
while Nature cures the disease.

—Voltaire

On a fine afternoon two days later, Lilly joined Christina Price-Winters for a drive through Berkeley Square in a sleek open landau. Tall trees stood sentry around the square, their trunks ringed by daffodils. The air was filled with low laughter and birdsong.

Christina joked and shared confidences as though the coachman were deaf, or as intelligent as the two horses he reined. Lilly shifted uncomfortably on the fine leather seat.

"Look!" Christina pointed across the square. "There's William!"

Christina waved and, beside her, Lilly followed suit. William came jogging across the green toward them. She was surprised to see Mr. Graves striding more sedately several yards behind.

"Hold there, Barker!" Will called to the driver, who halted the pair of bays. Reaching them, Will grasped the landau's door and beamed up at them. "I told Graves we'd find you two trolling the park for admirers."

"We are doing no such thing," Christina snapped playfully.

Mr. Graves joined them and appeared decidedly uncomfortable. Will looked at Lilly and teased, "Or has Miss Haswell been saving lives again?"

Lilly glanced at Mr. Graves, then away. "No, nothing of the kind."

Will did not seem to notice her discomfort. "We've just come from Father, who, I am happy to report, is in excellent health and spirits."

"Yes," Lilly said. "I paid a call this morning and was relieved to find him so."

Will grinned. "Checking on your patient, were you?"

Again she glanced at Graves, who had remained silent throughout the exchange.

"No. Simply to assure myself he is well."

"And he is, thanks to you." Will slapped the edge of the landau. "He confided he was perfectly able to be up and about, but was enjoying Mother fussing over him too much to make the effort. If Father's throat is sore, it is because he cannot cease singing your praises."

Lilly felt her cheeks flush.

"Do come down, and let us go into Gunter's for an ice," Will urged. "What do you say? Perfect weather for it."

Christina looked at Lilly, eyebrows raised hopefully.

"As you like."

Will opened the carriage door and offered a hand in helping the ladies down.

"Wait for us, Barker," he instructed the coachman. "We shall want the carriage for the return home."

"Very good, sir."

Mr. Graves stood awkwardly silent. Will glanced at him, then offered his arm to his sister. "Come, Chrissy. Let us you and I go in and purchase an ice for each of our friends here."

Lilly began to object. "You needn't—"

"The least we can do," Will assured her. "That is, unless you plan to send us a bill?"

Lilly again felt her cheeks burn. "Of course not."

Brother and sister left—Christina sending a look over her shoulder that was part confusion and part speculation over her brother's maneuverings.

Lilly prepared for an awkward wait.

"Shall we walk, Miss Haswell?" Mr. Graves asked suddenly.

She inhaled, relieved. "Thank you. Yes."

Carefully skirting parked carriages and sidestepping horse droppings, they left the paving and walked into the square's central garden. There they strolled under the scant shade of young maple trees, hands behind their backs.

After several minutes, Mr. Graves said, "You are to be commended for your quick actions the other night, Miss Haswell."

She looked up at his handsome, unreadable profile. "Thank you."

"May I ask how you knew what to do?"

Lilly hesitated. Her aunt had long counseled her not to offer details about her upbringing nor her father's trade. And who knew how this Oxford-trained physician would view an apothecary, let alone his daughter. Besides, her actions during the concert were not informed by her life as an apothecary's daughter. At least, not directly. Had the man's heart seized and she'd had to administer digitalis, that would have been another case entirely.

She settled for the most relevant truth. "My dearest friend suffers from falling sickness."

"Epilepsy?" His quick glance was grim. "I am sorry to hear it. Is she in an institution?"

"Heavens no. Why should she be?"

"It is very common here in London, depending on the severity of the fits."

"Well, it is *not* common in Bedsley Priors to lock away a lovely, clever person just because she has been, on rare occasion, seized by fits beyond her control."

Mr. Graves had to hurry to catch up with her agitated strides. "I did not mean to give offense."

"How can I not take offense at such an idea? Mary Mimpurse is a blessing to all who know her. She helps everyone and hurts no one."

He asked gently. "No one but herself?"

Lilly sighed and forced herself to slow down. "On occasion she has fallen and sprained or bruised a limb. Or has been eating and had something lodge in her throat. Twice I've had to pry out obstructions when her mother was not at hand."

"I see. That explains *how* you knew what to do for Mr. Price-Winters." He paused. "But not *why* you did so."

Lilly was confused by the question. "My friend's father needed help."

He stopped walking, and she halted as well, turning to face him.

"I think, Miss Haswell, that any friend of yours is lucky indeed."

She studied his expression and found it sincere. With his pale hair, perfect nose, and golden-lashed eyes of delft blue, Mr. Graves had the face of an angel. The only flaw she noticed was a pair of vertical lines between his eyebrows. He evidently squinted or frowned a great deal.

"I would have done the same for anyone," she said.

"Even someone like me?" Dimples framed each side of his wry grin.

"Even you." *Goodness.* If not for the unfashionable moustache, he might have been prettier than she was.

They resumed their stroll, walking in silence for several moments, relishing the sunshine and the fairlike atmosphere of the popular park.

He cleared his throat. "You were kind not to expose me."

"You were kind to defend me."

He breathed in through his nose. "I am not kind, Miss Haswell. I felt morally compelled to speak. Still, I almost did not, fearing recrimination for my inaction. I believe Dr. Porter was too angry with you to realize."

Or too intoxicated.

"Why was he so angry?"

"I fear most physicians are defensive these days. You are not likely aware, but there is a great deal of contention between the various branches of medicine—physicians, surgeons, apothecaries. Physicians are the most qualified to treat and prescribe, but that does not stop the others from horning in on physicians' rightful domain."

Lilly bit down on her lip, hard, to keep from speaking up, from defending her father's rights and skills.

"Even now," Mr. Graves continued, "Parliament is debating who should be allowed to do what. If men like Dr. Porter have their way, apothecaries will be able to do no more than fill the scripts given them by physicians. They can throw in their lot with the chemists."

Anger rose up in her, but she held it in check. "And do you agree with this assessment, sir?"

He lifted a shrug. "I am not yet certain what to think. Physicians alone are university-educated. Why, anyone with a mortar and pestle can hang a shingle and call himself an apothecary."

She shook her head. "But there are long traditions of apprenticeship, and training with a master at the Apothecaries' Society, which has its own laboratory and physic garden. . . ."

He stopped walking and stared at her.

"Or so I understand."

Quickly, she walked on and changed the subject. "May I ask . . . why did you *not* act when Mr. Price-Winters fell?"

He sighed. "Fear again—my old nemesis."

"Fear of what?"

He shrugged. "Fear of authority, fear of failing, fear of consequences . . . even fear of dancing with a beautiful woman."

Her stomach fluttered. "Goodness," she said breathlessly. "I wonder you want to be a physician at all."

"It is what my father wants. He determined each of our professions. My elder brother will take over the running of Father's estate, though he would have preferred the church. My second brother is a reluctant solicitor here in town. And I shall be a physician."

He took a deep breath before continuing. "I am not yet licensed, Miss Haswell. I resolutely grasp the hope that when that document is in my hand, proclaiming for all the world that I am a fully qualified, capable physician, I shall finally be just that."

Oh dear. She asked gently, "And if not?"

"It does not bear thinking about. My family, my father . . . No. I must overcome and succeed."

Dipping her head, she said, "Then I shall pray for you, Dr. Graves."

She saw him wince.

"Is it the prayer you object to, or the form of address?"

"Forgive me. You may address me as *doctor* if you like, but I fear it will be some time until I am accustomed to it."

Will Price-Winters hailed them, and she and Dr. Graves turned to join brother and sister, each bearing two glass licks of red barberry ice.

The following week, Lilly attended a rout with her aunt and uncle, and again wore the jonquille dress and topaz jewelry. The affair was grand, but her aunt was suffering from a headache, and Lilly from speculative and often cold glances, so they did not stay long. There seemed little point, as Roger Bromley was not in attendance.

Upon their return home, Lilly helped her aunt to her room before slipping downstairs to prepare a remedy. When she returned several minutes later, Dupree was just coming out, her aunt's dress in arms.

"Is she still awake?" Lilly asked.

"Yes, miss."

Seeing the tray in Lilly's hands, the maid knocked on the door for her. Lilly smiled her thanks and entered.

Ruth Elliott sat at her dressing table in her nightdress and dressing gown, brushing her long brown hair, which bore only a few strands of grey. When she laid down her brush and stood, Lilly swiftly set down her tray and took her aunt's arm to help her into bed.

"Thank you, my dear."

"How is your headache?"

"I shall be fine by morning."

"I hope you do not mind, but I have taken the liberty of preparing the Haswell remedy for headaches." *Peppermint, blessed thistle, feverfew, willow bark*. How long had it been since she'd thought in such terms?

Her aunt closed her eyes and released a breath. "My dear, you cannot have failed to notice the coolness, the speculation and gossip about your actions at the Willoughbys' last week. You know I would prefer—"

"I know you wish me to set aside that part of my life, but certainly it can do no harm here at home."

Her aunt looked up at her.

"Here in *your* home," Lilly awkwardly amended.

"No, my dear. I like hearing you saying that. This is your home now, for as long as you like."

"Thank you, Aunt. You are most kind." Lilly kissed her aunt's cheek. "Now, please, drink this." She handed her a teacup from the tray.

Accepting it, her aunt eyed the cup speculatively. "Dare I ask?"

"Merely peppermint and blessed thistle tea." Lilly held out two pills as well. "It is these you need worry about. Rather bitter, I am afraid."

"What are they?"

"Better not to know," Lilly teased. "Don't fret, I have put plenty of treacle in the tea to help you drink them down."

While her aunt swallowed the pills and sipped the tea, Lilly retrieved two cloth bundles from the tray. "And I've brought some wrapped ice."

Lilly arranged one bundle on the pillow and her aunt lay back against it. "There you are. One for your neck and another for your eyes." She settled the second iced cloth over her aunt's eyelids and temples.

"Heavenly," Ruth Elliott murmured.

Standing there, Lilly silently asked God to ease her aunt's pain. Touching her fingers to her throat and finding the necklace there, she said, "I had thought to return the topaz pieces to the jewel chest, but shall we leave it till morning?"

Her aunt's voice was drowsy. "Would you mind setting your things in there yourself, my dear? I prefer not to stir again this night."

"Of course. You rest. Shall I put your rings away as well?"

"If you would not mind. Thank you, Lillian. If you have any trouble, ask your uncle." She waved a limp hand toward the key on the bedside table. "He will likely be awake for some time yet."

"Very well. I shall."

Walking casually through her aunt's dressing room, Lilly opened the jewel chest with its many tiers of velvet-lined drawers—opening one, then another, looking for an empty compartment. Her hand froze. Her stomach lurched. *What on earth?*

Gingerly, she laid aside her jewelry and picked up what surely was a mirage. A specter of her imagination. Her fingers touched the cool metal, the glossy black onyx, and trembled. Her eyes widened and her heart pounded as she lifted the necklace with its unusual webbed, burnished chain and octagonal onyx pendant. She would have known it anywhere. It was the necklace her mother had always worn. The very one she was wearing the last time Lilly saw her. How had it come to be in the chest?

She longed to rush to Aunt Elliott and demand answers, but her aunt was feeling ill. Taking the necklace with her, she went to find her uncle, but contrary to her aunt's prediction, she found him asleep in his favorite chair in the library. Retracing her steps to the dressing room, she carefully returned each piece and locked the chest—its contents now more valuable and bewildering than before. Her questions could wait.

But not for long.

9

> Run into Bucklers bury, for two ounces of
> Dragon-water, spermaceti, and treacle.
>
> —*Westward Ho,* 1607

In the morning, her aunt was no better and stayed in bed.

"But you must still go shopping as we planned," she said. "Take Dupree with you."

"Shopping can wait." Lilly set aside her gloves and sat on the edge of her aunt's bed. "I shall stay and read to you."

Her aunt patted her hand. "Sleep is all I want, my dear. And I shall feel better if you are out enjoying yourself."

"Are you quite certain?"

"Yes, my dear. I am afraid your uncle has taken the carriage, but—"

"I shall hire a hackney. I do not mind in the least." In fact, she was relieved. This way only one servant would know where she'd spent her day.

With her aunt's maid to accompany her, Lilly climbed into a hackney coach and directed the jarvey to take them to Bucklersbury, to a row of shops known as Apothecaries Street.

Dupree looked at her in surprise. "I thought we were going shopping."

"We are. Just not for bonnets and ribbons and such."

"Are you unwell, miss?"

"I am quite well. Only curious."

She had thought of visiting the street once or twice before, though she had always dismissed the idea. But somehow her discussion with Dr. Graves about physicians and apothecaries—as well as the previous night's discovery—left her feeling unsettled and missing home.

When they reached Bucklersbury, near the east end of Cheapside, the two ladies alighted and Lilly paid the driver.

As she turned, she noticed Dupree craning her neck to look down a narrow street leading away from the shops.

"What is it, Dupree?"

"I know this place, miss. My sister lives just up that lane there."

"Does she indeed? Then you and she must have a nice visit while I peruse the row."

"On your own, miss?"

"I shall be quite safe and will venture no further. You can find me right here. Say, in an hour's time?"

"But the mistress . . ."

"We shall keep the specifics about how we spent the day to ourselves. Agreed?"

Dupree grinned. "Very good, miss."

Lilly watched as Dupree hastened up the narrow cross street. Then Lilly closed her eyes and breathed in deeply. Smells familiar and foreign reached her. Sounds too. Her father had told her about London's Apothecaries Street, where nearly every shop housed an apothecary, chemist, or grocer. He had spent a great deal of time on the street during the two years he had lived in London, apprenticed at the Worshipful Society of Apothecaries. She longed to see Apothecaries' Hall, as well as the society's garden in Chelsea, but would settle for Bucklersbury for now.

She began to slowly walk down the street, looking in bowed shopwindows so much like theirs at home. She took in signs advertising the latest patent medicines. She smiled in delight at the displays of the exotic—a shark hanging from one shop awning, a blowfish from another. There a statue of an Indian from the Americas, there a carved rhinoceros—one of the symbols on the

Society's coat of arms. A mother, in fine promenade dress and fruit-sprigged hat, held her toddler atop the wooden creature. The little boy grabbed for the horn on the rhino's back. A second horn graced its nose.

Unlike at home, she heard callers barking out their wares, offering free samples, and promising cure-alls. The further down the row she walked, the louder the clamor rose. She was about to turn back when a corner shop caught her eye. Its flaking window trim, its simple sign, reminded her very much of Haswell's. Stepping closer, she read the sign, *L. Lippert, Apothecary*, and peered through the window. Very similar indeed—traditional displays, neat counters, even an ancient alligator hanging from its beams. Her heart started at the sight of a young woman bent over a ledger at a tall clerk's desk in the corner. She was alone; there were neither customers nor an apothecary to be seen. Then, from the back, a man entered in waistcoat and apron. He wore spectacles and was older than her father but had the same competent bearing. When the man paused and spoke to the young woman, reached out and tugged affectionately at a loose strand of her hair, tears filled Lilly's eyes. She was happy with the Elliotts but suddenly felt nostalgic. How she missed her father. How she missed them all.

As she pushed open the shop door, the bell jangled, a slightly higher pitch than their own. The woman looked up with a pleasant expression. She had fair, delicate features and appeared to be only a year or so older than Lilly herself.

"Might I help you?" she asked.

"I am merely looking."

"You are most welcome."

The man stepped forward. "If I can answer any questions, do not hesitate to ask."

"Mr. Lippert, I presume?"

"The very same."

"I admire your shop. I was quite drawn to it."

"Well, you are alone in that, I am afraid." He stepped to straighten his already tidy counter.

"It reminds me of my father's."

"Ah! Well, I hope his is busier at least."

"Yes. But, after all, he is the only apothecary in our village."

"Indeed? And may I ask the name of this village?"

"Bedsley Priors. In Wiltshire."

"I know it!" He turned to the young woman. "Your grandparents live not far from there, Polly."

"In Little Bedwyn." The girl smiled. "Do you know it?"

"Indeed I do."

"Many a happy hour I spent with my grandparents in that beautiful valley."

Lilly smiled at the genuine warmth of her words.

"When I started out," Mr. Lippert said, brandishing an ancient pestle, " I thought I would return to Little Bedwyn. But the opportunities here in London were just too great. But now you see how it is." He gesticulated toward the window. "My son says that if I am to compete, I must change—update my equipment, displays, and labels; order the latest exotics from the East and West Indies; and stock all the popular patent medicines. Quite a head for business, my son. Unfortunately, prefers the shipping trade to medicine. Unlike Polly here. The draper offered her a position, but she won't hear of it."

"I like it here, Father. Are you wanting to be rid of me?"

"Of course not, my dear. In any case, I think the draper is in greater need of a wife than a clerk."

Polly smiled wryly. "I've no interest in that post either."

Lilly heard a voice shouting outside and walked to the window. She watched with interest a man with a market cart down the street, lifting a bottle high and proclaiming its virtues like a revivalist. "Who is he?"

Polly glanced up. "Just one of those irregular doctors."

"Irregular, indeed," Mr. Lippert said. "I'd call him a peddler at best, or a quack."

"What is he selling?"

"Lady Rutger's Restorative. Won't tell me what's in it. Declares it patent pending. Useless—as far as I can tell."

"You don't sell it here, do you?"

The old man looked chagrined. "I am afraid I do. My son says if customers want it, I should sell it." He walked across the small shop, selected a bottle from his display, and handed it to her. "The fool stuff is very popular."

She looked at the label. "No list of ingredients. No dosage instructions, no warnings."

"Just promises. I have done a bit of study on the stuff. It contains opium to be sure. Its aroma suggests rose, and something else. . . ." He opened the bottle and offered her the cork. She leaned close and sniffed gently.

"Rosemary," she said. "And peony. I'd know that fragrance anywhere."

He raised his brows, impressed. "No wonder Lady Rutger enjoys this restorative. Gets her foxed and fragrant all at once." He grimaced. "Forgive me, that was crude."

"But likely true." Lilly said. "You know, I believe I will trouble you for some feverfew and willow bark pills while I am here. My aunt suffers frequent headaches, and I have used nearly all the pills I brought from home."

"Of course. Though they will require a few minutes to prepare."

"I am happy to wait." She followed him to the back counter. "Have you sea feverfew?"

"No, only corn and common, I'm afraid." He glanced at her over his spectacles. "I am surprised you know the varieties."

"No matter. Common will do nicely. And white willow bark?"

"Very good."

"My goodness," Polly said. "You put this apothecary's daughter to shame."

"Not at all, my dear." Mr. Lippert assured her. Then to Lilly, explained, "Polly concentrates on the bookwork for me. She has no head for herbs and I've no head for numbers."

Lilly smiled. "Then you complement one another well."

The man began retrieving simples and readying his tools. As he worked Lilly noticed his gnarled, arthritic hands.

"I don't suppose you would allow me. I never thought I'd miss it, but . . . for old times' sake?"

"Of course, my dear, if you wish. That I should like to see." With a flourish of his arm, he invited her into his domain.

Setting aside her reticule, Lilly stepped behind the counter. In rapid motions she measured the powders and poured them into the mortar Mr. Lippert provided.

"And for the binding?" he asked.

"Vegetable gum, if you have it."

He handed it to her. Deftly, she added the liquid and picked up the pestle, turning and pressing. When the compound was the right consistency, she transferred it to the work surface, rolled it, then placed it across the grooves of an old gradated pill tile and cut the pills.

"She's a dab hand, she is," Polly said.

Mr. Lippert asked, "Talc, sugar, or silver coating?"

"Feverfew and willow bark are both terribly bitter," Lilly replied.

"Sugar it is."

Using the flat blade, she scooped the coarse pills into the spherical pill rounder, turning it to round the pills and coat them with sugar. After pouring the pills onto a screen to siphon off the extra coating, she scooped the finished pills into a packet.

"My goodness!" Mr. Lippert said. "If you were a lad, I would offer you a post. Oh. No offense, my dear."

She grinned. "None taken. But I should not accept a post in any case. Those days are past for me."

"I am relieved to hear it!" Polly said, but her smile indicated she had felt not the least threatened by her father's praise of Lilly.

"How much for the pills?" Lilly asked.

"Doesn't seem right to charge you full price when you did the work," Mr. Lippert said. "Shall we say sixpence?"

"That is very generous. I can see why you are not the wealthiest apothecary in the row—but I venture you are the kindest."

"Thank you, my dear. Please do come again."

"Oh yes, do," Polly said. "We close at four on Mondays. Come for tea."

"I should enjoy that. Thank you."

Slipping her little parcel into her reticule, she bid farewell to Polly and Mr. Lippert and left the shop, pausing once more to absorb the familiar jingle of the shop bell.

Then she crossed the street to listen to the irregular doctor preach his remedy.

The rotund man stood on a pallet near his cart. He lifted a paper-labeled brown glass jar before the small crowd gathered near. "Lady Rutger's Restorative. It restores the blood, balances the humours, brightens the complexion, and eases the mind."

"Does it balance ledgers?" a young dandy muttered sarcastically, and Lilly bit back a smile.

She raised her gloved hand and called out, "May I ask a question?"

The rotund man looked her way, eyes gleaming. "Of course, lovely lady. I have nothing to hide."

"What is the active ingredient?"

His eyes narrowed, but his smile widened. "Why? Do you plan to open your own laboratory?"

The crowd laughed.

"Not I," she said innocently.

"Of course not. A jest only. Well, miss, I would happily divulge the ingredients active and binding, but I am afraid such knowledge would be difficult to grasp. The world of medicine is the world of learned men, scientists, physicians, masters—"

"And which are you, sir?" the young dandy asked, thrusting his walking stick at the man for emphasis.

The peddler paused, his smile stiffening. "All of the above, I hope."

Lilly added, "And where did you receive your training?"

"The school of life, miss. I have traveled the world, discovered cures not yet known in England. I have treated patients in hut and castle. Farm and court."

"You speak very well, sir," Lilly said in mock admiration. "I should like to hear such a melodious, learned voice list the ingredients of Lady Rutger's Restorative."

"The language of medicine is Latin, miss. Even if I listed the *materia medica*, you would not understand."

"Might I at least try?" she asked.

"Very well." He spoke quickly and authoritatively, "This is a patented aromatic confection consisting of *Rosar*, *Poeniae*, *Anthos*, and *Bryonia dioica*."

He shuttered his brows and lifted one side of his mouth in a patronizing smirk.

She smiled sweetly in return and pronounced, "Or, in plain English—rosewater, peony, rosemary, and common bryony."

His nostrils flared and his mouth slackened.

She felt the stares of the crowd around her but kept her own gaze on the peddler. "In other words, plants these good people might find in their gardens or hedgerows. Or they could purchase from, say, Lippert's Apothecary for a mere fraction of what you are charging. Is that not so?"

The peddler stepped down from his pallet, stalked over, and dipped his face close to hers. "I don't know who you are," he hissed. "But you are coming dangerously close to irritating me. Who do you work for? Old Mr. Lippert? Is this some last-ditch effort to save that musty shop of his?"

She felt a prickle of fear and stepped back, but still projected her voice. "I work for no one and have had the privilege of meeting Mr. Lippert on only one occasion, this very day. But I can tell you, sir, there is not an apothecary—or irregular doctor—that I would trust as completely in all of Apothecaries Street."

"Hey, *Doctor* Poole," an old man called, "I'll have back my eleven shillings if you please."

"And mine as well," called a well-dressed matron.

Poole took a menacing step closer to Lilly, and she stifled the urge to run. She risked a hopeful glance at the dandy, but saw that he and his jaunty stick were backing off in retreat. *Stupid girl*, Lilly silently remonstrated. Why had she dared such a thing alone?

From out of the crowd, Dr. Graves appeared as if by magic, his face a mask of cool confidence. "Come now," he said officiously, "we really must go." He took her arm and led her smartly away from the peddler and the crowd.

Lilly did not resist.

When they had crossed the street, she whispered, "That will do, I think. Thank you."

He paused and released her, expelling a huff of breath. "I must say, Miss Haswell, that was a most foolish thing to do. Safer to stand between a wild dog and his bone. He will only be back again in an hour, and tomorrow and all next week. Do you plan to stand guard at every show?"

"No. But I could not stand by and let those people be taken in by that quack."

"As I saw. I had only come to purchase a few items for the hospital when I glimpsed you nose-to-nose with that mongrel. I could barely believe my eyes." He regarded her speculatively. "Nor my ears. I heard only a few scraps of what you were saying, but your Latin, Miss Haswell, is impressive indeed. I am surprised your tutor included the subject."

She hesitated. "I have learned a great many things since coming to London," she said, which was true enough. Though Latin had not been among them.

He glanced up the street, at the few waiting carriages. "You are not here alone, I trust?"

"No. I came with my aunt's maid in a hackney. She should return any moment."

He looked at her, eyes alight. "Then might I have the honor of delivering the two of you safely home?"

She smiled, relieved. "That you might, Dr. Graves." She cocked her head to one side to regard him. "For someone who owns numerous fears, may I say you acted very bravely today. I thank you for coming to my rescue."

His fair cheeks reddened with pleasure, and she thought his thin frame stood the taller for her praise.

"Well then," he said, "I am excessively glad I roused myself to the task."

10

> Give me an ounce of civit, good apothecary, to sweeten my imagination.
>
> —Shakespeare

When Lilly entered her aunt's room later that afternoon, Ruth Elliott smiled at her expectantly from the dressing table. "There you are, my dear." She patted the chair beside her. "Come. Show me what you have bought."

"I am afraid I found little I could not live without. Shopping was not the same without you. And you—how are you feeling?"

"A great deal better."

"I am relieved to hear it."

"Sleep is a powerful elixir. One they don't sell in shops. I think I shall even dress for dinner."

"Aunt, may I ask . . ." Lilly's heart began pounding at the mere thought of the black necklace. It was an effort to speak calmly. "May I ask about something I saw in your jewelry chest?"

Her aunt's eyes glinted. "Ah . . . Saw something that caught your fancy, did you?"

"Well, in a manner of—"

Her aunt rose. "Let us have a look. I am sure whatever it is, you shall be welcome to wear it. What is our next engagement? I forget. Dinner at Caldwells'?"

Thoughts elsewhere, Lilly vaguely replied, "I am not sure."

Ruth Elliott selected a key from the ornate chatelaine. "Here we are."

Lilly followed her into the dressing room and watched as her aunt opened the chest. "Now, what is it that has caught your eye, hmm?"

Lilly's palms were damp as she reached into the case and pulled open the compartment. Would it still be there, or had she dreamt it?

There it was. Black filigree. Black onyx. She lifted it reverently and turned to her aunt. Ruth Elliott took it from her gingerly, her brow furrowed. "I would not have guessed. This is rather severe, is it not? Elegant for mourning, I suppose. But not suitable, really, with any of your gowns. . . ."

"I do not wish to wear it. I wish to know how it came to be here."

Ruth Elliott looked at her, confused. Did her aunt truly not know this had been her mother's? Or was she hesitating, trying to figure out a plausible explanation?

"What do you mean, my dear?"

Lilly did not want to believe her aunt capable of deception, and the innocent question seemed genuine enough.

"Where did it come from?"

"I . . . I don't know. I think . . . if I remember correctly, it is a piece your uncle acquired."

"Acquired? From whom?"

The older woman stared at the necklace as though it held the answer, her face stretched in concentration. "I think he said he purchased it at auction. I don't recall where."

"Auction?" Was it possible? Lilly could hardly credit such a coincidence. Unless her uncle had bid on the piece *because* he had recognized it. "When? How long ago?"

"You will have to ask your uncle. But it seems to me that piece has been there for several years. I have never worn it. I really do not know what would possess him to buy such a thing, though I have never had the heart to tell him so."

Her aunt took her by the arms, concern deep in the lines of her face. "What is it, Lillian? Why do you want to know?"

It was on the tip of her tongue to say, *It was my mother's*. But she bit the words back. Should she tell her aunt if her uncle had never done so? Had he his reasons? Lilly swallowed. "It is an unusual piece, to be sure. You are right. I shall ask Uncle about it as you suggest."

"But—"

"Forgive me. I had better hurry or I shall never dress for dinner in time."

"Very well, my dear."

But she felt her aunt's concern follow her from the dressing room.

As they sat at the dining table that evening, each spooning spring soup in polite, silent sips, her aunt broached the subject.

"My dear. Lillian would like to ask you about a necklace in the chest."

"Oh?"

"The unusual black piece with the onyx pendant?"

Her uncle's face looked disturbed, his eyes stared at the tablecloth, unseeing. Or was she imagining this?

"I am afraid I do not have your every bauble memorized, my dear."

"Of course not. But you would remember this piece. Black filigree, octagonal pendant? I believe you said you purchased it at auction several years ago."

"Did I?" He set down his spoon with a clatter and leaned back heavily against the chair. "Let us finish our meal in peace—then you may show me the article in question. All right?"

Her aunt looked mildly stunned. "Yes, of course."

After dinner the Elliotts disappeared into her aunt's room, and Lilly retreated to her own, waiting anxiously. She found herself thinking back to the day her mother had disappeared. Of coming home to find her father pacing and Charlie hiding behind the draperies. She had gone into the bedchamber and begun searching through her mother's drawers and wardrobe, looking for a letter or for some clue as to why she had left and where she had gone. Lilly feared she knew the reason, at least in part. Even now, she couldn't quite dispel the guilt she felt, the awful notion that their argument had been the cause.

During her long ago search, Lilly had quickly surmised her mother had taken her jewelry and better dresses. Then she had realized the map was gone. The world map she and her mother had pored over on rainy afternoons—the rectangle of thick creased paper the color of a tea stain. The print dominated by two spheres—the eastern Old World. The western New. As a girl, Lilly could hardly believe the tiny rabbit-shaped island was England, its ears Scotland. How small her world was compared to the rest of the world. Mother had agreed, and together they dreamt for hours, their fingers tracing latitude lines, underscoring names of faraway places—the Canary Islands, Trinidad, Tobago, the Southern Icy Ocean—and imagining aloud what each might be like. Her mother seemed to know how long a sea journey might take to *Terra Australis*, where convicts were transported, or to the Cape of Africa, or to South America's Horn.

When she had left, Rosamond Haswell had taken the well-worn map with her. Where had *it* taken her? Was she even now using it to chart her course?

Lilly was pacing her room half an hour later when the housemaid knocked and asked her to join Mr. Elliott in the library. Lilly went down directly.

Her uncle stood alone, one hand on the fireplace mantel. "Come in, my dear. Be seated."

She sat in one of the chairs at the library table, hands clasped. An oil lamp glowed upon the table's gleaming mahogany surface.

He stepped quietly toward her, unfurling his palm, and the black necklace uncoiled from his hand. He laid it on the table between them.

He sighed, his eyes on the piece. "In all honesty, I had forgotten it was there—or at least put it from my mind."

She swallowed and whispered, "It was my mother's, was it not?"

He looked at her, sadness heavy in his hound dog eyes. "Yes, it was. Though I am surprised you remember it so clearly. Ah, I forget. Your infallible memory."

She hung her head. "Not *infallible* . . ."

"I meant no censure. I only wish my memory were half so keen." He sat down in the chair opposite and sighed again. "Your aunt did not know it was your mother's. I never told her before tonight."

While Lilly was relieved at her aunt's exoneration, confusion still plagued her. "Why?"

"Your mother did not wish for Ruth to know."

"I . . . I don't understand. What control would she have over an auction?"

"It was not a public auction, although I allowed Ruth to believe it so. Your mother came to see me privately."

"When?"

"Must be nearly four years ago now. I did not know then that she had left all of you. I arrogantly assumed your father had fallen on difficult times. Difficult indeed for her to be willing to come to me, to ask for money."

Lilly found it hard to breathe.

"She said she would rather offer the piece to me than some stranger, since I ought to value it more highly. I supposed she wanted to keep it in the family. Honorable enough, though it did strike me as cheeky to ask for money for something that our parents had given her."

"What else did she say? Where was she living?"

"As I said, I foolishly assumed she had merely come from Wiltshire seeking funds. I did not ask questions. Though I am afraid I said a few cruel things."

"Cruel?"

"About your father not being able to support her—how we had all been right in advising her not to marry him. I am ashamed to think of what I said then."

"I wonder if she was living in London or passing through . . . Was she alone?"

"Yes."

"And she asked you not to tell Aunt?"

"She and Ruth had been girlhood friends. I imagine it embarrassed her to think of Ruth knowing."

"Or perhaps she realized Aunt would ask more questions than you did. Questions she did not wish to answer."

"Perhaps."

"Did she ask for money on other occasions as well?"

He hesitated only a second. "No, my dear. That was the only money she ever asked for. I suppose she had nothing else of value and was too proud to ask for a handout."

Lilly shook her head, imagining the awkward scene between estranged brother and sister.

"I am sorry, Lillian. I never intended to deceive you. It is only that I knew it would upset you. Tell me you understand."

"I do." She stood slowly to her feet. "Does Aunt? Or is she angry with you?"

He shrugged. "Disappointed, perhaps."

Lilly walked to the window on wobbly legs. Outside on the street, lamplight gleamed on the rain-wet cobbles.

"Will you be all right?" he asked.

"Of course. Thank you for telling me."

Her uncle rose as well. "You are welcome to the necklace, Lillian. I am certain your mother would want you to have it."

Lilly was not so sure. Did anyone really know what her mother wanted? "Let us leave it locked away. For now."

In the morning, her aunt came to her room while Lilly was still in her dressing gown. She took Lilly's strong hands in her own delicate ones.

"My dear, I am sorry. I cannot imagine how you must be feeling."

"I don't know how to feel about it."

She squeezed her hands. "How can I help?"

Lilly took a deep breath. "By telling me everything you know."

Ruth Elliott hesitated. "Your mother and I confided a great deal to one another as girls, but I know very little about what happened after she married your father."

"And before?"

"Well, I don't think you . . . I don't think anyone enjoys hearing a parent's romantic history—that is, history not involving the other parent."

"Tell me anyway." Lilly seated herself on the made bed and patted the nearby chair.

Her aunt sat, though she looked far from comfortable. "Your mother fancied herself in love with a man before she met your father. Did she ever tell you?"

Lilly shook her head, and her aunt continued. "A very dashing man. A naval officer. And she believed he planned to marry her."

"What was his name?"

Ruth Elliott twisted her rings. "I suppose it can do no harm. A Captain Ernest Quincy. But everyone called him Quinn."

The name meant nothing to Lilly.

"She used to tell me that Quinn planned to have ships of his own one day and travel far and wide. And that he promised to take her with him."

Lilly nodded thoughtfully. She could understand how such a man—and such an offer—might appeal to her mother. Had she not spent hours dreaming over her prized world map?

"Rosamond was so happy in those days," Ruth continued. "Then, without warning, Quinn's betrothal was announced in the *Times*. He had engaged himself to Daisy Wolcott, a much better match, I suppose, as her father was quite wealthy. Rosamond was devastated.

"But then, not a fortnight later, she told me she had met another man and that this Charles Haswell was everything Quinn was not. Evidently, *he* thought Rosamond the most desirable and perfect creature ever to live. Balm to her wounded soul, no doubt. But as you know by now, the family thought Charles not at all suitable. No wealth. No family to speak of. No connections." She glanced at Lilly with sorrowful eyes. "I am sorry, but there it is." She took a deep breath. "Of course, Rosamond saw none of this. She argued that he would soon have a good income and good prospects. But more than this, she knew your father would take her from London, the scene of her disgrace, as she saw it, and I think this was his greatest attraction.

"He proposed in a matter of days, and Rosamond accepted. We all tried to dissuade her from such a course. Had your grandfather lived, he would never have allowed it, but he had already passed on by then. Rosamond begged Jonathan to purchase a special license so that she and Charles might marry as soon as possible. In the end, she married two days before Quinn's own wedding, with only her mother, Jonathan, and I in attendance. I think Rosamond spent a great deal of time imagining Quinn's remorse at discovering her wed to another. Several times during the wedding, I saw her glance toward the side door, as if she was sure Quinn would burst through it and object at any moment."

Ruth Elliott shook her head ruefully. "Your uncle determined that no one of our acquaintance should learn of your father's trade. When asked, we spoke in general terms of his 'holdings' somewhere in Wiltshire. After the wedding, the two departed almost immediately. Much to Rosamond's—and everyone's—relief, I am sorry to say."

Her aunt stopped speaking, and the room felt suddenly too silent. The clock above the mantel ticked, a door closed somewhere belowstairs, the faint sounds of hooves and passing carriages bled through the outside walls.

Lilly said, "I can see why you hesitated to tell me. It is not a romantic story, is it? I wonder if my poor father had any idea."

"I do not know, my dear."

Lilly rose, agitated, as all the new details struggled to fit themselves into the old and erroneous impressions in her mind. "So . . . did this Quinn ever buy his ships and sail away?"

Ruth remained seated. "Not that I know of. He is still married to the former Miss Wolcott. Though it does not appear to be a happy marriage. I see Daisy now and again, and she is almost always alone. The gossips claim, and I am among them now, I suppose, that he has kept a string of mistresses."

"You don't think Mother—?"

Aunt Elliott shifted, glanced at her, then away. "As far as I know, their connection was severed more than twenty years ago." She paused. "But I confess, when we received your father's letter telling us Rosamond had left him, I wasn't as surprised as I might have been, had I not known about Quinn. I had hoped Rosamond would be happy with your father. But I never really believed she would be." She sighed. "I am afraid I don't know any more, my dear. I have no idea where she went or where she is now."

Lilly stared out the second-floor window, at the passing traffic and the trees of Hyde Park beyond. "I have always imagined her sailing the high seas, or on a grand adventure somewhere."

"Have you indeed?"

Lilly turned and glimpsed some unfamiliar, dark emotion in her aunt's countenance.

"Then your imagination is far more generous than mine."

11

> But if the young are never tired of erring in conduct,
> neither are the older in erring of judgment.
>
> —Fanny Burney, *Cecilia*, 1782

Thoughts and questions coursed through Lilly all that day and night. In the morning, she felt quite restless. She wanted to run. Needed to run. But where in all of London could she do such a thing? Where were there no eyes ready to censure and report her unladylike conduct?

No place.

She sighed, took up the cup of chocolate from the tray on her bedside, and sipped. Chocolate had always helped her moods but did little to soothe her antsy limbs.

After breakfast, Lilly received a letter. She took it with her into the sitting room, planning to keep her aunt company while the dear woman did her daily hour of needlework. Her aunt smiled up at her, and Lilly smiled in return. No conversation was required. They were now comfortable enough with one another to enjoy silence as well as chatter.

The letter was from Mary. As she opened it, Lilly realized mildly that it was the first she had received from her old friend in several weeks.

When Lilly had first come to London, Mary had dutifully written every fortnight, if not weekly. And Lilly had written back, though not always as promptly as she should have. It was difficult that first year, when she was always so busy with her studies. And now . . . Well, she had time in the early mornings, surely, before the day's round of calls began, but then with taking exercise in the park, then tea, then endless evening and late-night social obligations, somehow she rarely made the time to write home.

She skimmed the few lines in Mary's small practiced hand, and experienced the pleasant warmth she always felt upon reading cheerful reports of new biscuit recipes, the topic of the Sunday sermon, or the latest village fete she had attended with Charlie, Francis, and Miss Robbins.

Lilly knew she should write back, but what could she say? She did not wish to describe the new gowns, the balls, shopping with Miss Price-Winters on Bond Street and Pall Mall, the museums, the concerts. She could not describe Roger Bromley nor his kind attentions—not when Mary had never known a suitor's regard.

"From home?" Aunt Elliott asked, eyes on her embroidery.

"Yes. From Mary."

Lilly would not demur and pretend her days were as ordinary as Mary's countrified life no doubt was.

She sighed.

Her aunt, pulling a thread of bishop's blue through the canvas, glanced up at the sound. "Everything all right?"

"Oh yes. The usual niceties." She began refolding the letter. "I like that blue."

I shall write back tomorrow, Lilly decided. *Or the next day.*

"Mr. Adam Graves," Fletcher announced and backed from the sitting room.

Startled, Lilly stood abruptly, the letter falling to the floor.

Dr. Graves entered and bowed. "Miss Haswell."

She curtsied and awkwardly swiped up the letter as she did so. "You remember my aunt, Mrs. Elliott?" Lilly hoped he would not mention their recent encounter on Apothecaries Street.

"I do indeed. Ma'am." He bowed again, a wave of blond hair falling forward and then returning to place as he straightened.

Her aunt nodded but remained seated with her needlework.

"By your leave, ma'am, I have come to ask if Miss Haswell might accompany me for a drive in the park. Perhaps tomorrow afternoon?"

Her aunt's expression was pleasantly bland, but the eyes she turned toward Lilly were full of both meaning and inquiry.

"I was certain we had an engagement for tomorrow afternoon. Are we not expected at the Langtrys', my dear? Do you recall?"

Lilly recognized her aunt's clever phrasing. She was giving Lilly an excuse—if she desired one. Lilly knew her aunt would prefer she not encourage the man, but she would not forbid her either. He was, at least, an Oxford man, and must therefore be from a family of at least modest wealth.

She swallowed. "I believe you are thinking of Friday, Aunt. I recall nothing on the schedule for tomorrow."

"Indeed? Well, you would know. That memory of yours. Sometimes I am not sure I should like to have one so keen."

Dr. Graves cleared his throat. "Excellent. I shall hire a carriage straightaway. I've not my own in town."

Aunt Elliott's eyebrows rose.

"I have use of my brother's, but it is engaged for the morrow."

Lilly bit her lip. Did he not know hacks were not allowed in Hyde Park? "Dr. Graves, you needn't bother. I would just as soon walk."

"Indeed? Are you quite sure?"

"Quite. At home there was only one thing I liked better than a country walk."

"And what was that?"

She glanced at her aunt, then changed the subject. "What time shall I expect you?"

Dr. Graves arrived promptly to take Lilly for the promised walk in Hyde Park, only a short distance from her aunt and uncle's home. He wore a morning coat of claret with a patterned waistcoat and buff trousers. Her aunt could not complain that his attire was not *de rigueur*.

Lilly wore a walking dress of ivory corded muslin with a lilac satin shawl. At her aunt's suggestion, she wore a large Oldenburg bonnet, perhaps to keep those of Mr. Bromley's acquaintance from seeing her out with another man.

Meeting anyone she knew seemed unlikely, however, as Hyde Park was sparsely populated in the early afternoon. The fashionable set did not show up until half past five, when they arrived en masse in fine carriages and finer carriage dress, and raced and ogled and flirted until it was time to return home and change into evening dress.

Nor were there any military reviews or driving meets to disturb their solitude as Lilly and Dr. Graves strolled along the web of walking paths and around manmade Serpentine Lake. As they did, Lilly did her best to conjure conversation, pointing out flowers in bloom, a chattering squirrel in a tree, and the occasional dandy in a high-perch phaeton. Dr. Graves would nod or murmur assent to whatever she said, but he was clearly distracted.

Finally he said, "Previously, Miss Haswell, you asked about my fears."

"You needn't—"

"I do," he insisted, then exhaled deeply. "I have diagnosed the underlying cause, I believe. Though not the prognosis, nor treatment. I am the youngest of three sons, as I believe I mentioned. We were all sent to a boarding school reputed for its unwavering discipline. But the stern headmaster was nothing to my father. We did as he said or the consequences were severe. To this day I struggle to confront authority or act in the face of opposition. I was five and twenty before I made a truly important decision on my own."

She looked at him and asked tentatively, "And what was it, if I may ask?"

He blinked his startling blue eyes. "Why . . . to court you."

She felt her face flush and her heart pound in sweet heavy beats. They walked in silence for several minutes before he spoke again.

He began abruptly, "I think it only fair to tell you that I was engaged once, but the lady broke it off."

"Oh." She was taken aback. "I . . . I am sorry."

He glanced at her briefly, then away. "She was my father's choice, but I am afraid neither she nor her mother approved of my chosen profession. The thought of hospitals, injuries and diseases . . . all quite disgusted them both."

Lilly nodded her understanding.

"I suppose medicine *is* rather distasteful," he continued. "Boils and growths. Infections and bodily fluids . . ." He stopped, turning to her, face stricken. "Forgive me!"

Lilly said mildly, "Do not be uneasy on my account."

"Such talk does not disturb you?"

"No. Though I own it is not my favorite mealtime topic."

"Of course. But you do not swoon nor faint nor sicken?"

Lilly shook her head.

He paused on the tree-lined path, regarding her with frank admiration. She was tempted to tell him the reason behind her understanding nature. But her aunt's cautioning voice whispered in her mind.

"In that case—" he gave a rare smile—"there is someplace I should very much like to show you."

His smile transformed his features. His frown lines disappeared, his eyes crinkled, his dimples deepened.

Oh my . . . Lilly felt her cheeks grow warm as she gazed at him, glad he could not read her thoughts.

12

Fade far away, dissolve, and quite forget
What thou among the leaves hast never known,
The weariness, the fever, and the fret
Here, where men sit and hear each other groan. . . .

—John Keats, poet & licensed apothecary, 1819

Dr. Graves hired a hackney to drive them to the southeast of London, to large and impressive Guy's Hospital.

"I would like you to see where I have spent my days and sometimes my nights this last year gone. This is where I 'walk the wards' as we say, to obtain practical experience. Officially I am a perpetual physician's pupil and pay handsomely for the privilege. Or rather, my father does." He gave a lopsided grin, blue eyes sparkling. "I have taken the examination for licentiateship and should learn very soon whether or not I have passed."

When they arrived, he paid the driver and helped Lilly down from the hired coach. She relished the excuse to place her gloved hand in his, however fleetingly.

He led her through the wrought-iron gates into the open courtyard, flanked on three sides by the four-story hospital of grey and drab-brown brick. In the center of the courtyard, they passed the statue of Thomas Guy himself, who founded the hospital nearly a century before.

"Do you know anything about Thomas Guy, Miss Haswell?"

She shook her head.

"I cannot but admire him. He was a man of humble beginnings—the son of a coal monger. He became a bookseller, and amassed his splendid fortune from the sale of Bibles, among other things. The list of all he did, all he gave, would run the length of a man's arm."

Passing between columns and beneath an archway, they entered the building. Dr. Graves seemed to come to life within its walls. Gone was the reticent man she had met at the ball. Eagerly, he led her on an enthusiastic tour of the main hall, the chapel, the lecture theatre, and two of the twelve wards.

"This is a teaching hospital," he explained. "Apothecaries, surgeons' apprentices, physicians' pupils, and dressers come here for courses of study."

Her attention was piqued by the mention of apothecaries, but this time she kept her mouth closed.

A young man bearing a stack of books and papers whipped around a corner and collided with Dr. Graves. Graves reached out his hands to prevent a blow, but still the young man's books and papers fell and scattered to the floor.

"I say, Keats, have a care."

"Sorry, old man." Young Mr. Keats sank to his haunches and began picking up his papers. Lilly did the same, picking up the sheet that had landed on the toe of her boot. She glanced at it, surprised to see, in a lovely hand, stanzas of a sonnet. A few phrases leapt off the page. *O SOLITUDE! . . . climb with me the steep . . . flowery slopes . . .*

As he rose, Lilly saw that the man, near her own age, seemed distracted and flighty as a sparrow.

She held out the paper toward him. Eyeing it, his frenetic movements stilled. He lifted his gaze to hers, warily. Without comment, she handed him the paper. He tucked it under the book on the top of his stack.

"Thank you, fair miss."

"Miss Haswell, may I present Mr. John Keats."

The young man bowed. "How do you do."

"Mr. Keats is training to become an apothecary. Are you not, Keats?"

He ducked his head. "Yes . . . and other pursuits as well."

Graves peered at the book Keats bore. "A volume of lyric poetry . . . I do not recall that in the curriculum."

"No, sir. Only in my spare time, sir."

Bowing again to Lilly, John Keats strode quickly down the corridor.

Watching him retreat, Dr. Graves shook his head. "Keen student. But a bit of a dreamer, I'm afraid. Fancies himself a poet. Writes such nonsense in the margins of his work . . ."

Graves then led her up two flights of stairs. "I would not bring you up here were any operations scheduled. But you might find the theatre itself interesting." He pushed the door open and ushered her inside. The air that met her held a sour, cloying odor, which she recognized instantly as blood. The theatre was horseshoe shaped with three rows of benches rising high on two curved sides.

He led her down the steep stairs to the operating pit below. A narrow wooden table stood at center. Light from a skylight and two gas lamps suspended from the ceiling illuminated the scene. Beneath the table was a box of sawdust for collecting blood, she guessed. Beside it was a common dining room chair and a sideboard of instruments. A mop and bucket stood at the ready against the wall.

From this lower vantage, Dr. Graves pointed up to the rows of benches rising around them. "The first two rows are for the dressers, and behind that partition sit the other pupils. All are required to attend, whether future surgeons, physicians, or apothecaries."

Suddenly the door above them, from which they themselves had entered, burst open, and a stream of young men rushed in, filing into the rows with friendly shoving and jocularity.

Graves frowned and looked at her apologetically. "Must be an operation after all. An emergency perhaps. Let us take our leave."

Before they could, the side door opened and two aproned men came in, carrying a draped figure on a litter.

Lilly climbed the steps quickly, but midway up, glanced back. Behind the two assistants came a man she identified as a surgeon by the old frock coat he wore, stained with blood, dried and fresh.

"Miss Haswell," Dr. Graves urged from behind. "Please."

She continued to the top, Dr. Graves at her heels. By now, the pupils were packed in as tight as pills in a bottle and pushing each other and maneuvering to see below.

Whenever their views were blocked, whether by fellow pupil or by surgeon below, calls of "Heads, heads," rang out. The air was filled with anticipation, laughter, and whistles to chums across the theatre—all of which seemed to belong not to this grave occasion, but to some macabre sporting event.

Once the door was closed behind them, her escort said earnestly, "Miss Haswell, please forgive me. If I had any notion they were operating today . . . I . . . I never meant to expose you to such sights."

Moved by the concern in his eyes and voice, she took a deep breath and considered what she had just seen. "I own I was relieved not to witness the operation itself, but I found the theatre, the wards, the dispensary . . . why, the entire hospital, quite interesting."

"Truly?"

"Yes."

He shook his head, eyes wide in amazement or disbelief, she could not tell.

As they walked on, leaving the din behind them, Lilly remarked, "Had I to require surgery, I should not like it above half to be observed by such a crowd."

"Nor I. It is mostly the poor who come here. They are willing to bear spectators because this is the only place they can afford treatment. Wealthier patients are operated on in their own homes. Usually on their kitchen tables, I understand."

She nodded without comment. In Bedsley Priors, people had to call upon the surgeon in Wilcot for such services. Her father did only minor procedures himself.

"Sadly the death rates are shockingly high. Therefore such operations are usually only performed as a last resort. I will be pleased to limit my practice to physic, if I may—though I suppose in smaller villages a medical man might need to do a bit of everything."

They descended the stairs and were once again in the long main corridor.

"*Do* you plan to establish yourself in a small village somewhere? I had not thought it of you."

He shrugged, then asked shyly, "Does the thought displease you?"

"Not at all. Why would it?"

He paused, examining her countenance closely. "Can you really be so perfect?"

Lilly felt her cheeks heat. She darted a look at him and saw his face redden as well.

"Hardly perfect, no." She was again tempted to disclose her father's trade and even her mother's disappearance. Certainly her aunt would not wish her to withhold the truth once a man was courting her, would she?

As they returned to the welcomed fresh air of the courtyard, he said, "If your father were alive, I should ask to meet him."

Confusion puckered her brow. "But he is alive."

He stared at her. "Is he? Well, dash it, what a blunder. I was given to understand that you were a ward of the Elliotts."

"I suppose I am. But not an orphan. My father is alive and well in Wiltshire."

"I see. Well, this changes everything. Do you think a letter would suffice?"

Here he was again, the timid man full of self-doubt.

She did not want to mistake his meaning. "What . . . sort of letter do you mean?"

Again, his face reddened. "I suppose a letter of introduction and, well, to . . . express my interest."

"In courting me?" she asked bluntly. How far afield she was from the subtle language of fans and flirting her aunt had paid so dearly for her to learn!

"Well, yes. For now."

"Then perhaps my uncle is the person to speak with in my father's stead." She thought once more of revealing her secrets. But if her uncle withheld his approval, might they both be spared the telling? "However, I must warn you that my aunt prefers I keep my distance from medical men."

"Why?"

"I am afraid in that, you will not find her much different from the mother of your previous fiancée."

"I see. I take it your aunt would be quite shocked to learn where you spent the afternoon?"

She shook her head. "Shocked, no. But certainly disappointed. I shall tell her the truth—" she grinned up at him—"that we enjoyed a most interesting walk."

He smiled back at her and again his features were transformed. He truly was a lovely man.

The shop bell jingled as Lilly and Dupree entered Monday morning. Polly Lippert looked up from her books and exclaimed, "Miss Haswell!" She rose, smoothing her apron over a patterned muslin frock. "How good of you to come again."

"I hope you don't mind my calling unannounced."

"No, you are most welcome. Any time."

"This is Miss Dupree. Dupree, this is Miss Lippert."

The maid bobbed a curtsy, then turned to Lilly. "Mind if I have a look around?"

"No. Go on."

Miss Lippert led Lilly back to the kitchen—far neater than theirs at home. Lilly realized the Lipperts must keep a separate laboratory.

"I am sorry my father is not here," Miss Lippert said. "He and my brother, George, have gone to the Docklands."

Lilly would have liked to meet George Lippert. A person like herself, skilled in physic but wanting little to do with it.

"Two colliers are just in from the Cape," Polly continued as she set a pot of water to boil. "The advertisement promised an immense shipment of new exotics and a *live* rhinoceros."

"I should have liked to see that," Lilly said, though she could just imagine how her aunt and uncle would cringe at the thought of her venturing to such a rough, dirty place.

Polly pulled two teacups from the cupboard and set out a pot of tea—infused with mint from their shop stores—and a plate of butter biscuits. The two young women enjoyed tea and half an hour's visit. As Lilly and Dupree prepared to take their leave, Polly wrapped up a new bottle of Warren and Rosser's Milk of Roses, which Dupree insisted Lilly use daily to diminish her freckles. Lilly was just tying the ribbons of her wrap when a startling crash rang out, quickly followed by the shattering of glass. Polly rushed to the shop-window, and Lilly and Dupree hurried to join her there. Through the wavy glass, Lilly saw a man in a blue gown standing in the threshold of a shop on the other side of the street. In his arms he held a crate of Lambeth pottery.

Lilly cried out in shock as he heaved the jars into the street.

The pottery exploded into pieces. Oils and syrups spilled like jeweled blood onto the beginnings of a pile in the street—wood from a broken medicine chest, perhaps, and shards of blue and brown glass.

"What is he doing?" Lilly exclaimed.

"Dash it. Father told Hetta to be careful."

A woman of middle years ran hysterically into the street, shrieked, then grabbed hold of the man's sleeve as he carried out another load. He did not even seem to notice her. This time he held a decorative blue and gold apothecary jar, nearly half his own height.

"No!" the woman cried.

The man seemed to hesitate for a moment, but perhaps it was only an illusion of the wavy glass. His expression stern, he heaved it onto the pile, the priceless piece shattering in a shower of blue and gold.

Lilly ran to the door and opened it. But Polly caught her arm and held her back. "Don't, Miss Haswell."

"Can we not do something?"

"What can we do? He is the beadle, and the man there"—Polly nodded toward an officious-looking man in black watching the proceedings with cool detachment—"is the master of wardens for the Apothecaries' Society."

Stunned into silence, Lilly watched from the open doorway.

"They are within their rights," Polly went on. "Everyone knows Hetta diagnoses and dispenses physic. Last week a boy nearly died from mislabeled medicine."

"Oh no."

"And it isn't the first time. There have been charges of selling inferior and adulterated medicine before."

"But why would they?"

Polly shrugged. "Mistakes. To save money. I don't know. Her poor husband."

Lilly looked at her, brows raised.

"He's under the cat's paw, that one is," Polly explained. "He's never been able to manage Hetta. Always insists she is as qualified as any man in the row."

The woman named Hetta covered her face and disappeared back into the shop. Finally the beadle brought out a large armful of dried herbs, stuck bunches in crevices among the rubble, and heaped the rest on top. A few seconds later he returned once more from inside the shop, this time bearing a smoldering stick of tinder, which he put to rapid use. The herbs smoked for a few seconds and then, fed by the alcohol in several of the syrups, leapt to angry life, the fire devouring the wood and filling the narrow street with pungent smoke.

Lilly stared. The flames and smoke rose to both frame and obscure the sign hanging above the desecrated shop. *J. W. Fry, Apothecary*. Though the heated air touched her skin where she stood, Lilly shivered.

13

> A certain noble lord had brought his health into a very critical state and the physicians recommended marriage as the most certain method of restoring his constitution.
>
> —*The Gentleman's Magazine,* 1769

Lilly flipped through the letters on the silver tray on the sideboard.

"Strange," she muttered.

Her aunt peered at her over the half-spectacles she wore for reading. "What is, my dear?"

"I wrote to my father nearly a fortnight ago and have yet to receive a response."

Lilly had at last written a few lines to her father the same day she had finally sent a note to Mary to wish her old friend a happy birthday.

Her aunt refolded her own letter. "Perhaps he is busy. Or the post was delayed."

"I do hope he is all right." Though she had not seen her father in over a year, they had corresponded regularly. Her planned visit last Christmas had been canceled when her aunt came down with a worrisome fever. Lilly had stayed in town to nurse her, and somehow the visit home had never been rescheduled.

"Of course he is. He would send word if there was anything amiss, would he not?"

"I hope so." Now that Lilly thought of it, his letters had become increasingly infrequent.

Her aunt slit open a second letter and began to read. She looked up at Lilly again, eyes bright.

"My dear, you will not believe it!"

"What is it? I have rarely seen you so animated."

"The Bromleys have accepted our invitation to dine with us on Saturday. They must realize Roger has selected you particularly. This is a most telling attention, to be sure."

"But we invited them."

Ruth Elliott went on undeterred, "Mark my words, Lillian. Roger Bromley will very soon be making you an offer."

"Oh, Aunt, I do not think so."

Lilly had hoped for such from Mr. Bromley since the end of last season. For beyond wishing to please her aunt by making a good match, she genuinely liked him. But now, with Susan Whittier on the scene, Lilly had all but given up that hope. Depressing though it was to lose the man's gallant addresses, Dr. Graves's attentions had served to lessen her disappointment.

"My dear . . ." Aunt Elliott removed her spectacles. "Tell me you will not reject Roger Bromley in favor of that Graves fellow."

Would she? Had she not given him leave to speak to her uncle on her behalf—believing Mr. Bromley lost to her?

Her aunt leaned closer. "Lillian, if Roger Bromley proposes, promise me you'll not let the likes of Dr. Graves spoil your chance at an excellent marriage. Your uncle and I are offering a substantial dowry and annual allowance. The Bromleys will have nothing to object to on that account."

Though on several others, Lilly thought, but forbore to say so. "That is very generous. I had no idea."

"What more can we do to show you our feelings?" Tears shimmered in her aunt's eyes. "We look upon you as our daughter and desire your every happiness. We will do all within our power to see you well wed."

Moved, Lilly reached across and squeezed her aunt's hand. "Very well. If Mr. Bromley proposes, I shall duly consider." Though she doubted she would need to, for despite the upcoming dinner, Lilly still believed Roger Bromley would soon be directing his addresses elsewhere.

"Wonderful girl!" Her aunt beamed. "Oh, you have a bright future ahead of you!"

On Saturday, Lilly was pacing the hall when she heard a carriage door close. Were the Bromleys early? She hoped not. Her aunt had not yet finished dressing and would want to greet their guests when they arrived. Lilly stepped to the hall window. The sight of the caller was worse than unfashionably early guests. Panicked, Lilly went to the door herself, opening it to the man before he even knocked.

"Dr. Graves! We were not expecting you."

He smiled at her seemingly enthusiastic greeting. "You suggested I call on your uncle. So, here I am."

"Did I? Well, I am afraid this is not a good time. We are expecting guests any moment."

"Oh?" He raised his brows in expectation, but she did not supply a name.

"Yes, so if you would be good enough to return another time?"

He frowned. "But I have spent the day rousing my courage and pressing my best frock coat. I hate the thought of having to start the whole dreadful process over again another day."

"I am afraid you must." She began to edge the door shut.

"Lillian?" Her uncle appeared in the entry hall behind her. "Where is Fletcher? You needn't . . . Oh, good day. Graves, is it?"

"Yes, sir. I had hoped to speak with you if you can spare a moment."

Lilly said, "I have just been telling Dr. Graves that we are expecting guests at any time."

"True, true," Jonathan Elliott said. "But, well, they are not here yet and you are. My wife is still dressing, but I am as good as I get, as you see." Her uncle chuckled. "Come back to the library, Graves, and tell me what this is about. . . ."

A quarter of an hour later, Lilly was still pacing the hall, but now for a different reason. She had hoped to see Dr. Graves out the door before the Bromleys arrived, but he and her uncle had tarried too long. Fletcher was just taking the Bromleys' coats and hats when Dr. Graves and her uncle reappeared in the hall.

"Graves?" Roger said. "I did not expect to see you here."

"Nor I you."

Roger turned to his parents. "May I introduce Mr. Graves, a new physician—attended the same college as Uncle Thomas, I understand."

Mr. Bromley smiled. "An Oxford man. Excellent."

"My parents," Roger continued. "Mr. and Mrs. Bromley."

"Perhaps you would like to join us for dinner, Dr. Graves," Uncle Elliott suggested kindly.

"Thank you, sir, but I would not wish to intrude."

Awkward silence filled the hall. Finally her aunt filled it, saying dutifully, but without warmth, "Of course you are welcome, Dr. Graves."

Mr. Bromley, senior, surveyed her from across the dining table. "Your parents, Miss Haswell. Would I know them?"

Wariness filled her. "I would not think so, Mr. Bromley. My father did live in London for a time, but that was many years ago now."

Her aunt deftly stemmed unwanted inquiries by adding, "And her mother has been gone these several years."

"Oh, I am sorry to hear it," Mrs. Bromley said. "And Mr. Haswell. He is . . . ?" The elegant woman raised her brows in expectation, too polite to ask if her father had a profession or, worse yet, a trade.

Ruth Elliott sweetly ignored the implied question. "I am sure he is faring as well as can be expected on his own."

Mr. Bromley skewered a hunk of roast pork from the nearby platter and set it on his plate. "How does he occupy his time, Miss Haswell?"

Lillian licked her suddenly dry lips.

Her aunt answered in her stead. "Missing our Lillian, no doubt. How long have you been with us now, my dear? Two years?"

"Not quite so long, but above a year, yes."

"And do you enjoy London?" Mrs. Bromley asked, taking the bait.

"Oh yes. The city is fascinating, and I have met so many wonderful people."

"The Price-Winters family have taken special interest in our niece," Ruth Elliott added. "Such close friends the girls are."

"Yes, but from where do you hail, Miss Haswell?" Mr. Bromley persisted, sawing at his meat with knife and fork.

"Wiltshire, sir."

"Wiltshire!" the man enthused. "I have been there. I shall never forget it."

Lilly smiled. "It warms my heart to hear you say so."

"Then you no doubt know of the Wiltshire miracle?"

Lilly's smile faded. "I am not sure . . ."

He set down his utensils and stared off into his memories. "Must be ten or twelve years ago now. Several of us gentlemen went to a house party there, to enjoy a bit of hunting in the country. Well, a bit of gaming, too, truth be known. One evening, after a long day of shooting very ill, we were all well in our cups and pipes, when the man of the house—my chum's father—died. Right there in front of us all. Thomas rushed to him, but said the old man was stone dead. Still, the servants scurried about and called for the local apothecary. In this fellow comes, and the servants carry the body away to another room, the apothecary and my chum following behind. Well, I have to admit, the rest of us returned to our cards and quite put it from our minds. Death making one want to eat, drink, and be merry.

"But then, lo and behold, not an hour later, my chum Marlow rushes back into the room and proclaims the apothecary had worked a miracle. His father was alive and well and asking for his supper! Well, that spoilt the weekend for the rest of us, I can tell you. Nothing like a miracle to sour the taste of port and pipe."

He lifted his glass to signify the end of his story. Murmurs of amused approval rose up from the others.

"Clearly the man was not dead," Dr. Graves declared. "Merely fainted or unconscious."

Mr. Bromley took a drink and set down his glass. "Normally I would agree with you, sir, and take first seat among the mockers, were it not for one fact. My own brother confirmed him quite dead."

"But anybody might mistake—"

"He is a physician, young man, a master at that college of yours."

Dr. Graves faltered. "Wait . . . Thomas Bromley?"

"That is what I've been telling you."

"He is very skilled, very knowledgeable, I admit," Graves said. "I sat under him for several courses."

Mr. Bromley nodded, sealing his point. He turned to Lilly. "Being from Wiltshire, I imagine you have heard the tale?"

Lilly had barely parted her lips when she saw her aunt's eyes flash warning. Ruth Elliott shook her head in the slightest of rebuttals, urging her to do the same.

"I forget the man's name," Bromley went on. "Something with an *H*, I believe. Howard, or Hatfield . . ."

Her aunt half rose from her seat. "Why do the ladies not withdraw and leave the men to their port?"

"Come to think of it, the apothecary had a scrap of a child with him. A little girl."

"Miss Haswell?" Dr. Graves turned to her, frowning deeply.

Lilly swallowed.

"Do you know this man, this apothecary?"

"Uhh . . . yes."

"Well, it sounds as if everybody in Wiltshire knows the man," her aunt said, stepping to the door. "Come, Lillian."

"But do you remember his *name*?" Mr. Bromley persisted. "I do so detest not remembering a name."

Lilly paused where she stood at her place. She glanced at her aunt, but Ruth Elliott looked away. There was nothing for it.

"His name is Charles Haswell, sir," Lilly said. "My father."

She glanced over and glimpsed Roger Bromley staring at her and Dr. Graves shaking his head.

At the conclusion of the unsettling evening, Lilly walked Dr. Graves to the door.

"Well, a night of surprises all around," he began. "An apothecary's daughter . . ." He took a breath. "It all makes sense now. Your actions with Mr. Price-Winters, your familiarity with Latin . . . Why did you not tell me?"

"My aunt prefers I not speak of it."

"Why? So you might capture a gentleman under false pretenses?"

She turned to look at him, anger and resolution kindling in her chest. "Please do not consider yourself captured, Dr. Graves. You are perfectly free."

He opened his mouth but closed it again, saying nothing. He seemed about to try again when Roger Bromley let himself from the dining room, quietly closing the door on the gentlemen still within. Her aunt and Mrs. Bromley were still in the drawing room, her aunt no doubt doing her best to minimize the damage.

Dr. Graves bowed stiffly. "Then I will bid you good-night. Miss Haswell. Bromley."

When the door shut behind Dr. Graves, Roger Bromley took her arm and gently led her to a padded bench near the stairs. Once she was seated, he sat beside her.

"Sorry about that. I don't think my parents meant to badger you. Big on pedigree, my mother. Father is actually impressed. 'The daughter of a real miracle worker,' he said. 'Handy to have one of those in the family.'" He glanced at her as the implication of his words registered. "I have to say I quite agree." He took her hand in his. "I don't care about any of it."

But he doesn't know it all, Lilly thought, *or he might care a great deal.*

"I like you as you are, Miss Haswell. So free from all the snobbery and airs of my set." He grinned. "And not a trial to look at either."

Her heart momentarily surged, but then she thought of her unspoken secrets, and his unresolved feelings for another. She smiled gently. "Mr. Bromley, thank you. But you said it yourself. You like me. And certainly I like you. But there is another, I think, whom you love."

"Miss Whittier, you mean?"

She nodded. "You cannot deny it. Your face gives you away whenever you look at her."

He grimaced. "But she will never accept me. She has already said as much."

"She might. You mustn't give up hope. She hasn't married anyone else, has she?"

He all but groaned, "No."

"You are a true gentleman, Mr. Bromley. Any woman would be blessed to own your heart."

"Miss Whittier would not agree with you."

"At least not yet."

She squeezed his hand before extracting her own. "Perhaps there is something we can do to help things along."

14

> The recipient paid dearly . . . there was a fourpenny charge for the typical letter consisting of one large sheet of paper folded several times and sealed with wax.
>
> —Sharon Laudermilk and Teresa Hamlin, *The Regency Companion*

Her uncle came into the library the following Monday and sat in the chair opposite her. His shoulders were hunched, elbows on his knees, and his face was wrinkled in deep thought.

She lowered *The Family Robinson Crusoe,* which she had acquired from the nearby circulating library, and steeled herself for another reprisal of Saturday night's failures.

For several moments, he seemed to study his clenched hands. "Lillian, when we spoke about the necklace, you made it clear you would like to know everything possible about your mother, even if it were . . . unpleasant?"

"Yes." Lilly leaned forward. "Have you heard something? Did she contact you again?"

He shook his head. "What I have to tell you happened some three years ago now." He held up his hand, forestalling her protest before it could form. "I know—but until the business with the necklace I never considered telling you."

He met her eyes directly. "I told you the truth, my dear. Your mother came to see me only that one time, but—"

"She wrote to you?"

"No, Lillian. If I had a letter from her in my possession I would not keep it from you. She did not write to me, but I did receive a letter concerning her. That is, concerning lodgings she was hoping to let. The landlord required a reference, and she must have given my name."

"Did you supply a reference?"

"I did. I made it clear I had no knowledge of her recent occupation or conduct, but that in her younger days she was a good girl from a respectable family."

"And that was all?"

He shrugged. "I assume she secured the lodgings but, of course, had no way of knowing."

"Have you the address of these lodgings?" Lilly's voice rose in excitement.

"I am getting to that, my dear. Before I brought this to your attention, I thought I had better see if I still had the letter. I could not find it, but my clerk did find, in an old ledger, a listing of the postage he paid to receive the reference request."

He handed her a slip of paper. "The street name and number of the lodging house."

Lilly stared down at the few numbers and words inked on the page in her uncle's small precise hand.

Her own hand trembled and her heart pounded. Could she really go and knock on her mother's door? Pay a call as to an old friend? Would she even be received? Her hand began perspiring at the thought of it, and she laid the paper on the table to keep from spoiling it.

"Will you go with me?" she asked in a voice she barely recognized—the voice of a very young girl.

The address was in a court off Fleet Street, in an area of narrow, modest houses.

Her uncle used his umbrella handle to rap on the door, as if he feared touching the surface would soil his gloves. Lilly held her breath. After a few tense moments, the door opened and a woman with silver-streaked black hair answered, dressed in a gown that had once been fine but appeared to Lilly to be nearly a decade out of fashion.

"Yes?"

"Good day, madam. We are looking for a lodger of yours, a Mrs. Rosamond Haswell?"

"No one 'ere by that name."

"Perhaps she used her maiden name, Elliott?"

"Look, this ain't no tenement slum, mind. We just has the one lodger at a time, see, in the rooms upstairs. Helps us live comfortable, now the children are gone."

"I understand, but you wrote to me and asked for a reference for Rosamond—"

"Oh, mayhap you mean Rosa? She is long gone. It's Tommy Baker now."

Rosa? Disappointment tinged with relief washed over Lilly. "How long ago did she leave?"

"Must be above two years now. Maybe more. Couldn't keep up with the rent, see. She took in pupils while she were here—merchants' daughters and the like—but the pay weren't much. She ain't in any trouble, is she?"

"Not that we are aware of. Do you know where she went?"

"Heavens no." The woman's brow wrinkled. "She got herself married, I believe. To some officer, I think it were."

Married? Then it cannot be her. Can it?

"This *husband* of hers," her uncle asked through gritted teeth. "Do you recall his surname?"

"I'm lucky to recall what I 'ad for tea, let alone something what happened years ago."

"Was it Quincy, perhaps?" Lilly asked, avoiding her uncle's startled look.

The woman's eyes narrowed in thought. "Don't ring no bells, no."

"Here is my card," Uncle Elliott said. "Should something come to you, please send word. I shall reimburse you for your trouble."

Lilly thought the woman's murmur of agreement lacked conviction.

As they walked away, Lilly's mind was reeling. Her mother, "married" to another man? She could not credit it. Her uncle strode stiffly at her side, face grim. If this was difficult for her to believe, what a blow it must be for a man such as he to learn that his sister may have sunk so low.

"Perhaps the woman had it wrong," Lilly began. "She said it herself, she has a poor memory. Perhaps 'Rosa' wasn't Mother at all."

He shook his head. "Do you now see why I was reluctant to come? Why I have avoided involving your aunt in these affairs?"

"I do see. Still, I am thankful to you. Painful as it was."

"Shall we speak of it no further?"

"Very well."

His eyes fixed on a shop across the street. "I know. Let us stop in that library there. I think you've read every novel in the one near us. A new book might be just the diversion we need after today's errand."

Lilly nodded her agreement. She already had a new book but could always use another. She gathered her uncle needed this diversion as much as she did.

He opened the door for her and she stepped inside. The lofty room was filled floor to ceiling with books. This library was not as elegant as the one they frequented, but it certainly held a wide selection.

In her peripheral vision, she saw a clerk hail her. "Mrs. Wells! How good to—Oh, forgive me." The thin young man faltered. "I thought you were someone else."

Lilly was instantly alert. "Who?" she prompted. "A Mrs. Wells, I believe you said?" *Who was Wells?*

He shook his head, bemused. "You do look a great deal like her. Henry?" he called to an associate who stood on a rolling ladder, replacing a book on a high shelf. "Come here, man."

The second clerk, somewhat older and rounder, clambered down and joined them.

"Does this lady not look a great deal like our friend Mrs. Wells?" the first asked.

"Indeed she does. Though younger to be sure."

Lilly met her uncle's gaze.

"Haven't seen that lady in some time, though," Henry said. "Have you?"

"No. Must be above a half year since I saw her. Thank you, Henry."

The second clerk returned to the shelves, and her uncle excused himself to peruse the history section.

"Now." The first clerk rubbed his palms together. "Is there something I can help you find, miss?"

Curious, Lilly asked, "What would your Mrs. Wells want?"

The young clerk thought. "Fanny Burney is a favorite of hers. Though she has also borrowed every volume of Scott and Coleridge we've had in. Never knew a keener reader. I believe she is a schoolmistress of some sort."

"And have you records of what she last read?"

He looked at her, clearly perplexed. "We have records, of course, but—"

Embarrassed, Lilly said quickly, "Never mind. I only thought that since I favoured her in appearance, I might enjoy reading what she did. That is all." She laughed sheepishly.

"Well, normally our records are private. But I do not see any harm in this case." He crooked a finger, and she followed him to the center desk. There he opened a wooden file box and walked his fingers through the cards inside. "Here she is. Last borrowed Fanny Burney's *The Wanderer*."

How apt, Lilly thought. "Well then, I shall have the same if I might."

The clerk was still skimming the card. "Oh dear, an outstanding balance of two p—"

Lilly lifted her reticule. "Allow me."

"No, miss, there's no need."

"Yes there is. It is the least I can do for her excellent book recommendation."

He dipped his chin in acquiescence. "That is very kind. When I see Mrs. Wells, whom shall I name as her benefactor?"

Lilly paused. It seemed unlikely Mrs. Wells, her mother or not, would return here, but even so, she hesitated. "You needn't say at all."

Her uncle reappeared beside her. "There you are, Lillian. Are you ready?"

The clerk grinned and made a note on the card.

"Actually, I have thought of one more thing," Lilly said. "Have you Steele's Navy Lists?"

The clerk's eyes widened. "Why, yes. The new one for this quarter has just arrived. Do you know, Mrs. Wells often had a look at those as well."

"Did she indeed?" Lilly was struck by the coincidence, if coincidence it was. "Do you keep older editions as well? From five or so years past?"

"I am afraid not. Only the most current editions. And here it is." He handed her the slim volume.

"Thank you. I shall borrow that as well."

Her uncle's eyebrows rose, but Lilly did not explain.

15

Men have the sword, women have the fan,
and the fan is probably as effective a weapon!
—Joseph Addison, eighteenth-century
English writer

Lilly was surprised when Dr. Graves paid a call a few days later. She had not expected him after their less-than-cordial parting. Her aunt was breakfasting in her own room, so Lilly was alone in the sitting room when Fletcher announced that a Dr. Graves was at the door. She was tempted to utter the socially acceptable prevarication "I am not at home at present" but could not bring herself to do so. While she dreaded seeing him again, she had lied more than enough to the man, even if in omission.

When Fletcher showed Dr. Graves in, he entered top hat in hand. Fletcher held out his hand to take it, but Dr. Graves did not seem to notice.

"Won't you sit down?" Lilly offered.

"Thank you, no." His gaze focused on the carpet. "Miss Haswell, I have been thinking. I wanted to say . . . that is, I believe I understand why you were not forthcoming about your background. Of course you would respect your guardian's wishes in the matter. I want to apologize for my . . . unfortunate reaction."

"I am sorry for keeping it from you for so long," she said. She was attempting to form the words to tell him of her other secret when he forged ahead.

"But now I think . . ." He looked at her. "Well, do you not see? It makes such sense. Is it any wonder I think you and I so perfectly suited?"

Lilly felt her mouth gape open and quickly closed it. She stared at him, saw his pale cheeks redden.

"That is . . . I do not view your father's trade as necessarily a disadvantage. Your experience lends you a level of understanding . . . of the hours and time away required of my profession."

It was not the most flattering of offers. *Was* he offering for her? Or merely expressing interest in continuing to court her?

On some level, the idea appealed to her. That she might be able to understand her husband's struggles and even help him in his work. Might this not make for the best of both worlds? Whom else could she marry and not count those years in her father's shop as absolute loss? As a physician, Dr. Graves would make a good living and still be considered a gentleman, welcome in her aunt and uncle's world. If not by Ruth Elliott herself.

"Speaking of my profession," he said awkwardly, "I had better take my leave. I do not wish to be late for my shift at hospital. But I do hope we might speak further soon. Will you be attending the Bromleys' rout and card party? They have kindly included me."

"I believe we will be," Lilly said. *If their invitation was not withdrawn after recent revelations.*

"Then I shall see you then."

Lilly had no interest in cards, but she was interested in the Bromley home, which the family seemed forever to be redecorating or improving—knocking down walls, adding or connecting chambers, retiling floors. Currently the home followed the Greek Revival style, though the gallery and main floor rooms also displayed exotic Egyptian art, Chinese lanterns, Italian oil paintings, silhouettes and etchings, all of which imbued the place with a museum-like atmosphere.

Lilly entered the crowded vestibule Friday evening in time to see Susan Whittier shake her head and turn from Roger Bromley. As the lovely blonde walked away, she slowly fanned herself, the gesture signaling, *Don't waste your time. I don't care about you.*

The pitiful look on Roger's face worked on Lilly's heart. She wove her way through the crowd and smiled at him in empathy. "At it again, is she?"

"Miss Haswell. What a delight." He sighed. "Yes, I am afraid so. If only every woman could be as agreeable as you are." He bowed deeply. As she curtsied in return, she felt her aunt and uncle's eager eyes upon them.

"Will you walk with me?" He indicated the long gallery with a sweep of his hand.

"Very well."

He offered his arm and she took it. She hoped Susan Whittier was watching.

He led her along the gallery, pointing out two new paintings his parents had purchased during their last holiday in Rome. "You are right, of course," Roger began quietly. "I cannot deny I have long and ardently admired Susan Whittier. I suppose everybody knows it and pities me. Including Miss Whittier herself, who seems to enjoy tormenting me."

Lilly could not contradict him.

Progressing further along the gallery, he paused to show her a primitive wood carving brought back from Jamaica by his mother's brother, Admiral Roth.

He then led her into the library, where woodwork and leather spines gleamed softly by the light of suspended oil lamps as well as two candle lamps on the desk.

He turned to face her, keeping hold of her hand. "But I do have a strong regard for you, Miss Haswell," he said in plaintive whisper. "I don't suppose you would accept my suit while my heart is fettered elsewhere?"

How kind he was. How gentleman-like. For a moment she was tempted, but then she thought of her mother and Quinn and felt a chill run up her neck. Sadly, she shook her head. She would not marry a man who would always pine for another.

"Roger, there you are."

Roger's mother stepped inside the library. Behind her, Susan Whittier entered the room and, seeing Lilly, hesitated. Lilly could well imagine the tableau she and Mr. Bromley made, standing hand in hand in a candlelit tête-à-tête. She hoped the scene had a desired effect.

Mrs. Bromley smiled thinly. "Susan and I wondered where you had gone."

Miss Whittier passed her fan from hand to hand. *I see you are looking at another woman.* Did Roger notice this expression of jealousy as well?

Mrs. Bromley begged Lilly's pardon, but insisted Roger come and stand with her to greet guests, as his father had already abandoned his post for a game of faro in the saloon.

Roger Bromley smiled apologetically and excused himself, both of them knowing that his mother was relieved to have reason to call him from her side.

Alone, Lilly slowly walked the perimeter of the library, pausing to admire a beautiful globe on an ornate wooden stand. As usual, the sight of a globe brought to mind the spheres on her mother's creased world map.

Moving on, she scanned the impressive collection of volumes, which would rival any subscription library, and was astonished to see an entire shelf of Steele's Navy Lists. Would the Bromleys mind if she perused them? She could not think of any reason why they should. Running her fingers along the narrow spines, she found the dates she was looking for. She pulled several from the shelf and carried them to the candle-lit desk. Opening the first volume, she skimmed the listing of commissioned officers of first one edition, then a second, then a third. In the last she found the name, Captain Ernest Quincy, and a number. Paging through, she found the corresponding ship name and its list of officers. Captain, Lieutenant, Paymaster, Surgeon, Gunner, Boatswain, Midshipman . . .

She returned the volumes to the shelf and pulled an older edition and repeated the process. Again she found the name Ernest Quincy and the corresponding ship upon which he had served. And there it was. Captain: Ernest Quincy. Lieutenant: James Wells.

Was this *the* Wells? Or was it merely coincidence that a Wells had served under Captain Quincy? Lilly was not sure she believed in coincidence anymore.

Footsteps startled her, and she closed the book as though a thief, caught.

"Miss Haswell." Dr. Graves bowed, looking quite dashing in his black tailcoat and white waistcoat. "Mrs. Bromley said I might find you here."

Lilly could well imagine the woman's eagerness to send another man to divert her attention. As she curtsied, she pressed the book against the folds of her skirt, hoping to conceal it.

"What is that you are looking at?" he asked. Reaching out, he turned the volume in her hand to better read its title, his fingers brushing hers.

She lifted it as though just remembering the book was there. "I was just curious," she said and backed away from him, returning the book to its place on the shelf. "Admiral Roth is uncle to Roger Bromley, you know."

"And what, may I ask, is Roger Bromley to you?"

Two aging spinsters entered the library, sparing her the need to reply. The four exchanged polite greetings and praised the Bromleys' collection for several moments, until Dr. Graves cleared his throat.

"Miss Haswell, I understand the Bromleys are eager for their guests to walk their maze. Would you like to give it a go?"

Understanding he wished to speak with her alone, she agreed. "Indeed. It sounds fascinating."

They excused themselves, then walked without speaking into the gallery and down a second corridor. While cards were being played in the saloon, in the other rooms—dining room, sitting room, and both drawing rooms—the furniture had all been taken away or moved to the walls, to allow hundreds of people to stand and mingle about. As they passed the open doors of the dining room, Lilly saw Roger Bromley hand Susan Whittier a glass of punch and stand close to her in intimate conversation.

When she and Dr. Graves neared their destination, they passed a couple just leaving, the man whispering in the lady's ear, the latter giggling. Dr. Graves frowned at the oblivious couple and ushered Lilly into the gothic conservatory. A dozen wax candles flickered in the darkness, reflecting back on the windows and illuminating the maze of red and black floor tiles.

Lilly looked with fascination at the pattern. "Where does one begin?"

"I am not certain. You begin there and I shall try from this point. Mind your gown near the candles." He walked around to the opposite side.

Lilly began tiptoeing the narrow path outlined by black tiles amid the red, arms gracefully extended as though she traversed a circus high wire. Dr. Graves's polished shoes filled the width of the path, and he took the corners none too neatly.

Lilly bit back a smile. "They say it is a rectangular version of the Hampton Court hedge maze. In miniature, of course."

He narrowly missed kicking over a candle lamp. "Do they. I say it is a colossal waste of time."

Keeping her focus on the tiles, she began, "I have thought about what you said, Dr. Graves. That with my background I might be of some help to you as you treat patients and seek to establish yourself in the medical profession."

"Well—dash it." He came to a dead end in the tiles and had to turn back around. "That is, of course, an agreeable, suitable wife can only help a man—medical or otherwise."

She felt an odd flutter at hearing him say the word *wife*.

She continued to delicately walk the line, reaching the center of the maze before he did. He retraced his steps, then chose another path. Realizing she had halted, he stopped where he was, a few steps away. He stood there, considering the tiles of the maze between them.

"Mustn't cross any lines," she warned in a whisper.

He looked at her intently. "Mustn't we?" He took a step closer.

Around them, the candles flickered, casting shadows on the perfect planes of his face and light on his golden hair and bottle-blue eyes.

Drawing near, he looked warmly at her, his gaze lingering on her hair, her eyes, her lips. She expected him to kiss her at any moment. Willed it. For though the lines of the maze were merely flat tiles on the floor, she felt something very real between them.

"What unusual eyes you have," he whispered. "Green and brown both."

He leaned closer still, and she felt her eyelids flutter closed of their own volition. *What would it be like to kiss a man with a moustache?* she wondered fleetingly. Or any man, for that matter?

A throat cleared. Lilly turned her head and saw Will Price-Winters in the doorway, watching them with marked interest. Lilly felt her entire face heat in a blush. Beside him was a tall, dark-haired man she recognized with a start.

"I thought I saw you passing by with golden boy here," Will began, barely suppressing an amused smirk. He turned to his companion. "May I introduce Sir Roderick Marlow."

Sir was his father's title, but Roderick did not correct him.

"This is Dr. Adam Graves," Christina's brother continued, and the men nodded to one another. "And this lovely creature is Miss Haswell."

She curtsied and Roderick Marlow bowed, though he kept his eyes on her all the while. "Miss Haswell and I are already acquainted."

"Well, dash it," Will said peevishly, "Then why did you insist we find her and beg an introduction?"

"I thought my eyes deceived me," Mr. Marlow said. "She is far more handsome than I recall."

"But how are you acquainted?" Will asked him. "You are not a London man, I understand?"

"Indeed no. I make it to town but rarely. Miss Haswell and I grew up together in the same village."

Together? Lilly thought incredulously. *Hardly that.*

"We be Wiltshire born and bred, ey?" Roderick Marlow's exaggerated accent surprised her, yet was music to her ears. "'Ow bis en', my lovely?"

She laughed appreciatively.

"Miss Haswell and her father have often been guests at Marlow House," Roderick Marlow explained to Will, with a pointed look at Dr. Graves.

Not unless one counted house calls, Lilly thought, but forbore to comment.

Will shook his head. "She and my sister have been friends for, what, well over a year now, and I had no idea."

"Well, Miss Haswell is known for her secrets," Marlow said, grinning wickedly. "And other crimes."

"Mr. Marlow," Lilly exclaimed. "I must protest."

"Very well, Miss Haswell, I shall keep your secrets for you. Though I suppose your Dr. Graves is already privy to all?"

She felt her lips part, but couldn't form an answer.

"No?" Marlow leaned closer but made no attempt to whisper. "P-W here hinted there might be something between the two of you. I am glad to hear that is not the case after all."

"I never said—"

In full view of the other men, Marlow tapped his forefinger against her lower lip. "Shh . . . Your secrets are safe with me, Lilly."

He turned and sauntered from the conservatory, Will Price-Winters at his heels.

She and Dr. Graves stared after them, both bewildered.

"Lilly?" Graves repeated the name with equal parts distaste and question.

"Yes," she said resignedly. "Lilly."

"A childhood pet name?"

She sighed, suddenly very weary. "My name, period. Until my aunt changed it."

"You have given that man leave to use your Christian name? Even I—"

"No one gives that man *leave* to do anything. He does as he pleases and always has. You need not mind anything he says."

He studied her face. "Indeed?"

16

WIDOW WELCH'S PILLS
The particular nature and symptoms of female complaints are given with every box of pills, and worthy the perusal of every person who has the care of young women. . . .

—*The Edinburgh Evening Courant,* 1815

When next Dr. Graves called, Lilly decided it was time to tell him all, though she feared the consequences. They were again alone in the sitting room, for Aunt Elliott was sleeping in after a late night at the theatre. Once he was seated, she began in low tones, "At the Bromleys' rout the other night, Mr. Marlow accused me of keeping secrets."

His raised his brows in expectation.

"There *is* another secret I should tell you." She pressed damp palms to her knees to still their trembling.

He nodded slowly, warily. "Something to do with that man?"

"No. Only that he knows of it." She took a deep breath. "It is about my mother."

His brow wrinkled. "Your mother is gone, I understand."

"Gone. But not dead. At least not as far as we know."

He stared at her, clearly stunned.

"She left us nearly five years ago now. Disappeared without word or letter. We don't know where she went or where she is." She glanced toward the door to make sure no one was listening, then said quietly, "My aunt and uncle prefer not to speak of her. They allow those of their acquaintance to believe she is still living in obscurity in Wiltshire—or dead. I cannot blame them. If it were generally known, their name and mine would be besmirched."

His expression was incredulous. "Simply because your mother disappeared? She might have been abducted—merely gone on some errand when unspeakable mishap befell her."

She raised one brow high. "Are you trying to make me feel better?"

His mouth drooped. "Forgive me."

"In any case, I doubt that." Swallowing a cinder of shame, Lilly whispered, "She was seen leaving Bedsley Priors with a uniformed man. It is only hearsay, and he may have simply been another passenger traveling on the same narrowboat, but as she was in love with a naval captain before she married my father, it seems too great a coincidence."

His expression grew serious, nearly alarmed, the lines deepening between his eyebrows. Still, she steeled herself and continued. "I have recently learned a few things about her. I know she came to London and saw my uncle. I know she lodged off Fleet Street for a time and took in pupils." A choked laugh escaped her. "I know which library she frequented, but I do not know"—her voice cracked—"why she left us, and if it was my fault, and why she never once wrote to tell us she was all right. . . ."

Her throat too tight to continue, she bit her lip to ebb the flow of tears. Finally, she continued. "I lied to you when you asked why I was looking at the naval lists. We believe my mother may be living under another name—as a *Rosa Wells*. It may simply be a false name, short for Haswell. But I wanted to see if a man by the name of Wells had served with the officer my mother once hoped to marry."

"And?" he asked, though a quick glance told her he dreaded the answer.

She exhaled deeply and nodded. "A James Wells did serve with him in at least one commission. I have no real proof he ever met my mother, but still it seems a strange coincidence."

"Will you contact this James Wells?"

She shifted, ill at ease. "I don't know. The connection seems so unlikely." She shrugged. "I don't even know how I would find him."

He nodded, and the two were shrouded in awkward silence for several moments.

"Well," Lilly said, squaring her shoulders. "I thought you had the right to know. Should my mother's desertion—or worse—become known, I would be tainted by scandal, as would my aunt and uncle. As would you, should you . . ." She let the thought trail away unfinished.

"My father detests scandal," Graves said, as though to himself. "Always has." He ran agitated fingers through his pale-blond hair and cleared his throat. "Well, thank you for telling me, Miss Haswell." He rose and eyed the door with apparent longing, his words coming in clipped phrases. "I had better take my leave. Much to ponder. Be in touch soon."

No you shan't . . . Lilly thought sadly, fatalistically, as the handsome golden man turned on his heel and hurried away. Hadn't she always known it would end this way, with any gentleman of quality? *I have finally succeeded in scaring off the last of my suitors*, she thought, and the realization pained her more than she would have guessed.

Fletcher handed Lilly a letter as she passed by him on her way upstairs. She needed to quickly finish dressing, for her aunt would soon be ready to begin paying calls.

But a quarter of an hour later, Lilly still sat on her bed, dressed only in her white muslin morning dress.

"Lillian?" her aunt called from the corridor. "Are you ready? I have the carriage waiting."

But Lilly remained where she was, the letter in her hands beginning to shake.

Her aunt let herself into the room, pulling on her gloves. She was fully dressed in striped carriage dress, vest, and cap. "Lillian? We are late, my dear. Lillian! What is the matter?"

She pushed the paper into her aunt's hand. Lilly already knew what it said, not because of her keen memory, but because of its cryptic brevity. *Come home. Your father is not himself.*

"But you do not know that anything dire has happened," Ruth Elliott insisted while Lilly paced the room. "Your father is 'not himself.' What does that mean?"

"I do not know."

"You do not even know who wrote the letter, if letter it can be called."

"I suppose it was Mrs. Mimpurse. Our neighbor."

"Then why did she not tell you what the matter is?"

"I don't know!" Lilly's voice rose, and her aunt winced at the unusual sharpness of her tone. "Forgive me, Aunt. I am only very worried. I have had no replies to my recent letters, and now this!"

Lilly bent and drew her valise from under the bed.

"What are you doing?"

"Of course I must go."

"But . . . what about Mr. Bromley?"

Lilly exhaled sharply. "Mr. Bromley hopes to engage the affections of Susan Whittier."

"Are you certain?"

Lilly nodded and threw back the lid of the worn valise. It was the only item her aunt and uncle had not thought to replace with a new one, perhaps hoping there would be no need.

"Oh no." Panic swelled in Ruth Elliott's voice and eyes. "There are only six weeks left in the season. Very little time to start again, and by next year they will say you have been passed over—on the shelf."

Lilly hesitated. "Is that really the end of the world?"

"No, my dear. Merely the end of your best opportunity for securing an advantageous match."

"I cannot think about that now." Beneath the brave words, these were the very thoughts plaguing her as Aunt Elliott's worries fed her own. For in spite of Lilly's ideals of marrying for love, or of using her skills to aid her husband, the truth was a good marriage was imperative to any woman's happiness and comfort, not to mention social standing.

She began to fold and pack her clothing—Dupree's job. Lilly knew how distressed her aunt was when she did not correct her.

But surely all was not lost. She would be back soon. She had not failed her aunt, nor her goal in coming to London. Not yet.

"Surely twenty or even one and twenty is not too old. Unless—Forgive me. I should not presume you would wish to host me here for another season."

For once, her aunt's perfect posture melted into a dejected slump. "In all truth, I am weary. And to see my hopes fall apart all over again. All the work, the expense . . ."

Lilly felt chastened. She said quickly, "Please forgive me. I did not realize I had become a burden, but of course I must be. I have been very selfish, and I am sorry for it."

Her aunt sighed. "I do not mean to threaten or frighten you, my dear. But with all our failures this season—the gossip, your father's trade becoming known, Susan Whittier diverting Mr. Bromley—I simply hold little hope for another season, when a whole new harvest of accomplished young ladies will come out to compete for the same string of gentlemen."

Lilly ceased her packing long enough to grasp her aunt's hand. "I am only going for a visit. A week, a fortnight at most. That will still give us the better part of a month when I return. Will it not?"

Her aunt looked into Lilly's eyes, her own brimming with unshed tears, as if she very much wanted to believe her, but could not quite succeed.

17

The human heart, at whatever age,
opens only to the heart that opens in return.
—Maria Edgeworth, 19th century novelist

If Lilly expected things to be the same as ever in Bedsley Priors, she was much mistaken. During the year and a half she had been gone, the village as well as neighboring Honeystreet had grown with the boom of canal traffic. New businesses and thatched cottages had been built to accommodate additional sawmill workers, barge builders, and their families. Huntley's Yard, bordering the canal, was now a bustling enclave of saw pits, paint shops, and even a cobbler and undertaker. The two villages had developed and spread until all that divided the once separate communities was the narrow Sands Road.

All this Lilly took in from the coach window, the startling scene narrated by a kindly passenger who introduced herself as the proprietor of a new millinery shop in town.

Lilly was too stunned to say much of anything. Was this why her father had not answered recent letters? Had his shop become so busy that he simply had no time to write?

Stepping down from the coach in front of the Hare and Hounds, she waited until the coachman handed down her valise and carpetbag. Then she walked around the tall coach, her eyes hungry for the first sight of her father's shop, the Haswell sign, the many-paned window. Eager, too, for the smells and sounds, the pleasant hum of cures discussed and remedies heeded. She walked quickly across the green, and there it was. The bowed window, flaking white paint, the sign hanging from one chain. She wondered when the other side had fallen. She hesitated at the window, noticing the display inside was sparse and dusty. Her brow furrowed. Where were all the customers, all the new villagers she'd heard about? It was not Sunday—why was the place empty?

Concern filtered through her mind. Her hand on the door latch, she breathed a prayer and then pushed the door open and closed her eyes to absorb the jangle of the bell. Same as always. She breathed in. Smells flooded her senses all right, but something damp and foul overrode the dried flowers and herbs.

"Hello?" she called tentatively, and then more loudly, "Father? Charlie?"

No answer. Alarm began pulsing in her veins.

She walked through the shop, noting with dismay the soiled dispensing counter, and the back counter cluttered with pill dust and used mortars, tools and tiles all in need of a good cleaning. *What on earth?* Why had Charlie let off with the sweeping and dusting?

A mouse skittered somewhere in the corner. She shivered. With mounting fear and dread, she opened the rear door into the laboratory-kitchen and private quarters. A foul smell charged out to repel her. Dirty dishes, scummy pots, dank mortars and funnels were piled in disarray on the sideboard. Had Mrs. Fowler given notice? Or been sacked? She had always kept their private rooms clean, if not orderly. She heard more skittering. Rodent or insect, she could not be certain.

"Fa-ther?" She tried again, her voice breaking. "It's Lillian—Lilly."

She passed the narrow chamber where Francis slept and peeked inside. Her heart lurched. The cot wore no bedclothes, the wall pegs were bare, as was the chest of drawers.

She called up the stairs but heard no answer. Remembering the surgery, she returned through the shop and pushed open the surgery door. Papers, bills, and parcels were piled high and obliterated the surface of her father's desk. Soiled plates and a half-eaten roll sat atop the highest stack.

Lilly stopped, hand over her breast. She had found her father at last. Lying on the surgery cot in shirtsleeves and rumpled breeches, jaw unshaven. His mouth hung open, drool forming rivulets at its corners. One arm was flung over his eyes, the other arm hung to the floor, hand clasping an empty bottle.

Dear Lord in heaven . . . "Father?" She tentatively touched his shoulder. She shook him gently, then with more urgency. "Father!"

He jerked. "What? What is it?" He wiped his mouth, then mumbled, "Be right with you."

His eyes were blurry slits, which opened wider at the sight of her. "Lilly?"

"Yes, of course it is me. What has happened, Father? Are you ill?"

He groaned. "Just a nap."

"It is more than that, clearly. Shall I call for Dr. Foster?"

"No. Not Foster." He rolled to his side and pushed himself up, only to fall back against the thin mattress.

Lilly's heart ached to see him in such a state.

"Just need to sleep."

To sleep it off? she wondered.

Her father had never been given to drink. What had happened to drive him to it? She hoped it had not been her long absence. But if so, why hadn't he written? Unbidden, she thought back to Mr. Bromley's declaration of "the Wiltshire miracle." Famed for having once raised a man from the dead, Charles Haswell could now not even raise himself from the bed.

"Where is Charlie, Father? And Francis?"

He mumbled something, his eyes halfway open and eerily unfocused.

"Where is Francis?" she repeated.

"Old tailor's shop."

"What?" Why would her father's apprentice be at the old haberdashery? It had been closed for years. Perhaps it had reopened during her absence. But even so, why would Francis be there?

Realizing she would get no more answers from her father for a few hours at least, she left him in the surgery, replaced her hat, and stepped back outside, careful to turn the shop sign to *Closed*.

She saw the coal monger walking on the green and hurried across the High Street to speak to him

"Pardon me, Mr. Jones," she said. "Have you seen Francis Baylor?"

"I did. In the apothecary's."

He must be mistaken, Lilly thought. She had just come from there.

Dipping her head politely, she walked on across the green, passed the coal merchant, and rounded the butcher's shop. Behind it, she turned down narrow Milk Lane, which housed the old haberdashery—and stopped midstride. Hanging there on two sturdy chains was a shiny new sign declaring, *Lionel Shuttleworth, Surgeon-Apothecary*.

Heart pounding, she forced one foot in front of the other until she stood just to the side of the big front window. She felt like an awkward spy as she leaned and peered inside. The scene that met her was very like the one she had imagined seeing at Haswell's. Ladies reading labels on blue bottles and brown jars. Men standing around the center counter, waiting to be advised or bled. The shelves spotless, the displays overflowing with patent medicines. From the ceiling hung a shark and a blowfish, glistening in magenta and gold.

She saw the back of a tall gentleman wearing a green fitted coat and buff trousers. He wore his brown hair short at the sides and back, his sideburns neatly trimmed. He cut a dashing figure, this man, who must be the new surgeon-apothecary. He turned, and she saw his profile was handsome indeed. . . .

Lilly put a hand over her mouth, catching a gasp. For the man was Francis Baylor—older and taller and better dressed—helping a customer as though he were a doctor himself.

She spun around, but not before she saw him glance up and his eyes widen. She strode away even as she heard the shop door open and rapid footfalls follow her. "Lilly! Miss Haswell!"

She'd wanted to see him, had she not? But perhaps what she had seen answered her questions without a single word being spoken.

Still, she took a deep breath and turned to face him. "Francis," she said coolly.

"Thank heaven you've come. You've seen your father?"

"Yes."

"So you know."

"Know what, exactly? That the apprentice he mentored for years has abandoned him? Gone to work for his competitor? Put Haswell's out of business?"

"No! It isn't like that!"

"Then what is it like? Were you forced to come here?"

"In a manner of speaking, I was. Your father was unable to pay me—"

"Fickle loyalty! You had a roof over your head, did you not?" She critically eyed the broad shoulders and chest beneath his fitted coat. "You don't look to be starving. Nor dressed in rags. Could you not extend a bit of grace?"

"I did. He hasn't paid me a farthing in six months. My apprenticeship is over. I am a journeyman now, entitled to wages. I stayed as long as I could, but I must have some means, mustn't I?"

"Why? Your mother makes a tidy living as tallow-chandler, I understand,

and she and your sister must have got by well enough all those years you earned nothing as an apprentice."

A young lady in fine flowered bonnet and gown came out of the shop and walked past, a brown-paper-wrapped parcel in her gloved hand. Lilly recognized her at once.

"Mr. Baylor. You disappeared before I could thank you. Most helpful as usual."

He cleared his throat. "You are welcome, Miss Robbins."

My goodness, she's prettier than ever, Lilly thought, relieved to be wearing her nicest carriage dress and fitted spencer. The girl looked her way and curtsied. Lilly stiffly returned the gesture.

"Miss Haswell, hello. Do you know what a wonderful dancer Mr. Baylor has become?"

Lilly dumbly shook her head.

"I have never enjoyed a village fete as well as I did the last. Well, until next time, Mr. Baylor."

He bowed briefly before returning his attention to Lilly.

Watching Dorothea Robbins saunter gracefully down the lane, Lilly shook her head in disgust. *Some things never change.*

She said, "I see why, or shall I say for *whom*, you are acquiring means." With that, she turned and stalked away.

She hurried back up Milk Lane and followed the High Street to the coffeehouse, hoping desperately that it too had not fallen into disrepair. What would she do if it were abandoned? If Mrs. Mimpurse and Mary were gone? *Please God, please God.*

She turned the corner and breathed a sigh of relief. Old Mrs. Kilgrove and another matron were coming from the coffeehouse, and candle lamps glowed in the windows. Walking quickly to the door, she pushed it open and stepped inside. She savored the sight of tables filled with customers, the stoked fire, the hum of conversation, the smell of coffee and cinnamon and life.

"Lilly Grace Haswell!"

And suddenly Mrs. Mimpurse was there, ample arms around her, floured bodice pressing close, aromas of nutmeg, ginger, and woodsmoke enveloping her. Lilly embraced her in return, feeling tears fill her eyes.

"I knew you would come, Miss Lilly. I knew it. Thank the good Lord."

Mary came out of the kitchen and stood on the threshold, wiping her hands on a cloth. She hung back, eyeing her almost warily. Lilly disentangled herself from Mrs. Mimpurse and walked close to Mary. "I have missed you."

"Have you?"

Lilly nodded and opened her arms, and Mary accepted her embrace. "And I you."

"Mary, my lovely," Mrs. Mimpurse said quietly, "I am afraid I must ask you to mind the place alone for a few minutes."

Mary nodded in grim understanding. Mrs. Mimpurse took Lilly's hand and led her up the stairs into their small sitting room. She moved with youthful energy and grace, though she was a contemporary of her father. "Be seated, my dear. Can I get you something to eat? Coffee? Tea?"

Lilly shook her head, a lump rising in her throat and hands perspiring at whatever news Mrs. Mimpurse hesitated to impart.

"You've been home?" she asked.

Lilly nodded.

Mrs. Mimpurse gave her head a stern little shake. "I would have written sooner, but your father forbade it. Said to leave you be, and not to worry you. But . . . well, have you seen him?"

Again Lilly nodded.

"The shop has been all but closed these last days. If you don't put it to rights, I fear Haswell's will never recover."

"So this has been going on for some time?"

"I am afraid so."

"What has brought it on?"

"I do not quite know. He hasn't been himself for months. Then the new surgeon-apothecary came, and it seemed to lay him very low."

"But, is he . . . Is he really . . . ?"

"Tippling? I don't know what all ails him. He refuses to see Dr. Foster."

"I know. I suggested it also, but he was quite adamant against it."

"Such bad blood between the two of them."

"And now Francis has left him. How could he?"

"Do not judge him harshly, my dear. Your father was very cross toward the end. I think he wanted to be rid of him. Let Mrs. Fowler go as well, so he could sink and stew himself in private. Wouldn't let anyone help."

"I don't understand."

"Well, you're home now." Mrs. Mimpurse smiled bravely. "And if anyone can set Haswell's to rights, it's you."

Lilly did not share the woman's confidence.

Mrs. Mimpurse insisted on going home with her, carrying a pot of stew while Lilly carried two loaves of cottage bread. They crossed the narrow mews between the two establishments and entered through the garden.

"Good *gracious*," Mrs. Mimpurse said, as they stepped into the laboratory-kitchen. "It is worse than I thought."

Lilly took off her hat as she made her way to the surgery. Her father sat on the edge of the cot, head in hands, in the same wrinkled clothes.

"Father, are you feeling any better?"

"As I said, I am quite well. Why have you come?"

She was taken aback by his dour demeanor.

Mrs. Mimpurse stood in the doorway behind her. "I've brought a nice chicken-and-leek stew for your supper."

"I've told you—don't fuss over me, Maude." Her father's voice was rough and sharp. "I don't need your charity."

Maude sniffed. "Charity, indeed. I'd not waste it on a sour cabbage like you. The food is for Miss Lilly here, home after these many months. And if you were half a gentleman, you would come to the table and take a proper meal with your daughter to welcome her home."

"I've never claimed to be a gentleman."

"As well I know, and no wonder."

He looked up at her, irritation and pain in his expression. Still, when Mrs. Mimpurse came and took one elbow, instructing Lilly to take the other, he allowed the two women to help him up and into the laboratory-kitchen. He sat heavily in the chair.

"Happy?" he asked.

"Deliriously." Mrs. Mimpurse matched her father's sarcasm.

"Now will you be gone, you meddlesome woman."

"With pleasure, you ungrateful ogre."

Mrs. Mimpurse hesitated at the door, looking back at them, the pained concern in her eyes not quite concealed by her tart barbs.

All the bowls were dirty, but Lilly managed to find two mugs that would suffice for their stew.

"She wrote to you, did she?" her father asked.

"Yes, and I am grateful she did."

"What did she say? Must have been pretty bad to bring you home with the season still on."

"She only said that you were not yourself. Which appears to be the understatement of all time. What is wrong, Father? What has happened?"

"Food is getting cold."

They ate a few bites in a silence broken only by the ticks of the clock. Lilly glanced up at the old wall-mounted timepiece. "Where is Charlie? Why is he not home for supper?"

Even as she asked, she guessed there hadn't been much supper to come home to for some time. Was he eating with Mary and Mrs. Mimpurse?

"Charlie doesn't live here anymore."

Her father could hardly have stunned her more. "What? Where is he?"

"Gone to Marlow House. Works as an undergardener there."

Her spoon clanked against the mug. She shuddered to think of her sweet, simple brother under the power of Roderick Marlow or his rough, angry gardener.

"But why, Father? When you obviously need his help more than ever. Especially with Francis gone."

He shrugged and laid aside his spoon.

"Eat more, Father. You are as thin as I've ever seen you."

He shook his head, his thoughts clearly far from food. "I am sorry you've come."

Her heart fell.

"Sorry and glad together," he amended. He reached across the small table toward her hand, then hesitated short of touching her. He pulled back and rose shakily from the table. She hurried to her feet and took his elbow to steady him, helping him back to his makeshift bed in the surgery.

"Father, I—" She determined to leave any judgmental words unspoken. "I have never seen you like this."

"I wish you had not. Or anybody else for that matter." He sat heavily on the cot. "I shall master it by and by. I must."

"Is there anything you need?" she asked.

"Just quiet. And time alone."

Lilly went to the door, then turned back to look at him. She saw him bring a new bottle to his lips, recork it, and hold it close to his chest as he lay back on the bed. The terrible act sliced at her. He embraced that bottle like a treasure. While he had not embraced her at all.

18

> The greatest pill taker on record appears to have been one Jessup, who died in 1814. He is stated to have swallowed 226,934 pills and 40,000 bottles of mixture, all supplied by an apothecary of Bottesford.
>
> —C. J. S.Thompson, *Mystery and Art of the Apothecary*

Lilly tossed and turned for hours, unable to sleep. At least her chamber was reasonably tidy, although she doubted anyone had dusted or aired the bed in some time. Still, she could not get comfortable. She had been spoiled, she supposed, by the high, luxurious feather bed she'd enjoyed in London. Or perhaps it was only that her mind could not rest. What was she to do about Charlie? About Father? About the shop—her father's only livelihood? If she spent a fortnight cleaning and restocking it, would it only fall to shambles again when she returned to London? Even if Charlie helped and she somehow convinced Francis to return, could they compete with the new surgeon-apothecary and his modern, fully stocked shop?

She sighed heavily, overwhelming dread filling her. There was just too much—too much uncertainty and too much to accomplish in too little time. A floor-to-ceiling cleaning of the shop and living quarters was needed, and who knew what shape the garden was in. There were many orders to be placed, but was there even money to pay for stock? Or had her father drunk it all away? It was too much for one person to manage. Too much for her at any rate. Finally, the heavy weight pressed down on her, and to escape it, she found sleep at last.

In the morning, she arose early, dressed in her simplest frock, pinned up her hair in a plain coil, and went downstairs. First things first. A great deal of hot coffee for her father and hot water for a bath and shave.

She walked quietly across the shop in the dim light of dawn. Again the enormity of the task ahead weighed on her. *Hopeless.*

She gingerly pushed open the surgery door. Her father lay sprawled on the cot, much as she had left him the night before. The bottle she had seen him clutch now lay empty beside him in bed. She crept closer. And in the light beginning to seep through the window, she noticed that the bottle bore no label. *What is his poison of choice?* she wondered. She bent low, gently tugged the bottle from his grasp, and brought it to her nose and sniffed. She knew little of liquor, but this biting acrid smell baffled her.

She heard a sound, the rattling of a door, and started. She was not ready to face any would-be patients yet—and the embarrassed explanations that would certainly follow. The door rattled again.

"Father? Father, wake up."

"Hmm?"

"Father, time to get up. Someone is at the door."

He did not respond.

Sighing, she stepped from the surgery into the shop, rehearsing the words to turn whomever it was away. Through the shopwindow, she saw Mrs. Mimpurse standing there. Why had she not come to the garden door as usual? As Lilly crossed the shop, she was surprised to glimpse two others, no three, no four others with her. Was Maude trying to help by bringing customers? Did she not realize neither the shop nor her father were in any condition to serve anybody?

She opened the door. Before she could say anything, Mrs Mimpurse bustled in, followed by her kitchen maid, Jane, each carrying a mop and bucket. Behind them, Mary bore a basket of biscuits and muffins. Then came sharp-tongued Mrs. Kilgrove; Mr. Baisley, the vicar; and old Arthur Owen with a hen under his arm.

"Put that bird in the garden, Mr. Owen," Mrs. Kilgrove ordered. "We are here to right the place, not foul it with fowl."

Lilly was too speechless to say anything at all.

Then came her brother, bounding through the door.

"Charlie!"

He stretched his arms as though he might embrace her, but ended by awkwardly patting her shoulders instead.

"Mrs. M. sent word you'd come home, Lilly. It's happy I am to see you."

"And I you, Charlie. How you have grown!"

"'At I have. And I am to see what I can do to right the garden. I've only my half day, but I'm a fast worker, I am."

There was so much she wanted to say to him, to ask him, but he was already walking through the shop on his way back to the garden. As he passed, Mrs. Kilgrove greeted him, her voice full of rare warmth.

Lilly was about to shut the door when one more caller approached. It was a sheepish Francis Baylor, hat in hand.

"Might I help as well?" he asked.

Again she marveled at how changed he was. Gone were the wild waves of hair in constant need of cutting. Gone the gangly limbs, the ill-fitting clothes. In their place stood a handsome, well-turned-out traitor.

She asked in her haughtiest voice, "What about Shuttleworth's?"

"I've asked for the day off. Mr. Shuttleworth is very obliging."

"Is he?"

He bit his lip. "I am sorry, Lilly."

"It is Miss Haswell, if you please, Mr. Baylor."

He tilted his head in question.

"We are too grown for Christian names."

"I do not expect you to call me *mister*."

"Why not? Miss Robbins did."

"You are not Miss Robbins."

"I am quite aware of that." He had never treated her with such gentlemanly deference. Nor such foolish awe.

"I meant only that you and I are old friends. At least I hope we are."

"Yes, well," she huffed. "I am in no position to refuse anybody's help, so do come in."

They worked steadily for several hours, Maude directing and Lilly answering questions as best she could as to where things went and what could be salvaged and what must be thrown away.

At one point the vicar asked quietly, "Your father, Miss Haswell. Is he ill, I wonder? He assures me he is perfectly well whenever I call but we have not seen him in church these many months."

"I am sorry to hear that." Though who was she to judge when she and her aunt and uncle had rarely attended church either, save for holidays. "Perhaps you would be so kind as to pray for my father, Mr. Baisley."

"Indeed I have. Is he here that I might pray for him now?"

She hesitated. "Well . . . Let me pop in first, to see if he is . . . dressed for callers."

She walked to the surgery door, then paused to paste on a false smile. "Father! It's wonderful," she said as she stepped inside. "Several of our neighbors have come to help tidy the place. Charlie is working in the garden, and Mr. Owen has even brought us a hen!"

"Has he an outstanding bill he cannot pay with coin?" he asked dully.

"No. Just being neighborly. And Mr. Baisley is here and would like to pray for you. May I send him in?"

He pulled a grimace. "I don't need some cleric mumbling incantations over me. I only need a few more days to get my strength back."

"But—"

"No."

She bit her lip but saw it was futile to argue further. She took a deep breath and let herself from the room.

She stepped toward the vicar. "He is not dressed for callers, I am afraid. But please, do include him in your prayers."

"Indeed I shall, Miss Haswell." He looked at her kindly. "And you as well."

After a long day of cleaning, sorting, and disposing of spoiled remedies and stale herbs, Lilly's back and neck ached. Mrs. Mimpurse invited the volunteers to the coffeehouse for an early supper, and they all filed out. Francis worked on, taking inventory and jotting in a small notebook. If she did not know him so well, Lilly might have thought him stealing the Haswell recipes.

Eyeing his list, she asked, "How bad is it?"

"You'll have several large orders to place, to bring the simples up to par—not to mention the patent medicines you've run out of."

"*I* have run out of nothing. It is not *my* shop." Still, she held out her hand, and he placed two sheets of paper on her waiting palm. The list was long indeed.

"So much?"

"The first column are necessities, I think. The second might wait if you don't have . . . if you don't have time to order all at once."

She understood his meaning. "Thank you."

"If there is anything else I can do, you need only ask."

Such as return to work here? she thought, but she could not ask it of him. She did intend to get Charlie back to the shop, however. He'd returned to Marlow House before she'd had a chance to talk with him at all.

"There is one thing you can do," she said, lifting a finger to indicate he should wait while she walked quietly to her father's surgery.

She returned directly, an empty bottle in her hand.

His eyebrows rose.

"Can you keep this between us?" she asked.

"Of course. Your father's?"

She nodded and held out the bottle. "What is it? Can you tell?"

With grim expectation, he accepted the bottle, regarded the unmarked surface, then swiped it quickly beneath his nose, as though assuming the smell would be readily identifiable. Instead he frowned and held it under his nose again, sniffing once, then again.

"I thought . . . But I don't know. What do you think?"

"I don't know either."

"I am no expert at this sort of thing. That is, assuming . . ." He broke off and began again. "I shall take this and see if either Freddy Mac or Mr. Shuttleworth can identify it."

Freddy McNeal was the proprietor of the Hare and Hounds, the village public house, a tiny place compared to The George on the canal in Honeystreet. "Do not say where it came from, all right?"

"You can trust me, Lill—Miss Haswell."

Already she felt foolish for insisting on her proper name.

"Are you coming to the coffeehouse?" he asked.

"No. But you go on. I had better stay and see if I can get Father to eat something."

He nodded, then cocked his head to look at her closely. "It is good to have you back."

"Not back, only visiting. For a fortnight."

He continued to study her, and she grew uncomfortable under his scrutiny. Had she changed so much? Was he about to tell her she looked well? "Is something amiss?" she asked.

Grinning a little, he said, "You have a bit of cobweb in your hair."

Embarrassed, she brushed at her temple. "Where?"

"Allow me." He reached out and gently drew his fingertips along her hairline. "There." He held up a wispy web and blew it from his fingers.

Her scalp tingled oddly from his touch. She did not even consider reprimanding him for blowing the web onto the just-cleaned floor.

19

Aloft in rows, large Poppy Heads were strung,
And near, a scaly Alligator hung. . . .
The Sage in Velvet Chair, here lolls at Ease,
To promise future Health for present Fees.
—Sir Samuel Garth, *Dispensary*

Using some of the money her aunt had given her for the journey home, Lilly hired a laundress to attack the pile of dirty clothes and linens in her father's room. She placed an order with the coal monger, then visited the chandler to replenish a few necessities—candles, soap, and such. She would worry about meals later. With the amount her father was eating, Mrs. Mimpurse's stew and Mary's bread would last a solid week in the cold cellar.

Late that afternoon, Francis returned to the shop and, seeing the surgery door ajar, gestured her over. "Mr. Shuttleworth would like to speak with you."

"Whatever for?"

"About"—he lowered his voice—"the bottle you gave me. Freddy Mac couldn't place it."

"And Mr. Shuttleworth?"

"Said he needed more information before he could hazard an assessment."

"A guess, you mean."

Francis shrugged. "You can come by the shop, or—"

"I cannot go there. It will look like I am spying, or worse, disloyal to my father."

Francis looked uncomfortable.

"And I cannot invite him here, for Father might hear us. Perhaps the coffeehouse?"

"Good. Mr. Shuttleworth frequents it."

"Does he?"

"He's a bachelor and keeps no servants."

For some reason his status surprised her. Still, she did not like the thought of Mrs. Mimpurse serving her father's rival.

Lilly was ill-prepared for the man who stood to greet her when she entered the coffeehouse and approached the table where he and Francis sat. He was not a tall man, but had a large presence. She guessed he might be as old as thirty, but it was difficult to tell. Though he was of average build, there was nothing else average about him. His black hair stood in three-inch prickles all over his head. His eyebrows formed sharp black peaks over dark eyes that sparkled impishly. His clothes were startling. A gold-and-black waistcoat shone between the lapels of a plush burgundy frock coat with yellow cuffs. His cravat was not white or ivory like every other she'd seen, but gold.

He followed her gaze. "Do you like it?" he asked, touching his cravat.

"Yes." She hesitated. "I have a gown that very hue."

"A lady with exquisite taste. How charming." His teeth, she noticed when he smiled, were quite long.

"Miss Lillian Haswell, may I present Mr. Lionel Shuttleworth."

She was surprised Francis thought to use her full given name.

She curtsied and Mr. Shuttleworth bowed. His grin, the light in his eyes, communicated deep delight. It gave her an odd feeling of warmth and discomfort at once.

"Miss Haswell. What a pleasure. I have been hearing such wonderful things about you, both from young Mr. Baylor here as well as the Mimpurse ladies."

Mary appeared, as if she'd heard her name. She set down a basket of breads and a pot of tea. "Chicken and vegetables will be coming out soon."

Lilly noticed Mr. Shuttleworth's eyes following Mary's every move. Her friend's fair round cheeks were flushed from more than just the kitchen fires, Lilly guessed. Dressed in her blue frock and white apron, with her hair loosely pinned, Mary might not be beautiful, but she made a pretty portrait indeed.

When Mary had disappeared back into the kitchen, Mr. Shuttleworth returned his attention to Lilly. "I do hope you will come by my little shop sometime. I would be honored to show you about the place. I have a new mounted tiger shark, a shrunken head, and several Egyptian scarabs. The colors, Miss Haswell, are like the finest gemstones. Really, quite exquisite."

"And do you use scarabs and sharks in your physic?" She did not ask about the skull; she knew all too well that many apothecaries used powdered bone—it was supposed to heal wounds and treat falling sickness. Her own father abhorred the practice, said it was blasphemous somehow. Lilly agreed. And it was certainly not something she wished to discuss while dining.

He ignored this question and went on, "I was right there on the deck when the crew hauled in the shark. No catalogue-purchased prize for me. And the scarabs I captured and lanced myself."

She could not keep the surprise from her tone. "You have been to Egypt?"

"Egypt, Italy, the West Indies, Africa."

"My goodness. May I ask how you came to travel so far?"

"Indeed you may." He leaned his elbows on the table. "I worked as a ship's surgeon on a merchant vessel for several years. My employer imported exotic things from exotic places. I found it all fascinating. Not only the unusual plants and animals—even people—but especially the healing practices of different cultures. Most interesting."

"Then I must ask the obvious question, sir," Lilly said. "How in the world—why in the world—would you choose to set up shop in a little inland village like Bedsley Priors? Have you family here?"

He shook his head. "I have no family." He stared off over her head, apparently in deep thought or memory. "I grew weary of shipboard surgery and living among coarse men. I quit my post and took passage on one of the canal boats transporting our wares from Bristol to London. There I served with a master apothecary for several months and then decided to stay a few years, London town having such a varied and rich culture."

"London I can understand, sir. But Bedsley Priors?"

She felt Francis's silent censure and amended, "It is a lovely place, and I am partial to it, having grown up here and having family here."

"You are fortunate to have family and friends, Miss Haswell. And indeed it is a lovely place, occupied by lovely people. In fact, when I passed Bedsley Priors on my way to London, I saw three reasons which compelled me to decide then and there that I would return to Bedsley Priors one day."

Lilly raised her eyebrows. "Three reasons, sir?"

Mary came out of the kitchen again, bearing a tray of dishes. Mr. Shuttleworth said softly, "And here comes one of those lovely reasons now." He rose. "May I assist you with that tray? Looks heavy."

Mary blushed. "I can manage, sir."

He beamed at them all. "And strong of limb as well." His gaze moved from Mary's face to Lilly's. "You might be sisters. So lovely are the both of you."

The platter of chicken clunked heavily onto the table. "Sorry," Mary mumbled. Biting her lip, Mary set out the bowls of vegetables with a return of her usual grace. Lilly hoped she wasn't about to have one of her bouts of falling sickness.

Breaking away from the man's steady gaze, Lilly asked, "Join us, Mary?"

"Can't now. Maybe for coffee and pudding later."

Lilly forked a piece of stewed chicken onto her plate and passed the platter to Mr. Shuttleworth. He stacked several pieces beside his mound of leeks and potatoes. "Well, now the food's arrived, let's dive into business, shall we?"

He leaned in close across the table. "The bottle. I extracted a few remaining drops of liquid. Definitely contains alcohol."

Her heart fell. She felt shame flush her features.

"As well as laudanum."

She looked down at her plate, all appetite fleeing.

"But I believe its primary purpose is not to intoxicate, but rather to tranquilize."

She looked over at the man.

"I surmise the bottle is your father's and is one of many?"

She darted a look at Francis, but Mr. Shuttleworth raised a hand. "Mr. Baylor did not tell me, but it seems fairly obvious. I have been aware of your father's reclusive state. Have even called in, only to have my concern rebuffed."

"I am sorry."

"Never mind." Mr. Shuttleworth dismissed her apology with a wave of his fork. "I saw him on the street several weeks ago, and his features were quite pinched. I wondered then if he was in a great deal of pain. And I am more convinced now. The mixture is a pain reliever to be sure, but what else it is, I am not completely certain."

"But it is physic, you think? Not simply . . . drink?"

"I believe so, yes. Perhaps some new patent medicine, or more likely, something of his own creation. You might look and see what simples he leaves about or is running low on." He leaned back expressively, "Or, you could simply ask him."

Lilly took a bite of chicken in lieu of answering. Mr. Shuttleworth did not know her father.

In the morning, Lilly observed her father carefully, more objectively, she hoped, now that the shock of so many changes had passed. He was unshaven, his cheeks bristling with a few days' worth of grey and ginger whiskers. The skin of his neck hung looser than she remembered, his jowls more slack. His hair was somewhat thinner and in disarray, with new strands of silver at his sideburns. His eyes had lost some of their blue color, it seemed, and much of their light. When she looked at him, she felt repelled and tender all at once. Even though she had not seen him for over a year, he was still the only parent in her life—her security, her constant. Her father had always been strong and capable. It unsettled her to see him seem so weak, so . . . diminished.

She approached and greeted him gently. She sat on the cot near his legs, so that she might speak with him nearer to his eye level.

"Morning." His voice was rough.

"And how are you today?" She found herself speaking to him in a calm, sweet tone one normally reserved for a child. He was no child. Neither was she, but still the thought of losing him filled her with the emptiest quiver of loneliness. She thought of the Chinese kites she had once seen in Hyde Park coming untied and floating away. Like she and her brother would. *Oh, Charlie . . . What would poor Charlie do without Father?*

She cleared her throat and tried again. "Are you very ill, do you think?"

He looked at her sharply.

"The bottles. I am ashamed to admit, but I at first believed you were foxed. And I doubt I am the only person in the village to think so."

"When have you ever known me to drink more than an occasional glass of port?"

"Never—before. But a great deal has changed since I've been away."

He looked away from her, shaking his head despondently.

"What is it, Father? Do you know?"

"No. Some days I am nearly myself, and others I can barely rise. The latter have become frightfully frequent. But I *know* I have only to come up with the correct combination of herbs and elixirs, and I shall conquer this thing."

"Without a diagnosis? When have you ever been successful treating an illness that way?"

"Rarely, but it does happen. Sometimes we are not sure what the underlying problem is, but we stumble upon a remedy after much trial and error."

"But this is foolishness! When you have not even consulted with another medical man. Let me send for Dr. Foster."

"That man! He would be the last I would crawl to for advice. He would waste no time advertising my weakness and failure—that I can tell you."

She knew old Dr. Foster had often resented her father for visiting and treating *his* patients. But bad blood notwithstanding, he was a professional, was he not?

"Mr. Shuttleworth, then."

"My new competitor? Shall I help him drive me from business once and for all? Shall I hand him the shovel to bury me?"

"I have met the man. He seems very decent. Besides, he is a fellow apothecary. He spent several months with the Worshipful Society, just as you did."

"I spent nearly two years there, between my time with the society and my summer working in the apothecaries' garden. Several months indeed."

"Father, please. I insist you see a doctor. If you refuse the two at hand, then I shall . . . I shall write to my uncle and ask him to bring a man from London."

"Your uncle? Who already believes me a useless failure? I'll not prove him right."

"You are not useless. Merely ill."

"Same thing."

"It isn't! Now, Father, I insist—"

He pinned her with an ice-blue gaze. "I am afraid, lass, that you have no right to insist upon anything."

"Do I not?" she asked, refusing to be cowed. "Is my father not acting irrationally? Damaging himself and his beloved shop, passed down from father and grandfather before him? A shop he would once have done anything to protect?"

"I am trying to protect it!"

"No, you are trying to protect your pride. And it is too late for that. I am calling for Dr. Foster or Mr. Shuttleworth—you have your choice."

"Just . . . just give me a little more time. I know I can get back on my feet. Just another month. By then I shall figure out what treatment I've overlooked . . ."

"Two days."

"A fortnight."

"A week—and no longer."

He sighed. "Very well."

"Good," she said briskly. But she wondered if they had that long.

20

> J. & A. PEPLER, beg respectfully to inform the Ladies of DEVIZES and its vicinity that J.P. is returned from London, where she has selected a choice assortment of MILLINERY DRESSES, Straws, & Fancy Bonnets.
>
> —*Devizes & Wiltshire Gazette,* 1833

In the morning, Lilly was just making up a breakfast tray for her father when a rap on the shop door startled her, causing her to spill hot tea on her hand. Blowing on the scorched skin, she walked from the laboratory-kitchen through the shop. She was surprised to see Francis at the door. She opened it and saw that he carried a crate in his hands.

"This is heavy. Might I . . . ?"

"Of course. Come in."

He carried the crate back and settled it gently on the counter.

"What is this?" she asked, eyeing the array of jars and packets.

"Bare basics. Hopefully enough to keep you going here until you can place and receive an order."

"But . . . how?"

"I made a second list for myself when I completed that inventory for you. I pulled this from Mr. Shuttleworth's stock."

"But we cannot accept this."

"This is not charity, Miss Haswell. It has all been accounted for. You will pay it back as you can."

"But I won't . . ." Why could she not finish the sentence, *I won't be here*? Dread and cold realization sifted through her. Orders to place, debts to pay, a shop to repair . . . but what of her plans for a stay of only a fortnight?

"Of course I shall see you are repaid," she said officiously. "Thank you." She turned abruptly and retreated to the laboratory-kitchen so he would not see her brave face fall.

The next day, Lilly and Charlie attended services together. How inviting the church looked that bright morning, sunshine streaming through colorful stained-glass windows, candles lit, happy voices filling the chapel. It felt good to be there, sitting in her old place, listening to the fine Kentish voice of Mr. Baisley.

During the singing of a hymn, Lilly was distracted by a deep male voice coming from somewhere nearby. The pleasing baritone filled in the reedy melody carried by so many women and old men. Lilly glanced discreetly over her shoulder and was surprised to see Francis Baylor two rows behind her, eyes on the vicar, singing intently and with feeling. *His voice has changed as well.*

After the service, many villagers made a point of coming over to greet Lilly and to welcome her home.

Undeniably handsome in his Sunday coat, Francis bowed briefly to her. "Miss Haswell. Charlie." He would have turned away without lingering had Charlie not called after him.

"I saw her again today, Francis."

Francis paused. "Who—the red-haired angel?"

My hair is not red, Lilly thought automatically. Russet brown or even ginger—the tawny brown spice—but not red. A moment later her cheeks were no doubt the very color she despised, for they were not speaking of her at all.

Charlie nodded. "Up early she were. I hoped maybe she were coming here."

"Ah well. Plenty of other angels about the place, Charlie."

Francis did not walk out with them but instead turned to greet Miss Robbins and her parents.

Once outside, Charlie put on a dingy hat. "I'd better to get back to Marlow House."

"Charlie, wait. Sit for a minute, will you?"

He hesitated but allowed her to lead him to a bench in the churchyard and sat down beside her.

She asked, "Do you not wish to return home and help Father and me?"

He shrugged.

"What is it, Charlie? Are you afraid? Has someone at Marlow House frightened you?" She resisted the urge to put her arms around him, to protect him from would-be bullies, as she had when he was a child.

"No. I like it 'ere, I do. Mr. Timms is a bit gruff, but I am learning ever so much from him."

"But Father needs you. You do want to help Father, don't you?"

"I do. But—" Charlie lowered his head. His wrists protruded from the sleeves of his old Sunday coat. Just as his ankles showed between trousers and boots. An overgrown little boy. But this streak of stubbornness was something new.

She forced a gentle tone. "I shall speak to Sir Henry, shall I? And explain?"

Again he shrugged. "He won't like it. And I don't like to break my word."

She hesitated. "You've an official agreement, then? A contract of some sort?"

"I'm an apprentice now, I am. Like Francis were." He sat up a little straighter, clearly proud of the fact.

Oh dear. That did complicate things.

She asked Charlie to come home for tea at least. He agreed, but as soon as they entered through the garden gate, he was distracted by a new hornets' nest hanging from the eaves near the back door. And there he sat. Lilly knew better than to try to cajole him while he was counting, especially objects in flight. She sighed. Maybe it was just as well. She could speak to Father alone first.

Over tea, she asked her father about Charlie's position.

Her father nodded. "I'd heard they were looking for a lad. Told Charlie he might try for it."

"But why?"

"I haven't been able to look after him properly, Lilly. Shames me to say it, but there it is." He rubbed a hand over his whiskered cheeks. "At least there I knew he'd not be wandering about the county, getting himself in some scrape or other with his strange ways and spying and I know not what."

"He does not mean to spy."

He waved her words away. "I know, but it does look it. Bedsley Priors has changed, Lilly. Lots of new people have moved here, some of them quite rough. Most don't know how harmless Charlie is. He might be caught eavesdropping on some shady affair and pay a high price for it. I don't so much mind if they say he's off in his attic, but I could not bear to see any harm come to the boy."

"Of course not."

"At least at Marlow House he's kept busy. And has regular meals, which is more than I can say here."

She pushed his plate of bread and jam nearer to him. "Go on."

He bit off a small morsel. "Mr. Timms took him on as an apprentice of sorts. Marlow waived the apprenticeship fee, in lieu of wages. Though he'll start earning after six months' time, and it's been nearly three already."

"But surely now—"

"I'd hate for him to break the contract. No telling what young Marlow might say to that. Might demand the forfeited apprenticeship fee since Charlie didn't earn out his service, at least some settling up for room and board. It isn't done, Lilly. It would look very bad if Charlie quit, especially without proper notice."

"But, perhaps if I talked with him."

"You are going to talk sense to Roderick Marlow?"

"I meant Sir Henry."

"He leaves all of that to his son." He lifted his cup with a shaky hand. "Sir Henry is in better health than I am at present. But during his last illness he gave up the running of things. Roderick Marlow is master of the estate for all intents and purposes."

"Well, even he can't be devoid of all natural feeling. Once I explain the situation."

"And exactly how will you explain the situation?"

"With great tact and discretion—you may depend upon it."

He shook his head. "I have no doubt you learned a fair dose of that in London, my dear. Go on then, but don't take it to heart if he isn't swayed."

She found Charlie still sitting beside the back door. "Charlie, I am going to see Mr. Marlow in a few minutes. See if we cannot work out some arrangement for a leave for you. Can you harness the gig, please?"

He hesitated, then nodded. "All right."

She stepped quickly across the mews to the coffeehouse. Mrs. Mimpurse and Mary were at the small kitchen table, enjoying a rare time of idle talk over tea.

"Mrs. Mimpurse, I'm riding out to Marlow House to see about getting Charlie released from his contract. Can you stop by and check on Father in the next hour or so? I shouldn't be gone long."

Mrs. Mimpurse looked her up and down. "You are going to Marlow House dressed like that?"

Lilly glanced down at the plain morning dress she had put on after church. "It isn't a social call. I merely wish to discuss business."

"Do you hope to sway Roderick Marlow with your words alone?"

"Well, yes."

Mrs. Mimpurse shook her head. "Tut, tut, Miss Lilly. Has your time in London taught you nothing?"

Two hours later, Lilly stood from her dressing table and pulled on her gloves. She wore one of her London gowns, a walking dress of jaconet muslin with lovely pink embroidery up the front and three flounces at the hem. Over it, she wore a cottage mantle of grey cloth lined with pink silk to cover the low neckline and provide some protection from the slight chill in the air. She had hoped to take care of her errand earlier in the day, but it had taken time to bathe and dress in her petticoat, stockings, and boned stays. Mary had come over to help tighten the stays and then remained to dress her hair. Now rich auburn curls showed at one temple beneath a straw gypsy hat trimmed with ribbon. Mary had wanted her to wear one boasting fruit or ostrich feathers, but Lilly would have felt too self-conscious driving through the village in either of those.

"Thank you, Mary."

"Nervous?"

"Definitely," Lilly allowed.

"The worst he can do is say no."

Lilly drew in a breath. "Is it?"

"And who could say no to you, looking as pretty as you do?" Mary hesitated, then added gently, "I know you and your father need help, but it wouldn't be so bad if Charlie stayed there. I think he likes it."

"You are trying to comfort me, should I fail, I know. But I worry for Charlie. Would worry for anyone under such masters."

"But . . . Well, never mind," Mary said and adjusted the curl nearest Lilly's cheek one last time.

Lilly descended the stairs and went out the back door, only to see Charlie sitting in the slanting rays of late afternoon sunlight, much as she had left him two hours before. She looked out into the mews but saw no sign of the gig.

"Have you harnessed Pennywort to the gig?"

"Wheel's broke."

"Is it?" She bit back her frustration. "But you knew I was hoping to take it. You might have said so before."

"You're only going to Marlows'. 'Tisn't far."

She huffed. "Oh, very well. I shall walk."

"Shall I come along?" He lurched to his feet. "'Ere's a pretty red-haired lady about the place now. Wouldn't mind clapping eyes on her again. All the lads say she's gurt handsome. Even Francis."

Lilly wondered if the red-haired lady was the woman she had seen with

Roderick Marlow in London. "Please stay with Father, Charlie. If he needs anything, run over and ask Mrs. Mimpurse."

"All right." Still, he looked uncomfortable.

"Come on, Charlie," Mary said, joining them outside and clearly sensing his unease. "How about a game of draughts before I go?"

Charlie looked up eagerly at this suggestion.

Lilly smiled her gratitude at Mary, then let herself from the gate.

Charlie was correct. Marlow House was not far. She had walked, even run that distance many times. But never in such fine dress, such delicate slippers, nor such tight stays.

She walked rather stiffly, hoping her hair, piled high on her head beneath her hat, would stay within its pins.

She approached Marlow House from the side and stopped abruptly. There, on the lawn, a man stood as still as a garden statue. She hesitated, then walked a few steps closer, staring at the man whose profile grew more familiar with each step.

No doubt hearing her footsteps on the gravel path, the man turned to look in her direction. "I say, you gave me a start."

Roger Bromley, here? In Bedsley Priors? Though she felt awkward and uncertain of how he might react to her presence, she was pleased to see him. She had always liked the man. She smiled at him, cocking her head to one side. Feeling the weighty crown of curls shift dangerously in that direction, she quickly righted it again.

"Miss Haswell?" Roger Bromley smiled in recognition and stepped to meet her. "I did not expect to see you here."

"Nor I you."

"What a pleasure." He bowed to her and she curtsied. "I have just come out for some air and a respite from silly females. I did not know you were joining the house party."

"Oh . . ." she faltered. "I am not. I live here—in the village, that is."

"That's right! I'd quite forgotten you were from the same rustic country as Marlow."

She took a breath, her anxiety rising at the mention of his name. Hoping to disguise it, she asked brightly, "Is Christina Price-Winters here?"

"No. She is busy buying wedding clothes. Engaged herself to Stanton. Had you not heard?"

Lilly shook her head. She had guessed Christina would not keep in touch. Still, it hurt that she had not written with such significant news.

"But there are at least two others here of your acquaintance," Mr. Bromley continued. "Toby Horton and Miss Whittier."

"How nice for you."

"Is it?"

"Oh dear. Has she thrown you over again?"

He eyed her wryly. "I would not say that, exactly, but yes, she has reverted to being quite cold to me."

"I am sorry to hear it. Perhaps you ought to invent another imminent engagement?" She bit back a smile. "Seemed quite effective the last time."

He laughed. "How deliciously forthright you are, Miss Haswell. I have missed you, though I know I have given little evidence of that."

"That is all right, Mr. Bromley," she said, relieved to feel no sting of regret. "I had no reason to expect correspondence."

"That's right, after throwing me over so heartlessly." He smiled at her, a teasing light in his eyes.

"Were you going in?" He offered her his arm.

"I do not wish to interrupt."

"No harm. Dinner will not be served for some time."

She had just laid her hand on his offered arm when Susan Whittier stepped out onto the veranda.

"Roger? I wondered where you had gone. Oh. Hello."

"You remember Miss Haswell, do you not?"

"Yes. How do you do," the pretty blonde said. "I did not know you would be joining us."

"I am not—"

"Miss Haswell is neighbor to Marlow. Why do you think I was so eager to come to . . . Where are we again?"

"Bedsley Priors."

"Bedsley Priors. Charming place." He winked at Lilly.

"Did you not find him?" The familiar voice of Roderick Marlow caused Lilly's smile to fade. Her heart began to pound uncomfortably when he strode out onto the veranda in evening dress, his cravat and dark hair in elegant disarray.

Susan Whittier said, "I did. But he is occupied, as you see, with your Miss Haswell."

Marlow turned to stare at her, dark eyebrows rising before lowering in perplexity . . . or was it annoyance? Lilly felt her cheeks redden.

"*My* Miss Haswell?" Mr. Marlow repeated.

"She is your neighbor, is she not?" Miss Whittier all but accused.

He cocked his head, considering. "Well, I suppose she is. Miss Haswell, what a surprise." He bowed.

"Forgive me. I did not know you had guests."

"No matter. I did not mean it was not a pleasant surprise. You are most welcome. I had forgotten you had friends among us."

"We enjoy only a limited acquaintance," Miss Whittier corrected. "Excuse me. I shall see you at dinner." At that, the blond woman turned and marched away.

Laying his hand over hers, Mr. Bromley escorted Lilly onto the veranda, where Mr. Marlow stood. There, Roger paused to beam down at her. "Miss Haswell quite broke my heart, Marlow. Did you not hear of it? She rejected me most cruelly."

"Did she?" Again Mr. Marlow's dark eyebrows rose.

Roger sighed dramatically. "Yes. But still, how pleased I am to see her again."

Feeling Mr. Marlow's eyes on her, she rushed to say, "I only wanted to speak with you for a few moments. I shall come again another time."

"Nonsense. You must stay," Roger insisted.

"Yes, of course," Marlow said politely. "Come, Miss Haswell." He gestured toward the door. "Shall we speak in the library? Then you may rejoin your most ardent admirer." Marlow cast a shrewd look at Roger Bromley. "Although I had hoped to win back my ten at whist."

"Another time, my friend." Roger grinned. "Who desires gaming when such beauty is before us?"

Lilly all but rolled her eyes.

"Come, Miss Haswell." Roderick Marlow opened the door for her with a flourish, as though welcoming the queen herself. Was he mocking her?

Once they were closed in the library, Lilly swallowed, wondering if seeking privacy had been a good idea.

Mr. Marlow remained standing but leaned back, propping himself against the edge of a massive desk, arms crossed. He dipped his chin, indicating a chair nearby. "What did you wish to speak to me about?"

She stepped closer but remained standing. "My brother, Charlie." When he appeared not to apprehend her meaning, she clarified, "Your new under-gardener?"

"Ah, yes. Stedman mentioned something. In fact, he reported the lad was working out rather well. Is there a problem?"

"Not a problem, exactly. But while I appreciate the offer of employment for him, Charlie is needed at home at present. Having both of us gone has left my father shorthanded, and there is much work to be done."

"Yes, I had heard something about Haswell's falling into disrepair."

She bit back a defensive rebuttal. He was right, after all, but it hurt her pride to hear him say it so matter-of-factly. "Yes, well. I understand you waived an apprenticeship fee, but my brother is very conscientious and doesn't want to break his contract, nor hinder his opportunities for future employment." She was relieved when he didn't ask why she was negotiating on her brother's behalf. Was he aware of Charlie's limitations?

He straightened to his full height and waved her concerns away as though a midge before his face. "Think no more of it, Miss Haswell. I understand. I will speak to Stedman and to Timms. Your brother may return to your father's shop without worry. He may even have a reference, if you like. And he will be welcomed back here, should the situation change and he is no longer needed at home."

She was stunned at how easily it was done. Was he really so kind, or simply eager to return to his guests? She had certainly asked at an opportune time.

"Thank you, sir. That is most magnanimous."

He stepped to the door, opened it, and looked back at her. Her invitation to leave.

She walked toward him but was surprised when he held out his arm. She looked up at him in question.

"May I escort you to the dining room?" he asked.

"But I . . . No. I did not intend nor presume . . ."

He looked at her closely. "Did you really refuse Roger Bromley?"

She took a deep breath. "I suppose I did. But only because I knew he loved another."

He nodded thoughtfully. "And you believe people should marry for love, Miss Haswell?"

"I do not know about all people, but I should."

"Shall we?"

"Shall we what?"

"Go in to dinner."

"Oh, of course." *Of course* he'd meant dinner, not *of course* she would stay for it.

Roger Bromley appeared in the corridor. "Enough village business. I'd hoped to escort Miss Haswell to the dining room."

"Too late, Bromley." Marlow actually took her hand and laid it on his arm. "I am afraid you shall have to escort Miss Whittier and her chaperone instead."

Across the hall, Susan Whittier stood with a faded, weary-faced woman of fifty or so years. Susan looked rather vexed. "Has everyone forgotten me?"

"There, there," Roger soothed, striding across the room and offering his arm. She actually smiled and laid her hand on his sleeve. Roger looked at Lilly over his shoulder and winked again.

Before she could protest further, Marlow was leading Lilly across the grand hall.

From above, a flash of green caught her eye. She looked up and saw a woman gliding down the staircase in gleaming layers of emerald silk. Her bearing was elegant, her crown of red hair regal, her porcelain features flawless. Yes, this was the woman she had seen on Roderick Marlow's arm at a London ball. How beautiful she was. Lilly felt horribly underdressed in her walking frock and straw bonnet.

The butler, Mr. Withers, appeared and offered to take her wrap. She swallowed. Should she stay? She wasn't properly dressed for dinner. Nor invited. Nervously, she removed her hat and handed it to Mr. Withers. Then she untied the bow that released the mantle from her neck and shoulders, and the butler took that from her as well. Roderick's gaze surveyed her throat and neckline before returning to her overheated face. Why did he want her to stay? Was not this woman, now pausing before them, his intended?

"Miss Lillian Haswell, Miss Cassandra Powell."

Miss Powell dipped her head politely but reservedly. Lilly returned the gesture. Closer now, Lilly realized that Miss Powell was older than she appeared from a distance. Perhaps a few years older than Roderick Marlow himself.

"I believe I saw the two of you in London together." Lilly meant it as an indication that she understood they were a couple and she posed no threat. But neither reacted as she'd expected.

Roderick cleared his throat, and Miss Powell looked away. "I do not recall such an occasion." She flipped open her lacquered fan. "Well, I shall just see myself in."

"Nonsense, Cass—Miss Powell." He offered her his left arm, his right still trapping Lilly's hand to his side. Miss Powell coolly accepted. And Lilly was taken in to dinner, feeling very much like the proverbial lamb being led to slaughter.

21

I will not dwell upon ragouts or roasts,
Albeit all human history attests
That happiness for man—the hungry sinner!—
Since Eve ate apples, much depends on the dinner.

—Lord Byron

The evening passed more pleasantly than Lilly would have guessed. Roderick Marlow was a gallant host, skillfully including everyone in a conversation that ranged from the London season to fashion, books, parliamentary affairs, and the war with France. Roger Bromley was also a master conversationalist, and managed to compliment both Lilly and Susan in equal measure, so that by the second course, Susan Whittier was smiling with genuine warmth at both Roger and Lilly. Miss Whittier's chaperone ate silently but voraciously for such a small woman. Toby Horton drank too much and spoke his opinions too loudly, but otherwise the meal passed very agreeably. Even red-haired Cassandra Powell made an effort to show interest in the others, as though she were already mistress of Marlow House.

The meal was finer by far than the plain fare—soups, stews, beef and kidney pies—she'd either prepared or been given since returning home. Finer even than most of the tables she had seen laid in London. For the first course they were served green-pea soup, crimped perch with Dutch sauce, stewed veal and peas, lamb cutlets and cucumbers. Then came a second course of haunch of venison, boiled capon in white sauce, braised tongue and vegetables. Finally, there arrived a third course of lobster salad, raspberry and currant tart, strawberry cream, meringues, and iced pudding. Lilly took only tiny portions from the serving dishes nearest her but still could not eat everything on her plate. Giving herself a respite, she paused to touch a linen serviette to her lips.

"Is the meal to your liking, Miss Haswell?" Roderick Marlow asked, raising his goblet.

"Indeed, sir. Mrs. Tobias is to be commended. I had not a finer meal in all my time in London."

Roderick Marlow dipped his head appreciatively.

"And how long were you in London?" Miss Powell asked. "A fortnight?"

Lilly ignored her pointed condescension. "A year and a half."

"Miss Haswell lived with her uncle and aunt, Jonathan and Ruth Elliott," Roger Bromley said warmly. "Fine people and friends of my parents."

Even Susan Whittier added a kind word. "Miss Haswell was quite a favorite with the Price-Winters family, Cassandra. You were guest in their grand home on at least one occasion."

Miss Powell nodded slightly but sipped from her wine glass in lieu of responding.

When the ladies withdrew to allow the men to drink port and smoke their pipes in private, Miss Powell led the way to the drawing room. Lilly followed reluctantly, knowing it would be rude not to join the ladies for at least a short time. Miss Powell went directly to the pianoforte and sat gracefully upon its bench. She ran her fingers over the keys with a flourish, then began playing a dramatic piece. Susan Whittier followed her chaperone's example and sat on one of the settees. She picked up a book lying on its arm but quickly laid it back down. She and Lilly exchanged an awkward smile. It was difficult to speak over the music, but Lilly sat on a chair near Susan and attempted it anyway.

"Your gown is lovely," Lilly said, eyeing the evening dress of willow-green crepe with gauze flowers around the hem.

"Do you think so? When I saw Cassandra's silk was green too, I feared we would clash horribly."

"It is beautiful, truly."

Miss Whittier smiled self-consciously. "Thank you."

Lilly could almost believe Susan an agreeable young woman, when not jealous, vexed, or bored. She hoped so, for Roger's sake.

Susan leaned closer. "Do not mind Cassandra. I am afraid she wields her disappointments like claws."

Her tongue as well, Lilly thought.

"She was engaged once, you see, but her fiancé was—"

Miss Powell halted mid-stanza, the chords fading under her words. "How amusing to see the two of you sitting together—all politeness. Two rivals under the same roof."

"One might say the same of two others, Cassandra," Susan said cryptically.

What did that mean? Lilly wondered. *Two sets of rivals?*

Miss Powell's eyes narrowed. "Careful, Susan dear."

Susan Whittier rose. "Please excuse me, ladies. I am just going to dash to my chamber and freshen my toilette."

"Good idea." Miss Powell smiled archly. When Susan and her matronly companion had gone, Miss Powell resumed playing—this time a quiet, moody piece. "Poor Susan. Only wants what she cannot have."

Lilly thought this quite perceptive. Susan Whittier certainly seemed to only want Mr. Bromley when she thought she could not have him.

"You are a shopkeeper's daughter, are you not?" Miss Powell asked.

"An apothecary's daughter."

Miss Powell lifted one hand from the keys in a dismissive wave. "That explains a great deal." She played a few more bars, then paused. "But not everything."

Lilly rose, deciding she had better take her leave before she said something foolish.

"I shall bid you good-night, Miss Powell."

Cassandra dipped her head slightly, but kept her eyes on the sheet music before her. "I shall be going up in a moment myself. I want to visit Sir Henry. The baronet was up and about all day yesterday. Bested us all at archery, went riding. Quite exhausted himself, I am afraid. Such a pity he was not feeling well enough to join us tonight."

"A great pity. Do greet him for me."

Cassandra paused in her playing. "You are acquainted with Sir Henry?"

"Yes, although I have not seen him in nearly two years."

She nodded, though Lilly had the distinct impression the woman would not bother to pass along the greetings of a mere *shopkeeper's* daughter.

Lilly let herself from the room, closing the door behind her.

She asked a housemaid, a girl she did not know, where Mr. Withers would have put her wrap. The girl bobbed a curtsy and ducked through a door. A moment later, the butler himself appeared, holding her mantle while she put on her straw hat. Roderick Marlow appeared in the hall and, seeing her there, quickly strode over.

"Leaving already, Miss Haswell?"

"Yes, I must be getting back."

He took her wrap from the butler and arranged it over her shoulders himself. She swallowed, uncomfortable with his familiarity, especially in front of Mr. Withers.

She self-consciously took a step away from Mr. Marlow as she tied the bow around her neck.

"Well, good evening," she said. "Thank you for including me so generously."

"You are more than welcome. Has Withers called for your carriage?"

Roger appeared in the hall and walked toward them just as Miss Powell came out of the drawing room. So much for slipping away quietly.

Lilly said, in what she hoped were low tones, "No. I walked actually. It is not far."

Even so, Roger heard her. "Marlow, send for your carriage, will you? I shall escort Miss Haswell home."

"Never mind, Bromley," Marlow said. "I shall see Miss Haswell home myself."

"Really, Roderick," Cassandra Powell said, passing by on her way to the stairs. "You have guests. The groom can take her perfectly well."

"Yes, please," Lilly urged. "I do not wish to trouble you further. I can walk, or if Cecil has time . . . ?"

"Cecil?" Cassandra swung back around, brow arched.

"Cecil Briggs. The groom."

"Ah," she said. "Do you know all the servants?"

Lilly lifted her chin. "Yes. I know everybody in the village. Or at least I did at one time."

"How quaint."

"As host, I insist on escorting you home," Roderick Marlow said. "Bromley, if you will be so good as to entertain Miss Whittier while I'm gone. Horton is out cold, I'm afraid. I shall have Withers and Stedman see to him."

"Oh, very well," Roger said, as though it were a burden to have Miss Whittier all to himself. His warm gaze fastened on Lilly. "I cannot tell you what a delight it has been to see you again, Miss Haswell. Shall we have the pleasure of your company again tomorrow?"

"No. But I do hope you enjoy the rest of your stay, Mr. Bromley." Lilly curtsied and he bowed.

Cassandra Powell was already halfway up the stairs without a backward glance.

Roderick called for his curricle and waved off the groom. "I'll handle the ribbons myself."

Discomfort flooded Lilly. Alone, unchaperoned with Roderick Marlow, at night? Did he not realize, or did he simply not care? She said, "I think, Mr. Marlow, that given the hour . . ."

"Of course. You are quite right. The landau, please, Withers, and Briggs to drive. No use rousing the coachman at this hour."

Lilly might have walked home in the time it took to harness the horses and bring the carriage around, but Mr. Marlow would not hear of it. When hooves sounded on the crescent drive out front, he escorted her outside. Cecil Briggs helped her up into the seat, and she did not miss the groom's speculative expression. He and Charlie had been boyhood friends. When Mr. Marlow leaned close to the groom and delivered some low instruction, Cecil darted a look at her that she could not quite decipher. Surprise? Worry?

As soon as Mr. Marlow was seated beside her in the front-facing bench, Cecil climbed up to his perch and started the horses into a mild pace, seeming in no great hurry. It was quite late, but the moon shone brightly on the summer night, and she could see both men quite clearly.

"When I first saw you in London," Roderick Marlow began, "I thought I was imagining things. Why did you run from me?"

"I should think that somewhat obvious."

"Is it?"

"Well, I worried you might . . ." She darted a look at him. "That is, I thought you would . . ."

"Ah." He nodded his understanding. "You thought I would stand on the orchestra stage and tell the venerable assembly that Miss Haswell was not the privileged, accomplished young lady they imagined her, but rather the cleverest, loveliest, most loyal lady in all of Wiltshire."

That was not the response she'd expected. What had come over the man? Was he foxed? Did she need remind him of the exquisite redhead waiting at Marlow House?

She acted on this notion. "And when I first saw you in London, you were with Miss Powell."

"I suppose she is rather hard to miss."

"She is very beautiful."

Marlow looked off into the passing countryside. "Yes, and very aware of that fact."

"All the lads in the village are quite agog, I understand. My brother and my father's apprentice—that is, his former apprentice—are both quite taken with her."

"I suppose the young men in this county have rarely seen such a woman."

"Will they be . . . seeing her often?" Lilly was curious about the former fiancé Miss Whittier had mentioned, but knew it would be impolite to ask him.

He looked at her and smirked. "If she has her way, yes. I believe they will see a great deal of her. You know we Marlows live to please the villagers."

She raised her eyebrows.

Feigning indignation, he said, "My father is highly respected among them—do you deny it?"

"Of course not. Sir Henry is admired by all."

"It is only me you take issue with?"

"You do seem improved with age. You certainly *appear* charming."

"You find me charming. I am pleased to hear it. But you think it only a surface charm? That beneath this façade, I am . . . ?"

He looked at her, waiting while she studied him. She thought of the pills they made in her father's shop, with their sugar pastes and silver coatings. Pretty to look at, sweet on the surface, but still just as bitter within.

"I pray I am wrong."

Surprisingly, he let that go. "Pray often, do you?"

"Not as often as I should." *Nor as often as I once did.*

Cecil turned the horses toward the north, she noticed, toward Alton. Why was he not simply driving straight into the village?

"What do you petition for, Miss Haswell? What worldly troubles press themselves upon your heart? Starving orphans in London? Slavery in Spain, perhaps? The war with France?"

"No, I am afraid my small prayers are of a far narrower scope. My father. Brother. My dear friend Mary." She did not mention her mother, though she could have. She was still distracted by the unexpected detour.

"What about *dear Mary* moves you to pray?"

"She struggles with epilepsy . . . falling sickness. Do you not remember?"

"Oh yes. That girl who has fits."

Her concern was instantly replaced with irritation. "She is not *that girl*. She is Mary Helen Mimpurse. The cleverest girl I know. The gentlest, truest friend. The daughter of a war hero and the finest woman in Bedsley Priors—well you are acquainted with her mother."

"Maude Mimpurse's daughter? I had forgotten. Forgive me, I meant no disrespect to your Miss Mary Mimpurse. My, how diverting to say that. Miss Mary Mimpurse. Miss Mary Mimpurse . . ."

She found herself chuckling with him and noted they were now driving on a narrow track east.

He suddenly sobered. "By your own admission, the list of beneficiaries of your prayers is quite small. Would you consider adding another?"

"You, sir?"

He pulled a frown, brows raised, "You think I need prayers?"

"We all do, sir. Some more than others."

"Miss Lillian Haswell, I do believe you are teasing me."

She grinned.

"Actually, I meant my father. He has fallen ill again. That smug Dr. Foster spent half the morning at his side."

How foolish she felt now. "Of course I shall pray for your father."

"Thank you." They rode on in silence for several moments. Lilly realized that after their brief detour, Cecil had again turned south toward Bedsley Priors.

Marlow said, "But if you happened to mention my name to God now and again, I should not object."

She smiled. "I shall ask Him to give you humility."

He cleared his throat. "Let us not ask for a miracle right off, shall we?"

She laughed.

"But of course . . . you Haswells call down miracles at will—is that not right? Your father, the legendary healer and all that. Bringing my own grandfather back from the dead, as they say."

Lilly bit her lip, then whispered, "That was a long time ago."

They made the final turning down the High Street.

"Well, here we are," he said. "I cannot remember when I've so enjoyed a carriage ride."

"Nor I. But then, we haven't a proper carriage."

He gave a dry bark of laughter. "Here I think I am about to receive a compliment, and she pulls the chair out from under me at the last."

Cecil reined in the horses in front of the shop.

"Hold there, Briggs." Marlow alighted from the carriage, lowered the step himself, and offered his hand to her. She swallowed but placed her gloved hand in his. With a gentle grip, he assisted her down and walked her to the front door.

Retrieving her hand, she looked up at him squarely. "Then here is a genuine compliment. Thank you for your fair treatment of my brother. More than fair. And for your gallant behavior toward me this very evening."

He bowed. "You are most welcome." He leaned near, and she felt his warm breath on her cheek. Quietly, he added, "Now go inside before I attempt something less than gallant."

She hurried to comply.

In the morning, Lilly walked over to the coffeehouse, letting herself in the kitchen door as she always had.

"How did it go last night?" Mary asked, pouring her a cup of coffee.

"It was really very pleasant. Mr. Marlow was quite gentlemanly, even though he had a house party in progress when I arrived uninvited. He even insisted I stay for dinner. I was so glad you'd dressed my—"

"I meant how did it go about Charlie?"

"Oh." Lilly felt foolish but continued on, "Fine. Perfect. He was quite magnanimous about the whole situation."

"Magnanimous," Mary repeated, somewhat skeptically.

"He said Charlie would be welcomed back at any time."

"*Roderick* Marlow said that?"

"Yes. He was very agreeable."

Mary narrowed her eyes. "Really."

Lilly stirred sugar into her coffee, waiting until young Jane passed by with brush and blacking before adding, "And a former suitor of mine was there as well—you remember the Mr. Bromley I told you about?"

Mary leaned her elbows on the worktable and studied her, slowly shaking her head. "I don't think Mr. Bromley put that blush in your cheeks, love."

"Mary, no. I can guess what you are thinking, but—"

"Can you? And worrying about?"

"Do not be uneasy. Roderick Marlow is a very handsome man—I do not deny it. And for some reason he was exceedingly charming last night. But I know what he's capable of. And I'm not foolish enough to think he'd have any serious intentions toward an apothecary's daughter. I experienced my share of that in London. Men happy to flirt and dance with me, all the while planning to marry another lady of their own class."

"Oh, you'll marry one day," Mary said wistfully. "Lovely, healthy girl like you."

Lilly looked up at her friend, sensing her sadness. "I could say the same of you, Mary. Mr. Shuttleworth can barely take his eyes off you."

Mary shrugged the idea away. "It is only because he doesn't know."

Seeing her discomfort and not knowing how to reassure her, Lilly changed the subject, telling all she had learned about Rosa Wells in London. She concluded by saying, "You and I have both seen unhappy marriages firsthand. I am in no hurry to end up in one of my own, no matter my aunt's machinations."

She rose and rinsed her coffee cup in the basin. "In any case, Mr. Marlow has all but said he will marry that red-haired beauty."

"Charlie will be brokenhearted," Mary said in jest.

"Probably." Lilly paused. "Cassandra Powell is a bit older, I think, than she looks. And I am told, suffered a broken engagement, poor thing."

"Poor thing, indeed. I cannot get over how sorry I'm feeling for the picture of perfection who's turned the head of the county's most eligible bachelor. Yes, I think I must take the poor thing to prayer."

Lilly bit back a smile. "Mary Helen Mimpurse! That is the first nearly unkind thing I believe I've ever heard you say about anyone."

Mary smirked and said dryly, "Stick around, love, stick around."

22

England is a nation of shopkeepers.
—Napoleon Bonaparte

With surprising reluctance, Charlie moved his things back into the bedchamber next to Lilly's. He resumed the sweeping up and his work in the physic garden. She would have liked to ask Mrs. Fowler back as well, and would, as soon as they could again afford to pay her wages.

Lilly was poring over ledgers and unpaid bills when Francis stopped in on his afternoon off. He hopped up onto the high counter, swinging his legs. It reminded her of the Francis of former days. All arms and legs and more energy for cricket than studying. Now those arms and legs had filled out with masculine muscle beneath his white shirt and breeches. He had certainly changed during her absence, but she wondered if the changes were only physical.

"How fares your mother, Francis?" she asked.

"Well enough."

"And your sister?"

"She has engaged herself to Tom Billings at last. That curate she had long pined for married someone else."

"Was your sister laid very low?"

He shrugged. "She caddled about for days at Christmas. But she seems to have recovered rather well."

Lilly closed the ledger and thought back. "I met your sister only the once, but I recall she was very pleasing in manner and countenance. Quite handsome."

"Do you think so?" He grinned. "You said *I* was very like her."

She chose to ignore this statement, true though it was. Thinking once more of her parents, she asked, "Does Mr. Billings know she preferred another?"

"He knows but overlooks her foolishness. That's the way love is, I suppose."

"Is it? I am not sure I would be as understanding if the man I loved pined for another."

His legs stopped swinging. "Do you . . . that is . . . did you form an attachment while you were in London?"

"Only two."

His eyebrows rose.

"But both ended just before I left. I doubt either will come to anything, even when—or if—I return."

He looked at her expectantly, clearly waiting for her to explain.

"One was a physician, of whom my aunt disapproved. He was reserved and uncertain. Still I thought, perhaps . . . The other was a gentleman whom my aunt advised me in the strongest terms to accept. Wealthy, an heir, good-looking, kind . . ."

"No wonder you refused that swell," Francis rued. "I detest him already."

Lilly shot him a wry grin. "No. I refused him because, while he admired me, he did not love me."

Looking at her, Francis said quietly, "He would have, in time."

She met his gaze for a moment, considering his words, then continued. "Perhaps—did he not love another."

"Is there no chance this other woman will accept him?"

"I believe there might be. If she believes she cannot have him."

"Ah . . . yes," Francis said. "I have seen that before—not realizing what one has until he—or she—has lost it."

Nodding thoughtfully, Lilly looked around the shop. "This feels very much like days gone, when you and I would sit here together, wondering where Charlie had got to, wagering on what he had found to count. Wondering where all the customers were, but glad for the respite too."

Francis picked up the thread, "Your father napping in his surgery or grumbling about something I'd forgotten to distill."

"And you forever teasing me. Like brother and sister, we were. I shall never forget it."

"I wonder," he said gently. "Do you remember, Lilly?"

She wrinkled her brow. "Of course I do."

"Clearly, I mean?"

She tilted her head and looked at him. "I am sure my memory will fail one day, but I am hardly in my dotage yet."

He hopped down from the counter, stepping closer as he continued, "What I mean is, you and I seem to remember those days differently. You could not leave here quickly enough when the chance came, but I hated to see those days end. I still remember being here with you . . . living under the same roof, taking meals together, talking and laughing together." He looked steadily into her eyes. "It was one of the happiest times of my life."

Charlie came in, the door slamming behind him. Lilly pulled her gaze from Francis to greet her brother as he carried in an armful of peppermint for her to bunch and dry. Francis moved to the door to take his leave.

Hand on the latch, Francis turned and looked at her. "And I never once thought of you as a sister."

Lilly stood upon the Honeystreet Bridge for the first time since she'd returned from London. She had crossed it several times, of course, but had never tarried. Yet she felt drawn to do so now, as though she might find answers in the slowly flowing water of the canal. She knew she must make a decision, difficult as it seemed. Her aunt's recent letter weighed on her mind. She had written to ask if Lillian would return in time to attend the Langtrys' annual ball.

> *Don't forget the new gown we had made for the occasion and how much we were all looking forward to it. And Mr. Alban has just acquired a new Italian novel he knows you will enjoy. It will sharpen your command of the language before we travel to Rome this winter. . . .*

How Lilly longed to travel to Italy! To see the Coliseum and Pantheon, the basilicas and squares, to stay in a little pension, to speak Italian with Italians. . . .

She sighed, knowing that if she stayed in Bedsley Priors any longer she risked her future with the Elliotts. She would forfeit her last season, her best chance of finding a proper husband and residing in London as a lady of quality.

Her aunt had also written a piece of unexpected news.

> *Your uncle insists I mention that Dr. Graves called. Seemed quite surprised to find you had quit London without a word. As you had not told him anything, I did not think it my place to do so and sent him on his way.*

Why had he called? Lilly wondered. She had guessed he would be relieved to be rid of her after the revelation about her mother. Had she been wrong? If she returned soon, might he still be interested in courting her?

Part of her was ready to jump aboard the next coach to London. After all, Haswell's was not her responsibility. She was only a young woman. Her father had made it clear he did not want her to give up her London life for him.

But she also knew that if she left again, there was little hope her father would survive. If nothing else, his shop—his only livelihood—would fail. And what about Charlie? Her father was in no condition to look after him.

Lilly detested the thought of disappointing her generous aunt and uncle. She felt disloyal, ungrateful. She cringed to imagine the hurt that would cloud their features. Would they feel as though they had wasted their time, money, and attentions on her, only for her to leave them without warning with a roomful of gowns, hats, and hopes that none of them had use for any longer? All so she could . . . what? Attempt to keep her father's shop going when it was obviously failing, along with her father's health? Everyone knew women were not allowed to be apothecaries.

"You are a picture, Miss Haswell."

Startled from her musings, she turned and saw Mr. Shuttleworth standing on the canal bank, this time wearing a red velvet frock coat over the same gold waistcoat and cravat. He circled his hands into a tube and looked at her through it, as a captain might look through a ship's glass. "This is exactly how you looked the very first time I saw you."

"You are mistaken, sir. You were not even living in Bedsley Priors the last time I stood here."

He walked up the bank and onto the bridge.

"Ah. But do you recall my telling you I traveled by narrowboat on this very canal from Bristol to London?"

She nodded.

"I passed Bedsley Priors, of course, and in fact we tied off there near The George for several hours. That's when I saw the first of the three enticements I mentioned."

He rested his elbows on the bridge a few feet from where she stood.

"She was a lovely young lady in white, strolling along the canal near the mill. A beauty among workmen. A blossom in the mud."

"Miss Robbins, no doubt," Lilly said. Did everyone idolize the girl?

"Yes, though of course I did not know her name at the time. I stood watching her until she disappeared. By then, the crew had all gone into The George, and I realized I needed a good meal more than a belly full of smoke and ale. I walked into Bedsley Priors. Into the coffeehouse. And there was served most kindly by the lovely Miss Mimpurse. Your oldest friend, I understand."

"She is indeed. We grew up together."

He nodded his understanding. "But it was only later, after a good meal, and back aboard that cramped narrowboat, that we passed under this bridge and I saw the loveliest enticement of all. Standing here, looking sad and a bit lost, much as you do now."

She felt her lips part in surprise, but before she could form any response, he continued.

"And then and there I decided that as soon as I could, I would return to this picturesque village. Maybe even set up shop here one day.

"But first, I served my term with the Apothecaries' Society, then I studied at St. Tom's Hospital for the poor, as well as a private institution, to update my surgical skills. I sold a great deal of my own exotics collection to raise funds to set myself up in a place. And in between, spent as much time as I could watching the ships come in. I often counted five or even six hundred collier ships waiting to discharge their cargo. Fruit from Kent and Spain, coal from Newcastle, huge Greenland whales . . . Do you know, I once even saw a group of porpoises come up with the tide nearly to London Bridge?"

She shook her head in wonder. "And after all that, you left London to settle here. I am still surprised you would."

"Are you? I understand you lived in London—experienced its delights—and yet you also have returned."

Have I? Lilly wondered. "I planned only a short visit. But, well . . ."

"Your father needs you."

"Yes."

"And so you will stay."

Holding a breath, she squeezed her eyes shut, then exhaled. "Yes."

"Well, I for one am pleased to hear it. I own I have never stayed in one place so long before. Even in London, I was forever moving from one lodging house to another." He looked at her closely. "Still, I wonder . . . Will you always wish, always imagine what you might be missing elsewhere?"

"Will you?"

He smiled shyly, then returned his gaze to the canal. "It is a bit early to tell."

"I warn you," Lilly said. "If I stay, Haswell's will give you a run for your money."

He grinned at her. "I have no doubt you will prove a worthy adversary—though I do not like to use that term to describe you, Miss Haswell. It will be a friendly competition, I hope. I for one believe there are plenty of patients for everybody, what with Honeystreet's labourers and canal traffic, and Alton so close by."

"You are surprisingly fair and generous, sir."

He shrugged. "I have no longing for great wealth. For great adventure, yes, to travel widely and love deeply—these things I value more than profits. Though certainly one needs enough of those to finance the former things."

She chuckled. "So I am learning."

"And you, Miss Haswell. What is it you want?"

She stared thoughtfully at the turbid water below. Once, she had wanted to experience life and love beyond Bedsley Priors. That, and to find her mother. In London, she had experienced a small measure of each. What *did* she want now? Instead of trying to verbalize her jumbled thoughts, she parroted his own words back to him. "It is a bit early to tell."

My dear Aunt & Uncle Elliott,

I am sorry to disappoint you, but I will be remaining here in Bedsley Priors for the foreseeable future. My father is quite ill and his shop failing. Though he does not ask it of me, and though much of my heart is still with you in London, I know I must stay to help Father and look after Charlie. It pains me to be apart from you and to miss all the events and travels we'd planned, but I hope you will understand my decision, painful as it is. I regret the great expense and trouble you have taken over me, but I for one do not count it wasted. My months with you will forever be a treasure in my memory and in my heart. While I enjoyed the education and all the entertainments, what I valued most was coming to feel as though I were truly part of your family. I love you both and always shall.

I plan to write to Christina P-W myself, but please give my regards to others of our acquaintance, as you judge best.

With love & gratitude,
Lillian

She did not write to Dr. Graves, knowing it was improper for an unmarried woman to write to any man not of her family, unless they were formally engaged. Had Dr. Graves asked, her uncle might have given him permission to write to her, though her aunt would not approve. But as the weeks passed without correspondence, she realized anew that Dr. Graves did not wish to continue their relationship, regardless of the call her aunt had mentioned. Lilly had already guessed as much but still felt the silence keenly.

She did write to Christina, congratulating her on her engagement and asking her to pass along her farewells and warm felicitations to her family. She knew Christina would not stay in touch. As much fun as they'd had together, their friendship was not deep like hers and Mary's. Lilly did not think the worse of Christina for it. Out of sight, out of mind, the saying went, and in Lilly's brief experience, this was a rule effortlessly observed by others. She sometimes wished she could do the same.

23

Desperate affairs require desperate measures.
—Admiral Horatio Nelson

Lilly asked Charlie to scrape the peeling paint from the many-paned shopwindow. He seemed to take to the repetitive task effortlessly. She purchased new paint from the ironmonger in Huntley's Yard, and arose early to paint the window frames herself. Her arms ached from the effort, but she felt satisfaction at doing the work on her own, saving money she desperately needed to restock the shop.

Most mornings, she and Charlie worked in the physic garden, harvesting all the flowers, seeds, and roots they could. She hung the flowers upside down to dry in the herb garret and shop rafters, and ground what root they needed immediately, while storing the rest in the cellar. When the shop bell rang, still unfortunately a rare occurrence, Lilly would hastily lay aside her garden work and jog into the shop, wiping her hands on her apron as she went, fretting over what each patron might require. Recommending remedies for everyday needs—headache powders, laxatives, hair and complexion creams, tooth sponges, and the like—was no problem. But when a person—especially a man—wanted medical advice, that sent her adrift in murky waters.

"Mr. Haswell is occupied in his surgery at present," she would say, "but I shall nip in and ask him what he would recommend." She would indeed ask, "Father, what would you recommend for Mr. James's rheumatism?" Her father would usually try to rouse himself, sometimes asking for clarification and offering sound advice. But when he could not, she would continue on as though he had. "Yes, the same symptoms as before. Do you think he ought to stay with Burridge's Specific, or try another? Very well, I shall let him know. . . ."

Fortunately, she had known what to dispense for the few ailments presented to her so far—mostly by patients they'd had for many years. She would not risk anyone's health. But neither would she send a paying customer to Shuttleworth's or Dr. Foster until absolutely necessary.

In the meantime, she wrote another letter.

Dear Miss Lippert,

I have returned to my father's apothecary shop in Bedsley Priors. Like you, we also now face greater competition. I am seeking to help my father compete against a young new surgeon-apothecary. I remember our discussion about your brother's keen business sense, and I myself witnessed your skills in displays and ladies' items. I wonder if I might I ask your advice—as well as that of your brother and father?

Polly Lippert wrote back promptly, including a kindly penned list of the most popular ladies' items, toilet articles, and perfumes in their shop. The letter included a few lines written in the shaky hand of Polly's father, saying he would be happy to offer what advice he could and that his son, George, would write to her directly. A few days later, she received a letter from George Lippert himself.

On his advice, she ordered new exotics, new patent remedies, and even an "electricity machine," reportedly highly effective in the treatment of epilepsy, gout, and other disorders of the nerves. Following Polly's list, Lilly ordered French perfumes and cosmetics and other pretty things London ladies liked. She got rid of the jar of putrid bear grease and in its place displayed fragrant Macassar oil from India, which promised to "bestow an inestimable gloss and scent, rendering the hair inexpressibly attracting."

She updated all the displays, adding feminine touches like a vase of flowers and a fabric runner in the window display. She set out bowls of dried flower petals and cinnamon to sweeten the air. She offered free samples of ready-made items like skin lotions and breath tablets. She prayed as she balanced the ledgers and then, prayed some more.

Francis Baylor opened Haswell's back door as he had without thought all the years he'd lived at the shop. He supposed he should have gone around to the front, but he already had his foot in the door and wanted to see how Mr. Haswell was faring. Mostly, however, he wanted to see Lilly.

When he stepped inside, he saw her standing before the laboratory-kitchen cupboards. She looked sharply at him over her shoulder. "Oh, Francis! You startled me."

"I should have knocked. Forgive me."

"That's all right . . ." She was clearly distracted, pawing through drawers, crates, and tins.

"What is it?" he asked. "What are you looking for?"

She hesitated, then sighed. He realized she was whispering. "I was sure Father would have plenty of calcium phosphate. I have already searched the drawers and jars in the shop. Have you any idea if he'd begun storing it elsewhere?"

"No. It was always in its jar on the shelves out front."

Lilly pressed her hands over her eyes.

"Lilly . . . ?" Francis grew concerned.

"A new family in Honeystreet has the ague. All six children. The mother is in the shop now. When I did not find any fever powder, I told her I would just step into the back to prepare some fresh for her. Now I shall have to send her to Shuttleworth's. Can you help her? A Mrs. Todd Hurst. In those new lodgings on Chimney Lane?"

"I know it."

Lilly shook her head. "Such a fine prospect. Her husband a trained barge builder. *Six children* . . . I dare not wait any longer. I must admit defeat and hand the family to you."

Francis had not seen Lilly so discouraged since the first few days after her return, and he did not like to see her so now. He held up his palm. "Don't say anything. Get the calcined antimony and sleeves ready."

"But we haven't—"

But Francis was already out the door.

Wringing her hands and pacing, Lilly tried to pray but only succeeded in worrying and feeling guilty. Treating the children promptly was so much more important than who provided the remedy. She should have sent Mrs. Hurst to Shuttleworth's directly. But she was sure her father would have the *materia medica*. Was it so wrong to want to prove Haswell's still viable? Make a sale? She chuckled dryly. If her London friends could see her now and witness her thinking like a tradesman! She should simply march back into the shop and explain to Mrs. Hurst that she would not be able to supply her needs after all.

The back door banged open and Francis barged in, pottery jar in arms. "Come on, we've powder to prepare. You can box my ears later."

"I was not going to box your ears," Lilly whispered. In fact she felt like embracing him. Instead, she turned her attention to the fever powder.

As the two worked side by side, Lilly surveyed his deft motions. "You have become quite good at this."

"You sound surprised."

"Well . . ."

He held out his hand for the sleeves. "I should be glad you went away to London."

The words startled her.

"Turns out your leaving was good for me," he continued. "I had to learn to do things myself. When you were here, it was easier to ask you rather than haul out those cumbersome tomes and find the answer myself. Took more time, but in the end, I remembered the answers."

"I am glad someone benefited from my absence."

"I did not say I was glad you went away. Nor am I sorry you've returned."

How final that sounded. Uncomfortable, she merely nodded.

"If only *you* were not sorry," Francis said wistfully.

She hesitated, but thought of no suitable answer.

Francis rubbed his palms together. "Now, what else do we need?"

In short order, they had the medicine in individual paper sleeves ready for Mrs. Hurst. She squeezed his arm and whispered, "Thank you."

With a faint smile, he covered her stained fingers with his own.

Lilly returned to the front of the shop to apologize for the delay and explain the dosages to the mother. Once Lilly had paid Mr. Shuttleworth for the calcium phosphate, she would make little profit on the sale, but hopefully Haswell's had gained a customer who would return often.

The following week, Lilly opened a letter from her aunt with some trepidation. How would she respond to the news that Lilly would not be returning after all?

Dear Lillian,

Your letter was both bane and balm. How your uncle and I feared you would be drawn in to your former life there. All our efforts in vain. I confess this is the second letter I have begun to you since reading yours. The first was a blatant attempt to convince you to return at once. Filled with details of all you were missing, of all that might be. Utterly selfish, I realize now. Well, not utterly—I sincerely believe you could be a success in town yet. But of course you must stay as long as your father needs you. I witnessed that noble quality in you when we first met—when you were so eager for your brother to have every advantage you have since enjoyed. We admired your selfless loyalty then. How could we think the less of you for the same honorable trait now?

My dear, what balm your kind words of affection delivered. I know I said this would very likely be your last season, but I certainly do not want you to imagine that you have spent your last days here with us. You are ever welcome, Lillian. We hope that when things with your father are in hand, you may yet return to us, if not for securing a suitor, then for enjoying the felicity of society with those here who love and admire you—your uncle and I chief among them.

What is the situation with your father? You were quite vague, my dear, and if that was your intention, I shall pry no further. But if there is anything we can do to help, you have only to ask.

In that light, I am enclosing a bank draft. Please do not refuse it. In all truth, I had every intention of sending this amount home with you to help address whatever situation you found there. But at the last, I withheld all but a token amount, scheming again, I confess, to keep you on a short tether in hopes of hastening your return. You see how we depend on your company! Please forgive my foolishness and gratify me by using the funds as will do you and your father the most good.

Do write back and keep us apprised of your situation there.

We remain,
Your loving aunt and uncle

How kind they were! How the affectionate words—even the admission of machinations—brought warmth and longing to Lilly's heart and made her miss her dear aunt and uncle all the more. And with the much-needed funds they enclosed, she could pay Francis back for the things he'd procured for them, place new orders, and begin chipping away at her father's other debts.

She would be so relieved to fulfill past obligations and start anew. Still, she could not deny that her aunt's letter stirred embers of longing for all she would miss in London. Besides the Elliotts, would anyone in London miss her?

24

A skillful leech is better far than half a hundred men of war.
—Samuel Butler, English satirist

Lilly was surprised a few days later when Mr. Shuttleworth knocked on the shop door with his walking stick—an affectation she knew to be all the crack in London.

"Mr. Shuttleworth! How do you do?"

He cleared his throat. "As a matter of fact, Miss Haswell, I am . . . concerned."

"Oh? Is there some way I might help?"

"Indeed there is." His signature smile was noticeably absent. "I understand Mr. Baylor has been securing powders and other simples for you from my shop."

She swallowed. "Yes, on a few occasions. When the need was urgent."

"Well, I do not like it at all. Quite insupportable."

She had never known the man to be so somber. Hadn't Francis told her his employer would not mind? "We did pay for the items—full price."

"Yes, yes. I am not accusing anyone of stealing. However, I cannot allow things to go on in this manner."

She felt truly chastened. A sneak—caught. "Please forgive me, Mr. Shuttleworth. You are quite right. I should have asked you first."

"Indeed you should. For I should never have allowed it."

She bit her lip. She had never seen this side of him before. She hated the thought of losing the man's goodwill. Of jeopardizing Francis's position. "It will never happen again," she assured him.

"I should hope not. Next time, come to me and I will give you whatever you need at wholesale. Full price indeed. Are we not colleagues? Part of the same professional society?"

There, she saw it. Just a hint of a twinkle in his dark eyes.

"Yes, I suppose we are."

He took a step closer, and grinned almost sadly. "Moreover, are we not friends? I had rather hoped we were."

She nodded. "You are right, Mr. Shuttleworth. Again, please forgive me."

"I shall. On one condition."

"Yes?"

"I have a proposition for you." He held up his hand. "A business proposition. You acquire what you need from me at cost—assuming you don't empty the crockery. And, in return, you sell me the herbs, flowers, and other garden stuff I need. I understand from Mr. Baylor you have an excellent physic garden."

"Not as fruitful as it once was. But we are working to revive it. In fact, we have been harvesting all week."

He pushed up his hat brim with the tip of his walking stick. "I own I have never been much of a gardener myself. I like clean hands and fine clothes too dearly. I must go to market for everything. It would be a great boon to have fresh Haswell herbs on hand."

"Truly?"

"Truly." He held out his hand. A gesture rare among unwed ladies and gentlemen, but common enough among tradespeople. Among business associates. "Have we a bargain?"

With a rueful grin, she smartly shook his hand. "Indeed we have."

The next day, her father did not even get out of bed. A fortnight had passed since she had made him promise to see a doctor, and still he refused. But she couldn't bring herself to force him against his wishes.

"I think I need to draw off some blood," he said. "Would you mind bringing the leech jar?"

Lilly felt uneasy. "Are you sure that is the best course?"

"I believe so. I would do it myself, but it's a dashed bother to position them from a supine position."

Lilly went to find the leech jar. The simple white pot had a tight-fitting lid and tiny air holes. *Hirudo medicinalis* were known to squeeze through the smallest of openings. An apothecary needed to take care when placing them on a patient's face that none found its way up a nostril.

She pried open the lid. A strong rotten fish smell rushed out and repulsed her. The water was dry. The leeches quite dead. How had she missed it during cleanup?

Lilly groaned. "I find we need to purchase some, Father. I shall help you as soon as I return." She did not wish to rile her father by admitting she planned to acquire the leeches from his competitor. She was relieved when he did not ask.

She went to find her reticule. "Aaron Jones is bringing a load of coal today," she called. "If he comes while I am out, tell him I shall settle up later."

"Very well. Don't be long."

Stashing a few bank notes into her reticule and sliding the small bag onto her wrist, Lilly hung the new hand-lettered *Returning Soon* sign on the door and let herself out. She walked briskly up the High Street and down narrow Milk Lane to Shuttleworth's. She did not like going there in the middle of the day, but it could not be helped.

"Miss Haswell!" Mr. Shuttleworth greeted her, looking up from his splendid central desk. "What a lovely surprise. Mr. Baylor is out, I am afraid."

"I came to see you, actually."

"Wonderful. How can I help?"

She took a deep breath. "I am in need of leeches."

"You and the entire medical profession. Did you know there is a shortage on? I had to order this last batch all the way from Germany. The French, it seems, are going through them by the barrelful."

"I had no idea."

"It does not signify, lovely lady. My leeches are your leeches." He chuckled. "Now if that is not the most gallant thing I have ever said."

She laughed. "Chivalrous, indeed."

Mr. Shuttleworth stepped over to his compounding counter, where stood an impressive leech jar nearly two feet tall and decorated with elegant floral and scroll work.

He paused to ask, "Have you milk at home?"

She nodded.

"Excellent. Encourages them to bite. Sometimes they seem capriciously determined to resist all attempts to adhere. If you ever have a great deal of trouble, you can always prick the skin with a lancet and draw a little blood. They cannot resist it. Has never failed me."

She hoped it would not come to that.

Seeing her stare at the ornate jar, he explained, "The most exquisite leech jars are made in Staffordshire. I can order one for you if you like."

"Oh. Thank you, no. I shall content myself to admire yours."

Mr. Shuttleworth opened the lid, extracted one wet leech, and held it aloft for her inspection. The wormlike body was murky green with yellow stripes and as thick and long as her forefinger.

"Humble but hardworking creatures like these deserve the most elegant of raiment." He gave a wink and a tug on his waistcoat. "Like me, ey? Now, how will you transport your new friends home?"

Chagrined, she lifted her reticule. "This is all I thought to bring."

He chuckled again. "Why not? I shall just pop a few into a small jar, and you can transfer them to a proper one at home."

"I am afraid our poor jar is nothing to yours."

His long teeth gleamed at her praise. "You are very kind to say so."

A quarter of an hour later, Lilly walked into her father's surgery with their own leech jar, cleaned and filled.

"Here we are. Five fat *H. medicalis*."

"Only five?"

"There is a shortage on. The French cannot get enough of them. Leeching is all the crack there—doctors using fifty at a time, then salting them."

He shook his head in disapproval. "Makes them regurgitate the blood so they can be used again. But kills them if you salt them too heavily."

"Right. So, we shall make do with five very hungry German leeches, shall we?"

"Very well."

He had already washed and rinsed his chest during her absence. She removed the leeches from their damp jar and let them crawl about on a cloth for a few moments to dry. At the surgery side table, she had a pot of milk, wine glasses, and a lancet at the ready.

She laid the first leech on her father's chest, then a second. She turned to pluck a third from the cloth, only to return to find the first two crawling away. One was heading for her father's neck, the other for his waistband.

Oh dear. The glasses. Right.

One by one she captured each leech under a small upturned wine glass, trapping it in the desired area. She felt as though she were performing a circus act in Astley's Royal Amphitheatre, hurrying to keep the plates spinning before they fell.

Finally, she stood still, both hands splayed. "There."

"Yes, as long as I don't make any sudden moves," her father said. "Or cough."

"Or talk. Steady on."

"Tickles devilish, but no bites."

Frowning, she removed the first wine glass and dabbed a bit of milk on the spot before replacing it.

No good. She hoped she would not need to resort to the lancet. The thought of drawing blood from her father, cutting him even superficially, made her queasy.

Remembering something she'd overheard in Mr. Lippert's shop in London, she turned and hurried to the door. "Don't move."

"Where are you going?"

"To the tea set."

"Tea . . . now?"

She returned with the sugar bowl and mixed a spoonful into the milk. The sugared milk did the trick, and one after another the leeches bit her father, evidenced by his five successive winces.

When she was sure they had each adhered, she removed the wine glasses, returning them to the side table.

"We'll let them take their fill," he said. "Let them fall off by themselves."

"Very well. Are you warm enough?" She picked up a lap rug hanging over a chair and laid it over his legs.

"Thank you, my dear." He sighed. "If only you had been a boy. The son I might have left my shop to."

"Shh. You will be back on your feet, running the shop in no time."

"For how long? For what reason? What good is a legacy with no one to leave it to? There has been a Haswell in this shop for nearly a hundred years. But now . . . ?"

"Father, Haswell's is not going anywhere. But for now you must regain your strength. Which you won't do by fretting."

"Bossy girl. Sound like a physician."

"No. I sound like you." She grinned. "Worse yet."

25

It has been recommended, to bleed people when they are lying down. Should a person, under these circumstances faint, what could be done to bring him to again?

—*Mrs. Beeton's Book of Household Management*

Lilly had never seen the woman before, yet there she sat in Haswell's surgery, boldly giving Lilly detailed descriptions of all her feminine flows and woes.

"I feel like a good bleedin' is all I need," the barge pilot's wife said. "There's nothin' like it to balance the humours, I always say. I've been to Dr. Foster, but that man is worse than a cross headmaster. I like the notion of a female apothecary. So much easier to discuss one's flux without embarrassment, if you know what I mean."

Lilly managed a meek smile. She had been the one to insist her father return to sleeping in his bedroom instead of the surgery. She had counted it a small victory when he had finally relented. Not only would he get more rest in his own bed, but it freed the surgery for private discussions and examinations. The idea had sounded appealing. In theory.

"So you have been bled before," Lilly began nervously. "Can you tell me if the blood was let from elbow, ankle, or throat?"

"Had my ankle opened once. If that didn't hurt devilish bad. Not the neck, either, if you please. Don't want to spoil my frock."

"The inside of the elbow it is." Lilly's pulse pounded in her ears. She began to perspire in a very unladylike fashion. Leeches, she could manage. Blisters and plasters, all well and good. But the lancet? Piercing a person? Drawing not a drop of blood but a veritable fount, were she to accomplish it correctly? Or a waterfall, should she use the many-razored scarificator. She winced at the thought.

She began by washing the woman's arm—that she could do. She had her recline in the bleeding chair, in case she swooned. Offered her a sip of water. Positioned her elbow on the small caster table for the purpose. Picked up the lancet and the double-handled bleeding bowl. Sat on the stool where her father always sat to do what she was about to attempt. If only her fingers would cease trembling.

She rose on shaky legs. "Will you excuse me one moment, Mrs. Hagar?"

The woman nodded, eyes closed. "If you have any blue ruin, I shouldn't mind a sniff. Takes the sting out."

Ignoring the request for strong drink, Lilly quickly padded up the stairs to her father's bedchamber. He looked up at her from over the top of a book. "Bloodletting, Father. I cannot do it."

"Of course you can. Seen me do it a thousand times."

"Seeing it done does not mean I can manage it myself." She suddenly thought of Mr. Shuttleworth. Perhaps he would perform the procedure for her.

"And you've no doubt memorized the prescribed method from one of the texts."

"Yes, but remembering the words is not the same as performing the act."

"Lilly, we cannot afford to refuse patients. Nor to send them to our competition."

So much for asking Mr. Shuttleworth. . . . "Then you come down and do it yourself."

He huffed. "Very well." He used one elbow to push himself into a sitting position on the bed. His arm shook from the effort. He sat on the bed, catching his breath, steeling himself for the energy and pain required to stand.

Her heart ached to see it. "Never mind, Father. You lie down. I shall take care of it."

He fell back, panting. "You can do it, Lilly. Just remember—"

"I remember. Now you rest."

Retreating back down the stairs, she prayed with each step. *Please help me, help me, help me . . .*

She started at the sight of a figure standing in the laboratory-kitchen. "Francis! You startled me."

"Forgive me. I hope you don't mind, but I—"

"No! I am so pleased to see you. Might you do me a favor?"

"Um . . . of course. Anything, if I am able." He grinned, eyes sparkling. "What do you need? Dragons slain, villains dueled? Alembics scoured?"

Grasping his wrist, she led the way to the surgery door. "Nothing so arduous, I assure you."

"What then?"

"Just one small hole."

"Who's this, then?" Mrs. Hagar asked when they entered.

"This is Francis Baylor. Our former apprentice. Now a journeyman at—"

"At your service, madam." Francis bowed to Mrs. Hagar and gave her a charming smile.

"My, my." The woman placed a hand over her chest.

"That is, if you do not mind my stepping in? I can understand why you might prefer Miss Haswell—"

She waved this away. "Oh, that don't signify. You will suit just fine, young man."

"You are most obliging, Mrs. Hagar. Now. Are you comfortable?"

"I am."

"Very good. Let's just tie a ligament here. Miss Haswell?"

She sprang to hand him the tie.

"Thank you." He tied the linen tape around the woman's fleshy upper arm. "Firm, but not too tight. How does that feel?"

"Fine."

"Excellent. Now, let us have a look at your veins. My goodness! When have I ever seen such lovely veins? Really, Mrs. Hagar. What a light task this shall be!"

The woman looked down at her arm with sheepish pride. "Indeed?"

Isolating the vein between thumb and forefinger of one hand, Francis held out his free hand toward Lilly. "The thumb lancet, I think, Miss Haswell. Only the finest instrument for such a fine vein."

The woman fairly blushed.

Lilly quickly handed him the thumb lancet with the ornate tortoiseshell case.

"Thank you. And the bowl is here at the ready. Well done, Miss Haswell. Now, Mrs. Hagar, do let me know the minute you feel light-headed or a swoon coming on."

"I own I feel on the verge already, young man, with you holding my hand that a'way."

Lilly met his eye and bit back a grin.

He chuckled. "You flatter me, ma'am. Now, do tell me where you were born."

"Stanton St. Bernard, but I don't see how that signifies."

"Not in the least. I just wanted to distract you from the prick."

"Ohh . . . I didn't even know you'd done it."

The blood ran in a thin, graceful stream into the waiting receptacle. Not a drop went astray nor soiled her frock. Lilly was impressed indeed. Not only at his skill, but at his warm and charming manner with the worn, plain Mrs. Hagar.

When the blood reached the first gradient line in the bleeding bowl, Francis asked. "And how are we feeling, Mrs. Hagar?"

"Floaty. Tingling. Dark."

"Excellent." With swift deft movements, he placed a lint pad on her wound, pressing it with his thumb and lifting her hand in the air. "There. You put pressure on that if you can."

"All right . . ." she said dreamily.

Lilly handed him the linen bandage and sling, and he skillfully wrapped the wound and secured the woman's arm in less than a minute's time. "Now you rest here, Mrs. Hagar. Until you are quite yourself again."

She nodded and asked, "Mr. Baylor, will you be here next I come?"

Francis again met Lilly's eyes. "Perhaps, Mrs. Hagar. But if I am not, either Miss Haswell or her father will be. And I have learned everything worth knowing from them."

Leaving the woman to rest, Lilly followed him from the surgery. "Francis," she called softly.

He turned.

"How can I thank you?"

His smile grew thoughtful. "Quite easily, Miss Haswell."

She tilted her head in question.

Looking at her, he slowly shook his head, lips quirked, brown eyes alight with equal parts humor and longing.

She stared back, eyes drawn to his full lower lip, and felt a shocking desire to touch it with her own. Where had *that* come from? Thank heaven he could not divine her thoughts!

I am merely grateful to him, she assured herself. If Aunt Elliott had disapproved of a physician, she would be scandalized to think her niece attracted to an apothecary's assistant!

The shop bell jingled, and she self-consciously took a step back, putting a proper distance between them.

The next morning, Lilly opened the door of the coffeehouse kitchen and stuck her head inside. "Hello, Mary."

"Come in, Lill. You've caught me elbow deep in flour, I'm afraid."

Lilly stepped to the worktable. "I would offer to help, but I know how you feel about my abilities in the kitchen."

"Indeed. You with your odd apothecaries' weights and measures with *our* recipes . . ." She feigned a shudder.

Grinning, Lilly sat and surveyed the assembled mixing bowls and ingredients. "A cake?"

Mary nodded. "And not just any cake, mind. A Rich Bride Cake."

"And who is the rich bride?"

With a glance toward the scullery door, Mary leaned across the worktable and lowered her voice. "One Miss Cassandra Powell."

Lilly felt an unexpected stab of regret. She had enjoyed Roderick Marlow's brief attentions. She had known he would never ask for her hand, yet could not help being disappointed at the news, for she could not like Miss Powell. "Well, I should be not be surprised. Mr. Marlow intimated they would marry."

Mrs. Mimpurse burst into the kitchen from the dining room, her face flushed. "Girls, you will be most surprised to hear what I have just learned. That bonny Miss Powell is going to marry—"

"Yes, Mamma. I was just telling Lill about the cake order."

"But we have had it wrong, Mary." Mrs. Mimpurse drew near and spoke in hushed tones. "Miss Powell *is* marrying one of the Marlows to be sure. But not Roderick, as we supposed. She is marrying Sir Henry himself."

"No!" Mary's small mouth fell open.

"How can that be?" Lilly asked, stunned. "I saw them together in London and at the house party at the manor. And when I spoke to Roderick Marlow, I had the distinct impression *he* was going to marry her." Lilly's mind whirled over their conversations. He had not actually said the words, but what he *had* said seemed clear enough.

"Maybe he planned to, but she threw him over," Mary suggested. "Why be Mrs. Marlow when you can be Lady Marlow?"

"But Sir Henry must be nearing sixty," Lilly said. "And not in the best of health."

"Still, a charming man," Maude offered. "Always so kind and attentive to the first Lady Marlow."

"Poor Roderick," Lilly breathed.

"Poor Roderick?" Mary repeated in wonder. "Now, there are two words I would never have imagined coming from your lips, Lilly Haswell."

Lilly ignored that. "I wonder if he is heartbroken."

"You allow he has a heart?"

"Of course he has, Mary," Mrs. Mimpurse said.

Lilly amended, "Though one capable of both extreme coldness as well as warmth."

"How warm?" Mary quirked a brow.

Lilly felt her cheeks heat and hurriedly asked, "When is the great day to be?"

"Thursday," Mary and her mother answered in unison.

Lilly shook her head. "Rich bride indeed. Or will be in two days' time."

Mrs. Mimpurse returned to the front room with a fresh pot of coffee, and Mary continued working, sprinkling liquid onto the mound of almonds she had pounded into a fine powder.

"What is that?" Lilly asked.

"Orange-flower water."

Mary left the almonds and began whisking a bowlful of egg yolks.

Lilly ran her gaze over the worktable. "Where is the recipe?"

Mary shrugged. "Around here somewhere. Slice those candied peels for me, would you?"

"How thin?" Lilly picked up a knife and made a trial cut.

"Like that, right. Mind you don't cut yourself."

"Yes, Mother."

Mary hesitated, looking cautiously at her. Lilly pulled a humorous face, surprised she could make such a joke without an answering sting of loss.

Clearly relieved, Mary said, "The Marlows will not want your blood in their cake."

"No indeed. What else does a rich bride get?"

"Five pounds of the finest flour; five pounds currants; three pounds fresh butter; two pounds loaf sugar; one pound sweet almonds; a half pound each of candied citron, orange, and lemon peel; sixteen eggs; one gill each of wine and brandy; two nutmegs; and a titch o' mace and cloves. And two layers of almond-and-sugar icing besides."

"Rich indeed."

"The ingredients alone cost us nearly ten pounds."

Lilly's eyes widened, and she popped a bit of orange into her mouth.

Mary again raised her brows, "Ten pounds tuppence now."

"It was only a *titch*." Lilly helped herself to a currant. "What is a titch, anyway?"

"A dessert-spoonful or quarter ounce, if I took the time to measure proper."

Two fluid drams. Of its own volition, Lilly's mind converted to the apothecaries' system, based on twelve ounces to a pound and eight drams to an ounce. "And you don't need a recipe?" Lilly asked again.

Mary shrugged.

"But you cannot make *this* cake very often."

"Indeed not. The last one I made was for the christening of the Robbins boy." Mary gave her a shrewd look. "Of course, then I called it a Christening Cake."

"How do you remember—not only what goes in it, but the mode of preparation?"

Mary tucked her chin. "An odd question coming from you, of all people."

Lilly chuckled. "We are alike in that ability it seems."

"True. But my concoctions don't save anybody's life."

Grinning, Lilly snitched another currant and popped it into her mouth. "Oh, I would not be too sure."

26

BITES OF DOGS
Keep the wound open as long as possible. This may be done by putting a few beans on it, and then by applying a large linseed-meal poultice.

—*Mrs. Beeton's Book of Household Management*

Her apron and gloves already black from cleaning the stove and alembic, Lilly decided she might as well clean the shop hearth also. She thought about her recent encounter with Francis, when he helped her with Mrs. Hagar, and realized she had never felt so flustered, so . . . feminine, in his presence before.

As she knelt to her task, she heard a dog barking outside. She thought little of it at first, but then the barking grew louder and more fevered.

"Down, I say!" She heard a man holler in false bravado. "Down!"

She hurried across the shop and unlatched the door, just as a man pushed it open, causing him to nearly topple into the shop, his hat dropping to the floor. She put out her hands to stop his fall—and to keep the man from falling into her.

The Fowlers' wolfhound tried to bound in behind the man, but Lilly forcibly shut the door on the long muzzle of the shaggy creature, which likely weighed more than she did. The dog raised itself on its rear haunches at the window and continued to bark.

"Go home, Bones!" she shouted. "Go home!"

The grey dog whimpered but dropped to all fours and trotted away.

She turned from the window to look at Bones's latest victim and started.

"Dr. Graves!" She was stunned to see him again. Especially here in their shop.

He cleared his throat. "Miss Haswell." He bowed awkwardly, and she belatedly curtsied. They both reached for his fallen hat at the same moment, their foreheads nearly colliding.

"Forgive me." She straightened. "Oh! *Forgive* me!" she repeated more vehemently. "I have blackened your coat!"

He looked down at his tawny frock coat, one shoulder and sleeve now marked with smeared black handprints, like the claw marks of a wild animal.

"My tailor admonished me to choose the dark green," he said dryly, "but I would have my way."

"I shall have it cleaned for you. I know an excellent laundress."

His blue gaze swept her person. "Take no offense, Miss Haswell, but you are in more need of a laundress than I."

She looked down at her own attire, the sooty apron, the blackened gloves. He took a handkerchief from his pocket and offered it to her. "You have some—ash, is it?—along your cheekbone."

She held up her soiled gloves. "Thank you, but I do not wish to blacken your handkerchief as well."

He hesitated. Was he about to wipe her cheek? Instead, he tucked the piece of fine linen back into his pocket.

"Could be worse," she said feebly. "At least it isn't on my nose."

"Actually—" he winced apologetically—"there is a smudge there as well."

She began to put a hand up to shield her face, but remembered her soiled gloves just in time. She rushed on nervously, "I am sorry about Bones. He is usually harmless but isn't fond of strangers. He did not bite you, I trust?"

"No. All bark and no bite, as they say. Although I rarely find solace in that morsel of wisdom."

"You have been bitten before?" she asked.

"Yes, and still bear the mark to prove it." He pointed to a scar above his upper lip and extending, though faintly, beneath his moustache and nearly to his nose. "It is why I've taken to wearing a moustache, unfashionable as it is."

She nodded, taking in the short golden hairs, a shade darker than the pale blond hair of his head and eyebrows. She *had* wondered.

"It isn't very noticeable," she said.

"The scar, or the moustache?"

She smiled to cover her embarrassment. "Neither one."

He chuckled dryly. "I must say, this is not at all how I imagined meeting you again."

She peeled off her filthy gloves. "I shouldn't think so. What brings you to Bedsley Priors?"

She wished the words back as soon as she'd said them. Her heart beat anxiously and her neck grew warm. She thought she had alienated him with the news of her mother. Had she mistaken the matter?

He ignored her question and looked around the shop, arms behind his back. "So, this is the famous Haswell's."

She sheepishly followed his gaze. "Well, yes. Though Tuesdays are a slow day for us."

"It is Wednesday."

"Oh. Right."

After a moment of awkward silence, a sudden thought came to her. "Might I take you into my confidence?"

He straightened, eyes alert. "Of course."

"My father is ill," she began quietly.

His brows rose. "Is he? I am sorry to hear it." He hesitated. "Is . . . that why . . . you left?"

When she nodded, he expelled a long breath. "I see."

"But he will see neither the village physician nor the new surgeon-apothecary," she continued, "for fear of his weakness becoming generally known."

"I don't follow."

"He believes it will steal his credibility. The proverbial 'Physician, heal thyself.'"

"Ah." He nodded his understanding.

"Would you look in on him? There is bad blood, I am afraid, between the local physician and my father."

"Dr. Foster?"

"You have heard of him?"

"Well, yes. I—"

"He can be difficult at times, I own," Lilly said. "He rather resents my father, I am afraid. And Father fears he would spread his plight only too eagerly."

"Miss Haswell, I think—"

"But if I explain that you are only visiting," she hurried on, "he might be willing to allow an examination."

"But I am not."

She stared at him, feeling slapped. "Not willing? But—"

"Of course I am willing," he rushed to amend. "But I am *not* only visiting. I am settling here."

"What?" Her heart hammered. She faltered, "But . . . oh . . ."

"Dr. Foster is taking a partner, with an eye to retiring in a year or two. I have accepted the situation. It's provisional for now, but if all goes well, I shall remain indefinitely."

"You and . . . Dr. Foster. Oh, dear. I am sure he is a most capable physician. It is only—"

"Miss Haswell, you needn't worry on my account. Your father's condition and your opinions are safe with me."

She sighed. "Thank you. So you are a licensed physician now?"

"Yes." He bowed once more. "Dr. Adam Graves, at your service."

Three-quarters of an hour later, Dr. Graves emerged from her father's surgery.

"Well?" Lilly asked, laying aside the blocks of Castile soap she had been wrapping in brown waxed paper.

He closed the door gingerly and joined her at the counter. "He is resting comfortably. I do not think there is cause for alarm at present."

"But what is it? Do you know?"

"I cannot discuss a patient's condition without his consent."

"He is my father."

"And a grown and, may I add, stubborn man."

That Lilly knew only too well.

"I *can* tell you he agreed that I might attend him now I am here," he said.

"I am relieved to hear it."

Dr. Graves turned his hat around in his hands. "Miss Haswell, there is something I would speak to you about. . . ."

Her nerves jingled and she felt a thrill of hope. Had he come to renew his suit? Her thoughts about Francis seemed foolish now.

He hesitated. "But I can see that you have a great deal on your shoulders, and on your mind, at present. I will not press you." He cleared his throat. "Well, I suppose I had better go and unpack. I will be lodging in one of Dr. Foster's spare rooms until things are . . . settled between us."

"Us" meaning he and Foster, or . . . ? She felt her palms grow damp at the thought.

When Dr. Graves had taken his leave, promising to return soon, Lilly knocked on the surgery door and warily let herself in.

"Father, how do you feel?"

He groaned and raised himself to a sitting position on the cot. "Like a lump of bread dough that Maude has kneaded while vexed."

"Thank you for seeing him."

"And to what do I owe such an honor? He said he made your acquaintance in London. Am I to understand he is here to court you?"

She shrugged. "He did once speak to Uncle on my account. But—"

"I thought as much." He chuckled. "I noticed your handprints on his coat."

Face burning, she hurried to change the subject. "I am not here to talk about me, rather you. Dr. Graves would not divulge a thing."

"I should hope not."

"Father, please."

"There isn't a great deal to tell. He spent most of his time diagnosing what it is *not*. Not brain fever, nor typhus, nor several other fates worse than death. He doesn't believe it is anything contagious, although he has not ruled that out completely. So you still need to keep your distance."

Is that why he's been so aloof? she wondered. "What does he think it might be?"

"Perhaps a compound of two fevers—lung fever and glandular."

She sucked in a breath. "Not lung *sickness*?"

"He does not think it the consumption, no."

"I am relieved to hear it."

"Don't go planning my sixtieth birthday party yet, my dear. Lung fever itself can be can be quite serious. But yes, there is reason to hope." He looked at her shrewdly. "And here I feared your London season in vain. A physician, ey? Ah well, as long as he is nothing like Foster."

27

A tincture of sage will give old men
the spirit and the advantages of youth.
—Dr. Hill, *The Old Man's Guide to Health and Longer Life,* 1764

On Thursday morning, before beginning her jaunt up Grey's Hill, Lilly stopped in at the coffeehouse to tell Mary the surprising news about Dr. Graves coming as prospective partner to Dr. Foster. She knew Mary was not fond of Dr. Foster, either, but whether out of loyalty to Mr. Haswell or for reasons of her own, Lilly could not say.

"Are you certain it's Foster he's come to partner with?" Mary asked, suggestively raising a brow in a manner that brought Christina Price-Winters to mind.

Lilly made no attempt to hide her bemusement. "I am not at all certain. I had thought things ended between us in London." Promising to tell Mary more later, Lilly continued on her way.

She reached the top of Grey's Hill and stood catching her breath, looking down at the village below. The church bells rang. She could see several fine carriages in front of the church, the first of which began to pull away. This was the morning Sir Henry and Miss Powell were to be married, she knew. Few had been invited to attend the wedding breakfast, which she supposed was not surprising. Considering Sir Henry's advanced years, a private affair was more dignified.

"Miss Haswell."

Lilly started and turned. "Mr. Marlow! I did not see you there."

He rose and dusted off his breeches. "Seems I am quite invisible these days."

"Is the wedding finished already?"

"It is finished. My role in any case, which was to appear publicly in full support of my father and his new bride. They shall now return home for the wedding breakfast, but I find I cannot stomach it."

"I did wonder how you must be feeling."

"Did you? Well, then you are the only one considering my feelings these days."

She took a tentative step closer. "You . . . did hope to marry her, then?"

He shrugged. "Perhaps." He added acrimoniously, "I certainly did *not* hope she would marry my father. Devilish humiliating."

"I am sorry."

"Never fear, Miss Haswell. I will forget by and by."

"Will you?" she asked, studying his dull expression.

"Yes, with concerted effort and time, I shall."

"Perhaps you might teach me that trick."

She had only been jesting, but he looked at her quite earnestly.

"It can be learned. I am quite the master of forgetting unpleasant things. When the memory raises its head, you force it down. It rises again, you supplant it with new and more vibrant memories. It tries once more, you intoxicate the mind, drown it out. You do not allow such thoughts to revisit themselves upon you."

"But then, do we never learn from our past mistakes? Is that not one reason God gave us memory?"

"I do hope not. Pleasant memories are well and good, but I prefer to banish the others. With practice and constant diligence, one may train a memory to remain cowering in the dark reaches of the mind, where it can no longer prick one's conscience. It may not be quite the same as truly forgetting, I grant you, but a near enough imitation."

"You sound as if you have had long practice. What is it you strive so hard to forget, I wonder?" She nodded toward the church below. "Besides recent events."

He hesitated, and a shadow of remorse flickered and quickly disappeared, replaced by a cavalier grin. "I am sure there must be something, Miss Haswell, but I *do not* remember."

Lilly found herself wondering if she ought to attempt the same method with her own memories that brought such disquiet. Of coming home and finding her mother gone, her father pacing and desperately pretending all would be well, that she would return in a few days. Charlie sitting behind the draperies in Mother's bedchamber, running his small fingers over the roses in the pattern, mumbling the same numbers over and over again—"*Seventy-four, five, six, seven . . . ty-four, five, six . . .*"

"In any event," Mr. Marlow continued, "I am certain there is a woman out there who will not throw me over for a man twice my age."

"I have no doubt there are many." She had only meant to console him, but a sudden gleam in his eye sent warning bells ringing in her mind.

He reached out and touched a tendril of hair against her neck. "You are a balm, Miss Haswell. A sweet balm."

She backed away. "I had better go." She turned and made her way down the hill at a rapid clip.

He jogged beside her. "May I walk with you?"

"I am on my way to visit a family recovering from the ague. I do not think you—"

"How noble you are." He captured her hand and tucked it beneath his arm.

Once they reached the village, she pulled away gently, putting a proper distance between them. As they passed the churchyard, now deserted, he suddenly veered through its gate, pulling her in his wake to stand behind the tall privet hedge. He pulled her close, one arm draped diagonally from her shoulder to waist, his jaw to her temple.

He was tall and strong and wounded, and for one brief moment she allowed herself to enjoy the warm strength of his arm around her, before pulling away once more. With his free hand, he tried to capture her chin, to angle her face toward his, but she turned away. "Mr. Marlow, please!"

"You are right. Forgive me."

"I realize you feel betrayed. But do you really think toying with a substitute will remedy your pain?"

"It would dull it, at least."

"For how long? And at what cost to me? If someone had seen us, just then—"

"Your brother, for example?"

She had been thinking of Dr. Graves. "Actually, I meant—"

"For there he sits."

She turned and stared, and there was Charlie reclining against Grady Milton's headstone. "Hallo, Lilly. Hallo, Mr. Marlow."

"What are you doing here?" she asked.

Charlie shrugged casually. "Countin' dead men."

Lilly sighed and thought, *It's the live ones I have to worry about.*

Still, she was relieved to see her brother there. Something told her Roderick Marlow would not have been as easily dissuaded had he not been.

True to his word, Dr. Graves returned late that afternoon to check on her father, promising to stop in regularly and oversee her father's progress. In fact, he seemed to relish the prospect. She supposed if Dr. Graves had come to Bedsley Priors to continue courting her, he could not have invented a more plausible excuse to see her so often. In any event, she was exceedingly grateful to him for taking over her father's care.

Charlie came in from the garden, and Lilly introduced her brother to the new doctor.

"Graves, is it?" Charlie repeated, confused. "I like graves. Queer name for a doctor though, innum?"

She was relieved when Dr. Graves took no offense.

Afterward, Dr. Graves asked her to recommend a hostelry where he might dine. She immediately suggested the coffeehouse, explaining the proprietress was a dear family friend.

He hesitated at the door. "Perhaps you would be so good as to show me the way?"

She bit back a smile. "Happily, sir."

Even taking the time to tie on her bonnet and retrieve her shawl, she stepped out onto the High Street as he held the door for her. He walked beside her across the narrow mews and progressed several steps before realizing she had already stopped at the next establishment.

"Here it is."

She smiled at him, and he smiled back. There were those dimples she remembered so fondly and the blue, blue eyes brightened by the afternoon sun.

She led him inside and introduced him to Mrs. Mimpurse and Mary—her friend studying the doctor with more than customary interest.

Mr. Shuttleworth was enjoying an early supper, and Lilly introduced Dr. Foster's new partner to him as well.

"Dr. Foster speaks highly of you, sir," Graves said to him.

"I am much obliged." Mr. Shuttleworth smiled. "He honors me with his trust."

Francis walked in, hat in hand. He drew up short at seeing the well-dressed man beside her.

"Mr. Baylor, will you join me?" Mr. Shuttleworth enthused. "You come here far too rarely."

"Many thanks, Mr. Shuttleworth, but I am only here to give you a message. Mr. Robbins asks you to call when you can. One of his workers injured his leg. May have broken it."

"I shall go directly." Mr. Shuttleworth rose, shook hands with Dr. Graves, and turned toward Francis. "Have you met Mr. Baylor here, my young right hand?"

Francis greeted the newcomer politely, but Lilly did not miss the speculative concern in his eyes as he looked from the good-looking stranger to her.

28

GOWLAND'S LOTION
Eruptive humours fly before its power,
Pimples and freckles die within an hour.
—*Ackermann's Repository advertisement*, 1809

The rain was relentless. A smoky grey sky poured leaden sheets of water on Bedsley Priors for three days without ceasing. Dr. Graves called on her father, who seemed to be steadily improving, but otherwise the shop and High Street were silent but for the pounding of rain on roof and cobbles. Rivulets streamed down the shop's windowpanes, and only occasionally did Lilly see some brave soul dash past on his way to the coffeehouse, where, by all appearances, half the men of Bedsley Priors were taking refuge.

Late on the third afternoon, the shop door burst open, startling Lilly as she sat at the dispensary counter reading a worn volume of Sterne's *A Sentimental Journey Through France and Italy*. Francis rushed inside, carrying a canvas-wrapped bundle. Water streamed from his coat and the brim of his sodden hat.

"My goodness," Lilly said, closing the book. "What has happened to bring you out in this?"

Instead of answering, he asked, "Are we quite sure God has promised never to flood the earth again?"

She smiled. "Quite sure. Not the entire earth."

"Only Bedsley Priors, it seems."

Her father appeared at the surgery door and leaned against the jamb. "Hello, Mr. Baylor. Communing with the ducks again, are we?"

Francis held up the bundle. "I am returning the text you lent me. I did not wish it to get wet."

Charles Haswell's face wrinkled in confusion. "And so you carried it outside in this . . . ?"

"It's the roof, you see. Now I understand why the old haberdashery remained vacant so long. The roof leaks during any hard rain. But after this storm, the ceiling has more holes than a sieve. I've had to roll up the carpets and pack away the bedding and all my clothes and papers. Mr. Shuttleworth is doing the same."

"And the shop?" her father asked.

"We've employed a score of basins and buckets abovestairs, and so far the shop below is fairly dry."

"Ah." It wasn't clear whether Charles Haswell was relieved or disappointed. He said, "You must bring over anything else you don't wish ruined. And you are more than welcome to stay here tonight."

Francis darted a look at Lilly. "I should not like to intrude, sir."

"No trouble. Unless you relish the prospect of sleeping in a puddle?"

Francis shook his head. "I *was* wondering how I would balance the stew pot on my abdomen all night. . . ."

"It's settled, then. You shall spend the night here." He hesitated, then added, "And do invite Shuttleworth as well. You are both welcome."

Three quarters of an hour later, both men rushed into the shop, bumping into each other with cases and bundles in their arms, hat brims pulled low and coat collars high. Their boots left a glistening trail of water on the floorboards.

"Not fit for man nor water buffalo," Mr. Shuttleworth panted.

Her father gingerly took the man's valise. "Come, Shuttleworth, bring your things up to Charlie's room. He's gone to Marlow House to help batten down the place. Can't say we've needed him here these last few days. Sold two liquorice draughts and one plaster. How is business for you?"

"Quiet as well."

"Good, good," her father said, leading the way with unusual vigor. "I know a father-son from Alton Barnes who can put your roof to rights at a fair price. Shall I give you their names?"

"Most obliging, Mr. Haswell."

Lilly was surprised by her father's warm reception. Was he so pleased to learn his rival's business fared no better than his own? He turned back at the threshold. "And you may have your old room, Mr. Baylor—if you do not mind the tight quarters."

"Not at all, sir."

As the two older men disappeared through the door, Lilly smiled up at Francis. "It will be just like old times."

His gaze lingered on her. "Will it?"

She hesitated. "Here, let me help you with your wet things." She took his hat while he hung his coat on a peg, then followed her through the laboratory-kitchen and into the stark former pantry. "I am afraid I have not had time to make this bed yet."

"Then I shall help you."

She reached down and picked up the edge of the dust cover. A bed of less than a yard's width lay between them. On its far side, Francis reached down and picked up the cloth's other edge. He brought up his two corners to meet hers. Their fingers grazed as she took the thin material from him. Then he moved to the foot of the bed and took one end while she took the other, and again they brought the corners toward each other, Francis stepping around the bed to close the gap between them. This time when she tried to take his corners, he held on, their hands touching, his face dipped close to look into hers. Taking a shallow breath, she tugged harder until he let go.

He helped her put on the fresh sheets, tucking the corners and spreading the blanket while she plumped the pillow.

The task accomplished, he thrust his hand toward her, as Mr. Shuttleworth might. "You are very kind, Miss Haswell. Thank you."

Hesitantly, she put her smaller hand in his. "You are very welcome, Mr. Baylor."

Instead of releasing her hand, he held it with gentle firmness. His large brown eyes seemed filled with some unspoken message as well as a glint of humor. "How *do* you make your hands colder than the outside air?"

She said with a shaky laugh, "It is a gift."

He lifted her hand and brought it to his lips, his eyes focused on hers. Her heart pounded as he pressed his warm lips to her cool fingers. She felt a rush of pleasure and nervous tension at the intimate act.

He straightened, but kept his eyes lowered. Quietly, he asked, "You and Dr. Graves were . . . acquainted in London?"

At the mention of Dr. Graves, Lilly blinked. The pleasure she felt dissolved. She shook her head to clear away the unsettling emotions.

He mistook the gesture and furrowed his brow. "No?"

"No. I mean, yes."

Tension stiffened his voice and posture. "The physician of whom your aunt disapproved?"

She nodded and gently pulled away her hand. "Well, I hope you will be comfortable. Do let me know if you want for anything."

He took a slow, deep breath, his broad chest rising and falling. "I want a great many things, Miss Haswell."

His eyes were strangely sorrowful.

She did not ask what he wanted. She was not sure she wished to know.

The rain and chilly weather of the previous week brought with it summer colds and ague, which kept Mr. Shuttleworth and Francis quite busy into the following week of sunny, warm days.

They had met Dr. Graves a few more times, when he had entered the shop in the company of Dr. Foster. The younger physician was a bit formal and starched, Francis thought, and suspected his stiff demeanor hid insecurities natural to any new medical man. Francis determined to be as kind and helpful as he could be, even though the new man was treating Mr. Haswell, which Francis could not help but consider a vague snub.

While Dr. Foster frequented Shuttleworth's, his new partner went more often to Haswell's. Francis knew *Mr.* Haswell was not the primary reason. Nor could he blame the man.

He thought back to that rainy night spent in his old bed beneath Lilly's room. What bittersweet memories that had evoked, of all the nights he had slept there before, comforted yet taunted by his awareness of her lying in her own bed above him. Should he have told her how she affected him?

She was so much the same, yet different too. Her face somewhat thinner, her curves somewhat fuller, though that might be due to the cut of the gowns she now wore. She was as clever and charming as ever, yet she seemed less approachable than before, as though painted with a shiny veneer that kept her true self out of reach. He realized dully that she thought herself above him. She likely always had, but her time in London had served to increase the perceived distance. *Maybe it is better this way,* he told himself. He could not allow her return to disturb his carefully laid plans. Besides, what chance did he stand against a handsome London physician?

Early one morning, a rap sounded from the shop door below, while Lilly was in her bedchamber. She ran lightly down the stairs to answer the door, dressed, but with her hair still down.

She unlocked the door and opened it to Dr. Graves. He stared at her, then away, clearing his throat.

She pushed her long hair behind her shoulder. "I was not quite finished dressing."

"No . . . um, your hair is beautiful," he faltered.

"Thank you," she said, self-consciously pleased, and gestured him inside. "Are you here to check on Father? I fear he is still sleeping."

"No. I shall come back later for that." Again he stared at her.

"Did you need something?"

Glancing around and seeing the shop empty, he went on in lower tones, "Miss Haswell, when I first arrived, I mentioned there was something I wanted to say to you."

Lilly's heart began to pound. "Yes?"

"I have been waiting for an opportune time. I did not wish to spring it upon you when I saw how ill your father was."

She nodded, mouth dry.

"I must tell you, Miss Haswell. I was disappointed when I called on the Elliotts and discovered you gone. Your aunt was rather vague about the reason."

Lilly could well imagine.

"But considering, well, everything," he continued, "I believe I understand why you left without a word of farewell."

"I did not think you would mind, after our last conversation about my mother."

"It is precisely that conversation I wish to speak of now."

Oh dear.

"The day after we spoke, I went to see my brother, a solicitor, as I believe I mentioned. He contracted a runner on my behalf to discover information about the former lieutenant James Wells."

Lilly was taken aback. This was not what she had expected him to say.

Dr. Graves continued, "It seems Wells now works aboard a convict transport ship, and maintains an address in Cheapside, though he can be home but rarely. He . . ."

He paused and Lilly held her breath, trying to guess the thoughts behind his grim mouth, his serious blue eyes.

"He was married two years ago." Graves extracted a small slip of paper from his pocket and glanced at it. "To a German woman, according to the record. A Gertrude Kistinger, now Wells."

He handed her the paper and she silently stared at it. He looked at her expectantly, then cocked his head to one side. Clearly she was not reacting as he had thought she would.

"Is that not good news? Your mother is not with Wells, as you feared."

Was it good news? Just because she was no longer with Wells, did that mean she never was? And where was she now? Her fragile link to her mother, if a link it could be called, had been broken as easily as a spider's web.

"Thank you for inquiring for me." She wondered, though, if he had done so to help her, or merely to gauge the threat of scandal for himself.

"I thought you would be pleased," he said hopefully. "It can no longer come between us."

She looked up into his warm blue eyes and angelic face and felt her own face—and heart—warm in response. Perhaps he was right. Perhaps nothing stood between them after all.

The door bell rang and Lilly stepped back. Hannah Primmel timidly entered the shop.

"Hannah, hello," Lilly said, striding to the counter. She hoped Hannah did not notice her blush, or would at least not read anything untoward in it if she did.

"Hello, Miss Haswell." The poor girl had the misfortune of skin continually plagued with blemishes and had therefore earned the monikers Carbuncle Face and Hannah Pimples from cruel lads. Seeing Dr. Graves, the girl hung her head, as she habitually did, as though that might keep people from noticing her face.

"I am very pleased to see you," Lilly said. "I hoped you would come in."

Hannah glanced up eagerly. "Did you?"

"Yes." Lilly leaned closer, speaking in confidential tones. "I have something I would very much like you to try."

Her eagerness faded. "I haven't much money."

"This is a complimentary sample. Apply it for a fortnight and report on its efficacy. Will you do that for me?"

Hannah smiled. "Of course I will. Thank you, Miss Haswell."

"Thank me later—if you are pleased with the results."

When Hannah left, Dr. Graves approached the counter and asked quietly, "What did you give her?"

Lilly sighed. "Neither Gowland's nor chamomile was bringing about the improvement I had hoped for. I have now given her an ointment of lemon juice, rose water, and silver supplement."

"Culpeper's Remedy," he said.

"Right. Of course, Culpeper also recommended rubbing fresh butter on one's face of a morning. But that always seemed to worsen the problem when I experienced bouts of the same."

"You, Miss Haswell? I would have thought you had always been perfect."

She glanced at him, surprised that his flattery was not delivered with a smile. Instead, his expression was oddly sober.

"By the way," he added, "you might wish to be careful about prescribing physic."

The warmth she felt turned to annoyance. "I was not *prescribing*. It is a simple, known remedy."

"I am only cautioning you. A woman compounding medicines is one thing, but prescribing is another. If Dr. Foster had seen that just now, he might think you were overstepping. He might . . ." He grimaced. "Just be careful."

29

I like dreams of the future better than the history of the past.

—Patrick Henry

Lilly received a letter from her uncle, which surprised and mildly alarmed her, for she had received a letter only a few days before. She hoped the Elliotts were both in good health.

My dear Lillian,

I know we agreed to speak no more on the subject of your mother, but still I thought you should know. I have received additional information. Do you remember Mrs. Browning, the lady who let rooms to "Rosa" off Fleet Street? And do you further recall that I left my card? I confess I believed that card would come to tinder and that I should never hear from her again. But, behold, I received a letter from her today—if such scrawl can be called such—and happily paid the fourpence postage.

As I understand it, Mrs. Browning had long ago given your mother—or at least "Rosa"—a letter of reference, and a prospective employer has recently written to Mrs. Browning to verify Rosa's suitability for the post. I suppose you will struggle to credit it as I did. Rosamond—a housekeeper? In any case, the trail is cold no longer, should you like to pursue it. Of course I cannot say for certain whether Rosa was given the post in the end, but it seems likely, given Mrs. Browning's confidence that she'd "writ a lettr shure to inpress and pleas." But perhaps a letter from you to the steward or butler would answer if you are so inclined. I've included the directions below. Do let me know if there is anything you would like me to do in this regard.

Most sincerely,
Mr. Jonathan Elliott

Lilly fingered the postscript, the name of the estate and its direction. In Surrey, south of London. Part of her longed to go. Another part said this was not a good time—her father was unwell, and she could ill afford to close the shop. Still, it would not be so long a journey. She could go by post and return in two days' time.

The hired hackney took her as far as the end of the lane. From there, she walked, through the gates and up the curved stone drive. Craybill Hall was grander than she had imagined. The estate further out in the countryside than she would have guessed.

Lilly clutched her reticule tightly, knowing her damp palms would likely mar the smooth satin but at that moment not caring. She took a deep breath. The nausea she felt, she tried to tell herself, was from the long day of travel—first the long coach journey, then the jarring ride in the old hackney. She pressed one hand to her stomach, hoping to calm her nerves. How would her mother react upon seeing her? At being tracked down when she had clearly made no effort to reconnect with the family she had left behind? Did her mother assume, perhaps, they wanted nothing to do with her? If so, surely her mother would, if not welcome a visit, be relieved to know her daughter wished her well.

Lilly paused at the bottom of the wide steps leading to the main entrance. She prayed for wisdom, for peace, for her legs to quit trembling. She heard a sound in the distance, several voices raised in laughter. Something about the sound was familiar. On impulse, she turned and walked around the manor house, the peals of laughter guiding her like a ship's bell in the fog.

At the rear of the house, she saw a low garden wall. On its other side, a small table and chairs were arranged on a manicured lawn. Two children sat at that table, a little boy with golden hair, and a girl a few years older with ginger curls. And there, standing between them—smiling—was her mother. She was singing along as the children clapped and sang "Pat-a-cake."

How young and pretty her mother looked. She wore a blue-and-white walking dress, and her dark hair was swept back in a high, fashionable coil. *Where is her hat?* Lilly wondered. *She ought not be out-of-doors without one.* Lilly chided herself for her inane observation at such a time. In the midst of their game, her mother looked up from the children and clearly saw her standing there. Saw *someone* standing there, at any rate. She ceased singing, and her expression sobered.

Taking a deep breath and fisting her hands, Lilly walked slowly to the garden wall. Would her mother recognize her as she drew near? Letting the reticule dangle at her wrist, Lilly laid both hands on the waist-high stone wall.

"Yes?" Rosamond Haswell asked, her tone officious.

"Hello, Mother," Lilly said quietly.

She only stared in response.

The little boy asked in an endearing lisp, "Who is da lady?"

The little girl hung her head, so Lilly could not make out her features.

"Sit up straight, dear, and greet our guest," her mother said to the girl. But the girl made no sign of hearing her. She was either very shy or very rude.

Swallowing hard, Lilly said the next thing that came to her mind. "I thought you were the housekeeper here?"

Her mother continued to survey her person, hat to waist and up again. "I was. The governess took ill." She shrugged. "Besides, I like children. Well, some children . . ."

Lilly felt as though she'd been struck in the chest by a heavy mallet.

The little girl looked up then, revealing a face eerily identical to Lilly's own at that age. The girl scowled and stuck out her tongue.

Lilly sat up in bed, breathing heavily and perspiring as the dream faded. Feeling ill, she arose, wrapped her dressing gown around herself, and stepped gingerly to Charlie's door. She opened it inch by creaking inch. In the moonlit chamber, Charlie slept soundly, hands clasped beneath one cheek, fair hair splayed on his pillow and over his brow.

Lilly tiptoed across the room and leaned low. She reached out and gently brushed the hair from his eyes.

She needed to touch someone real.

In the morning, Lilly went in search of her mother's miniature portrait. She found it in a drawer in the sitting room, shrouded in brown paper. Unwrapping it, she blew off the paper dust and looked at the lovely face, so like the one in her dream the night before. It had been painted before her marriage more than twenty years ago. Lilly wondered how much she had changed by now. And knew she would go on wondering.

Lilly slipped the small frame into her apron pocket, wanting it near. She *would* act upon the information her uncle had sent. She would write a letter to start. After that, she did not know.

An hour later, she was already in the shop, bent over stationery and quill, when Francis came by for the Haswell herbs Mr. Shuttleworth wanted. She had the herbs bunched, tagged, and ready in a crate.

"Excellent. This everything?" Francis asked.

"Hmm?" she murmured, distracted.

"Is this everything. For Mr. Shuttleworth . . . ?"

"Oh." She glanced up at him, then at the crate. "Yes." She looked back at the few lines she had written. "Francis, you never met my mother, did you?"

He wrinkled his brow, no doubt wondering why she had asked a question when she already knew the answer.

"No. She left not long before I arrived."

Lilly nodded, tapping the quill against the inkpot as she thought.

"I do remember a little portrait of her," Francis said. "You used to carry it about with you, until your father asked you to put it away."

Lilly nodded again, thinking how she had found the portrait wrapped and tucked in a drawer. Out of sight.

"I remember thinking she was quite lovely," Francis continued. "And that you were very like her."

Silently, she pulled the framed miniature from her apron pocket and slid it across the counter toward him. He leaned down and peered at it. "Very like her indeed."

She told him about her mother's necklace and *Rosa Wells*. As she spoke, he took her hand in his and pressed it, his brown eyes warm with compassion. The laboratory-kitchen door creaked open and Francis stepped back. Seeing her father in the doorway, Lilly slipped the miniature under her writing paper.

"Good morning, Mr. Haswell," Francis said. "You are looking better."

"I feel better. For now, at any rate. Tell me, Mr. Baylor, how is our new physician getting on in the village? Lilly's Dr. Graves?"

She saw Francis wince. His brow pucker. Uncomfortable, Lilly protested mildly, "Father . . ."

Francis glanced at her, then quickly away. "Well enough, I suppose, though you know how it is. Some are slow to accept a newcomer."

Her father nodded, then eyed the crate. "What's this, then?"

Fearing her father's response, Lilly answered, "Mr. Shuttleworth has asked for some of our famed Haswell herbs, Father. That should please you."

He was incredulous. "You are giving herbs to our competitor?"

"Selling, Father. Selling," Lilly said, realizing her father had resumed his curmudgeonly temper toward his rival. "And at a tidy profit." She gave Francis a look, and Francis took the hint.

"It's dear they are, but Bedsley Priors folk will have Haswell herbs if they can. Shuttleworth has little choice but to pay for the privilege."

Charles Haswell nodded, apparently satisfied. "I should think so."

"Well, I bid you both good day." Lips pulled tight in a resigned line, Francis bowed to Lilly, then to Mr. Haswell, and took his leave.

Her father tilted his head to view the paper before her. "Another order?"

She hesitated. "No, a letter. To Mother."

He looked stunned. "What?"

"At least to the estate where she is believed to have a situation."

"What are you talking about?"

"Come, Father," Lilly bid softly. "Sit down and I will tell you."

They seated themselves in the surgery, and Lilly explained once more about the discovery of the necklace and what she had learned about her mother in

London and since—in review, very little. Not wanting to hurt him more than he had already been, she did not include the details about her mother's first love.

She asked gently, "Why did she leave, do you know?"

He took a deep breath. "I thought she was happy, at least for a time." He stared out the surgery window. "When you were born, I thought everything would be all right. She was so delighted with you." He shifted in his chair. "But I believe she always regretted marrying me. I know she missed London, and I think she always wondered what might have been, whom she might have married had she stayed."

She squeezed his hand. "You are the best man I have ever met—in London or anywhere."

He uttered a dry laugh. "Did the Elliotts take you *nowhere*?" Shaking his head, he said, "No, my dear, I am afraid I am a very flawed man indeed. Perhaps even more than your mother knew. . . ."

He let the words fade away and then leaned forward earnestly. "I caution you, Lilly, in this search of yours. You may not like what you find."

30

> [The apothecary] is the physician to the poor at all times, and to the rich whenever the distress or danger is not great.
>
> —Adam Smith, 1776

As Lilly and her father lingered over breakfast the next day, Charlie came in and dropped one of their medical cases onto the table before her, nearly toppling her teacup. "Come with me to Marlow House, Lilly. Mr. Timms has a gurt boil and won't see a doctor."

Lilly grimaced. She no more wanted to lance that crass old man's boil than she wanted to manage her father's shop. "Perhaps Father might," she said, spooning jam onto her remaining crust of toast.

Charles Haswell looked up from his newspaper. "I don't think I am equal to it today, my dear."

How convenient, Lilly thought.

"Come on, Lilly," Charlie urged. "Man's hurtin' fierce."

"Oh, very well," she huffed, dropping the toast onto her plate and rising. Seeing brother's earnest face, she hesitated and added grudgingly, "It is kind of you to think of Mr. Timms."

Half an hour later, Lilly stood in Mr. Timms's small kitchen at one end of the Marlow row houses, where several of the oldest servants lived.

"You rest easy now, Mr. Timms," she advised, repacking instruments and vials.

"Rest? You'll not see me lolloping about. Think the goosegogs'll pick their selves? The deer'll overrun the galley-crow afore the day's out, and the garden be dry as a gix."

Sitting beside the man, Charlie said, "I can help, Mr. Timms."

"Nay, yer needed at home now, ey? But I sore miss ye. A good tasker ye are, Charlie Haswell, and don't ye forget it."

Charlie smiled and hung his head, sheepishly proud.

Lilly said, "I am sorry, Mr. Timms, but my father and I—"

"No need to be sorry, miss. I know how 'tis. Yer father's ailin', innum? I know how that is too."

She shut the case, preparing to take her leave. "I hope you shall be right as a trivet now."

"No doubt of it. I'm obliged to ye, I am. And glad to be shot of that gurt ol' boil."

They bid the wizened gardener farewell and let themselves out the door.

"See, I told you he weren't so bad," Charlie said.

"You were right, Charlie. And if he was surly, no wonder! To be in such pain day and night."

The weather was mild, so they strolled across the lawn to the formal gardens, Charlie pointing out this planting and that which he had helped tend. As they did, Lilly heard a dog bark—first a warning, then with more ferocity. A man called out in a stern voice laced with a telling note of fear.

"Back, I say. Back!"

"Oh no." Lilly ran down the lane, and around the bend spotted Dr. Graves, his back against a tree. The Marlows' large-headed mastiff, nearly the size of a pony, stood on its hind legs, massive front paws splayed against the man's chest.

"Dotty, no!" Lilly called with calm authority. "Down this instant!"

Dotty whined, drooled, and leapt down. Charlie jogged over and grabbed the collar of the brindled brown-and-black dog.

Lilly said, "Tether her in the stables, Charlie, will you?"

"Come on, Dotty-girl," Charlie urged and led the great dog away.

"Dotty?" Dr. Graves exclaimed. "Who in their right mind would name a monster of that size *Dotty*?"

"The Marlows have an uncommon sensibility when it comes to humor and most things," she said, stepping near to look him over. Besides two muddy pawprints on his tawny coat, he appeared unscathed. "Are you all right?"

"You mean beyond my utter mortification and the fact that my heart is beating like a cornered hare?"

"Yes."

He extracted a handkerchief from his pocket and wiped drool from his cheek. "I was only come to meet Sir Henry. I had no idea the act would prove so perilous."

She took the handkerchief from him. "You've a bit of mud . . ." She wiped the dirt from his neck and collar. His Adam's apple bobbed and his pupils dilated. Realizing what she had just done, she swallowed and handed back the handkerchief.

His eyes met hers, then darted away. She attempted to keep her expression impassive, lest he guess how forward she felt.

He cleared his throat. "You are a singular woman, Miss Haswell."

She licked her suddenly dry lips. An awkward silence followed. To break it, she said, "I am afraid your coat is spoiled."

In the act of dusting off the pawprints, he paused. "Are *you* afraid of nothing?"

She considered this. "Everybody is afraid of something. Or someone."

"What are you afraid of?"

She cocked her head to one side to look at him. "Why? Will it make you feel better to know?"

"Vastly." He stooped to pick up his hat and attempted to restore its shape. "Or at least distract me from my humiliation."

"Very well. But I tell you in confidence."

"Of course."

She grinned wryly. "I had rather face that great dog ten times over than his master once."

His hands stilled. "Roderick Marlow?"

She nodded.

He did not return her grin. Instead looked quite alarmed. "Has he threatened you? Harmed you?"

"Well, nothing of consequence, but—"

"He hasn't acted in an untoward manner toward you?"

"Dr. Graves. I meant to comfort you by my confession, not distress you further."

"But, Miss Haswell!"

"There have been a few occasions when I felt mildly . . . threatened, as you say. But these were long ago. Still, I suppose it is the same for me as for you—

one bite and I shall ever be wary." She hastened to add, "Of course I meant that figuratively. He did not *actually* bite me." Again she tried to lighten the moment with a smile, but he continued to look quite stern.

He said, "I understand he all but got a man killed once. In a brawl or duel or some such."

Had he? She had never heard such a tale.

"In any case, if he ever threatens or harasses you again, Miss Haswell, you must not allow it to pass. You must tell someone. Me, if no one else."

She wondered briefly what Dr. Graves would do. She could not fancy him fighting Roderick Marlow. Dr. Graves would surely lose any duel not fought with lancets or ear horns.

"Thank you. But as I said, it is in the past. Put it from your mind."

"Have you?"

"Absolutely. As long as he is out of my sight." She smirked. "Or chained up."

Blue eyes sparkling, he grinned—then actually laughed out loud. It was the first genuine sound of mirth she had ever heard him utter. She liked it very much indeed.

When the return letter arrived almost a week later from Craybill Hall, Lilly could not bring herself to open it. To face the rejection that might very well be contained within. How many times had she imagined the possible responses? The cool, detached words: *"I regret to inform you I have no interest in renewing our acquaintance."* Or *"I request that you no longer attempt to contact me; I do not wish to jeopardize my position."* Or even *"If I had wanted to see you, I knew where to find you, did I not?"*

But dared she hope for a warmer response? *"How I have longed to hear of you! But to receive a letter penned in your own hand—My, what a fine young lady you must have become! I would very much like to see you again. I feared to hope you would ever desire to see me. . . ."*

Which would it be?

Turning the shop sign, she jogged to the coffeehouse, barely noticing Jane hunched on the garden bench shelling beans. She dashed through the back door, and thrust the letter at Mary.

"Read it. I cannot."

Mary was grinding coffee beans but paused to study her. She turned to wipe her hands on a cloth. "What is it?"

"From my mother I think. I wrote to the house where she was said to have a situation."

Setting aside the cloth, Mary took the letter. "It is addressed to you."

"Please."

Mary held her gaze a moment longer, then nodded. She slit open the seal and unfolded the letter. As she quickly read the lines, her expression shifted from perplexity to concern.

"She does not wish to see me, does she?" Lilly braced herself.

Mary shook her head.

Lilly winced. *I knew it.*

"It isn't from your mother. It is from the housekeeper, a Mrs. Morton. Here, read it yourself."

Lilly took the letter from her friend and skimmed it quickly, then sank down onto her usual stool and read the critical portion again.

We've had no one here by the surname Haswell, but there was a housekeeper by the name Rosa Wells. However, she is no longer employed here, and I am the new housekeeper. I cannot tell you where she went, but I can tell you she left after only a few weeks, without proper notice and without references and that the coachman disappeared on the very same eve. Him, by the name of Stanley Dugan, in case you're wanting to know. If you find them, be sure and pass on that Mr. Dugan left without returning the livery that is rightly the master's property, though the master is a forgiving sort and pressed no charges. Rosa took nothing what didn't belong to her, and Cook tells me she was a fair worker, though not content in her post. This is all I can tell you, as she was gone before I come.

Mrs. Morton, Housekeeper
Craybill Hall

Gone. Again.

Did her mother have some inkling she was being sought? Or was it her nature to move on quickly from situations that did not suit?

"Might it have been someone else?" Mary asked. "With the name Wells, I mean. She could not have married again, could she? With your father still alive?"

Lilly shrugged, feeling numb and empty. "It could be a false name, short for Haswell. Or perhaps she took the name of the man she left us for, and has even now taken another *husband*. It would explain why she has cut all ties to an inconvenient family hidden away in Wiltshire."

"I cannot credit it," Mary said. "More likely it was some other woman."

Lilly said dully, "Perhaps." She crumpled the paper and tossed it among the embers in the cookstove. The paper flamed to life, then just as quickly extinguished.

Like her foolish, foolish hopes.

31

A man of very moderate ability may be a good physician,
if he devotes himself faithfully to the work.

—Oliver Wendell Holmes

The next morning, when Lilly entered the coffeehouse by the kitchen door as usual, she was surprised to see Mr. Shuttleworth there, seated in her customary stool at the worktable.

She hesitated. "Oh. Pardon me."

He rose and bowed. "Miss Haswell."

"Morning, Lill," Mary said pleasantly, looking pretty in a green frock and seeming perfectly at ease. She walked over to pick up the stool beside the hearth, but Mr. Shuttleworth, perceiving her intention, leapt to assist her, carrying the stool over and setting it not far from his own.

Both ladies thanked him at once. He beamed at them, his gaze lingering on Mary. "My pleasure, ladies."

Lilly perched herself up on the stool, feeling awkward. Mary poured a cup of coffee and placed it before her, then returned her attention to a large basin, stirring its contents with fluid, steady strokes.

"Miss Mimpurse was so obliging as to offer a poor bachelor a bite of breakfast," Mr. Shuttleworth said. "Though the establishment is not yet open."

"Mamma is just opening the shutters now, Mr. Shuttleworth, should you prefer the comfort of soft chairs not dusted with flour."

"And why should I prefer it? Have I not the best seat in the house?"

Lifting the coffee cup to her lips, Lilly said dryly, "I have always thought so."

"Indeed. I cannot imagine warmer fires nor warmer company in any other place in the world."

"And that is saying a great deal, is it not," Lilly said. "Considering all of the many places you have been."

"You are too kind to remember, Miss Haswell."

"Lilly remembers everything, Mr. Shuttleworth," Mary said. "Had you not heard?"

"Dear me. I am obliged to you for the warning."

He grinned, and Mary lifted her eyes from her work long enough to return the gesture.

Lilly smiled as well, though did wonder that Mary should raise the subject of her memory. Knowing how self-conscious Lilly felt about it, her friend usually avoided mentioning it to strangers. Of course, by all appearances, Mr. Shuttleworth was stranger no longer.

Suddenly a pained look pinched Mary's usually docile features, and she grasped her left hand with her right.

"Please excuse me," she said, and Lilly doubted anyone who did not know Mary so well would even notice the tension in her face. "I've just been reminded of something I must attend to."

Mr. Shuttleworth rose, mouth ajar. But Mary had already turned and fled the room before he could say anything.

Lilly rose beside him, concerned.

"I have clearly overstayed my welcome," he said sheepishly. "Do offer your friend a thousand apologies on my behalf."

"Not at all, sir. I am certain it is nothing you did."

"I shall see myself out." He opened the back door and bid her farewell.

As soon as he had gone, Lilly hurried toward the dining room, thinking Mary must have gone upstairs, but a flash of green caught her eye as she passed the pantry. There Mary half sat, half reclined on a ten-stone sack of flour.

"Mary, is a fit coming on?"

Jerking a nod, Mary held her arms tightly, clutching her abdomen as a wounded soldier might hold his innards. Her arms shook and the movement expanded, overtaking her until even her head began to wobble on her neck, tendons corded like angry claws lashing into her shoulders.

Lilly reached for Mary's apron pocket, for the leather scrap she kept there. Empty. "Hold on. I'll try and catch Mr. Shuttleworth."

"No!" Mary cried, voice trembling. "No . . . father."

"But my father is too ill. He has returned to his bed."

"My . . ." Mary began, then her body convulsed, rendering her unable to speak.

Lilly hesitated only a second, then dashed into the kitchen, grabbed the first wooden spoon she saw, and ran back with it. Mary winced but opened her mouth and Lilly slid the spoon between her teeth. Stepping to the door, she glanced into the dining room, where Mrs. Mimpurse was greeting a group of timber men and barge builders, Mr. Robbins among them.

Catching her eye, Lilly jerked her head toward the pantry, mouthing, "Mary." Her pained look must have communicated the rest, for Mrs. Mimpurse quickly but tactfully took her leave of the men and strode toward the kitchen.

Lilly did not wait. With her father ill, and Mary's clear command not to involve Mr. Shuttleworth, she could think of only one place to go for help.

She would even have asked Dr. Foster if need be, but when she pounded on the office door, she was relieved when Dr. Graves answered.

"Please come quickly. It's Mary Mimpurse. She's having a fit."

She half expected him to freeze in the face of an emergency as he had in London, but she silently thanked God when he bent immediately and picked up his case.

Adam Graves's heart pounded, but he did not hesitate. Miss Haswell's practical, no-nonsense commands pushed him into action, and his limbs obeyed her even while his mind struggled to catch up.

She asked, "Have you valerian, or should I run home for some?"

He opened his case and checked its contents. "I have all I need."

"Good. Hurry." She turned on her heel, giving him little choice but to follow.

He had to jog to keep up with her along Milk Lane and then down the High Street. She had somehow learned to run at an impressive pace while appearing merely to glide.

Rounding the coffeehouse, she opened the back door and gestured him inside ahead of her. Mrs. Mimpurse had swept the utensils from the worktable and managed to lay her daughter upon it. The poor girl convulsed, eyes rolled back, wooden spoon protruding from her mouth. Her mother did her best to hold her in place, with the help of a young maid. He surprised himself by immediately rushing forward to aid them.

"Father believes valerian to be the best remedy," Miss Haswell said, appearing beside him at the table. "The trick is to administer it while she's in this state."

"Give me two ounces of the extract, then."

"So much? Is not the regular dose one half to one dram?"

"We shall debate theories later, shall we? With all haste, Miss Haswell."

He continued to help the two women steady Miss Mimpurse while Lilly poured the liquid into a glass measure and handed it to him.

"Help me pry open her mouth." Using the wooden spoon as a lever, the two managed to open her mouth, pour in the foul liquid, and coax it to the back of her throat. Her swallowing reflex did the rest.

"Now, help us hold her until it takes effect. If it does . . ."

"It will. Always has."

Already, the young woman's seizures were gentling, whether from the dosage or the simple passage of time, he could not tell. He did not like that Miss Haswell felt she had to question him, that she could not trust his judgment.

While they held Miss Mimpurse, he endeavored to explain, "You are correct that the accepted *preventative* dose is one half to one dram three or four times as day. But more is required to calm an episode in full force."

"I see."

"In any case, I am not convinced valerian suppresses seizures, and it certainly does not cure the root of the disease."

"What is the cure?" she asked.

He glanced at the white-faced mother, then back at Miss Haswell. "I fear there is none."

Later, after he had helped Mrs. Mimpurse put her weakened daughter to bed, and accepted the woman's gratitude, Adam walked outside with Miss Haswell.

"Do you think she ought to take valerian on a daily basis?" she asked.

"Not at this point. I recommend an infusion of scullcap."

"Mad-dog weed?"

"It works as antispasmodic and relaxing nervine both. Perhaps you would be so good as to prepare it?"

"Of course," she said, clearly pleased to be called upon.

Reaching Haswell's, she paused to look up at him. How earnest her expression, her heart-shaped face wreathed by that splendid russet hair.

"May I ask you to keep this episode to yourself?" she began. "Mary is quite self-conscious about her condition. It has been so long since she's had a fit, the poor dear no doubt hoped she'd outgrown them."

He wondered how he could refuse Miss Haswell anything, when she captivated him so. Though she had not asked, she must know she was the reason he had pursued this partnership in Bedsley Priors.

"Dr. Foster may ask for an account of my time, but otherwise I shall keep it to myself as I would in any case."

"Thank you."

He thought then of the next call he must make. "May I ask a favor of you in return?"

At the cottage door, they were greeted by one of the nine Somersby children and a rush of sharp smells. Inside, Mr. and Mrs. Somersby sat at table, a spread of cheese, pickled herring, and mugs of ale before them. Two toddlers sat on the floor, banging wooden spoons against the floorboards. Four others were blowing and chasing a downy feather about the room, keeping it aloft. The family's cottage was small, their clothes old, but as Mr. Somersby was both poulterer and cheese monger, they always ate well. Perhaps, Lilly thought, too well.

"I beg your pardon. I am Dr. Graves, paying a call on behalf of Dr. Foster. And this is Miss Haswell."

Lilly knew the older physician rarely bothered with house calls now that he had Dr. Graves to send about.

"But we had no intention of interrupting your repast."

"Never ye mind." Mrs. Somersby, a plump woman of forty or so years, lifted her apron hem and wiped her mouth. "Chester here come home from market leer-starved. Why not sit yerselves? I've got a junk o' cheese, good an' aged. Chicken livers, too."

"Thank you, no," Dr. Graves said.

The feather landed on his shoulder, unnoticed by him. Lilly plucked it off and blew it in the air for the expectant children.

Mrs. Somersby rose. "Well then. Let's shut us in the bedchamber away from all these peepers. I'm much obliged to you fer comin' 'ere. Hard to get away with all these young ones aboot."

As she led the way to the cottage's sole separate room, Dr. Graves said, "Dr. Foster described several complaints of a female nature and I have therefore brought Miss Haswell along."

"As I see."

As soon as the three of them were inside the small bedchamber, Mrs. Somersby lowered herself heavily onto the edge of the bed, and Lilly sat beside her. "Now, tell me," Lilly asked gently. "What ails you?"

"I'm just not my old self of late. My poor nerves are givin' me quiy' a lot of trouble. My Chester don't like how I mump aboot. Seems we 'ave a shandy near ever' night for no good reason. And I'm 'aving pains in my stomach." She leaned toward Lilly and whispered, "And pains in my breast what don't bear speakin' of in a young man's 'earing."

Lilly smiled and said soothingly, "Well, he is a doctor after all, is he not?"

They gave the woman St. John's wort for her nerves and stomach, and a decoction of vervain for the breast pain.

"Now, if that does not bring you relief, you just come by the shop when you can and I shall give you a treatment of tempered figs." Lilly paused, then turned sheepishly to Dr. Graves. "Forgive me. You might prefer to do that yourself. She is your patient after all."

He hesitated, perhaps imagining the awkward scene—pressing figs, tempered as hot as a patient could endure, and applying them to Mrs. Somersby's breasts. He cleared his throat. "Not at all." He said to the woman, "Feel free to see Miss Haswell for that procedure."

They were packing their things away to take their leave when Mrs. Somersby pressed both hands to her temples. "Wha's this? I feel right queer all of a sudden."

Lilly hurried to her side. "What is it?"

"My 'ead . . . aches somethin' awful. Dizzy-like too." Mrs. Somersby used one arm to prop herself upright and moaned, "Wha's 'appenin'?" Then she collapsed onto the bed.

"Dr. Graves!" Lilly exclaimed.

Acting quickly and with surprising calm, Dr. Graves deftly gave Mrs. Somersby a dose of ipecacuanha, and once it had done its work, administered hawthorn and strong coffee.

Half an hour later, Mrs. Somersby was quite herself again, though shaken. Lilly prepared a cup of chamomile tea at Dr. Grave's request, then instructed Mr. Somersby to give another cup when his wife finished the first.

When they finally took their leave, Dr. Graves accompanied Lilly back to Haswell's.

"Do you think it was the St. John's wort?" she asked as they neared the shop. "I've never known vervain to produce such a dramatic reaction."

"Nor I."

He opened the shop door for her and followed her inside.

"A skin rash, perhaps," she continued, "but not collapse. Good heavens. I don't know what I would have done had you not been there. Well done, Dr. Graves."

In her relief, she forgot herself and held out her hand in a congratulatory gesture as Mr. Shuttleworth might have done. Instead of briefly pressing it, Dr. Graves took her hand in both of his own, his countenance quite serious.

"When you are with me, I feel as though I might do anything. You strengthen me, Miss Haswell."

She allowed him to hold her hand but shook her head slowly. "I cannot be your strength, Dr. Graves. That is God's role. I am not fit for it."

"Is it the role you object to, or the man asking it of you?"

She took a deep breath. "At present, I have all I can do to be my father's strength as well as my own."

He let go of her hand and drew himself up. "Of course you have. I would not blame you, in any case. You know my weaknesses too well."

"Have we not all some weakness, Dr. Graves?" Lilly said kindly. "Besides, you seem to be overcoming your weaknesses, as you call them, since coming to Bedsley Priors."

He lifted one side of his mouth in a rueful grin. "Which brings me back to my point, Miss Haswell."

She untied her bonnet and stepped away to hang it on a peg. "We certainly work well together," she allowed. "As evidenced this very day."

"Indeed, though I would certainly not expect you to work alongside me, were we to . . . That is, unless it were a simple case, or involved a female complaint like Mrs. Somersby's."

"Why? Do you not think a woman capable of grasping medical knowledge and skills?"

"Well, I do not say it is impossible, were universities to allow women to study. But . . . they do not."

"I help my father all the time." She moved to stand behind the dispensary counter.

"I understand that. And I admire your abilities." He stepped to the counter and stood looking down at her. "But, Miss Haswell, once you are—Once you are a married woman, you will no longer have need of such skills. Although, certainly as the lady of the house, a knowledge of basic injury care, invalid cookery and the like, will always be useful."

She should have been relieved he would not expect such from her. Had she not wanted to escape such a life? Then why did she feel discounted instead?

32

I try to avoid looking forward or backward,
and try to keep looking upward.
—Charlotte Brontë

Lilly stood on the back stoop. She looked out over the garden and breathed deeply of an English summer morn. It had rained in the night, and all smelled fresh and green. Grey's Hill—her hill—was just visible in the distance beyond the garden wall. She closed her eyes, enjoying the warm caress of the sun on her face and arms though she knew she ought not be out-of-doors without a hat. *Ah, what is one more freckle. . . .*

Songbirds chirped happily in the hornbeam and lime trees, and beyond her view, a single horse clip-clopped its way along the High Street. The church bells rang, and when their last peal faded away, all was quiet save birdsong.

She could not help but think back to where she had been and what she had been doing exactly one year ago. She knew she should not let the memory play itself out, knew she should not compare this year to the last, but she gave in and let the memories come.

Many hooves had beat the busy streets outside the Elliotts' Mayfair townhouse. Carriage wheels and church bells had sounded as well. Dupree brought up a breakfast tray bearing a vase of lemon-yellow lilies in honor of the day. Then she helped Lilly put on a new frock of sprigged muslin and dressed her hair with ribbons.

There had followed shopping with Aunt Elliott and Christina Price-Winters. Roger had sent a nosegay and a lovely new fan with his compliments. Later they dined at the Clarendon and then attended the Theatre Royal, sharing a box with Will Price-Winters and his then-fiancée, as well as Christina, Toby Horton, and Roger Bromley. There had been a pearl necklace from her aunt and uncle and a new shawl from Christina. She remembered the presents, of course, but it was not the presents themselves she longed for now. It was the feeling of being special she missed, of being cherished.

She recalled Mr. Marlow's advice on how to tame unpleasant memories and realized there were times when one might wish to stifle pleasant memories as well—when they dimmed the present by comparison.

Stop feeling sorry for yourself, Lilly Haswell, she warned sternly. Purposefully, she strode to the clump of lilies near the garden wall and plucked a lemony bloom. She tucked it behind her ear and felt better immediately.

"You're up early." Francis appeared above the garden wall, and her heart lightened further.

He pushed his way through the garden gate with his hip, his hands full. Spying the wrapped parcel in his arms, Lilly felt foolishly thrilled and bit back a smile.

"I've brought you something. I hope Dr. Graves won't mind."

He would, she thought, but forbore to comment. After all, she'd thought no one had remembered. Her father had not. Nor had Mary said a word. "How thoughtful, Francis. Do come in."

He followed her inside, and Lilly gestured uncertainly toward the kitchen table. "Here, or . . . ?"

"The shop, I think."

She led the way and stood aside as he laid the large parcel on the dispensing counter. He urged her forward with a sweep of his hand. "Go on."

Smiling, she gently ripped back the brown paper. She felt her eyes widen as she stared at what lay beneath. Not a gift box, but a cage. A cage inhabited by a hairy rodent.

She frowned. "It is a rat."

"Not a rat, a cavy. *Cavia porcellus*."

"Looks like a rat." She darted a glance at him. "Though more handsome, I grant you." This long-haired animal had white and caramel markings and close-set eyes.

"Dr. William Harvey himself used several in his research."

"Harvey . . ." Lilly thought. "The first to correctly describe the circulatory system?"

"Exactly."

"I do not recall any mention of . . . What did you call it—a cavy?"

"I believe he referred to them in his writings as *ginny-pigs*."

She peered into the cage. "This little thing is hardly a pig. How odd."

"Mr. Shuttleworth kept one in his ship's surgery. He believed in feeding it new remedies—especially materia acquired in foreign lands—before offering them to the ill among the crew."

"And you thought I could . . . ?"

"Well, since he was working on his own—without colleague to discuss treatments or dosages—he thought it a wise precaution."

Lilly felt herself growing piqued. "And has he a cavy now in that fancy shop of his?"

"No." Francis smiled ruefully. "He has me."

"You know perfectly well many poisons do not show up immediately."

"I do not suggest it as a foolproof measure. Only a precaution against the most harmful of substances."

She huffed and balled the paper tight.

"Come, Lilly, do not take offense. I only thought . . . I know you pretend otherwise, but you are essentially alone here. I know you remember everything you once learned, but some things have changed. There are new exotics, new materia, new methods."

Now she doubted Francis had remembered her birthday at all, but was too self-conscious to ask. Likely he had no idea, the date and the gift coming together in pure coincidence.

He tried another tack. "Mostly I thought he was a sweet little mite. Queen Elizabeth herself kept one as a pet."

"Did she indeed?"

He nodded.

She looked from him to the cavy, then back again. "I would have preferred a cat."

"But cats do not—"

"As a pet I mean. Not a royal taster."

"I did not think Haswells went in for cats."

"That was a long time ago. These days, Haswells are doing all sorts of things we never imagined we would."

His rueful smile returned. He reached out and gently touched her arm. "Well, happy birthday anyway."

Lilly closed the shop as usual that evening and retreated to the laboratory-kitchen to see what she might find in the larder to scrape together for supper. Very little, it appeared. A quarter loaf of bread. A scrap of Stilton. A jar of goosegog conserve and another of sardines.

She took herself upstairs to check on her father and ask if he felt up to eating. Lately, his condition seemed to vacillate by the hour. She knocked, but he did not answer. She opened the door to find the bedchamber empty, the bed made, if haphazardly so.

Where had he taken himself off to? Had he wandered down to the surgery without her noticing? She paused in her own room, to splash water on her face and check her hair in the small mirror. Still reasonably neat. She took off her apron, laid it in the laundry basket, and returned downstairs.

Her father was not in the kitchen, nor the surgery. Had he gone to see Dr. Graves? She stepped out the back door to check the garden. The air was still as warm and sweet as it had been that morning, and she took a moment to inhale it.

Charlie's head appeared over the garden wall, startling her.

"Lilly! Come quick."

Trepidation shot through her. "Is it Father?"

"Father too. Mary says hurry."

What now? Lilly rushed out the garden gate and across the mews to the coffeehouse. She burst through the kitchen door and hesitated in the threshold. Mary looked up at her from the hearth.

"What is it? Charlie said you and Father needed me."

"We do. We're missing something."

"Missing what?"

Mary straightened. "The guest of honor, you goose. Surely you guessed?"

Lilly shook her head.

Mary rolled her eyes, took her by the arm, and led her through the door into the coffeehouse dining room. Charlie followed behind. There, at the large center table were her father, clear-eyed and sitting upright, Mr. Shuttleworth, Francis, and Dr. Graves. Maude Mimpurse stood nearby, reaching over to set a platter of food on the table. An iced cake sat in the middle.

Lilly looked at Mary with surprise and saw her own pleasure mirrored in her dearest friend's face. She squeezed Mary's hand and whispered, "Thank you."

Mr. Shuttleworth cleared his throat. "In ancient Egypt," he began, "at least one pharaoh celebrated his birthday by doing away with his baker."

"Mr. Shuttleworth," Mary scolded, though Lilly did not miss the teasing lift of her mouth.

He winked at her. "No doubt his cakes were not as good as yours."

Charlie hurried over and took a seat next to Francis. "Mary's sittin' next to me," he said. "But your place is here, Lilly." He reached behind Francis and patted the back of a chair at the open place—the place between Francis Baylor and Adam Graves.

Francis met her gaze with a knowing look of his own.

Dr. Graves stood and pulled back her chair. "Felicitations, Miss Haswell."

Walking around the table, she placed her hand on her father's shoulder as she passed behind him. He reached up and grasped it with his own. She looked down at him, saw his eyes crinkle as he smiled up at her. "Happy birthday, my dear."

It was the loveliest gift she could imagine.

After supper, Maude rose to cut the cake. "Now, this is no ordinary cake," she said. "It's an olde English cake, baked with coins and other treasures inside, each one a symbol of something."

"Mind you don't break a tooth," Mary warned, handing plates with generous wedges to each of them.

Looking at each other with nervous anticipation and barely suppressed grins, they began to tentatively fork pieces of cake into their mouths and carefully chew. All except for Charlie, who shoveled in big hunks of cake with abandon.

In a matter of moments, Mr. Shuttleworth held up a coin.

"But not just any coin. Look again," Mary urged.

Squinting, he read, "*Italia*." He flipped it over. "Looks familiar."

"It ought to," Mary said. "It is the one I borrowed from you for the occasion. It means travels in your past or future."

"Ah . . ." He nodded his understanding.

"I also have a coin," Dr. Graves said, holding one up. "A shilling."

"Well then," Mary said, "you shall be wealthy one day."

He leaned in, his expression mock-serious. "Might I have that in writing?"

"I have a sweet!" Charlie triumphantly raised a cake-covered peppermint, then popped it into his mouth.

"What did you find, Charles?" Maude asked quietly.

Her father wiped the find with his handkerchief. "An old Roman coin. Plenty unearthed in these parts. Is this from Harold's collection, or a new find?"

Maude didn't respond to the query about her deceased husband, but Mary murmured, "Treasure from the past."

Lilly glimpsed the crumb-coated thimble on Mary's plate, but noticed she made no move to display it. Mrs. Mimpurse glanced over and clearly saw it as well. Looking worriedly at her daughter's face, she whispered, "I am sorry, my love. It is only a game after all."

Mary shrugged and attempted a smile.

"What is it you have, Miss Mary?" Mr. Shuttleworth asked eagerly.

Lilly sent him a warning look, but the man apparently did not notice or understand, for his long-toothed smile did not waver. He leaned closer. "A thimble, is it? What does it mean?"

An awkward silence filled the room.

Lilly opened her mouth but could not form the words.

Head high, Mary said briskly, "It means I shall never marry."

Mr. Shuttleworth tucked his chin. "What nonsense. You must have Graves's piece." He slapped Dr. Graves hard on the shoulder, causing the slighter man to jerk forward.

Lilly knew most people believed epilepsy rendered a woman ineligible for marriage and motherhood. But she did not agree. Hoping to direct the attention off her friend, Lilly asked, "And what did you find, Mrs. Mimpurse?"

Maude Mimpurse blushed and held up a ring. "I got the piece meant for one of you girls, no doubt."

They all chuckled politely.

"I have a key," Francis said. "What does it mean?"

They all looked at Mary.

"I don't know," she admitted. "Couldn't think of anything else to withstand the oven!"

Everyone laughed.

Everyone except Lilly, who was still forking through her piece. And though she looked and looked, she found nothing at all.

33

> I do not know of any remedy under heaven that is likely to do you so much good as the being constantly electrified.
>
> —John Wesley, 1781

When Lilly came downstairs the next morning, still securing a final pin into the plait coiled at the back of her head, she was pleased to see her father up and about already. Perhaps Dr. Graves's latest treatments were helping after all.

"I've made tea and toast," he announced with pride. "Had a taste for blood sausage, as well, so I'm frying a few slices if you'd care for any."

She shuddered. "You know I cannot abide the stuff. But tea and toast sounds just the thing." Watching her father potter about the kitchen, Lilly smiled to herself. "You must be feeling some better, Father."

"Indeed I am. And I've had a look at the ledgers, Lilly. First time I've had the courage to do so in months."

Scooping his sausage onto a plate, he joined her at the table. "I cannot express how proud I am. Well done, Lillian Grace Haswell. Well done, indeed."

She ducked her head, hiding her smile of pleasure. "Thank you, Father."

He picked up his fork. "No, my dear. Thank you."

"Shall we thank God, then?" she suggested. "I must say I am feeling quite grateful for His provision of late."

Charles Haswell paused, mouth ajar, and awkwardly lowered his forkful of sausage back down to his plate. "As you like."

Lilly bowed her head and offered a brief prayer of thanksgiving.

Afterward, her Father nodded and quickly moved on. "Once we've eaten, I'd like you to show me everything you've done in the shop. Went out there this morning and scarcely recognized the old place. Smells like a bakery, or a flower shop. But it looks fine, Lilly. Fine."

Lilly bit back another smile and echoed, "As you like."

"I also wonder if it might be time to ask Mrs. Fowler back," he said. "You do far too much on your own."

Lilly heard these words with great relief and pleasure. "I think that an excellent plan. I shall ask her this afternoon."

After they had eaten and done the washing up together, she led him into the shop, telling him about the Lippert family in London and pointing out the new patent medicines, the French perfumes, the ribbons, the rouge pots and other cosmetics.

"Here's one I used myself in London." She picked up a jar of Warren and Rosser's Milk of Roses and read from its label, "'The most delightful cosmetic in Europe. Recommended by females of distinction for removing freckles and rendering the complexion delicately fair.'"

He glanced at her and coughed. "I'd request my money back, were I you."

"Father," she scolded, but grinned in spite of herself.

He raised his hands in defense. "I like your freckles." He then paused before an unfamiliar contraption. "And what, pray, is this?"

The apparatus, standing on four glass legs, resembled a miniature table. Two wooden uprights stood atop it, holding aloft a cylinder with a crank handle on one side and, on the other, an arm extending to a a small metal ball.

"That is the latest thing in London. Supposed to be all the crack, according to George Lippert."

"But . . . what is it?"

"An electricity machine, reportedly highly effective in the treatment of paralysis, gout, and . . . perhaps even epilepsy."

"Indeed?"

"John Wesley himself called it 'the most efficacious medicine in nervous disorders of every kind.'"

"Ah, that's right. The good reverend fancied himself a healer as well as an evangelist."

She searched for censure in his expression, but saw only mild incredulity.

He asked, "How does it work?"

"The patient holds the ball and, when the arm contacts the rotating cylinder, receives a shock—the strength of which depends upon the vigor with which the handle is turned. I have an explanatory pamphlet, but I own I have not had the courage to try it."

He eyed the device warily. "Let us leave it for another day, shall we? Now, what else have you done?"

They moved on. "Charlie and I repainted the shopwindow. I updated all the displays, as you see. I have also been offering free samples of ready-made items. And . . ."

When she hesitated, he prompted, "And?"

"And I prayed. A great deal."

Lilly and Mary sat on a bench in front of the coffeehouse, half-heartedly watching a group of young men play a scrappy game of football on the village green, Francis among them.

Enjoying the fading afternoon sun, as well as the cheers and shouts of male camaraderie, Lilly and Mary discussed their plans for the coming Sunday.

Across the green, the door to the Hare and Hounds opened and a beefy young man wobbled out.

"There's Nick Clark," Lilly said quietly. "Still won't speak to me."

"No wonder," Mary said, giving a little snort. "He's not likely to forget how you laid him flat before the entire cricket team."

"It was only that once."

"Twice."

"Well, he should have learned the first time."

Lilly had first slugged the loud-mouthed lad for saying Mary's fits meant she was a witch. The second time occurred when they were girls of fifteen, and Nick Clark had said Lilly's mother was a doxy who had run off with the gypsies.

A few minutes after Nick Clark had gone, Roderick Marlow stepped out of the Hare and Hounds. Lilly knew villagers were shaking their heads, agreeing that the baronet's son had been spending too much time in that establishment since his father's marriage.

Lilly was relieved to see him walk quite steadily across the green, adroitly skirting a near collision with ball and player.

"Hello, Mr. Marlow!" Mary called before Lilly could silence her with an elbow in her side.

He crossed the High Street and bowed before them. "Miss Haswell. Miss . . ."

"Mimpurse."

"Of course. How fares your mother?"

"She is well, sir. I thank you," Mary said.

"Gentler on you than she was on me, I hope."

Mary bit back a grin. "I am sure my mother meted out whatever each of us deserved, sir."

"Ah, Miss Mimpurse, you wound me," he teased. "You are your mother's daughter."

Mary smiled, then turned to Lilly. "Perhaps Mr. Marlow would like to go along with us?"

Lilly gave a start. "Oh. . . . um. Well . . . yes," she faltered. "That is an . . . excellent . . . idea, Mary."

He raised his brows in mild expectation.

"We are to have a picnic, Mr. Marlow," Mary supplied, elbowing Lilly.

Lilly hastened to say, "I doubt it will be of a fashion you are used to, but you would be most welcome to join us." She stopped, but he still looked at her expectantly. "So . . . ?"

"When is it to be?" he asked.

"Oh." How foolish of her to leave out that detail. "Sunday afternoon. We are to climb Walker's Hill."

Mary added warmly, "And Mr. Shuttleworth is to bring his telescope, so we may determine if one can truly see the spire of the Salisbury Cathedral from there."

"And Mary is bringing along her famous cakes and sweets," Lilly said.

"Plenty for another," Mary assured him.

Mr. Marlow addressed Mary, "If I were sure Miss Haswell wished me to attend . . ."

They both turned toward her. Lilly swallowed. "Well, I . . . of course would be pleased. After all, you showed such kindness in inviting me to join your guests not long ago."

"True. And so I shall return the favor and accept, though clearly not your original intention nor, I daresay, preference."

"Well, I—"

"In fact, I shall bring a hamper," he interrupted. "I am sure it has been far too long since Mrs. Tobias has had the pleasure of preparing a proper picnic. What shall it be? Cold chicken? Roast of beef? Lobster salad?"

"All of the above!" Mary clapped her hands like a delighted child.

Mr. Marlow laughed. "All of the above, it is. How many shall I ask her to prepare for?"

Lilly answered, "We will be a party of seven or eight, I suppose. Mr. Shuttleworth, of course. And Francis Baylor."

"And Dr. Graves, I presume?" he added in exaggerated nonchalance.

She paused. Why did she feel awkward at his mention of Adam Graves? She lifted her chin. "If he is free." Lilly hurried to add, "And you are welcome to bring someone along if you like."

Charlie suddenly appeared in the open coffeehouse window behind them. "Bring Miss Powell, do. She is ever so nice to look at."

"Charlie," Lilly gently scolded. She had not even realized he was near. "She is Lady Marlow now, remember."

Marlow's jaw worked a few seconds and she feared Charlie had angered him. "Perhaps I shall," he said pleasantly enough. "I shall also bring round the landau—and the gill for the hampers and lads. Just name the time."

They settled the arrangements, and when he had left them, Mary snorted back a giggle.

"Mary Helen Mimpurse!" Lilly reprimanded.

Mary burst into laughter.

Lilly shook her head, biting back a grin of her own. "You are too bad."

A few minutes later, as Lilly knew he would, Mr. Shuttleworth came along after closing up the surgery for the day. Francis had the afternoon off, but he left the game and jogged over to join them as well, clad in grass-stained trousers and shirt-sleeves.

"We've invited Mr. Marlow to join us on Sunday," Mary announced.

"Roderick Marlow?" Francis was incredulous. He was still breathing hard from the game, and his damp white shirt outlined a well-formed chest.

"Take heart," Lilly said. "He may bring the new Lady Marlow you are always gaping at."

At the sound of her name, Charlie bounded outside. "I hope so."

Ankles crossed, Mr. Shuttleworth leaned on his walking stick and looked over at Francis. "Graves, and now Marlow as well. I cannot say I like our odds, Mr. Baylor."

"Nor I," Francis said. "What say you we invite another lady to improve our ratio? Miss Robbins would no doubt appreciate a little variety of society."

"Excellent idea, my boy," Mr. Shuttleworth agreed.

Francis gave Lilly a meaningful look. "And an invitation from Miss Haswell would no doubt come as quite an unexpected pleasure. Unless—is there some reason you would prefer she not come?"

Lilly felt trapped. Indignant. "What reason could I possibly have? Of course she may join us." Francis knew Lilly was now being courted by Dr. Graves. Why should she be surprised he had returned his attentions to Miss Robbins?

Francis nodded his approval, then clapped Charlie on the back. "Come on, Charlie. Come and join the lads."

"Aww. 'Em lads don't let me play," Charlie said.

"They do now."

Francis crooked his arm around Charlie's shoulder and led him to the green.

Lilly watched them go with a warmed heart, ready to forgive Francis his irritating habit of foisting unwanted creatures on her. *Ah well* . . . she could understand why Francis admired Miss Robbins. She was undeniably a lovely, accomplished girl.

"My, our little party is growing by the minute," Mary said, rising from the bench. "I had better bake another cake."

34

If thy heart fails thee, climb not at all.

—Queen Elizabeth I

On Sunday morning, Lilly greeted the vicar outside the church doors after the service.

"Good morning, Mr. Baisley."

"Miss Haswell. How fares your father?"

"A little better, I thank you."

Mr. Baisley nodded and cleared his throat. "You no doubt noticed my blunder this morning." He leaned closer. "I believe it startled you awake."

Lilly felt her neck grow warm. "Forgive me. It was only a slight misquotation. I happen to have learned that Scripture as a girl."

He shook his head in wonder. "What it must be like to remember everything you have ever seen or heard or read . . ."

Lilly fidgeted. "Not everything, really. Only what I truly attend to."

"If I had such a gift, what I would store away." He thumped a broad finger against his temple. "Scripture, hymns, my wife's birthday . . ."

She acknowledged his joke with a polite smile.

He studied her closely. "And what do you store away in that pretty head of yours, Miss Haswell?"

She shrugged dismissively, her discomfort increasing. "Whatever comes my way, I suppose."

A perplexed frown flickered across the kind man's features. "But whatever you take in or, as you say, attend to, it stays with you forever?"

"It seems so."

He shook his head solemnly. "Then, my dear, I hope you will be most careful what you allow in."

Lilly swallowed and attempted another smile, one she feared was quite stiff. *Well*, she bolstered herself, *what is church without a dose of conviction?*

At the appointed hour, Lilly, Mary, Charlie, and Francis were waiting before the coffeehouse when Miss Robbins arrived from neighboring Honeystreet in a lovely white-and-pink gown, French bonnet of tulle, and a parasol. Lilly bit her lip. That parasol would not withstand a half minute atop the wind-whipped pitch. She and Mary had settled for simple bonnets tied securely under their chins and long-sleeved spencers—for even on a summer day, the windy hills of Wiltshire could prove chilly.

The ladies exchanged polite greetings, and Lilly warmed to Miss Robbins when she saw how nervous the girl was.

A man on horseback rode up, and Lilly was surprised to recognize Mr. Marlow. Had he not said he would bring a carriage? It would be a long walk. And what of Mary's hamper?

Beside her, Miss Robbins sucked in her breath and squeaked, "Mr. Marlow!" She turned to Lilly, face stricken, and whispered tersely, "No one told me he was coming."

Was everyone afraid of this man?

Marlow dismounted. Seeing the girl, he hesitated, clearly surprised. "Miss Robbins?"

"I . . . I did not know you were coming," she said defensively.

"Nor I you." He paused, then seemed to recover. "But that doesn't mean it cannot be a pleasant surprise, does it?"

Her mouth hung loosely. "Oh. No . . ."

Francis stepped beside Miss Robbins and assumed a protective, proprietary posture, shoulders back, hands fisted at his sides. For a moment, Marlow regarded the younger man with cynical amusement, then turned at the sound of a carriage approaching.

Lilly heard Francis whisper to the girl, "Do not be uneasy. You shan't be alone."

Her attention was pulled away as a landau, driven by Marlow's coachman and with a footman in the rear, pulled up and halted in the street. The young footman hopped down and jogged over to open the door and lower the step.

But Lilly's eyes were fastened on the landau's sole occupant.

Beside her, Charlie breathed, "Miss Powell . . ." And from the corner of her eye, she glimpsed Francis elbowing him lightly in the ribs.

Lady Marlow was like a print from a ladies' magazine in a promenade dress with ribboned sleeves and a long green vest laced across her ample bosom. A hat of satin straw trimmed with feathers sat at a smart angle upon her head, showing a wealth of red ringlets at one temple.

Francis leaned close and whispered in Lilly's ear. "Now who is gaping?"

Mr. Shuttleworth drove up in his curricle, Dr. Graves beside him. At their arrival, Mr. Marlow made the introductions with practiced ease, as though he had socialized with them all many times before. "Well, now that we are all acquainted . . ."

As if on cue, Cecil Briggs drove up in the low four-wheel gill, hampers stacked in back.

"If the gentlemen would be so kind as to ride in the gill," Marlow said with a sweep of his arm, "the ladies may enjoy the comfort of fine springs and leather seats."

Francis and Charlie climbed in the back of the low wagon, but Mr. Shuttleworth said he and Dr. Graves would take his curricle.

Marlow nodded, then offered his hand to Lilly. "Miss Haswell."

Self-conscious at being singled out first, Lilly stole a sideways glance at the other two ladies. Mary looked as though she'd just sold a Rich Bride Cake—Miss Robbins as though she had a goosegog stuck in her throat.

As he helped her up into the landau, Marlow said quietly to Lilly, "What a diverting outing this is proving to be."

They quickly left the village behind, passing nearby Alton as well. The wild roses were all gone from the hedgerows, Lilly noticed, and the elderberry blossoms had given way to clusters of ripening fruit, which they would pick come October.

A few miles to the north, the carriages halted along the roadside at the foot of Walker's Hill. Mr. Marlow rode back to speak to his servants while the other men alighted. Dr. Graves offered Lilly his hand. Francis, she noticed, hurried over to help Miss Robbins down. She did not miss his reassuring smile nor the lingering press of hands.

Marlow directed the coachman to stay with his horse, the landau, and Mr. Shuttleworth's curricle. Cecil Briggs and the young footman would drive the wagon up the hill as far as they could, then haul the hampers and picnic blankets to the top from there.

While Mr. Shuttleworth transferred his telescope to the gill, the others stood clustered about, staring up at the summit.

"'At's a gurt big hill," Charlie breathed.

Lilly shielded her eyes with a gloved hand. "A fair pitch indeed."

Miss Robbins eyed the wagon with longing.

"You may ride up if you like, Miss Robbins," Lilly offered kindly.

"All of you mean to walk?" she asked timidly, her parasol already wavering in the breeze.

Lilly nodded. "I believe so."

"Walk?" Francis said as though scandalized. He turned to Mr. Marlow. "What say you, Marlow. Shall we peg it? Have a friendly race?"

"Race?" Marlow's lip curled distastefully.

"What—afraid you'll muss your cravat?"

Lilly winced. *Careful, Francis.*

But Marlow retaliated only with words. "No, afraid you will foul the air."

Francis said easily, "I do not plan on perspiring. Do you?"

Mr. Marlow held his gaze and loosened his cravat.

Francis turned to his employer. "What about you, Mr. Shuttleworth. Are you in?"

"Good heavens." He rubbed his palms together. "Sitting about the surgery all day as I do, I haven't a chance. But why not? I shall be a buck about it." He smiled shamelessly at Mary. "Am I not a jolly buck, Miss Mary?"

She smiled indulgently. "Indeed you are, Mr. Shuttleworth."

He took off his fine coat, folded it, and laid it neatly atop the hamper. Cecil Briggs clicked the horse into action and the gill pulled away. Miss Robbins watched it go with regret.

"If I am very lucky," Mr. Shuttleworth said, "I shall swoon at the top and have four lovely ladies falling to their knees beside me, waving their fans over me and I know not what."

"What a schemer you are, Mr. Shuttleworth," Mary teased.

Stuffing his cravat into his pocket, Marlow challenged, "What about you, Graves?"

Dr. Graves shook his head. "You may count me out. I shall escort the ladies."

"I for one look forward to the climb," Lady Marlow said. "I believe exercise is beneficial for the female figure. Do you not agree, Dr. Graves?"

Dr. Graves cleared his throat.

Lady Marlow surveyed the hill once more. "Pity my husband could not join us. Sir Henry is meeting with his solicitor today, or I know he would have enjoyed this."

Lilly would not have guessed Sir Henry equal to the climb. His health must be greatly improved. Evidently marriage suited him.

Lionel Shuttleworth rolled up his sleeves. "Come on, Graves, don't be a fribble. Give me someone to beat at least."

"I shall walk up and so you shall handily beat me," Graves said.

"Indeed I shall," Shuttleworth agreed with boyish earnestness.

"And I as well, Dr. Graves," Charlie said, adopting an awkward runner's crouch. "I own I'm hudgy, but even I can beat a fellow on a wander."

Lilly bit her lip. She hoped her brother was right.

Mr. Shuttleworth urged, "Start us off, Miss Mary."

"Very well. Ready?" She held up her handkerchief, then sliced the air with a flourish. "Let the race begin!"

The men scrambled forward, Marlow nearly losing his footing on the loose rock at the bottom of the hill. Francis shot forward into an early lead. Shuttleworth ran with an upright, rooster-like stance that threatened to topple him as the pitch steepened. Marlow's long loping strides quickly overtook him. Charlie ran behind, arms windmilling, gait awkward.

"Careful, Charlie!" Lilly called after him. "Mind you don't fall and wrick your ankle!"

The three other women accompanied by Dr. Graves began a leisurely pace up the circuitous path, which climbed the hill more gradually.

Watching them stroll languidly away, Lilly thought, *Fiddle!* She hiked up her hems and ran straight up after the men. She caught up with Charlie easily and had nearly reached Mr. Shuttleworth when she heard Charlie stumble and let out an "Oomph" behind her. She stopped and helped him up, keeping a hold of his hand, thinking to jog the rest of the way side by side. But Charlie pulled away and started off once more, on his own. It stung Lilly, though she knew it should not have.

Reaching the summit first, Francis called down, "Come on, you lollopers!"

"Go, Charlie, go!" Mary shouted her encouragement from the path below.

At that, her brother gave a great burst of speed and reached the top well before her. When she did reach the ridge of flat rocks between her and the summit, Francis reached out his hand to her. Their eyes met. She wondered what he had been thinking to challenge Roderick Marlow. She wondered, too, at the strange mixture of triumph and irritation and something else in his eyes now. Still, she took his offered hand and allowed him to help her safely up and over. Charlie was dancing an ungainly victory jig. Marlow and Shuttleworth were twin bookends, panting figures with hands on knees. She walked slowly over to join them, struggling to catch her own breath. It had been too long since she had run or climbed. Her heart pounded, her lungs burned, her side ached. She felt . . . wonderful.

35

Tears are often the telescope by which men see far into heaven.

—Henry Ward Beecher

Lilly and Mary directed the arrangement of blankets and provisions atop Walker's Hill.

"Join us, Mr. Briggs?" Mary asked the groom who helped carry the hampers.

"I thank you no, mum." Cecil Briggs jerked his thumb toward the waiting horses. "My place is with the gristle and rub."

"And mine is in the kitchen," Mary said matter-of-factly, and Lilly felt a pang at her friend's humble self-regard.

"Go on now, miss," Cecil urged. "Enjoy yourself."

Mary's eyes twinkled. "You would not refuse a leg of roast chicken and an apple crowdy, would you?"

He smiled and self-consciously tugged on the brim of his hat. "That I would not."

Mrs. Tobias, the Marlows' cook, had outdone herself. There was enough food for thirty, Lilly guessed. A joint of cold roast beef, four roast chickens, two ham and veal pies, two pigeon pies, and stewed fruit in glass bottles, as well as a basket of fresh fruit, lettuces, cucumbers, and the promised lobster salad. There were also cheeses, bread, butter and jam, three pots of tea, and another hamper filled with bottles of ginger-beer, ale, lemonade, and claret, which Roderick Marlow helped himself to early and often. In her hamper, Mary had brought a large plum pudding, lardy cakes, apple crowdies, jam puffs, and a tin of mixed biscuits.

After they had eaten their fill, the ladies sat primly on the wide blankets while the men lounged at their leisure with legs outstretched.

Francis groaned with satisfaction. "I do not think I can move."

"A fine meal, Miss Mary, Marlow," Mr. Shuttleworth acknowledged, patting the buttons of his snug waistcoat.

"Yes," Lilly added. "Do thank Mrs. Tobias for us."

Marlow nodded and lifted his glass.

Mr. Shuttleworth set up his long telescope, mounted on a tripod of poles, on the ridge facing south.

Mary leaned down, her cheek bunched up as she closed one eye to look with the other through its lens. Mr. Shuttleworth hovered close, a hand lightly on Mary's shoulder to position her just so for the best viewing, clearly enjoying his role as scientific explorer—as well as the excuse to stand so near the ladies.

"There it is!" Mary exclaimed, "At least I think it must be the Salisbury Cathedral, although I have never seen it before."

"I have. Allow me." Marlow bent at the waist and peered through the lens. "Indeed. The spire of Salisbury Cathedral. It is above twenty miles from here. I would not have believed it."

As Mr. Shuttleworth and Mary stood near one another, Lilly noticed his gaze resting upon Mary's profile. He frowned slightly and peered closer yet. "I have never noticed that before."

"What?" Mary asked self-consciously.

"That little scar along your jaw. A burn, was it?"

Lilly saw her friend nod, before looking away disconcerted. Lilly felt embarrassed on Mary's behalf. She was not certain of the burn's origin but could well guess.

"Forgive me, I did not mean to give offense," he said. "Why, it is barely noticeable. It is only my being a surgeon, you see."

"That's all right. It was a long time ago." Mary stepped away. "Who is next?"

They all took turns looking through the telescope—Lady Marlow, Miss Robbins, Charlie, Francis. Lilly hung back, watching the surprise and delight on each face. Charlie likely had no real idea what he was seeing, but he seemed as caught up in the moment as everyone else.

Dr. Graves paused before taking his place at the scope. "Miss Haswell? Will you not have a turn?"

"You go on. I do not mind waiting. I am enjoying seeing it through everyone else's eyes."

Finally it was Lilly's turn. She stepped close and leaned in. She was small enough not to have to lean down very far. "I don't—no . . ."

"Here." Mr. Shuttleworth stepped in very close, nearly cheek to cheek with her, as she tilted her head away so he might take a look. "Must have been jostled. Now, try again." She felt his hand touch her shoulder, much as he had Mary's, but did not mind. There was something likeable and comfortable about Mr. Shuttleworth. And there it was. Britain's tallest spire. Could it really be twenty miles away? She remembered a few years gone, standing on Grey's Hill, wanting to come here, to see this sight, wishing she could actually travel there—travel anywhere. Now she had. She had traveled far more than twenty miles. Had lived in magnificent London. What joys she had imagined in the great *out there*. Had she found them?

She looked up and realized she was alone with Mr. Shuttleworth. Chagrined, she said, "I did not mean to monopolize it. Here. Have a go."

"If you will stay and keep me company."

"As you like."

The others had wandered back to the picnic blankets. Cecil Briggs and the footman had carried the food hampers away, but the beverage hamper and Mary's sweets hamper remained. Shoulder to shoulder at the scope, she and Mr. Shuttleworth turned their heads to regard the rest of the group.

Mary was handing Charlie the biscuit tin, and Mr. Marlow was opening another bottle of claret. Dr. Graves and Francis sat near one another, forearms resting on raised knees. Though both men stared out at the horizon, they were deep in conversation, the light of the westerly afternoon sun turning their faces golden and causing them to squint as they spoke. Miss Robbins and Lady Marlow sat together on the opposite end of the blanket, talking and laughing like old friends. How very unexpected. What a strange party they were.

Quietly, Mr. Shuttleworth said, "We stand apart, do we not?"

She turned to look at him, to search his countenance for the meaning of his odd statement. But he turned as well, so that they faced one another, noses too close together. He did have a prominent nose. She backed up a step, leaving him at the telescope. "What do you mean?"

"We are here but not here," he said softly. He turned away from her to stare out to the west, past Milk Hill to the ridgeline diminishing into the distance, the narrow canal cutting through the vale, and the horizon beyond. He looked without aid of telescope, his hand resting on its surface, chin resting on his hand.

She spoke as quietly as he had, "What do you see?"

He stared without speaking, then took a slow, deep breath. "Tomorrow. The next day. Next year."

She studied him for several moments, then asked gently, "Are you leaving us, Mr. Shuttleworth?"

He inhaled again, seeming to return to himself. "Why would I? I have my work here. I have settled here. I like life in Bedsley Priors. It is what I wanted."

Still he looked off into the distance, and she felt she understood him.

She understood that he spoke to convince himself as well as her. She understood he spoke a truth beyond his grasp.

Adam Graves felt restless at the sight of Miss Haswell and Mr. Shuttleworth in such intimate conversation. He believed the man harmless but still resented him for monopolizing Miss Haswell. He would not be so obtuse as to join them, but nor could he sit there any longer, no matter how decent a chap Baylor seemed. He rose to stretch his legs and for respite from the incessant chatter of Lady Marlow and Miss Robbins, two lovely but vociferous creatures.

As he walked away from the group, a voice called after him. "Graves."

He looked back and saw Roderick Marlow rise a bit unsteadily to amble after him. Reaching and then passing him, Marlow climbed the steep incline to the ancient burial mound atop Walker's Hill.

He called down, "Do you know what this mound is called?" The man did not wait for a response. "Adam's Grave. Did you know it?"

"I have heard that, yes."

"Climb up with me, ol' boy."

Adam was instantly wary. "Why?"

"I want to show you something."

Adam frowned but climbed up anyway, his boots slipping on the grassy slope.

Atop the mound, Roderick Marlow flopped a heavy arm across his shoulders and laughed. "Adam Graves atop Adam's Grave. Is that not ironic? Mind you don't fall." Marlow crooked his arm around Adam's neck, an embrace bordering on a headlock. "What does Miss Haswell see in you, I wonder?" He leaned in close, nearly nose to nose with him. "You are a pretty quiz, I own."

How much claret has the man had? Adam wondered.

"You are devoted to her, are you not?" Marlow asked.

Adam pulled away, disgusted. "And you are devoted to claret."

"I am. It is my own prescription. Purely medicinal, I assure you." Marlow again peered at him. "Do you *love* Miss Haswell?"

The cheek! "That is none of your affair." He was affronted as well as perplexed. Was Marlow implying feelings toward Miss Haswell? When every patient gossiped about how the man pined for the former Miss Powell? Still, Marlow's question rang in his mind. Did he love her? He believed so. Did he not hope to marry her once he had established himself?

Adam glimpsed Lady Marlow approaching the foot of the mound. She called up to them coyly, "What are you two discussing, pray?"

"Not you, Cassandra," Marlow snapped. "Of that I can assure you."

Adam stepped nearer. "Might I offer you a hand up, Lady Marlow?"

"Thank you. At least there is one gentleman among us."

Adam gently pulled her atop the mound. The wind, even stronger at this height, threatened to loose her hat. Tendrils of red hair escaped from under it, blowing across her cheek. She was beautiful, indeed. No wonder Marlow was perturbed. He felt that man's glare upon him and turned.

Marlow looked from the lady to him. "Careful, Graves. That woman can knock the life out of you faster than any fall from Adam's Grave."

"Pay him no mind, Doctor," Lady Marlow said with a casual smile. "Mr. Marlow enjoys playing the heartbroken lover. But if you were to examine him, you would find he hasn't a heart to break."

"If I did," Roderick Marlow said, eyes hard, "you can be certain nothing you could say or do would touch it."

She seared him with a look that belied her sweet tone. "Indeed? I shall remember that, Roderick. I suggest you do so as well."

36

> AGAINST YE FALLING SICKNESS
> Take purple foxgloves and polipodium of the oak. Boil them in bear or ale and drinke ye decoction. One that fell with [this disease] 2 or 3 times in a month, had not a fitt for 16 months after.
>
> —17th century recipe, *Mystery and Art of the Apothecary*

At church a week later, Lilly sat with Mary and Mrs. Mimpurse. As usual, Lilly's father had not felt well enough to attend and Charlie was nowhere to be found, no doubt off on one of his wanders. Even had the male members of her family seen fit to join her, she thought the Mimpurse ladies might appreciate her company on this, the seventh anniversary of the death of Harold Mimpurse.

Mr. Shuttleworth, Lilly noticed, was seated on the other side of the church and often glanced their way. *Mary's way*, she corrected herself and secretly smiled.

As Mr. Baisley was winding down his sermon, Lilly noticed something unusual. Mary's posture, as she sat beside her, was erect yet unnaturally rigid. Even as those around her flipped pages to follow along in the Book of Common Prayer, Mary's book remained perfectly still in her hands. She stared ahead, pale blue eyes unblinking.

Lilly reached over and gently squeezed her wrist. No blink, no response. She squeezed again, harder. Nothing. Around them, people flipped pages to find the final hymn, cleared throats, and upon the vicar's signal, began to sing. Still Mary stared, unmoving. Lilly shuddered. How eerie those unseeing eyes were. As if someone had put out the candle behind them. She reached over Mary's lap to tap Mrs. Mimpurse, who was singing robustly. Mrs. Mimpurse glanced over and instantly became alert. She set aside her own book and gently removed the book from her daughter's stiff fingers. She sent Lilly a pleading look, and Lilly believed she understood it.

The song over, the benediction given, the congregants rose and began to follow the vicar down the aisle. She glimpsed Francis walking out with the Robbins family and Dr. Graves offering his arm to old Mrs. Kilgrove. Only Mr. Shuttleworth showed no sign of leaving, remaining no doubt to greet them. But Lilly knew Mary would not want him to see her in such a state.

She heard a long exhalation and felt Mary go limp beside her. Using her body, Lilly gently pushed Mary toward her mother, and Maude put her arm around her daughter and pressed her cheek close to hers as though deep in whispered conversation. Lilly rose and stepped across the aisle to distract Mr. Shuttleworth.

"Is Miss Mary all right?" he asked with concern.

"She will be. It is the anniversary of her father's death. I think they are both rather melancholy at present."

"I had no idea. I am sorry to hear it. Shall I—?"

"I think we ought to leave them for now."

"Very well. I am sure you know best."

Charlie burst through the doors at that moment, the door slamming against the rear pew like cannon shot.

"Sorry I'm late," he said.

Lilly noticed mud on his face and straw in his hair. "Church is over, Charlie. Perhaps you could show Mr. Shuttleworth where Mr. Mimpurse lies?"

Her brother didn't seem to find this request at all strange, and if Mr. Shuttleworth did, he was too polite to say so.

When they departed, Lilly hurried back to Mary and Mrs. Mimpurse.

She was relieved to see her friend had returned to her senses. "Are you all right?" Lilly whispered.

"I think so. Just tired," Mary said wanly.

Tears glimmered in her mother's eyes. "Oh, my dear girl."

Together they helped Mary to her feet and out into the churchyard.

"I'll be all right, Mamma," Mary said. "Am I not always?"

Lilly spent an hour with Mary in her bedchamber that afternoon. Mary leaned back against the headboard, hugging a pillow to her chest, while Lilly sat in a chair near the window, reading to her from Byron. Finally Lilly could stifle her curiosity no longer. She lowered the book and regarded Mary until her friend's eyes rose to meet hers.

"What is it like?" Lilly asked gently.

"Hmm?"

"You know, when it happens?"

Mary fidgeted atop the bedclothes. "You have seen it yourself."

"I know what it looks like, but what does it *feel* like?"

Mary exhaled sharply. "Oh, I don't know." She looked down at her hands.

"Come on. I want to know."

Mary said brusquely, "Thank the Lord you don't." She rose and went to stare out the other window, posture rigid.

Taking in her friend's grim countenance, Lilly said, "I am sorry."

Mary stood there silently for so long, Lilly wished she had not asked.

On Tuesday Lilly watched as Mary swiftly chopped several carrots at once. The carrots lay side by side, like logs in a raft, and were each as big around as a man's finger, yet Mary cut them as easily as if they were fingers of dough.

"If I could cut pills that swiftly, my father would be rich indeed."

Mary barely seemed to look at the vegetables as she made quick work of reducing the roots into even chunks for stewing. And then her hands stilled. "You asked what it was like."

Lilly had already determined not to raise the topic again and was surprised when Mary did. "I said I was sorry."

"Don't be. Only . . . I don't much like to talk about it." Mary paused, her eyes far away. "I feel as if to even speak the words might bring on . . . well, you know."

Lilly nodded.

Mary returned to her work, chopping in silence for several minutes until Lilly was sure she had said her final word on the subject.

"It is not always the same," Mary began abruptly. "At times, like on Sunday, I just . . . go away. I sit there, eyes open, but I am not there. I feel no pain, no sensation. It is as if I am watching myself from a short distance away. Then everything goes white. When I return to myself, I am left feeling weak and tired." Mary scooped up the chopped carrots and dropped them into a pot.

Tentatively, Lilly asked, "Do you never cut yourself?"

Her friend shrugged. "Rarely. I usually have a bit of warning."

Mary then moved on to a bunch of leeks. "Other times, like when Mr. Shuttleworth was here that day . . . my head begins to ache and my fingers to tremble—or they might go numb. Either way, I usually have time to call Mamma or get to my bed—so I don't fall and injure myself."

Mary leaned her elbows on the worktable. "But then, when that sort overtakes me, I feel as though I might be sick—hot, then cold. Then everything starts clamping up, shutting down, and I find it difficult to breathe." Mary straightened and continued with her chopping. "Then my vision goes black and I wake up a quarter of an hour later to find Mamma or your father looking down at me."

"How dreadful," Lilly murmured, but she could not stop staring at the long, sharp knife so close to her friend's pale fingers. She said quietly, "I pray for you, Mary."

Mary winced. "For what?"

Lilly was taken aback. "Well, for you to be healthy—healed, of course."

Mary shrugged. "You heard Dr. Graves. There is no cure. And Wiltshire has already had its miracle." A grin flickered across her face. "We needn't be greedy."

She chopped the leeks, then looked across at Lilly earnestly. "If you pray for me, pray that I would bear this cross cheerfully. That I would be a blessing to my mother and . . . everyone."

"You already are."

Mary acknowledged this with a nod. "I overheard Dr. Foster once tell Mamma she ought to send me to an asylum. *Once*. He has not been welcome here since."

"Your mother was right," Lilly said hotly. "You do not belong in an asylum—you belong here, with those who love you."

"I know, but . . ." Mary set down the knife and wiped her hands on a towel. "There are times I think it would help to talk with someone who knows how it is. Is my experience the same as theirs, or different? Am I really as strange as I feel?"

Realizing she needed to return to the shop, Lilly rose from her stool. "I can answer that myself." She said mischievously, "You are strange indeed, Mary Helen Mimpurse."

Mary grinned and swiped at her skirts with the towel.

37

> We must trust to the Great Disposer of all events and the justice of our cause.
>
> —Admiral Horatio Nelson

Later that day, Lilly was busy in the laboratory-kitchen preparing a strong decoction of chamomile, which they sold as a hair rinse and, separately labeled, as a wash for ailing teeth and gums. She heard Charlie rattling around in the shop, playing with the cavy most likely.

"Charlie!" she called, opening the large pot on the stove to see if the water was boiling. "Remember to take Mrs. Kilgrove her tablets. They are on the front counter."

"All right, Lilly." A moment later Charlie called, "Cavy likes chamomile, does he not?"

"What?"

"The cavy. Likes chamomile?"

Replacing the pot lid, she called back, "Yes."

Just that morning, she had pressed a bottle of chamomile tablets for Mrs. Kilgrove—they soothed her stomach and helped her sleep. Most people made a tea of the herb for this purpose, but Mrs. Kilgrove could not abide the taste. "Smells like tobacco, tastes like fodder," she always complained. Lilly did not ask the old woman how she knew.

"Give him some?" Charlie called.

"Yes, all right. Only a few tablets. From the drawer."

Since she had used the last of the dried chamomile they had on hand, she and Charlie had harvested a batch of chamomile flowers from their garden early that morning. Her back still ached from the tedious chore.

Lilly checked the stove. She added more coals to the fire to keep the water steaming. Now she would allow the tiny blossoms to steep for half an hour.

Just in time to give over the stove to Mrs. Fowler to prepare their dinner. She was so relieved to have the dear woman back in service. She not only cooked but also took in the laundry and cleaned their living quarters.

While the blossoms steeped, Lilly spread the remaining flowers on stretched-linen screens. Then she carried the first of them up the three flights of stairs into the stifling hot herb garret, where the flowers could dry out of direct sunlight. Later, she would store the dried blossoms in tightly sealed jars.

As she came back down the stairs, she heard the shop bell ring. Wiping her hands on her apron, she stepped into the shop. Glancing around, she was surprised to find the place empty. That was not Charlie just leaving, was it? She had imagined him ten minutes gone. She checked her memory—no, she had not heard the shop bell ring earlier. What had the lad been doing since she'd asked him to take Mrs. Kilgrove her tablets? Surely it hadn't taken so long to feed a bit of herb to a caged cavy.

Though she had not wanted the animal, Lilly actually enjoyed tending and feeding it. She grimaced wryly. Now she had three males in her care. Thinking of this, she turned and walked out the garden door, striding to the plot of carrots. The cavy would need more than a few bites of chamomile for his supper.

Francis's head and shoulders appeared over the garden wall. Eyeing the dirt-encrusted root in her hand, he asked skeptically, "Hungry?"

"I am, actually, but this is for that rodent you foisted upon me."

"Aww. Warms my heart to see you taking such good care of him."

She rinsed the carrot in the water pail. "I must. It would not help business should I fail to nurture life in any form."

"I see. Still. If you really don't want it, I suppose I could always give it to Mrs. Kilgrove. She has a cat who is ever hungry."

"You would not dare."

She shook the carrot in his direction, the wet greens splattering him with water. He ducked behind the wall and she returned to the house, swinging the carrot, humming as she went.

Undaunted, Francis followed. "Mind if I pop in and greet your father?"

She held the kitchen door open behind her. "You don't fool me. I know you really only want to see the cavy."

She thought of Charlie again. She hoped he had not gotten sidetracked on his way to Mrs. Kilgrove's. The woman would want her chamomile before supper.

"I have been reading up on lung fever," Francis said. "I trust Dr. Graves has ordered nitrate of potash or spirit of nitre?"

"Mmm . . ." she murmured noncommittally, too distracted to be impressed.

Striding back into the shop, Lilly examined the dispensing counter. The small jar of tablets she'd labeled for Mrs. Kilgrove had been taken—all seemed just as it should be.

Francis paused in the threshold. "Is your father in his surgery?"

She pointed without looking up. "Bedchamber."

Her eye was drawn to a new bottle of silvered pills at the end of the counter. The late afternoon sun shone on the glass and glimmering metallic pills. Then she noticed it. The lid askew, a disparate yellow tablet among the silver.

Dear Lord, no . . .

She turned toward the cage on the back counter. Frowning, she stepped closer. Shock drove a cry from her lips, and her hand flew over her mouth.

The cavy was dead.

Lilly ran.

Pausing only long enough to shout for Francis and grasp a vial of emetic tartar, she dashed down the High Street as fast as she could.

"Charlie!" she cried as she ran. She crossed the Sands Road and followed the narrow dirt track leading to Mrs. Kilgrove's cottage. "Charlie!"

She had to catch him before he delivered those tablets . . . before the woman took them, at any rate. She recalled the labeled dosage: *two tablets with supper.* Two tablets. Two chances. How long had she stood there, speaking foolishness with Francis, while Charlie may have carried the wrong remedy to an unsuspecting woman? *Lord, please. Please. . . .*

Francis caught up with her as she reached Mrs. Kilgrove's gate. There was Charlie just outside the door. How was it he was just now arriving? Had he stopped to visit Mary on his way? Normally, she would scold him for such. Today she thanked God.

"Charlie. Wait. Don't—"

Charlie spun toward her, pale-faced. "Lilly! Somefing's wrong. Mrs. K. is pigged. I don't know what to do. I was coming to find you."

Panic seized her. "Did you give her the tablets?"

He nodded. "She were waiting for 'em like you said."

Oh, God. Oh no.

"What did she take?" Francis asked, still panting from the run.

Lilly pushed through the cottage door without answering or knocking. Mrs. Kilgrove was on the settee, holding her abdomen and groaning. Lilly hurried to her side, and in the woman's pained and confused eyes there was not one spark of recognition. Was she already experiencing delirium?

Lilly opened the vial of prepared emetic tartar and tried to press it to Mrs. Kilgrove's mouth. The old woman batted at her hands, nearly knocking the fragile vial from Lilly's grasp.

"Away!" she cried, waving her hands wildly. "Yellow smart—away!"

"Mrs. Kilgrove," Lilly said officiously, "there are no bees in here. It is Lilly Haswell. You need to drink this. Now. Do you understand?"

Francis knelt beside the woman and put his arms around her in a firm but careful hold. This done, Lilly succeeded in administering a generous dose of the vomit-inducing preparation.

Francis rose and disappeared into the kitchen.

"Charlie, run and fetch Dr. Graves," Lilly said. "Or Dr. Foster. Tell him Mrs. Kilgrove's taken digitalis not meant for her."

Francis, returning with a basin, nearly tripped at the words. He quickly laid the vessel on the floor. "I'll go," he said soberly. "I'm faster."

She nodded and laid Mrs. Kilgrove back on the settee, holding the groaning woman on her side at its edge, knowing she would be sick any moment. Lilly prayed desperately. She prayed Francis would find Dr. Graves. Or even Dr. Foster, though the old man could not run and would take far too long in hitching his gig. Only later did she consider that in coming he would have to know everything.

Several minutes later, Francis ran back in, followed by Dr. Graves, bag in hand. Both men were breathing heavily.

"I've already administered emetic tartar," Lilly said. "Though likely she would have been sick enough without it, poor creature."

"How did it happen?" Dr. Graves asked.

"I am still trying to work that out for myself."

An hour later, Lilly gazed mournfully down at Mrs. Kilgrove. The woman's lined face was grey, her body so lifeless on the bed where Dr. Graves and Francis had lain her. With remorseful tears in her eyes, Lilly slowly lifted the blanket over Mrs. Kilgrove's legs, her torso, then under her chin.

Lilly whispered, "How long will she sleep?"

"She is not sleeping, Miss Haswell," Dr. Graves said sternly. "She has lost consciousness."

Lilly nodded, tears spilling down her cheeks.

"Her heart rate seems to have slowed to a more normal rate, but it is irregular. We can only hope this restful state will aid her recovery."

"Will she recover?" Francis asked.

"I cannot say. She is very weak. It is too early to know if she suffered a fatal disturbance of the heart. I've administered the *de viper* antidote. Now we shall have to wait and see."

When they had removed themselves to the woman's sitting room, Lilly sat down on Mrs. Kilgrove's settee, wadding and twisting a handkerchief in her hands. Mrs. Kilgrove's cat to curl up on her lap, but Lilly firmly returned him to the floor, feeling unworthy to be comforted by his warmth. Francis sat in an armchair across from her, elbows on his knees, leaning near. Dr. Graves stood, his hand on the mantel, staring into the empty fireplace.

"I think I know what must have happened." Tears made her cheeks wet and her throat tight. "You know how Charlie is. He would have to count the yellow chamomile tablets. Then the new silvered pills must have caught his eye. We don't often do silver coatings, but Dr. Foster ordered them for Mrs. Robbins's dropsy. Charlie must have poured the pills out and counted those as well. He could not have resisted all those pretty silver pills. When I reminded him to take the tablets over, he must have quickly tried to slide the pills back into their correct bottles. In his haste, he must have mixed one or two digitalis pills in with Mrs. Kilgrove's chamomile. She must not have even noticed. Her eyesight isn't keen, you know. Poor creature! And Charlie—" She suddenly realized she had not seen her brother this hour gone. She looked around the room. "Where is Charlie?"

Francis said, "He was pegging it down the road as we ran in. Thought you must have sent him on some errand or other. And with . . . well . . . everything, I quite forgot."

New tears filled her eyes. Her facial muscles strained. "Poor Charlie! He never meant to harm anyone."

Dr. Graves's expression remained somber, but Francis said quickly, "Of course not. We all know how fond he is of Mrs. Kilgrove."

"Charlie must be frightened to death by all this. Francis, please find him. This will lay him very low, and I fear what he might do."

Francis reached over and laid his hand on hers. "You mustn't think the worst. I am sure he is in the churchyard, or one of his other haunts. I shall find him."

He gave her hand a squeeze, his eyes wide with compassion. Lilly noticed Dr. Graves frown at their clasped hands just as Francis let go and took his leave.

38

> DEATH BY A POISONOUS HERB
> Wm. Ross had or pretended to have considerable skill in the administration of herbs. His daughter had got a root of monk's-hood in a neighbouring garden. He mistook it for some other plant, and commenced chewing it . . .
>
> —*Devizes & Wiltshire Gazette,* 1833

True to his word, Francis found Charlie—hunkered down in the churchyard—and gently escorted him home. He had twigs in his hair and torn breeches but was otherwise unharmed.

For two days, Lilly, Francis, Dr. Graves, and even Mr. Shuttleworth took turns sitting with Mrs. Kilgrove, spooning distilled water and broth into her dry mouth, turning her to prevent bedsores, doing whatever they could. By unspoken agreement, none of them mentioned the incident to Dr. Foster, but Lilly guessed it was only a matter of time until everyone in Bedsley Priors and Honeystreet knew of it.

Late that second day, just as Lilly feared, a sharp knock sounded on the door. Rising from Mrs. Kilgrove's bedside, she walked slowly, dreading to answer it. When she opened the door to Dr. Foster, his lip curled and he brushed past her without comment. He took himself into Mrs. Kilgrove's bedchamber, felt the woman's pulse, laid his ear on her chest, and lifted her eyelids, testing for responsiveness. All the while, Lilly hovered in the threshold.

"So. It has finally happened," he said. "The Haswells have killed someone."

Lilly sucked in her breath. "We have killed no one, sir, and I'll thank you to lower your voice." She was fleetingly tempted to tell him it had been the pills *he'd* ordered that had done this to Mrs. Kilgrove, but she knew that was irrational. If only Dr. Graves had taken Foster's order to Shuttleworth's instead!

"Yes, she lives, but barely. And not for long, I'd wager."

"Is there nothing you can do? Or advise me to do?"

"I will do what I can, but I would not waste my breath on you, girl. You already fancy yourself too much the medical man."

"No, I have—" She hesitated. Wasn't he right? To know that she had injured, possibly even taken the life of another person was the worst feeling she had ever known. Worse even than losing her mother.

"Unprescribed digitalis. Past time that brother of yours was put away somewhere, if you ask me."

Hot indignation rose up in her, only to be quelled by an icy chill as his words registered. This man held the power to do that very thing.

When Adam Graves came to take his shift, he immediately noticed that Miss Haswell's expression was somber indeed. He could easily guess the reason. "Dr. Foster came?"

She nodded and sat heavily on the settee.

Remorse filled him. "He heard it somewhere and asked me directly. I could not lie."

"Of course not." She sighed deeply. "He all but accused us of purposefully harming Mrs. Kilgrove. Charlie would never intentionally hurt a soul. And she, always so sharp with everybody else, dotes on Charlie."

She shook her head, over and over again. Clearly the reality of what they were facing had begun to sink in. "He is so innocent, so childlike. If they were to arrest him, to take him to . . . prison, or an institution . . . I could not bear it. *He* could not bear it."

Tears cascaded down her cheeks, and he felt powerless to comfort her. He recalled how Francis Baylor had so naturally taken her hand. Why could he not do the same?

She pressed a handkerchief against the corner of one eye, then the other. "I must protect him. I love him more than my own life. Please, Dr. Graves. Please, help him."

Dread gripped him. "I will try, Miss Haswell, but what can I do? You must know Foster will report this to the constable."

"That man! Everyone knows Bill Ackers will do the bidding of whoever puts a pound in his pocket."

"But will he not bring the case to the local magistrates to make any official ruling of wrongdoing?"

"But it was a mistake! An accident!"

"Neither of which are allowed in this profession," he said, as gently as he could. "You must know that."

She hung her head. "Tell them it was my fault, then. Charlie was only acting under my authority."

He sighed. "Miss Haswell, I hate to be blunt, but you have no authority. Do you not realize what could happen if you are found guilty of poisoning someone?"

"Poisoning . . . ? What a nightmare this is! But . . . may she not yet live? Oh, God, that she might live. For all our sakes."

He paced behind the settee. "I do not know. She may yet pull through, but you should not rely on it."

She hid her face in her hands. Finally, he reached over and touched tentative fingers to her shoulder.

"I can bear the punishment, whatever it is," she said. "But Charlie must be spared."

Foolish girl! He strode around the settee to stand before her. "You don't know what you are saying. Women have been transported or imprisoned for less. And should your part reach the ears of the Worshipful Society of Apothecaries, they would be well within their rights to tear apart your father's shop, burn everything, and put him out of business for good. The Haswell's you have been trying to save could very well be ruined forever."

"But Charlie is more important than the shop. Father would not disagree."

He stared at her. "You have not told him?"

"Not yet. I fear what it will do to him."

He knelt before her to look into her eyes and gripped her hand. This was not the topic he had imagined discussing from this position. "Tell him, Lillian. You cannot bear this on your own. I will do all I can to help, but I fear it is not a great deal."

Lilly was sitting in a chair beside Mrs. Kilgrove's bed when the woman's eyes fluttered opened at last.

"Mrs. Kilgrove?" Lilly reached out and grasped her spidery hand. The old woman turned watery eyes in her direction.

"Rosamond?" she whispered hoarsely. "I knew you'd return." Her head lolled to the side, and Lilly had to rise and lean over the bed to hear her murmur, "You did the first time, after all."

Lilly's heart hammered. "What do you mean, Mrs. Kilgrove?"

But the old woman did not answer, merely squinted toward the bedside table. "Why do the candles wear blue halos?" Her eyes closed and she said no more.

Mrs. Kilgrove was seeing things, Lilly realized. Had even mistaken her for her mother. No doubt what she had said about Rosamond's return had been wild imaginings as well.

Despite the poor woman's hallucinations, a tentative, fluttering hope filled Lilly's breast. She tamped it down, lest it fly away at any moment. Fearing the old woman might yet take a turn for the worse, she waited and prayed. Her father came, brought by Charlie's racked confession. There was nothing he could do, but it was still a relief to hear him confirm everything that could be done for Mrs. Kilgrove had been done. Later, the vicar came to pass an hour with her at Francis's behest, offering words of comfort and prayer in his mellifluous voice.

That evening, Mrs. Kilgrove again opened her eyes. She turned to Lilly with a weak smile. "How nice to wake with someone beside me. Haven't known that comfort since my John died a day back agone."

"I am glad to be here," Lilly said. "Do you know me?"

Mrs. Kilgrove frowned. "Foolish girl," she whispered. "Have I not known you since an infant?"

"Yes, but you've been unconscious." She did not add *delirious*. "How do you feel now?"

"Queer. My head aches." She slowly moved her gaze across the room. "And everything seems rather . . . yellow."

"Mrs. Kilgrove, do you remember the pills you took—the ones I sent over?"

She squinted in attempted concentration. "I don't . . . to help me sleep?"

"Just so, and to calm your stomach. I am afraid there might have been one or two wrong pills in the lot. Do you remember taking any silver pills?"

She winced. "Lass, I am near eighty years old. I am happy to remember my name, much less the color of a pill I took . . . when was it?"

"Three nights gone."

"Three nights? Some pills . . ." Her eyes drifted closed once more.

The next morning when Mrs. Kilgrove awoke, Lilly and Charlie were both with her. Charlie sat in a bedside chair, the woman's cat on his lap. When he saw her eyes open, his voice shook. "I am dreadful sorry, Mrs. K." Tears filled his wide blue eyes.

Mrs. Kilgrove turned her head toward him and reached out a shaky hand. "No need. I don't blame you, Charlie. You may be small in the attic, but you have a big heart."

Charlie bit his pronounced lip and ducked his head.

"Mrs. Kilgrove, will you take some water?"

The woman turned sharp eyes in her direction. "Why—is there no tea?"

Biting back a smile, Lilly rose to prepare some. While she was at it, she set a pan of broth to warming on the stove, broth Mrs. Mimpurse had kindly sent over, firmly believing the invalid would regain consciousness as well as appetite. Lilly certainly hoped she was right.

Francis Baylor was on his way to visit Mrs. Kilgrove and, if he were honest with himself, to see Lilly, who stayed so loyally by the woman's side. He knew he was a fool. Graves, a good-looking, Oxford-educated physician, was courting her, was he not? Francis sighed. Still, he would do anything to help her.

From the corner of his eye, he glimpsed Dr. Foster disappearing into Ackers Stables and Smithy, the establishment of Bill Ackers, the county-appointed constable of the neighbor villages.

His stomach seized at the thought of what trouble Ackers could bring down on the Haswells, and he knew the man was more than capable of doing so with relish. Francis changed course and crossed the road, stepping surreptitiously near the open stable door.

"Will you fail in your duty, Ackers?" He heard Foster say, voice sharp. "There has been a crime, man. A devilish crime."

Francis blew out a puff of air. *Worse than I feared.*

"You'd like 'at, would'n ye?" Bill Ackers spoke in a voice passed down from generations of family members who'd never ventured beyond Wiltshire. "Haswell's dippin' in yer pockets, innum?"

"No. He is nothing to me."

"Now, long as the woman lives, there's been no murder, mind. And no one's gawpus enough to believe 'at young dummel meant to harm the old ghel."

"It is a fine thing when a body can poison an innocent person in your village, Ackers."

"Now, Foster. Let's not jarl. You know I'll be watchin'. And when summateruther happens, I'll see to it, I will."

"I am very glad to hear it."

There was a pause. Thinking the conversation at an end, Francis was about to move away when Dr. Foster spoke again.

"Perhaps, Mr. Ackers, we might discuss this further at the Hare and Hounds? I for one grow thirsty standing here."

"If yer buying, I'll go along," Bill Ackers said. "Always were a fair-minded man."

39

A robin red breast in a cage
Puts all heaven in a rage.
—William Blake,
Auguries of Innocence

As Charlie was finishing his breakfast of eggs and sausages the next morning, Lilly slipped briefly from the kitchen, then returned with arms full. "I have something for you, Charlie."

Still chewing, Charlie's gaze tracked her progress across the room. At her mother's old place at the table, Lilly set down a bandbox with bored-out air holes. Anticipation prickled within her as she watched her brother's face. Though his memory was poor, she thought she saw a glint of recognition in his blue eyes.

He swallowed his bite and said, "I had somefing very like it once."

"Indeed you did. I am pleased you remember."

A flick of white batted against one of the holes and disappeared.

Charlie's eyes grew wide. "Am I to have a puss?"

With effort, she kept her voice calm. "Open it and see."

Still he hesitated.

"Go on."

Charlie carefully removed the lid. A young cat, older than a kitten but not fully grown, lifted his grey head and put two white paws on the edge of the box. He sniffed the air, and when Charlie offered him his fingers, sniffed those too.

"Hallo, boy." Charlie looked up at her anxiously. "He is a boy, innum?"

"I am no expert on such, mmm, identification, but Mr. Fowler assures me this is indeed a male."

"Good. 'Twould be a queer fing to call a girl-cat Jolly."

Her heart warmed and ached at once. "Is that what you will call him?"

He nodded. "Does he look like the first Jolly, Lilly? I can't remember."

"Well, I do remember, and he looks a great deal like your old Jolly. I daresay this lad is his grandson or grandnephew."

"Oh, 'at's fine! Fine!"

But then Charlie's smile faded. He faltered, "But she said I weren't ever to have another."

"She . . ." Lilly hesitated, then said gently, "Mother is gone. But Father and I want you to have it."

"But what if he runs away again?"

Lilly answered thickly, "Then I shall help you find him. And you will love him and care for him better than anyone in Bedsley Priors. As I love you."

The cat put its muzzle close to Charlie's face, sniffing his cheek and mouth.

Lilly smiled through her tears. "He seems to like you a great deal already."

Charlie stroked the cat. "I fink he does. Or the milk I drank wi' breakfast."

"Look how gentle you are with him."

"Mrs. K. taught me."

A movement caught her eye, and Lilly looked up to see her father leaning against the doorjamb. Their gazes met for several ticks of the clock, and she saw that hers were not the only eyes filled with tears.

Three days later, just before closing time, Bill Ackers strode boldly into the shop. Lilly felt her heart jerk as wildly as from foxglove itself. Ackers was a big, broad man in his late twenties with arms strong from his smithy work and years of starting and breaking up fights. Broom in hand, Charlie froze, staring up at the man.

"Charlie Haswell, there thee bist. I've come for ye."

Charlie's mouth drooped open. "She died, did she, Mr. Ackers? Poor Mrs. K. gone to the churchyard?"

"Not yet, she ain't. No thanks to you and yers."

"Thank God," Lilly breathed.

"There's still wrongdoin' to be answered for, lad. That's why I'm come to take ye in."

"To the blind house, Mr. Ackers?" Charlie asked.

"Aye."

"Mr. Ackers," Lilly protested, panic rising. "If anyone is to blame, it is I."

"You poisoned Mrs. Kilgrove then?"

"No one *poisoned* Mrs. Kilgrove. That word conveys such vile intent, does it not? A mistake has been made, I own. She swallowed one small pill of the wrong sort. Not poison. Not for a healthy stout person. But for an eighty-year-old woman . . ."

"I have it on good authority that givin' a person the wrong medcine is a crime, Miss Haswell, no matter the old ghel's age. And seein' how it might yet lead to her death, can ye deny it?"

"No. Of course it is wrong. And I do not expect all consequences to be waived. But it is *my* fault, the shop is my responsibility."

"Is it now? Might yer father have sumat to say about that?"

"Father is recovering from an illness, Mr. Ackers. In his stead, I have temporarily assumed responsibility. It was I who filled the pill bottle and I who left the wrong pills in proximity to the first. Charlie was only the delivery boy."

"Yer telling me *you* put the wrong pill in 'er bottle?"

She swallowed. "Well. Not actually physically put it there, but in effect, by my negligence, yes."

"And who actually, physically, put it there?" A dark glint lit his eyes.

She changed tack. "Am I to be brought before the magistrates, Mr. Ackers?"

"Might come to that, aye. Need to hold 'im till the next quarter session in Devizes. Though in yer brother's case, I'm thinkin' the JPs might forgo county gaol or transportation."

"Oh?" Tentative relief sprouted within.

"I understand there are places for imbeciles like Charlie. Where he'd be kept safe and do no harm to others."

Relief quickly withered. "He is not an imbecile, and he does no harm to others now!"

"I've got a woman courtin' death who just might jarl with'ee. If she lives, that is." He smirked at his macabre joke.

Suspicion filled her. She narrowed her eyes at the man, her head tilted to one side. "How would you know about such institutions? Dr. Foster put you up to this, did he not?"

"I may have asked the man's advice. But I act on my own authority. Maybe I ought to take ye both in till we get this sorted out. Fisherton Anger has a women's prison too."

"No!" The vehemence of Charlie's shout startled her and the broom handle cracked to the floor. "Lilly did nofing wrong. Never has. It was me what done it, Mr. Ackers. Don't know how, but must have done. Leave Lilly be."

"That's to yer credit, Charlie. I daresay there might be a jobbet of man in'ee after all."

As Charlie stepped forward, Lilly took his arm. "Charlie, no."

"Lilly?" Her father appeared in the doorway, fatigue and concern in his eyes.

"He's taking Charlie!" Her voice rose. "To the blind house."

"It's all legal, Haswell," Ackers said. "I'll be holdin' 'im till a hearing is set."

Father slumped against the doorjamb. "Take me, then, Ackers. It is my shop, after all."

"Don't look to me like ye can barely stand, let alone stand trial. Weren't even in the shop the day it happened, now were ye?"

"I . . . don't know. When was it?"

Lilly answered quietly, "You were abed all day, Father."

"Seems every Haswell's in an awful hurry to bear the blame," Ackers said.

"Would ye rather I locked yer ghel in the blind house, Haswell? We've only the one drunkard presently—might not go too hard on her."

"Of course not, man."

"It's all right, Father," Charlie said. "I don't mind. Mind less if 'ere were windows."

"Then it wouldn't be a blind house, now would it?" The constable turned harsh eyes on Lilly. "Not an imbecile, innum?"

Her father launched himself from the threshold but stumbled and nearly fell, barely managing to take hold of the dispensing counter for support.

Lilly ran to help him, and Ackers took advantage of the diversion. He grasped Charlie's arm and led him from the shop without interference. He wasn't violent but did stride rapidly, pulling gangly Charlie along behind him like a floppy fish on a line.

Trying to hold her father upright, Lilly called, "Charlie!"

Her brother looked back over his shoulder. "Take care of Jolly. And tell Mary, so she don't fret where I've gone."

"I'll come as soon as I can!" But the door was already closed, shop bell jingling, and she knew he could not have heard her.

Her father slipped lower, and taking his arm, she helped him onto the surgery cot without injury. She knelt beside him, dread filling her anew at the sight of his grey face and trembling limbs. "Are you all right?"

He fell back against the pillow. "So detestably weak . . ."

Indeed he seemed worse than ever. And now Charlie imprisoned—what a double blow this was! Covering her father with the lap rug, she tried to keep the panic from her voice. "What will they do to him? Will he be whipped? Put in an institution? Transported?"

"I do not know. Which is the least of evils? Which should we pray for?"

She noted his rare mention of prayer, and knew he must feel as desperate as she.

"A miracle. We need another Wiltshire miracle."

Grief and fear overwhelmed her. Tears streaming down her face, Lilly bolted from the shop. Her first impulse was to run to the arms of Mrs. Mimpurse and Mary, but she knew they were visiting Maude's sister in Wilcot. She thought of running up Grey's Hill, but for once the thought of its wild loneliness didn't draw her. She felt too alone already.

As she dashed through the village, the quiet churchyard called to her. She paused at its gate, then turned and walked up the stone path to the old church. The door creaked in her hands as it opened to the dim, quiet interior. She entered slowly, her boot heels disturbing the silence and echoing against the limestone walls. There seemed no one about, and that suited her. It was not a mere human's presence she sought. She stepped through the nave and into the chapel.

She sat in the front pew, where Haswells had sat for a hundred years. Where her mother had once sat in her fine frocks and plumed hats, and her father in his dark blue Sunday coat, Charlie on his lap, little eyes staring at the stained glass, counting the individual panes, no doubt. How long ago it seemed since they had all sat there as a family. They would never do so again.

Lilly fell to her knees on the stone floor, driven there by losses of the past . . . and by probable losses of the near future.

Oh, Lord, please spare my brother and father. I have already lost my mother. I cannot bear to lose them as well. . . .

How long she stayed like that, on her knees, head bent and eyes closed, she could not say. Vaguely, she heard a door open, footsteps echo in the nave, and the clank of something metallic. But the sounds took several seconds to fully register. When she came to herself with a start, embarrassed to be found in such a humble position, she tried to quickly rise. Only to realize she could not.

"Lilly?" a surprised voice asked.

The chapel seemed completely dark at first, but as her eyes adjusted, she saw the faint glow of a lantern or candle somewhere nearby.

Her discoverer knelt before her. Francis.

"Lilly!" Concern sharpened his voice, though it was still hushed in that reverent place. "Here, let me help you up."

"I am afraid my legs have fallen asleep. I cannot feel them."

He took her hands to pull her up but hesitated, holding her fingers more tightly. "Your hands are chilled!" He released them to grasp her arms. "A little at a time, all right?" Gingerly, slowly, he helped her up onto the bench. As he did, she realized the clank she had heard must have been the sound of a lantern being set hastily on the floor. Its light flickered dimly down the aisle.

"Here now, let's get some life into those limbs." He rubbed her hands, first briskly, then kneading them more deeply.

"My knees—"

She'd only meant to comment on how strange they felt, numb yet prickling with pins and needles at the same time. But Francis took her words as plea and began working on her knees as well, massaging her estranged appendages. Though his touch was professional and her modesty secure beneath her sturdy kerseymere frock, still the act felt unquestionably intimate. His administrations at first intensified the pain, but gradually the pins faded and warmth spread through her.

He returned his attention to her hands. "Still cold."

She allowed him to caress and knead her hands, sudden tears pricking her eyes. How nice to feel cared for. An old memory unwound itself in her mind's eye—her father cupping her little face with both palms. *"Patient has no fever, but suffers a fatal case of good looks and freckles."*

"Here." Francis dropped her hands and leapt to his feet. She missed his touch immediately.

He hurried down the aisle, retrieved his lantern, and sat beside her again. "Warm your hands over this."

She eagerly complied.

While she did so, he said, "May I ask what brings you here tonight? Your father?"

She nodded, tears filling her eyes anew. "And Charlie . . ." She told him about the constable taking him away and her father's recent collapse. She felt more than saw him grimly shake his head in the dim light, her hands masking much of the lantern's glow.

Setting the lantern on the floor before them, he pulled off his coat and laid it over her shoulders, enveloping her in warmth and lingering aromas of herbs and woodsmoke. He took her hand in his once more. "All right if I pray for you?"

She hesitated. "Now?"

He nodded.

"Aloud?"

He pursed his lips. "Unless you'd prefer to read my thoughts?"

She bit her lip. "Very well."

Francis bowed his head, the lantern light glimmering on his profile. When had his jaw become so square, and hints of a beard begun to show at the end of day?

"Gracious Father, please look with compassion upon the Haswell family. Have mercy upon Charlie in his present danger. Relieve the pangs of Mr. Haswell's disease, and avert from him all lasting harm. Give Lilly strength to bear these afflictions, and comfort them all. Grant this for the sake of our blessed Saviour, in whose holy name we pray. Amen."

"Amen," Lilly echoed softly, warmed by his words, lofty yet so sincere. She felt a new flutter of hope lift her spirits.

She soon became self-conscious, sitting so close to Francis in the dark, quiet place. Gently pulling her hand from his, she straightened and looked up at the chancel, shadowy in the flickering light. She asked lightly, "Have you not enough of this place on the Sabbath?"

He leaned back against the pew. "Well, with all the page turning and hymn singing and sermon listening—of which I approve, don't mistake me—little time remains for quiet reflection."

"Could you not do that in your lodgings? Now that the roof is repaired, I mean."

He laughed softly. "I attempt it. But as well as Mr. Shuttleworth and I get on, it is tiring to be always in the society of one's employer. And, well . . . the man does love to sing. Often. And with great enthusiasm."

Lilly chuckled. "Most men would flee to the Hare and Hounds or the coffeehouse."

"No doubt. But I cannot afford to go every night like Mr. Shuttleworth is wont to do. I keep a few eggs, bread, and cheese in the larder and do well enough on my own most meals."

"You seem quite concerned about money, Mr. Baylor. Is Mr. Shuttleworth not fair in your wages?"

"He is more than fair. I . . . well, my wages are not for spending."

"Then what?"

He took a deep breath and shifted on the bench. "Let's talk of something else."

"Very well. What do you reflect upon when you come here?"

She felt him shrug.

"Whatever is in my thoughts at the time. My father was such a man. He would always talk over his decisions before he made them."

"With your mother?"

"With her as well. My father was a North Somerset fisherman. He always said if the apostles needed the Lord to tell them where to cast their nets, then he could do no better than to ask the Almighty for direction as well." As the echo of his words faded, he looked over at her. "Do you feel ready to stand now?"

"Of course." She rose tentatively, and he took her hand, deftly moving it to his arm for support.

"I shall walk you home." He picked up his lantern.

"What of your time of quiet reflection?"

"Oh, I think I came here for a different reason tonight."

As they stepped out into the churchyard, she studied his profile in the moonlight. "Are you really so changed?" she asked.

"I hope I am more responsible than I was as a lad, but that is only to be expected." He walked beside her up the High Street. "You know, a decade ago, had a young man and woman been seen coming out of a dark building alone together . . . why, their parents would have seen them married by morning."

"Do not fret, Mr. Baylor," she said on a laugh. "No one will force you to the altar."

"I was not fretting in the least."

His tone was perfectly serious, and she felt oddly disoriented as their light banter fell away, replaced by an awkward silence.

He cleared his throat. "But I . . . understand that may soon be another man's privilege."

She let the comment fade away. It would be indiscreet and premature to confirm such a presumption. Dr. Graves *had* moved from London to be near her, had he not? She was grateful he was not pressing her with a declaration, instead giving her time to help her father, to see him well again. And now to help Charlie too. She was fond of Francis, but could not let him distract her from a gentleman like Dr. Graves.

When they reached Haswell's, Francis said, "I will continue to pray for you and every member of your family, dispersed as they are." He squeezed her hand. "I will also see what can be done."

40

I once was lost, but now am found,
Was blind, but now I see.

—John Newton,
Amazing Grace, 1772

The blind house was like a round, windowless granary with a cone-shaped roof. Most villages in Wiltshire and surrounding counties kept such a building to temporarily confine wrongdoers.

Lilly knocked on the locked door. "Charlie? Are you all right?"

Hearing nothing, Lilly pressed her ear to the door. She heard a shuffle, then Charlie's muffled voice. "'Tis awful dark, Lilly. Nofin' to see."

"We shall get you out, Charlie. As soon as we can."

"Nofin' to see . . ."

At the distress in her little brother's voice, she pressed her forehead to the wood, blinking back tears.

"Try counting sounds, Charlie," she said, injecting false calm into her voice. "Bird calls, passing horses. Whatever you hear, all right?"

No response. Then a feeble, "All right . . ."

Oh, God, Lilly prayed, *this will not do. Please help us.*

"It is a medical matter. An apothecary matter," Charles Haswell asserted, slowly shuffling across the surgery. "Perhaps we should suggest Ackers report it to the Society and let *them* dole out reprimand or consequence to me as they see fit."

"Would that satisfy Ackers?" Lilly asked, relieved to see her father on his feet. He had even felt strong enough to walk across the village that morning to speak with Charlie through the blind house door. Dr. Graves had given him sweet spirit of nitre, as Francis had suggested. The liquid preparation clearly had some effect, though it remained to be seen how long the improvement would last.

"I don't know. He'd like to get his own pound of flesh, I'd wager. Worse yet, if someone else is pulling his strings."

"Dr. Foster?"

"Would not surprise me in the least."

She'd had the same thought. "Should I call on Mr. Ackers and suggest he refer the case to the Society?"

Charles Haswell ran a weary hand over his stubbled cheeks. "Bill Ackers write a letter? I'd as soon believe the claims of a Cornhill quack."

Lilly was having her tea alone when Maude Mimpurse let herself in the kitchen door. She had been incensed when Lilly had told her the news and had promised to see Charlie just as soon as she could get away.

Over one arm Mrs. Mimpurse bore the straps of a worn leather market bag, in her free hand, a quart jar. A delicious smell of pastry and savory sauce emanated from the bag.

Seeing Lilly eye her burden, Maude explained, "Two gurt meat-and-potato pasties and a jar of honey tea. Charlie's favorite."

Lilly rose from the table. "But do you think Mr. Ackers will allow it?"

Mrs. Mimpurse snorted. "You leave Billy Ackers to me."

Her father was in his surgery with Mr. Fowler. But even if she'd had to leave the shop unattended, Lilly would not miss this chance to see Charlie face-to-face.

A quarter of an hour later, coat and blanket in arms, Lilly strode beside Mrs. Mimpurse as the woman marched smartly along the hedgerow. Lilly kept up easily, but Bill Ackers—whom Maude had cajoled from his smithy—trudged begrudgingly behind.

"Do keep up, Billy. These pasties won't stay warm forever."

Reaching the blind house first, Maude and Lilly waited for the constable to catch up. "Do hurry, Billy. My coffeehouse won't run itself."

"My smithy either," he grumbled. Taking out a pair of old heavy keys, Bill Ackers unlocked the blind house door. "Step back, Charlie," he called gruffly.

Incredulous, Maude said, "As though a lamb like Charlie would run away? Really, Billy."

"All right. Hand 'im 'is supper."

"Indeed I will not. Why can he not sit here in the sunlight and eat his meal with dignity?"

"He's not on holiday, mum."

"Nor is he an animal. Come out, Charlie. I have a nice supper for you."

Charlie emerged from the darkness and hesitated at the threshold, eyes squinting. Lilly's heart ached to see it.

"Poor love!" Mrs. Mimpurse tutted. "You come out nice and slowlike, Charlie. No hurry."

Bill Ackers sighed.

Glancing shrewdly at him, Mrs. Mimpurse handed him one of the pasties. "For your trouble, Billy."

Four days later, when the post came, Lilly received two letters. One was an all-too common request for payment, but the second set her palms to perspiring.

She found her father alone in the surgery, looking through the newest dispensatory Mr. Shuttleworth had loaned him.

"It is a letter, Father, as I feared. From the Worshipful Society of Apothecaries. It appears Mr. Ackers wrote to them after all."

"I cannot credit it."

"Who else could it be? Foster could have nothing to do with apothecaries, could he? When he so clearly loathes the lot of us?"

He shrugged uneasily. She held out the letter, but he waved it away. "You read it."

She broke the seal and unfolded the fine stationery. "'The Court of Examiners at Apothecaries' Hall, Blackfriars, London.'"

He frowned. "Spare me the friggling and just lay out the worst."

"Very well. 'It has been reported that one Charles Haswell III has dispensed an adulterated, potentially harmful drug.'"

Her father thundered, "They haven't even the facts!"

"'Upon receiving any further such reports, the Society will have no alternative but to pursue formal action. Proceedings will then be taken against said person.'"

"Said person? Formal action—all the way from London? Fuss and nonsense. What a narration about nothing."

"I am not so certain it is."

"Is that all it is to be, then? A threat? A slap on the wrist from afar?"

"I can hardly credit it," Lilly said. "Can this really be all?"

"I would wish it so."

"Wishing isn't enough, Father. We must pray it so as well."

Her father stared out the surgery window. "Now, if only we could convince Ackers."

The days passed slowly, and Lilly found the wait interminable. Rarely had she felt so helpless, so frustrated, so afraid. She visited Charlie every day, as did Mrs. Mimpurse, Mary, Francis, and her father, when he was able. And she prayed. But as Charlie's imprisonment approached a fortnight, she felt her faith flagging. Had she not prayed for her mother's return to no avail? Her father's healing? Did it really make any difference?

Then, in a moment, everything changed. One minute she and her father were despondently sitting before plates of food neither saw nor wanted, and the next there was Charlie in the doorway. Dirty, odiferous, and wonderful to behold.

"Enough for one more?" he asked, looking at their breakfast.

Lilly gasped, leapt to her feet, and grabbed her brother in a fierce hug. Her father raised himself on shaky legs and squeezed Charlie's shoulder before sinking heavily into his chair. His improvement had not lasted.

"Sit down, Charlie. I can barely believe it. Tell us what happened."

He sat, and they both looked at him expectantly. Charlie eyed her breakfast once more.

"Oh, here." She pushed her untouched plate before him.

They waited impatiently while he took several bites, and then Lilly prompted again. "What happened?"

Charlie shrugged, and said around a bite of cold ham, "Mr. Ackers comes in and says, 'Charlie lad, it's yer lucky day. Mr. Marlow says you work for him and he wants you back. He's responsible for you now, so no more nanny fudgin' about.'"

Lilly shook her head, stunned. "I cannot believe it. Mr. Marlow! And when he had already released you from your contract."

"Must need me straightaway for his gurt garden."

Lilly doubted the garden was in such dire need, but forbore to say so. She did not doubt Mr. Marlow's influence over the constable as leading landowner and future baronet. Beyond that, the two had been boyhood friends. She fleetingly wondered how she had not thought to request his help herself.

"Well," Lilly said, relief flooding her, "we shall have to go and thank Mr. Marlow personally."

After breakfast, she and Charlie hitched up Pennywort and drove the gig to Marlow House. As they drew near, Charlie saw Mr. Timms clipping privet near the fountain and asked to be let down to speak to him. "Very well. But come to the house as soon as you've done so."

She turned the horse toward the stables, but instead of Cecil Briggs coming to take the reins, Roderick Marlow himself strode out, dressed in riding coat and Hessian boots.

Flushed and breathless at his sudden appearance, she burst out, "Mr. Marlow, I have come to thank you."

A smile slowly formed on his aquiline countenance as he looked up at her. "Your brother has been released?"

"Yes, thanks to you."

"I am pleased to hear it." He led her horse and gig into the stable yard.

She stood, preparing to climb down. Lifting his hands, he grasped her by the waist and effortlessly carried her to the ground. She felt her cheeks flush anew. A simple hand down would have sufficed.

"You are very kind. Charlie is with Mr. Timms, but I know he will want to thank you. I'll—" She turned to fetch Charlie, but Mr. Marlow took hold of her wrist, halting her departure.

"Please wait." Hand still holding hers, he led her into the stable office. "I am glad for your brother, but do not paint me a saint. I confess I thought only of you."

She inhaled deeply. Her heart beat with heavy thuds. Would he always have such an effect on her?

"I don't know what to say."

"Miss Haswell, speechless?" He grinned. "I am all astonishment."

She tried to smile in return, but her awe was such that her lips only managed a tremble.

He slowly shook his head. "What a man would do, to have a woman forever look at him the way you are regarding me." He reached out and traced a finger along her jawline and chin. "I should very much like to kiss you, Miss Haswell."

She swallowed.

"I must also own that I have never before asked permission."

She said shakily, "You have kissed a great many women, then?"

He considered this. "I would not say a *great* many. But I have never kissed you, Miss Haswell. That I would remember."

She stared at him, mesmerized by his unusual eyes. One a shade darker than the other. Or was one green and the other brown?

"Miss Haswell?"

"Oh!" She started. "Forgive me."

He leaned down. "Here, now you may examine me more closely."

For a moment, she did just that. Studied his eyes, his dark lashes and brows. His prominent cheekbones and pinpricks of black whiskers beneath fair skin.

"Anything amiss?" he asked. "A sty, perhaps?"

She shook her head, still regarding him, his thin lips and sharp nose, the nostrils which seemed to flare at her close inspection.

When she returned her gaze to his eyes, she saw that they gleamed with suppressed laughter. "Have I need of an apothecary, or might a kiss suffice?"

She bit her lip. "I cannot give you leave to kiss me."

He sighed dramatically. "Which is why I never ask first."

She squared her shoulders. "But perhaps I might kiss your cheek, Mr. Marlow. For saving my brother."

His brows rose. "A gratitude kiss? Not my favorite sort."

Feeling foolish, she began to turn away. "Never mind, then."

He gently turned her back to face him. "No. Please never mind *me*. I dearly long for a gratitude kiss from you, Miss Haswell."

She realized he was likely mocking her, but her thankfulness overwhelmed every other emotion.

He bent low again, face near. She would not have reached him otherwise. His hands, she surmised, were now safely behind his back. Safe enough, she hoped.

She leaned forward slowly, aiming for his cheek. He shifted and she kissed his lips instead. Their lips touched for a lingering moment. One heartbeat, then two. When she pulled away, the laughter had altogether gone from his eyes.

41

> The fashion hails—from countesses to queens,
> And maids and valets waltz behind the scenes. . . .
>
> —Lord Byron

In the coffeehouse dining room, Lilly helped Mary with the heavy task of pushing all the tables to one side and stacking chairs, preparing to mop the entire floor. Surveying the open space, Lilly dramatically stood her mop straight, head up, and curtsied before it.

"I would be delighted to dance with you, sir," she said. With a bend of her elbow, the mop-haired "gentleman" tilted toward her in a bow. Grasping her stick-thin partner with both hands, Lilly performed a spinning dance around the cleared room.

Leaning on a second mop, Mary grinned and shook her head. “You can take the lady out of London . . .” She let the words trail away. She studied Lilly’s whirling steps. “I have not seen that dance before.”

“It is the dreaded turning waltz.”

“No,” gasped Mary in feigned shock. “Not the scandalous dance condemned by all the papers.”

Lilly halted and propped her mop against the wall. “The very same. Might I tempt you into learning it?”

“Never,” Mary said coyly. “I am far too proper for such wickedness.”

Lilly raised an eyebrow. “The Mary Mimpurse who spied the cricket team swimming in the Owens’ pond? I think not.”

Tugging the mop from Mary’s hand and standing it beside her own, Lilly grasped Mary about her waist and pulled and spun her around the room, until they nearly collided with the stacked chairs.

“Please, Lill, stop,” Mary gasped. “I am dizzy!”

Lilly halted abruptly, still holding on to Mary as her friend regained her balance and breath. “Are you all right?” she asked, concerned.

Breathing hard, Mary said, “I am not having a fit, if that is what you mean. Unless you mean a fit of the vapors.”

Assured her friend was all right, Lilly released her.

“That dance will *not* be performed at Wilcot, I assure you,” Mary said, refastening a hairpin that had come loose whilst spinning.

“Even so, how I look forward to the country dance.” Lilly retrieved her mop and dipped it into the bucket near the hearth. She slanted a glance at Mary. “And I know a certain surgeon-apothecary who looks forward to dancing with you.”

Mary bit back a smile of pleasure. “I own a certain gleeful anticipation of that myself.”

After the trying days of Charlie’s imprisonment, they were all looking forward to Wilcot’s end-of-summer fete, which was to include both a fair and a dance. She and Mary planned to attend with Charlie, Dr. Graves, and Mr. Shuttleworth. No doubt Francis and Dorothea Robbins would attend as well.

But on Saturday, her father awoke with a fever, and Lilly felt obliged to stay with him.

“Then I shall stay as well,” Mary said, though her countenance was decidedly downcast.

“And leave all those fine partners to Miss Robbins alone? I think not. You know Mr. Shuttleworth and Charlie will be exceedingly disappointed if you do not attend."

Mary grinned. "They would, would not they?"

"Of course. Now go and be danced off your feet, my lovely, as you well deserve."

Mary's eyes sparked with mischief. "I shall benefit from your absence in that regard, shan't I?"

"Oh!" Lilly winked. "I can see how much I shall be missed!"

That afternoon, Dr. Graves called on her father, prescribed fever powder, fluids, and bed rest. He was disappointed to learn she would not be attending the Wilcot fair. "I would not go either," he said sheepishly. "But Dr. Foster requests it. Says I should make the acquaintance of as many potential patients as possible. But I shall not dance, Miss Haswell—you may depend upon it."

"I do not wish to depend upon it! I hope you will dance, especially should gentlemen be scarce and ladies be in want of a partner."

She thought of her own first dance with Dr. Graves and hoped no lady would have to endure such a reluctant performance.

He said quietly, "I did not come all this way to dance with other ladies, Miss Haswell."

She smiled shyly up at him. "Just don't enjoy it overly much and I shall be satisfied."

He grinned. "When have I ever?"

Lilly looked up from her book to the sitting room clock once more. Two hours had slowly passed. It felt like more. Her father was sleeping peacefully and the novel was not engaging. Perhaps she should just give it up and go to bed.

An unexpected knock sounded on the sitting room door. Before she could react, Francis stepped in, looking masculine and handsome in his dark coat and trousers, hat in hand.

She rose. "Francis. What are you doing here?"

"I could not enjoy myself, knowing you were not."

She was pleased and anxious at once. "You needn't have come. There is no use in the both of us missing out."

"I don't mind."

"But Miss Robbins mentioned you were quite the accomplished dancer."

"Mr. Shuttleworth has taught me a few things, I own." His eyes gleamed. "Now, there's a sight not to be missed. Mr. Shuttleworth in purple coat and gold waistcoat, prancing the fancy steps of a cotillion."

She chuckled. "I can well imagine. But I should have liked to see you dance as well. No doubt Miss Robbins was counting on you as a partner."

He shrugged easily. "She was dancing with Mr. Marlow when I left, Mr. Shuttleworth awaiting the next."

She wondered if he was disappointed. Was that why he had returned?

He said kindly, "You have had little entertainment since returning, Miss Haswell, and far too much work. I am sorry *you* had to miss it. I hope your father is better."

"Yes, the fever has broken. He is resting comfortably."

"Good. Good."

They stood awkwardly for a few moments, until Francis said, "Mary told me about the dance lesson you gave her. That *I* was sorry to miss."

Lilly screwed up her face. "I would never have done so with an audience."

He smiled, a warm glint in his chocolate-brown eyes. "As you said, there is no point in both of us missing the evening's entertainment. We might have a dance here."

"Here?" She looked skeptically around the small room.

"Why not? We could try that turning waltz Mary described. Though I am surprised your aunt and uncle allowed such a scandalous dance."

Her cheeks heated. "There is really nothing scandalous in the side-by-side position, only in the closed."

He took a step nearer. "And what is the 'closed' position?"

She knew she ought to refuse and back away but felt oddly drawn to him, touched that he would return, surprised to find she wanted to touch him.

She tentatively reached out. "I would place my hands here. . . ." She lightly gripped his upper arms, feeling the firm muscles beneath his coat sleeves.

He looked into her eyes and asked in a low voice, "And where do I place mine?"

She drew in a long shallow breath, nerves tingling, throat tight. "On my . . . waist." She was relieved her hands were not in his, for he would no doubt have felt how damp they were.

His large hands pressed warmly around her waist, though his eyes never left her face. She had difficulty holding his gaze at such close proximity. "Then you would step forward, and I back."

He stepped forward as directed, but his hands held her fast, keeping her from stepping back, keeping her close to him. His jaw tensed, his brown eyes sparked with longing.

She looked away, focusing on her hand on his arm. "Partners must keep a proper distance apart," she said, parroting the admonition of the Viennese dancing master. "Bodies must not actually touch."

"Pity," Francis breathed, his sweet breath warm on her temple, her ear.

He leaned close, his face dipped toward hers, but still she averted her gaze. She did not want this, did she? This was Francis—what was she doing? She knew she had but to look up and he would kiss her. Her heart pounded at the thought.

"Lilly," he urged hoarsely. "Tell me it is not too late for us. That you and Graves are not—"

The door opened behind them, and Lilly pulled away.

Dr. Graves stood there, hand on the door latch, expression startled, bearing rigid. "I came to see how you and your father were faring, but I see I am interrupting." Eyes dull, he backed from the room.

"No, Dr. Graves, please come in! I was merely demonstrating the waltz to Mr. Baylor."

He stared at her, flicked a glance at Francis, then returned cool eyes to her. "Do you think that wise, Miss Haswell?"

The particular dance, or the partner? Lilly thought. "You must forgive us, Dr. Graves. Francis and I grew up together, and find it far too easy to slip back into our former foolish ways."

He stared at her a moment longer, then cleared his throat. "I see. Well." He bowed stiffly. "Good evening."

He did not acknowledge Francis in his farewell.

"Dr. Graves, you needn't leave," Lilly insisted.

"Miss Haswell has done nothing wrong." Francis gestured in vague motions between Lilly and himself. "I instigated this."

"No, Francis," Lilly said. "I have acted thoughtlessly. I ask you both to forgive me."

Her father's voice called from down the passageway, "Lilly? Everything all right?"

Lilly grimaced. "We've woken him."

Dr. Graves said icily, "I shall go and check on him. If you don't mind." He skewered Francis with a look.

"Yes, please do, Dr. Graves," Lilly quickly replied. "You are very kind to think of him. I thank you."

Graves nodded and pivoted on his heel. As soon as he had left the room, Lilly turned toward Francis feeling contrite and chagrined. "Francis," she whispered tersely, "I was wrong to allow this to happen. I don't know why I did."

"Because you feel something for me, Lilly. I know you do."

She exhaled. "Of course I do. But not what you might wish I would feel. Francis, please understand. I do not want the life you do. I do not want to spend mine in an apothecary shop. I never have."

He ran a hand through his thick brown hair. "It is all I know. All I *want* to know. Are you suggesting I give it up?"

"No. Stay. But all *I* want is to help my father regain his strength, put the place to rights, then leave it to him."

"But I've seen you, Lilly—helping people, easing their pain. . . . I know you derive as much satisfaction from it as I do."

She shook her head. "You are wrong. I have done what I've had to do, but I do not enjoy it. Nor do I aspire to any profession. I am, after all, a woman."

He winced. "I am aware of that. Painfully aware. But the Lilly Haswell I knew would never so belittle her sex."

"That Lilly Haswell is gone," she said, more sharply than she'd intended.

His eyes glittered with sadness and irritation both. "I for one am sorry to hear it." He picked up his hat. "I will trespass upon your time no longer. Good evening, Miss Haswell."

On his lips, the formal address sounded nearly derisive, and it delivered an unexpected prick of pain.

42

> I, being of a sound mind, memory and understanding, knowing the certainty of death when I shall be called to my wished-for-long home, do make my last Will and Testament. . . .
>
> —William Phillips, Gentleman, 1786

Francis opened the kitchen door to say hello to Mary—and hoping to apologize to Lilly, who was so often there in the mornings.

He had been tempted to give up hope when Dr. Graves first arrived in Bedsley Priors. But as the weeks passed and no engagement was announced, he'd allowed himself to believe he still had a chance with Lilly. After their last encounter, however, Francis was almost relieved he would soon be going away.

Mary stood at her worktable as usual, but she did not smile, or even acknowledge him. She seemed to be staring straight ahead. Her hands, still idly chopping something, slowed, then jerked.

"Mary!" He bolted across the room, but was too late. She collapsed where she stood, a sickening crack preceding the thud of her landing.

He knelt beside her on the hard brick floor. A deep gash on her forehead showed white, just before the blood began to flow profusely. There was blood between the fingers of one of her hands as well—the hand still clutching the knife.

Jane rushed in from the scullery and shrieked at the sight. Mrs. Mimpurse came running as well, no doubt hearing him shout her daughter's name. She gasped and covered her mouth with a trembling hand.

"Clean linen, and quickly!" Francis called.

The kitchen maid rushed to do his bidding while he ran his hands down Mary's limbs and checked her pupils. When Jane returned, he pressed a linen serviette to the gash on her forehead.

"She needs a surgeon. Send someone for Shuttleworth."

Lilly appeared at the back door, as he had hoped she would, though for far different reasons. "I will go." Her face was pale but resolute.

"Wait," Francis called. "I think he will attend her better in his surgery. She has no broken bones, I am sure. Help me wrap her hand, and I shall carry her."

Lilly nodded and deftly assisted him in wrapping Mary's cut palm and finger while Mrs. Mimpurse and Jane looked on, sobbing. Yes, it might be better to treat Mary elsewhere for several reasons.

Mary's eyes fluttered opened. "What's happened?" she mumbled, blue eyes clouded.

"You've cut yourself and need a surgeon," Francis said. "We're taking you to Mr. Shuttleworth."

He did not miss the look of pain, of mortification, which passed over her pale features. Why wouldn't Mary want to be helped by a man she so obviously admired, and who admired her in return? *Unless Mr. Shuttleworth does not know . . .*

Lilly glanced at him, then back to her friend. She said gently, "There's no help for it this time, love."

Resigned, Mary gave the briefest of nods and her eyes fluttered closed once more.

Please let the man be in his office, Francis prayed as he lifted Mary in his arms.

Lilly jogged beside Francis as he carried Mary with impressive strength. Mrs. Mimpurse scuddled behind them, hand to her heavy bosom, face stricken. Crossing Milk Lane, Lilly was relieved when Mr. Shuttleworth opened his door before they had even reached it, likely having seen them run across the lane. He appeared shocked and alarmed to see the patient Francis bore with such determination, the blood already seeping through white linen at her brow and hand.

"She fell. Holding a knife," Francis panted.

For a fraction of a moment, Shuttleworth found and held Lilly's gaze.

Lilly looked away first.

She waited while Mr. Shuttleworth skillfully stitched up the gash on Mary's forehead as well as one of the deeper cuts on her finger. Mary was in a strange dreamlike state, and did not even seem to feel the pain of the stitches, though he gave her laudanum to lessen the pain she was sure to feel soon.

He assured Mrs. Mimpurse that he expected both injuries to heal well in time. He asked Mary's mother more questions about how the injury occurred, and if the like had happened before. And as Mrs. Mimpurse began her quiet explanations, Lilly let herself from the surgery.

A few hours later, Mr. Shuttleworth sought Lilly out, as she had known he would. Finding her alone in the shop, he began in low tones, "I cannot believe I did not know. Does everybody?"

Lilly nodded. "Everyone from Bedsley Priors." She sighed. "We gossip among ourselves freely, but with outsiders, as you have been, we protect our own."

"Why did *you* not tell me?"

Lilly looked away from the hurt in his dark eyes. "She did not wish me to."

"But . . . that's not right. Nor fair."

She forced her eyes to meet his. "Was it so wrong that she wanted to enjoy your company without the knowledge tainting your opinion of her? To be just a lady with a gentleman? She's never had an admirer before."

He frowned. "Had I known, I might have been more circumspect. Not allowed myself to . . ." His words drifted off, but his meaning was clear.

"But why? It isn't really so dreadful, is it? It has been quite a rare occurrence, at least, until lately."

He blindly gripped the edge of the dispensing counter. "Miss Haswell. I served in an epileptic asylum, two years gone. Not to learn to treat epilepsy, for there is little treatment to speak of and certainly no cure. I was there because surgeons were always in demand in that place. I received a great deal of practical experience stitching cuts and cracked heads, splinting broken bones, and treating burns. . . ."

She thought back to Dr. Graves mentioning such institutions and her adamant rebuttal at the thought of sending her dear friend to such a place. Lilly found she had no strength for such a speech at present. Not with such deep disappointment in the man's voice and expression.

Mr. Shuttleworth took a deep breath and blew it out between his cheeks. "Epileptics were sent there to live. Permanently. And, Miss Haswell, patients beyond the age of thirty were exceedingly rare."

While Mary recovered from her wounds, Mrs. Kilgrove recovered her strength, relieving lingering fears of further penal action. Charlie, seemingly no worse for his captivity, spent all his spare time with the doting, forgiving woman, and with his cat, Jolly.

Lilly's gratitude toward Roderick Marlow did not flag. His father's health, however, did. After enjoying a brief return of vitality in the weeks prior to and after his marriage, Sir Henry had again fallen ill. Her father had been called in to see him a few nights before, and just that morning, Marlow's man had come to the shop to ask Mr. Haswell to come again. But her father had awoken quite weak that day, so Lilly had gone alone. This seemed to agitate Mr. Withers, and upon entering the ailing baronet's chamber, she'd understood why. Never had she seen Sir Henry in such a state. She had actually been relieved to hear Dr. Foster had been summoned as well.

Now, Lilly wearily made her way home from Marlow House, grieved at this latest turn in Sir Henry's health and her inability to help him. Ahead of her, Lilly heard someone cry out. Picking up her skirts, she ran through the trees separating the road from Arthur Owen's farm. In the clearing, she paused, stunned. There was Roderick Marlow in the Owens' market garden, kicking and punching first the galley-crow, then the fence post. He cried out in unintelligible grief or anger or both.

He must know, she thought.

Owen's pigs scrambled to the far end of the pen. Marlow's horse whinnied, ribbons dangling, trotting this way and that, clearly spooked by his master's behavior. Lilly was spooked as well.

"Mr. Marlow!" she called. "Mr. Marlow, pray calm down."

He spun to face her, expression wild. "Calm down? How can I?"

"Your father is ill, I know, but—"

"Father has been ill for years—in body, but never in mind. Until this!" He thrust a piece of paper high above his head, then crumpled it with both hands, hurtling it toward the pond, though the wad fell short of its mark.

Wary, Lilly walked closer. "What is it?"

"A copy of his new will. He has authored my ruin, or more accurately, the red witch has convinced him to do so. Now should my father die, *she* will take what is rightfully mine."

Her mind whirled. "But . . . I thought the law was quite clear. The eldest son is heir."

"I am to inherit the land, yes. It is entailed. But to raise the staggering amount specified for her jointure, I shall have to sell off the stock, the London house, and I know not what to satisfy it."

"But certainly you would not begrudge your father's widow something to live on."

"Something to live on, I would not begrudge. But the amount is far above that. I shall be unable to pay my steward, the servants, let alone afford to heat that huge place. Father no doubt allowed her to believe he was wealthier than he was when she married him. But in truth we have struggled for some time. You know we keep only two carriages, only a small London house—and that we let out for most of the year. We do not entertain often. We live quietly, and we retrench and retrench again. And so far we have managed, but this is the absolute end."

"But did your father not realize? He has been ill, perhaps—"

He went on as though he had not heard her, "I may even have to let the place out. My own home . . ."

"I am sorry. There must be some mistake. Some misunderstanding."

In two strides, he closed the remaining distance between them. "Perhaps I shall have to enter a trade as you have, Miss Haswell." He looped his arm around her and pulled her close, but the fire in his eyes was fueled by betrayal, not passion. "Do you think I should make a good butcher? Perhaps an apothecary. . . . You would teach me all I need know, would you not?"

"Mr. Marlow, please. I—"

No doubt seeing her stricken expression, he released her, the fire in his eyes fading to dullness. "Forgive my foolishness, Miss Haswell. You have come upon me at a most dark moment." He reached down, retrieved his fallen hat, and stepped toward his horse. "I beg your pardon. I must speak to my father and unwork the devilish persuasion that woman has wrought."

Lilly was confused. "But . . . I have just come from Marlow House. Your father lies in a coma. I thought you knew."

"No!" He whirled back around, hat forgotten. "I have been trapped with Father's solicitor all morning." Mr. Marlow sank to the ground and stared at her, stunned. "When?"

"He might have been in this state all night, but there's no way to know. Withers said he at first thought Sir Henry merely sleeping. When he did not rouse, he sent for my father. My father was indisposed, so I went in his stead."

Cautiously, she sat down on the ground near the stricken man, tugging her skirts around her. "Dr. Foster is expected any time, I understand," she added, hoping to comfort him. "He has long experience with your father."

He sat, elbows on his knees, staring blankly ahead. "Indeed my father has had long association with several of the medical profession, enjoyed their company, but with no benefit that I can see. And now this."

He shook his head. "I argued bitterly with Father when last we spoke. I have not quite managed to forget that, as is my wont. And now I shall never be able to make it right."

He laid his head down, face hidden within his arms. "A coma," he breathed. "Then it is too late. All is lost. . . ."

Impulsively, she laid a hand on his elbow. "Your father may yet rally. He has before, remember."

He lifted his head and regarded her, eyes alight. "Might he come to his senses, then, at any moment?"

"I don't know. But it is possible."

"Then I must be there should he awaken." He rose quickly. "Beg him to change his mind and . . . to forgive me."

With that he turned, leapt on his horse, and galloped away, without farewell or backward glance.

That evening, when Lilly confided Mr. Marlow's tidings in hushed tones to Mrs. Mimpurse, the Marlows' former nurserymaid shook her head, her mouth turned down in a rare frown.

"Him not even in his grave and already they're fighting o'er his money. Fuss and commotion."

"What's this about?" Mary asked, coming in from the dining room, her finger still wrapped but healing nicely.

"Sir Henry changed his will," Lilly explained once more. "So much money is to go to the new Lady Marlow that, in raising the sum, Marlow House may very well be ruined."

Mary's brow puckered. "If she wanted the money and title of Lady, " she began, "why not marry the heir and have both? She had to know Sir Henry could not be expected to live many years."

"Perhaps she really does love Sir Henry," Mrs. Mimpurse ventured. She sighed. "And now the poor man is senseless, and not two months gone since the honeymoon."

Lilly knew Maude was partial to her former employer, but she could not quite believe Cassandra Powell had married the sickly baronet for love alone. "Or perhaps she liked the thought of a widow's jointure to spend as she liked."

Mrs. Mimpurse shook her head. "Most widows get only a small portion of the dowry they brought to the marriage. Beyond that, they must depend upon the generosity of the husband's heir."

Lilly considered this. "Then perhaps Lady Marlow did not wish to depend upon Roderick's generosity, and that is why she worked on Sir Henry to change his will, as Roderick suspects."

That Lilly would believe. But she did not foresee the danger it would mean for them all.

43

Oh thou, to whom such healing power is giv'n
The delegate, as we believe, of heaven.
—Richard Cumberland,
Ode to Doctor Robert James

When the summons came the following afternoon, Lilly was not overly surprised. In the hastily written note, Roderick Marlow bid Charles Haswell to come directly, bringing all medical necessities.

"I did not think I would be summoned, not with Foster attending Sir Henry yesterday." Her father groaned and swung his legs off the side of the bed.

"I shall go again, Father. You are still not fit for it."

He lifted the piece of paper. "He asks specifically for me in the most pointed terms. I dare not refuse."

"Then I shall go with you."

She harnessed Pennywort to the gig and helped her father up into it, then set his largest medical case on the floor.

When they arrived, Mr. Withers opened the door to them. Lilly noticed the man still seemed agitated, and was surprised when he did not escort them up to his master's rooms as he had on previous calls.

She helped her father up the long staircase and down the corridor to Sir Henry's chambers. Holding his arm, she said, "Lean on me, Father. It is not much further."

She pushed open the first door and was surprised and perplexed to see Dr. Graves standing in Sir Henry's outer dressing room.

"We did not expect you to be here," she said.

"I was summoned by Mr. Marlow."

"As were we."

Before either of them could say anything further, her father's knees buckled. Dr. Graves rushed to take his arm, and together they helped him to the stuffed chair. With shaky hand, her father pulled a handkerchief from his pocket and mopped his perspiring brow. "A great many stairs, that."

Moments later, the door opened again, and Mr. Shuttleworth came in, stick in hand. He smoothed down his fine coat before realizing there were others already in the room. He seemed startled to see them there. "Good heavens. The old man must be very bad indeed."

Lilly nodded. Her heart pounded at the thought of the grief and rage she had witnessed in Roderick Marlow the previous day. Whatever was about to happen would not be pleasant.

The door to the inner room, Sir Henry's private bedchamber, opened and Roderick Marlow strode out. He stood, hands on hips, eyes blazing. His face seemed more gaunt than she remembered, and his strange eyes, unfocused and glowering, were like those of a mad dog.

When those eyes lit on her, he seemed to falter. "Miss Haswell . . . you should not be here." He swept his arm toward the door. "You may leave. Go."

She forced herself to hold his gaze without flinching. "I will stay and assist my father in whatever you have summoned us here to do."

He hesitated only a moment. "As you wish." He lifted his outstretched arm and scratched at the back of his neck. "I cannot say I am surprised. Everyone knows the apothecary's clever daughter is all but running Haswell's these days. The master to her father's impotent puppet."

The words felt like a slap after his recent kindnesses. Her father opened his mouth to protest, but then tucked his chin, defeated.

She squeezed her father's shoulder. "Charles Haswell is the greatest apothecary Wiltshire has ever known."

"So he would have us believe. Today, he shall have his chance to prove it. Or be ruined once and for all."

She opened her mouth—stunned—but no words came.

Marlow paced the room maniacally before them. "You medical sorts. You all pretend to such powers, such compassion, but really, all you care about are your own purses. I read the papers, I know about the posturing, the verbal battles about who should be allowed to treat what. You don't care about patients—you care only for your own livelihoods."

He jerked his thumb toward his father's bedchamber. "Dr. Foster was here last night and again this morning. It seems that each of you has treated my father—has filled him with potions that together have rendered him unconscious. You have all treated my father in the last week, have you not?" He paused, scorching each of them with his gaze.

Lilly was flummoxed. Aside from her father, she'd had no idea the others had so recently seen Sir Henry. Why had no one told her?

"Lady Marlow sent for me three days ago," Dr. Graves defended. "I did what I could for Sir Henry, which was little enough, but he was still lucid when I left."

Her father nodded. "I called on Sir Henry that same evening. I found him weak but stable."

Mr. Shuttleworth's dark eyebrows seemed unnaturally high on his forehead. "Sir Henry's solicitor asked me to render an opinion *two* days ago. Said he did not trust his client was getting the best care."

Lilly felt her face wrinkle in confusion. She said, "Mr. Withers summoned me—that is, my father—again yesterday. I came in his stead."

Mr. Marlow paced before them once more. "And so you each plied him with elixirs that in combination worked to send him into a coma. Now you will work together to revive him."

Lilly shook her head in dismay. Sir Henry was already unconscious when she arrived yesterday, but she made no attempt to exonerate herself. In her mind, if her father bore any responsibility, she did as well. When she had last seen Roderick Marlow, he had been looking for someone to blame. Now it appeared he had found his scapegoat. Several of them, in fact.

"I know you will not endeavor to revive my father for pity's sake," Marlow continued. "Nor for mine. Financial reward has not been sufficient motivation to this point, so instead I offer threat. Punishment. I have no power to cure my father, but I have enough to crush each of you. To bring ruination to your practices, your reputations. Is this motivation more suitable, more *efficacious*, as you say? Will you now heal my father?"

Dread filled her like bile. Roderick Marlow must be drunk. Perhaps even mad. She had never seen him like this. She barely recognized this furious, desperate man as the same one she had kissed not so long ago in the stables.

Marlow stopped before her father, shifting his weight to one hip. "Haswell, legend has it that you once raised my grandfather from the dead. How convenient for you—otherwise people would not have been so quick to overlook your fickle wife and idiot son. How the hordes have flocked to you, to lap up your counsel and supposed cures. You have lived off your fame long enough."

Marlow turned. "Shuttleworth, you came to town claiming your worldly experience, your remedies brought from distant lands. Here is your chance to show up your rivals."

"And Dr. Graves." Marlow's lip curled. "You with your privileged Oxford education—about which you constantly remind us. Here is your opportunity to prove your knowledge superior to the less-learned surgeon or apothecary."

His hands returned to his hips. "Personally, I do not care which one of you succeeds. But should you all fail, if my father dies without regaining consciousness, your livelihoods die with him." He looked once more at Lilly. "You should have left, Miss Haswell, when you had the chance."

The outer door slammed behind Roderick Marlow, and no one spoke or moved until the echo died away. Then together the four of them quietly entered Sir Henry's inner chamber and approached his bed. How still the man was. How grey.

"Good Lord," her father breathed. "He is far gone indeed."

Dr. Graves bent to listen to the old man's heart. Mr. Shuttleworth lifted

Sir Henry's sagging eyelids and palpated his abdomen. Her father took up his limp wrist. "Rapid, yet weak."

Together they discussed how each had treated Sir Henry, what medicines they had given him, and if any of these might have reacted adversely together.

"I gave him a very low dose of digitalis for dropsy," Dr. Graves said. "It would not have done this."

"Digitalis?" Shuttleworth asked. "When an infusion of juniper or briony would have been much less risky?"

"Gentlemen, please," Lilly said. "Let us not place blame. Let us together find a solution."

"Solution?" Dr. Graves's voice rose, incredulous. "The man is dying. There is no solution."

Lilly thought, flayed her memory for answers. Could she—could any of them—find a possible remedy for this impossible situation? Neither physician, surgeon, nor apothecary knew anything to do for Sir Henry. Nor for his desperate son.

They needed a miracle.

The door burst open behind them. Whirling about, Lilly saw Francis Baylor at the threshold, quite out of breath. She felt unaccountably relieved to see him. "Francis! Were you summoned as well?"

Francis surveyed the room and its occupants. "No. But Mrs. Mimpurse told me about the will. When I couldn't find Mr. Shuttleworth, or either of you, I became concerned. Thought I had better come. See how I might help."

"Have you some remedy in mind?" Mr. Shuttleworth asked.

Francis walked across the room and laid his hand on the baronet's pale brow. It seemed clear the old man was not long for the world. "I am afraid I don't. Though I may have let Withers believe I did, to gain entry."

Dr. Graves asked, "What's this about a new will?"

Lilly confided, in low tones, what she had learned from Mr. Marlow about the new will—the primary reason, she suspected, for today's threats. Unless . . . Could he really be so desperate to gain his father's forgiveness?

The outer door banged open again and Roderick Marlow strode in. "What is this about a remedy, Baylor?" he challenged.

Francis held up his hand. "I am afraid there is little any of us can do for Sir Henry but pray."

Marlow threw up his hands in angry disgust.

Francis said, "But I suggest you stay in here with your father, Mr. Marlow. Spend all the time you can at his side. Talk to him. He may very well be able to hear you."

For a moment, Marlow's eyes lit. "Do you really think he might?"

Francis nodded. "The rest of us will leave you and Sir Henry in peace."

Marlow crossed his arms, eyes narrowed. "None of you is going anywhere. Not until you have accomplished what I summoned you here to do."

"We are not leaving, sir. Only withdrawing to the dressing room." Francis held Marlow's glare without wavering. "You have my word—we shall not depart until you give us leave to do so."

Roderick Marlow hesitated, staring at Francis, sizing up the younger man. Lilly was surprised when he nodded and returned to his father's bedside.

The rest of them moved to the door. Dr. Graves took one of her father's arms, she the other, and together they helped him to the chair in the dressing room. Francis closed the bedchamber door behind him.

As he helped Mr. Haswell back into the stuffed chair, Adam Graves found himself remembering Lady Marlow's veiled threat to Roderick atop Adam's Grave. Was that somehow related to the present threat? Had the new will—her unexpectedly large jointure—been what she had referred to? If so, no wonder the man was incensed.

Adam forced himself to remain calm and think. Turning to Lillian's father, he began, "Mr. Haswell. If it is true that you once raised a man from the dead, might we ask for a repeat performance?"

"Indeed, Mr. Haswell," Shuttleworth added. "If you could get us out of this muddle, I would be much obliged."

Miss Haswell laid a hand on her father's arm. "We know the truth, do we not, Father? Perhaps it is time we admitted it."

Charles Haswell looked as though he might refuse, then sighed. "I don't do miracles. Never have."

"But word of it has spread as far as London and Oxford," Adam insisted. "It has become the stuff of legends. Dr. Thomas Bromley was here at the time, I understand, and witnessed the event. He attests the man was dead indeed."

Mr. Haswell nodded. "I tried everything I knew, but nothing had any effect. I devised no secret miracle cure. Rather, in desperation, I fell to my knees in this very room and prayed for his recovery." Haswell looked at his daughter, tears shimmering in his eyes. "My little girl beside me."

Miss Haswell took his hand, tears in her eyes as well.

"Perhaps that is what is needed again," Mr. Baylor quietly suggested.

Charles Haswell inhaled deeply. "I own it has been too long since I have done so."

Still holding his hand, Miss Haswell helped her father kneel beside the chair. Mr. Baylor joined them, and together the three bowed their heads.

Adam looked on, feeling sheepish. Beside him, Shuttleworth also looked uncomfortable. For an awkward moment their gazes met. Adam shrugged his response. He considered kneeling beside them, but felt too foolish at the thought. He noticed Shuttleworth had closed his eyes where he stood. He did the same.

Kneeling there beside her father, Lilly felt her legs begin to stiffen and guessed her father must be growing uncomfortable as well. She glanced over, but her father's eyes were still closed, his face wrinkled in concentration. On his other side, Francis also had his eyes closed, forehead resting on clasped hands. As if sensing her scrutiny, Francis looked at her. In silent agreement, they rose and, with a few whispered words, encouraged Mr. Haswell to rise and rest, and together they helped him regain his seat.

"What is happening here?" Lady Marlow asked, startling them all. She had entered without any of them hearing her. Wearing a reserved day dress, her red hair simply fashioned, she stood regally inside the dressing room door, looking from one face to another. Her gaze landed on Dr. Graves.

He cleared his throat. "We were each of us summoned by Mr. Marlow. To see what might be done for Sir Henry."

"Then what are you doing out here?"

When Dr. Graves hesitated, Francis answered, "Praying." He added gently, "I am afraid, Lady Marlow, there is little else to be done for your husband."

For a moment the woman froze, her mouth forming a pink oval of surprise.

"Mr. Marlow is in with Sir Henry now," Francis explained. "Saying his farewells."

Lady Marlow sighed as if suddenly weary, her face drooping into lines that added ten years to her apparent age. "Poor man," she murmured bleakly. And Lilly wondered which man she referred to.

The bedchamber door opened and, as one, they warily turned. Roderick Marlow appeared at the threshold, tears on his cheeks. Ignoring the others in the room, his gaze sought out Lilly's.

"I begged his pardon . . . and he . . . squeezed my hand." His face contorted with emotion. "He knew me. . . ."

Tears of understanding trailed down Lilly's own cheeks as her eyes held his.

The rest of the assembly were equally moved, as well as relieved, to realize Roderick Marlow had returned to his senses. In a matter of minutes, he gave them all leave to go, visibly chagrined at his reckless and irrational behavior. Given the distress of his father's condition, all seemed ready to forgive the future Sir Roderick, Baronet.

Sir Henry did not regain consciousness.

There had been no miracle, no answer to their prayer.

Or had there been? Lilly remembered the look of wonder, and relief on Roderick Marlow's face when he said, *"I begged his pardon and he squeezed my hand. He knew me."*

So perhaps there had been a miracle, after all.

44

What is a weed?
A plant whose virtues have not yet been discovered.
—Ralph Waldo Emerson

In the busyness that followed, getting her father home to bed, telling Mary and Mrs. Mimpurse all that had happened, and checking on Charlie, Lilly did not see Francis again. She wanted to thank him for coming to Marlow House and to talk over the events of the day. She had hoped he would come by the shop that evening, but now it was late and he no doubt thought she had already retired for the night. Or had he stayed away in deference to Dr. Graves?

When Lilly finally slipped into her nightdress and into bed, she still could not sleep. Beyond the stress of the day, she could not stop thinking about Francis Baylor. Though the youngest man there, he had been the one to take charge, and the one to suggest praying together. She thought back to his quick actions after Mary's fall and his many kindnesses to her since then.

She thought, too, of his tall, athletic figure, his strong jaw and cleft chin, his chocolate-brown eyes. As she had come to realize, Francis Baylor had changed a great deal since her return to Bedsley Priors. Or was it she who had changed?

She now understood what Miss Robbins had long seen in Francis, and felt that same admiration herself. When she thought of how she had so soundly rejected him, she was filled with wistful regret.

Lilly rolled over in bed. Still, he was only an assistant—a journeyman—in an apothecary shop. Dr. Graves was a physician and therefore a gentleman. Might he not move his practice elsewhere in a few years? Perhaps even return to London? Somehow, the inner arguments rang hollow now.

Even so, Lilly wondered why she should suddenly feel shy at the thought of seeking out her old friend. Francis would certainly come by the shop on the morrow, would he not? She would thank him then.

In the morning, someone did enter the shop and Lilly hurried out to greet him. But it was not Francis. Nor even Adam Graves. It was Dr. Foster.

He removed his hat and said, "I know it is early and you are no doubt recuperating from a trying day yesterday, but I am afraid I need you to dispense an order for me."

His tone was surprisingly polite.

"Of course." She moved to the dispensing counter and picked up her quill. "What is it you need?"

He fiddled with his hat brim. "A fortnight's worth of St. John's wort, powdered, five grains per day."

She nodded. "For?"

He looked up at her. "I am sure you, being a dab hand yourself, know what the herb is used for, Miss Haswell."

"I do, but—"

"Good. Now, can you figure the sum, or shall I?"

"I meant, who is the patient? For our records."

"My, my. Records too. Haswell's is better managed than I knew."

Was the man being sarcastic? She wasn't certain. "Thank you. We do our best."

He inhaled, then paused. "It is for Mrs. Chester Somersby of Honeystreet. Do you know the family?"

Lilly lowered her quill. "Indeed I do."

"She suffers from nerves, poor creature. Have you sufficient powder on hand, or shall I call round for it later?"

Lilly stared at the man. Did he really not know what he was asking?

"I don't mind stopping back," he said.

"You cannot."

"I can quite easily. It isn't far."

"I mean, you cannot give Mrs. Somersby St. John's wort. She had a violent reaction to it once before."

He regarded her placidly. "I know of no such reaction."

"I do. And Dr. Graves does as well. Ask him if you don't believe me."

His eyes met hers boldly. "Dr. Graves follows my directives and keeps me informed of all irregularities. You needn't trouble yourself, Miss Haswell. Shall I pick up the order at say, four o'clock?" He replaced his hat smartly, turned without awaiting her response, and strode from the shop.

She stared after the man. Anger and fear and dread balled in her stomach.

He was either ignorant or pretending to be for his own ends. Either way, Mrs. Somersby was not the only person about to be hurt.

The shop had been so busy that, when four o'clock came, she'd had no time to ask anyone for advice. Now Dr. Foster again stood before her, the dispensing counter between them like a futile shield.

"Are you refusing to fill my order?" he asked.

"You have not had an opportunity to confer with Dr. Graves, I see. If you will only speak with him—"

"Yes or no?" His voice rose. "Will you dispense my prescribed medicine for Mrs. Somersby or will you not?"

"I have no wish to quarrel with you, Dr. Foster. But I cannot in good conscience do what you ask."

"Once more, girl. Do you or do you not refuse to dispense the physic I ordered?"

She swallowed. "Yes. I refuse."

He nodded, clearly angry yet not surprised. And apparently satisfied as well.

Leaving the shop untended, though it was before five, Lilly hurried up the High Street and down narrow Milk Lane to Shuttleworth's. She wanted to make sure Dr. Foster did not turn there for the prescription he wanted for Mrs. Somersby. She found Mr. Shuttleworth standing at his large central desk, drying glass measuring jars with a clean white cloth. When she asked about Dr. Foster and learned he had not been there all day, she sighed with relief. She leaned her elbows on the high desk and confided her confrontation with the old physician.

Mr. Shuttleworth winced. "Oh dear. I am not certain that was wise."

She jerked back, stung. This wasn't the empathy she'd expected. "What was I to do?"

"But to refuse him?" Lionel Shuttleworth whistled under his breath.

"I had no choice."

"Do you not read the newspapers?"

"I barely have time to read bills of lading and ledgers, let alone news."

"You *have* heard about the recently passed Apothecaries Act?"

She frowned. "I believe Francis may have said something, but I own I paid little attention."

Mr. Shuttleworth leaned forward, sober concern in his dark eyes. "Among other things, a clause of this new act imposes severe penalties on any apothecary who refuses to dispense medicines on the order of a physician."

"You are joking."

"I am deadly serious."

"How long has this been generally known?"

"It's been before Parliament for quite some time, but came into effect the first of August."

How easily she had walked into his trap.

Adam Graves walked slowly down the High Street to Haswell's to pick up two prescriptions he had requested earlier. He knew Miss Haswell appreciated that he brought them to her though Shuttleworth's was nearer his offices. Normally he enjoyed the excuse to see her. But today he dreaded the coming encounter and the news he must impart.

When Adam had first learned of a possible partnership in Miss Haswell's home village, he had thought it a godsend. Now it was beginning to seem more like a test. One he appeared destined to fail.

He hesitated at the door to take a deep breath, then pushed his way inside. At the dispensing counter, Miss Haswell acknowledged him with a nod. He waited until Miss Primmel had paid for her purchases and said farewell to them both before approaching the counter himself.

Miss Haswell handed him his order without her usual smile, her features strained. She asked tensely, "Have you spoken to Dr. Foster about Mrs. Somersby? Tell me he did not procure the St. John's wort elsewhere."

"He has not. He pursued another course of treatment."

She released a breath. "I am relieved to hear it. He understood, then?"

"I would not say that." He found himself fidgeting with his parcel. "I did describe Mrs. Somersby's reaction, but he said it was more likely caused by the vervain you suggested for the . . . other complaint."

"But I asked Father, and he agrees. Vervain would not—"

"Yes, yes, I tried to explain that, but he would not hear me."

"You ought to have *made* him hear you."

He looked down at the counter. "Seems I fail at a great many things you believe I ought to do."

Her voice rose to a consolatory pitch. "Dr. Graves, I did not mean—"

"In any case"—he forced himself to continue—"I am afraid he has written to your own society, reporting your refusal."

"To the Apothecaries' Society?" she said. "I can hardly credit he'd waste the ink, so little does he respect the profession."

"I believe there you are wrong, Miss Haswell. It is not apothecaries in general he abhors."

He saw her bite her lip, clearly apprehending his meaning. "Surely nothing will come of it. The last time we heard from the Society, we received nothing more than a warning."

He shook his head. *Can she really be so naïve?* "The law has changed since then."

"What can he hope to accomplish?"

"I should think that all too evident. He wants to see Haswell's put out of business."

She blanched. "Could you not do something?"

There it was again. It was his fault. His failure. "What would you have me do?" His voice rose. "Pilfer his letter from the post?"

A quick glance revealed her chagrin. He took a deep breath and forced himself to speak calmly. "There is little I can do at this point. But I did want to warn you. And I shall apprise you of anything else I learn."

"Thank you," she murmured.

Feeling defeated and indignant both, he turned on his heel and left the shop. Why could she not leave the criticizing to Foster? It appeared neither of his provisional partnerships was working out as he had hoped.

On his way back to Dr. Foster's offices, he saw Bill Ackers leaving. What was the constable doing there? He then saw the man fold what looked to be several bank notes and tuck them into his pocket.

The following week, Dr. Foster brought two men with him into the office.

"Graves, come out here, man."

Adam did not appreciate the way the elder man ordered him about. Still, he put on his coat and stepped from his private office into the reception hall.

"Here you are." Foster addressed his guests, "This is Dr. Adam Graves, the young partner I was telling you about. Not quite seasoned, but working out rather well. So far."

Adam managed not to frown and bowed to the newcomers. One was a man near Foster's own age in dark double-breasted coat and pantaloons, his waistcoat festooned with a lacy cravat. His hair was far too black to be natural for a man of his fifty or more years. He affected both quizzing glass and walking stick.

"May I introduce Mortimer Allen, a very old friend indeed," Foster began. The man inclined his head but showed little interest in the introduction.

"And this is John Evans, his . . . associate."

Mr. Evans was in his forties, Graves surmised, and wore a serviceable but plain coat and trousers. He looked exceeding fit, with a wiry strength rather than bulk. His tawny hair was thin on his forehead.

"How d'you do?" Evans said. This man took his measure, and Graves felt himself standing up the taller under it.

"What brings you gentlemen to Bedsley Priors?" Graves asked politely.

Mortimer Allen parted his full lips, but turned toward Foster in lieu of answering.

Dr. Foster said, "Merely a visit. They are on their way to Bath to take the waters. I don't credit the medicinal benefits myself, but I give you leave to prove me wrong, Mortimer."

"A rare pleasure it would be to accomplish that, I assure you."

"Well, do come upstairs for port and cigars. I have some good cheese and herring as well."

"Lead the way," Mortimer said.

"Thaht's all right. You gentlemen go on," John Evans said. "I'll leave you two to visit."

The man had a mild accent that Graves could not place after such a brief sampling.

"Are you sure, Evans?" Mortimer Allen asked.

"Indeed. I'll do on my own. I expect there's a public house nearby."

"Don't be out late. We've an early start on the morrow."

"I haven't forgotten."

The two older men went up the stairs together to Foster's private living quarters.

Evans looked at Graves. "If you would kindly point me in the right direction, I shall disturb you no more."

"Mind a bit of company?" Graves asked, curious about the man.

"If you like."

As the two walked the short distance to the Hare and Hounds, Graves hit on the origin of the man's accent. The long vowels, the clipped staccato syllables, the *r*'s, nearly rolled. "Wales?" he asked.

Evans smiled. "God's country, yes."

They entered the small, dim public house and took stools at the polished wooden counter. Two old men, one Adam recognized as Mr. Owen, sat in chairs near the fire, their dogs lying at their feet. He was relieved when the curs paid him no mind.

Once Freddy McNeal had served them each a half pint, Graves asked Mr. Evans, "But you live in London now?"

"Had to find work, hadn't I?"

"And what is your work, if I may ask?"

The man paused, considering, an odd smile playing about his lips. "I serve a city livery company, like. But I *work* for Mr. Allen."

Before Graves could ask him to explain, Evans asked, "And you? Who do you serve?"

"I would like to say I serve my patients. But as you said, I *work* for Dr. Foster."

Evans nodded and took a sip of dark ale. "What's he like?"

"A man of strong opinions. An experienced physician."

Evans grimaced. "No offense, mind, but I've never cared much for physicians—and thaht's the truth."

"May I ask why not?"

"Comes to this. In plague years, when the rich fled London for the country, every physician followed, leaving the poor to suffer and die without care. Surgeons followed. But apothecaries all stayed—to a mahn."

"You admire them."

"I do. When a body's ailing, money or no, apothecaries turn up trumps. Which is why it rankles me to . . ."

"To what?"

"Never you mind. Thaht's the half pint of bitter talkin'." Evans rose. "I'm to bed now."

45

> All doctors are more or less Quacks! . . . and what they talk is neither more nor less than nonsense & stuff. . . .
>
> —The First Duke of Wellington

The next morning, Adam Graves jogged down the stairs from his third-floor rooms, but when he reached the ground floor, stopped, stunned. There stood John Evans. Gone were the congenial ale-warmed gaze and the unremarkable suit of clothes. In their place the man wore a gown of vibrant blue tufted with dozens of golden tassels. His eyes were stern, hard, and brooked no question.

What on earth?

Voices followed him down the stairs. There came Mr. Allen, dressed in an unadorned black gown. Dr. Foster followed him, breakfast teacup still in hand. Foster hesitated at seeing his young partner standing there, but the smile did not waver from his whiskered face.

"I shall bid you farewell here, Mortimer." Foster held out his free hand. "Thank you for coming to address the situation as only you can."

Mr. Allen shook his hand. "You are quite welcome. Again, I apologize for not being able to respond in person to your first letter. But I trust you will be more than satisfied by day's end."

What did it mean? Adam wondered, suspicion gnawing at him.

John Evans opened the door for Mr. Allen, but once they were outside, Graves saw that John Evans preceded the older man down the lane.

"It is going to be quite a day for medicine, Graves. Quite a day."

Adam turned from his place at the window. "How so?"

"Justice, my boy. Justice for the common man and the Royal College both."

"I have no idea what you mean, sir. Has this something to do with your friends?"

"Indeed. Though I count only one as friend. Mortimer and I have known one another since boyhood. His father would have gladly stood him at Oxford, as did mine. I suppose Mortimer had a taste for power—enjoys being a big fish among small. One would think he knew all along he'd end as Master of those beetle crushers and potion pushers."

"What?"

"Yes. Mortimer is Master of Wardens for the Apothecaries' Society."

Adam felt his stomach clench as alarm pulsed through his body.

"We both have well-placed friends in Parliament," Foster continued,"and have helped one another over the years, when a letter to a friend might sway the vote on one medical issue or another. Very broad-minded the both of us, I'd say. That other man is only the beadle of the beetle crushers, who does my friend's bidding."

"Mr. Evans seemed quite well-spoken. A gentleman, I'd say."

"A gentleman? A hired henchman." Foster all but shuddered.

Adam swallowed, his mind reeling. "What are they about?"

"Oh, merely righting wrongs left too long to fester. Really, when one *thinks* of it—the negligence, the arrogance. Refusing to dispense a physician's order? Unpardonable—as the new law makes quite clear." He chuckled into his teacup.

"If you are referring to the Haswells and that order of yours, you know very well they were justified in not filling it."

"So you say."

"I have the patient record to prove it."

"I have the law. And the Master of Wardens of pompous Haswell's very own society."

"The letter of the law, sir, perhaps, but not the spirit. Does not our Hippocratic oath rank supreme? To save a life must be the primary mandate, not the law."

"That's radical politic, young man."

"You brought them here for this purpose, did you not? Journey to Bath, indeed. They stray quite far afield from their jurisdiction, would you not agree?"

"Now who's holding to the letter of the law?"

"It isn't right. In this case, the Haswells have done no wrong."

"Do you not mean *she* has done no wrong? I have not missed your interest in the Haswell girl. But perhaps I *did* miss some new law allowing women to diagnose and dispense physic?"

Adam turned toward the door.

"Hold there, Graves. I advise you—do nothing to interfere. I promise you a bleak future if you do."

Adam Graves reached for the door latch, and felt its cold metallic reality in his hand.

Lilly opened the door to Shuttleworth's and leaned across its threshold. The surgeon-apothecary was alone with his ledgers.

"Mr. Shuttleworth, do you know where Francis might be? I have not seen him these two days gone."

He looked up at her blankly. "Do you not know?"

Her senses became instantly alert. "Know what?"

"Mr. Baylor has taken his leave. Quit my employ."

She was stunned. "But why?"

"He has other plans. Did he not tell you?"

"He told me nothing."

"Well . . ." Mr. Shuttleworth awkwardly straightened his cravat. "They're not my plans to tell."

"Lilly!" Charlie ran up Milk Lane toward her, arms windmilling. "Francis is leaving." He paused when he reached her, bending over and panting to catch his breath. "I just seen him . . . carryin' his bag to the canal."

Lilly stared at her brother, yet hardly saw him nor her surroundings as he spoke.

Charlie straightened. "Remember when he first come 'ere? And spoilt Father's shoes?"

Lilly ran.

She arrived at the canal, out of breath, lungs heaving, as much from emotion as the exertion of the run. There was Francis, stepping down onto the stern of his cousin's narrowboat, moored near the Honeystreet Bridge.

"Francis!"

When he saw her, he left his valise and hat on the deck and climbed back up the bank to where she stood, still trying to catch her breath.

"Where are you going?" she asked.

"London."

"London?" She stared at him in confusion, her mind whirling. Had he told her and she'd forgotten? Was this what it felt like to forget something? This disorientation, this disturbing, irrational dread?

He continued, "It is my turn to see something of the world, I suppose. Learn a few things. Better myself."

"Without saying good-bye?"

He nodded, sheepish.

"But I've wanted to talk to you, to thank you." She swallowed a rising wave of panic. "How long will you be away?"

His grin was rueful. "Do not fret, Lilly. You've not seen the last of me."

She thought of her mother's vain promise to Charlie. She thought of Mr. Lippert, the apothecary from Little Bedwyn, who had stayed in London where the opportunities were too great to give up for village life. "You cannot know that, Francis."

He tilted his head to the side, studying her.

She took a deep breath, forcing herself to remain calm. "If you are determined to go to London, I should like to give you the name of a kindly apothecary I met there."

"An apothecary? At one of your fine London balls?"

"No. In Bucklersbury, where every other shop is an apothecary's or chemist's."

Again she felt his inquiring look.

"I went there a few times, when I was feeling lonely, I suppose. Missing home."

"I am surprised you had the time to miss Bedsley Priors."

"Well, not only the village itself, but my father, of course. And Charlie and Mary and . . . you."

Eyes intent on hers, he took a step forward. "Lilly—"

"Mr. Baylor!" a feminine voice called. Glancing over, Lilly saw Miss Robbins smiling and waving from the lawn of Mill House. "Bon voyage!"

He waved back quickly before returning his attention to Lilly. It stung to realize he had shared his plans with Dorothea Robbins instead of her. Had the two an understanding? She felt her chin begin to tremble.

"In any case," she hurried on, determined not to cry, "the apothecary's name is Lippert. He and his son were very generous when I needed advice on reviving the shop." Lilly darted a glance at the retreating figure of Miss Robbins. "And he has a charming daughter as well."

He raised a skeptical brow. "What is that to me?"

"She is a lovely young woman who adores everything about an apothecary's shop. There is no place she would rather be."

He frowned. "And you wish me to meet her?"

Do I? Lilly hesitated. "Well, if you are ever in need of a friendly face in London."

He looked at her, slowly shaking his head. "Is that what you really want, Lilly? For me to find myself a charming London girl and never return?"

"No. I . . ." She faltered, confused. Of course she wanted him to come back—though not for Dorothea Robbins. *Have I mistaken the matter? Did Francis not renew his attentions to Miss Robbins after I refused him?* Tentatively she asked, "Do you plan to return?"

He expelled a dry puff of air, a bitter pull at his lips. "I don't know. Not until you . . . That is . . ." He ran a hand through his hair. "This is why I thought to leave without trying to say good-bye." He cleared his throat. "Lilly, I know Dr. Graves is a physician, and that he—"

"Come on, Francis!" his cousin called up from the narrowboat. "Must shove off and sharpish. The lockkeeper Reading way goes to bed at eight bells."

Francis lifted a hand to the man, then looked once more at Lilly. "I've got to go."

"But—"

"Francis! We can't wait any longer!"

Francis took Lilly's hand and pressed it with his larger one. "No matter what you decide, I hope we shall always be friends." He turned away and jumped aboard. The crew immediately began casting off.

"Write!" she called as the boat moved away from the bank.

But Lilly knew Francis had never been one to write. His poor mother had received a letter at Christmas and another on her birthday only when Lilly had been there to remind him.

She watched as Francis faded away. He lifted his hand in farewell, and the sight of it caused her chest to ache and tears to burn and well in her eyes. The canal had claimed another dear to her.

She felt bereft. Muddled. Aching. Was he implying what she thought—*hoped*—he was implying? But why did she—when she never wanted any part of the life Francis would likely lead? But she did hope. Too late, she realized she did. But what about Dr. Graves? He had uprooted himself and come to Bedsley Priors to pursue her. Had she not an obligation to him?

She groaned, her prayer inarticulate. She breathed in deeply, exhaled, then breathed in again. She paused. Sniffed the air gently, critically. What was it she smelled? Something sweet and mildly familiar yet too complex to identify. She closed her eyes and breathed in again, relishing the strange, sweet smell. But then something acrid joined the wispy odor.

"Lilly!" Charlie screamed. "Lillllll-leeeee!"

She spun around, eyes scanning the village behind her. A narrow spire of smoke rose above the rooftops, and below, Charlie bounded wildly down the Sands Road toward her.

Fire. Near the shop. Father in bed. *Dear God, no.* Lilly hurried to meet her brother.

"He's burning it, Lilly," Charlie cried. "Burning it all. Grandfather's pretty pots, all broken!"

Lilly ran.

Adam Graves turned the corner and dashed down the High Street. Smoke billowed from a mound in the street before Haswell's door. A small crowd of people had already gathered. Mortimer Allen stood on the opposite side of the High Street watching the proceedings with cool detachment. John Evans came out the shop door, heaved a crate onto the fire, then turned back and disappeared inside once more.

As Adam ran across the cobbles, he saw Mr. Shuttleworth cross the green in his odd upright trot.

Bill Ackers suddenly appeared before Adam, blocking his view and path. "Steady on."

He tried to step around the bulky man, but Ackers took his arm in an iron grip. "Stay back, Dr. Graves. Woe betide ye if Foster hears of ye meddlin' in this affair."

Ackers's bailiff, his brother in size and strength, held Shuttleworth as the surgeon, cravat askew, strained forward. His dark troubled eyes met Adam's over the bailiff's beefy shoulder. "Good heavens, man," he cried. "Do something."

"Nothin' he can do to puh a stop to it," Ackers said. "Haswell's in quiy' a lot of trouble. Gentlemen come down from London town with papers." He nodded toward John Evans, coming back out with an armload of dried herbs. "That man in the queer une-ee-form showed me. All legal an' so like."

"Foster paid you off," Adam said. "You knew what would happen today."

"I am only doin' my duty. Keeping the peace, innum? You'll keep yers, too, if yer a clever man."

Adam stopped resisting, stepping back from the constable's hold.

"That's it. Just go on to yer offices, now. Nothing to concern you here."

Adam stepped back, into the shadows beneath a lime tree on the green. Across the waves of heat and roils of black smoke he saw Miss Haswell, clutching a thick book in one arm, and with the other, holding her father back.

Their gazes caught, and for a moment hers alighted, but then, as he stood there, unmoving, her focus dimmed and finally fell away from him. Adam realized it was happening again. He was once more held in fear's grip. Frozen. He uttered a rare prayer, *Lord in heaven, help me!*

The beadle carried out a tall eighteenth-century jar bearing the Haswell crest, and seeing it sent a jolt through Adam's limbs. As if in boiled syrup, he strode heavily across the cobbled street and stood before John Evans. Recognizing him, the beadle hesitated. His hard eyes grew angry and his Welsh accent lilted his answer. "Not workin' fahst enough for you, is thaht it?"

"Please stop, Mr. Evans—John. The charges Dr. Foster brought are unjust."

"Thought you worked for the mahn?"

"Yes. But I can prove that a person would have died if Haswell's had filled Foster's order."

"Show it to the Master, then." He jerked his head toward Mortimer Allen, across the street.

"No, John. I am showing it to you—a man of honor. Your master and mine are in league together. Would you destroy the livelihood—the legacy—of an innocent man? A noble apothecary?"

Evans hesitated. "I've a writ with two charges—not just the one. Are you telling me there's no truth in either of them? Thaht . . . this"—he nodded toward the pile of broken rubble—"was unjust?" For a moment the man's green eyes looked bleak, urging him to deny it, to renounce his guilt.

"What other charge?" Adam asked warily.

"Thaht one Lillian Haswell, female, has been practicing as an apothecary, unlawfully diagnosing and dispensing physic without legal qualification to do so. Can you prove this charge false as well?"

Again Adam hesitated, held by the earnest, forthright eyes of the man staring back at him. "I . . . cannot."

Mr. Evans blinked.

"But this is a lesser charge, surely," Adam added. "Not requiring such a heavy toll. No charge of adulterated medicine, no harm done. Her father has been dreadfully ill—she has been nothing but a credit to him."

Something in the man's eyes glinted, as if he understood Graves's reasons for interfering were not merely professional. Evans stared at him a moment longer, then shoved the tall jar into his arms and turned away.

"Why do you stop?" the Master of Wardens called after him. "Who told you to stop?"

"We are well beyond our jurisdiction here. I've done all I will."

"We are not finished here!"

"We are."

John Evans strode down the street, his golden tassels flapping against his blue gown. On him, the effect was regal. Adam Graves had no doubt he had just been in the presence of a true gentleman. A man worth knowing.

The Master sputtered with anger and looked as though he might continue the dark task himself. But he seemed to consider the growing crowd of onlookers, and the fact that the burly constable was retreating with his bailiff, and instead followed after the beadle.

Standing there with smoke burning his eyes and lungs, Adam held the Haswell jar in his arms, feeling defeated and useless. He slowly walked toward Miss Haswell, who stepped forward to meet him as he drew near. Tears streamed down her cheeks. He met her eyes and held out the jar toward her. An offering. She took it mutely from him. For a moment, they both held it. Then he let go, turned, and walked away. Tears stung his own eyes, but that was only the smoke, doing what it would.

46

> The past is the beginning of the beginning . . .
> the twilight of the dawn.
>
> —H. G. Wells

Much had been lost. But they would have lost far more without Dr. Graves's interference.

Still, Lilly was not surprised when he appeared at the shop door two days later, carrying both valise and medical case. That he had shaved off his moustache did surprise her, and she regarded the pale exposed skin above his lip with a feeling of nearly maternal tenderness.

He cleared his throat. "As you know," he began quietly, "I came here to see if a provisional partnership would work out." He smiled wistfully. "It did not."

"I am sorry," she whispered.

He nodded. "I have given up my partnership with Dr. Foster, though he no doubt would have broken our agreement had I not done so first."

"I do not blame you, for that decision nor for that day."

He looked down at the floor. "There comes a time, Miss Haswell, when a man must admit defeat."

She knew he was speaking of more than his profession. "Of course you must not yoke yourself with Foster, but might you not set up on your own?" She attempted a wry grin. "I know where you might let a surgery very cheaply."

"Thank you. But I know this village cannot support two competing physicians."

"Does Foster not mean to retire after all?"

He shrugged. "It does not signify. I go to London."

"To practice there?"

"Not private practice. I own now, I am not fit for it." With a lift of his hand, he cut off her objections before she could voice them. "I intend to return to Guy's Hospital. I was offered a teaching post there before and turned it down. Now I shall take it. No doubt I shall be quite content. I excel in academia." He grinned bravely. "It is only real life I fail to master."

He bowed and took his leave of her. She watched him go, regretting that he had come there only to be disappointed. Yet she knew it was not within her power to make him happy. Nor whole.

The shop cleanup continued. Given her father's state of health and their shaky finances, they could no longer fool themselves that they could restore the shop to its former glory. Humpty Dumpty had taken too great a fall. Though clearly grieving its loss, her father seemed oddly resigned to the closing of Haswell's. Perhaps even relieved. Lilly felt a muddle of conflicting emotions herself.

It took days to sort through the rubble and salvage what they could, to sweep up the spilled powders and scrub away the syrups soiling the shop floor, and to make sense of the jumble which had been her father's surgery. Her father had always been disorganized. His desk and sideboard were forever piled high with papers, but now those papers carpeted the floor and were wedged between sideboard and wall, desk and window. Lilly piled and sorted and read and tossed until the dustbin threatened to overflow. *If the beadle must burn,* Lilly thought tartly, *why could he not have burned this lot?* Such calamity was likely the only thing that would have driven them to this frenzy of purging and cleaning.

Charlie's cat, Jolly, had fled the house during the fire, and had not been found. Though discouraged, Charlie did his best to help, splitting his time between Marlow House and home. At the moment he was sweeping the floor near the large front window, its display empty now save for the rescued apothecary jar.

Still in the surgery, Lilly reached down and pulled at a corner of paper sticking out from under the desk like a child sticking out its tongue.

"Charlie, come here a moment, please," she called.

Charlie was not clever, but he was very strong. When he appeared, she asked, "Do lift the corner of the desk for me, will you? Father's papers have flown everywhere, and knowing me, I'd miss the only one worth recovering."

Charlie heaved the heavy oak desk and Lilly snatched the paper out. "Well done, Charlie. Thank you."

He grinned meekly before returning to his task.

She began to put the letter on the stacks remaining to be sorted when the handwriting caught her eye. This was no bill of lading, no chemist's advertisement. Hairs prickled at the back of her neck. Her heart began to pound. She remembered this handwriting. Of course she would. It belonged to her mother.

Trembling, she sat on her father's desk chair and studied the letter. When had her mother written it? The paper was starting to yellow and bore deep indentations like a triangular leech bite, as though it had been pressed under that desk for a long time.

It had been directed to Charles Haswell without return address. The postal markings were faded and unreadable.

From where had she posted it? From someplace exotic, as Lilly had long imagined? From her London lodgings? Perhaps even from some nearby estate where she had a post? Lilly wondered if her father had read it and purposely hidden it from her all these years. Lilly ran a fingernail under the fold; the yellowed wax seal still held. It might very well have been lost in the chaos of her father's surgery, and lain there unread by anyone. Or perhaps the seal had become reaffixed from the pressure of the desk.

What answers did it hold?

Part of her longed to open it right then and there. Part of her was too exhausted to care. Did she really want to know?

She dutifully carried it up the stairs to her father's bedchamber. She was relieved to see him up and dressed, sitting at his little letter-writing desk, quill in hand.

He looked at her over his new spectacles, and she handed him the letter without comment. He turned it over in his hand, then sat still, staring at it, head bowed.

"I found it under your desk in the surgery."

He did not move.

"Do you know its contents?"

He gave a barely perceptible shake of his head.

"Father?"

"No, but I fear it."

"What more can she do to hurt us? After all this time?" Lilly held out her palm. He looked at her for a moment, blue eyes wide, before lowering his head again. He thrust the letter toward her without looking her way.

She took it from him and carried it to the window, where the light was better. She peeled open the shrunken wax seal and carefully unfolded the stiff yellowed paper.

A clue to the letter's age was given in its opening line.

A year has come and gone since I left Bedsley Priors.

Lilly read on silently. Finding out her mother was not traveling the continent nor the high seas as she had often imagined did not surprise her as it might once have done. At the time of this writing, her mother was living in London under another man's protection. But even that was not what shocked her.

"What can she mean?" Lilly murmured, and reread the section once more, this time aloud.

"I do not lay all the blame at your door, Charles. I know that as a wife, I was a disappointment, and that I broke our marriage vows even before you did, and in more respects. I had been unhappy for quite some time, as you well know.

"I release you to M., Charles. I know she is the wife of your heart. And if that poor afflicted girl can grow up with a father, then I shall take some comfort in that. Comfort I sorely need whenever guilt over leaving L. and C. rises to stab me in the heart. . . ."

Lilly felt frozen and overheated all at once. Nerves tingled down her spine and through her limbs. Her mind spun and spun again, down through the years of memories, trying to force it all to make sense. *It cannot mean what it appears to mean. It cannot.*

She looked at her father and saw the shame and grief in his eyes. For so long she'd assumed him innocent, the victim. She had blamed her mother alone! Blamed and empathized with and longed for. What good was an endless memory if what it remembered had all been a lie?

"Is it true?" Lilly asked. "You and . . . Mrs. Mimpurse?"

"It was a long time ago."

The hands holding the letter shook. "How long?"

"More than twenty years . . . long before your mother left us. I thought we had got past it."

"Where was Mr. Mimpurse?"

"Gone, as he often was, before he left for good."

"Before he died, you mean?"

"You had better ask Maude about that."

"You want me to ask your *lover*? I think not." Never had Lilly used such a cutting tone with her father.

He winced.

Her mounting anger suddenly faded into a cold, dizzy cloud that threatened to suffocate her. "What does she mean, 'if that poor afflicted girl can grow up with a father'? Did she mean she expected you to marry Mrs. Mimpurse and raise Mary as your own?"

Her father looked at her. Two seconds passed. Two ticks of the clock. Three. Four.

"She is my own."

47

The company of agreeable friends will be the best medicine.

—Dr. Hill, *The Old Man's Guide to Health and Longer Life,* 1764

Lilly burst into the coffeehouse—through the front door, not the kitchen. Mary glanced up at her from where she was wiping off a table, startled by the door banging against the wall. Vaguely, Lilly noticed tears in Mary's eyes, eyes that were bloodshot and miserable.

Lilly faltered, suddenly not sure if, or how, to reveal her own news. Instead she asked, "What is it?"

Mary wiped randomly at the table without seeing its surface. Her finger bore only the smallest bandage now. "I know it is foolish. Did I not tell you he would be quickly shot of me once he learned . . . ?"

Oh no. "I am so sorry to hear it."

"I do not blame Mr. Shuttleworth, poor man. It is my own fault for not telling him I was not the woman he thought I was."

Lilly took a deep breath. She said unsteadily, "You are not the woman I thought you were either."

Mary looked up at her sharply, searchingly.

Lilly crossed the room and stood before her. "What do you know of your father?"

Mary straightened. "My father? Do you mean . . . Harold Mimpurse?"

Lilly asked quietly, "Do I?"

Mary stood perfectly still, only her sad blue eyes blinked. Eyes so like Charlie's, Lilly realized.

"Do you know?" Mary tentatively asked.

Lilly nodded. "Do you?"

"Yes."

They heard a sudden scraping of chair legs on the floor above them, and as the two stood there, staring at one another, Maude Mimpurse trod heavily down the stairs. She halted at the bottom step, holding the rail for support, looking from one of them to the other.

Lilly stepped forward and held the letter out to her. She kept her face impassive as Mrs. Mimpurse's wide eyes tried to search her own. Maude's gaze fled to the letter instead, and after a few seconds of skimming its contents, the woman pressed a trembling hand over her heart. She looked again at Lilly, shamefaced. The eyes she turned toward her daughter were filled with trepidation.

"You know?" she asked Mary.

"That Charles Haswell is my father?" Mary said matter-of-factly. "Yes, I know."

"How? For how long?" Maude was clearly stunned.

"My room is above this one, as yours is, and sound carries in this house, as you've just witnessed. I heard the two of you talking once. Arguing actually, about what Dr. Foster said about me. But even if I hadn't overheard, I had the evidence of my eyes, hadn't I? I remember *Papa* well enough to know there was nothing of the man in my veins." She splayed her fingers in the air beside her head. "And where else did this ridiculous hair come from?"

"I never thought it. Not once," Lilly said breathlessly. "Have I not always said you were more clever than I?"

Maude said, "We didn't want anyone to know Mr. Mimpurse was not your father. Your reputation would have suffered."

"Mine, or Charles Haswell's?" At the unusual rancor in Mary's tone, Lilly winced. She could easily imagine her father putting his precious Haswell reputation—and that of his shop—above anything else.

"It's very natural you should be upset," Maude said.

Mary took a deep breath. "I am not. I am glad she knows."

Lilly stared at Mary, a girl she had always known, but had never really known at all.

"Lill finding out we are sisters is the only good thing this day has brought."

Sisters.

"*That*," Lilly said, "I have always known."

Mary looked skeptical, brows high. "Indeed?"

"Though I may have forgotten, for a year or two."

"Lilly Haswell forgetting," Mary said, smiling tremulously. "A day of firsts all around."

Maude, Mary, and Lilly sat in the kitchen near the hearth, all three indulging in a rare glass of honey wine.

"It was about a year after your father returned to Bedsley Priors with his new bride," Maude began. "I had loved Charles for years and, in truth, thought he would marry me when he returned from his apothecary's training in London. Instead he came home with a beautiful wife."

Tears brightened Maude's eyes even all these years later. "I could not blame him. We were not officially engaged. And Rosamond *was* very lovely, though she seemed to regret the marriage almost at once. I was heartbroken but decided I would go on as best I could. I married Harold Mimpurse, though I'd refused him once before. I had always wanted to open a coffeehouse once my days as a maid were behind me, and Harold promised to set me up. And that's the one promise he kept. He was a goodhearted man but had the constancy of a hound." She glanced at Mary. "Sorry, my dear."

Mary nodded.

"He was gone more often than not, peddling his copper wares once he'd been decommissioned from the army. Met up with a widow in Reading and spent more nights with her than with me. It was during one of these absences that your mother left the first time, before you were born."

"The first time?" Lilly interrupted. "She'd left before?" Lilly instantly recalled Mrs. Kilgrove's seemingly delirious words about her mother's first return.

Maude nodded. "Charles and I were both hurting and lonely, and temptation had its way. I thought perhaps we'd be together after all, Charles and I, after a fashion. But then, Rosamond came back only two days later. As though she'd only been gone shopping. I don't know that she ever told your father where she'd gone or who she'd been with, but I saw how shaken and repentant she was. Charles and I were mortified over what we'd done and didn't speak of it for years.

"Your parents had a real marriage after that, it seemed. For a time anyway. Mr. Mimpurse came back as well, though I cannot say with equal repentance. He soon left again, while Rosamond stayed. How could I tell Charles I was carrying his child? When his marriage looked to finally be on solid ground? Especially when Rosamond soon confided she, too, was carrying a child?" Maude paused to drain her glass.

How difficult that must have been for her, Lilly thought. She had always known her father and Mrs. Mimpurse were fond of one another beneath their sharp words and brusque ways, but she'd had no idea how deep those feelings went.

"When Rosamond was in her lying in, I admit I wondered if the child would look like Charles . . . and I wondered if he feared the child would not." She turned wine-warmed eyes on Lilly. "But one look at you and it was perfectly clear you were Charles Haswell's daughter, with tufts of his reddish hair already gracing your little head. As you grew older, you came to look more like your mother, but are still so like him in many ways.

"After that, I tried all the harder to be a friend to your mother. Both of us having wee girls so near in age gave us plenty in common we'd not had before. I cannot say I felt *no* resentment, but I prayed God would give me a love for her, and I think He answered."

Maude reached over and refilled their glasses, though hers was the only one empty.

"Things went along quite uneventfully until Charlie was born. Such a hard birth it was. Your poor father. He did all he knew how, but it wasn't enough. He even sent Mrs. Fowler to fetch Dr. Foster. The man was so long in coming, Charles thought he had refused. Foster never gave an excuse for his delay. I don't think your father has ever forgiven him for it."

Lilly shook her head. "I had no idea."

"Finally Foster did come with his gruesome forceps and cold condescension and pulled the child from your mother at last. To his credit, he also revived the babe. Poor Charlie was nearly blue at birth."

Thoughtfully, Maude shook her head. "Rosamond was cast down after that. Not even your sweet face could cheer her."

Lilly felt the familiar ache of rejection stir in her breast.

"By Charlie's first birthday, it was evident that something was not right with the lad. Very little could hold his attention. He did not want to be held or petted. Was slow to creep, stand, and walk. But still she stayed."

Maude sighed. "Harold did not. When Mary was twelve years old, he announced he would not be returning. I told no one. I confess I was tempted to announce that he had died on one of his trips. The status of widow so less shameful than abandoned wife. When I received a letter from the Reading widow a few months later, I thought I had brought his death down upon him. Killed in a fall from his horse. Can you imagine? Him, a war hero. I'd have sooner believed the pox." She took another sip and stared at the embers in the hearth.

"Rosamond did not leave until some three years later. I saw her walk away with her carpetbag, dressed for travel. I knew your father had gone to see Sir Henry, so I ran next door, to make certain Charlie was all right. You and Mary were already at Mrs. Shaw's. I asked Mrs. Fowler where your mother had gone, but she said the missus hadn't told her a thing, just bid her look after the lad till Charles come home. I hurried after Rosamond in the direction she'd gone. I did not actually see her on the narrowboat that was heading east on the canal, but Mrs. Kilgrove did. Said Mrs. Haswell had embarked with a tall, dark-haired man in naval dress. Of course, Mrs. Kilgrove's sight wasn't keen even then."

Quinn or Wells? Lilly wondered and shifted in her chair. "In London, I learned that Mother hoped to marry a naval captain before she met Father. But the man married another." She thought of what Dr. Graves had told her. Had first Quinn, then Wells disappointed her?

Mrs. Mimpurse nodded her understanding. She looked exhausted from the telling, eyes bleary and troubled. She glanced back at the letter, almost forgotten in her hand. "I always wondered if your mother knew, or guessed, about your father and I. If it had something to do with her leaving. But with so much time passing between, I hoped I was not to blame." She reached over and grasped Lilly's fingers with her free hand, eyes intense. "I promise you, Lilly, your father and I were together those two nights twenty years gone, and never again since."

Lilly nodded, feeling sick and dazed about the whole affair. "I always feared *I* was to blame."

"Oh, my dear, why?"

Lilly took a deep breath, trying to keep her voice steady. "We argued, you see, a few days before she left. She received a letter, which was rare for her, but would not tell me who it was from. She became angry when I kept asking her. Of course, now I wonder if the letter was from a man. This officer."

Mrs. Mimpurse considered this. "A letter might very well explain why she left when she did. But it wasn't your fault." Again she squeezed Lilly's hand. "Why, if every woman left after an argument with her daughter, there wouldn't be a mother left at home in all of England." Mrs. Mimpurse glanced at Mary, and mother and daughter shared a knowing look.

Lilly felt as if a stone had been lifted from her chest. She gently retrieved the letter from Maude's hand and reread its few lines. "It is as if she expected you and Father to marry. But how could you?"

Maude Mimpurse took a deep, shuddering breath. "How could we, indeed."

On a crisp autumn afternoon, Lilly saw Roderick Marlow standing before his father's grave, black mourning cloak about his shoulders. They had buried Sir Henry a fortnight before. The villagers had turned out in great numbers for his funeral, Lilly and her father among them. She had already given her condolences, which were civilly if awkwardly received. Still, seeing him standing there now, alone, she felt compelled to speak to him.

When he glanced over and noticed her beside him, he acknowledged her with a silent nod.

She stood there with him for several moments, looking at the freshly turned soil. The headstone would be several weeks or even longer in the making.

"What will you do now?" she asked gently.

He wiped his nose with a handkerchief and inhaled deeply. "I suppose I shall go forth and find a wealthy wife," he said archly. "So I can afford the widow's jointure and somehow manage to keep the place up. Father would no doubt haunt me if I let the place fall to ruin."

"And what will become of—" she hesitated—"the former Miss Powell?"

He shrugged. "She was my father's wife, no matter what else she be. She will have a place at Marlow House for as long as she wants one. Though I doubt it will be for long. Once she receives her portion, she will no doubt move on, perhaps even remarry. I wish her no ill will."

"You surprise me," she said. "I never took you for a merciful sort. Except when you secured my brother's release, of course."

He looked at her for a moment, then away, off into the distance. "That was your clever Mr. Baylor's doing. He brought to my attention how my old friend Ackers was having his ribbons yanked by Foster. Never liked the man. I suppose Baylor knew that and used it to goad me into action. Anything to put a fly in that man's ointment." He looked at her again. "Though had I known you'd kiss me for it, I might have done so anyway."

Francis.

"Truth is, I owe Cassandra a debt. I wronged her long ago and believe she married my father as revenge. She never admitted it, but . . ." He left the thought unfinished.

"What happened? How did you—?"

He tapped a finger against her lips. "Tut, tut, Miss Haswell. Have I taught you nothing? That memory is long gone, and I intend to keep it that way."

He glanced down once more at his father's bare grave beside his mother's ornate headstone. "I still regret my bitter words to him. How I wish I might see him again."

She said quietly, "But you can see him again someday. After all, you know where he is."

He shrugged. "I confess I have never shared your faith, Miss Haswell."

"I am sorry to hear it."

"I suppose I lost it when I lost my mother. Did not you?"

Lilly took a deep breath, considering. "For a time, perhaps."

He turned to her and gently gripped her shoulders. "Still, might we not share other things?"

Shaking her head, she pulled away. "Let me go, Sir Roderick. And I will do the same of you."

A week later, Lilly hatched her plan for a long-belated gift for Mary.

"It is all settled," she announced as soon as she stepped into the coffeehouse kitchen. "You and I shall go to London. It isn't right that I have been while you have not."

Mary's lips parted, but she quickly resumed her work. She kneaded the dough, turning the lump over and pressing it down with the butt of her palm. "No, Lilly. I don't need—"

"Yes you do. You deserve a holiday in London. My aunt has sent a far too generous gift of funds which will see us there in fine fashion."

"I don't know. What about the coffeehouse?"

"Father is doing well enough and has said he will help, as will Mrs. Fowler if need be. We have all conspired against you, Mary, so further objections will only prove futile."

As she separated and placed the dough in pans, Mary seemed lost in thought and Lilly was afraid she was formulating another argument. Instead she asked, "Could we eat somewhere very fine?"

Lilly smiled. "Of course."

"And see a palace or two?"

"Or three! And anything else you'd like."

"I would dearly enjoy that, I think."

"And I would dearly enjoy being there with you. Perhaps we might take in a play, or visit the museums, or the shops."

"And Francis?" Mary suggested.

The mention of his name turned Lilly's stomach into a ten-stone sack of wormwood and regret. "Oh. I am sure he is very busy . . . doing whatever it is he went to London to do."

"You've had no word?"

Lilly shook her head and forced a light tone. "I don't even know where his lodgings are. He did send Charlie a letter on his birthday, but it bore no address." Upon admitting she'd checked this, Lilly felt her ears burn and fiddled with her gloves.

"Never mind," Mary said. "We shall have plenty of other handsome sights to see, shall we not?" She grinned, and Lilly could not resist mirroring the gesture.

They settled on Friday of the following week for their departure, and Lilly posted a letter to her aunt and uncle, letting them know of their coming visit and asking to call at their convenience. She went through her wardrobe and pulled out two gowns she had barely worn since returning home, and two others she thought would do nicely for Mary.

They visited the new village milliner for hats and gloves and the dressmaker in Devizes for warm autumn cloaks. Together they planned an itinerary and packed.

On the night before their departure, they sat down to supper together. Her father looking younger than he had in months, Mrs. Mimpurse, rosy-cheeked and cheery. And Mary pretty in a new frock, her hair curled and pinned high on her head in a fashion they had seen in *La Belle Assemblée*. Even Charlie came, late and mussed, straight from the garden, and they had to send him to the well to wash.

"Goodness, Mary," he said upon his return. "You're as pretty as the portraits hangin' at Marlow House."

Mary smiled with no hint of blush. She clearly felt as lovely as she looked.

They dined on vegetable-marrow soup, fried soles, veal and ham pie, and all manner of vegetables, breads, sauces, and jams. The Mimpurse ladies had truly outdone themselves. But the biggest surprise came after, when Mary carried out a beautifully frosted Rich Bride Cake. Or, Lilly mused, was it a Christening Cake?

"What's this?" Maude asked, perplexed. "Is there something you are wanting to tell us?"

Now Mary blushed. "No. I have not gone and got myself a husband. Or a babe."

"Thank the good Lord for that," her mother murmured.

Mary remained standing at the table before them, and made the first speech Lilly could ever remember her giving. "But I do feel there is cause for celebration. For thanksgiving. For God has added greatly to my family, and I am thankful indeed."

"Here, here," Lilly said as she lifted her small glass. She glanced at her father and glimpsed tears rising to fill his blue eyes. She saw him glance at Maude, and answering tears brighten her eyes as well.

"I have always had the best of mothers . . ." Mary began.

Lilly found herself nodding to this. She too had gained the best of mothers. In many ways, Maude Mimpurse had long been a second mother to her.

"But now I have a brother—"

"Now, Mary, I ain't really." Charlie could still not grasp the change in their relationship, and Lilly could barely blame him, so recently had the facts come to light.

"And sister." She smiled at Lilly, eyes shining. Mary's voice was hoarse when she added, "And Father."

Tears spilled down Charles Haswell's freshly shaven cheeks. Lilly was distracted by Charlie, however, his face bunched up into a grimace of confusion and working himself up to a question. Hoping to divert him from asking about Mr. Mimpurse, Lilly said to him, "You don't like cake, do you, Charlie?"

He looked nearly indignant at this. "Indeed I do. You know I do. Father! Lilly forgot I like cake. Why, it's my favorite."

Sharing a knowing glance with Lilly, Mary said, "Then you shall have the first piece, Charlie. Would you like a little piece or a large one?"

"A gurt big one, Mary, if you please."

The moment was saved.

The evening was the most delightful in recent memory. They all stayed and did the washing up together, and then Mrs. Mimpurse shooed the girls off to bed, saying she would finish putting the dishes away on her own. She reminded them they had a big day ahead of them, and the London coach would not wait, should they oversleep. At the kitchen door, her father gently embraced Mary before bidding her a good night. Lilly wanted to throw her arms around her friend . . . no, sister . . . too, but Mary was already backing away, waving good-bye on her way up to bed. Ah, well. They would have a whole week together in London.

The next morning, Lilly awoke early, taking a great deal of time with her appearance. She felt unaccountably nervous about returning to London. Her gowns would no longer be the latest, and her hands were calloused from long hours with the pestle. Thank goodness for gloves. She wished she might have thought to ask Mary to come over and help her with her hair. Not as a servant might, but as sisters might help one another. She felt giddy at the thought, and at the adventure ahead. She packed the items she had just used—brush and comb, tooth sponge and alum—into her valise and checked once more to make certain her money was in her reticule. Putting on her hat and cloak, she slipped the reticule onto her wrist and left her bedchamber, descending the stairs with no effort to be quiet. If her father was not yet awake, he ought to be rising. He insisted he wanted to be there to see them off. But it was not her father who stood in the laboratory-kitchen, awaiting her noisy descent.

Mrs. Mimpurse stood there, a shawl thrown hastily over her nightdress, hair down, face . . . broken. Tears and anguish marred her countenance and Lilly froze in shocked horror. She knew the truth even before Mrs. Mimpurse could form the world-darkening words.

Part III

Thus ends the story of the apothecary. Although he has ceased to exist in name, his art still survives, and though stripped of much of its ancient mystery, it is likely to live, so long as suffering humanity has need of drugs and medicines to alleviate the ills to which the flesh is heir.

—C. J. S. Thompson, *Mystery and Art of the Apothecary*

Sweet Memory! wafted by thy gentle gale,
Oft up the stream of Time I turn my sail.

—Samuel Rogers

48

Remember Man as you Pasby
as You Are Now So once Was i
as i am Now so Must You Bee
Make Peace with Christ And
FOLLOW ME

—1715 epitaph,
Wiltshire Notes and Queries

Mary Helen Mimpurse had died in her sleep. And according to her mother, and to Mr. Shuttleworth who had attended her, peacefully. No sign of a fit marred her lovely, placid features, nor her pale fingers. Mr. Shuttleworth said he had seen the like before, in the asylum where he once worked, though he did not pretend to understand the cause of death.

Lilly did not think she could have loved Mary more for knowing they were sisters, but she did mourn her loss more deeply, more enduringly, for that knowledge.

How Lilly wished she had known the truth sooner, even while she understood her father's and Mrs. Mimpurse's reasons for keeping it secret. She wished she might have explored, embraced, relished the strange and wonderful fact that she had a sister. Had she not always longed for one? Someone with whom to share frocks and courtship confessions. Someone to favour.

Now Lilly longed to look once more into Mary's dear face and recognize all that she had been blind to. Charles Haswell's features softened by Maude Mimpurse's rounder ones. Charles Haswell's—and Charlie's—blue eyes. The ginger hue of the Haswell hair, though a lighter wash upon Mary's fine silken strands. And what of Mary's infallible memory for the most complex recipes? So like Lilly's with physic.

Now Lilly felt guilty for the slight superiority of situation, intellect, and even beauty she had felt toward Mary over the years. *How mistaken I was!* Mary, she concluded, was the wiser, lovelier woman twice over.

As the days, then weeks, then months passed, regret for the past transformed into pining for a future that would never be. Lilly thought of all she and Mary would miss together. They would have been aunts to each other's children. Their children close cousins. She thought of the hours they would have enjoyed, sitting together in Mary's coffeehouse—for it would have been hers—nibbling on scones and village news and the triumphs of their children and grandchildren.

What comfort there would have been in beholding that familiar face and seeing the lines and reeves there, as on her own. They would have grown old together, yet seen in each other the young women they had once been, long after everyone else saw but two grizzled crones. Long after their husbands were gone—men did seem to die the sooner—they would have bided together as they had "a day back agone," as Mrs. Kilgrove would say. Of course all of this was assuming Mary would have been allowed to wed.

Lilly would have seen to it somehow.

Charlie still visited the churchyard, as he always had. He no longer went to count dead men. He went instead to talk to Mary. He sat in the sun, his back resting against Sir Henry's headstone. Lilly did not think the old baronet would have minded.

Poor Charlie, Lilly thought. He had lost another woman he loved. Lilly prayed nothing would happen to her.

Since the fire, they had begun referring their patients to Shuttleworth's—or even to Dr. Foster, as the case required. Several of their oldest patients, Mrs. Kilgrove and Mr. Owen to name two, still insisted they would see a Haswell and no other, and she and her father did what they could for them.

That spring after Mary's death, Lilly and her father tended the physic garden together, and throughout the summer months, sold the herbs and simples to Shuttleworth and other medical men in the county, but also to the proprietor of The George, and other hostelries which had no kitchen-garden of their own. She—and even her father, when he was able—helped in the coffeehouse now that Mary was gone. Though neither her father nor Maude would likely admit it, Lilly thought the two old friends took great comfort in each other's company.

With the arrival of September, Lilly finally received a letter from Francis Baylor. Her heart squeezed at the sight of it and, hand to her chest, she stepped into the garden to read it.

Dear Miss Haswell,

I have only just learned of Miss Mary's death. I was stunned and deeply sorrowed as no doubt everyone in Bedsley Priors must be, but especially you and Mrs. Mimpurse. You have my deepest sympathies. Had I known in time, I would have returned for the funeral, in hopes of being some comfort to your families at such a dark hour.

Though my lodgings seem to change with much regularity, I know I ought to have given you or your father some way to contact me. I had my reasons for not doing so at the time, but they seem foolish now, given what has happened. I hope you will forgive me.

I am here in London studying to become a fully qualified apothecary. Under the Apothecaries' Act, I need to acquire a certificate from the Court of Examiners to practice as an apothecary. But I did not tell you my plans, because in all truth I was not certain I should be able to afford the schooling, nor that I would succeed in passing the examinations. You know I have never been a quick student. . . .

"Nonsense," she breathed. "That was only as a lad. When you did not apply yourself."

. . . But I am succeeding. Beyond my five-year apprenticeship with your father, the new Act requires instruction in anatomy, botany, chemistry, materia medica, and physic, in addition to six months' practical hospital experience. I am now undergoing the latter here at Guy's Hospital. God willing, I will set out my own shingle one day, if you can believe it. I occasionally see Dr. Graves about the place, though he is master to my pupil. I suppose his return to London means you will soon be returning as well?

I have taken your advice and made the acquaintance of Mr. Lippert and his son and daughter. They have made me most welcome on several occasions. Miss Lippert is quite as charming as you led me to believe, and I must thank you for making the family known to me. The felicity of their society has given my life in London a congeniality I had not hoped to find. Mr. Lippert has even offered to sell his shop to me, hinting that I might have a wife in the bargain. He is only jesting, of course.

Lilly inhaled sharply. *Is he?* she wondered.

Francis went on to describe his studies at both the laboratory and gardens of the Apothecaries' Society as well as his time spent "walking the wards" at Guy's. He ended by giving his address and asking how her father fared. He sent his best to Mr. Haswell and said he would write to Mrs. Mimpurse himself.

He signed it *FB*.

No *love*, no *warmly*, no *sincerely*. Her spirits sank. But after nearly a year, what had she expected?

Still, Lilly wrote back to Francis, at the address he had given, and described her father's ongoing symptoms. She also told Francis in the most dispassionate terms of the demise of Haswell's as he knew it. She was surprised when he wrote back directly and suggested her father come to London. Thomas Bromley and a master apothecary at the teaching hospital were working with glandular and lung fever and might be able to help him. He said he would have suggested it earlier, but believed Charles Haswell would never consider leaving his shop as long as its doors remained open. Francis even offered to share his lodgings. It seemed there was a small pantry her father might have for nothing. She expected he was teasing with this last part and doubted her father would be interested in submitting himself to hospital care in any case.

She was wrong.

Within a matter of days, she and her father had made plans to travel to London. Aunt and Uncle Elliott had extended several invitations over the preceding months and wrote to say they would be delighted to have her stay with them for as long as she liked, Charles as well. But her father was adamant about going to the hospital directly. He was tired of being ill and wanted to start treatment as soon as possible.

Lilly was relieved they would not be arriving during the height of the season, but rather the quiet of autumn. They traveled by post to London and, from the coaching inn, hired a hackney to take them the rest of the distance to Guy's.

Lilly had worn black and grey mourning clothes for six months, as custom decreed for the passing of a sister. But now, a year after Mary's death, she wore one of her more reserved promenade dresses from her London days, no longer in fashion and creased from the journey. She found she could not care. Her thoughts were of Francis. She longed to see him, but felt increasingly jittery and ill at ease as they neared the hospital.

There it was. The gate, the tan and grey building were familiar. Yet how long ago it seemed since she had been there with Dr. Graves. She wondered if she would see him again, and felt nervous at the prospect. She hoped he held no ill will toward her.

Taking her father's arm and a deep breath, they walked past the columns and arched doorway, and into the main corridor.

She was surprised to find Dr. Graves awaiting them in the receiving office. His smile was sincere, if reserved, as he stepped forward to greet them.

"Mr. Haswell." He shook her father's hand. "Welcome. And Miss Haswell." He bowed, then faltered. "I . . . trust you are well."

She nodded. "I am. And you?"

He pursed his lips, considering. "Like a fish tossed back in the pond."

She opened her mouth to reply but hesitated. Did he mean that he was relieved to be back in his element, or that he felt rejected? Before she could fashion some suitable reply, he returned his attention to her father.

"Dr. Bromley has been called away, I am afraid. But I have agreed to oversee your case until he returns." With that, Dr. Graves excused himself, saying he would see if the bed for Mr. Haswell was ready.

Francis appeared along the corridor. His pace hastened to a near-jog at seeing them, and he smiled broadly. Reaching them, he shook her father's hand vigorously. "Mr. Haswell, I am so glad you've come. You've arrived just when you wrote you would."

"Yes, we made good time by post."

He turned to Lilly, suddenly more reticent. "Miss Haswell." He bowed, and she curtsied stiffly, surprised at his cool greeting.

Graves rejoined them, and Lilly saw Francis hesitate. "Ah, here's Dr. Graves." She noticed him glance from the physician to her and back again.

"Dr. Bromley has quite a schedule of tests and treatments in store for you, Mr. Haswell," Dr. Graves said. "I trust we shall have you stronger very soon."

Her father nodded. "Excellent. When do we start?"

"Tomorrow morning. Let's get you settled into a room for a good night's sleep first."

Her father turned to her and said warmly, "I will bid you farewell here, my dear. I am sure you will not want to venture into the men's ward."

"Indeed no." She received her father's kiss and embraced him in return. She whispered, "I shall pray for you every day."

"I count on it." He held her at arm's length and looked directly into her face, as though committing her features to memory. As though in final farewell. Lilly felt her lips begin to tremble and forced them into a smile.

"Never fear," Francis assured her. She felt the barest graze of his hand at her elbow. "He will be in excellent hands with your Dr. Graves here."

She felt her smile falter and her brow pucker at his final words.

"Well," Dr. Graves said to her father. "Why don't I show you the way." He glanced back at Francis, brows raised. "Mr. Baylor?"

Francis was still looking at Lilly. "I shall be along directly. I shall just see Miss Haswell out. Hail a hackney for her."

Dr. Graves nodded, stiffly resigned. "Very well." And led her father away.

With a sweep of his hand, Francis gestured Lilly toward the entrance and walked beside her. She was filled with nervous anticipation at being alone with him. Would he say anything? Should she? Her palms were damp, while her mouth felt suddenly dry.

"Staying with your aunt and uncle?" he asked.

"Yes. In Mayfair."

He nodded. "How does Mrs. Mimpurse fare?"

"As well as can be expected. Still wearing her mourning, though."

Somberly, he reached over and pressed her hand. Her whole arm tingled. "Again, I am sorry I was not there."

She nodded her understanding, disappointed he had released her hand so quickly. An awkward silence followed, broken only by the sound of their echoing footfalls. They had never been so stiff and formal in one another's company before. Had it been too long? Were things irreparable between them?

As they emerged through the columns into the courtyard, Lilly asked too brightly, "And how are the Lipperts?"

He pursed his lips. "Fine, last I saw them." They reached the gutter and Francis hailed a hackney carriage approaching from up the street. "I am afraid I haven't visited of late. I've been busy preparing for exams." He turned to look at her, hesitated, then said, "Your Dr. Graves has never given his reason for leaving Bedsley Priors. I admit I wondered. When I received your letter, I deduced it was something to do with Foster and the fire. I suppose he is waiting until he fully establishes himself here before—"

The hackney driver reined in his horse beside them, the sound of hooves and his "Whoa now" interrupting their conversation.

The jarvey leapt down and opened the carriage door. Francis gave the driver the direction and handed him Lilly's valise. Francis offered her his hand.

She accepted it and stepped up into the carriage. She held on tightly for a fleeting moment, then let go. "Thank you," she murmured. Why could she not find the words? Tell him she'd been wrong?

The driver climbed back to his perch as Lilly took a seat and looked down at Francis from the open window.

Last chance, Lill, she thought. *Say something. Say something now.* Heart hammering, she opened her mouth and managed two breathless syllables. "Francis?"

He lifted his chin to meet her gaze, his brown eyes expectant.

She spoke the words before she lost her courage. "He isn't *my* Dr. Graves."

His eyes searched hers. The jarvey cracked his whip and the carriage lurched away.

When they reached Mayfair, the driver handed her down on her aunt and uncle's street. She tried to pay the jarvey, but he waved her away, saying the gentleman had already done so. Francis, who had always been so careful with his money. Now she realized he had been saving for his education all along. She picked up her valise and paused to take in the tall façade of the building. The stately white townhouse was still familiar, of course. Yet how long ago it seemed since she had thought of it as home.

She walked up the steps and was let in by stony-faced Fletcher, who barely concealed a smile at seeing her. Dupree dashed down the stairs and seemed about to embrace her, then thought the better of it and curtsied instead. Her aunt and uncle did embrace her and welcomed her warmly. How good it was to see them all again.

Stepping into her former room in the Elliotts' home was like visiting a museum of the past. Her best ball gowns, slippers, and hair ornaments were all as she had left them—relics of another age—*a day back agone*. On the dressing table was a clipping from the *Times*, which announced the wedding of Roger Bromley and Susan Whittier. Lilly grinned ruefully. She hoped Roger would finally be happy.

Before going to sleep, she slid to her knees beside the bed. Something, she realized, she had not done a single time while she had lived here those eighteen months. Now she couldn't imagine *not* doing so.

She prayed for her father, far from home, and for the doctors and apothecaries who would endeavor to help him. She prayed for Francis and Dr. Graves. She prayed for Charlie, Maude Mimpurse, and her mother, wherever she was.

Then she climbed into the soft, lofty featherbed with a sigh of pleasure.

Her aunt and uncle had planned a full week of events and outings. Lilly would have liked to visit Guy's again while she was in town, to see how her father was getting on. But he had been adamant that she not worry about him—that she allow the doctors to do their work while she enjoyed herself in London. She would do her best to honor his request.

The dear Elliotts no doubt hoped Lilly would yet return to them to stay. But Lilly knew then that she would not. Not for anything longer than a visit. As much as she enjoyed London, Bedsley Priors was, after all, home.

49

Remember, it's as easy to marry a rich woman as a poor woman.

—William Makepeace Thackeray

Several months later, on a wet day in late spring, Lilly stood upon Grey's Hill, taking in the damp vale, the canal and the village—her village—below. The bluebells and plum trees were in bloom, and the mist carried the honeyed scents of their blossoms.

She was mildly surprised to see Mr. Shuttleworth climbing the footpath toward her. Reaching the summit, he paused to catch his breath. "I've become too sedentary. This mound seems a veritable mountain this morning."

"Good day, Mr. Shuttleworth."

He bowed. "Miss Haswell. How fares your father?"

"He is doing quite well."

"I am pleased to hear it."

In London, her father had undergone several courses of treatment—aconite inhalation among them—and had returned home greatly restored. The demise of Haswell's had produced that silver lining at least. She returned her gaze to the village below, wearing a veil of mist.

"A haypenny for your thoughts," he said.

Quietly, she admitted, "I was thinking about Mary."

He nodded, his features pinched as if in sudden pain. "You must despise me, Miss Haswell. For I know I disappointed your friend."

He picked up a handful of chalk and pebbles in one hand, and with the other, tossed them as far as he could—not far at all. "I suppose I am a coward. But the thought of becoming attached to any woman, dear though she may be, who might succumb at any moment . . . I could not do it."

Do any of us know the number of our days? Lilly thought, but refrained from saying so. She watched as he dusted his hands, unaware that he had gotten chalk on his usually immaculate coat. "I believe I understand, Mr. Shuttleworth, and I know Mary did. But for my part, I would give anything to have a little more time with her, no matter the cost or risk."

He looked at her, then away again toward the village. He inhaled a long breath. "You were great friends."

"More than friends. Sisters."

He lifted his chin. "Ah. I heard the tale, but was not certain I was supposed to know."

"I am glad you know. Did you not once tell us we could be sisters?"

"Yes, angels the both of you. Sisters in spirit."

He was right in a sense. She and Mary had been like sisters even before they knew they were related by blood.

"She was an excellent girl. Truly. I regret I did not tell her so more often."

Tears brightened his dark eyes, and Lilly felt answering tears fill her own. Impulsively, she reached over and squeezed his hand. "So do I."

He looked down at their clasped hands, then turned his gaze to the canal below. "I should tell you I am leaving Bedsley Priors."

Lilly slowly shook her head. *Must everybody leave?* "I cannot say I am surprised, but I am sorry to hear it."

"Are you? Then perhaps you ought to come with me. See more of the world, as you once longed to do. I feel the sea calling to me and must visit her again. Why not come along? There is less to keep you here now, is there not?"

An incredulous laugh escaped her. "Mr. Shuttleworth! I know you have never concerned yourself with the rules of polite society, but even you must see the impropriety of such a suggestion."

He grinned ruefully, and she smiled in return.

"I do enjoy your company, Mr. Shuttleworth, and will miss it more than you know. But . . ." She sighed. "This is my home. I am at last content here. I wonder," she asked kindly, "if you shall ever be content anywhere?"

She spoke from genuine concern and was relieved when he seemed to take no offense.

"I wonder that as well." He looked out to the horizon. "But I cannot help thinking I will find it. Someday, somewhere, beyond that hill, or the next. In the next county or the next port. . . ."

She nodded thoughtfully. "For my part, I would not wish to live always on the move, a few years here and there. Perhaps once, but no longer. I have become quite attached to Bedsley Priors since my London days."

"Yes, sometimes we must lose something . . . someone . . . before we realize its worth."

She remembered Francis once saying something similar. They were silent several moments, each one thinking of his own losses. Finally she asked, "How soon do you leave?"

"As soon as I can manage it. I've received an offer from the advertisement I placed in the *Times*. If all goes as planned, I shall be selling out and moving on in no more than a fortnight."

She groaned inwardly. *Another new medical man to get used to*. "I daresay your replacement will not realize how fortunate he is with so much less competition now that Haswell's and Dr. Graves have gone."

"Has your father no plans to reopen?"

"None he will admit to. He is, however, expanding the physic garden. He likes the idea of making a tidy profit on his *famous* Haswell herbs."

Mr. Shuttleworth chuckled. "Perhaps he ought to stay on as a chemist, then."

"I think not. Haswells are apothecaries the way we are English. One cannot simply change citizenship at will."

Again he chuckled and nodded his understanding.

For several minutes they stood without speaking. Down on the canal, a narrowboat was slowly making its way under the Honeystreet Bridge. "I remember when I first arrived here and saw you standing on that bridge," Mr. Shuttleworth said. "One of the three lovely enticements to settle here."

She nodded at the memory.

"Do you know if Miss Robbins enjoys the sea?"

"Mr. Shuttleworth!" Lilly was incredulous and amused both. "Are you serious?"

"Why not?"

"She is daughter of a boat builder," Lilly allowed.

"My thoughts exactly."

Lilly thought about Francis. "Mr. Baylor seemed to think a lot of her as well."

"Do you think so? He was attentive to her, I own. But nothing to the attention he paid you. In any event, he departed, leaving the field open for me."

She shook her head, grinning in spite of herself.

"You judge me fickle, Miss Haswell? I protest your censure. I have always been completely loyal to whichever one of the three of you I could convince to fall madly in love with me—and did not tend toward seasickness."

Nor sickness of any kind, she thought sadly, but did not say so.

"Now . . ." He rubbed his hands together comically, looking down toward Mill House and the barge yard. "I wonder if Miss Robbins is in the mood for adventure."

Still shaking her head, Lilly watched him go.

Realizing she had lingered far too long, Lilly trotted down the damp, windswept hill to help Mrs. Mimpurse and Jane serve supper. She was enjoying helping at the coffeehouse. For all Mary's teasing, Lilly had learned to convert from her ingrained apothecaries' measurements to the standard with less trouble than she would have imagined. Still, many was the time Maude found her bent over the worktable with a frayed quill and scrap of paper, checking her sums. Lilly was still no great cook, but was steadily improving. She took to baking more naturally. She liked the careful measurements required, the level teaspoonfuls of leavening or pounds of fat. Not the "pinch of this and handful of that" mode Mrs. Mimpurse used to throw together stews, soups, and other dishes with such easy flair.

When she stood in Mary's place at the old worn worktable, Lilly felt closer to her sister-friend. She took pleasure and comfort in mixing, in kneading, in shaping dough. Not so different from mixing and cutting pills, really.

Still, she found herself unexpectedly missing the shop. She hadn't realized how much she had enjoyed knowing how to help people and doing so as confidently as Maude whipped up a suet pudding or pasty. Francis had been right. Lilly even missed the feel of the mortar and pestle in her hands, and when she brought a small one from the shop to use in mixing spices, she saw Maude bite her lip, but the dear woman had not protested.

Now, as Lilly rounded the corner of the vicarage, she slowed her pace according to long habit. When she reached the coffeehouse and opened its door, she paused as she usually did to inhale deeply of the sweet, familiar aromas. Freshly ground coffee beans, cinnamon, nutmegs, ginger, and cloves.

Smells like home . . .

She did not miss the alligator.

50

LOVAGE
A known and much praised remedy.
—*Culpeper's Complete Herbal*

Lilly remembered it clearly, although it was years ago now. For she remembered everything.

She remembered the day Francis arrived by narrowboat more than seven years before, as a seasick apprentice. She had been standing on the Honeystreet Bridge, as she often did, searching for her mother on every narrowboat that passed by on the canal.

She stood there now on a warm springtime evening, a fortnight after her meeting with Mr. Shuttleworth atop Grey's Hill. *One last time*, she told herself. Once more searching—searching God's will for the future, searching her memory for every moment spent with Francis Baylor, Mary Mimpurse, her mother—even Roger Bromley and Dr. Graves. Dear ones lost to her. Any day now, Mr. Shuttleworth would join that list.

She watched as a barge approached from the east, followed by a narrowboat.

She had given up standing there all those months she had tried to manage her father's shop. She hadn't the time for it then. Now it seemed she had a great deal of time.

Or do I? she wondered. She once thought she had all the time in the world to see the world, enjoy the world. Now she understood what far wiser people had long known—no one is promised the world, nor even the morrow.

Lilly used to long for travel and adventure far from Bedsley Priors. But death and loss had narrowed her sights. Her telescope no longer focused on the horizon, but rather on what was nearest and dearest to her heart. The rest was just so much water boiled away and gone—it might steam the glass and cloud one's view for a time, but in the end it vanished, leaving only the purest essence of life behind. Family. Faith. Friends and neighbors. Health. Things Mary would have given her last breath for, and perhaps had.

Lilly told herself all this, and yet she knew. She knew her heart had never gotten over the loss, the missing of one gone away from her. Should she return to London and begin a *new* search? No. She must let go. Again.

The barge passed under the Honeystreet Bridge, its load of coal sinking the vessel low in the canal's waters. A crewman lifted his hat to Lilly, and she dipped her head in acknowledgment. She knew she should be getting back. Her father and Mrs. Mimpurse were having a few neighbors in for whist and tea—an unofficial end to their mourning—and they were expecting Lilly to join them.

The narrowboat approached then, painted in shades of muted gold by the slanting rays of sunlight. Lilly saw two figures on its tiller deck. One hand rising in salute.

She felt a flicker of recognition. Strained forward to better see in the fading light.

It cannot be. . . .

But it was.

Finally, finally, Lilly saw that cherished face, the much-missed and loved person.

The hand waved. The well-known voice called, "Lilly!"

Her heart leapt within her.

It was Francis, coming back to Bedsley Priors.

Before the boat was even lashed to its moorings, Francis jumped from the deck and scrambled up the bank with no thought to his fine suit of clothes. At the end of the bridge, he stopped and looked at her, his earnest gaze reflecting all the longing she felt.

Lilly stood there, feeling stunned and oddly rooted where she was, some fifteen or so feet away from him.

"You can have no idea how much I have missed you," he said, the angles of his face more defined than ever, his brown eyes large and intense.

Lilly swallowed. "Have you?"

"I've thought of you every day. Why do you think I wanted so badly to succeed?"

Breathless, she could only stare at him.

"I have passed the examinations, Lilly," he said. "I am a certified apothecary."

Her throat was suddenly dry. "Congratulations," she managed.

"I am taking over Shuttleworth's. Did he mention it? He's let me have it for exceedingly generous terms."

"Shuttleworth's?" Lilly asked, feeling slow-witted. "*You're* the new apothecary?"

Francis nodded. "Though I do not plan to call it Shuttleworth's any longer. I was thinking . . ." He took a step forward. "That is . . . How does *Baylor and Haswell* sound?"

Lilly's heart, already beating at an alarming rate, felt as though it had taken a shock from the electricity machine. Dragging in a deep, shaky breath, she feigned a casual shrug. "Or *Haswell and Baylor*."

He grinned and opened his arms.

Lilly ran.

Francis caught her mid-air and held her tightly against his chest. Slowly, he let her slip down until her feet returned to the bridge. He released her only to cradle her face in his hands. Lilly looked up at him with all the love she felt, and his warm, chocolate eyes seemed to melt into hers. He leaned down as she reached up, and their lips finally met. She leaned into his embrace and together they stood, with no thought to passersby, nor to the canal, nor to a single boat upon it.

Epilogue

I walked, as I often did, to the churchyard. My brother, Charlie, was not there this time. He was likely off working in the gardens at Marlow House, counting weeds as he plucked them, or ladybird beetles, or emmets crawling about their hill. And I knew he was content in his own way.

I stood before a headstone, still new, not yet cankered by time and wind and lichen. But in my mind's eye, I was standing before another grave. Her grave.

Uncle Elliott had finally sent the letter I had once longed for: *We have found your mother.* Upon reading those words, I remember thinking that we ought to go to her quickly, before she moved again—again out of reach.

But Rosamond Haswell was not going anywhere. Ever again.

When the Elliotts took me "to her," they took me to a London cemetery. To a plot bearing a temporary cross marker with the name *R. H. Wells* inscribed.

Her searching, and mine, was over.

She died in hospital of consumption, her secrets with her. A scrap of paper with Jonathan Elliott's name and address was found among her things, and the hospital had sent a message—hoping, no doubt, for payment. Uncle Elliott had been away traveling, but upon his return he had paid what was due and located the gravesite, leaving the temporary marker until he might confer with me.

I could not protest that she was not buried here in the Bedsley Priors churchyard, when she had so long wanted to escape our village. But I agreed with the Elliotts' plan to purchase a headstone and have it engraved with her legal name. Rosamond Haswell had disappeared, and Rosamond Haswell had been found. If *Rosa Wells* wished a pauper's grave, we would not oblige her. Cemeteries and headstones are for the living, after all. The ones who need a place to mourn and visit and remember.

We held a brief funeral in London. The service was sparsely attended. Jonathan and Ruth Elliott, Charles and Charlie Haswell, Maude Mimpurse, Francis and I. A small announcement ran in the *Times*, but no unfamiliar men—men named Quinn or Wells or Dugan—appeared. In the end, it boiled down to blood and love.

It always did.

After the funeral, Uncle Elliott led me into the library, pressed something into my palm, and closed my fingers around it, saying only, "I found it among your mother's things." When he left me, I opened my hand. My heart lurched at the sight of my name written in a familiar though shaky hand, on a thrice-folded scrap of paper. I unfolded it and saw that it had been torn from the corner of a larger piece. The smeared ink words it bore swam before my eyes.

It is too late to undo what I have done.
Too late to plead forgiveness, or tell you I love you.
But I beg you, do not follow my course.

And please, tell Charlie I am sorry I never returned as I told him I would.

Squeezing my eyes shut, I clutched the paper to my breastbone, and held it there. Only when I held the note aloft once more, tears magnifying my vision, did I recognize the paper itself—the thick, creased paper the color of a tea stain. The curve of a sphere. Torn away . . .

To think I used to covet her *adventurous* life. Even wished she had taken me with her. How foolish I had been.

The memory of my mother's grave receded, and I focused on the one there before me in the Bedsley Priors churchyard. The large headstone my father had paid a dear sum to purchase and a dearer sum yet to have engraved. So many words and flowers and embellishments have not graced a headstone since the first Lady Marlow's. We had feared Mrs. Mimpurse might mind our involvement. But she, dear woman, seemed to understand my need to claim kinship and Father's need for atonement—for though kind to Mary, he had never publicly acknowledged her during her lifetime.

Now I traced gloved fingers along the grooves of the carved-out dates of my sister's life. *1795 to 1815*. Far, far too brief. I sank to my knees before the sun-warmed stone. Tears streamed down my face as I again read the words that ushered in such a bittersweet torrent of pain and pleasure and release.

Here lies
Mary Helen Mimpurse,
The Apothecary's Daughter

I felt a hand on my shoulder and looked up. Francis had come. He offered me his hand and helped me to my feet. In his dear brown eyes I saw love and empathy. He kissed me tenderly and then wrapped his arms around me. For a moment, we stood there, simply remembering. Then together we walked hand in hand back to our shop, back to the endless duties and joys of an apothecary, and his wife.

Author's Note

While most people visit the London Eye or Buckingham Palace, I dragged my long-suffering husband to less-visited places like the Worshipful Society of Apothecaries and a museum of pharmacy. While other tourists snapped pictures of the changing of the guard, he tirelessly photographed ancient mortars and leech jars. I appreciate his help very much. We did *not* visit Bedsley Priors, for the village exists only in my imagination, near the real places of Honeystreet and Alton Barnes, Wiltshire.

I am indebted to John Williams, Beadle of the Apothecaries' Hall, for his gallant and informative tour and for sharing a history of which he is justifiably proud. He even donned his ceremonial gown covered with golden tassels, which represent the posies that beadles of old pinned on to ward off the odors of the plague years. For fictional purposes, I took a few liberties with the information he gave us. I certainly hope Mr. Williams won't come after me wearing that gown.

I am also grateful to Julie Wakefield, Assistant Keeper of the Museum of the Royal Pharmaceutical Society of Great Britain, who gave us a detailed, fascinating tour through the changing medical treatments from early to modern times. She also took pity on my "poor soldier" husband, offering him a soft chair and a cool drink while I continued my barrage of questions.

I would also like to thank my colleagues and friends at Bethany House, especially Ann Parrish, Charlene Patterson, Jennifer Parker, and my editors, Karen Schurrer and Jolene Steffer. Deepest thanks to author Beverly Lewis, for her friendship and prayers.

Greetings to the ladies at Curves, who bought so many books, and to Sarah, the pharmacy technician who first brought the apothecaries' system of weights to my attention.

I appreciate all the readers who have taken time to visit my Web site and send kind e-mails about my first novel, *Lady of Milkweed Manor*. Your encouraging words have helped me through many late nights of writing.

Heartfelt thanks to Carlisa, first reader and dear sister-friend, as well as friends Teresa, Berit, Gina, Suzy, Betsey, Patty, Lori, and Mary, who have given me such support—and a great book party!

Finally, thanks again to my husband and sons, who have given me the time and quiet (usually!) to write. I thank God for you.

Reading Group Discussion Questions

1. What does the opening quotation, "Providence has made the most useful things most common, and for that reason we neglect them," mean to you?

2. When is it easy for you to neglect "the most useful things" in life? What distracts you from your priorities?

3. What surprised you about apothecaries in the early 1800s? How are apothecaries similar to and different from today's physicians, pharmacists, and herbalists?

4. Did you grow up "missing" someone in your life (mother, father, sister, brother, grandparents, etc.)? Did you find ways to fill this void?

5. Mary suffered from epilepsy. Do you know anything about epilepsy or anyone afflicted with it? How has public opinion about this condition changed since the 1800s?

6. Charles Haswell was too proud to ask for help. Do you ever struggle to reach out in times of need?

7. Did you want to know more about what happened to Lilly's mother, or were you satisfied?

8. Have you ever been guilty of wanting something (or someone) only when you cannot have it (or him or her)? Have you ever had to lose something before you appreciated its worth?

9. If you had a memory like Lilly's, what would you want to memorize or remember?

10. Which of Lilly's suitors did you most like? Did she choose as you would have?

The Silent Governess

To Carlisa,
treasured friend & first reader

The virtue of silence is highly commendable, and will contribute greatly to your ease and prosperity. The best proof of wisdom is to talk little, but to hear much. . . .

—Samuel & Sarah Adams,
The Complete Servant, 1825

Remember Who it is that has placed you in your present position; perhaps you have no home, perhaps you have experienced a reverse of fortune; no matter what! It is God who has willed it so, therefore look to Him for guidance and protection.

—*Hints to Governesses,*
By One of Themselves, 1856

Prologue

For years, I could not recall the day without a smoldering coal of remorse burning within me. I tried to bury the memory deep in the dark places of my mind, but now and again something would evoke it—a pulic house placard, a column of figures, a finely dressed gentleman—and I would wince as the memory appeared and then scuttled away, like a silverfish under the door. . . .

The day began wonderfully well. My mother, father, and I, then twelve, rode into Chedworth together and spent a rare afternoon as a harmonious family. We viewed many fine prospects and toured the Roman ruins, where my mother met by chance an old friend. I thought it a lovely outing and remember feeling as happy as I had ever been—for my mother and father seemed happy together as well.

The mood during the journey home was strained, but I chalked it up to fatigue and soon fell asleep in the gig, my head lolling against my mother's shoulder.

When we arrived home, I remained in such buoyant spirits that when my father dully proclaimed himself off to the Crown and Crow, I offered to go along, although I had not done so in many months.

He muttered, "Suit yourself," and turned without another word. I could not account for his sudden change of mood, but then, when had I ever?

I had been going with him to the Crown and Crow since I was a child of three or four. He would set me upon its high counter, and there I would count to a thousand or more. When one has mastered one hundred, are not two, five, and nine so much child's play? By the age of six, I was ciphering sums to the amusement and amazement of other patrons. Papa would present two or three figures and there before me, as if on a glass slate, I would see the totals of their columns.

"What is forty-seven and fifty-five, Olivia?"

Instantly the numbers and their sum would appear. "One zero two, Papa."

"One hundred two. That is right. That's my clever girl."

As I grew older, the equations grew more difficult, and I began to wonder if the weary travelers and foxed old men would even know if I had ciphered correctly. But my father did, I was certain, for he was nearly as quick with numbers as I.

He also took me with him to the race clubs—even once to the Bibury Racecourse—where he placed wagers entrusted to him by men from Lower Coberly all the way to Foxcote. Beside him, with his black book in my small hands, I noted the odds, the wins and losses, mentally subtracting my father's share before inscribing the payouts. I found myself caught up in the excitement of the race, the smells of meat pasties and spiced cider, the crowds, the shouts of triumph or defeat, and the longed-for father-daughter bond.

Mother had always disliked my going with Papa to the races and public house, yet I was loath to refuse him altogether, for I was hungry for his approval. When I began attending Miss Cresswell's School for Girls, however, I went less often.

In the Crown and Crow that day, being twelve years of age, I was too old to perch upon the high counter. Instead I sat beside my father in the inglenook before the great hearth and drank my ginger beer while he downed ale after ale. The regulars seemed to sense his foul temper and did not disturb us.

Then *they* came in—a well-dressed gentleman and his son, wearing the blue coat and banded straw hat of a schoolboy. The man was obviously a gentleman of quality, perhaps even a nobleman, and we all sat up the straighter in defense of our humble establishment.

The boy, within a year or two of my own age, glanced at me. Of course we would notice one another, being the only young people in the room. His look communicated disinterest and contempt, or at least that was how I ciphered his expression.

The gentleman greeted the patrons in gregarious tones and announced that they had just visited a lord somebody or other, and were now traveling back toward London to return his son to Harrow's hallowed halls.

My father, cheeks flushed and eyes suddenly bright, turned to regard the boastful gentleman. "A Harrow lad, ey?"

"Just so," the gentleman answered. "Like his old man before him."

"A fine, clever lad, is he?" Papa asked.

A flicker of hesitation crossed the gentleman's face. "Of course he is."

"Not one to be outwitted by a village girl like this, then?" Papa dipped his head toward me, and my heart began to pound. A sickening dread filled my stomach.

The gentleman flicked a look at me. "I should say not."

Father grinned. "Care to place a friendly wager on it?"

This was nothing new. Over the years, many of the regulars had made small wagers on my ability to solve difficult equations. And even fellows who lost would applaud and buy Papa ale and me ginger beer.

The gentleman's mouth twisted. "A wager on what?"

"That the girl can best your boy in arithmetic? They do teach arithmetic at Harrow, I trust?"

"Of course they do, man. It is the best school in the country. In the world."

"No doubt you are right. Still, the girl here is clever. Is she not, folks?" Papa turned to the regulars around the room for support. "Attends Miss Cresswell's School for Girls."

"Miss Cresswell's?" The gentleman's sarcasm sent shivers down my spine. "My, my, Herbert, we had better declare defeat before we begin."

My father somehow retained control of his temper. Even feigned a shrug of nonchalance. "Might make for a diverting contest."

The gentleman eyed him, glass midway to his lips. "What do you propose?"

"Nothing out of the ordinary. Sums, divisions, multiplications. First correct answer wins. Best of three?"

That was when I saw it—the boy's look of studied indifference, of confidence, fell utterly away. In its place pulsed pale, sickly fear.

The gentleman glanced at his son, then finished his drink. "I don't find such sport amusing, my good man. Besides, we must be on our way. Long journey ahead." He placed his glass and a gold guinea on the counter.

"I don't blame you," Papa rose and placed his own guinea on the bar. "A bitter pill, bein' bested by a girl."

"*Pu-ppa . . .*" I whispered. "Don't."

"Well, Herbert, we cannot have that, can we." The gentleman poked his son's shoulder with his walking stick. "What do you say, for the honour of Harrow and the family name?"

And in the stunned dread with which son regarded father, I saw the rest. I recognized the fear of disappointing a critical parent, the boy's eagerness for any morsel of approbation, and his absolute terror of the proposed contest. Clearly he was no scholar in mathematics, a fact he had perhaps tried desperately to conceal—and which was now about to be exposed in a very public and very mortifying manner.

"Excellent," my father said. "Ten guineas to the winner?"

"Per equation? Excellent," the gentleman parroted shrewdly. "Thirty guineas total. Even I am skilled in ciphering, you see."

I swallowed. My father had not meant thirty guineas. Did not *have* thirty guineas, as the gentleman must have known.

My father did not so much as blink. "Very well. We shall start out easy, shall we? First with the correct answer wins."

He enunciated two three-digit numbers, and the sum was instantly before me and out of my lips before conscious thought could curtail it.

I glanced at Herbert. A trickle of sweat rolled languidly from his hairline to his cheek.

"Come, Herbert, there is no need to act the gentleman in this instance. You may dispense with 'ladies first' this time, ey?"

Herbert nodded, his eyes focused on my father's mouth as though willing the next numbers to be simple ones, as though to control them with his stare.

Papa gave a division problem, not too difficult, and again the answer painted the air before me.

And again the young man did not speak.

Go on, I silently urged. *Answer.*

"Come, Herbert," his father prodded, features pinched. "We haven't all night."

"Would you mind repeating the numbers, sir?" Herbert asked weakly, and my heart ached for him.

I felt my father's pointed look and heard his low prompting, "Out with it, girl."

"Six hundred forty-four," I said apologetically, avoiding the gazes of all.

Murmurs of approval filled the room.

The gentleman stood, eyes flashing. "There is no way the girl could figure that in her head. I see what this is. A trick, is it not? No doubt we are not the first travelers to be taken in by your trained monkey who has memorized your every equation."

I cringed, waiting for my father to rise, fists first, and strike the man. Cheaters infuriated him, and many was the time I'd seen him fly into a rage over a thrown game or race. Yes, he'd take his share of other men's winnings, but not a farthing more.

"Let us see how she fares if *I* propose the question," the gentleman demanded. "And the first correct answer wins the *entire* wager."

Would my father abide such an insulting insinuation?

The proprietor laid a hand on his arm, no doubt fearing for the preservation of his property. "Why not, man?" he quietly urged. "Let Olivia prove herself the clever girl we all know she is."

My father hesitated.

"Unless you are afraid?" the gentleman taunted.

"I am not afraid."

My father's eyes bore into the face of the proud traveler, while I could not tear mine from the son's. Such humiliation and shame were written there.

It was one thing for a girl to be clever—it was unexpected. A parlor trick, however honestly come by. But for a son, his father's pride, and no doubt heir, to be proven slow, to be made a fool by a girl? I shuddered at the thought of the piercing reprimands or cold rejection that would accompany him on the long journey ahead. And perhaps for the rest of his life.

The gentleman eyed the hop-boughed beams as he thought, then announced his equation. No doubt one he knew the answer to, likely his acreage multiplied by last year's average yield. Something like it, at any rate. Against the background of the boy's pale face and bleak green eyes, the numbers appeared before me, but lacked their usual clarity. Instead they swayed and slithered like that old silverfish and slid beneath the door.

The young man's eyes lit up. He had likely hit upon the number by memory rather than calculation, but as soon as he proclaimed the answer, I knew he was correct. The relief and near-jubilation on his face buoyed me up for one second. The answering smile and shoulder-clap from his father, one second more. Then the disapproval emanating from my own father's eyes pulled me around, and I saw the terrible truth of what I had done. Too late, I saw. Never again would he take me with him. Never again would he call me his clever girl, nor even Olivia.

The gentleman picked up my father's guinea from the bar. "I will take only one guinea, and let that be a lesson to you. I shall leave the rest to cover your debts to the others you have no doubt tricked over the years." Turning with a flourish, the gentleman placed a gloved hand on his boy's shoulder and propelled him from the room.

I watched them go, too sickened to be relieved that all I had cost my father was one guinea. For I knew I had cost him far more—the respect of every person in that room.

Slowly I became aware of their hooded looks, their unconscious shrinking back from us. Now they would believe the traveler's accusation that my ability had been a trick all along. All their applause and ale and wagers accepted dishonestly. In his eyes—in theirs—they had all been made fools by us. By me.

By my silence.

1

It is nought good a slepyng hound to wake.
—Geoffrey Chaucer

Twelve years later
November 1, 1815

Heart pounding with fear and regret, Olivia Keene ran as though hellhounds were on her heels. As though her very life depended upon her escape.

Fleeing the village, she ran across a meadow, bolted over the sheep gate, caught her skirt, and went sprawling in the mire. The bundle in her cape pocket jabbed against her hip bone. Ignoring it, she picked herself up and ran on, looking behind to make sure no one followed. Ahead lay Chedworth Wood.

The warnings of years echoed through her mind. *"Don't stray into the wood at night."* Wild dogs stalked that wood, and thieves and poachers camped there, with sharp knives and sharper eyes, looking for easy game. A woman of Olivia's four-and-twenty years knew better than to venture into the wood alone. But her mother's cries still pulsed in her ears, drowning out the old voice of caution. The danger behind her was more real than any imagined danger ahead.

Shivers of fear prickling over her skin, she hurled herself into the outstretched arms of the wood, already dim and shadowy on the chill autumn evening. Beneath her thin soles, dry leaves crackled. Branches grabbed at her like gnarled hands. She stumbled over fallen limbs and underbrush, every snapping twig reminding her that a pursuer might be just behind, just out of sight.

Olivia ran until her side ached. Breathing hard, she slowed her pace. She walked for what seemed like an hour or more and still hadn't reached the other side of the wood. Was she traveling in a circle? The thought of spending the night in the quickly darkening wood made her pick up her pace once more.

She tripped on a tangle of roots and again went sprawling. She heard the crisp rip of fabric. A burning scratch seared her cheek. For a moment she lay as she was, trying to catch her breath.

The pain of the fall broke through the dam of shock, and the hot tears she had been holding back poured forth. She struggled up and sat against a tree, sobbing.

Almighty God, what have I done?

A branch snapped and an owl screeched a warning to his mate. Fear instantly stifled her sobs. Hairs prickling at the back of her neck, Olivia searched the moonlit dimness with wide eyes.

Eyes stared back.

A dog, wiry and dark, stood not twenty feet away, teeth bared. In silent panic, Olivia scratched the ground around her, searching for something to use as a weapon. The undergrowth shook and the ground pulsed with a galloping tread. Two more dogs ran past, one clenching something round and white in its jaws. The head of a sheep?

The first dog turned and bounded after the other two, just as Olivia's fingers found a stout stick. She gripped it tightly, wishing for a moment that she still held the fire iron. Shivering in revulsion, Olivia thrust aside the memory of its cold, hard weight. She listened for several tense seconds. Hearing nothing more, she rose, stick firmly in hand, and hurried through the wood, hoping the dogs wouldn't follow her trail.

The moon was high above the treetops when she saw it. The light of a fire ahead. *Relief.* Wild animals were afraid of fire, were they not? She tentatively moved nearer. She had no intention of joining whoever had camped there—perhaps a family of gypsies or a gentlemen's hunting party. Even if the rumors of thieves and poachers were stuff and nonsense, she would not risk making her presence known. But she longed for the safety the fire represented. She longed, too, for its warmth, for the November night air stole mercilessly through her cape and gown. Perhaps if another woman were present, Olivia might ask to warm herself. She dared move a little closer, stood behind a tree and peered around it. She saw a firelit clearing and four figures huddled around the flames in various postures of repose. The sound of men talking and jesting reached her.

"Squirrel again tonight, Garbie?" a gravelly voice demanded.

"Unless Croome comes back with more game."

"This time o' night? Not dashed likely."

"More likely he's lyin' foxed in the Brown Dog, restin' his head on Molly's soft pillows."

"Not Croome," another said. "Never knew such a monkish man."

Laughter followed.

Every instinct told Olivia to flee even as she froze where she stood. This was no family, nor any party of gentlemen. Fear slithering up her spine, she turned and stepped away from the tree.

"Wha's that?"

A young man's loud whisper stopped Olivia's retreat. She stood still, afraid to make another sound.

"What's what? I don't hear nofin'."

"Maybe it is Croome."

Olivia took a tentative tiptoe step. Then another. A sticky web coated her face, startling her, and she stumbled over a log onto the ground.

Before she could right herself, the sound of footsteps surrounded her and harsh lamplight blinded her.

"Well, kiss my bonnie luck star," a young man breathed.

Olivia struggled to her feet and pushed down her skirts. She brushed her fallen hair from her face and tried to remain calm.

"Croome's got a mite prettier since we saw 'im last," said a second young man.

Beside him, a bearded hulk glowered down at her. In the harsh, gravelly voice she had first heard, he demanded, "What are ya doin' here?"

Panic shot through her veins. "Na—nothing! I saw your fire and I—"

"Looking for some company, were ya?" The big man's leer chilled her to the marrow. "Well, ya come to the right place—hasn't she, lads?"

"Aye," another agreed.

The big man reached for her, but Olivia recoiled. "No, you misunderstand me," she said. "I simply lost my way. I don't want—"

"Oh, but we do want." His gleaming eyes were very like those of the wild dog.

The stout stick she had been carrying was on the ground, where it had landed when she fell. She lunged for it, but the man grabbed her from behind. "Where d'ya think yer going? Nowhere soon, I'd wager."

Olivia cried out, but did manage to get her hand around the stick as he hauled her up.

"Let go of me!"

The burly man laughed. Olivia spun in his arms and swung the stick like a club. With a *thwack*, it caught the side of his head. He yelled and covered the wound with his hands.

Olivia scrambled away, but two other men grabbed her arms and legs, wrestled the stick from her, and bore her back to the fire.

"You all right, Borcher?" the youngest man asked, voice high.

"I will be. Which is more'n I can say for her."

"Please!" Olivia implored the men who held her. "Release me, I beg of you. I am a decent girl from Withington."

"My brother lives near there," the youngest man offered.

"Shut up, Garbie," Borcher ordered.

"Perhaps I have met your brother," she said desperately. "What is his na—?"

"Shut yer trap!" Borcher charged forward, hand raised.

"Borcher, don't," young Garbie urged. "Let her go."

"After the hoyden hit me? Not likely." Borcher grabbed her roughly, pinning both arms to her sides with one long, heavy arm and pressing her back against a tree.

She tried in vain to stomp on his foot, but her kid slippers were futile against his boots. "No!" she shouted. "Someone help me. Please!"

His free hand flashed up and clasped her jaw, steely fingers clamping her cheeks in a vise that stilled her shouts. She wrenched her head to the side and bit down on his thumb as hard as she could.

Borcher yelled, yanked his hand away, and raised it in a menacing fist.

Olivia winced her eyes shut, bracing herself for the inevitable blow.

Fwwt. Smack. Something whizzed by her captor's ear and shuddered into the tree above her. She opened her eyes as Borcher whirled his head around. Across the clearing, at the edge of the firelight, a man stood atop a tree stump, bow and arrow poised.

"Let her go, Phineas," the man drawled in an irritated voice.

"Mind yer own affairs, Croome." Borcher raised his fist again.

Another arrow whooshed by, slicing into the tree bark with a crack.

"Croome!" Borcher swore.

"Next time, I shall aim," the man called Croome said dryly. Though he appeared a slight, older man, cool authority steeled his words.

Borcher released Olivia with a hard shove. The back of her head hit the tree, where long arrows still quivered above her. Even the jarring pain in her skull did not diminish the relief washing over her. In the flickering firelight, she looked again at her rescuer, still perched on the stump. He was a gaunt man of some sixty years in a worn hat and hunting coat. Ash grey hair hung down to his shoulders. A game bag was slung over one of them. The bow he held seemed a natural extension of his arm.

"Thank you, sir," she said.

He nodded.

Glimpsing the stout stick by the light of the forgotten lamp, Olivia bent to retrieve it. Then turned to make her escape.

"Wait." Croome's voice was rough but not threatening. He stepped down from the stump, and she waited as he approached. His height—tall for a man of his years—and limping gait surprised her. "Take the provisions I brought for these undeserving curs."

She accepted a quarter loaf of bread and a sack of apples. Her stomach rumbled on cue. But when he extended a limp hare from his game bag, she shook her head.

"Thank you, no. This is more than enough."

One wiry eyebrow rose. "To make up for what they did to you—and would have done?"

Olivia stiffened. She shook her head and said with quiet dignity, "No, sir. I am afraid not." She handed back the bread and apples, turned, and strode smartly from the clearing.

His raspy chuckle followed her. "Fool . . ."

And she was not certain if he spoke of her or of himself.

Olivia walked quickly away by the moonlight filtering through the autumn-bare branches, the stick outstretched before her like a blindman's cane. She stayed alert for any hint of being followed but heard nothing save the occasional *to-wooo* of a tawny owl or the feathery scurrying of small nocturnal creatures. Eventually her fear faded into exhaustion and hunger. *Perhaps I should not have been so proud,* she thought, her stomach chastising her with a persistent ache.

Finally, unable to trudge along any further, she curled into a ball beside a tree. She searched her cape pockets for her gloves, but only one remained—the other lost in the wood, no doubt. She again felt the firm bundle in her pocket but did not bother to examine it in the dark. Shivering, she drew her hooded cape close around herself and covered her thin slippers with handfuls of leaves and pine needles for warmth. Images of her mother's terrified eyes and of a man's body lying facedown on the dark floor tried to reassert themselves, but she pushed them away, escaping into the sweet forgetfulness of sleep.

2

> Send her to a boarding-school, in order to learn a little ingenuity and artifice. Then, Sir, she should have a supercilious knowledge in accounts . . .
>
> —R. B. Sheridan, *The Rivals,* 1775

The sunrise glimmered through the canopy of branches, beribboned with sparse, tenacious leaves. Her limbs were stiff, her toes numb from sleeping on cold, rooted ground. She rubbed warmth into her hands, then her feet, before replacing her shoes. If she had known what would happen yesterday, she would have taken time to lace on half boots instead of wearing her flimsy kid slippers.

The dreadful scene replayed in her mind.

She'd come home late from her post at Miss Cresswell's school. Found her father's coat on an overturned chair. Her slippers crunched on broken glass. What had he thrown this time? A drinking glass? A bottle? A shrill cry pulled her into the bedchamber, dark, but light enough to see a chilling sight—the back of a man with his hands around her mother's throat. Her mother's eyes wide, gasping for air . . .

Olivia had not thought, only reacted, and suddenly the fire iron was in her hand. She raised it high and slammed it down with a sickening clang, and he fell facedown on the floor. The force of the blow reverberated up her arm and into her shoulder. Numbing shock followed like an icy wave. She stared, unmoving, as her mother sucked in haggard draws of air.

Then her mother was beside her, pulling the fire iron from her stiff fingers, and drawing her from the room, through the kitchen to the front door, both of them trembling.

"Did I kill him?" Olivia had whispered, glancing back at the darkened bedchamber door. "I did not mean to do it. I only—"

"Hush. He breathes still, and may revive any moment. You must leave before he sees you. Before he learns who struck him."

By the light of the kitchen fire, Olivia glimpsed the welts already rising on her mother's neck. "Then you must come with me. He might have killed you!"

Dorothea Keene nodded, pressing shaky fingers to her temples, trying to concentrate. "But first I will go to Muriel's. She will know what to do. But he must never know you were here. You . . . you have left the village . . . for a post. Yes."

"But where? I don't know of any—"

"Far from here." Her mother squeezed her eyes shut, thinking. "Go to my . . . go to St. Aldwyns. East of Barnsley. I know one of the sisters who manage the school there. They may have a post, or at least take you in."

Her mother turned and hurried across the kitchen. Reaching up, she winced as she pulled a small bundle from behind a portrait frame.

"I cannot leave you, Mamma—you are hurt!"

Returning, her mother gripped her arm. "If he should die, it will be the noose for you. And that would kill me more surely than he ever could."

She shoved the bundle into Olivia's cape pocket. "Take this and go. And promise me you will not return. I will come to you when I can. When it is safe."

A low moan rumbled from the other room, and panic seized them both. "Go now. Run!"

And Olivia ran.

The scene faded from her mind, and Olivia shuddered. She drew forth the small bundle, studying it by morning's light. At first glance, it looked like an old, folded handkerchief, but on closer inspection, she saw that it had seams and a small beaded clasp.

Why had her mother made this? Had she foreseen last night's events and Olivia's need to flee? Or had she been prepared to make her own escape, from a husband whose violent temper had been escalating for months?

Olivia opened the concealed purse and examined its contents. Four guinea coins were tacked in with thread, to keep them from jingling and giving away their hiding place, she supposed. There was also a letter. She picked it up, but saw it was firmly sealed with wax. She turned it over and read the tiny script in her mother's fine hand: *To be opened only upon my death*. Olivia's heart started. *What in the world?* She thought once more of her father's jealous rages—the overturned chairs, the broken glass, the holes punched in the wall. Still, Olivia had never believed he would actually harm his own wife. Had her mother feared that very thing? Curiosity gnawed at her, but she quickly returned the letter to its place.

As she did, she felt a thin disk within the folds of fabric, apparently a fifth, smaller, coin. A small tear in the lining revealed its would-be escape route. Curious, she worked the coin with stiff fingers back to the hole. As she extracted the shilling, a scrap of paper came with it. It was an inch-by-three-inch rectangle, torn from a newspaper, yellowed with age. It appeared to be a brief portion of a marriage announcement.

. . . the Earl of Brightwell of his son,
Lord Bradley to Miss Marian Estcourt
of Cirencester, daughter of . . .

Brightwell . . . Estcourt . . . the names echoed dully in Olivia's mind. She could not recall her mother mentioning either name before. Why had she kept the clipping?

Her stomach growled and Olivia tucked away the paper—and her questions—for another time. Gingerly she rose and began pulling leaves and needles from her hair. Brushing off her cape and dress, she grimaced at a long tear in her bodice. Her shift and one strap of her stays showed. Thinking of her peril of the previous night, she shuddered, realizing the damage could have been far worse. She pulled up the hanging flap of bodice and tied it crudely to the strip of torn cloth at her shoulder. She hoped she didn't look as dreadful as she felt.

She tried to run her fingers through her hair and discovered it was a knotted mess, her neat coil long-since fallen. She longed for a bath and a comb. *No use in fretting about it now*, she told herself. *If I don't get moving, no one but the trees shall see me anyway.*

Olivia once more wove her way through the trees and underbrush, wondering if the schoolmistress her mother knew would really take in a stranger, and what Olivia would do if not. She bit the inside of her cheek to hold back self-pity and tears. She breathed a quick prayer for her mother and kept walking, her breath rising on the cold morning air.

The trees thinned as the sun rose higher in the sky, lifting her spirits with it. She saw a ribbon of road ahead and decided to follow it, knowing she could return to the shelter of the wood if necessary.

She walked along the road for several minutes, then accepted a ride in the back of a farmer's wagon. His wife looked askance at the stick in her hand but did not comment.

After many jostling, jerking miles, the farmer called a welcome "whoa" to his old nag and smiled back at Olivia. "That's our farm up the lane there, so this is as far as we can take you."

Thanking the couple, Olivia climbed stiffly from the wagon and asked the way to St. Aldwyns.

"Follow the river there," the farmer said, pointing. "It'll be quicker than the road, though you'll not meet another wagon."

Olivia followed the river as it passed through a rolling vale, skirted a tiny hamlet, then another. Soon after that, the river disappeared within a copse of trees. *Not another wood* . . . Olivia lamented. She did not wish to lose her way, so she took a deep breath and entered the copse.

The trees were not dense, and through them she saw an open field beyond. Having had her fill of trees the previous night, she walked faster.

A sound startled Olivia, and she stopped abruptly. Listening over her pounding heart, she heard it once more. Barking. Her stomach lurched. More wild dogs? Coming fast! She was running before she consciously chose to, stick banging against her leg. With her free hand, she hiked up her skirts and darted onto the field. Ignoring the cinder burning in her side, she ran on, not daring to pause to look behind her. Another sound joined the first—a low rumble, growing louder. Thunder? A search party?

The dogs drew closer—she could hear the barking distinctly now—they were nearly upon her. Panic gripped her. Something nipped at her skirts, and she spun around, swinging the stick and yelling at the top of her voice.

"Be gone! Go!" The barking dogs skidded and jumped. She grazed one on its rump, and it yelped and ran away.

Slowly the blur of mottled fur came into focus and she realized these were not wild dogs at all. Horse hooves thundered around her. She looked up in a daze as a small army of scarlet coats and black hats—men in hunting attire—charged up on all sides.

"Stand clear!" one of the riders shouted, his roan galloping dangerously close.

She leapt out of his way. Then she screamed and lifted her arms over her head—for she had jumped right into the path of an oncoming horse. Its rider pulled up sharply and the black horse skittered and reared up. Dirt flew, splattering Olivia's face. The horse's hooves flashed inches from her chin and then exploded onto the ground before her.

"What on earth do you think you are doing?" The rider of the black yelled down. "Are you mad?"

Other riders—whippers-in and gentlemen on field hunters of white, grey, and chestnut—circled around her, their voices raised and angry.

"You have spoilt an excellent hunt!" This from the elderly master of the hunt, silver side-whiskers showing beneath his telltale velvet hat. His lined, aristocratic face was nearly as red as his coat.

"She tried to kill the hounds!" another accused. "The lead dog is limping."

"I thought they were wild dogs!" Olivia sputtered in lame defense.

"Wild dogs!" the huntsman echoed, copper horn hanging from his neck. "I don't believe it. Are you daft?"

She wiped her sleeve across her eyes to clear the mud and her mind. "No. I . . . I—"

"I believe her, gentlemen." The rider of the black horse dismounted and grabbed the stick from her hand. "She is obviously armed to ward off wild dogs."

"From the looks of the chit," the stout rider of the roan called down, "I'd say she battled a mud puddle—and lost."

The other men laughed. Ignoring the jeers, Olivia kept her eyes on the tall young man before her. Though not the master of the hunt, and by all appearances no older than she was, he was clearly a leader of men and cut an imposing figure in his hunting kit and Hessian boots.

Forcing her voice into cool civility, she said, "I am sorry about the dog. Now kindly return my stick, sir."

His eyes were glittering blue glass in a face that would have been handsome were it not imperious and angry. "I believe not. You are far too dangerous."

Olivia could feel her anger mounting as the men continued their laughter and taunts. But it was the disdainful smirk of the young man before her that threatened her self-control, already worn thin by recent stress and lack of sound sleep. She thrust out her hand. "Return it to me at once."

The elderly master of the hunt called derisively, "Have you any idea whom you are addressing, *ghel*?"

Keeping her eyes on the haughty young man before her, she answered levelly, "Someone with very poor manners."

The others reacted with barely concealed snorts of laughter. *Good*, she thought. *See how he likes being laughed at.*

Some new emotion flickered across the man's face, but the expression was quickly overlaid with contempt. Broad shoulders strained against his close-fitting coat as he carelessly flung the stick into the brush some thirty yards away.

Olivia opened her mouth to protest, but the old master called down a steely warning. "Careful, ghel. Bradley there is magistrate as well as lord. You don't want to risk his wrath."

She looked once more at the young man called Bradley. Golden side-whiskers indicated fair hair beneath his hat. Under its brim, blue eyes rested on a bit of dirt on his coat sleeve. With the merest glance at her, he flicked it away with a finger, and in that one gesture Olivia knew she had been dismissed as thoughtlessly.

"Ross!" he called, and a younger man, by appearance his groom, jogged over. "How is Mr. Linton's hound?"

"He is well, my lord, merely bruised."

"Still, bear him on your horse. Linton's kennel-man will want to have a look at him."

"Yes, my lord."

"Thank you, Bradley," the master said. "I think we must call off the hunt for today."

The huntsman nodded and pocketed his horn. "That fox is in Wiltshire by now at any rate."

"Perhaps *she* could be our fox." The stout roan rider jeered, gesturing toward Olivia with his riding crop.

"Excellent plan," another said. "Quite sorry, constable. We thought the sorry creature a fox."

"No—a mad dog!" A second man poked Olivia on the shoulder with his crop, and soon three of them were circling her on their horses, laughing all the while.

"Gentlemen!" came a loud command.

The three men reined in and looked at Bradley.

"That is quite enough," he said. "Peasants are not for prodding."

"Just so," another snorted. "They are for paying rents."

Lord Bradley scowled, clearly not amused.

"Take heart, gentlemen," the master consoled. "The season has barely begun. We shall have many more hunts come winter."

Lord Bradley prepared to remount his tall black horse. He paused, his icy glare resting briefly on Olivia. "Are you still here?"

She expelled a dry puff of air. "No, sir. I have disappeared utterly."

His eyes narrowed. "Have you not somewhere to go?" It wasn't a question.

"I—"

"Go!" he commanded, jerking his crop to the south.

Olivia strode blindly across the field, humiliated and indignant. She was angry at herself for obeying, for fleeing in the exact direction he pointed. Was she a dog herself? He surely had not meant for her to go in any specific direction. Only away. *I was traveling in this direction at any rate,* she thought hotly, and trudged toward the river once more.

3

> Always remember to hold the secrets of the family sacred, as none may be divulged with impunity.
>
> —Samuel & Sarah Adams, *The Complete Servant*

The sun was high in the sky when Olivia knelt beside the river to wash her face and hands. She scrubbed at the stubborn dirt encrusted in the lines of her palms and beneath her nails. She hoped the dirt on her face did not cling as tenaciously. Nor the guilt she felt. Had there been no other recourse? Surely she might have thought of another way to stop her father. She might have called the constable or a neighbor. But it was too late now. Olivia splashed cold water on her face, wishing she could wash away the memory—the regret—as easily.

She found but two hairpins still tangled within her fallen curls and, in the end, tore a strip of ribbon edging from her shift and tied back her hair with it. She did not wish to enter the next village looking like a beggar. Or worse.

The water, while too frigid for comfortable washing, seemed inviting to her dry throat and she bent low to drink, using her now-clean hand as a cup. Cold and delicious. She bent low over the water once again.

"I say! Hello there! Don't—Are you all right?"

Still on her knees, Olivia turned at the call. A man in a black suit of clothes and tabbed white neckcloth briskly approached. Behind him followed a spotted dog and four young boys, a sight which put Olivia more at ease than she would otherwise have been.

"I am well. Only thirsty."

"Oh!" He stepped nearer. "I feared you might be about to do yourself harm. Though I suppose the river is too shallow and gentle here to pose much danger."

"No, sir. I was not."

"Of course not. Forgive me. A young lady such as yourself could have no reason to be so desperate, I trust."

She hesitated, her lips stiffening. "No reason . . ."

"I am Mr. Tugwell," he said, doffing his round, wide-brimmed hat of black felt. "Vicar of St. Mary's."

"How do you do." She guessed him to be in his midthirties, with light brown hair and soft, mobile face.

He extended his hand. "May I offer you a hand up?"

"I fear mine are wet and cold, sir," she apologized as she placed her hand in his.

He pulled her to her feet. "You were in earnest! A cold fish comes to mind." He grinned. "Never fear, I have handled far worse."

She found herself grinning in spite of her recent ordeal. "And my face. I suppose it is a fright?"

He cocked his head to the side and appraised her. "Your face is charming." He nodded toward his boys. "You fit right in with my lot here. These are my sons—Jeremiah, Ezekiel, Isaiah, and Tom. Amos, my eldest, is at school."

"Hello. I am Miss Keene." The name was out of her mouth before she could think the better of it. But how could she lie to four such angelic, albeit dirty, boys?

Mr. Tugwell handed her his handkerchief, then tapped a broad finger to a spot along his jaw.

Blushing, she wiped the same place on her own jaw. "I am afraid I have fallen and made a mess of myself."

"Have we not all done so, Miss Keene?" he asked, a twinkle in his kindly hazel eyes. "Have we not all?"

Not knowing how to respond, she returned the handkerchief and asked, "And who is this?" of the spaniel sniffing at her skirts.

"That is Harley," little Tom supplied.

"Harley likes these wanders as much as we do," Mr. Tugwell explained. "The lady of the house believes a great deal of exercise keeps male animals from tearing about the place." He grinned. "The dog as well."

She smiled. "Might you direct me to St. Aldwyns, sir?"

"With pleasure." Tucking the handkerchief back into his pocket, the vicar said, "We are for Arlington, which is on your way. May we escort you that far at least?"

"Thank you." She thought a moment. "I suppose my first task will be to repair my appearance. Is there someplace in Arlington where I might purchase a needle and thread and perhaps a pair of gloves?"

"Indeed there is. Eliza Ludlow's shop. Miss Ludlow is a friend of ours. Might we have the pleasure of introducing you?"

"Yes, that would be most kind. Thank you."

In company with Mr. Tugwell and his boys, Olivia crossed a stone bridge near the village mill and turned up the high street, passing the Swan Hotel and a row of weavers' cottages—evidenced by stone troughs for washing and dying cloth, and the narrow mill leat flowing past. They crossed the cobbled street and approached a cluster of shops—a chandler's, a wool agent's, and the promised ladies' shop with a display of hats and bonnets in its many-paned bow window.

"Please await me here, boys," Mr. Tugwell said. "And do keep Harley from the chandler's wares this time, hmm?"

The vicar opened the shop door for her. Quickly smoothing back the wisps of hair at her temples, Olivia stepped inside while the bell still jingled.

The shop was small, neat, and sweet-smelling. Shelves displayed gloves, scarves, stockings, fans, and tippets. A dress form wore a flounced walking dress of white cambric muslin. The front counter held fashion magazines and an assortment of cosmetics and perfumes.

A woman in her thirties, dressed in an attractive, vested gown of striped twill, stood at a tidy counter. She smiled brightly at the vicar. "Mr. Tugwell, what a lovely surprise."

Her ready smile dimmed only fractionally as Olivia stepped near.

"Good afternoon, Miss Eliza." He made a slight bow. "May I present Miss Keene, of . . . ?"

Olivia faltered. "Near Cheltenham."

"Who is in need of your services."

"Of course." Miss Ludlow turned warm brown eyes in Olivia's direction.

Mr. Tugwell straightened. "I shall leave you ladies to it. I know little of such falderals, and confess I prefer my ignorance." He smiled at Olivia. "But you may trust Miss Ludlow implicitly, I assure you."

The woman blushed at his praise.

Mr. Tugwell rubbed his lip in thought. "I don't wish to be presumptuous, Miss Keene, but it does grow late, and St. Aldwyns is still a few miles off. You would be most welcome to stay the night in the vicarage guest room. Miss Tugwell will make you quite welcome, I assure you."

"You are very kind. I . . . Perhaps I shall, indeed. If you are certain it is not too much of an imposition?"

"Not at all. And the boys and I promise to be on our best behavior. Though I cannot speak for Harley." He grinned, then turned once more to Miss Ludlow. "If you would be so good as to point out the way, Miss Eliza, once your business is concluded?"

"Of course."

"Then I shall bid you adieu for now." He bowed to both ladies and made his exit.

When the jingle of the shop bell faded, Eliza Ludlow asked kindly, "And how may I help you, Miss Keene?"

"I hope to find a situation, you see . . ." Olivia began.

The woman's dark eyebrows furrowed. "I am afraid this little shop barely provides for me."

"Oh no. Forgive me, I did not mean here. I understand there is a girls' school in St. Aldwyns."

"Yes, I have heard of it. Managed by a pair of elderly sisters, I believe. I cannot say whether they need anyone, but you might try."

"I plan to. But I should not go looking like this." Olivia pulled back one shoulder of her cape, exposing the crudely tied fabric of her frock. "I am afraid I suffered a mishap—a few of them, actually—on my way here."

Miss Ludlow tutted sympathetically. "You poor dear."

"Have you needle and thread I might purchase to put this to rights?"

"Indeed I have. Blue thread?"

Olivia nodded. "And, perhaps, a hairbrush and pins?" Her stomach rumbled a rude complaint, and Olivia ducked her head to hide a blush.

"Of course, my dear." Eliza Ludlow smiled sweetly. "And you must come up to my rooms and repair yourself properly. Perhaps you would join me for tea and cake?"

Tears pricked Olivia's eyes at this unexpected generosity. "You are very kind. I thank you."

An hour later, Olivia's hair was combed and securely pinned, and her gown repaired and brushed reasonably clean. She wore a new chip bonnet, two gloves, and a small reticule dangling from her wrist. She'd had money enough to purchase the bonnet, but Eliza had insisted on giving her a lone glove, saying she'd lost its mate and wasn't it nearly a perfect match? Not wanting to deplete her funds, Olivia had gratefully agreed and accepted. Now her mother's small purse, a new comb, and a handkerchief were encased within the reticule, which Miss Ludlow had sold her for a suspiciously low price.

Prepared to take her leave, Olivia listened as Eliza described the way to the vicarage. "Continue up the high street as it angles to the north. The vicarage is just past an old white house with a dovecote."

"Is it proper, do you think, for me to accept the vicar's invitation?" Olivia asked. "Mrs. Tugwell won't mind?"

"You mean *Miss* Tugwell, his sister."

"Oh. I thought—"

"Mrs. Tugwell died several years ago, poor soul."

"How tragic. Those poor motherless boys . . ."

"Yes." Miss Ludlow's brown eyes glowed sympathetically. "Still, I think it appropriate. Unless you would feel more comfortable in the Swan, though the inn might be more expense than you wish to bear."

"I am afraid it would be."

"Then we shall hope and pray the school has need of you directly."

Olivia pressed the shopkeeper's hand. "Thank you. You have been prodigiously kind, and I shall never forget it."

"You are more than welcome." Miss Eliza was suddenly distracted by a bandbox on the counter, her dark brows knit in perplexity or irritation. "Oh, fiddle . . ."

"Are you all right?"

The woman sighed. "I would be better had Mrs. Howe paid for this feathered cap she ordered. Said she wanted it for a party at Brightwell Court, but the party is this very evening, and still she has not sent anyone round to collect it. And *bon chance* trying to sell this piece of London frippery to anyone else in the village."

"I am sorry," Olivia murmured, but her mind had caught on something else Miss Ludlow had said. "Brightwell Court?" Olivia asked. She remembered the name *Brightwell* from her mother's newspaper clipping.

"Yes. Do you know it? The largest estate in the borough, save the Lintons'. There is a party there this very evening." She winked at Olivia. "But I seem to have misplaced my invitation."

Olivia grinned at her joke. "As have I."

Promising to call on her new friend when she was able, Olivia thanked her once again and let herself from the shop.

The evening was already growing dark, the hours of daylight quite abbreviated in the final months of the year. The wind pulled at her cape and she shivered. It was indeed too dark and cold to continue further. At least by foot.

She walked up the high street where it curved to the north, and passed the village square. She saw a stately church beyond it, which she supposed to be St. Mary's. Several fine carriages passed, and one coachman stopped to ask if she would like a ride.

"Are you for St. Aldwyns?" she asked hopefully.

He shook his head. "Not bound for Brightwell Court like every other fine lady in the borough? Big doings there tonight."

Brightwell . . . There it was again.

Olivia shook her head. "Thank you anyway."

She waited while the carriage passed, then watched as it turned through a gate and up a long, torchlit lane. Had her mother some connection to the place? Olivia felt compelled to lay eyes on this Brightwell Court. Then she would make her way directly to the vicarage.

Olivia walked through the gate, up the graveled lane, past several small outbuildings, and then, there it was. A tall, grey Tudor manor in an E-shape, with a many-peaked roof.

Had her mother friends here? Had she once visited or had a post here? Olivia certainly was not going to knock on the door and ask, especially while the owners were entertaining.

She started to turn back when the lively, happy music caught her attention. It swirled in her ears and swelled in her chest. She stepped carefully across the lawn, drawn by the light spilling from large mullioned windows. As she drew near she received her first good look into one of the grand rooms. Lovely women in fine gowns and distinguished gentlemen in black evening attire stood in groups, talking, laughing, bowing, eating, and drinking. A sigh escaped her.

Mesmerized, she slowly walked past the first wing, glimpsing a buffet graced by a life-size ice swan, towering jelly molds, a stuffed boar, and a huge golden bowl overflowing with fruits. She walked past the recessed courtyard of the shorter leg of the E, and then around the final wing, staring in each window, as if watching vivid tableaux lit by a hundred candles. As she rounded the manor, she walked by another window, open, she guessed, to release cigar smoke or the heat of the crowd. Her steps faltered. Inside what appeared to be a library, a dapper middle-aged gentleman embraced his middle-aged wife. They were alone. The man kissed the top of her head and stroked her back, murmuring some reassurance or encouragement near her ear. The gentle tenderness stung Olivia's heart. She knew she should turn away, respect their privacy. But she could not. Then the man put his hands on either side of her face and said something. The woman nodded, her pale cheeks wet with tears. The man brushed them away with his thumbs and kissed the woman full on the mouth.

Embarrassed, Olivia lowered her head and walked away. She leaned against a shadowed tree to catch her breath. If only her mother and father might have shown such affection to one other instead of brooding silences and heated arguments. If only she herself might one day know such tender love.

A side door opened. Olivia froze beside the tree. Footsteps sounded on the flagstones of the veranda, followed by another set.

"Edward, wait."

"This is not something I wish to discuss before the assembled company, nor the servants."

"Must we discuss it at all?"

Olivia peered from behind the tree, looking for a way of escape. The veranda was mottled shadow and moonlight. Upon it, she glimpsed the same older gentleman from the library standing before a taller man, whose back was to her.

The taller man sputtered, incredulous. "Am I to simply forget what I read?"

"No, I don't suppose you could. But it need not be a disaster, my boy."

"How can you say that?"

"I have known all along and it has not altered my feelings."

"But how did you . . . ? Where did I come from? Who was my mother, my—?"

"Edward, lower your voice. I will tell you one day if you really must know. But not today. Not on the eve of our departure."

Olivia was chagrined to overhear such a personal conversation. What should she do? If she moved at all, even to lift her hands to her ears, they would see her.

The elder man put his arm around the younger man's shoulder. "I am sorry you had to learn of it at all, and especially now, but nothing has changed. Nothing. Do you understand?"

The younger man slapped his chest, his voice hoarse. "Everything has changed. Everything. Or will. If . . ." His voice broke, and Olivia missed the rest of his sentence.

"There is nothing we can do about that now. Promise me you will not attempt to ferret out anything more until we return. Let it lie for now, Edward. Please. You have been given enough to adapt to already."

"That is an understatement indeed, sir."

The father turned his son back toward the manor. "Come inside, my boy. How cold it is. Your mother will wonder what became of us."

The young man muttered something inaudible as they stepped to the door and Olivia released a breath she had not realized she was holding.

"May we *not* burden your mother with this right now?" the older man asked. "I want nothing to spoil this journey for her."

His son sighed. "Of course. Her health must come first." He held the door for his father. "After you."

The older man pulled a sad smile and disappeared inside.

Olivia stepped from behind the tree, ready to make her escape at last. But the young man stopped suddenly, hand on the open door. He stood, staring blindly in her direction. Had he seen her? Heard her?

Her heart pounded. She took a step backward, hoping to further conceal herself in the shadows, and instead collided with something solid and warm. She cried out as a foul sack descended over her head and wiry arms grasped her by the shoulders and hauled her away.

4

> A poacher becomes an infirm old man if he be fortunate enough to escape transportation or the gallows. . . .
>
> —*The Gamekeeper's Directory*

When the sack was pulled from her head, Olivia found herself in a small parlor, staring at a bald man and a round, aproned woman. The man introduced himself. "I am John Hackam, village constable. Again."

"Again," the woman echoed. "No one else will take 'is term."

The constable nodded to the woman. "My good wife."

"What did the earl's man catch 'er at," Mrs. Hackam inquired. "Thievin'?"

"Mayhap," Hackam replied.

An earl? "No," Olivia protested. "I took noth—"

"No time to hear your tale o' woe now, girl. I've an inn to run, and we are full up tonight."

"Full up." His wife nodded.

Mr. Hackam took Olivia's elbow. "It's the lockup for you tonight, and we'll sort it in the morning."

The constable led her from the inn's parlor and out a side door to a windowless octagonal building some twenty yards distant.

"Court is held here at my humble inn regular-like, but the JPs are all at Brightwell Court tonight and can't hear your case at present."

He unlocked the heavy door and firmly, though not roughly, compelled her inside. The door shut behind her, enveloping her in darkness. She heard the key scrape in the lock and footsteps retreating. Weariness and fear competed for precedence within her.

Was this God's judgment for what she had done? She berated herself yet again for not going directly to the vicarage.

Olivia blinked, trying to adjust her eyes to the darkness. Not complete darkness after all—a small red glow shone several yards away. A rat's eye? No. A lit cigar. Suddenly a flame sputtered and sparked to life, illuminating a big man holding a candle stub in one hand and the cigar in the other.

Her heart lurched and stomach seized. Borcher!

The big man held up the candle and peered at her. She prayed he would not recognize her from Chedworth Wood.

"Well, well. What have we here?" He stepped closer and held the candle near her face. In the wobbling light, his fat lips curled into a feline smile. "The hoyden from the wood."

"No. I—"

Tossing aside the candle, he slammed her hard against the door. Pain shot up her spine. She turned and banged on the door. "Help! Please help me!" A scream caught in her throat as Borcher slapped one hand over her mouth and with the other gripped her arm, pulling her back against him. He laughed a ghoulish giggle in her ear, his foul breath making her gag.

"I told ya I'd get ya, girlie. And now I have done."

She struggled and tried to call out, but only a muffled murmur escaped his thick hand. Her mind reeled, *No, no, no!* She opened her mouth and tried to bite his hand.

"Not this time, pet." He released her mouth only to grasp her neck with both hands. He squeezed until Olivia thought his thumbs would crush her windpipe. Something popped within her throat.

Olivia choked and struggled against the pain and suffocation, panic soaring as she struggled to suck in the thinnest stream of air. Was this what her mother had experienced? At least Olivia had been able to save her. *Oh, God,* she prayed. *Please forgive me. I only meant to stop him. . . .* She hoped he would not try again. *Please watch over her,* Olivia silently pleaded as her mind clouded over, the shutters of her brain closing tight.

Blackness.

Vaguely she heard something. A key in the lock? The door banged open, though Olivia could see none of the lamplight that surely was flooding in. Borcher growled and pushed her roughly away as he released her. She would have fallen, but strong arms caught her. She tried to breathe through a throat that felt sealed off. Crushed. She gasped painfully and smelled a man's sweat and pipe smoke. Sputtering and sucking in panting breaths, her vision returned. The constable righted her, then scowled—first at her, then Borcher.

"You there." He glared at her attacker. "An extra fortnight for you. And you, come with me. There is someone to see you."

A fortnight? Olivia thought dumbly. *That is all my life is worth?*

Relieved to be leaving the lockup, she asked no questions. With a trembling hand, she tentatively reached up to survey her burning throat. She thought it a miracle her neck was not broken. As it was, her legs shook from the shock and violence of the ordeal. When she stumbled, the constable took her arm and pulled her along. She would not have remained upright otherwise.

"Lord Bradley wants to question you." The constable sighed in a long-suffering manner. "Wants to see the trespasser properly punished, no doubt." He whistled low. "Looks dreadful fierce, he does."

He led her back into the Swan, pushed open the door to the same parlor, and propelled her within.

She shrank at the sight of the tall man in full evening dress, his blue eyes intense with scrutiny and suspicion, but not, she thought, recognition. She, however, recognized him at once. The haughty young man from the hunt. Lord Bradley. His father was an earl? *Theirs* was the conversation she had overheard?

She looked down, hoping he would not remember her. She imagined she appeared quite altered with a clean face, her hair neatly pinned back—at least it had been—and a proper bonnet over all.

Olivia could feel his glare on her bowed profile. She registered his finely shod feet, then slowly raised her head. *I am not a dog to cower in the corner*, she encouraged herself, forcing her gaze to meet the man's icy blue eyes. He scowled, his countenance darkening. Had he just recognized her from the spoilt hunt?

Staring at the slight figure before him, Edward Stanton Bradley bade his heart rate to slow and his anger to calm. His mind still reeled, not only with the stunning sledgehammer of news he had barely had time to assimilate himself, but with the terrifying prospect that someone had overheard the tidings he hoped with all his being to bury forever. He fisted his hands, ineffectively trying to quench the irrational desire to squash this unknown foe, to silence her before she might open her mouth and devastate them all.

When she looked up at him, Edward felt the barest hint of recognition, but it quickly flitted away. He knew not this sorry creature. *Good heavens, what had befallen her?* She seemed barely able to walk, let alone stand. Had Hackam not held her arm, she seemed certain to fall. Her face was ashen, her neck . . . *What the plague?*

"Hackam, what have you done to the chit?"

"Nothing, my lord."

"Did my man do this to you?" he asked her directly, knowing Hackam would not hesitate to lay blame at the gamekeeper's feet.

Eyes glazed, the girl shook her head.

"Dash it, Hackam. Punishment before a hearing?"

"No, my lord. It was another prisoner. Gordon didn't tell me he'd put a poacher in the lockup. I thought it empty."

Biting back an oath, Edward grimly shook his head. Still, he believed Hackam. He was not a cruel man, but he was busy with his inn and held little patience for his secondary role as constable. The quarter sessions and more frequent petty sessions brought business to his establishment, so he begrudgingly took up the unpopular duty year after year when no one else stepped forward.

"Do you not wish to hear about the poacher, my lord?" Hackam asked. "Likely to be one of the lot what evaded us all summer. Is that not good news, my lord?"

Edward ignored the man's attempt at diversion. "The next session is not for a fortnight, and there is no question of calling an early hearing. My father is leaving the country on the morrow, and Farnsworth is already on the continent. If this is what happens in half an hour, what would become of her in a week?"

"I plan to send her up to Northleach. Let the justices up there deal with her."

Hackam referred to the new house of corrections—a fortresslike prison only about as old as Edward himself. An improvement over the gaols of old, where men and women were held together, but a prison just the same. "That will not be necessary."

"'Course it is. Your man said she were trespassing, maybe even a thief."

The young woman swayed, and Hackam tightened his grip.

"Have you any evidence she meant to steal anything?" Edward asked. He knew trespassing was a petty offense, unless accompanied by theft, nuisance to the land, or injury to a person. But could not great personal injury come of her eavesdropping? Not to mention the repercussions his father would face should his deception be made known?

"Well, she weren't an invited guest, now, were she? What else would she be doin' there?"

"That is what I should like to know." Edward turned to the pale-faced woman. "What is your name?"

She opened her mouth to speak, her small lips forming a silent O. Wincing in surprise, tears swamping her bright blue eyes, she raised thin fingers to her rapidly discoloring throat.

Could she really not speak, or was she a consummate actress?

"Could have her flogged on the pillory," the constable jovially suggested. "That would loosen her tongue."

The girl's pale skin blanched nearly white.

"Or hung in the stocks on the village green. An example to other would-be thieves." The constable rocked on his heels as he considered. "Or ducked on the ducking chair. Haven't used that contraption since my first term."

The woman's eyes flared, then drooped, her posture rigid. She was falling forward before he realized it, her eyes open but unseeing. Hackam's grip was insufficient to stop her fall, and she crumpled to the ground.

Returning to her senses sometime later, Olivia peered through her lashes to find a bespectacled middle-aged man leaning over her. She shrank back instinctively, only to realize she was lying flat while he sat peering down at her, touching her throat in the gentlest of palpations. An apothecary, she guessed. Or a surgeon. She closed her eyes once more and listened to the conversation above her.

"Such an injury could indeed render a person speechless for a time. Have you reason to think her pretending to muteness?"

"She was caught trespassing on our estate." Lord Bradley's voice.

"A great many people were at Brightwell Court this evening. Why do you think her intentions nefarious?"

Lord Bradley did not respond. Instead he asked, "Can she be moved?"

"I think so. Doesn't seem to have any broken bones. Even so, I have given her laudanum. That neck injury must be dreadfully painful."

"Moved, my lord?" The incredulous voice of the constable. "Moved where?"

"Clearly I cannot leave her here, Hackam. Nor do I wish her taken to Northleach for mere trespassing. Release her to my custody for now."

Hackam's voice rose. "Are you certain that is wise, my lord?"

"She doesn't look dangerous to me," the medical man offered.

"Is that your professional diagnosis?" Bradley's tone was acerbic. "I shall hold you to it."

"But—" Hackam tried once more. "She might turn out to be a thief, after all."

"Then you shall have your chance to flog her yet."

Olivia sank into darkness once more, from a hefty dose of laudanum. And fear.

Edward and the constable helped Dr. Sutton settle the young woman into the back of Sutton's cart.

"Speaking of moving," the doctor said. "I dearly hope the trip to Italy does your mother good."

"Thank you, Sutton. As do I."

"Many in my profession attest to the benefits of a warm Mediterranean winter for their patients."

"Do you concur?"

"What I *can* attest to are the benefits of avoiding a damp English winter. That I heartily recommend. When do they depart?"

"Tomorrow."

The doctor nodded. "Then I wish them Godspeed."

The constable had just bid them good-night and returned to the Swan, when the Reverend Mr. Charles Tugwell crossed the cobbles toward them. "Bradley. Sutton." His gaze flicked from the men to the prone girl, concern drooping his hound-dog eyes. "I say, what is happening here?"

"Mr. Tugwell," Edward said quickly. "I am afraid you have come upon me at an inopportune time. Might I come round the vicarage next week?"

"Of course. But that young woman. I know her."

Edward was stunned. "Do you?"

"That is to say, I met her today near the river. What has befallen her?"

"She was caught trespassing at Brightwell Court and, I am afraid, was injured in the lockup by a male prisoner."

"Good heavens!"

"Sutton here believes she will shortly recover."

"Thank God." The clergyman shook his head. "A young lady such as she, locked in with a criminal!"

"We do not know that *she* is not a criminal as well."

The clergyman shook his head. "She seemed a genteel, well-spoken young lady to me."

"Lady?" Edward sneered. "What sort of *lady* lurks behind trees, unchaperoned at night, eavesdropping on private conversations?"

"A desperate one, to be sure, but let us not be too quick to judge. I myself escorted her to Miss Ludlow's to replace the gloves she had lost in some mishap. I believe she said she was on her way to St. Aldwyns, seeking some post or other."

"And of course *you* believed her."

The clergyman eyed him speculatively. "Have you some reason to suspect her of more than curiosity? My own boys were tempted to sneak over and have a look-in at Brightwell Court tonight. All the fine carriages and horses, footmen and musicians, and I know not what. I had to send Zeke to bed without his supper and forbid Tom to leave his window open in hopes of hearing the music. Everyone in the village knew of the party. Why, I imagine Miss Ludlow mentioned it to her. The young lady was to come to the vicarage tonight and sleep in our guest room."

"Was she indeed?"

"I wondered what became of her and dropped by Miss Ludlow's just now to see if she had changed her plans. I imagine she took a brief detour to see the goings-on at the manor and that is all. Pray do not besmirch her reputation by calling her a criminal until she recovers and you learn her true intentions."

"Regardless of her *intentions*, she has likely—" Edward broke off, glancing at Sutton, and waited while the doctor climbed onto the bench of his cart.

"Likely what?" Tugwell urged.

Edward lowered his voice. "I cannot say. But it is imperative that I learn who she is, and whether she plans to use whatever she may have overheard for mercenary ends."

"Good heavens, Edward. What is it?"

"Forgive me, Charles. I am not at liberty to say."

His friend's eyebrows rose. "Even to me?"

Edward grimaced. "Even to you."

5

> People leave their native country, and go abroad for one of these general causes—Infirmity of body, Imbecility of the mind, or Inevitable necessity.
>
> —Stearne, *A Sentimental Journey through France and Italy*

It was nearly midnight when Edward faced his prim housekeeper. Fortunately she was still dressed, the party having only recently broken up. He held the young woman in his arms, still limp from laudanum. He found it ironic that a figure so light could weigh so heavily on his mind. His future.

"This girl was injured in the village," he began. "Attacked by a suspected poacher."

"In the village?" Mrs. Hinkley repeated, wide-eyed.

He hesitated, remembering Tugwell's request, and did not mention the arrest.

"Yes. I don't know all the details, because her injury—there you see her bruised throat?—seems to have rendered her unable to speak."

"Merciful heavens." She opened the door to her small parlor and gestured for him to lay the girl upon the settee.

"Her attacker is in the lockup, Mrs. Hinkley. There is no call for alarm."

"Shall I send Ross for Dr. Sutton?"

"Sutton has already seen her. In the Swan. In fact, we bore her here in his cart."

He could see her brain working, trying to add up his disjointed sentences and make them equal a reasonable explanation for bringing the young woman to Brightwell Court.

"And you thought I . . . could . . . ?"

"I want to see her recover. I feel some responsibility, as she was injured in our village. Being the new magistrate and all."

Again he could see the wheels of her mind turning. Could guess her thoughts. Would not the vicarage be better suited? Or Dr. Sutton's offices. Or even the almshouse? But the woman had not risen to her position by questioning her masters.

"Shall I see to her here in my parlor, my lord? The nurserymaid recovered here after she wricked her ankle."

"Excellent. Dr. Sutton will call tomorrow, but he does not believe her injury severe. In the meantime, I would rather not inform Lord or Lady Brightwell. I do not wish anything to spoil their departure in the morning."

"I see, my lord. As you wish."

After a fitful sleep, Edward bid a stilted farewell to his father, and warmly embraced his mother as they prepared to depart. Once the coach disappeared up the lane, Edward went directly to the housekeeper's parlor. He was determined to discover how much the girl had heard and if she had understood its import. He'd had insufficient time to grasp the potential consequences himself. He had barely slept for thinking of what might happen were she to sell such news to the highest bidder, or even to let it slip in company, where it would spread like barley fire through the county, through the London ballrooms and clubs, to the Harringtons, and the Bradley relatives. He would lose all—his reputation, inheritance, title, his very home.

Could one slip of a girl ruin his life as he knew it?

Mrs. Hinkley met him at the door with a curt nod and let him in, closing the door discreetly behind him. The young woman half reclined on the settee, some foul-smelling poultice wrapped around her neck. Whether the work of Dr. Sutton or Mrs. Hinkley he did not know or care. She wore the same light blue gown, neither that of a hussy nor a lady. A scratch marred one cheek. Her complexion was still pale, but not ashen as it had been the previous night. Her dark hair was neatly coiled at the back of her head. Her intense blue eyes regarded him levelly from between black lashes. She clasped and unclasped her hands, then stretched one out, indicating he should sit as though receiving guests in her very own drawing room.

He remained standing. "If you will excuse us, Mrs. Hinkley?"

The matronly housekeeper hesitated, pressing her thin lips into a disapproving line, but let herself from the room.

When she had gone, he said briskly, "Now that you are somewhat recovered, I must put several questions to you."

She hesitated slightly, then nodded her acquiescence.

"Have you regained the power of speech?"

Again she hesitated, then parted her small lips. A broken rasp came from her throat, and her eyes immediately filled with tears. She gingerly touched her wrapped neck and shook her head, her expression apologetic.

How convenient, he thought, far less than charitably. "Very well, then I shall pose questions and you will nod or shake your head as appropriate."

She nodded.

He took a deep breath. "Was it your intention to spy on us last night?"

She shook her head no.

Well, what would she say? "You overheard my father and I speaking to one another on the veranda?"

Shame flushed her pale cheeks, and she looked down at her clasped hands before nodding.

His heart hammered. "You heard . . . everything?"

Not meeting his eyes, she nodded once more.

Dread twisted his stomach. *Burn it, I am ruined.* "Were you here on anyone's behest?" He began pacing before her. "Did someone send you?"

The girl shook her head.

"Sebastian's solicitor? Admiral Harrington?" He leaned near and stared into her eyes, daring her to lie. Seeing her shrink from him, he pulled back quickly, trying to rein in his emotions. Never before had he dealt so harshly with anyone.

"Where do you . . . ? That is, do you live nearby or . . . ?" He ran agitated fingers through his hair. "Dash it, this is maddening."

She imitated the act of scribbling.

"You can write?"

She nodded and had the cheek to roll her eyes at his skepticism.

He helped himself to the small desk in the housekeeper's parlor and produced a piece of paper, quill, and pot of ink. He placed them on the low table before the settee and waited while she opened the ink and took up the quill. She looked up at him, expectant as a schoolgirl awaiting her tutor's instructions.

He asked, "What is your name?"

She dipped the quill but hesitated. She bit her lip, then wrote, *Miss Olivia Keene.*

Suspicion filled him. "Is that your real name?"

Avoiding his eyes, she merely nodded.

"And where do you come from, Miss Olivia Keene?"

Again, that slight hesitation. *Near Cheltenham.*

She was being purposely vague. But why? He was familiar with Cheltenham; a school chum had recently relocated to the area, but he had no enemies there. Did it signify?

"How old are you?" he asked.

She wrote, *24.*

His age. That surprised him. She looked younger.

"What brought you to our borough?"

I came seeking a post.

"So our good vicar said. Godly man. Always believes the best in people. Sometimes to his cost. Why did you come to Brightwell Court?"

Again that maddening hesitation as she apparently calculated her answer to best effect. She wrote, *Miss Ludlow mentioned the party. I only meant to glimpse the place.*

"And to eavesdrop?"

She shook her head. *That was a mistake. I regret it.*

"As well you might," he muttered. "Did you know of Brightwell before the helpful Miss Ludlow mentioned it?"

She nodded—sheepishly, he thought.

"Where had you heard of it?"

She reached for a folded handkerchief on the settee beside her and, from it, withdrew a yellowed newspaper clipping. She handed it to him.

Skeptically, he read the old type, taking several seconds to recognize the announcement for what it was. *What the devil?* "Where did you get this?"

She wrote, *I found it in Mamma's purse.*

"Did you indeed? How extraordinary. And why would *Mamma* have this in her purse?"

I don't know.

"Do not lie to me."

She shook her head, shrugged once more.

"And you wish me to believe you came here with no other motives? When you had the names Brightwell and Bradley in your possession?"

No other motives, my lord.

It was his turn to hesitate. He was surprised she addressed him thus. He was also surprised she wrote with such a fine hand, but of course did not verbalize the compliment.

Even if she were innocent of all but eavesdropping, what was he to do with her? Let her go? Extract a promise of silence from her? Bribe her?

She bent over the paper and wrote again. As she did, twin coils of hair came loose and fell forward. When she looked up once more, with dark curls framing her pale face, he recognized her with a start as the girl from the hunt. He had been ready to believe her—that she had stumbled upon his estate with no ulterior motives. But this . . . To have her interrupt the hunt and then appear outside his very door? The names Brightwell and Bradley on her person? It was too much of a coincidence. He looked from her face to the final words she had written. Words that pricked his pride.

You have nothing to fear from me.

"I, fear you? You will find, Miss Keene, that *you* had better fear me. As acting magistrate, I hold the power to see you imprisoned, or worse. Do I make myself clear?"

She nodded, but did not look as frightened as he might have wished.

When the housekeeper knocked and tentatively stepped back into her own parlor, Edward straightened and announced, "Mrs. Hinkley, good. It seems Miss Keene would like nothing more than a *trial* post at Brightwell Court. Three months. Is that not so, Miss Keene?"

Again, that irksome hesitation. Did the chit think he was giving her any choice? He glared at her as a myriad of thoughts passed wordlessly behind those bright blue eyes. What he would give for a transcript.

Finally, she nodded. Almost meekly, he thought.

"What is she fit for?" the housekeeper asked, clearly dubious about the notion.

"Emptying chamber pots?" Edward offered helpfully. "Or scrubbing laundry, perhaps?" He liked the idea of assigning Miss Keene to the laundry. She would spend her time in the washhouse and have little contact with the other servants, and none at all with the family.

Miss Keene narrowed her eyes at him.

"Look at them hands, my lord. She has never seen the inside of a laundry, and that's a fact."

"Well, it is never too late to learn a new skill, is it?"

Mrs. Hinkley tapped her chin in thought. "With Miss Dowdle gone and Becky still hobbling about on that ankle, the nursery is shorthanded. We could use an under nurse. One of the housemaids has been lending a hand, but none too happily."

"And what does an under nurse do, Mrs. Hinkley?" Though he addressed the housekeeper, his eyes held Miss Keene's.

"Why, she bathes and dresses the children. Carries up the breakfast and dinner trays, and attends the older children. Nurse Peale, of course, is chiefly engaged with the infant."

The idea of consigning Miss Keene to the nursery also appealed to him. High on the top floor, eating and sleeping separately from all the servants save a nurserymaid and old Nurse Peale, who had been his own nurse and was loyal to him to the last. And what of Judith? She went more rarely to the nursery than he privately thought she ought, but when she did, she was certainly not one to encourage the confidences of a servant.

Could he trust Miss Keene with the children? He believed so. He would have a word with Nurse Peale and ask her to keep a sharp eye on the new girl.

And when she did happen upon another servant or family member in the course of her duties, she was not likely to ask for a paper and quill, was she? Yes, the nursery seemed an excellent plan.

"Under nurse, it is, Mrs. Hinkley." He turned to the girl. "You shall not leave the premises until I give you leave to do so. Nor post any letters without my consent. I trust I make myself clear?"

She opened her mouth as if to reply—or protest—but closed it again and nodded.

So until her voice returned, he should be safe enough. At least until he could figure out if he could trust this secretive, silent newcomer.

6

A Young English Person wishes to obtain a SITUATION as NURSE, Lady's-maid, or Teacher in a school. No objection to travel.

—Advertisement in the *Times,* 1853

When Lord Bradley had skewered her with his shrewd, icy-blue glare and pronounced that she would like a trial post at Brightwell Court—*"Is that not so, Miss Keene?"*—Olivia had known it was a command, not a question. Still, she had hesitated.

A part of her panicked at the thought of staying there. She had not gotten far enough away from Withington. Nor had she made it to St. Aldwyns as planned; her mother would not find her at Brightwell Court. But in truth, she needed a post and bore only the faintest hope of finding one at an unfamiliar girls' school. With only a few coins left in her purse, and no character reference, she could ill afford to refuse a situation and a place to live. And really, had he given her any choice?

As soon as she was able, she would send word to the school, asking the proprietress to let her mother know where she was. What had she said? *"I will come to you when I can. When it is safe."*

But would Olivia be any safer here? For she had overheard a good deal of the conversation between Lord Bradley and his father and could piece together the rest. Could not such knowledge put her in more danger than ever?

Mrs. Hinkley had allowed Olivia a few more hours' rest, then removed the poultice. She gave Olivia a long white apron to wear over her gown—the sole dress in her possession. Only the footman and the coachman had livery, she explained. The female servants wore modest frocks and plain aprons.

Without ceremony, the housekeeper lifted Olivia's frayed hem, took one look at the thin, stained slippers, and said, "It'll have to be new half boots for you when you get your first wages. Eight guineas per annum, paid quarterly."

Eight guineas? A trifling sum indeed.

"You'll have your own small room off the nursery, once Doris moves her things out."

Olivia nodded, taking it all in. The fact that the young lord had children surprised her. *Was he the Lord Bradley mentioned in the marriage announcement Mother saved?*

"Come along. I shall help you get your bearings and introduce you to Miss Peale."

Olivia followed Mrs. Hinkley out of her parlor, where the woman paused. "To the left are the butler's pantry and serving room, which supply the dining and breakfast rooms there ahead of us. Below us are the menservants' quarters, kitchen, and servants' hall. You shall see those another time."

Mrs. Hinkley turned right, striding into the lofty central entry hall with its double front door, tall windows, and white-and-black marble floor. "On the other side of this hall are the library, billiards room, and drawing room. You'll not need to see those."

Olivia followed the housekeeper up the hall's stone, cantilevered staircase, gripping the carved banister to steady herself. When they reached the first floor up, Mrs. Hinkley did not pause. "The family bedchambers and Lord Bradley's study are on this floor."

Olivia was huffing by the time she reached the top floor, but Mrs. Hinkley marched up the stairs and along the corridor with a soldier's unaffected vigor. "And up here are the nursery, children's sleeping chamber, and schoolroom. The nurse and housemaids have rooms up here as well." She knocked on a pair of double doors and pushed both open without awaiting a reply from within. She gestured Olivia in beside her.

In the bright, cheery nursery, Olivia glimpsed a thin adolescent girl blackening the fireplace grate, and an elderly woman rocking a child. The woman rose gingerly at their entrance, the rocking chair still swaying behind her. The chubby baby in her arms sat upright of his own strength but was less than a year old. He wore a long white gown and had a halo of white-blond wisps about his head. The child did resemble his papa.

"Miss Peale. This is Olivia Keene, your new under nurse. She has not been in service before, so you will need to instruct her in her duties."

The old nurse frowned. "Never been in service? At her age? What has she been about all this time?"

The housekeeper pursed her lips. "I am afraid I do not know. My Lord Bradley offered her the post."

The grey eyebrows rose. "Did he indeed? Who recommended her?"

"No one that I am aware of. She presented no letter of character."

Both women looked at her as though she were a freak of nature. Even the adolescent maid paused in her work to stare.

Olivia attempted an apologetic smile.

Nurse Peale narrowed her eyes. "And what have you to say for yourself, my girl?"

Mrs. Hinkley cleared her throat. "Nor has she the ability to speak, I am afraid."

The old woman stared, incredulous. "What? A mute?"

"Only temporarily, or so Dr. Sutton says. She suffered an injury but should recover her voice in time."

"And *Master Edward* offered her a post?"

"Yes, as I believe I said. So. I will leave the two of you to become acquainted. Olivia does read and write, should you want to communicate that way."

The woman's eyes clouded briefly, then sparked. "I shall make myself understood, Mrs. Hinkley. Never fear. But the care of Master Andrew and Miss Audrey . . . without sayin' a word? What good she'll be, I shudder to think. It's children what is to be seen and not heard, not their nurses."

Mrs. Hinkley smiled stiffly. "Yes, well. I trust the two of you will come to a suitable arrangement."

Once Mrs. Hinkley left them, the old woman resumed rocking herself and the child, studying Olivia shrewdly. "I was Master Edward's own nurse. Did he tell you?"

Olivia shook her head, trying not to stare at the wiry, inch-long grey hairs poking this way and that from the vague arc of Miss Peale's eyebrows.

"Such a fine lad he was. And always so kind to me. It was me who looked after him and tended to all his wants. It was me he poured out his troubles to."

Uncertain how to respond, Olivia was relieved not to be expected to reply.

Nurse Peale tipped her head to the side, resting her silver hair against the baby's blond curls. "This is Master Alexander. Ten months old, he is. So like Master Edward at that age. Isn't it a wonder?"

Though she saw nothing to wonder at, Olivia smiled politely.

Nurse Peale lifted a hand toward the young maid. "And that's Becky, the nurserymaid what does the cleanin' and such."

Becky smiled across the room at her, still scrubbing away, and Olivia nodded in return. Olivia thought a girl so young should be in a schoolroom, not in service, but knew many girls were put out to work even younger.

With a bang and a shout, two brown-haired children burst into the room wearing coats, hats, and gloves. Their attire, as well as their red cheeks, proclaimed them just returned from out of doors. A young woman puffed in after them. She wore a grey cape over a plain green frock and an apron identical to Olivia's. A simple muslin cap and ginger hair framed a wide, freckled face, punctuated by bright green eyes and a squat nose.

Upon seeing Olivia, she halted and clapped her hands. "The new under nurse?"

When Olivia nodded, the maid rushed forward and took one of Olivia's hands in both of her own, squeezing it warmly. "Oh! I cannot tell you how relieved I am you've come! Now *you* may have charge of these wild animals and I shall enjoy the peace of cleaning perfectly quiet rooms."

"We are *not* wild animals, Dory," the girl said. "You oughtn't to say so."

"Are you not wild? I'll say you are. Lions and tigers the both of you."

At this, the little boy raised his "claws" in the air and let out a great roar. Olivia flinched.

"What did I tell you? Well, they're yours now, love. You've a friend in me forever. That scamp is Master Andrew and this is Miss Audrey."

The little boy was six or seven years of age and the girl eleven or twelve. Surely too old to be Lord Bradley's children. Unless he was older than he appeared. And besides, they looked nothing like him. They must favour his wife.

"And I'm Doris." The ginger-haired maid looked at Olivia expectantly. "What's your name, then?"

"This is . . . uhh, Olivia," Nurse Peale said. "Rather a fine name for an under nurse. We shall call her Livie."

Olivia parted her lips to object, but just as quickly pressed them closed. Even if she could speak, she had little grounds to insist on *Miss Keene*.

Doris was staring at her, her head tilted to one side. "You always this quiet?"

"She cannot speak at present," Nurse Peale explained. "She suffered an injury to her neck—so Mrs. Hinkley tells me."

Dory's eyes widened. "Are you the girl what got strangled in the lockup? I heard tell of it last night. A poacher, was it?"

Had the tale gotten round already? Lord Bradley would not be pleased. Nor was Olivia eager to spread word of her imprisonment.

"Or did it happen in the Swan?" Doris asked. "That's what Johnny said, but I heard the lockup."

Olivia lifted a faint shrug, and Doris's eyes narrowed.

She turned to the nurse. "Is she daft as well as dumb?"

"I shouldn't think so. Master Edward himself engaged her—with good reason, I don't doubt. Now, what are you standing there for? Do I not see muddy boots on the young ones' feet and coats what need airing out?"

In the tiny chamber that would be hers, Olivia placed her list of duties, which Nurse Peale had told Doris to write down for her, on top of the dressing chest. Olivia had been impressed the maid could read and write—until she had looked at the list. The scrawled hand—the spelling!

Opening the top drawer, she placed her reticule and her gloves inside. Then she hung her cape and new bonnet on a hook behind the door. She had ridiculously little to put away, to make the room her own.

The chamber was narrow, and the ceiling, which was high above the single bed, pitched steeply down to the outside wall, effectively reducing the walking space to half for anyone above three feet tall. The room was paneled in white, the cast-iron bed covered in white tufted cotton. One small dormer window offered the faint glow of afternoon sunlight. From it, she looked down onto a fallow field and the distant wood beyond. Which direction? From the angle of the light, she guessed her room faced northwest. The direction from which she'd come. The direction of home, though home no longer.

What was happening there now? Had her father regained consciousness? Had Muriel Atkins treated his injury and her mother's as well? Or had he . . . died? Was the constable even now mounting a search for her?

Why, oh why, had she given her real name? The shock and weariness had left her mind sluggish. She had not thought quickly enough. And once she had told the vicar her name, she dared not give another to anyone else. Could she hope to remain hidden here—a menial servant on the top floor of this great manor?

Pushing self-centered thoughts away, she contemplated once more what she had overheard and what it might mean for Lord Bradley and his wife and children. Was his wife very disappointed, assuming he had told her? And what of poor Andrew, the eldest son?

The sound of hooves and a shout brought Olivia to her small window once more. Through its wavy glass, she looked down upon the long lane below. A liveried footman hopped down and opened the carriage door, and Olivia watched as a woman appeared in the open frame, a small hat angled upon a head of blond curls. A dark cape flowed around her feet as she stepped gracefully down. The children's mother, Olivia guessed. *His* wife.

As if on cue, Lord Bradley entered the scene and greeted the woman a short distance from the carriage. The woman leaned close to his ear, perhaps to confide something or kiss his cheek; Olivia could not tell from this distance. Arm in arm, the two walked majestically toward the manor and out of view.

Olivia had not heard the nurse refer to a Mrs. or Lady Bradley. Only to Lady Brightwell—"gone to Italy, poor soul." But if this was the children's mother, Olivia knew she would meet her soon enough.

That very lady swept into the nursery a quarter of an hour later. She now wore a lace cap over the golden blond curls curtaining her brow. Her pale blue eyes were round and her cheeks rosy, giving her the look of an angelic little girl. That comparison ceased, however, when one's gaze lowered from her face to the generous curves evident beneath her close-fitting gown of dove grey.

Olivia felt far too shabby to stand in the same room with her.

The woman's large eyes fastened on the infant in Nurse Peale's arms. "There he is. How is my little man today?"

"He is well, madam," Nurse Peale said.

Audrey approached the woman almost shyly. "Alexander smiled at me," she said. "Look, I shall make him smile again."

"Never mind, Audrey. He is smiling at his mamma now."

Andrew left his toy soldiers and tugged on the blond woman's skirts, smiling up at her.

"Oh, Andrew, do wipe your nose," she said.

Before Olivia could move, the little boy obediently swiped his sleeve beneath his dripping nose.

The boy's mother winced, and looked heavenward as if for patience.

Olivia rushed forward with a handkerchief, helping the little boy tidy his sleeve and smeared cheek.

Nurse Peale lifted a spotted hand in Olivia's direction. "This is our new under nurse, Livie Keene."

Olivia curtsied and smiled politely at the woman.

The woman regarded her closely, and if Olivia wasn't mistaken, approval lit in her eyes. "Welcome. I trust I may depend upon you to tend well to Audrey's and Andrew's needs?"

Olivia nodded and curtsied once more.

The woman turned back to her youngest, hands extended. "Come, Alexander, come to mamma. Lord Bradley wishes to see how big you've grown."

Watching her, Olivia thought, *His wife is lovely indeed.* At closer inspection, she appeared to be in her late twenties, perhaps a few years older than Lord Bradley.

The woman took the child in her arms and strode from the room, babbling and cooing to her youngest as she went. Olivia closed the door after her, remembering Nurse Peale's admonition to keep the rattles and cries of the nursery well contained.

"That was Mrs. Howe," Nurse Peale said.

Mrs. Howe? Olivia tilted her head to the side in question.

"The earl's niece. A widow, I am afraid."

Ah. That explained the dull grey dress.

"Her husband died. . . . I forget exactly when, but more than a year ago, before Alexander was even born. Audrey and Andrew are her stepchildren, from his first marriage. That wife died in childbirth, I understand."

That explained why Audrey and Andrew looked nothing like either Lord Bradley or Mrs. Howe. Olivia nodded her understanding, readjusting her thoughts. Not Lord Bradley's wife, then, but his cousin. Living there out of necessity after the death of her husband. Or were there other reasons as well?

Olivia was relieved Lord Bradley was not married. This meant he had no wife and no future heir to disappoint. She found herself remembering what Nurse Peale had said about little Alexander looking like Lord Bradley and "wasn't it a wonder." Did it signify?

Doris stayed in the nursery the rest of that afternoon to explain Olivia's various duties, saying she was fortunate that Becky did most of the nasty work, the cleaning and the hauling of heavy bathwater. Still, how Olivia would miss her post at Miss Cresswell's.

Later, Doris brought up the dinner tray and they sat down together like an odd family—Nurse Peale, the venerable grandmother at the head of the table. Alexander had already been fed and sat on a quilt on the floor, shaking a well-chewed rattle.

After the meal of pea soup, cold beef, mashed potatoes, and carrot pudding, Becky rose and began stacking the dishes.

"Let's give these wild animals a good clean, hmm?" Doris said. "It's grotty, they are."

While Becky took the tray belowstairs and hauled up the water, Doris and Olivia got the children ready for their baths. As Becky filled the copper tub, Andrew ran across the room naked as God made him and splashed water about with a great *whoop*. Again Olivia flinched at the loud sound, so foreign in the sedate corridors of Miss Cresswell's. Boys would take some getting used to.

Doris managed Andrew with a good-natured firmness—that came from having a younger brother, she explained—and Olivia followed her lead as they bathed the children and helped them into their nightclothes.

From the corner of her eye, Olivia saw Doris yawn. Olivia pointed to herself, and gave Doris a gentle push toward the door. The maid squinted, somewhat bleary-eyed and not comprehending. Olivia pointed to Doris and then tilted her cheek against clasped hands, closing her eyes to mime sleep.

"Really? You'll put them to bed on your own?"

Olivia nodded.

"Thank you, love. I knew you were an angel the moment I laid eyes on you. Bless me, I am near off my feet. Be good for Livie, you lions and tigers. No eating your new under nurse on her first night, all right?"

Audrey nodded. Andrew roared.

After Doris left, Olivia pulled a chair before the fire, and there combed Audrey's damp brown hair until it hung straight and smooth. Andrew had settled down and now sat in his bed, looking through a picture book Olivia had found in the nursery. She wished she might read to them, as her mother had always read to her. A psalm, poem, or short tale, though nothing frightening before bedtime. There were no books on the stand between the two beds, which Olivia found odd. Did not Nurse Peale or Mrs. Howe read to the children?

Looking at Audrey and Andrew, Olivia put a finger to her lips, then lifted that same finger in the sign for "wait."

Taking a candle lamp with her, Olivia let herself from the sleeping chamber and back into the nursery. Holding the lamp high and looking about the room, it seemed Andrew's picture book was the only book to be found. She saw a child's table and chairs, a rocking horse in the corner, a chest of toys, and a line of pretty dolls sitting on the window seat, but no books.

She looked at the closed door at the other end of the nursery, which Nurse Peale had pointed to with a dismissive wave as "the schoolroom."

The schoolroom . . . Olivia had always adored its confines and endless horizons. The melodious purr of the teacher's voice rising up and down her lessons like a musical score. And the sight of book spines—black, blue, green—lined up side by side like London townhouses. Each leather rectangle a gift waiting to be opened and explored and savored.

Cautiously, Olivia tried the knob and opened the door with a creak. Though Nurse Peale had indicated the former governess had not been gone long, already the room held the cloying mustiness of disuse. But over this arose the fragrances Olivia loved. Chalk dust, old leather books, wilted wild flowers, paint and paste. Olivia closed her eyes and breathed deeply, transported back to her recent idyllic days as Miss Cresswell's assistant.

Raising the candle lamp, she swept the room with its light—the governess's desk, the chairs around a table set with slates, the world globe in one corner, the bookshelf in the opposite. She would have loved to take it all in, study the books and the prints on the walls, but the children were waiting. She lowered herself before the bookshelf and skimmed the spines. Aesop, Mangnall, Hannah More, Fordyce's *Sermons to Young Women*, Sarah Trimmer's *Fabulous Histories*, more commonly known as *The History of Robins*. And an elegant volume of the New Testament and Psalms.

She selected the latter two and bore them with her from the schoolroom, carefully closing the door behind her.

Back in the sleeping chamber, she listened to Audrey's and Andrew's prayers, surprised their stepmother did not come up to do so. Then she sat on Audrey's bed beside the girl and waved Andrew over to join them. The children seemed surprised by this, but did not object. The young maid, Becky, already lay on her pallet on the floor. She was supposed to be the first to hear if one of the children wanted for anything. But from the look of her, the poor thing would be sound asleep before a single sentence was read.

Olivia opened the book to Psalm 46 and followed along with her finger as Audrey read aloud. She encouraged Andrew to follow along as well, though she doubted the boy could read many of the words.

Then she opened *The History of Robins* and encouraged Audrey to read aloud once more.

> ". . . the Robins ate their meal with all possible expe . . . expe-dition, for the hen was anxious to return to her little ones, and the cock to procure them a

breakfast; and having given his young friends a serenade, he did not think it necessary to stay to sing anymore. . . ."

By the time Olivia closed the book, she realized Audrey was resting her head against her shoulder and Andrew was curled beneath her other arm. A small bittersweet pang struck her soul. *Thank you for delivering me to such a place, Almighty God.*

7

> Mrs. Goddard was the mistress of a . . . real, honest, old-fashioned boarding school, where a reasonable quantity of accomplishments were sold at a reasonable price.
>
> —Jane Austen, *Emma*

The following morning, Nurse Peale sent Olivia down to the kitchen for the breakfast tray. Olivia hoped she would not get lost. She jogged lightly down the many pairs of stairs until she reached the basement. There, she passed two closed doors, the open door of a larder, and a white-paneled stillroom with shelves of china and jarred preserves. The clank of pans and smells of savory sausage and warm bread led her to the kitchen, its small high windows proudly declaring it only mostly underground. A massive stove fitted with spit and pot hooks filled most of one wall, while the others held floor-to-ceiling cupboards and shelves of tins and utensils. A long worktable dominated the center of the room. From its head, a wide, well-padded woman in her fifties directed two thin young kitchen maids in a firm but kindly voice.

Mrs. Hinkley swept in from a second door, her face set in stern lines, her bearing one of clear authority. A tall footman followed in her wake.

"More coffee is needed abovestairs, Mrs. Moore. And why, may I ask, is breakfast not yet laid in the servants' hall?"

"Never fear, Mrs. Hinkley," the plump woman assured. "We are but one thin minute behind schedule. Here you are, Osborn." She handed the footman a silver coffee urn. "Take this upstairs. And, Edith, take this tray into the servants' hall before Mr. Hodges has an apoplexy."

Seeing Olivia hovering at the threshold, Mrs. Hinkley's stern countenance darkened further.

"Mrs. Moore," she said. "This is Olivia Keene, the new under nurse."

Mrs. Moore paused in her frantic preparations to give Olivia a friendly smile. "Aren't you a lovely one. Welcome, my dear. The nursery tray is right there all ready for you. Do let me know if you want something more than bread and milk. That is all the children want, but if you'd like porridge or eggs, you need only ask."

Olivia warmed to Mrs. Moore instantly, but Mrs. Hinkley soon dashed her spirits.

"This is not a hotel, Mrs. Moore," the housekeeper said. "She shall eat what you have provided and be grateful. Come, girl, let us introduce you to the others and have done." She lifted her hand and waited none too patiently as Olivia came forward.

As she stepped into the long narrow servants' hall ahead of Mrs. Hinkley, Olivia's nerves jingled and her ears heated, self-conscious at so many pairs of eyes turning to regard her.

Mrs. Hinkley stood at her place at the foot of the table. "If I may have your attention, please. This is Olivia Keene, the new under nurse."

"Nurse Peale said we are to call her Livie," Doris interjected.

Frowning at being interrupted, Mrs. Hinkley continued, "She is here on trial—new in service as of yesterday. Due to an injury she received before coming to us, she is unable to speak at present."

Doris leaned close to another maid and whispered loudly, "Did I not tell you?"

A young auburn-haired man grinned across the table. "Some of us might wish you were so afflicted, Dory."

Mrs. Hinkley silenced the two with an icy glare. "You are not to speak to her unless necessary to your duties. If she has a question, she will come to me with it."

"How will she ask, if she cannot speak?" the stodgy butler asked from the head of the table.

"She can read and write, Mr. Hodges, or so I understand." The housekeeper's skepticism was apparent, and Olivia felt her ears burn anew.

Mrs. Hinkley gestured with a snap of her wrist toward each in turn, rattling off a quick inventory of the gathered servants. On Mrs. Hinkley's left was a pretty lady's maid, Miss Dubois. Mrs. Moore, the rotund cook, set a platter of sausages on the table, then took her seat to the right of Mrs. Hinkley. Next to her were Doris and Martha, the two housemaids, and kitchen maids Edith and Sukey. At the other end of the table, Mr. Hodges nodded curtly to her. The male servants sat clustered at his end of the table—the coachman and hall boy, whose names she did not catch; Osborn, the snooty footman in livery, just returning from abovestairs; and the auburn-haired groom, who smiled shyly at her.

She doubted she would remember all the names, but as Nurse Peale had warned her, she "need not get chummy with the staff." Except for holidays, or when the children ate with the family, Olivia would take her meals in the nursery with only Nurse Peale, the nurserymaid, Becky, and the children.

Olivia attempted to direct a smile toward the table in general, but her face felt stiff and she was fairly certain her lips did not manage more than a quiver. Mrs. Hinkley sat and everyone bowed their heads while Mr. Hodges began the prayer. Olivia had been dismissed.

"I met the new under nurse last evening," his cousin Judith announced as she stepped into the library. "Have you seen her?"

Edward was instantly wary. "Yes." He slid the life-changing note beneath the cigar box on his father's desk.

"Most unusual, do you not think? That Mrs. Hinkley should engage such a girl, I mean." Judith bit her full lower lip. "Something isn't right there."

He stilled, pulse accelerating. He wondered what Judith had heard or guessed, but asked only, "What are you implying?"

"Only that there must be more going on than meets the eye." She seemed delighted at the prospect.

"I don't follow." He felt himself frowning. "Do you mean, because she cannot speak?"

"Of course. What did you think I meant?"

He did not respond to that. "Are you concerned about leaving the children in her care?"

"Not at all." She gazed above him, musing. "But it is interesting, is it not? Never been in service before. Doesn't speak a word." She returned her gaze to him. "Who wrote her character, do you know?"

"I do not." He hesitated. "I am surprised at you, Judith. You have never taken an interest in the servants before."

"You have never engaged a mute before, have you?" Her round blue eyes suddenly lit up. "Perhaps she is not mute at all but only pretends to be."

This snagged his interest, though he tried not to show it.

"What if she only pretends to be mute or dumb, or whatever the word is, so she need not reveal her secrets? She might be the daughter of some powerful lord who is bent on forcing her into an arranged marriage."

"Such marriages are no longer legal, Judith. As you well know."

"La! Fathers still wield a great deal of pressure—that I do know."

"All right. If she is nobility, why have we never seen her in London?"

Judith pursed her lips. "Locked in the tower, perhaps? Or . . . I know! She doesn't speak English!"

He leaned back in his chair. "I have seen her write perfectly good English, and she understands everything said to her."

Judith ran her finger along the table globe on his father's desk. "Then perhaps she speaks with an accent, and is afraid that if she spoke she would give herself away. She is a"—Judith twirled her slender hand with dramatic flair—"Prussian princess, escaping a cruel husband."

His interest lagged. "What nonsense, Judith. You read too many novels. I have always said so."

She sighed. "Ah, well. You are no doubt right." She poked through the dish of candies on the desk and changed the subject. "Did your parents depart without incident?"

"Yes, right on schedule."

"I was so sorry to miss their party. I intended to return in time but was delayed at Mamma's." Judith helped herself to a ginger drop. "Ah, Italy . . . Dominick and I took our wedding trip there, you know."

"Did you? Yes, I believe I do remember that."

"You were at Oxford at the time. Left us right after the wedding breakfast."

Dominick Howe had died only two years later, Edward recalled, from injuries received during the Peninsula War.

Judith sighed once more. "How I should love to visit Italy again. I do envy your parents."

"Don't. This trip is more about convalescence than pleasure. Though Father hopes that, should the climate improve Mother's health, they might take in some of the sights."

"It is their first time in Italy?"

"Yes."

"Did they not take a wedding trip?"

He inhaled, pursing his lips. "I do not know. A bit before my time."

She raised one perfect blond brow. "You have never asked?"

"No."

She studied him through narrowed eyes. "You certainly haven't much curiosity, cousin."

"Whereas, you, dear cousin, have enough for the both of us." He rose and the two left the library together.

"Would you be a dear and bring Alexander down to me?" she asked, pausing before the drawing room door. "I cannot face all those stairs at present."

"Of course. I thought to see how the children were getting on at all events.

Shall I bring all three? Perhaps I might give the older two a riding lesson, if you do not mind."

"If you like."

He bowed and stepped into the hall.

She called after him, "And do observe the new under nurse while you are there."

He turned back, brows raised. "And what shall I look for? A royal brooch she has forgotten to hide away? An indentation on her ring finger?"

She gave him a sidelong glance. "Mock me if you will, Edward. But in time, I shall discover her secret."

Olivia had just finished plaiting and securing a ribbon in Audrey's hair when the door to the nursery creaked open. Young Becky was out dumping the children's bathwater and Nurse Peale was still dressing little Alexander.

"Cousin Edward!" Andrew tossed his ball aside and ran across the room. Lord Bradley dropped to one knee as the boy launched himself into his arms.

He chuckled. "Good morning, Andrew. I take it you slept well."

"I dreamt I was a kite!"

Lord Bradley smiled good-naturedly. "You certainly fly about like one."

Audrey walked toward him as he rose but stopped several feet away, eyes both shy and admiring at once, tugging at the end of her plait and biting her chapped lip.

Lord Bradley smiled at Audrey, bestowing the attention she so obviously sought. "Good morning, Miss Audrey. Don't you look lovely today. I like your hair."

"Our new nurse did it."

He hesitated. "Did she indeed."

His eyes roved the room and met Olivia's where she stood in the doorway to the sleeping chamber. She dipped a curtsy. His eyes lingered on her a moment longer before returning to Audrey.

"Well, I've only come to see how you all were getting on." He laid a hand on each child's head.

"We are ever so happy, now Miss Dowdle has gone," Andrew said. "No schoolroom for us! No lessons for us!"

Olivia bit her lip.

"But Miss Livie did have us read our prayers before breakfast," Audrey said. "And one of *Aesop's Fables*."

"Oh, which?"

"'The Wolf in Sheep's Clothing.'"

One fair brow rose. "What an interesting choice. Do you recall its moral?"

"Frauds and liars are always discovered eventually," Audrey answered. "And pay accordingly for their deeds."

"Something I do hope each of you will remember." Again his gaze flickered to Olivia, and she felt herself flush self-consciously.

Andrew grinned. "Livie made Audrey start over when she tried to skip a whole line. Audrey thought she mightn't know, but she did!"

Audrey ducked her head.

"Well, do not become accustomed to life without lessons," Lord Bradley said. "For your mamma will no doubt engage another governess soon."

Andrew groaned.

"Now." Lord Bradley clapped his hands. "Who wants to ride today?"

Both children chimed in with great enthusiasm.

"Very well." He looked up, his smile disappearing, his eyes focusing somewhere over Olivia's head. "Please dress them in their habits and bring them to the stables at ten."

Olivia nodded, but inwardly, she sighed. As Lord Bradley took little Alexander down to his mamma, Olivia began the process of undoing all the bows and fasteners she had just done up.

At ten minutes before the appointed hour, Olivia ushered her young charges down the stairs and out the rear garden door. Or rather, her young charges ushered her. Audrey took Olivia's hand, as though directing a blind person instead of a mute. Meanwhile, Andrew bounded across the damp lawn, his little legs full of energy. He turned around, running backward to gauge their progress. She would have liked to urge him to be careful but, of course, could not.

He tripped over a tree root and would have toppled to the ground had not the auburn-haired man she'd seen at breakfast leapt forward and caught him. Olivia pressed a hand to her chest in relief and smiled at the groom.

His smile widened in return. He was nice looking—not too tall, but broad-shouldered, with fair freckled skin and brown eyes. The groom she had seen at the hunt, she now recalled.

"I'm Johnny Ross," he said. "And you're the girl who can't speak. Miss Livie, was it?"

She nodded.

"You can hear, though?"

She nodded again, trying not to grin. Of course she could hear—did he think she could read minds?

"Lots of fellows might like a girl who can't talk." He added hastily, "Not me, I mean, not that I mind if a girl can't, but I don't mind if she can do either." Flustered, his face reddened to match his freckles.

She bit her lip but could not hold back the smile this time. She dipped her head, then stepped around him to catch up with Audrey and Andrew. They had continued on to greet Lord Bradley, who stood in the stable yard, awaiting their arrival. It would not do for him to see her chatting, or rather not chatting, with the groom.

"I shall hope to see you later, miss," Ross called after her.

As she approached, Lord Bradley consulted his pocket watch. "Right on time. Excellent. I shall return them to the nursery when we are finished."

Olivia would have liked to stay and watch the children ride but understood a clear dismissal when she heard one.

With time on her hands, Olivia went to the kitchen, hoping for one of Mrs. Moore's smiles and an almond biscuit. She found the cook hunched over her worktable.

"Oh, fiddle," the woman murmured, clearly distressed. She squinted at the recipe in her fleshy hand, and Olivia wondered if the woman needed spectacles.

Mrs. Moore glanced up and met Olivia's quizzical look. "Hello, love. Don't mind me." She nodded toward the biscuit tin. "Help yourself."

Olivia removed her cape, then selected a biscuit and seated herself on a stool.

Mrs. Moore waved the recipe in the air. "You see, Lady Brightwell sometimes 'borrowed' the Lintons' French man-cook for parties and such," she explained, clearly offended by the practice. "All the best houses prefer a man-cook—a Frenchman most of all," she huffed. "Now Miss Judith wants me to make his *coq au vin* again, but bless me if I can read his French scrawl."

Olivia set down her biscuit and held out her hand.

The older woman hesitated, then handed over the grease-spotted paper. Olivia scanned the lines and nodded, gesturing for a quill. The cook quickly procured one, along with ink from her small escritoire and handed both to her.

Taking a moment to study the handwriting, Olivia dipped the quill and began rewriting the ingredients and mode in English.

"You've a lovely hand, Livie," Mrs. Moore said over Olivia's shoulder.

Olivia smiled up at her, then bent once more over the quill. Within a matter of minutes, she completed the translation and handed it to Mrs. Moore with an impish little bow.

Shaking her head and clucking her tongue, Mrs. Moore said, "Thank you, my dear. You've certainly earned that biscuit."

After her visit to the kitchen, Olivia went upstairs to the schoolroom, wanting to see it in the full light of day.

Stepping inside, she took a deep breath of chalk dust and memories.

Her mother had arranged their own schoolroom, in the attic of their cottage, and there had been her sole teacher until she had begun attending Miss

Cresswell's School for Girls. What a row her parents had fought over it too. In the end, her mother had appealed to her husband's pride. Did he want his neighbors to think he could not afford to educate his own child? Did he not want the pleasure of hearing his daughter touted as the top of her class? She had even vowed to pay for the school herself, out of her own wages from the needlework she took in each week and the occasional pupil.

She had won.

How Olivia had loved those hours at Miss Cresswell's, where adults spoke firmly but gently, even in reproof. Where students smiled in wonder as Miss Cresswell read to them from her favorite poems or novels or histories, bringing each character to life in her rich, musical voice. Yes, there were difficult hours too, of struggling to translate French and Italian or declining Latin verbs. The girls had performed plays together and went on nature walks and quizzed each other on spelling and vocabulary. They beamed at Miss Cresswell's praise and strived all the harder under her admonitions.

How Olivia longed to be a teacher like that. To inspire children to learn, to introduce the world of literature, the beauty of music and the music of mathematics, the wonder of creation in geography and the sciences, and so much more.

She had gotten a taste of it as Miss Cresswell's assistant, but now those dreams seemed further from her grasp than ever.

Sighing, she closed the door and returned to her duties as Brightwell Court's new under nurse.

8

> A POACHER generally exhibits characteristics of his profession; the suspicious leer of his hollow and sunken eyes, his pallid cheek, his wide, copious and well-pocketed jacket.
>
> —*The Gamekeeper's Directory*

That night, Olivia had just stripped down to her shift when a knock sounded on her door. Forgetting herself, she opened her mouth to call out, "Yes?" but only a croak emerged. Warily, she opened her door a crack and was relieved to see the friendly maid Doris standing there.

"Look slippy, love, and let me in," she whispered.

Olivia opened the door and then closed it softly behind the ginger-haired girl.

"Don't want me to get the push, do you? If Mrs. H. caught me in here talking to you . . . 'Course she can't do that, can she—you can't talk! I can barely imagine. Well, at least you don't rabbit on like Edith." She pressed a wadded bundle of cloth into Olivia's hand. "Here's an old nightdress a'mine. You can have what's left of it. Isn't much."

Thank you, Olivia mouthed, accepting it gratefully. She had not looked forward to sleeping in the same underclothes she'd worn for days. Now she could wash out her shift and let it dry overnight.

"Do you mind if I tell you something?" Doris asked. "I have to tell someone or I'll burst my stays. And you're a safe one, are you not?"

Olivia nodded, sure she would not get a word in even if she were able to speak.

Still fully dressed, Doris plopped down on the bed and crossed one leg under the other, patting the mattress. Olivia sat beside her.

"It's Martha, poor love. Got herself in a real muddle." Doris leaned closer. "She's going to have a babe, and her not married, nor even a sweetheart, far as I know. She won't say who the father is. Mrs. H. found out, and that means the master will hear soon enough. Do you know what happened the last time a maid got herself into trouble?"

Olivia shook her head.

"I heard the old master, the fourth earl—or was it the third?—put her out on her ear. Without a bean to her name. So, if you're a prayin' type, say one for Martha. If she's not past prayin' for."

Olivia's stomach dropped at the mere thought of finding herself in such a predicament. Poor Martha!

Doris cocked her head to the side and regarded her earnestly. "I been wonderin' about you, love. How you come to be here. No character. No valise. I suppose you run from home—is that it?"

Too stunned to deny it, Olivia nodded.

"Thought so from the first. A man, no doubt. A cruel husband, was it?"

Olivia shook her head.

"Your father, then. A mean crust? A scapegrace?"

Olivia nodded again, tears filling her eyes at this unexpected empathy. What a relief to talk with someone, even though she could not say a word.

Doris squeezed her hand. "Mine too. Ran out on my mum when my brother and sister was only babes. I've had to work since I was ten. Scoundrel." She cheered instantly. "There, there, ducky. That's the way of it. No use feelin' low. You and me get on well enough, don't we? A pigeon pair."

Olivia blinked back tears and grinned at the girl.

"Well, I had better dash to my room before Martha wonders where I've got to. Now not a word about what I told you. But you can't, can you?"

Doris threw her arms around Olivia in a stinging embrace before launching herself toward the door. Opening it a sliver, she paused to peer down the corridor, then smiled over her shoulder.

"Night, love." And she was gone.

Olivia did not pray as often as she should, but now, confronted with a young woman in worse straits than her own, she did just that.

The following afternoon was fine, so Olivia took the children out of doors for exercise. She and Audrey walked about the lawns while Andrew kicked a ball this way and that. After much cajoling on his part, she and Audrey gave in to a halfhearted game of football.

Olivia had little experience with such sport, and within a matter of moments, the ball flew right past her. Olivia turned to gauge its destination. The ball rolled to the edge of the wood, coming to a halt beneath a rowan sapling still bearing several fronds of bright red leaves. Olivia ran after it and bent low. She reached her hand beneath the sapling, where the ball lay amid a nest of fallen red leaves. She picked up the ball and rose, but then stopped, staring in dismay. The orb bore a red smear as if stained by the leaves themselves. Or was it . . . blood?

She looked up, over the sapling, and sucked in a silent shriek. A tall old man stood there, stone-still among the swaying tree limbs. His gaunt face was a stiff mask—a beak of a nose bracketed by deep scowl lines leading to a thin mouth. Long ash grey hair hung to his shoulders.

It was him. The old man from Chedworth Wood. Had he followed her? Had he saved her from Borcher only to track her down and harm her himself?

She felt rooted to the spot, afraid to turn her back on him. Beneath wiry, untamed brows, his narrow, silvery eyes stared at her, then down at the ball in her hand. He lifted a brace of dead birds by way of explanation. A reedy relief threaded through her. Only the blood of birds . . .

"Here," he rasped, holding out his hand for the ball.

Olivia was confused. Had he come to poach game and now wanted a child's ball as well? Numbly, she extended her gloved hand. He snatched the ball with stained, gnarled fingers.

She watched, still rooted, as he wiped the ball on his coat sleeve, inspected it again, then handed it back.

She accepted it and looked down at the ball, now unmarred. Andrew ran over to see what the matter was, but when she looked up once more, the man had utterly disappeared, only the merest swaying of a tree branch to testify that he had ever been there at all.

While the children played quietly in the nursery, Olivia paced. Should she tell Lord Bradley she had seen a poacher? Could she do so without admitting where she had seen him before? She had overheard something about the poacher problem in the area. As magistrate, he would want to know. Had the old man come to free Borcher from the lockup? Just thinking of those two men wandering the estate made her perspire. She had to tell someone.

Olivia penned a brief note.

When I was taking exercise with the children, I saw a strange old man in the wood, bearing a brace of dead birds. Possibly a poacher? I thought you would wish to know.

Leaving the children with Becky and Nurse Peale, Olivia carried the note to Lord Bradley's study, one floor down. She had seen him there from the landing when she had brought the children upstairs. Knocking on the open door, she stepped inside and handed him the note before he said a word. While he read it, she surveyed the room. It was like a small library, with fitted bookcases and a desk littered with ledgers, papers, and writing implements—quills and a wax jack for melting sealing wax. Statues of rearing horses stood atop the fireplace mantel.

He frowned as he read, but then his countenance cleared. "Man about sixty, very thin, long grey hair?"

She nodded.

"I daresay that was Croome."

Croome! Yes, that was his name, Olivia remembered. But how did Lord Bradley know? Was this Croome a wanted man? A known criminal?

Her stunned expression seemed to amuse him. "I do not blame you for being startled by old Croome. I grew up in fear and trembling of the man myself."

She stared at him, perplexed by his levity.

He sat forward, elbows on his desk. "Croome is our gamekeeper. Been with us for years."

Brightwell's gamekeeper?

He clearly misunderstood her uncomprehending look, for he explained, "As gamekeeper, he is responsible for the estate's preserved land. Stocking game, controlling vermin, predators, poachers . . . In fact, he is the man who caught you on the grounds and bundled you off to the constable."

Her mind was whirling so quickly she nearly missed the implication that she was of a kind with predators and poachers. *A gamekeeper in league with poachers?* It made no sense. Had he recognized her before he whipped that sack over her head? She had wondered why the "Brightwell man" had deposited her with the constable and departed before she had even laid eyes on her captor. Was he worried she would have recognized him? Reported him to the constable in turn?

Yet the man had saved her once and had done her no harm when he'd had the chance. She decided she would not reveal anything more about him for now. Lord Bradley had enough to worry about at present.

One further thought followed her back upstairs to the nursery. If she had overheard a conversation no one was meant to hear . . . had Croome heard it as well?

9

> There were always love affairs among servants, but if they came to the master's attention, instant dismissal was the rule.
>
> —*Upstairs & Downstairs,*
> *Life in an English Country House*

Mrs. Hinkley, looking rather put out, asked Olivia to come down to her parlor. It seemed the vicar wished to see her, and the housekeeper could not very well allow one of the servants to receive callers in the family's drawing room. But nor could she ask the good parson to descend belowstairs to the kitchen, where most servants received the occasional caller. Mrs. Hinkley sighed, and Olivia had the impression that the housekeeper thought the new girl more than a bit of bother.

"What does the parson want with you?" Mrs. Hinkley whispered.

Olivia shrugged.

"Said he met you when you first arrived in the village and wanted to see how you were getting on." She said it as though such a thing must be suspect indeed.

For her part, Olivia was pleased to know the man remembered her. She certainly recalled his kindness in introducing her to Miss Ludlow. She regretted that she had not gone to the vicarage that night as she'd intended. She hoped he and his sister had not laid a place for her at their table nor stayed up late expecting her. How sorry she would be if they felt their hospitality had been rejected.

Mr. Tugwell rose when she entered. "Miss Keene. How well you look! Much more fit than when I saw you last, I daresay! Are you well?"

She nodded, mildly taken aback. Had she looked so poorly at the river that day?

"Excellent. You do remember me, I hope? Charles Tugwell, vicar of St. Mary's?"

Again she nodded.

"When you did not come to us that night, I—"

She put her hand out in entreaty, eyes wide.

"Never mind, my dear. I understand completely. I learnt what befell you and was grieved indeed to hear it. In fact I saw you that very night, though you were not aware of my presence. The laudanum, you know. How I prayed for you."

Now she understood. He had indeed seen her at her worst. She felt tears misting her eyes at his kindness and managed a wavering smile.

"There, there, my dear. All is well now, yes? I had hoped to see you in church, but as I did not, here I am to see how you fare." He tilted his head to one side. "Your throat is bruised, I see. Am I to understand from your silence that your voice has yet to return? Or have I not allowed you to get a word in edgewise?"

She shook her head, biting back a grin.

"Your ability to walk seems unhindered, and it is a fine day. Might I interest you in a stroll?"

She looked at him, mouth ajar.

"Forgive me. You have a position here now, I understand. I confess I forget how blessed I am to be able to walk about whenever I desire, barring a christening or marriage to perform. I even compose my sermons whilst walking, did you know? Of course not—how could you? Yes, I find a brisk stroll just the thing to spur the mind and lift the spirits." He paused for a breath, then grimaced. "Forgive me. I do prattle on, I know. I warn you that when you do attend services you shall find my sermons much the same. I cannot seem to say anything succinctly. As several parishioners have been kind enough to point out most helpfully, I am sure."

She smiled.

"By the way. Miss Ludlow told me of your intention to seek a place at the girls' school in St. Aldwyns. I had thought to inquire on your behalf the next time I traveled that way. But I suppose that is no longer necessary, as you have found employment here?"

Eagerly, she gestured for him to wait, then sat down at Mrs. Hinkley's desk. Promising herself to reimburse the housekeeper out of her first wages, Olivia picked up a sheet of paper and wrote as concise a letter as she could.

Dear Madam,

My mother, Mrs. Dorothea Keene, recommended I contact you about a possible situation.

I have taken a temporary post at Brightwell Court, but if you have a position available after February 4th, kindly write to me here.

Also, should my mother call upon you, kindly inform her (and her alone, if you please) of my whereabouts.

Most gratefully,
Miss Olivia Keene

She folded the letter, rose, and was about to hand it to Mr. Tugwell when the parlor door opened and Lord Bradley strode in, suspicion evident in the set lines of his face.

"Ah, Edward," Mr. Tugwell said. "I had just called in to see how Miss Keene fares."

"So I heard." But Lord Bradley's gaze rested not on the vicar, but on the folded paper in Olivia's hand.

Mr. Tugwell followed the direction of his stare. "Oh. I have offered to deliver a note for Miss Keene when next I call in St. Aldwyns. She was bound for the girls' school there when her, um, mishap occurred. How good of you to offer her a post here instead."

Lord Bradley made no answer to this but instead pinned Olivia with a challenging glare.

The vicar held out his hand, but the note felt suddenly like a six-stone sack in Olivia's hand. She remembered Lord Bradley saying that she was allowed to post no letters without his approval and knew she was breaking that rule in asking the vicar to deliver a note. But did he really think she would divulge his secret in a letter to a schoolmistress . . . and through a man of God in the bargain?

Seeing the steely warning in his gaze, she swallowed.

Evidently he did.

She stepped forward and handed the letter to Lord Bradley instead. He unfolded it and began reading.

The vicar frowned. "Really, Edward, is that quite necessary?"

He made no answer to that either.

After skimming the hastily written lines, he looked up at her from over the top of the paper. "Do you really expect to gain a post with such a vague letter? With no offer of a character reference, nor even your qualifictions?"

She hesitated, then nodded.

He pulled a grimace. "Did you honestly come here on the faint hope of securing a post at a school where you don't even know the name of the proprietress, or even *if* they have a situation available?"

She stubbornly lifted her chin and nodded again.

He shook his head. "Incredible. And what is this about your mother? She has such confidence in the power of her recommendation that she has no doubt of finding you happily employed at the school whenever she happens to call?"

Olivia lifted a shrug.

"Why not write another letter to your mother directly? Let her know you have taken a post here instead. I shall approve it."

She hesitated, then slowly shook her head.

His pale blue eyes flicked over her clasped hands and hopefully benign expression before returning to the letter once more. "I wonder, *Miss Olivia Keene*—what are you hiding?"

She forced herself to hold his critical gaze without wavering.

He refolded the letter. "Thank you, Charles. But I shall have Hodges post this directly. No need to trouble yourself." He looked at her once again. "But I would not hold my breath awaiting a reply, were I you. Nor, of course, are you free to leave for another post until I give you leave."

Mr. Tugwell objected. "Edward, really. I don't see—"

He held up a halting hand. "Never mind, Charles. Miss Keene *does* see." He narrowed his eyes at her. "Does she not?"

She narrowed her own eyes in return, but nodded for the vicar's benefit.

"Very well. I shall leave the two of you to complete your visit." Lord Bradley turned on his heel and left the room as abruptly as he had entered it.

After an awkward pause, the parson picked up his hat from the settee. "Well, I had better take my leave and allow you to return to your duties." He hesitated, circling his hat by its brim. "I hope it will not make you uncomfortable if I tell you I am still praying for you, Miss Keene." He looked from her to the closed door and back again. "I sense there are things in your life that are not as they should be. I am asking God to 'work all things together for good,' as the Scripture says He will, for those who love Him and are called according to His purpose. Do you, Miss Keene?" he asked gently. "Do you love Him? Trust and serve Him?"

She stared, flummoxed. A man she hardly knew, posing such personal questions? She did not know whether to be touched or offended. His softly lined face blurred before her, and she was embarrassed to find tears once more filling her eyes and falling down her cheeks.

No . . . She shook her head. *I do not trust and serve God,* she thought. *Love him? Sometimes. Is my life as it should be? Am I? No, and again, no.*

He took her hand in his. "I shall pray for that as well."

A few days later, Olivia offered to help Becky give the nursery carpets a good beating. As she struggled to carry out one of the heavy carpets, Johnny Ross jogged over from the stables to the laundry yard.

"Might I help you with that, miss?" the groom asked. "It is no trouble."

She allowed him to help her hang the carpet on a line and in return gave him what she hoped was a grateful smile.

His smile widened. "I was wonderin' when you get your half day," he began. "If it is Sunday afternoon, like mine, might we walk into the village together?"

Slowly, she shook her head.

"No half day?"

She shook her head again.

"Good. Well, not good, but at least you ain't sayin' no to me in general. You ain't, are you?"

Olivia shook her head. But not wanting to encourage him, she began swatting the carpet with the paddle Nurse Peale had provided. She felt his brown eyes on her figure as she worked, but he must have given up, for when she glanced over her shoulder he was gone.

A few minutes later, she sensed a presence behind her once more. With a reproving smile, she turned around, expecting to see Johnny again. The smile fell from her lips.

"Expecting your admirer?" Lord Bradley sneered.

Olivia glanced around and realized they were shielded from the house by the hanging carpet. Perhaps he saw his opportunity to reinforce his threat without being seen with her and without the children present. She wished for the smiling Lord Bradley of the nursery and wondered where he had gone.

"I thought you understood you were not to talk with anyone."

Before she could respond, he continued, "From the smile on Ross's face, it seems you said a great deal with your eyes. Perhaps a promise for a later rendezvous?"

She shook her head.

"I hope not. If he is seen with you again, he might very well lose his position here."

She gasped. "That is not right!"

Her outburst surprised them both. Lord Bradley was momentarily stilled, but then continued evenly. "Your voice has returned, I see. What did you tell Ross?"

"Noth . . . ing," she rasped.

He stared at her, as though gauging her honesty. "Nor will you, until I give you leave."

She was indignant. "You cannot mean—" She swallowed, her throat dry and scratchy. "You cannot expect me to remain silent forever."

"You managed quite well at the Swan, when it was to your advantage."

"But I could not speak then," she argued hoarsely.

"Nor will you speak now."

"But for three months? Impossible!"

"For a woman I suppose it will be doubly difficult."

Olivia bit back a rebuke and instead reasoned, "It makes no sense. If I wanted to tell someone, I could"—she swallowed again—"all the while pretending to be mute before everyone else."

"Do you really think that in a household like this, word of your speaking would not reach me within minutes?"

She threw up her hands. "I promise you that I will not tell a soul what I heard."

"What is a promise from you worth?"

Olivia stared at him, feeling as though she'd been slapped.

He grimaced. "I am . . ." He rubbed the back of his neck. "I ought not to have said that. But—"

"If you think so poorly of my character," she said stiffly, "then why not send me away and have done?"

"Because I cannot risk having a loose tongue about." He added, as if to himself, "Especially now."

She wondered what that meant.

He straightened and continued briskly, "But in a few months, important matters should be settled. Perhaps then I can deal with the . . . the new information you overheard."

"But to pretend I cannot speak when I can, to deceive others . . . It is not right!"

"Neither is eavesdropping," he clipped, and stalked away.

10

> If the weather be favourable, the children are taken out by the assistant nurse for air and exercise. The day should be devoted, in bad weather, to such amusements as induce exercise, of dancing, the skipping-rope, and dumb-bells. . . .
>
> —Samuel & Sarah Adams, *The Complete Servant*

The housekeeper stood before Edward's desk. "The children would like to walk in the wood to collect autumn leaves or some such," Mrs. Hinkley began. "Might Livie take them?"

Miss Keene, Edward noticed, stood a respectful few steps behind the housekeeper. Why had she enlisted Mrs. Hinkley's help instead of writing another note? Did she guess he would refuse her?

He thought back to his harsh words to her the day before, regretting them yet again. But he did not regret his decision to keep her at Brightwell Court and to keep her quiet. After all, it was his future she held in her hands. His inheritance, his marriage prospects, his father's dreams and plans for him. His very home.

Edward looked directly into Miss Keene's eyes. Could she read his suspicious thoughts? For indeed, he suspected she might use such an opportunity to flee.

"If she is to walk out of view of the house, she must take another with her. Nurse Peale or one of the maids."

"Nurse Peale stays indoors these days, my lord. She hasn't the stamina she had when you were a boy."

This surprised Edward. Miss Peale would always seem a paragon to him. But he was four and twenty now, and his old nurse must be nearing seventy. "Of course. I forget. A maid, then."

"It is really necessary, my lord?"

Unaccustomed to having his orders questioned, he narrowed his eyes at the housekeeper. She would never have questioned his father so. "It is."

At Mrs. Hinkley's inquisitive look, Edward met Miss Keene's eyes once more and said glibly, "She is new, you see, and might *inadvertently* lose her way."

Wearing capes and gloves, Olivia and Doris followed behind as Andrew and Audrey tore down the path through the wood.

The autumn air was crisp, the wood a colorful fresco of flaming brown and orange beechwood trees, orange-red rowan trees, and the puckered berries of hawthorn. Leaves fell and twirled to the ground, revealing more of the pewter grey branches drop by drop. A pheasant skittered across their path, and from the direction of the river came a dipper's squeaking call.

As they walked, Dory kept up a cheerful prattle, unhindered by Olivia's lack of response.

Olivia was still thinking about Lord Bradley's reluctance to allow her to walk out of view of the manor alone. He had no way of knowing she had decided his estate afforded her a comfortable hideaway—until her mother came for her. She wondered if the schoolmistress at St. Aldwyns had yet received her letter.

A narrow track led from the main path to a clearing, where Olivia was surprised to see a snug stone cottage with a slate roof. A stack of chopped firewood, scratching chickens, penned pigs, and a wispy trail of chimney smoke declared the place lived in, while peeling paint, smeared windows, and one forgotten stocking swaying stiffly on a line bespoke recent neglect. Had they wandered outside the Brightwell estate?

Olivia paused and laid a hand on Dory's arm. Gesturing toward the place with her free hand, she gave the maid an inquisitive look.

"Oh. That's the gamekeeper's lodge," Dory said.

Olivia pointed to the frayed rope swing hanging listlessly from a tree.

"He hasn't any children, if that's what you mean. He lives alone out here and keeps to himself. Best place for him, I say."

Olivia lifted her brows expectantly.

Dory continued, "A rough old sod, from what I hear, though I have never spoken to the sourpuss. Looks as if he's lived on Tewksbury mustard his whole life." She shrugged. "Must be good at his post, though. Cook always has plenty of game. Though I grow tired of hare and snipes myself."

They walked on, quickening their pace to catch up with Audrey and Andrew.

"Stay to the path, dumplings!" Dory called ahead. To Olivia, she explained, "Never know where that man has laid his traps. And I for one don't wish to be caught in one."

Olivia shuddered. Neither did she.

The weather being rough and cold the next morning, Olivia kept the children indoors. She sat with Audrey at the old pianoforte in the corner, helping her reach the correct fingerings, and running her own fingers along the score during the more complicated phrases. Andrew, meanwhile, would not cease running about the nursery, kicking a ball and knocking down Alexander's wooden horses, making the ten-month-old cry. After a sharp word from Nurse Peale, Andrew picked up a battledore from an umbrella stand in the corner and began swinging the racquet like a cricket bat. He hit a wooden ball across the room, and it clunked against the wall perilously close to Olivia's head.

Rising from the bench, Olivia walked across the room to Andrew and held out her hand. Looking chastened, he laid the battledore onto it. She went to the umbrella stand, but instead of replacing the racquet, she picked up a second and rummaged around until she found a serviceable shuttlecock. Turning back to the gloomy-faced little boy, she presented him with the racquet and, armed with her own, stood facing him, several yards away.

His face instantly brightened.

She tinged the shuttlecock with a gentle underarm hit that sent the feathered birdie into the air. Andrew swung his battledore so vigorously that he spun a full turn in place, missing the object completely.

"Good heavens," Nurse Peale grumbled good-naturedly. "I had better remove Master Alexander before he becomes the next poor 'birdie.'" She groaned as she bent over, scooped up the little boy, and took him into her own room.

Andrew picked up the shuttlecock and whacked it back, this time into the toy trunk. But after a few more tries, they were able to keep up a volley of two or three hits before having to stop and retrieve the bird. Audrey looked over at them with interest.

"May I play?"

Olivia nodded.

"Two against one won't be fair," Andrew complained.

"Then I shall have to join you." The deep voice startled Olivia. She had not even noticed Lord Bradley standing in the partially open doorway. She hoped their tromping about had not disturbed him. But she thought he looked pleased or at least amused.

"Have you another battledore?" he asked, removing his coat.

Olivia found two more racquets, handing Audrey the sound one and her cousin the one with two tears.

He regarded it with a dubious expression, but murmured only, "Perfect."

The game commenced with much whooping and chasing. Olivia could barely reconcile this smiling, playful man with the haughty Lord Bradley she usually encountered.

"My, my, does this not bring back memories."

Olivia turned. Mrs. Howe now stood in the threshold, arms crossed beneath her bosom, a dimple beside her pink lips.

"Hello, Judith." Lord Bradley gave her a little bow, rendered less ceremonious in shirt sleeves.

She shook her head, amusement and annoyance sparking in her round china-blue eyes. "George Linton called. Hodges could not find you."

Lord Bradley leapt to return one of Andrew's wild shots. "Sorry."

"You are not the least bit sorry, and you know it."

He reached high and managed to bring one down from near the ceiling. The man had the wingspan of a crane.

"Do you remember how you, Felix, and I used to play in this very room," Judith asked. "With George Linton or even your father making up the fourth?"

He nodded, distracted by the game.

One of Audrey's shots went wide to the wall, and in reaching it Olivia stepped near to Mrs. Howe. Impulsively, she held out the battledore and shuttlecock.

The woman hesitated, looking down at her black-and-white-striped walking dress. "No thank you, I am not really—"

"Oh, come, Jude," Lord Bradley teased. "You are not in your dotage yet."

"Play with us. Do!" Audrey urged.

Judith Howe grinned. "Oh, very well. But if I muss my hair, and Dubois scolds me, it shall be on your head."

"You are on my side, Mamma," Andrew called.

Olivia watched for a few moments, and felt an odd emptiness steal over her as the game commenced without her.

Olivia was crossing the entry hall Friday afternoon when a young man sailed through the front doors, removing his greatcoat.

"Take this for me, will you?"

Olivia looked around and, seeing no sign of Osborn or Mr. Hodges, gingerly took the heavy coat from him. Beneath it, he wore a coat of blue velvet over a brightly patterned waistcoat, pantaloons, and tall boots. The youthful dandy had light reddish gold hair. *Titian hair*, she believed it was called, and green eyes. Eyes which lit upon closer inspection of her person. "And who are you?" He smiled. "I am quite certain I have never seen you before."

Olivia craned her head around, but there was no one about to help her.

"What is wrong, my dear—speechless? I never knew I could be quite so intimidating. I find I rather like the notion."

He appeared to be younger than she was, perhaps only nineteen or twenty, but possessed confidence, or at least bravado, beyond his years.

"Not that intimidating you was my intention." He leaned near. "I make it my business to know all of the maids, and I should dearly like to know you. Your name, my sweet?"

Olivia looked at him, brows high.

"Quite right. How rude of me. I am Felix Bradley, Judith Howe's brother and Lord Brightwell's nephew. And you are . . . ?"

Olivia could barely believe this expressive, brightly clad young man was Lord Bradley's cousin. But then . . . She let the thought go unfinished. From her pocket, she withdrew the small card upon which she had written her name, for just such an occasion.

"Love notes already? How delightful." He squinted at her script. "Lydia?"

She shook her head, amused. She found his friendly smile and elfin green eyes charming.

He looked once more. "Lilly?"

She wiggled her hand, signaling, close enough. He straightened and smiled again. Olivia noticed he was tall and thin—not as tall as Lord Bradley but appearing so due to his narrow frame. His features were fine, patrician even.

"Mr. Bradley! I did not hear you arrive." Mrs. Hinkley bustled across the hall and discreetly put a hand on Olivia's back and nudged her toward the staircase. "Lord Brightwell is abroad, as you know. Shall I have Hodges announce you to Lord Bradley?"

"No need, Mrs. H. I shall just pop up and see my sister."

"Very good, sir. The Chinese room is ready for you as always."

Olivia walked toward the stairs as directed, feeling Mrs. Hinkley's actions were more protection than rebuke. She could still hear their conversation over the padding of her slippers on the marble floor.

"Who is the new girl? Most unusual."

"Oh," Mrs. Hinkley said with evident nonchalance, "that is Livie, new to us since your last visit."

"Livie. Ah."

"You realized she is mute, of course."

"Mute? Really?" He spoke casually, as though Olivia were already absent—or deaf.

She felt his eyes on her back as she climbed the stairs.

"Come to think of it, she did not speak a word. Yet I could have sworn she had the most beautiful voice."

11

> If any one happens to drop the slipper in passing it,
> she must pay a forfeit.
>
> —Mrs. Child, *The Girl's Own Book*

Later that afternoon, Olivia sat beside Audrey as she read aloud from *Peter the Great*, following along and occasionally touching her fingertip to a word the girl had skipped over or mispronounced. If Audrey did not know the meaning of a word, Olivia would help her locate the definition in one of the volumes of Johnson's dictionary.

Bang. The nursery door hit the wall, startling them all. Andrew dropped his top and shouted, "Uncle Felix!"

Audrey squealed and jumped up from the settee, book forgotten. Both children ran to the man at the door.

"Hello, you ankle-biters," Felix Bradley teased. He patted his pockets and withdrew a peppermint for each of them. "Sweets for the sweet." His gaze sought and held Olivia's over their heads. He waved away their thanks. "I know my visits would not signify in the least were I not to bring you something."

He looked over at Olivia once more. "What is your new nurse tormenting you with?" He strolled to the settee and picked up the book. "Plague me. I remember this one. Devilish boring." He grinned at her censorious look. "Upon my soul, it was. Now. Who's for a game of hunt the slipper?"

His suggestion was met with cheers, and the children quickly cleared the toys from the worn circular carpet before the nursery hearth. Olivia rose to move the large wooden rocking horse, but Felix Bradley quickly came to her aid, stepping near and saying quietly, "Allow me, lovely Livie. And that is difficult to say, lovely Livie is, though I realize you shall have to take my word for it. I practiced saying it all the way up here."

She shook her head at his foolishness but could not help grinning.

Movement caught her eye, and she glanced over as a second figure appeared in the doorway. Lord Bradley stood, arms crossed, eyes narrowed. He looked from Felix to her and back again, seemingly annoyed to see his cousin standing so near to her. She felt defensive—she had not initiated the proximity. Still, she took a self-conscious step away.

"Felix. I am surprised to see you here."

"Are you? In the nursery, or in general?"

"Both, I suppose. Your term does not end for several weeks."

"That's right. Just before Christmas. I am only visiting. You do not mind, I trust?"

Lord Bradley regarded him speculatively, before his shoulders lifted slightly and his lips pulled down in a gesture of detached nonchalance.

"Come, Cousin Edward, do play with us," Audrey beseeched. "We haven't enough players for a proper game. And Nurse Peale says she is too old to sit on the floor."

"And what game are we playing?" he asked, eyes fixed on Felix.

"Hunt the slipper," Andrew answered. "Livie has never played it. Can you imagine?"

Lord Bradley feigned shock. "I cannot."

"Miss Livie, you are to stand in the center and try to guess which of us has the shoe," Audrey explained. "We shall use one of my doll shoes, for a real shoe would be too easily seen with so few players."

Andrew looked up at her soberly. "You are to say, 'Cobbler, cobbler, mend my shoe. Get it done by half past two.' But as you cannot speak, we shall say it for you."

Olivia dipped her head in appreciation.

"Whoever is caught with the slipper becomes the hunter, and pays a forfeit," Audrey explained. "One must sing a song, or dance, or tell a secret, or perform some trick."

"And, if anyone drops the slipper whilst passing it," Andrew added, "she must pay a forfeit as well."

"Why do you say 'she'?" Audrey demanded. "I shall not drop it."

"You always do."

"Do not."

While Olivia stood, the others sat on the floor—Audrey, Andrew, Becky, Felix, and Lord Bradley. She was surprised by his affability in joining the game. Evidently he was very fond of his young cousins.

The five sat, knees raised, in a boxy circle, and made a great show of passing the shoe under the tent of their bent legs. All fisted their hands and mimed the act of passing, trying to make the guessing more difficult. Still, they made a very small circle and Olivia was sure Andrew held the shoe, but then he passed it so quickly she could not be sure. A mischievous light gleamed in Felix's eyes.

She pointed to him with a suppressed smile.

He held forth empty hands and winked.

Olivia next guessed Audrey and, correct, was instructed to trade places with the girl—who had been seated directly beside Lord Bradley. Swallowing, Olivia sat down gingerly, careful to avoid grazing his knee with her own, and to keep her skirts tucked about her.

Audrey performed a pirouette for her forfeit, then lost no time in beginning another round, chanting, "Cobbler, cobbler, mend my shoe. Get it done by half past two."

Andrew passed the shoe to Lord Bradley, who reached for her hand to pass the shoe into hers. Olivia feared her palm would be damp with nerves at being so close to him. When his fingertips touched her palms she started, fumbled the shoe, and it fell to the floor.

"Now you've done it, Livie!" Felix said. "Got to pay your forfeit."

"Pay a forfeit, pay a forfeit!" Andrew chimed.

Olivia's heart pounded. She wiped her damp palms along the hem of her gown as it wrapped around her ankles. What should she do? What *could* she do?

She arose and stepped to the pianoforte and there played a few bars of one of Mozart's piano concertos, the festive "Turkish March" she had learnt at Miss Cresswell's. Afterward, she bowed with a flourish and reclaimed her spot on the floor.

Everybody clapped in delight except Lord Bradley. He merely stared. Had she overstepped by playing the pianoforte meant for the children's use?

Apparently she had, for he rose, smoothed his coat, and apologized to his cousins. "Forgive me, but I have forgotten an appointment with Father's clerk."

How foolish she felt, how chastened. The children groaned, but Felix watched him go as silently as she.

Olivia awoke, cold. Her small room had no fire of its own, but drew warmth from the hearth in the adjacent sleeping chamber. And that fire had no doubt smoldered to ash hours ago. She pulled her bedclothes over her head, attempting to warm herself and return to sleep. She heard something and stilled, ceasing to even shiver as she listened. Her door creaked slowly open, and Olivia sat upright, heart pounding.

As her eyes adjusted to the dark, she saw a figure tiptoeing into her room. A small figure.

Andrew.

"I had a bad dream," he muttered and audibly shivered.

Olivia turned down her bedclothes, and he immediately climbed in beside her. She realized she should return him to his own bed and find him an extra blanket, or rouse Becky to stoke the fire and warm another bed stone. Instead, she pulled the blankets up under his chin and asked God to send him sweet dreams. Andrew curled into her side with a little sigh, falling to sleep within seconds. *Ah, well* . . . she would rise early and carry him back to his bed.

Stroking his hair, Olivia wondered if this was what it felt like to be someone's mother—to possess the sweet, satisfying power to comfort and console. She wondered, too, if she would ever have children of her own. Considering she was unmarried at nearly five and twenty, it seemed unlikely. She thought fleetingly of the sole young man who had ever courted her and squelched the icy doubts that followed. Instead, she put her arm around Andrew, relishing his warmth, his nearness, and the sunny smell of his freshly washed hair as she drifted to sleep.

In the morning, Olivia awoke with Andrew still beside her and the discomfiting feeling of being watched.

She glanced toward her door and saw that it was still open from Andrew's entrance the night before. She gasped, startled to see Lord Bradley and Audrey in the threshold, peering at them. She jerked the bedclothes up over her thin nightdress.

"Forgive us," Lord Bradley murmured, averting his eyes. "Audrey was concerned when she could not find Andrew."

Olivia opened her mouth to defend herself, but remembered in time not to speak.

"Did he have a bad dream and ask to sleep with you?" Audrey asked.

Olivia nodded, realizing this was close enough to the truth and likely to assure their hastiest departure.

"There, Audrey, you see? Nothing to fear. Andrew is perfectly well."

He glanced at her, and Olivia felt her cheeks burn as she pulled the bedclothes higher.

Andrew opened his sleepy eyes and looked from Olivia to his sister and cousin, clearly confused to find himself in the under nurse's bed.

"You talked in your sleep, Miss Livie!" Andrew said, startling Olivia and their audience as well.

Olivia shook her head, but Andrew insisted, "You did! You said something about a comb and then, 'I should not have done it. I did not mean to.' You said that bit twice. What did you not mean to do?"

Olivia was dumbfounded and felt her face flush anew. She dared a glance up at Lord Bradley, knowing he would be displeased.

"Andrew, you must have been dreaming," Audrey said, stepping into the room. "Miss Keene cannot speak." She took Andrew's hand as he climbed out of bed and led him from the room. "You had another of your bad dreams last night, did you not?"

"I did, but—"

"See? That was all it was, then. Miss Keene talking in her sleep? What an imagination you have!"

After the children departed, Lord Bradley paused only long enough to nod curtly before pulling the door closed. Olivia sighed. Next time, she could most definitely *not* let Andrew share her bed.

On Wednesday morning, Olivia delivered the children to the stable yard for their riding lessons. When she arrived, Lord Bradley was nowhere to be seen, so she and the children went to the far stall and watched Talbot shoe a horse and then looked on as Johnny saddled up the small horse and pony Audrey and Andrew would ride. When a quarter of an hour had passed, and Lord Bradley still had not appeared, Johnny took pity on the antsy children.

"What say you, Miss Livie. These two beasts are raring to go. The horses too." He winked. "Why don't I lead them about the yard until Lord Bradley comes?"

Olivia nodded gratefully.

Smiling, Johnny put the horse and pony on leads. The children mounted, all enthusiasm, and the groom led them around the yard in a wide circle. Not as exciting as a ride with their cousin, but at least they were not sitting idle.

A few minutes later, Lord Bradley strode into the stables with the merest glance in Olivia's direction. He walked to one of the stalls and, over its gate, stroked the long muzzle of his tall black horse.

"Have you and the children been waiting long?" he asked, his gaze still on the horse. She was surprised he would initiate conversation with her.

Since no one was within earshot, Olivia answered quietly, "Not so long."

He nodded. And as no groom offered to do so for him, he opened the gate and began bridling the horse himself.

She waited, but when he did not scold her for speaking to him, she asked, "Pray what is his name, this beauty of a horse?" *That once nearly trampled me to death*, she added to herself.

"Guess." He pressed the bit between the horse's large teeth, then lifted the leather straps over the regal head and ears.

"Hmm . . ." she mused. "Considering his color, and your general demeanor, I would guess . . . *Black*."

"You wound me. Do you think me completely without imagination?"

"It is one's first impression." What was she thinking to tease him as she might tease Johnny? Was she so desperate for adult conversation?

Finished with the task, he narrowed his eyes at her. "Would you like to know what I am imagining right now?"

Throttling me? she thought, but whispered only, "No. Definitely not."

After the riding lesson, Olivia found herself in the uncomfortable position of walking back to the house beside Lord Bradley as the children, as was their wont, ran ahead. She slowed her pace to fall a respectful distance behind him, as befitted her station. He made no further conversation, and of course, neither did she.

She was startled when Croome rounded the corner of the manor. Evidently, Lord Bradley was startled as well, for he drew up sharply and she nearly collided with him.

"Ah . . . Mr. Croome." Lord Bradley's voice seemed suddenly unnatural and unsure. He turned to follow the man's hard gaze and for a moment, both men regarded her critically. Prompted to fill the awkward silence, Lord Bradley said, "This is . . . that is, you may recall Miss Keene."

"I recall," Croome muttered. "I recall I caught 'er snooping where she had no business."

"Yes, well. She has entered into service now. Helping with my young cousins."

Croome scorched her with a glare, but she doused it with an icy one of her own. For she remembered him as well, somewhere *he* had no business.

He looked away first and turned to Lord Bradley. "There's a polecat lurkin' about the place. I plan to set a trap for him, unless you prefer to leave him be. Keep the rats down, polecats do, but terrible destructive for game."

"I see. Well, whatever you think best, Mr. Croome. Father has always trusted your wisdom in these affairs."

Olivia studied Lord Bradley, perplexed. He was like a nervous schoolboy before an exacting headmaster.

Croome nodded and lurched away in his slightly limping gait, and they both turned to watch as the gamekeeper disappeared into the wood.

"You are still afraid of him," Olivia ventured quietly. "Has he ever harmed you?"

"No." He expelled a puff of breath. "Foolish, is it not? I think it has to do with my father. When I was a lad, he always seemed to stand closer to me whenever Croome was about."

How odd, Olivia thought. Aloud she said, "I wonder if Lord Brightwell knows something unsavory about the man's character." To herself she added, *Or about his dealings with poachers?*

"I don't know," Lord Bradley admitted. "But perhaps I shall ask him when he returns."

She was once again tempted to tell Lord Bradley where she had first seen Croome, but hesitated. She knew it would lead to more questions she was not prepared to answer.

Late in the afternoon, when Olivia went down to the kitchen for the nursery dinner tray, the kitchen maids were sitting on low stools, plucking feathers from a basketful of small birds. Seeing her stare, Mrs. Moore explained. "Grouse from the gamekeeper. Grouse pie will make for a nice change, will it not? Our neighbor George Linton filled our larder with partridges from his estate, and everyone is sick to death of them."

Mrs. Moore added a dish of suet dumplings to the nursery tray, then looked up at Olivia. "Have you met our Mr. Croome?"

Olivia gave a slight nod, which traveled into her shoulders as a shudder.

"Afraid of the man, are you? I shouldn't wonder. Looks a fright most days, doesn't he?"

Olivia nodded her agreement.

Mrs. Moore clucked her tongue. "He's as thin as I've ever seen him. What must he eat, I wonder? I doubt he's had a decent meal in years."

Olivia wondered at the sympathy in her tone. Of course she had been at Brightwell Court long enough to realize Mrs. Moore could not stand the thought of anyone going hungry.

"And too proud to take a meal with us," one of the kitchen maids piped up.

"Hush, Edith, and keep to your plucking," Mrs. Moore said. "Has his own house and fire ring, hasn't he? Not in service like the rest of us."

Mrs. Moore sighed. "And me with two perfectly good partridge pasties and no one to eat them." She lifted woeful eyes from the pasties to Olivia and back again.

No . . . Olivia thought, and slowly, emphatically, shook her head.

Sukey accompanied her as far as the narrow track but refused to go further. Swallowing, Olivia gripped the packet more tightly and stepped into the clearing.

Croome sat on the lodge stoop, stroking a long knife over a sharpening stone. When she stepped into the clearing, he jerked his head up.

"What do you want?" Croome's wiry brows formed an angry V over narrowed eyes. "Nothing to snoop around here for."

She recalled Mrs. Moore's admonition. *"Don't let him see your fear. Worse than the predators he keeps out of the wood, he is, when he smells weakness."*

He stared at her, and it was all she could do not to look away from the venom in his eyes.

Suddenly his gaze targeted the packet in her hands. "Whatever that is, you can take it right back with you. I don't need yer charity."

She lifted her chin and held out the paper-wrapped package upon which Mrs. Moore had written its contents: *Hashed Partridge Pasty*.

His scowl deepened to one of disgust, and Olivia was stunned when he rose and snatched the packet from her and threw it maliciously into the pigpen. The packet split open and the pasties spilled out, soon surrounded and disappearing under the grunting work of pigs.

She cringed, feeling the sting of her offering being rejected, even if Mrs. Moore had been the one to suggest it. Hashed partridge was considered a delicacy—a rare treat for any man. How ungrateful he was. How rude.

She had kept his secret and, against her better judgment, had allowed Mrs. Moore to persuade her to offer a gift. Well, she had done all she would to repay him for her rescue. All the way back to the manor, she fumed. She was done with the man. Croome could starve to death, and good riddance!

12

Avoid as much as possible being alone with the other sex:
as the greatest mischiefs happen from small circumstances.
—Samuel & Sarah Adams, *The Complete Servant*

The next morning, Olivia went downstairs to find Mrs. Hinkley, bearing a note Nurse Peale had dictated while she'd had her hands full with Alexander. The note requested the procurement of an ivory ring, and in the meantime, a crust of stale bread for the fussy, teething child to chew.

Olivia found the housekeeper sitting at the small desk in her parlor, bent over a lined book. She looked up when Olivia entered, and groaned. "I have spent the better part of three hours on the household accounts and cannot balance this ledger. Mr. Walters will want an accounting of every shilling tomorrow, and I cannot find where I have gone wrong."

Olivia bit her lip. Dared she offer? She touched a finger to her chest.

"You want to give it a go?" Mrs. Hinkley huffed a laugh. "Do you know anything about household accounts?"

Olivia lifted her shoulders, fluttered a hand.

Mrs. Hinkley rose. "Well, I suppose there is nothing confidential about how many rashers of bacon and pounds of sugar we buy or how much we pay the coal merchant."

She hovered behind the chair until Olivia shooed her gently away.

"Oh, very well. But if you don't find my error in half an hour, I shall have to try again."

Ten minutes later, Olivia rapped her knuckles against the desk. Mrs. Hinkley rose sprightly from the settee and hurried over. "Did you find something?"

Olivia nodded and pointed to an incorrect subtotal. She lifted a scrap of paper with the reworked sum.

"Bless me, you're right! How did I miss it?"

Olivia smiled and rose from the chair.

Still staring at the figures and shaking her head, Mrs. Hinkley said, "Sometimes a pair of fresh eyes is all that is needed, I suppose." Then she looked up at Olivia once more. "If you would not mind keeping this between us . . . ?"

Olivia nodded. She had no desire to tell a soul. She did not want anyone asking her how she came to know so much about account books.

She belatedly handed over Nurse Peale's note. Mrs. Hinkley skimmed it and sent Olivia down to the kitchen for the bread, promising to purchase the ring as soon as possible. Several minutes later, Olivia returned to the nursery with the crust of bread, only to have Miss Peale look at it blankly and say she was not hungry.

That afternoon, Edward was meeting in the study with his father's clerk when movement out on the lawn drew his attention. He paused in his dictation to Walters to look out the window. Miss Keene was outside, a red scarf tied across her eyes and bonnet, her arms outstretched in a game of hoodman blind. His young cousins, bundled head to toe, ran around her, evading her grasp. The children were laughing and calling out. Miss Keene was turning, her skirts and cape twirling about her, a wide smile lighting her face. He felt his own mouth turn up in response. He knew he should not find her attractive, but he did. He wished he knew if he could trust her. He thought of Sybil Harrington, whom his father hoped he would marry, with her classic features and rich dowry. She was more beautiful than any under nurse, surely.

Andrew ran too close, and Miss Keene grabbed him around his middle and lifted him, spinning him around and around until his hat flew to the ground. Andrew laughed with glee, the sound of it carrying through the glass. Miss Keene set him down and pulled down the blindfold. She mussed Andrew's hair affectionately before picking up his hat and replacing it on his head. Audrey joined them, sliding her gloved hand into Miss Keene's.

"Shall I repeat the last sentence, my lord?" the clerk asked.

"Hmm?" Edward murmured, returning to the business at hand. "Oh, yes please, Walters, if you would."

Olivia stuffed the red scarf into her cape pocket. She covered her eyes with her hands, then pointed toward the outbuildings.

"She wants to play hide-and-seek!" Andrew shouted.

Olivia nodded with a wry grin. She was becoming quite adept at charades.

"I am weary of childish games," Audrey grumbled.

"Come on, Aud," her brother urged. "I'll even seek first. Ready, steady, go!"

Giving in, Audrey ran off in the direction of the garden. Olivia followed more sedately, too self-conscious to run without the children at her side.

While Andrew counted, Olivia searched this way and that for a new hiding spot.

Johnny Ross stepped out of the stables, polish and brush in hand. "Here!" he called, waving her over. "I know a place those ankle-biters will never find you."

She hurried toward the groom, and when she smiled at him, his fair face broke into a blushing grin. "This way, miss."

Olivia followed him into the stables. There, he pushed at a section of wood walling that was actually a well-hidden door to a small closet.

"Don't use this anymore, not since the tack room was added."

Olivia stepped into the dark room, expecting Johnny to close the door from the outside. Instead, he stepped in after her and pulled the door shut against his back.

She felt suddenly ill at ease. She took a step toward the door, but he moved as well, blocking her path.

"You're a prime article," he whispered, gripping her waist. "A real beauty."

Olivia tried to pry his hands away. His grasp remained firm. By slim shafts of light filtering through cracks in the wall, she saw him lean his face toward hers. She turned her head so that his damp lips found only a bit of cheek and ear.

"Livie!" Andrew called from somewhere nearby. "Come out, come out, wherever you are!"

Olivia pushed Johnny away with all her strength and hurried out the door and into the stable yard, wincing in the bright sunlight. In a moment she could see, but dreaded what she saw.

Mrs. Hinkley.

The housekeeper's eyes slowly assessed her burning face.

Olivia looked away first.

Andrew, unaware of the awkward scene, explained. "Mrs. Hinkley came looking for you, so I said she could help me find you."

"I appreciate your assistance, Master Andrew," Mrs. Hinkley said dryly.

Johnny stepped out from the dim stables. Olivia darted a glance at him, then at Mrs. Hinkley. The older woman looked from one to the other. Olivia knew the shrewd housekeeper would not miss their guilty expressions.

"Might I steal you from your game, Livie?" she asked, all placid nonchalance. "Lord Bradley would like a word."

Olivia swallowed, but a ball of dread seemed lodged in her throat as she silently followed.

Lord Bradley sat behind his desk in a blue coat and white cravat, his golden hair brushed neatly forward. The strong lines of his face were set. His pale blue eyes stared, unwavering.

Once Mrs. Hinkley had closed the study door and her footfalls had retreated down the corridor, Olivia said stiffly, "You wanted to see me?"

"Yes. Please sit down," Lord Bradley's voice was formal and firm. He entwined his long fingers on the polished desktop. "I have learnt of your recent activities and must say I am surprised."

"It was nothing, really," she stammered, cheeks heating at the thought of being caught coming out of a closet with the groom. "Nothing happened."

"Nothing? Come, Miss Keene, the whole staff is talking about it. Why, I witnessed your activities myself this morning from this very window."

Olivia's stomach dropped. "Did you indeed?"

"Quite. Mrs. Howe is very impressed, and I must say I am as well." He paused. "I see I am making you uncomfortable." His tone softened; his eyes as well. "I simply asked you here to thank you for taking on the care of the children so admirably—going far beyond the duties of an under nurse. It is much appreciated, especially as they are without a governess at present." He picked up a letter from his desk and handed it to her. "And, to give you this."

The letter was addressed to her, and she was surprised to find the seal unbroken—he had not read it. She unfolded the single page and skimmed its contents. The brief letter was written in the arthritic hand of an older woman.

Miss Keene,

We are not seeking to hire anyone at this time. Nor has anyone called here inquiring after you.

Sincerely,
Miss Kirby, Proprietress
The Girls' Seminary,
St. Aldwyns

The curt reply held no warm remembrance or even acknowledgment of a former friendship with her mother. Had her mother put too much stock in the acquaintance?

"Any offer of a post?" he asked with apparent unconcern.

She shook her head.

"And have they told your mother where to find you?"

Again she shook her head, wondering what had delayed her mother.

"Perhaps it is just as well." He cleared his throat. "I have asked Mrs. Hinkley to give you a half day off per week—though I must still ask you to remain on the estate. I realize there is not much for a young woman to do here, especially this time of year, but—"

"I don't mind," Olivia interrupted, mustering a smile. "I could walk alone on the grounds or stay in my room and do a bit of reading. There are several books in the schoolroom—that is, if you do not mind."

He nodded. "By all means."

"Thank you, my lord." She straightened her shoulders and inhaled deeply. "I shall look forward to it. When is my half day to be? Sunday?"

His smile tightened. "Ross's half day is on Sunday, is it not?"

She hesitated, then nodded.

"Then yours shall be on Wednesday."

Taking the children for a turn around the shrubbery on Monday, Olivia glimpsed Lord Bradley walk past the stone gardening shed, then disappear behind a timber-framed outbuilding beside it. She would have liked to ask the children what the building was, but as she could not, she led the children toward it.

They turned the corner and saw Lord Bradley climb the two steps to the stoop and run his finger along a crack in the building's solitary window, then reach for the door handle. Seeing them, he abruptly drew his hand away and stood with his back to the closed door.

For once there was no welcoming smile for his young cousins. "Hello, Andrew. Audrey."

He did not address her, nor offer any explanation of why he stood there or what he was about.

"The gardener has just discovered a pure white cat living under the woodshed," he said to the children. "It has one green eye and one blue. If you hurry, he will no doubt show you."

Audrey and Andrew needed no further prodding and quickly ran off.

Olivia waited one moment more, wondering if he would say anything once the children were out of earshot. Instead, he just stood there, arms crossed, staring down at her in cool challenge.

"Had you not better follow your charges?"

Piqued, she turned and walked back in the direction she had come. Just as she turned the corner, she glanced back over her shoulder and saw Lord Bradley slip inside the building and shut the door firmly behind him. The message was clear. They were not welcome there. What was he doing within? Was he alone? She was tempted to peer in the window like the spy he already believed her to be, but recalling the challenge in his eyes, she resisted the impulse.

The next day, when Olivia delivered the children to the stables for their riding lessons, Lord Bradley had yet to return from his morning ride, so Johnny once again led the children around the yard on leads.

A few minutes later, Lord Bradley cantered in on his black horse. He reined in, swung his leg over to dismount, then tied the horse to the rail.

His eyes scanned the stable yard. "What is Ross about? This horse needs a good rubdown."

"Perhaps you could show me how it is done?"

One sardonic brow rose. "Protecting your lover again?"

Ignoring this, she said earnestly, "Actually, I dread the thought of going indoors on such a perfect autumn day. I would love to stay out here and give it a go."

He hesitated. "Have you ever done so?"

"No. But you shall not find a quicker student."

"Very well." He stepped into the tack room and returned directly. He laid a brush onto her waiting palm, tightening the strap over the back of her hand. Resting his free palm on the horse's damp withers, he lifted her equipped hand with his own and began guiding her through the brush strokes until she felt mesmerized by the rhythm and the firm hold of his hand on hers. She could almost feel the warmth of his body standing behind her, though he touched only her hand.

He cleared his throat. "There, I believe you have mastered the motion."

He stepped away, and the perfect autumn day felt suddenly quite chilly.

Lord Bradley leaned against the stable wall and gave her a shrewd look. He rapped his knuckles on the hidden door, producing a hollow knock. "I understand you have discovered the secret room here."

She looked up at him sharply.

"Yes, I know of it. I was underfoot as a lad when our old steward built it. I imagine he wanted a closet to nap in, or perhaps for some private assignation. It is perfectly suited for it, do you not think?"

He watched her closely. No doubt saw the blush warming her cheeks.

"Andrew mentioned last night that you hid in the stables with the groom. You were in here together, were you not?"

"Only for a moment," she whispered, wondering if he would retract his offer of a half day.

"And what, pray, did you do during that moment alone, in the dark?"

"Nothing."

"Why do I doubt that?"

"Perhaps you assume I share your own ill-intentions."

"Touché." He held up a consolatory hand. "Forgive me, Miss Keene. I meant no harm."

"I had better return to the nursery." Dropping the brush, she turned and strode away, chilled and flushed at once.

13

> The estate carpenter frequently made toys for the children in the nursery, furniture for the house, as well as carrying out repairs.
>
> —*Upstairs & Downstairs, Life in an English Country House*

On the first Wednesday afternoon in December, Olivia left the children under the care of Becky and Nurse Peale, donned her cape and gloves, and let herself out the rear door. Though the early December day was cold, the sun shone invitingly.

Walking around the manor toward the gardens, she saw Lord Bradley in coat and hat disappear once again behind the outbuilding near the gardening shed. Curiosity tugged at her, and she followed him around the building.

There Lord Bradley stood beside a tradesman as he packed his bag of tools. Both men stood for a moment, eyes trained on a small clear window as though a work of art. Then the tradesman lifted a hand in farewell and turned to go. The new window was certainly in better condition than the rest of the timber-framed structure, whatever it was. Wondering how she would be received this time, she whispered, "My lord."

He looked at her with mild surprise. "Miss Keene. What is it? The children all right?"

"Yes, my lord. It is my half day."

"Ah." He nodded. "That was the glazier just here. Replacing this window." He stepped to the door.

"What is this place?" she asked.

He hesitated at the threshold, then looked at her over his shoulder. "Come in and see for yourself."

She wondered if it was proper, but curiosity—and the longing to speak with the only person with whom she was allowed to do so—overrode her sense of propriety. She followed him inside.

"It is just a little carpentry shop," he said. "A workroom."

Sun shone in through the new window, illuminating a one-room interior of unfinished wood. A lamp glowed on the worktable, which held a large drape-covered object atop it. A small stove in the corner heated the space. Tools hung neatly from pegs on the walls, and planks of various sizes were stacked beneath. A chair, mid-repair, sat in one corner. The place smelled of wood shavings, smoke, and him, and she thought the fragrance quite pleasant.

Lord Bradley removed his coat and hung it on a peg. She was further surprised when he tied a leather apron around his waist.

"Our former steward did quite a bit of carpentry." Lord Bradley looked about him. "I used to come out here with him as a lad and tag along as he went about his duties. I had a small part—and many slivers—in the outbuildings, the arbor, and of course, the present stables of which you are so fond."

He gave her a knowing look, but she quickly averted her gaze.

He sighed. "Then Matthews died and I went away to school, and the place fell into disuse."

"It does not appear abandoned."

"I have cleaned it out and made repairs." He picked up a carpenter's plane and began stroking it across a pale piece of wood. "Matthews's tools were still here . . . like buried treasure for a man like me."

"What are you making?"

He shrugged. "Christmas gifts. A cricket bat for Andrew. Blocks for Alexander. Though a couple seem to have gone missing." He nodded toward the drape-covered object. "And something for Audrey. Attempting it, anyway. It must remain our secret, if you please, for I am dreadfully out of practice, and I don't wish to disappoint them if unsuccessful."

Another secret to keep . . . She looked with interest at the draped project. "Might I at least peek?"

He started to shake his head, then hesitated, regarding her with a gleam in his blue eyes. "You know, I could use an accomplice."

"An accomplice?" she said, her voice a little sharper than she intended, suspecting another reference to her "crime."

He held up one hand in entreaty. "Poor choice of words. But . . . you were a little girl once, were you not?"

"I should think so, yes." A little bubble of excitement rose in her chest.

"And you do sew?"

Her spirits quickly flagged. "You want me to *sew*?"

"Never mind."

She sighed. "Forgive me. It is only that I have a fair amount of sewing most evenings as it is, helping Becky keep the children's clothes repaired—especially Andrew's stockings and the knees of his breeches. But if you need something mended . . ."

"Not mended. Created."

"What?" She glanced at the chair in the corner. "A cushion for your chair, or . . ."

He followed her gaze. "Not a bad idea. But not for that chair." He pinched an inch of air between his thumb and finger. "Could you make one say, this big?"

She looked doubtful. "For a mouse?"

He cocked his head to the side. "You disappoint me, Miss Keene." His blue eyes twinkled as he pulled off the dustcloth from the large object on the worktable. "Have you *no* imagination?"

He revealed a three-story doll's house, a scale model of a manor very like Brightwell Court. Olivia drew in a breath of wonder. "*You* built this?"

"Your confidence astounds me."

"It is magnificent, truly."

"Do you think Audrey will like it?"

"How could she not?" Olivia said, though in truth, she wondered if Audrey was growing a little old for dolls. Still, she believed any girl would marvel at such a gift.

She pulled out a drawing peeking out from under the house and unfolded the thick paper to reveal the whole—a detailed drawing of the doll's house with measurements to scale. "You drew this as well?"

"Yes. So . . . will you?"

She dragged her gaze from the impressively drawn plan. "Hmm?"

"Help me make some draperies and cushions and bedclothes and such?"

She looked up at him, bewildered and touched that he would devote such time to amusing and delighting children who were not his own. "With pleasure, my lord."

He smiled down at her, his lips softening as his gaze seemed to fix on her mouth. She drew in a breath and turned away toward the doll's house. "Here is the nursery," she said quickly. "But you have not included my room, though you have been there." Her cheeks heated as she realized what she had said.

He stood beside her, bending near as they both pretended to study his handiwork. She felt his gaze on her profile, knew their faces were only inches apart.

A long curl of her hair came loose, a curtain falling between them. He slowly ran his finger along her temple and tucked the curl behind her ear. Her heart raced and her skin tingled at his touch. If she angled toward him, just a little, her lips might brush his. Did she want that? Did he?

The carpentry shop door creaked open and Olivia started. Beside her, Lord Bradley jerked upright. Croome stood framed in the threshold, eyes narrowed suspiciously, fowling piece in hand.

"Yes? What is it?" Bradley asked, somewhat defensively.

The man looked from Lord Bradley to Olivia. "I seen the door open to this ol' place and thought a raccoon or a tramp must have got inside." He pinned Olivia with a pointed look.

Lord Bradley replied, "As you can see, that is not the case."

Croome glared at Olivia a moment longer, then slowly lifted his gaze to survey the room. "You using ol' Matthews's shop again?"

"Yes, as you see."

Croome looked about at the neatly arranged tools, the sawdust, the work in progress.

"Have you some reason to object, Mr. Croome?" Lord Bradley asked with asperity.

The wiry brows rose. "Not my business, is it."

"Precisely."

"I'm setting rat traps in the outbuildings. Want one here as well?"

"Thank you, Mr. Croome."

He trained his eyes on Olivia once more. "Mind you don't get caught in it."

When Miss Keene left the shop, Edward took a deep breath and attempted to regain his composure. He should not, would not, be attracted to her. He brought Miss Harrington's image to mind once again, reminding himself that he would no doubt be seeing her at Christmas.

Christmas . . . His gifts would never be ready in time if he kept making a fool of himself over an under nurse. He was becoming as bad as Felix. He forced himself to return his attention to the blocks for Alexander. He had made ten of them, he was sure, with the numbers 1 through 10 rather crudely carved into one side and the letters A through J on the opposite. What had he done with blocks 1 and 2? They seemed to be missing. Being in close quarters with the woman had made sawdust of his brains. How had he mislaid them?

At that moment, Osborn knocked and announced that George Linton had just arrived. "Is my lord at home for callers?"

Stifling a groan, Edward untied his apron. The work—and the search—would have to wait.

That evening, Judith looked across the table at him as she cut her capon. She initiated their dinner conversation, as she often did, commenting on the exceptionally fine weather they had been having and could he believe December was already upon them?

Pushing away thoughts of Miss Keene, Edward murmured his agreement but knew himself to be distracted. He still found it strange to dine with only Judith, now that his parents were away and Felix had returned to Oxford. He supposed he should be used to Judith's company. She had lived with them since Dominick's funeral more than a year before. Judith's mother, who lived in a small townhouse in Swindon, had suggested the arrangement, and Lord Brightwell had quickly agreed, graciously offering a home to his then-expecting niece and her two stepchildren.

"I spoke with George Linton when he called for you," Judith said. "What did he want?"

"To boast about his new hunter." Edward guessed the call was only a ruse to lay eyes on Judith, whom George had admired in vain since boyhood.

She tried another topic. "Dominick's mother has written to ask if I have engaged a new governess for Audrey and Andrew." She paused to sip her wine. "I suppose I must, though I do so dread the prospect. Bringing in another creature like Miss Dowdle, who believes herself superior to me in education and my equal in station, were it not for her diminished means. Wanting to take meals with us, attend parties, and tempt the males of the family." She placed a dainty piece of capon in her mouth. "You saw how it was with Felix. I was never so relieved as when Miss Dowdle left—and not only because she was so stern with Audrey and Andrew. Even had the gall to lecture me on the proper manner of raising children."

Edward did not argue. He, too, had found Miss Dowdle most disagreeable and had worried where Felix's flirtation might lead.

Realizing he had left Judith to fend for herself in the conversation long enough, he wiped his mouth on a linen serviette and began a topic of his own. "What shall we do about Christmas?"

Picking at a sweetmeat, Judith said thoughtfully, "I suppose we must celebrate in some fashion, for the children's sake."

"I agree. But let us entertain modestly this year."

Judith nodded her assent.

Conscious of Lord and Lady Brightwell's absence, they together planned a smaller gathering than usual. No distant relations. No friends down from London. They would have only their neighbors—George Linton, his sister, Charity, and their parents—the vicar and his sister, and Admiral Harrington and his daughter. Edward would also invite his father's sisters, though he doubted their spinster aunts would make the trip from the coast this time of year. And Judith would invite her mother, though she believed Mrs. Bradley planned to spend Christmas with friends in Bath.

"But Felix will come, of course," Judith added.

Edward nodded. "When does he arrive?"

"Who can say with Felix? But he shan't miss Mrs. Moore's mincemeat pie, nor the opportunity to wear out his welcome at Brightwell Court—that I do know."

Inwardly, Edward sighed. That was what he was afraid of.

14

> I have been busily employed in preparing for passing Christmas worthily. My beef and mincemeat are ready (of which, my poor neighbors will partake), and my holly and mistletoe gathered.
>
> —letter from "a wife, a mother, and an Englishwoman," *Examiner,* 1818

Olivia witnessed the transformation of Brightwell Court with awe and delight. Mrs. Hinkley, with help from the housemaids and hall boy, dressed the mantels, windows, and doorframes with entwined greens of rosemary, bay, ivy, and yew. The housekeeper then twisted a long garland of holly down the stately staircase. "In remembrance of His crown of thorns," she whispered reverently. Soon, the entire manor was imbued with the spicy scent of greenery.

Doris, ever scheming, hung a kissing bow and a bunch of mistletoe above the threshold of the servants' hall. Mrs. Hinkley forbade that decoration in any of the public rooms upstairs, fearing the vicar would frown upon the pagan tradition.

In the nursery, Olivia guided the children in the cutting of silk and gold paper into stars and streamers with which they festooned their own hearth and walls. She wished she might purchase small gifts for her charges, and for Mrs. Moore besides. *Perhaps next year,* she thought and quickly chastised herself. She would not be at Brightwell Court next year. Her mother would come looking for her any day and only the Lord knew where they would be by next Christmas.

In her spare moments, when the children were otherwise occupied or sleeping, Olivia cut, pinned, and stitched in secret, creating miniature bedclothes, cushions, and pillows for the doll's house. She crafted a tiny embroidery hoop from a small strip of balsa wood, and wound miniature skeins of mending wool from embroidery floss. She painted several miniature landscapes with the supplies in the schoolroom and framed them in old shoe buckles. She even involved Audrey unknowingly, providing her with a tiny piece of canvas and suggesting she try to copy one of the prints on the nursery wall in miniature. Audrey had spent a pleasant afternoon doing so, none the wiser.

When the weather allowed, Olivia bore these small offerings out to the carpentry shop in her cape pocket and left them where Lord Bradley would discover them, both relieved and disappointed when he was not there to receive them in person. She hoped he would be pleased, and imagined the crooked smile that would lift one side of his mouth if he was.

One morning, she had that pleasure. She knocked softly and entered to find him examining one of the wooden blocks he had made for Alexander.

"Ah, Miss Keene," he said. "I was just thinking of you."

Her nerves tingled to attention. Thinking well of her, or . . . ?

"I seem to be missing a few of the blocks I made for Alexander. Have you seen any about?"

"No." She answered easily. Then she noticed he still studied her, as if testing her sincerity. The notion rankled. "Surely you do not accuse me of—"

He raised a placating hand. "I only thought you might have seen where I had mislaid them, or inadvertently picked a few up with a reel of cotton or some such."

"I did not."

He nodded, but he was still searching about the shop, distracted.

Disappointed, she set down the miniature paintings and carpets she had made and turned to go.

His voice stopped her at the door. "These are excellent, Miss Keene. Truly charming. And the cushions fit the settee perfectly. Well done."

She bowed her head in acknowledgment, but felt her pleasure dimmed by the nagging feeling that he had instantly assumed her—trespasser, eavesdropper, thief—responsible for the missing blocks.

On the morning of Christmas Eve, once Olivia had made her bed, washed and dressed, she opened her drawer and, from under a handkerchief, drew forth her mother's small purse. She sat on her bed and opened it on her lap. She picked up the sealed letter and held it up to the weak morning sunlight coming through her window. Nothing was discernable. She looked once more at the script on the outside and ran her fingers over her mother's fine hand. Replacing it, she picked up the old newspaper clipping. She realized this was the announcement of his father's wedding, not the current Lord Bradley's as she had originally guessed. Evidently, *Lord Bradley* was the title the eldest son used until his father died, and then that son became the next earl, the next *Lord Brightwell*. She wondered again why her mother had kept the clipping.

Someone scratched on her door and swung it open before Olivia could react. She quickly closed the purse and looked up to find Mrs. Howe regarding her with a lift of her brow.

Olivia rose, heart pounding. Now what had she done?

She belatedly saw the gown Judith Howe held over her arm. No doubt she needed a lace mended or seam sewn.

"Good morning, Miss Keene."

Olivia wondered again why her mistress addressed her so, but was pleased by this apparent sign of respect.

"I've noticed that you have only the one dress."

Olivia felt her lips part. She looked down, hoping to hide the blush heating her cheeks. Had she embarrassed the family?

Mrs. Howe continued, "As it is Christmas, I thought to give you one of mine."

A cast-off dress? Olivia's pride rebelled.

Her mistress lifted the dark blue gown on her arm. "I shall never again wear this. Once my mourning has passed, I shall need a whole new wardrobe."

The reserved gown certainly befitted Olivia's station. She could hardly imagine Mrs. Howe choosing to wear something so prim and plain before her mourning. Olivia's pride once more urged her to refuse it, but her practical nature compelled her to accept. It was Christmas, after all. And had not it stung when Croome refused her offering? She gave Mrs. Howe a quick smile and curtsy and held forth her hands to receive the gift.

Later that afternoon, Olivia paused at a tall window in the entry hall, drawn by the sounds of horse hooves and carriage wheels outside. It was not the Brightwell carriage, but rather a traveling coach. She watched as a liveried footman handed down an elegant young lady with a large ornate hat and fur-trimmed cloak. Behind her, a meek-looking woman followed, straightening the woman's cloak as she went. Her abigail, no doubt. Who was the lady? Someone invited to celebrate Christmas with the family of course, but who?

She had overheard Judith explain to Audrey plans for a more subdued Christmas this year. Lord Bradley would host in his father's stead while Judith, Olivia guessed, would act the part of hostess.

Someone grabbed her arm, and Olivia started, but it was only Doris, feather duster in hand.

"Come on, love," she whispered. "They don't want you greetin' their guest."

She pulled Olivia into a nearby closet, just as Hodges swept into the hall and opened the front doors. Dory closed the closet door, but for a few inches, and through it peered into the hall where the guest was being received.

With a sinking feeling, Olivia watched over Dory's shoulder as the elegant young lady slowly unfastened her cloak. The tall, graceful woman had caramel-brown hair, fine features, and large brown eyes.

The cape unfastened, Hodges took it from her. Her ivory gown shone with beadwork around a low-cut bodice. A large cameo necklace hung at her throat and sparkling gems encircled her gloved wrists.

Olivia almost whispered, "Who is she?" But before she slipped, Doris said in hushed tones, "That is Miss Harrington. Beautiful, is she not? Her father is an admiral and very wealthy. They say Lord Bradley will marry her for her dowry, even though she is beneath him."

Rich and beautiful . . . The thought pinched like a tight shoe. Olivia fidgeted behind the door. Perhaps Miss Harrington was the important matter Lord Bradley had mentioned, the one that ought to be settled soon—a matter that might be complicated by rumors and threats of exposure.

Suddenly Hodges opened the closet door and Olivia stifled a gasp. Dory put a finger to her lips. The man looked mildly startled to find them there, but as Doris and Olivia flattened themselves against the wall, he moved past them to hang up the lady's cloak. He then backed from the closet and shut the door without a word. They would be reprimanded later, no doubt.

"Don't worry, ducky," Doris whispered. "You're not in for it. Maids are supposed to make themselves invisible."

Doris cracked open the door again, and Olivia saw that Lord Bradley had joined Miss Harrington in the hall. He bowed before her, then took her hands in his.

"Where is the admiral?" he asked.

"Spending a few days with an ailing uncle, but he insisted I come as planned without him."

"I am very glad you did," Lord Bradley smiled warmly, and Olivia's stomach knotted. He offered Miss Harrington his arm and escorted her from view.

Watching them go, Doris said on a sigh, "A shame she's vain as an alabaster bust." She smirked. "And about as softhearted."

Olivia knew she should hope it wasn't true.

Soon after, the Tugwell family and the Lintons arrived to share in an evening of fireside festivities. When Olivia ushered Audrey and Andrew down to the drawing room, she paused in the threshold to admire the room. The walls were hung with gilt-framed portraits over panels of crimson and green silk. The high windows wore matching draperies, and the chairs and settees were upholstered in rich, apple green velvet. Candles and a crystal chandelier glowed and reflected in the large looking glass over the marble chimneypiece. The Tugwell boys sat clustered around a card-playing table and were beginning a game of oranges and limes while the adults took tea before a roaring fire. Mr. Tugwell smiled warmly at Olivia from across the room, but his sister's cool glance spoilt the pleasure of the moment.

Olivia recognized the elder Mr. Linton as the master of the hunt, and his stout son George as the taunting roan rider, but knew it unlikely that either man would recognize her. She turned to go, but Judith Howe asked her to stay to accompany the children on the pianoforte.

Mr. Tugwell's eldest son, Amos, was home from school, and he led his four younger brothers in a sweet harmonized performance of "Adeste Fideles," which brought tears to Olivia's eyes as she played. Audrey and Andrew, dressed smartly for the occasion, sang "While Shepherds Watched Their Flocks by Night." They matched the Tugwells' enthusiasm, if not their talent.

Afterward, Osborn brought in a tray laid with Christmas fare—widgeon, preserved ginger, black butter, sandwiches, and tarts. The adults sipped spiced cider and toddies, while the children drank milk punch and syllabub. Olivia could almost taste her mother's thick, sweet syllabub, though none was offered her now.

Olivia's Christmases at home had been much quieter affairs, but still, Olivia missed the warm comfort of Christmases past, of sitting beside the hearth with her mother and father, roasting chestnuts, talking, and opening small gifts. Her father had usually remained with them all night, rarely taking himself to the Crown and Crow on that holy eve. Sometimes he would give in to Mother's urging and sing "Adeste Fideles," and Olivia never ceased to be amazed at his sweet, haunting voice. If only all of their days could have been as pleasant.

Audrey begged for a Christmas ball, saying they had danced last year and could they not do so again?

Finally the adults roused themselves to the task. Lord Bradley, Felix, George Linton, and Mr. Tugwell made quick work of moving aside the heavy armchairs and rolling up the carpet, not wishing to give the servants extra work on Christmas Eve. Again, Olivia was asked to play. They made five couples, Edward and Miss Harrington, Felix and homely Miss Charity Linton, Mr. Tugwell and his sister, Augusta, George Linton and his mother, Amos Tugwell and Audrey. Judith, claiming her widowhood, and the elder Mr. Linton his gout, contented themselves to watch. Andrew and the younger Tugwell boys went back to their game of wind the jack.

Olivia wished her playing was better than it was. She had never played for a real ball before, only for the school's dancing master at Miss Cresswell's. She played a country dance and the heel-toe rigadoon, but then Miss Tugwell approached the pianoforte and said, "It would be so much easier to dance were the meter regular and the notes sharp. I shall relieve you, if you please."

Ears and cheeks heating, Olivia rose and dipped a brief curtsy and turned toward the door, hoping to make a quick escape. Mr. Tugwell's voice stopped her. "Miss Keene. Will you dance?"

An under nurse asked to dance with the family? Even she knew such a thing was not done. An awkward silence swelled. Olivia shook her head, her whole face burning now.

"But my partner has deserted me. Do have pity on me."

Several in the party exchanged scandalized glances, Miss Harrington among them.

Augusta Tugwell clanged a few sharp notes by way of introduction. "Do not be ridiculous, Charles."

"Oh, I shall take pity on you, Mr. Tugwell," Judith Howe said, rising. She gave Olivia a quick look of understanding, which eased Olivia's embarrassment. Mrs. Howe addressed the vicar once more. "That is, if you do not think it improper?"

"Not at all, madam. You are not so recent a widow." He bowed.

A widow and a widower, Olivia thought fleetingly, but could not envision the two as future husband and wife.

The next dance commenced with Miss Tugwell playing a vigorous and precise Scottish reel. Its militant pace put Olivia in mind of soldiers marching off to war.

Dismissed and feeling lonely, Olivia stole downstairs, hoping to find Mrs. Moore and share a glass of cider with the friendly woman by the warm kitchen hearth. As she passed the servants' hall, a figure shot out from the doorway and clasped her about the shoulders. Startled, she shrieked, just as Johnny kissed her full on the mouth.

He smiled impishly and looked above her head. "Yer under the kissin' bow, Livie. So don't slap me, like I see in yer eyes a mind to."

Her hand itched to do just that, but she resisted.

He frowned suddenly. "Did you make a sound just now?"

Oh, no . . . She hesitated, lifting a shrug.

He grinned. "Kissing you has made me addlepated, that's all." He leaned in to kiss her again, but she pulled away.

Shaking her head as she walked on, Olivia realized Johnny could not have known she would come belowstairs. For whom had he been lying in wait? Perhaps she should have slapped him after all.

Coming to the kitchen door, Olivia heard the hum of quiet voices. She paused to peek around the doorjamb. Mrs. Moore sat at a stool pulled up to the table, elbows resting atop it, hands around a large cup before her. Across from her sat Mr. Croome, taking the glass of cider Olivia had hoped for herself. She was stunned to see him there, head bowed, apparently listening to whatever Mrs. Moore was saying. Olivia's selfish disappointment gave way to a nobler emotion, and only the holy day could account for it. For she was glad the crusty hermit was not alone on Christmas Eve.

Suddenly the man flew to his feet, nearly toppling the stool he had so recently occupied. "I will thank you, madam, never to ask me again."

"Avery . . ." Mrs. Moore soothed, and in low tones attempted to cajole the man into sitting down once more. Olivia did not remain to see if she succeeded.

Giving up, Olivia climbed back upstairs. She wished nothing more than to go directly to her room and fall into bed, but knew she ought to check on the children. Returning to the withdrawing room, she peered in at the partially open doorway. The ball had apparently concluded. She heard only the hum of adult conversation and the occasional burst of youthful laughter. The adults were sitting once more before the fire, while at the table Audrey sat with the Tugwell boys, playing a game of dominoes. It was evident from her wide, adoring eyes that she thought Amos Tugwell a romantic figure.

But where was Andrew? Had he already gone upstairs?

Olivia turned back to the corridor and saw him. Curled up on the padded bench upon which the Tugwell boys had piled their coats, fast asleep. Poor lamb was exhausted. She lowered herself to her haunches before him. "Andrew?" she whispered, forgetting for a moment that she was not to speak. The boy didn't rouse. She gently stroked the brown hair from his forehead. She hated the thought of waking the child, but he was too heavy for her to carry up so many stairs.

"Shall I carry him?" a voice asked.

Startled, she looked up. Lord Bradley stood above her. She had not heard him step into the corridor. Had he heard her speak Andrew's name?

She nodded and silently mouthed, *Thank you.*

With gentle ease he bent and lifted the boy and carried him toward the stairs. Olivia followed.

On their way up to the nursery, Lord Bradley's breathing grew laboured, but he bore the child without pause. When they reached the sleeping chamber, Olivia hurried to assist, pulling back the bedclothes as he laid Andrew on his bed.

"Thank you," she whispered, this time aloud.

"A great many stairs, that," he said, unashamedly resting his hands on his knees to catch his breath.

"I am sorry. I should have tried—"

"No, of course you should not have. I am only sorry to be so woefully lathered. I shall have to take more regular exercise, I see."

Olivia removed Andrew's shoes, wondering where Becky was, but somehow glad the girl was not present just then.

She was surprised when Lord Bradley remained. "I shall see to him, my lord. I am sure you wish to return to your party."

He blew out a breath between his cheeks. "Not as much as I ought to."

He helped her remove Andrew's pantaloons and coat. His miniature neckcloth had long since been discarded somewhere. "Let us leave him sleep as he is," Lord Bradley whispered.

She nodded and loosened his shirt at the neck. The billowing white shirt, now untucked, resembled a nightdress at any rate. She pulled up the bedclothes under Andrew's chin. Still Lord Bradley lingered. He bent low and brushed the boy's forelock, much as she had done downstairs. How would it feel, she wondered, to be so gently touched by him? Or to stroke his fair hair with her fingers?

"He is very like his father," he said softly.

"Is he?"

"Yes. The dark hair, the cowlick, the impish face—all very like Dominick."

"You knew him well?"

"Fairly well, yes, though he was six or seven years older than I. Our London house was near to his, and we spent a great deal of time together during several seasons. Dominick was ever kind to me—even before he knew I had a beautiful cousin he might one day marry. He was in love with his Jeannette then and married her when he was still quite young. He was brought very low when she died. I admit I was surprised he rallied so quickly and married Judith only eighteen months later. I should not recover from such a loss so quickly."

Nor would I, she thought. "But then, he had two children who needed a mamma."

His expression darkened. "Yes." He hesitated, thought better of whatever he was about to say, and instead straightened. "I do appreciate the care you are giving my young cousins, Miss Keene. I am sure their stepmother does as well, if she has not said so."

"Thank you, my lord. It is my pleasure." She realized anew that Audrey and Andrew had lost both mother and father. Poor lambs! No wonder Lord Bradley felt so deeply for them.

He pursed his lips, then said quietly, "I find it interesting that you address me as 'my lord' when you know better."

Her heart pounded to hear him speak of the secret they never discussed. She said, "You call me Miss Keene."

He considered this. "A sign of respect, perhaps?"

She nodded, feeling warmth flood her body.

"How odd it is," he mused. "Carrying on . . . pretending everything is as it once was." He inhaled deeply, then stepped to the door. Once more he hesitated. "And for whatever it is worth, I thought your playing well. I am sorry you were so rudely dismissed."

She felt her ears heat at the recollection. "Think nothing of it. No doubt Miss Tugwell was right."

"Well, good night, Miss Keene. And happy Christmas."

A few minutes later, Olivia closed the door to the sleeping chamber quietly behind her, wondering how late Audrey would remain downstairs with the guests. Expecting the dark nursery to be empty, she started at the sight of a shadowy figure within. Had Lord Bradley not taken himself back down to his guests as she had thought?

But it was Felix's voice that rumbled through the darkness. "You know, Livie, when I came up here a few minutes ago, I could have sworn I heard two voices—in secret tête-à-tête. I waited in the shadows to see who would come out after my cousin and am confounded to find it was you."

Heart pounding, Olivia shrugged and shook her head.

"Not your voice?"

Olivia stared at him, nerves jangling.

Felix stepped closer. "Sticking to the mute bit, hmm?"

Olivia nodded.

His voice took on a silky sweetness. "So, if I were to, say, take your hands"—he pressed her hands in his—"you could not ask me to let you go?"

She stood stone-still, her whole body tensing.

"And if I wanted to hold you"—he pulled her against him, a surprisingly strong arm grasping her about the waist—"you could not refuse?"

She tried to pull free but could not break his grip.

"And if I were to kiss you . . . you could not protest?" He backed her against the wall, his voice a husky whisper now. "Don't protest, sweet Livie. Please. It is Christmas, after all." He leaned near, aiming for her mouth. She turned her face away, and he pressed a hard kiss against her neck. Olivia struggled, and finally, pulling one arm free, punched him in the eye.

Felix howled and cursed, releasing her to cover his face with his hands. "Livie!" he cried, incredulous.

She was already striding quickly from the room. His voice, calling after her, took on a pleading tone, "You needn't have done that. I was only teasing you. Don't go making a fuss!"

Was he afraid she would march straight to his cousin and report his behavior? Perhaps she should. She wondered briefly which man feared the other more. But who would believe her word against Felix's?

She would take Lord Bradley's secret to the grave, but if Felix Bradley dared touch her again, she would remain silent no longer.

15

> We had 12 dances & 5, 6, or 7 couples. We then had a game of Hunt the Slipper and ended the day with sandwiches and tarts . . . I must not omit saying that the little ones dressed up as usual and sang Christmas Carols.
>
> —Fanny Austen Knight, Christmas Eve, 1808

On Christmas morning, Olivia arose and ate a leisurely breakfast in her room while Becky, all apologies for disappearing the night before, bathed and dressed the children on her own. Olivia wondered where her mother was spending the day, and lifted her teacup in a silent Christmas salute.

She again eyed the dark blue gown hanging on the back of her door. She would wear it, she decided, and stood to dress. The gown fit her well, though she was more slender than Mrs. Howe. She guessed the woman had been thinner before her lying-in with Alexander. To make the gown her own, Olivia wore her new lace tippet—a Christmas present from Mrs. Moore—as a collar.

Stepping into the nursery, she saw Becky struggling to arrange Audrey's hair, so Olivia brushed and pinned it herself. Audrey wore a new long-sleeved pelisse over a printed muslin frock. Andrew wore his Sunday pantaloons, waistcoat, and new green coat.

Olivia escorted the children down to the breakfast room, where they were to join the adults before church.

After the tussle of the previous night, Olivia was relieved to find Felix conspicuously absent. Miss Harrington was not present either, though she was staying at Brightwell Court for several days.

Upon the sideboard rested a Christmas box for each child.

Opening it, Audrey's eyes grew as wide as the coins. "Two guineas."

"We are rich!" Andrew exclaimed, lifting his guineas high.

"Alexander has his as well," Judith explained. "But as he tried to eat them, I shall keep them until he is older."

Lord Bradley laid a hand on each child's head and added warmly, "From Lord and Lady Brightwell. Left especially for you before they departed."

"Ah . . . Christmas in Rome," Judith sighed. Then she turned to Olivia waiting by the door, the children's coats in her arms. She surveyed her figure, head to toe. "You look very well today, Miss Keene," she said.

Self-conscious, Olivia smiled and dipped a curtsy.

Lord Bradley surveyed her as well, but his expression was inscrutable. Olivia was relieved the woman did not announce to Lord Bradley and the hovering Osborn that Olivia wore one of her castoffs.

Felix stumbled in with rumpled hair and a hint of orange whiskers on his chin. The young man looked worse for drink from the night before. Olivia knew the look—greenish pale complexion, hollow eyes. She also noticed his bruised eyelid, which she could attribute to drink as well, at least indirectly.

Judith greeted her brother pleasantly. "Good morning, Felix. Mrs. Moore made mincemeat pie, your favorite."

"All I want is coffee."

"What happened to your eye, Felix?" Lord Bradley asked.

"Oh." Felix stole the briefest glance at Olivia. "I, uh, ran into an unexpected obstacle in the dark."

He poured coffee with less than steady hands. "I shall be my old self after coffee, a few more hours' sleep, a bath and shave. I won't manage church, I am afraid." He stirred sugar into his cup. "I would not wait for Miss Harrington either. To hear her father tell it, her little feet do not hit the floor until twelve most days."

Breakfast completed, Mrs. Howe, Lord Bradley, and the children rode in the carriage the short distance up the lane and around the high wall that separated Brightwell Court from St. Mary's. Glad to be allowed to attend, Olivia walked beside Doris along with the handful of other servants who could be spared from their duties.

Once inside the vestibule, Olivia followed Dory up into the gallery to sit with the other servants. She had never sat in a gallery before. At home, she and her mother sat on the main floor of the chapel with the small clutch of congregants who came out for Sunday services. Her father not among them.

Doris patted her knee and they settled in for the service. There was a feeling of camaraderie there in the gallery, the silent smiles shared among servants from different houses, who saw one another on occasional Sundays and rarely any other time. There were also winks and good-natured elbows in the side of a fellow groom or housemaid. Doris, she soon realized, attended only to flirt with menservants she would otherwise not see. The girl was fellow-mad.

Down below, on the second pew from the front, Olivia saw Lord Bradley, flanked by Audrey and Andrew. Beside Audrey, Judith stood in a black mantle and smart black hat with a half veil of silver gossamer lace. Alexander was too young to be quiet for church and had been left home with Nurse Peale. Olivia wondered how Andrew would manage to be still so long. How unlike his usual self he looked fidgeting in his Sunday coat, brown hair slicked down. Audrey, however, stood sedately and gracefully in her bonnet and gown, her gloved hand in Lord Bradley's. They looked like a family—husband, wife, children. Would they be one someday, once Judith's mourning was past?

Mr. Tugwell kept his sermon surprisingly brief, saying only thoughts of the sumptuous feast awaiting him could still his tongue on such a glorious day. He reminded the congregation that he and his good sister were once again holding an annual open hearth, and all were invited to drop in for a buffet meal.

At the close of service, Olivia stood and glanced once more down at Lord Bradley and the Howes, who were rising and gathering their things and smiling at their neighbors. Lord Bradley reached across the pew and shook hands with a man behind him. As the man turned, Olivia started. The man's profile struck her as familiar. She had seen him before. The man glanced up into the gallery, and Olivia quickly turned her head, hoping her bonnet would conceal her face. She did not wish to be recognized—could *not* be recognized. Who was the man? She wanted to look again, but dared not. Someone from home? Someone from Withington visiting family or friends? Someone who knew

Lord Bradley. . . . Olivia's heart pounded, and she prayed the man would not be following them home for Christmas dinner.

Feigning a search for something in her reticule, Olivia waved Doris on and managed to be the last person to exit the gallery. As she hoped, the familiar gentleman—along with most everyone else—was gone.

At the door, Mr. Tugwell exchanged well wishes or a "Happy Christmas" with the last few members of his congregation as they filed out. Miss Tugwell stood at his elbow, handing out small bags tied in rag ribbon. How generous. She noticed Miss Tugwell eyeing each person as she offered a gift. When she surveyed Olivia's new gown she whispered, "You haven't use for wheat, I trust, Miss Keene?"

Thinking of Mr. Croome, Olivia nodded and held out her hand.

Augusta Tugwell ignored it. "Foolish notion in these times. When I think of the price of wheat!"

Mr. Tugwell glanced over, eyes flicking from Olivia's extended hand to the bag in his sister's clutches. "Sister, Miss Keene is awaiting her gift." He smiled at Olivia while Augusta Tugwell only sniffed and relinquished the bag.

Edward found himself foolishly nervous while waiting for his young cousins to open their presents. He certainly hoped Miss Keene was correct and Audrey would like the doll's house, though she was not a little girl any longer.

"Mind your expectations," he said. "These are only things I made in the carpentry shop. Nothing new from the London shops, I am afraid."

Miss Harrington sat with perfect posture in the armchair beside his. She looked refreshed and elegant in a primrose gown with a white fichu tucked into the neckline. Felix sat slumped on the settee, more clear-eyed and certainly better groomed than he had been that morning. Judith perched on the settee's other end, little Alexander on the floor before her, sitting up of his own accord, but with his mamma nearby to catch him should he topple.

Judith set Edward's wrapped gift before the little boy, but Alexander seemed more interested in grabbing the silver buckles on his mother's slippers. Judith tore away the stiff paper for him, revealing the set of blocks, each carved with a letter, number, and animal.

"Look, Alexander. Cousin Edward has made such handsome blocks for you." She held one up. "What a charming fox, Edward. I am impressed. Look, Alexander, F for fox. And this one has a D on it and a very fine duckling."

Edward stared at the blocks as Judith fussed over them, still as confused as he had been when, two by two, they had reappeared in the shop. He had carved simple numbers and letters on each. But now they bore detailed images of animals as well.

Had Miss Keene carved the blocks as well as sewn all the cushions and draperies so skillfully? If so, she had never said a word. Somehow he could not imagine Miss Keene with a carving knife. But who else would have done so?

"Did you really make those yourself?" Miss Harrington asked.

Edward hesitated. "I had help with the carving."

Felix held up his hands. "Don't look at me."

"An anonymous Christmas elf," Edward said dryly.

Without waiting to be asked, Andrew ripped the paper from his elongated parcel. "Stab me!" he cried, mimicking his uncle Felix.

"Andrew, that is not polite," Judith admonished.

But the boy paid little heed. "A brand-new cricket bat! A ball too." He lifted the ball as if to give it a good whack.

Edward quickly stilled his small arms. "That is an outside gift, young man."

"Awww, but it is winter!"

"We shall bundle up tomorrow and see how it cracks, all right?"

Andrew dug the toe of his shoe into the carpet a bit sullenly. "All right . . ."

"Is it my turn?" Audrey asked quietly, looking up at her cousin with shy eyes.

Edward nodded, feeling his palms dampen as he watched the girl carefully begin to tug at the cloth covering her gift.

"I am afraid I hadn't enough paper for yours."

Slowly Audrey pulled the cover toward her.

"Just give it a good rip, Aud!" Andrew encouraged. "Shall I?"

"Leave your sister be, Andrew," Judith said.

Please let her like it, Edward thought. He almost wished sophisticated Sybil Harrington were not on hand to witness his failure, if failure it would be.

Audrey's eyes grew round and rather stunned as she took in the house, which came up nearly to her shoulders. "It is Brightwell Court," she breathed. She looked at him, uncertain.

His spirits fell. *She does not like it.*

"Is it really for me?" she asked.

"Yes, though if you are too old for dolls, I shall not be offend—"

"Look!" Audrey cried, kneeling before the open stories, the many chambers, and even a grand staircase. "There is the drawing room, where we are right now. And up there is the nursery!"

Edward felt the scrutiny of others and turned to find both Judith and Miss Harrington studying him with stunned incredulity.

"How long did it take you to build this?" Judith asked.

He waved aside her awe. "Oh, I have worked on it for several months, on and off, when I had the time."

Audrey looked up at her stepmother. "Look! It is the very settee you are seated upon. It even has a cushion!"

Judith's fair brows rose as she looked from the miniature piece of furniture to Edward. "If you tell me you made that as well, I shall not believe you."

"I had some help with the sewing and furnishings."

"The Christmas elf again?" Miss Harrington asked, one dark brow quirked high.

He thought it wiser not to mention any names.

Audrey looked up with wide eyes. "I painted this miniature landscape myself and never guessed what it was for!"

After several more minutes of exclaiming over favorite details, Audrey stood before him and made a graceful curtsy. "Thank you, Cousin Edward. It is the finest gift I have ever received."

Judith looked mildly offended, opened her pink lips, then shut them again.

Edward had not thought to outdo anybody. He simply wanted to please these children, these offspring of his friend, gone from this world. Did they not deserve some special happiness this day?

He bowed to Audrey in his best courtly manner, and then took her hand in his and pressed it. "You are most welcome, my dear Audrey."

When he looked up once more, Judith's expression had transformed into one of speculative approval. Miss Harrington looked from Judith to him, and appeared not pleased at all.

As the children began to play with the doll's house, Felix turned to him and asked, "Remember that raft you built, Edward?"

"Sink me, not that old yarn."

A mischievous sparkle lit Felix's green eyes. "You see, Miss Harrington, the great Noah here built us a fine raft when we were lads. Big enough to hold the two of us and that terrier—what was its name?"

"I don't recall."

"At all events, we put in near the Brightwell Bridge and the current bore us swiftly. Only when we passed the church, there where the river widens, did Edward realize he had neglected to fashion either rudder or oar!"

Self-conscious, Edward chuckled and shook his head.

"But the raft was seaworthy, I admit," Felix continued. "Took us all the way to the Arlington Mill and would have taken us further had Edward not grabbed hold of a low-lying branch and pulled us into the mill leat." He eyed his cousin. "Don't tell me you don't remember."

"I remember the miller was none too pleased. That I do recall."

"Whatever happened to that raft, I wonder?" Felix said. "I hope Andrew does not stumble upon it or we should never see that wag pirate again."

"Don't fear. I am sure that old thing has gone the way of most everything else I built in those days. Mother quietly disposed of it while I was at Oxford."

"Never say so! Such a work of art. Although after that excursion, I am quite sure you shan't have a career in shipbuilding."

"Nor would I want one."

Felix leaned back in his chair. "You have no need of a career, of course. It is only I who must find some way to eke out my existence."

"You make it sound as if you shall have to earn a living from the soil or some such," Miss Harrington said kindly. "Surely with a degree from Balliol it shall not come to that."

"No," he said. "I cannot fancy Felix Bradley, yeoman farmer."

"Nor I," Judith said.

"What will you take up?" Miss Harrington asked. "Have you decided?"

"I have not. I have no interest in the church. Detest the thought of fighting in a war. Haven't a head for the law. . . ."

"Come, now," Edward said. "You are as clever as the next fellow and will have your degree in due course. There must be something you are interested in."

"I am interested in a great many things. But none with prodigious remuneration. I suppose I had my heart set on remaining a gentleman, as my father and his father before him."

"And why not?" Judith said blithely.

"Because, as you well know, Jude, Father left us with very little but debts to live on. Uncle is generous indeed, but I cannot expect him to support a wife and children as well."

"Wife and children?" Judith straightened, suddenly alert. "My goodness, Felix, are you engaged? I had not the slightest notion you planned to marry soon."

Her brother flushed deeply. "No. Not engaged. No plans as yet. Only . . . hopes."

He smiled almost shyly at Miss Harrington. "I have not yet had the good fortune of meeting the perfect woman, as has Edward."

Miss Harrington's delicate complexion glowed pink while Edward grew uneasy.

Felix slapped Edward on the shoulder, then added with bravado, "But Edward won't be the only Bradley to marry well. Upon my soul he won't."

Olivia sneaked away to leave the bag of wheat on Croome's doorstep. As she turned to leave, she saw him bent low at the far edge of the clearing, laying a wreath of yew boughs on the ground. She wondered what he was about but, recalling his temper, decided not to interrupt him.

When she returned to the nursery, she was surprised to find Lord Bradley sitting on the settee beside Alexander and his new blocks.

He looked up when she entered. "I had no notion you could carve as well as sew, Miss Keene. Your talents are legion."

She frowned and, after glancing about to make certain no one else was in the nursery, whispered, "I am afraid you overestimate me, my lord. I carved nothing. I thought you did."

"I carved simple numbers and letters on each. And now they have animals carved into them as well. This H block has quite a detailed hound on it." He picked another block at random from the stack. "And the B has a bird of some type." He lifted the block toward her. "What do you make out?"

Olivia walked near and took the block from his outstretched hand, examining the skillful carving. To her, it looked very like a partridge.

The thought of animals brought the old gamekeeper to mind. "You don't think Mr. Croome . . . ?"

"I would be exceedingly surprised."

Olivia nodded. So would she.

Lord Bradley rose and cleared his throat. "Well, thank you again for all your assistance." He withdrew a folded bank note and extended it toward her. "Here is a little something for your trouble."

She ought to have been grateful but instead felt oddly deflated to be offered payment for what had been an act of friendship. To be reminded once more of the true nature of their relationship—that she was simply another servant in his employ.

"No thank you," she said, and turned away.

Olivia spent the afternoon helping the children fill Christmas boxes for the servants, which they would disperse on Boxing Day tomorrow. Then she took Audrey and Andrew down to the dining room, where the family gathered for Christmas dinner at the early hour of four o'clock.

After the meal, all of the servants were invited in to share a glass and toast the season. How strange it felt to stand in the dining room with Mrs. Moore, Doris, Johnny, and the others, as invited guests. Croome was not among them. Nor did anyone seem to miss him.

Audrey and Andrew sang carols once more, this time without accompaniment. As they sang, Olivia felt Johnny's eyes on her but did not look his way. She did peek at Doris, who winked at her. Martha, she noticed, watched the children with tears in her eyes.

When they finished, the menservants dipped into their coat pockets, and the women into their apron pockets, and the children collected the proffered coins. Perhaps seeing her confusion, Mrs. Moore leaned close and explained in a whisper that this money would later be given to the poor. Olivia wished she had known. She would have brought down one of her last remaining coins, still tacked inside the little purse. Olivia hoped her mother did not miss the money. Did her mother miss her?

This was the first Christmas the two of them had spent apart, but Olivia feared it only the beginning of many lonely Christmases to come.

Where was she?

Olivia lifted her glass to her mouth. She had no taste for wine, but she hoped the action would conceal the trembling of her lips.

16

> In your manner to your servants, be firm and kind, without being familiar. Never converse familiarly with them, unless on business, or on some point connected with their improvement.
>
> —Samuel & Sarah Adams,
> *The Complete Servant*

Twelfth-night festivities over, guests gone, and the house quiet once more, Edward sat down to enjoy his coffee and newspaper in peace. Hodges came in as stealthily as ever and held the letter tray before him.

Edward picked up the single piece of post and thanked the butler, who disappeared as silently as he had come. Glancing at the letter, Edward recognized the handwriting and noted the unfamiliar postal markings. The ink was smeared, but he believed it read, *Roma*.

Across the table, Judith eyed the letter over her teacup. "How exotic-looking. Who is it from?"

"Father."

Nibbling daintily at her toasted muffin, Judith regarded him with eager eyes. "I do hope they are enjoying their time abroad."

He hoped it wasn't bad news. With hands suddenly damp and clumsy, he broke the sealing wax and unfolded the letter.

My dear Edward,

I am grieved to inform you that your mother has left us—left her suffering and this world for brighter shores. She died peacefully in her sleep, with me holding her hand. I am returning home directly and should arrive by the tenth, God and tides willing.

Your loving father
BRIGHTWELL

A spear of grief pierced him. His mother . . . gone. Had she been frightened of dying . . . or accepting of her fate? Thank God she had died peacefully, and with her husband by her side.

Some adolescent part of him was relieved to have been spared the sight of his mother's death, but the nobler part of his heart wished he had been there. To have heard any last words she might have said to him. To have told her he loved her. No matter the past. No matter what. To say, "Until we meet again."

He recalled their tender parting as she left for Italy. How glad he was that he had kissed her cheek and bid her a fond farewell, not guessing it would be their last. *Almighty God,* he prayed, *please comfort my father.*

"Edward?" Judith asked. "What is it?"

He swallowed the lump in his throat. "Lady Brightwell has died."

Judith's hand flew to her heart. "Oh, Edward! I am sorry." She leapt to her feet and stepped around the table, laying a hand on his shoulder. He reached up and pressed it with his own.

"Thank you."

After a moment, he stood and excused himself, wanting to be alone. He went upstairs, shut himself in his study and there read the letter once more. He noticed that his father had ended with his title. A title Edward had once thought would be his one day. And now it might all be gone. His future. His very name. But at the moment, he could not care. He laid his forehead on his fist and wept, for his mother, for his bereaved father, for himself—a lost boy losing the only mother he had ever known.

News of Lady Brightwell's death spread quickly through the manor. Olivia ached over Lord Brightwell's loss of his wife. For Lord Bradley's loss as well. She wondered how he was. Wished she might somehow comfort him. If she were to receive such news of *her* mother, she knew she would be devastated indeed.

The following day dawned dreary and rainy, which seemed to echo the general mood of the house. In the afternoon, the melancholy children even succumbed to rare naps. Not allowed that luxury, Olivia searched the schoolroom for another book for Andrew. Finding none to suit, she wrote the title she sought on a piece of paper.

Mrs. Howe, dressed in dull black bombazine, entered the nursery, delivering Alexander back to Nurse Peale. Olivia politely held the note before her mistress with a questioning lift of her brows. Mrs. Howe assured her they'd had a copy of *The History of Little Goody Two-Shoes* in the nursery, but perhaps it had been returned to the library by an overzealous housemaid. Declaring her intention to return to her own room to nap as well, Judith stepped to the door.

"Has she your leave, then, to go into his lordship's library?" Nurse Peale asked.

"Yes, yes." Mrs. Howe waved her hand dismissively. "There is no one to disturb."

Lighting a candle lamp against the darkening rooms, Olivia made her way downstairs to the library. She knocked softly and, when no one answered, let herself in. The muted aromas of cigars, leather, and musty draperies greeted her.

Lifting her candle high, she surveyed the room. Tall bookcases were fitted between draped windows and across the entire rear wall. At the front of the room stood an impressive desk, and two high-backed chairs faced a dark fireplace.

Placing her candle on the table near the wall of books, Olivia began skimming the titles. She felt self-conscious and presumptuous about poking about the earl's library but reminded herself she was looking for a book for the children.

Suddenly the library door opened behind her, and Olivia whirled about. An older gentleman stumbled in with his own candle lamp, clearly exhausted and dressed in a rumpled suit of clothes. Setting down his lamp, he slumped into a chair and did not even seem aware that she was there. *Lord Brightwell*, she realized. For a long moment, Olivia found she could not move, could not take her eyes off the bent, blond-grey head, nor the agony etched in the wrinkled brow.

Remembered images filled her mind. She saw the earl holding his wife, comforting her with gentle words, tenderly stroking her cheek and kissing her. She had never known a husband could so love a wife, and now he had lost her.

Impulsively, Olivia ran to him. She knelt before his chair and gently took his limp hand in her own.

His eyes flew open in surprise.

"My lord," she whispered, all vows of silence forgotten. "I am so sorry." Tears blurred her vision, obscuring and then magnifying his reaction.

He squinted hard; then his eyes widened, and his mouth parted in shock. Olivia read his thunderstruck expression as revulsion that a servant should address him. Touch him.

She released his hand, her face growing hot, and lowered her eyes. "I am sorry," she whispered again, rising to her feet.

"Miss Keene!" came a stunned gasp. Judith Howe stood in the threshold, hand on the door latch. "What in the world are you doing? Return to the nursery at once!"

Head bowed, Olivia walked quickly toward the door, not missing the look of apologetic concern Judith gave Lord Brightwell. "I did not know you had returned, Uncle. I shall see that you are not disturbed further."

Olivia felt two sets of eyes follow her from the room.

When the summons came the next morning, Olivia stiffened, but was not surprised. She had been expecting it. *I acted on impulse*, she silently defended herself. *I meant no harm.* What would Lord Bradley be angrier about, she fretted, as she took the stairs down. That she had dared speak with his father, or that she had spoken at all?

She entered the study as bid, shut the door, and stood rigidly before his desk.

Lord Bradley rose. "I wish to speak to you about my father," he began evenly.

Olivia lifted her chin, holding her head high.

"Miss Keene?"

She met his gaze coolly, making a great effort to show no emotion.

"Though one might never guess it from looking at you," he said wryly, "my father seems to think you are quite a compassionate young woman. What did you say to him last night?"

She stared at him, bewildered.

"Yes, he told us you spoke to him. Judith assured him he must have been distraught—imagined it—because you are a *dumb mute*."

He pronounced the final words with relish.

"Tell me what you said to make such an impression."

Olivia felt her brow furrow, as perplexed by the earl's supposed reaction as Lord Bradley clearly was.

"All I said was how sorry I was."

He raised a brow. "What else?"

"Nothing." Her mind scrambled to recall further details.

An odd light crept into his eyes. "Then what did you *do*? Show me. Show me what you did, what you said, and how you said it."

She huffed in frustration. "But I cannot! He walked in and caught me unawares. The grief on his face was so devastating, his love for your mother so obvious, I was *moved* to act. It was an impulse. I did not think—"

He stepped around the desk and leaned back against it, arms crossed. "Show me."

"But you are not—" She stopped suddenly as a swift ache swelled in her chest. How could she be worried about defending herself when his mother had just died? The only mother he had ever known. She knew what it was like to love and miss a mother. It was ever-present pain.

Unbidden, tears filled her eyes. The man before her was pretending to be so hard, so aloof, but inside he was a boy who had just lost his mamma.

Edward saw the transformation cross her countenance and stared, mesmerized. When her eyes filled with tears, his chest tightened and his own eyes burned. He watched silently as she approached and stood before him, eyes wide, face pale and pained. She placed her slim fingers on his hand and drew it into both of hers, enveloping it in her warm grasp.

Edward drew in a shaky breath.

"I am sorry, my lord," she whispered, gaze locked into his. "I am so sorry."

Edward sank into her vivid blue eyes, finding beauty and empathy there, solace and peace. For a moment, he forgot his father, forgot his mother, forgot everything.

When he did not move or speak, Miss Keene laid her soft cheek against his hand. As Edward gazed down at her lovely profile, his free hand lifted of its own accord, as if to stroke her hair. He barely resisted the impulse.

"It must be so hard to lose your mother," she murmured.

He tensed immediately. This had been no ploy to seek her sympathy. He did not need a servant's pity or attentions, no matter how lovely she was.

He straightened and said sternly, "We were not speaking of me."

She quickly dropped his hand and stepped back, unable to meet his eyes, clearly embarrassed to find herself in such an intimate position—a position she had initiated.

He would not reveal how her nearness affected him. Would not be overcome as his father had been. "I must say," he began, hoping his voice would not waver and betray him. "I am very impressed with your acting ability. You might have a future in the theatre if you like. I can see why Father was taken with you, a woman half his age throwing herself at him."

"It was not like that."

"And you spoke to him!"

"I could not help it, I—"

"How many others have you spoken to?" Edward felt his anger rising but knew it had little to do with the fact that Miss Keene had spoken a few words to his father. It was his father's reaction to her that annoyed him. And if he were honest with himself, his own reaction as well.

"I am sorry—truly I am. But as Mrs. Howe said, your father was distraught. He may not remember clearly the events of last evening. He need never see me again and the whole business shall be forgotten."

"*Au contraire*," Edward drawled. "He wishes to see you tomorrow afternoon."

17

> The undertaker would provide professional mourners or "mutes" dressed in black to stand about and lend dignity to the affair.
>
> —Daniel Poole, *What Jane Austen Ate and Charles Dickens Knew*

Olivia smoothed the bodice of the dark blue dress with trembling fingers as she walked downstairs and across the hall to the library the next afternoon. Becky had taken the children outside for her, and Olivia would much rather have been with them than on her way to this appointed meeting with the Earl of Brightwell. What could the earl want with her? Certainly there was nothing to Lord Bradley's innuendo. She shuddered. No. It could not be. He could not have so misread her sympathy.

She took a deep breath and knocked.

"Come in."

She stepped in and closed the door behind her, heart pounding. Would he reprimand her, or worse?

The earl was sitting in one of the high-backed chairs near the fire, but he rose when she entered. "Please," he beckoned. "Come here, child. You have nothing to fear from me."

Olivia swallowed and walked forward. As she approached, Lord Brightwell watched her closely, his face wearing that same stunned expression of the first night. Had he not asked to see her?

He quietly bid, "Do sit down."

She complied and clasped damp palms in her lap.

He cleared his throat. "Miss Keene, my son has told me of the circumstances of your arrival. You need not keep silent with me." His voice was gentle, and she noticed his gracious choice of words.

She felt a new stab of regret. "My lord, it was not my intention to eavesdrop."

He lifted a hand. "That is not why I asked you here. And though I am not certain I approve of his actions, I know Edward has the family's best interests at heart. Miss Keene, when you spoke with me the other night—"

"I apologize for my familiarity, my lord."

"Do not apologize, please!" His vehemence surprised her. "My own family has been treating me like a leper. Yours was the only true warmth I received all day."

Olivia felt tentative pleasure at his words and studied her clasped hands. Feeling his gaze upon her profile, she looked up to find him studying her.

"We have not met?" he asked softly.

"No, my lord. I saw you and your wife from a distance the night I . . . the night before you left, but that is all."

"May I ask where you come from?"

She hesitated. "To the north and west of here. Near Cheltenham."

He watched her, slowly shaking his head in disbelief or some unfathomable wonder. Leaning forward, he rested his elbows on his knees and made a poor attempt to sound casual. "Miss Keene, may I ask about your . . . your family?"

She felt the old pain in her stomach, and twisted on her chair. "What would you like to know?"

"What your parents are like, where they are from . . . ?"

She latched on to the first part of his question. "My mother is a wonderful woman."

The earl's face brightened. "Yes?"

"She is kind and lovely. Intelligent and patient. She loves to laugh. . . ." Olivia hesitated, trying to remember the last time she had heard her mother laugh.

Lord Brightwell nodded, clearly eager for more information. *But why?* Olivia wondered.

"Go on."

But tears had filled her eyes and she bit her lip to hold them back.

The earl said quietly, "You miss her."

"Very much," Olivia whispered.

"And your father?"

She swallowed, lowering her gaze. "He is clever in his own way. Quick with numbers. Ambitious. Forthright."

"But?" he prompted.

She took a shaky breath. "He is . . . changeable. Often angry."

"Does he . . . ill-use you, my dear?"

"No, never."

"Your mother?"

She looked down at her hands. "He sometimes lashes out at her with harsh words—accusations and threats. But never with his hands, until . . ."

"Until?"

She looked away from his earnest eyes and changed the subject. "He was not always so. But now . . . now I am afraid there is not much warmth between us."

"I am sorry to hear it."

"Still, I never meant—" She stopped herself.

"Never meant what, Miss Keene?"

She saw the compassion in his eyes and was tempted to tell him the whole story. "Never mind."

He handed her his handkerchief. "Pray forgive me, Miss Keene. I did not mean to upset you."

"There is nothing to forgive," she said, wiping her eyes. "You are the one suffering the deepest loss."

Tears brightened his eyes. "Yes, a great loss. My wife was dear to me indeed. But there was a time when there was not much warmth between us either."

She wiped her eyes. "I struggle to credit it."

"It is true, but I confide it only to give you hope. Perhaps your father may warm to you in time, Miss—May I ask your Christian name? I am quite certain Edward never told me."

"My given name is Olivia, but most people here call me—"

"Olivia?" he breathed, visibly stunned.

"I know. I suppose it is rather lofty for a girl in service."

"Olivia . . ." he repeated. His eyes held both triumph and anguish. "Your mother, she . . ." He faltered. "Is her name . . . Dorothea Hawthorn?"

Olivia stared at him dumbly. "No." She slowly shook her head. "It is Dorothea Keene."

They stared into one another's eyes until Olivia whispered, "How do you know my mother?"

He shook his head in wonder. "I thought it must be so when first I saw you. I thought I was seeing a ghost. Or an angel. Dorothea's daughter. I can hardly believe it. How is she? When did you last see her?"

"It is above two months now."

He nodded. "Were you still under your parents' roof before you came here, or did you have a situation elsewhere?"

"I had a position, but I lived at home."

"Then, may I ask, why did you leave? Did something happen, or did you merely come seeking a situation?"

She hesitated. "I . . . I cannot tell you, my lord. You must forgive me."

Concern shone from his face. "But . . . she is well, I trust?"

Tears burned in her eyes once more. Her whisper was as hoarse as when her voice had first returned. "I do not know."

"Do you wish to return home? Edward would allow it, if I—"

She shook her head. "I cannot go back." Anxious to divert the conversation, Olivia asked again, "How are you acquainted with her? You never said."

"Do you not know?" Lord Brightwell's pale eyes twinkled. "She had a post here herself."

Olivia shook her head.

"Dorothea was governess to my half sisters—much younger than I. She was all the things you said—lovely, kind, clever." He looked as if he were about to say something else, then hesitated.

"I would like to talk further with you. But . . . considering the unfortunate circumstances, perhaps that discussion should wait."

Thinking of the funeral to come, Olivia nodded her solemn agreement. Questions trembled on her lips, but she held them back. She was not perfectly certain she wished to know the answers.

A dark cloud hung over Brightwell Court over the next days, rendering the place bright no longer. Judith Howe returned to full mourning attire of dull black bombazine and crepe. A horde of men in black coats, black hats, and armbands descended on the place like a flock of crows. Mr. Tugwell called in several times as well, pressing hands and murmuring condolences to family and servants alike.

In preparation for mourning, Judith Howe ordered a new black frock for Audrey from Miss Ludlow's shop. In the meantime, Olivia added several inches of black lace around the hem of Audrey's sole black dress, to accommodate the girl's added height since her father's death. She also removed the shiny buckles from Andrew's black shoes and replaced the gilt buttons on his dark coat with simple black ones.

The children would not be attending the funeral itself, but were asked to join the assembled company beforehand. When Olivia led the children downstairs to deliver them to the drawing room, she heard the low rumble of somber conversation from within, where mourners ate cold meat and pie and shared remembrances of the past and wonderings about the future.

In the corridor, Felix stood, wearing the black gloves and scarf of a pallbearer. He greeted her and the children with a solemn bow, his flirtations and winks for once blessedly absent. From Nurse Peale, Olivia had learned that Felix and Judith had spent a great deal of time at Brightwell Court as children—though their parents had not—and it was clear he felt the loss of his aunt keenly. The tentative, woebegone expression he wore made him look very like the little boy he must once have been.

Olivia, of course, would attend neither the service at the church nor the funeral. But from the nursery window, she watched the slow cortege of hearse and mourners make its way to St. Mary's and, afterward, the long procession of mourning carriages pulled by horses draped in black velvet, with black feathers on their heads, leave the drive on their way to the Estcourt family vault.

Olivia heard the church bells toll six times—to indicate the passing of a woman. Then after a pause, one peal for each year of Lady Brightwell's life. The slow regular succession of peals struck Olivia's heart, and she prayed comfort for Lord Brightwell and Lord Bradley long after the last echo died away.

18

> When one of the maids was found to be pregnant, although Parson Woodforde did not re-engage her at the end of her annual hiring, he gave her an extra 4s. "on going away," to supplement her wages.
>
> —Pamela Horn, introduction to *The Complete Servant*

Sitting with his father in the library on a quiet January evening, Edward once more read the brief, threatening note his father had first shown him on the eve of the ill-fated trip to Italy.

I know your secret. Tell him, or I shall.

The hand was fine, neat. Perhaps purposely ordinary and unadorned? *Who wrote it?* he wondered for the thousandth time. Not to mention the excruciating hours he'd spent pondering its ramifications.

He had been waiting for the proper time to raise the issue once again. And now that his father was home, and the funeral a week past, he thought the moment might be right.

He looked up when his father mumbled over some bit of parliamentary news in the *Morning Post*. Folding up the paper, the earl said, "Your mother's health being what it was this last year, I had no trouble receiving a leave for this session. How glad I am of that now."

Lord Brightwell rose and poured himself a glass of port. "I also appreciate your taking over the running of things here, Edward. During my absence and now. I own I am still not fit for it."

Edward nodded his understanding as his father flopped down in his favorite chair near the fire.

"Someday you will take my seat in parliament as well. How I wish I might be there when you receive your Writ of Summons, hear you read the oath, and see you sign the Test Roll. . . ." Lord Brightwell raised his glass in mock toast, then continued, "A young man with your mind, Edward, why, it is such a waste you must wait to serve your country until after I am dead and buried."

"At this point, it does not look as though I shall be taking your seat at all."

"Never say so, my boy. We are not undone yet. It was only one letter, and a vague one at that. Suspicions at best."

"Perhaps, but true nonetheless."

Lord Brightwell made no reply but only stared into the fire.

Seizing the lull, Edward took a deep breath and asked quietly, "Are you ready to tell me about it?"

"Tell you about what?"

"Everything. Where I came from. Who my mother was. My fa—"

The older man huffed, eyes still focused on the flames. "Your mother was Marian Estcourt Bradley, Lady Brightwell. The woman who *bore* you was an agreeable girl of humble birth."

"And my father . . . ? And do not say, 'Oliver Stanton Bradley,' for you have already admitted I am not your son."

"Of course you are."

"Are you telling me you are my father after all? Some poor dairymaid bore your child?"

"No. I was faithful to your mother. But you *are* my son—perhaps not legally speaking, not 'heirs-male of the body' and all that, but in every other way you are."

Edward slammed his fist on the desk. "Not good enough! Who am I? Who is my father? Who is the woman who bore me?"

"Do you really want to know, my boy? It does not signi—"

"Does not signify? Faith! Of course it does." Edward paced the room.

"You know I do not hold to all this fiddle-faddle about noble birth and blood. You have been raised by me; you are mine. You are just as much a Bradley as I am."

"Few in England would agree with you, sir. None in the peerage, I assure you." Edward dropped into the armchair beside his father's and leaned forward. "Who was she? What was her name?"

Lord Brightwell ran an agitated hand through his fair, thinning hair. "She was a modest, God-fearing young woman. Her father, a trusted man of . . . trade."

"How did you know her?"

He threw up his hand. "She was engaged as a kitchen maid. Happy? Or perhaps a housemaid. At any rate, I barely knew her."

Edward groaned. It was as he feared. He shook his head as though his brain refused the information. "My mother was a servant. And my father? Let me guess. The footboy? The coal monger? A poacher?"

"No." The earl clenched his jaw. "I am afraid it is worse than that."

Edward stared at him, stunned. But no matter how hard Edward pressed him, Lord Brightwell would tell him no more. "In due time" was all he would say.

Mrs. Hinkley stood at the study door, twisting her hands. "My lord, might I have a word?"

"Of course, Mrs. Hinkley, come in." Edward waited until she closed the door and approached his desk. "What is it?"

"It is about the maid. Martha. You said to ask after Christmas what was to be done about her. But then with Lady Brightwell passing and all . . ."

"Yes, I understand." Inwardly, Edward sighed under the burden of responsibility; the earl still insisted on delegating such decisions to him. "Has she told you who the father is?"

"No, my lord. She's too frightened to tell."

"Frightened, why?"

"She said if she tells, she shall have to leave and has no place to go. I told her if she *did* tell, perhaps you could make the man take responsibility, but she insists she can only stay if she does *not* tell."

Edward felt his brow wrinkle, wondering why on earth the girl would think such a thing and who might have given her that assurance. One of the menservants? Felix?

He looked up from his thoughts to see Mrs. Hinkley eyeing him speculatively.

"Now, Mrs. Hinkley. You know better than to suppose—"

"Of course not, my lord. The girl is just being foolish, no doubt."

"Foolish indeed. Does she think this an orphan asylum? A home for unwed mothers?"

Mrs. Hinkley dropped her head. "Am I to put her out then, my lord?" she asked, her voice reedy with fear. "It is what is done, I know."

Edward winced. How easily he would have done so only a few months before. He sat quietly for a moment and then exhaled a deep breath. "No, Mrs. Hinkley. You are not to put her out. Tell her she may stay as long as you are satisfied with her work, until the delivery of her child. If she can find someone to mind the child, she may return to her post in due time. Otherwise, she may leave with a reference. But, Mrs. Hinkley, assure the girl that her refusal to name the father had nothing to do with my decision. Is that clear?"

"Yes, my lord." Mrs. Hinkley expelled a rush of air and relief. "Thank you, my lord." She beamed at him as she backed toward the door. He realized he had never before seen her smile so warmly.

It was not until several weeks after the funeral that Lord Brightwell sent Osborn to once again ask Olivia to join him in the library at her earliest convenience.

Waiting only long enough to finish plaiting Audrey's hair and hand Andrew a book, she left the children with Becky and Nurse Peale and made her way downstairs. When she entered the hall, Osborn came forward from his post and opened the library door, but did not bother to announce her.

Stepping inside, she found the earl sitting at his desk, bent over a ledger. So focused was he that he did not look up when she entered. "Dash it," he muttered. "I cannot make out these figures."

She waited until Osborn had shut the door behind her, shielding her from his too-curious eyes and ears.

Lord Brightwell looked up when the door latched. "Ah, Olivia, my dear."

She approached his desk and offered quietly, "Might I help, my lord?"

He waved his hand dismissively over the ledger. "My eyesight is failing, and there is not a blind thing I can do about it."

"Except make bad puns?"

He chuckled. "At least my sense of humor is not failing me. Can you make this out?"

She peered over his shoulder. "Two thousand seventy-nine."

"And the profits from those acres last year?" He pointed at a figure in the adjoining column.

"One thousand nine hundred sixty-two. For a sum of four thousand forty-one."

"You ciphered that in your head?"

She shrugged. "I was always good with figures."

"Your mother taught you, I suppose. She was an excellent teacher, I recall."

Olivia did not say the ability had been honed by her father, nor in what manner. It would mortify her to speak of it to Lord Brightwell.

"Well, I did not ask you here to balance my accounts." He rose and indicated the two armchairs near the fire. "Please. Be seated."

She complied and looked up from smoothing her skirts to find him studying her.

"I find your presence quite comforting, Olivia. I suppose it is because you are so like your mother. And she was once a dear friend to me."

He looked down at his hands. "In fact, there was a time I had hoped to marry her. But my father would not allow it. In the end, I suppose he was correct, for Marian and I dealt well enough together over the years. But at the time, I was sorely vexed to have to give up Dorothea." He shook his head, chuckling at some scene in his memory. "Dorothea and I had even discussed names for our imagined children. Our son would be Stanton, after my grandfather, and our daughter would be Olivia, after me. Vain, I know." Lord Brightwell stopped, eyes distant.

"After you?" Olivia felt her brow pucker.

He glanced at her. "My name is Oliver, did you not know it?"

She drew in a sharp breath. Mutely shook her head.

"Oliver Stanton Bradley, Lord Brightwell."

What is he saying? she wondered. *Might he mean . . . ?* She could not voice such incredible questions. Instead she made a tremulous attempt at levity. "It appears you changed your mind, my lord, for your son is not named Stanton."

But he did not smile or rejoinder with an amusing anecdote of his wife trumping his chosen name with a favorite of her own. Instead his brow wrinkled and he murmured, "No. Edward was not my choice."

His somber tone invited no further inquiry. The earl looked away from her, through the rain-splattered window to the memories beyond.

Olivia sat staring into the fire, seeing her own memories. *What if . . . ?* Entertaining such thoughts of her mother, of herself, brought heat to Olivia's ears and shame to her heart. Still, it might certainly explain her father's coldness. And if he had only learned of it later, might it not account for the destruction of the bond they had shared in her youngest days? Or did he simply despise her for losing that odious contest? For losing his money and respect, as she had long thought? Yes, that was far easier to believe. For even if her mother had named her in honor of a former love, that did not necessarily mean . . . anything else.

For several moments, they both sat as they were, silent and lost in thought. But soon, doubts broke in on Olivia's mind like pounding waves. "How long ago, my lord, did you, ah, last see my mother?"

Lord Brightwell thought, "Dear me . . . Can it already be six and twenty years? Yes, it must be that or more."

Olivia felt equal portions of relief, vindication, and reluctance when she whispered, "I am not yet five and twenty."

He nodded thoughtfully. "Of course I may have summed the years incorrectly. My memory is not what it used to be. Nor my ciphering." He gazed at her intently and gave her a shaky smile. "You are so like her, my dear."

Olivia's eyes filled with answering tears that slipped down her cheeks. She grasped his hand in hers.

Edward gave the door a sharp rap and, not waiting for an answer, swung it open and strode in. He faltered, startled to see his father and Miss Keene sitting in intimate conversation, holding hands. Edward's heart sank while his anger rose.

"Sorry to interrupt your tête-à-tête, Father," he said acrimoniously. To himself he added, *And so soon after Mother's death!*

"Edward, you will never guess—"

"Try me," he snapped.

He noticed Miss Keene squeeze the earl's hand to gain his attention, her gaze pleading. His father lifted a brow, and she shook her head, *no*.

Edward witnessed their secretive exchange with disdain. "What?" he growled.

The earl hesitated and then said, "Miss Keene and I have discovered a mutual acquaintance."

"Really?" Edward doubted such a thing, if true, would bring about such fervent hand-holding. When neither offered to enlighten him, he said curtly, "Walters is ready to review the ledgers, Father. Would now be . . . inconvenient?"

"Actually I was enjoying my time with Olivia."

Olivia . . . ? He did not like the sound of her name on his father's lips.

Lord Brightwell sighed and straightened. "But if it cannot wait . . ."

"I should be returning to the nursery at all events, my lord," Miss Keene said, rising.

"But—" The earl started to protest but, seeing her expression, ceased. "Very well, Olivia. Um, Miss Keene."

The two shared a meaningful smile that filled Edward's gut with bile. Surely his father held no inappropriate interest in the girl. True, lords had been seducing maids for centuries, but he did not think his father such a man. He recalled his recent conversation with Mrs. Hinkley about one of the maids and felt a renewed rush of anger. Another emotion surged within him, but he did not stop to contemplate it.

19

> Unprotected by her own family the governess was vulnerable to sexual approaches.
>
> —Kathryn Hughes, *The Victorian Governess*

On her next half day, Olivia crunched through the newly fallen snow on the path through the wood. There was not enough snow for the children to play in, only a dusting on the ground and a thick coat of sugar icing on the branches, bushes, and berries. Tufts of grass and red and yellow leaves shone through the white glaze, reminding Olivia of an iced cake of dried fruits and nuts.

She walked further along the wooded trail—in the opposite direction from

Croome's lodge—and then, drawn by the slurry whisper of running water, strayed from the path and followed the sound. She saw two dippers on the riverbank, bobbing and dipping their heads in characteristic style. A woodcock, disturbed by her arrival, beat the air with panicked wings and whirred away.

Olivia brushed snow from a fallen log near the river's edge and sat down. How peaceful it was. Tipping her head back, she relished the unseasonably warm sun, which would melt away the snow far too soon.

As she sat there, Olivia realized she had reached the end of her three-month trial. Lord Bradley would allow her to go now, his father had said. Yet somehow the thought of leaving did not bring relief, but rather uncertainty. *Almighty God, show me what to do. . . .* She longed to know where her mother was and how she fared, but she had begged Olivia *not* to return—insisted that she would find *her* when it was safe to do so. But why had her mother not come? Had something happened to her, or had she stayed away for fear of leading the constable—or Simon Keene—to Olivia's door?

Another thought struck her then. Would Lord Bradley even allow her to stay longer? Suddenly she very much hoped so. At least then she would have a place to live while she waited, or until she found another post.

Edward walked through the wood, a gun held casually at his side. He had been scouting the far wood for wild dogs and poachers and now, on his return, paused at his favorite spot along the river. Looking up through the whitewashed canopy of branches, he saw a goose high overhead, flying alone. He found himself wondering how the creature had become separated from his flock. Where was it going? Would he find his way? There, surrounded by snow and silence, the sight filled Edward with a stinging loneliness.

He sensed movement nearby and tensed, searching the wood instead of the sky. Leaves crackled, and a woodcock took to flight, scattering snow in its wake. Surely there were no dogs this close to the house.

Then Miss Keene stepped into view on the far bank. She was humming quietly to herself and sat on a fallen log near the river. For several moments she simply tilted her head to the sunshine, eyes closed, dark curls framing her oval face. She was not as elegant as Miss Harrington or Judith, though of course she had neither cosmetics, fine gowns, nor a lady's maid, as they did. Still, Miss Keene was beautiful and—as Judith often alluded to—had a quiet nobility about her, a ladylike grace. He wondered again about the nature of his father's interest in the girl.

She stretched her legs out before her, and Edward glimpsed a sliver of stocking and tapered ankle. He averted his gaze. He was not a man to sneak a look at a woman's leg. He repeated this sentiment to himself once more. And then again.

Little flurries of snow began to fall, twirling and floating in the air like blossoms from a bird cherry tree. Returning his gaze to Miss Keene's face, he saw her open her mouth and hold forth her pink tongue, trying to catch snowflakes on it like a schoolgirl. He found himself smiling and had the urge to splash across the shallow river to join her. He wanted to share a smile with her, to share much more. But obstacles greater than an icy river stood between them. *I am a fool*, he admonished himself. *She would be mortified if she saw me and knew I had been watching her.*

He stayed where he was, reminding himself that his father had every intention of staying the course. He *would be* the next Earl of Brightwell and marry accordingly.

Miss Keene sat a moment longer, then rose from the log and turned from the river, brushing off her bottom with gloved hands as she went. Edward decided he would head back as well, and see if he might meet up with her at the Brightwell Bridge.

Olivia was surprised to see Johnny Ross sitting on the wooden bench at the top of the rise. She opened her mouth to admonish him, but remembered her charade just in time and quickly clamped her lips shut.

He looked up, rose, and came bounding down the path. "I surprised you, didn't I?" He laughed, putting his hands under her elbows. "I've been hoping to find you alone for days."

Olivia shook her head, gently pushing his hands away and heading up the frosted hill. They were so close to the manor. If someone saw them out there together, they would assume she and Johnny were . . . And if Lord Bradley saw them, Johnny would lose his place.

"Aw, come on," he urged, jogging to catch up with her. "At least sit with me on the bench a bit. I brushed the snow off."

Taking her arm, he pulled her down onto the bench beside him. She moved to its edge and took a deep breath. She didn't want to hurt his feelings, but nor did she wish to encourage him.

"Livie, you know I'm mad for you, do you not? Will you not give me a sign of affection?"

Oh, how frustrating! How could she explain without speaking? A simple shake of her head seemed so insufficient.

Johnny took her hesitation as his cue to convince her. He clutched her awkwardly by the shoulders and leaned forward to kiss her.

Turning her face away, Olivia glimpsed Lord Bradley on the path, and her immediate embarrassment flamed into irritation as she took in his arrogant stance. For a moment she was tempted to turn and kiss Johnny, show the haughty lord she was not intimidated by him. But she knew it would be unfair to use Johnny that way. For the briefest instant, she held Lord Bradley's cold gaze over Johnny's shoulder, unwilling to lower her eyes first. She had done nothing to be ashamed of.

Johnny pulled her closer, murmuring, "Come on, Livie. Just one kiss. You don't have to say a word. . . ." His razor-stubbled chin scraped her cheek as he pushed his face close.

Olivia held her tongue by the thinnest thread of self-will. She tried to pull away, but the groom was strong indeed. Would Lord Bradley just stand there? Was he no gentleman at all?

She thought, *I don't have to say a word, do I? Well, I am about to*. Olivia twisted in his grasp and opened her mouth to make very plain her ill-opinion of them both.

A gunshot exploded in the air. Johnny flew to his feet, sending Olivia tumbling from the bench onto the ground. His face went white as he whirled and saw Lord Bradley standing a few yards away, gun against his hip.

He strode toward them purposely, his face hard. "Back to the stables, Ross," he ordered as he bent toward Olivia and extended his hand to help her up. She ignored it and scrambled to her feet on her own, cheeks burning in indignation.

Johnny hesitated only long enough to glance her way without meeting her eyes and mumble a weak, "Sorry, miss." Then he all but ran up the path and out of sight.

As soon as he was out of earshot, Olivia hissed, "You needn't have done that. I could have managed on my own."

"That is not how it appeared."

"Perhaps you judged incorrectly. Perhaps I am sorry you interrupted us." She saw him hesitate, his jaw clench.

He said coldly, "Then you must excuse me. If you and your lover want privacy, I suggest you find a less public rendezvous. If Hodges had witnessed that little scene, Ross would be packing his bags as we speak. In the meantime, you ought to return to the house. It is not safe for you to be out in the wood alone."

"I am perfectly safe."

"Wild dogs have been spotted near Barnsley, Miss Keene. There is no guarantee they will not come here as well."

"You are only trying to frighten me."

"You should be frightened. You haven't your stick with you this time."

She stared, mildly stunned by his reference to their first meeting. So he did remember her from the hunt. Good. Maybe he would remember how rudely he and his friends had treated her.

"I appreciate your concern," she said coolly. "But I am certain you have more important things to do than protect me."

"You are correct. Therefore, I repeat—return to the house. Now."

"I have not finished my walk."

"Walk all you want in view of the house."

"I shall walk where I please."

"You forget your place."

"And you forget your promise of a half day to spend as I like. And your duty as a gentleman to treat me as a human being."

"Albeit a trespasser."

"You shall never let me forget my mistake, will you? *Forgive* and *forget* are not in your vocabulary. I am guilty of many things, but for the last time, I am neither spy nor thief. I foolishly trespassed upon your land, yes, but I would rather be a trespasser than an arrogant, unfeeling, ungentlemanly person like you!"

She turned her back on him, unwilling to allow him to see her tears.

"Miss Keene," he reprimanded.

She felt his gaze spear the back of her head but refused to turn around.

He raised his voice. "Miss Keene!"

She glanced at him over her shoulder. "I am not deaf, sir," she retorted. "Simply mute." And with that she lifted her skirts and ran down the path, deeper into the wood, choking back sobs as she ran.

Edward watched her go and realized with a prickling chill that it was the first time she had failed to address him by his courtesy title.

He sat down on the bench with a heavy sigh and held his head in his hands. Her words ricocheted inside his head and his stomach churned.

Well, she is wrong about one thing, he thought. *I am not unfeeling. I feel. I feel indeed.*

When Edward had spied her with Ross, he had been angry—but knew the emotion had little to do with the fact that fraternizing among servants was frowned upon. Hodges had let go more than one amorous footman and housemaid in the past.

In truth, he had been shot through with jealously, illogical though it was. Jealous . . . over attentions paid to an under nurse? He had never been attracted to one of the servants before, not even for a light flirtation as Felix often was. *Oh, how the mighty have fallen.*

When Ross had leaned forward to kiss Miss Keene, Edward's gut had clenched within him. He knew he should turn and quietly go—let Hodges deal with the groom later.

But I refuse to feel guilty, he thought. *Did she not spy on me?*

But instead of meeting Ross's kiss, Miss Keene had turned away. The flash of her eyes over Ross's shoulder told him she had seen him there and was not pleased. Still, he was relieved she had avoided the man's kiss.

Remorse filled him now as he replayed their recent exchange in his mind. *What am I doing?* He sat there trying to make sense of his turbulent thoughts and emotions. He knew he had no right to keep her there any longer, and no honest way to guarantee her silence. He ought to let her go.

In more ways than one.

He heard a sharp scream in the distance and knew instantly whom the voice belonged to. He jumped up, grabbed his gun, and flew down the path.

"Go! Be gone! Help . . . Lord Bradley!"

At her panicked cries, his legs flew faster. Branches cracked as he pushed his way through the underbrush in the direction of her voice. The sound of barking and growling reached him, chilling his blood. *Wild dogs . . .* He sprinted on, trying to load his gun as he ran.

Rounding a bend, his eyes registered the scene in an instant. Three dogs. One in a crouch, preparing to lunge. Edward snapped the gun chamber closed and raised the piece. *Too late . . .* The dog was midair, teeth bared. The moment slowed to a slogging dream. He saw a flash, heard a sharp report, and the dog's blazing eyes faded to grey, to emptiness, as the cur fell limply to the ground.

But Edward had yet to fire a shot.

Turning his head, he glimpsed Croome standing within a web of branches, arm outstretched and steady, fowling piece still smoking. Before Edward could respond, the second dog coiled to lunge. *Crack!* His own shot shuddered through the dog as it leapt. Olivia screamed as it landed in a heap at her feet. Before Edward could reload, the third dog flew forward and sunk its teeth into her skirts and gave a great jerk, pulling her feet out from under her, her head hitting the ground sharply as she fell. He saw Croome lift his fowling piece again and their eyes met. Croome did not shoot again. Why did the man not shoot? Fearing his own shot might miss its mark and hit Miss Keene, Edward charged forward, striking the dog with the butt of his gun. He shouted unintelligibly and struck again. Finally the dog unclamped its hold and scampered away. Croome's shot chased it into the wood.

Edward ran to where Olivia lay, silent and still.

"Miss Keene? Are you all right? Miss Keene?"

No response. He pressed trembling fingers to her neck and found a pulse. He gently rolled her by one shoulder to examine the back of her head where she had fallen. A jagged rock lay beneath her, smeared with blood.

Looking up, his gaze fell on the nearest dead dog. The dog's blank eyes were rheumy. Its tongue swollen. Foamy drool puddled beneath its mouth. Edward's heart thundered, ice formed in his stomach. He prayed the cur that escaped had only bitten her skirts, not her flesh. Jerking off his coat and bunching it to cushion her head, he rolled her gently back down. He was vaguely aware of Croome dragging the carcasses out of the way. Crawling to Miss Keene's feet, Edward pushed up her skirts only as far as necessary. He winced. Just below her knee, blood trickled red through her stocking. *God, no . . .*

He recalled too well his father's stories of the rampage of rabies through London in the days of his youth, when livestock and people died by the hundreds and lads earned five shillings for every dog they killed. The attacks of rabid dogs and foxes had become less common in recent years, but the disease—and dread of it—had never left England.

Edward rolled down the stocking and regarded the wound. The bite did not appear deep; the thickness of her skirts had no doubt hindered the cur's goal. Tossing aside her shoe, he yanked the stocking from that leg and wound it around the top of her calf, tying it tight. Croome reappeared, surveying his actions with wordless concurrence. The old man pulled his hunting knife from its sheath, uncorked his flask and poured some of the brandy over the blade, then handed the flask to him. Edward splashed the wound with the amber liquid. Croome offered him the knife, but when Edward hesitated, the man groaned to his knees and unceremoniously sliced the wound site. Olivia moaned but did not awaken. As the bleeding quickened, Edward rinsed it away with more of the brandy. He did not know if these actions would help, but it was all he knew to try. Once more he met Croome's eyes, deep in his skull beneath wiry grey eyebrows. The man's ever-present scowl offered him little hope.

Edward lifted Olivia in his arms and carried her as fast as he could up the path. Croome did not follow. When he reached the lawns, he saw Talbot and Johnny working a new horse in the gates.

"Talbot!" he yelled. "Send Ross on your fastest horse for Dr. Sutton. Miss Keene has been wounded!"

"Wounded?" Johnny's anxious eyes met his.

"Mad dogs," he gritted.

The young man paled and flew to his task.

20

To marry a member of one's household, even from its upper strata, was considered an appalling social misdemeanor.

—Mark Girouard, *Life in the English Country House*

Dr. Sutton arrived within the hour. With Mrs. Hinkley's assistance, he irrigated the wound with soap and warm water, then with diluted muriatic acid. When he commended Edward for his quick thinking with the knife and brandy, Edward credited his gamekeeper for knowing what to do.

"Avery Croome did this?" Sutton raised his brows and his lower lip protruded, but whether impressed or merely surprised, Edward did not know.

Dr. Sutton also bathed and bandaged Olivia's head wound, which he cited as the cause of her unconscious state—a bite, he said, even from a rabid dog, would not account for it.

"How long until we know if she has been infected?"

Sutton shrugged and pushed up his spectacles. "Symptoms may not appear for a week or more."

"What should we look for?" Mrs. Hinkley asked.

"Pain and itching at the wound site, headache, insomnia, nausea, refusal to eat or drink, agitation, aggression . . ."

Edward shuddered. "And if symptoms appear?"

"Then there is nothing we can do for her but keep her from passing the disease to others. Once symptoms are in full force, victims usually perish within the week."

A dull ache of dread pounded through Edward's body. "How long will she remain unconscious?"

"Only God knows. Head wounds are mysterious indeed. I shall arrange for a chamber nurse, shall I?"

"And I shall share that duty, if you don't mind," Mrs. Hinkley offered. "Even a chamber nurse needs rest from time to time."

Edward nodded his agreement and murmured dull thanks to them both.

Dr. Sutton continued his extensive irrigation of the wound, explaining that the best course was to do all in one's power to prevent the dog's saliva from making its way through the victim's body.

For the disease had no cure.

Edward returned to the sickroom later that night to ask the hired nurse if she would like a respite. He was surprised to find the earl sitting beside Miss Keene, and felt a renewed pinch of grief to see his father sitting at another sickbed so soon after his mother's death. The matronly chamber nurse sat off in the corner, working some embroidery by the light of a candle lamp.

"Any change?" Edward whispered, surveying Olivia's form shrouded by bedclothes.

"She grows restless," the older man answered softly.

As if hearing the words, Miss Keene's forehead puckered and she turned her face away from them, then back once more.

Edward recalled the list of symptoms the doctor had described and felt fear prick his gut. "I would be restless too, lying about all day," he said in mock confidence.

His father looked at him, then away. "No sign of nausea. Or"—he attempted a grin—"insomnia. And Nurse Jones here has got her to swallow some water. Another good sign, is it not?"

"I hope so," Edward answered.

As if sensing his son's discomfort, Lord Brightwell asked Nurse Jones to give them a few moments alone, suggesting she take herself down to the kitchen for some tea.

"Don't mind if I do, my lord." She rose stiffly and left them.

After a few moments of silence, Edward confessed, "It was my fault she ran into the wood."

The earl's eyebrows rose, but he didn't press Edward. "The important thing is that she get well."

"Yes. I am afraid I have much to apologize for."

"More than you know," the earl said, his eyes growing tender as he looked at Olivia's pale face.

"What do you mean?" Edward asked. His father's warm tone and mysterious words brought leaden dread to his stomach. Certainly his father had no designs on the girl.

When their gazes met, the older man's eyes were bright with unshed tears. "I think Olivia may be my daughter."

"What?" Edward thundered.

"Shh . . ." the earl admonished, and both turned their eyes back to Miss Keene's unconscious form.

"Olivia favours her mother a great deal," his father whispered with reverence. "It is why I was so startled when first I saw her. Her looks, her intelligence and warmth—so very like Dorothea."

"Who is Dorothea?" Edward demanded, a dark cloud building inside of him.

"She was governess to my half sisters, your aunts Margery and Phillipa." The earl frowned suddenly. "Do sit down, my boy. My neck grows stiff."

Edward complied, sitting in the last remaining chair, its hard wooden slats digging into his spine. Who had designed the torturous thing?

"Olivia's hair is darker, but still the resemblance is striking."

"And this Dorothea was . . . your mistress?"

The earl winced. "It was not as tawdry as all that. We fancied ourselves in love. I wanted to marry her, but as you might guess, my father would not hear of it."

Lord Brightwell rose and went to stand near the window, looking out at the moon pouring its waxy light over the white world below. "My father urged me to marry your mother, the Estcourts being such a well-connected and wealthy family." He sighed. "Of course none of us could have guessed that he would die before the year was out. In any case, I had barely agreed when the banns were read and the wedding set for three weeks hence. As soon as Dorothea heard, she resigned her post and left with no word of her destination. I never imagined she was with child, though perhaps I should have guessed. How irresponsible and selfish I was . . . how weak. I like to think I would have acted differently had I known. I did try to find her, but I own it was a halfhearted attempt at best. Even her family did not know where she was."

"Olivia," Edward whispered to himself, suddenly realizing the significance.

"Yes," the earl whispered.

Edward scowled. "Is she pushing for this, or are you?"

"I am. She doesn't want a shilling from me, if that is what you think."

"I did not think that," Edward muttered, though the thought had crossed his mind.

"I have not told Olivia outright what I suspect, though as intelligent as she is—and as *subtle* as I was—I believe she guessed. Being genteel, she is no doubt repulsed by the notion of being baseborn, as you can imagine."

"Yes, I can well imagine," Edward echoed wryly.

Lord Brightwell shot him a look. "You must know, Edward, Olivia is not convinced. My recollection of the timing and her age do not reconcile."

Edward shrugged. "Easily changed. No doubt many illegitimate children celebrate their first birthday a few months later than fact." Edward wondered for the first time what his real birth date might be.

The earl abruptly stood. "Dorothea would want to know. She would want to be here with her daughter. Did Olivia give you any direction beyond 'near Cheltenham'?"

Edward shook his head.

"Nor me. I wonder why. . . ."

The next day, Edward was just returning from the stables after exercising his horse when the shrill summons startled him.

"Master Edward! Come quickly!" Mrs. Hinkley stood at the garden door, waving wildly to him, her voice panicked. "It is Olivia. She is thrashing about and . . . and talking!"

She held the door for him as he strode toward her, pulling off his riding gloves and hat as he came. "Send for the doctor, Mrs. Hinkley. I shall go up and see what I can do."

"Yes, my lord," she answered, clearly relieved to have him take charge of the situation.

Tossing his things on a bench in the corridor, Edward took the stairs three at a time. He hurried into the sickroom, shutting the door behind him. Olivia's face was flushed, and she twisted about, the sheets and a long nightdress trapping her slender form. Her mouth twitched and her brows furrowed. Then she began muttering aloud, though her eyes remained closed.

"No! Be gone! Edward! Edward!"

His heart banged in his chest. He had never before heard her speak his Christian name. She was calling to him, no doubt reliving that horrible scene with the dogs.

Stepping to the bedside table, he wrung excess water from a cloth and then sat on the chair beside the bed. He held her face with one hand and with the other, gently touched the cool cloth to her cheeks and lips and brow. He murmured, "Shh . . . It is all right. I am here. The dogs are gone. You are safe now, Olivia. Perfectly safe."

She quieted almost immediately. He smoothed the cloth down her straight nose, dabbed her scratched chin, and then softly soothed the hot skin of her neck. Eventually he returned the cloth to the basin, and took one of her small hands in his own. He stroked her delicate fingers and spoke to her softly. "You are going to be all right, Olivia," he said, knowing his words were as much to reassure himself as her. He recalled the sound of her voice calling out his name. Not *my lord*, not *Lord Bradley*. Just *Edward*. He longed to hear her say it again, well and awake.

When Dr. Sutton came an hour later, he gave her chamomile and valerian to calm her and ordered she be helped to swallow more fluids. "It might just be a slight fever and not rabies, but it is too early to tell," he said. "There is little else to be done but wait."

Edward nodded. He would wait. But he would also pray. He sent Osborn with a note for Charles Tugwell, asking the man of God to join him.

21

Whenever you give any living creature cause to depend on you, be careful on no account to disappoint it.

—Sarah Trimmer, *Fabulous Histories Designed for the Instruction of Children*, 1786

When his cousin entered the sickroom, Edward was sitting in the armchair by the window, reading an old volume of Chaucer. Nurse Jones had taken herself belowstairs for dinner and Olivia slept quietly in bed.

"How is she?" Judith whispered.

"She grew restless several hours ago but has been quiet since."

Judith took several steps forward but did not draw near the bed, as though afraid to get too close. She looked down at Miss Keene, an inscrutable expression on her pretty face. "I was just speaking with your father. He seems quite concerned about her."

Edward shrugged uneasily. "He is . . . taken with her."

"Which I find a bit odd." She tilted her head to look at him. "Do you not?"

Uncomfortable, Edward only shrugged.

She studied him thoughtfully. "And here you sit like a faithful hound at her side. Are you not afraid of contracting rabies?"

He shook his head. "The doctor thinks it only a fever."

"Does it not concern you?"

"Of course, but Sutton—"

"I do not mean the fever," she interrupted. "I meant, does it not concern you that your father has developed a *tendre* for our under nurse?"

When Edward didn't respond, Judith asked, "And what did Mrs. Hinkley mean when she said, 'Is it not a miracle?'"

"Excuse me?"

"When I passed her just now, she said, 'Is it not a miracle about Olivia?'"

Edward nodded. "I suppose she means that Miss Keene has been talking in her sleep."

Judith's plump lips parted. "Has she indeed?" Her eyes flashed in triumph. "Did I not tell you she might be pretending to muteness?"

Edward felt annoyance rising. Yet had he not suspected the same at first?

"What does she say?" Judith asked eagerly.

Edward felt suddenly self-conscious. "Hmm . . . ?" he murmured, deliberately obtuse.

"What does Miss Keene say when she talks in her sleep?" Judith pressed.

He hesitated, not wanting to divulge the truth, but his eyes must have given something away.

Judith's fair brows rose, and the corners of her mouth twitched with humor. "Do *not* tell me she calls out for you."

Edward felt his neck heat. "She . . . mutters a good deal of nonsense—that is all."

His cousin's gaze was all too knowing, and disconcerted, Edward looked away.

Olivia opened her eyes and looked about her, quite bewildered to find herself in an unfamiliar room. A candle lamp burned on the bedside table and a fire in the hearth. A woman she did not recognize sat nodding off in an armchair near the fire, a wad of needlework in her lap.

Slowly, Olivia pulled herself into a sitting position, concerned to find the act quite taxing. Why was she so weak? At the movement, the bed ropes creaked and the unfamiliar woman roused herself and gaped at Olivia, eyes wide.

"Miss Keene? Are you . . . well?"

Olivia nodded, the memories of the attack slowly coming to mind.

The woman toddled to the bedside. "I am Mrs. Jones, chamber nurse. Do you need anything? Will you take some water?" Mrs. Jones brought the glass to her lips, but Olivia gently took the vessel from her and sipped from it herself. The nurse beamed at her as though she had just performed an amazing feat.

"You wait right there," she said. "The others will want to know you've come back to us."

Olivia wondered how long she had been abed and if she was fit for company. She looked down at herself, oddly touched to find herself clothed in a fine and modest nightdress. *Whose?* she wondered. Moments later, a voice rang out somewhere in the manor and echoed down the stairs and corridor.

"She's awake! She's awake!"

Doris, Olivia mused, and sat waiting. A few minutes later, the door opened and Doris poked her head inside the room. "Hello, love! Feeling well enough for visitors?"

Olivia nodded, feeling weak and a bit dazed, but otherwise well. Doris entered, followed by Mrs. Hinkley, both of them all eager expectation, which mildly confused her.

Doris fluffed two pillows behind her and straightened the bedclothes. "You've been asleep for two days, Livie. Did you know?"

Olivia shook her head.

Mrs. Hinkley smiled down at her. "You spoke in your sleep, my dear. I heard you myself."

Stunned, Olivia's mind reeled behind a stiff smile. What would Lord Bradley say? What had *she* said?

"You said a lot of balmy things, I hear," Doris chimed in. "I'd a paid two bob to hear 'em myself."

"Can you speak now?" Mrs. Hinkley's tone was gentle.

Olivia hesitated; they were both looking at her so expectantly. Lord Bradley slipped into the room behind them and held her gaze. He gave her a slight nod.

"I . . . ye-yes," Olivia stammered. "I believe I can."

"Ohh!" Doris exclaimed. "And don't she speak fine—just like a lady! Say my name won't you, love?"

"And mine?" Mrs. Hinkley added shyly.

Olivia chuckled. "My friend, Doris McGovern . . . and dear Mrs. Hinkley." Her eyes met those of the last person in the room, his expression inscrutable. She swallowed. "And . . . my lord Bradley."

A small smile curved his lips.

Doris and Mrs. Hinkley, suddenly self-conscious, murmured "Excuse me" and "God bless you" and hurriedly left the room.

"Perhaps she could speak all the time and didn't know it," Olivia heard Doris venture as the two women walked away down the corridor.

"Maybe so," Mrs. Hinkley agreed. "Or perhaps the sickness made her well."

When Olivia stepped into the nursery after her absence of several days, Andrew bounded across the room and threw his arms around her. Still weak and wobbly from her recent indisposition, Olivia had to grip the doorjamb to keep from falling backward.

"Hello, Miss Livie. Are you well now?"

"I am."

His little mouth dropped open. "Say that again."

Olivia smiled. "I am. I am well."

Audrey approached cautiously and Olivia held out a hand. The girl hurried forward then, biting back her shy smile. "Hello, Miss Keene," she said. "We have missed you."

"And I, you."

"I told you she could talk!" Andrew said. "I did hear her talk in her sleep, but you wouldn't believe me!"

"Perhaps I did, Andrew," Olivia soothed, "but did not realize I *could* speak while awake."

"I must say I am disappointed in you, Miss Keene."

Olivia looked up, disconcerted to see Judith Howe standing in the sleeping chamber doorway, little Alexander on one hip.

"I am sorry, madam. I don't—"

Judith glanced down and then up again. "You see, I had imagined you to speak with a Prussian accent, or German, perhaps. As would befit a foreign princess fleeing her home."

Olivia forced a laugh. "I am sorry to disappoint you."

Judith straightened. "You did not run away from a tyrannical father, forcing you into a despicable marriage?"

Olivia's mouth was dry. "No . . . forced marriage, no."

The woman sighed theatrically. "Ah, well. So be it."

Lord Brightwell knocked and stepped into the nursery. "Full house today."

"Hello, Uncle," Judith said. "Our under nurse is well, you see, but fails to be the foreign princess I had hoped for."

He patted his niece's shoulder, amused. "Life is full of such little disappointments, my dear." His eyes twinkled. "Though Miss Keene may surprise you yet."

"What does that mean?" Judith asked sharply.

Olivia tried to signal the earl, but Judith caught her shaking her head. Mrs. Howe looked from one to the other with mounting suspicion. "What is going on?"

"Not a thing, my dear. You must forgive the foolishness of an old man."

"Must I?"

Fearing Mrs. Howe might come to a more *imaginative* conclusion on her own, Olivia explained, "Lord Brightwell means only that he has realized my mother was once governess to his younger sisters."

"Indeed?" Judith Howe said, surprised. She nodded slowly and chewed her full lower lip as the news sunk in. She was clearly still considering the notion as she let herself from the room.

That night, when Olivia put the children to bed, they begged her to read to them and she happily obliged. She read Psalm 46, her favorite, and another chapter in *The History of Robins*.

Once more, Audrey leaned her head on Olivia's shoulder, while Andrew curled into her side, lifting Olivia's arm and draping it around himself like a human cloak.

> "When the mother-bird arrived at the ivy wall, she stopt at the entrance of the nest, with a palpitating heart; but seeing her brood all safe and well, she hastened to take them under her wings. . . ."

"I like your voice, Miss Keene," Audrey said.

"Me too," Andrew murmured, on the verge of sleep. "Is that what our *mamma's* voice sounded like?"

And from the reverence with which he spoke the word, Olivia knew he referred to their first mother. Olivia felt the tremble pass through Audrey's frame and rested her cheek atop the girl's head.

"I don't remember," Audrey whispered. "But I think it must be."

Olivia's throat tightened, and she could read no more.

22

> Wanted, a Governess—a comfortable home, but without salary, is offered to any lady wishing for a situation to instruct two [children] in music, drawing and English.
>
> —Advertisement in the *Times,* 1847

When Olivia stepped into the kitchen for the first time since the attack, Mrs. Moore opened wide her arms and enfolded Olivia in an embrace as sweet as the confections she prepared.

"Livie, my love, how I have been praying for you. I cannot tell you how good it is to see you up and about and in my kitchen once more. Now sit yourself down and I will pour you a cup of chocolate and we shall have ourselves a chat."

Olivia smiled and felt her insides warm before one sip of the hot drink had passed her lips.

Mrs. Moore bustled about, then set the cup of warm chocolate before her, and a buttery scone as well. She lifted her thin brows, eyes wide in expectation. "Well?"

"Well what, Mrs. Moore?"

"Ewww! I have been waitin' to hear you say my name. Say something else."

"Mrs. Moore, you embarrass me. I feel as though I am called before my French master, there to impress him with my command of a new language."

"Ahh!" She clapped her hands. "Doris said you spoke like a real lady, and bless me, but she was right."

Olivia laughed. "Is it so strange to hear me speak?"

"Strange and wonderful, my girl. Strange and wonderful."

A knock sounded on the kitchen door and Mrs. Moore rose. "You stay as you are and drink your chocolate. I shall return directly."

Olivia watched in silence as Mrs. Moore opened the door to the outside stairwell and accepted three hares from Mr. Croome. Over the mottled grey fur, the gamekeeper snared Olivia's gaze, gave one curt nod, then pivoted on his heel without a word of farewell.

"Thank you, Avery," Mrs. Moore called after him.

Without turning, the old man merely raised a hand in acknowledgment as he climbed back up the stairs.

Laying the hares in a basket beside the worktable, Mrs. Moore glanced at Olivia. "You know, he asked about you, while you were ill."

"Did he?"

Mrs. Moore nodded. "You really needn't be afraid of Mr. Croome, Livie. He's not so bad. Had a rough life, poor rogue."

Olivia tented her brows. "You are the first I've heard speak of him with any sympathy."

"How could I not? Lost his wife. My own sister, she was."

Olivia was stunned. For a moment she just sat there, staring at the woman. Then she reached out and laid her hand on Mrs. Moore's. "He was married to your sister?" Olivia could not imagine a hard, angry man like Croome deserving a woman anything like warm and kind Nell Moore. But then, did Simon Keene deserve Dorothea Hawthorn?

Mrs. Moore nodded. "But she died long ago. Lies in the churchyard now, she does." Tears misted the cook's eyes in spite of the passage of years. "They . . . oh, never mind me." She sniffed and forcibly brightened. "We are celebrating your return—from the sickbed and silence." Mrs. Moore squeezed her hand. "A very happy day indeed."

Olivia smiled and sipped her chocolate. "Do you know, Lord Bradley told me that Mr. Croome shot one of the dogs before it could attack me."

"Did he? Never said a word to me."

"I wonder if I ought to thank him."

Mrs. Moore's thin brows rose again, all innocence. "Do you think so?"

Olivia did not miss the twinkle in her eye. "I don't suppose you have any tidbits left over you cannot bear to waste?"

Olivia found Croome chopping wood and shivered at the sight of him wielding a sharp axe. At his feet, a grey bird with mottled orange-brown wings showed no such fear. It shadowed Croome as he set another hunk of wood on the tree stump and split it cleanly in two. *Clunk, chunk.*

He hesitated when he saw her. "What are ya doin' here, girl?"

"G-good day, Mr. Croome. I am Olivia Keene, as you may recall."

"I recall. The girl I caught snooping about where she had no business."

Clunk, chunk.

She remembered Mrs. Moore's admonition. *"Mind you give it right back to him."* Olivia steeled her voice. "And I recall you, Mr. Croome, where you had no business. In Chedworth Wood with an . . . interesting . . . group of acquaintances."

He let his axe fall to his side and split her with a sharp look. Even the bird's proud, roosterlike face seemed to sneer at her. "What I do when I'm away from here is none of yer concern, nor no one else's either."

"Very well."

He riveted his eyes on hers, and she forced herself to meet the glowering glare.

He bent and picked up another piece of wood. "Thought you'd tell the master 'bout that."

"I did not."

His eyes narrowed. "And why not?"

"Whatever else you be, you rescued me that night in the wood."

He lifted the axe again, but hesitated. "'Course I did. Young girl, at the mercy of a vile, debauched man . . ." He brought the axe down with a vicious blow, and she wondered if he spoke of Borcher alone.

She added, "And now, I understand, you have helped rescue me once again. This time from four-legged curs in this very wood."

He shrugged. "Only doin' my job, wasn't I?" He tossed the split logs onto the pile.

"Even so, I am grateful. I am afraid I do not recollect the events of that day very clearly, but Lord Bradley speaks highly of your quick actions."

Croome halted, peering at her. "Does he?" For a moment his expression cleared, but then his eyes alighted on the covered jar in her hands. He scowled once more.

"I told you before. I don' need yer charity."

"I am glad to hear it, for I have nothing to offer you. This is from Mrs. Moore. Jugged hare, I believe she said. She made more than can be used in the manor, and said if you were too mule-stubborn to accept it, you might feed it to your pigs again. It matters not to her."

"Said that, did she?" The faintest hint of a smile teased his lips, then fled to a tremor in his hand. "Sounds like Nell. Bossy bird."

"Will you take it, or shall I dump it in the wood on my way back? I for one hate to hurt her feelings."

"No call fer wastin' it. Shouldn't ha' brought it, but I do hate waste as well she knows, scheming woman. Leave it. I have dogs as well as pigs. Between us, we shall see it put to use."

"Very well." She set the jar on the stoop and turned without another word, holding her chin high as she marched away.

But it was several minutes before her heart beat normally once more.

At breakfast, Edward drank coffee while Judith took tea. His father had yet to join them. Hodges brought in the letter tray—bills for him, a letter from Swindon for Judith.

Setting down her teacup, Judith peeled open her letter and, after skimming a few sentences, said, "A letter from my mother. It seems my *dear* mother-in-law, Mrs. Howe, has written to her about the fact that the children have no governess at present. Meddlesome creature!"

She paused to sip her tea, then peered at the letter again. Edward guessed his cousin needed spectacles but she was too vain to admit it.

"Good heavens!" Judith's cheeks flushed. "Mamma offers—I'd say threatens—to engage my old governess if I am unable to find one on my own. The cheek!"

"I am sure my aunt Bradley only wishes to be of kind help to you."

"Kind!" Judith directed her stunned gaze at him. "Do you not *remember* Miss Ripley? I am sure you met her several times."

"I am afraid I do not recall that pleasure."

"She frightened me to death with her harsh ways and exacting nature. Miss Dowdle was a paragon next to *the Rip*. There was no pleasing the woman. I shudder at the thought of bringing such a creature under our . . . that is, your roof."

"Brightwell Court is your home now, Judith. You know that. For as long as you like."

"Thank you, but I should not presume—"

"Of course you must tend to the education of your children."

"But they are not my children."

"Judith"—his voice held mild reprimand and cajolery—"they are yours now. You know Dominick would want you to treat them as your own."

"I suppose. If his mother's gout were not so bad, I imagine she'd insist on raising them herself." Judith sighed. "Such a pity girls' seminaries have fallen out of fashion among persons of quality."

"But Audrey is still young. I hate the thought of sending her away at such a tender age."

"Do you?" Judith's eyes softened.

Edward looked away from her melting gaze. "Andrew will need be sent to school eventually, but I do hope it will not be too soon."

"How kind you are, Edward. Most men would not appreciate having another man's children underfoot."

"Judith, they are very welcome, as well you know."

She wrinkled her fair brow in thought. "There is a girls' boarding school in St. Aldwyns, I understand. Audrey would not be so very far away."

"Tugwell and I recently discussed that very place," he said dryly, but did not explain why. "Still, how much better to educate her here at home."

"It gives me such pleasure to hear you say that, Edward," Judith said, a slight blush in her cheeks.

Edward nodded, but felt uncomfortable under her praise. It was his father's generosity that housed them all. Not his.

Judith pensively studied the letter once more. "I don't suppose . . . No, I doubt it would be quite the thing."

"What?"

"I wonder . . . What about Miss Keene?"

"Miss Keene?"

"She is wonderful with the children and has none of the superiority and pretense I so despise in governesses."

Edward stared at her, rather taken aback and not sure if he should welcome or forbid such a course. He knew Miss Keene's "sentence" was over and he had no right to keep her any longer if she wished to leave. Might such a post entice her to stay on?

Judith continued, becoming more animated as she warmed to the notion. "I am already acquainted with her, as are the children. And she is very educated, you know. She has a fine hand and she speaks or at least writes French and Italian. And she plays. Well, a little."

He could not resist teasing her. "Are you so disappointed she turned out not to be a foreign princess that you shall make her governess instead?"

She wrinkled her nose at him, the expression reminding him of their days as childhood playmates.

He asked, "Has she ever been a governess before?"

"I don't believe so, but her mother was governess to Aunt Margery and Aunt Phillipa. And when I pressed her, she admitted she taught in a girls' school somewhere. I forget where. If they would provide a character reference for her, I should be well satisfied."

He studied her, perplexed. "Why are you doing this, Judith? Do you really so revile governesses in general, or have you some other reason for wanting Miss Keene in the post?"

"Many reasons. She is clearly an intelligent, patient young woman who adores children. Who adores *my* children. She has already taken it upon herself to begin teaching them their sums and to improve their reading. All the while performing her other duties quite admirably. What are the chances of finding some stranger who can do as well, and who would fit so well into our household? I own, the change would require a few adjustments. For one, we shall all of us have to call her Miss Keene, instead of her Christian name."

"You and I do so already."

Judith nodded. "I have never been comfortable using her Christian name," she said breezily. "There is such an air of the lady in her countenance. I am afraid she shall turn out to be nobility yet, and I want nothing to answer for." Her dimple showed. "But beyond that, I see no great obstacles."

"I must say, Judith. I am impressed . . . I can almost believe you care for the girl."

She shrugged. "Not a fig. I simply relish the thought of amusing my friends with tales of our once-silent governess."

Edward slowly shook his head and felt a grin stealing over his features. "I don't suppose a month's trial can lead to any harm. We can always engage another governess should Miss Keene not suit. Shall I have Mrs. Hinkley speak with her, or would you prefer to do the honours yourself?"

Olivia hesitated. "Governess? Good gracious. I don't know what to say. . . ." Was this an answer to her prayer for guidance? Or should she leave now that she could and risk going home, even though her mother had begged her not to return?

Sitting together in the housekeeper's parlor, Mrs. Hinkley handed Olivia a cup of tea. "I don't blame you, Olivia. It would mean quite a change for you. No more fraternizing with the servants, no tea and biscuits in the kitchen with Mrs. Moore . . ."

"But why?"

"My dear, are you not familiar with a governess's plight?"

"No." Her own mother had spoken little of those days.

"A governess is neither a servant, nor a member of the family. She must not socialize with either set. She is limited to the society of her pupils and the briefest contact with the children's parents, only as necessary to report any problems that arise."

"I do not presume myself part of the family, Mrs. Hinkley." The irony of that statement echoed in her ears. "But are you really telling me that, should I accept this situation, my dear friend Mrs. Moore will refuse to talk with me? That you would as well?"

Mrs. Hinkley fidgeted in her chair. "It is not that we would refuse outright, or be intentionally rude, but a very real wall will rise between us.

"I do not say this to discourage you from accepting, for you are no doubt doing those children more good than Miss Dowdle ever did, and I know you deserve the higher wages . . . but nor do I wish you to accept the situation unaware of what it will mean. We will very much lose you, my dear. And I for one will be sorry for it."

Olivia reached out and pressed Mrs. Hinkley's hand. "You are very kind to warn me. But I have always wanted to teach. I wish what you are saying were not true. For I shall be very lonely without all of you."

"Yes, my dear. I am afraid you most certainly will be." For a moment longer, the housekeeper regarded her with a gaze almost mournful. Then she drew herself up as sharply as if she had clapped her hands. "Well, if you have your heart set upon it, there is only one more thing to do."

Mrs. Hinkley rose and fetched quill, ink, and paper from her small desk. "Mrs. Howe would like to write to that school where you assisted and request a character reference."

Olivia's heart began to pound dully within her chest. Her brief joy fell away. She ought to have anticipated this. It was one thing to hire her without a character as a lowly under nurse, but as governess? Responsible for the education of two children?

"So, if you will just write down the direction, I will give it to Mrs. Howe." She handed Olivia the quill and paper.

Blood roared in Olivia's ears. Dared she? She had no doubt Miss Cresswell would write a fair and complimentary assessment—at least she would have been certain before recent events. Had Miss Cresswell heard what she had done? When she received the letter, Miss Cresswell would learn where Olivia was living. Would she feel obliged to share this information with her father, if he lived—or the constable, if he did not?

She thought once more of the silent schoolroom high in Brightwell Court, lying fallow as an unplanted field, just waiting to be brought to useful life once more. Nerves quaking, Olivia lifted the quill and dipped it in the ink. With trembling hands, she wrote the name and direction. Creating a connection with loops of mere ink that might one day form a noose.

23

Who as I scanned the letter'd page
Took pity on my tender age,
And made the hardest task engage?
My Governess

—William Upton,
My Governess, 1812

The aromas grew stronger as Olivia descended the stairs to the kitchen. Something spicy, sweet, and tangy, like autumn, which seemed so long ago now.

"What is that delicious smell?" she asked Mrs. Moore, who was busy filling jars with quartered apples.

"Hello, Olivia. Just preserving the last of the apples in ginger syrup. My dear, I have heard the news and must congratulate you."

"It is not official yet, Mrs. Moore. We still await a reference from my former schoolmistress."

"And she'll write nothing but the highest praise, I don't doubt."

"I hope you are right."

"Of course I am. Clever, kind young lady like you. No skeletons in your brief past, I shouldn't say."

"I don't know about that."

Mrs. Moore eyed her closely. "Then you and I would have something in common, love."

Olivia wanted to ask her what she meant, but the woman began bustling about in her usual way, bringing teacups and filling a plate with lemon biscuits. Her face while she worked was impassive and welcomed no inquiry.

"We shall sit and have ourselves a memorial tea, shall we? One last hurrah." Mrs. Moore sat beside her on a stool pulled up to the worktable. "Though I for one will be sorry for it."

Olivia could hardly believe she would no longer be welcome in Mrs. Moore's kitchen. Bravely, she sipped her tea and tasted the biscuit. "Delicious!"

Mrs. Moore smiled, but the expression did not quite reach her eyes.

"May I ask," Olivia ventured, "how long ago your sister passed on?"

The woman nodded as though she had expected the question, as though the topic had already been in her thoughts. "Must be eight and twenty years now. Alice was just fourteen."

"Alice? Is she . . . their daughter?"

Mrs. Moore nodded. "They had only the one child. What a dear girl she was, Alice. Never knew the kinder. Called me Aunt Nellie, though everybody else called me plain Nell. I can still hear her sweet voice and feel her arms around my neck. . . ." Mrs. Moore's eyes shone with tears once more, and she dug into her apron pocket for a handkerchief. "Avery was a different man then, I can tell you. What with Maggie to keep him fed and Allie to keep him tender." She smiled tremulously through her tears.

Olivia felt answering tears fill her own eyes. Fearing she already knew the answer, she asked quietly, "What became of Alice?"

Mrs. Moore sniffed and looked down at her hands. "They say she run off with a young man when she were eighteen, but . . ." She glanced up at Olivia, then away. "But between you and me," she whispered, "I know better."

"Have you never heard from her?"

Mrs. Moore shook her head, staring at some unseen point beyond the high windows. "She's with Maggie now, she is. I suppose that is some comfort."

"Poor Mr. Croome," Olivia breathed.

"Poor Mr. Croome, indeed." Mrs. Moore sighed, then straightened. "Well, that is enough of that. What a sorry last hurrah this is! But I will miss you, my girl, upon my soul, I will."

"And I you."

Olivia squeezed her friend's hand—too tightly she realized when the woman grimaced, but she could not help herself. Its impression had to last.

As she left the kitchen, Olivia crossed paths with Johnny Ross outside the servants' hall. His broad shoulders all but blocked the narrow passage, giving her little choice but to pause before him.

He shoved his hands into his pockets and stuck out his chin. "Governess, ey? I suppose that means you'll have no use for the likes o' me. Fancy yourself above me now, I'll wager."

"No, Mr. Ross, I don't—"

"Mr. Ross, is it? And I must call you Miss Keene now, and never more kiss you."

Glancing about and hoping no one was near, she whispered tersely, "Which you ought not to have done at any rate."

"Never said so before."

"I could not speak at the time, if you will recall."

His lip curled. "How high and mighty you've become already. I told the others that was how it would be."

She gaped. "Thank you very little. I prefer you not speak of me at all. What have I done to deserve your cruelty?"

"Me, cruel? It's you what used me ill."

She frowned. "How did I ever?"

"By throwing me over. You're too good for me now."

She shook her head. She had never thought of Johnny as a serious suitor. If she were honest with herself, she had always thought herself a little above him but could not admit such a thing now. He would never believe her rise in station was not what had come between them.

Doris scuttled toward them down the passage, laundry basket on her hip. She said tartly, "Let her be, Johnny. I'll have ya if she won't."

Doris winked at Olivia as she passed by.

Less than a week after Olivia had provided Miss Cresswell's direction, Judith Howe marched past her in the corridor, a letter in hand. "A glowing recommendation, Miss Keene." She waved the letter. "As I was certain it would be. I have wonderful instincts about people." Mrs. Howe headed for the stairs, to share the news with Lord Bradley, she guessed.

Olivia was relieved. She was also curious about Miss Cresswell's letter and wished she might read it herself. Would it contain any clue about what was happening at home?

She decided she would write to Miss Cresswell herself and ask. Now that she had revealed her whereabouts to her, what could it hurt? She wondered if she was still obligated to ask Lord Bradley to approve her letters now that her trial period was over.

While awaiting the reference, Olivia had prepared for her post as best as she could. There were several volumes in the schoolroom for use in instruction as well as books of advice, like: *Hints to Governesses* and *The Plan for the Conduct of Female Education*. The advice she read was often contradictory. Was a governess supposed to focus on making her pupil a "finished" lady, or a knowledgeable one?

Olivia did not wrestle with this issue for long and soon began developing her plans to help Andrew improve his reading, as well as introducing literature, poetry, French, Italian (it was the language of music after all), geography, the sciences, religion, and of course, arithmetic. According to the advice books, she must also teach Audrey plain and ornamental needlework, dancing, and drawing, as well as continuing the girl's lessons on the pianoforte. Later, a music master ought to be brought in, as well as a dancing master.

The list seemed endless. But instead of growing weary at the thought of the overwhelming work ahead of her, Olivia felt more alive and purposeful than ever before. She could hardly believe she would be instructing pupils in the very room where her mother had once taught. She hoped she might be half as good a teacher.

Olivia was both excited and nervous that first morning in the schoolroom. More nervous than she would have been, because Judith Howe joined them, saying she wanted to see how things got on. Audrey sat at attention at the table, hands clasped before her, posture erect. Andrew slumped beside her, eyeing Olivia warily, as if unsure about this new creature who looked a great deal like his under nurse but who now stood so officiously before them, iterating the rules of the schoolroom.

Mrs. Howe said in a loud whisper, "Do sit up straight, Andrew."

Olivia continued with the rules, much as Miss Cresswell had begun every term.

Judith Howe interrupted to say, "I do not allow any physical discipline, Miss Keene—just so we are clear. My own governess was a fiend, and I shall not have Dominick's children subjected to such."

Olivia nodded. She did not condone harsh tactics, but some form of discipline would likely be required, and she feared Mrs. Howe had already done a good deal to undermine her authority.

Rules dispensed with, Olivia decided to begin with the topic with which she was most comfortable. Arithmetic. She began by writing a few simple addition equations on Andrew's slate, and a few somewhat more difficult problems on Audrey's.

Audrey began to figure her answers speedily, but Andrew only sat, chalk still.

Judith walked over and stood beside him. "Andrew, those are so simple! You are not even trying."

"I am, Mamma, I am. You make me nervous. I wish you were not watching me."

Olivia wished it as well.

Andrew furrowed his little brow, his tongue protruding as he pressed the chalk hard on the slate, figuring one answer, then hesitating on the second. Olivia glimpsed Audrey writing a tiny number in the corner of her slate and tapping it lightly to draw his attention to it. No doubt she could have finished her equations already, but instead she was trying to help her brother. Olivia knew she ought to reprimand the girl but did not. She saw what Audrey was doing—trying to help her brother please a critical parent. For though generally kind to the children, Mrs. Howe did reprimand the boy a good deal more than she did Audrey.

Unbidden, Olivia was reminded of herself as a girl—of the time she let that Harrow boy win to spare him humiliation. Tears pricked her eyes, both at the pain of the memory and the pang of affection she felt for Audrey, trying to protect her brother. Olivia determined to do all in her power to fill the gaps in young Andrew's education . . . and in the attention paid him.

Eventually Mrs. Howe became bored and excused herself, telling Olivia with a flourish of her pale hand to "carry on."

When the door closed behind her, Olivia took a deep breath. Audrey and Andrew did the same.

Knowing the children were not used to attending for hours on end, Olivia declared a recess in lessons at two. She would have liked to take the children out of doors, but the weather was very rough—freezing rain *speck-speck*ed against the windowpanes.

So, instead, Olivia instigated a game of puss in the corner and felt her own spirits rise as she attempted to amuse her pupils.

Becky, who now filled the role of under nurse as well as nurserymaid, went downstairs to bring up the dinner tray. Olivia surprised the children by speaking French throughout the meal, encouraging them to repeat the names of simple objects, "*fourchette, poulet, pomme de terre*," and to ask for things to be passed with "*si'l vous plaît*," and "*merci*." Audrey took to the game immediately, but Andrew groused, wanting plain old chicken and potatoes and to eat with his fork and not his *fourchette*.

Olivia did not reprimand him. She understood how difficult it was to exercise one's brain all day when ill-used to doing so. She felt fatigued herself. After dinner, she allowed him to skip rope, while Audrey learned a few new dance steps.

That night, after Becky helped the children into their nightclothes, Olivia went into the sleeping chamber to hear their prayers. Because Audrey and Andrew had spent the day in the schoolroom, with much of that time devoted to reading, Olivia thought they might prefer to skip bedtime reading. Both insisted vociferously that this was not the case. Olivia was heartened that the children wished to continue their bedtime ritual even though she was now their governess. She remembered all too well what they—or at least Andrew—had said about their last governess.

24

> A governess must possess good sense enough not to intrude on domestic privacy. And, she must, of course, not make herself too familiar with the domestic servants.
>
> —Samuel & Sarah Adams, *The Complete Servant*

Before Olivia had a chance to write a letter to Miss Cresswell, she received one herself, which Becky brought upstairs to her at the request of Mr. Hodges. Apparently, Lord Bradley had no wish to review her incoming post. Accepting the letter, Olivia instantly recognized Miss Cresswell's fine decorative script and excused herself from the children to read the letter in private.

Dear Olivia,

I was pleased to write a reference to a Mrs. Judith Howe describing your superior suitability as a governess. I hope it will secure a situation for you that will be mutually beneficial to you and your pupils. I confess I was relieved to hear word of you, my dear, since you left so suddenly. I desponded of losing contact with you as well. Do you know

And there a word—*where*, she believed—was crossed out, quite unlike Miss Cresswell's normally exacting hand. The sentence continued

when you might visit us?

That is odd, Olivia thought. Perfectly polite, but not one mention of her father's fate, nor of her mother, though she and Miss Cresswell were longtime friends. Had Lydia Cresswell no reaction to her mother's leaving? Or had she not left after all? At least if her mother *were* still at home, Miss Cresswell was sure to tell her about the reference request, and her mother would learn of Olivia's whereabouts that way. When would she come?

At all events, Olivia was relieved the letter bore no word of condolence or censure. Surely Miss Cresswell would not write such a brief, polite letter had the worst happened.

Olivia began the afternoon lessons by posing questions from Mangnall's *Historical and Miscellaneous Questions, for the Use of Young People*. Miss Cresswell had used the text a great deal in her classes, and Olivia had been relieved to find a copy on the schoolroom bookshelf.

"Now, Andrew, you will not know these answers yet, but do attend just the same please." She cleared her throat and read, "'Name the significant events of the first century.'"

"I am afraid I don't know either, Miss Keene," Audrey said.

"Very well. Let us consider some of them." But before she could begin, Lord Bradley's deep voice filled the void.

"'The foundation of London by the Romans,'" he began, leaning against the back wall of the schoolroom. "'Rome burnt in the reign of Nero, and the Christians first persecuted by him.'"

Olivia watched him, lips parted.

"'Jerusalem destroyed by Titus, and the New Testament written.'"

"Bravo, my lord," Olivia acknowledged. "High honours for you. You forgot Britain's persecution of the druids, but, still, excellent."

He bowed.

Distracted from her course, and disconcerted by his blue eyes studying her impassively, she returned her gaze to the book and read another. "'Name some celebrated characters of the sixteenth century.'"

"Oh!" Audrey said. "I know. Christopher Columbus and . . . Martin Luther."

"Very good, Audrey."

Lord Bradley did not look as pleased. "But what about reformers Calvin, Melancthon, and Knox. Or the great navigators Bartholomew Gosnold and Sebastian Cabot, for whom Uncle Sebastian was named. And what of the astronomers Tycho Brahe and Copernicus?"

Olivia was beginning to feel piqued. "Well done, my lord, but you are not one of my pupils."

"Indeed I am not, and gratefully so. Might I have a word with you?"

She stared at him, uncertain.

"Alone?" he added.

She swallowed. "Andrew, please write the alphabet, and Audrey, as many first-century events as you can remember."

She followed Lord Bradley into the nursery, but Nurse Peale was snoring softly in her rocking chair, so he led the way out to the corridor instead.

"Miss Keene, are you trying to educate my young cousins or bore them to death?"

She gasped. "What do you mean?"

"*Mangnall's Questions*? That is nothing but rote memory. You've got to teach them to *think*, Miss Keene, to develop their logic and discernment."

"I plan to do that as well, my lord, but certain facts are essential and lay a foundation for future learning of politics, history . . . And Audrey is at a perfect age for memorizing facts. She is like a sponge."

"And Andrew like a dried bone."

"He is young, I admit, but I do give him other assignments that are more suited to his age."

"I should hope so. A boy of his energies cannot sit all day listening to you and his sister rattle off fact after fact about dead men and advanced concepts that are so much Latin to him."

"I understand your concerns. And, speaking of Latin, you will wish to engage a tutor for him soon. I do not claim to be an expert. Perhaps Mr. Tugwell?"

"Andrew is a bit young yet, do you not think?"

"Not if Mrs. Howe plans to have him educated at Harrow or Eton or the like."

"I do not believe she has any definite plans as yet, Miss Keene. I rely on you to educate him yourself, to the best of your ability. For now."

"I shall do my best, my lord, with what I have."

He studied her. "What is it you lack?"

"Texts suited to his age, a blackboard for geography . . ."

"A blackboard?"

"A wall-mounted slate. The invention of a Scots headmaster, I understand. Though I imagine large pieces of slate must be in short supply."

His mouth lifted sardonically. "Anything else?"

"A bit of patience on your part would be most welcome, I assure you."

"That too is in short supply." He gave her a long look, then turned on his heel, nearly colliding with Felix as he came up the corridor. She had not known he was again visiting for the weekend. Lord Bradley passed him without a word.

Felix watched him go, brows high, then turned to look at her. "He must think highly of you, Miss Keene, or he wouldn't push you so."

So Felix had heard Lord Bradley's reproof. She doubted his interpretation.

"It is true," Felix insisted. "My sister says you are an excellent teacher and very clever. Yes, I believe those were her words. Edward must see your potential and that is why he pushes you." He added good-naturedly, "And why he basically ignores me."

This caught her interest. "Does he?"

"Oh, do not mistake me. He is good to me. Just never satisfied. He is a dreadful perfectionist, as you must have realized by now. I have tried to dislike him but cannot quite stick to it. I should be terribly envious of him, and I suppose I am in some ways. . . . But I feel sorry for him at the same time. He has never really fit in, nor seemed happy. Not at Harrow, not at Oxford, not in London. Do you ever see him laugh?"

Olivia thought. "Sometimes, I think . . . with the children."

"If so, then it is only with them. At all events, when that green bug bites me, I say, Felix, which would you rather be? Unhappy heir to an earldom, or a jolly untitled man with decent means and an endless stack of invitations?"

Olivia smiled at him, touched by the vulnerability in his eyes.

"Ahh, Miss Keene. What a gem you are, listening to me prattle on. You know it is quite unusual for a man to take a governess into his confidence. Into his bed, yes, but not into his confidence. Not that you wouldn't be welcome in my bed—that is if you wanted to, which of course you don't. Do you?"

Olivia shook her head firmly, embarrassed. But she could not bring herself to be too angry at a suggestion so humbly presented.

"Ah well, never hurts to ask, as they say." He extracted a cigar from his coat pocket. "Now, you must excuse me. This cigar is demanding to be smoked, but my sister forbids me to do so indoors." He turned, then paused to add, "It has been a pleasure as always, Miss Keene, though I fear I dominated the conversation just as abominably as I did when you were mute."

The next morning, Edward gestured Miss Keene into his study and closed the door behind her. He began quietly, "Miss Keene, do be careful about my cousin."

"Mrs. Howe?"

He frowned. "I meant Felix. I have noticed the way the two of you . . . talk . . . together."

She lifted her chin. "I am allowed to talk now, am I not?"

He pursed his lips. "Yes, and you have obviously made quite an impression on him, but . . ." He took a step closer and lowered his voice. "Take no offense, Miss Keene, but you are not the first governess he has . . . shown interest in."

She lifted her stubborn chin. "Never fear, I did not flatter myself that I was. At all events, he seems a pleasant enough young man." She hesitated. "Most of the time. You might treat him more kindly."

"Kindly? Felix and I get on perfectly well."

"He thinks you disapprove of him."

"Disapprove of him?" Edward frowned. "He told you that?"

She nodded. "Though I ought not to have broken his confidence."

Edward admitted, "Some of his habits and manners are not to my liking. But I don't disapprove of him as a person."

When she didn't respond, he looked up and found her regarding him thoughtfully. "What?"

"Are you unhappy?"

Edward felt irritation surge. "Why would you ask that? Did Felix suggest it?"

She shrugged.

Edward detested the thought of Felix and Miss Keene discussing his character. And finding it lacking. "I may be a bit dour of late, what with . . . everything."

"But even before . . . everything . . . were you really happy?"

He thought for a moment and felt a wave of pain threaten to spill into consciousness. He pushed it away. "What an odd question, Miss Keene. And quite inappropriate, do you not think?"

He realized he was doing it again, referring to her status to put her in her place, to stop her provoking questions. He saw the quick look of hurt replaced by sparks of anger and, yes, disappointment in her eyes. She didn't say "hypocrite," but he heard it anyway and could not argue.

At the end of her first week as governess, Olivia made her way belowstairs in hopes of seeing Mrs. Moore, even though she knew she ought not do so. Doris and the hall boy stood in the passage, and Olivia heard the pleasant chatter of teasing voices and girlish giggles. Approaching them, Olivia saw kitchen maids Sukey and Edith in the stillroom, and realized the four of them were together enjoying a respite from their work.

"Careful, girls, there's a lady among us," Edith warned.

"Oh, shut up, Edie," Doris said. "She's only doing what any of us would do, given the chance."

"Wouldn't see me with my nose in the air, no matter."

Not knowing what else to do, Olivia walked past without a word.

"If she is standoffish, I don't blame her," Doris hissed. "She don't make the rules. How would you have liked it if that last governess, that sour-faced Miss Dowdle, had tried to join in with the lot of us belowstairs?"

"Not at all, but she was a regular governess. A right snob."

Dory's attempted whisper followed Olivia down the passage. "But Miss Livie is one too now. A governess, I mean, not a snob. And it isn't done, is it? She cannot have it both ways."

Though thankful for Dory's championing of her character, Olivia was relieved to enter the sanctuary of the kitchen.

There Mrs. Moore looked up from her receipt book and straightened. "Liv—Miss Keene. I am surprised to see you."

Olivia sighed. "I was afraid you would not be happy to see me. No one is, it seems."

"Now, now, love. No need to play the martyr. I am happy enough to see you, but governesses usually don't venture belowstairs."

"But I am not a usual governess, am I?"

"Certainly not. Never knew one so clever nor so kind." Mrs. Moore's eyes twinkled.

Olivia smiled. "Would you mind if I sat with you for a few minutes?"

Mrs. Moore patted the stool beside her. "A lonely life, is it? With only the young ones and Nurse Peale about."

Olivia nodded. "Nurse Peale isn't much for talking. When she does, she mostly repeats remembrances of the past. Tales of Lord Bradley from his nursery days."

"Not diverting?"

"A little. But not the same as talking with you." She squeezed the dear woman's plump hand.

Mrs. Moore winked. "What you won't say to get one of my lemon biscuits."

On her way back upstairs, Olivia walked directly into the path of Judith Howe. The woman looked from the door through which Olivia had just emerged to Olivia's no-doubt-telling red face.

"Miss Keene. I know you were one of the servants for a brief time, but I had hoped the experience had not affected you to a marked degree. I realize you have never been a governess before, so allow me to enlighten you on the proprieties. . . ."

Olivia swallowed as she listened, realizing she had paid her last visit to dear Mrs. Moore.

25

> The lower lake is now all alive with skaters, and by ladies driven onward by them in their ice-cars. Mercury, surely, was the first maker of skates. . . .
>
> —S.T. Coleridge, *The Friend,* 1809

One afternoon in February, Edward stepped into the schoolroom only to find Miss Keene and the children about to step out, bundled in coats, caps, mufflers, and gloves.

"Where are you all bound for?"

"We are going ice-skating," Audrey said. "Do come along!"

"Ice-skating? I have not strapped on skates in years."

Andrew tugged his hand. "Come along, Cousin Edward, do."

"I haven't the foggiest notion where my old skates might be."

Miss Keene pulled the largest blades from the trunk with a flourish and held them before him.

"How . . . fortunate," he grumbled.

A few minutes later, cocooned in his beaver hat, coat, and gloves, much like the children, Edward led the way as the small troupe tromped through the snow into the village, then along a well-trod path to the mill. He explained that the miller diverted water from the mill leat every year to fill a skating pond behind the mill.

"Very obliging of him," Miss Keene said.

Edward considered this. "I suppose it is. I have never thought of it before."

Using an old millstone as a makeshift bench, Miss Keene helped Audrey strap skates to her half boots while Edward assisted Andrew with the same.

"Wait for me, Andrew, and I shall come out and help you," Miss Keene called, tightening Audrey's final strap.

Edward eyed the blades still lying on the millstone. "Are you not skating, Miss Keene?"

"Oh no, my lord. I don't think it would be proper. I only brought that pair in case one of you tore a strap." She glanced around at the few skaters on the pond. "Besides, I shall be more surefooted in my boots, and more able to lend a steadying hand."

"Not fair of you at all," he said in mock sternness. "Insist I come, then sit out yourself? Come, now. What may not be proper in London or in your prim girls' school is perfectly proper here."

"I . . . Oh, very well. I shall give it a go."

"That is more like it."

She strapped on her skates before he finished his own, and hurried onto the ice to assist Audrey, who was flailing her thin arms and appeared about to fall. Andrew was busy chop-chopping the ice as he marched along, not falling, but not really skating either.

"Glide, Andrew, glide!" she called.

Edward skated to Andrew's side and held his mittened hand. Miss Keene took Audrey's arm and attempted to steady her while quietly instructing her on proper technique. Suddenly the girl's arms flailed again—her feet flew out before her and she fell back, taking Miss Keene down with her. They both slammed hard against the ice. Edward gave an empathetic wince and skated quickly over, leaving Andrew to his own devices. He crouched over their prone forms. "Are you all right?"

"Mortified and sore, nothing more," Miss Keene quipped, sitting up.

"I am sorry, miss," Audrey said, scrambling to her feet and wearing a pained expression.

"Never mind, Audrey. You shall master it by and by."

Edward offered Miss Keene his hand and, when she took it, gave a hard tug to pull her to her feet. The lurch propelled him backward, causing him to lose his balance and fall back. And as Miss Keene's hand was still captured in his, he pulled her forward with him before he could think to release her. He hit the ice first, and Miss Keene fell onto his chest, knocking the air from his lungs.

Edward opened his eyes, squinting at the blinding sunlight reflecting off snow, and at the disconcerting experience of having the governess draped over his body. If he could but breathe, he thought, the sensation would not be unpleasant in the least. Her blue eyes, wide with shock, met his. For a moment, they simply stared at one another.

Then Audrey giggled and Andrew laughed out loud, breaking the spell that held them. Miss Keene's face blushed deep pink and she averted her gaze, quickly pushing herself up and finding her feet with less than her usual grace.

Andrew, oblivious to their discomfort, continued to laugh.

"It is not kind to laugh at the misfortunes of others," Edward grumbled, pinning Andrew with a look of mock severity, which only sent his young cousin into a convulsion of guffaws.

A quarter of an hour later, Lord Bradley skated beside her. "I see you fooled us all by falling at the outset. You are quite graceful on the ice, Miss Keene."

"Thank you, my lord." Olivia had not skated since girlhood, and could still hear Miss Cresswell saying that in her day *ladies* did not participate in such sport. Pushed in an ice-car, perhaps, but skating . . . ?

The Tugwell boys arrived, waving and calling greetings. They invited Andrew to join them in a game which involved hitting a ball about the ice with brooms and sticks.

Audrey sat on a millstone beside George Linton's niece, who was near her own age, and soon the bonneted heads were close in confidences and chatter.

The children pleasantly occupied, Lord Bradley and Olivia continued to skate. She relished the gliding freedom, the crisp air, and the rare moment of no demands upon her person.

"I am glad to see you enjoying yourself, Miss Keene," he said.

She smiled up at him.

"Are we paying you for this?" he teased.

"Very little."

"Ah. Good."

"And you, my lord. Are you enjoying yourself?" she asked.

"I believe I am. The experience has become somewhat infrequent of late, but yes, I believe I recognize this emotion as enjoyment."

She shook her head and laughed. "Take no offense, my lord, but what else have you to do but enjoy yourself?"

He grimaced.

Realizing that she had annoyed him, she quickly changed the subject. "You are very involved with the children, more so than many *fathers* are, and they so enjoy your attention, but—"

"But it appears strange to you?"

"I am only curious, not criticizing in the least."

He nodded. "Their father was a good friend, as I mentioned, older though he was. A mentor, of sorts."

"You feel an . . . obligation, then?"

He lifted his shoulders as if to shrug off an uncomfortable garment. "Not directly, no. Though how can one help but feel some duty toward children who have lost both father and mother?"

"I think many 'help it' with ease. Look at the foundling homes."

He sighed. "You will think me stranger than you no doubt already do."

"Impossible," she teased.

He looked at her, as though to be sure she was jesting. "Well, nothing to lose, then. You see, when I was a boy of eleven, I made a promise to myself. Wrote it down even."

When he hesitated, she looked up expectantly.

"I know you admire my father, Miss Keene, and I do not deny he has always been exceedingly kind and generous. He is a good man, and I take nothing from him—do not mistake me."

"But?" She skated to the edge of the pond and stopped to give him her full attention.

He stopped beside her. "But he was away in London a great deal. As a member of parliament, he was obliged to spend January through June or even July there. Six or seven months a year. Sometimes longer. My mother and I did spend several seasons in London with him—it was there I first made the acquaintance of Dominick Howe—but still, we rarely saw Father. Even when he was in the townhouse with us, he was always busy with bills or correspondence or what have you. Mother soon grew weary of town life. I think her health was not very good even then. So we stayed home more and more. And even when Father returned to Brightwell Court, he spent more time with his clerk than with me." He held up his hand. "I am not criticizing, nor seeking pity, Miss Keene, merely showing the situation that inspired me to write a promise to my future adult self."

She nodded, and could not help compare his father to hers. He had spent many hours with her, though few of them idyllic—testing her in arithmetic, showing her how to balance the books, how to figure odds, and all those hours at the races and the Crown and Crow. . . .

"I can still see myself, a boy of nine, perhaps," Lord Bradley continued, "then a boy of ten, then finally eleven, standing with my fishing pole, waiting at the garden door for my father, who had promised yet again to take me fishing—'tomorrow,' 'tomorrow.'"

"He never did?"

Edward shook his head. "Hunting a few times, a game of chess now and again, but never fishing. I remember Croome came upon me waiting there, pole in hand, when my father finally came out—but only to tell me that he just could not get away. Croome offered to take me. But my father dismissed his offer. I remember feeling oddly sorry for the gamekeeper, though I had never felt anything but fear of the man before"—he grimaced—"or since."

Poor Mr. Croome, Olivia thought. An outcast even then.

"Forgive me. I am going on as endlessly as Mr. Tugwell. All this to say, after that I ran upstairs to the schoolroom, found paper and quill, and wrote myself a promise—to remember what it was like to be eleven years old, to remember what summertime was for, and when I had a boy of my own, to dashed well take him fishing." He glanced at her sheepishly. "I may have said something stronger, but you take my meaning."

She grinned. "Vividly."

"I know Audrey and Andrew are not my children, but they are under my roof without a father of their own."

"I think it wonderful," she said, and began skating again.

He skated after her. "Not every woman of my acquaintance would agree with you."

She guessed he referred to Miss Harrington.

"Have you?" she asked.

"Hmm?"

"Taken them fishing?"

He expelled a breath bordering on a groan. "Everything but that. I confess I never learnt how." Clearly uncomfortable, he quickly changed the subject. "And your father, Miss Keene? Did he take you fishing, or whatever the girlhood equivalent is?"

Olivia doubted horse races and taverns were the girlhood equivalent to anything as wholesome as fishing. "I had not really realized it until you described your own childhood, that while my father has many faults, he did spend time with me. Still, my father was . . ." She caught herself. "Is very different from yours. Were I you, I would be grateful indeed for such a father as Lord Brightwell."

"I am. But do not idealize him. You know him as he is now, the benevolent grandfatherly sort he has mellowed into."

"Are you saying he was once cruel?"

"No, never cruel. Just . . . imperious, busy, absent. And yours?"

She decided to risk telling him, realizing he might otherwise think she disapproved of her father for no very good reason. "He took me with him to the local public house and there had me display my arithmetic skills to entertain the other patrons."

"He was evidently proud of you. Wanted all the gents to know what a clever girl he had."

She bit her lip. That much was true.

"He also took me with him to horse races. Even to the Bibury Course, not far from here, I understand."

"Did he indeed? As a boy, I would have loved such an outing with my father above all things."

He was turning everything around on her. Confusing her. "He brought his clerking work home and had *me* balance the accounts for him. . . ."

"Astounding! Do you realize how rare a thing it is for a man to educate his daughter in his own profession? A son, yes. My father has groomed me to take over for him one day, so this is something our fathers have in common."

She felt her ire and incredulity rising. "Did the *Earl of Brightwell* teach you to accept wagers and take a handsome portion of men's winnings? Did he drink too much and throw things when angry?" She stopped herself. Did he not understand what kind of man Simon Keene was?

"No. That he did not do. Though he did take me to gentlemen's clubs in London where I was exposed to much the same."

Andrew skated between them, grasping a hand of each, and the conversation was abandoned.

Later, on the walk home, the children ran ahead, tossing snowballs at one another. Though Olivia had never told anyone the story of that most significant of wagers in the Crown and Crow, she felt compelled to do so now. Compelled to have another person judge the situation more objectively than she ever could. Had she really wronged her father? Or had he treated her unfairly? Lord Bradley listened with interest as she relayed the tale, doing her best to tell him the facts without coloring the story to put herself in better light, nor her father in worse. But Lord Bradley did not react as she might have guessed, or would have liked.

"The young man was a Harrow lad, you say?"

She shrugged. "Herbert something."

His eyes brightened. "Herbert? Herbert Fitzpatrick?"

"I never heard a surname. Nor his father's name at all." The name Fitzpatrick did seem mildly familiar, though she did not know why.

"I'd wager it was my old school chum Herbert." He laughed. "Boy never could conquer arithmetic. Pale boy. The blackest hair. How he would perspire during examinations! We teased him mercilessly."

"I cannot credit it. From London, was he?"

"You know, I just saw his father in church on Christmas. Visiting a sister or some such."

That was the man she had seen from the church gallery at Christmas?—the man she thought familiar but could not place?

"He lives in Cheltenham, I believe. But he mentioned Herbert is managing one of his interests in the north somewhere."

Olivia frowned, thinking back to what she remembered of the gentleman and his son. "I am not certain it can be the same Herbert. I distinctly remember they were merely passing through on their way home to Harrow and London."

"If memory serves, they moved to the Cheltenham area a year or two ago."

She did not respond to this, and after several minutes of silence, he said quietly, "It was not fair of your father to put you in such a position, Miss Keene. But do you not see what confidence he had in you? What pride? But he ought to have realized what you were about in allowing poor Herbert to win and been proud of you for that as well. It was very noble of you, especially for one so young."

"He was not in the least proud."

Lord Bradley looked at her, eyes soft in understanding. "I see that you did not have a typical upbringing, nor a typical father, Miss Keene. But as you have caused me to appreciate my father's qualities anew, I hope you will allow yourself to admit that your father has his good qualities as well."

"I don't want to admit it."

He looked at her, surprised. "Why? What do you risk in doing so?"

"More than you know." For if she admitted the good along with the bad, then how could she live with herself, knowing what she had done to him?

She did not tell him the most condemning charge against her father—what he had done, or at least tried to do, to her mother. She was too ashamed to form the words.

26

> Rebuked and saddened, I resigned myself with no good grace to my routine of instruction. Where were all the romantic fancies and proud anticipations with which I had accepted the position of governess . . . ?
>
> —Anna Leonowens, *The English Governess at the Siamese Court*

All that night, Miss Keene's words echoed over and over again in Edward's mind. "*What else have you to do but enjoy yourself?*"

The question goaded more than it should have.

Edward regarded himself in the looking glass above his washbasin. The face he always saw stared back at him, his fair hair darkening to a bronze in the long side whiskers, golden stubble glinting on his cheeks in the candlelight. His blond brows, a shade lighter than his hair. The pale blue eyes, so prevalent in the Bradley family, which he supposed was an ironic gift of fate. The nose, with the slight angle at its tip—a "gift" from Felix when they were boys and his cousin had rammed a sled right into his face. The snow had turned as bright red as cherry ice.

Edward had always assumed his looks came from his father. People had even commented on how Edward favoured Lord Brightwell—in looks, if not in character or temperament. His father had always been sanguine—an easy-going man who did not demand perfection in himself or others. He was at his ease in company, smiled often, and everybody liked him.

Edward, however, was not easily given to smiles. His neutral expression was intense, he knew, always seeming to waver on displeasure or disapproval. Why, he could not say. As Miss Keene had remarked so flippantly, what had he to do but enjoy life? At least until recently, he'd had no real reason not to smile throughout his days of blessing and ease. Yet, he had not. It was as if every minute he had been waiting for the fairy tale to end, for someone to disappoint him, to take it all away and destroy the grand illusion. But no, he could not factor recent revelations into a character formed over four and twenty years when he'd had not one inkling that he wasn't his father's boy. His mother's son.

His mother had known, however, and Edward found himself wondering if her awareness of his low birth had colored her perception, made her suspect his behavior and abilities were not all they should be. If she had sometimes been critical—*surely he might be further along in Latin,* and *what did he mean he had no ear for the Italian?* How his laugh *grated on her nerves* and his *table manners were low indeed.* Might not any mother have the same irritations with a son—boys being what they were, especially when young? Still, he knew she had loved him in her way. And he had loved her. Tears pricked his eyes at the thought. He would always miss her.

Perhaps he was more like his mother in temperament. More critical of others, never satisfied with his own performance. After all, he had spent more time in her company than in his father's, who was occupied with parliament so much of the year.

Parliament. Edward had known from boyhood that he would take his father's seat one day. He thought he might be good at lawmaking, since he tended to see things in black and white. Right or wrong. Good or bad. A person of quality or not. Educated or uneducated. Master or servant. But now . . . ? What sort of person was he?

If his secret was exposed, what then of his career in parliament, his marriage to Miss Harrington, his future as an earl? It was all at risk now. And if it all disappeared tomorrow . . . ? What then? What would he do with his life?

Olivia sat at the library table on Sunday afternoon, playing chess with Lord Brightwell. Winter sun spilled in through the library window through which she had first laid eyes on the earl and his wife. How long ago that seemed. Dust motes floated on the shaft of sunlight, which illuminated the ornate pieces and inlaid chessboard of the rosewood table. The earl seemed preoccupied, whether with his next move or something of greater import she did not know.

Lifting his queen, Lord Brightwell began, "Olivia, I must tell you something about your mother."

Olivia dropped her chess piece. "You have news of my mother?"

He nodded gravely. "I sent a man to search for her when you were ill. I thought she would want to know."

"A search?"

"You had been quite vague in your direction, if you will recall, something about 'near Cheltenham.'"

Olivia blushed.

"I am afraid he returned unsuccessful. When you finally named your village—for the school reference—I sent Talbot once again on horseback. Winter roads being what they are, he would never have made it in a carriage. As it was, he barely got through. In Withington, he located the constable, who was able to direct him to the home of Simon and Dorothea Keene."

Olivia nodded. "The cottage with the green door, just past the cobblers and beside the churchyard."

"Not any longer," he said quietly.

Olivia started to say Talbot must have missed it. It was a small cottage after all, but something in the earl's eyes stilled her tongue.

"He found the house, my dear, but no one was there."

Olivia swallowed, her mind working. "My father . . . was perhaps away at his work, and my mother gone. . . ."

"My dear, I do not mean that no one was home at that moment. I mean that no one had lived there for some time. The place was deserted. A neighbor confirmed it."

Olivia flinched. Was it as she feared, her mother gone and her father dead? But if her mother had left, why had she not gone to the school in St. Aldwyns and been directed to Brightwell Court? Or learnt her whereabouts from Miss Cresswell and come directly to find her?

Lord Brightwell scooted his chair closer to hers and held her hands in his. "Talbot spoke with several neighbors. While no one claimed personal knowledge, the rumor is that Simon Keene has fled the village to avoid arrest, and that your mother . . ."

Father is alive. I did not kill him. Her brain barely had time to register relief at this confirmation before a new fear swept in to take its place. "Yes?" she urged.

"There is a new grave in the churchyard, Olivia. I am deeply sorry to have to tell you that Dorothea Keene is believed dead."

Olivia stared with unseeing eyes. Her heart felt as if it had burst within her, and throbbed with the pain of it. Had her father lived only to end her mother's life?

"The constable would neither confirm nor deny anything. He told Talbot if he wanted to know who was buried in the churchyard, he would have to ask the church warden. That man referred him to the local midwife. A Miss . . ."

"Miss Atkins."

"That was it. But she would tell Talbot little. Seemed very suspicious of him and said she was under no compulsion to tell a stranger anything. When Talbot asked if she knew where Dorothea Keene was, the only answer she made was, 'She won't be coming back.'"

"I don't understand," Olivia said, voice trembling. "There must be some mistake. Miss Atkins would tell me everything. I know she would." Olivia leapt to her feet. "I shall have to go home."

His expression deeply apologetic, the earl said, "My dear, the roads are quite impassable at present after the recent snows. You shall have to wait for a thaw."

She bit her lip and blinked back tears. "At the first opportunity, then." She strode to the door, then forced herself to turn back, adding woodenly, "Thank you for telling me."

Edward found Miss Keene a short while later, sitting on the fallen log beside the river, crying into her hands. Scooping aside the wet snow, he sat down next to her on the log.

She looked up with red-rimmed eyes. "Did Lord Brightwell send you to find me? I am sorry to have troubled you."

"He did not send me, Miss Keene," Edward said gently. "But he is concerned about you. As am I."

She drew in a shaky breath. "I thank you, but I shall be well presently."

He tilted his head to regard her more closely. "Good. But I should like to stay with you, if I may."

"Have wild dogs been seen again?"

"No."

She nodded, tears trailing down her cheeks. Edward longed to touch her face, to wipe the tears from her eyes. But she turned away from him toward the river.

He said, "Lord Brightwell briefly described to me what Talbot learnt, and the rumors of your father's hand in your mother's disappearance. If true, how I regret defending him that day on the ice." Edward hesitated. "Do you . . . think such a thing possible?"

She inhaled. "A year ago I would not have believed it. But now . . . yes, it is possible, though I pray I am wrong."

He lifted her cold hand and placed it onto his palm. She had neglected to wear gloves. When she didn't stiffen, he began to softly stroke her knuckles with his free hand.

"I know," he murmured. "I know."

"Yes," she whispered, "you must know. You have lost two mothers yourself."

For the first time, he allowed himself to acknowledge that truth. "Yes, I suppose I have."

They sat in silence for a long moment.

Edward hesitated. "I am sorry I kept you here. Kept you from returning home."

She shook her head. "I could not have gone home then in any case. And now . . . if what Talbot discovered is true . . . there is nothing to go home for."

He didn't know how to respond. Simply held her hand.

After a moment she said, "Mr. Tugwell once told me he was praying that God would work 'all things work together for good.' But I do not see how that can be so now."

Nor I, Edward thought, but forbore to say so.

27

> I sit alone in the evening, in the schoolroom.
> Really I should be very glad of some society,
> it would be such an enjoyment.
>
> —Miss Ellen Weeton,
> *Journal of a Governess* 1811–1825

Tamping down her sadness, Olivia did her best to keep to a schedule, knowing children thrived under order and regularity. Bedtime promptly at eight was the rule, although Mrs. Howe often disturbed their routine, coming in after the wicks were extinguished to kiss Alexander "just once more."

While she was there, she would bid Audrey and Andrew "good night" or "sweet dreams," and how they, the boy, especially, would beam up at her. Now and then Judith would stop by his bed and lay her hand on Andrew's head, much as Lord Bradley often did, and ruffle his hair. The look of pleasure on the boy's face always pricked Olivia's heart. Did the woman not see the power she held to wield joy or pain?

Seeing how much these nighttime visits delighted her charges, Olivia did not think to complain about them, even had she dared.

And so they passed the next few weeks of winter in relative peace and tranquility, Olivia's uncertainty over her mother's fate wavering from grief to hope and back again. She kept busy, finding new and more active ways to teach Andrew, while Audrey continued to advance in her studies by the methods that had proved so effective at Miss Cresswell's.

Still, Olivia had never spent so much time alone in her life. When the children ate suppers with the family, and each evening after they were in their beds, Olivia spent time alone in the schoolroom, since it was larger and warmer than her room, and more private than the nursery, which was clearly Nurse Peale's domain. There, she read or sewed by candlelight. She thought back to the fine needlework her mother had done for Mrs. Meacham, the wife of her father's former employer, and more recently, for the wife of his new employer as well. Olivia had not such fine skills with the needle, nor such patience for the craft, but she could repair hems and darn socks, and that passed the time better than nothing.

She remembered with fondness the small cushions and bedclothes she had fashioned for the doll's house Lord Bradley had made. How she had enjoyed working on that clandestine project with him.

Lord Brightwell had extended an open invitation for her to sit with him in the library of an evening, but this she did but rarely, loath as she was to cause gossip among the servants.

In bed at night, the doubts would come, torturing her with endless scenarios of what might have happened after she left home. Feeding her worries over her mother's fate . . . and her own. And where was her father? A part of her longed for the roads to clear quickly, while another part dreaded the confirmation of her worst fears.

In the meantime, she arose each morning eager to return to the schoolroom, to lose herself and her worries to teaching once more. She even began teaching Becky to read and write whenever the maid's heavy workload allowed. She took great satisfaction from this. She thought Nurse Peale, who sometimes hovered nearby to watch when Becky bent her head over her slate or a simple book, would complain. But she did not.

On a day in early March, Olivia was listening to Becky read aloud from one of Andrew's books, helping her whenever she stumbled over a word. The two women froze when Lord Bradley strode into the nursery without knocking. He drew up short at seeing the two of them huddled together near the hearth, a candle lamp between them, for the evening was dark and rainy.

"A new pupil, Miss Keene?" he asked, and she could not tell if he was angry or simply curious.

She rose. "Yes, my lord. Becky is coming along nicely with her reading. But we only have lessons when Becky's duties are done, and Andrew and Audrey are with you or their stepmother."

"Where are they now? I have just returned from Northleach and can find no one about the place."

"Mrs. Howe took the children to visit their grandmother Howe."

"Dominick's mother? Good. And my father?"

"I am afraid I do not know."

"Well, the roads are finally becoming passable. Perhaps he has gone on some long-neglected errand or some such."

Olivia thought of the promised trip to Withington, once the roads had cleared. Surely he had not gone without her.

"Would you join me in the study, Miss Keene? When you are through here, of course."

"Certainly, my lord."

Becky looked at her apologetically, as though it was her fault Olivia was about to be reprimanded. She smiled at the girl, hoping to reassure her.

When Olivia stepped through the open study door a few minutes later, Lord Bradley rose from his chair near the fire.

"Please, be seated."

If she were about to be called to account, she would rather stand. "Do you not approve of my teaching Becky? As I said, I only do so when the both of us are—"

He lifted a hand to silence her. "I do not disapprove, Miss Keene. That would be rather hypocritical of me, would it not? But do be warned that Mrs. Howe might not be as liberal minded as I have recently become."

"Very well."

"Please sit down," he repeated. "I would ring for tea, but well, I think . . ."

She sat in the facing chair. "No, thank you, my lord. Nothing for me." She understood perfectly that a servant bringing tea to the young lord and the governess would set tongues to wagging in a hurry.

He sat down again as well. "I am curious, Miss Keene. I would think after teaching all day, taking on another pupil would be the last thing you would want to do."

She chuckled. "I believe it is the other way round. Becky is so exhausted by day's end, she can barely keep her eyes open to read."

He leaned back, steepling his fingers. "Do you really enjoy it so much?"

Olivia shrugged. "I know it may sound strange. But I believe God made me to teach, or at least gave me abilities that lend themselves to the calling. I have wanted to be a teacher—like my mother before me—since I was a little girl."

Tears pricked her eyes, and she quickly changed the subject. "What was it you wanted to be as a boy?" She studied his face as though the answer might be written there.

He looked away, uncomfortable. "Be? I wanted to be who I *thought* I was."

"Do, then. What did you want to do?"

It was his turn to shrug. "Gentlemen are not expected to work at much of anything. I was not born with a burning desire to accomplish something great *soli deo gloria*, like Bach or Beethoven, Rembrandt or Copernicus." He paused, thinking. "I did look forward to being Earl of Brightwell someday—peer of the realm, member of parliament, and all that—though *why* I looked forward to it, I could not say. I suppose because it was what I always expected to do."

He repositioned himself on the chair. "May I ask. Before you came here, what were your plans? Were you really going to teach at that little school in St. Aldwyns?"

"I hoped to."

"That was the dream I have kept you from?"

"No, my lord. A stepping-stone at best."

He looked at her expectantly.

"You will laugh."

"I will not."

"Very well. My dream is to have a school of my own one day. Ideally, with my mother as partner, though I have always known it was unlikely my father would allow her to do so. And now . . ." She clasped and unclasped her hands, taking a deep breath to steady herself. "But even on my own, I believe I could be mistress of a school one day. And I would love nothing more than to open its doors to all girls, regardless of their ability to pay."

One corner of his mouth lifted. "Only girls?"

"There are many more schools for boys, and as someone has so kindly pointed out to me, teaching boys is not my forte."

"I am sorry I said that."

"You were quite correct. At the time. But I believe Andrew is getting on famously these days."

"I believe you are right. What would we have done without you, I wonder."

She felt her cheeks heat. She had not meant to praise her own abilities. "No doubt some other governess would be performing as well, if not better. Never fear, I do not think myself irreplaceable."

He looked at her intently. "Oh, but there are those who would argue that."

She did not ask if he were among them.

Once Miss Keene had taken her leave, Edward resumed his seat by the fire, staring at the orange embers and the occasional flame that tongued to life. What he had said to Miss Keene was true enough. He felt no burning desire to do anything specific. Yes, he would have enjoyed the prestige and privilege of being lord of the manor—the running of the estate, investing in the property, and seeing the rewards of careful management. But even then, he would actually *do* very little. A clerk and perhaps a new steward would manage the daily affairs, while his tenants, workmen, and servants accomplished the actual work.

He did not enjoy managing people, and tensed whenever Mrs. Hinkley or Walters brought to him some concern with a servant or tenant. He did not mind hearing the problem, nor offering solutions, but was uncomfortable with tears and excuses.

He took well to his new role as village magistrate, which had seemed good practice for his service in the House of Lords yet to come. He had also enjoyed reading law at Oxford, though as a gentleman and future earl, he had never considered taking up the law as a profession—nor any profession for that matter. But now?

Miss Keene had said that she knew she wanted to be a teacher like her mother since she was a little girl. Charles Tugwell, a clergyman like his father before him. Was it not natural that he had planned to follow in his father's footsteps as well?

The only actual work he had enjoyed as a boy was building things with Mr. Matthews. The old steward had not been keen on accounts, but could repair a carriage wheel or a window casing with equal aplomb. He had often given Edward and young Felix scraps of wood, bent nails, and wooden mallets and had let them build whatever they willed. Felix had turned out boards with bent nails. Edward, a bench which stood in the stable yard to this day and a humble three-tiered bookcase, which had graced his bedchamber for several years, then disappeared while he was away at school. Become so much kindling, no doubt.

Mr. Matthews had built with stone or wood. From a drawn plan or from a scheme in his mind. And Edward had found great satisfaction in assisting him, especially during those long months his father was away.

But Edward had only helped, and boasted few real skills to speak of. He had given it all up as a young man. Carpentry and building had no place at Oxford. Architecture, perhaps. But he had no lofty dreams of building cathedrals or palaces. And he could not go into trade—building benches, bookshelves, and doll's houses—could he? How his supposed friends, even the villagers and his tenants, would scoff at the thought of Edward Stanton Bradley in such a humble profession.

Were other men so directionless? Of his peers, decidedly so. But, he reminded himself, they were his peers no longer.

28

In every town you go through, you may see written in letters of gold, "A Boarding-school for Young Ladies."

—Clara Reeve, 1792

The roads were slippery, muddy, and full of deep ruts. Olivia gripped the strap above the seat and hung on tightly as the carriage jerked and swayed. She had thought Lord Brightwell had been exaggerating the road conditions in order to put off this trip, to delay the inevitable disappointment he felt sure Olivia would suffer. Now she was suffering indeed on the tooth-jarring, stomach-churning journey, which seemed far longer than the sixteen miles it was. When Talbot stopped to water the horses, Johnny Ross let down the step so she and the earl might stretch their legs. Looking away from Johnny's cold glance, Olivia noted with dismay the mud-splattered coach and horses.

On their way once more, Olivia watched from the window as they passed through villages which became increasingly familiar with each mile. Fossebridge, Chedworth, and finally the outskirts of Withington itself, a grey-stone village on the river, sitting high on the Cotswold uplands. The closer they came, the closer her heartbeats seemed to sound until they were almost one atop the other in an erratic drumbeat. Beside her, Lord Brightwell squeezed her gloved hand.

When the carriage halted, Johnny once again lowered the step, opened the door, and gave her a hand down. She needed his assistance more than usual, for her legs felt suddenly weak and weightless. She looked about her and saw little had changed, except that the trees sported new buds where leaves of yellow and brown had been when she left. There stood the old mossy-roofed Mill Inn and, across the river, the Crown and Crow. And there the sleepy, slanting churchyard of St. Michael and All Angels.

Not ready to contemplate the churchyard, she quickly turned away. The cobbler's door was propped open to allow in the temperate breeze. And there, their low stone wall, her mother's bit of garden, their cottage of blond stone with its green door. The place looked much the same as ever, yet different somehow. Forlorn. No smoke rose from the chimneys, no welcoming light shone from the windows.

Olivia walked up the stone path and tried the door. Locked, as it rarely had been. She bracketed her eyes with gloved hands and, peering in the windows, saw that the place looked tidy but unlived in. No vase of early spring blooms graced the table, no kettle sat on the stove, no log glowed in the hearth. No . . . life. Her stomach twisted. Perhaps her mother really was dead.

"Have you a key?" Lord Brightwell asked. "Or perhaps a neighbor might?"

She shook her head. "Never mind." It was people she wanted to see, not empty rooms.

She crossed the lane and knocked on Muriel Atkins's door, but no one answered. Asking Lord Brightwell to wait for her, she walked across the village in hopes of seeing Miss Cresswell.

At the school, she let herself in and found the woman answering correspondence in her office. Olivia was relieved not to have to go looking about the schoolrooms for her. She was not ready to face her former pupils, nor to answer awkward questions.

"Olivia!" Miss Cresswell exclaimed upon seeing her. She rose quickly and hurried around the desk to embrace her. "My dear, how pleased I am to see you. I must tell you how relieved I was to receive that character request or I would never have known what became of you. Why did you leave so suddenly? I feared I had offended you somehow."

"Never, Miss Cresswell."

"You and your mother just seemed to disappear overnight!"

Olivia felt suddenly winded. "When did you last see her?"

"Not since you left in the fall. I thought . . . hoped . . . the two of you might have gone off together."

Olivia shook her head. So her mother had left . . . or been killed, right after Olivia fled?

Miss Cresswell's countenance dimmed, and she once more sat behind her desk, gesturing Olivia into the chair before it. "I was afraid to ask in my letter, not wanting to alarm you, in the event you did not know."

"Is it true what people are saying?" Olivia asked. "About the new grave in the churchyard?"

Miss Cresswell reached across the desk and touched her arm. "Oh, my dear. I had hoped you were spared that rumor. I avoided mentioning it when I wrote to you. The churchwarden will not say who is buried there. I believe Muriel may know, for she has been acting devilish queer for months, but she has told me nothing. You might ask her, but she is off attending a lying-in somewhere out in the country. I know not where."

"Where is my father now?"

Lydia Cresswell hesitated. "Have you not heard? There is a warrant out for his arrest."

Olivia swallowed. "For . . . murder?"

Her old mentor looked at her askance. "Murder? My dear, why would you think that? The specific charges have not been made public, but the rumor is embezzling."

"Embezzling?"

"That is what they are saying. Though some people still insist it relates to his part in your mother's disappearance, which I for one do not credit."

"I don't understand. . . ."

"You do know your father had been managing the spa Sir Fulke is developing near Cheltenham?"

Olivia shook her head. She knew her father clerked for a new employer, but not that he had been given such great responsibility. "I heard he fled the village to avoid arrest after he . . . after I left."

Lydia Cresswell pursed her lips in thought. "That was the rumor, but the warrant has only recently been issued. I believe he lived out at the construction site all winter. Though now . . . as he hasn't been seen there, nor here, for nearly a fortnight, he may very well have left to avoid whatever charges Sir Fulke is bringing against him."

Miss Cresswell interlaced her fingers on the desktop. "I gather Sir Fulke requested the charges be kept private, because if it is a case of mismanaged funds, and his investors hear of it, there will be a terrible scandal and they might all bail out."

Father, steal? Why could she not believe it, when she believed him guilty of far worse?

Olivia squeezed her eyes shut to clear the whirling confusion, then looked up at Miss Cresswell once more. "When you see Miss Atkins, will you ask her to write to me? With any word of my mother. Even . . . bad news?"

Lydia Cresswell squeezed her hand. "Very well, my dear. May I ask about your situation. It goes well?"

"Yes, I think so."

"And being a governess, it is to your liking?"

"I cannot say I would not prefer to be back in a school, but it is a satisfying, if sometimes lonely, post."

Miss Cresswell nodded. "I am afraid I have hired Mrs. Jennings, as you left with no word of returning, but if you are in need, perhaps—"

"Thank you, no, Miss Cresswell. You are very kind, but I am satisfied where I am. For now." She rose, and Miss Cresswell followed suit, promising to write and let Olivia know if she learnt anything new.

Olivia next visited the constable—ironmonger by trade. How strange to seek out one of the very men she had feared might come looking for her not long ago.

When she entered the shop, the tall bald man looked up from the nails he was sorting. "Miss Keene! It's glad I am to see you. We was worried some dire fate befell you as well."

"As well, Mr. Smith?"

He looked sheepishly troubled and pushed paint-stained hands into his pockets.

Olivia pressed her lips together. "I am well as you see, Mr. Smith, I thank you. But I am looking for my mother. Have you seen her?"

He shook his glistening head. "You ain't the only one. Several folks were here askin' after her last fall. Your own father amongst 'em. Devilish sorry to tell you he is a wanted man, miss. Did you know it?"

"I have just heard. Who else has been trying to find my mother?"

"Oh, there was a liveried man here some time ago, inquiring on behalf of a Lord somebody I never heard of, or so he said. I sent 'im on his way sharp-like. Sir Fulke asked after 'er as well. Seems yer mum did sewing for his missus or some-like. Took a hard fall down the stairs he did. Ears still ring fierce, I gather."

"I am sorry to hear it."

"Are you? Never liked the man myself. Surprised you would, after what he did to you and yer father."

"Do you mean, accusing Father of . . . some crime?"

"That too, but—do you not remember? In the Crown and Crow, that wager twixt you and his Harrow boy?"

"*That* was Sir Fulke?"

"Aye. Sir Fulke Fitzpatrick. Did you not know it?"

Fitzpatrick . . . Lord Bradley had been right. "We never learnt the gentleman's name at the time, and I have had little cause to see the new owner of Meacham's estate. He must not have recognized my father or he never would have kept him on as clerk."

"Oh, 'twas his steward what kept 'im on. Sir Fulke hasn't much to do with the day-to-day running of things."

"And his son, Herbert. Is he here as well?"

"He comes to visit his mother every month proper, but lives to the north somewhere, managing some interest of his father's."

Lord Bradley had been right again.

"I see." But Olivia didn't see. Her mind was whirling. Could it really be? That snobbish gentleman and his son who passed through the village more than ten years ago, had returned to the area, purchased Mr. Meacham's estate where her father worked, and kept him on as clerk, never knowing he was the same man he had humiliated before his peers? Accused as a cheat?

Had her father not recognized him? Surely they would have crossed paths at some point, even if the steward hired him. A chill prickled up Olivia's neck and scalp. Had her father recognized the gentleman all along, and kept the knowledge to himself, planning his revenge in the form of financial ruin? As logical as it sounded, something within Olivia rebelled at the thought.

"And Miss Cresswell was lookin' for you as well. Seemed fiendish odd that you would up and leave town without a word to yer father or your employer."

"I . . . needed to leave quickly."

His brows rose. "And why was that?"

Ignoring his question, she asked, "Did my mother . . . disappear . . . the same day?"

"I couldn't say, as I don't exactly know when you left or when she left, only that yer father first reported you both missing on—" he stepped to a corner desk and consulted a grimy notebook—"the second of November."

Olivia had left on the eve of the first, if she remembered correctly. "Morning or afternoon?"

"Evening, though I don't recollect the specific time. I gather he came home the night before and fell asleep, not knowing the house was already empty. He did not see either of you next morning, but thought maybe you'd gone out. And since he had to hurry to his post, he did not report the two of you missing until that evening. Sober as a puritan he was too. I remarked upon it at the time."

"Did you verify that—that he spent the day at his post?"

He narrowed his eyes. "Why would ya ask that? Suspect yer old man of having somethin' to do with yer mum's disappearance?"

Did she not? She shrugged. "Is not a spouse always suspect?"

He slowly shook his head, dark eyes glittering. "The man loves yer mother. I for one cannot imagine 'im harming her. You ought to have seen 'is face when he come and reported the two of you missing. Devilish white-faced, he were. Worried some evil had befallen the both of you."

Had Simon Keene been shaken to find his wife missing? Or because of what he had done to her?

"Yer tellin' me the two of you did not leave together?" Smith asked.

"No, sir," Olivia said. "She was still at home when I left."

"You still haven't told me why you had to leave."

Dare she tell him the whole truth? Would she be in trouble if she confessed striking her father in defense of her mother, even though she had not killed him as she once feared? Her father was already a wanted man. Did she really want to be responsible for suggesting him guilty of worse? To be responsible for his hanging? When she had not witnessed anything more than assault? When, in fact, Simon Keene had lain unconscious on the ground when last she saw him?

"I left for a post, sir. My mother thought I might obtain a place in a school she was familiar with in St. Aldwyns."

"That where you are presently?"

"No. But nearby."

"With that gentleman who accompanied you into the village?"

He evidently saw her surprised look. "Ah yes. I have eyes and ears everywhere, I do, miss. Had them that night as well."

What was he implying? That he knew or guessed her part in that night's violence? Or that he knew something else?

"Yes. He is my employer."

He proffered his notebook. "If you would be so good as to give me 'is name and direction? In case I have any further questions or hear anything about Mrs. Keene?"

Olivia swallowed, but complied. What had she been thinking in returning to Withington? Now her whereabouts would be common knowledge. But did it matter anymore? The constable was not trying to find her, nor, it seemed, was her father.

"And if you hear from either of your venerable parents, especially Mr. Keene, I trust you will be good enough to send me word?"

Olivia's throat seemed impossibly dry. She nodded wordlessly and took her leave.

The return journey to Brightwell Court was an exceedingly quiet one.

29

Few governesses could expect to obtain situations after the age of forty.

—Ruth Brandon, Governess, *The Lives and Times of the Real Jane Eyres*

The house had seemed empty while his father and Miss Keene were away, and Edward had been plagued with the notion that Miss Keene would not be returning to Brightwell Court. He was relieved to have been wrong.

His father confided the little he had learned from the venture, and Miss Keene, it appeared, had reverted to silence.

Three days after the trip, Edward was startled when Judith rushed into the study and took his arm. "Edward, do be a dear and come with me. My mother and mother-in-law are here—the both of them! I need moral support. A diversion. Reinforcements. Something."

He chuckled and rose. "I shall greet them, of course, but do not expect me to sit for hours of gossip, and talk of fashion, and I know not what."

He followed after her as she hurried out into the hall. She rushed to greet the ladies even before Hodges could escort them into the withdrawing room.

"Mamma! Mother Howe! What a surprise. I did not expect you. Certainly not at the same time. If I . . ." Judith hesitated, seemingly stunned to glimpse a third woman behind the first two.

Following her gaze, the elder Mrs. Howe said, "Your mother was kind enough to help me locate your own former governess."

Judith nodded stiffly to a plain, exceedingly thin woman in her mid to late forties. "Miss Ripley," she murmured, then quickly turned back to her mother. "But did you not get my letter, Mamma? I have engaged a new governess just as you suggested. It was not necessary to bring Miss Ripley here."

"Well, we are all here now," Judith's mother said. "Are we to be invited in, or shall we stand here in the hall?"

"Of course. Do come into the drawing room. I shall order tea."

While Osborn and Hodges took their wraps, Edward stood awkwardly, awaiting an opening to greet the women. Judith seemed to suddenly remember his presence, which a moment before had seemed so imperative. "You remember Lord Bradley, our cousin?"

"Indeed I do," the elder Mrs. Howe said. "A great friend to my poor Dominick, God rest his soul. How are you, dear boy?"

Edward pressed the woman's hand. "I am well, Mrs. Howe. Delighted to see you again. You are well, I trust?"

"Gouty leg, I fear. Otherwise quite well."

"And Aunt Bradley. What a pleasure." He kissed his aunt's powdered cheek.

"Upon my soul," Judith's mother said. "You look more like your father than ever."

"Indeed?" Edward hesitated. "I . . . thank you. You are very welcome here, ladies. I hope you have a pleasant visit."

"Will you not join us for tea?" Judith asked, her smile strained.

"Thank you, no. I must take my leave of you."

He bowed to the ladies, ignoring Judith's panicked expression. He would not be trapped in a room with this gaggle of females. Not for the world.

Osborn, breathing hard, beckoned Olivia to come down to the withdrawing room directly, explaining that Mrs. Howe and her guests desired her to attend them.

When Olivia entered a few minutes later, she quickly took in the scene. Judith Howe, hands fluttering nervously, stood beside the mantel. Two matronly women in their late fifties sat perfectly erect on the settee. One shabby, stick-thin woman a decade their junior sat on a chair in the corner.

As Olivia crossed the room, Judith's gaze swept her person with approval, and Olivia was glad she had taken a moment to re-pin her hair and smooth her skirts.

"Mother, Mother Howe, may I present Miss Olivia Keene, our new governess."

Mrs. Howe, the older of the two matrons, narrowed her eyes. "That gown. I have seen it before. Is it not one I recommended for your *trousseau*?"

"I do not think so," Judith forced a little laugh. "But I have been wearing mourning so long I cannot recall my former gowns. At any rate, I doubt I shall fit into any of them after having a child."

"Endeavor to eat less, my dear," Mrs. Howe said. "For economy's sake in both food and clothing."

Judith's smile grew tight. "How kind of you to offer advice, madam, but really, why do you concern yourself? It is not your money that pays for my clothes, nor feeds me and the children."

The older woman stiffened. "If you should like to live with me, Judith, you are welcome to do so. With economy, we should do well enough were we both to take in needlework."

"Thank you, no, madam. The children and I are quite comfortable here."

"For how long, I wonder?" The younger matron, Judith's mother, spoke up.

"What do you mean?" Judith asked.

"Lord Bradley is of an age, my girl. When he marries, the new mistress of the house may not look kindly upon sharing her husband's home, money, and . . . attentions . . . with you."

Mrs. Howe, continuing the previous topic, said, "Dear Jeannette, God rest her soul, went right back into her maiden gowns after Audrey was born."

"How nice for her," Judith said with acerbic sweetness.

Mrs. Bradley, still elegant and attractive as her daughter would no doubt remain, turned cool eyes back on Olivia. "Miss Keene, is it? From where do you hail? Would I know your family?"

"I would not think so, madam. I come from Withington."

"I do not know any Keenes. Has your family any connections to speak of?"

"I am not certain."

"And your father . . . what sort of gentleman is he?"

Olivia lifted her chin. "He is not a gentleman of any kind. He works as an estate clerk."

"A clerk? Really, Judith, where did you find this girl? What made you think her suitable?"

"She attended a very good school, Mamma. She reads and writes French, Italian, and I know not what."

"Does she indeed?"

"Yes, madam," Olivia answered for herself. "I attended Miss Cresswell's School for Girls. And after, Miss Cresswell was good enough to make me her assistant."

"Never heard of a Miss Cresswell," Judith's mother-in-law murmured, pulling a loose thread from her sleeve.

"And your mother, Miss Keene?" Mrs. Bradley asked. "I suppose it is too much to hope that she is a woman of gentle birth?"

"Indeed she was," the earl announced from the doorway. The ladies started. "Forgive me, ladies, but I could not help overhearing your, mmm, interview with Miss Keene."

"Lord Brightwell!" his sister-in-law exclaimed. "We did not intend to disturb you."

"You do disturb me, madam, if you question Miss Keene's suitability. Not only is she extremely clever and accomplished in her own right, but her mother is of the Cirencester Hawthorns, with whom I believe you are some acquainted."

"The Hawthorns?" the elder Mrs. Howe said. "Why, we have not seen that family in years, not since Thomas Hawthorn died and his wife and daughters moved away."

"Did your sisters not have a governess by the name of Hawthorn?" his brother's wife asked.

"Indeed, madam. Dorothea Hawthorn is Miss Keene's mother, and a finer governess I have never known."

His sister-in-law's brow puckered. "I seem to remember something about that governess. Now what was it? She left without notice, I believe. But there was something else. . . ."

The earl's warning look did not match his words. "What a keen memory you have, Mrs. Bradley."

"Do you know, I remember something of that family as well," the elder Mrs. Howe said, eyes alighting on the tea tray Osborn carried in, laden with cakes and tarts. "Of course they lost their home when Mr. Hawthorn died and the estate was entailed onto some cousin or other. But one of the sisters made an excellent match. Married a gentleman of means, a Mr. Crenshaw of Faringdon, and Mrs. Hawthorn, I understand, lives with her daughter on Crenshaw's estate."

Mrs. Bradley gestured for Osborn to lay the tea things on the table before her, as though mistress herself, then returned a cool gaze to Olivia. "While the other sister, your mother, married a . . . clerk?"

"Miss Keene," Lord Brightwell interjected, "if you have finished your visit with these fine *Christian* ladies, I wonder if you might join me in the library. I have hit another snag in the estate records and am in need of your skilled eye and mathematical prowess."

Olivia guessed he had fabricated the latter for the benefit of his hearers, but did not mind the pretense. In fact, she felt like kissing his hand.

After stopping briefly in Lord Brightwell's library for the requisite look at the records—in which she found a small error within a matter of minutes—Olivia excused herself, wishing to return to Audrey and Andrew. In the corridor, she found Miss Ripley sitting alone on a bench near the drawing room door. From within came the sounds of conversation and the musical ting of china, as the other ladies took tea together. Miss Ripley made a piteous figure, and Olivia, who had tasted a small sampling of a governess's lot, felt sorry for her.

"Miss Ripley. Would you care to join me in the schoolroom?"

The woman's drawn face brightened, then fell once more. "Thank you, miss, but you do not want me."

"Indeed I do. Did I not ask you?"

Compelled by Olivia's response, delivered more tartly than she had intended, the woman roused herself and followed Olivia up the many pairs of stairs to the schoolroom. Olivia opened the door with a flourish, secretly proud of the organization of the room. While Olivia added more coal to the stove, Miss Ripley surveyed the neat desk and table, maps and globe, easels and hung landscapes, books and slates with apparent approbation.

Rubbing skeletal fingers over the books on Olivia's desk, she asked, "What texts are you using?"

"*Mangnall's Questions*, primarily, as well as—"

"Excellent. Nothing better. And discipline, Miss Keene? Have you instilled proper discipline in your pupils?"

"I do not know. I own I sometimes struggle to command their attention."

"Never say so! You must rule with an iron fist—or rod, Miss Keene. A good boxing of the ears never goes awry either."

"I do not think . . ." Olivia decided nothing would be gained by voicing disagreement and said instead, "I am sure Mrs. Howe would never allow it."

"Miss Judith tasted her share of discipline as a girl, I can tell you, and it did her a world of good. I shall talk to her before I take my leave. Encourage her to be more stern with the children and allow you to be as well."

"Th-thank you, Miss Ripley. But that is not necessary. That is, I am finding my way."

"You shall never find your way without discipline, Miss Keene. Do not make the mistake of trying to befriend your pupils. You are not their friend; you are their governess, and so you must govern. They will not like you. Do not expect it. Expect them to show neither warmth nor appreciation, and you will not be disappointed."

Olivia stared at the older woman and saw a brittle façade formed by years of rejection and ill treatment. She said quietly, "It is a lonely way to live, is it not?"

"Of course it is. But any governess worth her salt knows so going in and expects no more."

"But . . . without friends, or warmth, or appreciation?"

The older woman looked at her then, as if for the first time. "It is our lot."

Olivia touched the woman's arm, and Miss Ripley jumped as if burned. "Would you take tea with me, Miss Ripley?"

The older woman's eyes glistened. "Thank you."

Becky brought them tea and a plate of Mrs. Moore's ginger biscuits, and the two governesses sat together at the schoolroom table.

"I was prepared to hate you, Miss Keene," Miss Ripley admitted over her teacup. "The inexperienced youth taking the post I wished for myself. I need a place, you see. No one wants a governess quite so old as I am, it seems."

Miss Ripley took a ladylike sip, then regarded Olivia earnestly. "I was not the only person surprised by your youth, Miss Keene. Before the ladies dismissed me, Mrs. Bradley commented on it to Miss Judith. She said you were altogether too young and pretty to be trusted. I gather she is concerned you will turn Lord Brightwell's head."

"Lord Brightwell?" Olivia assumed she had misheard.

"Yes." Miss Ripley took a delicate nibble of her biscuit. If she were not so homely, she might have been elegant. "Miss Judith asked her mother if she meant Lord Bradley, Lord Brightwell's son, but Mrs. Bradley was quite adamant. Then she realized I was listening and said no more."

"How strange. Lord Brightwell is old enough to be my . . ." The word stuck in Olivia's throat. "I assure you, Miss Ripley, that there is nothing of that sort going on."

Miss Ripley lifted one thin shoulder, her small smile a knowing one. "I would not blame you if there were. We must do what we can to secure our futures, I say."

Olivia gratefully took up this change of topic. "And what will you do now, Miss Ripley? Return home?"

"I haven't a home, Miss Keene. I have lived in other people's homes for more than twenty years. Sharing chambers with boys in nightdresses and curls, boys who have long since died in wars or had children of their own. Few remember me, and none fondly. I met a governess once—a Miss Hayes, who was so adored by her charges that she moved with them into adulthood, serving as governess for their children and then, when she was too old to work, lived with the family as a beloved friend. I have heard only one such story. More common are tales of governesses too old to work, or at least too old to be pleasant to look at and so not hired, begging menial work, living in a small rented room, and then on the streets, slowly starving to death." She took another bite of her biscuit. "No one is governess by choice, Miss Keene. It is a role of necessity. Of survival. A gentlewoman's only real means of putting a roof over her head and keeping herself clothed and fed."

Miss Ripley surveyed Olivia head to skirts. "I know what circumstances compelled me to enter the profession all those years ago, but I wonder at yours. I suppose your father could not, or would not, support you. But you are too pretty not to have offers of marriage, and you might have taught at a girls' school instead. May I ask what has driven you to this?"

Olivia stared at the woman, taken aback by her long and forthright speech. When was the last time Miss Ripley had had another adult to talk to, as an equal?

"I did assist in a girls' school," Olivia acknowledged, "but circumstances, as you say, compelled me here." Her father *had* supported her financially. Olivia could not say otherwise. But nor did she feel compelled to defend the man. He was a great part of the reason she was here after all.

30

> Take a lady in every meaning of the word, born and bred and let her father pass through [bankruptcy], and she wants nothing more to suit our highest beau ideal of a guide and instructress to our children.
>
> —Lady Elizabeth Eastlake, *Quarterly Review*

After Judith's mother, mother-in-law, and former governess had taken their leave, Judith cornered Edward in the billiards room, where he was enjoying a solitary game.

"Did I not tell you?" she exclaimed. "Miss Keene is granddaughter of a landed gentleman!"

"Hardly a Prussian princess, Judith."

"Still. I knew there was more to her than met the eye."

"Why are you elated? Are not most governesses gentlewomen of reduced circumstances?"

"Come, Edward, admit it. You thought her no better than a charwoman when she first arrived."

He shrugged. "Her grandfather might have been gentry and her mother of gentle birth, but as her mother married a clerk, Miss Keene is not even a gentleman's daughter."

"What a snob you are, Edward. Really, it is quite surprising."

He stilled. "What is?"

"Hmm?" Judith said, idly twirling a cue ball on the felt.

"You said it is quite surprising. What is? That I am a snob or that Miss Keene should be daughter of a clerk?"

There was laughter in her eyes and a touch of pique. "Both, I suppose." She turned and flounced from the room.

That evening, Olivia sat on her narrow bed and once again turned over the sealed letter she had found in her mother's purse. Should she open it? If her mother was dead, as a part of her feared, did not the brief directive inscribed upon it bid her to do so? And if she was not dead, as Olivia still hoped and prayed might be the case, then might whatever was inside help Olivia find her? She wondered yet again if she should have opened the letter sooner. Guilt and indecision pulled her this way and that. *Almighty God, what should I do? What is right? I wish to honour her request, but I want to help her if she needs me. . . .*

Hands trembling, she slid a fingernail under the seal and pried it open. She unfolded it only to find another letter within, this one sealed as well. It looked like an ordinary letter, directed to a *"Mrs. Elizabeth (or Georgiana) Hawthorn."* The surname rang in her memory. Had not Mrs. Howe and Mrs. Bradley discussed the Hawthorns as her mother's family? Her mother had said almost nothing about having family over the years, except to say that all ties had been cut between them. Now her mother was writing to them, but a letter meant to be delivered only after her death?

She would not open a letter directed to another. Nor could she post it in good conscience without knowing her mother's fate.

Needing counsel, she sought out Lord Brightwell and found him on the garden bench, smoking a cigar amid the budding trees and daffodils of an early springtime evening. She showed him both the outer and inner letters.

"You have had these all along?" He studied the outer letter more closely. "She must have feared something would happen to her. Forgive me, my dear—of course we still hope and pray that she is alive and well."

While Lord Brightwell considered the situation, Olivia prayed for wisdom for them both. After several moments, he set down the letters. "Well, there is nothing for it. You must go to Faringdon and see them."

Olivia's heart began to beat faster. "Will they receive me, do you think?"

"I do not know. But I hope they shall. You, after all, cannot help your mother's unfortunate marriage."

The words bit hard. She did not like to hear him say so, true though it was.

"Shall I accompany you?" Lord Brightwell asked.

"I don't wish to inconvenience you, my lord."

"It might be wise if I went along. At the risk of sounding proud, you may be better received."

Taking Lord Brightwell's card, the Crenshaws' footman went to ascertain if Mrs. Hawthorn was "at home" to visitors. Olivia's pulse raced and her hands grew damp within her gloves. She had taken extra time with her appearance, wearing half boots and a new spencer jacket, purchased from Miss Ludlow, over her dark blue gown, hoping it would give her the confidence she needed for the meeting ahead. She expected no warm reception from this woman, grandmother though she may be, since she apparently disowned her own daughter years before. Olivia took a deep and shaky breath, relieved Lord Brightwell had insisted on accompanying her.

They were shown into a formal drawing room. A dainty woman in her midsixties rose to greet them, and Olivia felt a start of recognition. The woman's nose was somewhat hawkish and her face lined but attractive. Lord Brightwell bowed and the woman gave a shallow curtsy, whether because of stiff limbs or lack of due respect Olivia did not know.

"Lord Brightwell, how do you do."

Olivia wondered if she might acknowledge that her daughter Dorothea had once had a situation with his family, but she did not.

"Mrs. Hawthorn. Thank you for seeing us."

At the word "us," Mrs. Hawthorn glanced at her. Olivia's heart lurched. Yes, there was a definite resemblance to her mother, in the eyes and high cheekbones. Was it her imagination, or did the woman falter as well?

"May I present Miss Olivia Keene," Lord Brightwell said.

Olivia dipped a low curtsy, and when she rose again, the woman had not moved, but was studying her. And not with a smile.

"I have not met Miss Keene, I do not think?"

"No, madam," Olivia said quietly.

"Do be seated." Mrs. Hawthorn regained her seat.

Lord Brightwell sat in a chair across the low table, while Olivia sat near the woman's left.

"Now, to what do I owe this visit?"

With fingers suddenly thick and clumsy, Olivia withdrew the inner letter from her reticule and handed it to the woman.

"What is this?" The woman's thin, kohl-darkened eyebrows rose. Then she squinted at the writing and Olivia wondered if her eyesight was poor. She turned it over, saw the seal. "Who has written this? I take it you know?"

Olivia nodded, somewhat surprised and disappointed that the woman had not recognized the hand. "Dorothea," she answered simply.

Whatever reaction she had expected, it was not this. The woman threw down the letter as if a venomous spider clung to it. "After all this time? She writes a letter and has *strangers* deliver it?"

Olivia withdrew the outer envelope and handed it to the woman. "It was sealed in this," she said quietly.

The woman stared at it, then brought it close to her face, until it touched her brow. When she lowered it again, Olivia saw tears in the woman's eyes. She grimaced and said bitterly, "I should have known. After more than twenty-five years, she would not contact me otherwise."

"We are not certain Dorothea is . . . has died," Lord Brightwell said. "But she has disappeared and we fear the worst. We are hoping that if we are wrong, something within might help us find her."

Still the woman hesitated.

"Please, madam." Olivia retrieved the rejected letter and handed it to her once more.

The woman swallowed, a bony ball moving within her thin, withered neck. She accepted the letter, eyeing Olivia once more before returning her gaze to the seal. She broke it with stiff fingers and unfolded the single sheet within.

Olivia waited, anxiety rising. What possible good could come from this? It had been a mistake to come here.

She felt Mrs. Hawthorn's penetrating look and forced herself to meet the woman's eyes.

"You are this Olivia. Her daughter?"

Olivia nodded.

Mrs. Hawthorn fixed her eyes on her a moment longer, then refolded the letter. Olivia fought to keep her face impassive. How she wanted to read it—any words her mother had written!

"I am afraid there is nothing here to help you," the woman said.

"Nothing?" Olivia asked, and in her own ears her voice sounded like that of a petulant child.

Mrs. Hawthorn laid the folded letter on the chair beside her and crossed her arms as though chilled. As though to protect herself. Did she fear Olivia had come to ask for money, or to be taken in like a poor destitute foundling?

"I want nothing from you, madam," Olivia said softly, "save any information about my mother. I had hoped she might have come to you when she . . . disappeared . . . and could not find me."

"She did not."

When the woman offered no more, Olivia rose and said somewhat frostily, "We shall trespass upon your time no longer."

The earl stood as well.

"I think it highly unlikely Dorothea would contact me," Mrs. Hawthorn said. "But if I am wrong, do I understand that you are . . . staying . . . at Brightwell Court?" She looked from Olivia to Lord Brightwell.

Lord Brightwell, perhaps roused to defend Olivia, to step in with a warm gesture when her maternal grandmother had not, said, "Yes, Miss Keene is living under my protection, and that of my son."

Olivia wondered why he had mentioned his son. Did he fear Mrs. Hawthorn might assume an inappropriate relationship between himself and her, had he not? She very well might, Olivia realized.

"It does not appear that you are friendless, after all," Mrs. Hawthorn said, leaving Olivia to wonder once more just what her mother had written, and concluding from the woman's words that she felt relieved of any obligation to aid or even contact her ever again.

Mrs. Hawthorn added, in an offhanded manner, "It might interest you to know . . . a man came here several weeks ago now, asking for Dorothea. I refused to see him and had my man send him away, though he did not go quietly."

Father? Olivia wondered. *The constable?* "What . . . sort of man?"

"A gentleman, by appearances, though certainly not by behavior. I own I glanced from the window and saw him as he swore at my footman and climbed back into his chaise. I did not see his face."

Not the constable. Her father, perhaps, in new clothes and a hired chaise? It seemed unlikely, but who else could it have been?

31

A chain of gold ye shall not lack, Nor braid to bind your hair;
Nor mettled hound, nor managed hawk, Nor palfrey fresh and fair.

—Sir Walter Scott, "Jock O'Hazeldean"

On a misty March morning, a basket over one arm, Olivia led the children through the wood. As they went, she pointed out primroses, wood anemones, and the last of the snowdrops with their modest, bowed heads. She identified many birds as well—flitting yellowhammers, jackdaws building nests, and a chain of rooks flying over the budding treetops.

When they neared the gamekeeper's lodge and stepped into the clearing, they found Croome slopping his pigs.

"What is it this time?" he asked in a long-suffering manner, as though it were a trial indeed to be given delicacies from the best cook in the borough.

Olivia lifted the basket on her arm. "Rump steak pie and canary pudding."

One wiry brow rose.

She chuckled at his scandalized expression. "There are no canaries in it, sir."

He reached for the basket, but Olivia turned as though she had not noticed. "We are learning about animals today, Mr. Croome," Olivia said. "And I thought you might be able to help us."

"What? Me do yer job fer you?"

"Who better? Who knows more about animals than you do?"

"I only know game, and cows and pigs and chickens and the like. And o'course all manner o' land fowl and waterfowl."

"And predators, Mr. Croome?"

"Oh, aye. A gamekeeper has to know his enemy, doesn't he? The owl, the raven, the wildcat, and weasel. But I'm no teacher. Never have been and never will be."

Olivia sighed. "Very well. Children, is a partridge a land fowl or waterfowl?"

"A bird?" Audrey guessed.

"A pigeon!" Andrew exclaimed.

Mr. Croome shook his head, not taking the bait.

"And what do wildcats eat?"

"Milk?" Audrey guessed.

"Pigeon!" Andrew exclaimed.

Croome threw up his bony hands in disgust. "Boy, have you ever seen a wildcat?"

Andrew shook his head.

"If you had, you'd know such a greedy beast would not bother with a tiny bird when the wood is filled with hares. That's his favorite, mind. Though he'll eat pheasant or partridge and all manner o' fowl if need be. It's why I keep Bob inside at night."

"Who's Bob?" Andrew asked.

When the man hesitated, Olivia sweetly supplied, "I believe he is Mr. Croome's pet partridge."

She was rewarded with a barbed glare.

"You keep a pet partridge?" Audrey asked in awe.

"I do, and don't be mockin' me."

"No, sir!" Andrew said. "May we see him?"

Audrey added, "May we feed him?"

Croome leveled a long look at Olivia, resentment fading to resignation. "Oh, very well, you rogues. I'll bring him out and show ya."

From the basket, Olivia lifted the stack of two covered plates. Croome reached for them, but Olivia held fast. "Mrs. Moore will need these returned. Have you something we might transfer the food into?"

His brows dropped darkly, but she thought she saw the faintest flash of humor in the silvery blue eyes. "You don't fool me, girl. Just want to nose about my place, don't ya?"

She only shrugged. "These dishes do grow heavy. . . ."

"Oh, come on, then. Wipe yer boots, Master Andrew—it isn't a pigpen."

Inside, Croome slid the pie and the lemon yellow pudding into basins of his own while the children fawned over Bob, who followed Croome about like a devoted hound. Olivia walked slowly about the room, taking in the dust, the cobwebs, a humble bookcase, and two colorful paintings on the wall, displayed in fine beech-wood frames as though in a portrait gallery. She bent closer to peer at them. Though the paper was coarse, the paintings themselves were surprisingly good. The first showed a man from the waist up, head tilted to look at a small bird in his hand. The man wore a hint of a smile as if he knew he was being observed. The artist had captured a put-out, though tolerant, expression.

"Why, this is you!" Olivia exclaimed. She had barely recognized Mr. Croome with a smile.

He scowled at her over his shoulder. "Stop yer pokin' about. I wouldn't keep a likeness o' me in plain sight, but Alice done it. Painted it, framed it, and hung it there. It pleased her, so I leave it. Now, leave it be."

Ignoring him, Olivia studied the second painting. It was of a woman—head and shoulders—surrounded by a border of colorful flowers and cherubim. Her face was not as clear as Mr. Croome's likeness, but held a vague, ethereal beauty.

"Is this your wife?" Olivia asked.

"Aye. That's my Maggie." Croome left the children feeding flies to Bob and joined her at the wall. "A decent likeness, though Alice painted it from memory after her mother was gone."

"She is beautiful."

He nodded. "I recollect she was even lovelier. Though I would think it."

"I am sorry for your loss," Olivia said. She would have liked to ask about Alice but did not dare.

"Not as sorry as I am." He stepped back to the table. "All right. Here's Nell's dishes. Now, quit yer meddling."

Edward strolled leisurely through the wood, intent on visiting his favorite spot near the river. The air was fresh and smelled of new grass and recent rain. Robins sang *twiddle-oo, twiddle-eedee* in a cheerful chorus around him. Into this chorus joined children's voices, and Edward paused. He heard laughter and an odd *fwwt, smack* sound. What in the world? Was Miss Keene in the wood with the children on one of her "nature expeditions"?

He followed the sound, at first eagerly, but then slowed as he realized it was leading him to the gamekeeper's lodge.

Approaching the clearing, he paused and looked through the trees at an unexpected scene.

Miss Keene sat on a stump. Audrey swung like a lazy pendulum on an old rope swing. Mr. Croome was helping Andrew position a bow on his small shoulder and showing him how to align the arrow on the bowstring. The boy released the arrow and it flew in a weak arc, landing shy of the straw-backed target across the clearing.

"Aww . . . it's too hard," Andrew moaned. "Why bother with arrows when you have your fowling piece, Mr. Croome? Let me get my hands on that, and I could shoot dead on, I know I could."

"Guns has their place, young man. But so does the bow and arrow."

"I don't see how. Why not just blast the game and be done?"

"Use yer head, boy. Blast the gun once and all the county knows it. All the game take off running or fly away. But with the bow and arrow, you have stealth, boy. You can bag a hare or down a buck before its neighbor is any the wiser."

"Ohh . . ."

"Now, try again, Master Andrew, and this time, pull back with every muscle God gave ya."

Andrew nodded and lifted the bow once more. Croome helped him level the arrow, whispered some direction in his ear, then placed his fingers over the boy's, helping him pull the cord further back.

"You can do it, Andrew," Miss Keene encouraged.

"Don't forget to aim," Audrey added.

Man and boy released the arrow. *Fwwt, smack.* The arrow pierced the outer ring of the paper target and shuddered into the straw barricade behind it.

Audrey and Miss Keene cheered. Croome slapped Andrew on his slight shoulder, causing the boy to jerk forward, but Andrew's smile only grew the wider. Edward felt conflicting emotions, remembering his father's long-ago warnings about their gamekeeper. Edward had even shared those concerns with Miss Keene, yet still she felt it safe, wise, to bring the children here?

Croome noticed him first. He darted a sharp look over his shoulder—his old ears evidently still keen, alert to approaching prey and predator alike. Which was he? Edward stepped forward, and the children rushed to greet him.

"I hit the target, Cousin Edward. Did you see?" Andrew asked.

"I did. Well done."

Audrey pouted. "You missed my turn. I hit the target once too, even closer to the center than Andrew did."

"I am sorry to have missed it. Perhaps you might try again?"

"Perhaps Lord Bradley would take a turn first, and show us how it is done?" Miss Keene suggested, blue eyes twinkling.

He narrowed his eyes at her. "You are too kind to offer, but I do not wish to interrupt the children's education, or whatever this is."

"It is sport. Good for the body and mind."

"Come, Cousin Edward. Do try," Andrew urged. "You cannot do any worse than Miss Keene did. She hit Mr. Croome's house!"

Miss Keene's cheeks pinked. Mr. Croome looked away and scratched the back of his neck.

"Did she indeed?" Edward said, barely suppressing a grin.

"Are we going to shoot or gad about all day?" Croome asked. "I've lines to set and eggs to hatch."

Edward swallowed. "Very well, I shall give it a go."

Croome handed him a second, larger bow, and then an arrow, his narrowed eyes fixed on Edward's face with disconcerting scrutiny. "Never done this before, have you?"

Was it so obvious? "No, sir."

Croome nodded and said in a low voice, "Place the arrow there and keep 'er level, both eyes open; pull back to your right shoulder, aim, then release."

Edward did so, the cord scraping his cheek as it released. The arrow smacked into the target, not far from Andrew's.

"Not bad for a first shot," Croome said. He eyed Edward's smarting cheek. "You'll live."

"Perhaps, Mr. Croome," Olivia said, "you might show us how it is done, for none of us has the way of it yet, I fear."

"Practice is all that's needed."

"We would like to see you shoot, Mr. Croome," Audrey said. "Are you very good?"

"Not bad, but don't like to make a coxcomb of myself either."

"We don't mind. We want to see," Andrew said. "Please?"

Croome gave Edward a glance, as if for his approval, which surprised him.

"By all means, Mr. Croome," he said.

"Do! Do!"

"Oh, very well, you little rogues, if only to still yer yappin' and give me peace."

Croome took up the stance and positioned the arrow in one smooth movement. He pulled the cord taut with practiced ease and sighted his target. *Fwwt, smack*. Dead center.

Edward decided he would not want this man for an enemy.

He was surprised when a bird came strutting across the clearing toward them, its grey neck stretched high and its broad belly balanced on peg legs, like a snobbish, well-fed footman. While not an experienced fowler, Edward guessed it a partridge.

Andrew, who was once again sighting the target, suddenly veered to the side, aiming at the partridge, making a mock *fwwt* sound between puffed cheeks.

Croome caught his arm in a blurred, razor-fast grab. "No, Master Andrew. Don't even pretend it."

Edward felt instantly defensive on his cousin's behalf, not liking the man's rough treatment of the boy. Over a game bird?

Andrew looked sheepish. "I am sorry, Mr. Croome. I was only fooling. I would never shoot Bob. Never."

Bob? The man had a pet partridge named *Bob*?

Perhaps he wasn't as fearsome as Edward had been led to believe.

32

The time I spend endeavoring to improve [my pupils] makes a small figure in my journal.
I trust it will turn out to their and to my benefit in the Book of Life, where all actions, thoughts and designs are registered by an unerring and gracious hand.

—*A Governess in the Age of Jane Austen: The Journals and Letters of Agnes Porter*

That evening, Edward stood in the doorway, amused by the scene in the drawing room. The carpets had been rolled back and some dancing master's text lay open on the floor. Andrew stood on a straight-back chair, face-to-face with the governess, who stood on the floor before him, hands in his. Audrey stood beside Miss Keene, an impish grin on her face. At Miss Keene's instruction, Andrew lifted one hand high, but before Miss Keene could turn beneath it, Audrey reached up and tickled him under his arm. Andrew doubled over and giggled.

Miss Keene sighed. It was clearly not the first time this had occurred.

Edward could not resist. He crossed the room to them, bowed, and asked formally, "May I cut in?"

With of whoop of relief, Andrew jumped from the chair and—after a running start—slid several yards across the polished floor in his stocking feet.

Shaking his head, Edward returned his gaze to Miss Keene and found her dubiously eyeing his offered hand.

She said, "I was only trying to demonstrate the nine positions of the German and French waltz."

"So I saw. Shall we continue?"

"You need not . . . That is, I am sure my lord is much too busy to—"

"Not at all. It is for the children's benefit, is it not? Their education?"

She opened her mouth to protest further, but before she could, Audrey said, "Show us position four, Cousin Edward. For neither Andrew nor I can master it."

Edward wondered if Audrey Howe fostered as many romantic fancies as did her stepmother. But he did not complain.

"You were doing fine, Audrey," Miss Keene said. "It was difficult without a proper partner. I am not very good at being the man."

Edward felt his brows rise.

"Please?" Audrey begged her governess.

Miss Keene sighed once more. "Very well. I shall be you, Audrey." She turned to Edward. "And you shall be the man."

He said dryly, "I can but try."

Edward raised his left arm over his head, and she, reluctantly, did the same. He grasped her uplifted hand in his own, creating an arch above them. "Position four requires, I believe, the woman to place her hand about the man's waist. And the man—that is me—to place his about hers. Is that not correct?"

She swallowed. "Yes."

Edward relished circling his arm around her and drawing her close to his side. Regarding her under the arch of their upraised arms, he noticed her pink, averted face. "To stand so close and yet ignore one's partner, Miss Keene? That will never do."

She tried to meet his gaze, but was clearly too self-conscious to do so.

Audrey dashed to the pianoforte and exclaimed, "I shall play and you two dance! I know I shall understand if I see the positions performed."

Little schemer, Edward thought, and felt his fondness for his young cousin grow.

Audrey began banging out a piece in three-quarter time, with none of the stately decorum the composer had intended.

Miss Keene gave him an apologetic look. "You need not. I—"

"Nonsense." He put both hands around her small waist—*Position seven or eight?* He did not care, only wanted to hold her close—and propelled her forward before she could object.

She grasped his upper arms and hung on desperately tight as he spun her around the room. He maneuvered her to his side—*position five?*—and whirled them both around, then lifted one arm and twirled her beneath it just as Audrey pounded out the final notes.

Still holding one of her hands, he bowed to her, the room spinning slightly. She seemed about to curtsy but instead swayed. He grasped both of her elbows to steady her. How desirable she was with her high color and coils of dark hair falling around her. Not to mention their entwined limbs. Standing this close to her, his face bent near hers, he wanted very badly to kiss her. Of course, he could not. Would not.

"Are you well?" he quietly asked.

"Besides breathless, dizzy, and embarrassed?"

He nodded.

"Perfectly."

Chuckling, his gaze roved her features—her bright blue eyes and parted lips, the rapid rise and fall of her chest—taking in every detail, but with none of the detachment his friend Dr. Sutton might have shown. He lifted her hand, still in his. She wore no gloves, and he felt an irrational urge to press his lips to her warm, bare skin.

"What is it?" she asked, concerned as he continued to inspect her fingers. "Is something wrong?" She tried to pull her hand away, but he held fast.

"I was only looking to see if your knuckles were white. You were holding my arms with impressive force."

Her mouth formed an O, and her blush deepened. He found her reaction quite charming.

"I am sure their impression will last several hours," he said, lifting one corner of his mouth in a half grin. "At least, I hope so."

He gave in to his impulse then and kissed the back of her hand. Warm and soft, as he'd imagined.

Audrey clapped, and Andrew came to a sliding stop beside them. "Is that a part of the dance too?" he asked.

"Perhaps," Edward said, reluctantly releasing Miss Keene. "When you are much older."

Audrey sat on a little stool in the garden, easel and watercolors before her, tongue poking between her lips as she concentrated. While the girl worked on a likeness of the arbor, Olivia walked back and forth a few feet behind her, Latin text in hand, now and again pausing to offer encouragement or suggestion.

Andrew sat cross-legged on the grass, capturing beetles in his hand and listening idly to Olivia as she attempted a Latin lesson.

A door in the churchyard wall squealed open, and Olivia started. Mr. Tugwell appeared in the narrow arched doorway. "Good day, ladies. Master Andrew." He bowed. "Was that you I heard declining Latin verbs, Miss Keene?"

Olivia's face suffused with heat. "I am sure my grasp of Latin is nothing to yours, Mr. Tugwell. I hope I did not disturb you."

"By no means. You have a lovely speaking voice. You know, I remarked upon it to Bradley when first you came. For I had met you once before that unfortunate . . . mmm, mishap stole your powers of speech. And from our brief meeting I knew you must be a woman of education and refinement."

"Did you indeed? Then I thank you. Lord Bradley, it seems, did not credit your assessment."

"No. He is a man to draw his own conclusions, and sometimes, I fear, all too quickly."

She grinned. "I believe he might say the same of you."

"You are no doubt right. Though I may be too quick to judge charitably and he harshly, I think mine the lesser flaw, if I do say so myself." His eyes twinkled.

"I quite agree with you. But to hear Lord Bradley tell it, you have often paid a high price for believing the best of people." She tilted her head and asked, "Perhaps you might relay such an instance?"

Mr. Tugwell tucked his chin. "Ah, you will join him in mocking me, I see."

"Not at all, sir. But it does arouse one's curiosity, naturally."

"Very well. If you consent to take a turn with me about the garden, I shall."

Olivia smiled and rose, encouraging Audrey to keep on with her painting and assuring both children she would return in a few minutes.

"I do hope such a tale will not discourage you from trusting people, Miss Keene," he began.

"I shall endeavor to keep an open mind."

"Good. Now, how shall I choose but one instance? Let me see . . . Of course I have had the odd problem at the almshouse. I thought the old gent on crutches really was a former soldier down on his luck. Stole every stick of furniture from his room and left only his crutches behind to spite me!"

Olivia laughed and quickly pressed a hand over her mouth.

"Then there was that young maid—a pretty lass, so Edward warned me especially against her. But I did trust her and there went a twelvemonth's worth of wine for the sacrament. Then, of course, there is my sister, but it would not be charitable to continue." He winked at her in a most unparson-like manner.

Olivia grinned. They took another turn around the garden, Audrey and Andrew ever in view at its center, and Olivia asked the vicar more questions. As Charles Tugwell shared about his work at the almshouse, Olivia felt drawn to help. Might it not make some small amends for her failings, bring good from all the bad that had brought her to this place?

In his study, Edward stared at Miss Keene incredulously. "You would like to spend your half day *where*?"

"In the almshouse. Mr. Tugwell said I might be of use."

"Mr. Tugwell invited you?"

"Yes. Surely you could have no objection? I understand the two of you are friends."

An unfair but clever tact, he thought as she continued.

"You do trust Mr. Tugwell, do you not?"

Did he? Trust Tugwell with his secret? Perhaps. Trust him with Miss Keene? The man had fathered five children in six years. No, he did not trust Charles Tugwell with Miss Keene.

"I thought his sister assisted him."

"She does what she can, but with the boys and a house to manage, she hasn't much time. Miss Ludlow helps as well, when she can get away from her shop. But there is always more to do. Your mother, I understand, was quite a patroness of the place."

"Yes, she was." Feeling a lingering ache over her loss, Edward stared off into the distance and said no more for several moments.

"You might . . . come along if you like," Miss Keene said.

He swiveled his head sharply and studied her face. Her cheeks were tinged with pink.

"To oversee my behavior, I mean," she hurried to amend. "Make sure I do not say or do anything I ought not."

With his secret, he wondered, or with Tugwell?

"You admire the man?"

Her eyes widened. Her lips parted, closed, then parted again. "I . . . I certainly have a great deal of respect for such a selfless clergyman. And he has been very kind to me since I arrived."

Far kinder than I have been, Edward thought with remorse.

"It is not as though I keep you prisoner here," he said. *Any longer.* "You attend services now and see the man every Sabbath. Are you certain there is not some other way you would like to spend your half day? Perhaps visiting a friend, or even the market in Cirencester?"

"You would give me leave to do so?"

He swallowed. Took a deep breath. "I believe I would. I would send someone to accompany you, of course. Just to see you return safely. Perhaps even I, should no one else be available."

She stared up at him with those mesmerizing blue eyes, and he felt as ensnared as a polecat in one of Croome's traps. His gaze caressed the curves of her face, her smooth fair cheek, and pointed chin.

Her voice was hushed and warm. "I should very much like to go to the market in Cirencester, if you, or someone, might accompany me."

He tried to nod but could not tear his gaze from hers. "I shall take you." He was tempted, sorely tempted, to tell her how beautiful she was. How sorry he was for the way he had treated her. To ask her to forgive him. To ask her to—

"There are several things I should like to buy for the almshouse," she continued brightly. "Mr. Tugwell mentioned a wheel of cheese would not go amiss and perhaps new gloves for the residents."

Hang the almshouse and hang Tugwell, Edward thought. The spell broken, he nodded curtly and stepped back. "Talbot can take you," he said, and strode away.

33

> The real discomfort of a governess's position arises from the fact that it is undefined. She is not a relation, not a guest, not a mistress, not a servant—but something made up of all. No one knows exactly how to treat her.
>
> —M. Jeanne Peterson, *Suffer and Be Still*

On her way to church that Sunday, Olivia walked a short distance behind the family, as was proper. As she entered the church behind the Bradleys and Howes, she noticed that many people smiled and quietly greeted them, while they ignored her.

Eliza Ludlow, however, grinned and patted the pew next to her. Gratefully, Olivia sat next to the woman.

Here it was again—she was not family and could not sit with them, but nor was her place in the gallery with the servants, though she would have been more comfortable there. As if sensing her unease, Miss Ludlow squeezed her gloved hand in one of hers and offered to share a prayer book with the other. What a dear she was.

After the service, Miss Ludlow walked down the aisle beside her.

"That spencer looks well on you, Miss Keene."

"Thank you. I like this maroon kerseymere you suggested. Much nicer than the puce I wanted."

"I am glad you are pleased with it." Eliza Ludlow smiled and took Olivia's arm. "I understand we may be seeing one another at the almshouse on Wednesdays?"

"Yes, if I can be of any use."

"I am sure of it. Mr. Tugwell speaks very highly of your generosity and willingness."

Olivia's heart sank to see the look of raw longing on the kind woman's face as she gazed across the chapel at the vicar, already shaking hands with his departing flock at the door. When they reached him, he smiled briefly at Miss Ludlow and then shifted his cherubic gaze to Olivia.

He took her hand in his. "Miss Keene. You are well, I trust?"

"I am, sir. I thank you."

Olivia did not miss Miss Ludlow's doe-eyed look swivel from Mr. Tugwell to her, nor the slight pinching of her smile as she registered the attention he paid the relative newcomer and the lingering press of hands. Was the man blind? Or did he choose to ignore Miss Ludlow, not realizing the worth of such a woman?

For her part, Olivia thought Eliza Ludlow a treasure. She had brown eyes, dimples, and a cheery, if mildly crooked, smile. Her dark hair was pulled back with a soft height, framing her face in a most attractive light. Eliza had not the across-the-room arresting beauty of a Judith Howe or Sybil Harrington, but a natural, sweet appeal. Miss Ludlow was also gentle, intelligent, charitable, and at ease with people. She would make a wonderful parson's wife. What did Mr. Tugwell find lacking in Eliza to so completely overlook her? Olivia hoped with all her heart that Mr. Tugwell's passing interest in her would not put a wedge between Miss Ludlow and herself. Friends were hard to come by in her position.

"Perhaps you might join me for tea on Wednesday," Miss Ludlow invited as they parted ways, "after our work at the almshouse?"

Olivia smiled. "I would be honoured."

A treasure indeed.

The Jesus Almshouse.

Olivia regarded the sign on the low white building with interest, taking in the engraved words and a fair likeness of a dove.

"Lady Brightwell commissioned that plaque," Charles Tugwell said, crossing the vicarage garden to join her. "I find it ironic, really. The almshouse was founded by a yeoman farmer who made his money dealing in land and property. He acquired quite a dubious reputation in the bargain. I wonder if he thought his good deed would make up for all his foul."

"You do not esteem good deeds?" She shifted the basket handle to both hands, just as a cool breeze blew a bonnet string across her face.

"My dear Miss Keene, what would the world be without them?" He brushed the string from her cheek. "Are we not admonished to be doers and not merely hearers of His word? Yet not on a mountain of good deeds can we climb our way to heaven."

She was confused by his words. Nothing she could do about her foul deeds? This was not what she wanted to hear. "You surprise me. If good deeds cannot move God to forgiveness, what will, then?"

"Not a thing. Which is why I find the name of this place so fitting. *We* cannot redeem our dark deeds, Miss Keene. Only the Lord can—and already has. All we can do is accept the merciful salvation He purchased for us on the cross long ago. But"—he smiled and rubbed his palms together eagerly—

"we can serve our fellow creatures and delight our heavenly Father's heart in so doing."

She found herself frowning. "Can one truly delight God? I own I do not think of Him that way."

"No? How do you think of Him?"

She shrugged, again shifting the heavy basket. "A God of wrath and judgment, I suppose. Cold and angry in the face of our wrongdoings."

He looked at her thoughtfully. "My dear Miss Keene. Is it possible you endow your creator with the attributes of your earthly father?"

The thought stilled her. Did she? But was it not natural to do so?

"God is holy and just, yes," Mr. Tugwell continued. "But He is infinitely loving and merciful as well. He loves you, Olivia, no matter what you do or fail to do."

If only her father could have loved in that manner. Did God truly love her—after what she had done?

"He does," Mr. Tugwell said, as if reading her thoughts.

She smiled feebly, touched yet unsure. He made it sound so simple. Could it really be so? She looked up to see him regarding her sheepishly.

"Now you shan't have to attend this week's service, having suffered through one of my sermons already! Do forgive me, Miss Keene."

She dipped her head. "There is nothing to forgive."

He eyed her basket. "May I ask what you have brought? Dare I hope for one of Mrs. Moore's seedcakes, perhaps?"

"I am afraid not, sir. Only cheese and gloves for the poor."

He heaved a shuddering breath. "You shall be good for me, Miss Keene. I have become too spoilt by widows plying me with cakes and sweets. We shall pour our energies into relieving the pangs of the poor, and not our earthly wants, shall we?"

She found his final statement mildly disconcerting. When she glanced up, he looked away, a boyish blush on his face, as though just realizing the implication of his words.

Inside, Olivia found Miss Ludlow sitting on the worn settee in the almshouse parlor, surrounded by yards of fabric.

"What are we working on today?" Olivia asked.

"New draperies for the parlor window. The old ones have grown shabby indeed. What think you of this corded muslin?"

"Lovely. So much lighter and cheerier than the present draperies."

Eliza smiled, dimples blazing. "I hoped you would like it."

Olivia helped Miss Ludlow take down the dusty old draperies and from them form a pattern to cut the new ones. Miss Ludlow announced that she would be more comfortable doing the sewing in her own home and reiterated her invitation to tea.

Mr. Tugwell was just bidding farewell to an elderly resident as the two ladies took their leave. All politeness, Miss Ludlow invited Mr. Tugwell to join them as well, and seemed surprised when he accepted. Olivia hoped he was not accepting on her account.

A short time later, ensconced in Miss Ludlow's sitting room, Charles Tugwell picked up his teacup and asked, "How goes governessing, Miss Keene?"

"Well, sir, I thank you. I still miss teaching in a school, but there is much to commend the profession."

"That reminds me. I called in at the school in St. Aldwyns last week, to see how the Miss Kirbys were getting on. I did inquire on your behalf, but it seems they have all the help they need at present."

"That's all right, Mr. Tugwell," Olivia said, resisting thoughts of her mother. "I am content where I am at present."

He nodded thoughtfully. "You know, I have an old friend—a friend of my late wife's, actually—who has a very successful girls' school in Kent. If you ever want a change, I should be happy to introduce you."

"Thank you. I shall keep that in mind."

The vicar studied Olivia over the tray of tea things. "You are what, Miss Keene, five and twenty?" he asked.

Olivia nodded. Her twenty-fifth birthday had recently passed with no one to recollect the date but herself.

"And not married?"

Self-conscious, Olivia shook her head. He must know this already. Did he think she was keeping a husband hidden along with her other secrets?

"It is a wonder a woman like you has not been swept off her feet by some worthy man long ago."

Olivia smiled weakly and nibbled her cake.

"Never been in love?"

She shrugged, increasingly uncomfortable with his line of questioning, especially under the vulnerable, watchful eyes of Eliza Ludlow.

"Surely you have been courted at least," he persisted.

She hesitated. "There was one young man who admired me," Olivia began, hoping to put off questions yet more personal. "He was kind and charming in his way, yet I could not fancy myself married to him. He worked as a panhand in a brushmaker's shop, hair-sorting and bundling bristles. He was proud of his pay, I recall. 'Twenty knots a penny-fourpence, halfpenny per good broom.'"

Miss Ludlow smiled encouragingly. The gesture brought the youth's image to mind—dark hair and warm brown eyes, a boy's impish smile. "He was the one young man in the village who did not mind my bluestocking speech and endless reading, although he had no interest in reading anything beyond the newspaper. We had so little in common."

Olivia thought back to how she had daily witnessed the frustration, the resentment, even the falsely awkward peace of a marriage between unsuited people. She'd had no wish to enter into one of her own.

Shaking her head, Olivia inhaled deeply and finished her tale. "I suppose the village girls were right. Perhaps I did think of myself too highly." *For who was I, after all?* she thought. *Merely the daughter of a clerk and a gentlewoman of reduced circumstances.*

Mr. Tugwell nodded his understanding but did not comment. His attention had suddenly shifted to Miss Ludlow as though he'd just remembered she was there. "And why did you never marry, Miss Eliza?"

Miss Ludlow tucked her chin, cheeks quickly reddening. "I don't know," she murmured with a lame little laugh.

"We all thought you would marry the miller," Mr. Tugwell said kindly. "A wealthy and influential man as ever there was."

"Perhaps I should have." Miss Ludlow's tone was nearly bitter, and Olivia's heart went out to her. The vicar had made her ill at ease with his awkward questions. Had he truly no idea how she felt about him?

His brows rose. "He offered marriage, then?"

Miss Ludlow gave a jerk of a nod.

"Forgive me, Miss Eliza. I did not intend to embarrass you. I own a parson's natural curiosity and concern for his flock. I am only surprised you did not marry."

She raised wounded brown eyes to his. "I did not love him."

"Ah . . ." He nodded thoughtfully, looking down into his teacup. "Never been in love . . . a good reason for remaining single."

She looked at him levelly. "I did not say that, sir."

He seemed unsure of her meaning but was finally aware that he had waded into murky, discomfiting waters. He finished his tea and straightened. "Well, thank you for tea, Miss Eliza. I shall trespass upon your hospitality no longer." He rose and bowed. "Good day, ladies." He avoided the eyes of both women as he stood and donned his hat.

34

> Governesses hold a place which varies according to the convenience and habits of the families in which they reside.
> This constantly subjects them to slights, wounding to the delicacy, and sometimes irritating to the temper.
>
> —*Advice to Governesses*, 1827

Charles Tugwell paid a morning call, and as was his habit, timed his visit to partake of a Brightwell breakfast. Hodges led him to the breakfast room, where Edward was sitting with coffee and newspaper.

The parson eyed the sideboard as if it were a lost soul. "Ah, my old friends crumpet and curd, how I have missed you."

Edward rolled his eyes with tolerant amusement. "Yes, I am well. Thank you, vicar."

"Do forgive me, Bradley. How are you? Look a bit tired, I will say."

"I am well enough." Edward flipped a page. "Now that you've dispatched with the niceties, do help yourself to breakfast."

"Don't mind if I do."

A few minutes later, Hodges returned with the tray and offered Edward his post. Ignoring his friend's moans of gourmand delight, Edward opened the first letter.

And froze.

His body broke out in a cold sweat. The script blurred and then focused once more.

> *Lady Brightwell has never borne a living child.*
> *You may be innocent, but your father has knowingly deceived the world at the cost of another. Where is justice?*

"My friend, what is it?" Mr. Tugwell asked around a bit of crumpet. "You look very ill."

Edward threw down his serviette and rose abruptly, toppling his chair in his wake and preparing to bolt from the room.

Tugwell rose as well. "Edward, wait!"

Edward pressed his eyes closed and took a deep breath.

"What is it? My dear friend, I have never seen you thus. You have come undone."

Panic rising, Edward paced the room liked a caged animal. "Exactly so. Undone, unwoven, unstrung."

"Edward, you alarm me! Do tell me what has happened."

"Have I your promise of secrecy?"

"Need you ask?"

Edward tossed him the letter, which the vicar read and read again, sitting slowly back down as he did so.

"Is it true?" he whispered, eyes wide.

Edward's pulse pounded in his ears. "I would not be this upset over a rumor."

"Lord Brightwell . . . ?"

"Admits it. This letter is not the first."

"I am sorry, my friend."

"You are sorry?" Edward bit back his frustration and lowered his voice. "Yes, well, so am I."

"Has he told you who or how . . . ?"

"Only that I was a foundling, taken in by them."

"Generous."

"Generosity was not the primary motivation. Rather, a determination that my uncle Sebastian never lay his hands on Brightwell Court."

"But he is dead now, is that not so?"

"Yes, which leaves Felix."

"Do you think—?"

"I don't know what to think." Edward raked agitated fingers through his hair. "Or who to blame."

Charles Tugwell stared at the letter once more. "And when this gets out . . . ?"

"*If* it gets out, I am ruined. My reputation . . . shot—baseborn nobody. Title, gone. Peerage to Felix. Political future . . . dead. Why do you think I was so determined to keep Miss Keene cloistered here?"

"She knows?"

"Yes. She overheard—the night she was arrested."

"Ahh . . ." The vicar slowly shook his head, eyes alight in deeper understanding.

"I stand to lose everything. My inheritance. My home. My very identity."

Charles set aside the letter and stood. "No, Edward. That you will not lose." He clasped Edward's shoulder. "Dear friend, whatever happens, you will always be God's child. 'And if children, then heirs; heirs of God, and joint-heirs with Christ.'"

Edward ran a weary hand over his face. "Cold comfort, Charles, when I believed myself heir to an earldom."

After Charles Tugwell took his leave, Edward sought his father in the library. Finding him at his desk, Edward carefully closed the door behind him and flopped down in a nearby chair. His father raised his eyes, taking in Edward's disheveled state.

"So much for parliament," Edward began.

"What are you talking about? Of course you will be summoned to take my seat after I am gone. It is what is done."

"Not in every instance, and certainly not in this."

"What has brought this on? You are my heir apparent—the next Earl of Brightwell. No one can take that from you."

"Are you sure about that, Father?" Edward tossed the note onto the desk.

"What is this? Hand me my spectacles."

Edward rose to deliver the wire frames and then watched as his father read the brief note. Lord Brightwell removed the spectacles and rubbed his eyes with thumb and forefinger. He sighed deeply. "When did this come?"

"This morning." Instead of resuming his seat, Edward resumed pacing.

"Have there been others?"

"This is the first directed to me. Have you received others?"

"Not since that first one before your mother and I departed for Italy."

"Who could have written this?"

"I don't know. I have never told anyone. I cannot speak for your mother, of course. I suppose it is possible she confided in someone—a friend or someone from her family." The earl looked far off for an answer. "Devil take it, who would do such a thing?"

He pulled the first letter from a desk drawer and laid both side by side. Edward looked over his shoulder and studied the handwriting.

His father asked, "Were both written by the same person, do you think?"

"I assume so. But it is difficult to tell—the first was so brief."

Lord Brightwell held the most recent letter at arm's length and regarded it, chin tucked. "Looks like a woman's hand to me."

Edward straightened. "But Felix is the obvious suspect."

"Felix? Felix can barely plan his attire, let alone a scheme like this." His father returned the letter to him.

"He has the most to gain."

"Not at present. Do not forget, Edward, the courtesy title you use is mine. Even if you *were* to give it up, Felix cannot use it in your stead. He would only be my heir presumptive, with no title and no inheritance until after my death."

Edward nodded and began pacing once more. "It may not change the present, but certainly his prospects for the future."

"I suppose you are right. Still I cannot credit it. From where was it posted?"

Edward turned the letter over. "Cirencester." The word echoed in his mind, and he recalled Miss Keene's recent trip there to "purchase cheese for the almshouse." Edward frowned. Just a coincidence surely.

"From so near!" Lord Brightwell said.

Should he tell his father? But no, it couldn't be Miss Keene . . . could it? He decided not to reveal, for the present, the fact of her being in Cirencester a few days ago.

"Is not Felix back at Oxford?" his father asked.

"Yes. But it is not so long a journey, if he wanted to throw us off the scent."

Restless and unable to focus on the accounts, Edward tucked the estate ledger under his arm and went to return it to Walters. When he could not locate the clerk, Edward took himself upstairs instead. He felt the need to see Miss Keene, to somehow reassure himself of her innocence.

Ledger still under his arm, Edward silently let himself in and stood at the back of the schoolroom. Audrey and Andrew, eyes forward, did not even notice him enter. Miss Keene did, however, and faltered in the lesson she was delivering. She glanced expectantly at him, but when he did not speak, she continued the Latin lesson, though clearly distracted by his presence.

"'Terms Seldom Englished,'" she read from the text. "'*Viva voce*, meaning by word of mouth. *Inter nos*, between ourselves.'"

Did she choose those terms for my benefit? Edward wondered. He thought back to the days when he alone heard Miss Keene's voice.

"'*Argumentum ad ignorantiam*, a foolish argument.'"

Oh yes, they'd had a few of those. Crossing his arms, Edward leaned against the wall, watching her closely.

"'*Alias*, otherwise.'"

Edward raised his brows. Had he not once accused her of giving an alias instead of her real name? Was it his imagination, or was a flush creeping up her neck?

"'*Alibi*, being in another place.'" She glanced up at him—guiltily, he thought. Had she need of an alibi? In his current state of mind, every word she spoke had some latent meaning, and seemed to accuse her. But she was innocent, was she not?

She cleared her throat, then continued, "'*Bona fide*, without fraud or deceit.'"

Was Miss Keene without deceit? His father believed she was. And Edward very much hoped he was right. But she *was* hiding something. She had never really explained how she had come to be at Brightwell Court with no belongings and no plans other than the name of a school, nor why she had initially concealed where she was from. No doubt it had something to do with her foul-tempered father. But even so, it did not mean she had anything to do with the letters. *Merciful Lord, let her have nothing to do with the letters. . . .*

"'*Extortus*, meaning extortion.'" Miss Keene glanced at him once more, clearly self-conscious, then closed the book.

Why was she so nervous?

"Well, I believe that is enough Latin for today. Let us move on to arithmetic. Your slates please, children."

She was turning to the shelter of the subject she knew best, he realized, recalling her tale of the public-house contest. Suddenly curious, he raised his hand. "May I pose a question?"

The children turned to smile at him, but Miss Keene looked anything but pleased. "Very well."

He opened the ledger and referred to one of the equations written in Walter's neat hand. "What is 4,119 multiplied by 4, then divided by 12?"

For a brief moment, she stared at something over his head. "It is 1,373. Why?"

He stared back, stunned. "I wonder . . . just how clever are you?"

35

Is it not the great end of religion . . .
to extinguish the malignant passions,
to curb the violence, to control the appetites,
and to smooth the asperities of man . . . ?
—William Wilberforce

Olivia had been sound asleep when her father's shout startled her awake. Had she really heard it, or merely had a nightmare? She listened, heart pounding. There it came again. All too real.

How did he find me? she frantically wondered. *Did Miss Cresswell tell him? Surely not the constable, when Father is a wanted man!*

Dare she pull the covers over her head and hope he would go away?

At a third shout, Olivia scrambled from bed, padded to her window, and looked down, but could not see the main doors from this angle. She unlatched the window and pushed it open. Through it, she could hear his voice more clearly—and hear him banging on the door as though to break it down.

"Dorothea! Dorothea . . ." It was half-rant, half-sob, and Olivia's heart seized to hear it, even as her mind clouded, cleared, and clouded again. He was not calling for her at all. If he was trying to find his wife, then he must believe her to be alive—had not knowingly brought about her end.

"Dorothea!"

Should she go down to him? Did he know she had been the one who struck him?

"Open up! I want to see my wife!" His voice was uncontrolled, slurred. She knew that tone, that cadence. He was foxed.

She heard the sound of a gun cocking and froze. Croome—she knew it instantly.

"On yer way, mister. Before I send you on yer way in a pine box."

Lord Bradley's voice joined in, though Olivia had not heard a door open. "Whom do you seek at this ungodly hour, man?" He had probably come out by one of the side doors and was likely bearing a pistol himself.

"I told you. Dorothea. My wife. She is here. I know she is."

"There is no one here by that name. Upon my honour, there is not."

"Who are you?"

"Lord Bradley."

"No . . . not Bradley. I want Brightwell."

"Lord Brightwell is my father."

"Your father? But you are so . . . grown. He must be old as I am and serves him right. Gone back to him, has she?" His voice rose again. "I mean her no harm. But I must see her. I must!"

"Do lower your voice, my good man. I promise you, my father has no woman here. He is in mourning for his own wife, only recently passed on."

"A widower, is he? How kind fate is to them! There is no hope for me, then. I have lost her. Well and truly lost her."

How defeated he sounded. How lost. Olivia steeled her heart. *This is remorse talking. And guilt. And perhaps fear of consequences. I must not forget—I saw him with his hands around her throat.*

But she could not fully reconcile this argument with the broken man she heard below.

Olivia threw her cape over her nightdress and ran down the stairs, suddenly determined to speak with him, to push confession or explanation from him, knowing she would be safe in the company of Mr. Croome and Lord Bradley.

But when she reached the front hall, she found Hodges and Osborn huddled at the door, holding it fast.

"Mrs. Hinkley pulled the curtain aside from the long-view windows. "He is gone."

All expelled a collective sigh of relief.

Even Olivia. He would not have given her trustworthy answers, she decided, foxed as he was. And with his passions so out of control, who knew how he might react to finding her there, in his enemy's abode? For clearly he did know of her mother's relationship with Lord Brightwell, long past though it was.

Even though it was not yet her half day off, Olivia left the children with Becky and Nurse Peale, donned her bonnet, and hurried up the lane and across the street to the almshouse. She was still unsettled from the late-night visit from her father and hoped a visit with calm Mr. Tugwell or cheerful Eliza Ludlow would soothe her. When she stepped inside and hung her bonnet, she saw no sign of Miss Ludlow. Hers was the lone article of feminine apparel on the pegs near the door. The parlor door was open and, hearing Mr. Tugwell's voice within, she went to greet him. She crossed the threshold and froze.

Charles Tugwell sat talking earnestly to Simon Keene, who was hunched in an armchair, head bowed, elbows on his knees. She was stunned to see him. It was such a collision of her old world and new . . . that for a moment she just stood there, stupefied.

Mr. Tugwell noticed her first and rose. "Miss Keene."

Her father's head jerked up. "Livie!" His hair, dark like hers, was in need of cutting. Stubble shadowed his cheeks. His suit of clothes was surprisingly fine, though somewhat rumpled.

He stood and took a step forward, as though to . . . what? A part of her longed to flee before she found out, but she felt rooted to the spot, as in a dream where one cannot run from danger. He stood where he was, staring at her. For a long moment she could not find her voice. When she remained silent, the light in his brown eyes faded and he sank back into the chair, thin mouth turned down.

Tugwell asked her quietly, "Shall I leave you?"

"Please stay."

"Come to rail at me?" her father asked. "I know I was a fool last night. I can hardly blame you for not coming to the door."

Mr. Tugwell said apologetically, "I am afraid I let it slip you were in residence."

Olivia lifted a stiff shrug, keeping her eyes on her father. "You did not ask for me."

"I would have, had I known. Thank God you are well."

He did not know, she realized, that she was the one who had struck him. All this time, living in fear . . .

He kneaded his hands as though they ached. "Your mother is . . . well, I trust?"

Olivia felt her brow furrow. *How could he ask such a thing, when he . . . ?*

"I have no idea," she said, more bitterly than she intended. "But if she is well, it is no thanks to you."

She felt Tugwell's look of surprise but ignored him. She wanted no sermons on forgiveness now.

Her father bowed his head. When he looked up, he did not quite meet her eyes. "The parson here assured me Dorothea is not at Brightwell Court, but I own I did not quite believe him."

"She is not. I have not laid eyes on her since I left. I have feared her dead these last months."

"Dead? Why?"

"*You* ask that?"

He grimaced. "You have heard the rumors about the grave?"

She nodded.

"I admit I too feared the worst when I awoke that morning and found broken glass and even a smear of blood. Figured I had come home foxed and had a terrible row with Dorothea." He sighed. "I did not realize the two of you were gone until the next day. I went to see Miss Atkins, but she would not even allow me into her house. She told me you had left to find a situation, and that Dorothea was gone and not coming back. She would not tell me more."

Had he really no recollection of trying to strangle his wife, of being struck himself? Had he been so drunk? How did he explain the large gash or lump that must certainly have risen on the back of his head?

She asked, "But what of the blood you mentioned?"

"I don't know." He held up his hands, turning them over. "Thought I must have punched a wall again, or cut myself on the glass, but I found no cuts on my hands."

It was on the tip of her tongue to ask if his head had bled. But then she would have to explain how she knew he had been injured. She was not ready to tell him, not now, when he knew where to find her. He seemed so peaceable and remorseful—so sober—at present, but for how long?

"I too heard the whispers about the new grave in the churchyard," he said quietly. "But I knew better—knew I had driven her away at last. Back to the arms of her *Oliver*."

Oliver? It jolted her to hear the name on her father's lips. Just how much did he know about his wife's long-ago relationship with the earl?

"I tried to let her go. . . . Moved to the spa site to better manage it, and to steer clear of that empty house and all the suspicious looks I was drawing about the village. All winter I was driven mad with missing her.

"Finally I could bear it no longer. I had to find her. It took some time to locate this man Oliver, for I had never known his surname. I tried to contact

Dorothea's family, but they would not see me. Finally someone I asked knew an Oliver and directed me to Brightwell Court." He shook his head regretfully. "I should never have stopped off at the inn last night. 'Just one cup for courage,' I told myself. But one led to two, then three . . ."

He winced his eyes shut. "For so long, I have imagined her with him, and how it has eaten at my soul. If she is not there, where on earth is she?"

"I do not know," Olivia said. "I thought she would come to find me, but she has not. Perhaps she feared *you* might find her if she did."

He shook his head. "The way you look at me, girl . . . Do you hate me so?"

"You ask me that? When you could barely stand the sight of me all these years? Not since that contest in the Crown and Crow. How you hated me for losing."

Simon Keene frowned. "Hated losing that contest, but never you."

She expelled a puff of air and disbelief. "You have never treated me the same since that day. You cannot deny it."

"I don't deny it. But not because of that plagued contest. Don't you know? That was the very day I learnt that you . . . that I . . ." He grimaced in his effort to find the words. "That your mother named you for this Oliver fellow."

Olivia shook her head. "I don't recall that. . . ."

"Do you not? When the three of us rode into Chedworth together, earlier that same day?"

"To see the Roman ruins—that I remember."

"And do you recall that woman who came up and greeted your mother like a long-lost friend?"

"Vaguely."

"I remember it perfectly. Your mother introduced me by name and then said, 'And this is our daughter.' She gave my name, see, but not yours. So like a fool I said, 'This is our Olivia.'

"'Olivia! After Oliver?' the woman says, then turned redder than a beetroot and tried to cover her tracks. Mumbled something like, 'Oh! Of course not. Only a coincidence, I am sure.'

"That's when I learnt the knob's name. *Oliver*. Dorothea denied the connection, said she had *always* liked the name Olivia. But what could she say? What more proof did I need?" His thin mouth twisted in disgust. "The cheek of her—naming the girl I fed and clothed after a man who never lifted a hand for either of you. It wasn't your fault, I know, but I could never look at you the same way again. Never look at myself the same. To think how idiotically proud of you I was when I had no right to be."

Olivia shot a glance at Mr. Tugwell, who seemed suddenly interested in the condition of his fingernails. If she had feared the parson admired her, this would certainly cure him of any lingering romantic notions.

Simon Keene shook his head again. "I knew she had a lover before I met her. And that she went to see the rake once, even after we were married. But then time went by, see, and we had a few good years, and I let myself think that maybe she had got over him—maybe she could love me after all. . . ." His voice broke. "Only to learn she had lied to me all those years. My own little girl, not mine after all. Named after the man she *really* loved, so she would never forget him."

An awkward silence followed, as her father tried to regain control of his emotions. Olivia felt torn between wanting to rail at him for attacking her mother, and confusion over his story. Her mind whirled, trying in vain to make it jibe with her own memories.

Simon rubbed a hand across his stubbled face. "It boiled my blood—and cut me deep, I own. How it galled me, the thought of her still pining for him. Still wishing she had never tied up with the likes of me."

Had this been behind his dark moods and fits of anger? Driven him to drink so heavily?

"Surely you know that is not why she left you," Olivia said. "I have never heard her speak of any other man, or seen anything that would make me think—"

"And why would you?" he interrupted. "Away at that school all day as you were? Your mother home alone, or so we thought. Did you never notice two glasses on the sideboard, or smell cigar smoke in the house?"

"Mother would never . . ." Olivia hesitated. Had she smelled cigar smoke? She could not be sure. Olivia *had* spent a great deal of each day and sometimes evenings at Miss Cresswell's. But to assume a caller was Lord Brightwell, after all these years? Ridiculous. "If someone was in the house, surely it was only a friend come to call," she said. "Or someone picking up needlework . . . or—"

"Then why would she not tell me who had called? Why did she act so nervous and secret-like? The more she lied about it, the angrier I got, until I thought I should explode!"

Had he snapped? Had his irrational jealousy led to that final act of violence?

The mantel clock struck the hour, and no one spoke while the bell chimed, then faded away.

The parlor door, which still stood ajar, opened a few inches further, and Lord Brightwell himself appeared in the gap. From his angle, Olivia realized, he could see only her, and perhaps Mr. Tugwell.

"Olivia, a puppeteer has arrived in the square and I thought the children might—" He pushed the door open further, and his gaze encompassed the entire parlor. "Oh, pardon me, I did not realize . . ."

Olivia panicked. These two men in the same room together? What dreadful timing! "Lord Brightwell. I . . ."

Simon Keene wiped his sleeve across his face and rose. "Speak of the devil. Oliver, is it?"

Mr. Tugwell laid a staying hand on her father's arm and in a low voice urged, "Steady . . ."

Olivia cleared her throat, finding it difficult to breathe in a room suddenly thick with tension. "Actually, it is Lord Brightwell. And this is Simon Keene, my . . ." Olivia swallowed, and before she could continue, the earl stepped to her side, assuming a protective stance.

Simon Keene looked from one to the other and slowly shook his head. "I see how it is." He shook off the vicar's hand and faced the earl squarely. "I will ask you, sir, man to man. Do you know where Dorothea is?"

Lord Brightwell stared coldly back. "And I will answer in all truth that I do not. But if I did, I should not tell you."

Olivia cringed, expecting her father to rage at this, to fly across the room and strike the earl . . . or strangle him.

But the fight seemed to have gone out of Simon Keene. "I see. Well." He picked up his hat and turned it in his hands. "I shall take my leave. Sorry to have bothered you."

Mr. Tugwell touched his arm once more. "Mr. Keene, wait. You are in no fair shape to sally forth. You are welcome to stay as long as you need."

The vicar glanced at the earl as though to gauge his reaction, but Lord Brightwell was looking at her. He offered his arm and together they exited the almshouse, leaving the two men where they were, Tugwell speaking gently to his visitor. Olivia guessed Simon Keene had never heeded a parson in his life, and doubted he would begin now.

It was only after she and Lord Brightwell had crossed the high street that Olivia realized she had not asked if her father knew he was a wanted man.

36

> Those ladies, who from the misfortunes of their families have been compelled to exchange happy homes and indulgent relations for the society of strangers, are objects of peculiar sympathy.
>
> —*Advice to Governesses,* 1827

For days, the meeting with her father revolved and replayed in her mind—what she should have said to him, the questions she ought to have asked, the truths she should have demanded. After torturing herself in this manner for several long, restless nights, Olivia decided to dwell on the positive aspect of the meeting. Simon Keene believed her mother alive. And Olivia would endeavor to believe it as well.

On her next half day, Olivia spent the afternoon keeping Eliza Ludlow company in her shop, and managed to enjoy herself quite convincingly.

She returned to Brightwell Court to find two letters awaiting her. One came with no return direction. The other bore the fine, artistic hand of Miss Cresswell. Olivia first opened the letter from her former teacher, feeling sixty percent eagerness and forty percent dread. Had Miss Cresswell heard from her mother? From Muriel Atkins, the midwife?

My dear Olivia,

Muriel has finally returned. After the birth in the country, it seems she went directly to her niece in Brockworth, whose time came early. It was a long and difficult lying-in (twins—both live, praise God), and rarely have I seen Muriel so exhausted.

When I told her of your visit, she said I was to tell you in confidence that your mother does not lie in the churchyard. Is that not good news? I am not to tell anyone but you. Muriel fears someone intends your mother harm, and if this person believes she might be, well, gone, then so much the better. She would not say who, but I am sure your guess is the same as mine. Sounds a desperate plan to me, when her own daughter is allowed to believe such a tragedy!

I understand your mother fell ill and stayed with Muriel's sister for much of the winter, but she has since fully recovered. Still, Muriel insists she knows nothing about where your mother is now, nor how she fares. She only hopes the ruse may have spared your mother from real harm. But as no letter has come, she begins to fear this is not the case. Still she and I hope every day for word from our dear friend Dorothea.

I am afraid my other news may be difficult for you to hear. Your father has been found and arrested. The specific charge has still not been made public, but rumors abound.

Do write and let me know that you are well. I am praying God's peace for you during such uncertain times.

Miss Lydia Cresswell

Arrested? He must have gone directly to Withington from the almshouse. Again, Olivia wondered what her father was accused of doing, and whether or not he was guilty. She felt an overwhelming ebb and flow of emotions, from vindictive satisfaction (did he not deserve some retribution for his violent act?) to embarrassment at having a parent in prison, to unexpected pity when she thought of the broken state in which she had last seen him. How strangely unsettling it had been to hear him acknowledge that he was not her father. It ought to have been a relief—even more so now after Miss Cresswell's tidings. Instead, she felt empty. Emotionally bankrupt. She thought back to Mr. Tugwell's words about a person's inability to pay for his own foul deeds, and felt spiritually bankrupt as well. For had she not committed her own offenses?

Olivia studied the outside of the second letter, noting the elegant seal and the fine stationery. She did not recognize the hand. Who else could be writing to her? Mrs. Hawthorn crossed her mind, but she quickly chastised herself for the foolish hope.

She pried open the seal and unfolded the letter, immediately looking at the signature. It *was* from her grandmother.

Dear Miss Keene,

Please forgive the delay. This is my fifth attempt at composing this letter.

I have given your visit a great deal of thought. In fact, I can think of little else, save occasionally fretting over what may have befallen Dorothea. You may think it cold of me to think of you instead of mourning my daughter, but you see, I mourned her loss more than five-and-twenty years ago, when she wrote to tell me she had married a man I could never approve of, nor accept. She said she knew she could expect no further relations between us and decided to spare me the trouble of severing ties myself. Still, I confess I have always held out hope that she would contact me again one day, to let me know where she was living and, if nothing else, that she was all right. Receiving such a letter from your hand was quite a shock.

When my daughter Georgiana returned from her shopping trip, she found me sitting where you left me, that letter still in my hand. She drew from me the events of the day and was quite vexed with me for not having asked you to stay long enough that she might have met you herself.

I regret not receiving you more warmly, my dear. Please, will you do us the honour of calling again?

Mrs. Elizabeth Hawthorn

Seeing the woman's name in her own hand caused Olivia's heart to contract as it had not done before she had met Mrs. Hawthorn. *Elizabeth*. Her own name was Olivia Elizabeth. Had her mother named her for her father and grandmother?

Another script, this one free and loopy, wrote an addendum beneath the precise formal hand:

Please do come, Olivia. Imagine! I have a niece!

Your Aunt,
Georgiana Crenshaw

(Mr. Crenshaw says you are most welcome.)

Olivia felt herself smiling, already drawn to this effervescent aunt she had never met.

Edward and Lord Brightwell made their way to the drawing room to greet Felix, who had returned to Brightwell for a weekend visit. Judith had arrived before them, evidenced by her voice sifting into the corridor from the open door.

"How go things at Oxford?" she asked.

Edward entered the room in time to see Felix shrug. He took up the refrain. "Yes, Felix, how go the studies?"

"Studies? Oh, is that what I am to be about at Oxford? I thought I was there for rowing and singing and impressing the ladies."

"Well, that too, of course," Edward said good-naturedly.

Felix selected a cigar from the wooden box on the sideboard and slipped it into his coat pocket. Then he helped himself to the decanter of port.

Lord Brightwell seated himself and asked Felix to pour him a glass as well. "Felix, I am happy to sponsor you at my old *alma mater*, but I did hope you would apply yourself."

Felix sighed and handed the earl a glass. "I am afraid I must disappoint you, Uncle. It seems success is beyond my reach. I have a mind to quit the whole business."

"What?" Edward exclaimed, trying but failing to keep the edge from his voice.

Felix threw up his hands. "Does it really matter? No one has ever expected much of me. Don't tell me you depend upon my having a brilliant career in the law, or the church, or politics or some such thing. It is ridiculous."

"No, it is not," Edward said.

"Why?"

"Why?" Edward faltered and felt Judith's curious glance. "Because . . . well, you never know what the future might bring, and well . . ."

His father joined in, "And Bradleys have always excelled at university. Even your father."

Edward was surprised to hear Lord Brightwell mention his long-estranged brother.

"My, we are all feeling charitable today, are we not?" Felix said. "Even my father, who is never praised here in his childhood home, was more intelligent than I, it seems."

"Your father was clever indeed," Lord Brightwell said. "But this is not about intelligence. You have perfectly good brains, my boy, you just lack . . . well . . ."

"Self-discipline," Edward offered.

"Ambition," Judith added.

Acrimony dripped from Felix's lips. "Well, thank you all very much."

"How bad is it?" Lord Brightwell asked, with an anticipatory grimace.

One hand on the mantel, neck bowed, Felix stared at the fire. "Not only will there be no honours, but I am on the cusp of failing out."

Lord Brightwell gaped. "Never say so!"

"I am afraid it is quite true, Uncle. I have come to grief at Oxford. I see no point in returning for the rest of the year and wasting more of your money."

Edward frowned. "You will not quit, Felix."

Felix stared at him, hard. "Why? Can't stand to see a blight on the Bradley pride?"

"What about *your* pride?" Edward said. "A man does not quit what he has begun. Now go back to Balliol, pass the examinations, and obtain your degree."

"To what purpose? I already told you I am not fit for the church or the law."

Edward felt Judith studying him, awaiting his answer just as her brother did.

"You have a bright future before you, Felix," he said, hedging. "I cannot say how it will come or what form it will take, but I would have you be prepared to rise to the occasion when it presents itself."

Brother and sister still stared at him, brows furrowed. Lord Brightwell stepped in to the unsettled void and slapped Felix on the back. "Come on, my boy. You can do it. We are all of us behind you."

37

When you set yourself on fire, people love to come and see you burn.

—John Wesley

The next morning, Olivia and the children played hide-and-seek amid a lifting grey fog and the hoarse call of ravens.

While Audrey covered her eyes and counted, Olivia stepped behind the carpentry shop. She was surprised Andrew had not followed and hidden near her as was his wont. Perhaps he had seen Johnny or Lord Bradley and had run off to join one of them.

Audrey made a great show of checking the garden and arbor, then ran across the lawn in her direction. Smiling, Olivia retreated behind the shop wall.

"I found you, miss. I found you!" Audrey happily announced.

Olivia smoothed a lock of hair from the girl's brow. "Yes, you did, my clever girl." Unexpected tears pricked her eyes, as thoughts of her father came unbidden. *"My clever girl"* had been his pet name for her in happier times.

"I am sorry I found you so quickly if it makes you sad," Audrey said, stricken.

"No, I am pleased you found me. Now, shall we go seek Andrew together?"

Audrey looked about her. "He isn't with you?"

"Not this time."

That was when Olivia heard it. The barked word "fire!" repeated again in a woman's shrill cry. "Fire! Fire in the stables!" The laundry maid, Olivia guessed, who worked near the stable yard.

Olivia's heart started. *The stables?* All that hay and straw. The poor horses! A dreadful thought struck Olivia's chest like an iron mallet. *Good Lord, no . . .*

"Andrew!" she cried, and ran headlong across the lawn. Audrey followed behind, shouting her little brother's name.

Reaching the stables, she called to the coachman, harried and single-handedly trying to herd the horses from harm.

"Mr. Talbot! Have you seen Andrew? We were hiding and—"

"No, miss. He isn't here."

Relief filled her. The coachman looped a rope around the neck of a grey gelding, and all but dragged the terrified animal from the stable. If only Lord Bradley would return from his morning ride!

"Audrey, run into the house and find Lord Brightwell," Olivia said. "And ask everyone you meet if they have seen Andrew."

The girl scurried to her bidding.

Johnny came on a run from the direction of the wood, a sheepish Martha trailing behind him.

"Have either of you seen Andrew?" Olivia called.

"No," Martha said, eyes wide. And she ran off to look for him while Johnny rushed to help Talbot with the horses.

Something compelled Olivia to stay where she was. She heard a terrified whinny and then another. *Bang!* The stable gate exploded outward, kicked hard by the rear hooves of a large black horse. Lord Bradley had not gone on his ride as she had thought. Where was he?

Instinctively, Olivia ran forward, skirting the horse's dangerous hind legs and stepping to its great head, trying to calm the horse as she had the day she had groomed it, with a firm hand and soothing words. The horse reared up and hit its head on the stable rafters, clearly disoriented by the smoke and too panicked to respond to her prodding.

Lord Bradley appeared through the smoke and whipped a hood over the horse's head in one deft throw. "Major, walk on!" And with a great heave, he pushed the stubborn horse through the broken gate and out into the yard.

Over his shoulder he called, "Miss Keene, get away from here!"

"Not until I know Andrew is safe. He was hiding and we have not found him. Have you seen him?"

Pulling the last of the horses free, Talbot scowled, "I told you he weren't here, miss. I checked the stables, the office, and the tack room." The coachman threw up his hands. "Now, get out the both of you before the roof falls down upon us."

Olivia and Lord Bradley swung around to look at each other, their gazes locking into place. The same thought—fear—in both of their minds. The little-known closet. What if Andrew had hidden there?

Olivia lurched forward, but Lord Bradley caught her by the arm. "Talbot, keep her back."

The coachman stepped forward and gripped her upper arms. Lord Bradley shrugged off his coat, bunched it over his nose and mouth, and disappeared into the smoke.

Olivia strained against Talbot. "Let me go!" Every maternal feeling swelled within her, overriding even her survival instinct. A little boy, her charge, might even now be overcome with smoke. "Let me go to him. Let me go."

The coachman's wiry strength was unyielding, and she was no match for a man who controlled horses six or seven times his weight.

Oh, God, please. This is my fault. Oh, please, spare them both!

The smoke roiled black and grey. With a loud crack, the far wall and roof crumbled—the section where the hay and straw were stored. The flames shot through the aperture, and the smoke rose even higher. People were running from all directions now, Mr. Croome leading the charge. Behind him, Hodges, Osborn, Mrs. Moore, Mrs. Hinkley, the gardener, hall boy, and maids, all formed a water brigade from the garden well. Grim-faced people sloshed bucket after bucket of water at the ravenous mouth of the fire. But Olivia could see it was futile. She scanned the growing crowd but saw no dear little brown mop of hair. No wide brown eyes. Now Lord Brightwell ran out of the house. And there, Judith, pulled along by Audrey. The girl's face was wild with fear. Olivia's heart sped within her. No Andrew.

Lord Brightwell reached them first. "Are the horses all out? The groom?"

Behind her, Talbot said, "All accounted for, my lord."

The earl looked at the coachman, still holding her fast, then searched her face. "What is it, Olivia?"

Stretching out her hands, she gripped Lord Brightwell's arm as tightly as Talbot held hers. "I could not find Andrew. Edward went in to make sure . . ."

"I told him not to, my lord," Talbot said.

Craning her neck, she asked the coachman, "Did you check the closet? The hidden door between the tack room and the saddle rack?"

"There is no closet there."

"But there is!"

Rumble . . . crack! The roof collapsed like a snake of dominoes from right to left.

"Edward!" Lord Brightwell lunged forward, loosing Olivia's hand as though a child's grip.

Through the black smoke, a figure materialized, black against black, like a specter. A beam fell and struck the dark figure, and Olivia screamed.

Lord Bradley, a burden in his arms, stuttered to the side and crashed to his knees just ahead of the weight of the wreckage. Olivia jerked away from Talbot's stunned grip and ran forward on the earl's heels, passing him and reaching Edward first. She pulled the small coat-shrouded body from him, and relieved of his burden, his duty, he fell face forward. His father caught him as he dropped, cushioning his fall. Croome appeared beside the earl, face ashen. Together they each took an arm and dragged Lord Bradley from the flames.

Watching from a point of relative safety, Andrew in her arms, Olivia's heart pounded, and new tears pooled in her eyes for reasons too numerous to sum.

In the library that evening, Lord Brightwell and Judith Howe sat in high-backed chairs very much like thrones. Olivia stood before them, hands clasped behind her back and head bowed—the posture of a criminal awaiting judgment. She felt she deserved the moniker. And worse.

Audrey stood behind her stepmother's chair, eyes red-rimmed. Olivia wished the girl need not be on hand to witness her dismissal.

Olivia forced her head up. "I am very sorry, Mrs. Howe. Lord Brightwell. I should never have allowed Andrew to run off on his own."

Judith Howe played with the worked lace on the arm of the chair. She looked up and said coldly, "I must say, Miss Keene, I am prodigiously disappointed in you."

"It was not her fault, Mamma," Audrey said. "We were only playing hide-and-seek. Miss Keene could not know a fire would start."

"How quick you are to defend your governess, Audrey," Mrs. Howe said. "You may leave us now."

Olivia's dear pupil gave her an apologetic glance and hurried from the room.

When the door closed behind Audrey, Mrs. Howe asked, "Are you in the habit of letting the children run wild about the estate, without supervision?"

"No, madam."

"Even that nurserymaid, who is little more than a girl herself, knows better. If anything had happened to Andrew . . ."

"I know. I know." Olivia pressed her eyes closed, miserable. "I would never have forgiven myself."

"Nor would you ever have the care of children again, had I anything to say about it." A new thought struck her mistress. "And why were *you* out with them instead of the girl?"

Olivia swallowed. "Becky has so much other work, and I enjoy playing with the children."

"It does not sound as if you were *with* them at all, but instead off on your own somewhere." She darted a glance at her uncle. "Perhaps meeting a lover?"

"No, madam. Nothing of—"

"Judith, please," Lord Brightwell admonished. "Such accusations are neither fair nor becoming."

Mrs. Howe gave him a sharp look. "Are you so quick to defend her as well?"

The earl spoke in moderating tones. "Of course I am. Miss Keene has been a marvelous addition to our household. I am sure she regrets this incident and will see that it does not happen again."

Judith looked from her uncle to Olivia and back again. "It seems, Uncle, that you would forgive her anything."

"It was an accident, Judith," he said. "And Dr. Sutton assures us Andrew will be fine. He did inhale a quantity of smoke and will cough for some days, but he is breathing well and will be his old mischievous self in no time."

Olivia dared ask, "And what of Lord Bradley?"

"He is badly injured," Mrs. Howe snapped. "Thanks to you."

"My dear Judith," Lord Brightwell said, "do you accuse her of starting the fire as well?"

Judith stubbornly lifted her chin but gave no answer.

"Judith, really! According to Talbot, there *were* two persons in the stables before the fire." He gave Judith a pointed look. "But neither was Miss Keene."

Mrs. Howe did not ask whom he meant, Olivia noticed. And wondered why.

After the interview, Olivia stepped into the sickroom. Andrew lay there, head raised on several pillows, eyes as red as the glass of berry ice he clutched in his hands.

Olivia felt her chest tighten. *Thank you for sparing him*, she breathed. "Hello, Master Andrew."

He smiled up at her, teeth and lips stained red. "Hello, Miss Livie."

"How are you feeling?"

"My eyes burn like the time I got Mamma's perfume in them. My throat hurts too, but Becky brought me an ice, which feels ever so good. Delicious too."

Olivia smiled. "I am very glad."

He scooped up another spoonful into his mouth, and several drips found their way onto his white nightgown.

"Might I help you with that?" she asked.

He shrugged good-naturedly and handed her the spoon as Olivia sat on the edge of the bed.

She gave him a spoonful and simply savored the sight and nearness of the dear little boy. A floorboard creaked and Olivia turned her head.

Judith Howe entered the dim room. "Miss Keene," she said officiously. "Why are you not in the schoolroom with Audrey? That is what Lord Brightwell is paying you for, I believe. I shall ask Mrs. Hinkley to sit with Andrew until the chamber nurse arrives."

Andrew's little brow furrowed, clearly hearing the restrained anger in his stepmother's voice. He asked, "Are you cross with Miss Livie, Mamma?"

"If I am, it is only because I am concerned about you, Andrew. You might have been killed in that fire."

"But *she* did not start the fire."

"She should not have allowed you to go into the stables alone."

Andrew shrugged his little shoulders again. "She did not 'low me, I just went. Saw Uncle Felix and wanted to talk to him."

"Did you? Still, she ought—"

"But he was already talking to Martha when I got there," Andrew continued. "So I just went into that hiding closet, like I seen Miss—"

"Saw."

"Saw Miss Keene coming out of that time."

Judith looked at her shrewdly. "Indeed?"

"I could see Uncle Felix and Martha through the cracks in the wall. He sounded angry, so I did not jump out and scare him as I planned to."

"Very wise," Judith murmured, distracted.

"He was smoking one of those cigars, Mamma—the ones you don't like? And he threw it down."

Judith darted a look at Olivia, then said agitatedly, "Yes, well, we cannot know if that is how . . . that is, you did not actually see the fire start?"

Again Andrew shrugged. "No. I went to look out the back of the closet to see if Audrey was coming to find me yet. I saw Martha run off into the wood and Johnny run after her. I smelled smoke and thought Uncle Felix must still be near, but that is all I remember. . . ."

"Poor boy."

"I am *well*, Mamma." He bestowed another of his cherry red smiles.

"I am relieved to hear you say so. Well, I am away to visit my mother. Miss Keene, you will return to your duties in the schoolroom promptly, I trust?"

"Yes, madam."

"At least . . . your duties for the present." Mrs. Howe nodded curtly and left the room.

Andrew opened his mouth for another bite and Olivia hurried to oblige him. He asked as though of a great adventure, "Did Cousin Edward really rescue me?"

"Yes, he did," Olivia said, and the little boy looked happier than he had opening gifts on Christmas morn.

38

> The governess ought never, under any possible circumstances, to allow herself to be either the source of family contention, or mixed up as a party in any domestic quarrel.
>
> —*The Guide to Service*, 1844

Olivia met Lord Brightwell coming out of the room next to the study. She waited until he closed the door, then whispered, "My lord, how is Ed—Lord Bradley?"

The earl's face was grim with exhaustion, but he managed a small smile for her. "Dr. Sutton has every confidence in a full recovery. The beam struck Edward across the nose and both brows. He has suffered minor burns around his eyes, but Sutton does not expect any long-term effect to his vision. His left arm is also injured. And two of his fingers burned, though not severely."

"How dreadful."

"He is well, Olivia." He lifted his chin toward the door he had just exited. "I was just in to see him, and his only concerns were for Andrew's well-being and your own."

"I am so sorry, my lord," Olivia said over the lump in her throat.

"My dear, those children have been running amuck since they came here, and if Judith has led you to believe they were under a watchful eye every moment before your arrival, then she has given you a false impression." He looked at her fondly and patted her hand. "You have given those children more attention and supervision than Judith ever has. Assure her it will not happen again and all will be well."

Olivia shook her head. "I believe I ought take my leave of you. I am certain Mrs. Howe would prefer it, and I do not blame her."

"Olivia, you are innocent in this, and I will make Judith see reason. But if it comes down to it, she is my niece, but you are my—"

She pressed his arm. "Don't say it."

"Very well, but if she will not have you as governess, you are welcome to stay as my . . . ward."

Olivia shook her head. "I am five and twenty, my lord, and, I pray, no orphan; surely this disqualifies me as anybody's ward."

"We shall see about that."

"I am grateful that you still want this . . . after everything," she whispered. "But I beg you, put the thought from your mind."

That night, once she had heard Audrey's prayers and kissed her brow, Olivia went downstairs to check on Andrew in the sickroom yet again. He lay so peacefully that for a moment she feared he did not breathe. She laid her ear close to his face, and feeling the warm breath on her cheek and seeing the gentle rise and fall of his chest, she kissed him and left the room. In the corridor, she noticed a door ajar—the door Lord Brightwell had indicated earlier.

She hesitated, knowing she should take herself upstairs and climb into bed. Yet she knew she would not, could not, sleep. Not without seeing Lord Bradley with her own eyes. To assure herself he was well, that he had all he needed, and that he did not blame her.

Surely Osborn was seeing to his every comfort—she was being foolish. Dr. Sutton had left half an hour ago and would have stayed were there any cause for alarm.

Then why did her heart beat so fast?

There was nothing for it. She stepped across the corridor, barely believing she was actually going to his bedchamber alone, at night. No, certainly she would *not* be alone. Lord Brightwell would be sitting at his bedside, Osborn at least.

She paused before the door, but heard nothing. Fearing to wake him should he be asleep, Olivia knocked softly. Receiving no response, she took a deep breath and opened the door several more inches. She would just look in on him. If he was asleep she would make sure he was breathing and then slip away. In and out. If Osborn was there, she would . . . what? Invent some excuse—Audrey could not sleep without first knowing if Lord Bradley was well? She hated to lie, but nor did she want every tongue in the servants' hall wagging by morning.

She hesitated in the threshold. Several lamps were lit, but she saw no one about. A black and gold Chinese screen stood in the middle of the room, blocking her view.

A giggle trickled down the corridor, and Olivia turned her head. At the far end of the dark passage, she saw snooty Osborn, footman and valet, pressing Doris against the wall and kissing her.

Quietly, Olivia slipped inside. As she began to pull the door, she saw the teakettle sitting beside the door and picked it up, then stepped gingerly into the room.

"Where the devil have you been, Osborn?" Lord Bradley mumbled dully.

Something in his voice worried her, and she walked quietly forward without identifying herself. Carrying the kettle—which Osborn must have been delivering when waylaid by Doris—she peeked around the screen, assuming she would find him awaiting tea. Stifling a gasp, she stopped midstride.

He was in a bathtub, his head resting against its high back, a large bandage across his eyes. Remnants of dark soot lingered along the hard line of his jaw and in the laugh lines around his mouth. His left hand, also bandaged, hung over the edge of the tub, propped on a nearby chair clearly put there for that purpose.

Her gaze traveled up from his swathed hand to his muscled forearm, bicep, and shoulder. His broad chest glinted with golden hair. Olivia felt herself flush, her heart thudding like the deepest bass drum.

"Let me know when an hour has passed. I wish to have done with this foul poultice." His voice was uncharacteristically languid, and she wondered how much laudanum the doctor had given him. She was thankful his eyes were covered and that no one was there to witness the burning of her face.

He huffed. "If you still insist on washing my hair again, let's have done. I could sleep for a fortnight."

Olivia's mouth went dry.

His hair needed another washing—the normally fair hair still bore streaks of ashy grey. What would it feel like to wash his hair? To entwine her fingers in the smooth blond strands? Imagining it, she released a shaky breath.

He lifted his head, brow furrowed. "Osborn?"

Caught. She froze, expecting any moment the poultice to drop and him to glare at her in shocked disgust at the vulgar intrusion. Dread seizing her, she set down the kettle with a splash and hurried from the room.

All the next morning Olivia berated herself. What had she been thinking to go into his bedchamber? From Audrey, she had learned Lord Bradley was up and about already. That was good news at least. Still, it was late in the afternoon before she finally roused the courage to walk down to his study. If she did not, would he not think her most ungrateful and unconcerned about his welfare? Would her absence not seal any suspicions he might have of the identity of his silent visitor the previous night? Pressing a hand to her chest to calm her beating heart, she knocked on his study door.

"Enter."

Wiping damp palms on her skirts, she pushed the door open and stepped inside.

"Ah, Miss Keene . . ." Lord Bradley, seated at his desk, laid down the letter he was reading. His coat hung over one shoulder, his injured arm not within its sleeve.

"My lord." She made a shallow curtsy, detesting the heat she felt infusing her face. For though he was now fully dressed, she involuntarily envisioned him as she had seen him last.

"You wanted to . . . see me . . . again?" he asked. Was that a twinkle in his blue eyes, or was she imagining it?

She licked her dry lips. "I wanted to make certain you were all right."

"And now that you have seen me, all of me, what is your prognosis?"

She felt heat creeping up her neck, though she had not, she told herself yet again, *not* seen all of him. So he did know. Or was very confident he did. She would not give him the satisfaction of admitting it.

His eyes flitted over her burning face and twisting hands with apparent amusement.

She pressed her jittery hands to her sides and cleared her throat. "Yes, that is . . . I wanted to thank you for rescuing Andrew so courageously."

"You are prodigiously welcome," he said. Rising, he stepped around the desk and leaned back against it. "Though why you should feel the need to thank me, I do not quite grasp."

"You know I adore Andrew, and if anything were to happen to him . . . And of course, I feel dreadfully responsible, letting him run off alone."

He nodded. "It is unfortunate Andrew learnt of your secret hiding place, and that Talbot did not know to look there, or this"—he raised his wrapped and slung arm—"might have been avoided."

She lowered her head, ashamed.

"Then again, I would not have earned your gratitude."

She looked up at him, uncertain whether he was being sincere or sarcastic. "If you wish to dismiss me, I understand and shall go at once."

He crossed his arms, quickly winced, and let go. "I hardly think it necessary. Nor am I ready to part with you. Judith was vexed, I know, but any mother—even stepmother—would be. Some of the steam went out of her when she learnt her darling brother was likely responsible for the fire—though, of course, Felix does not admit it."

He sighed. "At all events, it was an accident. In the meantime, we shall stable the horses at the Lintons, who have kindly offered, and rebuild. I for one look forward to the project and plan a few improvements and enlargements, though I was sorry to see our old steward's handiwork destroyed."

She looked at him more closely. "Will you be able to, do you think? How are you getting on? Does your arm not pain you?"

"It is naught. Aches a bit, but it is not broken as Sutton originally feared. Fingers itch like the blazes from whatever foul potion he applied. But otherwise I am well."

"And your face?"

He grimaced. "You tell me. I dared look in the glass and thought myself ridiculous with these singed brows and swollen nose. The thing was bent as a boy, and now has been bent yet again."

"You look . . . well, I think." She hurried on. "And your eyes?"

"My vision seems unhindered, thank the Lord." He studied her. "In fact, I believe I see more clearly now than I ever have before."

She swallowed. "Do you indeed?"

He held her gaze a moment longer, blue eyes to blue eyes, and his were alight with something inscrutable. "Indeed."

39

Between a governess and a gentleman there was no easy courtesy, attraction, or flirtation, because she was not his social equal.

—M. Jeanne Peterson, *Suffer and Be Still*

On Monday afternoon, Edward went out to the carriage to greet Judith, returning from another visit to her mother. She took his good arm and they walked companionably across the courtyard together, their pace made languid by the invitingly warm springtime air.

Miss Keene and the nurserymaid had brought the children outside to greet their stepmother. As usual Judith had eyes only for Alexander and took him from the maid, kissing and stroking the child.

Smiling at Audrey and Andrew in her stead, Edward thanked Miss Keene and then took his leave of his cousin, who broke off her cooing only long enough to smile at him before returning her gaze to her young son.

Edward returned to the library to see how his father was getting on. When he entered, he found the earl standing at the tall windows facing the lane. He did not turn when Edward entered.

"You are not thinking of marrying her, I trust?"

Edward stilled, instantly wary. "Why do you ask?"

"I have noticed the . . . change in your relationship of late. At least on her part."

Had she changed? Warmed to him? He had thought so, but wondered if he only imagined it.

"And if you are entertaining marriage, I must know."

Edward heard the concern in his father's voice. "You disapprove."

"Profoundly."

Irritation surged within Edward. "I am surprised, considering, well . . . everything." Had he not decided Olivia was his own daughter?

The earl looked out the window once more, rubbing his lip with thumb and forefinger. "I have my reasons."

"Even if she is related to you, I don't see how that signifies."

The earl turned to Edward, expression stern. "You don't see—that is exactly right. You don't. You must trust me in this, Edward. I have your best interests at heart. Hers as well."

"Her best interests? Which of us is beneath the other?"

"This is not about rank."

"But you think it in her best interests to have nothing to do with me?"

"Romantically speaking, yes."

Had *he* not loved Olivia's mother? "That is rich, coming from you, Father. You who have always been so *wise* in your love affairs."

"That is enough, Edward."

But Edward pressed on. "Even if she is who you think she is, I hardly think that raises her station of life beyond my own. Miss Keene is—"

"Miss Keene?" The earl eyed him speculatively, a strange stillness in his countenance.

"Were you speaking of someone else?" Edward asked, confused.

"Ah . . . well . . ." Lord Brightwell cleared his throat. "I am afraid you must excuse me. I spoke without thinking." The earl abruptly turned and strode across the room.

At the door, Lord Brightwell hesitated. "And you are quite right, Edward. I am not in the least qualified to give marital advice. You may disregard what I said."

Edward frowned, but his father—for there was no other way he could think of the man—was already out the door. Edward had the distinct impression he had not been worrying about Miss Keene at all. He replayed the exchange in his mind. If his father had not been speaking of Olivia, had he somehow been referring to Miss Harrington? But she was no relation of theirs. That left only Judith. And why should his father worry about her?

After the conversation with his father, Edward realized he had left things unsettled with Miss Harrington for too long. She might still be expecting an offer of marriage. How strange that an alliance he had recently contemplated with pleasure, or at least contentment, now filled him with misgiving.

Feeling restless, he asked Ross to saddle Major and took to the open road. His arm was still wrapped, but he no longer needed a sling. What he needed was to ride. To think.

He road south and west, giving Major his head, then reined him to a pace the well-conditioned animal could sustain for a longer journey.

When he trotted up the tree-lined avenue to Oldwell Hall, a young groom hurried out, and Edward flipped the lad half-a-crown, directing him to feed and water his horse.

Oldwell Hall was a large manse barely more than a decade old, with a central two-story block and two recessed wings. To Edward, the boxy grey building looked more like a military fortress than a home.

He was relieved to see Miss Harrington taking a turn about the lawn, a parasol on her shoulder. Still unsure of what he would say, Edward strode across the avenue to meet her.

She must have seen him, for she turned and waited until he reached her. "Bradley, what a nice surprise," she said with a warm smile. "I am afraid Father is gone to Bristol."

"That is just as well, Miss Harrington, for I hoped to speak with you."

A knowing smile lifted one corner of her mouth.

"May I walk with you?" he asked.

"Of course."

Shifting the parasol to her other hand, she took Edward's arm. Together they strolled across the lawn, damp from recent rains. The landscape was stark; only a few shrubs and a massive fountain ornamented the grounds. The temperature was mild, and the sun shone at intervals between passing clouds.

He cleared his throat and began in what he hoped was a nonchalant tone. "Do you recall you once said you wished your father would not pressure you, that you might"—he hesitated to verbalize the word—"marry as you pleased?"

She dipped her chin coyly, tentatively drawing out her reply, "Ye-ess . . ."

"Would you wish to marry a man, Miss Harrington, were he not heir to a title and peerage?"

She lifted her head and grinned. "Would this 'man' still be rich?" She laughed, but soon quieted. "Bradley, I am only teasing you. Has someone suggested I am only interested in you to become a countess?"

"Perhaps."

Her brow puckered. "But . . . how could I not admire you? You are the future Lord Brightwell . . . as well as young and handsome and attentive."

"And were I not?"

"My dear Bradley, we shall all grow older and less attractive in time. Though I shall find it a tedious bore not to have heads turn whenever I enter a room. . . ." She laughed again and awaited his chivalrous assurance.

"I meant, were I not a future earl," he persisted.

A spring breeze fluttered the parasol ruffle. "Really, you are in a strange mood. You know perfectly well that you are your father's heir. And if you were not, I would most likely have never even met you."

"Some other fortunate chap would be walking beside you now?"

She grinned again. "Some other fortunate *aristocratic* chap."

He nodded and walked on in silence.

She sent him a sidelong glance. "Why are we playing this game? Has your cousin Judith been riddling you with doubts about me?"

"Judith? What has she to do with it?"

Miss Harrington expelled a puff of dry laughter. "She wants you for herself, of course. Do not tell me you have never guessed."

Edward drew in a deep breath. Had he? Had this been what his father was hinting about? Cousins married often enough, he knew, but Judith was almost like a sister to him.

Sybil Harrington gave him a discerning look. "Tired of your game, Bradley?"

He managed a weak smile. "Yes, I suppose I am." He looked at her, then sighed. "Tired of the whole charade."

"Good," she said, blithely. "Are we . . . that is, will you be going to town after Easter?"

He shook his head and said quietly, "I will not."

She twirled the parasol on her shoulder. "Being in mourning, I did wonder. Still, what a bore to endure the season without you. Father hoped we might avoid it altogether this year, if . . ."

He knew what the "if" was. If he was going to propose marriage, then she need not go to London in hopes of securing a match.

As if suddenly aware of the change in him, she stopped walking and regarded him closely, cautiously. The earlier amusement faded from her brown eyes.

He turned to meet her somber gaze. "Miss Harrington, I think you should go. Enjoy yourself."

Her cheeks paled, but she masked her disappointment well. "Do you indeed?"

"Yes, in fact, I am convinced of it." He faced her earnestly. "Please. Do not forego anything on my account."

She smiled bravely, but he did not miss the trembling of her chin. "Very well, I shan't." She turned away and looked up at the cloudy sky. "Now, I am afraid I must return to the house. My slippers are soaked, and it looks very much like rain."

That evening after the children were in bed, Olivia sat with Lord Brightwell in the library. Edward was gone, she had heard—off to visit the Harringtons—and how the thought depressed her.

Silently, the earl withdrew a velvet box from his pocket and handed it to her.

She was instantly uncomfortable. "My lord, you should not—"

"It is something I gave your mother long ago. Something she returned before she left. I want you to have it."

Swallowing, Olivia opened the hinged box and gazed at the lovely cameo necklace nestled within. "It is beautiful. Thank you."

He pressed her hand. "Olivia, I have thought about this. I care about you, and your mother was a special person in my life. It would give me great joy to call you my daughter."

Olivia flushed and lowered her head. Then she closed the box and looked up at him earnestly. "But we are not at all certain, and now . . . now we may never know."

"I realize that, but I believe I owe it to your mother to care for you now that she is . . . gone."

Something like panic rose within her. "Pray take no offense, my lord, but I have little wish to be *anybody's* illegitimate daughter. Besides, I do not feel it would be right to proclaim I *am* your daughter, when that is far from definite."

He grinned. "A proclamation. Excellent notion. I shall proclaim my intention to adopt you as my ward. We need not mention the blood tie if you prefer."

"But . . . is not such a thing highly unusual?"

"Well, yes." The earl chuckled. "I can just hear the cronies talking now, 'gone and made a lovely young woman his ward, clever old fox.'"

"Oh!" Olivia exclaimed, flustered.

He leaned forward. "Olivia, should it matter what those old fools think? It matters not to me. We know the truth."

"But we don't," Olivia emphasized.

"Olivia . . ."

"Do not think me ungrateful. I am more thankful than I can say for your many kindnesses to me, but you need *not* recognize me."

"But I want to."

A part of Olivia was deeply moved to be so warmly cared for when her own father had become so cold. But another part of her recoiled. It was not right.

"But what would your family think?" she asked.

"I do not care what Judith and Felix think. Their father did far more scandalous things, I assure you."

"And your son? Do you not care for his opinion either?"

He nodded. "I do care what Edward thinks. When he returns, I shall have to ask him."

"Ask me what?" Edward said, striding into the room in time to hear his father's last sentence.

"Edward! You are returned early. We did not expect you."

Edward shrugged, not wishing to discuss the Harringtons in Miss Keene's presence.

"What did you want to ask me?" Edward repeated.

Miss Keene avoided his gaze and seemed to shrink in her seat as the earl explained his plan.

"You cannot be serious!" Edward exclaimed. "Why on earth would you? A ward, at her age?"

At his outburst, Miss Keene ducked her head, and his father reached over and grasped her hand. "Because, as I have told you, I believe she is my daughter."

"But it is madness—she is a grown woman!"

"I realize that."

Edward paced the library like a caged tiger. "Are you really so convinced she is your child?"

Lord Brightwell looked at Olivia's bowed head, before returning his gaze to Edward. "More so than Olivia is . . . but it does not matter to me if she is or not."

"How can it not matter?"

His father looked at him pointedly. Indeed, Edward already knew how little blood meant to the man.

Edward stewed in silence, his emotions quaking within him.

Miss Keene stood. "Pray excuse me," she said and turned toward the door.

"Very well, my dear," Lord Brightwell soothed. "We shall talk again tomorrow."

Edward rose, but Olivia refused to look at him as she swept past, cheeks mottled red and white.

When the door closed behind her, his father sighed. "That was badly done, Edward. Badly done indeed."

"I know." Edward hated that he had injured her feelings, but he had his reasons for objecting.

"Olivia was already reticent to accept my offer. In fact, eschews any public proclamation. Your little snit has not helped my cause."

Why would Olivia not want the protection, connections, and resources of the Earl of Brightwell? Edward wondered. Was she so loath to be thought illegitimate? If so, what must she think of him?

But he refused to voice the searing thought that caused his heart to lurch—for if Lord Brightwell acknowledged Olivia as his daughter, she and Edward would be half brother and sister in the eyes of the world.

40

> Governesses had a way of coping with status incongruity. This most often took place in a form of escape.
>
> —Carissa Cluesman, *A Historical View of the Victorian Governess*

At least, Olivia told herself, she had her answer to what Lord Bradley thought of her becoming the earl's ward. He thought her unworthy, would be ashamed of her—that seemed clear. She should not have been surprised, but witnessing his outburst had hurt more than she would have guessed, and she had blinked back tears all the way to the schoolroom.

She expected Lord Bradley to avoid her after that terrible clash. She certainly planned to avoid him. But two nights later, as she was writing a letter to the proprietress of the girls' school in Kent—the friend of Mrs. Tugwell—Lord Bradley threw back the schoolroom door.

It was difficult to say which startled her more, the thunderclap of door hitting the wall, or being caught writing a letter she meant to send in secret. She jumped, and reflexively covered the letter with Mangnall's text. The quill in her hand shook, and she quickly laid it down upon the desk.

His blue eyes darted from the quill to the book to her no-doubt-guilty face. His expression darkened. "Writing another already, I see."

He strode to the desk, face grim, eyes sparking dangerously. "'*Extortus*, meaning extortion,' hmm?" he sneered, parroting her Latin lesson back to her. "Did you really think you could get away with it?"

Confusion and dread filled her. "What are you talking about?"

He unfurled a letter clenched in his hand. "We received this note in the post, or so I thought. It bears no postal date stamp, and Hodges has no recollection of how it arrived."

"I wrote no note."

"Here. Perhaps this will jar your memory." He thrust the note toward her, and she took and read it. The harsh, vile words stunned her.

> *You tryd to hide yer secret, but I know what you did.*
> *Leave 50 ginny in the pozy urn on Ezra Sackville's grave*
> *on olde Lady Day and none shall be the wizer.*

"Oh . . ." Olivia breathed, feeling a smart punch to her stomach. She looked up into his face with concern, but at his contemptuous glare quickly angered.

"You don't believe I wrote this," she challenged, holding up the note.

"I don't want to believe it, but how can I ignore the evidence of my eyes?"

She sputtered, incredulous. "It is not even in my hand!"

"Easily disguised."

"And the abominable spelling . . ."

"Cleverly done, Miss Keene. I noticed that right off."

"I did not, could not, write such a thing."

"Your accomplice, then. The 'he' with poor spelling. For you are the only one who knew."

"Obviously not. Surely there were people who learnt of it at the time. Your birth mother or one of the staff or family."

"Someone who has held this information all these years only to reveal it now? I for one think that too great a coincidence."

"I admit it—"

"You admit it?" he roared.

"I admit it looks bad, but I did not do it."

He shook his head. "Has your time here been so intolerable? Is this your plan to exact revenge?"

"Revenge?" She shook her head in disbelief.

"Your motive. And why not pry a bit of coin from us in the bargain."

"Why indeed," she blustered. "But more than a bit of coin. A hundred guineas might do for starters."

He glared. "The letter says fifty."

She lifted her chin. "I have just raised the figure. A hundred guineas seems a small price to pay to keep the world from knowing what you *really* are."

He stared at her, momentarily stunned. He shook his head bleakly. "At long last speaks the true Olivia Keene. You really have made fools of us all."

His words stung deep, and her anger moldered into shame. She rose unsteadily.

"Forgive me," she choked out. "I had no right to say such a thing." Her voice grew haggard. "But I tell you, I have nothing to do with this, nor have I ever breathed one word of your secret to another soul. Give me leave to go and I shall be silent forever."

She abruptly turned and all but ran from the room.

Edward clomped back down the stairs, anger and suspicion giving way to regret and dejection. In truth, he had taken the extortion letter to the schoolroom not believing Miss Keene a party to it at all. But then he had seen her hide the letter she was writing and he'd jumped to conclusions.

He took himself to the library to join his father. Lord Brightwell was asleep in his favorite chair before the fire. He was startled awake when Edward closed the door.

"Hello, Edward," he said, straightening himself in the chair.

"Better remain seated," Edward advised. "We have had another letter."

The earl sighed wearily.

"From the hand, I assumed it was from a tradesman and opened it with the other estate correspondence, as you'd asked." Edward retrieved his father's spectacles and handed them and the note to him.

His father read, cursed under his breath, and dropped the letter to his knee, staring blindly at the fire.

"Who could have written this?" Edward asked. "I have accused Miss Keene, but—"

"Olivia? Are you serious? I cannot believe you!"

Edward squeezed his eyes shut. "I know, I know. I have made a muddle of it. I walked in while she was writing a letter—one she quickly hid from me. I suppose I snapped." He ran a hand through his hair. "All that plagued secrecy since she arrived. Her silence about her past and even where she lived. Is it any wonder I suspected her of some plot?" He shook his head. "I will apologize. I don't really believe she would do this. But who else knows? Perhaps someone who was there at the time?"

"It is possible. The girl's father knew, but he swore his secrecy. Nurse Peale attended your mother and must have known, though I don't recall her asking any questions."

"Loyal Nurse Peale. I cannot imagine her having anything to do with it."

"Nor I."

"Anyone else?"

"The physician and the midwife who told your mother she was unlikely to bear a living child must have suspected, but neither was actually present when I brought you here."

"When you switched a living infant for a stillborn, you mean? And passed me off as your own?"

"Yes. Do you judge us so harshly for it?"

Edward rubbed his eyes with his good hand and exhaled. "No. Forgive me. I am grateful you raised me as your son. But obviously, someone else is not."

Edward spent a restless night, tossing to and fro in his bed, tortured by echoes of his unforgivable words to Olivia.

In the morning, he dressed without care, not bothering with a cravat, and struggled into his boots without calling on Osborn. He trudged downstairs to the empty breakfast room. The thought of food sickened him, and even the coffee he poured was too bitter to drink. He slumped into a chair and rested his head in his hands.

A soft scratch on the door roused Edward from a doubt-induced fog. "Come."

Mr. Tugwell stepped in, hat in hand.

"Hello, Charles," Edward said bleakly, not bothering to rise.

"I am returned to see how you fare," the parson began, closing the door behind him. "I have been concerned about you, my friend, since the fire and"—he lowered his voice—"the letter. I have been praying, of course. Is there nothing more I can do?"

"Nothing. Unless you can rewrite the past. Unless you can conjure a father who was actually wed to the woman who bore me. A peer, ideally, that I might take his seat in the Lords and fulfill my life's ambition."

His friend regarded him with drooping hound eyes. "There is no need to conjure a father. For He already calls you His own. And no mere earl or duke, no. The very King who reigns forever."

Edward sighed. "Thank you, Charles. I know you mean well, but I am not talking about religion—"

The vicar's voice rose. "Neither am I!"

"Faith in God will not change the facts of my past."

"No, but it could make all the difference to your future."

Edward leaned back in his chair. "What future?"

"Oh, really, Edward. I have had quite enough. You are behaving like a spoilt child. Lord Brightwell will not leave you penniless, will he?"

"No, but—"

"Where has God promised to fulfill our every whim according to the minutia of our earthly desires? Where has He promised to keep us from suffering or disappointment? Things He did not spare His own Son? You were raised in one of the finest manors in the borough, by a man and woman who could not have loved you better. You have been given the best education, the best of everything. You are sound of mind and limb, and yet you dare to rail at God? I for one grow weary of it. Now leave off simpering like an ungrateful brat and make something of this new life you've been given."

Edward stared. His old friend, the docile Charles, had utterly disappeared. The man before him was suddenly every inch the Reverend Mr. Tugwell, someone to be revered indeed.

Emotions wrestled for preeminence within Edward. He rose, wanting to strike the man, stalk off, or . . . laugh. Absurdly, the latter won out, and he felt a smile crack his scowl and he chuckled.

"What?" Charles said peevishly.

Edward laughed, bent over, and laid his hands on his knees as he did so.

The vicar frowned. "I fail to see what I said that has so amused you."

Edward placed a hand on his friend's shoulder. "I wish you could have seen your face just then. I wish your father might have seen. How it shone with righteous wrath! He would have been proud indeed."

"You are mocking me."

"Not at all. Everything you said was quite true." Edward slapped his friend's back and the smaller man jerked forward. "You have woken me from my stupor, Charles, and I am grateful to you." He put his arm around the vicar and turned him toward the door. "You really ought to deliver your sermons in such a manner. The old men would stay awake and how the widows would swoon."

Charles Tugwell took his leave, but Edward saw not his friend's retreating figure. Instead, other scenes filtered past his mind's eye, bits of memory and conversations with Olivia. Finding Andrew in her bed, grooming his horse together, working on the doll's house in stolen moments in Matthews's shop, ice-skating with the children, hearing her speak his name in her sleep, that delicious dance lesson . . .

What a fool he had been, what an irrational fool. And he realized, there and then, that he could not do it anymore, he would not hold on to what was not his. It was making him a defensive, suspicious lout, snarling at everyone, dreading that at every turn his secret would be revealed. It had to stop. It was not worth it.

Edward strode quickly down the corridor with an urgent sense of purpose, realizing there was one benefit to the new life Tugwell referred to, the one thrust upon him. He was free to marry without regard to rank and connection.

He took the stairs up to the nursery by threes, ignoring the wide-eyed stare of a young maid, who was slowly making her way down. He knocked on Olivia's door and, when there was no response, stepped quickly down the corridor and pushed open the schoolroom door. He was startled to find his father there, standing at the window, peering out.

"She is gone, Edward."

Edward's heart lurched. "Gone? Run away?"

"Not 'run away.' I was able to prevent that, if barely. Patching up after you is not an easy task."

"I was wrong, I know. Utterly, unforgivably wrong. Did you not tell her I never really believed her responsible for those letters? I was angry, irrational, I did not mean—"

His father lifted his hand. "Yes, yes, but she wished to leave anyway."

Edward ran a hand over his face. "Where is she?"

The earl sat at the schoolroom desk, looking older than his age for the first time in Edward's memory. "I think it best not to tell you at present," he said. "I believe it would be unwise of you to go charging after her now, when she wanted quite desperately to get away from here."

"Away from me."

"Well, yes. And can you blame her, after you accuse her of extortion, not to mention your less-than-enthusiastic response to the notion of making her my ward?"

Edward groaned. "She can be your ward. She can be your daughter as far as I am concerned. I am ready to end this charade. Felix can have it all. The title, the estate, the peerage. I just want—"

When he broke off, the earl raised his brow. "Yes?"

Edward pressed a hooked finger to his lip. "There will be time enough for what I want later, Lord willing. In the meantime, let us figure out a way to let the wind out of our adversary's sails."

41

> Men . . . generally look with a jealous and malignant eye on a woman of great parts, and a cultivated understanding.
>
> —John Gregory, *A Father's Legacy to his Daughters,* 1774

Walking briskly, Edward led his father to his favorite spot in the wood. A branch snapped, and through the trees, Edward glimpsed Croome kneeling on the ground in the distance—doing what, he could not tell. Croome rose and walked away, disappearing into the wood.

"Why do you drag me all the way out here?" Lord Brightwell asked, out of breath.

"Shh. The walls have ears, as they say. Or might." Edward glanced around. Satisfied they were alone, he said, "Now. I have been thinking about our greedy adversary."

"Of course we shall not gratify such vile demands."

"Oh, but we shall."

"What? And have the fiend ask for a hundred the next week and a thousand next year?"

Edward shook his head. "We shall bag up a few shillings and leave them in Sackville's urn as bait. We shall wait and see who comes for it and then have our man. Or woman."

"And what are we to do with the wretch once we have caught him, or her?"

"I have not the slightest notion. But at least we shall know whom we are up against."

On the night of old Lady Day, Edward and his father slipped through the narrow door in the wall and into the churchyard. There, they positioned themselves on a granite bench behind the mausoleum of the second Lord Brightwell, a position which leant them a view of the Bradley and Sackville plots, across from a cluster of graves called the Bisley Piece.

"Do you see my mother's tomb, there?" the earl whispered. "And the flower urn beside it?"

Edward looked. "Yes?"

"That is where I buried our stillborn son."

Edward stared at the spot and felt a shiver run up his spine. It was eerie enough in the churchyard after dark without thoughts of late-night, clandestine burials.

"I bundled him well and buried him there beside his grandmother. I moved that urn over the spot to disguise the disruption of grass and soil."

Edward looked at the massive stone planter and could not imagine any man moving it. "Alone?"

"Yes . . . I was a younger man then, of course. And prodigious scared I would be caught."

They sat for several more minutes in silence, waiting, their eyes and ears alert for the extortioner's approach. An owl screeched and his father jerked. Edward laid a hand on his arm.

A cloud, masking the greater portion of the moon, rolled away on the wind whistling through the yew trees, and the moonlight illuminated Sackville's grave more clearly. A figure stood before it, though they had neither heard nor seen anyone enter the churchyard.

"What the devil . . ." his father whispered, but Edward shushed him with a squeeze to his arm.

They watched as the figure reached into the urn, but when he withdrew his hand, it held no white bag. His father made to rise, but Edward increased the pressure on his arm. "Wait."

Two things caused Edward to hesitate. First, he wanted to catch the person with bribe in hand to seal his guilt. And second, there was something familiar about the thin figure.

"It is Avery Croome," Edward whispered.

"What? I cannot believe it."

Surprisingly, Edward could not believe it either and sat where he was, deliberating.

Instead of reaching in again to try to find the money—perhaps they ought to have used a larger sack, as his father had suggested—or turning to leave, Croome crept around a carved, pre-Norman tombstone and disappeared.

"Where did he go? Is there another gate behind the Bisley Piece?"

"Not that I know of. Perhaps he is lying in wait?"

"For us? You think he knows we are here?"

"Shh . . ."

Footsteps approached through the churchyard gate, boot heels on the paving stones. Now who was coming? Edward feared it would be Charles Tugwell, come to pray, or worse yet the constable on his rounds. While the constable would no doubt be more adept at apprehending the extortioner, they did not want it done publicly.

The figure left the paved path and turned in their direction. Edward and his father sat utterly still, hidden by tombstones and shadows.

A bat flew low over them, brushing the hair on Edward's hatless head. He did not so much as flinch, so focused was he on the approaching figure. Whoever it was wore a hooded cape, as dark as the enveloping night. Beneath the black shadows of the hood, a crescent of face shone pale in the moonlight.

"Is it a woman?"

"Shh . . ."

Edward did not think it was a woman—the walk was a masculine lurch. *But it might be a ruse.*

The caped figure walked directly to Sackville's grave as if the way were familiar even in darkness. An arm lifted, and Edward saw the slight glimpse of a pale hand as it reached into the "pozy urn"—deeper, deeper . . .

Snap! A vicious metallic clang split the silence, and the figure screamed. For a second, Edward and his father sat frozen in shock. The perpetrator's hood fell back and Edward saw it was a white-haired man. Screaming again, the man snatched back his hand—and the steel trap which impaled it.

His father turned to him, eyes wide in the moonlight. "Did you . . . ?"

Rising, Edward shook his head. "Croome." He rushed forward, his bottled fury at this unseen enemy greatly deflated by the old man's pitiful cries. Croome reached the man before Edward did.

"Get it off me, get the fiend off me," the man begged.

"Tell me who sent you," Croome demanded in his gruff voice.

Did Croome know what was going on? How? Why did he assume the man was not acting on his own?

"For the love of Pete—get it off me! My arm's broke."

"Croome . . ." Edward quietly urged.

"Who told you to do this, Borcher?" Croome persisted. "Who?"

"Nobody."

Croome stuck a stake into the trap's release, but instead of springing it open, he levered up the pressure.

"Stop! All right!"

Croome lowered the stake.

"A woman come round," the man began breathlessly, "askin' questions 'bout Lady Brightwell's lyin'-ins, my missus bein' the midwife in those days, God rest her soul. I had not thought on it in years, until the lady put it into my head again. She let on that Lord Brightwell had a secret." He panted, perspiring profusely. "My boy Phineas figgered it might be worth a great deal to him to keep it quiet. He wrote the letter. Never learnt to write myself."

Croome released the trap. "Phineas Borcher. Figured he had somethin' to do with it."

Edward glimpsed the man's bleeding wound and dug into his pocket for a clean handkerchief. "Who was the lady who came to see you?" he asked.

"Oh, Lord Bradley! I . . ." The old man looked stricken to see him. "I don't know. She wore a black veil. I never saw 'er face."

Edward wordlessly handed him the handkerchief.

He pressed it to the wound. "I never meant you no harm. You—"

"Only me?" his father asked, coming to stand beside Edward.

The man's eyes widened even further. "Bless me. Lord Brightwell! I never meant to . . . I don't really know what it is all about."

Edward turned to Croome. "Did you overhear us in the wood?"

The gamekeeper gave a slight nod.

"Even so, how did you—"

Croome held up his hand. "Let's just say I have the misfortune o' being acquainted with this man's son. And I make it my business to know his. Heard him boastin' how he was gonna lighten yer purse, my lord."

"We didn't mean no harm," the man whined. "Phineas said we could get some blunt for nothing, and times is hard, you know."

Croome scowled. "And about to get worse."

42

My nurse was my confidante.
It was to her I poured out my many troubles.
—Winston Churchill, *My Early Life*

Despite her regret over abandoning Audrey and Andrew and leaving without saying farewell to those she had come to love at Brightwell Court—and Miss Ludlow and Mr. Tugwell, besides—the time with her mother's family had proved more pleasant than Olivia would have guessed. She had fretted how Mr. Crenshaw might react to her, considering her mother's unsuitable marriage, disappearance—and the potential scandal—might all one day be revealed. But Mr. Crenshaw, a small, balding, cheery-faced man with dancing brown eyes, warmly assured her that he had "got quite used to taking in scandalous Hawthorns, forced from their homes and down on their luck—and should like it above all things to take in another." It had been too many years since he had done so, he added with a wink and a smile for his wife. Olivia could not help but smile as well.

As Olivia had expected from the few lines Georgiana Crenshaw had penned within her grandmother's note, she liked her aunt immediately. She was warm and amiable, with easy, unaffected manners. Perhaps it was the likeness to her mother, but Olivia felt as if she had known Georgiana for years.

Her grandmother was somewhat tentative and staid at first, asking questions about Olivia's childhood and education. She avoided asking about Mr. Keene, for which Olivia was relieved. Still, Olivia realized that her grandmother was making a sincere effort to welcome this granddaughter she barely knew, and Olivia could not help but be touched.

The Crenshaws urged her to stay for as long as she liked. Olivia hoped to begin teaching school in the autumn but gratefully accepted their invitation to spend the summer at Faringdon.

Olivia had been with her relatives for less than a week when the Crenshaws' footman announced Lord Brightwell and showed him into the morning room. Olivia rose, suddenly nervous in his presence, as she had not been in some time. Her anxiety was heightened by the fact that his usually placid countenance was strained.

"Are the children well?" she asked.

"Yes, though disappointed, of course, to learn of your . . . leave."

"Is Mrs. Howe very angry?"

He chuckled mirthlessly. "I think my niece smells another mystery in the air and longs to get to the bottom of it."

Olivia longed to know how Lord Bradley had reacted to her departure but would not ask. Remembering her manners, Olivia said, "Please. Do be seated." She settled back into her own chair, but he remained standing. He pulled something from his coat pocket.

"Olivia. I have something for you."

"Not another gift! You have given me too much already."

"No. Not this time." His sober voice chilled her.

"What is it?"

He unfolded a rectangle of thick paper and held it before her. She accepted it gingerly, as though it were a coiled snake. Angling the printed notice to better catch the light from the window, she read quickly, gasped, then read it again.

Olivia Keene
24 years old, dark hair, blue eyes
Anyone with information please contact the
Girls' Seminary, St. Aldwyns

"Where did you get this?" Olivia breathed.

"It was delivered by a paid messenger who did not know, or would not say, whom it was from."

Olivia felt a painful mixture of fear and hope. "It looks somewhat faded—and I am five and twenty now. Perhaps my father posted this before he came to Brightwell Court."

"Do you think so? But why would he go through a school?"

"Because he is clever. He knew I would assume my mother was trying to find me. Or it could be her doing," she acknowledged. "Maybe she has come to find me at last."

"But you sent a letter to the school, letting them know your whereabouts."

"I did. But that was several months ago. Perhaps the mistress did not recall." She looked up from the notice and found him watching her closely. She asked, "Will you take me to St. Aldwyns?"

He nodded. "The carriage is just outside."

Asking Olivia to wait inside the closed carriage, Lord Brightwell strode the few feet from the lane to the seminary door. Peering discreetly from behind the curtained chaise window, Olivia watched as a thin, older woman came to the door. Lord Brightwell introduced himself, and the woman curtsied and identified herself as Miss Kirby, one of the mistresses of the seminary.

The earl pulled the notice from his pocket and held it before her. "I am here because of this."

She gave it a cursory glance. "Forgive me, my lord, but what has this to do with you?"

"Perhaps a great deal." He hesitated. "Can you tell me, are you acting on behalf of a family member?"

It was the woman's turn to hesitate. "I don't . . . that is, I am not at liberty to say."

"I would very much like to speak with this person."

"I am afraid my sister, who would know how to go about this better than I, is away at present. If you could return another time?" She began to close the door.

"Olivia will be disappointed," he said shrewdly, and the door opened once more.

The woman's face became animated. "You have seen her, my lord?"

"Yes. She has been at Brightwell Court these several months. I hope to make her my ward."

"She is there now?" Olivia heard the restrained excitement in the woman's voice.

Again the earl hesitated, likely not wanting to give away her location until he knew who was looking for her. "Not at present. But I know where she is."

"And she is well?"

Olivia missed the earl's reply.

"That is excellent news. I will pass along this information to . . . to the interested party."

"Thank you." The earl gave the woman his card.

"I think I should tell you, my lord," Miss Kirby said nervously, "that you are not the first person to inquire after Miss Keene."

A sense of foreboding filled Olivia as she listened. Had her father called at the seminary before he came to Brightwell Court?

"Oh? Who was it?" he asked.

"The woman did not give a name."

"A woman? How old? What did she look like?"

Hope and caution competed within Olivia. Had it been her mother, after all?

"I really could not say. She was heavily veiled. A well-to-do woman, I would guess. She had an upper-class voice at any rate. Not old, but not a girl either."

Was the veiled woman her mother? Disguising herself to avoid being recognized by Simon Keene, not knowing he had been arrested?

"What did she say?" the earl asked.

"She tried to persuade my sister to tell her who was looking for Miss Keene, and why. She said she would like to talk with this person on behalf of Miss Keene."

"You did not arrange such a meeting?"

"Sister was tempted. The woman seemed so sincere in her concern. But at the last minute sister felt it was not right."

"Thank the Lord for that."

"We expect the woman to return Friday at two."

"Then you may expect me Friday at one."

Determined to conquer his lowness of spirits, Edward dragged his weary limbs up the many stairs to the nursery. He had not gone as often as late, and he knew the reason. But a visit with his young cousins might cheer him.

He found only Nurse Peale, sitting motionless on her rocking chair, staring vaguely ahead.

"Hello, Miss Peale," he said kindly. "How are you getting on?"

"Master Edward, my dear boy."

"Where are the children?"

"Becky took the older two outside. Alexander is down for his nap."

He nodded, then asked, "You were here when I was born, is that not right?"

She smiled, her eyes strangely bright and distant. "That I was. Monthly nurse for your poor mamma. How is Lady Brightwell? Still sad as ever?"

He hesitated. It struck him hard to realize the mind of his stalwart nurse was failing, but on impulse he decided not to remind her of recent events. "Quite so. Why is she sad, Miss Peale?"

"Foolish boy, because her babies died." She looked past him at some unseen object or memory.

His breath caught. "All of them, Miss Peale?"

She sighed. "All of them."

He gently asked, "Did you mind when they took me as their own?"

"Why should I? They said I could stay on as your nurse and at quite high wages in the bargain." She glanced up at him. "Do you know I earn more than Hodges? Mrs. Hinkley once remarked upon it." She cackled. "I would have stayed for less. I loved ya the moment I saw ya. So like Alexander."

"Yes," he murmured, trying to keep the concern from his expression and tone. "You were a very good nurse and have served our family well."

She nodded, her eyes clouding in confusion. Had she just realized she had admitted something she was never to divulge?

Another thought startled him. Could she have written the letters? Confused as she was? He realized he would not know her writing if he saw it. Had he ever seen it? But something Miss Keene once said whispered in his mind.

He said, "Yes, you were an excellent nurse, but you never learnt to read and write, did you?"

She shook her head. "I can't lie to you, Master Edward." She winced. "But pray don't tell. It has been my shameful secret all these years."

That secret she kept, he thought, somewhat cynically.

"What was my mother's name?" he asked, deciding to take advantage of her current state of mind.

Nurse Peale shook her head slowly, eyes far away again. "Poor Alice Croome . . ."

His heart jerked. *Croome? It cannot be.* Had Croome a wife? Daughter? Niece? He had not thought it.

"Is that her name?" he pressed. "Is my mother Alice Croome?"

Nurse Peale looked up sharply, mouth stern and a fire in her eyes that would have set him quaking as a lad. "Your mother is Lady Brightwell, of course," she snapped. "'*Who is my mother . . . ?*' What nonsense!"

43

> The most fashionable [school] was Mrs. Devis's in Queen square, where dancing masters, music masters and drawing masters were much in evidence.
>
> —Ruth Brandon, *Governess, The Lives and Times of the Real Jane Eyres*

Olivia spent an anxious few days with her aunt and grandmother before Lord Brightwell came for the promised return to St. Aldwyns.

When the carriage arrived at the school and Lord Brightwell again went to the door alone, Miss Kirby seemed more agitated and nervous than ever. "Oh! It is you, Lord Brightwell. I feared it might be that veiled woman returning once more."

"She has already been here? It is not even one o'clock."

"She came early. And was very vexed when I would not tell her what she wished to learn. You have only just missed her."

Olivia, still ensconced in the nearby carriage, looked out the chaise's rear window and glimpsed a figure in a dark cape, hat, and full veil step into a waiting carriage parked along the high street. Her stomach lurched. Had she just missed her mother?

"My sister has gone to pick up a new pupil from the afternoon coach," Miss Kirby said. "If you would care to return in, say, an hour's time?"

"Thank you. Might my ward and I tour the seminary while we wait?"

Hearing her cue, Olivia let herself down from the carriage.

Miss Kirby watched her approach with owl eyes. She faltered. "I don't . . . That is, this is not really a convenient time, my lord. My sister not being here, you understand. And I am wanted in class in three minutes' time. The dancing master departs at one sharp."

Olivia offered her hand to the woman. "I am Olivia Keene," she said.

Miss Kirby's mouth gaped as she accepted Olivia's hand. "Is it you?" She bit her lip. "If only . . . But my sister left strict instructions. If perhaps Miss Keene would care to wait alone?"

"Miss Keene stays with me, under my protection," Lord Brightwell said. "You understand."

"I don't think, that is . . . Oh, I really must go in. Here. If you will follow me, I will show you to the parlor. If you will remain there, I shall send my sister in to you the moment she returns."

"You are too kind, Miss Kirby."

The woman's head swiveled side to side as she led them into the school and down a short passageway to a small, tidy parlor. "Wait right here," she said and closed the door firmly behind her.

"Cautious lady, our Miss Kirby," the earl remarked.

"I noticed that as well."

"I do hope they are not delousing pupils or some such thing they don't wish visitors to witness."

Olivia made no reply but walked slowly about the room. "This is where I was bound, before I diverted to Brightwell Court," she said. "I had hoped they might want another teacher."

"You hope it still, I see."

"Do not think me ungrateful."

"I don't. You are your mother's daughter. Of course you want to teach. Whenever I see you with Audrey and Andrew, why, it is like seeing Dorothea all over again."

"About that, my lord—are you thinking what I am thinking? About the veiled woman, I mean?"

He frowned. "I doubt it."

"You do not think it was my mother, come in disguise to find me?"

"No, I do not," he said flatly, with no hesitation.

She was about to ask him to explain when muffled laughter seeped beneath the closed door.

Olivia swung to face Lord Brightwell, grabbing his forearms. "It is Mother!" she whispered. Excitement pulsed in her veins.

The earl's eyes shone with sympathy. He shook his head and pleaded, "Olivia . . ."

Olivia hurried to the door and carefully opened it several inches, listening. The laughter rang out again from somewhere in the seminary.

"It is her! I know it!" Olivia bolted from the room. True, it had been a long time since she had heard her mother laugh, but the sound connected with her soul. She pushed open the first door she came to.

"Mother?"

A girl of thirteen or fourteen looked up from her desk, startled.

"Forgive me," Olivia mumbled and backed out, feeling the most foolish creature alive.

Lord Brightwell stood in the parlor doorway, silently beckoning her back inside. But Olivia heard the laugh again, from somewhere above her. She ran to the nearby staircase and, lifting her skirts, rapidly ascended the stairs. She hurried down the passageway to an open door and looked within. A woman sat at a low table, her back to the door. Before her were two girls near Audrey's age, playing a game with French vocabulary cards. The girls saw Olivia first.

"What is it?" The woman turned her slim shoulders and sable-brown head, revealing an infinitely familiar profile.

Olivia's stomach flipped and nerves shot through her body.

The woman's eyes widened, and she leapt to her feet, hand pressed to her heart. Olivia and her mother stood staring at one another in stunned silence.

"Olivia!" Dorothea Keene opened her arms and pulled her daughter close.

"Oh, Mamma, we have been so worried," Olivia said, tears filling her eyes. "We thought you were dead!"

"Olivia. Let me look at you. Until a few days ago, it was I who thought you were lost to me forever." Her mother pulled her close again. Then Olivia felt her stiffen. "Oliver . . ." she breathed.

Olivia turned and saw Lord Brightwell standing in the threshold, visibly shocked.

"It was Mamma I heard," Olivia said, out of breath. "Did I not tell you?"

"Yes . . ." the earl murmured, not taking his eyes from Dorothea's face. "Hello, ah . . . Mrs. Keene."

"My lord." Her mother bowed a jerky curtsy that lacked her usual grace. "I asked after Olivia in Arlington, but the only newcomer described to me was a dumb mute."

Olivia looked at Lord Brightwell and chuckled sheepishly. "It is a long story, Mamma. . . ."

Miss Kirby served them tea in the parlor, apologizing, but explaining that they had instructions to reveal Mrs. Keene's presence only to her daughter—and only if her daughter was alone.

"I am sorry I could not come sooner, Olivia," her mother said. "After you left, Muriel took me to her sister's in the country. I intended to stay only a few days while I recovered from my . . ." She darted a look at the others, then returned her gaze to Olivia. "But I am afraid I fell dangerously ill. Between that and impassable roads, I was forced to trespass upon her hospitality for several months. I only managed to come to St. Aldwyns in early March and posted the notices then." She smiled at Miss Kirby as the woman poured tea. "When I did not find you, the Miss Kirbys kindly offered me a situation here."

Olivia thought it a just fate that her mother had been given the post she herself had wanted. There was no one else more qualified or deserving.

"Did you send a copy of the notice to Lord Brightwell?" she asked.

She shook her head. "I had no reason to think you would go to Brightwell Court instead of here."

Politely, Olivia asked Miss Kirby if she recalled the letter she had sent, inquiring after a position, and giving her direction within, should her mother come looking for her.

The older woman winced in thought. "I vaguely recall Sister mentioning a letter from Brightwell Court some months ago, but nothing about Dorothea's daughter—that I would remember! Did you not mention your mother by name?"

"I am certain I mentioned Mrs. Keene."

"Ah! But you see, we knew her only as Miss Hawthorn. Sister no doubt failed to make the connection. We only learnt the name Keene upon your mother's arrival, and I suppose Sister had forgot all about the letter by then—her memory is not what it should be. Nor mine, I am afraid." She winced again. "I hope you will forgive us, my dear."

"Of course I shall."

When Miss Kirby left, the three of them began to fill in the details in an overlapping jumble of conversation.

"I sent a man to Withington a few months ago," Lord Brightwell explained. "But your neighbors led him to believe, or at least *allowed* him to believe, that you might very well occupy the new grave in the churchyard."

Dorothea nodded, shamefaced. "It was Muriel's idea. But I agreed. It was the only way I could think to escape him. I knew he would search for me otherwise."

Olivia blurted, "Father has been arrested. You are safe."

Instead of relief, her mother's face froze, then furrowed. "Your father?"

"Yes. At first we assumed he had been arrested for . . . bringing you harm, but Miss Cresswell—"

"Olivia, no," her mother interrupted. "Your father did not . . . Did you think it your father you struck that night?" Her face was white with shock.

Dread and confusion filled Olivia. "Yes."

"My dear. I don't deny your father has a violent temper and many faults. But he has never raised a hand against me. It never occurred to me you thought it was him."

"I . . . I know it was dark, but I saw glass smashed against the grate and his coat on the overturned chair. . . ."

Mrs. Keene shook her head, her expression pained and bewildered.

"Then . . . who was it, Mamma? Whom did I strike?"

Dorothea glanced at Lord Brightwell, and then down at her hands. "Perhaps we might discuss this later. We have only just been reunited. And . . . you say your father has been arrested?"

"Miss Cresswell thinks the charge embezzlement."

"Although others believe Mr. Keene responsible for your . . . disappearance," Lord Brightwell added. "Especially as he fled the village as if guilty."

Pain creased Dorothea's brow. "I could not bear it if he were punished for a crime he did not commit," she said. "Do you think any magistrate would convict him with no evidence?"

"Who *was* buried in the churchyard?" Olivia asked.

"A poor gypsy lady who died in childbirth, her infant with her. Miss Atkins knew the church warden would never allow such a woman to be buried in the churchyard if she asked permission. So she did not."

Olivia shook her head. Over and over again. "I have felt so guilty. So sickened. To think my own father . . ." Olivia paused, glanced from her mother to Lord Brightwell and back again. "*Is* Simon Keene my father?"

Her mother stared at her, uncomprehending. Then she looked at Lord Brightwell sitting beside her daughter, and understanding slowly dawned on her face. Still she hesitated.

"Lord Brightwell thought . . . that is, we . . ." Olivia stammered.

"We hoped," the earl added, taking Olivia's hand.

"Oh, Olivia." Uncertainty clouded Dorothea's features. "Miss Kirby told me Lord Brightwell had taken you under his protection, but I never dreamt—"

"You named her *Olivia*," the earl said, almost plaintively.

She winced as if in pain. "Very foolish, I know. But in truth I had always loved the name, and had planned it for my daughter since girlhood." She stole a sheepish glance at the earl. "And yes, I was fond of the name for other reasons as well."

Dorothea fixed her eyes on Olivia's hand clasped in Lord Brightwell's and her eyes filled with tears. "Good heavens . . ." She swallowed and ducked her head. "I had just learned I was with child when I left Brightwell Court," she quietly acknowledged, cheeks flushed. "And Simon married me, knowing it. I could think of no other alternative. My family would not, I knew, have anything to do with me if they learnt of my disgrace. I could not support myself, and moreover, I wanted my child to be born in wedlock. Legitimate." Dorothea looked into Oliver Bradley's eyes, and time seemed to slow down. "But I miscarried that child soon after the wedding."

"Then why did he despise me!" Olivia burst out, feeling suddenly very young indeed.

"Oh, Olivia. It was not your fault." Her mother's voice shook. "He was terribly jealous, and I made it worse by going back to Brightwell Court after the miscarriage. I should not have done so. I went only to see with my own eyes that he was well and truly married, gone from me forever."

Dorothea addressed Oliver, tears in her eyes. "I saw the two of you in the garden. Saw you embrace her. Kiss her. That was all I needed. It killed me and set me free at once."

The earl's eyes glistened. "I never knew you were there."

Dorothea returned her gaze to Olivia. "I returned home the same day and threw myself in Simon's arms, determined to make a new start. But then someone told him I had been seen on the eastbound coach, and he accused me of meeting a lover that day." She inhaled. "I assured him I had not. And for a time, I thought he believed me."

"But even he thinks Lord Brightwell is my father!"

Tears glistened on Dorothea's cheeks. "If only we had not gone to the Roman ruins that day." She shook her head. "Ruins, indeed."

"I thought if it were true, it might explain . . ." Olivia began, but tears closed her throat.

Lord Brightwell added, "I asked Olivia to allow me to publicly claim her as my ward, even knowing we could not be certain she was my daughter. But Olivia steadfastly refused. She must have known somehow, in her heart."

"Oh, Olivia." Her mother shook her head, contrite. "This is why I did not reveal myself when Lord Brightwell first called here. I thought perhaps you would be happier with him, instead of reuniting with me and my sordid lot."

"Olivia has been heartbroken over you," Lord Brightwell said. "I could never take your place."

Olivia felt tears streaming silently down her face.

"I am sorry all of this has befallen you, Olivia. Sorry most of all that you should think so ill of your father." Her mother cupped her chin. "Life was not always so bad, was it? We all got on reasonably well at times, when your father was sober. . . ."

Olivia felt numb. Her mother continued to speak, but the words grew indistinct.

Instead she heard the clink of glasses, the low rumble of men's voices, and her father's deep voice saying, "That's my clever girl." She felt the warmth of his praise wash over her again. An opaque web clouded her vision, and her mother and Lord Brightwell blurred. How long had it been since she'd thought back on the evenings around the fire, number games at the kitchen table, or listening to her father sing? Too long. Yes, there had been bad times. And she had tallied them like figures in a column, not remembering to factor in the good. She had doctored the books.

Suddenly Olivia felt embarrassed at having presumed on the earl's kindness. Yes, she had told him her reasons for doubting. But she had let him hope, had let their relationship grow.

Beside her, Lord Brightwell still held her hand. If anything he held it tighter. But Olivia could feel herself pulling away. Edward's face appeared in her mind. His expression full of disdain. How pleased he would be to know she had no claim on the earl after all.

Olivia wiped her eyes, realizing she had another confession to make. "When we feared the worst, Mamma," she said, "I opened that letter in your little purse. Lord Brightwell and I delivered it to your mother and sister."

Dorothea's eyes widened, and her countenance paled. "I wish you had not done so."

"You needn't worry," Olivia assured her. "Your mother and sister have welcomed me into their home. Aunt Georgiana's husband as well. They are very kind, Mamma, and Grandmother regrets the long separation between you. I know they would welcome you as well."

"Do you think so?"

Olivia had rarely seen her mother so uncertain. "Will you return to the Crenshaws' with me? It will be quite a shock to them, I own, for we thought never to see you again, but a wonderful shock, I assure you."

"I don't know. . . . Perhaps you might break it to them, and if they still wish to see me . . . you could write and let me know?"

"Are you certain? You could come back with me now and see them in person."

Her mother shook her head. "It is all too sudden. And I have my pupils here now. Perhaps another time?"

"Then, might I stay with you tonight?" Olivia asked. "Do you think the sisters would mind? It seems wrong to leave you so soon after finding you again."

Dorothea smiled. "You may share my room. They cannot mind that."

Lord Brightwell stood and suggested, "Why do I not send the carriage for you tomorrow, Olivia, to take you back to Faringdon. Or if you decide to stay here longer, you might send Talbot with a message for your grandmother so she does not worry."

"Thank you, my lord." Olivia rose, as did her mother. "You are always so thoughtful."

Dorothea curtsied before Lord Brightwell. "I am truly grateful for your watch-care over my daughter."

The earl bowed in return, but his farewell smile did not quite reach his eyes.

Olivia walked the earl to the seminary gate and there gently pulled her hand from his.

"What will you do now, my dear?" he asked.

She chewed her lip, then answered, "Spend time with Mother, of course, and learn what I can about my father's situation. I have been invited to spend the summer with my aunt and grandmother, and after, I hope to take a teaching post in Kent."

"But, Olivia, must you go so far away? Your mother will miss you, and so will I. And Edward."

"Well," Olivia faltered, and then pushed the thought of Edward from her mind. "I shall miss you as well. But I long for a new start."

He shook his head. "I know this has been quite a blow for you, Olivia. But it changes nothing."

"My dear Lord Brightwell, I disagree. We can no longer feign a relationship that we now know to be false. Your kindness has been my greatest solace these last months, and I will always be deeply grateful to you. But I must not depend upon you further." She leaned close and kissed his cheek. "Thank you for everything." She quickly pulled away, fearing yet more tears.

"Olivia . . ."

"Please, tell no one of my plans."

He looked incredulous. "But why?"

"I have but a few months before I leave for Kent, assuming they offer me a post, and I wish to spend every moment with my family."

He winced, stung. Olivia felt the sting in her own heart and instantly regretted her choice of words.

He asked, "But will you not at least come to Brightwell Court and say good-bye to everyone?"

"Well . . . I . . ." Olivia could not bring herself to admit the truth: that she did not want to see Edward. The earl must have seen her awkwardness, and the reason for it evidently dawned on him.

"Edward will be away tomorrow morning," he said quietly. "You might call in then, before you return to the Crenshaws'."

Olivia looked into Lord Brightwell's eyes and saw mournful understanding there. Her throat tightened. She whispered hoarsely, "Yes. Tomorrow morning will do."

She waved as he climbed into the carriage, and the equipage drove away. Then she turned toward the seminary. As she did, a thought that had been lurking in the back of her mind darted to the forefront at last. She recalled her hope that the veiled woman had been her mother, come to find her. Now Olivia felt a chill creep up her spine like a slithery silverfish. Her mother had been within the seminary when they arrived. Who, then, was the veiled woman Olivia had seen . . . and what did she want?

44

Scapegallows:
One who deserves and has narrowly escaped the gallows,
a slip-gibbet, one for whom the gallows is said to groan.
—Francis Grose, *The 1811 Dictionary of the Vulgar Tongue*

Edward found the gamekeeper on his stoop, sitting in a puddle of sunshine, pet partridge at his heels, whittling knife and wood in his hands.

"I have learnt some distressing news, Mr. Croome," Edward began somberly.

The old man shot him a hawk-eyed look. "I daresay I can guess who told ya. Whatever she said, I trust you'll hear my side o' the tale. Isn't as bad as it appears."

"She? Are you talking about Miss Keene?"

"Well, ain't you?"

"No. Should I be? What might Miss Keene have told me?"

Croome closed the knife with a snap. "You'll ask 'er now, so I'll tell ya myself, and you can put me out if ya have a mind to. She seen me once before she ever come here. With a bunch o' ne'er do wells in the Chedworth wood."

"Chedworth—? What was our gamekeeper doing there?"

"I take a day now and then. After more'n thirty years workin' for yer father and his before 'im, I have it comin', haven't I?"

"But what—?"

"These men be poachers, but not here, my lord. Not after I caught them the once. Netting partridges by the barrelful."

"When was this? I don't recall hearing of it. Did you take them in to the constable?"

"Long ago. And no I did not. One o' those men was no more'n a lad. Another had a new missus with 'er first babe on the way. I couldn't do it. So I struck up a bargain-like. They would never more set foot on Brightwell property, and I would not take them in."

"But to trust the word of poachers?"

"I don't say I trusted them. Not Borcher and that other scoundrel. Hard, uncouth dogs. So I followed them, see, and they none the wiser, all the way back to the Chedworth wood, where they camp."

Edward scratched the back of his head. "Are you telling me you happened upon Miss Keene the one time you went? Preposterous!"

"No. I go back every fortnight or so."

"Why? Are you in league with them? I cannot imagine another cause but profit to travel such distance."

"Can you not? I would have credited you with more imagination, lad. A man with a full belly is much less likely to poach, ain't he?"

Edward looked at the old gamekeeper sharply. Wanted to cut as he had been cut. "Who is Alice Croome?"

The man's face slackened, then stilled. A wary light came into his faded eyes. "What did yer father tell ya?"

"I don't know who my father is. Do you?" When Croome hesitated, Edward hissed, "Are you the man?"

The old man's eyes widened, and he gave a mirthless bark of laughter. "Seems you have imagination after all, be it twisted. If I knew who yer father was, I'd 'ave killed him long ago for what he did to my sweet Alice. But never would she tell me who used her ill. And her what never hurt a living soul."

"Alice was your . . ."

"My girl. My own daughter." His voice trembled. "The dearest creature God ever made."

Croome's daughter. From worse to worse. "Where is she now?"

"Where did Lord Brightwell tell you she were?"

"He told me nothing."

"Then how did you hear of her?"

Edward shook his head, snorted a laugh. "My old nurse. The venerable Nurse Peale forgets a great deal these days, but recalls things she was meant to forget."

Croome seemed deep in thought and nodded his understanding.

Edward studied him. "Seems she is not the only one who knows, for we have received more than one threatening letter. You wouldn't know anything about that, would you?"

Croome scowled. "I know naught of threatening letters, save the one from Borcher. Do you think I would raise a hand to harm you? Me? When yer all I've left in this world to show for me and mine? And sure and why did I refuse Linton's offer at twice the wages? Or Sackville's, for half again as much, and a lodge what's not falling down about me in the bargain? Why do I stay here? Where naught but me cares for the wood nor game? Not a sportsman on the place since the fourth earl. Did I stay bidin' my time so I might one day write you a threatening letter? Never."

Listening, Edward felt rattled, disconcerted to hear laconic Mr. Croome speak so many words together.

"Forgive me. I did not think you were behind the other letters. But you still have not told me where my . . . where your daughter is." Edward could not say nor even think the word. Lady Brightwell was his mother and always would be.

Croome stared off at the westerly sun, shining between the trees like a golden clockface framed in wood. "They say she run off with her young man."

"They? Who is they?"

"They what don't want people askin' questions 'bout her and what become of her."

"And what do *you* say?"

Croome narrowed his eyes until they all but disappeared beneath overgrown brows. "I say the Lord knows, and the earl knows, and one of them'll have to be the one to tell ya."

Olivia asked the coachman to first stop at the dress shop, where she bid an affectionate farewell to Eliza Ludlow. From there, she went to the vicarage, and found Mr. Tugwell in his garden.

"I have come to say good-bye."

He pressed her hand. "I heard you were leaving us. And very sorry I was too."

"Thank you." She hoped it was not obvious she had been crying and attempted a light tone. "Might I ask a favor, Mr. Tugwell?"

"Anything, Miss Keene."

"I have written to your late wife's friend—the mistress of the girls' school in Kent?"

He nodded.

"She has written back to offer me a post, on the condition you will provide a character reference. Will you?"

"Of course, my dear. Though I should very much dislike for you to move so far away."

She forced a smile. "No need to fear. Miss Ludlow will still be here. And the two of you deal very well together."

"At the almshouse, yes." He hesitated. "You have been . . . let go . . . from Brightwell Court?"

"Not exactly, but with all that has happened, I think it best I leave. In all truth, I miss a schoolroom full of pupils, the camaraderie of girls from near and far, the company of like-minds, the friendship of other teachers."

"As well you might. I have never envied the life of a governess. Such lonely hours. Betwixt and between the family and the servants. A school would be much more commodious. I confess I cannot abide being alone for more than a few hours. I become bored with my own company all too quickly."

Olivia shook her head, bemused and mildly frustrated. "I think you must be blind, Mr. Tugwell. Or only see what you wish to see."

His brow puckered. "What do you mean?"

What could one say to a parson? The vicar of prestigious St. Mary's? *Open your eyes, man. The woman loves you. If you don't make Eliza Ludlow the next Mrs. Tugwell, then you are foolish indeed.* It would not do. Men did not like to be pushed. She would need to appeal to his heart of faith. Speak his language. "I believe you ought to pray for Miss Ludlow."

"Oh?"

"Yes. I cannot divulge details, but there is cause to believe she shall soon marry, and she will need wisdom to choose her husband wisely."

"Choose? Do you mean to say she has more than one suitor? I did not know she had any."

"I cannot break a confidence, Mr. Tugwell. Only ask you to pray fervently for our dear Eliza and for God's will to be done in her life."

"I shall, of course." He looked pensive and disconcerted.

Olivia reckoned it a good sign.

Olivia felt a pang of regret as she made her rounds of the estate, saying farewell to one and all. She hugged Doris and held her close.

"I am ever so happy you found your mum," Doris said. "What about your nasty ol' papa?"

Olivia inhaled deeply. "I found that I had misjudged him. At least in part."

"Did you now—not a mean crust? A slip-gibbet scapegallows?"

The words stilled Olivia. Might Mr. Tugwell not say they were *all* scapegallows? Escaping the penalty for their deeds only through God's grace? She swallowed. "I am not certain *what* he is, but I plan to find out."

Doris sighed. "I don't hold much hope for people changin' their ways, but I'd be glad to be proved wrong. And no matter what, you've got a mum who loves ya, and that's more than most of us have, and don't you forget it."

Olivia smiled. "How I shall miss you, Dory."

In the kitchen, Mrs. Moore crushed Olivia in a warm embrace. "We shall all miss you, love. Mr. Croome as well, though he would never admit it. Have you been to see him?"

"No, but I shall."

Mrs. Moore nodded and pressed a wrapped bundle of biscuits into her hand. "Take this, my dear," she said, eyes glistening. "A piece of my heart goes with it."

In the nursery, Andrew threw his arms about her waist. When he loosened his hold at last, Olivia knelt down to his eye level.

"Why are you going away again, Miss Livie?" Andrew asked with a pout. "You have been gone too long already."

Audrey stood apart, and Olivia held out a hand to her. The girl came forward, crestfallen.

"I will miss the both of you very much," Olivia whispered. "But I find I must go."

"But we need a teacher!" Andrew complained.

Olivia forced a bright tone over the lump in her throat. "You shall have kind Mr. Tugwell for your Latin, I understand."

"Ugh. He's nothing like you, Miss Livie. He talks a great deal but teaches very little."

Olivia did not doubt his words were true, but she bit back a smile. "Be respectful and attentive, Andrew. He might improve on you."

She pressed Audrey's hand. "And lovely Audrey will have another governess, or perhaps attend the Miss Kirbys' seminary and have the best teacher of all—my own mother."

"Your mother is a teacher there?"

"Indeed she is. You would enjoy having Dorothea Keene as your teacher. I know I did."

Andrew dug his toes into the carpet. "Aud reads from the *Robins* book every night. But it isn't the same as having you read it."

Eyes burning, Olivia embraced each of them again, holding them under her wing one last time.

On her way down the stairs, she paused before Edward's study. She wondered if she ought to leave a note. But what could she say? How would she even begin to write down how she felt? She put her hand on the doorknob, running her fingers along the cool, smooth surface. Then she turned and walked away.

On her way to the gamekeeper's lodge, a quiet voice whispered in her mind. On its impulse she stopped in the garden, where the kindly gardener helped her cut a handful of lily of the valley. How sweet the aroma.

She found Mr. Croome sitting at the edge of the clearing beside a slight grassy mound, his back against a tree. Seeing her, he gave a little lurch as though to rise, but sank back, apparently resigned to being found in such a humble pose.

Stepping near, she glimpsed several flat, lichen-encrusted stones on the mound, in the shape of a cross. She said nothing. Nor did she meet his challenging look. She hadn't the strength to spar with him that day.

She bent, laid the lily of the valley on his daughter's grave, and walked away.

45

> Never keep servants, however excellent they may be in their stations, whom you know to be guilty of immorality.
>
> —Samuel & Sarah Adams, *The Complete Servant*

Edward found Lord Brightwell in the garden, smoking one of his cigars. He slumped onto the bench beside him, blind to the beauty of the arbor, trees, and flowers.

"I spoke with my *grandfather* yesterday," Edward began.

The earl looked up sharply. "Devil take it. He swore—"

Edward cut him off with a dismissive hand. "He has never breathed a word. It was Nurse Peale. Her mind is slipping. Her tongue as well."

Lord Brightwell groaned.

"Is that why you never wanted me to be alone with the man?" Edward asked. "Afraid he might try to take me back? Faith! I grew up in terror of my own grandfather."

"I did worry. But you were never to know. He was never to *be* your *grandfather*. He agreed to the arrangement—wanted the best for you." Lord Brightwell inhaled and exhaled a long stream of smoke. "I had no idea what a difficult thing I was asking at the time. Now, when I think about how I would feel giving up a grandson forever, for another man to claim as his own? Impossible! But at the time, I was only thinking of your mother and myself. And I knew that only by absolute secrecy could we raise you as our own flesh and blood and rightful heir."

Edward huffed. "Well, we see how well *that* has worked out." He rose, restless. "How did you manage the exchange?"

"Croome came to me several months into your mother's third lying-in. Your mother had already suffered two miscarriages during the first few months of our marriage. After the second, both the physician and midwife examined her and concurred that she was unlikely to ever bear a living infant. Still, when she was soon once again with child, we hoped they were wrong, that this time would be different. At all events, Croome asked if I had any idea who was responsible for his daughter being with child. As she worked in my house, he assumed I might be in the way of knowing. He did not accuse me, for I gather his daughter was good enough to exonerate me, even as she refused to name the man responsible.

"I did what I thought best. Assured him we could handle things quietly—his daughter would give notice before her condition became evident, and I would not tell a soul. I gave her an extra quarter's wages on going away, then put her from my mind.

"Months passed and Marian's lying-in seemed to be going miraculously well—her longest yet. The physician ordered bed rest and all manner of dietary precautions, but I could tell he did not hold out much hope. We called in only the physician that time, for after Marian's first two experiences, she did not want the blunt, coarse midwife to attend her again."

He paused for breath. "When Marian was seven or eight months along, she went into early labour and we sent for the physician. He assured us it was only a false labour, but when he tried to find the infant's heartbeat, he could not and told us to prepare for a stillbirth. Marian was terrified.

"She began having pains again a few days later, but we assumed it was another false labour and did not send for the physician right away. By the time we did send for him, the labour was hard and fast. But the doctor had been called away somewhere. I wanted to send for the midwife, but your mother refused. Miss Peale was already here, installed as the doctor's monthly nurse. In the end, she alone attended the birth, as I mentioned. A stillborn . . .

"We were devastated, Marian and I." He shook his head at the painful memory. "I had never seen your mother laid so low. When she finally fell into a grief-exhausted slumber, I left her in Nurse Peale's care and went out of doors. I needed air. And . . . to ask Matthews to fashion a tiny coffin.

"But near the carpentry shop, I paused. I heard wild keening from the direction of the wood and feared mad dogs or worse. I followed the sound to the gamekeeper's lodge. The keening grew louder until I thought some animal was tearing Croome limb from limb. But as I ran near, I found only Croome sitting beside a mound of dirt just beyond the clearing. He was rocking himself and wailing in a way that echoed my own lament.

"Croome saw me and waved me away, barking at me to leave him alone. I wanted nothing more than to do just that. But then you cried. There from the little basket where he'd placed you. I could not bear to look upon the grief-mad father and so I looked at you. At your bald, misshapen head and red face. And thought I had never seen anything so, well, pitiful and irresistible all at once." Lord Brightwell chuckled.

"He buried his daughter there, in the wood?" Edward was incredulous.

"He said he could not bear to have his Alice taken from him. Wanted her near. I feared he was a bit unhinged, and I suppose that was part of the reason I always cautioned you against him."

Edward nodded, remembering the protective gestures, the whispered warnings. But had they been justified? Would not any parent be as distraught, at least temporarily?

Lord Brightwell continued, "I wanted nothing more than to leave that makeshift grave, that scene of a parent's worst nightmare. But I realized I did not wish to leave alone. I asked him if a midwife had been called, if anyone else knew. He said only Mrs. Moore."

"Our cook? What on earth?"

"Croome's sister-in-law, I gather. Young Alice's aunt. I wonder if he blamed her."

"Blamed her? Why should he?"

"I take it she delivered the child the day before, when neither midwife nor doctor could be found. And when things went badly . . ." He lifted a hand expressively.

Edward nodded, his mind filling in the gruesome scene.

His father rose and went to stand beside the arbor, turning to face the sun. "I am not sure how rashly I behaved in insisting Croome not tell anyone his daughter had died. I suppose I thought, if people knew she died, they'd ask how. If they knew she died in childbirth, they'd want to know what became of the child."

The earl ran a hand over his face. "It was wrong of me to deny him his right to grieve openly. I was thinking only of my family. Me. I did not understand. I don't think I had ever loved anyone the way he loved his Alice. But all that changed in the course of days, hours even, once I held you."

"He agreed to give me to you?" Edward barely managed to keep the edge from the words. "Or did you pay him?"

"I own I asked if he required any remuneration, and I thought he would strike me down where I stood. He made it clear he was not 'selling the child,' but only giving you to me because he was not fit to raise you himself. He threatened me with violence if I ever mentioned money again." The earl shuddered. "I never did." He shook his head remembering. "I did ask if Mrs. Moore would feel the same way. How he glowered at me. He said, 'You leave her to me. She'll not say a word, she won't.' And to my knowledge she never has."

Edward's mind spun. Did Mrs. Moore know what became of the babe she delivered? How odd to think that his family's cook, and certainly their gamekeeper and his own nurse, had known the truth about him all these years, while he'd had not a clue. Had Mrs. Moore written the letters? He could not credit it. Why now, after so many years?

"And . . . Mother," Edward asked. "What did she think of it all?"

"She was hesitant at first. We would not have pursued such a course for many years, if ever, had opportunity—in this case, you—not landed in our laps. Providence, I say. There was little warmth between Marian and myself in the first year of our marriage, but we fell in love over you, my boy. And she did love you, Edward. Never doubt it. Though I admit she never liked your name."

Edward felt his brow rise in question.

"It was Croome's final word on the subject. He told me in his gruff voice, 'His name is Edward. *She* named him that. My father's name, and my second name as well. I'll not have you changing it.'" Lord Brightwell chuckled. "I did not dare."

Edward shook his head, failing to see the humor in the situation. *Edward* . . . How ironic. How strange. He had been named for his father's gamekeeper, a man he had spent his whole life avoiding.

When Edward walked into the kitchen, Mrs. Moore looked up, mouth slack, eyes wide. He almost never came belowstairs, save for Christmas carol singing and the like a few times each year. Any directions for the cook were delivered through the housekeeper or butler.

Two young kitchen maids stared up at him, one blushing profusely, the other daring a saucy look.

Edward asked, "Mrs. Moore, might I have a private word?"

The woman swallowed, evidently expecting news of the worst sort. "Of course, my lord."

She directed him to the stillroom off the kitchen, with its floor-to-ceiling shelves of blue-and-white china, jarred pickles and ruby red preserves, and the sharp, tangy aromas of beehive and gooseberry vinegars.

Once inside, he closed the door behind them, startling her further.

"I have been speaking with Mr. Croome. . . ." he began.

"Oh dear," she interrupted. "What has the old fool been up to now?"

"Nothing to fret over, I assure you. I was asking him about his daughter, Alice."

She frowned, clearly troubled. "Were you? I am surprised you even know of her. She . . . left us . . . before you were born."

"Did she?"

Mrs. Moore squinted in thought. "One or two days before, I believe. It is so long ago."

He nodded. "You delivered her of a child, I understand." He added gently, "It is all right, Mrs. Moore. I know she died."

Her mouth puckered, her round cheeks paled. "Avery told you that?" She looked stricken indeed. "I know he has never forgiven me . . . but to tell you? After all these years? When he swore me to secrecy?"

"I don't think he blames you. I suppose at the time, in his grief . . ."

She shook her head. "He planned to send her north to his family to have the child, but never did. Never could bear to part with her. When her time came, he asked me to stay with Alice while he went to find the doctor or midwife. I was only to sit with her. But he didn't return for hours, and when he did, he was alone. He could find no one to deliver her. I understand your father had the same problem when your mother's time came soon after."

Edward nodded. "Nurse Peale attended my mother."

She squinted once more. "Yes, I do remember hearing that." Mrs. Moore grimaced. "I did what I could for Allie, but I knew so little. I had never even had a child of my own. I have never felt so helpless. My own dear niece, my sister's lass, and I couldn't save her." She shook her head, clearly reliving those mournful images once more. Tears filled her small hazel eyes and rolled up and over her round cheeks. "Avery has never forgiven me. He sent me back to the house soon after, as if he couldn't bear the sight of me."

Mrs. Moore swiped at her tears with the back of a fleshy hand. "And the child . . . a little boy. He never would tell me what became of him. I suppose he took him to kin in the north, or found some family to take him in. I was surprised he could part with him, all he had left of his Alice. But he was in no fit shape to raise wolves, let alone a child in those days." Her lips trembled as she spoke. "He was mad with grief, repulsed my every effort to comfort him. Refused to speak of it. To tell me where the boy was." Her voice broke. "The boy she died bringin' into the world."

"Mrs. Moore," he said gently. "You will not believe it, I fear. But Alice died bringing *me* into the world."

She stared at him, brows furrowed, lips tight. She looked angry or at least frustrated and confused.

"Mr. Croome did not take Alice's son to the north," Edward continued quietly. "He gave that child to Lord and Lady Brightwell. To raise as their own."

Her small mouth slowly drooped into a sloppy O. She looked nearly comical, and he bit his lip to stay a rogue grin.

"I said you would not believe me."

She peered up at him, shaking her head in wonder. "I never saw it," she breathed. "You are not very like her."

"Ironic, isn't it, how I look so much the Bradley."

"God's hand, I should say."

"I don't know about that." He ducked his head, giving way to a sheepish smile.

"There. I see a hint of her." Mrs. Moore's hazel eyes twinkled. "Something around your mouth, when you smile. I can't remember seeing you smile, not since you were a lad."

"I shall have to work on that."

Her mouth dropped open again as a new thought struck her. "That must be why it was all such a secret! Why he refused to say what became of you." She sucked in a long breath. "And why he stayed on, when we all thought he would leave. Why does he stay, I used to wonder, since he had family in the north that would care for him in his old age. What keeps him here now his Maggie is gone and Alice too?" She stared at Edward, slowly shaking her head in amazement. "He couldn't bear to leave *you*."

Edward's chest tightened, and his throat followed suit.

"I cannot believe it." Tears sprung anew into her eyes, but the desolation of moments before was replaced by apparent joy. "Allie's boy." She reached out to him, but quickly caught herself as she realized what she was about to do. "Forgive me."

He took both of her hands in his own. "There is nothing to forgive, Mrs. Moore. After all, you are my great-aunt, are you not?"

She laughed and beamed up at him, squeezing his hands. "I suppose I am." She bit her lip. "Though I suppose it is all still a great secret?"

He inhaled deeply. "At present, yes, if you don't mind. But not forever."

"How long have you known that you are not . . ." She let the question go unfinished.

"I only learnt of it when Miss Keene arrived, last autumn."

"Miss Keene? What has she to do with it?"

He pulled an apologetic face. "It is a long story, I fear."

As if sensing a dismissal, she withdrew her hands and straightened. "I am sure you are quite busy, and I . . . well, supper will not cook itself."

She opened the stillroom door, but he stopped her with a gentle entreaty. "Mrs. Moore. Please."

She hesitated in the threshold.

He stepped near, closing the gap between them. "I should very much like to tell you all, but another time. Perhaps we might take tea together some afternoon? Say, in the gamekeeper's lodge?"

She gave him a sidelong glance. "He won't like that."

"You might be surprised. And I think it would do him a world of good."

"Do you indeed?" Her eyes twinkled once more. "Then I should like that above all things."

On impulse, he leaned down and kissed her cheek.

As he turned, he heard the kitchen maids gasp, followed by giggles and frenzied whispers.

Mrs. Moore's officious voice followed him as he ascended the stairs. "He was only thanking me for my best plum cake, and had you ever tasted it, you would buss me as well. Now, haven't you garden peas to shell?"

Edward smiled.

Edward Stanton Bradley knocked on the gamekeeper's lodge and held his breath, the tool case heavy in his hand.

After a long minute, Avery Croome opened the door, his silvery blue eyes narrow. "Hope you ain't come to ask me to break my word."

"I am asking you to break nothing, Mr. Croome," Edward said, feeling strangely buoyant. "I am here to repair what is already broken."

Croome's overgrown eyebrows rose. He looked from Edward's face to Matthews's tool case and back again. "You?"

Edward gestured toward one of the front windows, eyeing a deeply cracked pane. "I shall call out the glazier for that. Will Tuesday suit?"

Croome only peered at him, suspicion pinching his features.

"Now, let us take a look inside," Edward said, gesturing toward the door.

"Why?"

Edward said innocently, "Because I have it on good authority that the place is all but in ruins. I believe you spoke of wanting a lodge that is not falling down about you?"

Keeping his eye on Edward, Croome pushed open the door and stepped backward, as though not to turn his back on a potentially dangerous predator. He said, "I weren't expecting company, mind. Not since Miss Keene left. She's the only one what bothered to come out here."

"Was she indeed?"

"Up and left, ey?" Croome shook his head, mouth twisted in disapproval.

"I fear I am to blame," Edward confessed. "If it is any consolation, I miss her too."

Croome scowled. "Never said I missed her."

"Oh, and before I forget—" Edward pulled a wrapped bundle from the tool case—"Mrs. Moore sent along a slice of plum cake. Still warm."

Croome's eyes were mere slits now, and he gave his head a slow shake. "Got you in on it now, has she?"

Edward shrugged but bit back a grin when the old man accepted the bundle.

Edward followed him inside. A musty smell greeted him—damp, but not vile. The main room was relatively tidy, and only one dish and cup stood waiting to be washed on the sideboard.

"Does not look so bad," he said, surveying the room. "Where is the problem?"

Laying Mrs. Moore's offering on the table, Croome limped over to the far wall and pointed up to a ceiling water-stained and cracked.

Edward followed. Sinking to his haunches to lay the heavy tool case on the floor, he paused, his attention snagged by the bookcase standing against the wall.

His eyes roved over the three tiers crudely pieced and stained in his favorite shade. He had not laid eyes on it in a half-dozen years, but he knew it instantly.

Behind him, Croome muttered, "Saved it from the bonfire. Couldn't stand to see it wasted."

Edward nodded, chest tight.

"Well, let's get to it," Croome said brusquely. "I do hope yer skills 'ave improved since then."

46

The objects of the present life fill the human eye with a false magnification because of their immediacy.

—William Wilberforce

When the Crenshaws' footman held forth the silver letter tray, Olivia recognized Lord Brightwell's scrawl on a letter directed to her. Pleased to hear from him, she peeled open the seal and unfolded the single sheet. Her breath caught. For the words within were written in a different hand—a bold, masculine hand. His.

Her aunt Georgiana stepped into the room, pulling on her gloves. "Olivia my dear, are you ready?" she asked.

Olivia closed the note. "Forgive me, Aunt, but I have just received a letter. Would you mind very much if I stayed here? You go on without me."

"Are you certain, my dear?"

"Quite certain."

Reluctantly, her aunt agreed to pay morning calls without her.

Olivia hurried to her room and, with shaking fingers, unfolded the letter once more.

My dear Miss Keene,

There is so very much to tell you, I barely know where to begin. Except to say how profoundly sorry I am for how I have treated you. For the foolish accusations, and for what must have seemed a rejection of yourself when I objected to my father's plans to acknowledge you as his daughter or at least his ward. Please know I hold only the deepest respect and admiration for you. Although the motives which governed me may appear insufficient, I had a very good, albeit selfish reason for not wanting the world to believe you my sister. I will say no more about this herein, except to ask you to forgive me if you can.

I long to share with you, of all people, the facts which I have learnt since your departure. But I dare not do so in a letter, should it be misdirected. Therefore I write in vague terms which I know you, clever girl, will understand.

I have not learnt all I wish to know, but a great deal has recently come to light. I hope I might one day be able to tell you all in person. In the meantime, I pray that all goes well with you.

Again, I offer you my deepest apologies. And will only add, God bless you.

Edward S. Bradley

Her heart squeezed, even as questions began spinning through her mind. She read the signature once more and saw that his title was notably absent. What had he learned? What did it mean?

Johnny Ross stood before the desk, hat in hand. Beside him stood the maid Mrs. Hinkley had told Edward about, now noticeably with child. Hodges and Mrs. Hinkley awaited his verdict at the back of the room. Lord Brightwell stood behind Edward, still content to leave such decisions to him.

"I know we are not to marry while in service, my lord," Ross said. "But Martha here is expecting, so . . . we did."

"Are you the father?" Edward asked and instantly regretted it. He had thought another man responsible, but it was none of his business, and he certainly had not meant to mortify the young woman. He obviously had, however, for she bowed her head, a blush creeping up her neck. Even Ross's face burned red.

Behind Edward, Lord Brightwell cleared his throat. Edward opened his mouth to retract the question, but Ross answered before he could.

"No, my lord. But I love her just the same."

Edward noticed the young woman surreptitiously take the groom's hand in hers.

Ross continued, "Mr. Hodges said I am to be dismissed, unless you say otherwise. I was wonderin', my lord, if you might see your way to givin' me a character. Otherwise another post will be awful hard to come by."

Edward stared at the groom, stunned by his unexpected nobility. "No."

Ross looked down at the floor.

"No, you shall not be dismissed," Edward clarified, turning toward the earl. "That is, unless you disapprove, Father?"

Lord Brightwell hesitated. "Ah . . . no, Edward. Whatever you think best."

Ross beamed. "Thank you, my lord. Thank you!"

Even Martha gave him a shy smile, and Edward could not help but think of Alice Croome and wonder what she had looked like while carrying him.

Once the details and lodging arrangements had been discussed, the staff took their leave.

Edward shut the door behind them and turned to face Lord Brightwell with steely resolve. "Who was my father?" he asked quietly,

The earl began, "The girl never told anyone, so—"

"Who was he?" Edward persisted.

For a moment Lord Brightwell looked pugnacious, as if formulating another excuse, but then sighed. "I thought you might have guessed by now."

Frowning, Edward shook his head.

"Have I not always insisted you are a Bradley?"

Edward blinked and felt a chill run through his body. "Sebastian—*Uncle Bradley*—was my father?"

The earl nodded. "I believe so, yes."

Edward's mind whirled. He was a Bradley after all. Still illegitimate. Still rightful heir to nothing save shame and his adopted father's unmerited love.

He thought back to all he knew about Sebastian Bradley, dead these six or seven years.

He was aware, of course, of the long enmity between Lord Brightwell and his brother. Though Oliver was eldest and their father's heir, he had not left Sebastian to fend for himself, as perhaps he should have. He had set him up in a London house, furnished it, supplied him servants, a carriage, and horses. Most of which Sebastian had lost gaming or owed to debt collectors. Oliver, in turn, lost all respect for the younger man. Nor was uncontrolled gambling Sebastian's only sin. He had taken advantage of more than one young woman in his day, requiring sums to be paid and arrangements made.

The earl had confessed himself surprised when Sebastian announced his engagement to a respectable woman. He had even come to Oliver, hat in hand, and proclaimed himself a changed man. And Oliver had wanted to believe him.

Soon after his own marriage to Marian Estcourt, Oliver invited his brother and sister-in-law to visit Brightwell Court, which they did that summer and again in the fall, bringing with them their baby girl, Judith, and her nurse.

But that autumn visit was to prove the last for Sebastian. He was permitted at Brightwell Court no longer, though his wife and Judith, and eventually Felix, were still welcome. The reason was not specified. A falling out of sorts was assumed, some disagreement or one too many gaming debts to pay off . . . something.

Now Edward realized there was more to it than that.

"I came upon Sebastian one night, coming up from belowstairs," the earl began. "His face was scratched and his clothing disheveled. He seemed startled to see me, but quickly recovered. I asked what he was doing belowstairs, and he made an excuse about looking for something to eat, though he could easily have asked a servant to bring him a tray. I also asked about his face, and he said it must have gotten scratched in the wood or some such. I did not believe him.

"When he had taken himself up to bed, I went down to the kitchen, and there came upon Croome's daughter, sitting near the dying fire, face in her hands, thin shoulders quaking.

"I own I wanted nothing more than to turn back, but I was compelled by duty to speak to her. I hoped I was wrong in my suspicions. That Sebastian really *had* scratched his face in the wood.

"The girl jumped when she saw me. When I asked her what the matter was, she only gaped at me, apparently stunned or shaken. I took a step closer, lifted my lamp to better see her face, and asked if she was unwell. How wide her eyes were, I remember, and through them, I thought I witnessed some inner struggle, though perhaps my memory is now colored by later revelations.

"Thinking to encourage her, I said that I was acquainted with her father—a most trusted man. But at the mention of Mr. Croome, new tears filled her eyes. She assured me she was well, that she *had* been sad over some trifling matter but was better now. It was not a very convincing performance.

"I left the kitchen with a heavy heart, telling myself I had done my duty, had given the girl every opportunity to accuse my brother, but she had not. Perhaps nothing so terrible had happened. If it had, why had she not told? Was she so frightened of her father—afraid he would blame *her* for any wrongdoing? Perhaps the girl was a known flirt.

"With these paltry justifications, I dismissed the scene from my mind. Only later, when Croome came to me—devastated by his daughter's fallen state—did I realize Sebastian was the person she had feared, for her father clearly doted on the girl and believed her the very picture of innocence. I wondered if Sebastian had threatened to have Croome sacked should she tell. Sebastian had no authority to do such a thing, but a maid would have no way of knowing that, would have no reason to think the lord of the manor would believe her over his own brother.

"But I would have. Experience had taught me not to trust Sebastian. I was infuriated with myself for opening my heart and home for more disappointment and debauchery. That was the end. Nevermore was Sebastian welcome at Brightwell Court—no matter that it had been his childhood home. It was his home no longer.

"I did not admit my suspicions to Croome. Saw no reason to. Croome would likely have killed Sebastian and ended in a hangman's noose, and then where would his daughter have been? Alone in the world with a by-blow to raise on her own. I needed to let the girl go, of course—no master kept on an expecting girl in those days, no matter his charitable leanings. I gave her a quarter's wages and raised Croome's salary on the sly, to help him provide for her.

"I knew my brother would not do anything for the girl. It was left to me to make recompense. As it always was."

When his father finished speaking, Edward asked, "You never told him?"

"That he fathered a child? Do you think he would have welcomed the news? Done his duty by your mother—had she lived—and by you? Never. There had been rumors of other illegitimate children, but none had tempted him to duty before."

"But you did not go about the country taking in his other whelps?" Edward asked dryly.

"No. I confess the thought never crossed my mind. But then, I had never met one of his victims personally, witnessed her devastation, and that of her father—a man I respected as my father had before me. I was untouched by those other faceless women and rumored offspring. But not this time.

"Still, I had no intention of claiming or even supporting the child when first I learnt of its coming. It wasn't until months later, when your mother had given birth to a stillborn son . . . and I remembered the verdict the physician and midwife had given us—no children. No son and heir . . ."

Edward said, "You would not have been the first peer to face that disappointment."

Lord Brightwell sighed. "Indeed not. But who would inherit in a son's stead? None other than my brother, Sebastian, who would no doubt lose everything and ruin Brightwell Court—sell off anything not nailed down or entailed. Let the place out to strangers and I shudder to think what all."

"But what of Felix?"

"There was no Felix when I made my decision to make you my son and heir. And even if there had been, Sebastian would have been heir before him. I doubt there would have been much left to inherit after Sebastian had been Earl of Brightwell for a few years."

"But now Sebastian is dead."

Lord Brightwell inhaled deeply. "Yes."

"And so Felix is your rightful heir."

"Felix is a fool. And with that Titian hair and green eyes, he is likely less a Bradley than you are. My sister-in-law had her revenge, I daresay, though in the end it does not signify. She and Sebastian were married at the time of his birth, so in the eyes of the law, Felix is legitimate, no matter what is whispered about his mother and a certain ginger-haired duke."

His face weary, Lord Brightwell pressed his fingers against his eyelids. "Forgive me, Edward. I have never before joined in the rumor-mongering and am ashamed to have done so now." He ran a hand over his face. "I am not myself at present."

Edward attempted a grin. "Neither am I."

Lord Brightwell shook his head. "Felix is young and irresponsible, and already shows every likelihood of following Sebastian's dissolute ways. Still, he isn't the scoundrel my brother was. At least not yet. I will see him provided for. And Judith and the children, of course."

"Hmm," Edward muttered, shaking his head. "It is ironic. Judith has often commented that she and I looked more alike than she and Felix. I wonder if she had any idea how close to the truth she was."

"I doubt it."

"Now I see why you warned me against her romantic notions."

"Yes. You see, my dear boy, you really are a Bradley. My only son, and your uncle's eldest son—at least, as far as we know."

"But the law . . ."

"Dash the law."

"No, Father. It doesn't change what I am. In the eyes of the law, I cannot be your heir."

"Then the eyes of the law need not see."

Edward grimly shook his head. "The veiled woman would not agree with you."

47

Women saw the governess as a threat to their happiness.

—M. Jeanne Peterson, *Suffer and Be Still*

When the post came that day, Judith snatched a letter from Hodges and quickly took herself upstairs. Edward watched her go with fatalistic sadness.

A few minutes later, he stepped into Judith's private apartment for the first time in his adult life. And he did so without knocking.

Judith was seated at an elegant lady's writing table, bent over the missive.

"Hello, Judith. Another letter?"

She looked up sharply, searching his face. "Yes . . . but it is only from Mamma." She fluttered her fingers dismissively and began to refold the single sheet.

"May I?" he asked, feigning nonchalance as he held out his hand. Their gazes locked. When she did not release the letter to him, he pulled it from her grasp.

He removed the first threatening letter from his pocket and compared the two as if they were nothing more interesting than two newspaper accounts of the same story. "And how is *Mamma* keeping these days?" he asked idly.

She watched him, face stiff, eyes wary. She said in convincing disinterest, "She is well enough, I suppose."

"I imagine she is. Now that she has reason to believe her son will be heir to Brightwell Court."

"Will he be?" Judith asked, her voice revealingly high-pitched.

"It seems likely, as well you know. Here she says, and I find it most interesting, 'Do you see any sign of his giving way? Or need I write again?'"

Judith swallowed. "That could relate to any number of subjects."

Edward tucked both letters into his pocket. "How long have you known?"

She considered him with steady, round blue eyes. "We are not the ones who have done anything wrong, after all," she said, abandoning pretense.

"Nothing illegal, at any rate. Unless one counts your part in the extortion attempt."

Her fair brows rose high.

"Yes, the midwife's husband was inspired to attempt extortion after your visit, or was it your mother's?"

She shook her head, lips parted. "I would not have believed it. The doddering fool seemed barely to know his name when I called. He did recall his wife muttering about strange goings-on at Brightwell Court many years ago. Yes, it might have to do with a baby, but he could not say what it was." She lifted a shrug. "If I did hint at the secret, I certainly never suggested extortion."

"Still, I think the constable might find the connection most interesting. As magistrate, I know I do."

"I did not start this crusade," Judith defended. "Though I did insist Mamma leave off for a time after Lady Brightwell died."

She pushed back her chair and rose. "She says she and Father always suspected something. Doctor come and gone with no news of a birth. Everyone certain Lady Brightwell had suffered another 'mishap.' Then suddenly there appears a perfectly stout baby boy."

Judith walked languidly across the room. "It was only rumors, of course, and since you looked every inch a Bradley, nothing was done. But then your father took ill with the lung fever—when was that, seven, eight years ago? And my father thought the situation might bear looking into. He tried to locate the midwife, but she had already passed on. He next sought the doctor, but you know how physicians are, all gentlemanlike and professional and discreet. Too successful to be brought round by any small bribe my father might offer." She exhaled deeply. "So he let it lie again. And then died himself while your father fully recovered."

She turned and faced him. "But you see, Edward, your dear loyal nurse is getting on in years. Her mind is slipping. She prattles on about how my Alexander looks so like you at that age, and how can that be? I told her it was not surprising, considering you and I were cousins. 'Cousins?' said she, and laughed as though I had made a fine joke. The first time, I thought she was simply confused. Forgot that you and I were related, because of my married surname. But often she seems quite certain of herself. Quite clear."

"That is no proof, of course," Edward said, sounding, he believed, satisfactorily unconcerned.

"Do we need proof?" she asked rhetorically. "All we need do is pose the question to the House of Lords with enough circumstantial evidence that *they* ask your father. Would he lie to his countrymen? In deed, perhaps, but not in word, if asked directly."

Edward cringed at the thought of his father being publicly condemned by his peers.

"And then there is you, noble Edward. You would not take another man's rightful place, knowing as you now do that you have no claim to it."

"You flatter me, Judith. But can you think so highly of one of such low birth?"

"It is all in the rearing, I suppose."

"You sound like Father." Edward studied her, sadness stealing over him. "Why did you do it, Jude?"

She shrugged, said flippantly, "I was afraid of doing without. Of being embarrassed by reduced circumstances once more. You know I detested growing up with shopkeepers and bill collectors forever knocking on the door. My father gambled away all his money and then Mamma's, so that I could barely outfit myself for a proper coming out."

"You always looked well to me."

"Much good it did me. I married a dashing naval captain, sure he would make his fortune in the war. Instead I ended a widow with no fortune, and another woman's children to care for."

"But Father provides for you, does he not?"

"Yes, but for how long?"

He waited for her to explain. Now that she was talking, she seemed ready to reveal all.

"I admit a part of me was loath to learn of your base birth, for it fouled my plans. I had thought you and I might marry, once my mourning was past."

"Did you?"

She hurried on self-consciously, before he could confirm or deny having similar thoughts. "You are so fond of the children and, as a friend of Dominick's, felt some responsibility, I think."

"True."

She glanced at him, but then turned away once more. "But you *would* pursue Miss Harrington and even Miss Keene. If you were to marry another, your wife might not be so willing to have me under her roof and support the children. But if Felix were to become heir, as my brother, he would always be obliged to provide for me, would he not?"

"I am your brother, Judith. As much as Felix is."

She frowned. "What can you mean?"

"There is a reason Alexander resembles me. You do remember remarking how you and I favour one another more than you and Felix do? There is a reason for that."

She gaped at him, almost fearfully, he thought.

He continued evenly, "My mother was no one you would know. But you knew my father. For he was yours as well."

She stood perfectly still, as if holding her breath. Then her eyelids began to blink, a window shutter, opening and closing, trying to change the view or chop to pieces a hundred images of the past. But she did not try to refute it.

"Did he know?" she asked.

"Your father? I don't think so."

"I think he may have suspected it. . . . Perhaps that is the real reason he decided to let it lie."

Edward sighed, sick of the whole affair. "Well, it does not matter in the end, nor does it change anything. Does it, *dear* sister?"

She blinked again, this time to clear the tears at his biting tone. "Do you so despise me?"

He regarded her somberly. "I could never hate you, Judith. But I am disappointed. I had thought we were friends at least. You might have simply come to Father and me with what you had learned. There was no need for all this cloak-and-dagger business."

Edward stepped to Judith's wardrobe and opened its door casually, like a youth searching the cupboards for a late-night repast.

She lifted her chin. "He would never have admitted it, unless forced."

"You may be right. But I fear you may live to regret the cost of your little charade." He pulled down the veiled hat and tossed it on the dressing table. "The veiled woman, Judith? How gothic."

"It was Mother's idea. She thought Lord Brightwell's interest in Miss Keene might threaten our plans. When I showed her the notice from the seminary, she hoped we would discover something incriminating about her, which might sever their attachment."

"Why? Even if she had been his daughter, which she is not, she would inherit nothing, save perhaps a dowry or some small settlement."

She grimaced. "Daughter? We did not think that. We feared he might . . . that he had romantic intentions toward her."

"Ah." He nodded. "I confess I did as well for a brief time. But his interest in Miss Keene was of the most paternal, I assure you. However, that is not to say he will not marry another once his mourning has passed."

She cast him an anxious glance.

"You see, Judith, the risk you run? Instead of being content with a home in Brightwell Court and everything you should ever need, you have wagered it all on the chance my father will die without a legitimate son. You are furthermore gambling on Felix's willingness to be as generous as Father, which I doubt, but that is another matter. For if Father marries again, and his wife bears him a son . . . then you lose all. Do you not see, Judith? You turned out to be every bit the gambler your father was, though you say you despised him for it."

Her lips trembled. And though she glared rebelliously, her façade was beginning to crack.

Edward turned and walked slowly back across the room.

"Must I leave, then?" she called after him, her voice deceptively calm.

At the door, he turned and looked back. She stood, facing away from him, the sunlight from the window enshrouding her in an unmerited halo of gold. Perhaps, he thought, that was how God saw all His children. Selfish and fallen, yes. But in the forgiving light of His Son, each wore an unmerited halo.

"My father does not ask it of you. You are his niece. He will always love you."

Her rounded shoulders shook, but he felt no satisfaction, no victory. For whether she stayed or went, in his heart he had bid farewell to this woman he had loved since a boy, as playmate, cousin, confidante, and friend.

Three weeks later, Felix stood stiffly before them in the library, unable to meet Edward's gaze. Instead he trained his eyes on Lord Brightwell's cravat and pronounced as if by rote, " . . . If my uncle will publicly recognize me as his rightful heir and Edward agrees to rescind his claim and not challenge the resulting new will, then we shall take no further action and require no legal recompense for fraud."

Lord Brightwell's eyes blazed. "Recompense? As long as I live, you are entitled to nothing. Nothing."

Felix visibly shrunk at his uncle's outrage.

"Everything I have given you—your tuition and expenses, your annual allowance, all of these came out of generosity of feeling, not obligation."

"I—" Felix chanced to meet the earl's gaze, and any rebuttal quickly faded. Instead, he muttered, "I have always thought so, my lord."

"Then who wrote that little monologue for you? Your mother, I suppose?"

Sheepishly, Felix nodded. "She said that what you have done for me, you have done out of guilt. Not generosity."

"And have I taken in your widowed sister for this same reason? I am to be credited with no Christian charity?"

Felix's chin protruded stubbornly, defensively. "I did not say I concurred with Mamma, my lord. But when I am Lord Brightwell, I shall provide for Judith myself."

"Very proper," the earl drawled. "But are you not putting the mourning coach before the horse? As long as I live, you would only be heir presumptive—no title, no money, no privileges. And know this, nephew—I plan to live for a very long time."

Felix swallowed. "For my part I wish you would," he said earnestly. "I have no great longing to be a peer. Devilish lot of responsibility that."

"I am relieved to hear it. For who knows?" the earl said. "I may even remarry. Have a son of my own, and then *he* shall be my heir and you receive nothing."

"Mamma is afraid of that. She was ever so relieved to hear Miss Keene left."

"Was she indeed?"

"For my part, I had just as soon not be Lord anybody. Except . . . it would help me win the hand of a certain lady."

"Miss Harrington, I presume," Edward said.

The young man's face burned scarlet. "I am afraid so."

Ignoring his admission, Lord Brightwell asked, "Did you not read any law at Oxford, Felix? You must realize, my boy, that there is nothing but scandal to be gained by making this public while I live. There is nothing for Edward to rescind. He is just as much a commoner as you are. Only an eldest son can be heir apparent, and as such has *use* of the courtesy title through my lesser rank of Baron of Bradley, but I still hold the peerage. Do you understand? You can never be Lord Bradley. And would only become Lord Brightwell after my death."

His nephew's face fell.

"You will find, my boy, that not every worthy female requires a title to win her."

Felix's lower lip jutted forth. He was clearly unconvinced.

"Here is what I propose," Lord Brightwell said. "I will write within my will a full confession, disclosing my deception, and accepting full blame, so that any serious consequences befall *me*—I shall be too dead to care—but not Edward, who is innocent of any wrongdoing in this matter. He *will* lose the courtesy title, and many in society will rebuff him when the true nature of his birth is revealed. But as he plans to live quietly, apart from London society, I don't think the repercussions will be overly severe.

"After I am gone, you and the solicitors will take this proof to the Lord Chancellor." Here he put his arm around Felix's shoulder and said in a confidential aside, "You have no real proof at present, my boy. Save one senile old woman who would never betray us to strangers, even were she to live long enough to do so." He removed his arm and continued in his best parliamentary voice, "The Committee for Privileges will review the case and shall, I have every certainty, acknowledge your claim to the peerage." He gave Felix a shrewd look. "Remember, this assumes an absence of a new heir apparent. If I remarry and have a son, then such a will and confession would naturally place him in position to inherit. Do I make myself understood?"

A knowing gleam sparked in Felix's eyes. "Have you some lady in mind, Uncle?"

"Ah. That is my affair, is it not? Now. If you agree—and your mother and sister as well—to handle this quietly and avoid a scandal, then I will continue to provide a generous allowance which will give you the life of a gentleman you desire, and allow you to win the hand of any number of ladies of quality." He stood before his nephew and looked him directly in the eye. "If you do *not* agree and scandal erupts, then you shall not have one shilling from me until after my death and the legal case to follow. Do you agree or not?"

Felix swallowed once more. "I agree."

Lord Brightwell nodded his acknowledgment. "Good. Now. I may very well remarry, but at my age I cannot afford to lay all my eggs, as it were, in that basket. There is every chance you *shall* be the next Lord Brightwell, and if so, I want you to be well prepared to live up to the name. So—" He drew himself up and commanded briskly, "First, there will be no further improprieties with the servants. Second, you *will* finish your coursework and obtain your degree. And third, you shall begin your education in estate management and parliamentary affairs—in the library, Saturday week, nine o'clock. Do I make myself clear?"

"You do, my lord." Felix looked up at Lord Brightwell in wonder. "I must say you astound me, Uncle. I had not thought it of you."

"What had you thought?"

"That you would put me out. So I would not be tempted to . . ."

"Hasten my demise?"

Again Felix's face reddened. "Just so."

"I would never believe it of you, my boy, regardless of the schemers your mother and sister turned out to be. You may not be the most clever boy, nor the most prudent, nor the most gentlemanlike, nor . . ."

Edward cleared his throat.

"Right! But you have a good heart, and I have every hope that with proper education and mentoring you will be a credit to the family yet."

"And my sister?"

"I am sorry to tell you Judith has already left us."

"Left?"

"Yes, she has remarried and is even now on her wedding trip."

Felix gaped. "When was this?"

"Two days ago, I understand. By special license."

"Why was I not told?"

"You shall have to ask Judith that, when she returns from Italy. I did not forbid her to contact you, if that is what you are tempted to think."

"Who on earth did she marry?"

"George Linton."

"Linton? Thunder and turf, you must be joking! That dolt?"

"That dolt, indeed, with his handsome four thousand a year. It seems Judith was not content to wait for you to make good on your promise to provide for her."

Felix shook his head. "I'll be hanged. And not a word to her own brother. And what of the children?"

"They are all still here at present. After the wedding trip, Alexander alone will reside with the happy couple. It seems George Linton is willing to take on the one child, but not three."

Felix frowned. "I don't understand."

"Nor do I," Lord Brightwell said. "But Judith has decided to leave Audrey and Andrew here in my care. If you object, and prefer to engage some qualified person to house and care for them near you at Oxford, to provide for them yourself and see them properly educated, you are welcome to do so."

Felix pulled on the hem of his waistcoat and shifted his weight. "I am fond of them, of course," he faltered. "But I cannot afford . . . and truly, they are no relatives of mine. Not even my sister's, are they? Will not Dominick's mother take them in?"

"It seems the elder Mrs. Howe is stricken with such severe gout and tenuous finances—*her* words, you understand—that she will not be able to do so, much as she might wish it. She will not object to my raising them as my wards, with the stipulation that I bring them to visit her on occasion."

"Your wards?" Felix repeated.

"Yes."

Felix regarded his uncle with something akin to begrudging respect. "Taking in another's children again, are you?" he said drolly.

Lord Brightwell's eyes twinkled. "Yes," he drawled. "I seem to make a habit of it."

48

> HAINES George, for stealing a gun and a powder flask, the property of James Hickman; and a rabbit, the property of Henry Simcox. Three calendar months for 1st Offence; One calendar month for 2nd
>
> —Northleach House of Correction records, 1850
> (transcribed by Phil Mustoe)

When the Crenshaws' footman handed her Lord Bradley's card, emotions flared like Chinese rockets through her body—panic, fear, hope. She was tempted to refuse to see him but knew she could not do so. Not after his letter of apology. For what if Lord Brightwell was ill? Or something had happened to one of the children?

"Show him up, please."

The ensuing minute seemed an hour, but then she heard footsteps approaching all too soon. She swallowed and took several deep breaths to try to calm herself. To no avail.

When the door opened once more, Olivia rose unsteadily. "Lord Bradley. I . . . I did not expect you."

He bowed. "I am certain you did not." He looked down at his boots. "And I expected the footman to announce in no uncertain terms that you were not at home, whether you were or not."

"It did cross my mind, I own." Her chuckle sounded forced in her ears. "But I did not wish to cause a stir, when I am but a guest here."

He looked at her through his golden lashes. "An honoured guest, I hope?"

Olivia bit her lip, then smiled. "Rather, yes. My mother as well. They have all gone into Cirencester together or I would introduce you."

He nodded. They stood there awkwardly for a long moment. Finally he cleared his throat and twirled his hat in his hand.

"Oh! Forgive me," Olivia said. "Do be seated, please."

"Actually, I . . . I feel a bit like Andrew in the schoolroom. Too much energy to sit. Would you be so good as to walk with me? I saw a fine garden as I rode in."

"Of course . . . I shall just find my bonnet."

They strolled together through formal gardens enclosed by walls of mottled stone. The sun shone and the air was heavy with the fragrances of rose and lavender.

"You received my letter?" he asked.

"Yes. Though I saw your father added the direction."

He nodded. "I beseeched him to tell me where you were since the day you left, and he finally gave way."

Edward had been so nervous that he had not looked at her squarely, fully, until this moment. He stopped walking and stared. Her rose pink gown had a low square neckline which displayed delicate collarbone as well as a beguiling swell of femininity. A matching pink ribbon drew his attention upward to her long graceful neck. Beneath her bonnet, earrings dangled from small white earlobes, and gleaming coils of dark hair framed her face. Her lips shone and her cheeks blushed most becomingly. "What have they done to you?"

Her lips parted; her blush deepened.

"Forgive me, that came out very wrongly. I meant, well, you look beautiful. Always did, of course, but—I like your hair and . . . well . . . everything."

She dipped her head. "Thank you. My aunt insists on having her abigail arrange my hair and dress me. Takes far too long, I fear."

"Worth it, I assure you."

Her hint of a grin bloomed into a smile.

As they walked on, hands behind their respective backs, he told her about all that had recently happened at Brightwell Court. And all that he had learned.

Olivia stopped, eyes and mouth wide. "Avery Croome is your grandfather!" She shook her head. "I am astounded and yet . . . I should have guessed." She studied his countenance, her blue eyes sparkling. "Indeed I do see a resemblance."

He said dryly, "I don't know whether that is a compliment or not."

"It would not have been a few months ago, but since I have come to know him, it is."

As they walked on, he glanced at her, noticed from her furrowed brow that she was pondering still.

"That means Alice Croome was your mother," she said. "And Mrs. Moore . . . has she known about you all along?"

Edward shook his head.

"No, I did not think so. Did you tell her?"

"Yes."

"How did she react?"

Edward drew in a deep breath. "I am afraid I caused quite a stir belowstairs."

"Oh?"

"Two maids spied me kissing her cheek."

"No!" Olivia said, mock-scandalized, then laughed. "Pray tell me all."

He complied, and they walked and talked for the better part of an hour.

When he finished his tale, she asked, "What will you do now?"

"An excellent question. What will you do?"

She took a deep breath. "Spend the rest of the summer here. Then go to Kent and teach in a girls' school, as I have always longed to do."

"But that wasn't *precisely* what you longed for, was it?"

She shrugged. "Not precisely, no. I had dreamed of Mother and me opening our own school one day. But that must remain a dream for now." She sighed. "I will content myself to assist another experienced schoolmistress and learn all I can in the meanwhile."

"I cannot convince you to return to Brightwell Court?"

"No. As much as I adore Audrey and Andrew, I . . . cannot. I own I am not fit for it after all."

"Nonsense. You are the cleverest, kindest—"

"The solitary life, I mean. Ever only in the company of children. Long hours alone. Not really fitting anywhere. Never to have a true friend. . . . Forgive me! I am prattling on worse than Doris ever did."

He looked at her blankly. "Doris . . . ?"

She pressed her eyes closed. "Exactly."

They walked on, Edward aware that he had made a gaff but not knowing how to remedy it. Instead he said, "Surely you might teach somewhere closer than Kent."

"Perhaps. But there is something appealing about a fresh start far away, now that I know my mother is safe. I have written to the constable in Withington and am still awaiting word on my father's situation."

He cleared his throat. "You have not heard, then? Seeing you, I thought not. There is news, I am afraid—news I wished to deliver in person."

She looked up. "What is it?"

From his coat pocket, he withdrew a segment of newspaper and unfolded it. "Word of your father's trial, the specific charges and likely sentence."

He held it toward her, but she did not reach for it, only regarded it blankly. "Tell me what it says," she whispered.

He breathed deeply, hating to be the bearer of such tidings, guessing how conflicted she must feel. "Your father is being tried for embezzlement, as rumored, and as is the case with servant betraying master, and the staggering amount taken, they expect him to be hung, or at the very least transported for life."

"Dear Lord, no . . ."

"I am sorry, Olivia. Even with your father's failings, this must come as a terrible blow."

Her wide, panicked eyes beseeched his. "But he did not do it! I know he did not. He has been a lot of things, but never a cheat. Never a thief."

His heart clenched to see her so distressed. "I do not mean to cast aspersions, when I have encouraged you to see your father in a more charitable light, but could not a quest for revenge have tempted him to it, if greed would not?"

She nodded. That notion had crossed her mind.

They walked on for several minutes in silence, and then he turned to her once more. "Our solicitor is at your disposal, and whatever funds you need for—"

She gripped his arm. "Take me to him. Will you please? I must see him. Ask him."

He placed his hand over hers, unable to resist the chance to touch her. "I have another idea. You recall I am some acquainted with Sir Fulke and his son, Herbert. Perhaps I might appeal to them, ask for leniency, at least a lesser punishment."

"Do you think them capable of mercy?"

"Sir Fulke? Not likely. If Herbert were there, I might be able to sway him, but as far as I know he is still away. Yet, I would try."

"You would?"

"For you, yes. And I am certain Father would approve."

"Why should you?"

They looked at one another, blue gazes melding.

"Olivia . . ." he said, sounding almost offended. "I think you know the answer to that."

49

> Of my Arithmetic I was very fond, and advanced rapidly. Mensuration was quite delightful, Fractions, Decimals and Book keeping.
>
> —Miss Weeton, *Journal of a Governess* 1811–25

Olivia waited nervously in the entry hall of the former Meacham estate, now in the possession of Sir Fulke Fitzpatrick.

A quarter of an hour after he had been shown into a room down the corridor, Lord Bradley reemerged, in the company of two men. After a few low words were exchanged, the two men crossed the corridor with the merest glance in her direction and then disappeared into another room. Lord Bradley turned to face her, and she hurried across the marble floor to meet him.

He cleared his throat. "I have good news and rather trying news both, I am afraid. Herbert is in town for the trial. He and his solicitor have agreed to allow you to see the books in question."

"And the trying news?" Olivia whispered.

His blue eyes were somber. "You have one hour, Olivia. It is all I could manage."

She swallowed, then nodded. "Pray for me."

"I shall. I am." He squeezed her hand, then opened the door for her.

Olivia entered an ornate library, where alabaster busts stared blindly from atop tall bookcases of mahogany and brass. A claw-footed table sat at the middle of the room, while fringed chairs of velvet huddled closer to the marble chimneypiece. Above it reigned a gilt-framed portrait of a lace-bosomed dowager, who looked down at Olivia in marked disapproval. Ignoring her, Olivia stepped to the table and sat down. Three books lay before her, illuminated by four tall sash windows. She prayed that old glass slate in her mind, murky from lack of regular use, would come back to her once more. She opened the books in order and slowly ran her finger down the columns, figuring and checking as she went. Everything seemed in order. *Almighty God, please help me. . . .*

An hour later, the door opened. Olivia closed the last book and rose. Into the library walked not two men but seven. Lord Bradley; a black-haired young man she guessed must be Herbert Fitzpatrick; his father, Sir Fulke; the solicitor she had glimpsed earlier; Mr. Smith, the constable; the local magistrate; and another man she did not recognize.

Lord Bradley stepped in the breach between Olivia and the cluster of men. "Sir Fulke, this is Miss Keene, Simon Keene's daughter."

Standing before her was the proud gentleman from the Crown and Crow, now a dozen years older. The years had not been kind to him.

His thin lip curled. "Ah . . . the little trained monkey, all grown."

She felt Lord Bradley stiffen beside her. "Sir Fulke . . ."

Olivia doubted the man even heard Edward's steely warning.

"How fate played into his hands," Sir Fulke continued. "That I should purchase his master's estate and that my own steward would keep him on. How Keene bided his time, earning my steward's trust, learning his way about my business and about my books, then when he was confident in his position, he struck, thinking I would never be the wiser. Well, now fate delivers her cruel twist, and he is caught in his own trap."

Olivia met the man's gaze. "I might say the same of you, sir."

He smirked. "What is that supposed to mean?"

"I am very glad your solicitor and our constable are here today, as well as the local magistrate," Olivia said. "Fate, I believe, is still at work."

"You talk nonsense, ghel. If you think to confuse me with riddles, you are quite mistaken."

Olivia forced a smile and changed tack. "I am glad to see you looking so well, Sir Fulke," she began. "Mr. Smith told me you suffered a hard blow to your head. He thought you might have taken a fall. Down a pair of stairs, perhaps." The second smile came more easily. "It was kind of you not to inform the constable *where* you were injured. For that might have looked very bad for my father."

His eyes narrowed, but he said nothing.

"For the highly esteemed Mrs. Atkins says she found you in our home, unconscious."

As she'd hoped, he did not challenge Mrs. Atkins's word. Everyone in the village respected the midwife. Most had been delivered by her, or entered the world into her hands. Sir Fulke could not have lived in Withington long and not known how highly she was regarded.

Olivia said, "Is it not possible that you very naturally blame Simon Keene for that injury, and that is why you seek such a stern penalty? The very revenge you accuse my father of taking?"

"What are you talking about?"

"I suppose you might have fallen down our stairs, but why you would be abovestairs in our house, where the only rooms are my bedchamber and the old schoolroom, I cannot guess. Is there some reason?"

He stared at her coldly. "No reason I can think of."

"Then is not another explanation more plausible? Were you not, in fact, struck from behind? By some scoundrel too cowardly to fight you face-to-face?"

He made no answer, but there was a wary gleam in his eye.

"It would explain a great deal," Olivia continued. "It would explain why Simon Keene left the village so soon after, as though a guilty man. A fire iron can do a lot of damage. More than any fall down stairs."

"Perhaps, Davies," Sir Fulke said to his solicitor, though his eyes remained on Olivia, "we ought to add assault to our list of charges."

"He admits it, then?" Mr. Smith, the constable, asked.

"Actually, no," Olivia said. "Though I have blamed him these many months for a violent act. As you have blamed him."

"Ah!" Sir Fulke's muddy eyes lit. "Perhaps you seek a bit of revenge yourself. A cruel father, was he?"

She smiled sweetly. "Nothing to you, I am sure."

He studied her, uncertain of her meaning.

"I suppose you had just come to our house to bring my mother more needlework for your dear wife," Olivia continued. "And perhaps Simon Keene burst in and hit you from behind, driven by jealous rage. And you never knew what hit you. You awoke later to find yourself in Mrs. Atkins's office, where she had taken you to recover."

"She saw nothing?" he asked, selecting a cigar from a wooden box on the table and idly rolling it between his fingers.

"Do you mean, did she see my father strike you? Sadly, no."

"Miss Keene," Edward interrupted. "I do not see what . . . this cannot help your father."

"I only want the truth to be revealed," Olivia said. "Does not the truth set one free?"

"Yes, but—"

Sir Fulke interrupted, "My own memory of those events—head injuries being what they are—is vague, Miss Keene," he said dismissively. "When I awoke, I found myself rather in a fog. I thought Mrs. Atkins told me I had fallen down stairs, but I may have mistaken the matter. I later learnt I had been unconscious for more than a day."

With the help of copious amounts of laudanum, Olivia thought.

"It must have been as you said," Sir Fulke said, warming to the notion. "Your father found me in his home, assumed the worst, and struck me down like the coward he is."

Olivia grimaced. "But do not forget, sir, you gave your attacker just cause."

Again those muddy eyes narrowed. "What do you mean?"

"You see, the reason someone struck you from behind—I do not deny that part—was because when this person entered our home, he or she found you violently strangling my mother."

"Preposterous!"

"I agree it sounds so," Olivia said calmly. "And in fact, for the longest time, I believed this fiend, bent on destroying my dear mamma, was my own father, to my shame. But it was not. He was in Cheltenham, in the company of your own steward."

The seventh man, the one she had not recognized, nodded his agreement. "That's right, miss."

Sir Fulke's lip curved in a feline smile. "Miss Keene, your tale-bearing astounds me! You ought to be a writer of novels. You have missed your calling with all that arithmetic nonsense."

Olivia sighed. "If only it were a fiction. But for me it became a nightmare that has haunted me for months."

"If not your father, who?" Sir Fulke asked. "Do you claim some passing tramp or thief struck me?"

She stole a glance at Edward. "I have been mistaken for both in the past. But, no."

"Who, then?" Mr. Smith asked, while the magistrate leaned forward in his chair, watching her closely.

"I stayed late at Miss Cresswell's that evening, tutoring two pupils who had fallen behind. I came home to find chairs overturned and glass smashed against the grate. I heard my mother call out in panic and ran to her bedchamber. It was quite dark, but light enough to see a man with his hands around my mother's throat, squeezing hard. I know what that feels like now. Sharp pain, lungs burning, the surety of death any moment . . ."

"Rubbish, the lot of it!" Sir Fulke exclaimed.

"I did not think. I only knew I must stop the man and save my mother. Before I knew it, I had grasped the fire iron and struck for all I was worth. I thought I might have killed the man. But I did not. He breathed still."

"I was not that man," Sir Fulke said, with a pointed look at the magistrate. "You said yourself the room was dark and you suspected your own father. He must have heard your mother was entertaining gentleman callers. I had certainly heard the rumor myself, though I, of course, did not credit it."

Olivia said coldly, "You lie."

"And *you* would do anything, say anything, to try and spare that vile father of yours. Spin all the tales you like, my dear. But you have no *witness* save yourself."

"I am afraid I do." She nodded to Edward, who opened the door. Dorothea Keene walked in, regal in striped gown and hat, head held high.

Every head turned. The constable gaped like a beached fish.

Sir Fulke instantly paled. "Dorothea!"

Mr. Smith stammered, "Mrs. Keene, we thought . . . after you disappeared, well, everyone thought the worst. I told 'em Keene would never harm you, but few believed me."

"You were right, Mr. Smith," her mother began. "But Sir Fulke would and did. He tried to strangle me. And I was terrified that when he came to, he would try again—and take revenge on whoever struck him. I felt I had no choice but to send my daughter away that very night and to flee the village myself the next morning, though injured."

Sir Fulke's face was beetroot red. "What lies! Preposterous, the lot of it! The whole family is in on it. I know our magistrate and constable are wise enough to see the truth."

Mr. Smith looked like a confused boy. "Why would Sir Fulke mean you any harm, Mrs. Keene?"

Dorothea Keene took a deep breath and faced the constable and magistrate. "Because I refused his advances. Not once but over and over again for several months. He became . . . obsessed . . . with me, though I never gave him any encouragement."

"You did!" Sir Fulke exclaimed, ignoring his solicitor's staying hand and whispered warning.

Her mother continued, "He began coming to our house for his wife's needlework in her stead. I was quite uncomfortable with his calls, but he would not stop. He tried to push himself on me that night, and when I fought back, he . . . he . . . nearly killed me."

"Nonsense! Smith, it is all nonsense!"

Mr. Smith looked flabbergasted and uncertain how to proceed. Sir Fulke's steward sat silent, as did the magistrate, who watched the proceedings in calculated detachment.

Herbert Fitzpatrick rose. "I believe her," he said.

"Shut up, boy!" his father snapped. "Turn against your father, will you? Always were a weak, useless lad."

Herbert flinched, but when he spoke, his voice was calm and cool. "I did not witness the events of that evening, but I was aware of my father's increasingly frequent calls on Mrs. Keene, and my mother's distress because of it. It would not be the first time my father has pursued another woman, though I had never known him to pursue anyone so doggedly before."

"Shut your trap, boy. You are hereby disinherited. Davies! I want a new will." Sir Fulke turned toward the door.

"We are not finished here, Sir Fulke," Olivia said.

"Yes, we are," he said, jaw clenched.

"There is the matter of the embezzlement charge. I have reviewed the books, and my father did not embezzle from you."

"Right," Sir Fulke sneered. "Who did, then?"

Olivia looked at the young man beside the solicitor, his pale face framed by the blackest hair. And in his wary green eyes, she saw once more the dread of disappointing one's father that she recognized in herself, that she recognized from a boy in the Crown and Crow all those years ago. Would, could, this boy, grown now, dare disappoint his father? Own up to the truth which would surely earn his father's wrath and rejection a hundred times over what a lost contest would have done?

The young man looked at her then. Really looked. And whether he recognized her or something in himself, Olivia could not know, but he stood up the straighter for it, and his eyes lit with a strange determination, like a soldier marching into certain, but resigned-to, death.

"No one *embezzled* from you, Father," he began. "But I took it, to keep you from wasting the family's last shilling on gaming and women. You have not given Mother and me enough to live on these last years, so I felt within my rights to take what was needed to pay the bills and keep my mother in the comfort she deserves. Disinherit me if you like—here stands your solicitor at the ready. I have invested wisely. From the interest earned, I can now support Mother and myself—if not in grand fashion, respectable at least. Which is more than I can say for you. Your affairs are in a sorry state indeed, and it does not take an accomplished clerk to figure that out." He turned to Olivia. "Though it did take an accomplished young woman to discover I did it—and to give me the courage to own up to it."

"But . . . ! How dare you," the older gentleman blustered. "I shall disinherit you indeed. Cut you off!"

Herbert said dryly, "Disinherited twice in a single day. How extraordinary."

The steward cleared his throat. "Sir, if I may. The sum your son invested is all that is keeping the family from debtors' prison. Perhaps leniency is in order?"

"He shall never lay his thieving hands on my money."

"What money, Father?" Herbert said. "We have already established your debts outweigh your assets and the investors are dropping like scales off a rotting fish."

Sir Fulke glowered. "And whose fault is that?"

"Yours, sir."

"These rumors and now charges of embezzlement have done it. It is on your head. Yours!"

Herbert looked at his father coldly. "So be it. But Mr. Keene goes free."

"Why should he?"

"Because he is innocent," Olivia's mother said. "And because if you drop all charges, the rest of this sordid business will remain our secret."

The constable objected. "Mrs. Keene, are you sure you want to let him off? I could have him—"

"Quite sure, Mr. Smith." She turned cold eyes on Sir Fulke. "That is, unless he ever comes near me again."

Herbert Fitzpatrick offered Olivia his arm and escorted her from the room while the magistrate, Mrs. Keene, and Sir Fulke sealed the bargain, with Edward, the steward, and the solicitor acting as witnesses.

In the hall, Herbert withdrew a single gold guinea from his waistcoat pocket and pressed it into Olivia's gloved hand. "This is yours, I believe, Miss Keene. You won that long-ago contest and you won today."

"I think we both won," she said. "Thank you for speaking out."

Pulling his gaze from her hand, he looked up ruefully. "Would you have let me keep silent, had I not?"

She smiled gently but shook her head. "I have been silent long enough."

50

It was all the romance of the nursery and the poetry of the schoolroom.

—Henry James, *The Turn of the Screw*

The carriage made its way to the far end of Northleach, to the mottled greystone prison and magistrate building known as the House of Correction. The arched doorway was flanked on either side by imposing two-story walls.

Edward waited in the carriage with her mother, while Mr. Smith offered Olivia a hand down. The constable led Olivia through the magistrate's building and into a small visitors' room near the keeper's house. Then he disappeared, taking the magistrate's order with him.

Several minutes later, a keeper opened the door and Simon Keene shuffled into the room, head bowed and hands clasped together in front of him as though manacled, though no physical restraint bound him.

Her father looked up and started. Clearly no one had told him who had come to see him. Nor why.

"Livie! I did not think to ever lay eyes on you again."

Her heart was so full to see him that for a moment she could not speak. When she did not, his hopeful expression faded.

"Come to say good-bye?" he asked dully. "Or to rail at me once more?"

"Neither." She sat at the table and gestured her father toward the second chair across from her.

He slumped down. "Surely you've heard I'm done for. It's the noose for me. Or transportation. Fatal the both of them."

"No. You are being released. Did they not tell you?"

He frowned. "Are you dreamin', girl? Out to raise my hopes and dash them as I have disappointed you time and time again?"

"You are innocent."

"Ha! I did not embezzle a farthing, but I am guilty of far worse. It is why I don't care what they do to me now—I have made peace with my maker. I wish I might have told your mother how sorry I am. Begged her pardon—yours as well. If you might forgive me, I could die content enough."

"I do forgive you," Olivia said. "And I hope you will forgive me."

"Forgive you? For what?"

"For thinking the worst of you."

He looked away. "I have given you prodigious cause."

"Perhaps," she allowed. Later, she would confess all that she had thought him guilty of. But not now, not here. He looked low indeed, yet there was an odd new light in his eyes, a peace in his countenance she had not before seen. "Never mind that now. I have had a look at Sir Fulke's books and—"

"Did you indeed?" he interrupted, brows high. "And how did you accomplish that?"

"Lord Brightwell and his son are acquainted with Sir Fulke, and—"

"Brightwell again. I might have known. Has he claimed you as his own?"

"No. The point is they convinced Sir Fulke's son and solicitor to give me an hour with the account books, and do you know what I discovered?"

He shook his head absently, his eyes flitting about her face, as though taking an inventory and committing it to memory.

"The money had been taken over a period of only a few months, more than a year ago. It had been categorized as petty cash, yet withdrawn in large amounts which, when summed, rounded to the pound. Not the work of an accomplished clerk like you, even had you been working for Sir Fulke at the time, which you were not. You are far too clever for such a hack job."

"Who was it, then? Not his steward, I hope? Seemed a decent man to me."

She shook her head. "It was Herbert Fitzpatrick, Sir Fulke's own son. And with good cause, I gather. Do you remember him? The Harrow lad who won that contest in the Crown and Crow?"

"Won?" He humphed. "You let him win—that's what."

She leaned across the table and looked him in the eye. "You are right, I did. Will you never forgive me for it?" Tears blurred her vision, and she was twelve years old all over again.

Tears filled his drooping brown eyes, and her heart ached to see it. "Me forgive you? When it's I who was worse than the devil to you? You who never did me a wrong—well, if you don't count that one contest. . . ." He attempted a grin, which only served to push the tears from his eyes and down his cheeks, thinner than she had ever seen them.

He sighed and slumped back. "I have not had one drop to drink since that night I came the fool to Brightwell Court. I have been praying too, for the first time in my life. That parson, Tugwell, he helped me see—not the error of my ways, for I knew them all too well already—but what was wanting in me. I am far from perfect, I know, but I am changed and changing still. I know it is too late for Dorothea and me. When news of my hanging reaches her, wherever she is, she will no doubt wed her Oliver after all. I hope she will finally be happy."

Olivia shook her head. "She did not leave you for him. She felt she had to flee because someone was threatening her. Nearly killed her."

His face darkened, thunderstruck. "What? I shall kill the fiend! Who is he? Who?"

"This is exactly why she did not tell you. She knew you would murder the man and end up hanging for it, and she did not want that."

He shook his head regretfully. "Well, it is what I get in the end, at any rate, and I would have rather given my life to protect her." His voice grew thick with emotion. "I would, you know. I would give my life for her."

"I know you would," whispered Dorothea Keene.

Olivia looked over her shoulder. Her mother stood timidly in the threshold. When Olivia looked back at her father, his mouth was slack, expression stunned. He stared at Dorothea as though not believing his eyes. As though for the last time.

"You gave your life for me long ago," she said quietly. "When you married me, even knowing I carried another man's child."

He slowly nodded. "I loved you then, and I love you now. Livie too, though she don't belong to me."

Dorothea shook her head. "But she does. I did visit Brightwell Court once after I lost the first child, but I was never unfaithful to you. I have told you before, and I will tell you until you believe me. She is your daughter. *Yours*."

Still he stared at his wife, disbelief evident in his expression, but whether disbelief of her words or of her very presence, Olivia was not certain.

"Why are you here?" he asked breathlessly, "Why are you telling me this, when you had already made your escape? When you were already well and free of me?"

Tears brightened Dorothea's eyes. Her whisper grew hoarse. "Perhaps I do not wish to be free."

Hope flared and faded in his dark eyes. "Well, free you'll be, and soon now. I'm to be hung or transported, and men don't come back spry and whole, if they come back at all. Still, I am glad you've come. I asked God to let me see the both of you once more, and He has answered."

"Did you not hear a word I said, Papa?" Olivia exclaimed. "You have been exonerated."

He shook his head in wonder, a rare twinkle in his eyes. "Figured it out when neither the steward nor I could, did you? Caught that Harrow boy out at the last."

She nodded.

"That's my girl. My clever girl."

Olivia's throat tightened, and her heart squeezed to hear him say those long-missed words. She reached across the table and pressed the guinea into his hand, much as Herbert had done. "He returned this."

Simon Keene held the coin in his fingers, turning it this way and that. "Of all the things I have lost in my life, this is the very least I'd want returned to me."

He placed the coin back in her hand, pressing her fingers for a lingering moment.

"You are free to go, Father," she whispered. "We are all of us free."

Olivia finally understood what Mr. Tugwell had tried to tell her. This was how it was for every fallen creature. *Christ bore the penalty we each deserve, to purchase our freedom.*

He shook his head. "I cannot take it in. Free to go . . . where?"

Olivia glanced at her mother. It was not her place to invite him home.

"You will be going back to your Lord Brightwell with his riches and title, no doubt," he went on. "And I would not blame you. Not a bit of it."

"Listen to me," Olivia said. "Lord Brightwell is a very kind and generous man, but he is not my father. That is *your* title, whether you accept it or not."

He studied her, wanting to believe, she could tell, but afraid to do so.

"The man may be an earl," Olivia continued, attempting a grin, "but he is no scholar in arithmetic, I assure you. In fact, he makes rather a muddle of it." She slowly shook her head, looking him directly in the eye. "I long ago inherited your dark hair and mind for numbers. There is no disinheriting me now."

He lifted thin lips in a wobbly smile. "Never."

Edward was pacing outside the prison when Olivia emerged at last. Alone. He searched her face, relieved to see only a trace of the anxiety that had been there before. He exhaled deeply.

"They will be out soon," she said with a tremulous smile. "They wished to speak privately first, as you might imagine."

He nodded and pressed her hand, wondering what the outcome of that discussion would be.

Simon and Dorothea Keene emerged a few minutes later, not arm in arm, but side by side.

Edward stepped forward and shook Mr. Keene's hand. Olivia formally introduced the two men, though they had met under awkward circumstances once before.

Simon Keene thanked Edward for his part, then cleared his throat. "Thing is," he began awkwardly, "it would not be wise for either of us to return to Withington. Too near Fitzpatrick, you understand. And of course, I no longer have a post there. Dorothea here would like to return to the school—"

"Just for a time," Mrs. Keene hastened to clarify. "I feel I should finish out the term."

"And I feel I ought to return to the almshouse," Mr. Keene said, "to speak with that parson again. And then later . . ." He glanced at Dorothea, then away again. "Well, we shall see."

Edward looked at Olivia, who bravely nodded her understanding. He hoped she was not too disappointed there would be no instant reconciliation for her parents. But surely with wise counsel from Mr. Tugwell—and much prayer and patience—they might be reunited soon.

Edward directed the coachman first to St. Aldwyns, where Mrs. Keene bestowed a tentative smile on her husband and embraced Olivia with a promise to see her soon.

They then delivered Mr. Keene to the almshouse as he'd requested. But when they arrived, Charles Tugwell bustled out and insisted Mr. Keene stay in the vicarage guest room. A village shopkeeper, a Miss Ludlow, he believed, followed in the vicar's wake, smiling and waving to Olivia.

When Olivia stepped away to speak with her and Charles, Edward pulled Simon Keene aside.

"I wonder, Mr. Keene, if the position of clerk at Brightwell Court might interest you?"

The man frowned. "You don't want the likes of me in your house, not after everything."

"On the contrary," Edward said. "Father has promoted our man Walters to steward, leaving us without a clerk. And I understand you are very clever with accounts, as is your daughter."

"Are you offering for her sake?"

"And if I am?"

"Your father cannot want me."

"My father has more pressing things on his mind at present—a new will to draft, a new heir to groom, and new wards to oversee."

"And what does Liv—Olivia say to the notion?"

"Why not ask her yourself?" Edward looked over at Olivia, and his chest warmed to see her smiling at him, smiling at them both.

Simon Keene looked over as well, and a slow smile transformed his downturned features. "Perhaps I shall at that."

Late that evening, after lingering over tea and sandwiches with Lord Brightwell and the children, Edward and Olivia took Audrey and Andrew up to the nursery, bestowing many hugs and kisses before Becky swept them away for bed.

Together they descended the stairs once more, but instead of returning to the library, Edward stopped in the hall.

"Will you join me for a walk through the garden, Olivia?"

She felt a thrill of anticipation. "I will."

They walked along the church wall, through the arbor, and around the side of the house. Seeing the tree from which she had first overheard Edward's secret, she paused beside it, running her fingers over the rough bark and remembering.

As if reading her thoughts, Edward said, "Now this brings back memories. But this time, I shall hide behind the tree with you. Do you mind?"

Olivia shook her head, heart beating fast and her throat suddenly tight.

He stepped forward, and nervous, she stepped back. He stepped closer yet, and her back against the tree, she could retreat no farther, could not move. Did not want to move.

"You do know why I objected to Father claiming you as his daughter, do you not?"

She shrugged, guessing the answer but wanting to hear him say it.

"Because my feelings for you are . . . not at all brotherly."

He ran a finger along her cheek, and she shivered. Then he traced her lips with that same finger, and she could barely breathe. He whispered, "Do you know how long I have wanted to kiss you?"

She shook her head again, not trusting her voice.

"Not when I first saw you behind this tree, I admit. Then I wanted to strangle you." He grimaced. "Forgive me. Poor choice of words, that."

She managed a tremulous grin.

He placed his hands on her shoulders and slowly dragged his warm fingers down her bare arms and then up again. Shivers of pleasure fluttered up her spine.

"I believe it was when I saw you swinging Andrew about on the lawn. Or was it when I found you and Andrew asleep together, your hair down around you and wearing only the thinnest of nightdresses?" He gave her a roguish wink.

She whispered shakily, "Seems I have a great deal to thank Andrew for."

He smiled down at her. Ran his hands up her arms once more, then lifted them to her flushed cheeks. "You are burning."

"I know."

He framed her face with his hands and bent toward her, eyes fixed upon her eyes, then lowering to her mouth. At the last instant, as his lips touched hers, she closed her eyes, focusing her senses on him. The spicy, masculine scent of him, the cool fingers on her cheeks, his warm lips on hers, kissing her in whisper-soft caresses that deepened and intensified with passion.

When he finally broke the kiss, his breathing was haggard and his voice husky. "I love you, Olivia. Have you any idea how much?"

"No," she breathed. "But I hope the number is very, very high."

He kissed her once more, then lifted his head, his gaze caressing her bare neck, her face, her hair, her eyes. "Have I told you how beautiful you look tonight?"

"Several times, yes," she answered, her voice rather breathless.

"You look like a duchess . . . or a countess. I wish I might have made you one."

"I never wanted to be a countess."

"No?"

"All I have wanted, for the longest time now, was simply to be . . ."

When she hesitated, he guessed, "Free? A teacher? Reunited with your mother?"

Olivia shook her head. " . . . yours."

He bestowed upon her a smile so tender that her heart ached to see it.

Suddenly serious, he led her to the veranda, and there, under the light of several torches, looked intently down at her, eyes warm. "I have something for you."

He withdrew an object from his coat pocket. Not a ring, not a jewel box, but a folded piece of paper. He unfolded it with great care and held it out to her.

It took her eyes and mind several seconds to figure out what she was looking at. It was one of Edward's drawn plans for a building project, this one with a garden indicated behind and walking paths around. The scale drawing depicted a kitchen and laundry belowstairs, dining parlor, sitting room, and schoolrooms on the ground floor, and many bedchambers above.

He pointed to where he had labeled the plan in his bold, block printing.

Miss Keene's Boarding and Day School for Girls
All accepted, regardless of ability to pay.

Joy swelling within her, she smiled up at him.

He turned the paper over, revealing a second, similar plan. "This one has a few improvements over the original, which I hope you will approve."

The drawings themselves were identical, Olivia realized. Only the title had changed:

The Keene and Bradley School for Girls

"You wish to teach school?" she asked, brows high in feigned misunderstanding.

He stroked her chin. "Goose. The Keene refers to your mother. The Bradley refers to you. At least, I hope it will, very soon."

"Ah . . ." She slid her arms around his neck and lifted her face to receive his kiss. "A great improvement indeed."

Epilogue

Finally, I can think about that long-ago day in the Crown and Crow without the remorse that plagued me for so many years. Now I grin and sometimes laugh to think how God wove even that into something good. A sum far greater than its parts.

As I sit on a lawn rug on a warm summer's day and look at the dear ones gathered around me, my heart is light and joyful. And amazed.

I watch as Edward, my Edward, tries unsuccessfully to untangle line on a fishing pole, as though his hands are covered in schoolroom paste.

Shaking his head and wearing one of his famous scowls, Avery Croome limps over and takes the pole from Edward, muttering about the uselessness of modern youth. But beneath his gruff façade, there is a twinkle in his silvery blue eyes (so like Edward's, though I am determined his eyebrows shall never grow as wild), and I know Mr. Croome is thoroughly enjoying himself. I sometimes wish he and Mrs. Moore might wed, but they seem content to simply spend more time in one another's company, now that the hurt and misunderstandings of the past no longer stand between them.

Andrew's birch-bark float sinks into the river, and he calls out with glee. Mr. Croome hurries over, hand to the lad's shoulder, encouraging him and instructing him on how to land the fish. Drawn by Andrew's shout, Lord Brightwell saunters over from the garden in time to admire the brown trout. Edward ruffles Andrew's hair and grumbles good-naturedly about the boy catching three fish while Edward has yet to catch one.

Beside me on the lawn rug, Audrey cheers on her brother, adjusting her bonnet when it threatens to fall back. What a lovely young woman she is becoming. At thirteen, she is nearly my height, and her face has lost its childish roundness. Something tells me that when Amos Tugwell returns from school next term, he shall finally take notice of her.

Audrey bends low and tickles the infant lying on a soft hare rug before us, enjoying the warm breeze on his skin and cooing happily. Our son—Edward's and mine. We named him Avery S. Bradley. The S standing for Simon or Stanton, depending on which grandfather asks the question.

From behind, I hear a tap on the window glass and turn toward Brightwell Court. There at the library window stands my father. How handsome he looks in his clerk's coat and neckcloth. Sober as a Quaker. A flash of Titian red hair appears behind the wavy glass, and there is Felix, holed up with my father and Walters, learning all he can about the running of an estate.

My father lifts a hand in greeting, and I wave back. It does my heart good to have him here, to see him doing so well.

My mother is not numbered among us this afternoon, for she is busy at the school Edward built for us on the outskirts of Arlington, where she is proprietress and headmistress. How she loves the work and her pupils. I taught beside her the first year, until my Avery was born. Then, as unbelievable as it sounds, we hired Miss Ripley to assist her. The former governess is so pleased to have a place and be spared the workhouse that she follows my mother's edicts and manner of teaching, never once reverting to the harsh discipline she once described to me.

I still call-in at the school at least once a week, to teach arithmetic and to hear how the pupils are getting on. Becky attends there now, as does Dory's younger sister. How satisfying to see them learn and gain confidence as young women of worth.

To reach the school, I must pass by the village lockup. Whenever I do, I cannot help but look at that little place and remember. How long ago it seems. Thankfully so!

Shaking off thoughts of the past, I look at the riverbank once more and watch them—these men of my son's family. Mr. Croome, Lord Brightwell, Edward, Andrew. Great-grandfather, grandfather, father, and adopted brother. And a second grandfather inside. How blessed our Avery is. How blessed we all are.

As if sensing the direction of my thoughts, Edward, line in the water, looks over his shoulder, and our gazes catch. His knowing smile gladdens my heart.

Suddenly his line pulls taut and is nearly jerked from his hand. "I think I have one!" he calls, his voice as excited as a little boy's. Instantly, Mr. Croome is there beside him—hand on Edward's shoulder, leaning near, encouraging, and instructing him on how to land the prize. My heart aches and my eyes burn to see it.

And then the fish, a very tiny fish, is brought to shore to the cheers of Audrey and Andrew. Mr. Croome, his scowl noticeably absent, claps Edward on the back, and says in a hoarse voice, "Well done, lad. Well done."

When Edward looks across at me once more, there are tears in his dear blue eyes, and answering tears fill my own. I breathe another prayer of thanksgiving for all God has done in our lives.

Well done indeed.

Author's Note

The idea for this novel was inspired by Mahler's Third Symphony, which I heard many years ago on a road trip to Davenport, Iowa. I admit I rarely listen to classical music, but that day, as I did, whole scenes spun forth like a movie in my mind. Today, very little of that original story remains, which—hopefully—means that I have become a better researcher and writer since then. Still, Mahler's Third remains the "soundtrack" of the first two chapters.

Brightwell Court is not a real place, but it was loosely inspired by the very real, very picturesque Bibury Court in the Cotswold village of Bibury, which the artist William Morris called "the most beautiful village in England." Many thanks to author Davis Bunn for recommending that my husband and I take tea there during our first England trip. We happily did so. Not only did we enjoy the ivy-covered Tudor manor, the lovely grounds bordered by the curvy River Coln, and the greedy ducks that nipped at our scones, but I also realized it would make an ideal setting for *The Silent Governess*. I am not the first, nor will I be the last, to set a novel in that idyllic place. If you ever have the opportunity, I hope you will visit Bibury yourself.

I have been fascinated by governesses ever since my sixth-grade teacher read aloud *Jane Eyre* to us, in short increments over several weeks, with real emotion and even mascara-tears. My thanks to Ms. Rebecca Hayes, now Morgan, for sparking my lifelong love of British literature.

As always, heartfelt appreciation to my family, church-family, friends, and Bethany House colleagues for all their encouragement and support. Special thanks to my diligent and thoughtful editor Karen Schurrer and to author Laurie Alice Eakes for her gracious help with historical details.

And with deepest gratitude to God, the giver and fulfiller of dreams, and for His glory.

Soli Deo Gloria.

Reading Group Discussion Questions

1. Which character in the novel did you most like or relate to? What drew you to that character?

2. The book's opening quote says, "The best proof of wisdom is to talk little, but to hear much. . . ." Do you agree? Have you ever wished too late you had followed this advice?

3. Has a childhood regret remained with you into adulthood? What have you learned about getting past such regrets?

4. What did you learn about the life of governesses that surprised you? Do you think you would have enjoyed being a governess in the early nineteenth century?Why or why not?

5. Governesses were expected to teach literature, poetry, French, Italian, geography, the sciences, religion, arithmetic, needlework, dancing, drawing, and to play a musical instrument. How does this compare with your own (or your children's) education? Anything on the list you wish you'd had the chance to learn?

6. How might discovering that your origins are different from what you've always believed affect you? Would you have reacted differently than Edward?

7. Legal adoption as we know it was not practiced in Regency England. Unless a child was a peer's natural son born in wedlock, he might be

left some money but could not inherit his father's title or estate. Women could not usually inherit either. Did this surprise you? Strike you as unfair?

8. Where do you get your identity? From your parents, your profession, your kids, your church, your relationship with God? How has the source of your identity changed over the years?

9. Has your view of God been influenced by your earthly father or another person? Positively or negatively? If negatively, what ways have you found to overcome that influence?

10. Did any character or happening in the novel surprise you? How so? And did you enjoy the twist?

For additional book club resources, please visit *www.bethanyhouse.com/anopenbook*.

About the Author

JULIE KLASSEN loves all things Jane—Jane Eyre and Jane Austen. A graduate of the University of Illinois, Julie worked in publishing for sixteen years and now writes full time. Three of her books, *The Silent Governess*, *The Girl in the Gatehouse*, and *The Maid of Fairbourne Hall*, have won the Christy Award for Historical Romance. *The Secret of Pembrooke Park* was honored with the Minnesota Book Award for genre fiction. Julie has also won the Midwest Book Award, the Minnesota Book Award, and Christian Retailing's BEST Award, and has been a finalist in the Romance Writers of America's RITA Awards and ACFW's Carol Awards. Julie and her husband have two sons and live in a suburb of St. Paul, Minnesota.

For more information, visit www.julieklassen.com.

More From Julie Klassen

Visit julieklassen.com for a full list of her books.

After the man she loves abruptly sails for Italy, Sophie Dupont's future is in jeopardy. Wesley left her in dire straits, and she has nowhere to turn—until Captain Stephen Overtree comes looking for his wayward brother. He offers her a solution, but can it truly be that simple?

The Painter's Daughter

As secrets come to light at the abandoned manor house Pembrooke Park, will Abigail Foster find the hidden treasure and love she seeks . . . or very real danger?

The Secret of Pembrooke Park

With the help of the lovely Miss Midwinter, can London dancing master Alec Valcourt unravel old mysteries and bring new life to the village of Beaworthy—and to one widow's hardened heart?

The Dancing Master